ZORA NEALE HURSTON

ZORA NEALE HURSTON

NOVELS AND STORIES

Jonah's Gourd Vine
Their Eyes Were Watching God
Moses, Man of the Mountain
Seraph on the Suwanee
Selected Stories

THE LIBRARY OF AMERICA

Jonah's Gourd Vine copyright 1934 by Zora Neale Hurston,
renewed 1962 by John C. Hurston. *Their Eyes Were Watching
God* copyright 1937 by J.B. Lippincott Company, renewed 1965
by John C. Hurston and Joel Hurston. *Moses, Man of the
Mountain* copyright 1939 by Zora Neale Hurston, renewed
1967 by John C. Hurston and Joel Hurston. *Seraph on the
Suwanee* © 1948 by Zora Neale Hurston, renewed 1976 by
Everett E. Hurston, Sr. Reprinted by permission of
HarperCollins. Stories copyright © by Zora Neale Hurston.
Reprinted by permission of the Estate of Zora Neale Hurston.
See pp. 1033–34 for further acknowledgments.

The paper used in this publication meets the
minimum requirements of the American National Standard for
Information Sciences—Permanence of Paper for Printed
Library Materials, ANSI Z39.48—1984.

Distributed to the trade in the United States
by Penguin Books USA Inc
and in Canada by Penguin Books Canada Ltd.

Library of Congress Catalog Number: 94–25757
For cataloging information, see end of Notes.
ISBN 0–940450–83–6

First Printing
The Library of America—74

Manufactured in the United States of America

CHERYL A. WALL
SELECTED THE CONTENTS AND
WROTE THE NOTES FOR THIS VOLUME

*The publishers express their appreciation to
the Beinecke Library at Yale University for the use of
Zora Neale Hurston material.*

Contents

JONAH'S GOURD VINE

TO

BOB WUNSCH

WHO IS ONE OF THE LONG-WINGDED ANGELS
RIGHT ROUND THE THRONE
GO GATOR AND MUDDY THE WATER

THE AUTHOR

Chapter I

GOD was grumbling his thunder and playing the zig-zag lightning thru his fingers.

Amy Crittenden came to the door of her cabin to spit out a wad of snuff. She looked up at the clouds.

"Ole Massa gwinter scrub floors tuhday," she observed to her husband who sat just outside the door, reared back in a chair. "Better call dem chaps in outa de cotton patch."

"'Tain't gwine rain," he snorted, "you always talkin' more'n yuh know."

Just then a few heavy drops spattered the hard clay yard. He arose slowly. He was an older middle-age than his years gave him a right to be.

"And eben if hit do rain," Ned Crittenden concluded grudgingly, "ef dey ain't got sense 'nough tuh come in let 'em git wet."

"Yeah, but when us lef' de field, you tole 'em not to come till you call 'em. Go 'head and call 'em 'fo de rain ketch 'em."

Ned ignored Amy and shuffled thru the door with the chair, and somehow trod on Amy's bare foot. "'Oman, why don't you git outa de doorway? Jes contrary tuh dat. You needs uh good head stompin', dass whut. You sho is one aggervatin' 'oman."

Amy flashed an angry look, then turned her face again to the sea of wind-whipped cotton, turned hurriedly and took the cow-horn that hung on the wall and placed it to her lips.

"You John Buddy! You Zeke! You Zachariah! Come in!"

From way down in the cotton patch, "Yassum! Us comin'!"

Ned shuffled from one end of the cabin to the other, slamming to the wooden shutter of the window, growling between his gums and his throat the while.

The children came leaping in, racing and tumbling in tense, laughing competition—the three smaller ones getting under the feet of the three larger ones. The oldest boy led the rest, but once inside he stopped short and looked over the heads of the others, back over the way they had come.

"Shet dat door, John!" Ned bellowed, "you ain't got the sense you wuz borned wid."

Amy looked where her big son was looking. "Who dat comin' heah, John?" she asked.

"Some white folks passin' by, mama. Ahm jes' lookin' tuh see whar dey gwine."

"Come out dat do'way and shet it tight, fool! Stand dere gazin' dem white folks right in de face!" Ned gritted at him. "Yo' brazen ways wid dese white folks is gwinter git you lynched one uh dese days."

"Aw 'tain't," Amy differed impatiently, "who can't look at ole Beasley? He ain't no quality nohow."

"Shet dat door, John!" screamed Ned.

"Ah wuzn't de last one inside," John said sullenly.

"Don't you gimme no word for word," Ned screamed at him. "You jes' do lak Ah say do and keep yo' mouf shet or Ah'll take uh trace chain tuh yuh. Yo' mammy mought think youse uh lump uh gold 'cause you got uh li'l' white folks color in yo' face, but Ah'll stomp yo' guts out and dat quick! Shet dat door!"

He seized a lidard knot from beside the fireplace and limped threateningly towards John.

Amy rose from beside the cook pots like a black lioness.

"Ned Crittenden, you raise dat wood at mah boy, and you gointer make uh bad nigger outa me."

"Dat's right," Ned sneered, "Ah feeds 'im and clothes 'im but Ah ain't tuh do nothin' tuh dat li'l' yaller god cep'n wash 'im up."

"Dat's uh big ole resurrection lie, Ned. Uh slew-foot, drag-leg lie at dat, and Ah dare yuh tuh hit me too. You know Ahm uh fightin' dawg and mah hide is worth money. Hit me if you dare! Ah'll wash *yo'* tub uh 'gator guts and dat quick."

"See dat? Ah ain't fuh no fuss, but you tryin' tuh start uh great big ole ruction 'cause Ah tried tuh chesstize dat youngun."

"Naw, you ain't tried tuh chesstize 'im nothin' uh de kind. Youse tryin' tuh fight 'im on de sly. He is jes' ez obedient tuh you and jes ez humble under yuh, ez he kin be. Yet and still you always washin' his face wid his color and tellin' 'im he's

uh bastard. He works harder'n anybody on dis place. You ain't givin' 'im nothin'. He more'n makes whut he gits. Ah don't mind when he needs chesstizin' and you give it tuh 'im, but anytime you tries tuh knock any des chillun 'bout dey head wid sticks and rocks, Ah'll be right dere tuh back dey fallin'. Ahm dey mama."

"And Ahm de pappy uh all but dat one."

"You knowed Ah had 'm fo' yuh married me, and if you didn't want 'im round, whut yuh marry me fuh? Dat ain't whut you said. You washed 'im up jes lak he wuz gold den. You jes took tuh buckin' 'im since you been hangin' round sich ez Beasley and Mimms."

Ned sat down by the crude fireplace where the skillets and spiders (long-legged bread pans with iron cover) sprawled in the ashes.

"Strack uh light, dere, some uh y'all chaps. Hit's dark in heah."

John obediently thrust a piece of lightwood into the embers and the fire blazed up. He retreated as quickly as possible to the farther end of the cabin.

Ned smoked his strong home-grown tobacco twist for a few minutes. Then he thrust out his feet.

"Pour me some water in dat wash-basin, you chaps, and some uh y'all git de washrag."

There was a scurry and bustle to do his bidding, but the drinking-gourd dropped hollowly in the water bucket. Ned heard it.

" 'Tain't no water in dat air water-bucket, Ah'll bound yuh!" He accused the room and glowered all about him, "House full uh younguns fuh me to feed and close, and heah 'tis dust dark and rainin' and not uh drop uh water in de house! Amy, whut kinda 'oman is you nohow?"

Amy said nothing. She sat on the other side of the fireplace and heaped fresh, red coals upon the lid of the spider in which the bread was cooking.

"John!" Ned thundered, "git yo' yaller behind up offa dat floor and go git me some water tuh wash mah foots."

"You been tuh de house longer'n he is," Amy said quietly. "You coulda done been got dat water."

"You think Ah'm gwine take uh 'nother man's youngun and feed 'im and close 'im fuh twelve years and den he too good tuh fetch me uh bucket uh water?" Ned bellowed.

"Iss rainin' out dere, an' rainin' hard," Amy said in the same level tones.

"Dass right," Ned sneered, "John is de house-nigger. Ole Marsa always kep' de yaller niggers in de house and give 'em uh job totin' silver dishes and goblets tuh de table. Us black niggers is de ones s'posed tuh ketch de wind and de weather."

"Ah don't want *none* uh mah chilluns pullin' tuh no spring in uh hard rain. Yo' foots kin wait. Come hawg-killin' time Ah been married tuh you twelve years and Ah done seen yuh let 'em wait uh powerful long spell some time. Ah don't want mah chilluns all stove-up wid uh bad cold from proagin' 'round in de rain."

"Ole Marse didn't ast *me* ef hit wuz rainin' uh snowin' uh hot uh col'. When he spoke Ah had tuh move and move quick too, uh git uh hick'ry tuh mah back. Dese younguns ain't uh bit better'n me. Let 'em come lak Ah did."

"Naw, Ned, Ah don't want mine tuh come lak yuh come nor neither lak me, and Ahm uh whole heap younger'n you. You growed up in slavery time. When Old Massa wuz drivin' you in de rain and in de col'—he wan't don' it tuh he'p you 'long. He wuz lookin' out for hisself. Course Ah wuz twelve years old when Lee made de big surrender, and dey didn't work me hard, but—but dese heah chillun is diffunt from us."

"How come dey's diffunt? Wese all niggers tuhgether, ain't us? White man don't keer no mo' 'bout one dan he do de other."

"Course dey don't, but we ain't got tuh let de white folks love our chillun fuh us, is us? Dass jest de pint. We black folks don't love our chillun. We couldn't do it when we wuz in slavery. We borned 'em but dat didn't make 'em ourn. Dey b'longed tuh old Massa. 'Twan't no use in treasurin' other folkses property. It wuz liable tuh be took uhway any day. But we's free folks now. De big bell done rung! Us chillun is ourn. Ah doan know, mebbe hit'll take some of us genera-tions, but us got tuh 'gin tuh practise on treasurin' our

younguns. Ah loves dese heah already uh whole heap. Ah don't want 'em knocked and 'buked."

Ned raked his stubbly fingers thru his grisly beard in silent hostility. He spat in the fire and tamped his pipe.

"Dey say spare de rod and spile de child, and Gawd knows Ah ain't gwine tuh spile nair one uh dese. Niggers wuz made tuh work and all of 'em gwine work right long wid me. Is dat air supper ready yit?"

"Naw hit ain't. How you speck me tuh work in de field right long side uh you and den have supper ready jis az soon ez Ah git tuh de house? Ah helt uh big-eye hoe in mah hand jes ez long ez you did, Ned."

"Don't you change so many words wid me, 'oman! Ah'll knock yuh dead ez Hector. Shet yo' mouf!"

"Ah change jes ez many words ez Ah durn please! Ahm three times seben and uh button. Ah knows whut's de matter wid *you*. Youse mad cause Beasley done took dem two bales uh cotton us made las' yeah."

"Youse uh lie!"

"Youse uh nother one, Ned Crittenden! Don't you lak it, don't you take it, heah mah collar come and you shake it! Us wouldn't be in dis fix ef you had uh lissened tuh me. Ah tole you when dey hauled de cotton tuh de gin dat soon ez everything wuz counted up and Beasley give us share for yuh tuh take and haul it straight tuh dis barn. But naw, yuh couldn't lissen tuh me. Beasley told yuh tuh leave hit in *his* barn and being he's uh white man you done whut he told yuh. Now he say he ain't got no cotton uh ourn. Me and you and all de chillun done worked uh whole year. Us done made sixteen bales uh cotton and ain't even got uh cotton seed to show."

"Us et hit up, Major Beasley say. Come to think of it 'tis uh heap uh moufs in one meal barrel."

"No sich uh thing, Ned Crittenden. Fust place us ain't had nothing but meal and sow-belly tuh eat. You mealy-moufin' round cause you skeered tuh talk back tuh Rush Beasley. What us needs tuh do is git offa dis place. Us been heah too long. Ah b'longs on de other side de Big Creek anyhow. Never did lak it over heah. When us gather de crops dis yeah less move."

"Aw, Ah reckon we kin make it heah all right, when us don't have so many moufs in de meal barrel we kin come out ahead. 'Tain't goin' be dat many dis time when Ah goes to de gin house."

"How come?"

"Cause Ah done bound John over tuh Cap'n Mimms. Dat's uh great big ole boy, Amy, sixteen years old and look lak he twenty. He eats uh heap and den you won't let me git de worth uh mah rations out of 'im in work. He could be de finest plow-hand in Alabama, but you won't lemme do nothin' wid 'im."

"He don't do nothin'? He's uh better hand wid uh wide sweep plow right now dan you is, and he kin chop mo' cotton dan you, and pick mo' dan ah kin and you knows Ah kin beat you anytime." Then, as if she had just fully heard Ned, "Whut dat you say 'bout boundin' John Buddy over tuh Cap'n Mimms? You ain't uh gonna do no sich uh thing."

"Ah done done it."

In the frenzied silence, Amy noticed that the rain had ceased; that the iron kettle was boiling; that a coon dog struck a trail way down the Creek, and was coming nearer, singing his threat and challenge.

"Ned Crittenden, you know jes ez good ez Ah do dat Cap'n Mimms ain't nothin' but po' white trash, and he useter be de overseer on de plantation dat everybody knowed wuz de wust one in southern Alabama. He done whipped niggers nigh tuh death."

"You call him po' when he got uh thousand acres under de plow and more'n dat in wood lot? Fifty mules."

"Don't keer if he is. How did he git it? When Massa Pinckney got kilt in de war and ole Miss Pinckney didn't had nobody tuh look atter de place she took and married 'im. He wan't nothin' but uh overseer, lived offa clay and black m'lasses. His folks is so po' right now dey can't sit in dey house. Every time you pass dere dey settin' in de yard jes ez barefooted ez uh yard dawg. You ain't gwine put no chile uh mine under no Mimms."

"Ah done done it, and you can't he'p yo'seff. He gwine come git 'im tuhmorrer. He's gwine sleep 'im and feed 'im

and effen John Buddy's any account, he say he'll give uh suit uh close come Christmas time."

"Dis heah bindin' over ain't nothin' but uh 'nother way uh puttin' us folks back intuh slavery."

"Amy, you better quit talkin' 'bout de buckra. Some of 'em be outside and hear you and turn over you tuh de patter roller, and dey'll take you outa heah and put uh hun'ed lashes uh raw hide on yo' back. Ah done tole yuh but you won't hear."

The clash and frenzy in the air was almost visible. Something had to happen. Ned stood up and shuffled towards the door.

"Reckon Ahm gwine swill dat sow and feed de mules. Mah vittles better be ready when Ah git back."

He limped on out of the door and left it open.

"John Buddy," Amy said, "you and Zeke go fetch uh bucket full uh water and hurry back tuh yo' supper. De rest uh y'all git yo' plates and come git some uh dese cow-peas and pone bread. Lawd, Lawd, Lawd. Je-sus!"

There was a lively clatter of tin plates and spoons. The largest two boys went after water, Zeke clinging in the darkness to his giant of a brother. Way down in the cotton Zeke gave way to his tears.

"John Buddy, Ah don't want you way from me. John Buddy,—" he grew incoherent. So John Buddy carried him under his arm like a shock of corn and made him laugh. Finally John said, "Sometime Ah jes ez soon be under Mimms ez pappy. One 'bout ez bad as tother. 'Nother thing. Dis ain't slavery time and Ah got two good footses hung onto me." He began to sing lightly.

They returned with the water and were eating supper when Ned got back from the barn. His face was sullen and he carried the raw hide whip in his hand.

Amy stooped over the pot, giving second-helpings to the smaller children. Ned looked about and seeing no plate fixed for him uncoiled the whip and standing tiptoe to give himself more force, brought the whip down across Amy's back.

The pain and anger killed the cry within her. She wheeled to fight. The raw hide again. This time across her head. She charged in with a stick of wood and the fight was on. This

had happened many times before. Amy's strength was almost as great as Ned's and she had youth and agility with her. Forced back to the wall by her tigress onslaught, Ned saw that victory for him was possible only by choking Amy. He thrust his knee into her abdomen and exerted a merciless pressure on her throat.

The children screamed in terror and sympathy.

"Help mama, John Buddy," Zeke screamed. John's fist shot out and Ned slid slowly down the wall as if both his legs and his insides were crumbling away.

Ned looked scarcely human on the floor. Almost like an alligator in jeans. His drooling blue lips and snaggled teeth were yellowed by tobacco.

"Lawd, Ah speck you done kilt yo' pappy, John. You didn't mean tuh, and he didn't had no business hittin' me wid dat raw hide and neither chokin' me neither. Jesus, Jesus, Jesus, Jee-sus!"

"He ain't dead, mama. Ah see 'im breathin'." Zachariah said, "John Buddy sho is strong! Ah bet he kin whip ev'ry body in Notasulga."

Ned got up limpingly. He looked around and sat upon the bed.

"Amy, Ahm tellin' yuh, git dat punkin-colored bastard outa dis house. He don't b'long heah wid us nohow."

"He ain't de onliest yaller chile in de world. Wese uh mingled people."

Ned limped to the fireplace and Amy piled his plate with corn bread and peas.

"Git dat half-white youngun uh yourn outa heah, Amy. Heah Ah done took 'im since he wus three years ole and done for 'im when he couldn't do for hisseff, and he done raised his hand tuh me. Dis house can't hol' bofe uh us. Yaller niggers ain't no good nohow."

"Oh yes dey is," Amy defended hotly, "yes dey is—jes ez good ez anybody else. You jes started tuh talk dat foolishness since you been hangin' 'round ole Mimms. Monkey see, monkey do."

"Well, iss de truth. Dese white folks orta know and dey say dese half-white niggers got de worst part uh bofe de white and de black folks."

"Dey ain't got no call tuh say dat. Is mo' yaller folks on de chain-gang dan black? Naw! Is dey harder tuh learn? Naw! Do dey work and have things lak other folks? Yas. Naw dese po' white folks says dat 'cause dey's jealous uh de yaller ones. How come? Ole Marse got de yaller nigger totin' his silver cup and eatin' Berksher hawg ham outa his kitchin when po' white trash scrabblin' 'round in de piney woods huntin' up uh razor back. Yaller nigger settin' up drivin' de carriage and de po' white folks got tuh step out de road and leave 'im pass by. And den agin de po' white man got daughters dat don't never eben smell de kitchin at the big house and all dem yaller chillun got mamas, and no black gal ain't never been up tuh de big house and dragged Marse Nobody out. Humph! Talkin' after po' white trash! If Ah wuz ez least ez dey is, Ah speck Ah'd fret mahself tuh death."

"Ah naw," Ned sneered, "de brother in black don't fret tuh death. White man fret and worry and kill hisself. Colored folks fret uh lil' while and gwan tuh sleep. 'Nother thing, Amy, Hagar's chillun don't faint neither when dey fall out, dey jes have uh hard old fit."

"Dass awright, Ned. You always runnin' yo' race down. We ain't had de same chance dat white folks had. Look lak Ah can't sense you intuh dat."

"Amy, niggers can't faint. Jes ain't in 'em."

"Dass awright. Niggers gwine faint too. May not come in yo' time and it may not come in mine, but way after while, us people is gwine faint jes lak white folks. You watch and see."

"Table dat talk. Dat John is gwine offa dis place effen Ah stay heah. He goes tuh Mimms uh he goes apin' on down de road way from heah. Ah done spoke."

"Naw Ned," Amy began, but John cut her off.

"It's all right, mama, lemme go. Ah don't keer. One place is good ez 'nother one. Leave him do all de plowin' after dis!"

With his mouth full of peas and corn bread, Ned gloated, "De crops is laid by."

"Yeah, but nex' year's crops ain't planted yit," John countered.

So John put on his brass-toed shoes and his clean shirt and

was ready to leave. Amy dug out a crumpled and mouldy dollar and gave it to him.

"Where you goin', son?"

"Over de Big Creek, mama. Ah ever wanted tuh cross over."

"Ah'll go piece de way widyuh tuh de Creek, John. Gimme uh li'dud knot, dere, Zeke, so's Ah kin see de way back."

"Good bye, pap," John called from the door. Ned grunted over a full mouth. The children bawled dolefully when John called to them.

Amy threw a rag over her bruised head and closed the door after her. The night was black and starry.

"John, you wuz borned over de Creek."

"You wuz tellin' me dat one day, Ah 'member."

"Dey knows me well, over dere. Maybe Ah kin pint yuh whar some work is at."

"Yassum. Ah wants tuh make money, so's Ah kin come back and git yuh."

"Don't yuh take me tuh heart. Ah kin strain wid Ned. Ah jes been worried 'bout you and him. Youse uh big boy now and you am gwine take and take offa 'im and swaller all his filth lak you been doin' here of late. Ah kin see dat in yo' face. Youse slow, but wid him keerin' on lak he do now, hit takes uh Gawd tuh tell whut gwine happen in dat house. He didn't useter 'buke yuh lak dat. But his old mammy and dat ole cock-eyed sister uh his'n put 'im up tuh dat. He useter be crazy 'bout yuh. 'Member dat big gol' watch chain he bought fuh you tuh wear tuh big meetin'? Dey make lak he love you better'n he do de rest on 'count youse got color in your face. So he tryin' side wid dem and show 'em he don't. Ahm kinda glad fuh yuh tuh be 'way from 'round 'im. Massa Alf Pearson, he got uh big plantation and he's quality white folks. He know me too. Go in Notasulga and ast fuh 'im. Tell 'im whose boy you is and maybe he mought put yuh tuh work. And if he do, son, you scuffle hard so's he'll work yuh reg'lar. Ah hates tuh see yuh knucklin' under 'round heah all de time. G'wan, son, and be keerful uh dat foot-log 'cross de creek. De Songahatchee is strong water, and look out under foot so's yuh don't git snake bit."

"Ah done swum dat ole creek, mama—'thout yuh knowin'. Ah knowed you'd tell me not tuh swim it."

"Dat's how come Ah worries 'bout yuh. Youse always uh runnin' and uh rippin' and clambin' trees and rocks and jumpin', flingin' rocks in creeks and sich like. John, promise me yuh goin' quit dat."

"Yassum."

"Come tuh see me when yuh kin. G'bye."

Amy was gone back up the rocky path thru the blooming cotton, across the barren hard clay yard. For a minute she had felt free and flighty down there as she stood in the open with her tall, bulky son. Now the welts on her face and body hurt her and the world was heavy.

John plunged on down to the Creek, singing a new song and stomping the beats. The Big Creek thundered among its rocks and whirled on down. So John sat on the foot-log and made some words to go with the drums of the Creek. Things walked in the birch woods, creep, creep, creep. The hound dog's lyric crescendo lifted over and above the tree tops. He was on the foot-log, half way across the Big Creek where maybe people laughed and maybe people had lots of daughters. The moon came up. The hunted coon panted down to the Creek, swam across and proceeded leisurely up the other side. The tenor-singing hound dog went home. Night passed. No more Ned, no hurry. No telling how many girls might be living on the new and shiny side of the Big Creek. John almost trumpeted exultantly at the new sun. He breathed lustily. He stripped and carried his clothes across, then recrossed and plunged into the swift water and breasted strongly over.

Chapter II

THERE was a strange noise that John had never heard. He was sauntering along a road with his shoes in his hand. He could see houses here and there among the fields—not miles apart like where he had come from. Suddenly thirty or forty children erupted from a log building near the road-side, shouting and laughing. He had been to big meeting but this was no preaching. Not all them li'l' chaps. A chunky stern-faced man stood in the door momentarily with a bunch of hickories in his hand. So! This must be the school house that he had heard about. Negro children going to learn how to read and write like white folks. See! All this going on over there and the younguns over the Creek chopping cotton! It must be very nice, but maybe it wasn't for over-the-creek-niggers. These girls all had on starchy little aprons over Sunday-go-to-meeting dresses. He stopped and leaned upon the fence and stared.

One little girl with bright black eyes came and stood before him, arms akimbo. She must have been a leader, for several more came and stood back of her. She looked him over boldly from his tousled brown head to his bare white feet. Then she said, "Well, folks! Where you reckon dis big yaller bee-stung nigger come from?"

Everybody laughed. He felt ashamed of his bare feet for the first time in his life. How was he to know that there were colored folks that went around with their feet cramped up like white folks. He looked down at the feet of the black-eyed girl. Tiny little black shoes. One girl behind her had breasts, must be around fourteen. He looked at her again. Some others were growing up too. In fact all were looking a little bit like women—all but the little black-eyed one. When he looked back into her face he felt ashamed. Seemed as if she had caught him doing something nasty. He shifted his feet in embarrassment.

"Ah think he musta come from over de Big Creek. 'Tain't nothin' lak dat on dis side," the little tormenter went on.

Then she looked right into his eyes and laughed. All the others laughed. John laughed too.

"Dat's whar Ah come from sho 'nuff," he admitted.

"Whut you doin' over heah, then?"

"Come tuh see iffen Ah could git uh job uh work. Kin yuh tell me whar Marse Alf Pearson live at?"

The little girl snorted, "Marse Alf! Don't y'all folkses over de creek know slavery time is over? 'Tain't no mo' Marse Alf, no Marse Charlie, nor Marse Tom neither. Folks whut wuz borned in slavery time go 'round callin' dese white folks Marse but we been born since freedom. We calls 'em Mister. Dey don't own nobody no mo'."

"Sho don't," the budding girl behind the little talker chimed in. She threw herself akimbo also and came walking out hippily from behind the other, challenging John to another appraisal of her person.

"Ah calls 'em anything Ah please," said another girl and pulled her apron a little tight across the body as she advanced towards the fence.

"Aw, naw, yuh don't, Clary," the little black-eyed girl disputed, "youse talkin' at de big gate now. You jus' want somebody tuh notice yuh."

"Well, effen you calls 'em Mista, Ah kin call 'em Mista too," John talked at the little spitfire. "Whar at is Mista Alf Pearson's place?"

"Way on down dis road, 'bout uh mile uh mo'. When yuh git long dere by de cotton-gin, ast somebody and dey'll tell yuh mo' exact."

John shifted from one foot to another a time or two, then started off with the long stride known as boaging.

"Thankee, thankee," he threw back over his shoulder and strode on.

The teacher poked his head out of the door and all the other girls ran around behind the school house lest he call them to account for talking to a boy. But the littlest girl stood motionless, not knowing that the others had fled. She stood still akimbo watching John stride away. Then suddenly her hands dropped to her sides and she raced along the inside of the fence and overtook John.

"Hello agin," John greeted her, glad at her friendliness.

"Hello yuhself, want uh piece uh cawn bread look on de shelf."

John laughed boisterously and the girl smiled and went on in another tone, "Whyn't *you* come tuh school too?"

"'Cause dey never sont me. Dey tole me tuh go find work, but Ah wisht dey had uh tole me school. Whut Ah seen of it, Ah lakted it."

From behind her the irate voice of a man called, "Lucy! Lucy!! Come heah tuh me. Ah'll teach yuh 'bout talkin' wid boys!"

"See yuh later, and tell yuh straighter," John said and walked off.

John strode on into Notasulga, whistling; his tousled hair every which away over his head. He saw a group of people clustered near a small building and he timidly approached.

"Dis heah mus' be de cotton-gin wid all dem folks and hawses and buggies tied tuh de hitchin' postes."

Suddenly he was conscious of a great rumbling at hand and the train schickalacked up to the station and stopped.

John stared at the panting monster for a terrified moment, then prepared to bolt. But as he wheeled about he saw everybody's eyes upon him and there was laughter on every face. He stopped and faced about. Tried to look unconcerned, but that great eye beneath the cloud-breathing smoke-stack glared and threatened. The engine's very sides seemed to expand and contract like a fiery-lunged monster. The engineer leaning out of his window saw the fright in John's face and blew a sharp blast on his whistle and John started violently in spite of himself. The crowd roared.

"Hey, dere, big-un," a Negro about the station called to John, "you ain't never seed nothin' dangerous lookin' lak dat befo', is yuh?"

"Naw suh and hit sho look frightenin'," John answered. His candor took the ridicule out of the faces of the crowd. "But hits uh pretty thing do. Whar it gwine?"

"Oh eve'y which and whar," the other Negro answered, with the intent to convey the impression to John that he knew so much about trains, their habits and destinations that it would be too tiresome to try to tell it all.

The train kicked up its heels and rattled on off. John

watched after it until it had lost itself down its shiny road and the noise of its going was dead.

"You laks dat ole train Ah see," the Negro said to John, watching him as he all but fell down into the railroad cut, trying to keep sight of the tail of the train.

"Yeah, man, Ah lakted dat. It say something but Ah ain't heered it 'nough tuh tell whut it say yit. You know whut it say?"

"It don't say nothin'. It jes' make uh powerful racket, dass all."

"Naw, it say some words too. Ahm comin' heah plenty mo' times and den Ah tell yuh whut it say." He straightened up and suddenly remembered.

"Whar de cotton-gin at?"

"Hit's right over dere, but dey ain't hirin' nobody yit."

"Ain't lookin' tuh git hiahed. Lookin' fuh Mist' Alf Pearson."

"Dere he right over dere on de flat-form at de deepo', whut yuh want wid 'im?"

"Wants tuh git uh job."

"Reckon you kin git on. He done turned off his coachman fuh stovin' up one uh his good buggy hawses."

John stalked over to the freight platform.

"Is you Mist' Alf?" he asked the tall broad-built man, who was stooping over some goods.

"Why yes, what're you want?"

"Ah wants uh job uh work, please suh."

The white man continued to examine invoices without so much as a glance at the boy who stood on the ground looking up at him. Not seeing what he wanted, he straightened up and looked about him and saw John at last. Instead of answering the boy directly he stared at him fixedly for a moment, whistled and exclaimed, "What a fine stud! Why boy, you would have brought five thousand dollars on the block in slavery time! Your face looks sort of familiar but I can't place you. What's your name?"

"Mama, she name me Two-Eye-John from a preachin' she heered, but dey call me John Buddy for short."

"How old are you, John?"

"Sixteen, goin' on sebenteen."

"Dog damn! Boy you're almost as big as I am. Where'd you come from?"

"Over de Big Creek. Mama she sont me over here and told me tuh ast you tuh gimme uh job uh work. Ah kin do mos' anything."

"Humph, I should think you could. Boy, you could go bear-hunting with your fist. I believe I can make a lead plow-hand out of you."

"Yassuh, thankee, Mista Alf, Ah knows how."

"Er, who is your mama?"

"Amy Crittenden. She didn't useter be uh Crittenden. She wuz jes Amy and b'longed tuh you 'fo surrender. She say Ah borned on yo' place."

"Oh yes. I remember her. G'wan get in my rig. The bay horses with the cream colored buggy. Fetch it on over here and drive me home."

John went over by the courthouse to get the rig. It was some distance. As soon as he was out of earshot, one of Alf Pearson's friends asked him, "Say, Judge, where'd you get the new house-nigger from?"

"Oh a boy born on my place since surrender. Mama married some stray darky and moved over the Big Creek. She sent him over here to hunt work and he ran into me and I'm hiring him. Did you ever see such a splendid specimen? He'll be a mighty fine plow hand. Too tall to be a good cotton-picker. Sixteen years old."

"Humph! plow-hand! Dat's uh house-nigger. His kind don't make good field niggers. It's been tried. In his case it's a pity, because he'd be equal to two hands ordinary."

"Oh well, maybe I can do something with him. He seems willing enough. And anyway I know how to work 'em."

When John brought the horses to a satisfactory halt before the white pillars of the Pearson mansion, his new boss got down and said, "Now John, take those horses on to the stable and let Nunkie put 'em away. He'll show you where the quarters are. G'wan to 'em and tell old Pheemy I said fix you some place to sleep."

"Yassuh, thankee suh."

"And John, I might need you around the house sometimes, so keep clean."

"Yassuh."

"Where's the rest of your clothes?"

"Dese is dem."

"Well, you'll have to change sometime or other. I'll look around the house, and perhaps I can scare you up a change or two. My son Alfred is about your size, but he's several years older. And er, er, I'll fetch 'em down to the quarters in case I find anything. Go 'long."

Ole Pheemy gave John a bed in her own cabin, "Take dis bed heah if hit's good 'nough fuh yuh," she said pointing to a high feather bed in one corner.

"Yassum, thankee ma'am. Ah laks it jes fine, and dis sho is uh pritty house."

He was looking at the newspapers plastered all over the walls.

Pheemy softened.

"Oh you ain't one uh dese uppity yaller niggers then?"

"Oh no ma'am. Ahm po' folks jes lak you. On'y we ain't got no fine houses over de Creek lak dis heah one."

"Whus yo' name?"

"John, but Zeke and Zack and dem calls me John Buddy, yassum."

"Who yo' folks is over de Big Creek?"

"Mama she name Amy Crittenden—she—."

"Hush yo' mouf, you yaller rascal, you! Ah knowed, Ah seed reckerlection in yo' face." Pheemy rushed upon John, beating him affectionately and shoving him around. "Well, Lawd a'mussy boy! Ahm yo' granny! Yo' nable string is buried under dat air chanyberry tree. 'Member so well de very day you cried." (First cry at birth.) "Eat dis heah tater pone."

The field hands came in around dusk dark, eyeing John suspiciously, but his utter friendliness prevented the erection of barriers on his birth place. Amy's son was welcome. After supper the young folks played "Hide the Switch" and John overtook and whipped most of the girls soundly. They whipped him too. Perhaps his legs were longer, but anyway when he was "it" he managed to catch every girl in the quarters. The other boys were less successful, but girls were screaming under John's lash behind the cowpen and under the sweet-gum trees around the spring until the moon rose. John never for-

got that night. Even the strong odor of their sweaty bodies was lovely to remember. He went in to bed when all of the girls had been called in by their folks. He could have romped till morning.

In bed he turned and twisted.

"Skeeters botherin' yuh, John Buddy?" Pheemy asked.

"No'm Ahm jes wishin' Mist' Alf would lak mah work and lemme stay heah all de time." Then the black eyes of the little girl in the school yard burned at him from out of the darkness and he added, "Wisht Ah could go tuh school too."

"G'wan tuh sleep, chile. Heah 'tis way in de midnight and you ain't had no night rest. You gotta sleep effen you wanta do any work. Whut Marse Alf tell yuh tuh do?"

"He ain't tole me nothin' yit."

"Well, you stay heah tuh de house. Ontell he send fuh yuh. He ain't gwine overwork yuh. He don't break nobody down. Befo' surrender he didn't had no whippin' boss on *dis* place. Nawsuh. Come tuh 'membrance, 'tain't nothin' much tuh do now. De crops is laid by, de ground peas ain't ready, neither de cawn. But Ah don't speck he gointer put you in de fiel' nohow. Maybe you hand him his drinks uh drive de carridge fuh him and Ole Miss."

"Yassum," drifted back from John as he slid down and down into sleep and slumber.

That night he dreamed new dreams.

"John."

"Yassuh."

"I see the clothes fit you."

"Yassuh, Ahm powerful glad dey do, cause Ah laks 'em."

"John, I don't reckon I'll have you to drive us again. I thought to make a coachman out of you, but the mistress thinks you're too, er, er—large sitting up there in front. Can't see around you."

"Yassuh," John's face fell. He wasn't going to be hired after all.

"But I've got another job for you. You feed the chickens and gather the eggs every morning before breakfast. Have the fresh eggs in the pantry at the big house before seven o'clock so Emma can use some for our breakfast."

"Yassuh."

"And John, see to it that Ceasar and Bully and Nunkie keep the stables, pig pens and the chicken houses clean. Don't say anything to 'em, but when you find 'em dirty you let me know."

"Yassuh."

"And another thing, I want you to watch all of my brood sows. As soon as a litter is born, you let me know. And you must keep up with every pig on the place. Count 'em every morning, and when you find one missing you look around and find out what's become of it. I'm missing entirely too many shoats. I'm good to my darkies but I can't let 'em eat up all my hogs. Now, I'm going to see if I can trust you."

"Yassuh."

"Can you read and write, John?"

"Nawsuh."

"Never been to school?"

"Nawsuh, yassuh, Ah passed by dat one d'other day."

"Well, John, there's nothing much to do on the place now, so you might as well go on down to the school and learn how to read and write. I don't reckon it will hurt you. Don't waste your time, now. Learn. I don't think the school runs but three months and it's got to close for cotton-picking. Don't fool around. You're almost grown. Three or four children on this place go so you go along with them. Go neat. I didn't have slouchy folks on my place in slavery time. Mister Alfred, my son, is studying abroad and he's left several suits around that will do for you. Be neat. Let's see your feet. I don't believe you can wear his shoes but I'll buy you a pair and take it out of your wages. You mind me and I'll make something out of you."

"Yassuh, Mister Alf. Thankee. Youse real good tuh me. Mama said you wuz good."

"She was a well-built-up girl and a splendid hoe hand. I never could see why she married that darky and let him drag her around share-cropping. Those backwoods white folks over the creek make their living by swindling the niggers."

John didn't go to school the next day. He had truly been delighted at the prospect of attending school. It had kept him

glowing all day. But that night the young people got up a game of "Hide and Seek." It started a little late, about the time that the old heads were going to bed.

Bow-legged, pigeon-toed Minnie Turl was counting, "Ten, ten, double ten, forty-five, fifteen. All hid? All hid?"

From different directions, as the "hiders" sought cover, "No!"

> "Three li'l' hawses in duh stable,
> One jumped out and skint his nable.
> All hid? All hid?"

"No!" from farther away.

John ran down hill towards the spring where the bushes were thick. He paused at a clump. It looked like a good place. There was a stealthy small sound behind it and he ran on. Some one ran down the path behind him. A girl's hand caught his. It was Phrony, the womanish fourteen-year-old who lived in the third cabin from Pheemy's.

"Ah'll show yuh uh good place tuh hide," she whispered, "nobody can't find yuh."

She dragged him off the path to the right and round and about to a clump of sumac overrun with wild grape vines.

"Right under heah," she panted from running, "nobody can't find yuh."

"Whar you goin' hide yuhself?" John asked as he crept into the arboreal cave.

"Iss plenty room," Phrony whispered. "Us bofe kin hide in heah."

She crept in also and leaned heavily upon John, giggling and giggling as the counting went on.

> "Ah got up 'bout half-past fo'
> Forty fo' robbers wuz 'round mah do'
> Ah got up and let 'em in
> Hit 'em ovah de head with uh rollin' pin.
> All hid? All hid?"

"Yeah."

"All dem ten feet round mah base is caught. Ahm comin'!"

There were screams and shouts of laughter. "Dere's Gold-Dollar behind dat chany-berry tree. Ah got yuh."

"Whoo-ee! Ahm free, Minnie, Ah beat yuh in home."

"Less we run in whilst she gone de other way," John whispered.

"Naw, less we lay low 'til she git tired uh huntin' us and give us free base."

"Aw right, Phrony, but Ah loves tuh outrun 'em and beat 'em tuh de base. 'Tain't many folks kin run good ez me."

"Ah kin run good, too."

"Aw, 'tain't no girl chile kin run good ez me."

"Ah betcha 'tis. Lucy Potts kin outrun uh yearlin' and rope 'im."

"Humph! Where she at?"

"She live over in Pottstown. Her folks done bought de ole Cox place. She go to school. Dey's big niggers."

"She uh li'l' bitty gal wid black eyes and long hair plats?"

"Yeah, dat's her. She leben years ole, but she don't look it. Ahm fourteen. Ahm big. Maybe Ah'll git married nex' year."

"Ahm gwine race huh jes soon ez Ah gits tuh school. Mista Alf gwine lemme go too."

"Dat's good. Ah done been dere las' yeah. Ah got good learnin'. Reckon Ah'll git uh husban' nex'."

Cry from up the hill, "John and Phrony, come on in. You get free base!"

They scrambled out. John first, then Phrony more slowly, and trudged up the hill. A boy was kneeling at the woods chopping-block base when they came into the crowd. The crowd began to disperse again. John started off in another direction. He looked back and saw Phrony coming behind him, but Mehaley cut in from behind a bush and reached him first.

"Come on wid me, John, lemme show yuh uh good place." He started to say that he didn't want to hide out and talk as he had done with Phrony. He wanted to pit his strength and speed against the boy who was counting. He wanted to practise running, but he felt a flavor come out from Mehaley. He could almost sense it in his mouth and nostrils. He was cross with Phrony for following them. He let Mehaley take his hand and they fled away up the hill and hid in the hay.

"De hair on yo' head so soft lak," Mehaley breathed against his cheek. "Lemme smoothen it down."

When John and Mehaley came in, Minnie Turl was count-ing. Everybody was hid except Phrony who sat bunched up on the door step.

"Y'all better go hide agin," she said.

"Somebody else count and lemme hide," Minnie wailed. "Ah been countin' most all de time," she came and stood near John.

"G'wan hide, Minnie, Ah'll count some," John said.

"Heh! Heh!" Phrony laughed maliciously at Minnie. Min-nie looked all about her and went inside the house and to bed.

"Haley, where mah hair comb you borried from me las' Sunday? Ah wuz nice enough tuh len' it tuh yuh, but you ain't got manners 'nough tuh fetch it back." Phrony ad-vanced upon Mehaley and John.

"You kin git yo' ole stink hair comb any time. Ah'll be glad tuh git it outa mah house. Mama tole me not tuh comb wid it 'cause she skeered Ah'd git boogers in mah haid."

"Youse uh lie! Ah ain't got no boogers in mah haid, and if yo' mamy say so she's uh liar right long wid you! She ain't so bad ez she make out. Ah'll stand on yo' toes and tell yuh so."

"Git back outa mah face, Phrony. Ah don't play de doz-ens!" Mehaley shoved. Phrony struck, and John and all the hiders, who came running in at the sound of battle, had trouble stopping the rough and tumble.

"Did y'all had words befo' yuh fell out?" Charlie asked.

"We ain't had no words," said Mehaley.

"Whut y'all fightin' 'bout, if yuh ain't mad?"

"Aw, ole fish-mouf Phrony mad cause John wouldn't hide wid her and he took and hid wid me."

"Youse uh liar, madam! He did so hide wid me."

"He wouldn't stay, and Ah'll betcha Alabama wid uh fence 'round it he won't never hide wid yuh no mo'."

Mehaley preened herself akimbo and rotated her hips in-solently.

"Sh-sh—" Charlie cautioned, "de old heads liable tuh wake up, and dey'll haul off and take and frail everybody. Less all tip in tuh bed. Iss way after midnight anyhow."

So John overslept next morning and by the time that he had gathered the eggs and counted the hogs it was too late

for school. He didn't want to see Lucy anyway. Not the way he felt that day, but late in the afternoon as he wandered over the place, he found a tiny clearing hidden by trees.

"Dis is uh prayin' ground," he said to himself.

"O Lawd, heah 'tis once mo' and again yo' weak and humble servant is knee-bent and body bowed— Mah heart beneath mah knees and mah knees in some lonesome valley cryin' fuh mercy whilst mercy kinst be found. O Lawd! you know mah heart, and all de ranges uh mah deceitful mind— and if you find any sin lurkin' in and about mah heart please pluck it out and cast it intuh de sea uh fuhgitfullness whar it'll never rise tuh condemn me in de judgment."

That night John, deaf to Mehaley's blandishments, sat in the doorway and told tales. And Brer Rabbit and Brer Fox and Raw-Head-and-Bloody-Bones walked the earth like natural men.

Next morning, bright and soon he stood at the schoolhouse door. The teacher was a stodgy middle-aged man who prided himself on his frowns. Every few moments he lifted his head and glared about the room. He yearned to hold his switches in his hand. He had little ambition to impart knowledge. He reigned. Later John found out he was Lucy's uncle.

"Come heah, you," he pointed his ruler at John. "Don't you know no bettern to come in my school and sit yo'self down without sayin' a word to me?"

"Yassuh," he approached the deal table that went by the name of desk.

"If you know better, why did you do it? I ought to put forty lashes on yo' bare back. You come to school?"

"Yassuh."

"Don't say 'yassuh' to me. Say 'Yes suh.' "

The room tittered.

"What's yo' name?"

"John."

"John whut? You got some other name besides John."

"Mama, she name me Two-Eye John—"

They burst into loud laughter. John colored and he stole a glance at Lucy. She wasn't laughing. Her hands and lips were tense. She must be put out with him for being a fool. She wasn't laughing like the rest.

"But Mama and all of 'em at home calls me John Buddy."

"Buddy is a nick-name. What's yo' papa' name?"

John scratched his head and thought a minute.

"'Deed Ah don't know, suh."

There was another short silence.

"Where do you live?"

"On Mista Alf Pearson's place."

"Was you born there?"

"Yessuh."

"Well, Ah'll jus' put you down as John Pearson and you answer by that, you hear?"

"Yes suh."

"Ever been to school before?"

"Naw suh."

"Well, you get over there in de A B C class and don't let me ketch you talkin' in school."

John was amazed at the number of things to be learned. He liked to watch Lucy's class recite. They put so many figures on the board and called it long division. He would certainly be well learnt when he could do that. They parsed sentences. They spelt long words.

He studied hard because he caught Lucy watching him every time he recited. He wrote on the ground in the quarters and in a week he knew his alphabet and could count to a hundred.

"Whut you learnin' in school, John—A, B, Ab's?" Charlie asked him.

"Ah already know dat, Charlie. Ah kin spell 'baker' too."

"Don't b'lieve it. Not dis quick, yuh can't."

"B-a-k-bak-e-r-er baker."

"Boy, you sho is eatin' up dat school!"

"Ain't ez smart ez some. Take Lucy Potts for instink. She's almost uh 'fessor now. Nobody can't spell her down. Dey say she kin spell eve'y word in Lippincott's Blue-back Speller."

"Shucks! You ain't tryin' tuh buck up tuh her in book learnin', is yuh? Dey tell me she kin spell 'compresstibility,' and when yuh git dat fur 'tain't much mo' fuhther fur yuh tuh go."

"She sho kin spell it, 'cause Ah heered 'er do it. Some say she kin spell 'Constan-ti-nople' too."

"Ah b'lieve it. All dem Potts is smart. Her brother leads de choir at Macedony Baptis' Church, and she trebles right 'long wid dem grown women and kin sing all de notes—de square ones, de round ones, de triangles."

"Ah'll be dere tuh heah her do it nex' big meetin'. Charlie, Ah loves tuh heah singin'."

"Whyn't yuh join de choir? You oughter be able tuh sing lack git out wid all dat ches' you got."

"B'lieve Ah will, Charlie. Ah laks big meetin'."

It was three weeks from the time that John started to school 'til cotton-picking time. Prodded on all sides, he had learned to read a little and write a few words crudely.

He was sorry when school closed for the cotton-picking but he kept on studying. When the school re-opened for its final month he wanted to get promoted again. He found himself spelling out words on barns and wagons, almanacs, horse-medicine-bottles, wrapping-paper.

He had been to church; he hadn't enough courage to join the choir, but every meeting he was there. Lucy tossed her head and sang her treble and never missed a note.

When the cotton-picking began on his place, Alf Pearson said to John, "You better go across the Creek and let your mama know how you're getting along. If you see any good cotton pickers—anybody that can pick more than two hundred a day—tell 'em I need some hands, and you be back by tomorrow night. I bought a brood sow over round Chehaw and I want you to go get her."

There was great rejoicing in Amy's house when John climbed the hill from the Creek.

They didn't know him in his new clothes. They made great "'miration" over everything. Amy cried.

"Jes tuh think, mah boy gittin' book-learnt! Ned, de rest uh dese chillun got tuh go tuh school nex' yeah. Sho is."

"Whut fur? So dey kin lay in de peni'ten'ry? Dat's all dese book-learnt niggers do—fill up de jails and chain-gangs. Dese boys is comin' 'long all right. All dey need tuh learn is how tuh swing uh hoe and turn a furrer. Ah ain't rubbed de hair offa mah haid 'gin no college walls and Ah got good sense. Day ain't goin' tuh no school effen Ah got anythin' tuh say 'bout it. Jes' be turnin' 'em fools!"

Stormy weather. John cut in.

"Mama, Mista Alf say if Ah could find some good cotton-pickers tuh tell 'em he need hands. You know any? He payin' fifty cent uh hund'ed."

"Dat's more'n dey payin' over heah," Ned cut in eagerly, "Amy, whyn't you take Zeke and Zack and y'all g'wan make dat li'l' change? Ah'll take keer de li'l' chillun and pick up whut li'l' Ah kin git over heah. Cotton open dat side de Creek fust anyhow. By time y'all finish over dere hit'll jis' be gittin' in full swing over heah."

"Reckon us could make li'l' money. Tell 'im, 'Yeah,' John Buddy, we's comin'."

"Zack!" Ned called, "Take dis heah jug and run over tuh de Turk place and tell Ike tuh send me uh gallon. Pay 'im nex' week some time."

When the cotton was all picked and the last load hauled to the gin, Alf Pearson gave the hands two hogs to barbecue.

That was a night. Hogs roasting over the open pit of oak coals. Negroes from three other plantations. Some brought "likker." Some crocus sacks of yellow yam potatoes, and bushels of peanuts to roast, and the biggest syrup-kettle at Pearson's cane-mill was full of chicken perleau. Twenty hens and six water-buckets full of rice. Old Purlee Kimball was stirring it with a shovel.

Plenty of music and plenty of people to enjoy it. Three sets had been danced when Bully took the center of the hard-packed clay court upon which they were dancing. He had the whole rib of a two-hundred-pound hog in his hands and gnawed it as he talked.

"Hey, everybody! Stop de music. Don't vip another vop 'til Ah says so. Hog head, hog bosom, hog hips and every kind of hog there ever wuz is ready! Come git yourn. De chickens is cacklin' in de rice and dey say 'Come git it whilst iss fitten 'cause t'morrer it may be frost-bitten!' De yaller yams is spilin' in de ashes. It's uh shame! Eat it all up, and den we's gointer dance, 'cause we'll have somethin' tuh dance offa."

The hogs, the chickens, the yams disappeared. The old folks played "Ole Horse" with the parched peanuts. The musicians drank and tuned up. Bully was calling figures.

"Hey you, dere, us ain't no white folks! Put down dat

fiddle! Us don't want no fiddles, neither no guitars, neither no banjoes. Less clap!"

So they danced. They called for the instrument that they had brought to America in their skins—the drum—and they played upon it. With their hands they played upon the little dance drums of Africa. The drums of kid-skin. With their feet they stomped it, and the voice of Kata-Kumba, the great drum, lifted itself within them and they heard it. The great drum that is made by priests and sits in majesty in the juju house. The drum with the man skin that is dressed with human blood, that is beaten with a human shin-bone and speaks to gods as a man and to men as a God. Then they beat upon the drum and danced. It was said, "He will serve us better if we bring him from Africa naked and thingless." So the bukra reasoned. They tore away his clothes that Cuffy might bring nothing away, but Cuffy seized his drum and hid it in his skin under the skull bones. The shin-bones he bore openly, for he thought, "Who shall rob me of shin-bones when they see no drum?" So he laughed with cunning and said, "I, who am borne away to become an orphan, carry my parents with me. For *Rhythm* is she not my mother and Drama is her man?" So he groaned aloud in the ships and hid his drum and laughed.

"Dis is jes' lak when Ah wuz uh girl," Amy told Pheemy and offered her body to the voice.

Furious music of the little drum whose body was still in Africa, but whose soul sung around a fire in Alabama. Flourish. Break.

> Ole cow died in Tennessee
> Send her jawbone back to me
> Jawbone walk, Jawbone talk
> Jawbone eat wid uh knife and fork.
> Ain't Ah right?
>
> CHORUS: Yeah!
> Ain't I right? Yeah!

Hollow-hand clapping for the bass notes. Heel and toe stomping for the little one. Ibo tune corrupted with Nango. Congo gods talking in Alabama.

If you want to see me jabber
Set me down to uh bowl uh clabber
Ain't Ah right? Yeah!
Now, ain't Ah right? Yeah!

Ole Ant Dinah behind de pine
One eye out and de other one blind
Ain't Ah right? Yeah! Yeah!
Now, ain't Ah right? Yeah!

"Looka dat boy uh yourn, Amy!" Zeke Turk urged. "Didn't thought he knowed how tuh dance. He's rushin' de frog tuh de frolic! And looka 'Big 'Oman,' dat gal dancin' wid 'im. Lawd, she shakin' yonder skirt."

Wisht Ah had uh needle
Fine ez Ah could sew
Ah'd sew mah baby to my side
And down de road Ah'd go.

Double clapping—

Down de road baby
Down de road baby
It's killing mama
Oh, it's killing mama.

Too hot for words. Fiery drum clapping.

"Less burn dat ole moon down to a nub! Is dat you, Pheemy?"

"Yeah Lawd. Mah head is tilted to de grave, but Ah'll show y'all Ah ain't fuhgit how. Come on out heah, Dink, and help ole Pheemy do de Parse me lah."

"Heel and toe. Don't call no figgers."

"Aw yeah, less call figgers. Go 'head Bully, but don't call it lak you call for white folks and dey go praipsin' 'cross the floor lak dey steppin on eggs. Us kin dance. Call 'em, Bully."

"Awright, choose yo' partners."

"Couples tuh yo' places lak hawse tuh de traces."

"Sixteen hands up!"

"Circle four."

"Y'all ain't clappin' right. Git dat time.

> Raccoon up de 'simmon tree
> Possum on de ground
> Raccoon shake dem 'simmons down
> Possum pass 'em round."

The fire died. The moon died. The shores of Africa receded. They went to sleep and woke up next day and looked out on dead and dying cotton stalks and ripening possum persimmons.

As the final day of school closing drew near, John found life tremendously exciting. The drama of Pearson's plantation yielded to the tenseness around the school house. He had learned to spell his way thru several pages in his reader. He could add, subtract and divide and multiply. He proved his new power to communicate his thoughts by scratching Lucy's name in the clay wherever he found a convenient spot: with a sharp stick he had even scratched it on the back of Pheemy's chimney.

He saw Lucy at school every day. He saw her in church, and she was always in his consciousness, but he had never talked with her alone. When the opportunity presented itself he couldn't find words. Handling Big 'Oman, Lacey, Semmie, Bootsie and Mehaley merely called for action, but with Lucy he needed words and words that he did not have. One day during the practice for school closing he crowded near her and said, "Wisht Ah could speak pieces lak you do."

"You kin speak 'em better'n me," Lucy said evenly, "you got uh good voice for speakin'."

"But Ah can't learn no long ones lak you speaks. When do you learn 'em?"

"In de night time round home after Ah git thru wid mah lessons."

"You ain't got many mo' days tuh be studyin' of nights. Den whut you gwine do wid yo'self?"

"Mama always kin find plenty fuh folks tuh do."

"But Ah mean in de night time, Lucy. When youse thru wid yo' work. Don't you do nothin' but warm uh chair bottom?"

Lucy drew away quickly, "Oooh, John Buddy! You talkin' nasty."

John in turn was in confusion. "Whuss nasty?"

"You didn't hafta say 'bottom.'"

John shriveled up inside. He had intended to recite the rhymes to Lucy that the girls on the plantation thought so witty, but he realized that—

> Some love collards, some love kale
> But I loves uh gal wid uh short skirt tail.

would drive Lucy from him in disgust. He could never tell her that. He felt hopeless about her. Soon she was recalled to the platform to recite and John's chance was gone. He kept on thinking, however, and he kept on making imaginary speeches to her. Speeches full of big words that would make her gasp and do him "reverence." He was glad when he was selected as the soldier to sing opposite Lucy in the duet, "Oh Soldier, Will You Marry Me?" It meant something more than singing with gestures beside a girl. Maybe she would realize that he could learn things too, even if she could read the better. He meant to change all that as quickly as possible. One day he shyly overtook her on her way home.

"Dey tell me you kin run fast," he began awkwardly.

"Dey tole you right," Lucy answered saucily, "whoever tole you. Ah kin outrun most anybody 'round heah."

"Less we race tuh dat sweet-gum tree and see who kin beat," John challenged.

They were off. Lucy's thin little legs pumping up and down. The starchy strings of her blue sunbonnet fluttering under her chin, and her bonnet lying back of her neck.

"Ah beat yuh!" John gloated over the foot or two that he had gained with difficulty.

"Yeah, you beat me, but look how much mo' legs you got to run wid," Lucy retorted. "Bet if Ah had dem legs nobody couldn't never outrun me."

"Ah didn't mean tuh beat yuh. Gee, us done come uh good ways! How much further you live from heah, Lucy?"

"Oh uh little ways cross de branch."

"B'lieve Ah'll go see how yo' ole branch look. Maybe it got uh heap uh fish in it."

" 'Tain't got no fish in it worth talkin' 'bout. 'Tain't hardly knee deep, John, but iss uh great big ole snake down dere."

"Whut kinda snake?"

"Uh great big ole cotton-mouf moccasin. He skeers me, John. Everytime Ah go 'cross dat foot-log Ah think maybe Ah might fall in and den he'll bite me, or he might reah hisself up and bite me anyhow."

"How come y'all don't take and kill 'im?"

"Who you reckon goin' down in de water tuh strain wid uh moccasin? He got uh hole back under the bank where you kin see 'im, but you can't git 'im 'thout you wuz down in de branch. He lay all 'round dere on de ground and even on de foot-log, but when he see somebody comin' he go in his hole, all ready for yuh and lay dere and dare yuh tuh bother 'im."

"You jes show 'im tuh me. Ah can't stand tuh be aggravated by no ole snake and then agin Ah don't want 'im slurrin' *you*."

"Sh-sh, watch out, John! He 'round heah somewhere. Can't you smell 'im? Dere he is goin' in his hole!"

John took a good look at the snake, then looked all about him for a weapon. Finding none he sat down and began to remove his shoes.

"You ain't goin' in dat branch!" Lucy gasped.

"Turn me go, Lucy. If you didn't want yo' ole snake kilt yuh oughta not showed 'im tuh me." He exulted, but pretended not to see her concern was for him.

He looked carefully to see that no other snakes were about, then stepped cautiously down into the water. The snake went on guard, slowly, insolently. Lucy was terrified. Suddenly, he snatched the foot-log from its place and, leaning far back to give it purchase, he rammed it home upon the big snake and held it there. The snake bit at the log again and again in its agony, but finally the biting and the thrashing ceased. John fished the snake out and stretched it upon the grass.

"Ooh, John, Ahm sho glad you kilt dat ole devil. He been right dere skeerin' folks since befo' Ah wuz borned."

"He won't skeer nobody else, lessen dey skeered uh dead snakes," John answered in the tone that boys use to girls on such occasions.

"Reckon his mate ain't gonna follow us and try tuh bite us for killin' dis one?"

"Lucy, he can't foller bofe us, lessen us go de same way."

"Thass right, John. Ah done forgot, you live over on de Alf Pearson place."

"Yeah, dat's right."

"Where M'haley and Big 'Oman live."

"Unh hunh, Ah speck dey do live dere. Ah seen uh lot uh pullet-size girl chillun 'bout de place. Nearly uh hund'ed head uh folks on dat plantation."

A heavy silence fell. Lucy looked across the shallow stream and said,

"You ain't put de foot-log back, John."

"Dat's right. Sho nuff Ah done fuhgot. Lemme tote you 'cross den. Ah kin place it back for de other folks."

"Doncha lemme fall, John. Maybe 'nother ole snake down dere."

"How Ahm gonna let uh li'l' bit lak you fall? Ah kin tote uh sack uh feed-meal and dat's twice big ez you. Lemme tote yuh. Ah 'clare Ah won't drop yuh."

John bore Lucy across the tiny stream and set her down slowly.

"Oh you done left yo' book-sack, Lucy. Got tuh take yuh back tuh git it."

"Naw, you hand it tuh me, John."

"Aw, naw, you come git it."

He carried Lucy back and she recrossed the stream the third time. As he set her down on her home side he said, "Little ez *you* is nobody wouldn't keer how fur he hafta tote you. You ain't even uh handful."

Lucy put herself akimbo, "Ahm uh li'l' piece uh leather, but well put t'gether, Ah thankee, Mist' John."

"Mah comperments, Miss Lucy."

Lucy was gone up the hill in a blue whirlwind. John replaced the foot-log and cut across lots for home.

"She is full uh pepper," John laughed to himself, "but ah laks dat. Anything 'thout no seasonin' in it ain't no good."

At home, Lucy rushed out back of the corn crib and tip-

toed to see if her head yet touched the mark she had made three weeks before.

"Ah shucks!" She raged, "Ah ain't growed none hardly. Ah ain't never gointer get grown. Ole M'haley way head uh me!"

She hid and cried until Emmeline, her mama, called her to set the table for supper.

The night of school closing came. John in tight new shoes and with a standing collar was on hand early. Saw Lucy enter followed by the Potts clan. Frowning mama, placid papa, strapping big sister, and the six grown brothers. Boys with "rear-back" hair held down by a thick coating of soap. Boys hobbling in new shoes and tight breeches. Girls whose hair smelled of fresh hog-lard and sweet william, and white dresses with lace, with pink or blue sashes, with ruffles, with mothers searching their bosoms for pins to yank up hanging petticoats. Tearful girls who had forgotten their speeches. Little girls with be-ribboned frizzed-out hair who got spanked for wetting their starchy panties. Proud parents. Sulky parents and offspring. Whispered envy.

"Dere's Lucy Potts over dere in uh fluted dress. Dey allus gives her de longest piece tuh speak."

"Dat's 'cause she kin learn more'n anybody else."

"Naw 'tain't, dey muches her up. Mah Semmie could learn je' ez long uh piece ez anybody if de give it tuh her—in time. Ahm gwine take mah chillun outa school after dis and put 'em tuh work. Dey ain't learnin' 'em nothin' nohow. Dey makes cake outa some uh de chillun and cawn bread outa de rest."

Opening prayer. Song. Speech by white superintendent. Speeches rattled off like beans poured into a tin can.

"A speech by Miss Lucy Potts."

The shining big eyes in the tiny face. Lacy whiteness. Fierce hand-clapping. Lucy calm and self-assured.

"A chieftain to the highland bound, cried 'Boatman do not tarry' "—to the final. "My daughter, oh my daughter." More applause. The idol had not failed her public.

"She kin speak de longest pieces and never miss uh word and say 'em faster dan anybody Ah ever seed." It was agreed Lucy was perfect. Time and speeches flew fast.

Little fishes in de brook
Willie ketch 'em wid uh hook
Mama fry 'em in de pan
Papa eat 'em lak uh man.

"Duet—Miss Lucy Potts, bassed by Mr. John Pearson." They sang and their hearers applauded wildly. Nobody cared whether the treble was treble or the bass was bass. It was the gestures that counted and everybody agreed that John was perfect as the philandering soldier of the piece and that Lucy was just right as the over-eager maid. They had to sing it over twice. John began to have a place of his own in the minds of folks, more than he realized.

Chapter III

ONE MORNING in the early spring John found Amy sitting before the fire in Pheemy's house.

"Howdy, mam."

"Howdy, son."

She rubbed her teeth and gums with the tiny snuff-brush. She had something to say and John knew it.

"How's everybody makin' it over de Big Creek, maw?"

"Right middlin', John. Us could do better but yo' pappy always piddlin' from piller tuh post and dat keep de rest uh us in hot water."

"Yessum. Whut's de trouble now?"

"Yuh know Beasley took and beat us out uh our cotton and we ain't hardly had nothin' tuh eat, so day 'fo' yistiddy Ned took and kilt one uh Beasley's yearlings way down dere in de hammock and fetched it home dere and us cooked and et some of it and put some of it down in salt. We thinkin' nobody'd ever know de diffunce, but Beasley heard de cows bellerin' when dey smelt de blood where it wuz kilt and went down dere and found de hide. So us had tuh pack up our things in meal sacks and when it wuz black dark us went on over tuh de Shelby place, and us goin' work dere dis year."

"Dat's uh whole heap better'n Beasley's place, but 'tain't nigh good ez heah. Wisht y'all would come work fuh Mist' Alf."

"Ned, he too hard-headed tuh do dat. Ah done tried and tried but his back don't bend. De only difference 'tween him and uh mule is, de mule got four good foots, and he ain't got nairn. De minute anybody mention crossin' dat creek, he's good tuh make disturbiment and tear up peace. He been over dat creek all his life jes' ez barefooted ez uh yard dawg and know he ain't even got uh rooster tuh crow fuh day, yet and still you can't git 'im 'way from dere."

"How come you don't quit 'im? Come on, and fetch de chillun wid you!"

"You can't know intuh dat yit, John. In times and seasons,

us gwine talk dat, but Ah come tuh take you back wid me, John."

"Me, mama?" John asked in agonized surprise, "you know Ah don't want no parts of over dat Creek."

"Mama know, son, but Mist' Shelby asted where wuz you de fust thing and say he don't want us 'thout you."

"Mama, Ah don't wanta go 'way back over dere in dem woods. All you kin hear 'bout over dere is work, push-hard and pone-bread, ole cawn bread wid nothin' in it but salt and water! Ah laks it over here where dey talks about biscuit-bread some time."

"Yeah, John Buddy, mama know jes' how yuh feels and her heart is beatin' right wid yourn. Mama love flour bread too. But, you know, lots uh white folks ain't gwine be bothered wid Ned, and us got tuh find some place tuh lay our heads. Mist' Shelby ain't uh mean man, but he don't b'lieve us kin make de crop 'thout you. Reckon you better git yo' things and come 'long."

Amy got up wearily, the ruffles of her faded calico skirt sweeping the floor as she moved.

"Ahm goin' and see Marse Alf 'bout takin' yuh. Be ready ginst Ah git back, John Buddy."

John watched her out of the door, then slowly he went out himself and wandered about; but finally he was standing back of Pheemy's cabin and gazing at the rude scratching on the adobe chimney. "Lucy," "Lucy Ann," "Lucy Potts," "Lucy and John," "Lucy is John's girl," "No 'nife can cut our love into," "Lucy Pearson."

"Oh," John sobbed, "she ain't gonna want no over-de-creek-nigger."

He stood there a long time before he went inside and began to collect his things. Then he came upon the song book that Lucy's terrifying brother had given him when he joined the choir. There was a crude drawing of a railroad train on it. No, he couldn't leave Notasulga where the train came puffing into the depot twice a day. No, no! He dropped everything and tore out across the fields and came out at last at the railroad cut just below the station. He sat down upon the embankment and waited. Soon in the distance he heard the whistle, "Wahooom! Wahup, wahup!" And around the bend

came first the smoke stack, belching smoke and flames of fire. The drivers turning over chanting "Opelika-black-and-dirty! Opelika-black-and-dirty." Then as she pulled into the station, the powerful whisper of steam. Starting off again, "Wolf coming! Wolf coming! Wolf coming! Opelika-black-and-dirty, Opelika-black-and-dirty! Auh—wah-hoooon"—into the great away that gave John's feet such a yearning for distance.

The train had been gone a long time when Alf Pearson's buggy pulled up beside John.

"What are you doing down here, John, with Amy looking all over Macon County for you?"

"Jes' come down tuh hear whut de train say one mo' time, Mist' Alf."

"Get in and drive me down to get the mail, John. How's the hogs getting on?"

"Jes' fine, Mist' Alf. S'pectin' two mo' litters dis week. Dat make five litters since New Year's. Ain't lost one since Chris'mas, neither."

"Splendid, John, splendid."

"Mist' Alf, Ah don't treasure 'cross dat creek. Lemme stay heah wid you, please suh."

"John, I'm not sending you over there. Your mother is taking you. If you're ever in need of a job, come on back here and behave yourself and I'll look after you. No matter where you are, don't steal and don't get too biggety and you'll get along. Touch the horses up a little. I'm in a hurry."

Chapter IV

THERE was work a plenty on the Shelby place. John and Ned were plowing the rocky hillsides. As they turned the furrows John always strode several feet in advance of Ned. The older man limped behind his plow, stumbling now and then, slashing the mule and swearing incessantly.

"Gawd uhmighty! Git up heah, you hard-tailed bastard! Confound yuh, gee! John Buddy, whar you gwine?"

"Ahm goin'tuh git me uh sweat-rag tuh wipe mah face wid. Ahm tired uh sweat runnin' intuh mah eyes."

"You jes' tries tuh keep from workin', John. Out nearly all night proagin' over de Creek and now yuh don't wanta do nothin'."

"Ah done plowed uh acre and uh half tuh yo' one, and nowhere you put yo' foot down but whut 'tain't uh rock dere. Nobody can't make nothin' on dis place—look lak God jus' stood up and throwed uh handful uh rocks. If dis ain't work, 'tain' uh hound dawg in Georgy."

"Jes' you stay from over dat Creek, runnin' after all dem gals and git yo' night rest, dem rocks wouldn't be so worrysome."

"Ah do mo' of it than you right now. Dis ain't no slavery time," John flung back over his shoulder as he started towards the house.

"Yuh done got powerful biggity since yuh been on dat Pearson place," Ned muttered to himself, "Can't say uh word, 'thout he got tuh gimme two fuh one."

Amy stood trembling between her son and her husband. The other children were growing up and imitating everything that John did, as closely as possible. Zack and Zeke were already trying on John's hats and ties. Their whole talk was "over de Creek," and "man when us git on dat ole train." Amy had managed to keep things on an even keel by soothing John's feelings and reminding Ned that if John went over to Notasulga to choir practice and meeting, that he was now seventeen and ought to have a little freedom. So it had gone, and now the cotton was knee-high. The crops more than half

made. She breathed a little easier. She was at the house putting on a pot of collard greens when John came in for the sweat-rag.

"Mama, better tell Ned tuh leave me be. Tell 'im tuh stop his bulldozia. Ah done heered 'im lyin' tuh Mist' Shelby makin' out Ah don't do nothin'—hard ez Ah works."

"He be's drunk when he keer on lak dat and his likker tell 'im tuh talk. Don't pay 'im no mind."

"But, mama, ev'ry time Ah go cross de Creek he look lak he go crazy and git tuh blasphemin' 'bout no 'count gals. Ah don't keer if he do be peepin' through his likkers he got tuh quit dat. Sho ez gun's iron, he got tuh quit dat. He don't know nothin' 'bout—'bout no gal Ah keeps comp'ny wid."

"Heah de rag yuh wanted, John. Go 'long back tuh work and Ah'll give Ned uh straightenin'. Dat is if he kin stand uh straightenin'."

Ned was sullen when John returned but he said nothing. He took part of his humor out on the mule and held the other inside him. He said to himself as he stumbled along behind his plow, "Damn biggity rascal! Wisht Ah had 'im tied down so he couldn't move! I'd put uh hund'ed lashes on his bare back. He know he got de advantage uh me. He don't even know his pappy and he ought tuh be proud Ah took and married his ma and made somethin' out of 'im. He ought to be humble, but he ain't, and plenty folks right now on account uh his yaller skin will put 'im above me. Wisht Ah knowed somethin' that would crumple his feathers! But he sho' is makin' dis crop, though. Ah oughter clear more'n uh hund'ed dollars. Effen Ah do, Ahm gwine buy me uh hawse and buggy, and ain't gwine 'low nobody tuh hitch it up but me."

That evening the things unsaid laid a steamy blanket over talk. John made the long journey over the creek and Ned fumed.

"Whyn't you tell John whut yuh got tuh say, Ned?" Amy slapped back, "You *been* tellin' 'im."

"'Cause Ah don't want tuh hafta kill 'im, dat's how come. He must smell hisself—done got so mannish. Some fast 'omanish gal is grinnin' in his face and he tries tuh git sides hisself."

Amy smoked her pipe and went on to bed. The children too. Zeke and Zack were in the woods trying out a new coon dog and came in after moon-up. John came home later.

When Amy brought dinner to the field next day John took his bucket and went off alone to eat. With a huge hickory tree between him and the others, he pulled out the three cornered note and read again and again.

> Sweet Notasulga, Chocklit Alabama
> Date of kisses, month of love
> Dere John, you is my honey. I won't
> never love nobody else but you.
> I love choir practise now. Sugar
> is sweet, and lard is greasy, you
> love me, don't be uneasy.
> > Your darling,
> > LUCY ANN POTTS

Ned called several times before John heard him.

"John Buddy! You John! Come heah and take holt uh dese plow lines."

"Yes suh," John said at last.

"Don't set dere and answer me. When Ah speak, you move!"

"Ah, Ahm comin', but Ah ain't goin' tuh run fuh nobody."

"Looka heah, John, Ahm sick uh yo' sass. Ah got it in me tuh tell yuh and if Ah don't tell yuh, Ah'll purge when Ah die. Youse uh good fuh nothin' trashy yaller rascal—ain't fit tuh tote guts tuh uh bear." A sudden frenzy took Ned, "Anyhow, Ah done made up mah mind tuh beat you nelly tuh death. You jes' spilin' fuh uh good killin'! Drop dem britches below yo' hocks, and git down on yo' knees. Ah means tuh straighten you out dis day."

As he said this, Ned snatched off the trace-chain from the plow and turned upon John who was still twenty feet or more from his step-father. When Ned whirled about with the doubled trace-chain in his right fist he found not a cowering bulk of a boy but a defiant man, feet spread wide, a large rock drawn back to hurl.

"Don't you vary! Dog damn yuh!" John challenged. "Come uhnother step and Ah'll bust yuh wide open, wid dis

rock. You kin cuff and kick Zeke and them around but Ah done promised Gawd and uh couple uh other men tuh stomp yo' guts out nex' time you raise yo' hand tuh me."

For a throbbing space the two stood face to face. Ned turned and hobbled off.

"Stand dere! Jes' you stand dere till Ah go git mah double-barrel britch-loader and Ahm gointer blow yo' brains out!"

Ned limped off towards the house. John held his pose until the older man dipped below the first rise. Then he let fall his arm, and walked back towards the hickory tree.

"Ahm gointer git behind dis tree and if dat ugly-rump nigger come back here wid dat gun, Ahm gointer bust 'im wide open wid uh rock 'fore he know whut hit 'im. Humph! Ah don't b'lieve he gone at no brich-loader nohow. He gone 'cause he got skeered Ah wuz goin' take dat trace-chain 'way from 'im and lay it 'cross his own back."

John waited a long time. Ned could have gone twice the distance and returned with a gun. If he could have looked over the hill he would have seen Ned "proaging" off to the Turk place to get a gallon of red-eye-for-courage. Finally John came out from behind the hickory tree and loosed the mules from the plows and looped up the plow lines on the hames.

"Shucks! Ahm goin' 'way from heah." It came to John like a revelation. Distance was escape. He stopped before the burnt-off trunk of a tree that stood eight or ten feet high and threw the character of Ned Crittenden upon it.

"And you, you ole battle-hammed, slew-foot, box-ankled nubbin, you! You ain't nothin' and ain't got nothin' but whut God give uh billy-goat, and then round tryin' tuh hell-hack folks! Tryin' tuh kill somebody wid talk, but if you wants tuh fight,—dat's de very corn Ah wants tuh grind. You come grab me now and Ah bet yuh Ah'll stop *you* from suckin' eggs. Hit me now! G'wan hit me! Bet Ah'll break uh egg in yuh! Youse all parts of uh pig! You done got me jus' ez hot ez July jam, and Ah ain't got no mo' use fuh yuh than Ah is for mah baby shirt. Youse mah race but you sho ain't mah taste. Jus' you break uh breath wid me, and Ahm goin' tuh be jus' too chastisin'.

"Ahm jus' lak uh old shoe—soft when yuh rain on me and cool me off, and hard when yuh shine on me and git me hot.

Tuh keep from killin' uh sorry somethin' like yuh, Ahm goin' way from heah. Ahm goin' tuh Zar, and dat's on de other side of far, and when you see me agin Ahm gointer be some-body. Mah li'l' finger will be bigger than yo' waist. Don't you part yo' lips tuh me no mo' jes' ez long ez heben is happy—do Ah'll put somethin' on yuh dat lye soap won't take off. You ain't nothin' but uh big ole pan of fell bread. Now dat's de word wid de bark on it."

John stepped back a few paces, balanced his rock, hurled it against the stump with all his might and started across the field to the creek.

The involuntary beauty of sunset found him once again upon the plantation of his birth exulting among the herd, and finding Pheemy's cabin good to be in.

Chapter V

"HELLO, John."

"Hello, Bully."

"Whut you doin' back over here?"

"Come tuh git me uh job uh work again. Whuss de news?"

"Oh de white folks is still in de lead. Seen Mist' Alf yit?"

"Naw, goin' up tuh de big house now."

"Soon's yuh git back tuh de quarters Ah got uh bug tuh put in yo' ear."

"Awright, be back tuhreckly."

There were more used suits in Alf Pearson's clothes closet and John received them.

"My son, Mister Alfred's, clothes don't fit you now as well as they did last year, John. Too tight. Reckon I'll have to give you mine from now on. By the way, John, I've lost two hogs since you've been gone. Get back on your same job. Can you read and write fairly well now, John?"

"Yes suh."

"That's fine. I want you to take this note book and keep up with the groceries and fertilizer and feed that the folks in the quarters draw. It's hard for me to do it with running the bank and watching slick politicians. I had thought my son would have been home by now to help me, but it seems to take quite a long time to finish studying in Paris."

"Yes suh."

"You just take everybody's name on a separate page and put down everything they get the moment you hand it to 'em."

"Yes suh."

"And John, if you've been fooling around Duke's wife, leave her alone. He's been up here to me about it. Don't start no fight about it. There's plenty single girls around here."

"Ah ain't studyin' 'bout his Exie, Mist' Alf. He better talk tuh *her*. She de one come pullin' on me."

Alf Pearson laughed heartily and gave John a playful shove.

"Get along you rascal you! You're a walking orgasm. A living exultation."

"Whut's dat, Mist' Alf?"

"Oh never mind about that. Keep up with the pigs."

That night M'haley and Big 'Oman and Bootsie got up a game of "Hide and Seek" but John counted and let the other boys hide. The game ended fairly early. John had been around behind the house to look at his writing and the chimney and found it all defaced, so he didn't want to play. When the game was over he called Bully aside.

"Bully, Ah wrote some writin' on de back uh An' Pheemy's chimbley."

"Yeah, Ah know you did. Fack is, ev'rybody know yuh did, and dat's de very crow Ah wants tuh pick wid yuh."

"Is you heard who took and scratched it, and put smut out de chimbley all over it and mommucked it all up?"

"You ain't mad, is yuh?"

"Yeah, Ahm mad. Ahm jes' ez hot ez Tucker when de mule kicked his mammy, and any man dat tell me tuh mah face dat he done it he got tuh smell mah fist. You know who done it, Bully?"

"Don't yuh say Ah tole yuh and when you go tuh git atter her, don't you call my name, but M'haley took and done dat when she heered you wuz singin' in de choir. Some of 'em say you jes' done it so you could git a chance tuh see Lucy Potts."

"Whut M'haley got tuh do wid dat? Ah feel lak Ah could take and lam her wid lightnin'."

"Why doncher do it, John? If 'twas me felt bad lak you do, Ah'd beat her jes' ez long ez she last. Anyhow she takin' de under currents on you."

"Naw, Ah don't choose beatin' lady people. Uh man is crazy tuh do dat—when he know he got tuh submit hisself tuh 'em. Ahm gittin' sleepy. B'lieve Ah'll turn in."

Bully went away whistling, and John made to go inside to bed.

"John!" in a soft whisper from around the corner of the house. "Come heah, John."

John stepped to the corner, "Who dat callin' me?"

"Aw, you come see," the voice retreated into the shoulder-high cotton. John followed.

"Whut you want wid me, M'haley?"

"Look lak you ain't glad youse back."

"Yes Ah is, M'haley, but 'tain't lak de fust night Ah come. Ah reckon all de new done wore off de plantation."

"'Tain't de plantation. Dat's jes' de same. Ah reckon you jes' ain't got time tuh strain wid us quarters niggers now. You sings on de choir at Macedony."

"Whut's singin' notes got tuh do wid it? It jus' 'tain't new no mo'."

"Naw, you jes' stuck on dat li'l' ole Lucy Ann, and she ain't nothin' but uh baby. She ain't but leben years ole."

"She twelve now, goin' on thirteen. She had her birth night de day befo' mines. Her'n on December 31, and mine's January 1. Ain't dat funny?"

"Ahm fifteen, so goody, goody, goody."

John said nothing. After a while M'haley said, "John, Ah thought once me and you wuz gointer make uh wed." He stood stolid and silent.

In the silence she threw her arms about John's passive neck and swung herself off the ground, then lay still against him.

"John."

"Hunh."

"Feel mah heart. Put yo' hand right heah. Ain't it beatin' hard? Dat's 'cause Ahm so glad youse back. Feel it agin. My heart is rearin' and pitchin' fur you lak uh mule in uh tin stable. John, Ah loves you, Ah swear Ah does. You so pretty and you ain't color-struck lak uh whole heap uh bright-skin people. John?"

"Hunh."

"John, hug me till mah dress fit tight."

The next day John whitewashed Pheemy's chimney, and wrote Lucy's name in huge letters across it, and on Sunday he was at church far ahead of anybody else, with a three-cornered note in his hymn-book.

"Hope ole big-mouf M'haley don't come pukin' her guts 'round heah," he thought aloud. This was another day and another place. Pearson's quarters and M'haley had no business here. His eye wandered out of the window and down the dusty road. A bunch of girls approached in starchy elegance. "Lawd, dat look lak M'haley now—comin' heah tuh bull-doze and dominize."

John fell to his knees and prayed for cleansing. He prayed

aloud and the empty house threw back his resonant tones like a guitar box.

"Dat sho sound good," John exulted. "If mah voice sound *dat* good de first time Ah ever prayed in de church house, it sho won't be de las'." He arose from his knees and before the drove of girls had reached the steps John had forgotten all about his sins and fears, but he retreated to the choir-stand out of M'haley's reach.

As soon as Lucy took her seat before him he leaned forward and thrust his hymn-book into her hand. She coyly dropped hers, and he picked it up and pretended to search for a song. Lucy slyly did the same and read:

> Dere Lucy:
>> Whin you pass a mule tied to a tree,
>> Ring his tail and think of me.
>>> Your sugger-lump.
>>> JOHN

John read:

>> Long as the vine grow 'round the stump
>> You are my dolling sugar lump.
> Mama whipped me last night, because Bud told her we was talking to each other.
>>> Your sweet heart,
>>> LUCY ANN

John was so sweetly distracted by this note that he was blind and deaf to his surroundings. Bud Potts had rapped loudly and importantly and had gestured with his hands as if he were pushing a wash-basket of clothes up on a high shelf for the choir to rise. Everyone was standing but John. He never noticed this until Oral Johnson nudged him.

"Get yo' pitch!" Bud ordered as if he were giving the order to fire on Fort Sumter.

"Basses—duh-h-h-h. Y'all got it? Altos—fah-h-h—Trebles —me-e-e-e—. Pay 'tention dere, Lucy!"

Satisfied in the matter of the pitch, Bud took a full breath and broke out thru his nose—"Duh, duh, duh, duh! Dole la fee so lah so fee." The altos were right behind the basses and

fighting in haughty jerks for sound supremacy—"fah! fah! me! sol! fah-so-la-so-lah-so-fah!" The trebles pitched out in full, Ory behind the pack and keened furiously to make up for lost time, "—me, me, ray, do! Me-fah-lah-so-lah-so-fah! Oh me, me, me,—"

It was a hard race and hotly contended at the top of the lungs all the way. The trebles won because while altos, basses and even other trebles forgot their notes in confusion and fell by the wayside, Lucy never missed a note. Bud growled away in the bass but Lucy treed him and held him growling in discomfiture out upon a limb until the end of the piece cut him down.

John beat the bass notes by a vigorous side-to-side motion of his head and everybody in the audience thought they heard him singing them.

The preacher arose.

"Ah takes mah tex' and Ah takes mah time." He pursed up his wrinkled black face and glared all over the church. No one accepting the challenge he went on—"Ah takes mah tex' 'tween de lids uh de Bible," and slammed it shut. Another challenging glare about the room. Same results. "Don't you take and meddle wid *whar* Ah takes mah tex'. Long ez Ah gives yuh de word uh Gawd, 'tain't none uh yo' business whar Ah gits it from."

For two hours his voice beat about the ears of the people and the "Amen's" rocked and rolled back to the pulpit.

John heard little of it. He studied the back of Lucy's head and shoulders and the way the white rice buttons ran down her back and found plenty to entertain him the whole while.

When the cotton had been picked and ginned, Alf had John to pick out the hogs for the barbecue. The same elaborate preparations as usual. Same high laughter, but John sat passively in a doorway with Zeke who was getting tall and emitting ram odors.

"Less we dance, John Buddy. Ah wants tuh swing one dem gals."

John laughed scornfully, "Whut you know 'bout swingin' gals? You don't eben know how tuh dance."

"Dat's much ez *you* know. Ah done been tuh four, five frolics 'cross de Creek since you been gone."

Phrony came dashing up, hair wrapped with blue rag strings and reeking of lemon extract used as a perfume.

"John' how come you ain't dancin'?"

"Ah got uh bone in mah leg," John bantered.

"Aw come on, John."

"Go head on, Phrony. You got plenty boys 'sides me. Ah tell yuh Ah got uh bone in mah leg."

"Sho 'nuff, John? When did you git it in dere? You wuz walkin' all righ' jes' fo' dark."

"He jes' funnin' wid yuh," Zeke cut in, "'Course he got uh bone in his leg. How he goin'tuh walk if he ain't? Come on and lemme switch yo' coat."

Zeke grabbed Phrony by the point of her elbow and they plunged into the cauldron of sound.

John sat on, thinking of the words on the chimney back, but soon Exie found him.

"John, how come you ain't in de play party? M'haley dancin' wid Bully."

"She's uh much-right gal. Much right for Bully ez it is for me."

Exie laughed happily. "Big 'Oman huntin' you too and plenty mo'."

"Whut for?"

"Dey say de dance don't go so good 'thout you. Dey say de boys neither de gals don't do 'round when you ain't dere lak dey do when yo' is."

"Dey done 'thout me fo' dey seen me. Ah jes' don't feel lak no dancin' and whoopin' and hollerin' t'night."

"Me neither. Less we all jes' set and talk, John."

"Naw, Gawd! Ah don't want Duke pickin' no fight wid me over you. You his'n."

"Us ain't got no courthouse papers. Dat's commissary license us got. Ah kin quit anytime, and then agin effen Ah had courthouse license Ah got divorce in mah heels." She picked up John's hand and pulled it into her lap. Just then M'haley walked up to them.

"Oh 'scuse me," she turned away scornfully, "Ah didn't reckon you wuz so busy, John," she whirled and ran back to the dance.

"You better g'wan back tuh de play party, Exie. M'haley's goin' tuh tell Duke on you."

"Let her tell 'im, tell 'im, turn 'im up and smell 'im."

John rose. "Ah got tuh step off a li'l' piece. Ah'll be right back." He walked off and Exie started on back to the fire. Half way she met Duke, and John could hear the struggle of battle. He turned about and hurried to them.

"Whut you beatin' Exie 'bout? She ain't done nothin'."

"If she wan't doin' nothin', whut y'all doin' up heah in de dark?" He struck her violently in the face again. John stepped between them.

"Don't lam dis 'oman no mo', Duke. She ain't did a thing wrong. You wanta beat on somebody, hop me. Mah shoulders is broad."

Besides the ones who had heard M'haley say out loud that John and Exie were up the hill in the dark too busy to dance, there were others who had heard what Duke said when he left the fire-lit circle. So the crowd had surrounded the three. Exie, bruised but exultant, John and Duke standing face to face.

"Fight, fight, you no kin. Kill on 'nother 'twon't be no sin," Nunkie shouted.

Old Pheemy stepped between and scattered the crowd.

"Neb mind," Duke threatened as he was led away, "Ah ain't through wid you, John Pearson. Ahm goin' git yuh! Ahm goin'tuh git yuh if Ah have tuh steal yuh! Youse bigger'n me, but mah Barlow knife'll even us up."

The dance went on. John danced a little with Big 'Oman and Bootsie but he wasn't flamboyant.

In the bed with Zeke later he said, "Zeke, Ahm goin' 'way from here."

"You ain't skeered uh Duke, is yuh?"

"Naw, Duke cuts and shoots too, but all de shootin' he do is shoot fuh home if somebody git behind 'im, and cut fuh de nearest way. He don't fight no men-folks. He's uh woman-jessie. Beat up women and run from mens. Ah ain't got him tuh study 'bout, but Ah feel lak Ah weighs uh thousand pounds and it's mah heart make me feel that away."

"How come?"

"Y'know dat li'l' gal dat trebles in de choir at Mace-dony—de one whut don't wrop her hair, de onliest one up dere dat don't wrop her hair no time wid all dat cord-string lak de rest? Well, Ah loves her, and she say she love me too, and Ah betcha ole moufy M'haley uh some uh dese other niggers goin' make out Ahm goin' wid Exie, and dat's whut me and Duke lak tuh fought over, and then agin Mist' Alf done tole me not tuh fool wid Exie and Duke goin' up tuh de big house and tell uh lie on me."

"If yuh go off somewhere, John Buddy, lemme go wid yuh, heah, Please?"

"You too little. Ain't but fourteen, and if Ah go 'way from heah atall, Ahm goin' tuh de tie-camp and cut cross ties. Man asted me tuh go yistiddy in Notasulga. Yuh makes good money too."

"John Buddy, please. Heah?"

"Naw, you stay 'round heah and watch out for Lucy. Git word tuh me iffen any ole mullet-head tries tuh cut me out. Ahm gointer write tuh you and you way-lay her and git her tuh read it fuh yuh."

"Aw, Ah kin read too. Ah kin read some."

"Whut kin you read?"

"In de fust reader it say, 'This is Ned. He has a dog,' Ah kin read dat lak anything. Dat's uh heap, ain't it?"

"Dat'll do, but Ah ain't goin tuh write 'bout no Ned in de fust reader, and neither no dawg. You do lak Ah tell yuh, and if she say she don't pay dese niggers' talk no mind, you git de word tuh me quick ez yuh kin, heah, Zeke?"

"Unhunh."

"Yuh see, she got de advantage uh me 'cause she knows Ah love her, but Ah don't know whether she love me or not. Lots uh folks makes 'miration at her. You stay 'round heah and back mah fallin', and then nex' time Ah'll take you 'long."

"Aw right, John Buddy."

The next morning John was gone—walked to Opelika and on to the tie-woods on the Alabama River.

Chapter VI

IT WAS dusk-dark when John walked into the tie-camp. At some distance away he could see a group of men bunched on the ground beside a small fire. Gaming. They were so intent that John was right on them before they knew. When somebody saw him, there was a breathy cry, "De Buckra!" Somebody grabbed up the dice and everyone made to run. John laughed and stepped up among them.

"Ha, ha! Y'all thought Ah wuz white, didn't yuh?"

Everyone laughed except Coon Tyler. He was every bit as large as John and several years older. He looked up at John out of red, angry eyes and growled, "You oughter quit goin' 'round skeering folks. You better hail fo' you tuh walk up on *me* again."

John kept on laughing. "Lawd, y'all sho wuz snatchin' and grabbin'. Ah ought not tuh uh said nothin' and some uh y'all would uh been to Selma in five minutes."

Coon would not be amused, "You scoundrel-beast, you git from over de game!"

John stepped back a little, not in fear but in surprise.

"You ain't mad, is yuh?" he asked.

One of the men said, "Don't pay Coon no mind, he jes' funnin' wid yuh."

Seeing the passive attitude in John, Coon blazed, "Funnin'? Y'all know Ah don't joke and Ah don't stand no jokin'. 'Tain't nothin' in de drug store'll kill yuh quick ez me."

"Mah name is Ezeriah Hill, but de lady people calls me Uncle Dump," the oldest man in the group said to John, "Whuss yo' name, boy?"

"John. Where de boss at?"

"He gone intuh town. Be back tuhreckly. He goin' hiah yuh 'cause us needs help. Come on lemme show yuh uh place tuh sleep."

John followed him into the bunk house. "Heah whar you sleep at. Eve'ybody scorch up dey own grub. Be ready tuh hit de grit by daylight."

"Yes suh."

"Chaw tuhbacker uh smoke?"

"Naw suh."

"Wall you gwine learn 'cause you can't keep dis camp grub on yo' stomach lessen yuh do. Got tuh learn how tuh cuss too. Ah kin see you ain't nothin' but uh lad of uh boy. Mens on dese camps is full uh bulldocia 'til dey smell uh good size fist. Den dey dwindles down tuh nelly nothin'."

All next day John wielded a broad axe, a maul and pestle with the rest. He found that he liked the rhythmic swing, the chant "Cuttin' timber!" with the up stroke of the axe. Then the swift, sure descent, "Hanh!" Up again, "Cuttin' ties! Hanh." All day long, "Cuttin' timber! Hanh! Cuttin' ties, hanh!"

A boy called Do-dirty because of his supposed popularity with and his double-crossing of women, took John to town with him Saturday night. John was eager to go so he could buy writing paper and a pencil. He got it and then Do-dirty proudly showed him the town, and the town's women. It was late Sunday evening when they returned to camp and from one thing to another it was two weeks before John wrote to Ezekiel.

And when a month passed and he got no answer he began to feel that there would never be a word from Lucy. He went to town often. On the nights that he stayed in camp he was the center of camp life. He could chin the bar more times than anyone there. He soon was the best shot, the fastest runner and in wrestling no man could put his shoulders to the ground. The boss began to invite his friends out to watch the fun. John won his first match by pinning Nelse Watson from another camp to the ground, but his greatest stunt was picking up an axe by the very tip end of the helve and keeping the head on a level with his shoulders in his out-stretched arm. Coon could muscle out one axe, but John could balance two. He could stand like a cross, immobile for several seconds with an axe muscled out in each hand. Next to showing muscle-power, John loved to tell stories. Sometimes the men sat about the fire and talked and John loved that. One night Do-dirty began, "Y'all wanta heah some lies?"

"Yeah," said Too-Sweet, "Ah evermore loves lies but you can't tell none. Leave John tell 'em 'cause he kin act 'em out.

He take de part uh Brer Rabbit and Brer B'ar and Brer Fox jes' ez natche'l."

"Aw, 'tain't nothin' tuh 'im," Coon grumbled, "y'all make me sick."

Saturday afternoon Do-dirty looked off towards the West and cried, "Looka yonder! Who dat comin' runnin'?"

Everybody looked but John. He was inside getting ready to go to town.

"Do John Buddy work at dis heah camp?" he heard and recognized Zeke's voice.

"Come inside, Zeke!" he called out quickly.

Zeke came in and sat down on the bunk beside John. No words. Happiness radiated from one to the other.

"You seen Lucy?"

"Yeah, two times."

"Whut she say?"

Zeke tugged at a letter inside his clothes.

"She writ dis tuh yuh and tole me tuh mail it, but Ah run off and bring it tuh yuh. Yuh see Ah ain't got yo' letter till day befo' yestiddy. 'Cause pappy wouldn't leave me go tuh town tuh de Post Office. John Buddy, you goin' tuh leave me stay wid yuh? Hunh?"

John spelled slowly thru his letter and smiled, "Yeah, you kin stay whut li'l' time Ahm goin tuh be heah. Two mo' pay days and Ahm gone. Got tuh take uh birthday gif' tuh Lucy. Wisht Ah could give her Georgy under fence."

"John Buddy, Ahm hongry. Feel lak Ah ain't dirtied uh plate dis week."

"Wait uh minute. Ah'll stir yuh up uh Ash-cake and you kin sop it in some syrup. Maybe Ah ain't goin'tuh town nohow now."

John went outside and fixed the fire and put the bread in the hot ashes and covered it up.

"Reckon Ah better git uh bucket uh water, Zeke. You watch de bread. It's uh good li'l' piece tuh de spring."

Zeke watched the bread and took it out of the ashes when it was thoroughly brown. John had not returned. Most of the men lounged about outside. Finally Coon said to Zeke, "You better run down de hill dere and see whut's de matter wid yo' big buddy. Pant'er got 'im, maybe."

All alarm, Ezekiel leaped up and flew down the path he had seen John take. In a few minutes he saw John coming.

"Where you goin', Zeke?"

"Huntin' yuh. Skeered uh brute-beast had done kotched yuh."

When they got back to the bunk house, John gave Zeke his tin plate and set the gallon jug of syrup before him.

"He'p yo'self, Zeke, and grow hair on yo' chest."

Zeke poured a plate full of syrup and looked for the Ash-cake. "Whar at de bread is?" he asked John.

"You seen it since me," John answered. He looked about and seeing the suppressed laughter on the men's faces he asked, "Where de bread Ah took and cooked fuh mah li'l' bubber?"

General laughter. John got angry. "Ah say, who took and done 'way wid mah bread? Whoever done it mus' be skeered tuh own it."

Coon first, laughing instantly, "Ah et yo' damn bread. Don't you lak it, don't yuh take it, heah mah collar, come and shake it."

"Yeah and Ahm gointer shake it too dis day and year of our Lawd, and if Ah don't, Gawd knows, Ahm gointer give it uh common trial. My gal don't 'speck me tuh run."

They flew at each other and the others scrambled out of the way. Coon was too wise to clinch. He stayed his distance and slugged, but his wariness wore him out. Trying to hit and duck at the same time, he struck out ten or twelve times and landed one high on the enemy's head. John ran in and landed one smack in his enemy's mouth, and while Coon was spitting out his teeth, he ripped a mule-kicking right to the pit of Coon's stomach and the fight was over and done.

John felt good. His first real fight. Something burned inside him. He tasted blood in his mouth, but there was none actually. He wished somebody else would hit him. He wanted to feel himself taking and giving blows.

"You be keerful how you hit folks, Jawn," Uncle Dump cautioned, "you don't know yo' own strength. Dat man (indicating Coon) is hurt bad."

"He been pickin' on me ever since Ah been heah, and Ah been takin' and takin' 'til mah guts is full."

An hour before Lucy's letter had arrived Coon might have eaten John's Ash-cake and offered other insults safely. Now John was different. There was something about Lucy that stuck another and stiffer bone down his back.

He walked over and looked upon the fallen Coon. His surly black face was relaxed in a vacuous manner—blowing bloody foam out thru his swollen lips at every breath.

"Nex' time he fool wid me, Ah bet Ah'll try mah bes' tuh salivate 'im. He try tuh be uh tush hawg—puttin' out his brags everywhere."

He cooked Zeke more bread and soon the camp had settled down to normal. Somebody put Coon in his bunk, and he never spoke a word until after John had taken Zeke to town.

"Know whut," he lisped to the others, "dat boy slipped up on me, but Ahm gwine git even wid him. 'Tain't too late. Seben years ain't too long fuh uh coudar tuh wear uh ruffled bosom shirt. Ahm gwine gently chain-gang fuh dat same nigger."

"Aw," Dump disparaged, "you got uh belly full uh John. You ain't wantin' no mo' uh him."

"Yeah Ah wants tuh fight 'im, but not wid no fist. Ah flies hot quick but Ahm very easy cooled when de man Ahm mad wid is biggern me."

Chapter VII

JOHN and Zeke got back to Notasulga in time for the Christmas tree at Macedony, and John put a huge China doll on the tree for Lucy. She didn't know he had returned until he walked in during the singing and sat across the aisle from her.

At home, Emmeline Potts pounced upon the large package. "Dis is uh stray bundle dat didn't come from de Sunday School and it didn't come from dis house." She opened it. "Lucy Ann, read dis piece uh paper and tell me who give you dis great big play-pritty."

Lucy faltered. She turned the paper around two or three times.

"John Pearson."

"Dat big yaller boy from cross de Creek?"

"Yes ma'am."

"Whut he doin' givin' *you* uh present?"

"Ah don't know'm."

"Yes you do, madam. Dere's uh bug under dat chip. Mind yuh now, mah young lady; Ah ketch you foolin' wid boys, 'specially uh yaller bastard, Ahm uh goin'tuh put hick'ries tuh yo' back tuh set, Miss Potts. Ah done tole Artie Mimms he kin have yuh when yuh git sixteen."

Chapter VIII

ALF PEARSON welcomed John back with a bluff cursing out.

"I told you to leave Duke's woman alone. I didn't tell you to leave the place. Don't gimme excuses nor back talk. G'wan to work. I'll be glad when some good girl grabs you and makes something out of you. Stop running away. Face things out."

That Sunday Mehaley got two of her friends to go to Macedony with her, though they all belonged to Shiloh.

"Less go slur dat li'l' narrer-contracted Potts gal," she urged. "Somebody say John put uh great big doll-baby on de tree fuh her and den agin he bought her gold hoop ear-rings fuh her birthday. Course Ah don't believe he done no sich uh hot-do, but she fool wid me tuhday Ah means tuh beat her 'til she rope lak okra, and den agin Ah'll stomp her 'til she slack lak lime."

They crowded near Lucy after preaching, but old Emmeline was ever at Lucy's elbow. John had written Lucy to meet him at the spring, but Lucy was not permitted the liberty.

"Naw, you ain't goin' lolly-gaggin' down tuh no spring wid all dese loose gals. You goin' git in dis road 'head uh me and g'wan home."

Emmeline was most emphatic, but while she said her good byes to her friends, John came up and tipped his hat.

"How yuh do, Mis' Potts."

"Howdy John," she glared like noon.

"Mis' Potts, kin Ah scorch Mis' Lucy home?"

"Lucy ain't takin' no comp'ny yit. She ain't but fourteen and Ah don't turn mah gals loose tuh take comp'ny 'til dey sixteen, and when Ah does Ah picks de comp'ny mahself. Ah ain't raisin' no gals tuh throw way on trash."

Richard Potts spoke up. "Whut make you got tuh plow so deep, Emmeline? Ack lak 'tain't nobody got feelings but you. All right, son, Ah reckon it won't hurt nothin' if yuh walk 'long wid Lucy jes' ahead uh us. But she too young tuh court."

The world turned to red and gold for Lucy. She had read
the jealousy and malice in Mehaley's face, and John had asked
for her company right in front of Mehaley and her crowd! He
had faced her hard-to-face mama! She stretched up another
inch. There was little to say on the way home, but she had
made those big girls stand back. There was one moment
when they reached the bend in the road a moment before
Richard and Emmeline and John had squeezed her arm. The
whole world took on life. Lucy gave no sign that she noticed
the touch but in one flash she discovered for herself old
truths.

John noted the prosperous look of the Potts place. It was
different from every other Negro's place that he had ever
seen. Flowers in the yard among whitewashed rocks. Tobacco
hanging up to dry. Peanuts drying on white cloth in the sun.
A smoke-house, a spring-house, a swing under a china-berry
tree, bucket flowers on the porch.

"Stay and have dinner wid us," Richard Potts invited.

John stayed but ate little, and in his presence Lucy cut peas
in two and split grains of rice, for which she was coarsely
teased by her brothers until John left her, shamefaced.

Another look from his gray eyes that Lucy knew was her
look and nobody else's, and John loped on off to Pearson's.

The next morning Lucy found a hair upon her body and
exulted.

"Ahm uh woman now."

The following Saturday when she stripped to bathe in the
wooden wash tub, she noted that tiny horizontal ridges had
lifted her bust a step away from childhood.

She wrote John a long letter and granted him her special
company.

Chapter IX

"Y OU LUCY!" Emmeline scolded as she struggled along be-
hind John and Lucy on the way from church, "Ain't Ah
done tole yuh and tole yuh not tuh let no boys be puttin' dey
hand all over yuh? You John! You stay arm-length from dat
gal and talk it out. You got uh tongue."

Lucy and John sniggered together slyly and walked an inch
or two farther apart.

"Good Gawd, dey could drive uh double team between us
now," John complained.

"Talk loud, Ah don't 'low no whisperin' tuh no gal uh
mine."

They talked about the preaching and the new hymn-books
and the proposed church organ. Some were for the innova-
tion but the majority of the congregation thought that kind
of music in a church would be sinful to the extreme. Emme-
line stayed close enough to hear every word.

At home Lucy's married sister, Dink, sympathetically in-
veigled Emmeline into the kitchen where she was dishing up
dinner. Lucy and John sat in the parlor with the crayon en-
largements on easels and the gilded moustache-cups and sau-
cers on wire props and the religious mottoes on the wall.

John cleared his throat to speak, but Emmeline popped in
at that moment and took her seat beside the center table.
John was on one side of the room behind her and Lucy was
on the other side facing her.

"Ah been keepin' comp'ny wid you uh long time, ain't Ah,
Lucy?"

"Yeah, mighty nigh uh year now."

"And you ain't never had manners 'nough tuh ast *me* fuh
her comp'ny reg'lar," Emmeline snapped.

Conversation died. On the lower shelf of the center table
John spied Lucy's double slate with the slate-pencil suspended
from it by a string.

"Dis de same slate you use in school, ain't it, Lucy?"

"Unhunh."

John opened the slate and wrote a few words in it as softly

as possible. Emmeline seemed neither to see nor hear the scratching of the pencil, but when John leaned forward and tried to hand the slate past Emmeline to Lucy, Emmeline's hand flew out like a cat's paw and grabbed the slate. She looked on both sides and saw no writing, then she opened it and looked hard at the message, "I got something to tell you. Less go for a walk." Emmeline couldn't read a word and she was afraid that no one would read it correctly for her, but one thing she was sure of, she could erase as well as the world's greatest professor. She spoiled out the words with a corner of her apron, and put the slate back under the table. Not a word was passed.

"Mama!" from the kitchen.

"Whut you want, Dink?"

"Come turn dis sweet bread out on uh plate. Ahm skeered Ah'll make it fall uh tear it, tryin' tuh git it out de pan."

Emmeline went grumbling to the rear.

"Less set on de piazza," John suggested, "Maybe us kin git uh word in edgeways fo' she git back."

"Aw right."

They went out on the porch and sat slyly side by side— Lucy in the old red rocker, and John on a cow-hided straight chair.

"Lucy, Ah loves yuh."

Emmeline burst out of the parlor.

"Lucy! Whut you doin' settin' on top uh dat boy?"

"Ah ain't settin' on top of 'im. Uh milk cow could git between us."

"Don't you back talk *me*. When Ah speak you *move*. You hear me Lucy?"

"Yessum."

"How come you ain't movin'? Mah orders is five feet apart. Dink know befo' she married Ah never 'lowed her tuh set closer dan five feet and you know it and when Ah don't 'low tuh one, Ah ain't gwine 'low tuh de other. Heifer! Move dat chear 'way from dat boy!"

Silence.

"Lucy!"

"Yessum."

"Is you deef?"

"No'm."

Richard came in from the barn at that moment and called his wife.

"Aw, Emmeline, don't plow so deep. You puts de shamery on folks. Come on inside and hep Dink fix de dinner. Ahm hongry."

"Naw, Ah see she done got hard-headed, and Ahm gwine pray fuh her. Hard-headed chillun never come tuh no good end. Mind whut Ah say! Ahm gwine tell God about *you*, madam."

She pulled back the curtain in the parlor so that she could see every move on the porch and prayed.

"O Lawd and our Gawd, You know Ah tries tuh raise mah chillun right and lead 'em in de way dat dey should go, and Lawd You know it 'tain't right fuh boys and gals tuh be settin' on top one 'nother; and Lawd You know You said You'd strike disobedient chillun dead in dey tracks, and Lawd make mine humble and obedient, and tuh serve Thee and walk in Thy ways and please tuh make 'em set five feet apart, and when Ah done sung mah last song, done prayed mah last prayer, please suh, Jesus, make up mah dyin' bed and keep mah chillun's feet p'inted tuh de starry pole in glory and make 'em set five feet part. Dese and all other blessin's Ah ast in Jesus name, Amen, and thang Gawd."

"Aw Emmeline, dat prayer uh yourn ain't got out de house," Richard commented, "it's bumblin' 'round 'mong de rafters right now and dat's fur as it'll ever git."

Out on the porch John said softly, "Meet me tuhmorrer 'cross de branch by dat swee' gum tree 'bout fo' o'clock."

"Aw right. Aincha goin'tuh stay and have some dinner wid us?"

"Naw, Ah don't choose none. Dey got baked chicken at de big house and Ah eats from dere whenever Ah wants tuh. You gointer be sho' tuh be at our tree?"

"Unhunh."

"Sho now?"

"Unhunh."

"S'pos'n yo' mah uh some of de rest of 'em ketch yuh?"

Lucy threw herself akimbo. "Humph, dey can't do nothin' but beat me, and if dey beat me, it sho won't kill me, and if

dey kill me dey sho can't eat me. Ah'll be dere jus' as sho as gun's iron."

"'Bye den, Lucy. Sho wisht Ah could smack yo' lips."

"Whut's dat you say, John?"

"Oh nothin'. 'Bye. Doan let de booger man ketch yuh."

"Don't let ole Raw-Head-and-Bloody-Bones waylay yuh neither."

John was at the tree long before Lucy. He was sitting on the knurly-roots tying his handkerchief into a frogknot when he saw her coming diffidently down the hill on the Potts side of the branch. Presently she was standing before him.

"'Lo, Lucy."

"Hello, John. Ah see you fixin' tuh make soap."

"Whut make you say dat, Lucy?"

"Ah see yuh got yo' bones piled up."

She pointed to his crossed legs and they both laughed immoderately.

"Miss Lucy, uh Lucy, whyn't yuh have some set down?"

"Unrack yo' bones den and make room."

Lucy sat down. John untied his handkerchief and Lucy plaited rope-grass. John attempted another knot but fumbled it nervously. Lucy caught hold of the handkerchief also.

"Lemme he'p yuh wid dat, John. Ah know how tuh tie dat. Heah, you take dem two corners and roll 'em whilst Ah git dese fixed."

They both held the handkerchief taut between them. But before the knot could be tied John pulled hard and made Lucy lean towards him.

"Lucy, something been goin' on inside uh me fuh uh long time."

Diffidently, "Whut, John?"

"Ah don't know, Lucy, but it boils up lak syrup in de summer time."

"Maybe you needs some sassafras root tuh thin yo' blood out."

"Naw, Lucy, Ah don't need no sassafras tea. You know whuss de matter wid me—but ack lak you dumb tuh de fack."

Lucy suddenly lost her fluency of speech. She worked furiously at the love-knot.

"Lucy, you pay much 'tention tuh birds?"

"Unhunh. De Jay bird say 'Laz'ness will kill you,' and he go to hell ev'ry Friday and totes uh grain uh sand in his mouf tuh put out de fire, and den de doves say, 'Where you *been* so long?' "

John cut her short. "Ah don't mean dat way, Lucy. Whut Ah wants tuh know is, which would you ruther be, if you had yo' ruthers—uh lark uh flyin', uh uh dove uh settin'?"

"Ah don't know whut you talkin' 'bout, John. It mus' be uh new riddle."

"Naw 'tain't, Lucy. Po' me, Lucy. Ahm uh one wingded bird. Don't leave me lak dat, Lucy."

Suddenly Lucy shouted, "Look, John, de knot is tied right, ain't it pretty?"

"Yeah, Lucy iss sho pretty. We done took and tied dis knot, Miss Lucy, less tie uh 'nother one."

"You got mo' han'kerchiefs in yo' pocket?"

"Naw. Ah ain't studyin' 'bout no hankechers neither. De knot Ah wants tuh tie wid you is de kind dat won't come uh loose 'til us rises in judgment. You knows mah feelings."

"How Ah know whut you got inside yo' mind?"

"Yeah yuh do too. Y'all lady people sho do make it hard fuh us men folks. Look at me in de eye Lucy. Kiss me and loose me so Ah kin talk."

There was an awkward bumping of mouths. Lucy had had her first kiss.

"Lucy, Ah looked up intuh Heben and Ah seen you among de angels right 'round de throne, and when Ah seen *you*, mah heart swole up and put wings on mah shoulders, and Ah 'gin tuh fly 'round too, but Ah never would uh knowed yo' name if ole Gab'ull hadn't uh whispered it tuh me."

He extended his hands appealingly.

"Miss Lucy, how 'bout changin' frum Potts tuh Pearson?"

"Yeah, John."

"When?"

"Whenever you ready fuh me. You know mo' 'bout dat dan Ah do."

"How 'bout on yo' birthday, Lucy? Us kin make merry fuh uh heap uh things den at de same time."

"Aw right, John."

It was coldish on the December night, as Lucy made ready to meet John at the church. She had only finished her wedding-dress the day before, and only her father had seemed to care whether she had one or not. Now the puffed and laced little dress of light gray cashmere lay across the bed with her new shoes and six starchy petticoats loaded down with lace of her own making.

"Lucy Ann!" Emmeline bawled from the kitchen.

"Whut, mama?"

"Don't you answer *me* no 'whut'! Ah'll come in dere and stomp yo' guts out. Whut you got all dis fiah goin' fuh?"

"Mama, you know Ah got tuh bath mah self 'fo' Ah put on dese clothes."

"Ah keers nothin' 'bout no bathin'. 'Nother thing, you done kilt up fo' uh mah fryin'-size chickens, madam, and got 'em all cooked."

"No'm, Ah ain't kilt none uh yo' chickens. Dem wuz mah own Ah kilt fuh mah weddin'."

"How come dey yourn? You stinkin' li'l' heifer you!"

"'Cause dem is some uh Lay-Over's biddies dat Ah raised. Papa gimme dat hen las' year, and tole me tuh start raisin' mahself some chickens, so's Ah have uh good start when Ah git married, and you know Ah got twenty odd from her now."

"Youse uh lie, madam. Eve'y chicken on dis place is mines. Ah woulda give yuh uh few fuh seed if you wuz marryin' anybody. Here Artie Mimms is wid sixty acres under plow and two mules and done ast me fuh yuh ever since yuh wuz ten years ole and Ah done tole 'im he could have yuh and here you is jumpin' up, goin' over mah head, and marryin' uh nigger dat ain't hardly got changin' clothes."

"He is got changin' clothes."

"Hush up! Maybe he got clothes, but he ain't got uh chamber pot tuh his name nor uh bed tuh push it under. Still he kin take you outa uh good home and drag yuh off tuh Pearson's quarters."

"Mama, yuh been hell-hackin' me eve'y since us tole yuh us wuz gointer git married. Whut Ah keer 'bout ole Artie Mimms?"

"He ain't ole!"

"He is so ole, too. Ah looked at 'im good last big meetin'. His knees is sprung and his head is blossomin' fuh de grave. Ah don't want no ole springy-leg husband."

"You better want one dat kin feed yuh! Artie got dat farm and dem mules is paid fuh. He showed me and yo' paw de papers las' week."

"Whut Ah keer how many mules he got paid fuh? Ah ain't speckin' tuh live wid no mules. You tryin' tuh kill me wid talk. Don't keer whut yuh say, Ahm gointer marry John dis night, God bein' mah helper."

Lucy had been fixing her bath all during the talk. She now closed the room door, flung off her clothes with a savage gesture and stepped into the tub.

Instantly Emmeline's angry hand pushed against the latched door. "Whose face you slammin' uh door in, madam? Ah means tuh bring you down offa yo' high horse! Whar dem peach hick'ries? Somebody done done 'way wid mah switches. Aaron! You go cut me five uh six good peach switches and don't bring me nothin' dat ain't long ez mah arm. Dis gal done provoked me. Ah been tryin' tuh keep offa her back 'til dat trashy yaller bastard git her outa dis house, but she won't lemme do it. Go git dem hick'ries so Ah kin roast 'em in dis fiah. Ah birthed her, she didn't birth me, and Ah'll show her she can't run de hawg over me."

"Yessum, mama, Ahm gwine."

"Make haste, Aaron. Go in uh speedy hurry!"

Lucy spoke from the wash-tub, "Mama, 'tain't no use in you sendin' Aaron out tuh be cuttin' and ruinin' papa's peach trees, 'cause Ahm tellin' anybody, ole uh young, grizzly or gray, Ah ain't takin' no whippin' tuhnight. All mah switches done growed tuh trees."

"Whuss dat you say in dere, madam?"

Richard drove 'round to the front and hitched the horse and buggy at that moment.

"Whut's all dis racket gwine on in heah?" he demanded.

"Dat youngest gal uh your'n done sassed me out, and darted me tuh hit uh. Ah birthed uh but now she's older'n me. She kin marry dat yaller wretch, but Ah means fuh her tuh tote uh sore back when he gits uh."

"Aw dry up, Emmeline, dry up! She done done her pickin',

now leave her be. If she make her bed hard, she de one got tuh lay on it. 'Tain't you. Git yo' clothes on fuh de weddin'. Us Potts can't leave our baby gal go off tuh git married by herself."

"Me! Ah ain't gointer put mah foot in de place. Ahm gointer let folks see whar Ah stand. Ah sho ain't gwine squench mah feelin's fuh Lucy and dat John and you and nobody else—do Ah'll purge when Ah die."

Richard tucked Lucy into the buckboard and drove the silent little bundle to the church huddled against him. His arm about her gave his blessing but he knew that she would have gone anyway. He but made the way easier for her little feet.

To Lucy, Macedony, so used to sound and fervor, seemed cold and vacant. Her family, her world that had been like a shell about her all her life was torn away and she felt cold and naked. The aisle seemed long, long! But it was like climbing up the stairs to glory. Her trembling fear she left on the climb. When she rode off beside John at last she said, "John Buddy, look lak de moon is givin' sunshine."

He toted her inside the house and held her in his arms infant-wise for a long time. "Lucy, don't you worry 'bout yo' folks, hear? Ahm gointer be uh father and uh mother tuh you. You jes' look tuh me, girl chile. Jes' you put yo' 'pendence in me. Ah means tuh prop you up on ev'y leanin' side."

Chapter X

A MONTH after he was married John had moved up into the house-servants' quarters just back of the big house. John had achieved a raise in his wages. Alf Pearson had given them among other things a walnut bed with twisted posts, as a wedding present, and Lucy loved it above all else. She made it a spread and bolster of homemade lace.

After a few months Mehaley began to waylay John at the pig pens and in devious ways to offer herself. John gradually relaxed and began to laugh with her. She grew bolder. The morning after Lucy's first son was born, when he found her at the chicken house before him, he said, "Mehaley, Ah ain't gonna say Ah ain't laked you 'cause youse soft and nice, but Ah got Lucy, and Ah don't keer how she feel uh nothin', Ah'll want her right on. Ah tastes her wid mah soul, but if Ah didn't take holt uh you Ah'd might soon fuhgit all 'bout yuh. Pomp love you—you go marry Pomp. He'll do fuh yuh lak uh man. You better take and marry 'im."

"Ah don't want no Pomp! John Buddy, you know'd me 'fo' yuh knowed Lucy. If y'all wuz ever tuh quit would yuh marry me, John Buddy?"

"Us ain't never gonna do no quittin' 'til one uh us is six feet in de ground, and if you git de notion tuh run tell her a whole mess tuh back her feelin's and tear up peace, you better take wings and fly 'fo' Ah find it out. You hear me? Nothin' ain't gointer part us."

So when Pomp Lamar, the new hoe hand, fell beneath Mehaley's mango call—exotic, but fibrous and well-bodied —she answered "Yes" quickly with a persuasive kiss.

"But Ahm got tuh be married real, Pomp."

"And dat's whut Ah means tuh do, M'haley, come nex' pay-day."

"And less we g'wan off dis farm, Pomp. You know is too much back-bendin' and mule-smellin' on cotton plantations. Less go on some public works, lak uh sawmill uh sumpin'. Ah kin git 'long wid anybody any whar so long ez you half-way treat me right."

"M'haley, you might no know it, but youse gittin' uh do-right man. Whenever you needs somebody tuh do uh man's part Ah'll be 'round dere walkin' heavy over de floor."

Next pay-day the quarters was gathered at Mehaley's mother's cabin. Quantities of sweet biscuits had been cooked up along with the chickens. The wedding was set for eight o'clock and the crowd was there—all except Pomp. People began to ask questions that had no answers. Mehaley didn't get dressed. She was asked why she was still in her working clothes.

"Humph! Y'all think Ahm gwine put mah trunk on mah back and de tray on mah head, and dat man don't never come? Naw indeed! Ah ain't gwine tuh dress tuh marry no man 'til unless he be's in de house."

"You reckon he done run off?" Nunkie asked.

"Aw naw," Duke dissented. "He tole me he wuz crazy tuh marry Haley. He jus' keepin' colored folks time. When white folks say eight o'clock dey mean eight o'clock. When uh colored person say eight o'clock, dat jes' mean uh hour ago. He'll be heah in plenty time."

It was after nine when the bridegroom arrived. "Where you been at all dis time?" Mehaley's mother wanted to know.

"Ah couldn't stand on de flo' wid M'haley in dem ole sweaty britches. Ah been off tuh borry me some clothes tuh git married in."

Mehaley began to dress with the interference of ten or more ladies. Finally she was ready, but a quarrel arose as to whom was to perform the ceremony. Mehaley's father wanted to do it, but her mother had invited the pastor.

"Ah don't keer if you *is* her pappy," the mother stated, "you ain't nothin' but uh stump-knocker and Ah wants dis done real. Youse standin' in uh sho 'nuff preacher's light. G'wan set down and leave Elder Wheeler hitch 'em right. You can't read, nohow."

"Yes, Ah kin too."

"Naw, you can't neither. G'wan sit down. If us wuz down in de swamp whar us couldn't git tuh no preacher, you'd do, but here de pastor is. You ain't nothin' but uh jack-leg. Go set in de chimbley corner and be quiet."

"You always tryin' tuh make light uh mah preachin'," the

husband defended, "but Gawd don't. Dis de fust one uh mah chillun tuh jump over de broomstick and Ah means tuh tie de knot mah own self."

Around eleven o'clock, the pastor, worn out by the stubbornness of the father, retired from the field, and the couple stood upon the floor.

"Whar yo' shoes, Pomp?" Mehaley asked. "You ain't gwine marry me barefooted, is yuh?"

"Dey over dere under de bed. Yo' paw and the preacher argued so long and dem new shoes hurted mah foots so bad, Ah took 'em off. Now Ah can't git 'em back on. Dat don't make uh bit uh diff'rence. You gointuh see mah bare foots uh whole heap after dis."

So Mehaley Grant stood up to marry Pomp Lamar and her father Woody Grant, who had committed the marriage ceremony to memory anyway, grabbed an almanac off the wall and held it open pompously before him as he recited the questions to give the lie to the several contentions that he could not read.

"Ah now puhnounce you man and wife."

"Bus' her, Pomp, bus' her rat in de mouf. She's yourn now, g'wan Pomp. Les see yuh kiss her!"

After many boisterous kisses, the women took Mehaley by the arm and led her off.

"Us goin' and bath M'haley fuh huh weddin'-night. Some uh y'all men folks grab Pomp, and give him uh washin' off."

Mehaley got out of bed that night after the guests had all gone home.

"Whar yuh gwine, Haley?"

"Huntin' fuh mah box uh snuff."

"Yo' box uh snuff? Gal, don't you know you jes' got done married tuh uh husband? Put out dat light and come git back under dese kivvers."

"Naw, Pomp, not 'til Ah gits uh dip uh snuff. Ah wants it real bad."

She hunted about until she found it. "Lawd," she cried, "you see some dem women done messed 'round and spilt soap suds in mah snuff!"

She sat down before the fireplace and wept, hard racking sobs. Pomp's assurance that she would have a dozen boxes

from the Commissary first thing in the morning did not comfort her, and it was only when her stormy tears had exhausted her that she let her new husband lead her back to bed. In his arms, she said, "Pomp, don't fuhgit you said you wuz gwine take me 'way fuhm heah."

"Cose Ah is, Haley. Nex' pay-day, sho." He kept his word.

At sundown on the evening of their leaving, Lucy was on her knees at the praying ground, telling God all her feelings.

"And oh, Ah know youse uh prayer-hearin' God. Ah know you kin hit uh straight lick wid uh crooked stick. You heard me when Ah laid at hell's dark door and cried three long days and nights. You moved de stumblin' stone out my way, and now, Lawd, you know Ahm uh po' child, and uh long ways from home. You promised tuh be uh rock in uh weary land—uh shelter in de time uh storm. Amen."

Lucy and John raced around their house in the later afternoons playing "Hail Over" and "Hide the Switch," and Lucy grew taller. The time came when she could no longer stand under John's outstretched arm. By the time her third son was born she weighed ninety-five pounds.

John had added weight to his inches and weighed two hundred and fifteen pounds, stripped. There was no doubt about it now. John was foreman at Pearson's. His reading and writing had improved to the degree where Alf could trust him with all the handling of supplies.

"John," Alf said to him one day, "you damn rascal! that girl you married is as smart as a whip and as pretty as a speckled pup. She's making a man of you. Don't let her git away."

"Oh good Lawd, naw! Mist' Alf, she even nice. Don't talk 'bout her never partin' from me. Dat sho would put de affliction on me."

"Well, John, you'd better keep Big 'Oman out of that Commissary after dark. Aha! You didn't think I knew, did you? Well, I know a lot of things that would surprise folks. You better clean yourself up."

The hand of John's heart reached out and clutched on fear. Alf Pearson shoved him on out of his office and returned to work, chuckling. Two days later Big 'Oman was gone. It got

said that she was shacked up with somebody in a tie-camp on the Alabama River.

A month later John said, "Lucy, somebody done wrote Mist' Alf 'bout uh drove uh cows dey wants tuh sell 'im. He say fuh me tuh go look over 'em and see whut dey worth. Be back Sad'day."

"Iss been rainin' uh lot fuh you tuh be goin' uh long way, John."

"Goin' on horse-back, Lucy. De water ain't goin' bother me."

Lucy said no more. John didn't notice her silence in the haste of his departure, but a few miles on down the road he said, "Humph! Lucy ain't frailed me none wid uh tongue. Wonder how come dat?"

On Thursday John was cheerfully riding away from Lucy, but at daybreak on Saturday he was dressed and ready to ride back.

"John, you ain't gwine leave me, is yuh?" Big 'Oman sobbed, "thought you come to stay. De big boss say you kin git uh job right heah."

"Ah got uh job, Big 'Oman. Done been off too long now."

The weeping girl clung to his stirrup. "When you comin' back tuh me, John?"

"In times and seasons, Big 'Oman. Lemme go now. All dat rain yistiddy and las' night makes bad travelin'. Bad 'nough when Ah wuz comin'. De later it gits, de higher de river."

He dashed off quickly and rode hard, counting the miles as he went.

"Eighteen miles from home. 'Leben mo' miles. Heah 'tis de river—eight mo' miles."

The river was full of water and red as judgment with chewed-up clay land. The horse snorted and went mincing down to the bridge. Red water toting logs and talking about trouble, wresting with timber, pig-pens, and chicken coops as the wind hauls feathers, gouging out banks with timber and beating up bridges with logs.

"Git up, Roxy! Us got tuh cross dis river, don't keer if she run high ez uh bell-tower, us got tuh cross. Come on up dere. Let de damn bridge shake, bofe us kin swim."

Midway over, a huge log struck the far end of the bridge and tore it loose from the shore and it headed down stream. The whole structure loosened, rolled over and shot away.

John freed himself and struck out for shore. Fifty feet or more down stream Roxy landed, snorting her loss of faith in the judgment of man. John felt himself being carried with the stream in spite of his powerful stroke, but inch by inch he was surely gaining land. The neighing of Roxy had attracted the attention of a white squatter on the farther shore and John saw people looking on his fight with the Alabama.

There was a cry from the shore, a thud at the back of his head and he sank.

John strode across infinity where God sat upon his throne and looked off towards immensity and burning worlds dropped from his teeth. The sky beneath John's tread crackled and flashed eternal lightning and thunder rolled without ceasing in his wake.

Way off he heard crying, weeping, weeping and wailing— wailing like the last cry of Hope when she fled the earth. Where was the voice? He strained his eye to see. None walked across the rim bones of nothingness with him, but the wailing wailed on. Slowly John saw Lucy's face. Lucy wept at a far, far distance, but the breath of her weeping sent a cold wind across the world. Then her voice came close and her face hung miserably above his, weeping. She brought the world with her face and John could see without moving his head the familiar walls of their house.

Gradually things came closer. The gourd dipper, the water-bucket, the skillets and spiders, and his wife so close above him, forearm across her face, retching in tears.

"Whuss de matter, Lucy? You thought Ah wuzn't never comin' back? Don't you know nothin' couldn't keep me 'way from you?"

"John! Ah thought you wuz dead."

"Naw, Ah ain't dead. Whatever give you de idea Ah wuz dead, Lucy?"

"Dey brought yuh home fuh dead dis mawnin' and iss nelly sundown now and you ain't moved, and you ain't spoke 'til jus' now."

"Who brung me home?"

"De Bickerstaffs. Say de bridge washed uhway wid yuh and de hawse on it, and you got hit by de timber. Yo' lip is cut deep and yo' head is hurted in de back and uh bad place right dere side yo' nose."

"Umph, umph, umph! Lawd have mussy. Ah thought Ah been sleep. So dat's how come Ahm all wet up and mah face hurt me so, eh?"

"Yeah, and John, Ahm so glad you ain't dead 'way from me and mah li'l' chillun, and then agin Ah hated tuh think 'bout you herded tuh judgment in yo' sins."

A silent wait.

"You can't lay on dis floor all night. Ah got tuh git yuh in de bed some way uh 'nother. Lemme go call somebody tuh he'p me muscle yuh. Ah sent fuh mah folks but 'tain't been nobody from dat side yet."

The next day John called Lucy to him.

"Lucy."

"Yeah, John."

"Dey done tole you 'bout Big 'Oman and me?"

"Yeah, John, and some uh yo' moves Ah seen mahself, and if you loves her de bes', John, you gimme our chillun and you go on where yo' love lie."

"Lucy, don't tell me nothin' 'bout leavin' you, 'cause if you do dat, you'll make two winters come in one year."

There was a feeling silence.

"Lucy, Ah loves you and you alone. Ah swear Ah do. If Ah don't love you, God's gone tuh Dothan."

"Whut make yuh fool wid scrubs lak Big 'Oman and de rest of 'em?"

"Dat's de brute-beast in me, but Ah sho aim tuh live clean from dis on if you 'low me one mo' chance. Don't tongue-lash me—jes' try me and see. Here you done had three young-uns fuh me and fixin' have uh 'nother. Try me Lucy."

The next big meeting John prayed in church, and when he came to his final:

> You are de same God, Ah
> Dat heard de sinner man cry.
> Same God dat sent de zigzag lightning tuh

Join de mutterin' thunder.
Same God dat holds de elements
In uh unbroken chain of controllment.
Same God dat hung on Cavalry and died,
Dat we might have a right tuh de tree of life—
We thank Thee that our sleeping couch
Was not our cooling board,
Our cover was not our winding sheet . . .
Please tuh give us uh restin' place
Where we can praise Thy name forever,

<div align="right">Amen.</div>

"Uh prayer went up tuhday," Deacon Moss exulted to
Deacon Turl. "Dat boy got plenty fire in 'im and he got uh
good strainin' voice. Les' make 'im pray uh lot."

Deacon Turl agreed and went on home to his chicken
dumplings.

John never made a balk at a prayer. Some new figure, some
new praise-giving name for God, every time he knelt in
church. He rolled his African drum up to the altar, and called
his Congo Gods by Christian names. One night at the altar-
call he cried out his barbaric poetry to his "Wonder-workin"
God so effectively that three converts came thru religion
under the sound of his voice.

"He done more'n de pastor," Moss observed. "Dat boy is
called tuh preach and don't know it. Ahm gwine tell him so."

But Moss never did. Lucy's time was drawing nigh and a
woman named Delphine drifted into town from Opelika.
John was away from both home and church almost continu-
ally in the next month.

Alf went to see Lucy.

"Lucy Ann, where's that husband of yours?"

"He's out 'round de barn somewhere's, ain't he, Mist'
Alf?" Lucy asked. She knew he was not there. She knew that
Alf Pearson knew he was not there and that Alf Pearson knew
that she knew he was not there, but he respected her reti-
cence.

"Lucy, you oughta take a green club and frail John good.
No matter what I put in his way to help him along, he flings
it away on some slut. You take a plow-line and half kill him."

When Alf was gone Lucy looked drearily up the path for her husband and saw her oldest brother coming with his double team.

"Lawd a mussy!" She groaned and dropped into a chair. A heavy knocking at the door.

"Who dat?"

"Iss me, Bud. Lemme come in right now. Ahm in uh big hurry."

Lucy opened the door feebly and Bud's stumpy figure thrust itself inside aggressively as if it said in gestures, "Who you tryin' tuh keep out?"

"Lucy, Ah come tuh git dat three dollars you borried offa me."

"Well, Bud, tuh tell yuh de truth, Ah ain't got it right dis minute. Mah husband ain't here, but he'll be here pretty soon, then he'll pay yuh sho, Bud."

"Who don't know he ain't here? How he gointer be here, and layin' all 'round de jook behind de cotton gin wid Delphine?"

"You better come back, Bud, when he's here and tell 'im all dat tuh his face."

"And whut it takes tuh tell 'im, Ah got it! He ain't nothin' but uh stinkin' coward or he wouldn't always be dodgin' back uh yuh. Ah'll tell 'im all right. 'Tain't no fight in him."

"G'wan home, Bud. If papa wuzn't dead you wouldn't come heah lak dis—and me in mah condition."

"Ah know you done wished many's de time you had married Artie Mimms."

"Naw. Not nary time."

"Gimme mah money and lemme go 'fo' Ah git mad agin."

"Ah tole you Ah ain't got no money and won't have none till John come."

"You ain't gonna git none den—dat is if he ever come. Some folks say he done quit you fuh dat Delphine. She strowin' it herself all over Macon County and laffin' at yuh. You jes' dumb tuh de fact."

"You can't pay no 'tention tuh talk. Dey's talkin' everywhere. De folks is talkin' in Georgy and dey's talkin' in Italy. Ah don't pay dese talkers no mind."

"Gimme de money, Lucy, and lemme go."

"Done tole yuh Ah ain't got no money. Come back heah when John is home."

"Naw, Ah ain't gonna do nothin' lak dat. Ah come heah wid de determination tuh git mah money uh satisfaction, one."

"But, don't you see Ah ain't in no fix tuh be fretted all up this uh way? G'wan leave me uh lone."

Bud looked around him contemptuously. "Humph! Here mah sister is cooped up wid three li'l' chillun in uh place ain't big uhnough tuh cuss uh cat in 'thout gittin yo' mouf full uh hair."

"G'wan way from me, Bud. Ahm too sick tuh be worried."

"Naw, Ah means tuh have something fuh mah money. Gimme dat bed."

"Dat big one wid de knobs on it?"

"Yep. Who you reckon want de tother one dat dem chillun done wet in? Move! Don't you git in mah way. Move! If you wuz married tuh anybody you wouldn't be in no sich uh fix."

The bed was down in a twinkling, the feather mattress and bolster heaped upon the floor, while Bud dragged out the head and foot pieces. Lucy sank down upon the mattress and fought the lump in her throat. When her brother returned for the rails and slats, Lucy was crumpled in a little dark ball in the center of the deep mound of feathers.

"Bud, you ought'n tuh take dat bed. Mist' Alf give it tuh us. Dat's our weddin' bed."

"He oughta give 'im mo'. Git up offa dat air mattress!"

"Ah ain't, and if you don't git offa dis place Ah'll call Mist' Alf. Ah bet you'll leave here then."

"Aw Ah ain't skeered uh no white man. Ah been free ever since Grant took Richmond."

But in a few moments Bud was gone and Lucy was shivering and weeping upon the feather mattress.

"Hezekiah," she called to her oldest boy, "run down tuh de quarters lak uh li'l' man and tell An' Pheemy tuh come quick. Run on, son. Youse five years ole now, youse uh great big boy. Hurry up."

"Mama, Ahm hungry."

"Mama know it too. Run on now. Run fast, Hezekiah! Show mama how fas' you kin run. Oh Gawd have mercy on me! Have mussy in uh mos' puhticular manner. Have mussy on mah ever-dyin' soul!"

Before midnight Lucy in awful agony upon her pallet on the floor had given birth to her first daughter.

The odor of airless childbirth hung over the stuffy room. Pheemy with the help of Old Edy and Della performed the ancient rites.

Edy and Della sweetened the mother and put a clean meal-sack sheet beneath Lucy, but only Pheemy could handle the after-birth in the proper way, so that no harm could come to Lucy. That is she buried it shoulder deep to the east of the house beneath a tree, then she returned and attended to the navel string of the baby and adjusted the belly-band.

"Della, you and Edy kin go 'long now. Ah kin see after Lucy."

They went reluctantly. As soon as the sound of their feet died away Pheemy asked, "How you feelin' inside, Honey?"

"Lawd, An' Pheemy, Ah got somethin' in mah heart ain't got no name. Ah layin' here right now tryin' tuh find some words for feelin's. Look lak mah right heart ain't beatin' no mo'."

"Neb mine, Lucy, 'bout de words. You needs sleep and rest and some chicken gruel. Ah gwine bring yuh some. Ahm gwine find some sheep pills so de baby kin have some sheep shadney."

That night Pheemy fell asleep in a chair before the fire. The children full of corn pone and buttermilk had been asleep since early night. Lucy alone saw John when he crept in towards morning. She shut her eyes and pretended sleep. John stood looking down upon her for a long time. Lucy, later, thru the crack of her eye saw him examining the new-born baby, and felt him timidly tucking the covers under her feet, and heard him stretching himself on the floor beside the mattress; heard the deep breathing of his sleep. She raised herself upon her elbows and looked at him hard. She looked at the flickering fire, the rude dingy walls and everything in the room and knew that she'd never lose the picture as long as

she lived. She stretched out her hand nearest her husband and rested the fingers on his tousled head. With her other arm she cuddled her baby close, and fell into a deep, healthful sleep.

When Lucy woke up, old Hannah was riding high. The light was strong in her face. She looked about and asked Pheemy, "Where John?"

"He at de barn—done chopped up uh tree for wood. Oughter be 'bout through wid his work by now. You better suckle dat chile."

John crept in and stood before Lucy while her fat daughter searched hungrily for the nipple.

"Lucy, whut you doin' sleepin' on de floor?"

"Dat's all Ah got tuh sleep on, John Buddy."

"Where de weddin' bed at?"

"Bud come took it fuh dat li'l' change us owe 'im fuhm las' year."

"When he come got it?"

"Yistiddy."

He hung his head a moment.

"Lucy, kin Ah see de baby?"

"She nussin' now, John. Soon's she git through."

"Dat ain't no trouble." He stooped and picked up mother and child and sat with them in his lap. "Lucy, Ahm sho proud uh dis li'l' girl chile you done had. Dat's jus' whut Ah wanted—uh girl so us could have it fuh uh doll-baby. An' Pheemy, don't Lucy have de biggest babies? Dis chile it almost big as her. She so little Ah hafta shake de sheets tuh find her in de bed."

She slapped him feebly.

"Ain't you got no better sense dan tuh set in uh man's lap and box his jaws? He's liable tuh let yuh fall thru his legs." He stopped laughing abruptly. "An' Pheemy you fed mah wife and slopped mah three li'l' pigs?"

"Look in de meal-barrel and see."

John didn't look. Pheemy's words told him. He laid Lucy again upon the pallet and left. As he stepped thru the wire fence gap at Bud's place he saw Bud riding up the path behind him on his mule, his huge bull whip coiled upon his saddle-horn.

"Gid up dere, Sooky!" Bud Potts held his eyes stubbornly

before him. John Pearson's hand flung out, grasped the mule's bridle close to the bit, and shoved the animal back upon its haunches.

"Gid down, Bud. You might kin beat me, but if you do, eve'ybody goin tuh know you been in uh fight. So good uh man, so good uh man."

"Whut you mean, John, comin' here pickin' uh fuss lak dat?"

"Ah ain't come tuh pick no fuss, Ahm come tuh fight. God bein' mah helper Ah means tuh teach yuh how tuh go proagin' 'round takin' folkses weddin' beds when dey ain't home and flinging dey wives on de floor. Gid down!"

"If you wuz any kind uh man, all dis wouldn't come tuh pass. De white folks and ev'ybody is sick and tiahed uh de way you keerin' on. Nohow you can't beat *me*. Ahm uh *man*."

"Maybe Ah can't, but Ahm sho goin'tuh give it uh common trial. Hit de ground! If Ah don't beat yuh, you kin go and tell de word Ah give it uh po' man's trial."

Bud tried to ride off, but he was snatched scuffling to the ground and hammered to his knees time and time again. When he swore no more, when he begged for mercy no more, John picked him up and heaved him across the rump of the mule and recrossed the branch.

Almost home he remembered the empty meal-barrel and swerved off into the Weens' wood lot where droves of piney wood rooters nosed for ground nuts. John laid a shoat by the heels and stuck it expertly before it had squealed more than three or four times. Looking all about to see if he was seen, he swung the hog over his shoulder and took the back way home.

By that time the sun was washing herself in the bloody sea and splashing her bedclothes in red and purple. John built a fire under the washpot, and dressed his meat before he came inside the house. When Lucy opened her eyes from a nap, crude slabs of pork steak were sizzling in the skillets.

"Where you git all dat fresh meat from, John?"

"Neb' mind where Ah got de meat from. You jes' eat 'till you git plenty. Ah'll get out and throw uh natural fuh you any time. You got uh *man* tuh 'fend fuh yuh."

"Lawd knows Ah do needs one. Me and mah po' li'l' chillun been singin' mighty low 'round here."

"Now, Lucy, don't start dat talk 'bout breakin' up and quittin' 'cause Ah ain't goin' tuh hear dat. Youse mah wife and all Ah want you tuh do is gimme uh chance tuh show mah spunk."

"Good Lawd, John, dat's all justice been beggin' righteous tuh do—be uh *man*. Cover de ground you stand on. Jump at de sun and eben if yuh miss it, yuh can't help grabbin' holt uh de moon."

"Li'l' Bit, please don't tongue lash me," there was a short pause, "'cause Ah done beat Bud nelly tuh death, and dat's plenty tuh think uhbout—by rights Ah oughta kilt 'im." He rubbed his swollen knuckles.

"Oh mah Gawd! When?"

"Dis evenin'—Jus' 'fo' Ah come home, Lucy. Ah wouldn't be no man atall tuh let yo' brother uh nobody else snatch uh bed out from under you, mo' special in yo' condition."

"John dat's goin' tuh cause trouble and double, Bud hate you and now you done hit 'im he ain't goin' tuh let his shirt-tail touch 'im till he tell it tuh de white folks. Lawd, me and mah po' chilluns. If dey ever git yuh on dat chain-gang Ah never speck tuh see you live no mo'."

"Ah ain't goin' tuh no chain-gang. If dey ever git in behind me, Ah'll tip on cross de good Lawd's green. Ah'll give mah case tuh Miss Bush and let Mother Green stand mah bond."

"Dey liable tuh grab yuh, 'fo' yuh know it."

"Aw les' squat dat rabbit and jump uh 'nother one. You ack lak you done cut loose."

"Naw, Ah ain't cut loose but look lak wese tied tuhgether by uh long cord string and youse at one end and Ahm at de other. Way off."

"You kin take in some de slack."

"Don't look lak it."

"Aw, lemme see de caboose uh dat. Less eat dis hog meat and hoe-cake. Jes' 'cause women folks ain't got no big muscled arm and fistes lak jugs, folks claims they's weak vessels, but dass uh lie. Dat piece uh red flannel she got hung 'tween her jaws is equal tuh all de fistes God ever made and man ever seen. Jes' take and ruin a man wid dey tongue, and den dey kin hold it still and bruise 'im up jes' ez bad."

"Say whut yuh will or may, you tryin' tuh loud talk me,

but, John, you gives mah folks too much tuh go on. Ah wants mah husband tuh be uh great big man and look over 'em all so's Ah kin make 'em eat up dey talk. Ah wants tuh uphold yuh in ev'ything, but yuh know John, nobody can't fight war wid uh brick."

Chapter XI

DUKE came panting up to Lucy's late the next afternoon. Lucy was propped up in a rocker and Pheemy was washing baby rags.

"Hates tuh tell yuh, Lucy, but dey done got 'im."

"Do, Jesus."

"Yessum, de high sheriff put his hand on his shoulder down dere by de deepo' 'bout uh hour uh go. Bud Potts swo' out de warrant, and den Weens say he goin' have 'im bound over tuh de big cote. Sho is bad, and you in yo' condition."

"Where dey got 'im, Duke?"

"In de big jail. Cy Perkins, Jestice uh de Peace, goin' tuh bind 'im over. Den Judge Pearson'll set on de case nex' cote day."

Lucy rose abruptly, "Ahm goin', Pheemy. You take keer mah chillun."

"Lucy, yo' body ain't healed up yit. You can't go."

"Ah specks tuh be back 'fo' dark, An' Pheemy."

"Gal, you ain't but three days out uh labor. De elements is pizen tuh yuh, and effen yuh git lated 'til after sundown, de pizen night air sho will be de last uh you."

Lucy flung the plaid shawl about her head and shoulders. "And, An' Pheemy, if de baby cries tuh nuss 'fo' Ah git back, jus' give her uh sugar-tit tuh suck on and keep her pacified."

Lucy stepped out of the cabin door and was gone. In due time she stood in Cy Perkins' office where he was holding court. She saw her brother's bruised and beaten face. She saw her husband handcuffed and humble, his eyes turned away from the world.

The court had not set. She still had time if she worked fast. She held her shawl under the chin with the frail fingers of one hand as she went and stood before her brother.

"Don't come puttin' up no po' mouf tuh me, Lucy. Git out mah face," Bud shouted before she could speak. "Dis case ain't uh goin' tuh be nol prossed uh nothin' else. Ah wouldn't squash it fuh mah mammy. You made yo' bed now lay in it."

She turned away. Cy Perkins called her.

"Howdy, Lucy."

"Well, Ah thankee, Mist' Perkins. Ah come tuh see 'bout mah husband."

"Got any bail money, Lucy? That's what you need."

"Naw suh. Ah come wid jus' whut ah stand in, 'cause Ah ain't got nothin' else, but Ah come."

Cy Perkins looked hard at the forlorn little figure. Lucy stood before him with her large bright eyes staring and not knowing she stared. Suddenly she sat down because she couldn't stand any more.

"Look like you're sick, Lucy."

"Mah troubles is inward, Mist' Perkin."

"Her new baby ain't but three days old," Duke volunteered.

Perkins fumbled with his papers, never looking at Lucy the while. John remained with head hung down and face averted except for one begging glance at Lucy. Finally the Justice of the Peace arose and beckoned Lucy into his back office.

"Don't try to stand up, Lucy. Set down before you fall down. It's too bad that you are out at a time like this. Listen, Lucy, this is serious. Your family is well thought of 'round here and lots of folks think John needs a good whipping before he goes to the gang. If he's got any friends he better call on 'em now. Tell you the truth, Lucy, if it wasn't for you, and me knowing your papa so well, I wouldn't have parted my lips, but your husband is in a mess of trouble."

"Thankee, Mist' Perkin. Ah got fo' li'l' chillun 'round mah feet; if dey send John off Ah don't know whut'll 'come uh us all."

"Have you been to Judge Alf yet?"

"Naw suh. Ah hates tuh go 'cause he done cautioned John good tuh behave hisself, but Ah reckon Ah better."

"Hurry across there to his office. I won't set court until you get back."

Lucy didn't come back. She all but collapsed on the steps of Pearson's office, and he sent her home in his buggy. Alf Pearson strode across to Perkins' office and asked that the prisoner be released in his charge and it was done. Weens was paid for his hog, but John was bound over to the big court

for the assault upon his brother-in-law. There was a great deal of loud whispering about night-riders and the dark of midnight, but nobody touched John as he drove Judge Pearson home.

"John, I'm not going to ask you why you've done these things, partly because I already know, and partly because I don't believe you do."

"If Ah had uh knowed 'twuz gointer raise all dis rukus."

Alf laughed sardonically, "Of course you did not know. Because God has given to all men the gift of blindness. That is to say that He has cursed but few with vision. Ever hear tell of a happy prophet? This old world wouldn't roll on the way He started it if men could see. Ha! In fact I think God Himself was looking off when you went and got yourself born."

"Yes suh, Ah speck so."

They turned into the cedar-lined drive that led up to the big, columned veranda.

"John, distance is the only cure for certain diseases. Here's fifty dollars. There are lots of other towns in the world besides Notasulga, and there's several hours before midnight. I know a man who could put lots of distance between him and this place before time, even wearing his two best suits—one over the other. He wouldn't fool with baggage because it would hold him back. He would get to a railroad twenty-five or thirty miles off."

John assisted Alf Pearson to alight.

"Good bye, John. I know how to read and write and I believe Lucy does too."

He strode up the steps of his veranda very straight and stiff, as if he had an extra backbone in his back.

In the early black dark John was gone. Lucy feverishly peeped thru first one crack then another, watching up the big road after him.

"Lucy, whyn't you stay in dat bed?" Pheemy grumbled. "You look lak youse jes' determined tuh be down sick and Ah already got mah hands full wid dese chilluns."

"An' Pheemy, Ahm standin' on de watch wall. Reckon de patter rollers'll ketch 'im?"

"Lawd naw. He pitched out towards Chehaw and dem folks is in Notasulga waitin' fuh midnight."

The hours went past on their rusty ankles and midnight stood looking both ways for day.

"Hush!" said Lucy, "dey's comin'!"

Pheemy listened hard but couldn't hear a thing.

"Dat's all right, An' Pheemy, Ah don't zakly hear nothin' neither, but uh far uhway whisper look lak it's puttin' on flesh."

They stood peering for a quarter of an hour or more at the narrow slit of the big road visible from the cabin. Then sure enough as silently as horsemen can, rode twenty or thirty men in the cloud-muddied moonlight. Slowly, watchfully, as they passed the big gate that led to the quarters and on past the stately cedar drive.

"How come dey ain't turned in?" Lucy asked, a tremble.

"Dey ain't gwine set foot on Judge Alf Pearson's place, if dey run on 'im outside dey'd grab 'im. Dey might go in some folks' quarters, but 'tain't never no patter roller set foot on dis place. Dey know big wood from brush."

Pheemy told the truth, but she was only embolden to speak after the last rider had passed the big gate, and faded into the distance.

"Maybe dey already got 'im."

"Aw naw, gal, g'wan tuh rest. Dey jes' bluffin' tuh skeer us black folks."

The next day Chuck Portlock met Alf Pearson and tried to say casually, "Say, Judge dey tell me dat nigger run off. You got any notion which way he went?"

"Afraid not, Chuck, I've treed many a coon in my time, but I don't believe I've got a drop of bloodhound in me."

Chapter XII

JOHN'S destination was purely accidental. When he came out upon the big road to Chehaw, he overtook another Negro. They hailed each other gladly in the early dawn.

"Where you bound fuh?" John asked.

"Tuh ketch me uh high henry."

"Whuss dat?"

"Uh railroad train, man, where you been all yo' days you don't know de name of uh train?"

"Oh, 'bout in spots and places. Where you bound fuh when you git on de train?"

"Tuh Florida, man. Dat's de new country openin' up. Now git me straight, Ah don't mean West Florida, Ah means de real place. Good times, good money, and no mules and cotton."

"B'lieve Ah'll go 'long wid yuh."

"Man, dat calls fuh more'n talk. Dat calls fuh money."

"How much?"

"Twenty odd dollars. 'Cordin' tuh where at you goin'."

"Where you goin'?"

"Tuh uh town called Sanford. Got uh sister dere. She keepin' uh boardin' house," he looked John over, "she's uh fine lookin', portly 'oman; you better come 'long."

"Um already married, thankee jes' de same. Man, Ah got uh putty 'oman. Li'l' bitsa thing. Ahm sho tuh send fuh her soon ez Ah git settled some place."

"Aw shucks man, you ain't lak me. Ah don't take no women no place. Ah lets every town furnish its own."

They bought their tickets and John sat in a railway coach for the first time in his life, though he hid this fact from his traveling mate. To him nothing in the world ever quite equalled that first ride on a train. The rhythmic stroke of the engine, the shiny-buttoned porter bawling out the stations, the even more begilded conductor, who looked more imposing even than Judge Pearson, and then the red plush splendor, the gaudy ceiling hung with glinting lamps, the long mournful howl of the whistle. John forgot the misery of his

parting from Lucy in the aura of it all. That is, he only re-membered his misery in short snatches, while the glory lay all over him for hours at the time. He marvelled that just any-body could come along and be allowed to get on such a glo-rified thing. It ought to be extra special. He got off the train at every stop so that he could stand off a piece and feast his eyes on the engine. The greatest accumulation of power that he had ever seen.

Chapter XIII

As John and his mate stepped off the train at Sanford, they were met by a burly, red-faced white man who looked them over sharply—which gave them both the fidgets. Finally he asked, "Where y'all come from?"

"Up de road uh piece in Wes' Florduh," John's partner answered, much to his relief.

"Want work?"

"Ah kinda got uh job promised tuh me already," John's mate answered again.

"How 'bout you, Big Yaller?"

"Nawsuh, Ah ain't got no job. Sho would love tuh hear tell uh one."

"Come along then. Ever done any work on uh railroad?"

"Nawsuh, but Ah wants tuh try."

"Git yo duds then. We going over to Wildwood. Dollar a day. Seaboard puttin' thru uh spur."

That night John slept in the railroad camp and at sun-up he was swinging a nine-pound hammer and grunting over a lining bar.

The next day he wrote Lucy and sent her all of his ready money.

All day long it was strain, sweat and rhythm. When they were lining track the water-boy would call out, "Mr. Dugan!"

The straining men would bear down on the lining bars and grunt, "hanh!"

"Hanh!"

"Got de number ten!"

"Hanh!"

"Got de pay-car!"

"Hanh!"

"On de rear end."

"Hanh!"

"Whyncher pick 'em up!"

"Hanh!"

"Set it over."

"Hanh!"

And the rail was in place. Sometimes they'd sing it in place, but with the same rhythm.

> "When Ah get in Illinois
> Ahm gointer spread de news about de Floriduh
> boys
> Sho-ove it over
> Hey, hey, can't you line it?"

Then a rhythmic shaking of the nine-hundred-pound rail by bearing down on the bars thrust under it in concert.

"Ah shack-uh-lack-uh-lack-uh-lack-uh-lack-uh-lack-uh-hanh!"

Rail in place.

"Hey, hey, can't you try?"

He liked spiking. He liked to swing the big snub-nosed hammer above his head and drive the spike home at a blow. And then the men had a song that called his wife's name and he liked that.

"Oh Lulu!"

"Hanh!" A spike gone home under John's sledge.

"Oh, oh, gal!"

"Hanh!"

"Want to see you!"

"Hanh!"

"So bad."

"Hanh!"

And then again it was fun in the big camp. More than a hundred hammer-muscling men, singers, dancers, liars, fighters, bluffers and lovers. Plenty of fat meat and beans, women flocking to camp on pay-day.

On Sunday John and his breaster went into town to church. The preacher snatched figure after figure from the land of images, and the church loved it all. Back in camp that night, John preached the sermon himself for the entertainment of the men who had stayed in camp and he aped the gestures of the preacher so accurately that the crowd hung half-way between laughter and awe.

"You kin mark folks," said Blue. "Dass jes' lak dat preacher fuh de world. Pity you ain't preachin' yo'self."

"Look, John," said his breaster, "dey's uh colored town out

cross de woods uh piece—maybe fifteen tuh twenty miles, and dey's uh preacher—"

"You mean uh whole town uh nothin' but colored folks? Who bosses it, den?"

"Dey bosses it deyself."

"You mean dey runnin' de town 'thout de white folks?"

"Sho is. Eben got uh mayor and corporation."

"Ah sho wants tuh see dat sight."

"Dat's jes' whar Ah wants tuh take yuh nex' Sunday. Dey got uh Meth'dis' preacher over dere Ah wants yuh tuh mark. He talk thru his nose and he preaches all his sermons de same way. Sho would love tuh hear you mark 'im."

"Ah'll sho do it. Whut's de name uh dat town?"

"Eatonville, Orange County."

The Negro mayor filled John with almost as much awe as the train had. When he was leaving town that Sunday night he told his friend, "Ahm comin' back tuh dis place. Uh man kin be sumpin' heah 'thout folks tramplin' all over yuh. Ah wants mah wife and chillun heah."

There were many weeks between John and the little Negro village. He would resolve to move there on next pay-day, but trips to town, and visitors to camp defeated his plans.

But a letter from Lucy nerved him and he found work pruning orange trees in Maitland, the adjacent white town and went to live in Eatonville.

He had meant to send for Lucy within the month, but one thing and another delayed him. One day, however, in a fit of remorse he went and drew down a month's wages in advance and sent the money to Judge Pearson for his wife because he was ashamed to write to her.

He was working for Sam Mosely, the second most prosperous man in Eatonville, and borrowed his team to meet Lucy at the train.

He wouldn't let her walk down the coach steps, but held wide his arms and made her jump into his bosom. He drove the one mile from the depot in Maitland to the heart of Eatonville with a wagon full of laughter and shouts of questions.

"Glad tuh see me, Lucy?" John asked as soon as he had

loaded the battered tin trunk and the feather bed on the wagon and sprung into the driver's seat.

"'Course, John."

"Is you only mouf glad or yuh sho nuff glad?"

"Sho nuff, but one time Ah thought you sho took uh long time tuh write tuh me and send fuh us."

"You looks lak new money 'round heah, honey. Ah'd send fuh you, if Ah didn't had bread tuh eat. Look how our li'l gal done growed."

"Yeah she walkin' and talkin'. You been 'way from us might nigh uh yeah."

The children exclaimed at the fruit clustered golden among the dark glistening foliage.

"Ah got y'all plenty oranges at de house, y'all chaps. Yo' papa lookin' out fuh yuh."

"You got us uh house, John?" Lucy asked happily.

"Ah mean where Ah been stayin' at. Ah reckon us all kin git in dere."

"'Tain't no mo' houses in town?"

"Yeah, two, three vacant, but us ain't got much money. Sendin' fuh y'all and all, and den us ain't got nothin' tuh go in uh house but ourselves."

"Dat ain't nothin'. You go git us house of our own. 'Tain't nothin' lak being yo' own boss. Us kin sleep on de floor 'til we kin do better."

Lucy sniffed sweet air laden with night-blooming jasmine and wished that she had been born in this climate. She seemed to herself to be coming home. This was where she was meant to be. The warmth, the foliage, the fruits all seemed right and as God meant her to be surrounded. The smell of ripe guavas was new and alluring but somehow did not seem strange.

So that night John and his family were house-keeping again. John went to the woods at the edge of town and filled three crocus sacks with moss and each of the larger children had a sack apiece for a mattress. John and Lucy took the baby girl upon the feather mattress with them.

Next morning Lucy awoke at daylight and said to John in bed, "John, dis is uh fine place tuh bring up our chillun. Dey

won't be seein' no other kind uh folks actin' top-superior over 'em and dat'll give'em spunk tuh be bell cows theyselves, and you git somethin' tuh do 'sides takin' orders offa other folks. Ah 'bominates dat."

"Whut's it goin' tuh be, Lucy?"

"You knows how tuh carpenter. Go ast who want uh house built, and den you take and do it. You kin prop up shacks jus' as good as some uh dem dat's doin' it."

And to John's surprise people wanted houses built all over Orange County. Central Florida was in the making.

"And now less don't pay Joe Clarke no mo' rent. Less buy dis place, John."

"Dat's uh bigger job than Ah wants tuh tackle, Lucy. You so big-eyed. Wese colored folks. Don't be so much-knowin'."

But the five acre plot was bought nevertheless, and John often sat on Joe Clarke's store porch and bragged about his determination to be a property owner.

"Aw, 'tain't you, Pearson," Walter Thomas corrected, "iss dat li'l' handful uh woman you got on de place."

"Yeah," Sam Mosely said earnestly, "Anbody could put hisself on de ladder wid her in de house. Dat's de very 'oman Ah been lookin' fuh all mah days."

"Yeah, but Ah seen uh first, Sam, so you might jus' ez well quit lookin'," John said and laughed.

"Oh Ah knows dat, John. 'Twon't do me no good tuh look, but yet and still it won't hurt me neither. You might up and die uh she might quit yuh and git uh sho nuff husband, and den she could switch uh mean Miss Johnson in dat big house on Mars Hill."

"Hold on dere uh minute, Sam," John retorted half in earnest amid the general laughter, "less squat dat rabbit and jump uhnother one. Anyhow mah house liable tuh be big ez your'n some uh dese days."

"Aw, he jes' jokin' yuh, Pearson," Joe Clarke, the mayor intervened, "I god, you takin' it serious."

When John got home that night Lucy was getting into bed. John stopped in the hallway and took his Winchester rifle down from the rack and made sure that it was loaded before he went into the bedroom, and sat on the side of the bed.

"Lucy, is you sorry you married me instid uh some big

nigger wid uh whole heap uh money and titles hung on tuh him?"

"Whut make you ast me dat? If you tired uh me, jus' leave me. Another man over de fence waitin fuh yo' job."

John stood up, "Li'l' Bit, Ah ain't never laid de weight uh mah hand on you in malice. Ain't never raised mah hand tuh yuh eben when you gits mad and slaps mah jaws, but lemme tell you somethin' right now, and it ain't two, don't you never tell me no mo' whut you jus' tole me, 'cause if you do, Ahm goin' tuh kill yuh jes' ez sho ez gun is iron. Ahm de first wid you, and Ah means tuh be de last. Ain't never no man tuh breathe in yo' face but me. You hear me? Whut made you say dat nohow?"

"Aw, John, you know dat's jus' uh by-word. Ah hears all de women say dat."

"Yeah, Ah knows dat too, but *you* ain't tuh say it. Lemme tell you somethin'. Don't keer whut come uh go, if you ever start out de door tuh leave me, you'll never make it tuh de gate. Ah means tuh blow yo' heart out and hang fuh it."

"You done—"

"Don't tell me 'bout dem trashy women Ah lusts after once in uh while. Dey's less dan leaves uh grass. Lucy do you still love me lak yuh useter?"

"Yeah John, and mo'. Ah got mo' tuh love yuh fuh now."

John said, "Neb mine mah crazy talk. Jus' you hug mah neck tight, Ah'd sweat in hell fuh yuh. Ah'd take uh job cleaning out de Atlantic Ocean jus' fuh yuh. Look lak Ah can't git useter de thought dat you married me, Lucy, and you got chillun by *me!*"

And he held Lucy tightly and thought pityingly of other men.

The very next Sunday he arose in Covenant Meeting and raised the song, "He's a Battle-Axe in de time Uh Trouble," and when it was done he said, "Brothers and Sisters, Ah rise befo' yuh tuhday tuh tell yuh, God done called me tuh preach."

"Halleluyah! Praise de Lawd!"

"He called me long uhgo, but Ah wouldn't heed tuh de voice, but brothers and sisters, God done whipped me tuh it, and like Peter and Paul Ah means tuh preach Christ and Him

crucified. He tole me tuh go, and He'd go with me, so Ah ast yo' prayers, Church, dat Ah may hold up de blood-stained banner of Christ and prove strong dat Ah may hold out tuh de end."

The church boiled over with approval, "Ah knowed it! Tole 'im long time uhgo dat's whut he wuz cut out fuh. Thang God. He's goin'tuh be uh battle-axe sho 'nuff— Hewin' down sinners tuh repentance."

His trial sermon had to be preached in a larger church—so many people wanted to hear him. He had a church to pastor before the hands had been laid on his head. The man who preached his ordination sermon was thrown in deep shadow by the man who was to be ordained.

The church he pastored at Ocoee did all they could to hold him, but the membership was less than a hundred. Zion Hope, of Sanford, membership three hundred, took him to her bosom, and her membership mounted every month.

John dumped a heavy pocketbook into Lucy's lap one Monday morning before he took off his hat.

Lucy praised him. "We goin'tuh finish payin' fuh dis place wid dis money. De nex' time, us buy de chillun some changin' clothes. You makin' good money now, John. Ah always knowed you wuz gointuh do good."

He wore the cloak of a cloud about his shoulders. He was above the earth. He preached and prayed. He sang and sinned, but men saw his cloak and felt it.

"Lucy, look lak Ah jus' found out whut Ah kin do. De words dat sets de church on fire comes tuh me jus' so. Ah reckon de angels must tell 'em tuh me."

"God don't call no man, John, and turn 'im loose uh fool. Jus' you handle yo' members right and youse goin' tuh be uh sho 'nuff big nigger."

"Ain't Ah treatin' 'em good, Lucy? Ah ain't had no complaints."

"Naw, you wouldn't hear no complaints 'cause you treatin' 'em too good. Don't pomp up dem deacons so much. Dey'll swell up and be de ruination of yuh. Much up de young folks and you got somebody tuh strain wid dem ole rams when dey git dey habits on. You lissen tuh me. Ah hauled de mud tuh make ole Cuffy. Ah know whuts in 'im.

"Don't syndicate wid none of 'em, do dey'll put yo' business in de street." Lucy went on, "Friend wid few. Everybody grin in yo' face don't love yuh. Anybody kin look and see and tell uh snake trail when dey come cross it but nobody kin tell which way he wuz goin' lessen he seen de snake. You keep outa sight, and in dat way, you won't give nobody uh stick tuh crack yo' head wid."

As he swaggered up to Joe Clarke's store porch in his new clothes, putting and taking with his yellow cane, Sam Mosely teased, "Well, John done got tuh be uh preacher."

"Yeah Ah is, and Ah ain't no stump-knocker neither. Ah kin go hard."

"Maybe so, John, but anybody kin preach. Hard work and hot sun done called uh many one. Anybody kin preach."

"Naw dey can't neither. Take you for instance."

"Don't want tuh. Ahm de mayor."

"You ain't goin' tuh be it after de 18th day of August. Watch and see."

"Who gointer be it; Joe Clarke? He said he wuzn't runnin'."

"Naw, Ahm gointer be de mayor."

"YOU runnin' fuh mayor?"

"Not now but Ahm goin' tuh run when de time come, and if you want tuh be mayor agin you better *run*. Don't fool wid it—run! Go hard uh go home. You and Clarke ain't had nobody tuh run aginst, but dis time big Moose done come down from de mountain. Ahm goin' tuh run you so hard 'til they can't tell yo' run-down shoe from yo' wore out sock."

General laughter.

"I God," Joe Clarke declared, "Ah never seen two sworn buddies dat tries tuh out do on 'nother lak y'all do. You so thick 'til one can't turn 'thout de other one, yet and still you always buckin' ginst each other."

"'Tain't me," Sam Mosely defended, "Iss him, but he can't never ekal up tuh me 'cause Ah come heah from Wes' Floriduh uh porpoise, but look whut Ah got now. Ahm uh self-made man."

"Ah come heah right out de tie woods in uh boot and uh shoe, but Ah got proppity too. Whut you goin' tuh call *me*?" He thrust out his chest.

"Uh wife-made man," Mosely retorted amid boisterous laughter, "if me and him wuz tuh swap wives Ah'd go past 'im so fast you'd think it wuz de A. C. L. passin' uh gopher."

"Better say joe, 'cause you don't know. Anyhow when you run for mayor next time git ready tuh take yo' whippin'. De time done come when big britches goin' tuh fit li'l' Willie."

And Rev. Pearson did win. He was swept into office by the overwhelming majority of seventeen to three.

"Tell yuh how yuh beat me, John," Mosely said on the store porch that night, "course 'twan't fair, but it wuz de way you and Lucy led de gran' march night 'fo' las' at de hall, but by rights uh preacher ain't got no business dancin'."

"Grand marchin' ain't dancin'. Ah never cut uh step."

"Dat's right too, y'all," Joe Lindsay put in, "you ain't dancin' 'til yuh cross yo' feet, but Rev. John, no sinner man couldn't uh led dat march no better'n you and Lucy. Dat li'l' 'oman steps it lightly, slightly and politely."

"Tuh make short talk outa long," added Walter Thomas, "Sam, youse uh good man. Ah don't know no better conditioned man in dese parts. Yo' morals is clean ez uh fish—and he been in bathin' all his life, but youse too dry fuh de mayor business. Jes' lak it 'twuz wid Saul and David."

Lucy was going to have another baby and in her condition she missed John a lot. Now that he was called here and there over the state to conduct revivals, she knew that he must go. She was glad to see him in new suits that his congregation proudly bestowed upon him without his asking. She loved to see him the center of admiring groups. She loved to hear him spoken of as "The Battle-Axe." She even loved his primitive poetry and his magnificent pulpit gestures, but, even so, a little cold feeling impinged upon her antennae. There was another woman.

Time and time over the dish-pan, she'd find herself talking aloud.

"Lawd lemme quit feedin' on heart meat lak Ah do. Dis baby goin' tuh be too fractious tuh live." And then again, "Lawd, if Ah meet dat woman in heben, you got tuh gimme time tuh fight uh while. Jus' ruin dis baby's temper 'fo' it git tuh dis world. 'Tain't mah fault, Lawd, Ahm jus' ez clean ez yo' robes."

This was her second baby since coming to Florida, and she remembered how happy he had been at the coming of the fourth boy. A new baby might change things, perhaps, and she was right. When the new little girl was a month old, he took the lacy, frilly little bundle out of Lucy's arms and carried it out to the waiting horse and buggy.

"You ain't got time tuh fool wid dat youngun, John. You goin' up tuh Sanford tuh preach, ain't yuh?"

"Yeah, and de church got tuh see dis baby. Dis is sho mah work. De very spit uh me. 'Cep'n—"

"'Cep'n what? Dem sho yo' gray eyes."

"Dey ain't whut Ah wuz fixin' tuh say. Dat's mah eye color alright but her eyes look at yuh lak she know sumpin. Anybody'd think she's grown. Wonder whut she thinkin' 'bout?"

"Take uh God tuh tell. Ah toted de rest uh de chillun in mah belly, but dat one wuz bred in mah heart. She bound tuh be diffunt."

"Git yo' things on, Lucy, and come on tuh Sanford wid me. De church ain't seen mah wife in six months. Put on dat li'l' red dress and come switchin' up de aisle and set on de front seat so you kin be seen. Ahm goin' tuh tote de baby, lessen you want me tuh tote bofe of yuh."

"Go 'way, Ah don't hafta wear dat ole red dress 'cause Ah got uh brand new Princess, laced down de back wid uh silk cord wid tassels on it."

With her bangs above her shining eyes and the door-knob knot of hair at the back, Lucy sat on that front seat in church and felt a look strike her in the back and slide off helplessly. Her husband's glance fell on her like dew. Her look and nobody else's was in his gray eyes, and the coldness melted from the pit of her stomach, and at the end of the sermon John came down from the pulpit and took the baby from her arms and standing just before the pulpit proudly and devotedly called, "Come heah eve'ybody, one at de time and pass by and look on yo' pastor's baby girl chile. Ah could shout tuh-day." And they came.

There came other times of cold feelings and times of triumphs. Only the coldnesses grew numerous.

Once she had sent him off to Alabama when she felt such a

coldness that it laid her in a sick-bed. She knew that the glory of his broadcloth and Stetson would humble Bud, chagrin old Ned and make Amy happy, and in his present glory the "leaf of grass" would wither. Lucy prayed often now, but sometimes God was tired and slept a little and didn't hear her. Maybe He had other Johns somewhere that needed His ear, but Lucy didn't get too tired. She didn't worry God too much. She had her husband and seven children now and her hands were kept busy. John had to be pushed and shoved and there was no one to do it but Lucy.

There came the day, with Lucy's maneuvering, when John stood up in the State Association and was called Moderator. "Wisht ole Ned and Bud could see me now," John gloated, "always makin' out Ah wuzn't goin' tuh be nothin'. Ah uh big nigger now. Ain't Ah Lucy?"

"You sho is. All you got tuh do now is tuh *ack* lak one."

"Don't you reckon Ah know how tuh ack, Lucy? You ain't out dere wid Brown and Battle and Ford and all dem big mens, lak Ah is. You always tryin' tuh tell me whut tuh do. Ah wouldn't be where Ah is, if Ah didn't know no more'n you think Ah do. You ain't mah guardzeen nohow."

John strode off in his dark blue broadcloth, his hand-made alligator shoes, and his black Stetson, and left Lucy sitting on their porch. The blue sky looked all wrinkled to Lucy thru the tears.

And soon Lucy knew who the woman was, and once or twice the thought troubled her that John knew she knew, but didn't care.

One night as she sang the sleep song to the younger children she noticed a sallow listlessness in Isis, her younger girl. The next day she knew it was typhoid. For a week she fought it alone. John was down the East Coast running a revival and didn't come at once. When he did come, the doctor said, "Well, Reverend, I'm glad you're here. If she can last 'til midnight she's got a chance to get over it, but—but I doubt if she will live till dark."

The restrained Lucy stood at the far side of the bed looking at her child, looking at John. The agony of the moment sweated great drops from his forehead. He would have fallen on the bed but Lucy led him outside.

"Ah can't stand 'round and see mah baby girl die. Lucy! Lucy! God don't love me. Ah got tuh go 'way 'til it's all over. Ah jus' can't stay."

So John fled to Tampa away from God, and Lucy stayed by the bedside alone. He was gutted with grief, but when Hattie Tyson found out his whereabouts and joined him, he suffered it, and for some of his hours he forgot about the dying Isis, but when he returned a week later and found his daughter feebly recovering, he was glad. He brought Lucy a new dress and a pineapple.

Chapter XIV

PEOPLE in Sanford began to call Lucy aside. There was much under-voice mention of Hattie Tyson, Oviedo and shame, Gussie, Tillie, Della, church court, making changes in the pulpit and monthly conference.

"John," Lucy began abruptly one day, "you kin keep from fallin' in love wid *anybody*, if you start in time."

"Now whut you drivin' at?"

"You either got tuh stop lovin' Hattie Tyson uh you got tuh stop preachin'. Dat's whut de people say."

"Ah don't love no Hattie Tyson. De niggers lyin' on me."

"Maybe so, but if you don't you oughta stay from 'round her. Ah done seen de green tree ketch on fire, so you know uh dry one will burn."

"Lawd how some folks kin lie! Dey don't wait tuh find out a thing. Some of 'em so experk on mindin' folks' business dat dey kin look at de smoke comin' out yo' chimbley and tell yuh whut yuh cookin'."

"Yo church officers is talkin' it too, John."

"Sho 'nuff, Lucy?"

"Dey talkin' 'bout settin' you down."

"Lawd have mussy! You ain't ginst me too, is yuh Lucy?"

"Naw, Ah'll never be ginst yuh, John, but Ah did thought you done strayed off and don't love me no mo'."

"You musta thought it, Lucy, 'cause nobody sho didn't tell yuh. If you don't know, ast somebody."

"John, now don't you go 'round dat church mealy-moufin 'round dem deacons and nobody else. Don't you break uh breath on de subjick. Face 'em out, and if dey wants tuh handle yuh in conference, go dere totin' uh high head and Ah'll be right dere 'long side of yuh."

Conference night came and the church was full. It was evident that the entire congregation was keyed up. The routine business was gotten out of the way quickly. Beulah Tansill flung her low look at the pastor and then at Deacon Tracy Patton. Deacon Patton cleared his throat and did a great deal of head scratching. The look on the pastor's face didn't seem

to belong there. It was bold and unusual. It sort of dared him and the words he had brought there with him wouldn't slide off his tongue. He scratched his head some more. He had stirred up the side front the first time, he tried the opposite side back.

"Uh, ruh, uh ruh, any onfinished business?" prompted Deacon Harris.

Deacon Patton almost rose that time. Another look at Pearson and Lucy and he laid down his hat and scratched with both hands. Gave his entire head a thorough scratching and held his mouth open in sympathy.

"Shet yo' mouf, Tracy Patton!" Sister Berry cautioned. "De flies will blow yo' liver tuhreckly."

"Shet your'n. You tries tuh be so much-knowin'. You got tuh learn how tuh speak when you spokin to, come when youse called."

"Ah ain't got tuh do but two things—stay black and die," Sister Berry snapped.

"Less stand adjourned," Deacon Harris hurried, "us don't want no fight."

That was as far as the conference went. The Chairman realized that the Chief spokesman was not going to speak, hastily adjourned, hoping that Beulah and Tracy wouldn't implicate him if they talked it. He made it his business to walk home with the pastor and drop a defensive suggestion in his ear in advance.

"Rev. Ahm diggin' mah sweet pitaters tuhmorrer. Goin'tuh bring you some too."

"Thanks, Aleck. Mah wife and chillun all loves dem good ole yeller yams, good ez Ah do."

"Dey sho gointer git some. Look heah, Elder Pearson Ah reckon you done heard dat some dese niggers is throwin' lies 'bout you and some woman over 'bout Oviedo. Ah ain't tole yuh nothin', and you be keerful uh dese folks dat totes yuh news. Uh dog dat'll bring uh bone will keerp one. You know dat's de truth. Good night."

John had read the hostility in the meeting and his relief at his temporary deliverance was great. He said nothing to his wife, but he bought a dozen mangoes and thrust the bag into her hand.

As they undressed for bed Lucy asked in a matter of fact tone, "Whut tex' you goin' tuh preach on Sunday comin'?"

"Iss Communion so Ah reckon Ah'll preach de Passover Supper in de upper room."

"Don't you preach it. Dis thing ain't thru wid yit. 'Tain't never goin' tuh be finished 'til you tackle dey feelings and empty out dey hearts—do, it'll lay dere and fester and after while it would take God hisself tuh clean up de mess."

"Whut mo' kin Ah do? Ah wuz dere fuh dem tuh handle me and dey didn't do it."

"Dat wuz 'cause de folks didn't have no leader. They wuz plenty fight in dere. All dey needed wuz uh lead hound. You git yo'self out dey mouf and stay out of it, hear me?"

"Whut mus' Ah do?"

"You preach uh sermon on yo'self, and you call tuh they remembrance some uh de good things you done, so they kin put it long side de other and when you lookin' at two things at de same time neither one of 'em don't look so big, but don't tell uh lie, John. If youse guilty you don't need tuh git up dere and put yo' own name on de sign post uh scorn, but don't say you didn't do it neither. Whut you say, let it be de truth. Dat what comes from de heart will sho reach de heart agin."

"Mah chillun, Papa Pearson don't feel lak preachin' y'all tuh day," he began on Sunday after he had sung a song, "y'all been looking at me fuh eight years now, but look lak some uh y'all been lookin' on me wid unseein' eye. When Ah speak tuh yuh from dis pulpit, dat ain't me talkin', dat's de voice uh God speakin' thru me. When de voice is thew, Ah jus' uh-nother one uh God's crumblin' clods. Dere's seben younguns at mah house and Ah could line 'em all up in de courthouse and swear tuh eve'yone of 'em, Ahm uh natchel man but look lak some uh y'all is dumb tuh de fack.

"Course, mah childun in Christ, Ah been here wid y'all fuh eight years and mo'. Ah done set by yo' bedside and buried de dead and joined tuhgether de hands uh de livin', but Ah ain't got no remembrance. Don't keer if Ah laugh, don't keer if Ah cry, when de sun, wid his blood red eye, go intuh his house at night, he takes all mah remembrance wid 'im, but

some yuh y'all dat got remembrance wid sich long tangues dat it kin talk tuh yuh at a distance, when y'all is settin' down and passin' nations thew yo' mouf, look close and see if in all mah doin's if dere wuz anything good mingled up uh-moungst de harm Ah done yuh. Ah ain't got no mind. Y'all is de one dat is so much-knowin' dat you kin set in judgment.

"Maybe y'all got yo' right hand uh fellership hid behind yuh. De Lawd's supper is heah befo' us on de table. Maybe mah hands ain't tuh break de bread fuh yuh, maybe mah hands ain't tuh tetch de cup no mo'. So Ahm comin' down from de pulpit and Ah ain't never goin' back lessen Ah go wid yo' hearts keepin' comp'ny wid mine and yo' fire piled on mah fire, heapin' up."

He closed the great Bible slowly, passed his handkerchief across his face and turned from the pulpit, but when he made to step down, strong hands were there to thrust him back. The church surged up, a weeping wave about him. Deacons Hambo and Harris were the first to lay hands upon him. His weight seemed nothing in many hands while he was roughly, lovingly forced back into his throne-like seat.

After a few minutes of concerted weeping, he moved down to the Communion table and in a feeling whisper went thru the sacrifice of a God.

Chapter XV

A N' DANGIE DEWOE'S hut squatted low and peered at the road from behind a mass of Palma Christi and elderberry. The little rag-stuffed windows hindered the light and the walls were blackened with ancient smoke.

She had thrown several stalks of dried rabbit tobacco on the fire for power and sat with her wrinkled old face pursed up like a black fist, watching the flames.

Three quick sharp raps on the door.

"Who come?"

"One."

"Come on in, Hattie." As the woman entered An' Dangie threw some salt into the flame without so much as a look at her visitor. "Knowed you'd be back. Set down."

Hattie sat a moment impatiently, then she looked anxiously at An' Dangie and said, "He ain't been."

"He will. Sich things ez dat takes time. Did yuh feed 'im lak Ah tole yuh?"

"Ain't laid eyes on 'im in seben weeks. How Ahm goin' do it?"

"Hm-m-m." She struggled her fatness up from the chair and limped over to an old tin safe in the corner. She fumbled with the screw top of a fruit jar and returned with a light handful of wish-beans. "Stan' over de gate whar he sleeps and eat dese beans and drop de hulls 'round yo' feet. Ah'll do de rest."

"Lawd, An' Dangie, dere' uh yard full uh houn' dawgs and chillun. Eben if none uh dem chillun see me, de dawgs gwine bark. Ah wuz past dere one day 'thout stoppin'."

"G'wan do lak Ah tell yuh. Ahm gwine hold de bitter bone in mah mouf so's you kin walk out de sight uh men. You bound tuh come out more'n conquer. Jes' you pay me whut Ah ast and 'tain't nothin' built up dat Ah can't tear down."

"Ah know you got de power."

"Humph! Ah reckon Ah is. Y' ever hear 'bout me boilin' uh wash-pot on uh sail needle?"

"Yas ma'am and mo' besides."

"Well don't come heah doubtin' lak you done jes' now. Aw right, pay me and g'wan do lak Ah tell yuh."

Hattie took the knotted handkerchief out of her stocking and paid. As she reached the door, the old woman called after her. "'Member now, you done started dis and it's got tuh be kep' up do hit'll turn back on yuh."

"Yas'm."

The door slammed and An' Dangie crept to her altar in the back room and began to dress candles with war water. When the altar had been set, she dressed the coffin in red, lit the inverted candles on the altar, saying as she did so, "Now fight! Fight and fuss 'til you part." When all was done at the altar she rubbed her hands and forehead with war powder, put the cat-bone in her mouth, and laid herself down in the red coffin facing the altar and went into the spirit.

Chapter XVI

LUCY was lying sick. The terrible enemy had so gnawed away her lungs that her frame was hardly distinguishable from the bed things.

"Isie?"

"Yes ma'am."

"Come give mama uh dose uh medicine."

"Yes'm."

The skinny-legged child of nine came bringing a cheap glass pitcher of water. "Ah pumped it off so it would be cool and nice fuh yuh."

"Thankee, Isie. Youse mah chile 'bove all de rest. Yo' pa come yet?"

"Yes'm, he out 'round de barn somewhere."

"Tell 'im Ah say tuh step heah uh minute."

John Pearson crossed the back porch slowly and heavily and entered the bedroom with downcast eyes.

"Whut you want wid me, Lucy?"

"Here 'tis Wednesday and you jus' gittin' home from San-ford, and know Ahm at uh mah back too. You know dat Hezekiah and John is uhway in school up tuh Jacksonville, and dese other chillun got tuh make out de bes' dey kin. You ought tuh uh come on home Monday and seen after things."

He looked sullenly at the floor and said nothing. Lucy used her spit cup and went on.

"Know too Ahm sick and you been home fuh de las' long-est and ain't been near me tuh offer me uh cup uh cool water uh ast me how Ah feel."

"Oh you sick, sick, sick! Ah hates tuh be 'round folks al-ways complainin', and then agin you always doggin' me 'bout sumpin'. Ah gits sick and tired uh hearing it!"

"Well, John, you puts de words in mah mouf. If you'd stay home and look after yo' wife and chillun, Ah wouldn't have nothin' tuh talk uhbout."

"Aw, yes you would! Always jawin' and complainin'."

Lucy said, "If you keep ole Hattie Tyson's letters out dis house where mah chillun kin git holt of 'em and you kin stop

folkses mouf by comin' on home instid uh layin' 'round wid her in Oviedo."

"Shet up! Ahm sick an' tired uh yo' yowin' and jawin'. 'Tain't nothin' Ah hate lak gittin' sin throwed in mah face dat done got cold. Ah do ez Ah please. You jus' uh hold-back tuh me nohow. Always sick and complainin'. Uh man can't utilize hisself."

He came to the bed and stood glaring down upon her. She seemed not to notice and said calmly after a short pause, "Ahm glad tuh know dat, John. After all dese years and all dat done went on dat Ah ain't been nothin' but uh stumblin'-stone tuh yuh. Go 'head on, Mister, but remember—youse born but you ain't dead. 'Tain't nobody so slick but whut they kin stand uh 'nother greasin'. Ah done told yuh time and time uhgin dat ignorance is de hawse dat wisdom rides. Don't git miss-put on yo' road. God don't eat okra."

"Oh you always got uh mouf full uh opinions, but Ah don't need you no mo' nor nothin you got tuh say, Ahm uh man grown. Don't need no guardzeen atall. So shet yo' mouf wid me."

"Ah ain't goin' tuh hush nothin' uh de kind. Youse livin' dirty and Ahm goin' tuh tell you 'bout it. Me and mah chillun got some rights. Big talk ain't changin' whut you doin'. You can't clean yo' self wid yo' tongue lak uh cat."

There was a resounding smack. Lucy covered her face with her hand, and John drew back in a sort of horror, and instantly strove to remove the brand from his soul by words, "Ah tole yuh tuh hush." He found himself shaking as he backed towards the door.

"De hidden wedge will come tuh light some day, John. Mark mah words. Youse in de majority now, but God sho don't love ugly."

John shambled out across the back porch, and stood for an unknowing time among the palmetto bushes in a sweating daze feeling like Nebuchadnezer in his exile.

Lucy turned her face to the wall and refused her supper that her older daughter Emmeline cooked and that Isis brought to her.

"But mama, you said special you wanted some batter-cakes."

"You eat 'em, Isie. Mama don't want uh thing. Come on in when you thru wid yo' supper lak you always do and read mama something out yo' reader."

But Isis didn't read. Lucy lay so still that she was frightened. She turned down the lamp by the head of the bed and started to leave, but Lucy stopped her.

"Thought you was sleep, mama."

"Naw, Isie, been watchin' dat great big ole spider."

"Where?"

"Up dere on de wall next tuh de ceilin'. Look lak he done took up uh stand."

"Want me tuh kill 'im wid de broom?"

"Naw, Isie, let 'im be. You didn't put 'im dere. De one dat put 'im dere will move 'im in his own time."

Isis could hear the other children playing in the back room.

"Reckon you wanta go play wid de rest, Isie, but mama wants tuh tell yuh somethin'."

"Whut is it, mama?"

"Isie, Ah ain't goin' tuh be wid yuh much longer, and when Ahm dead Ah wants you tuh have dis bed. Iss mine. Ah sewed fuh uh white woman over in Maitland and she gimme dis bedstead fuh mah work. Ah wants you tuh have it. Dis mah feather tick on here too."

"Yes'm mama, Ah—"

"Stop cryin', Isie, you can't hear whut Ahm sayin', 'member tuh git all de education you kin. Dat's de onliest way you kin keep out from under people's feet. You always strain tuh be de bell cow, never be de tail uh nothin'. Do de best you kin, honey, 'cause neither yo' paw nor dese older chillun is goin' tuh be bothered too much wid yuh, but you goin' tuh git 'long. Mark mah words. You got de spunk, but mah po' li'l' sandy-haired chile goin' suffer uh lot 'fo' she git tuh de place she kin 'fend fuh herself. And Isie, honey, stop cryin' and lissen tuh me. Don't you love nobody better'n you do yo'self. Do, you'll be dying befo' yo' time is out. And, Isie, uh person kin be killed 'thout being struck uh blow. Some uh dese things Ahm tellin' yuh, you won't understand 'em fuh years tuh come, but de time will come when you'll know. And Isie, when Ahm dyin' don't you let 'em take de pillow from under mah head, and be covering up de clock

and de lookin' glass and all sich ez dat. Ah don't want it done, heah? Ahm tellin' you in preference tuh de rest 'cause Ah know you'll see tuh it. Go wash yuh face and turn tuh de Twenty-Sixth Chapter of de Acts fuh me. Den you go git yo' night rest. If Ah want yuh, Ah'll call yuh."

Way in the night Lucy heard John stealthily enter the room and stand with the lamp in his hand peering down into her face. When she opened her eyes she saw him start.

"Oh," he exclaimed sharply with rising inflection. Lucy searched his face with her eyes but said nothing.

"Er, er, Ah jus' thought Ah'd come see if you wanted anything," John said nervously, "if you want anything, Lucy, all you got tuh do is tuh ast me. De favor is in me."

Lucy looked at her husband in a way that stepped across the ordinary boundaries of life and said, "Jus' have patience, John, uh few mo' days," and pulled down her lids over her eyes, and John was glad of that.

John rushed from Lucy's bedside to the road and strode up and down in the white moonlight. Finally he took his stand beneath the umbrella tree before the house and watched the dim light in Lucy's room. Nothing came to him there and he awoke Emmeline at daybreak, "Go in yo' ma's room Daught' and come back and tell me how she makin' it."

"She say she ain't no better," Daught' told him.

The spider was lower on the wall and Lucy entertained herself by watching to see if she could detect it move.

She sent Isis to bed early that Thursday night but she herself lay awake regarding the spider. She thought that she had not slept a moment, but when in the morning Isis brought the wash basin and tooth brush, Lucy noted that the spider was lower and she had not seen it move.

That afternoon Mrs. Mattie Clarke sat with her and sent Isis out to play.

"Lucy, how is it 'tween you and God?"

"You know Ah ain't never been one to whoop and holler in church, Sister Clarke, but Ah done put on de whole armor uh faith. Ah ain't afraid tuh die."

"Ahm sho glad tuh hear dat, Sister Pearson. Yuh know uh person kin live uh clean life and den dey kin be so fretted on dey dyin' bed 'til dey lose holt of de kingdom."

"Don't worry 'bout me, Sister Clarke. Ah done been in sorrow's kitchen and Ah done licked out all de pots. Ah done died in grief and been buried in de bitter waters, and Ah done rose agin from de dead lak Lazarus. Nothin' kin touch mah soul no mo'. It wuz hard tuh loose de string-holt on mah li'l' chillun." Her voice sank to a whisper, "but Ah reckon Ah done dat too."

"Put whip tuh yo' hawses, honey. Whip 'em up."

Despite Lucy's all-night vigil she never saw the spider when he moved, but at first light she noted that he was at least a foot from the ceiling but as motionless as a painted spider in a picture.

The evening train brought her second son, John, from Jacksonville. Lucy brightened.

"Where's Hezekiah?" she asked eagerly.

"He's comin'. His girl is gointer sing uh solo at de church on Sunday and he wants to hear her. Then he's coming right on. He told me to wire him how you were."

"Don't do it, John. Let 'im enjoy de singin'."

John told her a great deal about the school and the city and she listened brightly but said little.

After that look in the late watches of the night John was afraid to be alone with Lucy. His fear of her kept him from his bed at night. He was afraid lest she should die while he was asleep and he should awake to find her spirit standing over him. He was equally afraid of her reproaches should she live, and he was troubled. More troubled than he had ever been in all his life. In all his struggles of sleep, the large bright eyes looked thru and beyond him and saw too much. He wished those eyes would close and was afraid again because of his wish.

Lucy watched the spider each day as it stood lower. And late Sunday night she cried out, "O Evening Sun, when you git on de other side, tell mah Lawd Ahm here waitin'."

And God awoke at last and nodded His head.

In the morning she told Emmeline to fry chicken for dinner. She sent Isis out to play. "You been denyin' yo' pleasure fuh me. G'wan out and play wid de rest. Ah'll call yuh if Ah want yuh. Tell everybody tuh leave me alone. Ah don't want no bother. Shet de door tight."

She never did call Isis. Late in the afternoon she saw people going and coming, coming and going. She was playing ball before the house, but she became alarmed and went in.

The afternoon was bright and a clear light streamed into the room from the bare windows. They had turned Lucy's bed so that her face was to the East. The way from which the sun comes walking in red and white. Great drops of sweat stood out on her forehead and trickled upon the quilt and Isis saw a pool of sweat standing in a hollow at the elbow. She was breathing hard, and Isis saw her set eyes fasten on her as she came into the room. She thought that she tried to say something to her as she stood over her mother's head, weeping with her heart.

"Get her head offa dat pillow!" Mattie Mosely ordered. "Let her head down so she kin die easy."

Hoyt Thomas moved to do it, but Isis objected. "No, no, don't touch her pillow! Mama don't want de pillow from under her head!"

"Hush Isie!" Emmeline chided, "and let mama die easy. You makin' her suffer."

"Naw, naw! she said *not* tuh!" As her father pulled her away from her place above Lucy's head, Isis thought her mother's eyes followed her and she strained her ears to catch her words. But none came.

John stood where he could see his wife's face, but where Lucy's fixed eyes might not rest upon him. They drew the pillow from beneath Lucy's head and she gulped hard once, and was dead. "6:40" someone said looking at a watch.

"Po' thing," John wept. "She don't have tuh hear no mo' hurtin' things." He hurried out to the wood pile and sat there between two feelings until Sam Mosely led him away.

"She's gone!" rang out thru the crowded room and they heard it on the porch and Mattie Mosely ran shouting down the street, "She's gone, she's gone at last!"

And the work of the shrouding began. Little Lucy, somewhat smaller in death than she had been even in life, lay washed and dressed in white beneath a sheet upon the cooling board when her oldest son arrived that evening to break his heart in grief.

That night a wind arose about the house and blew from the

kitchen wall to the clump of oleanders that screened the chicken house, from the oleanders to the fence palings and back again to the house wall, and the pack of dogs followed it, rearing against the wall, leaping and pawing the fence, howling, barking and whining until the break of day, and John huddled beneath his bed-covers shaking and afraid.

Chapter XVII

THEY put Lucy in a little coffin next day, the shiny coffin that held the beginning and the ending of so much. And the September woods were ravished by the village to provide tight little bouquets for the funeral. Sam Mosely, tall, black and silent, hitched his bays to his light wagon and he bore Lucy from her house and children and husband and worries to the church, while John, surrounded by his weeping family, walked after the wagon, shaking and crying. The village came behind and filled the little church with weeping and wildflowers. People were stirred. The vital Lucy was gone. The wife of Moderator Pearson was dead.

"There is rest for the weary" rose and fell like an organ. Harmony soaked in tears.

"She don't need me no mo' nohow," John thought defensively.

"On the other side of Jordan, in the sweet fields of Eden—where the tree of life is blooming—"

And the hot blood in John's veins made him deny kinship with any rider of the pale white horse of death.

"Man born of woman has but a few days."

Clods of damp clay falling hollowly on the box. Out of sight of the world, and dead men heard her secrets.

That night they sat in the little parlor about the organ and the older children sang songs while the smaller ones cried and whimpered on. John sat a little apart and thought. He was free. He was sad, but underneath his sorrow was an exultation like a live coal under gray ashes. There was no longer guilt. But a few days before he had shuddered at the dread of discovery and of Lucy's accusing eye. There was no more sin. Just a free man having his will of women. He was glad in his sadness.

The next day John Pearson and Sam Mosely met on Clarke's porch. Sam remarked, "Funny thing, ain't it John— Lucy come tuh town twelve years uhgo in mah wagon and mah wagon took her uhway."

"Yeah, but she b'longed tuh me, though, all de time," John said and exulted over his friend.

Chapter XVIII

Deacons Hambo, Watson, Hoffman and Harris waited on Rev. Pearson in his study at the parsonage.

"No mealy-moufin, Harris. No whippin' de Devil 'round de stump. He got tuh be told." Hambo urged.

"Ahm goin' tuh tell 'im how we feel. You too hot tuh talk. You ain't in yo' right mind."

"Oh yes, Ah is too, Ahm hot, though. Ahm hot ez July jam. Jee-esus Christ!"

John entered the room radiating cheer.

"Hello, boys. How yuh do?"

"Don't do all dey say, but Ah do mah share," said Hambo quickly, "and damned if you don't do yourn."

Pearson didn't know whether it was one of the bluff Hambo's jokes or not. He started to laugh, then looked at the men's faces and quit.

"Oh."

"Now lemme handle dis, Hambo, lak we said," begged Harris.

"Naw, lemme open mah mouf 'fo' Ah bust mah gall. John, is you married tuh dat Hattie Tyson?"

"Yeah."

"De G— D— hell you is, man! Yo' wife ain't been dead but three months, and you done jumped up and married befo' she got col' in her grave!"

"Ah got dese li'l' chillun and somebody got tuh see after 'em."

"Well de somebody you got sho ain't seein' after 'em. They's 'round de streets heah jes' ez raggedy ez jay-birds in whistlin' time. Dey sho ain't gittin' uh damn bit uh 'tention."

"Course Ah didn't marry her jus' tuh wait on de chillun. She got tuh have some pleasure."

"Course she is! Dat strumpet ain't never done nothin' but run up and down de road from one sawmill camp tuh de other and from de looks of her, times was hard. She ain't never had nothin'—not eben doodly-squat, and when she gits uh chance tuh git holt uh sumpin de ole buzzard is gone

on uh rampage. She ain't got dis parsonage and dem po' li'l' motherless chillun tuh study 'bout."

"Hold on dere, Hambo, y'all. Dat's mah wife."

"Sh-h-ucks! Who don't know dat Hattie Tyson! Ah ain't gonna bite mah tongue uh damn bit and if you don't lak it, you kin jus' try me wid yo' fist. Ahm three times seben and uh button! And whut makes me mad 'nough tuh fight uh circle-saw is, you don't want uh yo'self. You done got trapped and you ain't got de guts tuh take uh rascal-beater and run her way from here. She done moved you 'way from Eatonville 'cause 'tain't 'nough mens and likker dere tuh suit her."

"Wait uh minute, Hambo."

"Ain't gonna wait nothin' uh de kind. Wait broke de wagon down. Ah jes' feel lak takin' uh green club and waitin' on dat wench's head until she acknowledge Ahm God and besides me there's no other! Gimme lief, John, and Ah'll make haste and do it. Ah feels lak stayin' wid yo' head uh week. Dey tell me you eben drawed uh knife on yo' son John, 'cause he tried tuh keep dat strumpet out his mama's feather bed dat she give tuh li'l' Isis on her death-bed, and nobody but uh lowdown woman would want you scornin' yo' name all up lak dat."

Pearson hung his head.

"If y'all come heah tuh 'buke me, g'wan do it."

Hoffman spoke up.

"We ain't come to 'buke you, Reverend, but de church sho is talkin' and gittin' onrestless 'bout yo' marriage."

"Yeah, dat's jus' whut Ah come fuh—tuh 'buke yuh. Ah ain't come tuh make yuh no play-party. Stoopin' down from where you stand, fuh whut?" Hambo broke out again, "Jus' 'cause you never seen no talcum powder and silk kimonos back dere in Alabama."

Harris and Hoffman took him by the arms and led him forth, and John went back upstairs and wept.

Hattie had heard it all, but she stayed out of sight until the rough tongued Hambo was gone. She went to John, but first she combed her hair and under-braided the piece of John-de-conquer root in her stiff back hair. "Dey can't move me—not wid de help Ah got," she gloated and went in to John where he lay weeping.

"Thought you tole me dat Hambo wuz yo' bosom friend?"

"He is, Hattie. Ah don't pay his rough talk no mind."

"Ah don't call dat no friend—comin' right in yo' house and talkin' 'bout yo' wife lak she wuz uh dog. If you wuz any kind of uh man you wouldn't 'low it."

"Uh preacher can't be fightin' and keerin' on. Mo' special uh Moderator. Hambo don't mean no harm. He jus 'fraid de talk might hurt me."

"Him and them sho treats me lak uh show man treats uh ape. Come right in mah house and run de hawg over me and tryin' tuh put you 'ginst me. Youse over dem and you ought not tuh 'low 'em tuh cheap, but 'stid uh dat they comes right to yo' face and calls yo' wife uh barrel uh dem things. Lawd knows Ah ain't got no puhtection uh tall! If Miss Lucy had tuh swaller all Ah does, Ah know she glad she dead."

"Lucy ain't never had nobody to call her out her name. Dey better not. Whut make *you* call her name? Hambo is de backbone uh mah church. Ah don't aim to tear de place tuh pieces fuh nobody. Put dat in yo' pipe and smoke it."

Hattie heard and trembled. The moment that John left town to conduct a revival meeting, she gathered what money she could and hurried to the hut of An' Dangie Dewoe.

Chapter XIX

THE LORD of the wheel that turns on itself slept, but the world kept spinning, and the troubled years sped on. Tales of weakness, tales of vice hung about John Pearson's graying head. Tales of wifely incontinence which Zion Hope swallowed hard. The old ones especially. Sitting coolly in the shade of after-life, they looked with an utter lack of tolerance upon the brawls of Hattie and John. They heard her complaints often and believed her and only refused action because they knew the complainant to be equally guilty, but less popular than the man against whom she cried. Besides, the younger generation winked at what their elders cried over. Lucy had counselled well, but there were those who exulted in John's ignominious fall from the Moderatorship after nine years tenure, and milled about him like a wolf pack about a tired old bull—looking for a throat-hold, but he had still enough of the former John to be formidable as an animal and enough of his Pagan poesy to thrill. The pack waited. John knew it and was tired unto death of fighting off the struggle which must surely come. The devouring force of the future leered at him at unexpected moments. Then too his daily self seemed to be wearing thin, and the past seeped thru and mastered him for increasingly longer periods. He whose present had always been so bubbling that it crowded out past and future now found himself with a memory.

He began to remember friends who had lain back on the shelf of his mind for years. Now and then he surprised them by casual visits, but the pitying look would send him away and it would be a long time before he made such a call again.

He began to see a good deal of Zeke who had moved with his family to Florida, a year or two before Lucy died. He loved seeing Zeke because he was just as great a hero in his brother's eyes as he had been when he was the biggest Negro Baptist in the State and when Zion Hope had nine hundred members instead of the six hundred now on its roll. Zeke talked but always spared him.

Yes, John Pearson found himself possessed of a memory at a time when he least needed one.

"Funny thing," he said sitting in Zeke's kitchen with his wife, "things dat happened long time uhgo used to seem way off, but now it all seems lak it wuz yistiddy. You think it's dead but de past ain't stopped breathin' yet."

"Eat supper wid us, John Buddy, and stay de night."

"Thankee, Zeke. B'lieve Ah will fuh uh change." He went to bed at Zeke's after supper. Slept a long time. He awoke with a peculiar feeling and crept out of the house and went home.

"Hattie, whut am Ah doin' married tuh you?" John was standing in his wife's bedroom beside her bed and looking down on her, a few minutes later.

Hattie sat up abruptly, pulling up the shoulder straps of her nightgown.

"Is dat any way fuh you tuh do? Proagin' 'round half de night lak uh damn tom cat and den come heah, wakin' me up tuh ast uh damn fool question?"

"Well, you answer me den. Whut is us doin' married?"

"If you been married tuh uh person seben years and den come ast sich uh question, you mus' be crazy uh drunk one. You *is* drunk! You oughta know whut us doin' married jus' ez well ez Ah do."

"But Ah don't. God knows Ah sho don't. Look lak Ah been sleep. Ah ain't never meant tuh marry you. Ain't got no recollection uh even tryin' tuh marry yuh, but here us is married, Hattie, how come dat?"

"Is you crazy sho 'nuff?"

"Naw, Ah ain't crazy. Look lak de first time Ah been clothed in mah right mind fuh uh long time. Look lak uh whole heap uh things been goin' on in mah sleep. You got tuh tell me how come me and you is married."

"Us married 'cause you said you wanted me. Dat's how come."

"Ah don't have no 'membrance uh sayin' no sich uh thing. Don't b'lieve Ah said it neither."

"Well you sho said so—more'n once too. Ah married yuh jes' tuh git rid of yuh."

"Aw naw. Ah ain't begged you tuh marry me, nothin' uh

de kind. Ah ain't said nothin' 'bout lovin' yuh tuh my knowin', but even if Ah did, youse uh experienced woman—had plenty experience 'fo' Ah ever seen yuh. You know better'n tuh b'lieve anything uh man tell yuh after ten o'clock at night. You know so well Ah ain't wanted tuh marry you. Dat's how come Ah know it's uh bug under dis chip."

"Well—if you didn't want me you made lak yuh did," Hattie said doggedly.

"Dat sho is funny, 'cause Ah know Ah wanted Miss Lucy and Ah kin call tuh memory eve'y li'l' thing 'bout our courtin' and 'bout us gittin' married. Couldn't fuhgit it if Ah wuz tuh try. Mo' special and particular, Ah remember jus' how Ah felt when she looked at me and when Ah looked at her and when we touched each other. Ah recollect how de moon looked de night us married, and her li'l' bare feets over de floor, but Ah don't remember nothin' 'bout *you*. Ah don't know how de moon looked and even if it rained uh no. Ah don't 'call to mind making no 'rangements tuh marry yuh. So you mus' know mo' 'bout it than Ah do."

Hattie pulled her long top lip down over the two large chalky-white false teeth in front and thought a while. She sank back upon her pillow with an air of dismissal. "Youse drunk and anybody'd be uh fool tuh talk after yuh. You know durned well how come you married me."

"Naw, Ah don't neither. Heap uh things done went on Ah ain't meant tuh be. Lucy lef' seben chillun in mah keer. Dey ain't here now. Where is mah chillun, Hattie? Whut mah church doin' all tore up? Look at de whiskey bottles settin' 'round dis house. Dat didn't useter be."

"Yeah, and you sho drinks it too."

"But Ah didn't useter. Not in Lucy's time. She never drunk none herself lak you do, and she never brought none in de house tuh tempt me."

"Aw g'wan out heah! Don't keer if Ah do take uh swaller uh two. You de pastor uh Zion Hope, not me. You don't hav' to do lak me. Youse older'n me. Hoe yo' own row. De nig-gers fixin' tuh put yuh out dat pulpit 'bout yo' women and yo' likker and you tryin' tuh blame it all on me."

"Naw it's jus' uh hidden mystery tuh me—whut you doin' in Miss Lucy's shoes."

And like a man arisen, but with sleep still in his eyes, he went out of the door and to his own bedroom.

Hattie lay tossing, wondering how she could get to An' Dangie Dewoe without arousing suspicion.

"Wonder is Ah done let things go too long, or is de roots jus' done wore out and done turn'd back on me?"

There was no sleep in either bedroom that night.

Hattie crept into John's bed at dawn and tried her blandishments but he thrust her rudely away.

"Don't you want me tuh love yuh no mo'?"

"Naw."

"How come?"

"It don't seem lak iss clean uh sumpin."

"Is you mad cause Ah learnt tuh love yuh so hard way back dere 'fo' Miss Lucy died?"

"Ah didn't mind you lovin' me, but Ah sho is mad wid yuh fuh marryin' me. Youse jus' lak uh blowfly. Spoil eve'y thing yuh touch. You sho ain't no Lucy Ann."

"Naw, Ah ain't no Miss Lucy, 'cause Ah ain't goin' tuh cloak yo' dirt fuh yuh. Ah ain't goin' tuh take offa yuh whut she took so you kin set up and be uh big nigger over mah bones."

"'Tain't no danger uh me bein' no big nigger wid *you* uhround. Ah sure ain't de State Moderator no mo'."

"And dat ain't all. You fool wid me and Ah'll jerk de cover offa you and dat Berry woman. Ah'll throw uh brick in yo' coffin and don't keer how sad de funeral will be, and Ah dare yuh tuh hit me too. Ah ain't gonna be no ole man's fool."

"You know Ah don't beat no women folks. Ah married Lucy when she wuzn't but fifteen and us lived tuhgether twenty-two years and Ah ain't never lifted mah hand—"

Suddenly a seven-year-old picture came before him. Lucy's bright eyes in the sunken face. Helpless and defensive. The look. Above all, the look! John stared at it in fascinated horror for a moment. The sea of the soul, heaving after a calm, giving up its dead. He drove Hattie from his bed with vile imprecations.

"You, you!" he sobbed into the crook of his arm when he was alone, "you made me do it. And Ah ain't never goin' tuh git over it long ez Ah live."

During breakfast they quarreled over the weak coffee and Hattie swore at him.

"No woman ain't never cussed me yet and you ain't gonna do it neither—not and tote uh whole back," he gritted out between his teeth and beat her severely, and felt better. Felt almost as if he had not known her when Lucy was sick. He panged a little less. So after that he beat her whenever she vexed him. More interest paid on the debt of Lucy's slap. He pulled the crayon enlargement of Hattie's out of its frame and belligerently thrust it under the wash-pot while she was washing and his smoking eyes warned her not to protest.

"Rev'und," she began at breakfast one morning, "Ah needs uh pair uh shoes."

"Whyn't yuh go git 'em den?"

"Where Ahm goin' tuh git 'em from?"

"Speer got plenty and J. C. Penney swear he sells 'em."

"Dat ain't doin' me no good lessen Ah got de money tuh buy 'em wid."

"Ain't yuh got no money?"

"You ain't gimme none, is yuh? Not in de last longest."

"Oh you got shoes uh plenty. Ah see yuh have five uh six pairs 'round out under de dresser. Miss Lucy never had nothin' lak dat."

"Miss Lucy agin! Miss Lucy dis, Miss Lucy dat!"

"Yeah Miss Lucy, and Ahm gointer put uh headstone at her grave befo' anybody git shoes 'round heah—eben me."

"Mah shoes is nelly wore out, man. Dat headstone kin wait."

"Naw, Hattie, 'tain't gonna wait. Don't keer if youse so nelly barefooted 'til yo' toes make prints on de ground. She's gointer git her remembrance-stone first. You done wore out too many uh her shoes already. Here, take dis two bits and do anything you wanta wid it."

She threw it back viciously. "Don't come lounchin' me out no two bits when Ah ast you fuh shoes."

Hattie reported this to certain church officers and displayed her general shabbiness. Harris sympathized.

"Iss uh shame, Sister. Ah'd cut down dat Jonah's gourd vine in uh minute, if Ah had all de say-so. You know Ah would, but de majority of 'em don't keer whut he do, some

uh dese people stands in wid it. De man mus' is got roots uh
got piece uh dey tails buried by his door-step. Know whut
some of 'em tole me? Says he ain't uh bit worse dan de rest
uh y'all 'round de altar dere. Y'll gits all de women yuh kin.
He jus' de bes' lookin' and kin git mo' of 'em dan de rest. Us
pays him tuh preach and he kin sho do dat. De best in de
State, and whut make it so cool, he's de bes' lookin'. Eben
dem gray hairs becomes 'im. Nobody don't haft do lak he *do*,
jus' do lak he *say* do. Yes ma'am, Sister Pearson 'twon't do
fuh us tuh try tuh handle 'im. He'd beat de case. De mo' he
beat you de better some of 'em laks it. Dey chunkin stones at
yo' character and sayin' you ain't fit. Pot calling de kittle
black. Dey points de finger uh scorn at yuh and say yo' eye is
black. All us kin do is tuh lay low and wait on de Lawd."

"Sho wisht Ah could he'p mahself," Hattie whimpered.

"They *is* help if you knows how tuh git it. Some folks kin
hit uh straight lick wid uh crooked stick. They's sich uh thing
ez two-headed men."

"You b'lieve in all dat ole stuff 'bout hoodoo and sich lak,
Brer Harris?" Hattie watched Harris's face closely.

"Yeah, Ah do, Mrs. Rev'und. Ah done seen things done.
Why hit's in de Bible, Sister! Look at Moses. He's de greatest
hoodoo man dat God ever made. He went 'way from
Pharaoh's palace and stayed in de desert nigh on to forty years
and learnt how tuh call God by all his secret names and dat's
how he got all dat power. He knowed he couldn't bring off
all dem people lessen he had power unekal tuh man! How you
reckon he brought on all dem plagues if he didn't had nothin'
but human power? And then agin his wife wuz Ethiopian. Ah
bet she learnt 'im whut he knowed. Ya, indeed, Sister
Pearson. De Bible is de best conjure book in de world."

"Where Ahm goin' ter fin' uh two-headed doctor? Ah
don't know nothin' 'bout things lak dat, but if it kin he'p
mah condition—"

"An' Dangie Dewoe wuz full uh power, but she dead now,
but up t'wards Palatka is uh 'nother one dat's good. He calls
hisself War Pete."

The old black woman of the sky chased the red-eyed sun
across the sky every evening and smothered him in her cloak
at last. This had happened many times. Night usually found

John at his brother's house until late or at the bluff Deacon Hambo's who kept filthy epithets upon his tongue for his pastor, but held down the church with an iron hand.

A fresh rumor spread over the nation. It said war. It talked of blood and glory—of travel, of North, of Oceans and transports, of white men and black.

And black men's feet learned roads. Some said good bye cheerfully . . . others fearfully, with terrors of unknown dangers in their mouths . . . others in their eagerness for distance said nothing. The daybreak found them gone. The wind said North. Trains said North. The tides and tongues said North, and men moved like the great herds before the glaciers.

Conscription, uniforms, bands, strutting drum-majors, and the mudsills of the earth arose and skipped like the mountains of Jerusalem on The Day. Lowly minds who knew not their State Capitals were talking glibly of France. Over there. No man's land.

"Gen'l Pushin', Gen'l Punishin', Gen'l Perchin', Gen'l Pershin'. War risk, war bread, insurance, Camp dis-and-dat. Is you heard any news? Dead? Lawd a mussy! Sho hope mah boy come thew aw-right. De black man ain't got no voice but soon ez war come who de first man dey shove in front? De nigger! Ain't it de truth? Bet if Ole Teddy wuz in de chear he'd straighten out eve'ything. Wilson! Stop dat ole lie. Wilson ain't de man Teddy Roosevelt wuz. De fightin'est man and the rulin'est man dat God ever made. Ain't never been two sho 'nuff smart mens in dese United States—Teddy Roosevelt and Booger T. Washington. Nigger so smart he et at de White House. Built uh great big ole school wuth uh thousand dollars, maybe mo'. Teddy wuz allus sendin' fuh 'im tuh git 'im tuh he'p 'im run de Guv'ment. Yeah man, dat's de way it 'tis—niggers think up eve'ything good and de white folks steal it from us. Dass right. Nigger invented de train. White man seen it and run right off and made him one jes' lak it and told eve'ybody he thought it up. Same way wid 'lectwicity. Nigger thought dat up too. DuBois? Who is dat? 'Nother smart nigger? Man, he can't be smart ez Booger T.! Whut did dis DuBois ever do? He writes up books and papers, hunh? Shucks! dat ain't nothin', anybody kin put down

words on uh piece of paper. Gimme da paper sack and lemme see dat pencil uh minute. Shucks! Writing! Man Ah thought you wuz talkin' 'bout uh man whut had done sumpin. Ah thought maybe he wuz de man dat could make side-meat taste lak ham."

Armistice. Demobilized. Home in khaki. "Yeah man, parlez vous, man, don't come bookooin' 'round heah, yuh liable tuh git hurt. Ah could uh married one uh dem French women but shucks, gimme uh brown skin eve'y time. Blacker de berry sweeter de juice. Come tuh mah pick, gimme uh good black gal. De wine wuz sour, and Ah says parlez vous, hell! You gimme mah right change! Comme telly vous. Nar, Ah ain't goin' back tuh no farm no mo'. Ah don't mean tuh say, 'Git up' tuh nary 'nother mule lessen he's setting down in mah lap. God made de world but he never made no hog outa me tuh go 'round rootin' it up. Done done too much bookoo plowing already! Woman quick gimme mah sumpin t'eat. Toot sweet."

World gone money mad. The pinch of war gone, people must spend. Buy and forget. Spend and solace. Silks for sorrows. Jewels to bring back joy. The factories roared and cried, "Hands!" and in the haste and press white hands became scarce. Scarce and dear. Hands? Who cares about the color of hands? We need hands and muscle. The South—land of muscled hands.

"George, haven't you got some relatives and friends down South who'd like a job?"

"Yes, suh."

"Write 'em to come."

Some had railroad fare and quickly answered the call of the North and sent back for others, but this was too slow. The wheels and marts were hungry. So the great industries sent out recruiting agents throughout the South to provide transportation to the willing but poor.

"Lawd, Sanford gettin' dis Nawth bound fever lak eve'y-where else," Hambo complained one Sunday in church. "Elder, you know we done lost two hund'ed members in three months?"

"Co'se Ah knows it, Hambo. Mah pocketbook kin tell it, if nothing else. Iss rainin' in mah meal barrel right uh long."

"Dat's awright. De celery farms is making good. All dese folks gone Nawth makes high wages 'round heah. Less raise de church dues," and it was done.

But a week later Hambo was back. "Looka heah, John, dis thing is gittin' serious sho 'nuff. De white folks is gittin' worried too. Houses empty eve'ywhere. Not half 'nough people tuh work de farms—crops rotting in de ground. Folks plantin' and ain't eben takin' time tuh reap. Mules lef' standin' in de furrers. Some de folks gone 'thout lettin' de families know, and dey say iss de same way, only wurser, all over de South. Dey talkin' 'bout passin' laws tuh keep black folks from buying railroad tickets. Dey tell me dey stopped uh train in Georgy and made all de colored folks git off. Up dere iss awful, de pullman porters tell me. Ride half uh day and see nothin' but farms wid nobody on 'em."

"Yeah," Pearson answered, "had uh letter from mah son in Tennessee. Same way. In some parts de white folks jails all them recruitin' agents so dey hafta git de word uhround in secret. Folks hafta slip off. Drive off in cars and ketch trains further up de line."

"Tell yuh whut Ah seen down tuh Orlando. De man wuz skeered tuh git offa de train, but he seen uh colored man standin' 'round de deepo', so he took and called 'im and he says, 'Ahm uh labor agent, wanta work?' He tole him, 'Yes suh.' 'Well git some mo' men and have 'em down heah tuh meet de Nawth bound train at 2:40 o'clock. Ah'll stick mah hand out de winder and show wid mah fingers how many Ah got transportation for. Y'all watch good and count mah fingers right,' and he done it. Wanted sixteen. He beckoned one of 'em onto de train and fixed up wid him fuh de rest and dey all went wid' im. Dat's all yuh kin heah. On de streets—in de pool-room—pickin' beans on de farm—in de cook kitchen—over de wash board—before dey go in church and soon ez dey come out, tellin' who done already went and who fixin' tuh go."

"Yeah," agreed Rev. Pearson, "we preachers is in uh tight fix. Us don't know whether tuh g'wan Nawth wid de biggest part of our churches or stay home wid de rest."

"Some of 'em done went. Know one man from Palatka done opened up uh church in Philadelphy and most of 'em is

his ole congregation. Zion Hope sho done lost uh many one. Most of 'em young folks too."

"Well maybe they won't stay Nawth. Most of 'em ain't use-ter col' weather fuh one thing."

"Yeah, but dey'll git used tuh it. Dey up dere now makin' big money and livin' in brick houses. Iss powerful hard tuh git uh countryman outa town. He's jus' ez crazy 'bout it ez uh hog is 'bout town swill. Dey won't be back soon."

Do what they would, the State, County and City all over the South could do little to halt the stampede. The cry of "Goin' Nawth" hung over the land like the wail over Egypt at the death of the first-born. The railroad stations might be watched, but there could be no effective censorship over the mails. No one could keep track of the movements of cars and wagons and mules and men walking. Railroads, hardroads, dirt roads, side roads, roads were in the minds of the black South and all roads led North.

Whereas in Egypt the coming of the locust made desolation, in the farming South the departure of the Negro laid waste the agricultural industry—crops rotted, houses careened crazily in their utter desertion, and grass grew up in streets. On to the North! The land of promise.

Chapter XX

Hattie was rubbing in the first water and dropping the white things into the wash-pot when Deacon Harris hurried up to her back gate.

"Mawnin', Sister Pearson," opening the gate.

"Howdy do, Deacon?"

"Ain't got no right tuh grumble. How you?"

"Not so many, dis mawnin'. You look lak you in uh kinda slow hurry."

"Nope, jes' anxious tuh tell yuh uh thing uh two."

"If is sumpin tuh better mah condition, hurry up and tell it. God knows Ah sho needs somebody tuh give aid and assistance. Reverend and his gang sho is gripin' me. Ah feels lak uh cat in hell wid no claws."

"First thing, Ah got uh man Ah b'lieve, if de crowd ever git tuh hear 'im, dey'd lak 'im better'n de Rev'und."

"Where he come from?"

"Wes' Floriduh. Man he kin cold preach! Preached over in Goldsborough las' night and strowed fire all over de place. Younger man dan Pearson too."

"Can't you fix it fuh 'im tuh speak at Zion Hope?"

"Sho. Done 'bout got it fixed fuh de fourth Sunday night. Dat ain't Pastoral Sunday, but it's de nex' bes'. De crowd'll be almos' ez big."

"Dat's fine! Some uh dem niggers don't b'lieve nobody kin preach but John Pearson. Let 'em see. Den maybe dey'll set 'im down. Ah don't keer whut dey do wid 'im. Ah do know one thing, Ah sho got mah belly full. Whus de other things you wuz goin' tuh tell me 'bout?"

"Well, in looking over de books, I saw where mos' of the folks whut would stand up for Rev'und so hard, is gone. If we wuz tuh bring de thing tuh uh vote Ah b'lieve we kin dig up de hidden wedge. Ah been sorta feelin' 'round 'mong some de members and b'lieve de time done come when we kin chop down dis Jonah's gourd vine."

"Dat sho would be all de heben Ah ever want to see. How

kin we bring it uhbout? You got tuh have plenty tuh show do some uh dat crowd won't hear it."

"You git uh divorce from 'im. You kin git plenty witnesses tuh bear yuh out in dat. Ah'll be one mahself."

"Chile, he wouldn't keer nothin' 'bout dat. He'd be glad, Ah speck, so he kin run loose wid dat Gertie Burden. Dat's de one he sho 'nuff crazy 'bout."

"Who you tellin'? Ever since she wuz knee high. Us knowed it all de time, but thought yuh didn't."

"He don't try tuh keep it out mah sight. He washes mah face wid her night and day."

"You jokin'!!"

"Know whut he tole me las' time Ah got 'im 'bout her? Says, 'Don't be callin' dat girl all out her name, Miss Lucy didn't call *you* nothin'.' Deacon Harris, Ah wuz so mad Ah could uh lammed 'im wid lightnin', but how de divorce goin' set 'im down?"

"Yuh see de church punishes fuh things de law don't chastize fuh, and if iss so bad 'til de law'll handle it, de church is bound tuh. Don't need no mo' trial."

"But Ah can't eben start uh divorce trial jus' dry long so."

"You kin pick uh fight outa Sister Berry uh Gertie Burden, can't yuh? Dat'll th'ow de fat in de fiah, and bring eve'ything out in de day light, and when iss all over wid, he'll be uh lost ball in de high grass. Ah sick and tiahed uh all dese so-called no-harm sins. Dis ain't no harm, and dat ain't no harm, and all dese li'l' no-harm sins is whut leads folks straight to hell."

"De one Ah wants tuh beat de worse is dat ole Beery Buzzard. Right on de church ground she ast me one Sunday, if Miss Lucy's bed wudden still hot when Ah got in it."

"Jump on her, den."

"She's rawbony, but she look real strong tuh me. Ole long, tall, black huzzy! Wisht Ah could hurt 'er."

"She don't eat iron biscuits and she don't sop cement gravy. She kin be hurt, and den agin, you kin git help—not open, yuh know, but on de sly. Somebody tuh hand yuh sumpin jes' when you need it bad."

"When mus' Ah tackle de slut?"

"De very nex' time Rev'und goes off somewhere tuh

preach. If he's dere he'd git it stopped too quick. Befo' it make uhnough disturbment."

Two incidents nerved Hattie's hand. The first, that same evening Rev. Pearson came in from some carpentry work he had been doing out around Geneva, obviously crestfallen, but nothing she did succeeded in making him tell her the reason.

If she could have seen her husband at noon time of that very same day she would have seen him seated beside the luscious Gertie on a cypress log with her left hand in his and his right arm about her waist.

"John, Ah b'lieve Ahm goin ter marry."

"Please, Gertie, don't say dat."

"You married, ain'tcha? Ahm twenty-two. Papa and mama spectin' me tuh marry some time uh other and dey think Ah oughter take dis chance. You know he got uh big orange grove wid uh house on it and seben hund'ed dollars in de bank."

"Dat's right, Gertie. Take yo' chance when it comes. Don't think—don't look at me. Ahm all spoilt now. Kiss me one mo' time. Den Ah got tuh go back tuh work. Lawd, Ah hope you be happy. Iss wonderful tuh marry somebody when you wants tuh. You don't keer whut you do tuh please 'em. Some women you wouldn't mind tearin' up de pavements uh hell tuh built 'em uh house, but some you don't give 'em nothin'. You jes' consolate 'em by word uh mouf and fill 'em full uh melody."

Therefore the next morning at breakfast when John grumbled about the scorched grits and Hattie threatened to dash hot coffee in John's face, he beat her soundly. The muscular exercise burnt up a portion of his grief, but it urged Hattie on. A few days later, when she learned of Gertie's engagement, she was exultant. "Now maybe, it'll hurt 'im, if Ah quit 'im. Gittin loose from me might gripe 'em now—anyhow it sho ain't gwine he'p 'im none wid Gertie."

Hattie knew, as do other mortals, that half the joy of quitting any place is the loneliness we leave behind.

Chapter XXI

THE FOURTH SUNDAY came shining with the dangerous beauty of flame. Between Sunday School and the 11:00 o'clock service, Andrew Berry called Rev. Pearson aside.

"Is de deacon board tole yuh?"

"'Bout whut?"

"De new preacher dey got here tuh try out tuhnight?"

"Naw, but Hambo did tell me tuh strow fire dis mawnin'. Reckon he wuz throwin' me uh hint right den."

"Ahm sho he wuz. De Black Herald got it dat dey got *you* on de let-loose and de onliest thing dat keeps some of 'em hangin' on is dey don't b'lieve nobody kin preach lak you, but if dis man dey got here tuhday kin surpass yuh, den dere'll be some changes made. Harris and de Black Dispatch say he kin drive all over yuh."

"Maybe he kin, Andrew. Ain't dat him over dere, talkin' tuh Sister Williams?"

"Yeah. He'll be tuh de service tuh hear *you* so he kin know how tuh do tuhnight when he gits up tuh preach."

John Pearson shook hands politely when he was introduced to Rev. Felton Cozy when he entered the church. Rev. Cozy was cordially invited to sit in the pulpit, which he did very pompously. All during the prayer service that led up to the sermon he was putting on his Oxford glasses, glaring about the church and taking them off again.

Rev. Pearson preached his far-famed, "Dry Bones" sermon, and in the midst of it the congregation forgot all else. The church was alive from the pulpit to the door. When the horse in the valley of Jehoshaphat cried out, "Ha, ha! There never was a horse like me!" He brought his hearers to such a frenzy that it never subsided until two Deacons seized the preacher by the arms and reverently set him down. Others rushed up into the pulpit to fan him and wipe his face with their own kerchiefs.

"Dat's uh preachin' piece uh plunder, you hear me?" Sister Hall gloated. "Dat other man got tuh go some if he specks tuh top dat."

"Can't do it," Brother Jeff avowed, "can't be done."

"Aw, you don't know," contended Sister Scale. "Wait 'til you hear de tother one."

"Elder Pearson ain't preached lak dat in uh long time. Reckon he know?"

"Aw naw. Dey kep' it from 'im. When he know anything, de church'll be done done whut dey going tuh do."

When Rev. Cozy arose that night the congregation slid forward to the edge of its seat.

"Well, y'all done heard one sermon tuhday, and now Ah stand before you, handlin' de Alphabets." He looked all about him to get the effect of his statement. "Furthermo', Ah got uhnother serus job on mah hands. Ahm a race man! Ah solves the race problem. One great problem befo' us tuhday is whut is de blacks gointer do wid de whites?"

After five minutes or more Sister Boger whispered to Sister Pindar, "Ah ain't heard whut de tex' wuz."

"Me neither."

Cozy had put on and removed his glasses with the wide black ribbon eight times.

"And Ah say unto you, de Negro has got plenty tuh feel proud over. Ez fur back ez man kin go in his-to-ree, de black man wuz always in de lead. When Caesar stood on de Roman forum, uccordin' tuh de best authority, uh black man stood beside him. Y'all say 'Amen.' Don't let uh man preach hisself tuh death and y'all set dere lak uh bump on uh log and won't he'p 'im out. Say 'Amen'!!

"And fiftly, Je-sus, Christ, wuz uh colored man hisself and Ah kin prove it! When he lived it wuz hot lak summer time, all de time, wid de sun beamin' down and scorchin' hot—how could he be uh white man in all dat hot sun? Say 'Amen'! Say it lak you mean it, and if yuh do mean it, tell me so! Don't set dere and say nothin'!

"Furthermo' Adam musta been uh colored man 'cause de Bible says God made 'im out de dust uh de earth, and where is anybody ever seen any white dust? Amen! Come on, church, say 'Amen'!

"And twelfth and lastly, all de smartest folks in de world got colored blood in 'em. Wese de smartest people God ever made and de prettiest. Take our race—wese uh mingled

people. Jes' lak uh great bouquet uh flowers. Eve'y color and eve'y kind. Nobody don't need tuh go hankerin' after no white womens. We got womens in our own race jes' ez white ez anybody. We got 'em so black 'til lightnin' bugs would follow 'em at twelve o'clock in de day—thinkin' iss midnight and us got 'em in between.

"And nothin' can't go on nowhere but whut dere's uh nigger in it! Say 'Amen'!"

"Amen! He sho is tellin' de truth now!"

At the close of the service, many came forward and shook Cozy's hand and Harris glowed with triumph. He was dry and thirsty for praise in connection with his find so he tackled Sisters Watson and Boger on the way home.

"How y'all lak de sermon tuhnight?"

"Sermon?" Sister Boger made an indecent sound with her lips, "dat wan't no sermon. Dat wuz uh lecture."

"Dat's all whut it wuz," Sister Watson agreed and switched on off.

Harris knew that he must find some other weapon to move the man who had taken his best side-girl from him.

Chapter XXII

HARRIS, Hattie and one-eyed Fred Tate went on with their plans for the complete overthrow of Rev. Pearson thru the public chastisement of Sister Berry, but things began to happen in other directions.

While she held a caucus one afternoon with supporters, Hambo sat at Zeke's house and sent one of Zeke's children to find John.

"John, youse in boilin' water and tuh you—look lak 'tain't no help fuh it. Dat damn 'oman you got b'lieves in all kinds uh roots and conjure. She been feedin' you outa her body fuh years. Go home now whilst she's off syndicatin' wid her gang—and rip open de mattress on yo' bed, de pillow ticks, de bolsters, dig 'round de door-steps in front de gate and look and see ain't some uh yo' draws and shirt-tails got pieces cut offa 'em. Hurry now, and come back and let us know whut you find out. G'wan! Don't stop tuh race yo' lip wid mine, and don't try tuh tell me whut you think. Jes' you g'wan do lak Ah tell yuh."

John Pearson went and returned with a miscellany of weird objects in bottles, in red flannel, and in toad-skin.

"Lawd, Hambo, here's uh piece uh de tail uh—uh shirt Ah had 'fo' Lucy died. Umph! Umph! Umph!"

"Ha! Ah wuz spectin' dat!"

"Whut kin Ah do 'bout it, Hambo?"

"Give it here. Less take it tuh uh hoodoo doctor and turn it back on her, but whut you got tuh do is tuh beat de blood outa her. When you draw her wine dat breaks de spell—don't keer whut it is."

"Don't you fret 'bout dat. Ah 'bominates sich doings. She gointer git her wine drawed dis day, de Lawd bein' mah helper. Ahm goin' on home and be settin' dere when she come."

Hattie saw the hole at the gate and the larger one at the front steps before she entered the yard. Inside, the upturned rugs, the ripped-up beds, all had fearful messages for her. Who had done this thing? Had her husband hired a two-

headed doctor to checkmate her? How long had he been suspecting her? Where was he now?

"Hattie," John called from the dining-room. She would have bolted, but she saw he made ready to stop her. She stood trembling in the hallway like a bird before a reptile.

"Whut you jumpin' on me fuh?" she cried out as he flung himself upon her.

"You too smart uh woman tuh ast dat, and when Ah git th'ew wid you, you better turn on de fan, and make me some tracks Ah ain't seen befo' do Ahm gointer kill yuh. Hoodooin' me! Stand up dere, 'oman, Ah ain't hit you yet."

And when the neighbors pulled him from her weakening body he dropped into a chair and wept hard. Wept as he had not wept since his daughter's serious illness, emptying out his feelings.

Hattie fled the house, not even waiting to bathe her wounds nor change her clothes. When John's racking sobs had ceased, the stillness after the tumult soothed him. He bathed and slept fourteen hours. In the morning he wrote to each of his children a shy letter. On the third day Hattie struck. He was sued for divorce.

"Ahm sho glad," he told Zeke and Hambo, "she made me jes' ez happy by quittin' ez Lucy did when she married me."

"Yeah, but if she prove adultery on you in de cotehouse, you sho goin' tuh lose yo' church," Hambo warned. "You got tuh fight it."

Chapter XXIII

TIME is long by the courthouse clock.

John Pearson sat restlessly in his seat. Sitting alone except for Zeke's oldest son. Zeke had to work that day and his sister-in-law excused herself on the grounds that she "never had been to any courthouse and she didn't want no bother with it. Courthouses were back luck to colored people—best not to be 'round there." Many of the people John had approached for witnesses had said the same thing. "Sho, sho," they wanted him to win, but "you know dese white folks—de laws and de cotehouses and de jail houses all b'longed tuh white folks and po' colored folks—course, Ah never done nothin' tuh be 'rested 'bout, but— Ah'll be prayin' fuh yuh, Elder. You bound tuh come out more'n conquer."

So John sat heavily in his seat and thought about that other time nearly thirty years before when he had sat handcuffed in Cy Perkins' office in Alabama. No fiery little Lucy here, thrusting her frailty between him and trouble. No sun of love to rise upon a gray world of hate and indifference. Look how they huddled and joked on the other side of the room. Hattie, the destroyer, was surrounded by cheer. Sullen looks his way. Oh yes, she had witnesses!

Mule-faced, slew-foot Emma Hales was there—rolling her cock-eye triumphantly at him. Why should she smite out at his head? He remembered the potato pones, the baked chicken with corn-bread dressing, the marble cake, the potato pies that he had eaten in her house many times. He had eaten but never tarried. Never said a word out of the way to her in all his life. He wondered, but Emma knew. She remembered too well how often he had eaten her dinners and hurried away to the arms of the gray-eyed Ethel.

Deacon Harris now outwardly friendly, but he had been told weeks before of Harris's activity against him. Harris should not be hostile, he had taken no woman who loved Harris, for none had wanted him. His incompetence was one of the behind-hand jokes of the congregation. He was blind

to human motives but Harris hated him with all the fury of the incompetent for the full-blooded lions.

The toadies were there. Armed with hammers. Ever eager to break the feet of fallen idols. Contemptuous that even the feet of idols should fall among them. No fury so hot as that of a sycophant as he stands above a god that has toppled from a shrine. Faces of gods must not be seen of him. He has worshipped beneath the feet so long that if a god but lowers his face among them, they obscene it with spit. "Ha!" they cried, "what kind of a divinity is this that levels his face with mine? Gods show feet—not faces. Feet that crush—feet that crumble—feet that have no eyes for men's suffering nor ears for agony, lest indeed it be a sweet offering at God's feet. If gods have no power for cruelty, why then worship them? Gods tolerate sunshine, but bestir themselves that men may have storms. From the desolation of our fireplaces, let us declare the glory. If he rides upon the silver-harnessed donkey, let us cry 'hosanna'. If he weeps in compassion, let us lynch him. The sky-rasping mountain-peak fills us with awe, but if it tumbles into the valley it is but boulders. It should be burst asunder. Too long it has tricked us into worship and filled our souls with envy. Crush! Crush! Crush! Lord, thou hast granted thy servant the boon of pounding upon a peak."

So the toadies were there. Vindictively setting the jaw-muscles. Taking folks for fools! But, yes they would testify. Their injury was great. Let his silk-lined broadcloth look to itself. They meant to rip it from his back today. Think of it, folks! We rip up broadcloth and step on Stetsons. Costly walking-sticks can be made into wood for the cook stove.

Hattie was a goddess for the moment. She sat between the Cherubim on the altar of destruction. She chewed her gum and gloated. Those who held themselves above me, shall be abased. Him who pastored over a thousand shall rule over none. Even as I. His name shall be a hissing, and Hattie's shall be the hand that struck the harp. Selah. Let the world hiss with Hattie. If he but looked with longing! But no, only hurt and scorn was in his eyes. Hurt that so many of his old cronies surrounded her and scorn of herself. Let him ache! If she could but ache him more!

Court was set. The waves of pang that palpitated in the

room did not reach up to the judge's bench. No. His honor took his seat as a walrus would among a bed of clams. He sat like a brooding thought with his eyes outside the room. It was just another day with the clerk and the stenographer.

"Hattie Pearson, pwop wah blah!"

John saw the smirking anticipation on the faces of the lawyers, the Court attendants, the white spectators and felt as if he had fallen down a foul latrine.

"Now, how was it, Hattie?" The look around the room at the other whites, as if to say, "Now listen close. You're going to hear something rich. These niggers!"

"So you wanta quit yo' husband, do you, Hattie? How come? Wasn't he all right? Is *that* him? Why he looks like he oughta be okeh. Had too many women, eh? Didn't see you enough, is that it? Ha! ha! couldn't you get yo'self another man on the side? What you worrying about a divorce for? Why didn't you g'wan leave him and get yourself somebody else? You got divorce in yo' heels, ain't you? You must have the next one already picked out. Ha! ha! Bet he ain't worth the sixty dollars."

So it went on with each of the witnesses in turn. John laughed grimly to himself at the squirming of prospective witnesses who would have fled but found it too late. One by one he saw four of his erstwhile intimates take the stand against him.

Finally the Clerk cast about for defense witnesses, "Say, Reverend, where's *yo'* witnesses?"

"Ain't got none."

"Why? Couldn't you find anybody to witness for you?"

"Yes suh, but who kin tell de truth and swear dat he know uh man ain't done nothin' lak dat?"

The Court laughed, but sobered with a certain respect.

"You want to enter a plea of denial?"

"Naw suh. Ahm goin' tuh say Ah did it all."

"You don't care, then, if Hattie has her freedom?"

"Naw suh, Ah sho don't. Matters uh difference tuh me whut she do, uh where she go."

The fun was over in the Court. Whisperings. Formalities. Papers. It was all over. He saw former friends slinking off to avoid his eye. Hattie was outside, flourishing her papers with

over-relish. Loud talking and waving them as if they were a certificate of her virtue.

Hambo's short sturdy legs overtook John as he went down the marble steps, and Hambo's big hand smacked his shoulders.

"Well, you, ole mullet-headed tumble-bug, you!"

John eyed him wearily, "How come didn't but four uh y'all testify aginst me? Ah thought Ah had five friends."

"You——!" Hambo went into a fit of most obscene swearing, "why didn't you call me fuh uh witness? Didn't Ah tell yuh to?"

"Yeah, but—"

"Take yo' but out my face. Ah wanted tuh git up dere and talk some chat so bad 'til de seat wuz burning me. Ah wanted tuh tell 'bout de mens Ah've knowed Hattie tuh have. She could make up uh 'scursion train all by herself. Ah wanted tuh tell de judge 'bout all dat conjure and all dem roots she been workin' on you. Feedin' you outa her body—."

"And dat's how come Ah didn't have 'em tuh call yuh. Ah didn't want de white folks tuh hear 'bout nothin' lak dat. Dey knows too much 'bout us as it is, but dey some things dey ain't tuh know. Dey's some strings on our harp fuh us tuh play on and sing all tuh ourselves. Dey thinks wese all ignorant as it is, and dey thinks wese all alike, and dat dey knows us inside and out, but you know better. Dey wouldn't make no great 'miration if you had uh tole 'em Hattie had all dem mens. Dey spectin' dat. Dey wouldn't zarn 'tween uh woman lak Hattie and one lak Lucy, uh yo' wife befo' she died. Dey thinks all colored folks is de same dat way. De only difference dey makes is 'tween uh nigger dat works hard and don't sass 'em, and one dat don't. De hard worker is uh good nigger. De loafer is bad. Otherwise wese all de same. Dass how come Ah got up and said, 'Yeah, Ah done it,' 'cause dey b'lieved it anyhow, but dey b'lieved de same thing 'bout all de rest."

It was late afternoon when John stumbled out of the courthouse with his freedom that had been granted to Hattie.

"You tellin' de truth, John," Hambo agreed at last, "but don't you come puttin' me in wid dem other crabs. Don't you come talkin' tuh *me* lak dat! Ah knock yuh so dead dat yuh can't eben fall. Dey'll have tuh push yuh over. Pick up

dem damn big foots uh your'n and come on up tuh mah house. Ah got barbecued spare-ribs and death puddin' ready cooked."

On the way over there was a great deal of surface chatter out of Hambo. John kept silent except when he had to answer. At Hambo's gate he paused. "Ain't it funny, Hambo, you know all uhbout me. Us been friends fuh twenty years. Don't it look funny, dat all mah ole pleasures done got tuh be new sins? Maybe iss 'cause Ahm gittin' ole. Havin' women didn't useter be no sin. Jus' got sinful since Ah got ole."

"'Tain't de sin so much, John. You know our people is jus' lak uh passle uh crabs in uh basket. De minute dey see one climbin' up too high, de rest of 'em reach up and grab 'em and pull 'im back. Dey ain't gonna let nobody git nowhere if dey kin he'p it."

Chapter XXIV

S ECOND Sunday in the month came rolling around. Pastoral day. Covenant meeting. Communion service. But before all this must come Conference meeting on the Saturday night before, and John knew and everybody knew what the important business of the meeting would be. Zion Hope, after seventeen years, was going to vote on a pastor. Was John Pearson to be given a vote of confidence? Not if Hattie's faction prevailed. Would Felton Cozy receive the call? Not if Hambo and the John Pearson faction was still alive.

Everybody was there. John opened the meeting as usual, then stepped down and turned the chair over to Deacon Hoffman. "I know we all come here tuhnight tuh discuss some things. Ah'd ruther not tuh preside. Deacon Hoffman."

Hoffman took the chair. "Y'all know whut we come here for. Less get thru wid de most urgent business and den we kin take up new business."

He fumbled with the pile of hymnals on the table and waited. There was an uneasy shuffling of feet all over the room, but nobody arose to put a motion. Finally Hattie got up about the middle of the center aisle.

"Brother Cherman."

"Sister Pearson."

"Ah wants tuh lay charges 'ginst mah husband."

Hambo was on his feet.

"Brother Cherman! Brother Cherman!"

"Sister Pearson got de flo', Brer Hambo."

"She ain't got no business wid it. She's entirely out uh order."

"She ain't. She says she got charges tuh make uhginst her husband. Dat's whut uh Conference meetin' is for in uh Baptis' Church—tuh hear charges and tuh rectify, ain't it?"

"Yeah," Hambo answered, "but dis woman ain't got no husband in dis church, Brother Cherman. We ain't got no right listenin' tuh nothin' she got tuh say. G'wan back where you come from, Hattie, and try to improve up from uh turpentine still."

"Dat's right, too," shouted Sister Watson, "been divorcted two weeks tuh mah knowin'."

"Better set down, Sister Pearson, 'til we kin git dis straight," Hoffman said, reluctantly.

"Iss straight already," Andrew Berry shouted, "when uh woman done gone tuh de cotehouse and divorcted uh man she done got her satisfaction. She ain't got no mo' tuh say. Let de mess drop. Ah ain't goin' tuh hear it."

"And another thing," Hambo put in. "Elder Pearson, you oughta git up and tell whut you found in yo' bed. Course he beat uh, and 'tain't uh man under de sound uh mah voice but whut wouldn't uh done de same. G'wan tell it, Rev'und."

"Naw, no use tuh sturry up de stink. Let it rest. Y'all g'wan do whut yuh want tuh."

There was a long, uncomfortable silence.

"G'wan talk, Harris, you and de rest dat's so anxious tuh ground-mole de pastor, but be sho and tell where *you* wuz yo'self when you seen him do all of dis y'all talkin' 'bout. Be sho and tell dat too. Humph! Youse jes' ez deep in de mud ez he is in de mire."

Another long silence. Finally Hoffman said, "De hour is growin' late. Less table dis discussion and open up de house fuh new business."

Soon the meeting was over. John, Hambo and Berry walked home together.

"If Harris and dem had uh called dat meetin' de nex' day after cote, it would a been uh smuttie rub, nelly eve'ybody would have been uhginst yuh, but two weeks is too long fuh colored tuh hold onto dey feeling. Most of 'em don't keer one way uh 'nother by now."

"Still plenty of 'em is 'ginst me," John spoke at last. "It made mah flesh crawl—Ah felt it so when Ah wuz in dere."

"But dey ain't got no guts. Dey wants tuh do dey work under cover. Dey got tuh fight war if dey wants tuh win dis battle, and dey needs cannon-guns. You can't fight war wid uh brick."

John said nothing. His words had been very few since his divorce. He was going about learning old truths for himself as all men must, and the knowledge he got burnt his insides like acid. All his years as pastor at Zion Hope he had felt borne up

on a silken coverlet of friendship, but the trial had shown him
that he reclined upon a board, thinly disguised. Hambo had
tried vainly to bring him around. A few others had done their
share. A few he recognized among the congregation as foes,
avowedly; a few friends in the same degree. The rest he saw
would fall in line and toady if he triumphed, and execrate him
if he failed. He felt inside as if he had been taking calomel.
The world had suddenly turned cold. It was not new and
shiny and full of laughter. Mouldy, maggoty, full of suck-
holes—one had to watch out for one's feet. Lucy must have
had good eyes. She had seen so much and told him so much
it had wearied him, but she hadn't seen all this. Maybe she
had, and spared him. She would. Always spreading carpets for
his feet and breaking off the points of thorns. But and oh, her
likes were no more on this earth! People whom he had never
injured snatched at his shoddy bits of carpet and sharpened
the thorns for his flesh.

Nobody pushed him uphill, but everybody was willing to
lend a hand to the downward shove. Oh for the wings, for
the wings of a dove! That he might see no more what men's
faces held!

Sunday afternoon, the sunlight filtered thru the colored
glass on the packed and hushed church. Women all in white.
Three huge bouquets of red hibiscus below him and behind
the covered Communion table. As he stood looking down
into the open Bible and upon the snow-white table, his feel-
ings ran riot over his body. "He that soppeth in the dish with
me." He knew he could not preach that Last Supper. Not
today. Not for many days to come. He turned the pages while
he swallowed the lump in his throat and raised:

> "Beloved, Beloved, now are we the sons of God
> And it doth not yet appear what we shall be
> But we know, but we know
> When He shall appear, when He shall appear
> We shall be like Him
> We shall see Him as he is."

The audience sang with him. They always sang with him
well because group singers follow the leader.

Then he began in a clear, calm voice.

"Brothers and Sisters: De song we jus' sung, and seein' so many uh y'all out here tuh day, it reaches me in uh most particular manner. It wakes up uh whole family uh thoughts, and Ahm gointer speak tuh yuh outa de fullness uh mah heart. Ah want yuh tuh pray wid me whilst Ah break de bread uh life fuh de nourishment uh yo' souls.

"Our theme this morning is the wounds of Jesus. When the father shall ast, 'What are these wounds in thine hand?' He shall answer, 'Those are they with which I was wounded in the house of my friends.' Zach. 13:6.

"We read in the 53rd Chapter of Isaiah where He was wounded for our transgressions and bruised for our iniquities, and the apostle Peter affirms that His blood was spilt from before the foundation of the world.

"I have seen gamblers wounded. I have seen desperadoes wounded; thieves and robbers and every other kind of characters, law-breakers and each one had a reason for his wounds. Some of them was unthoughtful, and some for being overbearing, and some by the doctor's knife, but all wounds disfigures a person.

"Jesus was not unthoughtful. He was not overbearing. He was never a bully. He was never sick. He was never a criminal before the law and yet He was wounded. Now, a man usually gets wounded in the midst of his enemies, but this man was wounded, says the text, in the house of His friends. It is not your enemies that harm you all the time. Watch that close friend. Every believer in Christ is considered His friend, and every sin we commit is a wound to Jesus. The blues we play in our homes is a club to beat up Jesus, and these social card parties.

Jesus have always loved us from the foundation of the world
When God
Stood out on the apex of His power
Before the hammers of creation
Fell upon the anvils of Time and hammered out the ribs of
 the earth
Before He made any ropes
By the breath of fire

And set the boundaries of the ocean by the gravity of His
 power
When God said, ha!
Let us make man
And the elders upon the altar cried, ha!
If you make man, ha!
He will sin
God my master, ha!
Father!! Ha-aa!
I am the teeth of time
That comprehended de dust of de earth
And weighed de hills in scales
That painted de rainbow dat marks de end of de parting
 storm
Measured de seas in de holler of my hand
That held de elements in a unbroken chain of
 controllment.
Make man, ha!
If he sin I will redeem him
I'll break de chasm of hell
Where de fire's never quenched
I'll go into de grave
Where de worm never dies, Ah!
So God A'mighty, Ha!
Got His stuff together
He dipped some water out of de mighty deep
He got Him a handful of dirt
From de foundation sills of de earth
He seized a thimble full of breath
From de drums of de wind, ha!
God, my master!
Now I'm ready to make man
Aa-aah!
Who shall I make him after? Ha!
Worlds within worlds begin to wheel and roll
De Sun, Ah!
Gethered up de fiery skirts of her garments
And wheeled around de throne, Ah!
Saying, Ah, make man after me, ha!
God gazed upon the sun

And sent her back to her blood-red socket
And shook His head, ha!
De Moon, ha!
Grabbed up de reins of de tides.
And dragged a thousand seas behind her
As she walked around de throne
Ah-h, please make man after me
But God said "NO"!
De stars bust out from their diamond sockets
And circled de glitterin' throne cryin'
A-aah! Make man after me
God said, "NO"!
I'll make man in my own image, ha!
I'll put him in de garden
And Jesus said, ha!
And if he sin,
I'll go his bond before yo' mighty throne
Ah, He was yo' friend
He made us all, ha!
Delegates to de judgment convention
Ah!
Faith hasn't got no eyes, but she' long-legged
But take de spy-glass of Faith
And look into dat upper room
When you are alone to yourself
When yo' heart is burnt with fire, ha!
When de blood is lopin' thru yo' veins
Like de iron monasters (monsters) on de rail
Look into dat upper chamber, ha!
We notice at de supper table
As He gazed upon His friends, ha!
His eyes flowin' wid tears, ha! He said
"My soul is exceedingly sorrowful unto death, ha!
For this night, ha!
One of you shall betray me, ha!
It were not a Roman officer, ha!
It were not a centurion
But one of you
Who I have chosen my bosom friend
That sops in the dish with me shall betray me."

I want to draw a parable.
I see Jesus
Leaving heben with all of His grandeur
Dis-robin' Hisself of His matchless honor
Yielding up de scepter of revolvin' worlds
Clothing Hisself in de garment of humanity
Coming into de world to rescue His friends.
Two thousand years have went by on their rusty ankles
But with the eye of faith, I can see Him
Look down from His high towers of elevation
I can hear Him when He walks about the golden streets
I can hear 'em ring under His footsteps
Sol me-e-e, Sol do
Sol me-e-e, Sol do
I can see Him step out upon the rim bones of nothing
Crying I am de way
De truth and de light
Ah!
God A'mighty!
I see Him grab de throttle
Of de well ordered train of mercy
I see kingdoms crush and crumble
Whilst de archangels held de winds in de corner chambers
I see Him arrive on dis earth
And walk de streets thirty and three years
Oh-h-hhh!
I see Him walking beside de sea of Galilee wid His disciples
This declaration gendered on His lips
"Let us go on to the other side"
God A'mighty!
Dey entered de boat
Wid their oarus (oars) stuck in de back
Sails unfurled to de evenin' breeze
And de ship was now sailin'
As she reached de center of de lake
Jesus was sleep on a pillow in de rear of de boat
And de dynamic powers of nature became disturbed
And de mad winds broke de heads of de Western drums
And fell down on de lake of Galilee
And buried themselves behind de gallopin' waves

And de white-caps marbilized themselves like an army
And walked out like soldiers goin' to battle
And de zig-zag lightning
Licked out her fiery tongue
And de flying clouds
Threw their wings in the channels of the deep
And bedded de waters like a road-plow
And faced de current of de chargin' billows
And de terrific bolts of thunder—they bust in de clouds
And de ship begin to reel and rock
God A'mighty!
And one of de disciples called Jesus
"Master!! Carest Thou not that we perish?"
And He arose
And de storm was in its pitch
And de lightnin' played on His raiments as He stood on the
 prow of the boat
And placed His foot upon the neck of the storm
And spoke to the howlin' winds
And de sea fell at His feet like a marble floor
And de thunders went back in their vault
Then He set down on de rim of de ship
And took de hooks of His power
And lifted de billows in His lap
And rocked de winds to sleep on His arm
And said, "Peace, be still."
And de Bible says there was a calm.
I can see Him wid de eye of faith.
When He went from Pilate's house
Wid the crown of seventy-two wounds upon His head
I can see Him as He mounted Calvary and hung upon de
 cross for our sins.
I can see-eee-ee
De mountains fall to their rocky knees when he cried
"My God, my God! Why hast Thou forsaken me?"
The mountains fell to their rocky knees and trembled like a
 beast
From the stroke of the master's axe
One angel took the flinches of God's eternal power
And bled the veins of the earth

One angel that stood at the gate with a flaming sword
Was so well pleased with his power
Until he pierced the moon with his sword
And she ran down in blood
And de sun
Batted her fiery eyes and put on her judgment robe
And laid down in de cradle of eternity
And rocked herself into sleep and slumber
He died until the great belt in the wheel of time
And de geological strata fell aloose
And a thousand angels rushed to de canopy of heben
With flamin' swords in their hands
And placed their feet upon blue ether's bosom, and looked
 back at de dazzlin' throne
And de arc angels had veiled their faces
And de throne was draped in mournin'
And de orchestra had struck silence for the space of half an
 hour
Angels had lifted their harps to de weepin' willows
And God had looked off to-wards immensity
And blazin' worlds fell of His teeth
And about that time Jesus groaned on de cross, and
Dropped His head in the locks of His shoulder and said, "It is
 finished, it is finished."
And then de chambers of hell exploded
And de damnable spirits
Come up from de Sodomistic world and rushed into de
 smoky camps of eternal night,
And cried, "Woe! Woe! Woe!"
And then de Centurion cried out,
"Surely this is the Son of God."
And about dat time
De angel of Justice unsheathed his flamin' sword and ripped
 de veil of de temple
And de High Priest vacated his office
And then de sacrificial energy penetrated de mighty strata
And quickened de bones of de prophets
And they arose from their graves and walked about in de
 streets of Jerusalem
I heard de whistle of de damnation train

Dat pulled out from Garden of Eden loaded wid cargo goin'
 to hell
Ran at break-neck speed all de way thru de law
All de way thru de prophetic age
All de way thru de reign of kings and judges—
Plowed her way thru de Jurdan
And on her way to Calvary, when she blew for de switch
Jesus stood out on her track like a rough-backed mountain
And she threw her cow-catcher in His side and His blood
 ditched de train
He died for our sins.
Wounded in the house of His friends.
That's where I got off de damnation train
And dat's where you must get off, ha!
For in dat mor-ornin', ha!
When we shall all be delegates, ha!
To dat Judgment Convention
When de two trains of Time shall meet on de trestle
And wreck de burning axles of de unformed ether
And de mountains shall skip like lambs
When Jesus shall place one foot on de neck of de sea, ha!
One foot on dry land, ah
When His chariot wheels shall be running hub-deep in fire
He shall take His friends thru the open bosom of an un-
 clouded sky
And place in their hands de "hosanna" fan
And they shall stand 'round and 'round his beatific throne
And praise His name forever,
<div align="center">Amen.</div>

There had been a mighty response to the sermon all thru its
length. The "bearing up" had been almost continuous, but as
Pearson's voice sank dramatically to the final Amen, Anderson
lifted a chant that kept the church on fire for several seconds
more. During this frenzy John Pearson descended from the
pulpit. Two deacons sprang to assist him at the Communion
table, but he never stopped there. With bowed head he
walked down the center aisle and out of the door—leaving
stupefaction in his wake. Hoffman and Nelse Watson posted
after him and stopped him as he left the grounds, but he
brushed off their hands.

"No, Chillun, Ah—Ah can't break—can't break de bread wid y'all no mo'," and he passed on.

"Man, ain't you goin' on back tuh yo' pulpit lak you got some sense?" Hambo asked that night. "If you don't some of 'em is sho tuh strow it uhround dat you wuz put out."

"Naw, Hambo. Ah don't want y'all fightin' and scratchin' over me. Let 'em talk all dey wanta."

"Ain't yuh never tuh preach and pastor no mo'?"

"Ah won't say never 'cause— Never is uh long time. Ah don't b'lieve Ahm fitted tuh preach de gospel—unless de world is wrong. Yuh see dey's ready fuh uh preacher tuh be uh man uhmongst men, but dey ain't ready yet fuh 'im tuh be uh man uhmongst women. Reckon Ah better stay out de pulpit and carpenter fuh mah livin'. Reckon Ah kin do dat 'thout uh whole heap uh rigmarole."

But after a while John was not so certain. Several people who formerly had felt that they would rather wait for him several weeks to do a job now discovered that they didn't even have time to get him word. Some who already had work done shot angry, resentful looks after him and resolved not to pay him. It would be lacking in virtue to pay carpenter-preachers who got into trouble with congregations. Two men who had been glad of a chance to work under him on large jobs kept some of his tools that he had loaned them and muttered that it was no more than their due. He had worked them nearly to death in the damp and cold and hadn't paid them. One man grew so indignant that he pawned a spirit-level and two fine saws.

John was accused of killing one man by exposure and over-work. It was well known that he died of tuberculosis several months after he had worked a day or two for John, but nobody was going to be behind hand in accusations. Every bawdy in town wept over her gin and laid her downfall at John's door. He was the father of dozens of children by women he had never seen. Felton Cozy had stepped into his shoes at Zion Hope and made it a point to adjust his glasses carefully each time he saw John lest too much sin hit him in his virtuous eye. John came to recognize all this eventually and quit telling people his troubles or his plans. He found

that they rejoiced at the former and hurried away to do what they could to balk the latter.

As one man said, "Well, since he's down, less keep 'im down."

He saw himself growing shabby. It was hard to find food in variety.

One evening he came home most dejected.

"Whuss de matter, big foots?" Hambo asked. "You look all down in de mouf."

"Look lak lightnin' done struck de po' house. Dey got me in de go-long Ah reckon. All de lies dese folks strowing 'round 'bout me done got some folks in de notion Ah can't drive uh clean nail in they lumber. Look lak dey spectin' uh house Ah build tuh git tuh fornication befo' dey could get de paint on it. Lawd Jesus!"

"Come in and eat some dese snap peas and okra Ah got cooked. It'll give you mo' guts than uh goat."

"Naw thankee, Hambo. Ahm goin' lie down."

He went into his room and shut the door. "Oh Lucy! Lucy! Come git me. You knowed all dis—whut yuh leave me back heah tuh drink dis cup? Please, Lucy, take dis curse offa me. Ah done paid and paid. Ah done wept and Ah done prayed. If you see God where you is over dere ast Him tuh have mercy! Oh Jesus, Oh Jesus, Oh-wonder-workin' God. Take dis burden offa mah sobbin' heart or else take me 'way from dis sin-sick world!"

He sought Lucy thru all struggles of sleep, mewing and crying like a lost child, but she was not. He was really searching for a lost self and crying like the old witch with her shed skin shrunken by red pepper and salt, "Ole skin, doncher know me?" But the skin was never to fit her again. Sometimes in the dark watches of the night he reproached Lucy bitterly for leaving him. "You meant to do it," he would sob. "Ah saw yo' eyes."

By day he gave no sign of his night-thoughts. His search and his tears were hidden under bed quilts.

When Hambo woke him for breakfast next morning he didn't get up.

"Don't b'lieve Ahm goin' out tuhday, 'cause if Ah meet

Cozy wid dat sham-polish smile uh his'n de way Ah feel tuh-day, dey'll be tryin' me fuh murder nex' time."

His courage was broken. He lay there in bed and looked back over days that had had their trial and failure. They had all been glorious tomorrows once gilded with promise, but when they had arrived, they turned out to be just days with no more fulfillment—no more glad realities than those that had pre-ceded—more betrayal, so why look forward? Why get up?

His divorce trial stayed with him. He saw that though it was over at the courthouse the judge and jury had moved to the street corners, the church, the houses. He was on trial everywhere, and unlike the courthouse he didn't have a chance to speak in his own behalf.

Sisters White and Carey came over around sundown with a gingerbread and melon-rind preserves.

"Always remembered you had uh sweet tooth," Sister Carey said.

They wanted to know if he was thinking of pastoring again. Certain people had crowded Cozy in, but the real folks had "chunked him out again. His shirt-tail may be long but we kin still spy his hips."

"He never could preach, nohow," Sister White complained, "and he been strainin' hisself tryin' tuh be stronger wid de women folks than you wuz. Settin' 'round de houses drinkin' and sayin' toastes 'bout, 'Luck tuh de duck dat swims de pond—' Bet if some dese men folks ketch 'im dey'll luck his duck fuh 'im. Since you won't consider, us callin' uh man from Savannah."

"Oh, he's more'n welcome to all de women folks," John rejoined.

"Where you keepin' yo'self dese days, anyhow, and whut you doin'?"

"Oh well, Sister White, since yuh ast me, Ah do any kind of uh job Ah kin git tuh make uh dollar, and Ah keeps mahself at home. Sometimes Ah reads de Bible and sometimes Ah don't feel tuh. Den Ah jus' knock uhround from pillar tuh post and sort of dream. Seem lak de dreams is true sho 'nuff some-time—iss so plain befo' me, but after while dey fades. But even while they be fadin', Ah have others. So it goes from day tuh day."

One night John had a dream. Lucy sat beside a stream and cried because she was afraid of a snake. He killed the snake and carried Lucy across in his arms to where Alf Pearson stood at the cross roads and pointed down a white shell road with his walking cane and said, "Distance is the only cure for certain diseases," and he and Lucy went racing down the dusty white road together. Somehow Lucy got lost from him, but there he was on the road—happy because the dead snake was behind him, but crying in his loneliness for Lucy. His sobbing awoke him and he said, "Maybe it's meant for me tuh leave Sanford. Whut Ahm hangin' 'round heah for, anyhow?"

At breakfast he said to Hambo, "Well, Hambo, Ah been thinkin' and thinkin' and Ah done decided dat Ahm goin' tuh give you dis town. You kin have it."

"You better say Joe, 'cause you don't know. Us been here batchin' tuhgether and gittin' 'long fine. Ahm liable not tuh let yuh go. Me, Ahm in de 'B' class, be here when you leave and be here when you git back."

"Oh yeah, Ahm goin'. Gointer spread mah jenk in unother town."

"Where you figgerin' on goin'?"

"Don't know yet. When Ah colleck dem few pennies Ah got owing tuh me, iss good bye Katy, bar de door. Some uh dese mawnin's, and it won't be long, you goin' tuh wake up callin' me and Ah'll be gone."

And that is the way he went. It was equally haphazard that he landed in Plant City and went about looking for work.

Several times he passed the big white building that Baptist pride had erected and that he had been invited as Moderator to dedicate, but he passed it now with shuttered eyes. He avoided the people who might remember him.

A week and no work. Walking the streets with his tool kit. Hopeful, smiling ingratiatingly into faces like a dog in a meat house. Desperation nettling his rest.

"How yuh do, suh? Ain't you Rev'und Pearson?"

He looked sidewise quickly into the face of a tall black woman who smiled at him over a gate. Yard chock full of roses in no set pattern.

"Yes ma'am. Well, Ah thank yuh."

"Thought Ah knowed yuh. Heard yuh preach one time at our church."

"Pilgrim Rest Baptis' Church?"

"Dat's right. Dat wuz uh sermon! Come in."

John was tired. He sat heavily upon the step.

"Don't set on de do' step. Elder, heah's uh chear."

"Iss all right, Sister, jus' so Ahm settin' down."

"Naw, it 'tain't. If you set on de steps you'll git all de pains in de house. Ha, ha! Ah reckon you say niggers got all de signs and white folks got all de money."

He sat in the comfortable chair she placed for him and surrendered his hat.

"You got tuh eat supper wid me, lessen you got somewhere puhticklar tuh go. Mah dead husband said you wuz de best preacher ever borned since befo' dey built de Rocky Mountains."

Rev. Pearson laughed a space-filling laugh and waited on her lead.

"You goin' tuh be in our midst uh while?"

"Don't know, Sister—er—"

"Sister Lovelace. Knowed you wouldn't know me. Maybe you would eben disremember mah husband, but Ah sho is glad tuh have yuh in our midst. 'Scuse me uh minute whilst Ah go skeer yuh up suppin' tuh eat."

She bustled inside but popped out a moment later with a palm-leaf fan.

"Cool yo'self off, Rev'und."

She was back in a few minutes with a pitcher clinking with ice.

"Have uh cool drink uh water, Elder—mighty hot. Ain't aimin' tuh fill yuh up on water, ha! ha! jes' keepin' yuh cool 'til it git done."

From the deep porch, smothered in bucket flowers the street looked so different. The world and all seemed so different—it seemed changed in a dream way. "Maybe nothin' ain't real sho 'nuff. Maybe 'tain't no world. No elements, no nothin'. Maybe wese jus' somewhere in God's mind," but when he wiggled his tired toes the world thudded and throbbed before him.

"Walk right intuh de dinin'-room and take uh chear, Rev'und. Right in dis big chear at de head uh de table. Maybe you kin make uh meal outa dis po' dinner Ah set befo' yuh, but yuh know Ahm uh widder woman and doin' de bes' ah kin."

"Dis po' dinner," consisted of fried chicken, hot biscuits, rice, mashed sweet potatoes, warmed over greens, rice pudding and iced tea.

"You goin' tuh set down and eat wid me, ain't yuh Sister Lovelace?"

"Naw, you go right uhead and eat. Ahm goin' tuh fan de flies. Dey right bad dese days. Ah been laying off tuh have de place screened, but jes' ain't got 'round tuh it. De wire is easy tuh git but dese carpenters 'round heah does sich shabby work 'til Ah ruther not be bothered."

"Ahm uh carpenter."

"You ain't got time tuh fool wid nothin' lak dat. Youse too big uh man."

"Oh, Ah got plenty time."

John felt warm heart-beats that night in his room. He decided to drop a line or two to Sanford. He sent a cheerful line to Hambo first of all.

He wrote to Mamie Lester for news and comfort. She never answered. She felt injured that he should ask such a thing of her. Her indignation burst out of her. She asked many people, "Who do John Pearson think Ah am to be totin' news for him? He ain't nothin'." She said "nothin'" as if she had spat a stinking morsel out of her mouth.

After a long time, when he didn't get an answer, John Pearson understood, and laughed in his bed. The virtuous indignation of Mamie Lester! He could see her again as he had first seen her twenty years ago, as she had tramped into Sanford as barefooted as a yard dog with her skimpy, dirty calico dress and uncombed head; and her guitar hanging around her neck by a dirty red ribbon. How she had tried to pick him up and instead had gotten an invitation to his church. Respectability and marriage to a deacon. She, who had had no consciousness of degradation on the chain-gang and in the brothel, had now discovered she had no time for talk with fallen preachers.

Now that he had work to do, he wrote to George Gibson, asking him to return his tools that George had borrowed.

George ignored the letter. He was really angry, "The son of a bum! Won't pay nobody and then come astin' me 'bout dem tools. Ah wish he would come to my face and ast me for 'em."

"Do Pearson owe you too?" another impostor asked.

"Do he? Humph!" he left the feeling that if he only had the money that John Pearson owed him, he need never worry any more.

George was indignant at being asked favors by the weak. His blood boiled.

It became the fashion that whoever was in hard luck, whoever was in debt—John Pearson had betrayed him. Gibson habitually wore a sorrowful look of infinite betrayal. In the meanwhile he used John's tools and came finally to feel that he deserved them.

The next day after the chance meeting John began his task of screening the house of Sally Lovelace, and when he was thru he hesitated over taking the money agreed upon.

"You done fed me more'n de worth uh de job," he said.

"Aw shucks, man, uh woman dat's useter havin' uh man tuh do fuh got tuh wait on somebody. Take de money. You goin' tuh be tuh church dis Sunday?"

"Er—er—Ah don't jus' exactly know, tuh tell yuh truth, Sister Lovelace."

"You jokin', Ah know. Whut you goin' tuh do, if you don't go?"

"Not tuh turn yuh no short answer, Ah don't know."

"Oh come uhlong wid me. Deacon Turner and dem wuz overglad tuh know youse in town. Dey wants yuh tuh run our revival meetin' and dey did say suppin' 'bout yuh preachin' Communion Service."

John flinched, and Mrs. Lovelace saw it. He had to stay to supper then, and at eleven o'clock that night she knew everything. He had not spared himself, and lay with his head in her lap sobbing like a boy of four.

"Well, youse gointer pastor right here at Pilgrim Rest and none of 'em bet' not come 'round here tryin' tuh destroy yo' influence!" Sally blazed. "Ain't doodley squat dey self and goin' 'round tromplin' on folks dat's 'way uhbove 'em." She ran her fingers soothingly thru John's curly hair, and he fell asleep at her knee.

John escorted Sally to church on Sunday and preached.

"Man, you preached!" Sally said warmly during dinner—"only thing Ah heahed so many folks wuz shoutin' Ah couldn't half hear whut you wuz sayin'. You got tuh preach dat at home some time. Special fuh me."

"Preach it anytime you say, but sho 'nuff Ah felt lak ole times tuhday. Felt lak Samson when his hair begin tuh grow out agin."

"Dat's de way fuh yuh tuh feel, John. Oh yeah, 'fo' Ah fuhgit it, dere's uh lady got twenty-seben houses. She wants you tuh look over and patch up wherever dey needs fixin'. Ain't been nothin' done on 'em in two years. 'Bout two weeks steady work and den de Meth'dis' parsonage got tuh have new shingles all over and me and de pastor's wife stands in. Oh you goin' tuh git 'long good in this town."

John had finished the work on the houses before he found out that they belonged to Sally. The Methodist preacher had paid him. He found himself displeased when he heard of Sally's ownership. What would she with all that property, want with him?

"John, dey's fixin' tuh loose de pastor uh Pilgrim Rest and Ahm quite sho dey's 'bout tuh call you. So go git yo' things tuhgether and less git married tuhday so nobody can't start no talk."

"Thank yuh, Sally."

"You wuz aimin' tuh ast me anyhow, wuzn't yuh?"

"Sho wuz, jus' ez soon ez Ah could git tuh de place where Ah could make support fuh yuh."

"Well, den eve'ything is all right between us. We ain't no chillun no mo', and we don't need tuh go thru uh whole lot uh form and fashion—uh kee-kee-in' and eatin' up pocket handkerchers. You done got de church and dat calls fuh over uh hund'ed dollars uh month and besides whut you got comin' in from carpenterin', and Ah got three hund'ed dollars eve'y month from de rent uh dem houses. Ahm gointer marry you, 'cause Ah love yuh and Ah b'lieve you love me, and 'cause you needs marryin'."

"Ah sho do, Sally. Less go git married and den got set on de fish pond and ketch us uh mess uh speckled perches fuh supper. Iss uh heap mo' fun than buyin' 'em."

"Less do. Ah always wanted tuh go sich places, but Oscar never would take me. He wuz uh good puhvider tho'."

Sally went to bed as a matter of course that night, but John was as shy as a girl—as Lucy had been. His bride wondered at that. He stayed a long time on his knees and Sally never knew how fervently he prayed that Sally might never look at him out of the eyes of Lucy. How abjectly he begged his God to keep his path out of the way of snares and to bear him up lest he bruise his feet against a stumbling-stone, and he vowed vows, if God would only keep his way clean. "Let Lucy see it too, Lawd, so she kin rest. And be so pleased as to cast certain memories in de sea of fuhgitfullness where dey will never rise tuh condemn me in de judgment. Amen and thang God."

Chapter XXV

"SALLY, you never ought tuh bought me no car. Dat's too much money tuh take out de bank."

"Who else Ahm goin' tuh spend it on? Ah ain't got uh chick nor uh chile 'ceptin' you. If us ever goin' tuh enjoy ourselves, dis is de world tuh do it in."

"But uh Chevrolet would uh done me. You didn't hafta go buy no Cadillac."

"Wanted yuh tuh set up in uh Cadillac. Dat's yo' weddin' present and our first anniversary present all two together."

"Don't look lak us been married no year, Sally."

"But us is. Dat's 'cause we happy. Tuh think Ah lived tuh git forty-eight 'fo Ah ever knowed whut love is."

"Ah love you de same way, Sally."

"Look here, John, you ain't been back tuh Sanford since yuh lef' dere."

"Don't keer if Ah never see it no mo' 'twill be too soon."

"Yeah, but honey, yo' buddy Hambo done been down here and paid you uh visit. You oughter go up and spend uh few days wid him, and let dem niggers see how well you gittin' uhlong."

"Awright; when you wanta go?"

"Me? Ah ain't goin'. Ah got mah guava jelly tuh put up. Ah don't trust ridin' so fur in dese cars, nohow. You go and tell me all uhbout it. You been right up under me ever since us been married. Do yuh good tuh git off uh spell."

"Naw, Sally, Ah don't want tuh go 'thout you."

"Fool, how you goin' tuh git uh rest from me and take me wid yuh? You jes' lak uh li'l' boy and dass whut make Ah love yuh so, but you g'wan."

"Naw, Ah promised mahself never tuh sleep uh night 'way from you. Ah don't wanta break mah vow."

Sally exulted in her power and sipped honey from his lips, but she made him go, seeing the pain in John's face at the separation. It was worth her own suffering ten times over to see him that way for her.

The next morning he turned the long nose of his car north-

wards and pulled up at Hambo's gate. He was affectionately called every vile name in the language and fed on cow peas, but it seemed good to be there.

Three girls in their late teens stood about his gleaming chariot when he emerged towards sundown to visit the new pastor of Zion Hope church. They admired it loudly and crudely hinted for rides, but John coolly drove off without taking any hints. He was used to admiration of his car now and he had his vows.

Sanford was warm. From what he heard now as he sat under the wheel of his car, Sanford had had not a moment of happiness since he left. Zion Hope was desolate. The choir in heaven had struck silence for the space of half an hour. Wouldn't he consider a recall?

"Naw, it would be de same ole soup-bone—jus' warmed over—dat's all. Ah got uh church bigger'n dis one."

"You could give dem two Sundays and us two, couldn't yuh?" Trustee John Hall pled.

"Ah couldn't see de way tuh be 'way from home dat much. We got too much proppity down dere fuh me tuh look after."

"You got proppity?"

"Yep. Thirty houses tuh rent. Three of 'em brand new. Ah jus' finished 'em off las' week and dey was rented 'fo' de roof got on." He pulled out the huge roll of bills in his pocket, "And Ah jus' got th'ew collectin' de month's rent 'fo' Ah come off."

"God uhmighty man, youse rich! You got bucks above suspicion! Oh shucks, Ah lak tuh fuhgit. Here's dat fo' dollars Ah owe you fuh buildin' dat shed-room 'fo' you went away from here. Ah could uh been done paid yuh, but Ah let talk keep me from it."

John pocketed the money without thanking him. He was grinning sardonically inside, thinking of the heat of the pavements and empty belly, the cold cruelty of want, how much men hit and beat at need when it pleads its gauntness.

But Hall was looking upon plenty and heard no miserable inside gnawings. He heard not John's cold lack of courtesy.

"But you got tuh preach for us dis comin' Sunday. Dat's Communion service. Nobody in de world kin preach dat lak

you. Lemme go put it out right now, so's de whole church will know."

"You reckon Ah'd fine uh welcome, Hall?"

"Lawd yes, Rev. Pearson. You left a welcome at Zion Hope when you left here, and you kerried a welcome wid yuh where you went and you brought a welcome back wid you. Come preach for us one mo' time. God a'mighty man, Zion Hope couldn't hold all de folks dat would be dere. We'd lift a collection lak on big rally day."

But John was fingering the four dollars in his mind. He would buy a chicken for supper. Hambo would like that. He would still have enough left over to service the car and take him home.

"Nope, Brother Hall. Thankee for de invitation, but Ah feels to get on back home tuh mah wife. Can't be off too long."

He went on thinking how to show Sally how he could guard their money. Sure three dollars and a quarter would take him home. Maybe less. He wrote Sally about it, wrote her some kind of a letter every day.

While he and Hambo ate supper he heard voices on the porch—gay giggling. He motioned to see who it was.

"Aw, don't go," Hambo continued, "'Tain't nobody but dem three li'l' chippies from up de street. Dey gone crazy 'bout dat car. Dat kinda plump one is Ora Patton— Jes' ez fresh ez dishwater. Always grinnin' up in some man's face. She's after yo' money right now. I seen her pass here eve'y few minutes—switchin' it and lookin' back at it. Set down and finish yo' supper man. Ah wouldn't pay her no rabbit-foot. She ain't wuth it."

"Oh, Ah ain't studyin' 'bout dem gals. Jus' don't want nobody tuh mess wid dat car. Dat radiator cap cost twenty-six dollars. Soon ez Ah git th'ew supper Ahm goin' tuh put de car up."

"You better, dey steal gas 'round here too, but dat Ora is hot after yuh. Her egg-bag ain't gonna rest easy 'till she git nex' tuh yuh. Money crazy. Don't give'er uh damn cent. Be lak me. Ah wouldn't give uh bitch uh bone if she treed uh terrapin."

"She won't git nothin' outa me. Ahm lak de cemetery.

Ahm takin' in, but never no put out. 'Ceptin' tuh Sally. She come tuh me in hell and Ah love her for it."

When John stepped to the door of his car he found Ora on the running-board.

"Hello, daddy."

"Oh, er, hello, daughter."

"Don't call me no daughter. Take me fuh uh short ride."

"Ahm jus' goin' tuh de garage. Two—three blocks, you kin ride dat fur if you wanta."

"Okay, stingy papa. You eben wear uh stingy-rim hat." As the car moved off silently, "Lawd! Ah wonder how it feels tuh be drivin' uh great big ole 'Kitty'."

"Kin you drive?"

"Yeah. Lemme take de wheel jes' uh minute. Every body in town is talkin' 'bout dis blue and silver 'Kitty.' You mus' got money's mammy, and grandpa Change."

"Nope, broke ez uh he-ha'nt in torment. All dis b'longs tuh mah wife. Here's de garage. Youse goin' on past it."

"Aw, gimme uh li'l' bit uh ride, daddy. Don't be so mean and hateful."

"Nope, Ahm goin' home tuhmorrer and Ah got tuh be in bed so Ah wont go tuh sleep drivin'. Move over."

He reached for the wheel and Ora shot down on the gas. They had nosed out on the road to Osteen before John dared to struggle for possession of the wheel. He hated to think of even a scratch on his paint. Then Ora pulled to the side of the road and parked and threw her arms about his neck and began to cry.

"Ora so bad and now, big, good-looking daddy is mad wid her! Po' Ora can't he'p who she like. Please don't be mad, you pretty, curly headed man."

John unwrapped her arms from 'round his neck gently.

"Well, Ah'll give you uh li'l' short ride, if thass all yuh want. Can't burn up too much gas."

Ora kissed him fleshily, "Dat's right sweet daddy. Let de wheels roll, Ah loves cars. Ride me 'til Ah sweat."

In twenty minutes John was back at the garage and Ora got out pouting. "You mus' figger Ah sweats mighty easy, papa. Ah ast yuh fuh uh ride, but you ain't gimme none hardly."

Friday came and John was glad. He was going home and

Ora had failed of her purpose. He was convincing himself that God and Sally could trust him.

Friday night Ora waited for him outside the garage. Standing in the dark of a clump of hibiscus.

"Thought you wuz goin' home Tuesday?" she accused. "Here 'tis Friday night and you ain't gone yet. Ah know you jes' wants tuh git rid uh me."

"Naw, 'tain't dat. First place Ah got uh wife and second place Ahm goin' home sho 'nuff tuhmorrer and therefo' Ah ain't got no time tuh talk. Needs mah sleep. Ahm gittin' ole."

"Aw, naw, you ain't. Come on less take uh good bye ride. Less don't make it stingy lak de las' time. Less ride out tuh Oviedo and back."

She climbed in beside him and put her hands on top of his wheel and eye-balled him sweetly.

"Don't go in dis ole garage. Drive on."

Chapter XXVI

TWO HOURS later when John found himself dressing in a dingy back room in Oviedo he was mad—mad at his weakness—mad at Ora, though she did not know it as yet. She was putting on her shoes on the other side of the bed.

"Daddy, you got twenty dollars you kin gimme? Ah needs so many things and you got plenty."

"Naw, Ah tole you befo' Ah didn't have nothin'. Anything you see on me b'longs tuh Sally." He laced his shoes and put on his vest, then he remembered the remainder of the four dollars he had collected. He pulled it out of his pocket and threw it at her, "Here! Take dat. Iss all Ah got, and Ah hope you rot in hell! Ah hope you never rise in judgment!" He seized his coat and put it on as he hurried out to the car. Ora grabbed up her dress and dashed after him, but he was under the wheel before she left the room, and the motor was humming when she reached the running-board. John viciously thrust her away from the car door without uttering a word. He shoved her so hard that she stumbled into the irrigation ditch, as the car picked up speed and in a moment was a red eye in the distance.

"Well, de ole gray-head bastard! Wonder whut got intuh him? Dis li'l' ole three dollars and some odd change is gonna do me uh lot uh good. Ah been strainin' up tuh git tuh Oviedo fuh de last longest and here Ah is, but Ah wisht Ah knowed whut he flew hot over. Sho do. He done lef' me right where Ah wants tuh be, wid pay-day at de packin' house tuhmorrer. Jes' lak de rabbit in de briar patch.

"Bright and soon tuhmorrer Ah means tuh git me uh bottle uh perfume and some new garters—one red one tuh draw love and one yeller one tuh draw money. Hey, hey, Ah can't lose—not wid de help Ah got."

When Hambo awoke John was gone. Ten dollars was on the dresser beside the clock, and a couple of brand new night-shirts were on a chair.

"Well de hen-fired son-of-a-gun done slipped off and never tole me good bye again! Bet de wop-sided, holler-headed ——

thought Ah wuz gointer cry, but he's uh slew-footed liar!" Whereupon Hambo cried over the stove as he fried his sow-bosom and made a flour hoe-cake. Then he found he couldn't eat. Frog in his throat or something so that even his coffee choked him.

The ground-mist lifted on a Florida sunrise as John fled homeward. The car droned, "ho-o-ome" and tortured the man. False pretender! Outside show to the world! Soon he would be in the shelter of Sally's presence. Faith and no questions asked. He had prayed for Lucy's return and God had answered with Sally. He drove on but half-seeing the railroad from looking inward.

The engine struck the car squarely and hurled it about like a toy. John was thrown out and lay perfectly still. Only his foot twitched a little.

"Damned, if I kin see how it happened," the engineer declared. "He musta been sleep or drunk. God knows I blowed for him when I saw him entering on the track. He wasn't drunk. Couldn't smell no likker on him, so he musta been asleep. Hell, now I'm on the carpet for carelessness, but I got witnesses I blowed."

Sally wept hard. "Naw, Ah don't want de seben thousand dollars from de railroad. Ahm goin' tuh give it tuh his chillun. Naw, Ah don't want none of it. Ah loved 'im too much tuh rob his chillun. Jes' lemme be buried right side uh him when Ah die. Us two off by ourselves. Dass how come Ah bought uh new burial lot. Ah can't git over it, people. Jes' ez he wuz gittin ready tuh live, he got tuh git taken uhway, but Ah got one consolation, he sho wuz true tuh me. Jes' tuh think Ah had tuh live fifty years tuh git one sweet one and it throwed de light over all de other ones. Ah'll never regret uh thing. He wuz true tuh me." She said it over and over. It was a song for her heart and she kept singing it.

She sat shining darkly among the multitudes from all over the State who had come to do John Pearson homage. She sat among his children and made them love her, and when he was laid to rest she was invited to attend memorial services in twenty or more cities.

Sanford was draped in mourning on the second Sunday when Zion Hope held her memorial for John Pearson. The high-backed, throne-like chair was decorated. Tight little sweaty bouquets from the woods and yards were crowded beside ornate floral pieces. Hattie in deep mourning came back to town for the service.

She would have seated herself on the front seat before the flower-banked chair that represented the body of Rev. Pearson, but someone stopped her. "His wife is in de seat," they whispered and showed her to a place among the crowd.

Hambo rolled his eyes at the black-veiled Hattie and gritted his teeth, and whispered to Watson:

"Uhhunh, Ah done heered she wuz comin' back tuh ast us all tuh he'p her git his lodge insurances. Wisht Ah wuz God. Ah'd take and turn her intuh uh damn hawg and den Ah'd concrete de whole world over, so she couldn't find uh durned place tuh root."

And the preacher preached a barbaric requiem poem. On the pale white horse of Death. On the cold icy hands of Death. On the golden streets of glory. Of Amen Avenue. Of Halleluyah Street. On the delight of God when such as John appeared among the singers about His throne. On the weeping sun and moon. On Death who gives a cloak to the man who walked naked in the world. And the hearers wailed with a feeling of terrible loss. They beat upon the O-go-doe, the ancient drum. O-go-doe, O-go-doe, O-go-doe! Their hearts turned to fire and their shin-bones leaped unknowing to the drum. Not Kata-Kumba, the drum of triumph, that speaks of great ancestors and glorious wars. Not the little drum of kidskin, for that is to dance with joy and to call to mind birth and creation, but O-go-doe, the voice of Death—that promises nothing, that speaks with tears only, and of the past.

So at last the preacher wiped his mouth in the final way and said, "He wuz uh man, and nobody knowed 'im but God," and it was ended in rhythm. With the drumming of the feet, and the mournful dance of the heads, in rhythm, it was ended.

September 6, 1933

Glossary

BIG BRITCHES GOIN' TUH FIT LI'L' WILLIE, he who was small
 is now grown. The underdog is now in position to fight
 for topdog place. 98

BITTER BONE, the all-power black-cat bone. Some hoodoo
 doctors select it by boiling the cat alive with appropriate
 ceremonies. (See "Hoodoo in America," Journal of
 American Folk-Lore, Vol. 44, No. 174, p. 387) and passing
 the bones thru the mouth until one arrives at the bitter
 bone. 106

CAT-BONE, same as above, though some doctors do not seek a
 bone by taste (See "Hoodoo in America," Vol. 44, No.
 174, p. 396). 107

GOD DON'T EAT OKRA, Okra when cooked is slick and slimy,
 i. e. God does not like slickness, crooked ways. 109

The pillow is removed from beneath the head of the dying
 because it is said to prolong the death struggle if left in
 place. All mirrors, and often all glass surfaces, are covered
 because it is believed the departing spirit will pause to
 look in them and if it does they will be forever clouded
 afterwards. 110

DOODLEY-SQUAT, nothing more valuable than dung. Hence
 the person is in extreme poverty. 116

"COLD" PREACH, cold used as a superlative to mean unsur-
 passed. Very common usage. 129

BLACK HERALD, BLACK DISPATCH, Negro gossip. 132

In his cooler passages the colored preacher attempts to achieve
 what to him is grammatical correctness, but as he warms
 up he goes natural. The "ha" in the sermon marks a
 breath. The congregation likes to hear the preacher
 breathing or "straining." 145–151

SOW-BOSOM, salt pork, a very important item in the diet of
 both negroes and poor whites in the South. 167

THEIR EYES WERE
WATCHING GOD

TO

HENRY ALLEN MOE

I

S HIPS at a distance have every man's wish on board. For some they come in with the tide. For others they sail forever on the horizon, never out of sight, never landing until the Watcher turns his eyes away in resignation, his dreams mocked to death by Time. That is the life of men.

Now, women forget all those things they don't want to remember, and remember everything they don't want to forget. The dream is the truth. Then they act and do things accordingly.

So the beginning of this was a woman and she had come back from burying the dead. Not the dead of sick and ailing with friends at the pillow and the feet. She had come back from the sodden and the bloated; the sudden dead, their eyes flung wide open in judgment.

The people all saw her come because it was sun-down. The sun was gone, but he had left his footprints in the sky. It was the time for sitting on porches beside the road. It was the time to hear things and talk. These sitters had been tongue-less, earless, eyeless conveniences all day long. Mules and other brutes had occupied their skins. But now, the sun and the bossman were gone, so the skins felt powerful and human. They became lords of sounds and lesser things. They passed nations through their mouths. They sat in judgment.

Seeing the woman as she was made them remember the envy they had stored up from other times. So they chewed up the back parts of their minds and swallowed with relish. They made burning statements with questions, and killing tools out of laughs. It was mass cruelty. A mood come alive. Words walking without masters; walking altogether like harmony in a song.

"What she doin' coming back here in dem overhalls? Can't she find no dress to put on?— Where's dat blue satin dress she left here in?— Where all dat money her husband took and died and left her?— What dat ole forty year ole 'oman doin' wid her hair swingin' down her back lak some young gal?— Where she left dat young lad of a boy she went off

here wid?— Thought she was going to marry?— Where he left *her*?— What he done wid all her money?— Betcha he off wid some gal so young she ain't even got no hairs—why she don't stay in her class?—"

When she got to where they were she turned her face on the bander log and spoke. They scrambled a noisy "good evenin'" and left their mouths setting open and their ears full of hope. Her speech was pleasant enough, but she kept walking straight on to her gate. The porch couldn't talk for looking.

The men noticed her firm buttocks like she had grape fruits in her hip pockets; the great rope of black hair swinging to her waist and unraveling in the wind like a plume; then her pugnacious breasts trying to bore holes in her shirt. They, the men, were saving with the mind what they lost with the eye. The women took the faded shirt and muddy overalls and laid them away for remembrance. It was a weapon against her strength and if it turned out of no significance, still it was a hope that she might fall to their level some day.

But nobody moved, nobody spoke, nobody even thought to swallow spit until after her gate slammed behind her.

Pearl Stone opened her mouth and laughed real hard because she didn't know what else to do. She fell all over Mrs. Sumpkins while she laughed. Mrs. Sumpkins snorted violently and sucked her teeth.

"Humph! Y'all let her worry yuh. You ain't like me. Ah ain't got her to study 'bout. If she ain't got manners enough to stop and let folks know how she been makin' out, let her g'wan!"

"She ain't even worth talkin' after," Lulu Moss drawled through her nose. "She sits high, but she looks low. Dat's what Ah say 'bout dese ole women runnin' after young boys."

Pheoby Watson hitched her rocking chair forward before she spoke. "Well, nobody don't know if it's anything to tell or not. Me, Ah'm her best friend, and *Ah* don't know."

"Maybe us don't know into things lak you do, but we all know how she went 'way from here and us sho seen her come back. 'Tain't no use in your tryin' to cloak no ole woman lak Janie Starks, Pheoby, friend or no friend."

"At dat she ain't so ole as some of y'all dat's talking."

"She's way past forty to my knowledge, Pheoby."

"No more'n forty at de outside."

"She's 'way too old for a boy like Tea Cake."

"Tea Cake ain't been no boy for some time. He's round thirty his ownself."

"Don't keer what it was, she could stop and say a few words with us. She act like we done done something to her," Pearl Stone complained. "She de one been doin' wrong."

"You mean, you mad 'cause she didn't stop and tell us all her business. Anyhow, what you ever know her to do so bad as y'all make out? The worst thing Ah ever knowed her to do was taking a few years offa her age and dat ain't never harmed nobody. Y'all makes me tired. De way you talkin' you'd think de folks in dis town didn't do nothin' in de bed 'cept praise de Lawd. You have to 'scuse me, 'cause Ah'm bound to go take her some supper." Pheoby stood up sharply.

"Don't mind us," Lulu smiled, "just go right ahead, us can mind yo' house for you till you git back. Mah supper is done. You bettah go see how she feel. You kin let de rest of us know."

"Lawd," Pearl agreed, "Ah done scorched-up dat lil meat and bread too long to talk about. Ah kin stay 'way from home long as Ah please. Mah husband ain't fussy."

"Oh, er, Pheoby, if youse ready to go, Ah could walk over dere wid you," Mrs. Sumpkins volunteered. "It's sort of duskin' down dark. De booger man might ketch yuh."

"Naw, Ah thank yuh. Nothin' couldn't ketch me dese few steps Ah'm goin'. Anyhow mah husband tell me say no first class booger would have me. If she got anything to tell yuh, you'll hear it."

Pheoby hurried on off with a covered bowl in her hands. She left the porch pelting her back with unasked questions. They hoped the answers were cruel and strange. When she arrived at the place, Pheoby Watson didn't go in by the front gate and down the palm walk to the front door. She walked around the fence corner and went in the intimate gate with her heaping plate of mulatto rice. Janie must be round that side.

She found her sitting on the steps of the back porch with the lamps all filled and the chimneys cleaned.

"Hello, Janie, how you comin'?"

"Aw, pretty good, Ah'm tryin' to soak some uh de tiredness and de dirt outa mah feet." She laughed a little.

"Ah see you is. Gal, you sho looks *good*. You looks like youse yo' own daughter." They both laughed. "Even wid dem overhalls on, you shows yo' womanhood."

"G'wan! G'wan! You must think Ah brought yuh somethin'. When Ah ain't brought home a thing but mahself."

"Dat's a gracious plenty. Yo' friends wouldn't want nothin' better."

"Ah takes dat flattery offa you, Pheoby, 'cause Ah know it's from de heart." Janie extended her hand. "Good Lawd, Pheoby! ain't you never goin' tuh gimme dat lil rations you brought me? Ah ain't had a thing on mah stomach today exceptin' mah hand." They both laughed easily. "Give it here and have a seat."

"Ah knowed you'd be hongry. No time to be huntin' stove wood after dark. Mah mulatto rice ain't so good dis time. Not enough bacon grease, but Ah reckon it'll kill hongry."

"Ah'll tell you in a minute," Janie said, lifting the cover. "Gal it's *too* good! you switches a mean fanny round in a kitchen."

"Aw, dat ain't much to eat, Janie. But Ah'm liable to have something sho nuff good tomorrow, 'cause you done come."

Janie ate heartily and said nothing. The varicolored cloud dust that the sun had stirred up in the sky was settling by slow degrees.

"Here, Pheoby, take yo' ole plate. Ah ain't got a bit of use for a empty dish. Dat grub sho come in handy."

Pheoby laughed at her friend's rough joke. "Youse just as crazy as you ever was."

"Hand me dat wash-rag on dat chair by you, honey. Lemme scrub mah feet." She took the cloth and rubbed vigorously. Laughter came to her from the big road.

"Well, Ah see Mouth-Almighty is still sittin' in de same place. And Ah reckon they got *me* up in they mouth now."

"Yes indeed. You know if you pass some people and don't speak tuh suit 'em dey got tuh go way back in yo' life and see whut you ever done. They know mo' 'bout yuh than you do

yo' self. An envious heart makes a treacherous ear. They done 'heard' 'bout you just what they hope done happened."

"If God don't think no mo' 'bout 'em then Ah do, they's a lost ball in de high grass."

"Ah hears what they say 'cause they just will collect round mah porch 'cause it's on de big road. Mah husband git so sick of 'em sometime he makes 'em all git for home."

"Sam is right too. They just wearin' out yo' sittin' chairs."

"Yeah, Sam say most of 'em goes to church so they'll be sure to rise in Judgment. Dat's de day dat every secret is s'posed to be made known. They wants to be there and hear it *all*."

"Sam is *too* crazy! You can't stop laughin' when youse round him."

"Uuh hunh. He says he aims to be there hisself so he can find out who stole his corn-cob pipe."

"Pheoby, dat Sam of your'n just won't quit! Crazy thing!"

"Most of dese zigaboos is so het up over yo' business till they liable to hurry theyself to Judgment to find out about you if they don't soon know. You better make haste and tell 'em 'bout you and Tea Cake gittin' married, and if he taken all yo' money and went off wid some young gal, and where at he is now and where at is all yo' clothes dat you got to come back here in overhalls."

"Ah don't mean to bother wid tellin' 'em nothin', Pheoby. 'Tain't worth de trouble. You can tell 'em what Ah say if you wants to. Dat's just de same as me 'cause mah tongue is in mah friend's mouf."

"If you so desire Ah'll tell 'em what you tell me to tell 'em."

"To start off wid, people like dem wastes up too much time puttin' they mouf on things they don't know nothin' about. Now they got to look into me loving Tea Cake and see whether it was done right or not! They don't know if life is a mess of corn-meal dumplings, and if love is a bed-quilt!"

"So long as they get a name to gnaw on they don't care whose it is, and what about, 'specially if they can make it sound like evil."

"If they wants to see and know, why they don't come kiss and be kissed? Ah could then sit down and tell 'em things. Ah

been a delegate to de big 'ssociation of life. Yessuh! De Grand Lodge, de big convention of livin' is just where Ah been dis year and a half y'all ain't seen me."

They sat there in the fresh young darkness close together. Pheoby eager to feel and do through Janie, but hating to show her zest for fear it might be thought mere curiosity. Janie full of that oldest human longing—self revelation. Pheoby held her tongue for a long time, but she couldn't help moving her feet. So Janie spoke.

"They don't need to worry about me and my overhalls long as Ah still got nine hundred dollars in de bank. Tea Cake got me into wearing 'em—following behind him. Tea Cake ain't wasted up no money of mine, and he ain't left me for no young gal, neither. He give me every consolation in de world. He'd tell 'em so too, if he was here. If he wasn't gone."

Pheoby dilated all over with eagerness, "Tea Cake gone?"

"Yeah, Pheoby, Tea Cake is gone. And dat's de only reason you see me back here—cause Ah ain't got nothing to make me happy no more where Ah was at. Down in the Everglades there, down on the muck."

"It's hard for me to understand what you mean, de way you tell it. And then again Ah'm hard of understandin' at times."

"Naw, 'tain't nothin' lak you might think. So 'tain't no use in me telling you somethin' unless Ah give you de understandin' to go 'long wid it. Unless you see de fur, a mink skin ain't no different from a coon hide. Looka heah, Pheoby, is Sam waitin' on you for his supper?"

"It's all ready and waitin'. If he ain't got sense enough to eat it, dat's his hard luck."

"Well then, we can set right where we is and talk. Ah got the house all opened up to let dis breeze get a little catchin'.

"Pheoby, we been kissin'-friends for twenty years, so Ah depend on you for a good thought. And Ah'm talking to you from dat standpoint."

Time makes everything old so the kissing, young darkness became a monstropolous old thing while Janie talked.

II

JANIE saw her life like a great tree in leaf with the things suffered, things enjoyed, things done and undone. Dawn and doom was in the branches.

"Ah know exactly what Ah got to tell yuh, but it's hard to know where to start at.

"Ah ain't never seen mah papa. And Ah didn't know 'im if Ah did. Mah mama neither. She was gone from round dere long before Ah wuz big enough tuh know. Mah grandma raised me. Mah grandma and de white folks she worked wid. She had a house out in de back-yard and dat's where Ah wuz born. They was quality white folks up dere in West Florida. Named Washburn. She had four gran'chillun on de place and all of us played together and dat's how come Ah never called mah Grandma nothin' but Nanny, 'cause dat's what everybody on de place called her. Nanny used to ketch us in our devilment and lick every youngun on de place and Mis' Washburn did de same. Ah reckon dey never hit us ah lick amiss 'cause dem three boys and us two girls wuz pretty aggravatin', Ah speck.

"Ah was wid dem white chillun so much till Ah didn't know Ah wuzn't white till Ah was round six years old. Wouldn't have found it out then, but a man come long takin' pictures and without askin' anybody, Shelby, dat was de oldest boy, he told him to take us. Round a week later de man brought de picture for Mis' Washburn to see and pay him which she did, then give us all a good lickin'.

"So when we looked at de picture and everybody got pointed out there wasn't nobody left except a real dark little girl with long hair standing by Eleanor. Dat's where Ah wuz s'posed to be, but Ah couldn't recognize dat dark chile as me. So Ah ast, 'where is me? Ah don't see me.'

"Everybody laughed, even Mr. Washburn. Miss Nellie, de Mama of de chillun who come back home after her husband dead, she pointed to de dark one and said, 'Dat's you, Alphabet, don't you know yo' ownself?'

"Dey all useter call me Alphabet 'cause so many people had

done named me different names. Ah looked at de picture a long time and seen it was mah dress and mah hair so Ah said:

"'Aw, aw! Ah'm colored!'

"Den dey all laughed real hard. But before Ah seen de picture Ah thought Ah wuz just like de rest.

"Us lived dere havin' fun till de chillun at school got to teasin' me 'bout livin' in de white folks back-yard. Dere wuz uh knotty head gal named Mayrella dat useter git mad every time she look at me. Mis' Washburn useter dress me up in all de clothes her gran'chillun didn't need no mo' which still wuz better'n what de rest uh de colored chillun had. And then she useter put hair ribbon on mah head fuh me tuh wear. Dat useter rile Mayrella uh lot. So she would pick at me all de time and put some others up tuh do de same. They'd push me 'way from de ring plays and make out they couldn't play wid nobody dat lived on premises. Den they'd tell me not to be takin' on over mah looks 'cause they mama told 'em 'bout de hound dawgs huntin' mah papa all night long. 'Bout Mr. Washburn and de sheriff puttin' de bloodhounds on de trail tuh ketch mah papa for whut he done tuh mah mama. Dey didn't tell about how he wuz seen tryin' tuh git in touch wid mah mama later on so he could marry her. Naw, dey didn't talk dat part of it atall. Dey made it sound real bad so as tuh crumple mah feathers. None of 'em didn't even remember whut his name wuz, but dey all knowed de bloodhound part by heart. Nanny didn't love tuh see me wid mah head hung down, so she figgered it would be mo' better fuh me if us had uh house. She got de land and everything and then Mis' Washburn helped out uh whole heap wid things."

Pheoby's hungry listening helped Janie to tell her story. So she went on thinking back to her young years and explaining them to her friend in soft, easy phrases while all around the house, the night time put on flesh and blackness.

She thought awhile and decided that her conscious life had commenced at Nanny's gate. On a late afternoon Nanny had called her to come inside the house because she had spied Janie letting Johnny Taylor kiss her over the gatepost.

It was a spring afternoon in West Florida. Janie had spent most of the day under a blossoming pear tree in the back-yard. She had been spending every minute that she could steal

from her chores under that tree for the last three days. That was to say, ever since the first tiny bloom had opened. It had called her to come and gaze on a mystery. From barren brown stems to glistening leaf-buds; from the leaf-buds to snowy virginity of bloom. It stirred her tremendously. How? Why? It was like a flute song forgotten in another existence and remembered again. What? How? Why? This singing she heard that had nothing to do with her ears. The rose of the world was breathing out smell. It followed her through all her waking moments and caressed her in her sleep. It connected itself with other vaguely felt matters that had struck her outside observation and buried themselves in her flesh. Now they emerged and quested about her consciousness.

She was stretched on her back beneath the pear tree soaking in the alto chant of the visiting bees, the gold of the sun and the panting breath of the breeze when the inaudible voice of it all came to her. She saw a dust-bearing bee sink into the sanctum of a bloom; the thousand sister-calyxes arch to meet the love embrace and the ecstatic shiver of the tree from root to tiniest branch creaming in every blossom and frothing with delight. So this was a marriage! She had been summoned to behold a revelation. Then Janie felt a pain remorseless sweet that left her limp and languid.

After a while she got up from where she was and went over the little garden field entire. She was seeking confirmation of the voice and vision, and everywhere she found and acknowledged answers. A personal answer for all other creations except herself. She felt an answer seeking her, but where? When? How? She found herself at the kitchen door and stumbled inside. In the air of the room were flies tumbling and singing, marrying and giving in marriage. When she reached the narrow hallway she was reminded that her grandmother was home with a sick headache. She was lying across the bed asleep so Janie tipped on out of the front door. Oh to be a pear tree — *any* tree in bloom! With kissing bees singing of the beginning of the world! She was sixteen. She had glossy leaves and bursting buds and she wanted to struggle with life but it seemed to elude her. Where were the singing bees for her? Nothing on the place nor in her grandma's house answered her. She searched as much of the world as she

could from the top of the front steps and then went on down to the front gate and leaned over to gaze up and down the road. Looking, waiting, breathing short with impatience. Waiting for the world to be made.

Through pollinated air she saw a glorious being coming up the road. In her former blindness she had known him as shiftless Johnny Taylor, tall and lean. That was before the golden dust of pollen had beglamored his rags and her eyes.

In the last stages of Nanny's sleep, she dreamed of voices. Voices far-off but persistent, and gradually coming nearer. Janie's voice. Janie talking in whispery snatches with a male voice she couldn't quite place. That brought her wide awake. She bolted upright and peered out of the window and saw Johnny Taylor lacerating her Janie with a kiss.

"Janie!"

The old woman's voice was so lacking in command and reproof, so full of crumbling dissolution,—that Janie half believed that Nanny had not seen her. So she extended herself outside of her dream and went inside of the house. That was the end of her childhood.

Nanny's head and face looked like the standing roots of some old tree that had been torn away by storm. Foundation of ancient power that no longer mattered. The cooling palma christi leaves that Janie had bound about her grandma's head with a white rag had wilted down and become part and parcel of the woman. Her eyes didn't bore and pierce. They diffused and melted Janie, the room and the world into one comprehension.

"Janie, youse uh 'oman, now, so—"

"Naw, Nanny, naw Ah ain't no real 'oman yet."

The thought was too new and heavy for Janie. She fought it away.

Nanny closed her eyes and nodded a slow, weary affirmation many times before she gave it voice.

"Yeah, Janie, youse got yo' womanhood on yuh. So Ah mout ez well tell yuh whut Ah been savin' up for uh spell. Ah wants to see you married right away."

"Me, married? Naw, Nanny, no ma'am! Whut Ah know 'bout uh husband?"

"Whut Ah seen just now is plenty for me, honey, Ah don't

want no trashy nigger, no breath-and-britches, lak Johnny Taylor usin' yo' body to wipe his foots on."

Nanny's words made Janie's kiss across the gatepost seem like a manure pile after a rain.

"Look at me, Janie. Don't set dere wid yo' head hung down. Look at yo' ole grandma!" Her voice began snagging on the prongs of her feelings. "Ah don't want to be talkin' to you lak dis. Fact is Ah done been on mah knees to mah Maker many's de time askin' *please*—for Him not to make de burden too heavy for me to bear."

"Nanny, Ah just—Ah didn't mean nothin' bad."

"Dat's what makes me skeered. You don't mean no harm. You don't even know where harm is at. Ah'm ole now. Ah can't be always guidin' yo' feet from harm and danger. Ah wants to see you married right away."

"Who Ah'm goin' tuh marry off-hand lak dat? Ah don't know nobody."

"De Lawd will provide. He know Ah done bore de burden in de heat uh de day. Somebody done spoke to me 'bout you long time ago. Ah ain't said nothin' 'cause dat wasn't de way Ah placed you. Ah wanted yuh to school out and pick from a higher bush and a sweeter berry. But dat ain't yo' idea, Ah see."

"Nanny, who—who dat been askin' you for me?"

"Brother Logan Killicks. He's a good man, too."

"Naw, Nanny, no ma'am! Is dat whut he been hangin' round here for? He look like some ole skull-head in de grave yard."

The older woman sat bolt upright and put her feet to the floor, and thrust back the leaves from her face.

"So you don't want to marry off decent like, do yuh? You just wants to hug and kiss and feel around with first one man and then another, huh? You wants to make me suck de same sorrow yo' mama did, eh? Mah ole head ain't gray enough. Mah back ain't bowed enough to suit yuh!"

The vision of Logan Killicks was desecrating the pear tree, but Janie didn't know how to tell Nanny that. She merely hunched over and pouted at the floor.

"Janie."

"Yes, ma'am."

"You answer me when Ah speak. Don't you set dere poutin' wid me after all Ah done went through for you!"

She slapped the girl's face violently, and forced her head back so that their eyes met in struggle. With her hand up-lifted for the second blow she saw the huge tear that welled up from Janie's heart and stood in each eye. She saw the terrible agony and the lips tightened down to hold back the cry and desisted. Instead she brushed back the heavy hair from Janie's face and stood there suffering and loving and weeping internally for both of them.

"Come to yo' Grandma, honey. Set in her lap lak yo' use tuh. Yo' Nanny wouldn't harm a hair uh yo' head. She don't want nobody else to do it neither if she kin help it. Honey, de white man is de ruler of everything as fur as Ah been able tuh find out. Maybe it's some place way off in de ocean where de black man is in power, but we don't know nothin' but what we see. So de white man throw down de load and tell de nigger man tuh pick it up. He pick it up because he have to, but he don't tote it. He hand it to his womenfolks. De nigger woman is de mule uh de world so fur as Ah can see. Ah been prayin' fuh it tuh be different wid you. Lawd, Lawd, Lawd!"

For a long time she sat rocking with the girl held tightly to her sunken breast. Janie's long legs dangled over one arm of the chair and the long braids of her hair swung low on the other side. Nanny half sung, half sobbed a running chant-prayer over the head of the weeping girl.

"Lawd have mercy! It was a long time on de way but Ah reckon it had to come. Oh Jesus! Do, Jesus! Ah done de best Ah could."

Finally, they both grew calm.

"Janie, how long you been 'lowin' Johnny Taylor to kiss you?"

"Only dis one time, Nanny. Ah don't love him at all. Whut made me do it is—oh, Ah don't know."

"Thank yuh, Massa Jesus."

"Ah ain't gointuh do it no mo', Nanny. Please don't make me marry Mr. Killicks."

"'Tain't Logan Killicks Ah wants you to have, baby, it's protection. Ah ain't gittin' ole, honey. Ah'm *done* ole. One mornin' soon, now, de angel wid de sword is gointuh stop by

here. De day and de hour is hid from me, but it won't be long. Ah ast de Lawd when you was uh infant in mah arms to let me stay here till you got grown. He done spared me to see de day. Mah daily prayer now is tuh let dese golden moments rolls on a few days longer till Ah see you safe in life."

"Lemme wait, Nanny, please, jus' a lil bit mo'."

"Don't think Ah don't feel wid you, Janie, 'cause Ah do. Ah couldn't love yuh no more if Ah had uh felt yo' birth pains mahself. Fact uh de matter, Ah loves yuh a whole heap more'n Ah do yo' mama, de one Ah did birth. But you got to take in consideration you ain't no everyday chile like most of 'em. You ain't got no papa, you might jus' as well say no mama, for de good she do yuh. You ain't got nobody but me. And mah head is ole and tilted towards de grave. Neither can you stand alone by yo'self. De thought uh you bein' kicked around from pillar tuh post is uh hurtin' thing. Every tear you drop squeezes a cup uh blood outa mah heart. Ah got tuh try and do for you befo' mah head is cold."

A sobbing sigh burst out of Janie. The old woman answered her with little soothing pats of the hand.

"You know, honey, us colored folks is branches without roots and that makes things come round in queer ways. You in particular. Ah was born back due in slavery so it wasn't for me to fulfill my dreams of whut a woman oughta be and to do. Dat's one of de hold-backs of slavery. But nothing can't stop you from wishin'. You can't beat nobody down so low till you can rob 'em of they will. Ah didn't want to be used for a work-ox and a brood-sow and Ah didn't want mah daughter used dat way neither. It sho wasn't mah will for things to happen lak they did. Ah even hated de way you was born. But, all de same Ah said thank God, Ah got another chance. Ah wanted to preach a great sermon about colored women sittin' on high, but they wasn't no pulpit for me. Freedom found me wid a baby daughter in mah arms, so Ah said Ah'd take a broom and a cook-pot and throw up a highway through de wilderness for her. She would expound what Ah felt. But somehow she got lost offa de highway and next thing Ah knowed here you was in de world. So whilst Ah was tendin' you of nights Ah said Ah'd save de text for you. Ah been waitin' a long time, Janie, but nothin' Ah been through

ain't too much if you just take a stand on high ground lak Ah dreamed."

Old Nanny sat there rocking Janie like an infant and think-ing back and back. Mind-pictures brought feelings, and feel-ings dragged out dramas from the hollows of her heart.

"Dat mornin' on de big plantation close to Savannah, a rider come in a gallop tellin' 'bout Sherman takin' Atlanta. Marse Robert's son had done been kilt at Chickamauga. So he grabbed his gun and straddled his best horse and went off wid de rest of de gray-headed men and young boys to drive de Yankees back into Tennessee.

"They was all cheerin' and cryin' and shoutin' for de men dat was ridin' off. Ah couldn't see nothin' cause yo' mama wasn't but a week old, and Ah was flat uh mah back. But pretty soon he let on he forgot somethin' and run into mah cabin and made me let down mah hair for de last time. He sorta wropped his hand in it, pulled mah big toe, lak he al-ways done, and was gone after de rest lak lightnin'. Ah heard 'em give one last whoop for him. Then de big house and de quarters got sober and silent.

"It was de cool of de evenin' when Mistis come walkin' in mah door. She throwed de door wide open and stood dere lookin' at me outa her eyes and her face. Look lak she been livin' through uh hundred years in January without one day of spring. She come stood over me in de bed.

" 'Nanny, Ah come to see that baby uh yourn.'

"Ah tried not to feel de breeze off her face, but it got so cold in dere dat Ah was freezin' to death under the kivvers. So Ah couldn't move right away lak Ah aimed to. But Ah knowed Ah had to make haste and do it.

" 'You better git dat kivver offa dat youngun and dat quick!' she clashed at me. 'Look lak you don't know who is Mistis on dis plantation, Madam. But Ah aims to show you.'

"By dat time I had done managed tuh unkivver mah baby enough for her to see de head and face.

" 'Nigger, whut's yo' baby doin' wid gray eyes and yaller hair?' She begin tuh slap mah jaws ever which a'way. Ah never felt the fust ones 'cause Ah wuz too busy gittin' de kivver back over mah chile. But dem last lick burnt me lak fire. Ah had too many feelin's tuh tell which one tuh follow so Ah

didn't cry and Ah didn't do nothin' else. But then she kept on astin me how come mah baby look white. She asted me dat maybe twenty-five or thirty times, lak she got tuh sayin' dat and couldn't help herself. So Ah told her, 'Ah don't know nothin' but what Ah'm told tuh do, 'cause Ah ain't nothin' but uh nigger and uh slave.'

"Instead of pacifyin' her lak Ah thought, look lak she got madder. But Ah reckon she was tired and wore out 'cause she didn't hit me no more. She went to de foot of de bed and wiped her hands on her handksher. 'Ah wouldn't dirty mah hands on yuh. But first thing in de mornin' de overseer will take you to de whippin' post and tie you down on yo' knees and cut de hide offa yo' yaller back. One hundred lashes wid a raw-hide on yo' bare back. Ah'll have you whipped till de blood run down to yo' heels! Ah mean to count de licks mah-self. And if it kills you Ah'll stand de loss. Anyhow, as soon as dat brat is a month old Ah'm going to sell it offa dis place.'

"She flounced on off and left her wintertime wid me. Ah knowed mah body wasn't healed, but Ah couldn't consider dat. In de black dark Ah wrapped mah baby de best Ah knowed how and made it to de swamp by de river. Ah knowed de place was full uh moccasins and other bitin' snakes, but Ah was more skeered uh whut was behind me. Ah hide in dere day and night and suckled de baby every time she start to cry, for fear somebody might hear her and Ah'd git found. Ah ain't sayin' uh friend or two didn't feel mah care. And den de Good Lawd seen to it dat Ah wasn't taken. Ah don't see how come mah milk didn't kill mah chile, wid me so skeered and worried all de time. De noise uh de owls skeered me; de limbs of dem cypress trees took to crawlin' and movin' round after dark, and two three times Ah heered panthers prowlin' round. But nothin' never hurt me 'cause de Lawd knowed how it was.

"Den, one night Ah heard de big guns boomin' lak thun-der. It kept up all night long. And de next mornin' Ah could see uh big ship at a distance and a great stirrin' round. So Ah wrapped Leafy up in moss and fixed her good in a tree and picked mah way on down to de landin'. The men was all in blue, and Ah heard people say Sherman was comin' to meet de boats in Savannah, and all of us slaves was free. So Ah run

got mah baby and got in quotation wid people and found a place Ah could stay.

"But it was a long time after dat befo' de Big Surrender at Richmond. Den de big bell ring in Atlanta and all de men in gray uniforms had to go to Moultrie, and bury their swords in de ground to show they was never to fight about slavery no mo'. So den we knowed we was free.

"Ah wouldn't marry nobody, though Ah could have uh heap uh times, cause Ah didn't want nobody mistreating mah baby. So Ah got with some good white people and come down here in West Florida to work and make de sun shine on both sides of de street for Leafy.

"Mah Madam help me wid her just lak she been doin' wid you. Ah put her in school when it got so it was a school to put her in. Ah was 'spectin' to make a school teacher outa her.

"But one day she didn't come home at de usual time and Ah waited and waited, but she never come all dat night. Ah took a lantern and went round askin' everybody but nobody ain't seen her. De next mornin' she come crawlin' in on her hands and knees. A sight to see. Dat school teacher had done hid her in de woods all night long, and he had done raped mah baby and run on off just before day.

"She was only seventeen, and somethin' lak dat to happen! Lawd a'mussy! Look lak Ah kin see it all over agin. It was a long time before she was well, and by dat time we knowed you was on de way. And after you was born she took to drinkin' likker and stayin' out nights. Couldn't git her to stay here and nowhere else. Lawd knows where she is right now. She ain't dead, 'cause Ah'd know it by mah feelings, but sometimes Ah wish she was at rest.

"And, Janie, maybe it wasn't much, but Ah done de best Ah kin by you. Ah raked and scraped and bought dis lil piece uh land so you wouldn't have to stay in de white folks' yard and tuck yo' head befo' other chillun at school. Dat was all right when you was little. But when you got big enough to understand things, Ah wanted you to look upon yo'self. Ah don't want yo' feathers always crumpled by folks throwin' up things in yo' face. And Ah can't die easy thinkin' maybe de menfolks white or black is makin' a spit cup outa you. Have some sympathy fuh me. Put me down easy, Janie, Ah'm a cracked plate."

III

THERE are years that ask questions and years that answer. Janie had had no chance to know things, so she had to ask. Did marriage end the cosmic loneliness of the unmated? Did marriage compel love like the sun the day?

In the few days to live before she went to Logan Killicks and his often-mentioned sixty acres, Janie asked inside of herself and out. She was back and forth to the pear tree continuously wondering and thinking. Finally out of Nanny's talk and her own conjectures she made a sort of comfort for herself. Yes, she would love Logan after they were married. She could see no way for it to come about, but Nanny and the old folks had said it, so it must be so. Husbands and wives always loved each other, and that was what marriage meant. It was just so. Janie felt glad of the thought, for then it wouldn't seem so destructive and mouldy. She wouldn't be lonely anymore.

Janie and Logan got married in Nanny's parlor of a Saturday evening with three cakes and big platters of fried rabbit and chicken. Everything to eat in abundance. Nanny and Mrs. Washburn had seen to that. But nobody put anything on the seat of Logan's wagon to make it ride glorious on the way to his house. It was a lonesome place like a stump in the middle of the woods where nobody had ever been. The house was absent of flavor, too. But anyhow Janie went on inside to wait for love to begin. The new moon had been up and down three times before she got worried in mind. Then she went to see Nanny in Mrs. Washburn's kitchen on the day for beaten biscuits.

Nanny beamed all out with gladness and made her come up to the bread board so she could kiss her.

"Lawd a'mussy, honey, Ah sho is glad tuh see mah chile! G'wan inside and let Mis' Washburn know youse heah. Umph! Umph! Umph! How is dat husband uh yourn?"

Janie didn't go in where Mrs. Washburn was. She didn't say anything to match up with Nanny's gladness either. She just fell on a chair with her hips and sat there. Between the

biscuits and her beaming pride Nanny didn't notice for a minute. But after a while she found the conversation getting lonesome so she looked up at Janie.

"Whut's de matter, sugar? You ain't none too spry dis mornin'."

"Oh, nothin' much, Ah reckon. Ah come to get a lil information from you."

The old woman looked amazed, then gave a big clatter of laughter. "Don't tell me you done got knocked up already, less see—dis Saturday it's two month and two weeks."

"No'm, Ah don't think so anyhow." Janie blushed a little.

"You ain't got nothin' to be shamed of, honey, youse uh married 'oman. You got yo' lawful husband same as Mis' Washburn or anybody else!"

"Ah'm all right dat way. Ah *know* 'tain't nothin' dere."

"You and Logan been fussin'? Lawd, Ah know dat grass-gut, liver-lipted nigger ain't done took and beat mah baby already! Ah'll take a stick and salivate 'im!"

"No'm, he ain't even talked 'bout hittin' me. He says he never mean to lay de weight uh his hand on me in malice. He chops all de wood he think Ah wants and den he totes it inside de kitchin for me. Keeps both water buckets full."

"Humph! don't 'spect all dat tuh keep up. He ain't kissin' yo' mouf when he carry on over yuh lak dat. He's kissin' yo' foot and 'tain't in uh man tuh kiss foot long. Mouf kissin' is on uh equal and dat's natural but when dey got to bow down tuh love, dey soon straightens up."

"Yes'm."

"Well, if he do all dat whut you come in heah wid uh face long as mah arm for?"

"'Cause you told me Ah mus gointer love him, and, and Ah don't. Maybe if somebody was to tell me how, Ah could do it."

"You come heah wid yo' mouf full uh foolishness on uh busy day. Heah you got uh prop tuh lean on all yo' bawn days, and big protection, and everybody got tuh tip dey hat tuh you and call you Mis' Killicks, and you come worryin' me 'bout love."

"But Nanny, Ah wants to want him sometimes. Ah don't want him to do all de wantin'."

"If you don't want him, you sho oughta. Heah you is wid de onliest organ in town, amongst colored folks, in yo' parlor. Got a house bought and paid for and sixty acres uh land right on de big road and . . . Lawd have mussy! Dat's de very prong all us black women gits hung on. Dis love! Dat's just whut's got us uh pullin' and uh haulin' and sweatin' and doin' from can't see in de mornin' till can't see at night. Dat's how come de ole folks say dat bein' uh fool don't kill nobody. It jus' makes you sweat. Ah betcha you wants some dressed up dude dat got to look at de sole of his shoe everytime he cross de street tuh see whether he got enough leather dere tuh make it across. You can buy and sell such as dem wid what you got. In fact you can buy 'em and give 'em away."

"Ah ain't studyin' 'bout none of 'em. At de same time Ah ain't takin' dat ole land tuh heart neither. Ah could throw ten acres of it over de fence every day and never look back to see where it fell. Ah feel de same way 'bout Mr. Killicks too. Some folks never was meant to be loved and he's one of 'em."

"How come?"

"'Cause Ah hates de way his head is so long one way and so flat on de sides and dat pone uh fat back uh his neck."

"He never made his own head. You talk so silly."

"Ah don't keer who made it, Ah don't like de job. His belly is too big too, now, and his toe-nails look lak mule foots. And 'tain't nothin' in de way of him washin' his feet every evenin' before he comes tuh bed. 'Tain't nothin' tuh hinder him 'cause Ah places de water for him. Ah'd ruther be shot wid tacks than tuh turn over in de bed and stir up de air whilst he is in dere. He don't even never mention nothin' pretty."

She began to cry.

"Ah wants things sweet wid mah marriage lak when you sit under a pear tree and think. Ah . . ."

"'Tain't no use in you cryin', Janie. Grandma done been long uh few roads herself. But folks is meant to cry 'bout somethin' or other. Better leave things de way dey is. Youse young yet. No tellin' whut mout happen befo' you die. Wait awhile, baby. Yo' mind will change."

Nanny sent Janie along with a stern mien, but she dwindled

all the rest of the day as she worked. And when she gained the privacy of her own little shack she stayed on her knees so long she forgot she was there herself. There is a basin in the mind where words float around on thought and thought on sound and sight. Then there is a depth of thought untouched by words, and deeper still a gulf of formless feelings untouched by thought. Nanny entered this infinity of conscious pain again on her old knees. Towards morning she muttered, "Lawd, you know mah heart. Ah done de best Ah could do. De rest is left to you." She scuffled up from her knees and fell heavily across the bed. A month later she was dead.

So Janie waited a bloom time, and a green time and an orange time. But when the pollen again gilded the sun and sifted down on the world she began to stand around the gate and expect things. What things? She didn't know exactly. Her breath was gusty and short. She knew things that nobody had ever told her. For instance, the words of the trees and the wind. She often spoke to falling seeds and said, "Ah hope you fall on soft ground," because she had heard seeds saying that to each other as they passed. She knew the world was a stallion rolling in the blue pasture of ether. She knew that God tore down the old world every evening and built a new one by sun-up. It was wonderful to see it take form with the sun and emerge from the gray dust of its making. The familiar people and things had failed her so she hung over the gate and looked up the road towards way off. She knew now that marriage did not make love. Janie's first dream was dead, so she became a woman.

IV

LONG BEFORE the year was up, Janie noticed that her husband had stopped talking in rhymes to her. He had ceased to wonder at her long black hair and finger it. Six months back he had told her, "If Ah kin haul de wood heah and chop it fuh yuh, look lak you oughta be able tuh tote it inside. Mah fust wife never bothered me 'bout choppin' no wood nohow. She'd grab dat ax and sling chips lak uh man. You done been spoilt rotten."

So Janie had told him, "Ah'm just as stiff as you is stout. If you can stand not to chop and tote wood Ah reckon you can stand not to git no dinner. 'Scuse mah freezolity, Mist' Killicks, but Ah don't mean to chop de first chip."

"Aw you know Ah'm gwine chop de wood fuh yuh. Even if you is stingy as you can be wid me. Yo' Grandma and me myself done spoilt yuh now, and Ah reckon Ah have tuh keep on wid it."

One morning soon he called her out of the kitchen to the barn. He had the mule all saddled at the gate.

"Looka heah, LilBit, help me out some. Cut up dese seed taters fuh me. Ah got tuh go step off a piece."

"Where you goin'?"

"Over tuh Lake City tuh see uh man about uh mule."

"Whut you need two mules fuh? Lessen you aims to swap off dis one."

"Naw, Ah needs two mules dis yeah. Taters is goin' tuh be taters in de fall. Bringin' big prices. Ah aims tuh run two plows, and dis man Ah'm talkin' 'bout is got uh mule all gentled up so even uh woman kin handle 'im."

Logan held his wad of tobacco real still in his jaw like a thermometer of his feelings while he studied Janie's face and waited for her to say something.

"So Ah thought Ah mout as well go see." He tagged on and swallowed to kill time but Janie said nothing except, "Ah'll cut up de p'taters fuh yuh. When yuh comin' back?"

"Don't know exactly. Round dust dark Ah reckon. It's uh

sorta long trip—specially if Ah hafter lead one on de way back."

When Janie had finished indoors she sat down in the barn with the potatoes. But springtime reached her in there so she moved everything to a place in the yard where she could see the road. The noon sun filtered through the leaves of the fine oak tree where she sat and made lacy patterns on the ground. She had been there a long time when she heard whistling coming down the road.

It was a cityfied, stylish dressed man with his hat set at an angle that didn't belong in these parts. His coat was over his arm, but he didn't need it to represent his clothes. The shirt with the silk sleeveholders was dazzling enough for the world. He whistled, mopped his face and walked like he knew where he was going. He was a seal-brown color but he acted like Mr. Washburn or somebody like that to Janie. Where would such a man be coming from and where was he going? He didn't look her way nor no other way except straight ahead, so Janie ran to the pump and jerked the handle hard while she pumped. It made a loud noise and also made her heavy hair fall down. So he stopped and looked hard, and then he asked her for a cool drink of water.

Janie pumped it off until she got a good look at the man. He talked friendly while he drank.

Joe Starks was the name, yeah Joe Starks from in and through Georgy. Been workin' for white folks all his life. Saved up some money—round three hundred dollars, yes indeed, right here in his pocket. Kept hearin' 'bout them buildin' a new state down heah in Floridy and sort of wanted to come. But he was makin' money where he was. But when he heard all about 'em makin' a town all outa colored folks, he knowed dat was de place he wanted to be. He had always wanted to be a big voice, but de white folks had all de sayso where he come from and everywhere else, exceptin' dis place dat colored folks was buildin' theirselves. Dat was right too. De man dat built things oughta boss it. Let colored folks build things too if dey wants to crow over somethin'. He was glad he had his money all saved up. He meant to git dere whilst de town wuz yet a baby. He meant to buy in big. It

had always been his wish and desire to be a big voice and he had to live nearly thirty years to find a chance. Where was Janie's papa and mama?

"Dey dead, Ah reckon. Ah wouldn't know 'bout 'em 'cause mah Grandma raised me. She dead too."

"She dead too! Well, who's lookin' after a lil girl-chile lak you?"

"Ah'm married."

"You married? You ain't hardly old enough to be weaned. Ah betcha you still craves sugar-tits, doncher?"

"Yeah, and Ah makes and sucks 'em when de notion strikes me. Drinks sweeten' water too."

"Ah loves dat mahself. Never specks to get too old to enjoy syrup sweeten' water when it's cools and nice."

"Us got plenty syrup in de barn. Ribbon-cane syrup. If you so desires—"

"Where yo' husband at, Mis' er-er."

"Mah name is Janie Mae Killicks since Ah got married. Useter be name Janie Mae Crawford. Mah husband is gone tuh buy a mule fuh me tuh plow. He left me cuttin' up seed p'taters."

"You behind a plow! You ain't got no mo' business wid uh plow than uh hog is got wid uh holiday! You ain't got no business cuttin' up no seed p'taters neither. A pretty doll-baby lak you is made to sit on de front porch and rock and fan yo'self and eat p'taters dat other folks plant just special for you."

Janie laughed and drew two quarts of syrup from the barrel and Joe Starks pumped the water bucket full of cool water. They sat under the tree and talked. He was going on down to the new part of Florida, but no harm to stop and chat. He later decided he needed a rest anyway. It would do him good to rest a week or two.

Every day after that they managed to meet in the scrub oaks across the road and talk about when he would be a big ruler of things with her reaping the benefits. Janie pulled back a long time because he did not represent sun-up and pollen and blooming trees, but he spoke for far horizon. He spoke for change and chance. Still she hung back. The memory of Nanny was still powerful and strong.

"Janie, if you think Ah aims to tole you off and make a dog outa you, youse wrong. Ah wants to make a wife outa you."

"You mean dat, Joe?"

"De day you puts yo' hand in mine, Ah wouldn't let de sun go down on us single. Ah'm uh man wid principles. You ain't never knowed what it was to be treated lak a lady and Ah wants to be de one tuh show yuh. Call me Jody lak you do sometime."

"Jody," she smiled up at him, "but s'posin'—"

"Leave de s'posin' and everything else to me. Ah'll be down dis road uh little after sunup tomorrow mornin' to wait for you. You come go wid me. Den all de rest of yo' natural life you kin live lak you oughta. Kiss me and shake yo' head. When you do dat, yo' plentiful hair breaks lak day."

Janie debated the matter that night in bed.

"Logan, you 'sleep?"

"If Ah wuz, you'd be done woke me up callin' me."

"Ah wuz thinkin' real hard about us; about you and me."

"It's about time. Youse powerful independent around here sometime considerin'."

"Considerin' whut for instance?"

"Considerin' youse born in a carriage 'thout no top to it, and yo' mama and you bein' born and raised in de white folks back-yard."

"You didn't say all dat when you wuz begging Nanny for me to marry you."

"Ah thought you would 'preciate good treatment. Thought Ah'd take and make somethin' outa yuh. You think youse white folks by de way you act."

"S'posin' Ah wuz to run off and leave yuh sometime."

There! Janie had put words to his held-in fears. She might run off sure enough. The thought put a terrible ache in Logan's body, but he thought it best to put on scorn.

"Ah'm gettin' sleepy, Janie. Let's don't talk no mo'. 'Tain't too many mens would trust yuh, knowin' yo' folks lak dey do."

"Ah might take and find somebody dat did trust me and leave yuh."

"Shucks! 'Tain't no mo' fools lak me. A whole lot of mens will grin in yo' face, but dey ain't gwine tuh work and feed

yuh. You won't git far and you won't be long, when dat big gut reach over and grab dat little one, you'll be too glad to come back here."

"You don't take nothin' to count but sow-belly and corn-bread."

"Ah'm sleepy. Ah don't aim to worry mah gut into a fiddle-string wid no s'posin'." He flopped over resentful in his agony and pretended sleep. He hoped that he had hurt her as she had hurt him.

Janie got up with him the next morning and had the breakfast halfway done when he bellowed from the barn.

"Janie!" Logan called harshly. "Come help me move dis manure pile befo' de sun gits hot. You don't take a bit of interest in dis place. 'Tain't no use in foolin' round in dat kitchen all day long."

Janie walked to the door with the pan in her hand still stirring the cornmeal dough and looked towards the barn. The sun from ambush was threatening the world with red daggers, but the shadows were gray and solid-looking around the barn. Logan with his shovel looked like a black bear doing some clumsy dance on his hind legs.

"You don't need mah help out dere, Logan. Youse in yo' place and Ah'm in mine."

"You ain't got no particular place. It's wherever Ah need yuh. Git uh move on yuh, and dat quick."

"Mah mama didn't tell me Ah wuz born in no hurry. So whut business Ah got rushin' now? Anyhow dat ain't whut youse mad about. Youse mad 'cause Ah don't fall down and wash-up dese sixty acres uh ground yuh got. You ain't done me no favor by marryin' me. And if dat's what you call yo'self doin', Ah don't thank yuh for it. Youse mad 'cause Ah'm tellin' yuh what you already knowed."

Logan dropped his shovel and made two or three clumsy steps towards the house, then stopped abruptly.

"Don't you change too many words wid me dis mawnin', Janie, do Ah'll take and change ends wid yuh! Heah, Ah just as good as take you out de white folks' kitchen and set you down on yo' royal diasticutis and you take and low-rate me! Ah'll take holt uh dat ax and come in dere and kill yuh! You better dry up in dere! Ah'm too honest and hard-workin' for

anybody in yo' family, dat's de reason you don't want me!"
The last sentence was half a sob and half a cry. "Ah guess
some low-lifed nigger is grinnin' in yo' face and lyin' tuh yuh.
God damn yo' hide!"

Janie turned from the door without answering, and stood
still in the middle of the floor without knowing it. She turned
wrongside out just standing there and feeling. When the
throbbing calmed a little she gave Logan's speech a hard
thought and placed it beside other things she had seen and
heard. When she had finished with that she dumped the
dough on the skillet and smoothed it over with her hand. She
wasn't even angry. Logan was accusing her of her mama, her
grandmama and her feelings, and she couldn't do a thing
about any of it. The sow-belly in the pan needed turning. She
flipped it over and shoved it back. A little cold water in the
coffee pot to settle it. Turned the hoe-cake with a plate and
then made a little laugh. What was she losing so much time
for? A feeling of sudden newness and change came over her.
Janie hurried out of the front gate and turned south. Even if
Joe was not there waiting for her, the change was bound to
do her good.

The morning road air was like a new dress. That made her
feel the apron tied around her waist. She untied it and flung it
on a low bush beside the road and walked on, picking flowers
and making a bouquet. After that she came to where Joe
Starks was waiting for her with a hired rig. He was very sol-
emn and helped her to the seat beside him. With him on it, it
sat like some high, ruling chair. From now on until death she
was going to have flower dust and springtime sprinkled over
everything. A bee for her bloom. Her old thoughts were
going to come in handy now, but new words would have to
be made and said to fit them.

"Green Cove Springs," he told the driver. So they were
married there before sundown, just like Joe had said. With
new clothes of silk and wool.

They sat on the boarding house porch and saw the sun
plunge into the same crack in the earth from which the night
emerged.

V

O N THE TRAIN the next day, Joe didn't make many
speeches with rhymes to her, but he bought her the
best things the butcher had, like apples and a glass lantern full
of candies. Mostly he talked about plans for the town when
he got there. They were bound to need somebody like him.
Janie took a lot of looks at him and she was proud of what
she saw. Kind of portly like rich white folks. Strange trains,
and people and places didn't scare him neither. Where they
got off the train at Maitland he found a buggy to carry them
over to the colored town right away.

It was early in the afternoon when they got there, so Joe
said they must walk over the place and look around. They
locked arms and strolled from end to end of the town. Joe
noted the scant dozen of shame-faced houses scattered in the
sand and palmetto roots and said, "God, they call this a town?
Why, 'tain't nothing but a raw place in de woods."

"It is a whole heap littler than Ah thought." Janie admitted
her disappointment.

"Just like Ah thought," Joe said. "A whole heap uh talk
and nobody doin' nothin'. I god, where's de Mayor?" He
asked somebody. "Ah want tuh speak wid de Mayor."

Two men who were sitting on their shoulder-blades under
a huge live oak tree almost sat upright at the tone of his voice.
They stared at Joe's face, his clothes and his wife.

"Where y'all come from in sich uh big haste?" Lee Coker
asked.

"Middle Georgy," Starks answered briskly. "Joe Starks is
mah name, from in and through Georgy."

"You and yo' daughter goin' tuh join wid us in fellowship?"
the other reclining figure asked. "Mighty glad tuh have yuh.
Hicks is the name. Gov'nor Amos Hicks from Buford, South
Carolina. Free, single, disengaged."

"I god, Ah ain't nowhere near old enough to have no
grown daughter. This here is mah wife."

Hicks sank back and lost interest at once.

"Where is de Mayor?" Starks persisted. "Ah wants tuh talk wid *him*."

"Youse uh mite too previous for dat," Coker told him. "Us ain't got none yit."

"Ain't got no Mayor! Well, who tells y'all what to do?"

"Nobody. Everybody's grown. And then agin, Ah reckon us just ain't thought about it. Ah know Ah ain't."

"Ah did think about it one day," Hicks said dreamily, "but then Ah forgot it and ain't thought about it since then."

"No wonder things ain't no better," Joe commented. "Ah'm buyin' in here, and buyin' in big. Soon's we find some place to sleep tonight us menfolks got to call people together and form a committee. Then we can get things movin' round here."

"Ah kin point yuh where yuh kin sleep," Hicks offered. "Man got his house done built and his wife ain't come yet."

Starks and Janie moved on off in the direction indicated with Hicks and Coker boring into their backs with looks.

"Dat man talks like a section foreman," Coker commented. "He's mighty compellment."

"Shucks!" said Hicks. "Mah britches is just as long as his. But dat wife uh hisn! Ah'm uh son of uh Combunction if Ah don't go tuh Georgy and git me one just like her."

"Whut wid?"

"Wid mah talk, man."

"It takes money tuh feed pretty women. Dey gits uh lavish uh talk."

"Not lak mine. Dey loves to hear me talk because dey can't understand it. Mah co-talkin' is too deep. Too much co to it."

"Umph!"

"You don't believe me, do yuh? You don't know de women Ah kin git to mah command."

"Umph!"

"You ain't never seen me when Ah'm out pleasurin' and givin' pleasure."

"Umph!"

"It's uh good thing he married her befo' she seen me. Ah kin be some trouble when Ah take uh notion."

"Umph!"

"Ah'm uh bitch's baby round lady people."

"Ah's much ruther see all dat than to hear 'bout it. Come on less go see whut he gointuh do 'bout dis town."

They got up and sauntered over to where Starks was living for the present. Already the town had found the strangers. Joe was on the porch talking to a small group of men. Janie could be seen through the bedroom window getting settled. Joe had rented the house for a month. The men were all around him, and he was talking to them by asking questions.

"Whut is de real name of de place?"

"Some say West Maitland and some say Eatonville. Dat's 'cause Cap'n Eaton give us some land along wid Mr. Laurence. But Cap'n Eaton give de first piece."

"How much did they give?"

"Oh 'bout fifty acres."

"How much is y'all got now?"

"Oh 'bout de same."

"Dat ain't near enough. Who owns de land joining on to whut yuh got?"

"Cap'n Eaton."

"Where *is* dis Cap'n Eaton?"

"Over dere in Maitland, 'ceptin' when he go visitin' or somethin'."

"Lemme speak to mah wife a minute and Ah'm goin' see de man. You cannot have no town without some land to build it on. Y'all ain't got enough here to cuss a cat on without gittin' yo' mouf full of hair."

"He ain't got no mo' land tuh give away. Yuh needs plenty money if yuh wants any mo'."

"Ah specks to pay him."

The idea was funny to them and they wanted to laugh. They tried hard to hold it in, but enough incredulous laughter burst out of their eyes and leaked from the corners of their mouths to inform anyone of their thoughts. So Joe walked off abruptly. Most of them went along to show him the way and to be there when his bluff was called.

Hicks didn't go far. He turned back to the house as soon as he felt he wouldn't be missed from the crowd and mounted the porch.

"Evenin', Miz Starks."

"Good evenin'."

"You reckon you gointuh like round here?"

"Ah reckon so."

"Anything *Ah* kin do tuh help out, why you kin call on me."

"Much obliged."

There was a long dead pause. Janie was not jumping at her chance like she ought to. Look like she didn't hardly know he was there. She needed waking up.

"Folks must be mighty close-mouthed where you come from."

"Dat's right. But it must be different at yo' home."

He was a long time thinking but finally he saw and stumbled down the steps with a surly " 'Bye."

"Good bye."

That night Coker asked him about it.

"Ah saw yuh when yuh ducked back tuh Starks' house. Well, how didju make out?"

"Who, me? Ah ain't been near de place, man. Ah been down tuh de lake tryin' tuh ketch me uh fish."

"Umph!"

"Dat 'oman ain't so awfully pretty nohow when yuh take de second look at her. Ah had to sorta pass by de house on de way back and seen her good. 'Tain't nothin' to her 'ceptin' dat long hair."

"Umph!"

"And anyhow, Ah done took uhlikin' tuh de man. Ah wouldn't harm him at all. She ain't half ez pretty ez uh gal Ah run off and left up in South Cal'lina."

"Hicks, Ah'd git mad and say you wuz lyin' if Ah didn't know yuh so good. You just talkin' to consolate yo'self by word of mouth. You got uh willin' mind, but youse too light behind. A whole heap uh men seen de same thing you seen but they got better sense than you. You oughta know you can't take no 'oman lak dat from no man lak him. A man dat ups and buys two hundred acres uh land at one whack and pays cash for it."

"Naw! He didn't buy it sho nuff?"

"He sho did. Come off wid de papers in his pocket. He done called a meetin' on his porch tomorrow. Ain't never seen no sich uh colored man befo' in all mah bawn days. He's

gointuh put up uh store and git uh post office from de Goven'ment."

That irritated Hicks and he didn't know why. He was the average mortal. It troubled him to get used to the world one way and then suddenly have it turn different. He wasn't ready to think of colored people in post offices yet. He laughed boisterously.

"Y'all let dat stray darky tell y'all any ole lie! Uh colored man sittin' up in uh post office!" He made an obscene sound.

"He's liable tuh do it too, Hicks. Ah hope so anyhow. Us colored folks is too envious of one 'nother. Dat's how come us don't git no further than us do. Us talks about de white man keepin' us down! Shucks! He don't have tuh. Us keeps our own selves down."

"Now who said Ah didn't want de man tuh git us uh post office? He kin be de king uh Jerusalem fuh all Ah keer. Still and all, 'tain't no use in telling lies just 'cause uh heap uh folks don't know no better. Yo' common sense oughta tell yuh de white folks ain't goin' tuh 'low him tuh run no post office."

"Dat we don't know, Hicks. He say he kin and Ah b'lieve he know whut he's talkin' 'bout. Ah reckon if colored folks got they own town they kin have post offices and whatsoever they please, regardless. And then agin, Ah don't speck de white folks way off yonder give uh damn. Less us wait and see."

"Oh, Ah'm waitin' all right. Specks tuh keep on waitin' till hell freeze over."

"Aw, git reconciled! Dat woman don't want you. You got tuh learn dat all de women in de world ain't been brought up on no teppentine still, and no saw-mill camp. There's some women dat jus' ain't for you tuh broach. You can't git *her* wid no fish sandwich."

They argued a bit more then went on to the house where Joe was and found him in his shirt-sleeves, standing with his legs wide apart, asking questions and smoking a cigar.

"Where's de closest saw-mill?" He was asking Tony Taylor.

"'Bout seben miles goin' t'wards Apopka," Tony told him. "Thinkin' 'bout buildin' right away?"

"I god, yeah. But not de house Ah specks tuh live in. Dat

kin wait till Ah make up mah mind where Ah wants it located. Ah figgers we all needs uh store in uh big hurry."

"Uh store?" Tony shouted in surprise.

"Yeah, uh store right heah in town wid everything in it you needs. 'Tain't uh bit uh use in everybody proagin' way over tuh Maitland tuh buy uh little meal and flour when they could git it right heah."

"Dat would be kinda nice, Brother Starks, since you mention it."

"I god, course it would! And then agin uh store is good in other ways. Ah got tuh have a place tuh be at when folks comes tuh buy land. And furthermo' everything is got tuh have uh center and uh heart tuh it, and uh town ain't no different from nowhere else. It would be natural fuh de store tuh be meetin' place fuh de town."

"Dat sho is de truth, now."

"Oh, we'll have dis town all fixed up tereckly. Don't miss bein' at de meetin' tuhmorrow."

Just about time for the committee meeting called to meet on his porch next day, the first wagon load of lumber drove up and Jody went to show them where to put it. Told Janie to hold the committee there until he got back, he didn't want to miss them, but he meant to count every foot of that lumber before it touched the ground. He could have saved his breath and Janie could have kept right on with what she was doing. In the first place everybody was late in coming; then the next thing as soon as they heard where Jody was, they kept right on up there where the new lumber was rattling off the wagon and being piled under the big live oak tree. So that's where the meeting was held with Tony Taylor acting as chairman and Jody doing all the talking. A day was named for roads and they all agreed to bring axes and things like that and chop out two roads running each way. That applied to everybody except Tony and Coker. They could carpenter, so Jody hired them to go to work on his store bright and soon the next morning. Jody himself would be busy driving around from town to town telling people about Eatonville and drumming up citizens to move there.

Janie was astonished to see the money Jody had spent for

the land come back to him so fast. Ten new families bought lots and moved to town in six weeks. It all looked too big and rushing for her to keep track of. Before the store had a complete roof, Jody had canned goods piled on the floor and was selling so much he didn't have time to go off on his talking tours. She had her first taste of presiding over it the day it was complete and finished. Jody told her to dress up and stand in the store all that evening. Everybody was coming sort of fixed up, and he didn't mean for nobody else's wife to rank with her. She must look on herself as the bell-cow, the other women were the gang. So she put on one of her bought dresses and went up the new-cut road all dressed in wine-colored red. Her silken ruffles rustled and muttered about her. The other women had on percale and calico with here and there a head-rag among the older ones.

Nobody was buying anything that night. They didn't come there for that. They had come to make a welcome. So Joe knocked in the head of a barrel of soda crackers and cut some cheese.

"Everybody come right forward and make merry. I god, it's mah treat." Jody gave one of his big heh heh laughs and stood back. Janie dipped up the lemonade like he told her. A big tin cup full for everybody. Tony Taylor felt so good when it was all gone that he felt to make a speech.

"Ladies and gent'men, we'se come tuhgether and gethered heah tuh welcome tuh our midst one who has seen fit tuh cast in his lot amongst us. He didn't just come hisself neither. He have seen fit tuh bring his, er, er, de light uh his home, dat is his wife amongst us also. She couldn't look no mo' better and no nobler if she wuz de queen uh England. It's uh pledger fuh her tuh be heah amongst us. Brother Starks, we welcomes you and all dat you have seen fit tuh bring amongst us—yo' belov-ed wife, yo' store, yo' land—"

A big-mouthed burst of laughter cut him short.

"Dat'll do, Tony," Lige Moss yelled out. "Mist' Starks is uh smart man, we'se all willin' tuh acknowledge tuh dat, but de day he comes waggin' down de road wid two hund'ed acres uf land over his shoulder, Ah wants tuh be dere tuh see it."

Another big blow-out of a laugh. Tony was a little peeved at having the one speech of his lifetime ruined like that.

"All y'all know whut wuz meant. Ah don't see how come — "

" 'Cause you jump up tuh make speeches and don't know how," Lige said.

"Ah wuz speakin' jus' all right befo' you stuck yo' bill in."

"Naw, you wuzn't, Tony. Youse way outa jurisdiction. You can't welcome uh man and his wife 'thout you make comparison about Isaac and Rebecca at de well, else it don't show de love between 'em if you don't."

Everybody agreed that that was right. It was sort of pitiful for Tony not to know he couldn't make a speech without saying that. Some tittered at his ignorance. So Tony said testily, "If all them dat's gointuh cut de monkey is done cut it and through wid, we'll thank Brother Starks fuh a respond."

So Joe Starks and his cigar took the center of the floor.

"Ah thanks you all for yo' kind welcome and for extendin' tuh me de right hand uh fellowship. Ah kin see dat dis town is full uh union and love. Ah means tuh put mah hands tuh de plow heah, and strain every nerve tuh make dis our town de metropolis uh de state. So maybe Ah better tell yuh in case you don't know dat if we expect tuh move on, us got tuh incorporate lak every other town. Us got tuh incorporate, and us got tuh have uh mayor, if things is tuh be done and done right. Ah welcome you all on behalf uh me and mah wife tuh dis store and tuh de other things tuh come. Amen."

Tony led the loud hand-clapping and was out in the center of the floor when it stopped.

"Brothers and sisters, since us can't never expect tuh better our choice, Ah move dat we make Brother Starks our Mayor until we kin see further."

"Second dat motion!!!" It was everybody talking at once, so it was no need of putting it to a vote.

"And now we'll listen tuh uh few words uh encouragement from Mrs. Mayor Starks."

The burst of applause was cut short by Joe taking the floor himself.

"Thank yuh fuh yo' compliments, but mah wife don't know nothin' 'bout no speech-makin'. Ah never married her for nothin' lak dat. She's uh woman and her place is in de home."

Janie made her face laugh after a short pause, but it wasn't too easy. She had never thought of making a speech, and didn't know if she cared to make one at all. It must have been the way Joe spoke out without giving her a chance to say anything one way or another that took the bloom off of things. But anyway, she went down the road behind him that night feeling cold. He strode along invested with his new dignity, thought and planned out loud, unconscious of her thoughts.

"De mayor of uh town lak dis can't lay round home too much. De place needs buildin' up. Janie, Ah'll git hold uh somebody tuh help out in de store and you kin look after things whilst Ah drum up things otherwise."

"Oh Jody, Ah can't do nothin' wid no store lessen youse there. Ah could maybe come in and help you when things git rushed, but—"

"I god, Ah don't see how come yuh can't. 'Tain't nothin' atall tuh hinder yuh if yuh got uh thimble full uh sense. You got tuh. Ah got too much else on mah hands as Mayor. Dis town needs some light right now."

"Unh hunh, it *is* uh little dark right long heah."

"'Course it is. 'Tain't no use in scuffin' over all dese stumps and roots in de dark. Ah'll call uh meetin' bout de dark and de roots right away. Ah'll sit on dis case first thing."

The very next day with money out of his own pocket he sent off to Sears, Roebuck and Company for the street lamp and told the town to meet the following Thursday night to vote on it. Nobody had ever thought of street lamps and some of them said it was a useless notion. They went so far as to vote against it, but the majority ruled.

But the whole town got vain over it after it came. That was because the Mayor didn't just take it out of the crate and stick it up on a post. He unwrapped it and had it wiped off carefully and put it up on a showcase for a week for everybody to see. Then he set a time for the lighting and sent word all around Orange County for one and all to come to the lamp-lighting. He sent men out to the swamp to cut the finest and the straightest cypress post they could find, and kept on sending them back to hunt another one until they found one that pleased him. He had talked to the people already about the hospitality of the occasion.

"Y'all know we can't invite people to our town just dry long so. I god, naw. We got tuh feed 'em something, and 'tain't nothin' people laks better'n barbecue. Ah'll give one whole hawg mah ownself. Seem lak all de rest uh y'all put tuhgether oughta be able tuh scrape up two mo'. Tell yo' womenfolks tuh do 'round 'bout some pies and cakes and sweet p'tater pone."

That's the way it went, too. The women got together the sweets and the men looked after the meats. The day before the lighting, they dug a big hole in back of the store and filled it full of oak wood and burned it down to a glowing bed of coals. It took them the whole night to barbecue the three hogs. Hambo and Pearson had full charge while the others helped out with turning the meat now and then while Hambo swabbed it all over with the sauce. In between times they told stories, laughed and told more stories and sung songs. They cut all sorts of capers and whiffed the meat as it slowly came to perfection with the seasoning penetrating to the bone. The younger boys had to rig up the saw-horses with boards for the women to use as tables. Then it was after sun-up and everybody not needed went home to rest up for the feast.

By five o'clock the town was full of every kind of a vehicle and swarming with people. They wanted to see that lamp lit at dusk. Near the time, Joe assembled everybody in the street before the store and made a speech.

"Folkses, de sun is goin' down. De Sun-maker brings it up in de mornin', and de Sun-maker sends it tuh bed at night. Us poor weak humans can't do nothin' tuh hurry it up nor to slow it down. All we can do, if we want any light after de settin' or befo' de risin', is tuh make some light ourselves. So dat's how come lamps was made. Dis evenin' we'se all assembled heah tuh light uh lamp. Dis occasion is something for us all tuh remember tuh our dyin' day. De first street lamp in uh colored town. Lift yo' eyes and gaze on it. And when Ah touch de match tuh dat lamp-wick let de light penetrate inside of yuh, and let it shine, let it shine, let it shine. Brother Davis, lead us in a word uh prayer. Ask uh blessin' on dis town in uh most particular manner."

While Davis chanted a traditional prayer-poem with his own variations, Joe mounted the box that had been placed for the purpose and opened the brazen door of the lamp. As the word Amen was said, he touched the lighted match to the wick, and Mrs. Bogle's alto burst out in:

> We'll walk in de light, de beautiful light
> Come where the dew drops of mercy shine bright
> Shine all around us by day and by night
> Jesus, the light of the world.

They, all of them, all of the people took it up and sung it over and over until it was wrung dry, and no further innovations of tone and tempo were conceivable. Then they hushed and ate barbecue.

When it was all over that night in bed Jody asked Janie, "Well, honey, how yuh lak bein' Mrs. Mayor?"

"It's all right Ah reckon, but don't yuh think it keeps us in uh kinda strain?"

"Strain? You mean de cookin' and waitin' on folks?"

"Naw, Jody, it jus' looks lak it keeps us in some way we ain't natural wid one 'nother. You'se always off talkin' and fixin' things, and Ah feels lak Ah'm jus' markin' time. Hope it soon gits over."

"Over, Janie? I god, Ah ain't even started good. Ah told you in de very first beginnin' dat Ah aimed tuh be uh big voice. You oughta be glad, 'cause dat makes uh big woman outa you."

A feeling of coldness and fear took hold of her. She felt far away from things and lonely.

Janie soon began to feel the impact of awe and envy against her sensibilities. The wife of the Mayor was not just another woman as she had supposed. She slept with authority and so she was part of it in the town mind. She couldn't get but so close to most of them in spirit. It was especially noticeable after Joe had forced through a town ditch to drain the street in front of the store. They had murmured hotly about slavery being over, but every man filled his assignment.

There was something about Joe Starks that cowed the

town. It was not because of physical fear. He was no fist fighter. His bulk was not even imposing as men go. Neither was it because he was more literate than the rest. Something else made men give way before him. He had a bow-down command in his face, and every step he took made the thing more tangible.

Take for instance that new house of his. It had two stories with porches, with bannisters and such things. The rest of the town looked like servant's quarters surrounding the "big house." And different from everybody else in the town he put off moving in until it had been painted, in and out. And look at the way he painted it—a gloaty, sparkly white. The kind of promenading white that the houses of Bishop Whipple, W. B. Jackson and the Vanderpool's wore. It made the village feel funny talking to him—just like he was anybody else. Then there was the matter of the spittoons. No sooner was he all set as the Mayor—post master—landlord—storekeeper, than he bought a desk like Mr. Hill or Mr. Galloway over in Maitland with one of those swing-around chairs to it. What with him biting down on cigars and saving his breath on talk and swinging round in that chair, it weakened people. And then he spit in that gold-looking vase that anybody else would have been glad to put on their front-room table. Said it was a spittoon just like his used-to-be bossman used to have in his bank up there in Atlanta. Didn't have to get up and go to the door every time he had to spit. Didn't spit on his floor neither. Had that golded-up spitting pot right handy. But he went further than that. He bought a little lady-size spitting pot for Janie to spit in. Had it right in the parlor with little sprigs of flowers painted all around the sides. It took people by surprise because most of the women dipped snuff and of course had a spit-cup in the house. But how could they know up-to-date folks was spitting in flowery little things like that? It sort of made the rest of them feel that they had been taken advantage of. Like things had been kept from them. Maybe more things in the world besides spitting pots had been hid from them, when they wasn't told no better than to spit in tomato cans. It was bad enough for white people, but when one of your own color could be so different it put you on a wonder. It was like seeing your sister turn into a 'gator. A

familiar strangeness. You keep seeing your sister in the 'gator and the 'gator in your sister, and you'd rather not. There was no doubt that the town respected him and even admired him in a way. But any man who walks in the way of power and property is bound to meet hate. So when speakers stood up when the occasion demanded and said "Our beloved Mayor," it was one of those statements that everybody says but nobody actually believes like "God is everywhere." It was just a handle to wind up the tongue with. As time went on and the benefits he had conferred upon the town receded in time they sat on his store porch while he was busy inside and discussed him. Like one day after he caught Henry Pitts with a wagon load of his ribbon cane and took the cane away from Pitts and made him leave town. Some of them thought Starks ought not to have done that. He had so much cane and everything else. But they didn't say that while Joe Starks was on the porch. When the mail came from Maitland and he went inside to sort it out everybody had their say.

Sim Jones started off as soon as he was sure that Starks couldn't hear him.

"It's uh sin and uh shame runnin' dat po' man way from here lak dat. Colored folks oughtn't tuh be so hard on one 'nother."

"Ah don't see it dat way atall," Sam Watson said shortly. "Let colored folks learn to work for what dey git lak everybody else. Nobody ain't stopped Pitts from plantin' de cane he wanted tuh. Starks give him uh job, what mo' do he want?"

"Ah know dat too," Jones said, "but, Sam, Joe Starks is too exact wid folks. All he got he done made it offa de rest of us. He didn't have all dat when he come here."

"Yeah, but none uh all dis you see and you'se settin' on wasn't here neither, when he come. Give de devil his due."

"But now, Sam, you know dat all he do is big-belly round and tell other folks what tuh do. He loves obedience out of everybody under de sound of his voice."

"You kin feel a switch in his hand when he's talkin' to yuh," Oscar Scott complained. "Dat chastisin' feelin' he totes sorter gives yuh de protolapsis uh de cutinary linin'."

"He's uh whirlwind among breezes," Jeff Bruce threw in.

"Speakin' of winds, he's de wind and we'se de grass. We bend which ever way he blows," Sam Watson agreed, "but at dat us needs him. De town wouldn't be nothin' if it wasn't for him. He can't help bein' sorta bossy. Some folks needs thrones, and ruling-chairs and crowns tuh make they influence felt. He don't. He's got uh throne in de seat of his pants."

"Whut Ah don't lak 'bout de man is, he talks tuh unlettered folks wid books in his jaws," Hicks complained. "Showin' off his learnin'. To look at me you wouldn't think it, but Ah got uh brother pastorin' up round Ocala dat got good learnin'. If he wuz here, Joe Starks wouldn't make no fool outa him lak he do de rest uh y'all."

"Ah often wonder how dat lil wife uh hisn makes out wid him, 'cause he's uh man dat changes everything, but nothin' don't change him."

"You know many's de time Ah done thought about dat mahself. He gits on her ever now and then when she make little mistakes round de store."

"Whut make her keep her head tied up lak some ole 'oman round de store? Nobody couldn't *git* me tuh tie no rag on mah head if Ah had hair lak dat."

"Maybe he make her do it. Maybe he skeered some de rest of us mens might touch it round dat store. It sho is uh hidden mystery tuh me."

"She sho don't talk much. De way he rears and pitches in de store sometimes when she make uh mistake is sort of ungodly, but she don't seem to mind at all. Reckon dey understand one 'nother."

The town had a basketful of feelings good and bad about Joe's positions and possessions, but none had the temerity to challenge him. They bowed down to him rather, because he was all of these things, and then again he was all of these things because the town bowed down.

VI

EVERY MORNING the world flung itself over and exposed the town to the sun. So Janie had another day. And every day had a store in it, except Sundays. The store itself was a pleasant place if only she didn't have to sell things. When the people sat around on the porch and passed around the pictures of their thoughts for the others to look at and see, it was nice. The fact that the thought pictures were always crayon enlargements of life made it even nicer to listen to.

Take for instance the case of Matt Bonner's yellow mule. They had him up for conversation every day the Lord sent. Most especial if Matt was there himself to listen. Sam and Lige and Walter were the ringleaders of the mule-talkers. The others threw in whatever they could chance upon, but it seemed as if Sam and Lige and Walter could hear and see more about that mule than the whole county put together. All they needed was to see Matt's long spare shape coming down the street and by the time he got to the porch they were ready for him.

"Hello, Matt."

"Evenin', Sam."

"Mighty glad you come 'long right now, Matt. Me and some others wuz jus' about tuh come hunt yuh."

"Whut for, Sam?"

"Mighty serious matter, man. Serious!!"

"Yeah man," Lige would cut in, dolefully. "It needs yo' strict attention. You ought not tuh lose no time."

"Whut is it then? You oughta hurry up and tell me."

"Reckon we better not tell yuh heah at de store. It's too fur off tuh do any good. We better all walk on down by Lake Sabelia."

"Whut's wrong, man? Ah ain't after none uh y'alls foolishness now."

"Dat mule uh yourn, Matt. You better go see 'bout him. He's bad off."

"Where 'bouts? Did he wade in de lake and uh alligator ketch him?"

"Worser'n dat. De womenfolks got yo' mule. When Ah come round de lake 'bout noontime mah wife and some others had 'im flat on de ground usin' his sides fuh uh wash board."

The great clap of laughter that they have been holding in, bursts out. Sam never cracks a smile. "Yeah, Matt, dat mule so skinny till de women is usin' his rib bones fuh uh rub-board, and hangin' things out on his hock-bones tuh dry."

Matt realizes that they have tricked him again and the laughter makes him mad and when he gets mad he stammers.

"You'se uh stinkin' lie, Sam, and yo' feet ain't mates. Y-y-y-you!"

"Aw, man, 'tain't no use in you gittin' mad. Yuh know yuh don't feed de mule. How he gointuh git fat?"

"Ah-ah-ah d-d-does feed 'im! Ah g-g-gived 'im uh full cup uh cawn every feedin'."

"Lige knows all about dat cup uh cawn. He hid round yo' barn and watched yuh. 'Tain't no feed cup you measures dat cawn outa. It's uh tea cup."

"Ah does feed 'im. He's jus' too mean tuh git fat. He stay poor and rawbony jus' fuh spite. Skeered he'll hafta work some."

"Yeah, you feeds 'im. Feeds 'im offa 'come up' and seasons it wid raw-hide."

"Does feed de ornery varmint! Don't keer whut Ah do Ah can't git long wid 'im. He fights every inch in front uh de plow, and even lay back his ears tuh kick and bite when Ah go in de stall tuh feed 'im."

"Git reconciled, Matt," Lige soothed. "Us all knows he's mean. Ah seen 'im when he took after one uh dem Roberts chillun in de street and woulda caught 'im and maybe trompled 'im tuh death if de wind hadn't of changed all of a sudden. Yuh see de youngun wuz tryin' tuh make it tuh de fence uh Starks' onion patch and de mule wuz dead in behind 'im and gainin' on 'im every jump, when all of a sudden de wind changed and blowed de mule way off his course, him bein' so poor and everything, and before de ornery varmint could tack, de youngun had done got over de fence." The porch laughed and Matt got mad again.

"Maybe de mule takes out after everybody," Sam said,

"'cause he thinks everybody he hear comin' is Matt Bonner comin' tuh work 'im on uh empty stomach."

"Aw, naw, aw, naw. You stop dat right now," Walter objected: "Dat mule don't think Ah look lak no Matt Bonner. He ain't dat dumb. If Ah thought he didn't know no better Ah'd have mah picture took and give it tuh dat mule so's he could learn better. Ah ain't gointuh 'low 'im tuh hold nothin' lak dat against me."

Matt struggled to say something but his tongue failed him so he jumped down off the porch and walked away as mad as he could be. But that never halted the mule talk. There would be more stories about how poor the brute was; his age; his evil disposition and his latest caper. Everybody indulged in mule talk. He was next to the Mayor in prominence, and made better talking.

Janie loved the conversation and sometimes she thought up good stories on the mule, but Joe had forbidden her to indulge. He didn't want her talking after such trashy people. "You'se Mrs. Mayor Starks, Janie. I god, Ah can't see what uh woman uh yo' sability would want tuh be treasurin' all dat gum-grease from folks dat don't even own de house dey sleep in. 'Tain't no earthly use. They's jus' some puny humans playin' round de toes uh Time."

Janie noted that while he didn't talk the mule himself, he sat and laughed at it. Laughed his big heh, heh laugh too. But then when Lige or Sam or Walter or some of the other big picture talkers were using a side of the world for a canvas, Joe would hustle her off inside the store to sell something. Look like he took pleasure in doing it. Why couldn't he go himself sometimes? She had come to hate the inside of that store anyway. That Post Office too. People always coming and asking for mail at the wrong time. Just when she was trying to count up something or write in an account book. Get her so hackled she'd make the wrong change for stamps. Then too, she couldn't read everybody's writing. Some folks wrote so funny and spelt things different from what she knew about. As a rule, Joe put up the mail himself, but sometimes when he was off she had to do it herself and it always ended up in a fuss.

The store itself kept her with a sick headache. The labor of getting things down off of a shelf or out of a barrel was

nothing. And so long as people wanted only a can of tomatoes or a pound of rice it was all right. But supposing they went on and said a pound and a half of bacon and a half pound of lard? The whole thing changed from a little walking and stretching to a mathematical dilemma. Or maybe cheese was thirty-seven cents a pound and somebody came and asked for a dime's worth. She went through many silent rebellions over things like that. Such a waste of life and time. But Joe kept saying that she could do it if she wanted to and he wanted her to use her privileges. That was the rock she was battered against.

This business of the head-rag irked her endlessly. But Jody was set on it. Her hair was NOT going to show in the store. It didn't seem sensible at all. That was because Joe never told Janie how jealous he was. He never told her how often he had seen the other men figuratively wallowing in it as she went about things in the store. And one night he had caught Walter standing behind Janie and brushing the back of his hand back and forth across the loose ends of her braid ever so lightly so as to enjoy the feel of it without Janie knowing what he was doing. Joe was at the back of the store and Walter didn't see him. He felt like rushing forth with the meat knife and chopping off the offending hand. That night he ordered Janie to tie up her hair around the store. That was all. She was there in the store for *him* to look at, not those others. But he never said things like that. It just wasn't in him. Take the matter of the yellow mule, for instance.

Late one afternoon Matt came from the west with a halter in his hand. "Been huntin' fuh mah mule. Anybody seen 'im?" he asked.

"Seen 'im soon dis mornin' over behind de schoolhouse," Lum said. "'Bout ten o'clock or so. He musta been out all night tuh be way over dere dat early."

"He wuz," Matt answered. "Seen 'im last night but Ah couldn't ketch 'im. Ah'm 'bliged tuh git 'im in tuhnight 'cause Ah got some plowin' fuh tuhmorrow. Done promised tuh plow Thompson's grove."

"Reckon you'll ever git through de job wid dat mule-frame?" Lige asked.

"Aw dat mule is plenty strong. Jus' evil and don't want tuh be led."

"Dat's right. Dey tell me he brought you heah tuh dis town. Say you started tuh Miccanopy but de mule had better sense and brung yuh on heah."

"It's uh l-l-lie! Ah set out fuh dis town when Ah left West Floridy."

"You mean tuh tell me you rode dat mule all de way from West Floridy down heah?"

"Sho he did, Lige. But he didn't mean tuh. He wuz satisfied up dere, but de mule wuzn't. So one mornin' he got straddle uh de mule and he took and brought 'im on off. Mule had sense. Folks up dat way don't eat biscuit bread but once uh week."

There was always a little seriousness behind the teasing of Matt, so when he got huffed and walked on off nobody minded. He was known to buy side-meat by the slice. Carried home little bags of meal and flour in his hand. He didn't seem to mind too much so long as it didn't cost him anything.

About half an hour after he left they heard the braying of the mule at the edge of the woods. He was coming past the store very soon.

"Less ketch Matt's mule fuh 'im and have some fun."

"Now, Lum, you know dat mule ain't aimin' tuh let hisself be caught. Less watch *you* do it."

When the mule was in front of the store, Lum went out and tackled him. The brute jerked up his head, laid back his ears and rushed to the attack. Lum had to run for safety. Five or six more men left the porch and surrounded the fractious beast, goosing him in the sides and making him show his temper. But he had more spirit left than body. He was soon panting and heaving from the effort of spinning his old carcass about. Everybody was having fun at the mule-baiting. All but Janie.

She snatched her head away from the spectacle and began muttering to herself. "They oughta be shamed uh theyselves! Teasin' dat poor brute beast lak they is! Done been worked tuh death; done had his disposition ruint wid mistreatment, and now they got tuh finish devilin' 'im tuh death. Wisht Ah had mah way wid 'em all."

She walked away from the porch and found something to busy herself with in the back of the store so she did not hear Jody when he stopped laughing. She didn't know that he had heard her, but she did hear him yell out, "Lum, I god, dat's enough! Y'all done had yo' fun now. Stop yo' foolishness and go tell Matt Bonner Ah wants tuh have uh talk wid him right away."

Janie came back out front and sat down. She didn't say anything and neither did Joe. But after a while he looked down at his feet and said, "Janie, Ah reckon you better go fetch me dem old black gaiters. Dese tan shoes sets mah feet on fire. Plenty room in 'em, but they hurts regardless."

She got up without a word and went off for the shoes. A little war of defense for helpless things was going on inside her. People ought to have some regard for helpless things. She wanted to fight about it. "But Ah hates disagreement and confusion, so Ah better not talk. It makes it hard tuh git along." She didn't hurry back. She fumbled around long enough to get her face straight. When she got back, Joe was talking with Matt.

"Fifteen dollars? I god you'se as crazy as uh betsy bug! Five dollars."

"L-l-less we strack uh compermise, Brother Mayor. Less m-make it ten."

"Five dollars." Joe rolled his cigar in his mouth and rolled his eyes away indifferently.

"If dat mule is wuth somethin' tuh *you* Brother Mayor, he's wuth mo' tuh me. More special when Ah got uh job uh work tuhmorrow."

"Five dollars."

"All right, Brother Mayor. If you wants tuh rob uh poor man lak me uh everything he got tuh make uh livin' wid, Ah'll take de five dollars. Dat mule been wid me twenty-three years. It's mighty hard."

Mayor Starks deliberately changed his shoes before he reached into his pocket for the money. By that time Matt was wringing and twisting like a hen on a hot brick. But as soon as his hand closed on the money his face broke into a grin.

"Beatyuh tradin' dat time, Starks! Dat mule is liable tuh be dead befo' de week is out. You won't git no work outa him."

"Didn't buy 'im fuh no work. I god, Ah bought dat varmint tuh let 'im rest. You didn't have gumption enough tuh do it."

A respectful silence fell on the place. Sam looked at Joe and said, "Dat's uh new idea 'bout varmints, Mayor Starks. But Ah laks it mah ownself. It's uh noble thing you done." Everybody agreed with that.

Janie stood still while they all made comments. When it was all done she stood in front of Joe and said, "Jody, dat wuz uh mighty fine thing fuh you tuh do. 'Tain't everybody would have thought of it, 'cause it ain't no everyday thought. Freein' dat mule makes uh mighty big man outa you. Something like George Washington and Lincoln. Abraham Lincoln, he had de whole United States tuh rule so he freed de Negroes. You got uh town so you freed uh mule. You have tuh have power tuh free things and dat makes you lak uh king uh something."

Hambo said, "Yo' wife is uh born orator, Starks. Us never knowed dat befo'. She put jus' de right words tuh our thoughts."

Joe bit down hard on his cigar and beamed all around, but he never said a word. The town talked it for three days and said that's just what they would have done if they had been rich men like Joe Starks. Anyhow a free mule in town was something new to talk about. Starks piled fodder under the big tree near the porch and the mule was usually around the store like the other citizens. Nearly everybody took the habit of fetching along a handful of fodder to throw on the pile. He almost got fat and they took a great pride in him. New lies sprung up about his free-mule doings. How he pushed open Lindsay's kitchen door and slept in the place one night and fought until they made coffee for his breakfast; how he stuck his head in the Pearsons' window while the family was at the table and Mrs. Pearson mistook him for Rev. Pearson and handed him a plate; he ran Mrs. Tully off of the croquet ground for having such an ugly shape; he ran and caught up with Becky Anderson on the way to Maitland so as to keep his

head out of the sun under her umbrella; he got tired of listen-
ing to Redmond's long-winded prayer, and went inside the
Baptist church and broke up the meeting. He did everything
but let himself be bridled and visit Matt Bonner.

But way after a while he died. Lum found him under the
big tree on his rawbony back with all four feet up in the air.
That wasn't natural and it didn't look right, but Sam said it
would have been more unnatural for him to have laid down
on his side and died like any other beast. He had seen Death
coming and had stood his ground and fought it like a natural
man. He had fought it to the last breath. Naturally he didn't
have time to straighten himself out. Death had to take him
like it found him.

When the news got around, it was like the end of a war or
something like that. Everybody that could knocked off from
work to stand around and talk. But finally there was nothing
to do but drag him out like all other dead brutes. Drag him
out to the edge of the hammock which was far enough off to
satisfy sanitary conditions in the town. The rest was up to the
buzzards. Everybody was going to the dragging-out. The
news had got Mayor Starks out of bed before time. His pair
of gray horses was out under the tree and the men were fool-
ing with the gear when Janie arrived at the store with Joe's
breakfast.

"I god, Lum, you fasten up dis store good befo' you leave,
you hear me?" He was eating fast and talking with one eye
out of the door on the operations.

"Whut you tellin' 'im tuh fasten up for, Jody?" Janie asked
surprised.

"'Cause it won't be nobody heah tuh look after de store.
Ah'm goin' tuh de draggin'-out mahself."

"'Tain't nothin' so important Ah got tuh do tuhday, Jody.
How come Ah can't go long wid you tuh de draggin'-out?"

Joe was struck speechless for a minute. "Why, Janie! You
wouldn't be seen at uh draggin'-out, wouldja? Wid any and
everybody in uh passle pushin' and shovin' wid they no-
manners selves? Naw, Naw!"

"You would be dere wid me, wouldn't yuh?"

"Dat's right, but Ah'm uh man even if Ah is de Mayor. But
de mayor's wife is somethin' different again. Anyhow they's

liable tuh need me tuh say uh few words over de carcass, dis bein' uh special case. But *you* ain't goin' off in all dat mess uh commonness. Ah'm surprised at yuh fuh askin'."

He wiped his lips of ham gravy and put on his hat. "Shet de door behind yuh, Janie. Lum is too busy wid de hawses."

After more shouting of advice and orders and useless comments, the town escorted the carcass off. No, the carcass moved off with the town, and left Janie standing in the doorway.

Out in the swamp they made great ceremony over the mule. They mocked everything human in death. Starks led off with a great eulogy on our departed citizen, our most distinguished citizen and the grief he left behind him, and the people loved the speech. It made him more solid than building the schoolhouse had done. He stood on the distended belly of the mule for a platform and made gestures. When he stepped down, they hoisted Sam up and he talked about the mule as a school teacher first. Then he set his hat like John Pearson and imitated his preaching. He spoke of the joys of mule-heaven to which the dear brother had departed this valley of sorrow; the mule-angels flying around; the miles of green corn and cool water, a pasture of pure bran with a river of molasses running through it; and most glorious of all, *No* Matt Bonner with plow lines and halters to come in and corrupt. Up there, mule-angels would have people to ride on and from his place beside the glittering throne, the dear departed brother would look down into hell and see the devil plowing Matt Bonner all day long in a hell-hot sun and laying the raw-hide to his back.

With that the sisters got mock-happy and shouted and had to be held up by the menfolks. Everybody enjoyed themselves to the highest and then finally the mule was left to the already impatient buzzards. They were holding a great flying-meet way up over the heads of the mourners and some of the nearby trees were already peopled with the stoop-shouldered forms.

As soon as the crowd was out of sight they closed in in circles. The near ones got nearer and the far ones got near. A circle, a swoop and a hop with spread-out wings. Close in, close in till some of the more hungry or daring perched on

the carcass. They wanted to begin, but the Parson wasn't there, so a messenger was sent to the ruler in a tree where he sat.

The flock had to wait the white-headed leader, but it was hard. They jostled each other and pecked at heads in hungry irritation. Some walked up and down the beast from head to tail, tail to head. The Parson sat motionless in a dead pine tree about two miles off. He had scented the matter as quickly as any of the rest, but decorum demanded that he sit oblivious until he was notified. Then he took off with ponderous flight and circled and lowered, circled and lowered until the others danced in joy and hunger at his approach.

He finally lit on the ground and walked around the body to see if it were really dead. Peered into its nose and mouth. Examined it well from end to end and leaped upon it and bowed, and the others danced a response. That being over, he balanced and asked:

"What killed this man?"

The chorus answered, "Bare, bare fat."

"What killed this man?"

"Bare, bare fat."

"What killed this man?"

"Bare, bare fat."

"Who'll stand his funeral?"

"We!!!!!"

"Well, all right now."

So he picked out the eyes in the ceremonial way and the feast went on. The yaller mule was gone from the town except for the porch talk, and for the children visiting his bleaching bones now and then in the spirit of adventure.

Joe returned to the store full of pleasure and good humor but he didn't want Janie to notice it because he saw that she was sullen and he resented that. She had no right to be, the way he thought things out. She wasn't even appreciative of his efforts and she had plenty cause to be. Here he was just pouring honor all over her; building a high chair for her to sit in and overlook the world and she here pouting over it! Not that he wanted anybody else, but just too many women

would be glad to be in her place. He ought to box her jaws! But he didn't feel like fighting today, so he made an attack upon her position backhand.

"Ah had tuh laugh at de people out dere in de woods dis mornin', Janie. You can't help but laugh at de capers they cuts. But all the same, Ah wish mah people would git mo' business in 'em and not spend so much time on foolishness."

"Everybody can't be lak you, Jody. Somebody is bound tuh want tuh laugh and play."

"Who don't love tuh laugh and play?"

"You make out like you don't, anyhow."

"I god, Ah don't make out no such uh lie! But it's uh time fuh all things. But it's awful tuh see so many people don't want nothin' but uh full belly and uh place tuh lay down and sleep afterwards. It makes me sad sometimes and then agin it makes me mad. They say things sometimes that tickles me nearly tuh death, but Ah won't laugh jus' tuh dis-incourage 'em." Janie took the easy way away from a fuss. She didn't change her mind but she agreed with her mouth. Her heart said, "Even so, but you don't have to cry about it."

But sometimes Sam Watson and Lige Moss forced a belly laugh out of Joe himself with their eternal arguments. It never ended because there was no end to reach. It was a contest in hyperbole and carried on for no other reason.

Maybe Sam would be sitting on the porch when Lige walked up. If nobody was there to speak of, nothing happened. But if the town was there like on Saturday night, Lige would come up with a very grave air. Couldn't even pass the time of day, for being so busy thinking. Then when he was asked what was the matter in order to start him off, he'd say, "Dis question done 'bout drove me crazy. And Sam, he know so much into things, Ah wants some information on de subject."

Walter Thomas was due to speak up and egg the matter on. "Yeah, Sam always got more information than he know what to do wid. He's bound to tell yuh whatever it is you wants tuh know."

Sam begins an elaborate show of avoiding the struggle. That draws everybody on the porch into it.

"How come you want me *tuh* tell yuh? You always claim

God done met you round de cornder and talked His inside business wid yuh. 'Tain't no use in you askin' *me* nothin'. Ah'm questionizin' *you*."

"How you gointuh do dat, Sam, when Ah arrived dis conversation mahself? Ah'm askin' *you*."

"Askin' me what? You ain't told me de subjick yit."

"Don't aim tuh tell yuh! Ah aims tuh keep yuh in de dark all de time. If you'se smart lak you let on you is, you kin find out."

"Yuh skeered to lemme know whut it is, 'cause yuh know Ah'll tear it tuh pieces. You got to have a subjick tuh talk from, do yuh can't talk. If uh man ain't got no bounds, he ain't got no place tuh stop."

By this time, they are the center of the world.

"Well all right then. Since you own up you ain't smart enough tuh find out whut Ah'm talkin' 'bout, Ah'll tell you. Whut is it dat keeps uh man from gettin' burnt on uh red-hot stove—caution or nature?"

"Shucks! Ah thought you had somethin' hard tuh ast me. Walter kin tell yuh dat."

"If de conversation is too deep for yuh, how come yuh don't tell me so, and hush up? Walter can't tell me nothin' uh de kind. Ah'm uh educated man, Ah keeps mah arrangements in mah hands, and if it kept me up all night long studyin' 'bout it, Walter ain't liable tuh be no help to me. Ah needs uh man lak you."

"And then agin, Lige, Ah'm gointuh tell yuh. Ah'm gointuh run dis conversation from uh gnat heel to uh lice. It's nature dat keeps uh man off of uh red-hot stove."

"Uuh huuh! Ah knowed you would going tuh crawl up in dat holler! But Ah aims tuh smoke yuh right out. 'Tain't no nature at all, it's caution, Sam."

"'Tain't no sich uh thing! Nature tells yuh not tuh fool wid no red-hot stove, and you don't do it neither."

"Listen, Sam, if it was nature, nobody wouldn't have tuh look out for babies touchin' stoves, would they? 'Cause dey just naturally wouldn't touch it. But dey sho will. So it's caution."

"Naw it ain't, it's nature, cause nature makes caution. It's

de strongest thing dat God ever made, now. Fact is it's de onliest thing God ever made. He made nature and nature made everything else."

"Naw nature didn't neither. A whole heap of things ain't even been made yit."

"Tell me somethin' you know of dat nature ain't made."

"She ain't made it so you kin ride uh butt-headed cow and hold on tuh de horns."

"Yeah, but dat ain't yo' point."

"Yeah it is too."

"Naw it ain't neither."

"Well what *is* mah point?"

"You ain't got none, so far."

"Yeah he is too," Walter cut in, "de red-hot stove is his point."

"He know mighty much, but he ain't proved it yit."

"Sam, Ah say it's caution, not nature dat keeps folks off uh red-hot stove."

"How is de son gointuh be before his paw? Nature is de first of everything. Ever since self was self, nature been keepin' folks off of red-hot stoves. Dat caution you talkin' 'bout ain't nothin' but uh humbug. He's uh inseck dat nothin' he got belongs to him. He got eyes, lak somethin' else; wings lak somethin' else—everything! Even his hum is de sound of somebody else."

"Man, whut you talkin' 'bout? Caution is de greatest thing in de world. If it wasn't for caution—"

"Show me somethin' dat caution ever made! Look whut nature took and done. Nature got so high in uh black hen she got tuh lay uh white egg. Now you tell me, how come, whut got intuh man dat he got tuh have hair round his mouth? Nature!"

"Dat ain't—"

The porch was boiling now. Starks left the store to Hezekiah Potts, the delivery boy, and come took a seat in his high chair.

"Look at dat great big ole scoundrel-beast up dere at Hall's fillin' station—uh great big old scoundrel. He eats up all de folks outa de house and den eat de house."

"Aw 'tain't no sich a varmint nowhere dat kin eat no house! Dat's uh lie. Ah wuz dere yiste'ddy and Ah ain't seen nothin' lak dat. Where is he?"

"Ah didn't see him but Ah reckon he is in de back-yard some place. But dey got his picture out front dere. They was nailin' it up when Ah come pass dere dis evenin'.".

"Well all right now, if he eats up houses how come he don't eat up de fillin' station?"

"Dat's 'cause dey got him tied up so he can't. Dey got uh great big picture tellin' how many gallons of dat Sinclair high-compression gas he drink at one time and how he's more'n uh million years old."

"'Tain't *nothin'* no million years old!"

"De picture is right up dere where anybody kin see it. Dey can't make de picture till dey see de thing, kin dey?"

"How dey goin' to tell he's uh million years old? Nobody wasn't born dat fur back."

"By de rings on his tail Ah reckon. Man, dese white folks got ways for tellin' anything dey wants tuh know."

"Well, where he been at all dis time, then?"

"Dey caught him over dere in Egypt. Seem lak he used tuh hang round dere and eat up dem Pharaohs' tombstones. Dey got de picture of him doin' it. Nature is high in uh varmint lak dat. Nature and salt. Dat's whut makes up strong man lak Big John de Conquer. He was uh man wid salt in him. He could give uh flavor to *anything*."

"Yeah, but he was uh man dat wuz more'n man. 'Tain't no mo' lak him. He wouldn't dig potatoes, and he wouldn't rake hay: He wouldn't take a whipping, and he wouldn't run away."

"Oh yeah, somebody else could if dey tried hard enough. Me mahself, Ah got salt in *me*. If Ah like man flesh, Ah could eat some man every day, some of 'em is so trashy they'd let me eat 'em."

"Lawd, Ah loves to talk about Big John. Less we tell lies on Ole John."

But here come Bootsie, and Teadi and Big 'oman down the street making out they are pretty by the way they walk. They have got that fresh, new taste about them like young mustard greens in the spring, and the young men on the porch are just bound to tell them about it and buy them some treats.

"Heah come mah order right now," Charlie Jones announces and scrambles off the porch to meet them. But he has plenty of competition. A pushing, shoving show of gallantry. They all beg the girls to just buy anything they can think of. Please let them pay for it. Joe is begged to wrap up all the candy in the store and order more. All the peanuts and soda water—everything!

"Gal, Ah'm crazy 'bout you," Charlie goes on to the entertainment of everybody. "Ah'll do anything in the world except work for you and give you mah money."

The girls and everybody else help laugh. They know it's not courtship. It's acting-out courtship and everybody is in the play. The three girls hold the center of the stage till Daisy Blunt comes walking down the street in the moonlight.

Daisy is walking a drum tune. You can almost hear it by looking at the way she walks. She is black and she knows that white clothes look good on her, so she wears them for dress up. She's got those big black eyes with plenty shiny white in them that makes them shine like brand new money and she knows what God gave women eyelashes for, too. Her hair is not what you might call straight. It's negro hair, but it's got a kind of white flavor. Like the piece of string out of a ham. It's not ham at all, but it's been around ham and got the flavor. It was spread down thick and heavy over her shoulders and looked just right under a big white hat.

"Lawd, Lawd, Lawd," that same Charlie Jones exclaims rushing over to Daisy. "It must be uh recess in heben if St. Peter is lettin' his angels out lak dis. You got three men already layin' at de point uh death 'bout yuh, and heah's uh-nother fool dat's willin' tuh make time on yo' gang."

All the rest of the single men have crowded around Daisy by this time. She is parading and blushing at the same time.

"If you know anybody dat's 'bout tuh die 'bout me, yuh know more'n Ah do," Daisy bridled. "Wisht Ah knowed who it is."

"Now, Daisy, *you* know Jim, and Dave and Lum is 'bout tuh kill one 'nother 'bout you. Don't stand up here and tell dat big ole got-dat-wrong."

"Dey a mighty hush-mouf about it if dey is. Dey ain't never told me nothin'."

"Unhunh, you talked too fast. Heah, Jim and Dave is right upon de porch and Lum is inside de store."

A big burst of laughter at Daisy's discomfiture. The boys had to act out their rivalry too. Only this time, everybody knew they meant some of it. But all the same the porch enjoyed the play and helped out whenever extras were needed.

David said, "Jim don't love Daisy. He don't love yuh lak Ah do."

Jim bellowed indignantly, "Who don't love Daisy? Ah know you ain't talkin' 'bout me."

Dave: "Well all right, less prove dis thing right now. We'll prove right now who love dis gal de best. How much time is you willin' tuh make fuh Daisy?"

Jim: "Twenty yeahs!"

Dave: "See? Ah told yuh dat nigger didn't love yuh. Me, Ah'll beg de Judge tuh hang me, and wouldn't take nothin' less than life."

There was a big long laugh from the porch. Then Jim had to demand a test.

"Dave, how much would you be willin' tuh do for Daisy if she was to turn fool enough tuh marry yuh."

"Me and Daisy done talked dat over, but if you just got tuh know, Ah'd buy Daisy uh passenger train and give it tuh her."

"Humph! Is dat all? Ah'd buy her uh steamship and then Ah'd hire some mens tuh run it fur her."

"Daisy, don't let Jim fool you wid his talk. He don't aim tuh do nothin' fuh yuh. Uh lil ole steamship! Daisy, Ah'll take uh job cleanin' out de Atlantic Ocean fuh you any time you say you so desire." There was a great laugh and then they hushed to listen.

"Daisy," Jim began, "you know mah heart and all de ranges uh mah mind. And you know if Ah wuz ridin' up in uh earoplane way up in de sky and Ah looked down and seen you walkin' and knowed you'd have tuh walk ten miles tuh git home, Ah'd step backward offa dat earoplane just to walk home wid you."

There was one of those big blow-out laughs and Janie was wallowing in it. Then Jody ruined it all for her.

Mrs. Bogle came walking down the street towards the porch. Mrs. Bogle who was many times a grandmother, but

had a blushing air of coquetry about her that cloaked her sunken cheeks. You saw a fluttering fan before her face and magnolia blooms and sleepy lakes under the moonlight when she walked. There was no obvious reason for it, it was just so. Her first husband had been a coachman but "studied jury" to win her. He had finally become a preacher to hold her till his death. Her second husband worked in Fohnes orange grove—but tried to preach when he caught her eye. He never got any further than a class leader, but that was something to offer her. It proved his love and pride. She was a wind on the ocean. She moved men, but the helm determined the port. Now, this night she mounted the steps and the men noticed her until she passed inside the door.

"I god, Janie," Starks said impatiently, "why don't you go on and see whut Mrs. Bogle want? Whut you waitin' on?"

Janie wanted to hear the rest of the play-acting and how it ended, but she got up sullenly and went inside. She came back to the porch with her bristles sticking out all over her and with dissatisfaction written all over her face. Joe saw it and lifted his own hackles a bit.

Jim Weston had secretly borrowed a dime and soon he was loudly beseeching Daisy to have a treat on him. Finally she consented to take a pickled pig foot on him. Janie was getting up a large order when they came in, so Lum waited on them. That is, he went back to the keg but came back without the pig foot.

"Mist' Starks, de pig feets is all gone!" he called out.

"Aw naw dey ain't, Lum. Ah bought uh whole new kag of 'em wid dat last order from Jacksonville. It come in yistiddy."

Joe came and helped Lum look but he couldn't find the new keg either, so he went to the nail over his desk that he used for a file to search for the order.

"Janie, where's dat last bill uh ladin'?"

"It's right dere on de nail, ain't it?"

"Naw it ain't neither. You ain't put it where Ah told yuh tuh. If you'd git yo' mind out de streets and keep it on yo' business maybe you could git somethin' straight sometimes."

"Aw, look around dere, Jody. Dat bill ain't apt tuh be gone off nowheres. If it ain't hangin' on de nail, it's on yo' desk. You bound tuh find it if you look."

"Wid you heah, Ah oughtn't tuh hafta do all dat lookin' and searchin'. Ah done told you time and time agin tuh stick all dem papers on dat nail! All you got tuh do is mind me. How come you can't do lak Ah tell yuh?"

"You sho loves to tell me whut to do, but Ah can't tell you nothin' Ah see!"

"Dat's 'cause you need tellin'," he rejoined hotly. "It would be pitiful if Ah didn't. Somebody got to think for women and chillun and chickens and cows. I god, they sho don't think none theirselves."

"Ah knows uh few things, and womenfolks thinks sometimes too!"

"Aw naw they don't. They just think they's thinkin'. When Ah see one thing Ah understands ten. You see ten things and don't understand one."

Times and scenes like that put Janie to thinking about the inside state of her marriage. Time came when she fought back with her tongue as best she could, but it didn't do her any good. It just made Joe do more. He wanted her submission and he'd keep on fighting until he felt he had it.

So gradually, she pressed her teeth together and learned to hush. The spirit of the marriage left the bedroom and took to living in the parlor. It was there to shake hands whenever company came to visit, but it never went back inside the bedroom again. So she put something in there to represent the spirit like a Virgin Mary image in a church. The bed was no longer a daisy-field for her and Joe to play in. It was a place where she went and laid down when she was sleepy and tired.

She wasn't petal-open anymore with him. She was twenty-four and seven years married when she knew. She found that out one day when he slapped her face in the kitchen. It happened over one of those dinners that chasten all women sometimes. They plan and they fix and they do, and then some kitchen-dwelling fiend slips a scrochy, soggy, tasteless mess into their pots and pans. Janie was a good cook, and Joe had looked forward to his dinner as a refuge from other things. So when the bread didn't rise, and the fish wasn't quite done at the bone, and the rice was scorched, he slapped Janie until she had a ringing sound in her ears and told her about her brains before he stalked on back to the store.

Janie stood where he left her for unmeasured time and thought. She stood there until something fell off the shelf inside her. Then she went inside there to see what it was. It was her image of Jody tumbled down and shattered. But looking at it she saw that it never was the flesh and blood figure of her dreams. Just something she had grabbed up to drape her dreams over. In a way she turned her back upon the image where it lay and looked further. She had no more blossomy openings dusting pollen over her man, neither any glistening young fruit where the petals used to be. She found that she had a host of thoughts she had never expressed to him, and numerous emotions she had never let Jody know about. Things packed up and put away in parts of her heart where he could never find them. She was saving up feelings for some man she had never seen. She had an inside and an outside now and suddenly she knew how not to mix them.

She bathed and put on a fresh dress and head kerchief and went on to the store before Jody had time to send for her. That was a bow to the outside of things.

Jody was on the porch and the porch was full of Eatonville as usual at this time of the day. He was baiting Mrs. Tony Robbins as he always did when she came to the store. Janie could see Jody watching her out of the corner of his eye while he joked roughly with Mrs. Robbins. He wanted to be friendly with her again. His big, big laugh was as much for her as for the baiting. He was longing for peace but on his own terms.

"I god, Mrs. Robbins, whut make you come heah and worry me when you see Ah'm readin' mah newspaper?" Mayor Starks lowered the paper in pretended annoyance.

Mrs. Robbins struck her pity-pose and assumed the voice.

"'Cause Ah'm hongry, Mist' Starks. 'Deed Ah is. Me and mah chillun is hongry. Tony don't fee-eed me!"

This was what the porch was waiting for. They burst into a laugh.

"Mrs. Robbins, how can you make out you'se hongry when Tony comes in here every Satitday and buys groceries lak a man? Three weeks' shame on yuh!"

"If he buy all dat you talkin' 'bout, Mist' Starks, God knows whut he do wid it. He sho don't bring it home, and

me and mah po' chillun is *so* hongry! Mist' Starks, please
gimme uh lil piece uh meat fur me and mah chillun."

"Ah know you don't need it, but come on inside. You ain't
goin' tuh lemme read till Ah give it to yuh."

Mrs. Tony's ecstasy was divine. "Thank you, Mist' Starks.
You'se noble! You'se du most gentlemanfied man Ah ever did
see. You'se uh king!"

The salt pork box was in the back of the store and during
the walk Mrs. Tony was so eager she sometimes stepped on
Joe's heels, sometimes she was a little before him. Something
like a hungry cat when somebody approaches her pan with
meat. Running a little, caressing a little and all the time mak-
ing little urging-on cries.

"Yes, indeedy, Mist' Starks, you'se noble. You got sympa-
thy for me and mah po' chillun. Tony don't give us nothin'
tuh eat and we'se *so* hongry. Tony don't fee-eed me!"

This brought them to the meat box. Joe took up the big
meat knife and selected a piece of side meat to cut. Mrs. Tony
was all but dancing around him.

"Dat's right, Mist' Starks! Gimme uh lil piece 'bout dis
wide." She indicated as wide as her wrist and hand. "Me and
mah chillun is *so* hongry!"

Starks hardly looked at her measurements. He had seen
them too often. He marked off a piece much smaller and sunk
the blade in. Mrs. Tony all but fell to the floor in her agony.

"Lawd a'mussy! Mist' Starks, you ain't gointuh gimme dat
lil tee-ninchy piece fuh me and all mah chillun, is yuh? Lawd,
we'se *so* hongry!"

Starks cut right on and reached for a piece of wrapping
paper. Mrs. Tony leaped away from the proffered cut of meat
as if it were a rattlesnake.

"Ah wouldn't tetch it! Dat lil eyeful uh bacon for me and
all mah chillun! Lawd, some folks is got everything and they's
so gripin' and so mean!"

Starks made as if to throw the meat back in the box and
close it. Mrs. Tony swooped like lightning and seized it, and
started towards the door.

"Some folks ain't got no heart in dey bosom. They's willin'
tuh see uh po' woman and her helpless chillun starve tuh

death. God's gointuh put 'em under arrest, some uh dese days, wid dey stingy gripin' ways."

She stepped from the store porch and marched off in high dudgeon! Some laughed and some got mad.

"If dat wuz *mah* wife," said Walter Thomas, "Ah'd kill her cemetery dead."

"More special after Ah done bought her everything mah wages kin stand, lak Tony do," Coker said. "In de fust place Ah never would spend on *no* woman whut Tony spend on *her*."

Starks came back and took his seat. He had to stop and add the meat to Tony's account.

"Well, Tony tells me tuh humor her along. He moved here from up de State hopin' tuh change her, but it ain't. He say he can't bear tuh leave her and he hate to kill her, so 'tain't nothin' tuh do but put up wid her."

"Dat's 'cause Tony love her too good," said Coker. "Ah could break her if she wuz mine. Ah'd break her or kill her. Makin' uh fool outa me in front of everybody."

"Tony won't never hit her. He says beatin' women is just like steppin' on baby chickens. He claims 'tain't no place on uh woman tuh hit," Joe Lindsay said with scornful disapproval, "but Ah'd kill uh baby just born dis mawnin' fuh uh thing lak dat. 'Tain't nothin' but low-down spitefulness 'ginst her husband make her do it."

"Dat's de God's truth," Jim Stone agreed. "Dat's de very reason."

Janie did what she had never done before, that is, thrust herself into the conversation.

"Sometimes God gits familiar wid us womenfolks too and talks His inside business. He told me how surprised He was 'bout y'all turning out so smart after Him makin' yuh different; and how surprised y'all is goin' tuh be if you ever find out you don't know half as much 'bout us as you think you do. It's so easy to make yo'self out God Almighty when you ain't got nothin' tuh strain against but women and chickens."

"You gettin' too moufy, Janie," Starks told her. "Go fetch me de checker-board *and* de checkers. Sam Watson, you'se mah fish."

VII

THE YEARS took all the fight out of Janie's face. For a while she thought it was gone from her soul. No matter what Jody did, she said nothing. She had learned how to talk some and leave some. She was a rut in the road. Plenty of life beneath the surface but it was kept beaten down by the wheels. Sometimes she stuck out into the future, imagining her life different from what it was. But mostly she lived between her hat and her heels, with her emotional disturbances like shade patterns in the woods—come and gone with the sun. She got nothing from Jody except what money could buy, and she was giving away what she didn't value.

Now and again she thought of a country road at sun-up and considered flight. To where? To what? Then too she considered thirty-five is twice seventeen and nothing was the same at all.

"Maybe he ain't nothin'," she cautioned herself, "but he is something in my mouth. He's got tuh be else Ah ain't got nothin' tuh live for. Ah'll lie and say he is. If Ah don't, life won't be nothin' but uh store and uh house."

She didn't read books so she didn't know that she was the world and the heavens boiled down to a drop. Man attempting to climb to painless heights from his dung hill.

Then one day she sat and watched the shadow of herself going about tending store and prostrating itself before Jody, while all the time she herself sat under a shady tree with the wind blowing through her hair and her clothes. Somebody near about making summertime out of lonesomeness.

This was the first time it happened, but after a while it got so common she ceased to be surprised. It was like a drug. In a way it was good because it reconciled her to things. She got so she received all things with the stolidness of the earth which soaks up urine and perfume with the same indifference.

One day she noticed that Joe didn't sit down. He just stood in front of a chair and fell in it. That made her look at him all over. Joe wasn't so young as he used to be. There was already something dead about him. He didn't rear back in his knees

any longer. He squatted over his ankles when he walked. That stillness at the back of his neck. His prosperous-looking belly that used to thrust out so pugnaciously and intimidate folks, sagged like a load suspended from his loins. It didn't seem to be a part of him anymore. Eyes a little absent too.

Jody must have noticed it too. Maybe, he had seen it long before Janie did, and had been fearing for her to see. Because he began to talk about her age all the time, as if he didn't want her to stay young while he grew old. It was always "You oughta throw somethin' over yo' shoulders befo' you go outside. You ain't no young pullet no mo'. You'se uh ole hen now." One day he called her off the croquet grounds. "Dat's somethin' for de young folks, Janie, you out dere jumpin' round and won't be able tuh git out de bed tuhmorrer." If he thought to deceive her, he was wrong. For the first time she could see a man's head naked of its skull. Saw the cunning thoughts race in and out through the caves and promontories of his mind long before they darted out of the tunnel of his mouth. She saw he was hurting inside so she let it pass without talking. She just measured out a little time for him and set it aside to wait.

It got to be terrible in the store. The more his back ached and his muscle dissolved into fat and the fat melted off his bones, the more fractious he became with Janie. Especially in the store. The more people in there the more ridicule he poured over her body to point attention away from his own. So one day Steve Mixon wanted some chewing tobacco and Janie cut it wrong. She hated that tobacco knife anyway. It worked very stiff. She fumbled with the thing and cut way away from the mark. Mixon didn't mind. He held it up for a joke to tease Janie a little.

"Looka heah, Brother Mayor, whut yo' wife done took and done." It was cut comical, so everybody laughed at it. "Uh woman and uh knife—no kind of uh knife, don't b'long tuh-gether." There was some more good-natured laughter at the expense of women.

Jody didn't laugh. He hurried across from the post office side and took the plug of tobacco away from Mixon and cut it again. Cut it exactly on the mark and glared at Janie.

"I god amighty! A woman stay round uh store till she get

old as Methusalem and still can't cut a little thing like a plug of tobacco! Don't stand dere rollin' yo' pop eyes at me wid yo' rump hangin' nearly to yo' knees!"

A big laugh started off in the store but people got to thinking and stopped. It was funny if you looked at it right quick, but it got pitiful if you thought about it awhile. It was like somebody snatched off part of a woman's clothes while she wasn't looking and the streets were crowded. Then too, Janie took the middle of the floor to talk right into Jody's face, and that was something that hadn't been done before.

"Stop mixin' up mah doings wid mah looks, Jody. When you git through tellin' me how tuh cut uh plug uh tobacco, then you kin tell me whether mah behind is on straight or not."

"Wha—whut's dat you say, Janie? You must be out yo' head."

"Naw, Ah ain't outa mah head neither."

"You must be. Talkin' any such language as dat."

"You de one started talkin' under people's clothes. Not me."

"Whut's de matter wid you, nohow? You ain't no young girl to be gettin' all insulted 'bout yo' looks. You ain't no young courtin' gal. You'se uh ole woman, nearly forty."

"Yeah, Ah'm nearly forty and you'se already fifty. How come you can't talk about dat sometimes instead of always pointin' at me?"

"T'ain't no use in gettin' all mad, Janie, 'cause Ah mention you ain't no young gal no mo'. Nobody in heah ain't lookin' for no wife outa yuh. Old as you is."

"Naw, Ah ain't no young gal no mo' but den Ah ain't no old woman neither. Ah reckon Ah looks mah age too. But Ah'm uh woman every inch of me, and Ah know it. Dat's uh whole lot more'n *you* kin say. You big-bellies round here and put out a lot of brag, but 'tain't nothin' to it but yo' big voice. Humph! Talkin' 'bout *me* lookin' old! When you pull down yo' britches, you look lak de change uh life."

"Great God from Zion!" Sam Watson gasped. "Y'all really playin' de dozens tuhnight."

"Wha—whut's dat you said?" Joe challenged, hoping his ears had fooled him.

"You heard her, you ain't blind," Walter taunted.

"Ah ruther be shot with tacks than tuh hear dat 'bout mah-self," Lige Moss commiserated.

Then Joe Starks realized all the meanings and his vanity bled like a flood. Janie had robbed him of his illusion of irresistible maleness that all men cherish, which was terrible. The thing that Saul's daughter had done to David. But Janie had done worse, she had cast down his empty armor before men and they had laughed, would keep on laughing. When he paraded his possessions hereafter, they would not consider the two together. They'd look with envy at the things and pity the man that owned them. When he sat in judgment it would be the same. Good-for-nothing's like Dave and Lum and Jim wouldn't change place with him. For what can excuse a man in the eyes of other men for lack of strength? Raggedy-behind squirts of sixteen and seventeen would be giving him their merciless pity out of their eyes while their mouths said something humble. There was nothing to do in life anymore. Ambition was useless. And the cruel deceit of Janie! Making all that show of humbleness and scorning him all the time! Laughing at him, and now putting the town up to do the same. Joe Starks didn't know the words for all this, but he knew the feeling. So he struck Janie with all his might and drove her from the store.

VIII

AFTER that night Jody moved his things and slept in a room downstairs. He didn't really hate Janie, but he wanted her to think so. He had crawled off to lick his wounds. They didn't talk too much around the store either. Anybody that didn't know would have thought that things had blown over, it looked so quiet and peaceful around. But the stillness was the sleep of swords. So new thoughts had to be thought and new words said. She didn't want to live like that. Why must Joe be so mad with her for making him look small when he did it to her all the time? Had been doing it for years. Well, if she must eat out of a long-handled spoon, she must. Jody might get over his mad spell any time at all and begin to act like somebody towards her.

Then too she noticed how baggy Joe was getting all over. Like bags hanging from an ironing board. A little sack hung from the corners of his eyes and rested on his cheek-bones; a loose-filled bag of feathers hung from his ears and rested on his neck beneath his chin. A sack of flabby something hung from his loins and rested on his thighs when he sat down. But even these things were running down like candle grease as time moved on.

He made new alliances too. People he never bothered with one way or another now seemed to have his ear. He had always been scornful of root-doctors and all their kind, but now she saw a faker from over around Altamonte Springs, hanging around the place almost daily. Always talking in low tones when she came near, or hushed altogether. She didn't know that he was driven by a desperate hope to appear the old-time body in her sight. She was sorry about the root-doctor because she feared that Joe was depending on the scoundrel to make him well when what he needed was a doctor, and a good one. She was worried about his not eating his meals, till she found out he was having old lady Davis to cook for him. She knew that she was a much better cook than the old woman, and cleaner about the kitchen. So she bought a beef-bone and made him some soup.

"Naw, thank you," he told her shortly. "Ah'm havin' uh hard enough time tuh try and git well as it is."

She was stunned at first and hurt afterwards. So she went straight to her bosom friend, Pheoby Watson, and told her about it.

"Ah'd ruther be dead than for Jody tuh think Ah'd hurt him," she sobbed to Pheoby. "It ain't always been too pleasant, 'cause you know how Joe worships de works of his own hands, but God in heben knows Ah wouldn't do one thing tuh hurt nobody. It's too underhand and mean."

"Janie, Ah thought maybe de thing would die down and you never would know nothin' 'bout it, but it's been singin' round here ever since de big fuss in de store dat Joe was 'fixed' and you wuz de one dat did it."

"Pheoby, for de longest time, Ah been feelin' dat somethin' set for still-bait, but dis is—is—oh Pheoby! Whut *kin* I do?"

"You can't do nothin' but make out you don't know it. It's too late fuh y'all tuh be splittin' up and gittin' divorce. Just g'wan back home and set down on yo' royal diasticutis and say nothin'. Nobody don't b'lieve it nohow."

"Tuh think Ah been wid Jody twenty yeahs and Ah just now got tuh bear de name uh poisonin' him! It's 'bout to kill me, Pheoby. Sorrow dogged by sorrow is in mah heart."

"Dat's lie dat trashy nigger dat calls hisself uh two-headed doctor brought tuh 'im in order tuh git in wid Jody. He seen he wuz sick—everybody been knowin' dat for de last longest, and den Ah reckon he heard y'all wuz kind of at variance, so dat wuz his chance. Last summer dat multiplied cock-roach wuz round heah tryin' tuh sell gophers!"

"Pheoby, Ah don't even b'lieve Jody b'lieve dat lie. He ain't never took no stock in de mess. He just make out he b'lieve it tuh hurt me. Ah'm stone dead from standin' still and tryin' tuh smile."

She cried often in the weeks that followed. Joe got too weak to look after things and took to his bed. But he relentlessly refused to admit her to his sick-room. People came and went in the house. This one and that one came into her house with covered plates of broth and other sick-room dishes without taking the least notice of her as Joe's wife. People who

never had known what it was to enter the gate of the Mayor's yard unless it were to do some menial job now paraded in and out as his confidants. They came to the store and ostentatiously looked over whatever she was doing and went back to report to him at the house. Said things like "Mr. Starks need *somebody* tuh sorta look out for 'im till he kin git on his feet again and look for hisself."

But Jody was never to get on his feet again. Janie had Sam Watson to bring her the news from the sick room, and when he told her how things were, she had him bring a doctor from Orlando without giving Joe a chance to refuse, and without saying she sent for him.

"Just a matter of time," the doctor told her. "When a man's kidneys stop working altogether, there is no way for him to live. He needed medical attention two years ago. Too late now."

So Janie began to think of Death. Death, that strange being with the huge square toes who lived way in the West. The great one who lived in the straight house like a platform without sides to it, and without a roof. What need has Death for a cover, and what winds can blow against him? He stands in his high house that overlooks the world. Stands watchful and motionless all day with his sword drawn back, waiting for the messenger to bid him come. Been standing there before there was a where or a when or a then. She was liable to find a feather from his wings lying in her yard any day now. She was sad and afraid too. Poor Jody! He ought not to have to wrassle in there by himself. She sent Sam in to suggest a visit, but Jody said No. These medical doctors wuz all right with the Godly sick, but they didn't know a thing about a case like his. He'd be all right just as soon as the two-headed man found what had been buried against him. He wasn't going to die at all. That was what he thought. But Sam told her different, so she knew. And then if he hadn't, the next morning she was bound to know, for people began to gather in the big yard under the palm and china-berry trees. People who would not have dared to foot the place before crept in and did not come to the house. Just squatted under the trees and waited. Rumor, that wingless bird, had shadowed over the town.

She got up that morning with the firm determination to go

on in there and have a good talk with Jody. But she sat a long time with the walls creeping in on her. Four walls squeezing her breath out. Fear lest he depart while she sat trembling upstairs nerved her and she was inside the room before she caught her breath. She didn't make the cheerful, casual start that she had thought out. Something stood like an oxen's foot on her tongue, and then too, Jody, no Joe, gave her a ferocious look. A look with all the unthinkable coldness of outer space. She must talk to a man who was ten immensities away.

He was lying on his side facing the door like he was expecting somebody or something. A sort of changing look on his face. Weak-looking but sharp-pointed about the eyes. Through the thin counterpane she could see what was left of his belly huddled before him on the bed like some helpless thing seeking shelter.

The half-washed bedclothes hurt her pride for Jody. He had always been so clean.

"Whut you doin' in heah, Janie?"

"Come tuh see 'bout you and how you wuz makin' out."

He gave a deep-growling sound like a hog dying down in the swamp and trying to drive off disturbance. "Ah come in heah tuh git shet uh you but look lak 'tain't doin' me no good. G'wan out. Ah needs tuh rest."

"Naw, Jody, Ah come in heah tuh talk widja and Ah'm gointuh do it too. It's for both of our sakes Ah'm talkin'."

He gave another ground grumble and eased over on his back.

"Jody, maybe Ah ain't been sich uh good wife tuh you, but Jody—"

"Dat's 'cause you ain't got de right feelin' for nobody. You oughter have some sympathy 'bout yo'self. You ain't no hog."

"But, Jody, Ah meant tuh be awful nice."

"Much as Ah done fuh yuh. Holdin' me up tuh scorn. No sympathy!"

"Naw, Jody, it wasn't because Ah didn't have no sympathy. Ah had uh lavish uh dat. Ah just didn't never git no chance tuh use none of it. You wouldn't let me."

"Dat's right, blame everything on me. Ah wouldn't let you

show no feelin'! When, Janie, dat's all Ah ever wanted or de-
sired. Now you come blamin' me!"

"'Tain't dat, Jody. Ah ain't here tuh blame nobody. Ah'm
just tryin' tuh make you know what kinda person Ah is befo'
it's too late."

"Too late?" he whispered.

His eyes buckled in a vacant-mouthed terror and she saw
the awful surprise in his face and answered it.

"Yeah, Jody, don't keer whut dat multiplied cock-roach told
yuh tuh git yo' money, you got tuh die, and yuh can't live."

A deep sob came out of Jody's weak frame. It was like beat-
ing a bass drum in a hen-house. Then it rose high like pulling
in a trombone.

"Janie! Janie! don't tell me Ah got tuh die, and Ah ain't
used tuh thinkin' 'bout it."

"'Tain't really no need of you dying, Jody, if you had
of—de doctor—but it don't do no good bringin' dat up
now. Dat's just whut Ah wants tuh say, Jody. You wouldn't
listen. You done lived wid me for twenty years and you don't
half know me atall. And you could have but you was so busy
worshippin' de works of yo' own hands, and cuffin' folks
around in their minds till you didn't see uh whole heap uh
things yuh could have."

"Leave heah, Janie. Don't come heah—"

"Ah knowed you wasn't gointuh lissen tuh me. You
changes everything but nothin' don't change you—not even
death. But Ah ain't goin' outa here and Ah ain't gointuh
hush. Naw, you gointuh listen tuh me one time befo' you die.
Have yo' way all yo' life, trample and mash down and then
die ruther than tuh let yo'self heah 'bout it. Listen, Jody, you
ain't de Jody ah run off down de road wid. You'se whut's left
after he died. Ah run off tuh keep house wid you in uh won-
derful way. But you wasn't satisfied wid me de way Ah was.
Naw! Mah own mind had tuh be squeezed and crowded out
tuh make room for yours in me."

"Shut up! Ah wish thunder and lightnin' would kill yuh!"

"Ah know it. And now you got tuh die tuh find out dat
you got tuh pacify somebody besides yo'self if you wants any
love and any sympathy in dis world. You ain't tried tuh pacify
nobody but yo'self. Too busy listening tuh yo' own big voice."

"All dis tearin' down talk!" Jody whispered with sweat globules forming all over his face and arms. "Git outa heah!"

"All dis bowin' down, all dis obedience under yo' voice — dat ain't what Ah rushed off down de road tuh find out about you."

A sound of strife in Jody's throat, but his eyes stared unwillingly into a corner of the room so Janie knew the futile fight was not with her. The icy sword of the square-toed one had cut off his breath and left his hands in a pose of agonizing protest. Janie gave them peace on his breast, then she studied his dead face for a long time.

"Dis sittin' in de rulin' chair is been hard on Jody," she muttered out loud. She was full of pity for the first time in years. Jody had been hard on her and others, but life had mishandled him too. Poor Joe! Maybe if she had known some other way to try, she might have made his face different. But what that other way could be, she had no idea. She thought back and forth about what had happened in the making of a voice out of a man. Then thought about herself. Years ago, she had told her girl self to wait for her in the looking glass. It had been a long time since she had remembered. Perhaps she'd better look. She went over to the dresser and looked hard at her skin and features. The young girl was gone, but a handsome woman had taken her place. She tore off the kerchief from her head and let down her plentiful hair. The weight, the length, the glory was there. She took careful stock of herself, then combed her hair and tied it back up again. Then she starched and ironed her face, forming it into just what people wanted to see, and opened up the window and cried, "Come heah people! Jody is dead. Mah husband is gone from me."

IX

J OE'S FUNERAL was the finest thing Orange County had ever seen with Negro eyes. The motor hearse, the Cadillac and Buick carriages; Dr. Henderson there in his Lincoln; the hosts from far and wide. Then again the gold and red and purple, the gloat and glamor of the secret orders, each with its insinuations of power and glory undreamed of by the uninitiated. People on farm horses and mules; babies riding astride of brothers' and sisters' backs. The Elks band ranked at the church door and playing "Safe in the Arms of Jesus" with such a dominant drum rhythm that it could be stepped off smartly by the long line as it filed inside. The Little Emperor of the cross-roads was leaving Orange County as he had come—with the out-stretched hand of power.

Janie starched and ironed her face and came set in the funeral behind her veil. It was like a wall of stone and steel. The funeral was going on outside. All things concerning death and burial were said and done. Finish. End. Nevermore. Darkness. Deep hole. Dissolution. Eternity. Weeping and wailing outside. Inside the expensive black folds were resurrection and life. She did not reach outside for anything, nor did the things of death reach inside to disturb her calm. She sent her face to Joe's funeral, and herself went rollicking with the springtime across the world. After a while the people finished their celebration and Janie went on home.

Before she slept that night she burnt up every one of her head rags and went about the house next morning with her hair in one thick braid swinging well below her waist. That was the only change people saw in her. She kept the store in the same way except of evenings she sat on the porch and listened and sent Hezekiah in to wait on late custom. She saw no reason to rush at changing things around. She would have the rest of her life to do as she pleased.

Most of the day she was at the store, but at night she was there in the big house and sometimes it creaked and cried all night under the weight of lonesomeness. Then she'd lie awake in bed asking lonesomeness some questions. She asked

if she wanted to leave and go back where she had come from and try to find her mother. Maybe tend her grandmother's grave. Sort of look over the old stamping ground generally. Digging around inside of herself like that she found that she had no interest in that seldom-seen mother at all. She hated her grandmother and had hidden it from herself all these years under a cloak of pity. She had been getting ready for her great journey to the horizons in search of *people*; it was important to all the world that she should find them and they find her. But she had been whipped like a cur dog, and run off down a back road after *things*. It was all according to the way you see things. Some people could look at a mud-puddle and see an ocean with ships. But Nanny belonged to that other kind that loved to deal in scraps. Here Nanny had taken the biggest thing God ever made, the horizon—for no matter how far a person can go the horizon is still way beyond you—and pinched it in to such a little bit of a thing that she could tie it about her granddaughter's neck tight enough to choke her. She hated the old woman who had twisted her so in the name of love. Most humans didn't love one another nohow, and this mis-love was so strong that even common blood couldn't overcome it all the time. She had found a jewel down inside herself and she had wanted to walk where people could see her and gleam it around. But she had been set in the market-place to sell. Been set for still-bait. When God had made The Man, he made him out of stuff that sung all the time and glittered all over. Then after that some angels got jealous and chopped him into millions of pieces, but still he glittered and hummed. So they beat him down to nothing but sparks but each little spark had a shine and a song. So they covered each one over with mud. And the lonesomeness in the sparks make them hunt for one another, but the mud is deaf and dumb. Like all the other tumbling mud-balls, Janie had tried to show her shine.

Janie found out very soon that her widowhood and property was a great challenge in South Florida. Before Jody had been dead a month, she noticed how often men who had never been intimates of Joe, drove considerable distances to ask after her welfare and offer their services as advisor.

"Uh woman by herself is uh pitiful thing," she was told

over and again. "Dey needs aid and assistance. God never meant 'em tuh try tuh stand by theirselves. You ain't been used tuh knockin' round and doin' fuh yo'self, Mis' Starks. You been well taken keer of, you needs uh man."

Janie laughed at all these well-wishers because she knew that they knew plenty of women alone; that she was not the first one they had ever seen. But most of the others were poor. Besides she liked being lonesome for a change. This freedom feeling was fine. These men didn't represent a thing she wanted to know about. She had already experienced them through Logan and Joe. She felt like slapping some of them for sitting around grinning at her like a pack of chessy cats, trying to make out they looked like love.

Ike Green sat on her case seriously one evening on the store porch when he was lucky enough to catch her alone.

"You wants be keerful 'bout who you marry, Mis' Starks. Dese strange men runnin' heah tryin' tuh take advantage of yo' condition."

"Marry!" Janie almost screamed. "Joe ain't had time tuh git cold yet. Ah ain't even give marryin' de first thought."

"But you will. You'se too young uh 'oman tuh stay single, and you'se too pretty for de mens tuh leave yuh alone. You'se bound tuh marry."

"Ah hope not. Ah mean, at dis present time it don't come befo' me. Joe ain't been dead two months. Ain't got settled down in his grave."

"Dat's whut you say now, but two months mo' and you'll sing another tune. Den you want tuh be keerful. Womenfolks is easy taken advantage of. You know what tuh let none uh dese stray niggers dat's settin' round heah git de inside track on yuh. They's jes lak uh pack uh hawgs, when dey see uh full trough. Whut yuh needs is uh man dat yuh done lived uhround and know all about tuh sort of manage yo' things fuh yuh and ginerally do round."

Janie jumped upon her feet. "Lawd, Ike Green, you'se uh case! Dis subjick you bringin' up ain't fit tuh be talked about at all. Lemme go inside and help Hezekiah weigh up dat barrel uh sugar dat just come in." She rushed on inside the store and whispered to Hezekiah, "Ah'm gone tuh de house.

Lemme know when dat ole pee-de-bed is gone and Ah'll be right back."

Six months of wearing black passed and not one suitor had ever gained the house porch. Janie talked and laughed in the store at times, but never seemed to want to go further. She was happy except for the store. She knew by her head that she was absolute owner, but it always seemed to her that she was still clerking for Joe and that soon he would come in and find something wrong that she had done. She almost apologized to the tenants the first time she collected the rents. Felt like a usurper. But she hid that feeling by sending Hezekiah who was the best imitation of Joe that his seventeen years could make. He had even taken to smoking, and smoking cigars, since Joe's death and tried to bite 'em tight in one side of his mouth like Joe. Every chance he got he was reared back in Joe's swivel chair trying to thrust out his lean belly into a paunch. She'd laugh quietly at his no-harm posing and pretend she didn't see it. One day as she came in the back door of the store she heard him bawling at Tripp Crawford, "Naw indeed, we can't do nothin' uh de kind! I god, you ain't paid for dem last rations you done et up. I god, you won't git no mo' outa dis store than you got money tuh pay for. I god, dis ain't Gimme, Florida, dis is Eatonville." Another time she overheard him using Joe's favorite expression for pointing out the differences between himself and the careless-living, mouthy town. "Ah'm an educated man, Ah keep mah arrangements in mah hands." She laughed outright at that. His acting didn't hurt nobody and she wouldn't know what to do without him. He sensed that and came to treat her like baby-sister, as if to say "You poor little thing, give it to big brother. He'll fix it for you." His sense of ownership made him honest too, except for an occasional jaw-breaker, or a packet of sen-sen. The sen-sen was to let on to the other boys and the pullet-size girls that he had a liquor breath to cover. This business of managing stores and women store-owners was trying on a man's nerves. He needed a drink of liquor now and then to keep up.

When Janie emerged into her mourning white, she had hosts of admirers in and out of town. Everything open and

frank. Men of property too among the crowd, but nobody seemed to get any further than the store. She was always too busy to take them to the house to entertain. They were all so respectful and stiff with her, that she might have been the Empress of Japan. They felt that it was not fitting to mention desire to the widow of Joseph Starks. You spoke of honor and respect. And all that they said and did was refracted by her inattention and shot off towards the rim-bones of nothing. She and Pheoby Watson visited back and forth and once in awhile sat around the lakes and fished. She was just basking in freedom for the most part without the need for thought. A Sanford undertaker was pressing his cause through Pheoby, and Janie was listening pleasantly but undisturbed. It might be nice to marry him, at that. No hurry. Such things take time to think about, or rather she pretended to Pheoby that that was what she was doing.

"'Tain't dat Ah worries over Joe's death, Pheoby. Ah jus' loves dis freedom."

"Sh-sh-sh! Don't let nobody hear you say dat, Janie. Folks will say you ain't sorry he's gone."

"Let 'em say whut dey wants tuh, Pheoby. To my thinkin' mourning oughtn't tuh last no longer'n grief."

X

One day Hezekiah asked off from work to go off with the ball team. Janie told him not to hurry back. She could close up the store herself this once. He cautioned her about the catches on the windows and doors and swaggered off to Winter Park.

Business was dull all day, because numbers of people had gone to the game. She decided to close early, because it was hardly worth the trouble of keeping open on an afternoon like this. She had set six o'clock as her limit.

At five-thirty a tall man came into the place. Janie was leaning on the counter making aimless pencil marks on a piece of wrapping paper. She knew she didn't know his name, but he looked familiar.

"Good evenin', Mis' Starks," he said with a sly grin as if they had a good joke together. She was in favor of the story that was making him laugh before she even heard it.

"Good evenin'," she answered pleasantly. "You got all de advantage 'cause Ah don't know yo' name."

"People wouldn't know me lak dey would *you*."

"Ah guess standin' in uh store do make uh person git tuh be known in de vicinity. Look lak Ah seen you somewhere."

"Oh, Ah don't live no further than Orlandah. Ah'm easy tuh see on Church Street most any day or night. You got any smokin' tobacco?"

She opened the glass case. "What kind?"

"Camels."

She handed over the cigarettes and took the money. He broke the pack and thrust one between his full, purple lips.

"You got a lil piece uh fire over dere, lady?"

They both laughed and she handed him two kitchen matches out of a box for that purpose. It was time for him to go but he didn't. He leaned on the counter with one elbow and cold-cocked her a look.

"Why ain't *you* at de ball game, too? Everybody else is dere."

"Well, Ah see somebody else besides me ain't dere. Ah just sold some cigarettes." They laughed again.

"Dat's 'cause Ah'm dumb. Ah got de thing all mixed up. Ah thought de game was gointuh be out at Hungerford. So Ah got uh ride tuh where dis road turns off from de Dixie Highway and walked over here and then Ah find out de game is in Winter Park."

That was funny to both of them too.

"So what you gointuh do now? All de cars in Eatonville is gone."

"How about playin' *you* some checkers? You looks hard tuh beat."

"Ah is, 'cause Ah can't play uh lick."

"You don't cherish de game, then?"

"Yes, Ah do, and then agin Ah don't know whether Ah do or not, 'cause nobody ain't never showed me how."

"Dis is de last day for *dat* excuse. You got uh board round heah?"

"Yes indeed. De men folks treasures de game round heah. Ah just ain't never learnt how."

He set it up and began to show her and she found herself glowing inside. Somebody wanted her to play. Somebody thought it natural for her to play. That was even nice. She looked him over and got little thrills from every one of his good points. Those full, lazy eyes with the lashes curling sharply away like drawn scimitars. The lean, over-padded shoulders and narrow waist. Even nice!

He was jumping her king! She screamed in protest against losing the king she had had such a hard time acquiring. Before she knew it she had grabbed his hand to stop him. He struggled gallantly to free himself. That is he struggled, but not hard enough to wrench a lady's fingers.

"Ah got uh right tuh take it. You left it right in mah way."

"Yeah, but Ah wuz lookin' off when you went and stuck yo' men right up next tuh mine. No fair!"

"You ain't supposed tuh look off, Mis' Starks. It's de biggest part uh de game tuh watch out! Leave go mah hand."

"No suh! Not mah king. You kin take another one, but not dat one."

They scrambled and upset the board and laughed at that.

"Anyhow it's time for uh Coca-Cola," he said. "Ah'll come teach yuh some mo' another time."

"It's all right tuh come teach me, but don't come tuh cheat me."

"Yuh can't beat uh woman. Dey jes won't stand fuh it. But Ah'll come teach yuh agin. You gointuh be uh good player too, after while."

"You reckon so? Jody useter tell me Ah never would learn. It wuz too heavy fuh mah brains."

"Folks is playin' it wid sense and folks is playin' it without. But you got good meat on yó' head. You'll learn. Have uh cool drink on me."

"Oh all right, thank yuh. Got plenty cold ones tuhday. Nobody ain't been heah tuh buy none. All gone off tuh de game."

"You oughta be at de next game. 'Tain't no use in *you* stayin' heah if everybody else is gone. You don't buy from yo'self, do yuh?"

"You crazy thing! 'Course Ah don't. But Ah'm worried 'bout you uh little."

"How come? 'Fraid Ah ain't gointuh pay fuh dese drinks?"

"Aw naw! How you gointuh git back home?"

"Wait round heah fuh a car. If none don't come, Ah got good shoe leather. 'Tain't but seben miles nohow. Ah could walk dat in no time. Easy."

"If it wuz me, Ah'd wait on uh train. Seben miles is uh kinda long walk."

"It would be for you, 'cause you ain't used to it. But Ah'm seen women walk further'n dat. You could too, if yuh had it tuh do."

"Maybe so, but Ah'll ride de train long as Ah got railroad fare."

"Ah don't need no pocket-full uh money to ride de train lak uh woman. When Ah takes uh notion Ah rides anyhow— money or no money."

"Now ain't you somethin'! Mr. er—er— You never did tell me whut yo' name wuz."

"Ah sho didn't. Wuzn't expectin' fuh it to be needed. De name mah mama gimme is Vergible Woods. Dey calls me Tea Cake for short."

"Tea Cake! So you sweet as all dat?" She laughed and he gave her a little cut-eye look to get her meaning.

"Ah may be guilty. You better try me and see."

She did something half-way between a laugh and a frown and he set his hat on straight.

"B'lieve Ah done cut uh hawg, so Ah guess Ah better ketch air." He made an elaborate act of tipping to the door stealthily. Then looked back at her with an irresistible grin on his face. Janie burst out laughing in spite of herself. "You crazy thing!"

He turned and threw his hat at her feet. "If she don't throw it at me, Ah'll take a chance on comin' back," he announced, making gestures to indicate he was hidden behind a post. She picked up the hat and threw it after him with a laugh. "Even if she had uh brick she couldn't hurt yuh wid it," he said to an invisible companion. "De lady can't throw." He gestured to his companion, stepped out from behind the imaginary lamp post, set his coat and hat and strolled back to where Janie was as if he had just come in the store.

"Evenin' Mis' Starks. Could yuh lemme have uh pound uh knuckle puddin'* till Saturday? Ah'm sho tuh pay yuh then."

"You needs ten pounds, Mr. Tea Cake. Ah'll let yuh have all Ah got and you needn't bother 'bout payin' it back."

They joked and went on till the people began to come in. Then he took a seat and made talk and laughter with the rest until closing time. When everyone else had left he said, "Ah reckon Ah done over-layed mah leavin' time, but Ah figgured you needed somebody tuh help yuh shut up de place. Since nobody else ain't round heah, maybe Ah kin git de job."

"Thankyuh, Mr. Tea Cake. It is kinda strainin' fuh me."

"Who ever heard of uh teacake bein' called Mister! If you wanta be real hightoned and call me Mr. Woods, dat's de way you feel about it. If yuh wants tuh be uh lil friendly and call me Tea Cake, dat would be real nice." He was closing and bolting windows all the time he talked.

"All right, then. Thank yuh, Tea Cake. How's dat?"

"Jes lak uh lil girl wid her Easter dress on. Even nice!" He locked the door and shook it to be sure and handed her the

*A beating with the fist.

key. "Come on now, Ah'll see yuh inside yo' door and git on down de Dixie."

Janie was halfway down the palm-lined walk before she had a thought for her safety. Maybe this strange man was up to something! But it was no place to show her fear there in the darkness between the house and the store. He had hold of her arm too. Then in a moment it was gone. Tea Cake wasn't strange. Seemed as if she had known him all her life. Look how she had been able to talk with him right off! He tipped his hat at the door and was off with the briefest good night.

So she sat on the porch and watched the moon rise. Soon its amber fluid was drenching the earth, and quenching the thirst of the day.

XI

JANIE wanted to ask Hezekiah about Tea Cake, but she was afraid he might misunderstand her and think she was interested. In the first place he looked too young for her. Must be around twenty-five and here *she* was around forty. Then again he didn't look like he had too much. Maybe he was hanging around to get in with her and strip her of all that she had. Just as well if she never saw him again. He was probably the kind of man who lived with various women but never married. Fact is, she decided to treat him so cold if he ever did foot the place that he'd be sure not to come hanging around there again.

He waited a week exactly to come back for Janie's snub. It was early in the afternoon and she and Hezekiah were alone. She heard somebody humming like they were feeling for pitch and looked towards the door. Tea Cake stood there mimicking the tuning of a guitar. He frowned and struggled with the pegs of his imaginary instrument watching her out of the corner of his eye with that secret joke playing over his face. Finally she smiled and he sung middle C, put his guitar under his arm and walked on back to where she was.

"Evenin', folks. Thought y'all might lak uh lil music this evenin' so Ah brought long mah box."

"Crazy thing!" Janie commented, beaming out with light.

He acknowledged the compliment with a smile and sat down on a box. "Anybody have uh Coca-Cola wid me?"

"Ah just had one," Janie temporized with her conscience.

"It'll hafter be done all over agin, Mis' Starks."

"How come?"

"'Cause it wasn't done right dat time. 'Kiah bring us two bottles from de bottom uh de box."

"How you been makin' out since Ah seen yuh last, Tea Cake?"

"Can't kick. Could be worse. Made four days dis week and got de pay in mah pocket."

"We got a rich man round here, then. Buyin' passenger trains uh battleships this week?"

"Which one do *you* want? It all depends on you."

"Oh, if you'se treatin' me tuh it, Ah b'lieve Ah'll take de passenger train. If it blow up Ah'll still be on land."

"Choose de battleship if dat's whut you really want. Ah know where one is right now. Seen one round Key West de other day."

"How you gointuh git it?"

"Ah shucks, dem Admirals is always ole folks. Can't no ole man stop me from gittin' no ship for yuh if dat's whut you want. Ah'd git dat ship out from under him so slick till he'd be walkin' de water lak ole Peter befo' he knowed it."

They played away the evening again. Everybody was surprised at Janie playing checkers but they liked it. Three or four stood behind her and coached her moves and generally made merry with her in a restrained way. Finally everybody went home but Tea Cake.

"You kin close up, 'Kiah," Janie said. "Think Ah'll g'wan home."

Tea Cake fell in beside her and mounted the porch this time. So she offered him a seat and they made a lot of laughter out of nothing. Near eleven o'clock she remembered a piece of pound cake she had put away. Tea Cake went out to the lemon tree at the corner of the kitchen and picked some lemons and squeezed them for her. So they had lemonade too.

"Moon's too pretty fuh anybody tuh be sleepin' it away," Tea Cake said after they had washed up the plates and glasses. "Less us go fishin'."

"Fishin'? Dis time uh night?"

"Unhhunh, fishin'. Ah know where de bream is beddin'. Seen 'em when Ah come round de lake dis evenin'. Where's yo' fishin' poles? Less go set on de lake."

It was so crazy digging worms by lamp light and setting out for Lake Sabelia after midnight that she felt like a child breaking rules. That's what made Janie like it. They caught two or three and got home just before day. Then she had to smuggle Tea Cake out by the back gate and that made it seem like some great secret she was keeping from the town.

"Mis' Janie," Hezekiah began sullenly next day, "you oughtn't 'low dat Tea Cake tuh be walkin' tuh de house wid yuh. Ah'll go wid yuh mahself after dis, if you'se skeered."

"What's de matter wid Tea Cake, 'Kiah? Is he uh thief uh somethin'?"

"Ah ain't never heard nobody say he stole nothin'."

"Is he bad 'bout totin' pistols and knives tuh hurt people wid?"

"Dey don't say he ever cut nobody or shot nobody neither."

"Well, is he—he—is he got uh wife or something lak dat? Not dat it's any uh mah business." She held her breath for the answer.

"No'm. And nobody wouldn't marry Tea Cake tuh starve tuh death lessen it's somebody jes lak him—ain't used to nothin'. 'Course he always keep hisself in changin' clothes. Dat long-legged Tea Cake ain't got doodly squat. He ain't got no business makin' hisself familiar wid nobody lak you. Ah said Ah wuz goin' to tell yuh so yuh could know."

"Oh dat's all right, Hezekiah. Thank yuh mighty much."

The next night when she mounted her steps Tea Cake was there before her, sitting on the porch in the dark. He had a string of fresh-caught trout for a present.

"Ah'll clean 'em, you fry 'em and let's eat," he said with the assurance of not being refused. They went out into the kitchen and fixed up the hot fish and corn muffins and ate. Then Tea Cake went to the piano without so much as asking and began playing blues and singing, and throwing grins over his shoulder. The sounds lulled Janie to soft slumber and she woke up with Tea Cake combing her hair and scratching the dandruff from her scalp. It made her more comfortable and drowsy.

"Tea Cake, where you git uh comb from tuh be combin' mah hair wid?"

"Ah brought it wid me. Come prepared tuh lay mah hands on it tuhnight."

"Why, Tea Cake? Whut good do combin' mah hair do *you*? It's *mah* comfortable, not yourn."

"It's mine too. Ah ain't been sleepin' so good for more'n uh week cause Ah been wishin' so bad tuh git mah hands in yo' hair. It's so pretty. It feels jus' lak underneath uh dove's wing next to mah face."

"Umph! You'se mighty easy satisfied. Ah been had dis same hair next tuh mah face ever since Ah cried de fust time, and 'tain't never gimme me no thrill."

"Ah tell you lak you told me—you'se mighty hard tuh satisfy. Ah betcha dem lips don't satisfy yuh neither."

"Dat's right, Tea Cake. They's dere and Ah make use of 'em whenever it's necessary, but nothin' special tuh me."

"Umph! umph! umph! Ah betcha you don't never go tuh de lookin' glass and enjoy yo' eyes yo'self. You lets other folks git all de enjoyment out of 'em 'thout takin' in any of it yo'self."

"Naw, Ah never gazes at 'em in de lookin' glass. If anybody else gits any pleasure out of 'em Ah ain't been told about it."

"See dat? You'se got de world in uh jug and make out you don't know it. But Ah'm glad tuh be de one tuh tell yuh."

"Ah guess you done told plenty women all about it."

"Ah'm de Apostle Paul tuh de Gentiles. Ah tells 'em and then agin Ah shows 'em."

"Ah thought so." She yawned and made to get up from the sofa. "You done got me so sleepy wid yo' head-scratchin' Ah kin hardly make it tuh de bed." She stood up at once, collecting her hair. He sat still.

"Naw, you ain't sleepy, Mis' Janie. You jus' want me tuh go. You figger Ah'm uh rounder and uh pimp and you done wasted too much time talkin' wid me."

"Why, Tea Cake! Whut ever put dat notion in yo' head?"

"De way you looked at me when Ah said whut Ah did. Yo' face skeered me so bad till mah whiskers drawed up."

"Ah ain't got no business bein' mad at nothin' you do and say. You got it all wrong. Ah ain't mad atall."

"Ah know it and dat's what puts de shamery on me. You'se jus' disgusted wid me. Yo' face jus' left here and went off somewhere else. Naw, you ain't mad wid me. Ah be glad if you was, 'cause then Ah might do somethin' tuh please yuh. But lak it is—"

"Mah likes and dislikes ought not tuh make no difference wid you, Tea Cake. Dat's fuh yo' lady friend. Ah'm jus' uh sometime friend uh yourn."

Janie walked towards the stairway slowly, and Tea Cake sat

where he was, as if he had frozen to his seat, in fear that once he got up, he'd never get back in it again. He swallowed hard and looked at her walk away.

"Ah didn't aim tuh let on tuh yuh 'bout it, leastways not right away, but Ah ruther be shot wid tacks than fuh you tuh act wid me lak you is right now. You got me in de go-long."

At the newel post Janie whirled around and for the space of a thought she was lit up like a transfiguration. Her next thought brought her crashing down. He's just saying anything for the time being, feeling he's got me so I'll b'lieve him. The next thought buried her under tons of cold futility. He's trading on being younger than me. Getting ready to laugh at me for an old fool. But oh, what wouldn't I give to be twelve years younger so I could b'lieve him!

"Aw, Tea Cake, you just say dat tuhnight because de fish and corn bread tasted sort of good. Tomorrow yo' mind would change."

"Naw, it wouldn't neither. Ah know better."

"Anyhow from what you told me when we wuz back dere in de kitchen Ah'm nearly twelve years older than you."

"Ah done thought all about dat and tried tuh struggle aginst it, but it don't do me no good. De thought uh mah youngness don't satisfy me lak yo' presence do."

"It makes uh whole heap uh difference wid most folks, Tea Cake."

"Things lak dat got uh whole lot tuh do wid convenience, but it ain't got nothin' tuh do wid love."

"Well, Ah love tuh find out whut you think after sun-up tomorrow. Dis is jus' yo' night thought."

"You got yo' ideas and Ah got mine. Ah got uh dollar dat says you'se wrong. But Ah reckon you don't bet money, neither."

"Ah never have done it so fur. But as de old folks always say, Ah'm born but Ah ain't dead. No tellin' whut Ah'm liable tuh do yet."

He got up suddenly and took his hat. "Good night Mis' Janie. Look lak we done run our conversation from grass roots tuh pine trees. G'bye." He almost ran out of the door.

Janie hung over the newel post thinking so long that she all

but went to sleep there. However, before she went to bed she took a good look at her mouth, eyes and hair.

All next day in the house and store she thought resisting thoughts about Tea Cake. She even ridiculed him in her mind and was a little ashamed of the association. But every hour or two the battle had to be fought all over again. She couldn't make him look just like any other man to her. He looked like the love thoughts of women. He could be a bee to a blossom—a pear tree blossom in the spring. He seemed to be crushing scent out of the world with his footsteps. Crushing aromatic herbs with every step he took. Spices hung about him. He was a glance from God.

So he didn't come that night and she laid in bed and pretended to think scornfully of him. "Bet he's hangin' round some jook or 'nother. Glad Ah treated him cold. Whut do Ah want wid some trashy nigger out de streets? Bet he's livin' wid some woman or 'nother and takin' me for uh fool. Glad Ah caught mahself in time." She tried to console herself that way.

The next morning she awoke hearing a knocking on the front door and found Tea Cake there.

"Hello, Mis' Janie, Ah hope Ah woke you up."

"You sho did, Tea Cake. Come in and rest yo' hat. Whut you doin' out so soon dis mornin'?"

"Thought Ah'd try tuh git heah soon enough tuh tell yuh mah daytime thoughts. Ah see yuh needs tuh know mah daytime feelings. Ah can't sense yuh intuh it at night."

"You crazy thing! Is dat whut you come here for at daybreak?"

"Sho is. You needs tellin' and showin', and dat's whut Ah'm doin'. Ah picked some strawberries too, Ah figgered you might like."

"Tea Cake, Ah 'clare Ah don't know whut tuh make outa you. You'se so crazy. You better lemme fix you some breakfast."

"Ain't got time. Ah got uh job uh work. Gottuh be back in Orlandah at eight o'clock. See yuh later, tell you straighter."

He bolted down the walk and was gone. But that night when she left the store, he was stretched out in the hammock on the porch with his hat over his face pretending to sleep. She called him. He pretended not to hear. He snored louder.

She went to the hammock to shake him and he seized and pulled her in with him. After a little, she let him adjust her in his arms and laid there for a while.

"Tea Cake, Ah don't know 'bout you, but Ah'm hongry, come on let's eat some supper."

They went inside and their laughter rang out first from the kitchen and all over the house.

Janie awoke next morning by feeling Tea Cake almost kissing her breath away. Holding her and caressing her as if he feared she might escape his grasp and fly away. Then he must dress hurriedly and get to his job on time. He wouldn't let her get him any breakfast at all. He wanted her to get her rest. He made her stay where she was. In her heart she wanted to get his breakfast for him. But she stayed in bed long after he was gone.

So much had been breathed out by the pores that Tea Cake still was there. She could feel him and almost see him bucking around the room in the upper air. After a long time of passive happiness, she got up and opened the window and let Tea Cake leap forth and mount to the sky on a wind. That was the beginning of things.

In the cool of the afternoon the fiend from hell specially sent to lovers arrived at Janie's ear. Doubt. All the fears that circumstance could provide and the heart feel, attacked her on every side. This was a new sensation for her, but no less excruciating. If only Tea Cake would make her certain! He did not return that night nor the next and so she plunged into the abyss and descended to the ninth darkness where light has never been.

But the fourth day after he came in the afternoon driving a battered car. Jumped out like a deer and made the gesture of tying it to a post on the store porch. Ready with his grin! She adored him and hated him at the same time. How could he make her suffer so and then come grinning like that with that darling way he had? He pinched her arm as he walked inside the door.

"Brought me somethin' tuh haul you off in," he told her with that secret chuckle. "Git yo' hat if you gointuh wear one. We got tuh go buy groceries."

"Ah sells groceries right here in dis store, Tea Cake, if you

don't happen tuh know." She tried to look cold but she was smiling in spite of herself.

"Not de kind we want fuh de occasion. You sells groceries for ordinary people. We'se gointuh buy for *you*. De big Sunday School picnic is tomorrow—bet you done forget it—and we got tuh be dere wid uh swell basket and ourselves."

"Ah don't know 'bout dat, Tea Cake. Tell yuh whut you do. G'wan down tuh de house and wait for me. Be dere in uh minute."

As soon as she thought it looked right she slipped out of the back and joined Tea Cake. No need of fooling herself. Maybe he was just being polite.

"Tea Cake, you sure you want me tuh go tuh dis picnic wid yuh?"

"Me scramble 'round tuh git de money tuh take yuh—been workin' lak uh dawg for two whole weeks—and she come astin' me if Ah want her tuh go! Puttin' mahself tuh uh whole heap uh trouble tuh git dis car so you kin go over tuh Winter Park or Orlandah tuh buy de things you might need and dis woman set dere and ast me if Ah want her tuh go!"

"Don't git mad, Tea Cake, Ah just didn't want you doin' nothin' outa politeness. If dere's somebody else you'd ruther take, it's all right wid me."

"Naw, it ain't all right wid you. If it was you wouldn't be sayin' dat. Have de nerve tuh say whut you mean."

"Well, all right, Tea Cake, Ah wants tuh go wid you real bad, but,—oh, Tea Cake, don't make no false pretense wid me!"

"Janie, Ah hope God may kill me, if Ah'm lyin'. Nobody else on earth kin hold uh candle tuh you, baby. You got de keys to de kingdom."

XII

IT WAS after the picnic that the town began to notice things and got mad. Tea Cake and Mrs. Mayor Starks! All the men that she could get, and fooling with somebody like Tea Cake! Another thing, Joe Starks hadn't been dead but nine months and here she goes sashaying off to a picnic in pink linen. Done quit attending church, like she used to. Gone off to Sanford in a car with Tea Cake and her all dressed in blue! It was a shame. Done took to high heel slippers and a ten dollar hat! Looking like some young girl, always in blue because Tea Cake told her to wear it. Poor Joe Starks. Bet he turns over in his grave every day. Tea Cake and Janie gone hunting. Tea Cake and Janie gone fishing. Tea Cake and Janie gone to Orlando to the movies. Tea Cake and Janie gone to a dance. Tea Cake making flower beds in Janie's yard and seeding the garden for her. Chopping down that tree she never did like by the dining room window. All those signs of possession. Tea Cake in a borrowed car teaching Janie to drive. Tea Cake and Janie playing checkers; playing coon-can; playing Florida flip on the store porch all afternoon as if nobody else was there. Day after day and week after week.

"Pheoby," Sam Watson said one night as he got in the bed, "Ah b'lieve yo' buddy is all tied up with dat Tea Cake sho-nough. Didn't b'lieve it at first."

"Aw she don't mean nothin' by it. Ah think she's sort of stuck on dat undertaker up at Sanford."

"It's somebody 'cause she looks mighty good dese days. New dresses and her hair combed a different way nearly every day. You got to have something to comb hair over. When you see 'uh woman doin' so much rakin' in her head, she's combin' at some man or 'nother."

"'Course she kin do as she please, but dat's uh good chance she got up at Sanford. De man's wife died and he got uh lovely place tuh take her to—already furnished. Better'n her house Joe left her."

"You better sense her intuh things then 'cause Tea Cake can't do nothin' but help her spend whut she got. Ah reckon

dat's whut he's after. Throwin' away whut Joe Starks worked hard tuh git tuhgether."

"Dat's de way it looks. Still and all, she's her own woman. She oughta know by now whut she wants tuh do."

"De men wuz talkin' 'bout it in de grove tuhday and givin' her and Tea Cake both de devil. Dey figger he's spendin' on her now in order tuh make her spend on him later."

"Umph! Umph! Umph!"

"Oh dey got it all figgered out. Maybe it ain't as bad as they say, but they talk it and make it sound real bad on her part."

"Dat's jealousy and malice. Some uh dem very men wants tuh do whut dey claim deys skeered Tea Cake is doin'."

"De Pastor claim Tea Cake don't 'low her tuh come tuh church only once in awhile 'cause he want dat change tuh buy gas wid. Just draggin' de woman away from church. But anyhow, she's yo' bosom friend, so you better go see 'bout her. Drop uh lil hint here and dere and if Tea Cake is tryin' tuh rob her she kin see and know. Ah laks de woman and Ah sho would hate tuh see her come up lak Mis' Tyler."

"Aw mah God, naw! Reckon Ah better step over dere tomorrow and have some chat wid Janie. She jus' ain't thinkin' whut she doin', dat's all."

The next morning Pheoby picked her way over to Janie's house like a hen to a neighbor's garden. Stopped and talked a little with everyone she met, turned aside momentarily to pause at a porch or two—going straight by walking crooked. So her firm intention looked like an accident and she didn't have to give her opinion to folks along the way.

Janie acted glad to see her and after a while Pheoby broached her with, "Janie, everybody's talkin' 'bout how dat Tea Cake is draggin' you round tuh places you ain't used tuh. Baseball games and huntin' and fishin'. He don't know you'se useter uh more high time crowd than dat. You always did class off."

"Jody classed me off. Ah didn't. Naw, Pheoby, Tea Cake ain't draggin' me off nowhere Ah don't want tuh go. Ah always did want tuh git round uh whole heap, but Jody wouldn't 'low me tuh. When Ah wasn't in de store he wanted me tuh jes sit wid folded hands and sit dere. And Ah'd sit

dere wid de walls creepin' up on me and squeezin' all de life outa me. Pheoby, dese educated women got uh heap of things to sit down and consider. Somebody done tole 'em what to set down for. Nobody ain't told poor me, so sittin' still worries me. Ah wants tuh utilize mahself all over."

"But, Janie, Tea Cake, whilst he ain't no jail-bird, he ain't got uh dime tuh cry. Ain't you skeered he's jes after yo' money—him bein' younger than you?"

"He ain't never ast de first penny from me yet, and if he love property he ain't no different from all de rest of us. All dese ole men dat's settin' round me is after de same thing. They's three mo' widder women in town, how come dey don't break dey neck after dem? 'Cause dey ain't got nothin', dat's why."

"Folks seen you out in colors and dey thinks you ain't payin' de right amount uh respect tuh yo' dead husband."

"Ah ain't grievin' so why do Ah hafta mourn? Tea Cake love me in blue, so Ah wears it. Jody ain't never in his life picked out no color for me. De world picked out black and white for mournin', Joe didn't. So Ah wasn't wearin' it for him. Ah was wearin' it for de rest of y'all."

"But anyhow, watch yo'self, Janie, and don't be took advantage of. You know how dese young men is wid older women. Most of de time dey's after whut dey kin git, then dey's gone lak uh turkey through de corn."

"Tea Cake don't talk dat way. He's aimin' tuh make hisself permanent wid me. We done made up our mind tuh marry."

"Janie, you'se yo' own woman, and Ah hope you know whut you doin'. Ah sho hope you ain't lak uh possum—de older you gits, de less sense yuh got. Ah'd feel uh whole heap better 'bout yuh if you wuz marryin' dat man up dere in Sanford. He got somethin' tuh put long side uh whut you got and dat make it more better. He's endurable."

"Still and all Ah'd ruther be wid Tea Cake."

"Well, if yo' mind is already made up, 'tain't nothin' nobody kin do. But you'se takin' uh awful chance."

"No mo' than Ah took befo' and no mo' than anybody else takes when dey gits married. It always changes folks, and sometimes it brings out dirt and meanness dat even de person didn't know they had in 'em theyselves. You know dat. Maybe

Tea Cake might turn out lak dat. Maybe not. Anyhow Ah'm ready and willin' tuh try 'im."

"Well, when you aim tuh step off?"

"Dat we don't know. De store is got tuh be sold and then we'se goin' off somewhere tuh git married."

"How come you sellin' out de store?"

"'Cause Tea Cake ain't no Jody Starks, and if he tried tuh be, it would be uh complete flommuck. But de minute Ah marries 'im everybody is gointuh be makin' comparisons. So us is goin' off somewhere and start all over in Tea Cake's way. Dis ain't no business proposition, and no race after property and titles. Dis is uh love game. Ah done lived Grandma's way, now Ah means tuh live mine."

"What you mean by dat, Janie?"

"She was borned in slavery time when folks, dat is black folks, didn't sit down anytime dey felt lak it. So sittin' on porches lak de white madam looked lak uh mighty fine thing tuh her. Dat's whut she wanted for me—don't keer whut it cost. Git up on uh high chair and sit dere. She didn't have time tuh think whut tuh do after you got up on de stool uh do nothin'. De object wuz tuh git dere. So Ah got up on de high stool lak she told me, but Pheoby, Ah done nearly languished tuh death up dere. Ah felt like de world wuz cryin' extry and Ah ain't read de common news yet."

"Maybe so, Janie. Still and all Ah'd love tuh experience it for just one year. It look lak heben tuh me from where Ah'm at."

"Ah reckon so."

"But anyhow, Janie, you be keerful 'bout dis sellin' out and goin' off wid strange men. Look whut happened tuh Annie Tyler. Took whut little she had and went off tuh Tampa wid dat boy dey call Who Flung. It's somethin' tuh think about."

"It sho is. Still Ah ain't Mis' Tyler and Tea Cake ain't no Who Flung, and he ain't no stranger tuh me. We'se just as good as married already. But Ah ain't puttin' it in de street. Ah'm tellin' *you*."

"Ah jus lak uh chicken. Chicken drink water, but he don't pee-pee."

"Oh, Ah know you don't talk. We ain't shame faced. We jus' ain't ready tuh make no big kerflommuck as yet."

"You doin' right not tuh talk it, but Janie, you'se takin' uh mighty big chance."

" 'Tain't so big uh chance as it seem lak, Pheoby. Ah'm older than Tea Cake, yes. But he done showed me where it's de thought dat makes de difference in ages. If people thinks de same they can make it all right. So in the beginnin' new thoughts had tuh be thought and new words said. After Ah got used tuh dat, we gits 'long jus' fine. He done taught me de maiden language all over. Wait till you see de new blue satin Tea Cake done picked out for me tuh stand up wid him in. High heel slippers, necklace, earrings, *everything* he wants tuh see me in. Some of dese mornin's and it won't be long, you gointuh wake up callin' me and Ah'll be gone."

XIII

JACKSONVILLE. Tea Cake's letter had said Jacksonville. He
had worked in the railroad shops up there before and his
old boss had promised him a job come next pay day. No need
for Janie to wait any longer. Wear the new blue dress because
he meant to marry her right from the train. Hurry up and
come because he was about to turn into pure sugar thinking
about her. Come on, baby, papa Tea Cake never could be
mad with you!

Janie's train left too early in the day for the town to witness
much, but the few who saw her leave bore plenty witness.
They had to give it to her, she sho looked good, but she had
no business to do it. It was hard to love a woman that always
made you feel so wishful.

The train beat on itself and danced on the shiny steel rails
mile after mile. Every now and then the engineer would play
on his whistle for the people in the towns he passed by. And
the train shuffled on to Jacksonville, and to a whole lot of
things she wanted to see and to know.

And there was Tea Cake in the big old station in a new blue
suit and straw hat, hauling her off to a preacher's house first
thing. Then right on to the room he had been sleeping in for
two weeks all by himself waiting for her to come. And such
another hugging and kissing and carrying on you never saw.
It made her so glad she was scared of herself. They stayed at
home and rested that night, but the next night they went to a
show and after that they rode around on the trolley cars and
sort of looked things over for themselves. Tea Cake was
spending and doing out of his own pocket, so Janie never
told him about the two hundred dollars she had pinned inside
her shirt next to her skin. Pheoby had insisted that she bring
it along and keep it secret just to be on the safe side. She had
ten dollars over her fare in her pocket book. Let Tea Cake
think that was all she had. Things might not turn out like she
thought. Every minute since she had stepped off the train she
had been laughing at Pheoby's advice. She meant to tell Tea
Cake the joke some time when she was sure she wouldn't

hurt his feelings. So it came around that she had been married a week and sent Pheoby a card with a picture on it.

That morning Tea Cake got up earlier than Janie did. She felt sleepy and told him to go get some fish to fry for breakfast. By the time he had gone and come back she would have finished her nap out. He told her he would and she turned over and went back to sleep. She woke up and Tea Cake still wasn't there and the clock said it was getting late, so she got up and washed her face and hands. Perhaps he was down in the kitchen fixing around to let her sleep. Janie went down and the landlady made her drink some coffee with her because she said her husband was dead and it was bad to be having your morning coffee by yourself.

"Yo' husband gone tuh work dis mornin', Mis' Woods? Ah seen him go out uh good while uh go. Me and you kin be comp'ny for one 'nother, can't us?"

"Oh yes, indeed, Mis' Samuels. You puts me in de mind uh mah friend back in Eatonville. Yeah, you'se nice and friendly jus' lak her."

Therefore Janie drank her coffee and sankled on back to her room without asking her landlady anything. Tea Cake must be hunting all over the city for that fish. She kept that thought in front of her in order not to think too much. When she heard the twelve o'clock whistle she decided to get up and dress. That was when she found out her two hundred dollars was gone. There was the little cloth purse with the safety pin on the chair beneath her clothes and the money just wasn't nowhere in the room. She knew from the beginning that the money wasn't any place she knew of if it wasn't in that little pocket book pinned to her pink silk vest. But the exercise of searching the room kept her busy and that was good for her to keep moving, even though she wasn't doing anything but turning around in her tracks.

But, don't care how firm your determination is, you can't keep turning round in one place like a horse grinding sugar cane. So Janie took to sitting over the room. Sit and look. The room inside looked like the mouth of an alligator — gaped wide open to swallow something down. Outside the window Jacksonville looked like it needed a fence around it to keep it from running out on ether's bosom. It was too big to

be warm, let alone to need somebody like her. All day and night she worried time like a bone.

Way late in the morning the thought of Annie Tyler and Who Flung came to pay her a visit. Annie Tyler who at fifty-two had been left a widow with a good home and insurance money.

Mrs. Tyler with her dyed hair, newly straightened and her uncomfortable new false teeth, her leathery skin, blotchy with powder and her giggle. Her love affairs, affairs with boys in their late teens or early twenties for all of whom she spent her money on suits of clothes, shoes, watches and things like that and how they all left her as soon as their wants were satisfied. Then when her ready cash was gone, had come Who Flung to denounce his predecessor as a scoundrel and took up around the house himself. It was he who persuaded her to sell her house and come to Tampa with him. The town had seen her limp off. The under-sized high-heel slippers were punishing her tired feet that looked like bunions all over. Her body squeezed and crowded into a tight corset that shoved her middle up under her chin. But she had gone off laughing and sure. As sure as Janie had been.

Then two weeks later the porter and conductor of the north bound local had helped her off the train at Maitland. Hair all gray and black and bluish and reddish in streaks. All the capers that cheap dye could cut was showing in her hair. Those slippers bent and griped just like her work-worn feet. The corset gone and the shaking old woman hanging all over herself. Everything that you could see was hanging. Her chin hung from her ears and rippled down her neck like drapes. Her hanging bosom and stomach and buttocks and legs that draped down over her ankles. She groaned but never giggled.

She was broken and her pride was gone, so she told those who asked what had happened. Who Flung had taken her to a shabby room in a shabby house in a shabby street and prom-ised to marry her next day. They stayed in the room two whole days then she woke up to find Who Flung and her money gone. She got up to stir around and see if she could find him, and found herself too worn out to do much. All she found out was that she was too old a vessel for new wine. The next day hunger had driven her out to shift. She had stood on

the streets and smiled and smiled, and then smiled and begged and then just begged. After a week of world-bruising a young man from home had come along and seen her. She couldn't tell him how it was. She just told him she got off the train and somebody had stolen her purse. Naturally, he had believed her and taken her home with him to give her time to rest up a day or two, then he had bought her a ticket for home.

They put her to bed and sent for her married daughter from up around Ocala to come see about her. The daughter came as soon as she could and took Annie Tyler away to die in peace. She had waited all her life for something, and it had killed her when it found her.

The thing made itself into pictures and hung around Janie's bedside all night long. Anyhow, she wasn't going back to Eatonville to be laughed at and pitied. She had ten dollars in her pocket and twelve hundred in the bank. But oh God, don't let Tea Cake be off somewhere hurt and Ah not know nothing about it. And God, please suh, don't let him love nobody else but me. Maybe Ah'm is uh fool, Lawd, lak dey say, but Lawd, Ah been so lonesome, and Ah been waitin', Jesus. Ah done waited uh long time.

Janie dozed off to sleep but she woke up in time to see the sun sending up spies ahead of him to mark out the road through the dark. He peeped up over the door sill of the world and made a little foolishness with red. But pretty soon, he laid all that aside and went about his business dressed all in white. But it was always going to be dark to Janie if Tea Cake didn't soon come back. She got out of the bed but a chair couldn't hold her. She dwindled down on the floor with her head in a rocking chair.

After a while there was somebody playing a guitar outside her door. Played right smart while. It sounded lovely too. But it was sad to hear it feeling blue like Janie was. Then whoever it was started to singing "Ring de bells of mercy. Call de sinner man home." Her heart all but smothered her.

"Tea Cake is dat you?"

"You know so well it's me, Janie. How come you don't open de door?"

But he never waited. He walked on in with a guitar and a

grin. Guitar hanging round his neck with a red silk cord and a grin hanging from his ears.

"Don't need tuh ast me where Ah been all dis time, 'cause it's mah all day job tuh tell yuh."

"Tea Cake, Ah—"

"Good Lawd, Janie, whut you doin' settin' on de floor?"

He took her head in his hands and eased himself into the chair. She still didn't say anything. He sat stroking her head and looking down into her face.

"Ah see whut it is. You doubted me 'bout de money. Thought Ah had done took it and gone. Ah don't blame yuh but it wasn't lak you think. De girl baby ain't born and her mama is dead, dat can git me tuh spend our money on her. Ah told yo' before dat you got de keys tuh de kingdom. You can depend on dat."

"Still and all you went off and left me all day and all night."

"'Twasn't 'cause Ah wanted tuh stay off lak dat, and it sho Lawd, wuzn't no woman. If you didn't have de power tuh hold me and hold me tight, Ah wouldn't be callin' yuh Mis' Woods. Ah met plenty women before Ah knowed you tuh talk tuh. You'se de onliest woman in de world Ah ever even mentioned gittin' married tuh. You bein' older don't make no difference. Don't never consider dat no mo'. If Ah ever gits tuh messin' round another woman it won't be on account of her age. It'll be because she got me in de same way you got me—so Ah can't help mahself."

He sat down on the floor beside her and kissed and playfully turned up the corner of her mouth until she smiled.

"Looka here, folks," he announced to an imaginary audience, "Sister Woods is 'bout tuh quit her husband!"

Janie laughed at that and let herself lean on him. Then she announced to the same audience, "Mis' Woods got herself uh new lil boy rooster, but he been off somewhere and won't tell her."

"First thing, though, us got tuh eat together, Janie. Then we can talk."

"One thing, Ah won't send you out after no fish."

He pinched her in the side and ignored what she said.

"'Tain't no need of neither one of us workin' dis mornin'. Call Mis' Samuels and let her fix whatever you want."

"Tea Cake, if you don't hurry up and tell me, Ah'll take and beat yo' head flat as uh dime."

Tea Cake stuck out till he had some breakfast, then he talked and acted out the story.

He spied the money while he was tying his tie. He took it up and looked at it out of curiosity and put it in his pocket to count it while he was out to find some fish to fry. When he found out how much it was, he was excited and felt like letting folks know who he was. Before he found the fish market he met a fellow he used to work with at the round house. One word brought on another one and pretty soon he made up his mind to spend some of it. He never had had his hand on so much money before in his life, so he made up his mind to see how it felt to be a millionaire. They went on out to Callahan round the railroad shops and he decided to give a big chicken and macaroni supper that night, free to all.

He bought up the stuff and they found somebody to pick the guitar so they could all dance some. So they sent the message all around for people to come. And come they did. A big table loaded down with fried chicken and biscuits and a washtub full of macaroni with plenty cheese in it. When the fellow began to pick the box the people begin to come from east, west, north and Australia. And he stood in the door and paid all the ugly women two dollars *not* to come in. One big meriny colored woman was so ugly till it was worth five dollars for her not to come in, so he gave it to her.

They had a big time till one man come in who thought he was bad. He tried to pull and haul over all the chickens and pick out the livers and gizzards to eat. Nobody else couldn't pacify him so they called Tea Cake to come see if he could stop him. So Tea Cake walked up and asked him, "Say, whut's de matter wid you, nohow?"

"Ah don't want nobody handin' me nothin'. Specially don't issue me out no rations. Ah always chooses mah rations." He kept right on plowing through the pile uh chicken. So Tea Cake got mad.

"You got mo' nerve than uh brass monkey. Tell me, what post office did *you* ever pee in? Ah craves tuh know."

"Whut you mean by dat now?" the fellow asked.

"Ah means dis—it takes jus' as much nerve tuh cut caper

lak dat in uh United States Government Post Office as it do tuh comes pullin' and haulin' over any chicken Ah pay for. Hit de ground. Damned if Ah ain't gointuh try you dis night."

So they all went outside to see if Tea Cake could handle the boogerboo. Tea Cake knocked out two of his teeth, so that man went on off from there. Then two men tried to pick a fight with one another, so Tea Cake said they had to kiss and make up. They didn't want to do it. They'd rather go to jail, but everybody else liked the idea, so they made 'em do it. Afterwards, both of them spit and gagged and wiped their mouths with the back of their hands. One went outside and chewed a little grass like a sick dog, he said to keep it from killing him.

Then everybody began to holler at the music because the man couldn't play but three pieces. So Tea Cake took the guitar and played himself. He was glad of the chance because he hadn't had his hand on a box since he put his in the pawn shop to get some money to hire a car for Janie soon after he met her. He missed his music. So that put him in the notion he ought to have one. He bought the guitar on the spot and paid fifteen dollars cash. It was really worth sixty-five any day.

Just before day the party wore out. So Tea Cake hurried on back to his new wife. He had done found out how rich people feel and he had a fine guitar and twelve dollars left in his pocket and all he needed now was a great big old hug and kiss from Janie.

"You musta thought yo' wife was powerful ugly. Dem ugly women dat you paid two dollars not to come in, could git tuh de door. You never even 'lowed me tuh git dat close." She pouted.

"Janie, Ah would have give Jacksonville wid Tampa for a jump-back for you to be dere wid me. Ah started to come git yuh two three times."

"Well, how come yuh didn't come git me?"

"Janie, would you have come if Ah did?"

"Sho Ah would. Ah laks fun just as good as you do."

"Janie, Ah wanted tuh, mighty much, but Ah was skeered. Too skeered Ah might lose yuh."

"Why?"

"Dem wuzn't no high muckty mucks. Dem wuz railroad hands and dey womenfolks. You ain't usetuh folks lak dat and Ah wuz skeered you might git all mad and quit me for takin' you 'mongst 'em. But Ah wanted yuh wid me jus' de same. Befo' us got married Ah made up mah mind not tuh let you see no commonness in me. When Ah git mad habits on, Ah'd go off and keep it out yo' sight. 'Tain't mah notion tuh drag *you* down wid me."

"Looka heah, Tea Cake, if you ever go off from me and have a good time lak dat and then come back heah tellin' me how nice Ah is, Ah specks tuh kill yuh dead. You heah me?"

"So you aims tuh partake wid everything, hunh?"

"Yeah, Tea Cake, don't keer what it is."

"Dat's all Ah wants tuh know. From now on you'se mah wife and mah woman and everything else in de world Ah needs."

"Ah hope so."

"And honey, don't you worry 'bout yo' lil ole two hundred dollars. It's big pay day dis comin' Saturday at de railroad yards. Ah'm gointuh take dis twelve dollars in mah pocket and win it all back and mo'."

"How?"

"Honey, since you loose me and gimme privilege tuh tell yuh all about mahself, Ah'll tell yuh. You done married one uh de best gamblers God ever made. Cards or dice either one. Ah can take uh shoe string and win uh tan-yard. Wish yuh could see me rollin'. But dis time it's gointuh be nothin' but tough men's talkin' all kinds uh talk so it ain't no place for you tuh be, but 'twon't be long befo' you see me."

All the rest of the week Tea Cake was busy practising up on his dice. He would flip them on the bare floor, on the rug and on the bed. He'd squat and throw, sit in a chair and throw and stand and throw. It was very exciting to Janie who had never touched dice in her life. Then he'd take his deck of cards and shuffle and cut, shuffle and cut and deal out then examine each hand carefully, and do it again. So Saturday came. He went out and bought a new switch-blade knife and two decks of star-back playing cards that morning and left Janie around noon.

"They'll start to paying off, pretty soon now. Ah wants tuh

git in de game whilst de big money is in it. Ah ain't fuh no spuddin' tuhday. Ah'll come home wid de money or Ah'll come back on uh stretcher." He cut nine hairs out of the mole of her head for luck and went off happy.

Janie waited till midnight without worrying, but after that she began to be afraid. So she got up and sat around scared and miserable. Thinking and fearing all sorts of dangers. Wondering at herself as she had many times this week that she was not shocked at Tea Cake's gambling. It was part of him, so it was all right. She rather found herself angry at imaginary people who might try to criticize. Let the old hypocrites learn to mind their own business, and leave other folks alone. Tea Cake wasn't doing a bit more harm trying to win hisself a little money than they was always doing with their lying tongues. Tea Cake had more good nature under his toe-nails than they had in their so-called Christian hearts. She better not hear none of them old backbiters talking about *her* husband! Please, Jesus, don't let them nasty niggers hurt her boy. If they do, Master Jesus, grant her a good gun and a chance to shoot 'em. Tea Cake had a knife it was true, but that was only to protect hisself. God knows, Tea Cake wouldn't harm a fly.

Daylight was creeping around the cracks of the world when Janie heard a feeble rap on the door. She sprung to the door and flung it wide. Tea Cake was out there looking like he was asleep standing up. In some strange way it was frightening. Janie caught his arm to arouse him and he stumbled into the room and fell.

"Tea Cake! You chile! What's de matter, honey?"

"Dey cut me, dat's all. Don't cry. Git me out dis coat quick as yuh can."

He told her he wasn't cut but twice but she had to have him naked so she could look him all over and fix him up to a certain extent. He told her not to call a doctor unless he got much worse. It was mostly loss of blood anyhow.

"Ah won the money jus' lak ah told yuh. Round midnight Ah had yo' two hundred dollars and wuz ready tuh quit even though it wuz uh heap mo' money in de game. But dey wanted uh chance tuh win it back so Ah set back down tuh play some mo'. Ah knowed ole Double-Ugly wuz 'bout

broke and wanted tuh fight 'bout it, so Ah set down tuh give 'im his chance tuh git back his money and then to give 'im uh quick trip tuh hell if he tried tuh pull dat razor Ah glimpsed in his pocket. Honey, no up-to-date man don't fool wid no razor. De man wid his switch-blade will be done cut yuh tuh death while you foolin' wid uh razor. But Double-Ugly brags he's too fast wid it tuh git hurt, but Ah knowed better.

"So round four o'clock Ah had done cleaned 'em out complete—all except two men dat got up and left while dey had money for groceries, and one man dat wuz lucky. Then Ah rose tuh bid 'em good bye agin. None of 'em didn't lak it, but dey all realized it wuz fair. Ah had done give 'em a fair chance. All but Double-Ugly. He claimed Ah switched de dice. Ah shoved de money down deep in mah pocket and picked up mah hat and coat wid mah left hand and kept mah right hand on mah knife. Ah didn't keer what he *said* long as he didn't try tuh *do* nothin'. Ah got mah hat on and one arm in mah coat as Ah got to de door. Right dere he jumped at me as Ah turned to see de doorstep outside and cut me twice in de back.

"Baby, Ah run mah other arm in mah coat-sleeve and grabbed dat nigger by his necktie befo' he could bat his eye and then Ah wuz all over 'im jus' lak gravy over rice. He lost his razor tryin' tuh git loose from me. He wuz hollerin' for me tuh turn him loose, but baby, Ah turnt him every way *but* loose. Ah left him on the doorstep and got here to yuh de quickest way Ah could. Ah know Ah ain't cut too deep 'cause he was too skeered tuh run up on me close enough. Sorta pull de flesh together with stickin' plaster. Ah'll be all right in uh day or so."

Janie was painting on iodine and crying.

"You ain't de one to be cryin', Janie. It's his ole lady oughta do dat. You done gimme luck. Look in mah left hand pants pocket and see whut yo' daddy brought yuh. When Ah tell yuh Ah'm gointuh bring it, Ah don't lie."

They counted it together—three hundred and twenty-two dollars. It was almost like Tea Cake had held up the Paymaster. He made her take the two hundred and put it back in the secret place. Then Janie told him about the other money she had in the bank.

"Put dat two hundred back wid de rest, Janie. Mah dice. Ah no need no assistance tuh help me feed mah woman. From now on, you gointuh eat whutever mah money can buy yuh and wear de same. When Ah ain't got nothin' you don't git nothin'."

"Dat's all right wid me."

He was getting drowsy, but he pinched her leg playfully because he was glad she took things the way he wanted her to. "Listen, mama, soon as Ah git over dis lil cuttin' scrape, we gointuh do somethin' crazy."

"Whut's dat?"

"We goin' on de muck."

"Whut's de muck, and where is it at?"

"Oh down in de Everglades round Clewiston and Belle Glade where dey raise all dat cane and string-beans and tomatuhs. Folks don't do nothin' down dere but make money and fun and foolishness. We must go dere."

He drifted off into sleep and Janie looked down on him and felt a self-crushing love. So her soul crawled out from its hiding place.

XIV

To Janie's strange eyes, everything in the Everglades was big and new. Big Lake Okechobee, big beans, big cane, big weeds, big everything. Weeds that did well to grow waist high up the state were eight and often ten feet tall down there. Ground so rich that everything went wild. Volunteer cane just taking the place. Dirt roads so rich and black that a half mile of it would have fertilized a Kansas wheat field. Wild cane on either side of the road hiding the rest of the world. People wild too.

"Season don't open up till last of September, but we had tuh git heah ahead uh time tuh git us uh room," Tea Cake explained. "Two weeks from now, it'll be so many folks heah dey won't be lookin' fuh rooms, dey'll be jus' looking fuh somewhere tuh sleep. Now we got uh chance tuh git uh room at de hotel, where dey got uh bath tub. Yuh can't live on de muck 'thout yuh take uh bath every day. Do dat muck'll itch yuh lak ants. 'Tain't but one place round heah wid uh bath tub. 'Tain't nowhere near enough rooms."

"Whut we gointuh do round heah?"

"All day Ah'm pickin' beans. All night Ah'm pickin' mah box and rollin' dice. Between de beans and de dice Ah can't lose. Ah'm gone right now tuh pick me uh job uh work wid de best man on de muck. Before de rest of 'em gits heah. You can always git jobs round heah in de season, but not wid de right folks."

"When do de job open up, Tea Cake? Everybody round here look lak dey waitin' too."

"Dat's right. De big men haves uh certain time tuh open de season jus' lak in everything else. Mah bossman didn't get sufficient seed. He's out huntin' up uh few mo' bushels. Den we'se gointuh plantin'."

"Bushels?"

"Yeah, bushels. Dis ain't no game fuh pennies. Po' man ain't got no business at de show."

The very next day he burst into the room in high excitement. "Boss done bought out another man and want me

down on de lake. He got houses fuh de first ones dat git dere. Less go!"

They rattled nine miles in a borrowed car to the quarters that squatted so close that only the dyke separated them from great, sprawling Okechobee. Janie fussed around the shack making a home while Tea Cake planted beans. After hours they fished. Every now and then they'd run across a party of Indians in their long, narrow dug-outs calmly winning their living in the trackless ways of the 'Glades. Finally the beans were in. Nothing much to do but wait to pick them. Tea Cake picked his box a great deal for Janie, but he still didn't have enough to do. No need of gambling yet. The people who were pouring in were broke. They didn't come bringing money, they were coming to make some.

"Tell yuh whut, Janie, less buy us some shootin' tools and go huntin' round heah."

"Dat would be fine, Tea Cake, exceptin' you know Ah can't shoot. But Ah'd love tuh go wid *you*."

"Oh, you needs tuh learn how. 'Tain't no need uh you not knowin' how tuh handle shootin' tools. Even if you didn't never find no game, it's always some trashy rascal dat needs uh good killin'," he laughed. "Less go intuh Palm Beach and spend some of our money."

Every day they were practising. Tea Cake made her shoot at little things just to give her good aim. Pistol and shot gun and rifle. It got so the others stood around and watched them. Some of the men would beg for a shot at the target themselves. It was the most exciting thing on the muck. Better than the jook and the pool-room unless some special band was playing for a dance. And the thing that got everybody was the way Janie caught on. She got to the place she could shoot a hawk out of a pine tree and not tear him up. Shoot his head off. She got to be a better shot than Tea Cake. They'd go out any late afternoon and come back loaded down with game. One night they got a boat and went out hunting alligators. Shining their phosphorescent eyes and shooting them in the dark. They could sell the hides and teeth in Palm Beach besides having fun together till work got pressing.

Day by day now, the hordes of workers poured in. Some

came limping in with their shoes and sore feet from walking. It's hard trying to follow your shoe instead of your shoe following you. They came in wagons from way up in Georgia and they came in truck loads from east, west, north and south. Permanent transients with no attachments and tired looking men with their families and dogs in flivvers. All night, all day, hurrying in to pick beans. Skillets, beds, patched up spare inner tubes all hanging and dangling from the ancient cars on the outside and hopeful humanity, herded and hovered on the inside, chugging on to the muck. People ugly from ignorance and broken from being poor.

All night now the jooks clanged and clamored. Pianos living three lifetimes in one. Blues made and used right on the spot. Dancing, fighting, singing, crying, laughing, winning and losing love every hour. Work all day for money, fight all night for love. The rich black earth clinging to bodies and biting the skin like ants.

Finally no more sleeping places. Men made big fires and fifty or sixty men slept around each fire. But they had to pay the man whose land they slept on. He ran the fire just like his boarding place—for pay. But nobody cared. They made good money, even to the children. So they spent good money. Next month and next year were other times. No need to mix them up with the present.

Tea Cake's house was a magnet, the unauthorized center of the "job." The way he would sit in the doorway and play his guitar made people stop and listen and maybe disappoint the jook for that night. He was always laughing and full of fun too. He kept everybody laughing in the bean field.

Janie stayed home and boiled big pots of black-eyed peas and rice. Sometimes baked big pans of navy beans with plenty of sugar and hunks of bacon laying on top. That was something Tea Cake loved so no matter if Janie had fixed beans two or three times during the week, they had baked beans again on Sunday. She always had some kind of dessert too, as Tea Cake said it give a man something to taper off on. Sometimes she'd straighten out the two-room house and take the rifle and have fried rabbit for supper when Tea Cake got home. She didn't leave him itching and scratching in his work clothes, either. The kettle of hot water was already waiting when he got in.

Then Tea Cake took to popping in at the kitchen door at odd hours. Between breakfast and dinner, sometimes. Then often around two o'clock he'd come home and tease and wrestle with her for a half hour and slip on back to work. So one day she asked him about it.

"Tea Cake, whut you doin' back in de quarters when everybody else is still workin'?"

"Come tuh see 'bout you. De boogerman liable tuh tote yuh off whilst Ah'm gone."

"'Tain't no boogerman got me tuh study 'bout. Maybe you think Ah ain't treatin' yuh right and you watchin' me."

"Naw, naw, Janie. Ah *know* better'n dat. But since you got dat in yo' head, Ah'll have tuh tell yuh de real truth, so yuh can know. Janie, Ah gits lonesome out dere all day 'thout yuh. After dis, you betta come git uh job uh work out dere lak de rest uh de women—so Ah won't be losin' time comin' home."

"Tea Cake, you'se uh mess! Can't do 'thout me dat lil time."

"'Tain't no lil time. It's near 'bout all day."

So the very next morning Janie got ready to pick beans along with Tea Cake. There was a suppressed murmur when she picked up a basket and went to work. She was already getting to be a special case on the muck. It was generally assumed that she thought herself too good to work like the rest of the women and that Tea Cake "pomped her up tuh dat." But all day long the romping and playing they carried on behind the boss's back made her popular right away. It got the whole field to playing off and on. Then Tea Cake would help get supper afterwards.

"You don't think Ah'm tryin' tuh git outa takin' keer uh yuh, do yuh, Janie, 'cause Ah ast yuh tuh work long side uh me?" Tea Cake asked her at the end of her first week in the field.

"Ah naw, honey. Ah laks it. It's mo' nicer than settin' round dese quarters all day. Clerkin' in dat store wuz hard, but heah, we ain't got nothin' tuh do but do our work and come home and love."

The house was full of people every night. That is, all around the doorstep was full. Some were there to hear Tea

Cake pick the box; some came to talk and tell stories, but most of them came to get into whatever game was going on or might go on. Sometimes Tea Cake lost heavily, for there were several good gamblers on the lake. Sometimes he won and made Janie proud of his skill. But outside of the two jooks, everything on that job went on around those two.

Sometimes Janie would think of the old days in the big white house and the store and laugh to herself. What if Eatonville could see her now in her blue denim overalls and heavy shoes? The crowd of people around her and a dice game on her floor! She was sorry for her friends back there and scornful of the others. The men held big arguments here like they used to do on the store porch. Only here, she could listen and laugh and even talk some herself if she wanted to. She got so she could tell big stories herself from listening to the rest. Because she loved to hear it, and the men loved to hear themselves, they would "woof" and "boogerboo" around the games to the limit. No matter how rough it was, people seldom got mad, because everything was done for a laugh. Everybody loved to hear Ed Dockery, Bootyny, and Sop-de-Bottom in a skin game. Ed Dockery was dealing one night and he looked over at Sop-de-Bottom's card and he could tell Sop thought he was going to win. He hollered, "Ah'll break up *dat* settin' uh eggs." Sop looked and said, "Root de peg." Bootyny asked, "What are you goin' tuh do? Do do!" Everybody was watching that next card fall. Ed got ready to turn. "Ah'm gointuh sweep out hell and burn up de broom." He slammed down another dollar. "Don't oversport yourself, Ed," Bootyny challenged. "You gittin' too yaller." Ed caught hold of the corner of the card. Sop dropped a dollar. "Ah'm gointuh shoot in de hearse, don't keer how sad de funeral be." Ed said, "You see how this man is teasin' hell?" Tea Cake nudged Sop not to bet. "You gointuh git caught in uh bullet storm if you don't watch out." Sop said, "Aw 'tain't nothin' tuh dat bear but his curly hair. Ah can look through muddy water and see dry land." Ed turned off the card and hollered, "Zachariah, Ah says come down out dat sycamore tree. You can't do no business." Nobody fell on that card. Everybody was scared of the next one. Ed looked around and saw Gabe standing behind his chair and hollered,

"Move, from over me, Gabe! You too black. You draw heat! Sop, you wanta pick up dat bet whilst you got uh chance?" "Naw, man, Ah wish Ah had uh thousand-leg tuh put on it." "So yuh won't lissen, huh? Dumb niggers and free schools. Ah'm gointuh take and teach yuh. Ah'll main-line but Ah won't side-track." Ed flipped the next card and Sop fell and lost. Everybody hollered and laughed. Ed laughed and said, "Git off de muck! You ain't nothin'. Dat's all! Hot boilin' water won't help yuh none." Ed kept on laughing because he had been so scared before. "Sop, Bootyny, all y'all dat lemme win yo' money: Ah'm sending it straight off to Sears and Roe-buck and buy me some clothes, and when Ah turn out Christ-mas day, it would take a doctor to tell me how near Ah is dressed tuh death."

XV

JANIE learned what it felt like to be jealous. A little chunky
girl took to picking a play out of Tea Cake in the fields and
in the quarters. If he said anything at all, she'd take the oppo-
site side and hit him or shove him and run away to make him
chase her. Janie knew what she was up to—luring him away
from the crowd. It kept up for two or three weeks with
Nunkie getting bolder all the time. She'd hit Tea Cake play-
fully and the minute he so much as tapped her with his finger
she'd fall against him or fall on the ground and have to be
picked up. She'd be almost helpless. It took a good deal of
handling to set her on her feet again. And another thing, Tea
Cake didn't seem to be able to fend her off as promptly as
Janie thought he ought to. She began to be snappish a little.
A little seed of fear was growing into a tree. Maybe some day
Tea Cake would weaken. Maybe he had already given secret
encouragement and this was Nunkie's way of bragging about
it. Other people began to notice too, and that put Janie more
on a wonder.

One day they were working near where the beans ended
and the sugar cane began. Janie had marched off a little from
Tea Cake's side with another woman for a chat. When she
glanced around Tea Cake was gone. Nunkie too. She knew
because she looked.

"Where's Tea Cake?" she asked Sop-de-Bottom.

He waved his hand towards the cane field and hurried
away. Janie never thought at all. She just acted on feelings.
She rushed into the cane and about the fifth row down she
found Tea Cake and Nunkie struggling. She was on them be-
fore either knew.

"Whut's de matter heah?" Janie asked in a cold rage. They
sprang apart.

"Nothin'," Tea Cake told her, standing shame-faced.

"Well, whut you doin' in heah? How come you ain't out
dere wid de rest?"

"She grabbed mah workin' tickets outa mah shirt pocket

286

and Ah run tuh git 'em back," Tea Cake explained, showing the tickets, considerably mauled about in the struggle.

Janie made a move to seize Nunkie but the girl fled. So she took out behind her over the humped-up cane rows. But Nunkie did not mean to be caught. So Janie went on home. The sight of the fields and the other happy people was too much for her that day. She walked slowly and thoughtfully to the quarters. It wasn't long before Tea Cake found her there and tried to talk. She cut him short with a blow and they fought from one room to the other, Janie trying to beat him, and Tea Cake kept holding her wrists and wherever he could to keep her from going too far.

"Ah b'lieve you been messin' round her!" she panted furiously.

"No sich uh thing!" Tea Cake retorted.

"Ah b'lieve yuh did."

"Don't keer how big uh lie get told, somebody kin b'lieve it!"

They fought on. "You done hurt mah heart, now you come wid uh lie tuh bruise mah ears! Turn go mah hands!" Janie seethed. But Tea Cake never let go. They wrestled on until they were doped with their own fumes and emanations; till their clothes had been torn away; till he hurled her to the floor and held her there melting her resistance with the heat of his body, doing things with their bodies to express the inexpressible; kissed her until she arched her body to meet him and they fell asleep in sweet exhaustion.

The next morning Janie asked like a woman, "You still love ole Nunkie?"

"Naw, never did, and you know it too. Ah didn't want her."

"Yeah, you did." She didn't say this because she believed it. She wanted to hear his denial. She had to crow over the fallen Nunkie.

"Whut would Ah do wid dat lil chunk of a woman wid you around? She ain't good for nothin' exceptin' tuh set up in uh corner by de kitchen stove and break wood over her head. You'se something tuh make uh man forgit tuh git old and forgit tuh die."

XVI

THE SEASON closed and people went away like they had come—in droves. Tea Cake and Janie decided to stay since they wanted to make another season on the muck. There was nothing to do, after they had gathered several bushels of dried beans to save over and sell to the planters in the fall. So Janie began to look around and see people and things she hadn't noticed during the season.

For instance during the summer when she heard the subtle but compelling rhythms of the Bahaman drummers, she'd walk over and watch the dances. She did not laugh the "Saws" to scorn as she had heard the people doing in the season. She got to like it a lot and she and Tea Cake were on hand every night till the others teased them about it.

Janie came to know Mrs. Turner now. She had seen her several times during the season, but neither ever spoke. Now they got to be visiting friends.

Mrs. Turner was a milky sort of a woman that belonged to child-bed. Her shoulders rounded a little, and she must have been conscious of her pelvis because she kept it stuck out in front of her so she could always see it. Tea Cake made a lot of fun about Mrs. Turner's shape behind her back. He claimed that she had been shaped up by a cow kicking her from behind. She was an ironing board with things throwed at it. Then that same cow took and stepped in her mouth when she was a baby and left it wide and flat with her chin and nose almost meeting.

But Mrs. Turner's shape and features were entirely approved by Mrs. Turner. Her nose was slightly pointed and she was proud. Her thin lips were an ever delight to her eyes. Even her buttocks in bas-relief were a source of pride. To her way of thinking all these things set her aside from Negroes. That was why she sought out Janie to friend with. Janie's coffee-and-cream complexion and her luxurious hair made Mrs. Turner forgive her for wearing overalls like the other women who worked in the fields. She didn't forgive her for marrying a man as dark as Tea Cake, but she felt that she

288

could remedy that. That was what her brother was born for. She seldom stayed long when she found Tea Cake at home, but when she happened to drop in and catch Janie alone, she'd spend hours chatting away. Her disfavorite subject was Negroes.

"Mis' Woods, Ah have often said to mah husband, Ah don't see how uh lady like Mis' Woods can stand all them common niggers round her place all de time."

"They don't worry me atall, Mis' Turner. Fact about de thing is, they tickles me wid they talk."

"You got mo' nerve than me. When somebody talked mah husband intuh comin' down heah tuh open up uh eatin' place Ah never dreamt so many different kins uh black folks could colleck in one place. Did Ah never woulda come. Ah ain't useter 'ssociatin' wid black folks. Mah son claims dey draws lightnin'." They laughed a little and after many of these talks Mrs. Turner said, "Yo' husband musta had plenty money when y'all got married."

"Whut make you think dat, Mis' Turner?"

"Tuh git hold of uh woman lak you. You got mo' nerve than me. Ah jus' couldn't see mahself married to no black man. It's too many black folks already. We oughta lighten up de race."

"Naw, mah husband didn't had nothin' but hisself. He's easy tuh love if you mess round 'im. Ah loves 'im."

"Why you, Mis' Woods! Ah don't b'lieve it. You'se jus' sorter hypnotized dat's all."

"Naw, it's real. Ah couldn't stand it if he wuz tuh quit me. Don't know whut Ah'd do. He kin take most any lil thing and make summertime out of it when times is dull. Then we lives offa dat happiness he made till some mo' happiness come along."

"You'se different from me. Ah can't stand black niggers. Ah don't blame de white folks from hatin' 'em 'cause Ah can't stand 'em mahself. 'Nother thing, Ah hates tuh see folks lak me and you mixed up wid 'em. Us oughta class off."

"Us can't *do* it. We'se uh mingled people and all of us got black kinfolks as well as yaller kinfolks. How come you so against black?"

"And dey makes me tired. Always laughin'! Dey laughs too

much and dey laughs too loud. Always singin' ol' nigger songs! Always cuttin' de monkey for white folks. If it wuzn't for so many black folks it wouldn't be no race problem. De white folks would take us in wid dem. De black ones is holdin' us back."

"You reckon? 'course Ah ain't never thought about it too much. But Ah don't figger dey even gointuh want us for comp'ny. We'se too poor."

"'Tain't de poorness, it's de color and de features. Who want any lil ole black baby layin' up in de baby buggy lookin' lak uh fly in buttermilk? Who wants to be mixed up wid uh rusty black man, and uh black woman goin' down de street in all dem loud colors, and whoopin' and hollerin' and laughin' over nothin'? Ah don't know. Don't bring me no nigger doctor tuh hang over mah sick-bed. Ah done had six chillun—wuzn't lucky enough tuh raise but dat one—and ain't never had uh nigger tuh even feel mah pulse. White doctors always gits mah money. Ah don't go in no nigger store tuh buy nothin' neither. Colored folks don't know nothin' 'bout no business. Deliver me!"

Mrs. Turner was almost screaming in fanatical earnestness by now. Janie was dumb and bewildered before and she clucked sympathetically and wished she knew what to say. It was so evident that Mrs. Turner took black folk as a personal affront to herself.

"Look at me! Ah ain't go no flat nose and liver lips. Ah'm uh featured woman. Ah got white folks' features in mah face. Still and all Ah got tuh be lumped in wid all de rest. It ain't fair. Even if dey don't take us in wid de whites, dey oughta make us uh class tuh ourselves."

"It don't worry me atall, but Ah reckon Ah ain't got no real head fur thinkin'."

"You oughta meet mah brother. He's real smart. Got dead straight hair. Dey made him uh delegate tuh de Sunday School Convention and he read uh paper on Booker T. Washington and tore him tuh pieces!"

"Booker T.? He wuz a great big man, wusn't he?"

"'Sposed tuh be. All he ever done was cut de monkey for white folks. So dey pomped him up. But you know whut de

ole folks say 'de higher de monkey climbs de mo' he show his behind' so dat's de way it wuz wid Booker T. Mah brother hit 'im every time dey give 'im chance tuh speak."

"Ah was raised on de notion dat he wuz uh great big man," was all that Janie knew to say.

"He didn't do nothin' but hold us back—talkin' 'bout work when de race ain't never done nothin' else. He wuz uh enemy tuh us, dat's whut. He wuz uh white folks' nigger."

According to all Janie had been taught this was sacrilege so she sat without speaking at all. But Mrs. Turner went on.

"Ah done sent fuh mah brother tuh come down and spend uh while wid us. He's sorter outa work now. Ah wants yuh tuh meet him mo' special. You and him would make up uh swell couple if you wuzn't already married. He's uh fine carpenter, when he kin git anything tuh do."

"Yeah, maybe so. But Ah *is* married now, so 'tain't no use in considerin'."

Mrs. Turner finally rose to go after being very firm about several other view-points of either herself, her son or her brother. She begged Janie to drop in on her anytime, but never once mentioning Tea Cake. Finally she was gone and Janie hurried to her kitchen to put on supper and found Tea Cake sitting in there with his head between his hands.

"Tea Cake! Ah didn't know you wuz home."

"Ah know yuh didn't. Ah been heah uh long time listenin' to dat heifer run me down tuh de dawgs uh try tuh tole you off from me."

"So dat whut she wuz up to? Ah didn't know."

"'Course she is. She got some no-count brother she wants yuh tuh hook up wid and take keer of Ah reckon."

"Shucks! If dat's her notion she's barkin' up de wrong tree. Mah hands is full already."

"Thanky Ma'am. Ah hates dat woman lak poison. Keep her from round dis house. Her look lak uh white woman! Wid dat meriny skin and hair jus' as close tuh her head as ninety-nine is tuh uh hundred! Since she hate black folks so, she don't need our money in her ol' eatin' place. Ah'll pass de word along. We kin go tuh dat white man's place and git good treatment. Her and dat whittled-down husband uh

hers! And dat son! He's jus' uh dirty trick her womb played on her. Ah'm telling her husband tuh keep her home. Ah don't want her round dis house."

One day Tea Cake met Turner and his son on the street. He was a vanishing-looking kind of a man as if there used to be parts about him that stuck out individually but now he hadn't a thing about him that wasn't dwindled and blurred. Just like he had been sand-papered down to a long oval mass. Tea Cake felt sorry for him without knowing why. So he didn't blurt out the insults he had intended. But he couldn't hold in everything. They talked about the prospects for the coming season for a moment, then Tea Cake said, "Yo' wife don't seem tuh have nothin' much tuh do, so she kin visit uh lot. Mine got too much tuh do tuh go visitin' and too much tuh spend time talkin' tuh folks dat visit her."

"Mah wife takes time fuh whatever she wants tuh do. Real strong headed dat way. Yes indeed." He laughed a high lung-less laugh. "De chillun don't keep her in no mo' so she visits when she chooses."

"De chillun?" Tea Cake asked him in surprise. "You got any smaller than him?" He indicated the son who seemed around twenty or so. "Ah ain't seen yo' others."

"Ah reckon you ain't 'cause dey all passed on befo' dis one wuz born. We ain't had no luck atall wid our chillun. We lucky to raise him. He's de last stroke of exhausted nature."

He gave his powerless laugh again and Tea Cake and the boy joined in with him. Then Tea Cake walked on off and went home to Janie.

"Her husband can't do nothin' wid dat butt-headed woman. All you can do is treat her cold whenever she come round here."

Janie tried that, but short of telling Mrs. Turner bluntly, there was nothing she could do to discourage her completely. She felt honored by Janie's acquaintance and she quickly forgave and forgot snubs in order to keep it. Anyone who looked more white folkish than herself was better than she was in her criteria, therefore it was right that they should be cruel to her at times, just as she was cruel to those more negroid than herself in direct ratio to their negroness. Like the pecking-order in a chicken yard. Insensate cruelty to those you can whip, and

grovelling submission to those you can't. Once having set up her idols and built altars to them it was inevitable that she would worship there. It was inevitable that she should accept any inconsistency and cruelty from her deity as all good worshippers do from theirs. All gods who receive homage are cruel. All gods dispense suffering without reason. Otherwise they would not be worshipped. Through indiscriminate suffering men know fear and fear is the most divine emotion. It is the stones for altars and the beginning of wisdom. Half gods are worshipped in wine and flowers. Real gods require blood.

Mrs. Turner, like all other believers had built an altar to the unattainable—Caucasian characteristics for all. Her god would smite her, would hurl her from pinnacles and lose her in deserts. But she would not forsake his altars. Behind her crude words was a belief that somehow she and others through worship could attain her paradise—a heaven of straight-haired, thin-lipped, high-nose boned white seraphs. The physical impossibilities in no way injured faith. That was the mystery and mysteries are the chores of gods. Beyond her faith was a fanaticism to defend the altars of her god. It was distressing to emerge from her inner temple and find these black desecrators howling with laughter before the door. Oh, for an army, terrible with banners *and swords!*

So she didn't cling to Janie Woods the woman. She paid homage to Janie's Caucasian characteristics as such. And when she was with Janie she had a feeling of transmutation, as if she herself had become whiter and with straighter hair and she hated Tea Cake first for his defilement of divinity and next for his telling mockery of her. If she only knew something she could do about it! But she didn't. Once she was complaining about the carryings-on at the jook and Tea Cake snapped, "Aw, don't make God look so foolish—findin' fault wid everything He made."

So Mrs. Turner frowned most of the time. She had so much to disapprove of. It didn't affect Tea Cake and Janie too much. It just gave them something to talk about in the summertime when everything was dull on the muck. Otherwise they made little trips to Palm Beach, Fort Myers and Fort Lauderdale for their fun. Before they realized it the sun was cooler and the crowds came pouring onto the muck again.

XVII

A GREAT DEAL of the old crowd were back. But there were
lots of new ones too. Some of these men made passes at
Janie, and women who didn't know took out after Tea Cake.
Didn't take them long to be put right, however. Still and all,
jealousies arose now and then on both sides. When Mrs.
Turner's brother came and she brought him over to be intro-
duced, Tea Cake had a brainstorm. Before the week was over
he had whipped Janie. Not because her behavior justified his
jealousy, but it relieved that awful fear inside him. Being able
to whip her reassured him in possession. No brutal beating at
all. He just slapped her around a bit to show he was boss.
Everybody talked about it next day in the fields. It aroused a
sort of envy in both men and women. The way he petted and
pampered her as if those two or three face slaps had nearly
killed her made the women see visions and the helpless way
she hung on him made men dream dreams.

"Tea Cake, you sho is a lucky man," Sop-de-Bottom told
him. "Uh person can see every place you hit her. Ah bet she
never raised her hand tuh hit yuh back, neither. Take some uh
dese ol' rusty black women and dey would fight yuh all night
long and next day nobody couldn't tell you ever hit 'em.
Dat's de reason Ah done quit beatin' mah woman. You can't
make no mark on 'em at all. Lawd! wouldn't Ah love tuh
whip uh tender woman lak Janie! Ah bet she don't even
holler. She jus' cries, eh Tea Cake?"

"Dat's right."

"See dat! Mah woman would spread her lungs all over Palm
Beach County, let alone knock out mah jaw teeth. You don't
know dat woman uh mine. She got ninety-nine rows uh jaw
teeth and git her good and mad, she'll wade through solid
rock up to her hip pockets."

"Mah Janie is uh high time woman and useter things. Ah
didn't git her outa de middle uh de road. Ah got her outa uh
big fine house. Right now she got money enough in de bank
tuh buy up dese ziggaboos and give 'em away."

"Hush yo' mouf! And she down heah on de muck lak any-body else!"

"Janie is wherever *Ah* wants tuh be. Dat's de kind uh wife she is and Ah love her for it. Ah wouldn't be knockin' her around. Ah didn't wants whup her last night, but ol' Mis' Turner done sent for her brother tuh come tuh bait Janie in and take her way from me. Ah didn't whup Janie 'cause *she* done nothin'. Ah beat her tuh show dem Turners who is boss. Ah set in de kitchen one day and heard dat woman tell mah wife Ah'm too black fuh her. She don't see how Janie can stand me."

"Tell her husband on her."

"Shucks! Ah b'lieve he's skeered of her."

"Knock her teeth down her throat."

"Dat would look like she had some influence when she ain't. Ah jus' let her see dat Ah got control."

"So she live offa our money and don't lak black folks, huh? O.K. we'll have her gone from here befo' two weeks is up. Ah'm goin' right off tuh all de men and drop rocks against her."

"Ah ain't mad wid her for whut she done, 'cause she ain't done me nothin' yet. Ah'm mad at her for thinkin'. Her and her gang got tuh go."

"Us is wid yuh, Tea Cake. You know dat already. Dat Turner woman is real smart, accordin' tuh her notions. Reckon she done heard 'bout dat money yo' wife got in de bank and she's bound tuh rope her in tuh her family one way or another."

"Sop, Ah don't think it's half de money as it is de looks. She's color-struck. She ain't got de kind of uh mind you meet every day. She ain't a fact and neither do she make a good story when you tell about her."

"Ah yeah, she's too smart tuh stay round heah. She figgers we'se jus' uh bunch uh dumb niggers so she think she'll grow horns. But dat's uh lie. She'll die butt-headed."

Saturday afternoon when the work tickets were turned into cash everybody began to buy coon-dick and get drunk. By dusk dark Belle Glade was full of loud-talking, staggering men. Plenty women had gotten their knots charged too. The police chief in his speedy Ford was rushing from jook to jook

and eating house trying to keep order, but making few arrests. Not enough jail-space for all the drunks so why bother with a few? All he could do to keep down fights and get the white men out of colored town by nine o'clock. Dick Sterrett and Coodemay seemed to be the worst off. Their likker told them to go from place to place pushing and shoving and loud talking and they were doing it.

Way after awhile they arrived at Mrs. Turner's eating house and found the place full to the limit. Tea Cake, Stew Beef, Sop-de-Bottom, Bootyny, Motor Boat and all the familiar crowd was there. Coodemay straightened up as if in surprise and asked, "Say, whut y'all doin' in heah?"

"Eatin'," Stew Beef told him. "Dey got beef stew, so you *know* Ah'd be heah."

"We all laks tuh take uh rest from our women folks' cookin' once in uh while, so us all eatin' way from home tuhnight. Anyhow Mis' Turner got de best ole grub in town."

Mrs. Turner back and forth in the dining room heard Sop when he said this and beamed.

"Ah speck you two last ones tuh come in is gointuh have tuh wait for uh seat. Ah'm all full up now."

"Dat's all right," Sterrett objected. "You fry me some fish. Ah kin eat dat standin' up. Cuppa coffee on de side."

"Sling me up uh plate uh dat stew beef wid some coffee too, please ma'am. Sterrett is jus' ez drunk ez Ah is; and if he kin eat standin' up, Ah kin do de same." Coodemay leaned drunkenly against the wall and everybody laughed.

Pretty soon the girl that was waiting table for Mrs. Turner brought in the order and Sterrett took his fish and coffee in his hands and stood there. Coodemay wouldn't take his off the tray like he should have.

"Naw, you hold it fuh me, baby, and lemme eat," he told the waitress. He took the fork and started to eat off the tray.

"Nobody ain't got no time tuh hold yo' grub up in front uh yo' face," she told Coodemay. "Heah, take it yo'self."

"You'se right," Coodemay told her. "Gimme it heah. Sop kin gimme his chear."

"You'se uh lie," Sop retorted. "Ah ain't through and Ah ain't ready tuh git up."

Coodemay tried to shove Sop out of the chair and Sop

resisted. That brought on a whole lot of shoving and scrambling and coffee got spilt on Sop. So he aimed at Coodemay with a saucer and hit Bootyny. Bootyny threw his thick coffee cup at Coodemay and just missed Stew Beef. So it got to be a big fight. Mrs. Turner came running in out of the kitchen. Then Tea Cake got up and caught hold of Coodemay by the collar.

"Looka heah, y'all, don't come in heah and raise no disturbance in de place. Mis' Turner is too nice uh woman fuh dat. In fact, she's more nicer than anybody else on de muck." Mrs. Turner beamed on Tea Cake.

"Ah knows dat. All of us knows it. But Ah don't give uh damn how nice she is, Ah got tuh have some place tuh set down and eat. Sop ain't gointuh bluff me, neither. Let 'im fight lak a man. Take yo' hands off me, Tea Cake."

"Naw, Ah won't neither. You comin' on outa de place."

"Who gointuh make me come out?"

"Me, dat's who. Ah'm in heah, ain't Ah? If you don't want tuh respect nice people lak Mrs. Turner, God knows you gointuh respect me! Come on outa heah, Coodemay."

"Turn him loose, Tea Cake!" Sterrett shouted. "Dat's *mah* buddy. Us come in heah together and he ain't goin' nowhere until Ah go mahself."

"Well, both of yuh is goin'!" Tea Cake shouted and fastened down on Coodemay. Dockery grabbed Sterrett and they wrassled all over the place. Some more joined in and dishes and tables began to crash.

Mrs. Turner saw with dismay that Tea Cake's taking them out was worse than letting them stay in. She ran out in the back somewhere and got her husband to put a stop to things. He came in, took a look and squinched down into a chair in an off corner and didn't open his mouth. So Mrs. Turner struggled into the mass and caught Tea Cake by the arm.

"Dat's all right, Tea Cake, Ah 'preciate yo' help, but leave 'em alone."

"Naw suh, Mis' Turner, Ah'm gointuh show 'em dey can't come runnin' over nice people and loud-talk no place whilst Ah'm around. Dey goin' outa heah!"

By that time everybody in and around the place was taking sides. Somehow or other Mrs. Turner fell down and nobody

knew she was down there under all the fighting, and broken dishes and crippled up tables and broken-off chair legs and window panes and such things. It got so that the floor was knee-deep with something no matter where you put your foot down. But Tea Cake kept right on until Coodemay told him, "Ah'm wrong. Ah'm wrong! Y'all tried tuh tell me right and Ah wouldn't lissen. Ah ain't mad wid nobody. Just tuh show y'all Ah ain't mad, me and Sterrett gointuh buy everybody somethin' tuh drink. Ole man Vickers got some good coon-dick over round Pahokee. Come on everybody. Let's go git our knots charged." Everybody got in a good humor and left.

Mrs. Turner got up off the floor hollering for the police. Look at her place! How come nobody didn't call the police? Then she found out that one of her hands was all stepped on and her fingers were bleeding pretty peart. Two or three people who were not there during the fracas poked their heads in at the door to sympathize but that made Mrs. Turner madder. She told them where to go in a hurry. Then she saw her husband sitting over there in the corner with his long bony legs all crossed up smoking his pipe.

"What kinda man is *you*, Turner? You see dese no count niggers come in heah and break up mah place! How kin you set and see yo' wife all trompled on? You ain't no kinda man at all. You see dat Tea Cake shove me down! Yes you did! You ain't raised yo' hand tuh do nothin' about it."

Turner removed his pipe and answered: "Yeah, and you see how Ah did swell up too, didn't yuh? You tell Tea Cake he better be keerful Ah don't swell up again." At that Turner crossed his legs the other way and kept right on smoking his pipe.

Mrs. Turner hit at him the best she could with her hurt hand and then spoke her mind for half an hour.

"It's a good thing mah brother wuzn't round heah when it happened do he would uh kilt somebody. Mah son too. Dey got some manhood about 'em. We'se goin' back tuh Miami where folks is civilized."

Nobody told her right away that her son and brother were already on their way after pointed warnings outside the café. No time for fooling around. They were hurrying into Palm Beach. She'd find out about that later on.

Monday morning Coodemay and Sterrett stopped by and begged her pardon profusely and gave her five dollars apiece. Then Coodemay said, "Dey tell me Ah wuz drunk Sat'day night and clownin' down. Ah don't 'member uh thing 'bout it. But when Ah git tuh peepin' through mah likker, dey tell me Ah'm uh mess."

XVIII

SINCE Tea Cake and Janie had friended with the Bahaman workers in the 'Glades, they, the "Saws," had been gradually drawn into the American crowd. They quit hiding out to hold their dances when they found that their American friends didn't laugh at them as they feared. Many of the Americans learned to jump and liked it as much as the "Saws." So they began to hold dances night after night in the quarters, usually behind Tea Cake's house. Often now, Tea Cake and Janie stayed up so late at the fire dances that Tea Cake would not let her go with him to the field. He wanted her to get her rest.

So she was home by herself one afternoon when she saw a band of Seminoles passing by. The men walking in front and the laden, stolid women following them like burros. She had seen Indians several times in the 'Glades, in twos and threes, but this was a large party. They were headed towards the Palm Beach road and kept moving steadily. About an hour later another party appeared and went the same way. Then another just before sundown. This time she asked where they were all going and at last one of the men answered her.

"Going to high ground. Saw-grass bloom. Hurricane coming."

Everybody was talking about it that night. But nobody was worried. The fire dance kept up till nearly dawn. The next day, more Indians moved east, unhurried but steady. Still a blue sky and fair weather. Beans running fine and prices good, so the Indians could be, *must* be, wrong. You couldn't have a hurricane when you're making seven and eight dollars a day picking beans. Indians are dumb anyhow, always were. Another night of Stew Beef making dynamic subtleties with his drum and living, sculptural, grotesques in the dance. Next day, no Indians passed at all. It was hot and sultry and Janie left the field and went home.

Morning came without motion. The winds, to the tiniest, lisping baby breath had left the earth. Even before the sun gave

light, dead day was creeping from bush to bush watching man.

Some rabbits scurried through the quarters going east. Some possums slunk by and their route was definite. One or two at a time, then more. By the time the people left the fields the procession was constant. Snakes, rattlesnakes began to cross the quarters. The men killed a few, but they could not be missed from the crawling horde. People stayed indoors until day-light. Several times during the night Janie heard the snort of big animals like deer. Once the muted voice of a panther. Going east and east. That night the palm and banana trees began that long distance talk with rain. Several people took fright and picked up and went in to Palm Beach anyway. A thousand buzzards held a flying meet and then went above the clouds and stayed.

One of the Bahaman boys stopped by Tea Cake's house in a car and hollered. Tea Cake came out throwin' laughter over his shoulder into the house.

"Hello Tea Cake."

"Hello 'Lias. You leavin', Ah see."

"Yeah man. You and Janie wanta go? Ah wouldn't give nobody else uh chawnce at uh seat till Ah found out if you all had anyway tuh go."

"Thank yuh ever so much, Lias. But we 'bout decided tuh stay."

"De crow gahn up, man."

"Dat ain't nothin'. You ain't seen de bossman go up, is yuh? Well all right now. Man, de money's too good on the muck. It's liable tuh fair off by tuhmorrer. Ah wouldn't leave if Ah wuz you."

"Mah uncle come for me. He say hurricane warning out in Palm Beach. Not so bad dere, but man, dis muck is too low and dat big lake is liable tuh bust."

"Ah naw, man. Some boys in dere now talkin' 'bout it. Some of 'em been in de 'Glades fuh years. 'Tain't nothin' but uh lil blow. You'll lose de whole day tuhmorrer tryin' tuh git back out heah."

"De Indians gahn east, man. It's dangerous."

"Dey don't always know. Indians don't know much uh nothin', tuh tell de truth. Else dey'd own dis country still. De white folks ain't gone nowhere. Dey oughta know if it's dan-

gerous. You better stay heah, man. Big jumpin' dance tuh-night right heah, when it fair off."

Lias hesitated and started to climb out, but his uncle wouldn't let him. "Dis time tuhmorrer you gointuh wish you follow crow," he snorted and drove off. Lias waved back to them gaily.

"If Ah never see you no mo' on earth, Ah'll meet you in Africa."

Others hurried east like the Indians and rabbits and snakes and coons. But the majority sat around laughing and waiting for the sun to get friendly again.

Several men collected at Tea Cake's house and sat around stuffing courage into each other's ears. Janie baked a big pan of beans and something she called sweet biscuits and they all managed to be happy enough.

Most of the great flame-throwers were there and naturally, handling Big John de Conquer and his works. How he had done everything big on earth, then went up tuh heben without dying atall. Went up there picking a guitar and got all de angels doing the ring-shout round and round de throne. Then everybody but God and Old Peter flew off on a flying race to Jericho and back and John de Conquer won the race; went on down to hell, beat the old devil and passed out ice water to everybody down there. Somebody tried to say that it was a mouth organ harp that John was playing, but the rest of them would not hear that. Don't care how good anybody could play a harp, God would rather to hear a guitar. That brought them back to Tea Cake. How come he couldn't hit that box a lick or two? Well, all right now, make us know it.

When it got good to everybody, Muck-Boy woke up and began to chant with the rhythm and everybody bore down on the last word of the line:

> Yo' mama don't wear no *Draws*
> Ah seen her when she took 'em *Off*
> She soaked 'em in alco*Hol*
> She sold 'em tuh de Santy *Claus*
> He told her 'twas aginst de *Law*
> To wear dem dirty *Draws*

Then Muck-Boy went crazy through the feet and danced himself and everybody else crazy. When he finished he sat back down on the floor and went to sleep again. Then they got to playing Florida flip and coon-can. Then it was dice. Not for money. This was a show-off game. Everybody posing his fancy shots. As always it broiled down to Tea Cake and Motor Boat. Tea Cake with his shy grin and Motor Boat with his face like a little black cherubim just from a church tower doing amazing things with anybody's dice. The others forgot the work and the weather watching them throw. It was art. A thousand dollars a throw in Madison Square Garden wouldn't have gotten any more breathless suspense. It would have just been more people holding in.

After a while somebody looked out and said, "It ain't gitting no fairer out dere. B'lieve Ah'll git on over tuh mah shack." Motor Boat and Tea Cake were still playing so everybody left them at it.

Sometime that night the winds came back. Everything in the world had a strong rattle, sharp and short like Stew Beef vibrating the drum head near the edge with his fingers. By morning Gabriel was playing the deep tones in the center of the drum. So when Janie looked out of her door she saw the drifting mists gathered in the west—that cloud field of the sky—to arm themselves with thunders and march forth against the world. Louder and higher and lower and wider the sound and motion spread, mounting, sinking, darking.

It woke up old Okechobee and the monster began to roll in his bed. Began to roll and complain like a peevish world on a grumble. The folks in the quarters and the people in the big houses further around the shore heard the big lake and wondered. The people felt uncomfortable but safe because there were the seawalls to chain the senseless monster in his bed. The folks let the people do the thinking. If the castles thought themselves secure, the cabins needn't worry. Their decision was already made as always. Chink up your cracks, shiver in your wet beds and wait on the mercy of the Lord. The bossman might have the thing stopped before morning anyway. It is so easy to be hopeful in the day time when you can see the things you wish on. But it was night, it stayed

night. Night was striding across nothingness with the whole round world in his hands.

A big burst of thunder and lightning that trampled over the roof of the house. So Tea Cake and Motor stopped playing. Motor looked up in his angel-looking way and said, "Big Massa draw him chair upstairs."

"Ah'm glad y'all stop dat crap-shootin' even if it wasn't for money," Janie said. "Ole Massa is doin' *His* work now. Us oughta keep quiet."

They huddled closer and stared at the door. They just didn't use another part of their bodies, and they didn't look at anything but the door. The time was past for asking the white folks what to look for through that door. Six eyes were questioning *God*.

Through the screaming wind they heard things crashing and things hurtling and dashing with unbelievable velocity. A baby rabbit, terror ridden, squirmed through a hole in the floor and squatted off there in the shadows against the wall, seeming to know that nobody wanted its flesh at such a time. And the lake got madder and madder with only its dikes between them and him.

In a little wind-lull, Tea Cake touched Janie and said, "Ah reckon you wish now you had of stayed in yo' big house 'way from such as dis, don't yuh?"

"Naw."

"Naw?"

"Yeah, naw. People don't die till dey time come nohow, don't keer where you at. Ah'm wid mah husband in uh storm, dat's all."

"Thanky, Ma'am. But 'sposing you wuz tuh die, now. You wouldn't git mad at me for draggin' yuh heah?"

"Naw. We been tuhgether round two years. If you kin see de light at daybreak, you don't keer if you die at dusk. It's so many people never seen de light at all. Ah wuz fumblin' round and God opened de door."

He dropped to the floor and put his head in her lap. "Well then, Janie, you meant whut you didn't say, 'cause Ah never *knowed* you wuz so satisfied wid me lak dat. Ah kinda thought—"

The wind came back with triple fury, and put out the light for the last time. They sat in company with the others in other shanties, their eyes straining against crude walls and their souls asking if He meant to measure their puny might against His. They seemed to be staring at the dark, but their eyes were watching God.

As soon as Tea Cake went out pushing wind in front of him, he saw that the wind and water had given life to lots of things that folks think of as dead and given death to so much that had been living things. Water everywhere. Stray fish swimming in the yard. Three inches more and the water would be in the house. Already in some. He decided to try to find a car to take them out of the 'Glades before worse things happened. He turned back to tell Janie about it so she could be ready to go.

"Git our insurance papers tuhgether, Janie. Ah'll tote mah box mahself and things lak dat."

"You got all de money out de dresser drawer, already?"

"Naw, git it quick and cut uh piece off de tablecloth tuh wrap it up in. Us liable tuh git wet tuh our necks. Cut uh piece uh dat oilcloth quick fuh our papers. We got tuh go, if it ain't too late. De dish can't bear it out no longer."

He snatched the oilcloth off the table and took out his knife. Janie held it straight while he slashed off a strip.

"But Tea Cake, it's too awful out dere. Maybe it's better tuh stay heah in de wet than it is tuh try tuh—"

He stunned the argument with half a word. "Fix," he said and fought his way outside. He had seen more than Janie had.

Janie took a big needle and ran up a longish sack. Found some newspaper and wrapped up the paper money and papers and thrust them in and whipped over the open end with her needle. Before she could get it thoroughly hidden in the pocket of her overalls, Tea Cake burst in again.

" 'Tain't no cars, Janie."

"Ah thought not! Whut we gointuh do now?"

"We got tuh walk."

"In all dis weather, Tea Cake? Ah don't b'lieve Ah could make it out de quarters."

"Oh yeah you kin. Me and you and Motor Boat kin all lock arms and hole one 'nother down. Eh, Motor?"

"He's sleep on de bed in yonder," Janie said. Tea Cake called without moving.

"Motor Boat! You better git up from dere! Hell done broke loose in Georgy. Dis minute! How kin you sleep at uh time lak dis? Water knee deep in de yard."

They stepped out in water almost to their buttocks and managed to turn east. Tea Cake had to throw his box away, and Janie saw how it hurt him. Dodging flying missiles, floating dangers, avoiding stepping in holes and warmed on the wind now at their backs until they gained comparatively dry land. They had to fight to keep from being pushed the wrong way and to hold together. They saw other people like themselves struggling along. A house down, here and there, frightened cattle. But above all the drive of the wind and the water. And the lake. Under its multiplied roar could be heard a mighty sound of grinding rock and timber and a wail. They looked back. Saw people trying to run in raging waters and screaming when they found they couldn't. A huge barrier of the makings of the dike to which the cabins had been added was rolling and tumbling forward. Ten feet higher and as far as they could see the muttering wall advanced before the braced-up waters like a road crusher on a cosmic scale. The monstropolous beast had left his bed. The two hundred miles an hour wind had loosed his chains. He seized hold of his dikes and ran forward until he met the quarters; uprooted them like grass and rushed on after his supposed-to-be conquerors, rolling the dikes, rolling the houses, rolling the people in the houses along with other timbers. The sea was walking the earth with a heavy heel.

"De lake is comin'!" Tea Cake gasped.

"De lake!" In amazed horror from Motor Boat, "De lake!"

"It's comin' behind us!" Janie shuddered. "Us can't fly."

"But we still kin run," Tea Cake shouted and they ran. The gushing water ran faster. The great body was held back, but rivers spouted through fissures in the rolling wall and broke like day. The three fugitives ran past another line of shanties that topped a slight rise and gained a little. They cried out as best they could, "De lake is comin'!" and barred doors flew open and others joined them in flight crying the same as they went. "De lake is comin'!" and the pursuing waters growled

and shouted ahead, "Yes, Ah'm comin'!", and those who could fled on.

They made it to a tall house on a hump of ground and Janie said, "Less stop heah. Ah can't make it no further. Ah'm done give out."

"All of us is done give out," Tea Cake corrected. "We'se goin' inside out dis weather, kill or cure." He knocked with the handle of his knife, while they leaned their faces and shoulders against the wall. He knocked once more then he and Motor-Boat went round to the back and forced a door. Nobody there.

"Dese people had mo' sense than Ah did," Tea Cake said as they dropped to the floor and lay there panting. "Us oughta went on wid 'Lias lak he ast me."

"You didn't know," Janie contended. "And when yuh don't know, yuh just don't know. De storms might not of come sho nuff."

They went to sleep promptly but Janie woke up first. She heard the sound of rushing water and sat up.

"Tea Cake! Motor Boat! De lake is comin'!"

The lake *was* coming on. Slower and wider, but coming. It had trampled on most of its supporting wall and lowered its front by spreading. But it came muttering and grumbling onward like a tired mammoth just the same.

"Dis is uh high tall house. Maybe it won't reach heah at all," Janie counselled. "And if it do, maybe it won't reach tuh de upstairs part."

"Janie, Lake Okechobee is forty miles wide and sixty miles long. Dat's uh whole heap uh water. If dis wind is shovin' dat whole lake disa way, dis house ain't nothin' tuh swaller. Us better go. Motor Boat!"

"Whut you want, man?"

"De lake is comin'!"

"Aw, naw it 'tain't."

"Yes, it is *so* comin'! Listen! You kin hear it way off."

"It kin jus' come on. Ah'll wait right here."

"Aw, get up, Motor Boat! Less make it tuh de Palm Beach road. Dat's on uh fill. We'se pretty safe dere."

"Ah'm safe here, man. Go ahead if yuh wants to. Ah'm sleepy."

"Whut you gointuh do if de lake reach heah?"

"Go upstairs."

"S'posing it come up dere?"

"Swim, man. Dat's all."

"Well, uh, Good bye, Motor Boat. Everything is pretty bad, yuh know. Us might git missed of one 'nother. You sho is a grand friend fuh uh man tuh have."

"Good bye, Tea Cake. Y'all oughta stay here and sleep, man. No use in goin' off and leavin' me lak dis."

"We don't wanta. Come on wid us. It might be night time when de water hem you up in heah. Dat's how come Ah won't stay. Come on, man."

"Tea Cake Ah got tuh have mah sleep. Definitely."

"Good bye, then, Motor. Ah wish you all de luck. Goin' over tuh Nassau fuh dat visit widja when all dis is over."

"Definitely, Tea Cake. Mah mama's house is yours."

Tea Cake and Janie were some distance from the house before they struck serious water. Then they had to swim a distance, and Janie could not hold up more than a few strokes at a time, so Tea Cake bore her up till finally they hit a ridge that led on towards the fill. It seemed to him the wind was weakening a little so he kept looking for a place to rest and catch his breath. His wind was gone. Janie was tired and limping, but she had not had to do that hard swimming in the turbulent waters, so Tea Cake was much worse off. But they couldn't stop. Gaining the fill was something but it was no guarantee. The lake was coming. They had to reach the six-mile bridge. It was high and safe perhaps.

Everybody was walking the fill. Hurrying, dragging, falling, crying, calling out names hopefully and hopelessly. Wind and rain beating on old folks and beating on babies. Tea Cake stumbled once or twice in his weariness and Janie held him up. So they reached the bridge at Six Mile Bend and thought to rest.

But it was crowded. White people had preempted that point of elevation and there was no more room. They could climb up one of its high sides and down the other, that was all. Miles further on, still no rest.

They passed a dead man in a sitting position on a hummock, entirely surrounded by wild animals and snakes. Common

danger made common friends. Nothing sought a conquest over the other.

Another man clung to a cypress tree on a tiny island. A tin roof of a building hung from the branches by electric wires and the wind swung it back and forth like a mighty ax. The man dared not move a step to his right lest this crushing blade split him open. He dared not step left for a large rattle-snake was stretched full length with his head in the wind. There was a strip of water between the island and the fill, and the man clung to the tree and cried for help.

"De snake won't bite yuh," Tea Cake yelled to him. "He skeered tuh go intuh uh coil. Skeered he'll be blowed away. Step round dat side and swim off!"

Soon after that Tea Cake felt he couldn't walk anymore. Not right away. So he stretched long side of the road to rest. Janie spread herself between him and the wind and he closed his eyes and let the tiredness seep out of his limbs. On each side of the fill was a great expanse of water like lakes—water full of things living and dead. Things that didn't belong in water. As far as the eye could reach, water and wind playing upon it in fury. A large piece of tar-paper roofing sailed through the air and scudded along the fill until it hung against a tree. Janie saw it with joy. That was the very thing to cover Tea Cake with. She could lean against it and hold it down. The wind wasn't quite so bad as it was anyway. The very thing. Poor Tea Cake!

She crept on hands and knees to the piece of roofing and caught hold of it by either side. Immediately the wind lifted both of them and she saw herself sailing off the fill to the right, out and out over the lashing water. She screamed terri-bly and released the roofing which sailed away as she plunged downward into the water.

"Tea Cake!" He heard her and sprang up. Janie was trying to swim but fighting water too hard. He saw a cow swimming slowly towards the fill in an oblique line. A massive built dog was sitting on her shoulders and shivering and growling. The cow was approaching Janie. A few strokes would bring her there.

"Make it tuh de cow and grab hold of her tail! Don't use yo' feet. Jus' yo' hands is enough. Dat's right, come on!"

Janie achieved the tail of the cow and lifted her head up along the cow's rump, as far as she could above water. The cow sunk a little with the added load and thrashed a moment in terror. Thought she was being pulled down by a gator. Then she continued on. The dog stood up and growled like a lion, stiff-standing hackles, stiff muscles, teeth uncovered as he lashed up his fury for the charge. Tea Cake split the water like an otter, opening his knife as he dived. The dog raced down the back-bone of the cow to the attack and Janie screamed and slipped far back on the tail of the cow, just out of reach of the dog's angry jaws. He wanted to plunge in after her but dreaded the water, somehow. Tea Cake rose out of the water at the cow's rump and seized the dog by the neck. But he was a powerful dog and Tea Cake was over-tired. So he didn't kill the dog with one stroke as he had intended. But the dog couldn't free himself either. They fought and somehow he managed to bite Tea Cake high up on his cheek-bone once. Then Tea Cake finished him and sent him to the bottom to stay there. The cow relieved of a great weight was landing on the fill with Janie before Tea Cake stroked in and crawled weakly upon the fill again.

Janie began to fuss around his face where the dog had bitten him but he said it didn't amount to anything. "He'd uh raised hell though if he had uh grabbed me uh inch higher and bit me in mah eye. Yuh can't buy eyes in de store, yuh know." He flopped to the edge of the fill as if the storm wasn't going on at all. "Lemme rest awhile, then us got tuh make it on intuh town somehow."

It was next day by the sun and the clock when they reached Palm Beach. It was years later by their bodies. Winters and winters of hardship and suffering. The wheel kept turning round and round. Hope, hopelessness and despair. But the storm blew itself out as they approached the city of refuge.

Havoc was there with her mouth wide open. Back in the Everglades the wind had romped among lakes and trees. In the city it had raged among houses and men. Tea Cake and Janie stood on the edge of things and looked over the desolation.

"How kin Ah find uh doctor fuh yo' face in all dis mess?" Janie wailed.

"Ain't got de damn doctor tuh study 'bout. Us needs uh place tuh rest."

A great deal of their money and perseverance and they found a place to sleep. It was just that. No place to live at all. Just sleep. Tea Cake looked all around and sat heavily on the side of the bed.

"Well," he said humbly, "reckon you never 'spected tuh come tuh dis when you took up wid me, didja?"

"Once upon uh time, Ah never 'spected nothin' Tea Cake but bein' dead from the standin' still and tryin' tuh laugh. But you come 'long and made somethin' outa me. So Ah'm thankful fuh anything we come through together."

"Thanky, Ma'am."

"You was twice noble tuh save me from dat dawg. Tea Cake, Ah don't speck you seen his eyes lak Ah did. He didn't aim tuh jus' bite me, Tea Cake. He aimed tuh kill me stone dead. Ah'm never tuh fuhgit dem eyes. He wuzn't nothin' all over but pure hate. Wonder where he come from?"

"Yeah, Ah did see 'im too. It wuz frightenin'. Ah didn't mean tuh take his hate neither. He had tuh die uh me one. Mah switch blade said it wuz him."

"Po' me, he'd tore me tuh pieces, if it wuzn't fuh you, honey."

"You don't have tuh say, if it wuzn't fuh me, baby, cause Ah'm *heah*, and then Ah want yuh tuh know it's uh man heah."

XIX

AND THEN AGAIN Him-with-the-square-toes had gone back to his house. He stood once more and again in his high flat house without sides to it and without a roof with his soulless sword standing upright in his hand. His pale white horse had galloped over waters, and thundered over land. The time of dying was over. It was time to bury the dead.

"Janie, us been in dis dirty, slouchy place two days now, and dat's too much. Us got tuh git outa dis house and outa dis man's town. Ah never did lak round heah."

"Where we goin', Tea Cake? Dat we don't know."

"Maybe, we could go back up de state, if yuh want tuh go."

"Ah didn't say dat, but if dat is whut you—"

"Naw, Ah ain't said nothin' uh de kind. Ah wuz tryin' not tuh keep you outa yo' comfortable no longer'n you wanted tuh stay."

"If Ah'm in yo' way—"

"Will you lissen at dis woman? Me 'bout tuh bust mah britches tryin' tuh stay wid her and she heah—she oughta be shot wid tacks!"

"All right then, you name somethin' and we'll do it. We kin give it uh poor man's trial anyhow."

"Anyhow Ah done got rested up and de bed bugs is done got too bold round heah. Ah didn't notice when mah rest wuz broke. Ah'm goin' out and look around and see whut we kin do. Ah'll give *any*thing uh common trial."

"You better stay inside dis house and git some rest. 'Tain't nothin' tuh find out dere nohow."

"But Ah wants tuh look and see, Janie. Maybe it's some kinda work fuh me tuh help do."

"Whut dey want you tuh help do, you ain't gointuh like it. Dey's grabbin' all de menfolks dey kin git dey hands on and makin' 'em help bury de dead. Dey claims dey's after de un-employed, but dey ain't bein' too particular about whether you'se employed or not. You stay in dis house. De Red Cross

is doin' all dat kin be done otherwise fuh de sick and de 'fflicted."

"Ah got money on me, Janie. Dey can't bother me. Anyhow Ah wants tuh go see how things is sho nuff. Ah wants tuh see if Ah kin hear anything 'bout de boys from de 'Glades. Maybe dey all come through all right. Maybe not."

Tea Cake went out and wandered around. Saw the hand of horror on everything. Houses without roofs, and roofs without houses. Steel and stone all crushed and crumbled like wood. The mother of malice had trifled with men.

While Tea Cake was standing and looking he saw two men coming towards him with rifles on their shoulders. Two white men, so he thought about what Janie had told him and flexed his knees to run. But in a moment he saw that wouldn't do him any good. They had already seen him and they were too close to miss him if they shot. Maybe they would pass on by. Maybe when they saw he had money they would realize he was not a tramp.

"Hello, there, Jim," the tallest one called out. "We been lookin' fuh you."

"Mah name ain't no Jim," Tea Cake said watchfully. "Whut you been lookin' fuh *me* fuh? Ah ain't done nothin'."

"Dat's whut we want yuh fuh—not doin' nothin'. Come on less go bury some uh dese heah dead folks. Dey ain't gittin' buried fast enough."

Tea Cake hung back defensively. "Whut Ah got tuh do wid dat? Ah'm uh workin' man wid money in mah pocket. Jus' got blowed outa de 'Glades by de storm."

The short man made a quick move with his rifle. "Git on down de road dere, suh! Don't look out somebody'll be buryin' *you*! G'wan in front uh me, suh!"

Tea Cake found that he was part of a small army that had been pressed into service to clear the wreckage in public places and bury the dead. Bodies had to be searched out, carried to certain gathering places and buried. Corpses were not just found in wrecked houses. They were under houses, tangled in shrubbery, floating in water, hanging in trees, drifting under wreckage.

Trucks lined with drag kept rolling in from the 'Glades and other outlying parts, each with its load of twenty-five bodies.

Some bodies fully dressed, some naked and some in all degrees of dishevelment. Some bodies with calm faces and satisfied hands. Some dead with fighting faces and eyes flung wide open in wonder. Death had found them watching, trying to see beyond seeing.

Miserable, sullen men, black and white under guard had to keep on searching for bodies and digging graves. A huge ditch was dug across the white cemetery and a big ditch was opened across the black graveyard. Plenty quick-lime on hand to throw over the bodies as soon as they were received. They had already been unburied too long. The men were making every effort to get them covered up as quickly as possible. But the guards stopped them. They had received orders to be carried out.

"Hey, dere, y'all! Don't dump dem bodies in de hole lak dat! Examine every last one of 'em and find out if they's white or black."

"Us got tuh handle 'em slow lak dat? God have mussy! In de condition they's in got tuh examine 'em? Whut difference do it make 'bout de color? Dey all needs buryin' in uh hurry."

"Got orders from headquarters. They makin' coffins fuh all de white folks. 'Tain't nothin' but cheap pine, but dat's better'n nothin'. Don't dump no white folks in de hole jus' so."

"Whut tuh do 'bout de colored folks? Got boxes fuh dem too?"

"Nope. They cain't find enough of 'em tuh go 'round. Jus' sprinkle plenty quick-lime over 'em and cover 'em up."

"Shucks! Nobody can't tell nothin' 'bout some uh dese bodies, de shape dey's in. Can't tell whether dey's white or black."

The guards had a long conference over that. After a while they came back and told the men, "Look at their hair, when you cain't tell no other way. And don't lemme ketch none uh y'all dumpin' white folks, and don't be wastin' no boxes on colored. They's too hard tuh git holt of right now."

"They's mighty particular how dese dead folks goes tuh judgment," Tea Cake observed to the man working next to him. "Look lak dey think God don't know nothin' 'bout de Jim Crow law."

Tea Cake had been working several hours when the thought of Janie worrying about him made him desperate. So when a truck drove up to be unloaded he bolted and ran. He was ordered to halt on pain of being shot at, but he kept right on and got away. He found Janie sad and crying just as he had thought. They calmed each other about his absence then Tea Cake brought up another matter.

"Janie, us got tuh git outa dis house and outa dis man's town. Ah don't mean tuh work lak dat no mo'."

"Naw, naw, Tea Cake. Less stay right in heah until it's all over. If dey can't see yuh, dey can't bother yuh."

"Aw naw. S'posin' dey come round searchin'? Less git outa heah tuhnight."

"Where us goin', Tea Cake?"

"De quickest place is de 'Glades. Less make it on back down dere. Dis town is full uh trouble and compellment."

"But, Tea Cake, de hurricane wuz down in de 'Glades too. It'll be dead folks tuh be buried down dere too."

"Yeah, Ah know, Janie, but it couldn't never be lak it 'tis heah. In de first place dey been bringin' bodies outa dere all day so it can't be but so many mo' tuh find. And then again it never wuz as many dere as it wuz heah. And then too, Janie, de white folks down dere knows us. It's bad bein' strange niggers wid white folks. Everybody is aginst yuh."

"Dat sho is de truth. De ones de white man know is nice colored folks. De ones he don't know is bad niggers." Janie said this and laughed and Tea Cake laughed with her.

"Janie, Ah done watched it time and time again; each and every white man think he know all de GOOD darkies already. He don't need tuh know no mo'. So far as he's concerned, all dem he don't know oughta be tried and sentenced tuh six months behind de United States privy house at hard smellin'."

"How come de United States privy house, Tea Cake?"

"Well, you know Old Uncle Sam always do have de biggest and de best uh everything. So de white man figger dat anything less than de Uncle Sam's consolidated water closet would be too easy. So Ah means tuh go where de white folks know me. Ah feels lak uh motherless chile round heah."

They got things together and stole out of the house and

away. The next morning they were back on the muck. They worked hard all day fixing up a house to live in so that Tea Cake could go out looking for something to do the next day. He got out soon next morning more out of curiosity than eagerness to work. Stayed off all day. That night he came in beaming out with light.

"Who you reckon Ah seen, Janie? Bet you can't guess."

"Ah'll betcha uh fat man you seen Sop-de-Bottom."

"Yeah Ah seen him and Stew Beef and Dockery and Lias, and Coodemay and Bootyny. Guess who else!"

"Lawd knows. Is it Sterrett?"

"Naw, he got caught in the rush. 'Lias help bury him in Palm Beach. Guess who else?"

"Ah g'wan tell me, Tea Cake. Ah don't know. It can't be Motor Boat."

"Dat's jus' who it is. Ole Motor! De son of a gun laid up in dat house and slept and de lake come moved de house way off somewhere and Motor didn't know nothin' 'bout it till de storm wuz 'bout over."

"Naw!"

"Yeah man. Heah we nelly kill our fool selves runnin' way from danger and him lay up dere and sleep and float on off!"

"Well, you know dey say luck is uh fortune."

"Dat's right too. Look, Ah got uh job uh work. Help clearin' up things in general, and then dey goin' build dat dike sho nuff. Dat ground got to be cleared off too. Plenty work. Dey needs mo' men even."

So Tea Cake made three hearty weeks. He bought another rifle and a pistol and he and Janie bucked each other as to who was the best shot with Janie ranking him always with the rifle. She could knock the head off of a chicken-hawk sitting up a pine tree. Tea Cake was a little jealous, but proud of his pupil.

About the middle of the fourth week Tea Cake came home early one afternoon complaining of his head. Sick headache that made him lie down for awhile. He woke up hungry. Janie had his supper ready but by the time he walked from the bedroom to the table, he said he didn't b'lieve he wanted a thing.

"Thought you tole me you wuz hongry!" Janie wailed.

"Ah thought so too," Tea Cake said very quietly and dropped his head in his hands.

"But Ah done baked yuh uh pan uh beans."

"Ah knows dey's good all right but Ah don't choose nothin' now, Ah thank yuh, Janie."

He went back to bed. Way in the midnight he woke Janie up in his nightmarish struggle with an enemy that was at his throat. Janie struck a light and quieted him.

"Whut's de matter, honey?" She soothed and soothed. "You got tuh tell me so Ah kin feel widja. Lemme bear de pain 'long widja, baby. Where hurt yuh, sugar?"

"Somethin' got after me in mah sleep, Janie." He all but cried, "Tried tuh choke me tuh death. Hadn't been fuh *you* Ah'd be dead."

"You sho wuz strainin' wid it. But you'se all right, honey. Ah'm heah."

He went on back to sleep, but there was no getting around it. He was sick in the morning. He tried to make it but Janie wouldn't hear of his going out at all.

"If Ah kin jus' make out de week," Tea Cake said.

"Folks wuz makin' weeks befo' you wuz born and they gointuh be makin' 'em after you'se gone. Lay back down, Tea Cake. Ah'm goin' git de doctor tuh come see 'bout yuh."

"Aw ain't dat bad, Janie. Looka heah! Ah kin walk all over de place."

"But you'se too sick tuh play wid. Plenty fever round heah since de storm."

"Gimme uh drink uh water befo' you leave, then."

Janie dipped up a glass of water and brought it to the bed. Tea Cake took it and filled his mouth then gagged horribly, disgorged that which was in his mouth and threw the glass upon the floor. Janie was frantic with alarm.

"Whut make you ack lak dat wid yo' drinkin' water, Tea Cake? You ast me tuh give it tuh yuh."

"Dat water is somethin' wrong wid it. It nelly choke me tuh death. Ah tole yuh somethin' jumped on me heah last night and choked me. You come makin' out ah wuz dreamin'."

"Maybe it wuz uh witch ridin' yuh, honey. Ah'll see can't

Ah find some mustard seed whilst Ah's out. But Ah'm sho tuh fetch de doctor when Ah'm come."

Tea Cake didn't say anything against it and Janie herself hurried off. This sickness to her was worse than the storm. As soon as she was well out of sight, Tea Cake got up and dumped the water bucket and washed it clean. Then he struggled to the irrigation pump and filled it again. He was not accusing Janie of malice and design. He was accusing her of carelessness. She ought to realize that water buckets needed washing like everything else. He'd tell her about it good and proper when she got back. What was she thinking about nohow? He found himself very angry about it. He eased the bucket on the table and sat down to rest before taking a drink.

Finally he dipped up a drink. It was so good and cool! Come to think about it, he hadn't had a drink since yesterday. That was what he needed to give him an appetite for his beans. He found himself wanting it very much, so he threw back his head as he rushed the glass to his lips. But the demon was there before him, strangling, killing him quickly. It was a great relief to expel the water from his mouth. He sprawled on the bed again and lay there shivering until Janie and the doctor arrived. The white doctor who had been around so long that he was part of the muck. Who told the workmen stories with brawny sweaty words in them. He came into the house quickly, hat sitting on the left back corner of his head.

"Hi there, Tea Cake. What de hell's de matter with *you*?"

"Wisht Ah knowed, Doctah Simmons. But Ah sho is sick."

"Ah, naw Tea Cake. 'Tain't a thing wrong that a quart of coon-dick wouldn't cure. You haven't been gettin' yo' right likker lately, eh?" He slapped Tea Cake lustily across his back and Tea Cake tried to smile as he was expected to do. But it was hard. The doctor opened up his bag and went to work.

"You do look a little peaked, Tea Cake. You got a temperature and yo' pulse is kinda off. What you been doin' here lately?"

"Nothin' 'cept workin' and gamin' uh little, doctah. But look lak water done turn't aginst me."

"Water? How do you mean?"

"Can't keep it on mah stomach, at all."

"What else?"

Janie came around the bed full of concern.

"Doctah, Tea Cake ain't tellin' yuh everything lak he oughta. We wuz caught in dat hurricane out heah, and Tea Cake over-strained hisself swimmin' such uh long time and holdin' me up too, and walkin' all dem miles in de storm and then befo' he could git his rest he had tuh come git me out de water agin and fightin' wid dat big ole dawg and de dawg bitin' 'im in de face and everything. Ah been spectin' him tuh be sick befo' now."

"Dawg bit 'im, did you say?"

"Aw twudn't nothin' much, doctah. It wuz all healed over in two three days," Tea Cake said impatiently. "Dat been over uh month ago, nohow. Dis is somethin' new, doctah. Ah figgers de water is yet bad. It's bound tuh be. Too many dead folks been in it fuh it tuh be good tuh drink fuh uh long time. Dat's de way Ah figgers it anyhow."

"All right, Tea Cake. Ah'll send you some medicine and tell Janie how tuh take care of you. Anyhow, I want you in a bed by yo'self until you hear from me. Just you keep Janie out of yo' bed for awhile, hear? Come on out to the car with me, Janie. I want to send Tea Cake some pills to take right away."

Outside he fumbled in his bag and gave Janie a tiny bottle with a few pellets inside.

"Give him one of these every hour to keep him quiet, Janie, and stay out of his way when he gets in one of his fits of gagging and choking."

"How you know he's havin' 'em, doctah? Dat's jus' what Ah come out heah tuh tell yuh."

"Janie, I'm pretty sure that was a mad dawg bit yo' husband. It's too late to get hold of de dawg's head. But de symptoms is all there. It's mighty bad dat it's gone on so long. Some shots right after it happened would have fixed him right up."

"You mean he's liable tuh die, doctah?"

"Sho is. But de worst thing is he's liable tuh suffer somethin' awful befo' he goes."

"Doctor, Ah loves him fit tuh kill. Tell me anything tuh do and Ah'll do it."

"'Bout de only thing you can do, Janie, is to put him in

the County Hospital where they can tie him down and look after him."

"But he don't like no hospital at all. He'd think Ah wuz tired uh doin' fuh 'im, when God knows Ah ain't. Ah can't stand de idea us tyin' Tea Cake lak he wuz uh mad dawg."

"It almost amounts to dat, Janie. He's got almost no chance to pull through and he's liable to bite somebody else, specially you, and then you'll be in the same fix he's in. It's mighty bad."

"Can't nothin' be done fuh his case, doctah? Us got plenty money in de bank in Orlandah, doctah. See can't yuh do somethin' special tuh save him. Anything it cost, doctah, Ah don't keer, but please, doctah."

"Do what I can. Ah'll phone into Palm Beach right away for the serum which he should have had three weeks ago. I'll do all I can to save him, Janie. But it looks too late. People in his condition can't swallow water, you know, and in other ways it's terrible."

Janie fooled around outside awhile to try and think it wasn't so. If she didn't see the sickness in his face she could imagine it wasn't really happening. Well, she thought, that big old dawg with the hatred in his eyes had killed her after all. She wished she had slipped off that cow-tail and drowned then and there and been done. But to kill her through Tea Cake was too much to bear. Tea Cake, the son of Evening Sun, had to die for loving her. She looked hard at the sky for a long time. Somewhere up there beyond blue ether's bosom sat He. Was He noticing what was going on around here? He must be because He knew everything. Did He *mean* to do this thing to Tea Cake and her? It wasn't anything she could fight. She could only ache and wait. Maybe it was some big tease and when He saw it had gone far enough He'd give her a sign. She looked hard for something up there to move for a sign. A star in the daytime, maybe, or the sun to shout, or even a mutter of thunder. Her arms went up in a desperate supplication for a minute. It wasn't exactly pleading, it was asking questions. The sky stayed hard looking and quiet so she went inside the house. God would do less than He had in His heart.

Tea Cake was lying with his eyes closed and Janie hoped he
was asleep. He wasn't. A great fear had took hold of him.
What was this thing that set his brains afire and grabbed at
his throat with iron fingers? Where did it come from and why
did it hang around him? He hoped it would stop before Janie
noticed anything. He wanted to try to drink water again but he
didn't want her to see him fail. As soon as she got out of the
kitchen he meant to go to the bucket and drink right quick
before anything had time to stop him. No need to worry Janie,
until he couldn't help it. He heard her cleaning out the stove
and saw her go out back to empty the ashes. He leaped at the
bucket at once. But this time the sight of the water was
enough. He was on the kitchen floor in great agony when she
returned. She petted him, soothed him, and got him back to
bed. She made up her mind to go see about that medicine from
Palm Beach. Maybe she could find somebody to drive over
there for it.

"Feel better now, Tea Cake, baby chile?"

"Uh huh, uh little."

"Well, b'lieve Ah'll rake up de front yard. De mens is got
cane chewin's and peanut hulls all over de place. Don't want
de doctah tuh come back heah and find it still de same."

"Don't take too long, Janie. Don't lak tuh be by mahself
when Ah'm sick."

She ran down the road just as fast as she could. Halfway to
town she met Sop-de-Bottom and Dockery coming towards
her.

"Hello, Janie, how's Tea Cake?"

"Pretty bad off. Ah'm gointuh see 'bout medicine fuh 'im
right now."

"Doctor told somebody he wuz sick so us come tuh see.
Thought somethin' he never come tuh work."

"Y'all set wid 'im till Ah git back. He need de company
right long in heah."

She fanned on down the road to town and found Dr. Sim-
mons. Yes, he had had an answer. They didn't have any serum
but they had wired Miami to send it. She needn't worry. It
would be there early the next morning if not before. People
didn't fool around in a case like that. No, it wouldn't do for

her to hire no car to go after it. Just go home and wait. That was all. When she reached home the visitors rose to go.

When they were alone Tea Cake wanted to put his head in Janie's lap and tell her how he felt and let her mama him in her sweet way. But something Sop had told him made his tongue lie cold and heavy like a dead lizard between his jaws. Mrs. Turner's brother was back on the muck and now he had this mysterious sickness. People didn't just take sick like this for nothing.

"Janie, whut is dat Turner woman's brother doin' back on de muck?"

"Ah don't know, Tea Cake. Didn't even knowed he wuz back."

"Accordin' tuh mah notion, you did. Whut you slip off from me just now for?"

"Tea Cake, Ah don't lak you astin' me no sich question. Dat shows how sick you is sho nuff. You'se jealous 'thout me givin' you cause."

"Well, whut didja slip off from de house 'thout tellin' me you wuz goin'. You ain't never done dat befo'."

"Dat wuz cause Ah wuz tryin' not tuh let yuh worry 'bout yo' condition. De doctah sent after some mo' medicine and Ah went tuh see if it come."

Tea Cake began to cry and Janie hovered him in her arms like a child. She sat on the side of the bed and sort of rocked him back to peace.

"Tea Cake, 'tain't no use in you bein' jealous uh me. In de first place Ah couldn't love nobody but yuh. And in de second place, Ah jus' uh ole woman dat nobody don't want but you."

"Naw, you ain't neither. You only sound ole when you tell folks when you wuz born, but wid de eye you'se young enough tuh suit most any man. Dat ain't no lie. Ah knows plenty mo' men would take yuh and work hard fuh de privilege. Ah done heard 'em talk."

"Maybe so, Tea Cake, Ah ain't never tried tuh find out. Ah jus' know dat God snatched me out de fire through you. And Ah loves yuh and feel glad."

"Thank yuh, ma'am, but don't say you'se ole. You'se uh lil girl baby all de time. God made it so you spent yo' ole age

first wid somebody else, and saved up yo' young girl days to spend wid me."

"Ah feel dat uh way too, Tea Cake and Ah thank yuh fuh sayin' it."

"'Tain't no trouble tuh say whut's already so. You'se uh pretty woman outside uh bein' nice."

"Aw, Tea Cake."

"Yeah you is too. Everytime Ah see uh patch uh roses uh somethin' over sportin' they selves makin' out they pretty, Ah tell 'em 'Ah want yuh tuh see mah Janie sometime.' You must let de flowers see yuh sometimes, heah, Janie?"

"You keep dat up, Tea Cake, Ah'll b'lieve yuh after while," Janie said archly and fixed him back in bed. It was then she felt the pistol under the pillow. It gave her a quick ugly throb, but she didn't ask him about it since he didn't say. Never had Tea Cake slept with a pistol under his head before. "Neb' mind 'bout all dat cleanin' round de front yard," he told her as she straightened up from fixing the bed. "You stay where Ah kin see yuh."

"All right, Tea Cake, jus' as you say."

"And if Mis' Turner's lap-legged brother come prowlin' by heah you kin tell 'im Ah got him stopped wid four wheel brakes. 'Tain't no need of him standin' round watchin' de job."

"Ah won't be tellin' 'im nothin' 'cause Ah don't expect tuh see 'im."

Tea Cake had two bad attacks that night. Janie saw a changing look come in his face. Tea Cake was gone. Something else was looking out of his face. She made up her mind to be off after the doctor with the first glow of day. So she was up and dressed when Tea Cake awoke from the fitful sleep that had come to him just before day. He almost snarled when he saw her dressed to go.

"Where are you goin', Janie?"

"After de doctor, Tea Cake. You'se too sick tuh be heah in dis house 'thout de doctah. Maybe we oughta git yuh tuh de hospital."

"Ah ain't goin' tuh no hospital no where. Put dat in yo' pipe and smoke it. Guess you tired uh waitin' on me and doing fuh me. Dat ain't de way Ah been wid *you*. Ah never is been able tuh do enough fuh yuh."

"Tea Cake, you'se sick. You'se takin' everything in de way Ah don't mean it. Ah couldn't never be tired uh waitin' on you. Ah'm just skeered you'se too sick fuh me tuh handle. Ah wants yuh tuh git well, honey. Dat's all."

He gave her a look full of blank ferocity and gurgled in his throat. She saw him sitting up in bed and moving about so that he could watch her every move. And she was beginning to feel fear of this strange thing in Tea Cake's body. So when he went out to the outhouse she rushed to see if the pistol was loaded. It was a six shooter and three of the chambers were full. She started to unload it but she feared he might break it and find out she knew. That might urge his disordered mind to action. If that medicine would only come! She whirled the cylinder so that if he even did draw the gun on her it would snap three times before it would fire. She would at least have warning. She could either run or try to take it away before it was too late. Anyway Tea Cake wouldn't hurt *her*. He was jealous and wanted to scare her. She'd just be in the kitchen as usual and never let on. They'd laugh over it when he got well. She found the box of cartridges, however, and emptied it. Just as well to take the rifle from back of the head of the bed. She broke it and put the shell in her apron pocket and put it in a corner in the kitchen almost behind the stove where it was hard to see. She could outrun his knife if it came to that. Of course she was too fussy, but it did no harm to play safe. She ought not to let poor sick Tea Cake do something that would run him crazy when he found out what he had done.

She saw him coming from the outhouse with a queer loping gait, swinging his head from side to side and his jaws clenched in a funny way. This was too awful! Where was Dr. Simmons with that medicine? She was glad she was here to look after him. Folks would do such mean things to her Tea Cake if they saw him in such a fix. Treat Tea Cake like he was some mad dog when nobody in the world had more kindness about them. All he needed was for the doctor to come on with that medicine. He came back into the house without speaking, in fact, he did not seem to notice she was there and fell heavily into the bed and slept. Janie was standing by the stove washing up the dishes when he spoke to her in a queer cold voice.

"Janie, how come you can't sleep in de same bed wid me no mo'?"

"De doctah told you tuh sleep by yo'self, Tea Cake. Don't yuh remember him tellin' you dat yistiddy?"

"How come you ruther sleep on uh pallet than tuh sleep in de bed wid me?" Janie saw then that he had the gun in his hand that was hanging to his side. "Answer me when Ah speak."

"Tea Cake, Tea Cake, honey! Go lay down! Ah'll be too glad tuh be in dere wid yuh de minute de doctor say so. Go lay back down. He'll be heah wid some new medicine right away."

"Janie, Ah done went through everything tuh be good tuh you and it hurt me tuh mah heart tuh be ill treated lak Ah is."

The gun came up unsteadily but quickly and levelled at Janie's breast. She noted that even in his delirium he took good aim. Maybe he would point to scare her, that was all.

The pistol snapped once. Instinctively Janie's hand flew behind her on the rifle and brought it around. Most likely this would scare him off. If only the doctor would come! If anybody at all would come! She broke the rifle deftly and shoved in the shell as the second click told her that Tea Cake's suffering brain was urging him on to kill.

"Tea Cake put down dat gun and go back tuh bed!" Janie yelled at him as the gun wavered weakly in his hand.

He steadied himself against the jamb of the door and Janie thought to run into him and grab his arm, but she saw the quick motion of taking aim and heard the click. Saw the ferocious look in his eyes and went mad with fear as she had done in the water that time. She threw up the barrel of the rifle in frenzied hope and fear. Hope that he'd see it and run, desperate fear for her life. But if Tea Cake could have counted costs he would not have been there with the pistol in his hands. No knowledge of fear nor rifles nor anything else was there. He paid no more attention to the pointing gun than if it were Janie's dog finger. She saw him stiffen himself all over as he levelled and took aim. The fiend in him must kill and Janie was the only thing living he saw.

The pistol and the rifle rang out almost together. The pistol just enough after the rifle to seem its echo. Tea Cake

crumpled as his bullet buried itself in the joist over Janie's
head. Janie saw the look on his face and leaped forward as he
crashed forward in her arms. She was trying to hover him as
he closed his teeth in the flesh of her forearm. They came
down heavily like that. Janie struggled to a sitting position
and pried the dead Tea Cake's teeth from her arm.

It was the meanest moment of eternity. A minute before
she was just a scared human being fighting for its life. Now
she was her sacrificing self with Tea Cake's head in her lap.
She had wanted him to live so much and he was dead. No
hour is ever eternity, but it has its right to weep. Janie held
his head tightly to her breast and wept and thanked him
wordlessly for giving her the chance for loving service. She
had to hug him tight for soon he would be gone, and she had
to tell him for the last time. Then the grief of outer darkness
descended.

So that same day of Janie's great sorrow she was in jail. And
when the doctor told the sheriff and the judge how it was,
they all said she must be tried that same day. No need to
punish her in jail by waiting. Three hours in jail and then they
set the court for her case. The time was short and everything,
but sufficient people were there. Plenty of white people came
to look on this strangeness. And all the Negroes for miles
around. Who was it didn't know about the love between Tea
Cake and Janie?

The court set and Janie saw the judge who had put on a
great robe to listen about her and Tea Cake. And twelve more
white men had stopped whatever they were doing to listen
and pass on what happened between Janie and Tea Cake
Woods, and as to whether things were done right or not.
That was funny too. Twelve strange men who didn't know a
thing about people like Tea Cake and her were going to sit on
the thing. Eight or ten white women had come to look at her
too. They wore good clothes and had the pinky color that
comes of good food. They were nobody's poor white folks.
What need had *they* to leave their richness to come look on
Janie in her overalls? But they didn't seem too mad, Janie
thought. It would be nice if she could make *them* know how
it was instead of those menfolks. Oh, and she hoped that
undertaker was fixing Tea Cake up fine. They ought to let her

go see about it. Yes, and there was Mr. Prescott that she knew right well and he was going to tell the twelve men to kill her for shooting Tea Cake. And a strange man from Palm Beach who was going to ask them not to kill her, and none of them knew.

Then she saw all of the colored people standing up in the back of the courtroom. Packed tight like a case of celery, only much darker than that. They were all against her, she could see. So many were there against her that a light slap from each one of them would have beat her to death. She felt them pelting her with dirty thoughts. They were there with their tongues cocked and loaded, the only real weapon left to weak folks. The only killing tool they are allowed to use in the presence of white folks.

So it was all ready after a while and they wanted people to talk so that they could know what was right to do about Janie Woods the relic of Tea Cake's Janie. The white part of the room got calmer the more serious it got, but a tongue storm struck the Negroes like wind among palm trees. They talked all of a sudden and all together like a choir and the top parts of their bodies moved on the rhythm of it. They sent word by the bailiff to Mr. Prescott they wanted to testify in the case. Tea Cake was a good boy. He had been good to that woman. No nigger woman ain't never been treated no better. Naw suh! He worked like a dog for her and nearly killed himself saving her in the storm, then soon as he got a little fever from the water, she had took up with another man. Sent for him to come there from way off. Hanging was too good. All they wanted was a chance to testify. The bailiff went up and the sheriff and the judge, and the police chief, and the lawyers all came together to listen for a few minutes, then they parted again and the sheriff took the stand and told how Janie had come to his house with the doctor and how he found things when he drove out to hers.

Then they called Dr. Simmons and he told about Tea Cake's sickness and how dangerous it was to Janie and the whole town, and how he was scared for her and thought to have Tea Cake locked up in the jail, but seeing Janie's care he neglected to do it. And how he found Janie all bit in the arm, sitting on the floor and petting Tea Cake's head when he got

there. And the pistol right by his hand on the floor. Then he stepped down.

"Any further evidence to present, Mr. Prescott?" the judge asked.

"No, Your Honor. The State rests."

The palm tree dance began again among the Negroes in the back. They had come to talk. The State couldn't rest until it heard.

"Mistah Prescott, Ah got somethin' tuh say," Sop-de-Bottom spoke out anonymously from the anonymous herd.

The courtroom swung round on itself to look.

"If you know what's good for you, you better shut your mouth up until somebody calls you," Mr. Prescott told him coldly.

"Yassuh, Mr. Prescott."

"We are handling this case. Another word out of *you*; out of any of you niggers back there, and I'll bind you over to the big court."

"Yassuh."

The white women made a little applause and Mr. Prescott glared at the back of the house and stepped down. Then the strange white man that was going to talk for her got up there. He whispered a little with the clerk and then called on Janie to take the stand and talk. After a few little questions he told her to tell just how it happened and to speak the truth, the whole truth and nothing but the truth. So help her God.

They all leaned over to listen while she talked. First thing she had to remember was she was not at home. She was in the courthouse fighting something and it wasn't death. It was worse than that. It was lying thoughts. She had to go way back to let them know how she and Tea Cake had been with one another so they could see she could never shoot Tea Cake out of malice.

She tried to make them see how terrible it was that things were fixed so that Tea Cake couldn't come back to himself until he had got rid of that mad dog that was in him and he couldn't get rid of the dog and live. He had to die to get rid of the dog. But she hadn't wanted to kill him. A man is up against a hard game when he must die to beat it. She made them see how she couldn't ever want to be rid of him. She

didn't plead to anybody. She just sat there and told and when she was through she hushed. She had been through for some time before the judge and the lawyer and the rest seemed to know it. But she sat on in that trial chair until the lawyer told her she could come down.

"The defense rests," her lawyer said. Then he and Prescott whispered together and both of them talked to the judge in secret up high there where he sat. Then they both sat down.

"Gentlemen of the jury, it is for you to decide whether the defendant has committed a cold blooded murder or whether she is a poor broken creature, a devoted wife trapped by unfortunate circumstances who really in firing a rifle bullet into the heart of her late husband did a great act of mercy. If you find her a wanton killer you must bring in a verdict of first degree murder. If the evidence does not justify that then you must set her free. There is no middle course."

The jury filed out and the courtroom began to drone with talk, a few people got up and moved about. And Janie sat like a lump and waited. It was not death she feared. It was misunderstanding. If they made a verdict that she didn't want Tea Cake and wanted him dead, then that was a real sin and a shame. It was worse than murder. Then the jury was back again. Out five minutes by the courthouse clock.

"We find the death of Vergible Woods to be entirely accidental and justifiable, and that no blame should rest upon the defendant Janie Woods."

So she was free and the judge and everybody up there smiled with her and shook her hand. And the white women cried and stood around her like a protecting wall and the Negroes, with heads hung down, shuffled out and away. The sun was almost down and Janie had seen the sun rise on her troubled love and then she had shot Tea Cake and had been in jail and had been tried for her life and now she was free. Nothing to do with the little that was left of the day but to visit the kind white friends who had realized her feelings and thank them. So the sun went down.

She took a room at the boarding house for the night and heard the men talking around the front.

"Aw you know dem white mens wuzn't gointuh do nothin' tuh no woman dat look lak her."

"She didn't kill no white man, did she? Well, long as she don't shoot no white man she kin kill jus' as many niggers as she please."

"Yeah, de nigger women kin kill up all de mens dey wants tuh, but you bet' not kill one uh dem. De white folks will sho hang yuh if yuh do."

"Well, you know whut dey say 'uh white man and uh nigger woman is de freest thing on earth.' Dey do as dey please."

Janie buried Tea Cake in Palm Beach. She knew he loved the 'Glades but it was too low for him to lie with water maybe washing over him with every heavy rain. Anyway, the 'Glades and its waters had killed him. She wanted him out of the way of storms, so she had a strong vault built in the cemetery at West Palm Beach. Janie had wired to Orlando for money to put him away. Tea Cake was the son of Evening Sun, and nothing was too good. The Undertaker did a handsome job and Tea Cake slept royally on his white silken couch among the roses she had bought. He looked almost ready to grin. Janie bought him a brand new guitar and put it in his hands. He would be thinking up new songs to play to her when she got there.

Sop and his friends had tried to hurt her but she knew it was because they loved Tea Cake and didn't understand. So she sent Sop word and to all the others through him. So the day of the funeral they came with shame and apology in their faces. They wanted her quick forgetfulness. So they filled up and overflowed the ten sedans that Janie had hired and added others to the line. Then the band played, and Tea Cake rode like a Pharaoh to his tomb. No expensive veils and robes for Janie this time. She went on in her overalls. She was too busy feeling grief to dress like grief.

XX

BECAUSE they really loved Janie just a little less than they had loved Tea Cake, and because they wanted to think well of themselves, they wanted their hostile attitude forgotten. So they blamed it all on Mrs. Turner's brother and ran him off the muck again. They'd show him about coming back there posing like he was good looking and putting himself where men's wives could look at him. Even if they didn't look it wasn't his fault, he had put himself in the way.

"Naw, Ah ain't mad wid Janie," Sop went around explaining. "Tea Cake had done gone crazy. You can't blame her for puhtectin' herself. She wuz crazy 'bout 'im. Look at de way she put him away. Ah ain't got anything in mah heart aginst her. And Ah never woulda thought uh thing, but de very first day dat lap-legged nigger come back heah makin' out he wuz lookin' fuh work, he come astin' me 'bout how wuz Mr. and Mrs. Woods makin' out. Dat goes tuh show yuh he wuz up tuh somethin'."

"So when Stew-Beef and Bootyny and some of de rest of 'em got behind 'im he come runnin' tuh me tuh save 'im. Ah told 'im, don't come tuh *me* wid yo' hair blowin' back, 'cause, Ah'm gointuh send yuh, and Ah sho did. De bitches' baby!" That was enough, they eased their feelings by beating him and running him off. Anyway, their anger against Janie had lasted two whole days and that was too long to keep remembering anything. Too much of a strain.

They had begged Janie to stay on with them and she had stayed a few weeks to keep them from feeling bad. But the muck meant Tea Cake and Tea Cake wasn't there. So it was just a great expanse of black mud. She had given away everything in their little house except a package of garden seed that Tea Cake had bought to plant. The planting never got done because he had been waiting for the right time of the moon when his sickness overtook him. The seeds reminded Janie of Tea Cake more than anything else because he was always planting things. She had noticed them on the kitchen shelf when she came home from the funeral and had put them in

her breast pocket. Now that she was home, she meant to plant them for remembrance.

Janie stirred her strong feet in the pan of water. The tiredness was gone so she dried them off on the towel.

"Now, dat's how everything wuz, Pheoby, jus' lak Ah told yuh. So Ah'm back home agin and Ah'm satisfied tuh be heah. Ah done been tuh de horizon and back and now Ah kin set heah in mah house and live by comparisons. Dis house ain't so absent of things lak it used tuh be befo' Tea Cake come along. It's full uh thoughts, 'specially dat bedroom.

"Ah know all dem sitters-and-talkers gointuh worry they guts into fiddle strings till dey find out whut we been talkin' 'bout. Dat's all right, Pheoby, tell 'em. Dey gointuh make 'miration 'cause mah love didn't work lak they love, if dey ever had any. Then you must tell 'em dat love ain't somethin' lak uh grindstone dat's de same thing everywhere and do de same thing tuh everything it touch. Love is lak de sea. It's uh movin' thing, but still and all, it takes its shape from de shore it meets, and it's different with every shore."

"Lawd!" Pheoby breathed out heavily, "Ah done growed ten feet higher from jus' listenin' tuh you, Janie. Ah ain't satisfied wid mahself no mo'. Ah means tuh make Sam take me fishin' wid him after this. Nobody better not criticize yuh in mah hearin'."

"Now, Pheoby, don't feel too mean wid de rest of 'em 'cause dey's parched up from not knowin' things. Dem meatskins is *got* tuh rattle tuh make out they's alive. Let 'em consolate theyselves wid talk. 'Course, talkin' don't amount tuh uh hill uh beans when yuh can't do nothin' else. And listenin' tuh dat kind uh talk is jus' lak openin' yo' mouth and lettin' de moon shine down yo' throat. It's uh known fact, Pheoby, you got tuh *go* there tuh *know* there. Yo' papa and yo' mama and nobody else can't tell yuh and show yuh. Two things everybody's got tuh do fuh theyselves. They got tuh go tuh God, and they got tuh find out about livin' fuh theyselves."

There was a finished silence after that so that for the first time they could hear the wind picking at the pine trees. It made Pheoby think of Sam waiting for her and getting fretful.

It made Janie think about that room upstairs—her bedroom. Pheoby hugged Janie real hard and cut the darkness in flight.

Soon everything around downstairs was shut and fastened. Janie mounted the stairs with her lamp. The light in her hand was like a spark of sun-stuff washing her face in fire. Her shadow behind fell black and headlong down the stairs. Now, in her room, the place tasted fresh again. The wind through the open windows had broomed out all the fetid feeling of absence and nothingness. She closed in and sat down. Combing road-dust out of her hair. Thinking.

The day of the gun, and the bloody body, and the courthouse came and commenced to sing a sobbing sigh out of every corner in the room; out of each and every chair and thing. Commenced to sing, commenced to sob and sigh, singing and sobbing. Then Tea Cake came prancing around her where she was and the song of the sigh flew out of the window and lit in the top of the pine trees. Tea Cake, with the sun for a shawl. Of course he wasn't dead. He could never be dead until she herself had finished feeling and thinking. The kiss of his memory made pictures of love and light against the wall. Here was peace. She pulled in her horizon like a great fish-net. Pulled it from around the waist of the world and draped it over her shoulder. So much of life in its meshes! She called in her soul to come and see.

MOSES

Man of the Mountain

Introduction

Moses was an old man with a beard. He was the great law-giver. He had some trouble with Pharaoh about some plagues and led the Children of Israel out of Egypt and on to the Promised Land. He died on Mount Nebo and the angels buried him there. That is the common concept of Moses in the Christian world.

But there are other concepts of Moses abroad in the world. Asia and all the Near East are sown with legends of this character. They are so numerous and so varied that some students have come to doubt if the Moses of the Christian concept is real. Then Africa has her mouth on Moses. All across the continent there are the legends of the greatness of Moses, but not because of his beard nor because he brought the laws down from Sinai. No, he is revered because he had the power to go up the mountain and to bring them down. Many men could climb mountains. Anyone could bring down laws that had been handed to them. But who can talk with God face to face? Who has the power to command God to go to a peak of a mountain and there demand of Him laws with which to govern a nation? What other man has ever seen with his eyes even the back part of God's glory? Who else has ever commanded the wind and the hail? The light and darkness? That calls for power, and that is what Africa sees in Moses to worship. For he is worshipped as a god.

In Haiti, the highest god in the Haitian pantheon is Damballa Ouedo Ouedo Tocan Freda Dahomey and he is identified as Moses, the serpent god. But this deity did not originate in Haiti. His home is in Dahomey and is worshipped there extensively. Moses had his rod of power, which was a living serpent. So that in every temple of Damballa there is a living snake, or the symbol.

And this worship of Moses as the greatest one of magic is not confined to Africa. Wherever the children of Africa have been scattered by slavery, there is the acceptance of Moses as the fountain of mystic powers. This is not confined to Negroes. In America there are countless people of other races

depending upon mystic symbols and seals and syllables said to have been used by Moses to work his wonders. There are millions of copies of a certain book, *The Sixth and Seventh Books of Moses*, being read and consulted in secret because the readers believe in Moses. Some even maintain that the stories of the miracles of Jesus are but Mosaic legends told again. Nobody can tell how many tales and legends of Moses are alive in the world nor how far they have travelled, so many have collected around his name.

So all across Africa, America, the West Indies, there are tales of the powers of Moses and great worship of him and his powers. But it does not flow from the Ten Commandments. It is his rod of power, the terror he showed before all Israel and to Pharaoh, and THAT MIGHTY HAND.

<div align="right">THE AUTHOR.</div>

In all the signs and wonders which the Lord sent him to do in the land of Egypt to Pharaoh, and to all his servants and to all his lands, and in that mighty hand *and in* all the great terror *which Moses showed in the sight of all Israel!*

Deuteronomy 34:11–12

I

HAVE MERCY! Lord, have mercy on my poor soul!"
Women gave birth and whispered cries like this in caves and out-of-the-way places that humans didn't usually use for birthplaces. Moses hadn't come yet, and these were the years when Israel first made tears. Pharaoh had entered the bedrooms of Israel. The birthing beds of Hebrews were matters of state. The Hebrew womb had fallen under the heel of Pharaoh. A ruler great in his newness and new in his greatness had arisen in Egypt and he had said, "This is law. Hebrew boys shall not be born. All offenders against this law shall suffer death by drowning."

So women in the pains of labor hid in caves and rocks. They must cry, but they could not cry out loud. They pressed their teeth together. A night might force upon them a thousand years of feeling. Men learned to beat upon their breasts with clenched fists and breathe out their agony without sound. A great force of suffering accumulated between the basement of heaven and the roof of hell. The shadow of Pharaoh squatted in the dark corners of every birthing place in Goshen. Hebrew women shuddered with terror at the indifference of their wombs to the Egyptian law.

The province of Goshen was living under the New Egypt and the New Egyptian and they were made to know it in many ways. The sign of the new order towered over places of preference. It shadowed over work, and fear was given body and wings.

The Hebrews had already been driven out of their well-built homes and shoved further back in Goshen. Then came more decrees:

1. Israel, you are slaves from now on. Pharaoh assumes no responsibility for the fact that some of you got old before he came to power. Old as well as young must work in his brickyards and road camps.
 a. No sleeping after dawn. Fifty lashes for being late to work.
 b. Fifty lashes for working slow.

 c. One hundred lashes for being absent.

 d. One hundred lashes for sassing the bossman.

 e. Death for hitting a foreman.

2. Babies take notice: Positively no more boy babies allowed among Hebrews. Infants defying this law shall be drowned in the Nile.

Hebrews were disarmed and prevented from becoming citizens of Egypt, they found out that they were aliens, and from one new decree to the next they sank lower and lower. So they had no comfort left but to beat their breasts to crush the agony inside. Israel had learned to weep.

II

THE SUN was setting. Under the brilliant, cloudless Egyptian sun thousands of Hebrew workers were struggling with building stones. Some of their backs were bloody from the lash; many of them were stoopy from age and all of them were sweaty and bent and tired from work. The Egyptian foreman gazed at the drooping sun in awe and breathed with reverence: "Ah, Horus, golden god! Lord of both horizons. The weaver of the beginning of things!"

Amram, struggling with the help of another man to move a heavy stone into place in the foundation, heard him and looked up.

"Horus may be all those good things to the Egyptians, brother, but that sun-god is just something to fry our backs."

"I heard him what he said," the other worker whispered back. "If Horus is the weaver of the beginning of things, he's done put some mighty strange threads in his loom."

"And still and all I used to admire him too, before this new government come in, didn't you?"

"Uhuh. I used to admire everything in Egypt. But the palms and the plains ain't scenery to me no more. They just look like suffering to me now."

"They look that way to me too, now," Amram whispered back, "and the worst part about it is, my wife is going to have another baby."

"I heard about it, Amram. What you going to do? Take her off in the wilderness like I did mine?"

"Don't know exactly, Caleb. One man was telling me he hid his wife out in a boat until it was all over. Turned out to be a girl so it was all right."

"How soon you expecting?"

"Of course you can't never be sure exactly, but we figure in two or three days more. I'm planning on hunting up some good cave or some place like that the secret police don't know about yet. Thought I'd take tonight to locate a place. Will you go along with me?"

"Sure I will. You got the midwife engaged?"

"Yes, that's all fixed up. Going to send my boy Aaron and my girl Miriam along to help around generally. They can do little things around and watch out for spies. Old Puah, the midwife, knows her business all right and she's just as loyal as she can be, but she's getting kind of old, you know."

"That's right. It's good you got a sizeable boy and girl to run errands and to stand watch. It's liable to happen while we are at work, you know."

"Oh, yes, and that's how come I want to find a place and get it sort of fixed up with a quilt or two for my wife to rest on and some water and things like that so when the time comes I won't need to worry. It's a sin and a shame our wives can't even have a baby in peace."

"And that's just the reason I want to go with that delegation to see old Pharaoh tonight. You know a bunch of us are going tonight to him to protest these new decrees, don't you?"

"Sure, but I don't believe it'll do a bit of good. Still and all I want to go just to see what he's going to say this time. But it makes me fighting mad to see him sit up there, him and his so-called advisors, and laugh right in our faces. Reckon we'll get back from our little cave hunt in time to go along with the rest?"

"Hope so. I just don't see how he can keep on putting out all these decrees and making 'em meaner all the time. He's got to give us some kind of a justice sooner or later."

"You think so, Caleb? I don't. I saw his eyes last time. That man loves to see us suffer. He loves to see us hurt and ache. That's how come he lets us come — to be sure he's griping us good. I've about made up my mind that these protests ain't doing us no good at all."

"You reckon, Amram?"

"Sure. You all talk like somebody else made these laws and Pharaoh don't know nothing about 'em. He makes 'em his own self and he's glad when we come tell him they hurt. Why, that's a whole lot of pleasure to him, to be making up laws all the time and to have a crowd like us around handy to pass all his mean ones on. Why, he's got a law about everything under the sun! Next thing you know he'll be saying cats can't have kittens. He figures that it makes a big man out of

him to be passing and passing laws and rules. He thinks that makes him look more like a king. Long time ago he done passed all the laws that could do anybody good. So now he sits up and studies up laws to do hurt and harm, and we're the only folks in Egypt he got the nerve to put 'em on. He aims to keep us down so he'll always have somebody to wipe his feet on. He brags that him and the Egyptian nation is eating high on the hog now."

"Well, it's his time now, be mine after while, maybe."

"Maybe is right. He's got us in the go-long and I just don't see no way out unless he was to die and a better man come along."

"It certainly is hard, Amram, getting use to being a slave."

"And look what he done done! Passed a law we can't go in the temples no more. He says their gods ain't our gods."

"Like what other gods do we know anything about. It gives you a real empty feeling not to have no gods anymore. If we can't go to the temples in Thebes and Memphis and Luxor, we could build us one in Goshen and sacrifice, Amram. Maybe if we do that they might help us to get our rights back again."

"Caleb, those temples were built by Egyptians and those gods were made by Egyptians. Gods always love the people who make 'em. We can't put no faith in them."

"Don't say that, Amram. That don't leave me no way to turn at all. Makes me feel like my insides been ripped out."

"Well, Caleb, I'm giving it out just like I figured it out. We just ain't got no out that I can see. Anybody depending on somebody else's gods is depending on a fox not to eat chickens. I don't see no way out but death and, Caleb, you are up against a hard game when you got to die to beat it."

The foreman was coming so they quit whispering and speeded up their work for a while. It was about dark and they knew they couldn't work much longer anyway. The foreman glanced at them in passing and went on. They began to whisper again right away, under pretense of adjusting a rope for lifting a stone.

"Caleb?"

"I hear you, Amram."

"Wouldn't it be swell if some of us hid knives in our clothes when we went to see Pharaoh?"

"It sure would. But they always search us, don't they, before they let us in."

"I know, but it is something nice to think about, ain't it?"

"Sure is."

"Right now, everybody's nerve is gone, but someday, maybe not in our time, but, he's bound to meet his match first and last."

"That's a long time to wait, Amram, but I reckon it is the best we can do. I hate myself for not trying it even if they all kill me for it."

"That's what I hate 'em for too, making me scared to die. It's a funny thing, the less people have to live for, the less nerve they have to risk losing—nothing."

"Where'd you get that good word from, Amram? It sure is the truth. I know it by myself."

"Oh, you learn things as you go along. I hope I don't have another boy, Caleb. Even if the soldiers don't find him and kill him, I don't want him feeling like I feel. I want him to be a man."

III

A MRAM and Caleb got off and plodded on home. Amram was full of feelings about his wife's condition and Caleb talked about the protest meeting. He wanted Amram to go if he could.

"I guess you're right about it not doing no good and I reckon we all know it. But I guess the reason we go is it makes us feel like we still got some say-so over our life. In that way we don't feel quite so much like mules."

Amram said, "Eat your supper just as quick as you can if you going with me and let's go locate a hiding place for my wife."

They said goodbye at the door of Amram's hut and Caleb went on home. Amram stepped inside to fate. Jochebed's water had broken and she was in labor. Old Puah was in the back room squatting down by the straw pallet of Jochebed whispering to her to "bear down!" in her harsh old voice.

Amram knelt by his wife and kissed her. She lifted her arms about his neck and hung there.

"Amram," she whispered, "you won't have no time to move me at all. But you mustn't let me scream, hear? No matter how hard the pain gets you mustn't let me scream. Pharaoh's secret police don't never stop prowling."

"I know that. Oh, honey, I hate for our child to come like this. I don't feel like no man at all."

"You can't help it, honey. You done the best you could. Just don't let me scream out when I get so bad I don't know what I'm doing. Hold my mouth good, Amram. Don't let me expose our child to murder, in case it's a boy."

"I promise, Jochebed, but this is a mean moment in life."

She hugged him faintly and smiled up. "The pains took me hard once or twice. I was afraid it was going to come before you got here," she said with a sort of happiness in her voice because her husband was there at her time.

In a little while Amram started to eat his supper. But no sooner did he begin than Jochebed uttered a cry. He flew back to her side and lifted her head in his arms and put one

347

hand over her mouth. She tried hard to scream, but Amram was there.

The back of Amram's hard hand filled her mouth. His rough hand clamped down fiercely over her lower face. Jochebed fought for her breath and for the boon of shrieking out her agony and suffering.

"Shhh! The Egyptians will hear you!"

The woman may have heard, but she struggled harder to release the agony of her loins through cries. Her lungs almost exploded with the pent-in air. She clawed at her husband's hands which so relentlessly smothered her gasping cries. She drew up her knees violently and arched her back.

Now old Puah, the midwife, knelt over Jochebed and laid helping hands upon her belly. "Bear down!" the midwife commanded sternly. "Bear down, Jochebed, and have done with this birthing. It is taking much too long. Bear down, I tell you!" The command was stern but whispered. It was muted by fear like every other sound in the house. Old Puah put her lips to the other's ear and beseeched, "Ah, Jochebed, will you not hurry up with this child before the soldiers pass again?"

"Shut up, woman," Amram began, but had to turn all of his attention and strength to muffling the agony of his wife. She was flinging her head from side to side to wrench free of the hands that gripped her lower face like a vice. Finally the pain wave passed and she subsided on the straw limp and white.

"Ah, it is awful when a woman cannot even cry out in childbirth," Puah said. "When will these Egyptians be punished for their crimes?"

"Hush! Mouth almighty!" Amram said. "The very air in Goshen has ears. Have you got the medicine fixed for her and ready?"

"Certainly, Amram. I didn't start to delivering babies just yesterday. As soon as I know a woman's time is near, I boil the herbs for her."

"Where is it, then?" Amram whispered anxiously.

"In that pot over against the wall. But do you think it is safe to give it now? It will speed up her labor but—" She looked fearfully over her shoulder towards the dark door of the outer room.

Jochebed set her teeth and hissed a groan. Instantly her husband's hands flew to her mouth. From his kneeling position he looked over his shoulder into the outer room and whispered "Aaron."

A young voice charged with fear whispered back from the dark outer room. "Yessir, papa."

"Don't stand there yelling back and forth with me! Come and hear what I have to say."

Aaron the boy entered the back room lit dimly by the crude oil lamp on the floor and stood timidly back of the squatting Puah. The lamp shone between the pale face of his mother on the straw pallet and the tortured features of his father kneeling over her. He didn't feel so much like a coward as he had out there in the dark front room for he saw the fear on the faces of the three grown folks in the room.

"Yessir, papa, what you want with me?"

"Where is your sister?"

"Miriam is out there — " indicating the outer room.

"Tell her to come here."

Aaron tiptoed back into the other room without a sound and came back shoving Miriam before him. They knelt before Amram and presented their ears.

"Miriam, you go and squat just inside the front door and watch. If anyone approaches come quickly. Do not call out."

"Yessir, papa."

"Aaron, you go outside."

"Not outside, papa. Please don't make me go outside," Aaron gasped in terror. "The secret police!"

"Yes, outside!" Amram answered sternly. "These Egyptian scoundrel-beasts must be overcome somehow. There ain't but a few of us Hebrews. We ain't got nothing to fight with. Do as I tell you. Go out to the main street and watch. When you see a band of the plug-uglies coming, run back and whisper to Miriam. She will give us the sign."

"But I ain't but twelve years old. All them Egyptian soldiers — "

"Go on! It's done got so that Israelite boys can't wait to get grown to be men. You will have to be a man right now." Amram gestured towards the pallet, the midwife and the room and Aaron stumbled out into the Egyptian darkness to

watch. Miriam took her post by the house door and Puah
gave Jochebed the drink she called the "friend of women"
while Amram knelt in love and fear beside her head. He
looked down on the thick red hair of his wife, her white face
with the eyes closed in weariness, the hollows in her neck and
her breasts. He saw the tracks of time over all and thought,
"Of course, Jochebed ain't a girl no more. We got a son
twelve years old and a daughter who is nine. Girl-wives must
turn into women some time or other."

The oil in the lamp was getting low and Amram moved to
replenish it. Old Puah measured and folded swaddling clothes
and the night kept its silence outside the house.

Suddenly screams full of terror, sounds of strife and things
overthrown came from another quarter of the village. Screams,
gagging cries, metal on metal, metal on softer substances.

Amram rushed to the middle door. "Where is that,
Miriam?"

"Beyond the house of Hur," the girl sobbed. "Oh, please
let me call in Aaron and let's bar the door, papa. The soldiers
will kill us!"

A great scream of pain burst from the throat of Jochebed
and Amram flew to her bedside and silenced her as before.
The struggle was brief and fierce. Then it all ended with a
little sigh of relief at the momentary cessation of pain. Amram
smoothed back her hair and put his palm soothingly upon his
wife's head.

"You, you let me scream," Jochebed accused Amram weakly
between subsiding gasps.

Amram thought to quiet her fears with soothing words,
but just then Aaron plunged through the front door, stum-
bling over Miriam's knees and flung his ghastly face into the
back room.

"Papa! Mama! Puah! They had a baby at Jacob's house and
the soldiers took it and killed it! It was a boy baby, papa, so
the Egyptians took it and killed it. Jacob tried to save his baby
so they killed him too. I saw it all from the darkness outside."

"How did they know the child was there?" Amram asked.

"They have been skulking around the neighborhood since
yesterday, someone told me. Maybe they heard it cry. Perhaps
somebody told on them."

Three pairs of eyes sought the midwife at once.

"We know your loyalty, Puah," Amram said, "but some of the midwives have been known to go from the confinement to the Egyptians."

"And, papa," Aaron went on, "the soldiers also killed Jacob's wife. Was it because she cried so loud?"

For a space they all swam in the silence in the room. All their bodies leaned forward as if in flight. The midwife, the husband and the woman on the straw, these were crumbling bags of fear. The naked flame of the rush light on the floor even tried to flee before the tiny breeze from the door. Then suddenly Jochebed clenched her fists and groaned like the earth birthing mountains, and the body and feel of the sound threatened them like a sword until the cry of the newborn baby ended it all.

Old Puah was squatted on her haunches to receive the child. The man heard the cry but did not look behind him. He looked at the pain-struck face of his wife and she begged him with her looks. Puah busied herself around behind him for a minute and then she spoke.

"Amram, your wife has borne you a son."

IV

Amram bowed his head for a space, then straightened tensely as if he listened to every sound in Egypt, however distant. As if he gazed and saw every sight and scene in the Kingdom from end to end. As if he felt every throb and tasted every draught.

"A son?" he gasped at last.

"A son," Puah answered him, "and a beautiful child."

"It must not live to cry again. Give it to me."

Jochebed roused herself upon her elbows.

"No."

"Give me the child, Puah," Amram said with a fearful calm in his voice. "It is a whole lot better for it to stop breathing in my hands than for those—"

Jochebed had struggled to her knees. "No! My son is going to live. If the Egyptians come to kill it, then they got to kill me before they do him. If Pharaoh done scared all the love out of its papa, then let all Egypt come against me. I can't die but one time nohow, and it might as well be now. Puah, hand me my son!"

Amram turned his stricken face upon his wife. "Jochebed, there are different kinds of courage. Sometimes ordinary love and courage ain't enough for the occasion. But a woman wouldn't recognize a time like that when it come."

"Is my son got a Hebrew for a father or a Pharaoh?"

"But you heard what Aaron said."

"What of it? Pharaoh may be dead tomorrow. Who knows? Let's take a chance."

Amram looked about him wearily. "Well, if we must fool the crocodiles, let us begin and do it right. Aaron, go and watch up and down the road while I dig out a cave under the inside wall of the house. It must be large enough to hold the child."

Aaron arose sullenly. "But, papa, the soldiers may come along and kill me. They'll ask me what I'm doing out there."

"Go on! As soon as I have finished I will come and stand

guard myself and you can go to bed. The sound of my battle with the soldiers will warn you all to hide the child."

Jochebed, clutching her new son to her breast, threw her husband a look so full of love and happiness that Amram felt for the moment that the sacrifice of his own body was a little thing.

The police, the secret police. That was what worried the people of Goshen. Just to look around, they were nowhere, but from the effects they were everywhere. Were ears pressed to their walls at night? It seemed so. A casual conversation might bring a public whipping and extra hours of work. How did Pharaoh find out so much? Hebrew began to suspect Hebrew. Men were accused of treason and revolt for saying Pharaoh was not kind. Everything was treason and subject to labor fines and lashings. No one except women were sent to jail. Pharaoh said it was a waste of man power and groceries to fasten up able-bodied Hebrews in jail. Every crime not punishable by death could be worked out in the brickyards, the stone quarries or on buildings. A beautiful new city bore his name and more were being planned. The Hebrews did not know all this about new plans. They talked together and said that when the new city of Rameses was finished, that Pharaoh would be satisfied. Some of them even thought that they might get back their houses and lands.

But Pharaoh took counsel with his servants. Week after week he called them to listen to his newest ideas that he was going to work into plans. The servants told Pharaoh that all of his thoughts had genius and after ten meetings they told him his plans were perfect. So he called the Hebrew elders together to listen. He was going to speak to them in the public place. His messengers went all through Goshen and they went on all the public works telling them to come to the meeting. Pharaoh was going to be good and kind enough to appear before them in person and speak to them of his own free will. Three days after the announcement he was going to speak on the Hebrew future.

The people in Goshen were excited. Hope burst its binding string and gushed over the province.

Jochebed held her baby on her lap and smiled at her husband.

"Maybe we won't have to hide our baby no more, Amram. Maybe we can circumcise it and hold a christening."

"Maybe."

"I could make some little honey cakes and have palm wine and beer. That would be just like old times, wouldn't it?"

"Yes, it would. Like when Aaron and Miriam come."

"Only this baby is so much prettier than either one of them ever was, ain't he?"

"I think so. He's awful fine looking. Too bad we can't show him around some. Finest looking baby in Egypt."

"You know, Amram, I just felt all along that Pharaoh couldn't keep up his meanness. It was too awful to last."

"What makes you think he's changed his mind? Him sending for us got everybody to hoping and wishing, but it don't have to be what we hope at all."

"Oh, there you go again! Amram, what makes you always looking for the dark side of everything? I declare to my rest you just like an old sorehead bear. Naturally, Pharaoh is fixing to free us and leave our boy babies alone. He couldn't do nothing else."

"Oh, yes, he could, too. Everybody to their own nature. He don't have to smell through our nose at all, and I don't believe nothing until I see it."

"Aw, Amram, you wrong this time. I done talked to a heap of people and they all think like I do."

"You all ain't thinking, you wishing. Anyhow, keep our baby in the hole just like we been doing for the last three months. Keep him hid till we hear further. 'Tain't no use in taking chances."

"He's getting so strong! Look at him trying to sit alone! Look at him! He's mad now cause he can't quite make it. Listen at the voice he's got on him!"

"That's just the thing I'm scared of. I can't half work for worrying. Some of them secret spies is bound to hear him before long. Then what we going to do, honey? I thought they had us last night."

"Oh, a couple of days more and we won't have to worry."

"I hope you know what you hoping about, but old Pharaoh is mighty hard, honey, mighty hard."

"You just wait till the meeting and you going to see I'm

right. God wouldn't let this thing we're under keep on like it's going. It's bound to come a change."

"What god you talking about, Jochebed? These gods was here in Egypt long before we ever thought of coming here. Don't look to them for too much, honey. Then you won't be disappointed."

Jochebed made to lay the child down on the pallet and it burst into lusty crying. Instantly the woman and her husband became hunted beasts. She grabbed the baby up and pressed its face into her soft bosom and glared towards the window and the door like something at bay. Amram crept to the door and looked around outside. When he returned the child had vanished into the dark hole under the wall, and the hole covered with a mat, but its voice could be heard nevertheless.

"See what I told you?" Amram gasped. "First and last we're all going to be butchered without mercy. Oh, Lord! why didn't I die before I cried? Why did I have to live for this?"

Jochebed seized the child again and pacified him quickly.

"Well, we got by again," she sighed with relief.

"But for how long?" Amram demanded. "Tomorrow, maybe, or in the next half an hour."

"You didn't see no spies around outside, did you?"

"Jochebed, you don't have to see spies for them to see you. Maybe the soldiers are on the way already."

Jochebed started to say something, but her husband shut her off with a gesture. His head hung down and for several minutes the thud-thud-thudding of his fists against his breast were like a funeral march in drum tones; a tearless sorrow throbbing over death; a muted wail without words. Finally he could bear his feelings and he stopped.

"You oughtn't to carry on like that, Amram, when Pharaoh done sent for you. Maybe things will be all right after you all talk with him and explain things."

"Listen, woman, Pharaoh is a flesh and blood man just like you and me, strange as it may seem. This won't be the first of his hearing how bad off we is here in Goshen. We ain't in the fix we're in by no accident, neither. He knows the feelings of a husband and a father. It is a terrible thing to strip a man of his meaning to his wife and children. Pharaoh knows all that. He means to do all that he is doing and maybe more. He has

hunted around in his own heart for something to measure one's feelings by and the things that would hurt us the most. Then when he found them, he has done those things with calculated spite. You're just dumb to the fact. And another thing, he ain't sending for us to better our condition. He hates the very sight of us. The only reason he consents to look at us at all is because he wants to destroy us some more and enjoy seeing it gripe us."

The woman bent like a willow and cried softly over the child like a thin soprano sob song. Amram carried the bass part with his fists against his chest. Finally they crept to bed without eating. But all night the woman soothed herself by thinking "maybe." Amram dreamed dreams of smiting out with a bloody sword. Then it was time for him to get up and go to work again.

Everybody at work was whispering about the meeting with Pharaoh and everybody had made up their minds what would happen there, each one according to his courage. Some rolled over and over in a wallow of hope and scratched their backs with wishes. These men were afraid to think. Some stared in the face of probabilities and braced themselves for the shock.

So the meeting came. The Hebrew Elders went and stood in the public place that was full of soldiers fully armed. Then Pharaoh came in surrounded by his high-born servants and took his place. After his chief scribe got through telling the Hebrews what a blessing it was for Pharaoh to not only let them see his sacred body, he was actually going to let them listen to his voice. He was going to speak to them, using his own sacred voice and lips. They had done nothing to deserve such a great blessing. It just went to show how very kind and gentle and gracious great Pharaoh was. Always considering others before he did himself, and so on and so forth. Then Pharaoh himself rose to speak.

He said that his goodness and mercies were too well known to waste time talking about. The only reason he mentioned it at all was because he could see all over Goshen that it was not appreciated as he had hoped and expected. Here they were, Hebrews, who had come down into Egypt as the allies and aides of those oppressors of the Egyptian people, and as such had trampled on the proud breast of Egyptian liberty for

more than three hundred years. But the gods had used the magnificent courage of the real Egyptians to finally conquer and expel those sheep-herding interlopers whom the Hebrews had aided in every way they could to deprive the real Egyptians of their homes and their liberties. And now that they, the Hebrews, were conquered and beaten, he might have killed them all. That would have been right and just, seeing the great injury his beloved country had suffered at their hands. But did he do that? No! He was gentle and he spared them and allowed them to continue to live in the country. All he had required of them was that they work and build him a few cities here and there to pay back in a small way for all the great benefits they had received in their long residence in Egypt and also to give back some of the wealth they had so ruthlessly raped from the helpless body of Egypt when she was in no position to defend herself.

And now, what does he discover? He finds that these same Hebrews, instead of setting to work with glad hearts, happy that they have been given a chance, even in a small way, to make some sort of pay back on their huge debt to Egypt, and to redeem themselves in the eyes of the world, were congregating in Goshen and planning protests against his mild and beneficent decrees! It was hard to believe, but he happened to have the facts. So what did it prove? It was too plain for even the most merciful to ignore that these Hebrews whom he had saved from the fury of his people and against the advice of his wise counsellors, did not want to pay their debt to Egypt and decency. They were doing all they could to evade it. This show of ingratitude and hardness of heart was bound to arouse the mild but courageous Egyptian nation to fury unless something was done to show the loyal nation, who had suffered so much already, that its ruler would not further encourage such iniquities. His piercing eyes and all-hearing ears had discovered a well-organized plot to swindle Egypt out of her just amount of work out of them, by slowing up their work—a most reprehensible and low-down trick worthy only of Hyksos and Hebrews! But he had a remedy for this. The overseers had been instructed to use the lash more freely to speed up work and to rub salt in the welts raised by the whip. But still that did not repay poor suffering Egypt for the work

they had lost in the past. So he now decreed that Hebrews must begin work one hour earlier in the morning and work one hour more in the evening.

Furthermore, the dishonesty and general wickedness of the Hebrews had reached the gods in their remote retreats and the gods had cried out for cleansing. The gods had announced emphatically that they would visit no altars which Hebrews were allowed to approach. Hebrews must not approach a single temple in Egypt. Neither must they build temples to Egyptian gods in Goshen. The gods were forbidden the boundaries of Goshen.

Just in passing he wanted to acknowledge a petition with many signatures that had reached him. In it the Hebrews had again raised that question of leaving Egypt. He just wanted to say neither in this generation nor yet in the generations of their great grandchildren would they be allowed to escape their just punishments. Did the Egyptians run away when they were being robbed and oppressed by these same malefactors and their friends? No!

Then he went on to say that even greater wickedness had been uncovered. His laws and most royal decrees were being flouted. He, after taking counsel with his wise advisors, had decreed that all boy babies born to the Hebrews must be destroyed. But he found that certain people were plotting together to make his laws come to nothing. And something was going to be done about it. The strong arm of Pharaoh had never failed against his enemies, in spite of his merciful nature.

Pharaoh paused and looked at the faces of the Hebrew Elders grouped below and before him. He saw the uncomfortable stir that moved them almost imperceptibly. The slight shifting of feet; the nervous movements of hands, the gaping, stricken faces of the less wary among them, and he smiled.

"I see that I got you by the short hair when I told you I know what is going on about those boy babies. That is not the worst yet. My police have captured several of those midwives who have been waiting on your womenfolks in secret. They claimed that they wouldn't talk, but when my men got through with them they talked and talked aplenty, from old Puah on down."

Amram started violently and then hated himself for his weakness, but he couldn't help himself. It looked like Pharaoh was looking straight at him. He could see the gleam in Pharaoh's eyes as he went on. "So now I know all about those births behind rocks and in caves and such as that. And I know all about those babies hidden out in the woods and in holes dug under house walls. My soldiers will be around to call on you, and when they come to call, they won't miss nobody. I done told you."

The Elders looked at one another and finally Hur spoke up. "Give us a chance, Great Pharaoh. We proved ourselves builders and generally constructive under the last regime. We love Egypt. It is the only home we know. Trust us and see if we are good citizens or not."

"Why should I trust people without monuments and memories? It looks bad to me—a people who honor nobody. It is a sign that you forget your benefactors as soon as possible after the need is past."

"We don't build monuments, but we do have memories."

"How is anyone to know that? Take for instance your great man Joseph. As long as you have been in Egypt you have not raised one stone to his memory."

"Look at it another way. Perhaps we do not need stones to remind us. It could be that some folks need stones to remind them. It could be that memorial stones are signs of bad memories. We just don't trust our memories to stones."

Pharaoh's face darkened at this. He laughed in a harsh way.

"Well, anyway, you won't need no stones to remind your children and your great-great-grandchildren of the punishment that Rameses put on you. You are going to work and work and work. You are going to weep and you are going to bleed and bleed until you have paid in a measure for your crimes against Egypt. I done told you now. Don't give me no trouble unless you want to make me mad."

The Elders shuffled out of the place somehow and started on home. "No rest, no property, no babies, no gods," Amram gasped. "Why would anybody want to live? Why don't we kill ourselves and be done with the thing?"

"Maybe we hope we'll beat the game somehow without dying. That's human, ain't it?" somebody said and so they

dragged themselves on home to tell what was said. They ground their souls between their teeth as they went but there was nothing to spit out. It was just a grinding and an aching.

Jochebed was asleep when Amram got home, so he wouldn't wake her to hear what he had to say. Tomorrow was time enough to start the weeping. So he stepped over the straw bed of his two older children and stretched out beside his wife till daylight. Then he told her.

She didn't say anything and she didn't stand up. She took the sleeping baby in her arms and sat there on the straw pallet staring down in its face. Amram squatted down before her and stared down at the baby too. Its little hands and feet and the helpless soft body was between the man and the woman and they huddled over it in silence for a long time. Then Amram said huskily, "Shall we grant it merciful escape, Jochebed?" and felt in her lap for her hand and pressed it. He could not bear to look at her eyes.

"No, Amram."

"Those brutal soldiers, Jochebed, grin with pleasure when they hunt down one of our children like hounds after rabbits."

"I don't care, honey. If my child is murdered, old Pharaoh has got to do the murdering his own self. I ain't going to allow him to make me do his murdering for him. If the gods want the life of my innocent boy, then they got to make a move and show me. I mean to hold out till they do. Let's hide it on the river like some others I know."

"All right, honey. I sure do want him to live and do well."

Impulsively he caught the child up in his arms.

"To think that we have not had the joy of giving it a name, nor fondling it, nor circumcising it lest it cry out and be found."

"It sure is sad. But you hurry on to work, Amram, before the soldiers come to hunt you up. It sure would hurt me to my heart to have to see 'em lay that salted lash on your back."

"But what will you do about this big, fat son of ours?"

"Go on to work, Amram, and I will find some way. One of the children is always on guard."

Amram hurried off and Jochebed called the children to her. "Go and cut me rushes from the marshes," she told them.

"Go and hurry back fast. I got to make a good basket. Get me the best rushes you can."

The basket was scarcely started when Amram reached home after dark. Jochebed had given way to her despair more than once and crumpled on the straw beside her growing child. Twice he had cried so loud that Jochebed knew he could be heard all over the neighborhood and prayed that no prowling Egyptians were near.

So four people forgot hunger that night and sleep was not present in them. Four pairs of ears strained towards the night outside the house and four hearts fainted at every creeping sound as four pairs of fingers toiled over the basket until it was woven strong and tight and daubed and calked with pitch and mud.

"You think, Amram, if I took the baby before Pharaoh and begged him, he might get sorry for me and let me keep my child?"

"Get sorry for you? No. He plans harsher measures for us. The horn that is hooking us gets stiffer day by day. If you could only run away with him or hide him for a while!"

"There ain't no other way then, but the river. All the roads is full of spies. Goshen is ringed with steel. Amram, do you think this basket will be safe?"

"I hope so, Jochebed. It is a real good basket, even if we was in a hurry. I don't believe the water will get in to it. Hand me the baby and let us see how he fits in it."

Jochebed lined the basket lovingly with one of her garments and then with goose feathers before she laid the child inside. Then she knew the basket was ready, so it was the time for tears. There was nothing any more with which to busy her hands and brace her spirits. She beat her breasts and wept without restraint for several minutes. Amram bowed his head in silence. Aaron and Miriam sat in dumb terror watching their parents and occasionally smiting their breasts to show their sympathy of grief.

"We must put him on the river, Amram," Jochebed said at last. "That is why I made the boat—the basket for him."

"But why upon the river?"

"We ain't never been nowhere, Amram, so we don't know. It could be other people besides those we know live along the

Nile. It may even run outside of Egypt. Maybe someone among them may find him and love him. Maybe even in Egypt there might be somebody with a heart." She broke down into sobbing again. "Anyway, there ain't nothing left for us to do. One thing I know Pharaoh can't make out of me. He can't take my son away from me and make me a murderer at the same time. That's one thing I don't aim to let him do."

Amram looked at his wife's face and was fed inwardly by her look. So the night of the morning found them with the basket moving stealthily down to the Nile. At the river, Amram withdrew with Aaron and Miriam to watch. Jochebed fed the child copiously from her breasts and put him back into the basket. Then the thought assailed her that perhaps her basket was not seaworthy after all. She took him out again and held him across her knees as she tried her woven boat upon the water. It floated dry and lightly upon the stream. She drew it back to her and placed her baby in it for the last time and covered it with the lid. The little bark was propelled out from the shore among the tall bulrushes and rested there with the Nile lapping it gently and lulling the child to sleep.

Jochebed squatted there watching until her husband sent Miriam to call her lest she be found there by some Egyptians. She rose stiffly after a while and closed her bosom slowly. She spoke to Miriam and told the girl to station herself beneath the clump of palms not too far away to see what happened to the child. She must go home and sprawl on the earthen floor with her fears. Then she spoke to the morning, and the Nile: "Nile, youse such a great big river and he is such a little bitty thing. Show him some mercy, please."

V

ALL the little stars crept back into heaven and the sun rose.
Miriam, standing on the watch wall among the palms,
calmed herself and sat down. Her eyes wandered from the
particular spot among the bulrushes to bulrushes in general.
Then she regarded the river and the activities on the river. Far
up-stream, several fishing boats were out. A group was draw-
ing water with oxen for the fields. Water birds swooping and
diving, and occasionally feeding-fishes, flinging their bodies
out of the water in the exultation of the kill. Then Miriam
went to sleep.

She woke up with a guilty start and looked for the little ark
on the river which contained her baby brother. It was not
there. She looked all around her to see if anyone was watch-
ing her and feeling sure on that score, she crept down to the
spot where the basket had been and parted the bulrushes. The
child and his basket were gone, that was all. And she had not
the least idea of where he had gone, nor how. What should
she tell her parents? She began to cry.

But her tears did not flow long. Down-stream at some dis-
tance she saw a glorious sight. A large party of young women
dressed in rich clothing was clustered on the bank. The morn-
ing sun struck against shining metal ornaments and drew
Miriam away from her search for her brother and from her
tired and frightened self. She crept down-stream, keeping as
close to the shrubbery growing along the river as best she
could.

Ten young women stood out in the stream holding up a
long piece of cloth that shielded another young woman from
public view, or almost shielded her. Two others washed and
massaged her for several minutes while Miriam watched
from her hiding place. It was a marvelous scene to her and
she felt uplifted from gazing on it. This could be nobody
else but the Princess Royal—only daughter of Pharaoh,
newly widowed by the death of the Assyrian crown prince
and returned to Egypt. Miriam noted her person, her trap-
pings and her attendants and said to herself: "Royalty is a

wonderful thing. It sure is a fine happening. It ought to be so that everybody that wanted to could be a queen. I wish I could get close enough to touch that princess. I wish I was one of those girls waiting on her, even."

The Princess came up out of the river. The girls holding the screening cloth moved up with her on dry land and kept shielding her until she was rubbed down, oiled and dressed. There was chatting and laughter. The lift of a thin, sweet tone came to where she crouched in the bushes and the child Miriam stood up and craned her neck to see where it came from. And now she saw two black eunuchs squatting on their heels at a distance from the bathing party playing, one on a flute and the other on a stringed instrument. Some of the girls took positions and began to dance. The others went on folding garments, packing caskets with toilet articles and generally preparing to leave the bathing place. The dance ended and then the music. The Princess rose from the stool placed for her and was instantly surrounded by her party. One eunuch carried a sunshade over her head. Two girls waved ornate fans on long handles. Miriam's heart beat fast as she realized that they were coming in her direction. Now she would be able to see them at close range.

But the party did not move off at once. Something in the water had attracted the attention of the Princess. She was directing someone in the party to it. One of the girls removed her sandals and went down into the stream and came out with a dark, oval object. "Aha!" thought Miriam, "they had forgotten the casket in which is kept the things for washing the Princess. They will get a good scolding for that. But I wish they had left it so I could have seen what was in it. That would have been wonderful! I could have run after her and returned it to her and maybe she might have made me one of her ladies in waiting. Oh, a lady in waiting to the Princess! Nothing could be greater than that."

The party moved off leisurely and came abreast of Miriam. They were not more than thirty feet from where she hid. She was so entranced that she stood up, the better to see, and one of the ladies saw her.

"It is a Hebrew!" she all but screamed. "What is she doing here? Catch her!"

"She is only a child," the Princess said lightly. "She can do nothing harmful."

"But she might be a spy," one of the ladies pointed out.

"Yes, these Hebrews may be planning to assassinate you."

The eunuchs drew their swords at this and looked threateningly at Miriam.

"Nonsense!" the Princess rejoined. "No one knew we were coming here today and no one—not even I—knows where we go tomorrow."

"Still she should be questioned. Never can tell what these Hebrews might do to overthrow the government."

"Governments are not overthrown by little girls," the Princess retorted, and the party swept on its way towards the palace of Pharaoh.

Miriam stood blinking for a long time. She was completely beside herself with ecstasy. She had seen the daughter of Pharaoh. The daughter of Pharaoh had spoken to her. Well, anyhow she had spoken of her. All her life she was going to remember the gait of the Princess when she walked. She wondered if that movement was a special gift to royalty or if people like her could copy it. She certainly meant to try it before her playmates. "This is the way the Princess walks," she would tell them. "I know, because I saw her and she spoke to me." She flew home as fast as her legs could move to tell what she had seen.

She burst into the house and found her mother stretched upon the floor facing the little cave where she had hidden the baby so often, and her mother was holding one of his little garments and weeping bitterly. Then Miriam remembered, not just that she had seen the Princess and heard her speak, but why she had been posted at that lonely place on the bank of the Nile at all. She recoiled from her mother's face in panic.

"What happened to my child, Miriam?"

"Oh—er—" Miriam came back to herself from her dreams of the palace. "I—I don't know, mama."

"You don't know?" Jochebed sprang to her feet in fury. "You don't know when you were left there to find out? You stupid dunce! Why *don't* you know? Didn't you stay where I put you?"

"Yes. Yes, mama, but I—I went to sleep. I was so tired from last night that I couldn't help it. I went to sleep after sun-up."

Seeing her frenzied mother searching for something with which to strike her made Miriam come alive inside more thoroughly than she ever had done before in her life and suddenly an explanation flashed across her brain.

"You see, mama, while I was asleep, the basket with your baby in it floated down-stream and the Princess saw it and took him home to the palace with her."

"The Princess? You mean Pharaoh's daughter?"

"Yes, mama, she's the very one. She was bathing herself in the river down below me and the basket with the baby in it floated down to where she was after she had finished her bath and was perfumed and anointed and dressed with a whole heap of pretty things in her hair. Then when she was ready to go she saw the baby and sent and took it with her. I met the party on the road and tried to ask 'em what they was doing with your child, but they took and drawed a sword on me and made like they was going to kill me."

Jochebed wept bitterly. She felt her heart crowding her throat. She felt like the whole of Egypt was crowded into her middle and still she felt empty of joy.

"Now I know my poor little baby will be killed," she wailed and bowed herself again upon the floor. "The sea-buzzards will kill it just for fun."

"No, mama, she was real nice. She walked like this and smiled at me. And when some of her servants threatened me she told them to leave me alone. She had music played when she found the child and took it to the palace like she was proud. I love the Princess, mama. I wish she would take me to the palace too."

"Miriam, I ain't to be fooled with today: is you telling me the truth, or is you trying to dodge a whipping for not minding the baby?"

"But, mama, I *did* see her send for the casket and take it home with her. One of her ladies in waiting carried it herself."

"Oh, I am so sorry that I did not stay myself to watch! Maybe I won't never know what become of my baby. Miriam,

are you sure it was the same basket which we made to hold the baby?"

"Yes, ma'am. I could see them get it even from a distance. And the Princess had on red sandals and her toe-nails was red."

"And how did she treat the baby?"

"She made them play music and they danced for her because she was so glad because she had found the child. I could see everything they did, mama. I wasn't far from the Princess. She told 'em she loved the child a lot already."

Jochebed stiffened her back and stood up suddenly. "I ain't a bit surprised to hear the Princess loved him. He is a mighty pretty child, and smart as a whip for his age." A glow began to gleam through her seamed face. "So my child is in the palace! I'll go let the neighbors know." She tied her best shawl over her head and got as far as the door and stopped. "No, I reckon I ought to tell my husband about our son getting to be a Prince of the house of Pharaoh before I tell the others." She took off her shawl and turned back. "Get busy, Miriam, folks will be coming in to see us when they hear. The house must look better than it's looking now for big doings like this. We is kinfolks to the Pharaohs now." She thrust the broom into Miriam's hands and herself began to make up a batch of honey cookies.

Jochebed began to mix the dough. She took great care with it and all the time laboring Miriam for more detail.

"Miriam."

"Yes, mama."

"Come here to me. You didn't tell me whether the baby cried or not when the Princess opened the basket."

"No, ma'am. I did not hear him cry at all. And, mama, the Princess had a headdress of blue feathers that fell down over her shoulders in a real pretty way like this." Miriam grabbed a shawl and draped it over her head and strutted about.

"What did she *say*, Miriam, when she saw him? Tell me her exact words."

"She said, 'What a beautiful child!'"

"Did she say that? She must be a real fine Princess sure enough."

"Oh, she is. Maybe if I was to go and ask her, she might take me for a nurse to the baby."

"Hush up talking foolish! Youse too young. She would need a woman with breast milk. I will go myself tomorrow to the palace and find out if they need anybody."

Jochebed kneaded dough vigorously and bustled about.

"Blow up the fire, Miriam. I want a bed of coals to bake these hot cakes." She patted out the little honey cakes and put them on the fire. "Think I *will* run over to Rachel's, Hur's wife, and tell her about it. We have always been the best of friends and she would feel hurt if I kept anything secret from her like this. I'll tell her it's a secret and she won't tell a soul. Mind you now, Miriam, don't let them cakes burn."

When Amram entered the door that night, very tired and sore from work, he greeted his wife with "What is this I hear about the daughter of Pharaoh adopting our son?"

"Oh, you done heard it already?" Jochebed asked with a pleased air.

"Who in Goshen ain't heard? That is all the folks are talking about. Well, is it so?"

"Certainly, it is so."

"How do you know? Did the palace say anything to you?"

"Why, no. Reckon they didn't count us enough to tell us, us being Hebrews. But Miriam saw her bathing party at the river and saw them take the child."

"Humph! Pharaoh's killing every Hebrew boy child he can get his hands on and his daughter taking one home for a son. Ridiculous!"

"Oh, the Egyptians may not be as cruel as you make them out to be. Come here, Miriam, and tell your pa what you saw and what you heard."

Miriam told again what she had told her mother and added, "And she wanted me to come to the palace to take care of the child for her."

"See, Mr. Smarty!" Jochebed cried triumphantly. "Always hunting for something mean and low. You don't even believe butter is greasy."

"Oh, I'm willing enough to believe if you give me something to go on. I still want to ask Miriam some questions. For instance, if Miriam was *not* close enough to make out any special marks on the casket, how can she know it was the same one? Millions like that been made in Egypt. If Miriam

didn't hear the baby cry how could she tell *what* was in the basket? It might have been the toilet articles of the Princess or a hundred other things. And then again even if she had heard a baby cry unless she was close enough to see the baby, how does she know it was the same one? Couldn't the party have brought a baby with them from the palace?"

Jochebed lost her good nature at that. Possibly he touched upon fears already hidden in her heart so she flew hot and turned upon Amram.

"Oh, you make me sick with your doubts and your suspicions! Always looking for a bug under every chip! Throwing cold water on everything! As if your own daughter couldn't tell the truth! I suppose you would rather believe that a crocodile come along while Miriam closed her eyes for a minute and et up our poor child."

"It could have happened, you know."

"Shut up!" Jochebed screamed. "You ain't human! You ain't got no feelings! First you wanted to kill the child yourself and—"

"No, Jochebed, I didn't want to kill my boy. Pharaoh passed that law, not me. I just wanted to keep the soldiers from having the satisfaction of murdering it, that was all."

"And when I wouldn't let you, you, its papa, I stopped you from killing it, you want to believe now that the crocodiles et it up or either the soldiers found it after all and drowned it. Amram, youse as hard as a flint inside. I hate you."

"Jochebed," Amram said patiently, "I don't want to rob you out of your hope. I dread to think myself. But don't let us not raise up our hope to the throne of truth. Let us go ask at the palace tomorrow. Anyway, you had no business telling this thing all around until you had talked with me."

They had to stop quarreling because people began dropping in. Soon the house was full of people gloating inwardly and chuckling out loud. "Ho, ho! Pharaoh hates Hebrews, does he? He passes a law to destroy all our sons and he gets a Hebrew child for a grandson. Ain't that rich?"

And Amram hated it all. It made him feel flimsy and artificial. He felt worse because he could hear Miriam outside, the center of a large crowd, telling and retelling her story. "The child was crying and that is how she found him. So Pharaoh's

daughter asked me to bring mama to the palace to be a nurse for the child."

"And why not?" one elder asked. "There is plenty of Hebrew blood in that family already. That is why that Pharaoh wants to kill us all off. He is scared somebody will come along and tell who his real folks are. The country can't get along without us. Take Joseph for example now: Did Egypt ever amount to anything until he took hold of things? I ask you, did it now? Tell me! We are going to have another great man in the palace when this boy they just took in grows up. This country can't make out without us."

"You said something just now, but you didn't know it," another added. "The higher-ups who got Hebrew blood in 'em is always the ones to persecute us. I got it from somebody that ought to know, that the grandmother of Pharaoh was a Hebrew woman."

"Why, they tell me that the new commissioner of finance is an out-and-out Hebrew who renounced his race. He won't even be seen speaking to one of us."

"That would be just like him to do a trick like that. Afraid of being recognized, that's why."

"For my part," one of the women said, "I think the Princess is a very fine woman. It is time we quit straining against the new order and took a active part in it." There was hearty agreement from many women with this viewpoint.

"Oh, you women!" Amram snorted. "You are always ready to go with the conqueror. You recognize nothing but power. If it is a woman, a cow, a ewe, a doe or whatever female it is—let the male fight and die for her, and the moment that he is thoroughly beaten or killed, she gives herself to his conqueror. Talk about men being hard! We are the sentimental fools and you are the realists. Phooey!"

The little cakes were finally all gone and the crowd talked far into the night of the Hebrew victory over Pharaoh and went home. They did not question too closely for proof. They wanted to believe, and they did. It kept them from feeling utterly vanquished by Pharaoh. They had something to cherish and chew on, if they could say they had a Hebrew in the palace.

So the next day, Jochebed washed herself and walked the

long and dusty way to the palace gate to offer herself as nurse to the baby, but they would not let her in. There was no new baby to be nursed, they told her. The Princess had been summoned home from Assyria on the death of her husband and had brought her infant son with her several months ago. But what is that to you, Hebrew woman? Anyway, no Hebrew servants were being used in the palace. Begone with you!

Still and all, Goshen never gave up their belief in the Hebrew in the palace. It was something for men to dream about. Jochebed became a figure of importance—the mother of our Prince in the palace. Miriam told her story again and again to more believing ears. It grew with being handled until it was a history of the Hebrew in the palace, no less. Men claimed to have seen signs at the birth of the child, and Miriam came to believe every detail of it as she added them and retold them time and time again. Others conceived and added details at their pleasure and the legends grew like grass.

VI

INSIDE the royal palace affairs went on unconscious of the legends of Goshen. The Pharaoh had his programs, national and international. At home he worked to reorganize the country into a unit intensely loyal to the new regime. Externally he strove to bulwark the country against outside attack. Force was his juices and force was his meat. It was his boast that his reign should make it so that outsiders trembled when they breathed the mighty name of Egypt. The very rims of the earth should bear the spread wings of the Hawk-god Horus, who signified the sun in Egypt and should bear its light to all the world.

Inside the palace was Pharaoh's son and daughter. The son Ta-Phar had all the self-assurance of the actual ruler without his father's ability. He was impatient of the day when he should take hold of the rod of state. Ah, then Egypt and the world would see a Pharaoh! Crowns, state and personal robes would take on new glory. Finer chariots and horses and many more dinners of state. His tomb should outdo every pyramid that had been built or ever would be built. The stumbling stones in the path of doing these things had never occurred to him. What was the use of being a Pharaoh if one could not be lavish? Why should the wishes of a Pharaoh be opposed? So none about the court dared oppose him. In the chase and other tests of strength and skill, the courtiers learned to be a poor second to his poorer first. The arrow of the Suten-Rech, Ta-Phar, was somehow found in a vital spot in every dead lion or antelope.

Inside the palace also was the Pharaoh's widowed daughter who was not expected to do any more than she did. She must lend her support to the female robes of state. She must lend her ears to the sounds of mighty words boiling out of futile men. She must bear something in male form, for after all that is what she was born for—a passageway for boy children. If she seemed too attentive to her son and a little blank while her brother, the heir apparent, poured out his boasts, he attributed it to her jealousy that she would not be sharing the

throne with him when the time came to share or not to share. She had been mated with a foreign prince and since she had the misfortune to become a widow, she must not be allowed the notion that living in the palace meant advancing the position of that mis-fit son of hers. Ta-Phar did not intend to break his neck in the chase nor expose himself too much in battle. Just to make way for that Moses, that little smart-aleck who was always nosing among the papyrus rolls in the library.

Inside the palace walls was Moses, son of the Princess and second in line for the throne of Egypt. To his mother he was the most beautiful child in all Egypt. He was considered a handsome child by all. And everyone who came inside the royal enclosures was conscious of him. At first he followed the household servants about asking what and how and why until they tried to devise means of directing his attention elsewhere.

Then it was the gardeners and the grooms who caught his imagination. He was always wanting to know about plants. Was a frog a plant? Well, if a frog was not a plant, why was it in the garden? Who put it there? Why did frogs want to come in the garden? Why was the sky blue? Who bent it up like that? Did it ever fall down? If the sun could come up by itself and could roost on the high perch of noon, why did it fall down in the evening? Where did it go at night? Where was the river going and what were the sounds it said? Who made the first day? When? Why? Some of these questions went unanswered, but not all. There was one old man who tended the horses. He had answers in the form of stories for nearly every question that Moses asked and he told stories unasked because they just came to him to tell. They were unexpected visitors, those stories were, he explained to the eager little boy, and they stood outside his door until they were asked to come in. He did not know why they called upon him and did not call on many others. They tortured him at times, these people and events who came unasked and walked about in his mind. They always seemed to want to get out where people could see them. That had puzzled the old stableman a great deal because they were not always beautiful nor their behavior pleasant. Nevertheless one and all wanted to get out as soon as ever they could to show themselves. They always departed

about their own business once they had been given outside life by his lips—for he could not write at all. So they had no home in the papyrus rolls like others who spring from the minds of scribes. These, his images and happenings of the mind, scrambled from his lips and entertained the listeners for a day, then went to join the thousands of other dreams where they dwelt. Where did they hide? He did not know. But he believed that they did not die. They were stronger and more enduring than men.

So Moses learned how God made that first day. He had ordered the covering robe stripped from the sun. Why had He done so? Well, you see, He had made the world and the firmaments. He had hammered out the great bowl of investing firmament and starred it with rivets. Then the company of heaven had asked to see the work of His hands and He had said, "Let there be light" and flung back the blanket from the sun and the world stood revealed.

"Then why do we have nights between days?" Moses asked.

"Well, He is still working on the world and He must hide His hand from us humans. That is why things grow at night. Most things are born in the mothering darkness and most things die. Darkness is the womb of creation, my boy. But the sun with his seven horns of flame is the father of life."

Hours and hours they sat, the old hostler and the little boy behind the royal stables, in the shade of the structure. And the images arose in the brain chamber of Mentu, the stableman, and stumbled off his lips and became real creatures to Moses—to live in his memory forever.

"You see, male man was made with five strong senses to gather the truth of things and his mind is a threshing floor to clean his truth in. This is often an unhappy thing, for man sees himself as he really is. Thus he is made very miserable. But he does not destroy himself because the female man was made with squint eyes so that she sees only those things which please her. And her threshing floor is cramped and cluttered. She cannot separate the wheat from the chaff. But she achieves a harvest that makes her happy. When she sees man fleeing from his bowl in horror of himself, she feeds him from her own dish and he is blindly and divinely happy. Ah,

yes, the female companion of man has the gift of the soothing-balm of lies."

From old Mentu Moses learned much about the ways of animals. The old man interpreted their noises and told Moses what they said. It was very amusing to the boy to hear the comments of all the birds and the beasts on human conduct and appearances. In fact, they were human by Mentu's interpretations. Tara the monkey, for example, was he not the smart-aleck person of no importance always trying to imitate his betters and making a mess of things? Why, certainly! Some folks said that monkeys were old folks and that all old folks turned to monkeys, when they got old. Possibly they did, but Mentu was not old enough yet to find out for sure. But he thought it just as well when Moses should be old enough to hunt seriously, that he refrain from shooting those monkeys with his arrows. "You might kill an old friend or two among those monkeys, Moses. And I know you don't want to do a thing like that."

"I certainly don't," Moses said emphatically. "Least of all would I want to kill *you*, Mentu. But how would I know?"

"If, when age comes upon me to the stage when I find myself a monkey, I would let you know."

"But how could you, Mentu? You couldn't talk to me like you do now, you know."

"That's right, too."

Both the little boy and the old man fell into a gloomy mood for a moment.

"I have it!" Mentu finally shouted. "You know how I always tease you by running my hand down your collar?"

"Yes."

"Well, if ever you come upon a company of monkeys and one should spring upon your shoulder and thrust its paw down your neck, you can be sure it's me."

They were both very happy at finding a solution. Moses leaned his head on the bosom of the old man and said, "Then I would take you into the palace as my pet and you would have a fine gold collar for your neck and plenty of fruits and nuts to eat, and sleep right on the bed with me."

"It would be lovely if I were a monkey now, to enjoy all of that."

"Wouldn't it, though? I wish you were a monkey right now so I could take you inside with me and give you things."

Mentu sighed heavily. So they decided to hunt the little birds that live in the tall grass by the river. They took a number of throw-sticks and set out. On the way Moses led the old man to the spot where he was trying to build a playhouse of bits of stone. A lizard peeped out from behind a rock nearby and looked at them with a long, earnest stare.

"That same lizard is there every day when I play here," Moses told Mentu.

"He thinks you are acting crazy," Mentu told him.

"Why? Why is it crazy for me to build a playhouse like the cities of Rameses and Pithom that the Hebrews are building for Pharaoh?"

"The lizard does not understand it that way. He thinks all structures are made for nesting. He thinks you have been building a nest for your mate to lay eggs in. He says you take too long about it so that your mate must be ready to bust from holding her eggs so long. He asks why do men build such high nests for their mates? Are they afraid that their eggs will be stolen?"

Moses laughed heartily at that, and he suspected that the grimace on the face of the old man was more of a laugh than a sign of serious thought.

"Did he say all of that, Mentu? How do you know?"

"You are too young to understand now, but when you are older I will tell you how it is that men can understand the language of the birds and the animals and the plants."

"You are not teasing me, Mentu? The lizard really said that?"

"Why, certainly he did. I explained to him that humans do many things in their nests besides lay eggs. He says he cannot understand such doings but perhaps it is just as well. He asks if you will be good enough to stun a few flies for him so that he can catch them."

"But, Mentu," Moses objected, "you told me once that lizards liked to catch their flies alive and vigorous. You said it was a point of pride with him to use his speed and cunning."

"So I did, little Suten-Rech. So I did, and they do when they are young and virile. But this lizard complains that he is

old like me and a little hungry like me. He says that he has been driven out of the company of the females by younger males. He has lost the power that once resided in his mighty hind legs so that he cannot spring so far nor so quickly as before. So he cannot catch enough flies to support himself. And what is worse, he cannot catch the females any longer. He is much too slow. A sad, sad situation. He fears he will father no more families."

"Why doesn't he ask some of them to wait for him?" Moses asked full of sympathy.

"It is sad but true that females seeking love do not wait for the weak and the aged. When the power to spring is gone — when you are older you will understand such things. A very trying period in a male thing's life."

"He could lie in wait and seize him a wife as she passed. Then he wouldn't have to run after her and he would not need so much strength to overcome her struggles," Moses offered.

"He says he had a fight about that yesterday. He ambushed a female, a handsome young thing, but a young buck heard the struggle and attacked him in his weak moments, and drove him off. He is quite lame from the mauling he took. So it would be nice if you crippled some flies so that he might eat a dinner. When one is too old for love, one finds great comfort in good dinners."

Moses obliged the lizard with some flies and said to Mentu, "Maybe you would like something to eat, too. I think I could get you something from the palace kitchen without too much trouble."

"Of course I would, Prince Moses. You have a big heart in that young body of yours. Of course, I would like something to eat. It would be ridiculous for the stableman to pretend that the food of Pharaoh was not good enough for his belly. Food makes people what they are. If the palace food makes a god out of high-born Pharaoh, it ought at least to make a man out of me."

"Then I will go and get you something from the cook."

"Thanks, Prince Moses, but be very careful that nobody finds out the food is for the stableman. The scraps from Pharaoh's table are set aside and dedicated to the stomachs of

Pharaoh's dogs. Don't be caught in the misuse of the dogs' dishes. Sacrilege is a terrible crime."

Moses hurried to embrace the old man.

"Why do you embrace me, Prince Moses?" Mentu asked.

"Because I love you better than anyone, except my mother," Moses answered with his face pressed against the cheek of Mentu.

"Why do you love me? It is natural for the stableman to love a prince, but why should a prince love a stableman?"

"I love you because you know all about the beginnings of things and you tell me about them. You tell me such nice lizard-talk."

"Well, all love is tempered with something, so it might as well be lizard-talk as plenty and power. Run along now and fetch me some meat. The food of Pharaoh has a lovely after-taste."

Moses hurried off towards the kitchens and brought back a filling snack for his friend. Day after day he kept this up until old Mentu ceased to struggle with the other yard servants for bits of the hog head when roast pork was on the palace table. This was always an occasion with yard help. Roast pork at Pharaoh's table meant boiled hog head for the help. And old Mentu used to struggle mightily for such bits as he could get. But now he loftily stood aside from the struggle and explained to the others mysteriously, "I am eating further back on the hog now."

And Mentu continued to charge the imagination of the boy with his tales of creation. Those first days of the world, which he called the "Kingdom Age," when people lived as long as trees.

"In the beginning," Mentu would say, "there was neither nothing nor anything. Darkness hid in darkness—shrouded in nothingness." Or he would talk at length on the seven rays of time; on fire, the father of the sacrifice who was the triple-formed messenger of men to the gods—as fire on earth, as lightning in the air and as the sun in heaven.

It was the talk of Mentu which stirred the inquisitive Moses to stealing into the enclosure of the priests. After that first time, he would slip away from his tutors and attendants and go softly into the temples and into the forbidden precincts

behind the temples where the priests lived and worked. And always he came out with more details of the home life of the gods when they were not attending their altars and being the inexpressible to men. In vain did the priests try to discourage him. They set magic tricks to awe and frighten him, but he would not stay away. He learned to feed the sacred snakes and handle the altar fires without hurt to himself. He begged to be taught the mysteries of signs and omens and the power of sayings and seals until the priests despaired. "What power will we have over the Suten-Rech if they are going to know as much as we do?" they asked themselves and put him off on account of his age. "Come back to us after you have had your manhood ceremony and we will teach you," they told him. When he was gone they said, "Oh, he will be far too interested in war and women to bother with temple magic by that time. Who would bother with being a priest if he could be a prince anyway? All young boys have silly notions. Five years from now he will laugh at the idea. Our Pharaoh, when he was a boy, begged to be allowed to be a charioteer."

"So it goes," a priest devoted to Rah concluded. "But the contributions at the altars are getting thin. Let us make a new sun-god to renew the devotions of the people. I have just invented a new incense that shall be known as his breath and indication of his presence at the altar."

VII

THE SEVEN red mares rushed the sun across the sky, the infinite expanse and the dawns made companies and formed years and the years brought Moses to young manhood and gave him bone and muscle. Mentu had taught Moses about horses. He showed him what made a fine horse and he showed him how to ride and sit.

"Further up towards his shoulders, Prince Moses, and bring up those knees. You can't lead an army until you can ride a horse."

"But my uncle, Pharaoh's son, leads his men with his chariot."

"A war chariot is a splendid vehicle, Prince Moses, but there is more action on the back of a horse. You fight down on the enemy then, and not among them. There are too many sides to a war chariot anyway. Men can surround it and trap you. They can break off wheels from the clumsy thing. But on horseback now, your chariot is a living thing and quick to answer your impulses. Speed is vital in war."

"My mother says she will order a splendid chariot for me."

"Keep it for parades, but fight on horseback and win your wars. Your uncle is Pharaoh's son and eighteen years older than you. He will be head of state and the nominal head of the army. But you shall be the first man of Egypt in war."

The men of war also loved the avid attention that Moses gave to their advice. They need not fear to differ with him nor scold him. He was a born trooper, they all agreed, as they watched his quick grasp of intricate problems and his tendency to experiment with troop placement and maneuvers. There was something about him, outside of being the grandson of Pharaoh, that made men listen to him with respect. There was something about him that assured them he was a companion to be relied on in times of danger. They wanted to follow him into whatever escapade he thought up. He was the young men's choice for a leader. To the old officers he was an upstart who tried to think and every statesman knew that thinking was not for soldiers.

For a long time his activities made no impression upon his young uncle, the Pharaoh apparent, because he was busy with affairs of his own. There was palace etiquette to struggle with; robes of state to be fitted and worn properly. Royal visits from other countries, hunts and ceremonies. Then there were the intrigues inside the palace and council to make sure that the woman who was his sister and the mother of Moses should not herself encroach upon her brother's future power and prestige, and that she should not persuade their father to harbor any such foolish notions about Moses. Ta-Phar jealously guarded his prerogative and that took time and energy. He felt that he was already something of a statesman and gave time now and then to thinking up new strictures for the Hebrews. It was his definite impression that the nation as a whole was softening towards these people and tending towards their attitude of before the revolution. Such laxness might give the Hebrews their opportunity to invite foreign allies to come in and send his family packing again and he had no taste for foreign travel under such circumstances. He wanted to rule and be King. The palace, to him, was not so much a residence as it was the seat of authority. He was more relieved than worried at the zest of Moses for the outdoor life. If he got any pleasure out of excelling with the bow and arrow and hurling spears at marks, let him do it. There were plenty of spears in Egypt to be hurled by others for the heir of Pharaoh. In the hunt, the game was always prepared for his final thrust so why spend hours in practice? Moses was merely lacking in appreciation of his position of a prince, the more fool, he.

Then came the day of the bi-annual military maneuvers. This was a happy day for the Crown Prince. This was the day he would appear in his new chariot and armor with the Egyptian force behind him. The last maneuver had been led by his father and he and Moses had played minor roles in the pageant. But this time his father was suffering from an injury to his hip and had decided to watch the action from a reviewing stand, in company with a visiting king and his retinue. The Prince would be King for the day.

All day there had been the rumble of war chariots past the palace and out to the great field that bordered the Nile.

Drums shouted and rumbled; bands blared, a thousand deco-
rated floats were moored on the Nile opposite the parade
ground to await the wives and daughters of nobles and offi-
cers out on the field in mock battle. Two sets of tents faced
each other at opposite ends of the field and at right angles to
the river so that the action would be visible to the reviewing
stand and the flower-decked barges on the Nile.

The hawk of Horus, the sun-god, mounted to his noon
perch and flew down the western sky for two hours, his blaz-
ing eyes fixed on the horizon of night. The men had been
ordered to their tents since dawn. The princes and nobles
now repaired to their decorated pavilions to dress. The barges
with their ornate and brilliant-colored awnings filled and Pha-
raoh took his seat upon his open-air throne. The six royal
trumpeters took their places before Pharaoh and at a sign they
began the salute to Pharaoh in his incarnation of the sun-god.

Then from their rich pavilions issued the princes and nobles
of Egypt and mounted their chariots. Martial music played
and the parade of the nobles before the throne of Pharaoh
began. Shouts and cheers came from the barges and the
standing people as each beautifully caparisoned war chariot
with its three steeds passed in review and saluted the throne as
they passed. First came the empty chariot of Pharaoh, the
horses led by grooms in the livery of the palace. Then came
the chariot of Egypt's Crown Prince with Ta-Phar the son of
Pharaoh at the reins. He was followed by Moses in a chariot
less richly worked and draped. Then all the other chariots
filed past four abreast, wheeled about the field and returned
to their tents to get ready for the maneuvers in earnest.

While they made ready, a company of dancers from the
royal ballet leaped out from behind the reviewing stand and
danced for the entertainment of the throne and the barges.
The activities of the gods was the theme of the ballet and it
was well received.

The trumpeters again. This time they announced the ma-
neuvers and the order. His Majesty's forces were divided into
the blues and the reds. The reds would be led by that em-
bodiment of all that was pure and noble, the image of Pha-
raoh himself, Suten-Rech Ta-Phar. The blues were nobly led
by the slightly lesser sun of the world and grandson of

Pharaoh, Suten-Rech Moses, son of the daughter of Pharaoh. They saluted in every direction and retired.

Out upon the field rode the ranks of red charioteers with the Prince at the head. They came out in perfect formation, massed close together and chanting, "Who is so great as Pharaoh, and who can meet his glance?"

"A truly magnificent force!" a visiting dignitary said to Pharaoh. "Magnificent?" Pharaoh retorted. "Why, man alive! You are looking at the finest chariot force in the world. It's stupendous! There never was such a fighting machine in the history of warfare. And it will be a long time before its equal will be seen again. It was our highly developed war chariots which swept out the Hyksos. They are unbeatable."

The red force had reached the center of the field and all eyes looked towards the blue camp for the defending force, but not a single chariot emerged. There was a thick brush back of the camp. Suddenly a hundred soldiers mounted on camels trotted from the camp and rode, none too hastily, towards the chariot force with lifted spears. The Prince and his men were too startled for a moment to move. People did not know what to think. Some of them laughed.

"What kind of a stupid joke is this?" the Prince sneered. "Bear down on them, my men, surround them and capture them."

The chariots got into furious motion. But as the horses got wind of the camels they began to rear and snort. At that precise moment a thousand horsemen burst from the wood and raced through the camp like lightning. As they cleared the tents a blood-chilling war whoop burst from the riders. They brandished their spears and bore down upon the chariots like so many fiends from hell. But they did not make a direct charge as their frenzied speed indicated. When almost near enough for hand-to-hand conflict, the horsemen split into two parties and executed a lightning-swift flanking movement and attacked the chariots from the side and rear. With quick jabs and thrusts, the charioteers were hurled from their machines. Bridles were seized. A wave of foot soldiers followed the cavalry and the charioteers struggling on the ground with their heavy armor and weapons, and often tangled in the reins of their chariots were overcome and taken prisoner. It was a

rout. The throne and barges were on their feet first in sur-
prise, then in alarm. Some asked, "Are those horsemen Egyp-
tians or are they Hebrews and their allies, the hated Hyksos?
Only men of the desert ride like that!"

And on the field the action went on furiously. Two thirds
of the chariots were empty. The field was full of plunging
horses, tangled harness and shouting men. It looked as if God
were stirring up hell with a pitchfork. But in a little while it
was evident that order was emerging out of the tangle. Pris-
oners were tied to the tails of chariots and the foot soldiers
were springing into the chariots and taking the reins to quiet
the horses. Out in front of the struggling mass a horseman
with his knees almost under his chin was brandishing his spear
and riding around the chariot of Ta-Phar the Crown Prince,
feinting at him from all sides as he circled the chariot with the
confidence and speed of a hawk. The horseman circled the
chariot six times, keeping the Prince in the chariot constantly
off-balance trying to defend himself with his shield and spear
from all sides before the horseman sent in the thrust that
toppled the Prince out of the chariot. He did not dismount to
secure the prisoner. Ta-Phar's personal attendants rushed for-
ward to lift him up. Moses seized the bridle of the three
horses hitched to the chariot and led them away from the
fallen Prince, helpless on the ground. Then only did a cry go
up from the blue forces. "Moses! Moses!" The grandstands
and barges took it up and shouted with delight. "It is Moses.
What a soldier!"

An elderly Egyptian statesman sitting directly behind Pha-
raoh leaned forward and whispered, "Did you see what I saw?
I believe we have a great military leader on our hands."

"Don't I know it? I intend to keep working on that boy
until I make a great soldier out of him. My mind never
sleeps," Pharaoh said in a manner to give the impression that
he had planned the whole thing, himself. "It won't be long
now before we punish those Ethiopians for inviting refugee
Hyksos and Hebrews into their country to plot against Egypt.
We have a military genius in Moses. I shall instruct him
further."

Solemnly walking his horse, Moses led the parade of the
victors around the field and up to the dais of Pharaoh to re-

ceive the trophy of the victor. He leaped off his horse, bowed himself to the ground and said, "As you have seen today, so will we do to the enemies of Pharaoh." Pharaoh acknowledged the salute and presented the trophy. Receiving it, Moses whirled his horse and gave a magnificent display of horsemanship before he led his lightly clad troops back to their tents.

The visiting dignitary leaned towards Pharaoh again and said: "I thought you said your chariot force was the finest in the world."

"I did and it is," Pharaoh said with some heat.

"What inspired rabble was it that defeated them out there, then?" the dignitary asked with a trace of malice in his voice.

"Rabble? You must be crazy in the head. That was strategy. Why, man alive, you were privileged to look on the world's finest cavalry and infantry forces. I have merely been keeping it under cover. It's something new in tactics. The newest development in warfare will always arise in Egypt. Rabble indeed! Don't get silly in your old age."

Back in his pavilion Prince Ta-Phar, unaware of his father's sentiments, was beating his attendants and swearing. "Treason! Treachery! and all of you knew of this heathenish trick that was to be played on the army of Egypt and kept a vile silence."

"But the blues are part of the army, too. It was just one side against the other," one young officer tried to explain while dodging cuffs and blows. "Everybody knew the riding practices were going on. You said — "

"Shut up! You bitch's baby you! When I reveal to Pharaoh the intrigue and treachery in his own army, everyone even suspected of guilty knowledge shall be whipped like slaves. Camels! Half-naked soldiers on horseback! What kind of an army is this? That Moses! When the time comes he is going to feel the weight of my hand. Nothing different! But what can you expect of a Suten-Rech who takes sides with Hebrews and hangs around the stables with grooms?"

As Moses entered his pavilion he saw a figure squatting in the far corner with a court wig lopsided over one eye and a hit-or-miss collection of garments on. A general's tunic, the shenti of a priest, the headdress of a high state official. It was

not until Moses' eyes traveled to the worn-out sandals that he received a clue to the puzzle. Then he looked up at the face in the midst of this costume mixture and burst out laughing.

"Mentu!"

"I—I know I have no business on the parade grounds. I am little better than a Hebrew or a swineherd in Pharaoh's eyes, but—"

"Shut up! You old monkey you! Where on earth did you get those clothes?"

"Oh, a piece here and a piece there. Everybody, even the servants, were gone to the maneuvers and so it was easy."

They fell upon each other laughing. Moses straightened up the wig and the headdress and held the old man off at arm's length to survey him.

"Not so bad," he laughed. "If they don't get too close. It got you inside anyway. Why didn't you ask me for a pass?"

"It seemed too much for a stableman to ask. And I wanted to see you ride."

"Did I do all right?"

"It could not have been better. Your seat, your knees, your hands, all perfect. You were a horse and the horse was a prince. Did Pharaoh approve?"

"I don't know yet. I'll find that out tomorrow at breakfast. Tonight is the great banquet. No personal matters taken up then."

"Well, anyhow, the Prince and those old-time army men have found out that they over-sported themselves with their war chariots just like I told you."

"My Mentu, if ever I become King you shall be Grand Advisor to the throne with eating privileges at my table."

"May you soon be Pharaoh! But long before that time I will have gone to join the monkeys or the snakes, if I learn more than I do now."

"Snakes?"

"Didn't you know that wise men do not die? When they have attained a certain stage of wisdom they enter the serpents."

"I did not know that. The priests never told me."

"They tell nothing that doesn't pay. Their business is like the cemetery. They take in but they never put out."

"Some day I shall look into their business and find out why they control rulers."

"Oh, they bite the rulers and everybody else with the tiny teeth of fear. Then rub ointment on the sore. Now, I had better go before I am seen."

"Take my own horse and ride him to the stables, Mentu, and may the forty-two gods in the hall of the double Maati find you just."

"May the deathless serpent that guards the book of Thoth whisper in your ears, my Suten-Rech. You are a man conferring with destiny."

Moses rushed to the door of the tent and seized Mentu by the shoulders and dragged him back.

"Come back here, Mentu."

"Why, Suten-Rech! In a few minutes your tent will be full of admirers and—er—some of them might recognize their clothes."

"Never mind that. I'll slip you out the back way if it comes to that. What about this deathless snake guarding the book of Thoth?"

"To tell you the truth, I don't know anything about it. All I know is what I have heard. It was told by the father of the father of my father to the father of my father and the father of my father has told it to my father."

"It is a really old story then."

"Sure. And the cry of it is that there is a book which Thoth himself wrote with his own hand which, if you read it, will bring you to the gods. When you read only two pages in this book you will enchant the heavens, the earth, the abyss, the mountain, and the sea. You will know what the birds of the air and the creeping things are saying. You will know the secrets of the deep because the power is there to bring them to you. And when you read the second page, you can go into the world of ghosts and come back to the shape you were on earth. You will see the sun shining in the sky, with all the gods, and the full moon."

"Where is this book, Mentu? Do the priests know it?"

"The priests have heard of it, of course, and now and then some one of them will pretend that he has read a page. But if they had read from that book, Suten-Rech, they would never

remain a priest in Pharaoh's temples. They would be too powerful for the place."

"The priests are men of learning, Mentu. They must be wise."

"They don't just have to be. Certainly they know what is in the books. That is learning, not wisdom. Learning without wisdom is a load of books on a donkey's back. I want *you* to understand."

"Where is this book, I ask you, Mentu? I mean to read it."

"The cry of it is that it is in the middle of the river at Koptos, in an iron box; in the iron box is a bronze box; in the bronze box is a sycamore box; in the sycamore box is an ivory and ebony box and in the ebony box is a silver box; in the silver box is a golden box and in that is the book. And there is a deathless snake by the box to guard it. That is all that they told me so I don't know any more."

"If it were not for the feasts and the entertainments, and the announcements of the promotions in the army, I would start out for Koptos tomorrow, Mentu. It may be only an old tale, what you told me, but I mean to search the river at Koptos for that snake and that book. Even if they are not there and never were there, it will be an interesting trip. When I go, you are going along. I will ask Pharaoh for you as my special attendant tomorrow. And if the box is there, Mentu, if it is only there!"

"If it is there and the snake is overcome, you will be the greatest priest the world will ever know. So far as I am concerned, if you take me with you, I won't be nothing but your shadow, and you'll be my boss. But I bet you I'll be the top pauper in all Egypt. I'll bet you that."

The old man went out full of joy. Moses stood in the door of his tent and the sun went down in an Egyptian way— without a memory in the sky.

VIII

THE ANNOUNCEMENTS were made. The very next day after the maneuvers, they were made before all the big men of the army in their uniforms and armor. The men who sat in big chairs around the throne were there with the officers, for they were the ones who made the wars for the generals to fight. Pharaoh told the announcements to the scribe and he wrote them down, and a man with a loud voice for speaking read them out to the people. The Suten-Rech, Moses, was Commander-in-Chief of the armies of Egypt by reason of what had happened the day before. He was the chief commander for life or until Pharaoh could see further, that is, until somebody could show a better way to win battles than Moses had. In reply, Moses begged that the honor be given to somebody else, somebody more worthy than he was. He gave as a reason, in addition to his unworthiness, that he wanted to go traveling into foreign countries and see how they lived and made war there. But Pharaoh was not interested in the ways of other peoples. He was not interested in their wars and warfare unless they were the enemies of Egypt or Egypt's allies. All that could wait. He was interested in winning wars at home and abroad. It would be time enough to consider how the people in those far-off countries lived after he had conquered them. Moses felt twisted and torn by his elevation. He had worked hard for more than three years to earn it, and now he didn't want it. He couldn't say to Pharaoh, "You are breaking into my arrangements with your old decorations." He had to pretend he liked it.

His Uncle Ta-Phar hated it too, but his personal feelings could not stand in the face of the enthusiasm of the military bloc and the intensified nationalism which had been whipped up for a generation by his father. Egypt was spreading by conquest and alliances based on force. If they didn't keep on getting more they would begin to look weak. So Ta-Phar had to swallow the elevation of Moses and make out he liked it. But after all, he was the heir to the throne and when the armies went out, he could always ride in front, if he wanted to. And

then again, the time would come when he would be Pharaoh himself and then other arrangements could be made. The old folks had a saying that the belt that went over the devil's back had to buckle under his belly. He could wait old Moses out and when his time came, that upstart was going to catch it. "Your hands must knead everybody's dough, and every shirt is too tight for you," he said to Moses time and again when they quarreled. "You are my father's first grandson, and so he dotes on you; and you are my sister's only child and so she spoils you. Just wait until they are gone and see what *I* do for you. I mean to make you catch me a natural hurry, and don't you forget it."

So this was the way he spoke to Moses in the corridor of the palace after the announcements were over, and Moses laughed in his face.

"I wouldn't let on if I were you, Ta-Phar. Somebody might hear you and laugh at you. Then you will have to get a law passed that people can't laugh at Princes."

"Another bit of impudence out of you and I'll whip you."

"No, you won't whip me, Uncle Ta-Phar, but there might be a fight. But there would have to be some good running done before that fight comes off."

"And why?"

"Because in the language of the soldiers' camps, I'd have to run you down and hem you up before I could get a fight out of you. You don't want no parts of me, and I know it; and you know it, and you know that I know you know it."

Moses strolled on off and joined his military escort and left Ta-Phar standing where he was. So Moses forgot all about him in a few minutes because his heart in all its height was far from the palace and armies and honors and hopes of honors. He was in his private suite with Mentu who was in the new clothes of his new job as personal attendant to the new commander of the Egyptian armies. But, they were not talking about troops and munitions and strategy. They were deep in the mysteries of life and magic. Moses had decided to go to Koptos at the first opportunity.

But years and wars and years of wars stood between him and his journey. The might of Egypt was stretching across the world. Ethiopia was conquered; Assyria kept in fear, Bab-

ylonia was terrorized. All tributes flowed towards Rameses and
Memphis. No one knew how the Egyptian armies would strike
nor when. The men were permanently in barracks. Once war
was decided upon, Moses was on the march and they did not
know whom they marched against until they were past the
boundaries of Egypt. Against some nations they fought in for-
mal battle formation and crushed them by sheer weight and
numbers; another time, they lured out the main army of the
enemy by sending an inferior force before the gates. When the
attacking Egyptian forces retreated before the defenders, the
swift-striking horsemen and foot soldiers of Moses fell upon
them from ambush and cut off their retreat, and hewed them
down like saplings. The returning armies of Egypt staggered
home under the weight of booty and led slaves in hordes. The
streets of the cities teemed with strange nationalities and
tongues. From the Sudan, all Asia and Greece.

So always Moses was asking himself, "When will there be
enough of conquests? When will I follow my own mind and
read the pages of Thoth?"

He came to feel, somehow, that he would never die until
he had read that book hidden in the river at Koptos. So he
was reckless in his daring. The huge hope of audacity spurred
him and he took chances to win that no other leader would
have dared, and won because his men had come to believe
that he could not fail, so they fought like fiends from hell.

He knew what sorrow meant because old Mentu died.
"Please give me the funeral and tomb of a priest," he begged
Moses at the last. "That is what I wanted to be. But I wanted
to be a great one—not just another one to light fires and
burn incense. I couldn't make it from where I started. You
have the power to insist—bury me as a priest."

"Don't you worry, Mentu. It is going to be done just like
you want it. You have been my best friend. I am very sorry
you will not be going to Koptos with me as we had planned,
for I shall go."

"Maybe I will, who knows? And, Suten-Rech, don't forget
what I told you about the monkeys and the snakes. It might
be true, you know. The old folks often know things you can't
find in a book."

"Oh, I won't forget. I won't forget anything that you have

ever taught me, the sayings, and the proverbs and all. They
have helped me a lot."

"You are right to listen to proverbs. They are short sayings
made out of long experience. Goodbye, son. I wanted a long
life, but I didn't mean to get old. Look out for the snakes and
monkeys and find out what they say."

Moses astonished the court by the elaborate burial of his
servant Mentu. Everything needful was inside the tomb for
the Ka of Mentu, even to the picture of a Prince and his
groom on a river journey to a place where a serpent lived in
the water. And no one knew why it was there but Moses.
The tomb was surrounded on the outside by a fenced-in
garden, and Moses ordered that no creature that entered that
enclosure was to be killed at any time, especially if it were
a monkey or a snake.

Sitting alone in his quarters he would picture Mentu in the
Hall of the double Maati, justifying his life before the forty-
two gods and crying:

"Hail, thou who eatest shades, who cometh forth from the
place where the Nile riseth, I have not committed theft.

"Hail, Leg of Fire, who comest forth from Akhekky, I have
not eaten my heart [harbored malice]."

And so on to the forty-two deities, and Moses felt that if he
could only be as pure as old Mentu when it came his time to
enter the court of Osiris Nu, he would be satisfied.

So these thoughts reminded Moses keenly of his days
among the priests and he took to visiting them again. Now,
he was the great soldier and a powerful Prince, and the priests
behaved accordingly. By his own inclination he was better
educated than any scribe in Egypt. He had read all of the
books in the library, and all of the priests knew that he had
read them. They were proud and happy to have him come
among them. It gave new prestige to the priesthood which
had declined considerably under the war party now in power.

"Tell me, and then again show me, so I can know," was
what Moses said to them about every bit of magic in the
temples. "Never mind the ceremonies. They are not impor-
tant. I can learn them from the other side of the altar. They
are nothing anyway, but the dressing for what goes on behind
the scenes. Make me know."

Some of them thought that Moses took seriously the things that meant so much to them, but he didn't. He learned all of their tricks as he went along, but only to sift them through his mind to see if any of them led towards real knowledge, or the book in the river. At last he knew all that there was to be known and still he found no doors that either hinged on hell nor heaven. He called the names a thousand times, but saw no faces of gods. But he learned many things to distract the minds of unthinking people from their real troubles, and to taint men with the fear of life. In this he saw a certain mastery over people if one cared to use it or needed to use it.

Then his mother died and he missed her very much. The Ethiopian Princess who had been brought to the palace as his wife as a sign of peace between Egypt and Ethiopia, meant nothing to him. Perhaps that was because he meant nothing to her other than what had been arranged for in the treaty. He looked at her face that seemed to come to a point at her nose like a fox and wondered if he would have loved her if he had been allowed to win her as lesser men won their wives. But it wasn't worth thinking about too much, and so he didn't think.

But he knew it was not because he did not feel. Long ago, before he was twenty, he had found out that he was two beings. In short, he was everybody boiled down to a drop. Everybody is two beings: one lives and flourishes in the daylight and stands guard. The other being walks and howls at night. He could be a lot of things to some woman when he found the right one. But the eye-looks of this treaty-wife in the palace was as impersonal as his own. She did not awaken the urge in him to give her the pain and tenderness that make up a marriage. He was always polite and kind. Whatever secrets her body held were no concern of his. And she was happy at being part of the court life. Some day, sometime, he would find a woman and crush from her body that essence that made men live. He would rouse her tears and her tenderness and he would give her something that she could not live without, of which his property and position was only a sign of his inward giving.

In the meanwhile, he had a great struggle on his hands. As the actual chief of the army he was demanding that Hebrews

be included in the forces of Egypt. But he was being strenu-
ously opposed by most of the court and a large part of the
officers. They argued that they were not citizens of Egypt, but
enemy-prisoners, and as such, it would be rash to put arms
into their hands again. Who knew when they might rise up
against their conquerors and turn the tables? Moses argued
that they were enemies certainly, because they were treated as
such. More than a generation of years had passed since the
revolution and it was time that these people either be restored
to citizenship or sent out of Egypt. It was a weak spot in any
nation to have a large body of disaffected people within its
confines. And then again, civilization and decency demanded
less harsh treatment for human beings. If they could not vote
and bear arms at once, then shorten their hours of work and
repeal the law that said their boy babies must be killed. It was
not being obeyed anyway, and since it put Egypt in a bad
light before other nations, why not strike it from the books?
The anti-Hebrew party led by Ta-Phar shouted "No" to all of
these proposals. If the Hebrews were sent out, wouldn't they
go and join themselves with some enemies of Egypt and re-
turn as invaders? They knew all of the back roads and the
weak spots of the country. They would know when and where
to strike. No, not one Hebrew was going to escape from
Egypt. Pharaoh receded from his former position a little. He
took off two hours from their working day and rescinded the
order on boy babies. Moses took this as a hopeful sign and
waited for a chance to demand other changes in the status of
Goshen.

The Hebrews heard of his efforts in their behalf and sent
little presents to him in secret to return him some thanks. He
took occasion to slip down into Goshen once or twice to see
their actual conditions and to talk with some of the leaders.
What he saw touched him so that he resolved in his heart to
do whatever was in his power to better their condition. He
went directly to Pharaoh for a talk, and told him what was in
his mind.

"To outside nations, Pharaoh, we seem better than we are.
My idea is, if we wish to be really great is to be better than we
seem."

"Don't be too brash, Moses. I have been thinking too. But

it is hard to go against public opinion. The Hebrews are thoroughly hated in Egypt. I don't say that I did not intensify the feeling to a degree when I came to the throne. But I only played on the instrument I found already. Be patient and some further changes might be decreed on my death."

"Let us hope that might be a long time off. In the meantime their misery is awful. It is too terrible to look at. Go see for yourself."

"I am old and sick and a trip like that would have me flat on my back for months. I don't believe the country in general would want my days shortened for the sake of those people. They brought it all on themselves anyway. Now, let's table that subject and get back to these Persians. Do you think we got a chance against them if we invade them? Or do you think we ought to work them up to attack us?"

"I'll think it over and let you know. It's a ticklish question whichever way you take it. If we go there we've got to figure out how to carry enough supplies for a long journey and a long stay. This living off of the countries we pass through calls for a lot of extra fighting and we lose men and animals. If they invade us, even if we win, they destroy too much property and lives. Can't we rest from wars and turn to home problems for a while?"

"Egypt has no home problems that I can see," Pharaoh said coldly and turned over in bed. "What internal problems we had, got settled before you were born. Send in my nurse as you go out, and report on the Persian campaign tomorrow."

IX

MOSES didn't have any more notion of killing that Egyptian overseer than he did of flying. It just happened. The whole thing started in the chambers of his wife. He had made his report to Pharaoh on the conduct of the Persian war and went on to his own house to tell the Princess that he was going away on a campaign. When he entered her bedroom she had shrunk away from him as if he had been a crocodile. She ran across the room to the farthest wall and covered her face. Moses stopped dead in his tracks and looked at her.

"What is the matter with you, woman? Are you crazy?"

"You kissed me."

"I kissed *you*?"

"Yes, you did!"

"When?"

"Don't stand there and make out you don't know what you did. You kissed me when we—when you received me as your wife two years ago."

"Oh, I had to do it then. What is wrong with that?"

"You Hebrew! putting your hands on *me*!"

"Hebrew? I a Hebrew? What ever put that notion in your head?"

"Get out of my room. The very idea of me being married to a Hebrew makes me sick at the stomach. Don't you dare to come near me. That gang of rapists and slaves."

"I am not a Hebrew. I am not a slave. And so far as that treaty-kiss is concerned, if you can call that rape you have plenty of imagination. If my indifference to you in the past isn't enough, you can take my word for it, you are absolutely safe from me."

"It is rape for you to even look at me. Get out of my bedroom. This is no place for Hebrew slaves. Get back to your place in Goshen."

"Do you realize what you are saying? As Mentu would have said, you must be blind in one eye and can't see out of the other one. This is Prince Moses, Commander-in-Chief of the Egyptian armies, standing before you. You are here in my

palace because I beat your father in Ethiopia, remember? Not because *I* sought you as a wife."

"I don't care how many wars and battles you have won. Bragging of your conquests does not excuse you for being a Hebrew."

"Why do you call me a Hebrew all of a sudden?"

"Because everybody connected with the court is calling you a Hebrew. Your Uncle Ta-Phar says so himself."

"But everybody around here, and Ta-Phar especially, knows who I am—my mother, my father and my grandfather. So if I am a Hebrew they are Hebrews, and that goes for Ta-Phar too."

"Oh, no, they are not your relations. Your mother did have a son by the Prince of Assyria, but he died and your mother wanted to guarantee an inheritance with Pharaoh, so she took a Hebrew child and passed it off as her own. Nobody ever would have known why you are always hanging around in Goshen and upholding those Hebrews and trying to put weapons in their hands so they can slaughter the rest of us. But now we know why. You are one of them."

"I can prove that these are all lies whispered around by my enemies out of jealousy, no doubt."

"How? How can you prove it? Your so-called mother is dead. A Hebrew woman came to the palace gates yesterday and demanded an audience with Prince Moses, stating emphatically that she was your sister."

"*My* sister?"

"Yes, your sister. She came to the palace gates and asked to see you. Of course, they wouldn't let her in. They asked her what she, a Hebrew, wanted with a Prince of the royal house and she said that she wanted to let you know that her father had been killed by the soldiers in some sort of an uprising. She thought you would do something about it—you being her brother."

"My sister in Goshen? Ridiculous!"

"Yes, your sister. What a filthy trick has been played on me and my country! She says she remembers when you were born and how you were put on the river in an ark and that is how the Princess got hold of you in the first place."

"If you and Ta-Phar despise Hebrews so much, how is it

you are so willing to take the unsupported word of one of them as gospel truth? My word ought at least to be as good as hers."

"Just about. One Hebrew's word against another."

Moses strode out of the room. He was angry. He never remembered being so angry before in his life. This was the work of Ta-Phar. This was the answer of the court to his plea for justice against oppression. This was mob malice. He made up his mind to go straight to Pharaoh and say that since they claimed that he was a Hebrew, they did not need his despised services in the Egyptian army. Let Ta-Phar or some of the other silly, useless nobles do for Egypt what he had done. But a second thought came to him. Perhaps he ought to wait until he was calm before he went to his grandfather. One thing was certain—that Persian war could wait until he came to himself again. It would never do to take the field in his present state of mind. He decided to take a walk and think things over. Then he would ask for an audience with Pharaoh and explain his situation and his feelings. Him a Hebrew? "That is the way with people. I am finding out," he was saying aloud to himself and the Infinite Expanse. "If they do you wrong, they invent a bad name for you, a good name for their acts and then destroy you in the name of virtue." He kept on walking and thinking. The idea of calling him, Prince Moses, a He-brew! If Ta-Phar thought so, why had he been so hush-mouth about it all these years? For it was no secret that Ta-Phar had never loved him. He had openly resented both his mother and him. So why did he bring the mess up now? Had some Hebrew really made such a claim? He didn't believe it. It was too much to believe. More likely Ta-Phar had thought it up himself since his mother's death, realizing the difficulty of proof, and the harm it would do before the proof could be had. So! The court was really angry with him for asking jus-tice for Hebrews. "They have decided to destroy me out of hand," Moses reflected. "They are ready to do anything to confirm them in their position, and to do that, they have to prostitute the language. They must blow out the sun and switch on a spot-light."

He walked and thought and felt and walked. He was out-side the new city of the King, the towered city of Rameses,

named for his grandfather, before he realized where he was. He was upon the new public works, a causeway, splendidly conceived, which was being built with forced Hebrew labor. He saw the men straining and striving and the Egyptian boss-man striding among them and striking out with his bull whip without regards to whom he hit nor why. Moses stopped in his tracks and looked on. He looked at the straining backs of the workmen and then at the face of the foreman, and suddenly he saw all Egypt in that face. The newness come to power, the cruelty and greed. And he thought, "I have risked my life and exposed myself to a thousand dangers for such as him. Only some of them strut around the capitol in robes of state. But the same faces. And their faces got that way from keeping company with their souls."

The foreman saw Moses and knew him. Who was it in Egypt that did not know that face and figure? It was Moses, the Suten-Rech, the mighty man of arms. The singers said that he was the savior of Egypt, the conqueror of the world. Both oceans knew him, the ocean of the sea and the ocean of the air. His name and fame were great, his clothes were fine. It was not often that a prince looked on a foreman nor the foreman on a prince. So the foreman wanted a smile of notice and a nod of approval from so rich and just a man. He must do something to attract his eye. Aha! there was a weazly Hebrew straining with a rock that was too heavy for him. Look at him, now! His knee joints were sprung and his back was humped. His neck was stringy from straining. The lash spat derisively in the air and wrapped around the Hebrew's shoulders, and bit into his short ribs. The sudden pain made him drop the stone he was lifting and it crushed his foot.

"Pick it up!" snarled the foreman and hit him again. By this time the foreman felt as mighty as the reputation of Moses. He fought a hundred battles on the Hebrew's back and the Hebrew grovelled on his all-fours begging for mercy. But that did not save him. The whip kept singing. He crawled between the knees of the overseer to protect his head and face. He was too close in for the lash to strike him but still he could not save himself. He begged for mercy, and it made a whining obbligato to go with the rhythm of the blows because the foreman turned the stock of the whip in his hand and beat

him about his head and shoulders. Other workmen cowered in fear and wailed in sympathy and terror.

Moses heard the wails and woke out of his nausea at what he was seeing. He leaped upon the foreman and snatched the whip away. With his right arm, so famous in Asia and Africa, he swung and struck the foreman between the eyes and staggered him. A terrible surprise crept to the eyes of the man and peeped out at Moses. Twice again he struck the creature of Pharaoh's hatred and intolerance and the man lay on the sand without a quiver. Moses stooped down and saw the man was dead.

Moses straightened up and thought came back. "I didn't mean to kill him," he said softly.

"You didn't kill him, Suten-Rech." The Hebrews all crowded about the Prince and wept for joy. "You didn't kill him. You just hurt him and he died from being hurt."

"Anyway, he is dead," Moses said with more calm than he felt. "Bury him well in the sand and keep your mouths shut about it. Pharaoh would be angry if he knew."

Moses stayed until the overseer was buried and the place smoothed over. "Go on about your work as if nothing had happened. If anybody asks you what became of your foreman say that a dignitary passed and called him away, and he has not returned. That is all you know."

The physical exertion had given Moses a sort of release from his turmoil of spirit. He turned back feeling better. He went to see his grandfather and arranged to have the war put off for another week. He was not sorry the foreman was dead; he was only sorry that he had had to get mixed up in it at such a time and under such circumstances. If Ta-Phar and some others heard about it, they would use it to bolster up the stories they were circulating about him. He felt reasonably safe that the Hebrew workmen would not expose him. He had jeopardized his future for their sake. It would be both graceless and foolish for them to spread the report around.

He felt lonely in the palace and he felt lonely in the camp. So he went to visit the tomb of Mentu the second day after the killing of the foreman. "Am I a Hebrew?" he asked himself there, but found nothing to convince him that he was. But one thing had come out of it—he found a new sympathy

for the oppressed of all mankind. He lost his taste for war. Warfare, under the fanfare and flattery of the court, had been his outlet. And now it had lost its glamor. He was saying to the glory of struggle and victory, "Go away, honey, you have lost your sweetness." He was denying what he had held to be the truth. Well, he thought, he was twenty-five. His youth was behind him. Henceforth he was a man of thought.

A week later he was drawn to pass the place where he had killed the foreman. He was surprised to find that a Hebrew foreman had been appointed to take the dead man's place. But things were going little better than before. Two of the workmen were having a fist-fight and paying no attention to the foreman.

"What is the trouble?" Moses asked. "What's the matter with you men?"

The foreman approached Moses respectfully and shook his head sadly as he explained, "Some of them want to knock off work early to hold a protest meeting, and the others agree with me that it just wouldn't do. It would look very bad to my over-boss that just as soon as a Hebrew got to be foreman, the men left work whenever they got ready to hold meetings."

"Your foreman is right," Moses agreed, speaking to the men. "This sort of thing is what I am working for. Hebrew foremen first and keeping on up the line until you have Hebrew state officials. But if you start leaving work and creating disturbances, you will find yourselves worse off than you were, instead of better."

"That is what I tell them," the foreman said, "but being one of them, my people despise me so much that they won't pay me no mind."

"They had better if they know what is good for them." Moses spoke firmly. "You must be united among yourselves and you must obey your foreman. You must respect yourselves if you want others to respect you. Now you get back to work, all of you, and do what your foreman tells you." Moses spoke in a military tone of voice.

"And why do we have to be taking orders from him?" one of the men asked scornfully, pointing at the Hebrew foreman. "I don't intend to let no Hebrew boss me around."

"And why not?" Moses asked in surprise.

"He ain't no better than I am. I don't mean to take nothing off of him at all."

"Oh, but you are wrong there, all of you. You ought to be glad to have one of your own over you."

One of the men who had been fighting turned to Moses with a sneer on his lips. "We thought that this was Prince Moses, chief of the Egyptian army. We did not know that you was straw-boss of public works. In fact we didn't know that you was our bossman at all. Nobody ain't told us you was suppose to come round here acting like a overseer."

"I am not your bossman at all. I am your friend. I want you to act in such a way that I can help you," Moses replied patiently.

"And how come you want to help *us*? How much are you getting out of it? Perhaps it is just like the people say. A cousin of mine who talks with a man who has a friend who talks with a palace guard says that all the people of the court say that youse jealous of Suten-Rech Ta-Phar and that you go around stirring up trouble to make yourself a King. You want to be everybody's boss."

Moses shrunk up inside like darkness at dawn. Such misunderstanding of motives! Such a will to see evil where only good was meant. Such a trampling on his sacrifices, for he had all but decided to resign from the army and to devote his time to bettering the condition of the Hebrews.

"I don't want to be anybody's boss. In fact, that is the very thing I want to do away with," he said quietly.

"Don't look like it," one of the men retorted. "If what you are doing ain't bossing then there ain't a crocodile in the Nile! Calling yourself our friend, and liable to get anybody in Goshen killed if ever they find —"

"Sh-sh-sh!"

Everybody looked scared and glanced about them fearfully.

"Don't you people see that I am trying to help you? Being a bossman is the last thing on earth I want to do. I want you —"

"Oh, yeah! We're mighty proud to hear all of them sentiments out of you. Cause some of us was scared you was trying to get to be our boss. And since we ain't heard tell of nobody

putting you over us, so far as I'm concerned I'd rather have a enemy overseer that just beat me and sent me on home with a sore back than one of them friends that might kill me and bury me in the sand."

For a moment Moses stood hurt at the lack of appreciation of his behavior and of the motives that prompted him. Then he was afraid of what might happen if such talk reached Pharaoh. Then he saw the gloating look on the face of the one who was talking, and a brother gloat on the face of several others. So! The will to humble a man more powerful than themselves was stronger than the emotion of gratitude. It was stronger than the wish for the common brotherhood of man. It was the cruelty of chickens—fleeing with great clamor before superior force but merciless towards the helpless. It made him feel cruel himself for a moment. Then his anger passed and he felt sad again. Well, anyway, the Hebrew who had been made overseer understood. Moses could tell by his face. The whole thing was too big and sudden for quick words from him. He turned abruptly and walked away.

"Did I tell that Prince something?" he heard the voice of a man behind him. "I told his head a mess!"

"You sure did. I'll bet you he won't come messing around here no more. Ha! Many dogs are the death of the lion."

"So they think I could not have answered them, or that I was afraid," Moses mused as he strode on off. "They don't realize that it all would have been too easy for me."

Thinking and walking and feeling, he was at home before he knew it. He did not follow his usual pattern by stopping in the big reception hall and sending word by one of his servants to the Princess that he had arrived. He went straight to his private suite and sat down to think. But this was not the place. Observing that the door between his apartment and that of the Princess was firmly closed for the first time, it brought back all of his unpleasant happenings of the week. So he summoned his steward and commanded him to follow to his quarters in the barracks.

"You are to bring several changes of clothes to me here," Moses told the steward, "and a well-filled purse and the most necessary ornaments. I am going to live with my men for a long while. Hurry and do as I tell you."

"I have something to tell you, Suten-Rech, if you will listen."

"First go and get me what I told you and then tell me whatever you want to."

The steward hurried off in the new darkness and Moses sat and thought, and grew by inches as he thought. "The time has come for a decision in my life. I'm going to sit right here until my whiskers touch the ground, if I don't come to some decision as to which way my life is going and why." He sat motionless with his hands joined behind his head until the steward returned with his things.

"Suten-Rech, there are some who say that you are an enemy of Egypt."

"They do?"

"Yessir, they say that you are stirring up the Hebrews to rise against the country."

"They wish to destroy me, and so they have quit using sense and taken to using phrases. Slogans can be worse than swords if they are only put in the right mouths."

"Yessir. And they say that you are going about secretly killing off the overseers who have charge of large groups of Hebrews to give them a chance to kill us."

"They said I killed overseers? Who said that? When?"

"I think the word was sent secretly to Pharaoh today telling him when and how you killed this particular man and where his body can be found."

"Oh."

"It is said that Pharaoh is very angry with you and plans to have you seized tomorrow morning when you go to that conference about troop movement. Suten-Rech, I love you and I love to serve you. It would have been better if you had not declared yourself a Hebrew."

"I never did."

"There are several people who swear that you told them that you were a Hebrew and would do anything at all to serve them."

"Just one lie after another one. Somebody wants me out of the way and they are not missing a trick to get rid of me. But it does not distress me as much as it would have done a

month ago, now that I have made up my mind to leave Memphis and perhaps leave Egypt."

"But why?"

"For one thing, I suppose it is the easiest thing for me to do right now. Property always rewards its defenders and the property owners now believe that I am plotting with the Hebrew slaves against their possessions. So the people who are lying against me are in high favor now according to the signs. So I am going away."

"When?"

"Before the old man becomes a child again." When Moses said that, he was telling his thoughts by pictures. The people said that Horus, the sun-god, the god of the two horizons, became a baby each morning at sunrise and grew older all day long. By sundown he was an old man with a beard. But during the night his youth returned and he rose the next morning in his red glory and with his watchful eye drove away all darkness.

"Oh, Suten-Rech, please take me with you."

"No, I am going alone. I want to leave all that I was behind me for a while—perhaps forever."

"Oh, Prince Moses! Egypt could not spare you. You are part of the King himself and he is descended from Ra. You must not think of leaving the country. Justice will win."

"That may be so, and then again you may be right. But I'm going just the same. You must tell my wife, the Princess, first of all. Get the news to her tomorrow after breakfast, will you?"

"Oh, yes, sir, I will."

"I trust you to do exactly as I tell you. She must be told first of all. Announce to her ladies in waiting that you have come with a message from me. Then wait until you deliver the news to her in person."

"Where will you go?"

"To the desert, I reckon, to think. I feel something I have never been conscious of before, and I must find out from within myself what to do about it."

"What is that?"

"I feel the cursing thought of the law and power. I had

always felt the beneficence of law and power and never stopped to consider that it had any other side. It is a sword with two edges. Never mind whether it is directed against me honestly or not. That has nothing to do with its power to injure me."

Moses kept his steward with him until he was ready to go. His signet, his state ring, his other rings and necklaces he hid about his person with his money and went out into the darkness. He knew the steward would do as he was told to because he was afraid not to. He knew that the steward would wait a long time before the Princess would receive that message from him in the morning, and so it would be very late before anyone else knew that he was running away. He would be beyond the borders before they suspected that he was not in his quarters, or somewhere around the palace.

X

ALL NIGHT he traveled and thought. He found his unformed wishes taking shape. He was wishing for a country he had never seen. He was seeing visions of a nation he had never heard of where there would be more equality of opportunity and less difference between top and bottom.

Out under the late moonlight he could see chickens roosting along the ridgepoles of barns with the arrogant tail feathers of roosters sticking out against the sky, and that brought his thoughts around to the hundreds of questions he wanted to ask of Nature. It gave him a freshening hope, as he fled for his life from Rameses. "The man who interprets Nature is always held in great honor. I am going to live and talk with Nature and know her secrets. Then I will be powerful, no matter where I may be. And now that I am free from wars and warfare, I shall go to Koptos. Not at this very moment, for if I am found in Egypt they will kill me sure. Wait a little while and grow whiskers and they won't know me from the next one, especially if I stay away from certain vicinities. I am going to answer the questions that Mentu raised in me. Is there a box in the middle of the river at Koptos? Does it contain a book? Was the book written by the god Thoth, whose messenger is the Ibis? Is it guarded by a snake? Is the snake really deathless? These were the questions that hurt him to hold inside him because the saw-teeth of his curiosity and impatience gave him no peace. From now on his sword should cease to think for him. He would spend the rest of his life asking Nature the why of her moods and measures. As he sailed swiftly down the river Nile, he saw many things in the water and along the banks which he would like to investigate and which he now regretted to leave. He realized now how Mentu had aroused his thought, and that once you wake up thought in a man, you can never put it to sleep again. He saw that he had merely been suppressing himself during his military period. That was over and gone. Everybody has some special road of thought along which they travel when they are

alone to themselves. And his road of thought is what makes every man what he is.

Bright and soon three mornings later, Moses was standing beside the Red Sea. What he wanted was a large boat to cross over into Asia. He talked to first one man and another about renting a boat, but with no success. It was early for the rest of the world, but late so far as the fishermen were concerned. Three hours before every available boat had gone out to catch fish. So Moses finally sat down to wait until a seaworthy craft should come in with its load, or without one as the luck might be. So that is how he got to talking with the old man who said he was too old to go out with his boy any longer.

While he waited he noticed what he had not noticed before—that whoever was about the water front had left off what they were doing and were collected about him. They were respectful, even reverential to a degree, but everybody's thoughts and actions were influenced by his presence. Under the circumstances it began to worry him a little. Several of the men withdrew into a knot down the beach a little way. Then the old man crept up to him.

"Suten-Rech," he said in a low tone, "them men is figuring out how to make some money out of you."

"They do? And how do they plan to do it?"

The old man scratched his head and regarded Moses shrewdly. "We don't see a Prince in a hurry often."

"How do they know that I am a Prince? And why do they think I am in a hurry?"

"All anybody needs to do is to look at you and they would know you was a Prince. The way you act proves that you're in a big hurry to cross over on the other side. So them men—yonder, Suten-Rech—done agreed not to find you a boat until you are ready to pay a large price for it. None of us ain't got nothing, you know."

"I wish they would hurry and make up their minds on the price."

The old man crept closer and murmured in the ear of Moses.

"Some folks got minds already made up that could help you."

"Why don't they let me know, then? I am really in a big hurry to cross over."

"Take me for instance—I am poor and old too, so that the money would do me more good than anybody else around here."

"Have you a boat?"

"No, my Prince. But I have something to tell you which you don't need a boat to do if you will give me the money whilst the others are too far off to hear what we are saying."

Moses reached for his purse and gave generously. The man kissed the money in a sort of ecstasy and hid it in his clothes.

"I never expected to be so rich!" he said in an exalted tone. "Now, I can have a funeral of the second class with a tomb. Oh, yes, my Prince, it is all a matter of the hour and the tide and you can wade across the sea."

"The Red Sea is a mighty place of waters. You are joking with me and I am in no mood for jokes."

"Don't kill me, Suten-Rech, I wouldn't dare to joke with such a big man as you. Look, you walk down the beach about two miles north and you come to a narrow neck of water, where the Red Sea joins the outer sea. It ain't never very deep there at no time, and at certain times at low tide, the strait is just about dry. If a man started at the hour when the tide is lowest, before it rushes back he could be on the other side—if the man was right peart in his walking. A sort of light trot would put you across there in no time."

Moses hurried away and broke into a run as soon as he was out of sight. The tide was receding, but he did not stand and wait for it. He pulled off his shoes and his shenti, the short skirt worn by the military men and began to wade across. All the time the water was shrinking away before him. So Moses felt himself moving Godward with an understanding of force and time. So he walked out with clean feet on the other side.

Moses had crossed over. He was not in Egypt. He had crossed over and now he was not an Egyptian. He had crossed over. The short sword at his thigh had a jewelled hilt but he had crossed over and so it was no longer the sign of high birth and power. He had crossed over, so he sat down on a rock near the seashore to rest himself. He had crossed over so he was not of the house of Pharaoh. He did not own

a palace because he had crossed over. He did not have an Ethiopian Princess for a wife. He had crossed over. He did not have friends to sustain him. He had crossed over. He did not have enemies to strain against his strength and power. He had crossed over. He was subject to no law except the laws of tooth and talon. He had crossed over. The sun who was his friend and ancestor in Egypt was arrogant and bitter in Asia. He had crossed over. He felt as empty as a post hole for he was none of the things he once had been. He was a man sitting on a rock. He had crossed over.

XI

W HICH WAY he was going when he got rested, Moses didn't know. He knew where he had come from and what it meant, but where he was going was something else again. Oh, well, he had the rest of his life to strain with that subject. So he sat on a rock in the morning sun on the far side of the Red Sea and conferred with the Never Untrue, which in a common way of speaking people call Experience. In this way he walked backwards over his road from the palace to the seat on the rock in a strange nation. He looked back and the glance changed him like Lot's wife.

"How was a young man to know these things?" he thought out loud. "You have to go to life to know life. God! It costs you something to do good! You learn that by experience, too. If you want that good feeling that comes from doing things for other folks then you have to pay for it in abuse and misunderstanding. It seems like the first law of Nature is that everybody likes to receive things, but nobody likes to feel grateful. And the very next law is that people talk about tenderness and mercy, but they love force. If you feed a thousand people you are a nice man with suspicious motives. If you kill a thousand you are a hero. Continue to get them killed by the thousands and you are a great conqueror, than which nothing on earth is greater. Oppress them and you are a great ruler. Rob them by law and they are proud and happy if you let them glimpse you occasionally surrounded by the riches that you have trampled out of their hides. You are truly divine if you meet their weakness with the sword to slay and the dogs to tear. The only time you run a great risk is when you serve them. The most repulsive thing to all men is gratitude. Men give up property, freedom and even life before they will have the obligation laid on them. Yet they make offerings at every altar and pray fervently to every god they have ever made to make them thankful. But no god has ever twisted Nature to that extent. So they often rush out of temples to destroy those who have served them too well.

Two hours passed by Moses and gave him eye-looks. Then

the strange sun drove him from his rock to find some shelter and some food. And since everything moves ever west, Moses buckled on his shoes and his shenti and went on across the world with the sun.

That night he came to a place where caravans rested for the night. There was a squat stone and mud house and several tents. Men from the four directions gathered around a fire outside and let their night selves live. They laughed a lot and drank to bring on feelings and talked. Many races and tongues like the streets of Memphis and Rameses. One woman particularly was conscious of the approval of men. She had fine eyes and she rocked her upper body in the saddle of her hips as she walked about the fire from group to group, feinting at men with her eyes and attacking them with her body. One man played upon a stringed instrument and finally the woman danced in a way that Moses liked. The man played again and another man sang a song with sad words but funny gestures and intonations. "I had a good woman but the fool laid down and died—" and the audience made him sing the details over and over and over.

Late in the night two camel drivers got into a quarrel over their beasts. They drew knives but did not use them. They grabbed up rocks and made all the motions of throwing but didn't throw. Their threats were terrible. They had everything for a good fight except the courage. They imitated a frenzy to rush upon each other so successfully that they actually did. The shock of actually having to do what they had threatened to do was too much. They sprang apart and ran several yards in opposite directions before they went back into character.

"Ha!" one screamed back, "it is a good thing you didn't catch me. If you had they would have toted you across three yards—this yard, the church yard and the graveyard."

"I don't beat up bums like you. I pass you up and call you lucky. I'm bad! and if you hit me they'll give you four names—Nubby, Peggy, Bad-eyed and Shorty, cause you'll look like all of them."

"Humph! Nobody is scared of you. They tell me you sticks pegs in tigers' hips, but I'll make you pull this peg out."

"Oh, you're not so bad! If I jump on you I might not beat you but scarce as people is around here, we'll draw a crowd."

They kept this up at a safe distance from each other until they both ran out of threats. Then they returned to the circle about the fire and drank together as if not a word had passed between them. When they turned in to sleep they rolled themselves in their separate blankets and slept side by side.

Moses took no active part in anything that went on though he was interested and entertained by all that he could understand. After the passage of threats between the camel drivers Moses thought: "Here it is just like it is in Egypt—the scared people do all of the biggest talk."

A party of travelers from the Sudan played their drums and danced. One man with a dirk in his hand danced a marvelous pantomime of a hunter going through a jungle. He trod the jungle path. He was on the lookout for sudden death from the brush and the trees. He thought he heard sounds and stopped to listen. He suddenly hid himself behind a tree. False alarm. He proceeded swiftly and leaped over impediments in his path. He carefully parted shrubbery and looked for danger before he ventured further. He whirled about when he sensed danger behind him. A leopard! It attacked and he fought it off and killed it after a terrible struggle and ended the dance with a triumphant flinging of his shiny black body about. It was so realistic that Moses felt he could hear the snarl of the beast as it fought.

Late that night when most of the travelers were asleep the chief of an Arab caravan of traders called across the fire to Moses.

"Well, how do you do, soldier?" he asked.

Moses listened to his mode of speech and decided the man had been educated by books or travel, probably both. He was well-dressed in a manner and bore himself with an air that proved he was accustomed to commanding others. Moses noted all this quickly, in the space of time it took to form an answer.

"Why do you call me a soldier?" Moses countered.

"Because you look like one. But like an officer soldier more than the common kind."

"Well, I have seen some service."

"Egyptian soldiers are very good fighters. I know from experience."

"Not the worst in the world."

"Well, what is on your mind?"

"Oh, nothing much. This place and the next one I suppose. I am just on the loose for a while."

"That is fine. I have a job for you."

"What kind of a job is it?"

"Right in your line—fighting."

"Where is the war?"

"Anywhere that we find booty that is takeable. Can you ride?"

"Anything with four legs under it."

"Better come along then. A lot of stuff could be picked up along the route, by fighting men."

"Thanks, but I've just made up my mind to never fight again except in self-defense. It seems that fighting is a game where everybody is the loser. I have simply abandoned the idea of force. I want to sit and think."

"That is a crying shame with the build you got on you. Great big frame, fine legs, beautiful muscles—perfect fighting machine."

"Thanks. I've been told that before and I have led many a battle and chopped down my share of men. But I doubt that any life I have ever taken benefited anybody. The property I took from conquered countries didn't make anybody rich. It just whetted their appetites for more. No, no more soldiering for me."

"Where are you headed for now? It is odd to see a high-born Egyptian around here. That outfit you got on cost aplenty, too."

"Just walking away, and following my toes."

"You can ride in my caravan tomorrow morning. Ride as far as you like and leave us whenever you want to. Of course, I'm hoping you will stay. We need a man like you for both offensive and defensive fighting. But you can have your way."

"Thanks. Believe I will ride with you for a while. No telling what I might think by tomorrow this time."

All day the next day Moses rode in the caravan of the desert Nomads. He sat a fine stallion and rode with pleasure. Everybody in the band seemed eager to win him over. As they went on, however, he became a little ill at ease. Too many of the

men wanted to feel the texture of his fine linen with their rough hands. Too many of them wanted to heft the fine steel of his jewelled sword, which he never presented by its hilt. Always he held it by the hilt and let them pass their hands along its beautiful blade. Then again there was too much curiosity about the jewels on his hands and neck. He felt the bite of the tiny fear known as suspicion. If he did not join the robber-traders, they but waited until night to take him. He could picture his stripped corpse being casually left behind at the next encampment. The prospect did not worry him too much because he knew that he didn't have to make that encampment. So long as they were on the march, he had a distinct advantage, mounted the way he was. The chief thought that he was at his mercy. All right, let him think it. But when he got ready to leave the caravan, nothing could be done about it. The first large settlement that they passed he would rein in and announce off-hand that he was stopping there.

But early in the afternoon he saw his first mountain. It made him feel as if he had been lacking in something vital to life all along. He saw the great mountain at a distance lifting its rocky crown above the world and he was dumb-struck with awe. To him it had its being in grandeur, so it was right and proper to draw itself apart from the surrounding country and hide its mysteries in its heart. It was near; it was far. It called. It forbade. It was all things to his inner consciousness. He must believe in gods again, for here was the tomb of a god a thousand greater than the pyramids. No, it was not a negative and vain thing like a pyramid, whose builders were puny pigmies about the toes of this mountain. This was not a mere pile of stone. It had an aura of clouds upon its brow. This sublime earth form was the living place of a god, certainly. It had peace and fury in its face. Moses slowed his mount to gaze on the eminence.

"What is the name of that mountain?" he asked the man nearest him.

"It's according to where you live. The people on one side of it call it Horeb. On the other side they call it Sinai."

For more than an hour the train of men and animals wound close to the mountain and it changed its aspect every

few minutes as it drew near, but gaining in glory and never losing. Then the way veered off to the right and the distance.

So Moses got down off his horse suddenly and walked away by himself and the riders nearest him were too surprised to act until he had gained ground in rocky territory. So Moses walked towards the mountain for some time. When he found water he quenched his thirst and sat down by the well.

XII

Moses sat there by the spring of water. He saw well-trod paths leading away in several directions. So people lived hereabouts—people with cattle. He began to wonder where he would sleep that night and how. Tomorrow he would visit the mountain. That was settled in his mind. But he was tired now and he wanted a good night's rest. He wondered if the people who made those paths were neighborly folks or would he have to fight for his life before he found a resting place. The cool of the trees surrounding the spring was homey enough to suit him.

Here came sheep and cattle down one path driven by young voices. All of the animals crowded around the watering trough in eager thirst, stamping and looking for someone to draw the water for them. Down the path came a troop of seven girls who looked to Moses to range in years from about six to seventeen or so. They could not see him so easily from where he sat on the ground at the foot of a sycamore tree. So the girls came with their water jars and filled them first. He watched their happy ways as they spilled little splashes of water on each other in fun. One girl about twelve splashed water from a pot into the face of an older girl and turned to run away. The other one chased her and both of them came tearing towards the spot where Moses sat on the roots of the tree. They both saw him at the same time and halted dead in their tracks with little screams of alarm. They whirled as quickly as they could and ran back to the well. He could see them telling the rest of them about finding him. They pointed the place out to the tallest of the girls. They all looked worried for a moment and seemed about to go away without watering the stock at all. At this Moses stood up and made a gesture of friendliness and sat down again. They set down their water jugs and began to draw water for the cattle and to laugh and talk again.

Then from another direction came bursting three young men who were, Moses estimated, between seventeen and twenty-one years old. They rushed down upon the little party

about the well, whooping, driving off the cattle and scattering them all about. The girls ran in fright and began to hide wherever they could—all except the tallest one. She stood her ground at the well where she was pulling up a bucket of water and looked at what was going on with a great hatred in her eyes. She stood there until she saw one of the boys deliberately trip up one of her sisters as she ran from him in terror. She heard his big ugly laugh as the girl fell sprawling on her face. Then she set down the bucket and flew at him with her little fists. The other two boys were scattering stock and little girls in every direction.

Moses forgot the resolve he had made in Egypt to mind his own business and leave other folks' affairs alone. He leaped from his place and rushed to the aid of the girl who was being shaken violently by the man whom she had tried to chastise for hurting her little sister. Moses sent in a smashing blow to the head that sent him to his knees. As he was rising, Moses slapped his face with the flat of his sword and sent him down again. This time he did not try to get up. He looked at the sword first and then Moses and saw him all over. He stayed on his knees and raised his hands for mercy. Moses' scorn of the bully mounted at his cowardice so he snatched him to his feet and knocked him down again. Pick on little girls, would he, then just as soon as he faced a man, beg for mercy! He left the man on the ground and went after the others and chased them completely away.

The girls crowded around him, all talking at once and acting out their gratitude. He could not understand a word they said but he read their gestures. So he helped them to round up their cattle again and to water them. Then they waved shy little goodbye gestures and followed their stock back up the way they had come.

Moses sat back down under the sycamore tree. He still didn't know where he was going to sleep that night and the sun was setting. It went down and down and at last it hung like a big gold dishpan against the wall of God. Just then the tallest of the girls came back down the path and motioned him to follow her home. He got up and walked behind her at a respectful distance for fear that she might not feel safe with him. In less than half a mile of walking they came out in a big

clearing, with a huge tent under shade trees and cattle pens and all the things that make up the household of a patriarch.

The master of the place met him at the gate and made him welcome. He was an oldish man with a gray beard. But his eyes were large and dark and they had power in them. Moses felt his personality before he spoke. To the surprise of Moses he could speak Egyptian well.

"Come right in, Moses, and make yourself at home."

"How did you know my name was Moses?"

"I don't know it. But that is what you were thinking when you came up."

"That certainly is the truth. I was wondering whether to tell you my real name or not. You have the advantage of me now, because you know my name, but I don't know yours."

"Jethro is the name my father named me. As chief of my clan I am chief Jethro. Otherwise, I am Ruel. Among the Kenites a priest has a ceremonial name, too. Pretty general habit all over the land of Midian. But I guess you already know that."

"Well, I tell you, it's like this. Over there where I come from, news from this side of the Red Sea don't get around very fast."

"Let's table that discussion and take up one more important. I certainly am mighty much obliged to you for looking out for my girls down at the well this evening—but wait, don't say a word till I get you inside on a couch so you can slip out of those shoes and rest your feet. The womenfolks are out there around the cook pots stirring up something to eat."

Moses sat down on a low couch and took off his shoes. A servant brought a basin of water to wash his feet. So he took off his sword and headdress and made himself comfortable.

"Now to go back to this business of my daughters at the well."

"That was no more than decency demanded. No man would stand and let a gang of ruffians mistreat girls."

Moses looked at Jethro and saw a man dignified and graying. He looked as if he was supposed to be listened to, but there was no insistence in his face. He looked capable of guiding people, but he didn't look as if he were determined to do it. Wisdom and a kind of strength were gathered together in

the man, but his self-confidence had not driven off simplicity. He knew little sorrows and joys as well as big ones. He looked as if he could understand and talk with shepherds as well as kings. So Moses was not surprised when he spoke to hear him dropping into idiom of the simple people. It took nothing from his majestic bearing, and somehow it fitted him. Moses was constrained to meet him on his level as they talked.

"But, Moses, it didn't just happen today. Nearly every day those same rough varmints annoy my children. Law and order is in a terrible state in Midian."

"If what I saw today is a sample, it sure is," Moses agreed.

"Oh, you don't know the half of it. I am getting along in years, you know. Not the man I once was at all. It hurts me to see my girls shoved around every time they go to water the cows."

"It's none of my business, but why do you send the girls? Why not send your sons and your menservants?" Moses asked.

"It is a shameful situation, Moses. I hate to talk about it, but my wife don't have nothing but girls. Seven children and not a boy! Why, I can't hold up my head around here. They say I am too weak to father boys."

"Nothing to be ashamed about at all, Jethro. Why don't you send your menservants to water the cows? Send somebody that can strain with those hoodlums."

"They have run away, my menservants, all but one and he is old. Those wretches would kill him sure if he went down to the well."

"But, Jethro, why do they run off your cattle and bother your girls?"

"Well, I tell you, Moses, my house has always been powerful. From generation to generation it was that way. Right and justice prevailed in all Midian. But for the last few years a weak King has been on the throne and the robbers and thugs are just about to take us. Nobody is afraid of the King so people do not respect their chiefs and the country is gone to the dogs. Nobody can have any more than he has the might to protect. It all started with the downfall of the Hyksos in Egypt many years ago. Bands of them retreating before the Egyptians' army overran this country and got things so upset

we just haven't been able to get straight since. No real unity any more. If a chief hasn't got an army of his own, he's in a mighty poor fix. Our menservants ran off and joined up with gangs who live in caves and what not. They drive off cattle and raid encampments. My own herds have been raided until I am a poor man. The three men you whipped yesterday are runaway servants turned bandits. Because I am a priest they are afraid to come up here. But they hang around the well, terrify my girls and stampede the cattle. Each day or so we lose another beast which I reckon they have killed to eat." There was a sad resignation in the voice of Jethro. "So I reckon the day will come when we won't have any stock to water."

"Not necessarily so. They could be stopped," Moses said belligerently.

Jethro shook his head slowly. "No, I am afraid it's too late. We have no man power to fight and that is what it takes."

The tallest girl came into the tent and began to put the food before her father and Moses. She arranged lamps to the best advantage and this time Moses happened to look up and see her squarely in the face. To him her eyes looked so large and brilliant that the rest of her face was a suburb. Her whole body was extremely pleasant to look at and something about her made every cell in his body thrust out its head.

Moses turned to Jethro after the girl went out of the tent and said, "If they come around stealing cattle while I am here they better bring their good luck charm along because they are going to need it."

"Oh, you mustn't let my talk drag you into something that may get you hurt. By the way, that oldest girl of mine is named Zipporah. You must excuse me for running my mouth so much that I haven't introduced you to the family."

"That is the second time that you have read my mind, Jethro. You must teach me how to do that."

"It is a gift and not a learning, Moses. But to get back to this cattle business, I can't thank you enough for what you did down at the well. The girls came home and told me about the high-class Egyptian sitting by the well who fought the boys with the strength of ten men."

"How did they know I was a high-born Egyptian? I might have been anybody at all from anywhere."

"Moses, I never saw anybody who looked more like what he was than you do. You are the quality, and no mistake about it. I asked the girls why they had left a stranger who had protected them so unselfishly, sitting by a well. Zipporah said that in her excitement she forgot her manners. So you must excuse her, Moses. She is very young."

"That is natural and neither of you need to apologize for your manners nor your hospitality."

The two men ate alone with the three oldest girls serving them. There was some music and laughter after supper and Moses forgot that he ever had been tired or unhappy in his life. He went to bed and slept soundly and was up with the sun and walking over the place. He hoped that Zipporah would be around early too. He felt strongly the need of the sight of her. There was no thought of the adventures of the open road in his head that morning.

And there was the mountain to see and to feel. No, he did not desire to go away from here. His cells had the memory of this locality. It was easy for Moses to conceive that the dust that he was made from came off of that mountain there. This was the place that had called him in his unfinished dreams since childhood. He had been here often, by some mysterious forecast of dreams. Nobody here seemed strange and everything seemed familiar. He even found it natural and easy to drop into the dialect of the people with Jethro and the others whom he met. He talked it deliberately to put everybody at their ease. It was only in moments of stress in the times that were to come that he instinctively reverted to the language of the court. But here he blended into the background. This was his resting place, his eternal niche in infinity. The mountain hovered over him and called him as a mother would. He must go up and embrace his mother. He told Jethro how he felt while Jethro showed him over the place after breakfast.

"I know it," Jethro said, "and I beg you to stay here with me. In fact, I felt you coming somehow. I was not a bit surprised when the girls got back with the cows and told me about you. I feel a great power in you that you don't know

anything about as yet. I really hope that you will make up your mind to stay here."

"Oh, I like it here," said Moses.

"I'm glad to hear that, Moses. I hope you won't find things too uncomfortable around here. Of course I'm a chief and a Prince in Midian, but I realize that's not like being a Prince in Egypt. We don't have any court life and no formality. A Prince in Midian can herd his own sheep if he has a mind to and nothing said about it."

"That sounds just fine. Formality can get too burdensome."

"Well, you see in Egypt the rulers don't have to go near the people, but here a chief is looked on as the sort of father of his tribe. He can go without sandals and most of us just talk the language of the people. I have traveled some and that is how I learned Egyptian, but I don't get a chance to use it much around here."

"I want to talk the dialect of your people. It's no use of talking unless people understand what you say."

"That's right, Moses. Well, we'll get in a lot of practice on it if you stay around here. We won't have a chance to talk our high Egyptian except when we're off by ourselves. And then it's always a great advantage when you're managing people to be able to speak their kind of language. Stiff words frighten poor folks. I hope you stay here, Moses. You will make a fine friend for a man."

"I thank you for your compliments, Jethro. When you don't know anything about me or nothing. I ought to tell you about myself before I accept your home as my own."

"Plenty of time for the little details of your life. I know that you are brave and honest. Everything else about a person is garnishment."

"Thanks for your confidence. Look here, Jethro, where do those thugs hang out around here?"

"Oh, in a big cave about two miles off. There are around a dozen or so in the bunch from what I can learn."

"Is that all?" Moses asked.

"That's about right from what I can learn. But that's too many for us to strain with in the fix we're in. It's awful, the way they go around bulldozing and running over helpless

people. And what makes me so mad is, some of those same men were under my shelter all their lives until they got this notion of living by grabbing."

Jethro looked sad and frustrated and the face of Moses hardened when he saw it. The older man tried to look away quickly, but Moses saw it and stiffened himself a little.

"Do you reckon they have destroyed all the cattle that they have driven off your place?" Moses asked.

"Couldn't possibly have eaten up all those cows and things. Why, they have a big herd grazing around there that they have taken from different people. I have suffered the most since they know that we can't put up a fight."

"Oh, yes, we can and we will. Got any weapons around here?"

"Yes, I have some good blades—spears and swords—but nobody to use them. It's a sin and a shame too, the way those thugs take advantage of our helplessness. Why, as I said, some of those same robbers used to work for me."

"No later than tomorrow we are going to get back some of your stuff. We are going to attack their hide-out."

"We?" Jethro exclaimed in alarm. "Who do you mean by we?"

"Me and you and that one manservant you have left and Zipporah. We will dress her up like a man."

"But, Moses, she is nothing but a woman. She wouldn't be a bit of service in a fight."

"Yes, she will, too. All I want her to do when the fight gets hot is to stand at my back with an extra spear and sword in her hands. Then they can't surprise me from the rear and I will have plenty tools to fight with. You and the servant must drive off the herds while I fight and keep them from stopping you. Once we get them back they would not dare to come here to start anything. They must be badly armed else they would have attacked your camp before now. As you said, they are a bunch of run-off servants who have neither the guts nor the steel to make a bold strike. Besides, they don't know how to fight. Let's see after our weapons today and take the brigands an hour before dawn tomorrow. They won't be able to see us too clearly and they will think that we are a big fighting force. Are you for it?"

"I'll have to be. I can't let you be more willing to fight for my stuff than I am myself. But it's mighty risky, Moses."

"Oh, not so risky as you think. We will have the advantage of surprise and the half darkness. Besides we have right on our side. If I don't teach those cur dogs something about shoving girls around and stealing their cows, I hope I don't sleep another night. Tomorrow before dawn then?"

"You are the soldier man so you must know what you are talking about. We are going to do like you say, that is on condition that you promise to stay here with us."

"I promise since you ask me the third time as I know you mean it. You are my father from now on."

"Thank you. It's grand to have a son even though my wife didn't bear you. Now let's go get out those fighting tools and clean 'em up. I am beginning to get sort of bloodthirsty myself. Those skunks have run me ragged in the last six months. I am good to my servants, too, and that is what makes it so bad, what they have done to us. And that puts me in mind of my manservant. He is a dead shot with a bow and arrow."

"That's fine then. So then we can take your wife and that second biggest girl along."

"What for? My wife can't fight and she makes a poor out running. She's fat right where a cow is—under her tail."

"She'll do for what I want," Moses said confidently; "you just tell her to mind me. We are going to carry some firewood up there and sneak up near the mouth of the cave and light a fire of fat pine wood that will burn fast and bright."

"What for?"

"When the noise of the cattle being driven off wakes up those in the cave they will rush out to protect what they have stolen. Then you and I and your man will drive them back with a shower of arrows. If any of them break out anyway we will fight it out with spears first and if that does not stop them, it will have to be swords."

"So you mean for the women to drive off the cattle ahead of the fight?"

"That's it. They must wait until they see the fire start before they stampede the herd. But they must not walk those cows off. They must run them off in a hurry or else they will get mixed up in the fight and we will have to leave our posts

and rescue them. This is one time your wife has got to keep up with those who *can* run."

"But, Moses, the question that is sticking in my craw is, who is going to make that fire?"

"I'm going to do it myself. Your shooting man is going to cover me while I get it done. Now, get it straight. The whole idea is to bottle those skunks up in that cave. Put the fear of force into them so that all we don't kill and maim will be glad to leave the neighborhood."

"Moses, you got leader-blood in you. Just full of that old monarch stuff. You got me so I'm ready to tackle a den of lions. Let me go stir my wife and children up."

That night Moses took the servant and scouted the vicinity of the cave. They found vantage points in absolute silence and watched the camp in the cave put out their fire and go into the black hole of the cave to sleep. Then the two wrapped themselves in their blankets and went to sleep also. Moses woke first and saw the light of the false dawn in the sky and made ready. He knew that Jethro and the women would be there soon. Presently he saw them moving towards him like shadows, so silently they moved. So Moses sent everybody to their posts and crept up to start his fire. He soon had the kindling crackling. Then he fled back to his vantage point and the cattle began to jump up from where they were lying and thunder off before the women's blows and cries.

A face with a questioning voice appeared at the door of the cave and got an arrow in his chest. Another and another arrow sped into the mouth of the cave from the bows of the three men. Several men approached the door of the cave with various weapons in their hands. A shower of arrows drove them back with loud shouts and screams and excited jibbering talk. Nobody ventured to show themselves for a long while.

"This is the time for us to make our get-away," Moses counselled. "The firelight makes them a good target and hides us where we are. But daylight will change it around. And that is what they are waiting for. We got somebody in there. Maybe two or three. Let's go while the going is good."

They melted into the grayness and went on home. As they entered the compound, some tired gray clouds were resting on the ground but the sun came up and drove them off. The

household all went to work penning up the big new herd before they thought about breakfast.

"Honey," Jethro's wife said as they looked over the herd, "looks like we've got a few cows here that we didn't have before. Them speckled cows, for instance. I disremember us having any cows like that."

"Well, I am not going to tote a casket in my pocket about it," Jethro said with a cheerful tone of voice. "I don't expect to take to bed sick over it for even one day. It just makes me and my son Moses hungry for our breakfast. You women get to doing around."

XIII

THAT EVENING it was Moses and Jethro, armed to the teeth, who drove the cattle to water. No troublesome ruffians appeared, however. The next morning Moses, instead of the girls, took over the task of herding the cattle to grazing ground, but he was not challenged. They heard nothing at all from the cave of the robbers. But the second morning, two dirty ragged men came shuffling up to the tent of Jethro and asked to see him.

"Oh, so you come back to steal more cattle, do you?" Jethro snarled at them when he saw them. "Look, Moses, these men are two of my servants who ran off and turned bandit. Now they say they want to come back to work. What must we do with them?"

"Oh, no, we didn't run off, boss. We was carried off by them robbers and we couldn't get loose from them until the leader and three more got shot the other night in a raid. Them others that didn't get killed that was holding us run off and so we had our chance to come on home and that's what we did."

Jethro looked at the raggedy men before him and over his shoulder at Moses. "What must we do with 'em, son? I know they are lying about being carried off by force, but they might behave decently if we gave them another chance. What do you say?"

"Give them the old army discipline and put them to work. I'll be seeing them if they start any more cattle stealing around here."

So every morning Moses drove out the flocks to graze and brought them home in the evening. There was no more trouble at the well nor anywhere else. The women went to work on suitable clothes for Moses, and he put his jewelry away until the family should need it. He and Jethro spent hours together talking over symbols and meanings and Jethro was the teacher. Moses told him about what he had learned among the priests in Egypt. He had met the bull of the sacred

428

marks and the unknown history* and Jethro was eager to hear all he had to say. But in nearly every case he had knowledge and methods far beyond anything that Moses had seen in Egypt. He forbade Moses to go up on the mountain until he gave him permission, and that made Moses a little unhappy. But he reasoned that the time would come when Jethro would take him to the mountain and so he was patient. In the meanwhile he was mastering the language of the Midianites as if he had been born to it. After all, he found it was close to the Egyptian so it made few difficulties for him.

He was glad one day when Jethro told him, "Moses, to-morrow night there is going to be a big clothes-putting-on and eating down the road a piece here and these two biggest girls have been harassing me and their mama to go. Reckon you better come go along. I'm not so much at these shindigs these days."

"I'd love to go," Moses said and looked across at Zipporah.

"That's mighty nice because you can go along with my wife and the girls. I'll stay home with the little children. I don't like to leave them by themselves."

"I'll do the best I can to look after them."

"Oh, I have every faith in you. Let's eat. Herding sheep and cattle is a mighty hungry job to my experience."

Moses went to bed rather surprised at how often he was thinking about Zipporah. He felt rather inadequate in dealing with her. She was no woman to be ordered into his tent at his pleasure and ordered out again at his will. He was not a military officer on a campaign to acquire his women by a nod. He had affairs around the court, of course, but not love affairs. He did not want any more treaty wives by arrangement. He wanted to win a woman and hold her by love. The matter was smooth and round like a ball. There was his heart's desire inside the sphere but the outside presented no place of entry, and Moses yearned for some progress in the matter with all his heart.

The next night, mounted on camels, they set out for the celebration. The two girls rode on the same camel. Their

*The priests in selecting the young bull for worship always pretended that it had appeared in their midst mysteriously, by divine guidance. No one was supposed to know anything about its origin. Divine origin was claimed for it.

mother said she would feel better with Moses driving her than one of the girls. Her bones were too old to be falling off of camels. So they set out in the dark. The girls began a repetitious little folk tune and after a while Moses could join in the refrain. It was too early for the moon and the darkness seemed to snuggle them all together in a sweet world all to themselves until they rode into the light of the celebration.

Moses was never to forget that party as long as he lived. There was feasting, music and games where everybody took part. But Moses felt lonesome and out of things. People treated him like he was some great lord. They were too deferential and impressed. Nobody ran up and grabbed him and pulled him into a game. They served him before anyone else was given a mouthful. And a barrel-shaped man kept choosing Zipporah for a partner in the games. Moses never realized that fat-faced men looked so much like fiends before. He caught himself feeling for his sword before he realized what he was doing. He was almost sorry that he had ceased to wear it with his new clothes. And Zipporah, the little devil, looked him right in the eye and kept on laughing happily and encouraging that fat-faced fool. He was glum all the way home, but the girls kept up their chatter and singing. He felt like slapping their faces, especially Zipporah's and he wanted to scold the moon for shining and somehow adding to his misery.

When they rode into the yard a servant came out with a light to help them dismount. As Moses walked towards the other camel to help the girls to dismount Zipporah feinted at him with her eyes and jumped down and started off. Her sister romped after her and her mother waddled behind them towards the big tent. Moses stood for a moment like a blazing tree on the plains, burning fiercely with the pitch from his own heart. Then for some reason Zipporah turned back from the door of the tent and came back in the moonlight towards the grunting camels.

"Come here, Zipporah!" Moses said tensely but in a low voice.

She looked up as if she was surprised to find him there. "What do you want with me?" she asked casually.

"Come here to me, woman. I know exactly what to do with you."

"Oh, you do, do you?"

"I certainly do. Come here."

"No."

"Yes! I want you."

"I don't come running like that. Even a hen must be sought after, Mister Moses, and I won't be less than a chicken."

"Oh, you are going to be run after, young lady. Don't be so hard to get. Come farther away from that door before I come after you."

He didn't wait. He rushed over and seized her girdle and snatched her towards him. And now that he had his hands on her, all the words that he had been preparing to say to her vanished from his tongue. He crushed her body against his and kissed her with as much energy as he needed for a cavalry charge. These were his words for her. When he finally let her go she ran into the big tent a few steps ahead of him and sat down by her mother.

Moses followed her more slowly and went to where Jethro was lying on a couch.

"Have a good time, Moses?" Jethro asked with his eyes closed. Moses was frightened inside but he answered calmly. "Oh, yes, it was a rather nice party."

"I thought you might like it, though it was not one of the really big local affairs. But when you and Zipporah get married you are going to see a real celebration."

Moses was dumbfounded. "Then I can really have her, sir?" he stammered like a schoolboy.

"I took you for my son, didn't I? And now if my daughter wants to take you for a husband, why should I object?"

"She told you that, Jethro? She said she wanted me?"

"She didn't need to tell me. She has been thinking it for weeks and somehow other people's thoughts are like glass to me, especially those who are close to me. When she came in the door just now she was determined to have you for a husband before another week was over. You are of the same mind and I know it, so there is no need of beating around the bush.

I was never more pleased about anything in my life. Now I know you will stay here with me."

Zipporah was clinging to her mother and weeping the tears all girls weep when they have captured the man of their choice. Jethro's wife was hugging her daughter and weeping in sympathy with her. She too had recollections of a night and an hour. She too had won the one man in all the world for her. She had had her ecstasy. So she rocked herself back and forth and cried tears.

Moses crossed and knelt before Jethro who placed his hand on Moses' head.

"My son, I hope."

"I will never fail her, father. I will hunt up new roads to heaven for her to go by. I mean to share every pleasure. And then again I will stand by her to the seventh sorrow. I love her."

He rose and went out of the tent door without speaking another word. And Zipporah rose from beside her mother and followed him to his sleeping tent.

XIV

ZIPPORAH of the tawny skin. Zipporah of the flowing body. Zipporah of the night-black eyes. Zipporah of the luxuriant, crinkly hair that covered her shoulders like a great ruff of feathers. Zipporah of the full, dark red lips. Zipporah of the warm, brown arms. These were the pictures that went with Moses all day long as he herded Jethro's sheep. Night and the time to go home was always too long coming. He loved her little songs, her childish delight in the Egyptian ornaments he had given her and others he bought for her from traders. She was beautiful when she was weaving. She was irresistible when she danced and played. She was always doing something that kept him enthralled. He spent no more evenings in the big tent with Jethro any more.

One morning Jethro was standing at the gate of the corral when Moses came there to let out the sheep.

"Just thought I'd go along with you today, Moses."

"That's fine. In fact, it's a high honor."

"No, just a lonely old man wanting a chance to talk, I reckon. I don't see very much of you these days, you know."

Moses blushed from the guilty feeling inside that he had been neglecting his friend of late. He herded the sheep before them for a long time before they found a good grassy spot. Then they sat down on the slope side by side.

"Moses," Jethro began a little sadly, "when you came here you were a man with a mission. I felt it in you strong."

"Did you? I sort of had the feeling that I had given up all missions. The life of a missionary seemed hard."

"Oh, you were out of dreams for the moment, but the great dreamer, the great leader was there. You have a great soul and something down in Egypt had waked it up. And you can't wake up thoughts in men and put them back to sleep again."

"I have a wife now and I have you and the mountain for a friend and that seems to be all that I need."

"Moses, what about the book in the box in the river at Koptos?"

"That is only a myth, perhaps."

"I notice you say perhaps, Moses. Look in front of you, son. That is a sacred mountain before you, Moses, and once you felt it, but no more. Once we had long talks in the evening that I meant should lead to something important later on, but you don't inquire of me any more."

"Jethro, you are still my best friend. But I have a woman now."

"Have you never had a woman before?"

"No. Not like this one. I have been as most soldiers among women, but not one was ever able to make me lose an hour from a campaign. But with Zipporah it seems that a whole lifetime would be too short to search out all her wonders. Why, her feet and supple toes are worth hours of watching. I have a consuming greed to absorb her inside of me so that I can possess her completely, but she seems to escape away from me all the time. Maybe my whole life will be necessary for the pursuit."

Jethro gave a grunt and fell back on his homely philosophy.

"You have more greatness about you than any man I ever heard of, Moses. Don't over-pull your belly on this love business and destroy it. Love some and think some."

Moses thought to himself, "If he only knew what a mess I have made of my life so far, he wouldn't think I am so great." Out loud he said, "Jethro, you see all that in me because you love me. I'm nothing but a happy man having the wisest man and the finest man on earth for my friend, and having my home with my wife. You probably look down on that as nothing but desire."

"No, I don't, Moses. I don't fault you for that. Everybody has to be young a while before they get old. It's too bad, but it's so. What you're feeling now has got its place in life. Desire is the germ of the mind. There is no creation without it. Desire is a woman who is little understood and much slandered when her back is turned. She is a woman with a beautiful face and an ugly back. She drives a strong-legged crowd before her, gilded with the light from her face, and pushing the world before it. Behind her is a limping horde with the cawing black bird of age sitting on its shoulders, screaming imprecations at her back. They are renegades who do not

deserve their past. Those who say desire is ugly have poor memories."

"Then you approve of my love?"

"Yes, I do, Moses, and then again I don't."

"Why?"

"You are an over-average man, Moses, and I hate to see you wasted on a woman. What goes for the everyday men does not apply to you. You have something that spoke to me from a distance. It can't die and it can't be hidden. You can't run away from it and you can't do away with it. It is a glory and a tragedy. You are sentenced by fate to lead."

"Lead who and what?"

"Men. In some way or another, whatever men you are thrown in with, you will lead. I am sorry for you, but that is true."

"There is no comfort in that. All I ever want to do is to herd your sheep, talk with you and take comfort in the arms of my wife, and bring up the sons, which I hope for in abundance, to be good and gentle. I want to sit on the side of Mount Horeb and ask Nature some questions."

"No use talking to you right away, I see. But you have a great call and some day you will have to answer. You can wring and twist all you want to, but when the hour comes you will have no choice but to go."

A long, thoughtful silence fell between them. After a while Jethro said, "I had thought to take you to the mountain soon, but — "

"That is where I want to go. Why do you forbid me to go?"

"Because you are not ready to go, Moses. That mountain is holy ground. Our people have worshipped on that mountain for many generations. So many that I don't know my own self. But God and the mountain can wait. You are still a young man."

"Why do you say that mountain is holy, Jethro? Why did the Kenites start to worshipping there in the beginning?"

"Why did you feel something about it, Moses? Perhaps they felt just as you did."

"Yes, Jethro, I have a feeling, but perhaps it's only a feeling because the mountain has the size and shape of majesty. That might be all. I don't know."

"No, there is a god up there, Moses. I have heard voices."

"Voices, Jethro?"

"Yes, Moses. But I am not so sure I make out exactly what they say. Perhaps it calls for more power than I have to really understand. But I *feel* the command to bring other people besides the Kenites to know this god and worship him. Besides, I am too old for missionary work now. But over and above all that, I feel that the call was never meant for me. I know now that the God of the mountain has been waiting for you."

"For me? Why, Jethro, I am nothing but your sheep-herder who has the honor to be married to your daughter. If this god found you not strong enough with all your great knowledge and power, then I—why, you are the greatest man who ever lived."

"No, Moses. You are a hundred times my superior. The great I AM took the soul of the world and wrapped some flesh around it and that made you. You are the one being waited for on this mountain. You have the eyes to see and the ears to hear. You are the son of the mountain. The mountain has waited for the man."

Moses frowned a little and sat quiet for a long while. Jethro studied his face and said nothing more while he watched the movements of the flocks. Finally Jethro said, "There are lots of plants and things that you ought to study so you can know their habits."

Jethro picked up his staff and walked off a short distance and came back to where Moses sat with a plant and began to teach him its properties. Moses was so interested that they spent the rest of the day that way. The older man went home feeling close to his pupil again and warm inside.

Mrs. Jethro had supper ready. She never asked Jethro where he had been after long absences. She was used to it and besides she knew she would get no answer. But Zipporah questioned Moses, and Jethro answered for him by telling her to work harder on the weaving of the new tent of camel's hair and not to be so talkative. She pouted at this and said, "I just wanted to tell you a message came for you today. We are going to have company tomorrow."

"Who is it that's coming?"

"Oh, that rascal from the other side of the mountain that comes over here with his gang every time they run out of rations and eat us out of house and home," Mrs. Jethro broke in with resentment. "But you just *will* feed him every time."

"Oh, you mean Chief Zeppo," Jethro said, laughing.

"I don't mean nobody else," Mrs Jethro went on. "Some day he is going to over-pull that belly of his and die with the colic and I sure won't care. Killing up our beef and mutton to fill that desert that he calls a stomach!"

"Well," Jethro temporized, "we have to be neighborly. And then again I am a chief and we just have to set a table accordingly."

"And, Moses, dear," Zipporah said, "you must let the servants look after the sheep tomorrow. You must stay home and put on your fine Egyptian linen and ornaments."

"But I gave you all that jewelry except my belt and sword, dear. You put it on. I like to see you all dressed up."

"No, you put it on, darling. I want them all to see you in it, all looking like a King or something like that."

"Why, darling? I'm just your father's herdsman."

"Because she wants all the rest of the women to envy her, that's why," her father snapped.

"Now, papa."

"Pay her no mind, Moses," Jethro said, dropping into the vernacular. "She is just like all the rest of the women. She wants to make out to the rest that you were some big high muck-de-muck back there in Egypt so she can put on side as Mrs. Muck-de-Muck, and earn some envy out of the rest of the women around here. She wants to make a Prince out of you so all the other women can suffer envy of the Princess Zipporah. Don't blame her for it. She's a woman, isn't she?"

Moses thought that Jethro had come close to doing what he had avoided doing before, that is, asking him who he really was. And now Moses felt that he must tell him everything. So he set the very next night for his time. He needed the day to bring himself to open the door that he had closed on his feelings. Since he had been with Jethro he had achieved a certain calm by forcing an internal silence on his soul. Sud-

denly it came to him that his new happiness had washed him out. He no longer cared. Tonight was as good as any other time. So he sat down and told his family everything that mattered.

"You are not to be blamed for anything, Moses. Your youth couldn't tell you that you couldn't make big men out of bigots. Urging compassion on your grandfather was useless because he did not have any place inside of him to put it. In my experience I have found out it is no more use to give advice to an old man than to give a tonic to a corpse."

"But his own grandfather ought to have had more feeling for him," Jethro's wife objected. "Don't those people in Egypt have no heart at all?"

"Oh, yes, there are plenty of fine, generous people in Egypt," Moses told her. "But Pharaoh is a man of great ambition. He does not have sons and grandsons in his heart. He has only connections who win honors and wars in his name."

"He is not by himself in that, I am sorry to say," Jethro said. "His feeling is very common on thrones."

"Well, all that is behind me and I have found a real father and a real home at last. I don't say anything about my beautiful wife. But if you all would rather not have me here after what I told you—"

"Don't even say what you started to say," Jethro said earnestly. "We all love you, each one of us in the way that is right and proper. And look what you have done for us. You came and found us in a pretty low state. Me a chief that had next to no power and now you have built me up around here. You found our cattle gone and got us more than we had. Why, we are eating high on the hog now, and all because you are here with us. No, Moses, you are never to consider leaving us. The bonds you have here are never to be broken as long as any of us are alive. Tomorrow we take the blood oath together and then I am going to open things to you that I have kept closed up to now."

"Thank you, Jethro. You are truly a generous man and I love you like my own self."

"More than me?" Zipporah pouted.

"No, silly. You are myself and the best-loved part of me, too."

"How can I believe that, Moses, when here you are a Prince and never told me a word about it."

"How did I know that a wonderful girl like you would stoop to marry a mere Prince? Especially a Prince without power and wealth. A miserable exile."

Zipporah was very pleased at this but she pretended to pout. "Don't try to flatter me, Moses. Here I am married to a Prince of the blood royal and the neighbors don't know a thing about it. Is that nice?"

"Very nice, being married to you."

"Moses, you must take me to Egypt."

"Why, dear?"

"Don't you want to show me our palace and all those places and people that you told us about?"

"Yes, I do, but I wouldn't want you to feel as I felt in those palaces and places. It might not be so wonderful as you think."

"Oh, I think you are mean! I don't believe you want that— that Ethiopian, that other Princess to know about me."

"Oh, don't be silly. I never even kissed her, really. That wasn't love, that was a treaty we were carrying out. I think she liked being a part of the court more than she did your husband. Several times I had the feeling that she was disappointed because she was not married to my Uncle Ta-Phar instead of me. She would have been a step nearer the throne as his wife. But he was already married at the time."

"I want to go and lay my eyes on that female," Zipporah said from the fountain of assurance of being desired, "and let her see *me*."

"But it would be worth my life to be caught in Egypt," Moses said. "As long as my grandfather lives it would be certain death. He believes that I am trying to undo his conquest and so he hates me. Ta-Phar took care of that. He figures Pharaoh is about to die and he is afraid the army might substitute me for him on the throne."

"You ought to let them do it, too," Zipporah said with shining eyes. "You were born to be a King, like papa says. I'll be very happy when we can go home."

"This is my home now, darling. Positively. I am through

with palaces and Kings and wars of Kings. Such things don't seem to be worth all they cost. Give me the black tent of Jethro with his wisdom and faith and the sheltering mountain and you and I can't imagine anything more worth having. They can have the palaces."

"Moses, darling, you can't talk like that. You have a wife to look after now. If you don't want such things for yourself, you ought to claim them for—for others."

"Oh, leave the man alone!" Jethro snapped. "You are just like all the rest of the women—ready to upset the whole world to make an opportunity to dress yourself up in ornaments. That is all women around Kings are good for. Put on more ornaments than anybody else and make more chances to wear 'em. Fix it so you won't have no competition, then parade your swag in front of the others and let 'em look on and envy you. You make property-grabbers out of otherwise good men. Leave Moses alone. There is something bigger in store for him than being a mere king."

Then Moses asked a bold question.

"One thing, Jethro, I ask you as my father and my friend. Will you go down into Egypt for me and renew the offerings at the tomb of my mother and my friend, Mentu? I will give you all directions."

"I will go," Jethro said simply.

"She might not be my actual mother as they say. She might have adopted me from Assyria, or found me on the Nile or borne me. It doesn't matter to me for she was a real mother, loving and kind. I prefer to think that she bore me, and I do not want her tomb neglected. Mentu was a servant who became a friend. Renew the offerings at his tomb."

"I will do all of that."

"Some day, you shall go with me to Koptos. Further than that I am not concerned with Egypt. Your house is mine. Your gods are my gods and your ways are mine. My life, so far as it is any use to you, is yours."

XV

THE YEARS went by with a loping gait and left tracks all over the place. A profound calm took up in the face of Moses. It grew rugged like the mountain but held its power inside. He loved his wife and their two sons, but there was no more ecstasy. He spent his days with Jethro's flocks and Nature. He learned the secrets of plants and animals, and the living and the giving earth. Long years had passed since he embraced the religion of Jethro. He had learned to build the altars of uncut stone or earth and make the offerings, and the tribesmen had come to accept him, both as a chief second only to Jethro and as a priest. He practically lived on the mountain, in the desert, beside streams, feeding his mind on Nature. Sometimes he would be absent for days and sometimes weeks in seeking answers to questions that Nature put to him. Jethro now sat at his feet in all things except one. Jethro was still his master in magic but Moses steadily closed the gap between them and that delighted old Jethro more than his grandsons.

Time put tracks on Zipporah. She came to know that she still had a certain power over Moses, but that she could not follow him past the door of the tent. He loved her and the children and was gentle with them, but Jethro was his company. Her flowing body had taken to bulging here and there so she quit putting accent on her body and took pride in her two growing sons. Now and then she recalled her dreams of the palaces of Egypt and was a little petulant with Moses. But he had made her feel that tears and pleas were no good. She had gone down into Egypt and with her father each year when he went to renew the offerings of light and incense and each time she had had a fit of despondency on her return. The glory of her husband's feats of arms were not forgotten in Egypt and she would hear of it while she was there, and it made her regret what might have been. If Moses only had the proper ambition, she might be mistress of the palace someone had pointed out to her. And her sons might be Princes near the throne.

Time left its footprints all over Jethro, too. He had shrunk up in his skin considerably, so that it no longer fitted his frame. But a hopeful light had come in his eyes. He was making of Moses what he himself had wanted to be—a great priest. Moses had the genius for leadership which he lacked. Moses had comparative youth and he had fire. Moses had education and breeding and Moses had soul in soul. All he needed to do was to point the direction and Moses passed him in accomplishment with a leap. Here was the man of science such as the world had never seen. But his beloved son-in-law had a serious failing. He had no mission in life except to study. Jethro with the help of Moses had become the wealthiest man in Midian. With his wealth and backing and Moses' own popularity, Moses could become King over all the local chiefs, but he made no move in that direction even when he was urged. He just had no wish to govern his fellow men.

The quick grasp of things that Moses had and his talent for developing what he found always amazed Jethro as well as delighted him. He had shown Moses how to effect a sending of flies upon an enemy and the next month Moses had produced such a swarm that the whole household had to work furiously for days to get rid of them. But he had not stopped at that. Moses went out into the wilderness alone and stayed for weeks without letting him know what he was about. When he returned he produced swarms of every insect and reptile at will. He drove off a wandering band of vagrants with a plague of snakes. Once when Zeppo sent word that he would accept Jethro's invitation to come over and eat meat with him for a few days, Moses laughed. Zeppo came with his huge family and lit down off his donkey and made straight for the cook tent to get "a little something to give him an appetite." Moses stood and watched him until he flopped down on a seat by the cook tent door. Then Moses lifted his right hand and extended it before him and frogs literally rained about Zeppo. His mouth was crawling with them and they were everywhere. Frogs swarmed over the family and they swarmed over beasts. Zeppo and his family screamed and fled in every direction till they were safely off the place. His womenfolks kept up with him as best they could. He did not

desert his youngest granddaughter because she could keep up with him. Next day he sent back for his donkeys. He also sent back a note which obviously had taxed Zeppo's small education a lot to write. It read like this:

"DEAR COUSIN JETHRO:

I take my seat and take my pen in hand to write you a letter. I want to know where is your raising that you ain't got no more manners than to let frogs be hopping all over people when they come to visit you? I have been a good and faithful cousin to you. I have always been kind enough to drop whatever I was doing and accept your invitation to bring my family and pass a few days with you and eat meat. But I know when I been insulted and I'll never accept another invitation to pass a week with you, not even if you ask me. But if you insist I will not refuse the meat you offer me. You can send it by my messenger when he comes.

Your loving cousin,

ZEPPO.

P.S. I'll bound you all them frogs was the work of that son-in-law of yours, Moses. Nobody else could have done it."

So Jethro wrote back a letter like this:

"DEAR COUSIN ZEPPO:

All the manners I ever had you done et it up long ago. So I reckon there just ain't no more. You will have to refuse my offer of beef because I am not slaughtering today. All my cows have a bone in their legs. All of my beds are full of folks so you can't snore in my ears no more.

Your loving cousin,

JETHRO.

P.S. Yes, my son Moses is the finest hoodoo man in the world and my wife says that stopping you from eating somebody else's groceries is his greatest piece of work. But she may be wrong.

Have you ever seen his sendings of snakes and lice?"

Time left his signs in Egypt, too. Death came and startled old Pharaoh. So Moses heard about it in Midian and came to Jethro one day ready to travel. He and Jethro dropped into the dialect of the people as they often did at times.

"My grandfather is dead and I am going down into Egypt."

"You going to the funeral?"

"No. I am going to Koptos at last."

"So you didn't forget, did you?"

"No."

Jethro thought a while then he said, "It's funny how long wishes will last, isn't it?"

"Sure is. Come to think of it, I've been with you twenty years."

"Did it seem very long to you, Moses?"

"No, Jethro, that is, in general it didn't. I have been happy about everything. And I have tried to deserve my memories. It was just my wish that worried me. Sometimes it looked like time was going to mock it to death. Twenty years is a long time to wait."

"Yes, I know by myself, Moses. I got a wish that's forty years old. Ever notice how long wishes can last?"

"It all depends on what sort of stuff they are made out of. You know about me, but I didn't know you had one living with you, too. What is it?"

"Oh, I've always meant to tell you about it first and last. Fact of the matter is I tried to tell you once or twice. But I figured you wasn't ready for it yet, because I could see you straining against understanding. Maybe I'll broach it when you get back from Koptos. By the way, while you are down in Egypt, why don't you look in on them Hebrews and see how they are making out? Things might be different with them now that they got a new King."

"All right, I will, though I have no way of helping them at all, now. I don't know as I rightly understand them and I feel sure they don't understand me. I'm sure they didn't twenty years ago. It wouldn't be a bit of use for me to go among them, I'm afraid."

"Oh, I don't know, now. Do you reckon your uncle, the new Pharaoh, will try to put you under arrest?"

"I am not going near the palace. Anyway, few people would know me, now. I am going straight to Koptos and when I return I will come with a forked stick in my hand and a fire pan on my head."

"The symbols of the hundred-bolt lightning and the sun, eh?"

"That's right."

"Let me go with you, Moses. Maybe I ain't too old for the journey."

"It will be a hard journey. Maybe Mentu's story is only a myth. Even if it is true, we might lose our lives in the attempt."

"I guess you're right, Moses. You go down and come back with the power, if it is to be had. It might come in handy some time. I used to teach you but now you can tell me and then again you show me about the God of our mountain. Your brain leaps past my stumbling mind to the inside meaning of things. But I don't lose a thing by it. Through you, I just got better eyes and ears and legs than I used to have. And that right hand of yours!"

So Moses went on down into Egypt and left Jethro sitting on the side of the mountain, back-thinking on his twenty years with Moses. And the more he thought the bigger Moses got in his sight.

Moses had lifted his right hand in Midian and the people feared it. The first few times that he made the gesture before a miracle nobody noticed it particularly. But when it kept on happening, that right hand became a symbol of terror and wonders. Then it quit being a sign of power to the people; it became to them power in itself. He lifted it and they experienced the miracle of water turned to blood. It had been done in a small way by the Cushite priests for a long time. But Moses lifted his hand and extended it imperiously and the rivulets and springs and wells and streams ran blood all that day. Moses lifted his hand and a malicious gossip was struck with leprosy. It was Moses who learned the secret power to command the power of flame. It was Moses who could bring on or drive off the cattle disease.

It was Moses, too, who saw in the little puff of white smoke that rose from the incense on the altar the symbol of the Presence behind the clouds on the crest of the holy mountain and he developed the smoke into a thick white mass that hung stationary and huge above the altar for as long as the ceremony lasted. It rested there in volume and mystery like the Presence it symbolized. It made the voice of the unseen Moses speaking behind the altar seem like the voice of God. It seemed to the people that Moses but lifted his right hand

and the cloud from Mount Horeb appeared upon the altar. From so many signs and wonders that they had witnessed when Moses extended that right hand before him, they came to believe that the hand of Moses held all of the powers of the supernatural in its grasp. It had a separate existence from the rest of his body. So when Moses lifted his hand the smoke of the incense ceased to be smoke. It became the Presence. If it was not the actual Presence, then it enclosed and clothed the Presence. Finally the smoke itself was deified. It was not understood so it became divine.

Now Moses found out how to make the excrescence that he called Manna appear on a certain plant. So Jethro himself began to be in awe of him. "No use talking," Jethro said to his wife. "Moses done found out something we others don't know about. Looks like he done found them secret words that's the keys to God that we all been looking for. I figure he's about ready to go to work."

XVI

ONE DAY Moses came walking up and looking tired and lean for his height.

"Well, I see you got back," Jethro said off-hand.

"Yes, back after a whole long year," Moses said, dropping his walking stick and taking off his shoes.

"It seemed like it too, Moses. You was mighty missed around here."

"I'm glad to hear it. I missed being here with all of you too."

"Once in a while I would get to fretting about you. I didn't know whether you would make it back or not."

"I wondered the same thing my own self a heap of times."

"Well, if I ain't too previous, Moses, did you get your wish?"

"I sure did. That's why I'm so wore out like I am."

"Do you care if I ask you how it was?"

"No, I don't. In fact, I don't intend to eat nor sleep until I tell you. I have been needing your ear and your advice for so long."

So Moses stretched himself upon the couch and told Jethro how he had passed through lower Egypt like a shadow of a cloud and hurried on to the Thebiad, where Koptos is.

He had gone into the temple of Isis at Koptos and brought an ox and a goose and some wine and made a burnt offering and a drink offering before Isis of Koptos. He spent four days with the priests of the temple.

On the morning of the fifth day he had called a priest to him and with his powers had commanded the priest to make a magic cabin that was full of men and diving tackle. Moses himself put the spell on it and put life in it and gave the men breath and said to them, "Workmen, go to the place in the river where the book is, and work for me." Then he had sunk the cabin in the water. In three days they had come to the place in the river where the box was and made a shoal out of sand to make the water shallow. They worked night and day.

Then he found the box all wrapped around with scorpions

and snakes and different other kinds of reptiles. But he knew what to do for them so that they all laid sleeping as if they were dead. Then he met the deathless snake. So the snake got ready for a hard fight and Moses fought him all the next day. Moses did not win over the deathless snake but then the snake did not beat him, so they met and fought again the next day. At sundown Moses felt that he had the advantage of the snake to a certain degree, so he called up all of his power of mind as well as his body, for if he won he would have more power than any man on earth and also the deathless snake would come under his command. And he wanted the obedience of the snake. So late in the third day, he beat the snake and commanded the snake to meet him anywhere in the world that he might call. So the snake did not appear to resist him any more.

Then Moses took the book out of the golden box that was closed in all the other boxes. And when he went with the book Light went before him and Darkness after. He knew the ways and the meaning of Light and he heard the voice of Darkness and knew its thoughts.

So Moses read the book and then he was able to command the heavens and the earth, the abyss and the mountain, and the sea. He knew the language of the birds of the air, the creatures that people the deep and what the beasts of the wilds all said. He saw the sun and the moon and the stars of the sky as no man had ever seen them before, for a divine power was with him.

When he had read the book, he took a new piece of papyrus and copied the words of the book on it. Then he washed off the writing with beer and drank the beer for then he knew he would never forget what he had read. So he put the book back in the golden box and put the golden box back inside the other boxes at the bottom of the river and commanded the snake to guard it until he should come again. And if he never returned, no man was ever to see the book until the end of Time. And the deathless snake took up his watch beside the box.

So then Moses broke a seal and read a spell over the workmen that he had made and told them, "Work for me back to the place from which you brought me." They toiled night

and day and that is how Moses came back to the harbor in Koptos. From one thing and another he found out that he had been nearly a year about the business of the book. The priests of Ra, suspecting his success, tried to stop him, but he proved himself top-superior to all that they did, and came out of Egypt with a high hand. So then there was nothing for him to do but to come on home and be with his folks.

"Then you are ready for the big job," Jethro said with an inside force that just barely grazed his face.

"What big job are you talking about, Jethro?"

"That big job I been saving up to get done for over forty years. I knowed all along I couldn't do it myself."

"What kind of a job is it, Jethro? Maybe I can do it if it ain't too big for me."

"There ain't no jobs too big for you, now, Moses. Not with the help you got."

"Tell me then, Jethro, so I can know what it is."

"It's my wish, Moses. You got yours now and you know how a wish is with you. It will keep on plaguing you till you get it. Ain't that right?"

"It sure is."

Jethro fumbled with his clothes a minute or so. Then he asked, "Oh, er—Moses, did you ask about them Hebrews while you was knocking around in Egypt?"

"Sure did, Jethro. I thought they was in a bad fix when I used to live down there. But they are in a sure enough bad fix now. Ta-Phar is bearing down on them in a big way."

"You don't tell me!"

"That's right. He claims they didn't do no work under his father. They were just fooling around with tools. So the first thing he did was to put them on double shift, working night and day. Why, he's got more government projects going on than you can shake a stick at. Those poor devils are building a brand-new Egypt under the lash."

Jethro smoothed his beard down for a while and thought.

"You know, Moses, I been thinking we're kind of selfish. Here we done found out about the one true God. The others been grabbing hold of little parts of Him and calling all of them parts a god by itself. It's like calling each limb of a

person a man. I been sort of thinking we ought to let more
people know about what we done found."

"They all know by now, don't they? That is, everybody
round here already knows about Jehovah, don't they?"

"That's just the point I'm coming out on. Not enough
folks know about him. We ought to spread it around. And
that's the wish I been nursing for forty-odd years."

"But, Jethro, everywhere you go, the people got gods al-
ready. They won't hear about no more. In my travels I been
way past the Jordan into the land of the Amorites, and the
Canaanites and the Philistines and they all got gods that suit
them. Who would listen to us? Where would you get the
people to make converts out of?"

"How about them Israelites? They're down there in Egypt
without no god of their own and no more protection than a
bareheaded mule. How come you can't go down there and
lead them out?"

"Who, me? I tried some missionary work down there
twenty-odd years ago and that is just how come I got to be an
exile. No, I'm satisfied with things the way they are going."

"You still letting love run you after all these years?"

"No, it ain't that, Jethro. I think the world of my wife. But
it ain't love I feel for her no more. It's the recollection of love
that comforts me and makes me want her to be happy."

"Well, what is it then, Moses, that you don't want to go?"

"I'm just satisfied with my life right here. I got everything
that a man could want. I've been to Koptos. I just want to sit
on the mountain and ask God some questions about life."

"You won't go?"

"Not to turn you a short answer, Jethro, but I'm through
messing in other folks' business. I can't go, no."

Jethro's feelings took his features and formed a face that
was wretched. "I sort of counted on you, Moses. In fact, all
my dependence was in you."

"I just couldn't do it, nohow. I'm not cut out for that. I
love silence and quiet places. I want to enquire. I don't want
to be enquired of. With a mob of people around me like that
I couldn't hear my ears."

"Those people, I mean those Hebrews, need help, Moses.
And besides, we could convert 'em, maybe. That really would

be something—a big crowd like that coming through religion, all at one time."

"I don't say it wouldn't. But I don't want to be the preacher. I'm through trying to regulate other folks' business. There ain't no future to it at all—just a whole lot of past. If you find a cow stuck in the mire, and pull her out, she'll hook you sure. I just want to practice up on all this new stuff I done learned."

"Get them folks out of Egypt and use them to practise on, why don't you?"

"How am I going to do that, Jethro? Pharaoh is getting too much benefit out of those Hebrews. He wouldn't let them leave. And another thing, why should they trust me? They don't know anything about me. They wouldn't believe I meant them any good. They wouldn't follow me."

"You could try. It would make a mighty big man out of you, Moses, if you did. You could even be King if you wanted to."

"I don't want other folks' property enough for that."

"You wouldn't have to call yourself a King. You could just sort of rule along without taking on the title."

"Jethro, it's not the title I am afraid of, it's the thing itself. It makes no difference what he calls himself, king or ruler, who sends the young men out to be killed and takes the people's cattle away from them. Titles ain't nothing but nicknames."

So Moses went back to herding sheep on Mount Horeb and went on asking Nature her secrets. He was at peace with himself, but not for long. The spirit of Jethro's tongue was docile, but he never let up on the subject. Moses kept on refusing but it got harder and harder to do so. Jethro had a feather touch but he crowded Moses farther and farther into a corner until Moses went around with a harried look. To make it worse the whole family was of the same mind. It followed him around the place and went to bed with him. One night he felt that he couldn't bear it any longer so he gave Jethro and his wife a flat refusal, and went off to bed.

Jethro and the full-bloomed Zipporah sat looking after him until he was out of hearing.

"Well, that's the end, I reckon," Zipporah sighed. "If he

won't, he won't. But I can't see to my soul how come he don't want to be a King. I don't ask for much. I don't bother him when he stays off on that mountain days at a time. I don't part my lips when he prowls all over Asia and Africa from one nation to another fooling with bugs and worms. All I ever asked for myself was to be Queen and he won't do it. Me with my two boys getting grown—it's hard on me."

"And a better piece of ruling material ain't never been born on earth," Jethro agreed. "It's a sin and a shame. He is a great priest. Jehovah went out of His way to make him. His kind may never be seen no more on earth. He could call sinners to repentance, he could preach the socks off of sin if he only would. If he don't want to be a King, that's all right. But he sure ought to go get that passel of Hebrew people and convert 'em to Jehovah. He could do it easy, with the power he's got. The man is just running over with spirit."

"Just a fine King going to waste," Zipporah said bitterly. "Look at the shape the man's got on him! Portly and strong and everything. He sure would look noble in a crown. So far as the Queen is concerned, I would do just as well as the next one with the right clothes on. It's a shame that Moses is that stubborn."

"Well, he might think I'm through with the thing, but first and last he's going to find out different. I ain't been to Koptos, it is true, and had no fight with no never-dying snake, but maybe there is still something about snakes that he can learn. The backside of that mountain may get too hot to hold him yet."

XVII

M OSES sat up on the mountain passing nations through his mind. Way late in the day he climbed up to a place where he had been resting every afternoon for a long time. He was watching the development of a family of reptiles under a rock beneath a bushy growth. So he went on up putting words into the mouths of the various little creatures that he saw on the way. What these creatures had to say about people had plenty of seasoning.

Moses rounded a large boulder in sight of the spot where he was going and went on easily. There was the bush, and there was the rock under it. He was within a few feet of it when the bush burst into furious flame. Moses could not believe his eyes, but neither could he shut them on the sight. Because the bush was burning brightly but its leaves did not twist and crumple in the heat and they did not fall as ashes beneath charred limbs as they should have done. It just burned and Moses, awed though he was, could no more help coming closer to try and see the why of the burning bush than he could quit growing old. Both things were bound up in his birth. Moses drew near the bush.

"Moses," spoke a great voice which Moses did not know, "take off your shoes."

"How come, Lord? I know no voice like that can't be like mine."

"This ground you are walking on is holy ground. Take off those shoes."

"Yes, sir, Lord." Moses loosened his shoes and took them off without once taking his eyes off of the burning bush that did not wither. Moses stood barefooted and bareheaded and trembled with awe.

"Moses!"

"Yes, sir!"

"Come closer, Moses. There is something that you must hear."

"I'm coming." Moses faltered nearer the flame and stood. For the first time in all his life he felt naked, meek and void.

"Moses, look on the ground in front of you."

Moses looked down, and started back in terror.

"What is it you see, Moses?"

"It's a snake! It's a deadly poison snake," Moses said in fear, and started to run away down the mountain.

"Moses!"

"Yes, sir, Lord."

"Come back here." Moses came because the mysterious voice commanded, but he came in fear. "Moses," the voice ordered, "pick up that snake." Moses shrivelled and shrank from the order. "Pick it up by the tail."

Moses gathered his strength and stooped. He seized the snake by the tail expecting to be bitten immediately. But except for a curious tremor of life that somehow communicated itself to the hand of Moses and from his hand to his arm and from his arm throughout his body, it might have been the wooden image of a snake. It was heavy for its length in wood, but it was stiff and motionless like stone. Moses was amazed that the writhing serpent on the ground could have become so quickly the lifeless thing in his hands. It was a walking stick carved in imitation of a snake.

"Moses, put it down." Moses dropped the rod and it became a living snake again. Suddenly his fear left him. He picked up the snake in that certain way again and it became again a rod to his right hand. It was his, he knew by the feel of it. It was the rest of him. But the voice came again.

"Moses, I want you to go down into Egypt."

"Into Egypt? How come, Lord? Egypt is no place for me to go."

"I said Egypt, Moses. I heard my people, the Hebrews, when they cried, when they kept on groaning to me for help. I want you to go down and tell that Pharaoh I say to let my people go."

"He won't pay me no attention, Lord. I know he won't."

"Go ahead, like I told you, Moses. I am tired of hearing the groaning in my ear. I mean to overcome Pharaoh this time. Go on down there and I'll go with you."

"And those people, Lord, they won't believe in me. I don't talk their kind of talk in the first place and then again, I got a

stammering tongue. I never could make a speech. Send somebody else, Lord."

"You go on; I'll go with you. Open your mouth and I'll speak for you."

"Well, Lord, if I go, tell me what to say; they won't believe in me," Moses said with hopeless resignation. "I don't even know your name. Who must I tell them sent me?"

"Tell them I AM WHAT I AM."

"Yes, sir, I'll go tell them, but I know it won't do any good."

"Somebody with a speaking mouth will be provided to talk for you. Go down into Egypt, Moses, and lead my people to the place I have provided for them. I AM WHAT I AM."

The Voice was hushed. The bush no longer burned. In fact, it looked just like it had yesterday and the day before and the day before that. The mountain was just as usual with the wind yelling "Whoo-youuu" against its rocky knots. There was nothing to speak to the senses of Moses and verify what he had heard and to hold him to what he had so unwillingly promised. That is, nothing but the rod he held in his hand. Therefore it was not a vision and neither was it a dream. This bush had blazed with fire before his eyes, but it had not burned as was natural. A serpent had become a rod to his hand and a rod had become a serpent and back again. Life could never be again what it once was. He had promised a god to go down into hated Egypt and command a man whom he hated and who hated him to permit a people whom Pharaoh hated to leave his servitude and go free. Moses dropped to a shady rock and sat with his face covered until the sun got low and red. Then he dragged himself home behind his mumbling sheep.

XVIII

JETHRO was very helpful when Moses told him about it. In fact he seemed to Moses to glow and to swell with pleasure. "No need in you taking the thing so serious, Moses. It might not be as hard to do as you think."

"No, it's just ten times as hard. I can't do it, and that I AM WHAT I AM ought to know it. It's going to be just about as hard to talk to them Hebrews as it is to Pharaoh. But the promise done been made, so—"

"Oh, I don't know, Moses. It stands to reason that anybody in slavery would be glad to be free."

"Humph!"

"And when you look at it again, a nation of folks with no particular god would naturally be glad for a god to choose them for his own and then pick out a land to give them."

"When they can get loose from slavery in Egypt and fight the folks that already got the land and lick 'em, they got it. It don't seem such a much to me—that land part don't."

"Oh, I don't know, now. With a good military leader, they might make out top-superior to everything they meet."

"Did you ever lead an army? It takes more than promise of some land to make a fighting army out of folks that just got free. Men fight with more than their hands."

"Well, anyhow, Moses, I can help you out some."

"How?"

"On one of those trips down into Egypt I met up with some of those Hebrews and I think I could maybe find a sort of headman among them who could help you out some."

"That would be mighty convenient if you could. Why, I don't talk their language. I don't talk with their thoughts. I don't know the first thing about them and they know next to nothing about me. I just can't go."

"How about your promise on the mountain?"

"It wasn't so much my promising as it was a command. I got to go, but I feel like the job don't belong to me. I never could talk to crowds, and least of all these people that is so strange to me."

456

"I'll go down into Egypt, Moses, and bring out a man to help you handle the people until you feel you can manage. His name is Aaron."

"And what am I going to say to him, Jethro, to get him to work with me?"

"Why can't I tell him the Voice mentioned him by name?"

"Tell him whatever you want to, Jethro," Moses said and walked away with his head hung down. "I'm going off to the wilderness to think. I am a man that has been called."

XIX

MOSES talked with Aaron and got more aggravated and put out every time they sat down together to plan. This Aaron was a short, squatty man who wanted things. First he wanted clothes like an Egyptian noble with ornaments. Then he wanted titles. Then Moses must recognize him as a brother. Moses refused at first to even listen, but Jethro persuaded him that the connection might be useful down in Egypt. He could make the old legend serve him. So Moses consented by a freezing silence. Then he wanted things for him family, and then he wanted things for his tribe. He was a Levite and the Levites must lead in all things or he could not consider a thing.

"This sounds like the very kind of a thing I hate," Moses said with some heat, "and before I'll be bogged down in a lot of politics, I'll call the whole thing off."

"But the Voice," Jethro reminded him quickly.

"Oh, I'll go back and ask that Voice again. I'll find out if I have to go through all this to save people that think more of personal preference than they do of rescuing a whole people and making up a nation."

So Jethro convinced Aaron that he really must give up some of his demands, or he would find himself back in Egypt and in the same fix he was before he, Jethro, had smuggled him out. This frightened Aaron and no more was said about his offices and prerogatives for a while. He did mutter something about people who wanted to make kings out of themselves, but didn't want anybody else to advance themselves the least bit. But Moses ignored all this and finished his plan of campaign.

It wasn't long after that he was saying goodbye to Midian and to his family. Jethro and the family mounted camels and went with Moses and Aaron for a day's march.

"It may be a month and it may be a year, but I won't be back until I march out with the children of Israel. We have no army to face Pharaoh with. I got to fight all Egypt with my right hand."

Jethro had dismounted and stood by Moses, showing all the old affection he felt.

"Be sure and come back, son. I hope you don't come by yourself, but come back home." He leaned his old head on Moses' broad chest like a child. "I wish I was in your shoes, Moses. Going on missions is a great privilege."

"I thought you was over-anxious for me to go, Jethro. That feeling helped me to consent to the Voice. I could feel how much it meant to you."

"I'm anxious for you to go, but I'm more anxious for you to come back. I realize it now when you are going. Don't let old Pharaoh kill you. You got power. Use it. Nothing can stand against your hand when you lift it up. All my love and all my powers go with you, son. And don't hold my impatience against me. You will know what it is to get tired of waiting on visions when you get old like me."

Moses looked past the outline of Aaron mounted on a camel toward the Red Sea, and for a moment he wavered. Then he looked back at the shape of Mount Sinai with its shoulder-wrapping of clouds and heard the mutter of thunder from its throat. He embraced Jethro affectionately and turned his feet resolutely towards Egypt. Jethro stood watching him for a long time, but Moses was on his way. He never looked back.

XX

MOSES was back in Egypt and the people of Goshen knew it. The leaders in Israel had known that Aaron had slipped out of Egypt to meet him, and they had been listening and looking for his return. Aaron had sent the tremor along the grapevine immediately after he returned—"our man of god is in Egypt."

Tremendous excitement rippled down the secret ways of Goshen.

"They say he owns a god" was whispered in hopeful emotion.

"Sure enough?" others questioned. "Wonder how do folks get hold of gods?"

"That's more than I can tell you because it's more than I know. But that ain't the point. The point I'm coming out on is, this god wants to work in our behalf. He aims to put us in power with the Egyptians."

"Hush your mouth! You don't mean to tell me that!"

"That's what he claims."

"It sure is something if it's so."

"They say he can really do what he says."

"What you say his name is?"

"The new god or the man—which one you talking about?"

"The man, fool."

"They call him Moses, because they say he came out of the water in some way or other. So they call his name Moses."

The other man paused and scratched his head and thought. "Look like to me I heard that name before somewhere a long time ago. Wasn't there a Prince of Egypt named Moses?"

"This is the same one."

"Well, what is he doing with a strange god and how come he wants to help us out? I ain't never seen no Egyptian with that sort of a notion."

"It seems like that's how come he had to leave Egypt a long time ago—because he had sympathy for us. He took and killed an Egyptian overseer for beating on Hebrews, so

old Pharaoh, I don't mean this Pharaoh we got now, I mean the old gentleman, got in behind him to kill him, so he had to run on off."

"Well, if he did that he's a friend of the race, and that's something we ain't got too much of. When can I meet him and see him? I wants to shake his hand."

"He was at the house of Aaron, they tell me, but he's hard to locate. Don't stay in one spot too long. That's to keep them secret police all fuddled up in case they try to grab him. But they tell me everybody is going to have a chance to meet him, first and last."

Other whisperers were asking, "Now this god that Aaron says Moses has got, where do he come from and what is his sign?"

"Nobody ain't seen no sign yet. Ain't even made no motion to build him a temple yet. It seems funny a god without a place to stay or anything."

And as for Moses himself, now that he had accepted the call and was down in Egypt, a sort of grim and stony peace came to him. He set himself to his task with determination.

Immediately after his arrival in Goshen he told Aaron to summon the Elders of the tribes to meet him, and anyone else of influence. When they came, Moses was surprised to find a woman among them.

"Who is this woman, Aaron?" Moses asked.

"That's Miriam, my sister."

"But what is she doing here? I have called the Elders to me on serious business."

Aaron showed irritation, pointed up by a certain arrogance.

"My sister Miriam is a great prophetess, Moses. Talking about influence, she's got plenty. We couldn't make out without her, that's all. Everybody comes to her to get things straightened out. She's a two-headed woman with power." He looked at Moses and challenged him with his eyes.

"She can hit a straight lick with a crooked stick, just the same as you can do."

Moses closed his eyes for a moment so that Aaron could not look through them into his mind and said simply, "In that case we need her. Tell her to stay. She would be useful in handling the women."

"Oh, she can handle the women, all right. In fact she can handle anybody. We ought to call a meeting of all the people right away and let her speak before everybody for you."

"No, Aaron," Moses said positively, "this is not the time I have appointed for speech-making. It is too soon. First we have to organize the Elders, then let the Elders prepare the people for us." He saw the petulant look on the goat-like face of Aaron and asked, "When did Miriam address the whole congregation of Israel last?"

"Oh, she ain't never done it yet," Aaron stammered.

"Did she ever speak to your whole tribe of Levi?"

"No, she ain't, not yet. She ain't never needed to, that's all. But she could really do it if she wanted to."

"Then what makes you so sure she could do all this speaking and influencing if you never have seen her do it?"

"Because her house is full every night of the people who come to her house to get help. Miriam got a certain little bundle that she makes, that ain't no bigger than a man's thumb. You put that around your neck and wear it, and nothing can't do you no harm."

"Hmm! It's a wonder every Hebrew in Egypt wouldn't have one of them. Pharaoh and his overseers wouldn't be a bit of trouble then. Why haven't you and Miriam done that on a large plan and freed Israel long ago?"

"We haven't considered like that and if we did, we might say that we, that is, Miriam, was called to prophesy to the people and not to save 'em."

"Oh, I see," Moses said significantly. "It's nothing for us to get angry about anyway."

"Who said I was mad?"

"I wouldn't say you were mad exactly, but we do seem to argue a lot about everything, Aaron, and none of it is necessary. The point I want to get clear in your mind is that if you, I mean Miriam, is called to prophesy to Israel and I am called to save Israel, our paths don't conflict at all."

Aaron was caught off guard by this statement and he didn't like it, and Moses saw it. Finally he said sullenly, "That ain't the point at all."

"What is the point?" Moses persisted.

"Well, er—the point is, I don't see how come she, that is,

both of us, can't get credit for what we got to do in saving Israel. And that is mighty important."

"Oh, you will be of great help in gathering the people and explaining my plans and you will get proper recognition for it, too. But we don't need to worry about recognition right now. What we need to worry about is the success of the plan. It's a mighty big project we got on our hands, Aaron. Let's bury ourselves in it, Aaron, and give it our whole devotion. It's too big for us to be mere people. We've got to give up being people and feel like the tools of destiny, that's a big honor in itself, Aaron. I want you to think it over."

A certain good humor was restored and Moses went on working out his plans and passing them out through Aaron, until finally the meeting of the Elders of Israel took place. When Moses spoke to them he said nothing about his whole plan. He merely said to them, "I come to bring you a message from a god who has chosen you as his people to love and protect."

"How did this god hear about us?" the Elders wanted to know. "You say he spoke to you in a far-away mountain. How did he hear about us here in Egypt?"

"You cried out for deliverance in your great sufferings, didn't you?" Moses asked.

"We sure did. We been crying a long, long time, but no gods, least of all the very ones we worship, didn't hear us at all," the Elders told Moses with suffering in their eyes and hopelessness in their voices.

"But this god of the mountain has ears," Moses said with conviction. "He heard your cries and sent me to tell you that he has chosen you and that he has the power to save you, even in spite of Pharaoh."

There was great excitement at this.

"What is the sign of this god?" they wanted to know.

"His sign is power," Moses answered with assurance.

"What we want to know is, What is his messenger?"

"I am his messenger," Moses answered with equal assurance.

"We want to know how we can recognize his signs when we meet 'em. What animal does he live in? Is he a bull like Apis, a cow like Isis, a cat like—"

"This god never shows himself through any animal. He has no representation on earth in any form. He speaks in fire and smoke, but the fire and the smoke are not god. He has no images and wants none made in his name."

"What is the name of this god, Moses? Maybe he is a god of Egypt who has left Egypt and sends to us from some place away off."

"No, he is no Egyptian god. He has not uttered his name as yet."

"You must not know a whole heap about this god your own self, Moses, if you don't even know his name. Didn't you even find out that much about him?"

"I asked him his name."

"And what did he tell you?" the Elders asked.

" 'I am what I am,' is all he said, but that is a great answer. It takes in the whole world and the firmaments of heaven."

That was a great mouthful for the people and they went off muttering to themselves in their unlettered tongues "I am what I am" over and over and blowing in the ashes of their hopelessness to kindle hope. They had intended to ask many more questions about this strange god who had sent to them—about his wife, and his food and his children, and what especial sin he punished, but all these questions had been smothered. So the Elders went off from the meeting to begin to spread the word to the people to meet Moses in a secret grove for a ceremony.

There, deep in the forest and amid the silences, Moses built the altar of rough stone as Jethro had taught him and performed the sacrifice as he had come to do for so long on the mountain with Jethro. And the people began to catch fire and worship.

Moses instituted the ceremonies to the god of the mountain and established altars and more and more the people came to them and began the new practices.

"The god of the mountain detests the flesh of hogs," Moses told them. "No worshipper of I AM WHAT I AM may eat pork," Moses commanded, and people began to give it up. He taught them many other laws. His god loved justice, he taught them justice and right among peoples, more than obligations to altars.

"When do we bear down on Pharaoh and this freedom?" Aaron asked impatiently.

"One thing at a time," Moses told him. "We have to lay a foundation before we try to build."

After several weeks had passed the Elders asked Moses, "When will we be free?"

"You will be free when you hear the thunder," Moses told them. "Pharaoh will issue a decree and you will think that you are free. You will march out and you will think that you are free. But one day, after you have suffered many things, when the thunder is heard from the mountain, you will be free, if you have courage."

"You can see further with your eyes closed than we can with ours wide open," some of the people clung about Moses and told him. "You're our rod of salvation, Moses. Lie down and sleep and dream for us."

And the Hebrews, working and suffering, and wondering about the nature of thunder, went through their days holding their hearts still against the present, prayed for the day of thunder.

XXI

THEREFORE Moses took his rod in his hand and went to see Pharaoh. He took Aaron along for his dressing. It looked better to the people anyway for Aaron to go. Suspicion was too easy to arouse if Moses went alone. Some would think he had only stirred them up in order to betray them to Pharaoh. He had heard hints and whispers that maybe he was buying his way back in with Pharaoh by stirring them up to show what was in them so Pharaoh could have an excuse to butcher them all. Pharaoh had done everything else that could be done. Nothing else for him to do but kill them and they didn't put that past him for a minute. Anyway, Moses had reason to believe that few if any accepted the story of his kinship with Miriam and Aaron. He was still an Egyptian noble to them. If he wanted to cast in his lot with them, well and good. But blood was thicker than missionary zeal and he would bear watching. Why should he serve them anyway? It looked mighty funny when you come to think of it, at that.

Now Moses was at the palace with Aaron.

Pharaoh took his seat and had his Queen with him so that Moses could see that she was the Ethiopian Princess who had once been his wife away back there when he was a Prince in Egypt and wore a jewelled sword at his side. Moses could see that it was supposed to hurt him and he was sorry for them a little. She had been all these years living off of more treaty kisses and Pharaoh had been living off of power, when he had gotten hold of it at last. Moses could picture just how fretful Ta-Phar and his wife had been while they waited for Rameses the Great to die. Moses could see Ta-Phar's old face slipping down into his neck. His Queen's hips looked like they had moved round in front of her, or more like they had abdicated in favor of her stomach. No, he still didn't care, no matter how much he saw that they wished he would. He stood with his rod in his hand and measured them. He stood before Pharaoh and felt as if he stood in the presence of the evil dead. And he was glad that he stood facing them at last. The past and the future were pouring out of time.

Pharaoh let Aaron stand before him and say what Moses had told him to say. He listened to the end, but he paid little attention to the ex-slave who he saw was quaking inside while he tried to put on a show of arrogance. At the same time Pharaoh kept looking to Moses for confirmation and assurance. So he listened casually to the voice of Aaron. But he paid strict attention to Moses. When Aaron had finished he ignored him and acted just as if Moses had spoken directly.

"Well, Moses, so you are back again doing your best to destroy the country."

"No, I leave that job to you. I am here by divine command to save a people, not to destroy."

"Oh, yes, I know. You are bent on being King of something, even if it is nothing but the Hebrews."

"No, Pharaoh, my call is higher than that. I am commanded to lead them out of their suffering to something better. And I'm going to carry them off."

Pharaoh laughed without moving his features. But Moses could see the formal set of his expression change to scornful banter. "And how do you aim to do that, Moses? Those Hebrews are mighty poor fighting material, and you ought to know what my army is."

"You have your army and I have my powers. I mean to attack you with what I have. Our side is stronger than yours."

"Since when?"

"Since a new and a stronger god has called them through me to his service. Your gods never were anything more than a deification of the forty-two judges of the forty-two Nomes of Egypt, and they are still servants to be ordered. The god I represent is one who commands. We shall win."

"With what?"

"With my uplifted right hand. If you can stand that, you can stand the flood."

Pharaoh indulged in a broad sneer. "Oh, you are still messing around with hoodoo, eh? You ought to know better than to come back here depending on that."

"And why not, Pharaoh?"

"You forget, Moses, that the priests of Pharaoh are the greatest priests on earth."

"I don't forget any such a thing, because I never knew it. I do remember though that I could surpass any priest in Egypt long before I left here."

"That's rich! First you come here pretending that you can't talk—bringing a slave to do your talking. Then you open your mouth in the wrong place. I'm going to call your bluff so these Hebrews can see what a friend they are trusting. And then I'm going to show you up for the pleasure of the thing."

"You mean we are going to show each other up. You fear me more than I do you and with good reason, too."

"Moses, I could call the palace guard and have you dead in a few minutes. I am going to do something worse. I am going to expose you first and then leave you to the people." He turned to a guard. "Call the priests from the temple. I want them here right now."

While they waited Ta-Phar smiled at Moses with utter cruelty in his face.

"You see, Moses, I know why you have come back to Egypt and it is not to rescue these miserable Hebrews. You are merely trying to use them to frighten Egypt into making you a King. I'm glad that you have come in the way you did. I intend to keep you at your activities so that Egypt can see you as the country's worst enemy—trying to arouse the slaves against the people."

"To me, Ta-Phar, the Hebrews are people."

"To me, Moses, slaves are slaves."

Moses could see Aaron wilting and he could see Pharaoh gloating at the sight. The priests came in, never missing a convention sacred nor civil until Pharaoh told them to rise and listen to what he had to say.

"This fraud and hypocrite was run out of Egypt around thirty years ago, after trying to be a priest, a soldier and a Prince, and first one thing and another. Now he's back trying to tote off our slaves on some religious cock and bull story. He claims he has enough magic in his right hand to outdo all my army and all my priests and the Hebrews are stupid enough to believe him, it seems. Go ahead with your skill and make a fool of him so the people can go on back to work and he can go on back wherever he has been hiding out all these years."

The chief priest bowed and announced the marvelous feat of turning their rods into snakes and back again.

Moses said, "Excuse me, Pharaoh, but I don't believe I want to be bothered with such children's foolishness. I won't work on that trick at all. Let Aaron do it. I'll wait till they do something worth noticing."

"Oh, you won't get out of it that easy," Pharaoh sneered. "Go ahead, men, and make him show you. We'll give him something to do besides brag on himself."

So the priests manipulated their rods and danced and finally threw them down on the floor before Pharaoh and they began to writhe and crawl. Pharaoh looked triumphantly at Moses. But Moses was looking all around the throne room in unconcern. So Pharaoh sent him a challenging snort. Moses merely handed his rod to Aaron and said, "Throw the rod down, Aaron, if that is the only thing that will pacify Pharaoh. Throw it down and get back out of the way."

Aaron dropped the rod of Moses to the floor with a "plop" and stepped back. The rod of Moses came alive. Its head darted out and seized the snake nearest it and swallowed it. The next one and the next one was run down and disappeared head first down the throat of Moses' living rod.

"Is that all you got to show me?" Moses asked casually.

"Show him something else!" Pharaoh ordered angrily.

"Er—er—Pharaoh, we didn't prepare anything more for right now, but if you have him back here later on we'll guarantee to show him."

"Oh, I'll have him back here and you are going to show him," Pharaoh retorted.

"Well, let me know when you get ready," Moses said. "And if that is all for right now, Aaron, go pick up that rod and show it to Pharaoh."

Aaron picked up the rod and found it a budding stick. So he showed it to Pharaoh and the priests and the sight of it made their eyes pop.

"You see what power I got behind me, Pharaoh. Will you let my people go?" Moses asked earnestly.

"No! I got work for those Hebrews to do, and they are going to do it, too."

"But the god of the mountain told me to tell you to let them go regardless."

"Moses, do you think you can come back here and scare me with a jumped-up tale about a mountain god and a few tricks and make me change my plans?"

"Pharaoh, do you think you can holler loud enough to break into a god's arrangements? *Will you let those Hebrews go?*"

"No! I won't."

"I see you call yourself a hooking-bull at the landing. You don't aim to let nothing pass."

"That's right, Moses. And certainly I won't let those Hebrews go."

"You're right sure about that, I take it?"

"Just as sure as you snore."

"One of us is bound to be wrong because I am just as sure that you will."

"The will of a Pharaoh and the might of Egypt says I won't."

"Somebody is lying and I know it's not me. I bid you a pleasant evening."

Moses left the palace but the news of what had happened in the palace was spreading over the city of ear. Egyptians collected in little knots and talked. The story of the rod that was a snake, and a budding bough became a legend overnight. People recalled the glory of Moses as a soldier and waited to catch glimpses of him on the streets.

But the court and the people of wealth sneered at his ambitions.

"So he is going to carry off our slaves by hoodoo, is he? Well, well, well! Pharaoh knows what to do with men like him. He is playing with that Moses like a cat with a mouse. When he is tired of the game he'll clamp down on him like a trap."

"I don't believe that snake story, but it is funny, isn't it? What would slaves want to be free for anyway? They are being fed and taken care of. What more could they want? I am off for a little trip down the Nile; let me know when Pharaoh closes in on Moses. I want to be in at the death."

Moses was satisfied so long as the people talked. For what he had to do concerned all Egypt and not just Pharaoh alone.

XXII

GOSHEN was a land of moving feet. Feet, torchlights and whispers. The news of what went on that day in the palace was traveling. Shadowy figures spoke out of darkened doors. Messages were sent by smoke and fire.

That was the work of Moses' helpers. Moses himself sat in his house and planned with Aaron and others.

"You got Pharaoh on a wonder, all right," Aaron gloated. "Reckon he won't switch around by tomorrow and let us go?"

"I hope not," Moses answered earnestly. "That would ruin us."

"How come, Moses? I thought that was what we was working after."

"It is, but I hope he don't give in right away."

"Why? It would save us a heap of work and worry."

"No, it wouldn't either. That would be the best way to beat us. You see, Aaron, we have come and demanded the people in the name of a god that neither Pharaoh nor the Hebrews ever heard about before. He has got to prove himself before them all to make folks believe. They have heard of God by ear but they don't know. If they went out from Egypt before I showed them signs and wonders it wouldn't be a week before they would be building altars to Egyptian gods. So what would be a better chance to show his powers than for Pharaoh to refuse and for me to beat him down with powers? That's what I aim to do. I don't want his consent, really. It would spoil everything I planned. I mean to whip his head to the ground and then lead out with a high hand."

"So that's why you talked to him so biggity like you did, eh?"

"That's just why I did. I know I got the power to bring him low. So the more he rears and pitches the more the people will believe when I whip him down. It ain't just to get you all out of Egypt, it's to make something out of you afterwards. That's the main idea. If Pharaoh lets the Hebrews go peaceably it won't be six months before they will be back here

ready to serve him again. If I'm to make a nation of you, you've got to be cut loose forever."

"I guess you know your business, Moses, but it seems like if we was to present a petition to Pharaoh, now that we got him worried—"

"I see you don't know people, Aaron. Pharaoh is not worried at all. He's not taking this serious yet, but he will when he has to. Now let's get back to our next visit to Pharaoh. One week from today we're going to call on him again. By that time his priests will have something ready that they think I can't do. He'll be glad to see me about that time."

"What we going to do next time?"

"Oh, that is all according to how I feel that day. Nothing too important. I'm saving the best for the last. Aaron, that's about all for now."

Aaron went on out with the other heads of the tribes and Moses was glad to be alone. He went and sat in the door and studied the night. Timid crowds collected at a little distance and watched him. He paid no attention to them really for his heart was in Midian, and his thoughts were walking the road in that direction. Jethro his father and friend. Zipporah and the numerous comforts and pleasures that flowed from her. His sons that were young men now and just as puzzling to him as young men have always been to their parents. The whispering crowds studying him from dark doorways were not on his mind nor heart. Nothing in Egypt was close to him. They could keep their distance forever.

But one person was bold enough to break in on his reverie. A curly headed boy in his mid-teens came up and stood smiling timidly at Moses.

"Hello," Moses said. "And what do they call you around the house?"

"Joshua. I live down the road there a piece. I expect you know who my papa is. He's always at the meetings. His name is Nun. Sort of bushy black beard and all."

"Oh, yes, so you are the son of Nun."

"Yep. I want to work for you."

"Oh, you do, do you? And why do you want to work for me?"

"Because you are great—greatest man that ever lived, I think, and then besides that I like you."

"Why, Joshua?"

"Oh, just 'cause, I reckon. I wish I was big and strong like you and I wish I was brave and great and I just like to be round you, that's all."

"That is a searching speech you made, Joshua, and I think we ought to clinch it in some way. We ought to do something so folks will know we are friends. What would you suggest?"

"I reckon I'm sort of big for it, but I think a neck-hug would be just fine."

"That was just what I was going to say. Come on!"

Joshua jumped forward and flung himself on Moses' neck and the leader of men clasped the boy to him until it hurt. Moses thought of his own sons back home and he thought of this welcome bit of warmth in Egypt.

"Joshua, you are the first person to come to me since I started out on this mission that didn't want something for himself."

"Oh, yes, I do. I want something too." Moses' arms relaxed and his face fell.

"Well, what is it that you want, Joshua—a high office for your papa if we succeed?"

"No, I want to be the one to wait on you right now."

Moses' arm tightened about him again. "You are the first to offer me your services, and I am going to remember it. Go get your things and come sleep in this house right away."

"Oh, I couldn't do that. Miss Miriam might not like it. She don't like many things that go on, you know."

"You leave Miss Miriam to me, Joshua. Go get your things and move in on us. I can use you."

Joshua bolted off like a roebuck and Moses sighed happily, "God even found me in Egypt. If I make no mistake, there's a real man in that boy."

XXIII

MOSES walked up the high steps of the palace next Wednesday with Aaron right behind him, and they told him Pharaoh was in the parlor waiting on him to come. The whole temple of priests were standing around just as Moses expected. He saw the expression of the face of Pharaoh and knew that Ta-Phar was treating the whole thing as a farce.

"Well, Moses, what you got to say today?" Pharaoh asked sort of offhand like he already knew the answer.

"The Lord says, 'Pharaoh, let my people go.'"

"And I say they won't."

"We beg to differ with you, Pharaoh, and that's why we are here."

"Don't make a bit of difference to me and that's why I am here."

"You know, Pharaoh, I figgered you was going to say that, because you and your servants and friends are trying to take us for a joke, so I better give you a sign and something to wonder about."

"Go right ahead, Moses. But I'm telling you in advance that anything you do, I, that is, my priests, are prepared to turn it right back on you."

"Well, that is your privilege. Anyhow the Lord told me to lift my right hand against you."

Moses walked to the center of the room and turned his face to the east and lifted his hand. He turned to the north and lifted his hand again. He turned to the west and last to the south and did the same. Then he stood perfectly motionless facing Pharaoh and lifted his right hand stiffly with his rod extended and held the position solemn and motionless for a space. Then he lowered it and said, "The Lord has spoken."

"Is that all?" Pharaoh sneered.

"Just ask for a drink of water and you will find out."

Pharaoh immediately ordered a glass of water. The attendant came in, bowed and hurried out after the drink of water. But in a minute he was back followed by the steward and the

whole palace staff. They knelt in terror and told Pharaoh that all the water around the palace had turned to blood.

"Well, get off the palace grounds and find me some that isn't blood. I don't want no foolishness about my drinking water."

In a short space of time they were back saying that every well and spring in the city was flowing blood. Through the windows came the sounds of terror and dismay. People were running to the palace and to the temples. They wanted water. Their beasts wanted water. Carriers were sent to the river and came back screaming that the Nile was running blood. Fish were dying and floating on the bloody stream. Pharaoh commanded men to dig wells lest all Egypt perish for want of water. Pharaoh went outside himself to witness this thing of Egypt running down in blood as if it had been wounded like a beast.

He saw and he heard the dismay of the people. Quickly he assembled the court and sat in council.

"What is it?" everybody wanted to know.

"Oh, some trick of Moses'," Pharaoh answered. "He's trying to scare us into elevating him to power. What else could he want?"

"Arrest him!"

"No, that wouldn't do."

"Why?"

"If I do that," Pharaoh explained, "the people will hear about it and believe in him."

"That would be terrible. Why, that man is a radical. He would have the common people talking about equality."

"Yes, and he would free the Hebrews."

"And what would we do without slaves?"

"Oh, that would never do. We must not let that happen."

"Don't you worry about that," Pharaoh assured them. "I'll see to that; we must beat him at his own game."

"But how? And we've got to have water to drink. Blood won't do."

"Yes, indeed we must have water."

"How are we going to get it?"

"Let Pharaoh go out and command the river to run water. It can't fail to obey."

Everybody looked towards Pharaoh and an embarrassing pause fell on the room as he hesitated. Finally he spoke.

"That will hardly be necessary. I have a better plan."

"What is it?"

"I shall trick Moses into turning this blood into water again. I'll promise to do what he wants—that is, let the Hebrews leave Egypt."

"No! No! we need our slaves."

"But I don't intend to deprive ourselves. When he has done his work, we'll change our minds and laugh at him."

Everybody beamed and grew calm.

"That is a splendid idea, Pharaoh. Meet trickery with tricks. Serve that radical just right, too."

"But what about the people? Won't they go over to him when they find out we had to go to him and make him promises?"

"They need never know. Listen, each of you must go out and spread reports that I, Pharaoh, turned the waters of Egypt into blood to prove my powers, and turned it back into water to prove my will. The priests will never deny it. They feel ashamed as it is."

"Sounds reasonable. Where is this Moses?"

"In Goshen, but we must pretend to ignore his existence. This is a strictly Egyptian affair. Don't mention his name at all."

"We'll all go out and calm the people."

"Fine, and I'll send secretly for Moses and trick him. By tomorrow night everything will be as it was."

"Perhaps we had better give him some sort of office to keep him quiet."

"No!" Pharaoh said with fury in his voice. "Never! and those priests had better do something to take the edge off of this thing or they are going to hear from me."

The priests went to the temple in a body. The next morning they sent word to Pharaoh that they could also cause streams to bleed like a wound. Pharaoh sent for Moses and Aaron and they and the priests assembled about a well that had been sunk in the palace grounds. The priests huddled about it and performed a ceremony. Finally they announced

that they had produced blood by magic and Moses and Aaron looked down and saw it was red.

"So you admit my priests have turned your trick back on you," Pharaoh asked scornfully.

"Yes, they really did," Moses said meekly.

"So your god can't be very original, Moses, and I can't see any reason for letting him change my plans. Bring me a better trick than that one before you come back here wasting my time."

"Well, one bellyful won't fatten you. How about next Wednesday at the same time?"

"Good. My priests will be ready and waiting. You amateurs need a good straightening out and we might as well give it to you. Guards, see that these men get off the place."

Pharaoh flouted his skirt contemptuously as he mounted the steps and went inside. Moses walked away without breaking another breath with him, and Aaron brushed past him and passed out of the palace gates before him.

He let Moses overtake him down the road a piece and fell in beside him. "Moses," he said, "it looks like your project got a back-set today."

"You think so?"

"I couldn't help it from what happened. Looks like those priests know just as much as you do."

"You reckon?"

"Seems so, don't it? You think it's any use in us going back to see Pharaoh any more?"

"He'll be looking for us next Wednesday for sure. We couldn't hardly back out of it now, do you think?"

"Oh, I don't know. Well, this is your movement and if you want to go back it's up to you."

"I'll be going back all right. Don't you worry about that."

So next Wednesday Moses and Aaron went up the steps to the palace again.

"Well, what did your Lord say today, Moses?" Pharaoh asked.

"He said to tell you, 'Let my people go.'"

"And what do you aim to do about it?"

"What He told me to do. Just a little sign to let you know that He means business."

"Well, my priests are here to teach you some more."

"I can't learn no younger, so I might as well begin. Let's all go outside for my lesson this time."

Pharaoh got right up and went outside where his flower garden was and Moses and the priests went out behind him.

Moses didn't lose any time. He walked to the made pond in the garden and lifted up his rod in his right hand and frogs swarmed out of the pond all over the garden. They filled the garden and the grounds and still they poured out of the fish pond. Hundreds and thousands and millions struggled over each other in the shallow water, clambered to the stone wall about the pond and leaped off in all directions. Moses still stood with his right hand lifted and the frogs kept on coming. Little frogs, big frogs, green frogs, toad frogs, rain frogs, bull frogs, every kind of frog that ever leaped or hopped. The foundation of the world seemed made of frogs and they came pouring out of that pond. The world croaked and leaped. The party fled inside but the palace was full of frogs. The streets and the cisterns were full. They leaped all over everywhere. They poured their millions out of the Nile, and every other stream and spring and still Moses held up his hand. The frogs kept coming till sundown. By that time the palace was besieged by citizens crying for relief from frogs. So Pharaoh commanded his priests to dispel them. They begged for time, so Pharaoh asked Moses to do away with the things.

"I'll be back tomorrow and talk it over," Moses said and went home.

The next morning streets, yards, fields and gardens held mounds of dead and stinking frogs. Moses saw piles and furrows of dead frogs as he made his way to the palace through a terrified populace.

"What! Your priests haven't done anything about this plague of frogs yet?" Moses demanded of Pharaoh.

"The worthless creatures who live in wealth off my bounty have done nothing yet," Pharaoh admitted as he hurled a cup of water full of tadpoles out of the window.

"Then I reckon the Lord with my poor help will have to do it," Moses said. He lifted up his rod and went outside and the millions of frogs began their march to the Nile. From all over the city and the province they hopped solemnly riverward and

leaped in till only the dead and rotting heaps and furrows were left in streets and fields. Moses ordered these to be buried. Men, women and children worked all day and all night and by mid-afternoon the third day of the plague of frogs, Egypt was free of the sending. So Moses went home again.

But the next day a messenger came hurriedly for him and Aaron.

"We fixed him that time," Aaron gloated on the way. "I'll bet he wants to tell us he's glad to let us Hebrews go."

"That may be so, Aaron, but I doubt it."

"Why?"

"Because, if Pharaoh lets me lead off the Hebrews, he will be driven from his throne by the nobles. They think they can't exist without slaves and Pharaoh wouldn't dare to go against them, not that he wants to anyway."

"He sent us a mighty nice message to come."

"Yes, to come and be assassinated in secret, but by now he knows that won't do."

"Why?"

"Because my death wouldn't do him any good if the common people knew why, and I have taken pains to let them know how all those frogs happened in Egypt and Pharaoh knows that they know."

"Moses, I hope this time he means to set us free. I don't want to believe nothing else."

"You are going to find out you are wrong."

"What else could he want with us? We beat him and he wants to give up, that's all."

"I hope not. I want to show that man a thing or two."

When they got to the palace, fresh and clean again, Pharaoh and the priests were assembled.

"Did you want to see me about something?" Moses asked.

"Yes, I want to see you about that frog trick you pulled," the King said shortly. "My priests want to teach you their version of the same thing. In fact, one of the priests says he remembered teaching you that stunt some years back when you used to hang around the temple so much."

"He never did," Moses retorted. "But I am here to be taught."

They went outside and the frogs poured again. When they

began to be plentiful in the garden, Pharaoh held up his hand and said, "That's aplenty—a gracious plenty. Now send them on off like Moses did."

The officiating priest stopped in his tracks and looked right sheepish at Pharaoh. The frogs kept on coming.

"I said stop," Pharaoh said coldly. The frogs kept on coming.

"You heard me!" Pharaoh roared. "I said stop those frogs and I mean stop. That's too many frogs already. Enough is enough and more than that is nothing but a nuisance."

The frogs kept right on coming.

"You chuckle-headed fool! Head those frogs for the river!"

The chief priest made motions, he waved his wand, he chanted something and the whole college of priests began to whirl. But the frogs kept right on coming and filling up the grounds. The priest pointed his rod towards the river but the frogs hopped in every other direction. They had to bring something for Pharaoh to stand on.

Finally Moses lifted his hand and the frogs in solemn procession and in a sort of rhythm moved on to the river as the others had done.

"I'll have another message for you next Wednesday this time," Moses said with a bow and walked off with Aaron at his heels.

Pharaoh didn't send for the court and the nobles, and this time they sent to him asking for an audience.

"The people are holding meetings and protesting against frogs," they told Pharaoh.

"But the frogs are all gone. Not a frog, well, no more than the usual amount to be found anywhere."

"They think you sent them."

"But why would I want to plague my people with frogs?"

"Oh, they remember about the bloody streams and they think you sent frogs to show your power again."

"Oh."

"I don't see why the army couldn't be called out to put a stop to things like that."

"How?"

"Well, er—"

"It's getting around that a great man is doing these things and people want to know him."

"I think it would be a good thing to order that Moses to leave Egypt before sundown. Get rid of him!"

"No!" Pharaoh said forcefully. "He'll go off as he did before and come back to make more trouble. I want to beat him at his own tricks and ruin him forever. Finish him! That's my will and intention. Besides, he might have an army somewhere outside the country. Humble him and then destroy him. That's my plan and I mean to go through with it if it is the last thing I do."

"No more frogs, I hope," said one courtier wearily.

"What must we tell the people?"

"Tell them that we are forever striving for their good. We will pass a law: frogs must stay out of the houses of the people."

The people thought that Pharaoh was very thoughtful of their comfort and needs when they heard about the law.

The very next week on Wednesday, Moses went to the sitting room of the palace and Pharaoh was waiting.

"I have a little sign from the Lord to let you know He says, 'Let my people go,'" Moses stated as soon as they had gotten through with the manners necessary around the court.

"I'm not letting them go, so you better show me your sign. But I'm telling you right now, no more frogs, Moses."

"This sign is also for your counsellors and judges. So you better call them in, too."

Pharaoh pointed out that he made a habit of making up his own mind, but if Moses wanted to entertain some more people with his tricks he would have them called. Moses had to wait for a long time before they all got there.

When the chairs were all full of nobles with their shaved heads and shoulders wrapped in cloaks, Moses lifted his right hand with his rod and all the others in the room began first to twitch, then to squirm and then to scratch and claw madly at their persons. One aged noble picked something off the edge of his cloak and gasped in disgusted surprise. "A louse! No, I mean lice!" But he could have saved his breath, for everyone present from Pharaoh down to the palace cat had made the same discovery.

"I pronounce on all Egypt, except Goshen, the plague of lice," Moses said solemnly and turned to go.

Pharaoh screamed at his college of priests. "Do something about this plague of lice and do it quick. And another thing, don't you dare scratch yourselves in front of me. Do something!"

The itching, twitching college of priests stood before Pharaoh as solemn as they could and the chief priest said, "Pharaoh, this plague is the finger of God. We don't know how it is done at all." But as they hurried out as fast as the priestly gait would allow, the chief priest said to his associates, "I mean to know this trick by next planting season."

"Moses!" Pharaoh called after him down the long corridor. "Moses!"

"Don't know just when I'll be back," Moses said over his shoulder, "but I'm coming."

A little further down the hall he called back, "I'd let them children of Israel go if I were you, but don't let *me* over-persuade you." Then he went on home to think.

And behind Pharaoh's outward show of indifference, he was beginning to worry a little. The thought came to him that if he issued a public order expelling the Hebrews from Egypt it would save his face and rid him of the harassment of Moses. He hinted as much to his courtiers, but they refused to listen. They had no intention of depriving themselves of their slaves like that. So Pharaoh issued a statement that the people themselves had brought on the plague of lice. The gods of Egypt had noticed their vice and loose living and had punished them. The people were silenced by the surprise of the thing.

"I haven't slept with more women than usual," one farmer asserted. "The gods are getting very strict these days."

XXIV

MOSES made no move to see Pharaoh for a whole month. Aaron and the council of the Elders of Israel were jubilant and urged Moses to press the issue but he would not be hurried. All Egypt was whispering and he pointed out that the Egyptian people would be begging Pharaoh to send them out before long. So let things rock on as they were for a while.

But he was not sleeping. He was coaching Joshua who was learning to read and write. Moses had placed him at the head of the boys' military society, and nearly every night there were drills and marchings. Caleb, a few years older than Joshua, was heading the young men's battalions, and Hur headed the older men. Moses was impressing upon them the necessity of military training and what he was doing with them was intensive. Their drill grounds were secret places and their hours of gathering changed often enough to be confusing to spies. Moses was particularly pleased with Joshua. Here was a person of action. No great talent for thinking, but a wizard in action. And his loyalty was so great that Moses would catch him studying his face trying to anticipate the wishes of Moses so he could hurry to do them. Moses was absolutely satisfied with him. Here was the perfect instrument to his hand. Give him time and growth, that was all. Israel, if it escaped Egypt, was going to have to do some fighting on its way to becoming a nation and here was hope. His eyes and ears served Moses well.

"Chief," Joshua whispered to Moses one morning, "a lot of the old heads are complaining because you make 'em drill."

"What do they say about it, Joshua?"

"They say they was under the impression that you had found some god who was going to save us. They didn't know they had to join the army."

"Don't they know, Joshua, that God Himself can't save people who won't try to save themselves?"

"They say that Pharaoh's army is too terrible for them to

483

face. They'd rather stay in slavery if they got to stand up before those soldiers and get killed."

"I know just how they feel, Joshua. I've been noticing things. And they don't need to worry about Pharaoh and his army. I'll take care of that part. But what is to become of them when we get out of Egypt? Do they think the world will be full of angels when they get out of here?"

"I reckon so. That's the way they talk anyhow. A lot of them are real discouraged."

"Pay 'em no mind and keep right on drilling and practicing with your spears and arrows. Somebody got to have some sense. I'm depending on you and Caleb to pull this thing off right."

"Oh, we will keep our part moving along. I got six thousand boys fifteen to seventeen years old and all of them want to fight just as quick as they can. Caleb's young men are all right too. It's just them old folks that's grumbling. We ought to march off and leave 'em here."

"No, Joshua, we can't do that, nice as it would be. They just don't think. They are trying to go on what they know and that ain't enough. So many more people know things than think things. One thought can put thousands to knowing, but knowing one thing don't put many to thinking. You see how it is?"

"Yes, sir. They know so much already they don't do no more thinking."

"That's just the point. What them old folks know is a stumbling stone to their thinking. But just for that we can't leave 'em behind. Joshua, when you find a man who has lost the way, you don't make fun of him and scorn him and leave him there. You show him the way. If you don't do that you just prove that you're sort of lost yourself. Remember that, son, if you ever get in the lead of people."

"Yes, sir. I mean I won't forget."

"Good for you. Now, Joshua, I think we're about ready to go see old Pharaoh again. He thinks we done forgot him, I reckon. But we ain't. Tomorrow is Wednesday. The Lord got a few more suggestions to make to that man by now. I better go see him tomorrow afternoon."

"I wish I could go with you sometimes. Oh, yes, Miss

Miriam says I am in her way around here. She told me to stay away and quit talking so much out of my mouth."

"Don't let Miss Miriam worry you. Just agree with her and go on like I told you. Let her lead work for the present. You won't lose nothing in the long run. I don't forget a thing."

XXV

NEXT DAY at the palace Moses told Pharaoh, "The Lord told me to tell you He said, 'Let my people go.'"

Pharaoh said, "We here in Egypt have known gods for thousands of years. I can't see why I should pay this new voice you talk about any mind at all. Who is He anyhow?"

"Why should I lose time talking to deaf ears?" Moses retorted. "The question before the house is will you let the Israelites go?"

"No."

"Well, it's mighty bad news for you, because if you don't, you're going to be plagued with flies."

With no more talk than that Moses lifted his rod with his right hand and flies seemed to pour out of the sleeves of his garments. The hum from their wings filled the room. The number of them darkened the rooms and Pharaoh and priests fought to flee the place. But it was no better outside. The city of the Pharaohs was smothered with flies. Moses changed his rod to his left hand and walked on out of the palace. All around him and Aaron was a space free from flies. So they went on back to Goshen and the people heard about it and hoped.

There was no mistaking the public panic this time. The public besieged the nobles and the nobles waited on Pharaoh. Their faces were long and haggard. Some retched with nausea as they waited.

"We realize that we have held you back too long, Pharaoh. We stopped you when you would have done something to put an end to these calamities. You must not let us interfere with you any further."

"It is good to feel your confidence and co-operation, but what can be done?"

"Find out what office that Moses is after and give it to him. Do something. We couldn't live through another plague of flies. We just couldn't!"

"I'll find out, but he claims he doesn't want anything in Egypt except the freedom of the slaves."

"That is not to be even discussed. Our work must go on. We can't let ourselves be robbed like that. I don't believe that Moses wants a thing like that himself. He's a Prince! He is one of us. He is being clever to get back his titles and his property. Let him have them. It would be cheap at that."

"Yes, tell him he need not carry those Hebrews off in order to have somebody to rule over. Make him governor of a province. The Nome of the Thebiad has no ruler at present. Give him that."

"Something must be done, Pharaoh. Our Hebrews are getting impudent and restless. Why, only this morning my steward was knocked down by one of my slaves because he tried to chastise the Hebrew for impertinence. It's awful! They are beginning to be bold and important. I heard of several instances of resistance to discipline. The idea of Egyptians having to fight with Hebrews!"

"Why not bribe him to go back where he came from?"

"He is despicable," Pharaoh said. "But I don't believe that he could be bribed. Remember he walked off and left wealth and position before. It is something else he wants. I don't see what he wants with our Hebrews, but if that is not his real aim, I don't know yet what it is he wants."

"Anything but our slaves. That is, anything in reason."

"Well, I'll send for him and put a stop to his nuisances."

"Do! This thing is not as funny as it was."

The next day Pharaoh sent for Moses and asked, "Moses, what is it you want for these Israelites anyway?"

"We want to go out of Egypt where we can worship in our own way."

"All of the Hebrews at one time?"

"Every last one of them from gray beard to battle heights. Every sheep and cow, even. That's what we want."

"Well, do away with these blasted flies and I'll let them go. That is provided you don't take them very far."

"How far do you mean?"

"Oh, not out of Egypt. A couple of hours' march ought to do."

"No, that is not enough, Pharaoh."

"It will have to do. I can't let my work be neglected while my slaves go too far away. No, indeed."

"The flies stay, then."

"Oh, no, Moses, do away with these flies and I'll let them go."

Moses said, "I'll go home and at five o'clock sharp, the flies shall vanish from Egypt."

"All right, Moses, you do away with this plague of flies and go on home. I'll send word tomorrow what day you can lead the people off to serve their god in the wilderness."

Moses changed his rod from his left hand to his right and lifted it and went on home and at five o'clock sharp the plague of flies disappeared from Egypt as they had come. The people of Goshen had a torchlight parade that night to celebrate the end of slavery.

But Moses waited a week and no messenger came to tell them. So the next Wednesday Moses went to the palace and Pharaoh laughed at him.

"Pharaoh, you made a fool out of me before all the people in Goshen."

"That's a fact, Moses, I sure did," Pharaoh said, laughing fit to kill himself, "but you have to admit I couldn't have done it if you hadn't furnished the material."

"Well, the Lord says that you are going to have a cattle murrain all over Egypt, except in Goshen. All your cattle are going to die. See if you can laugh that off. Why don't you kill me? I'll tell you why. Your will is paralyzed by power and your fear."

Moses changed hands on his rod and lifted it and turned to go. "One thing only can save you—when you come to know that justice is greater than pride. You know where I live when you get ready to talk sense."

And Moses walked away.

Moses walked out of the palace of Pharaoh knowing that he carried Pharaoh's peace and security in his hand.

If Pharaoh relented and let the Hebrews go, he would rid himself of the worry and humiliation he was suffering. But on the other hand he would have to face a danger more sure and certain right away. The nobles would never permit him to save his face at their expense. Even the servants who served about him personally belonged to that ruling class and so he could not even hope to escape with his life. If the house of

Pharaoh had not preached and practiced hatred and vengeance for generations, he could save himself by a show of generosity and dismiss the slaves. But the intolerance of Pharaoh and his fathers was fighting against him. Pharaoh was locked up in his own palace and inside himself. Moses walked out of the palace with a sense of power.

And in the privacy of his retiring room, Pharaoh was thinking the same thing, but in a different mood. After hours of seclusion and thought he still did not have the answer. So he set his face in stiff, proud lines and went among his courtiers expressing indifference and scorn. He wanted Moses dead, but he wanted it done by his own hand. And the people harassed Pharaoh with their fears and apprehensions, and the Princes worried him, so he had to make a gesture, but he did it with a growing feeling of desperation and frustration.

"Moses had courage," he thought grimly. "He walked away from it all."

Pharaoh had dreamed of making his name and fame greater than that of his father. How could he do it and abandon the public works? And how could he carry on the public works without the Hebrews? Even his military strength rested on these slaves. For, without them men would have to be taken from other things to fill their places. He had too often boasted of this advantage of holding the Hebrews for the army to forget it. They would resist him too. Nothing to do but wait until the gods favored his cause.

The third day Pharaoh sent for Moses and begged him to take off the plague and he would let the people go. Moses stopped what few cattle that were left from dying, but Pharaoh went back on his word again. Moses knew why he did it, and Pharaoh suspected that Moses knew, but neither of them gave a sign that they knew. When Moses went to see him he said, "Moses, these people must not have much to do if they got time to be planning camp meetings and barbecues. I just gave orders to all my foremen to double their tasks. The old folks always said that an idle mind is the devil's workshop and this just goes to prove it."

"That's very serious talk you are doing, Pharaoh," Moses said. "The Lord don't love ugliness and He usually does something to let you know. Now, you done promised and

took back your word so much till I reckon I'll have to send you another plague. You have got to learn that there is something in the world bigger than your pride and vengeance."

The chief priest stood up and said, "It's hard on the people, all these plagues and things. Why not let those Israelites go, Pharaoh? This Moses is threatening us with another plague."

"Oh, nothing but tricks," Pharaoh sneered. "He's bound to run out of tricks after a while."

Moses looked behind the mask of Pharaoh and was almost sorry for him. Then he remembered what he had to do. He handed Aaron his rod and walked to the fireplace and took up a handful of ashes and in the presence of Pharaoh, his court and the priests he said, "I am sending you a plague of boils on everybody in Egypt except Goshen." He threw the handful of ashes toward heaven and kept his hand lifted until the light air had scattered the ashes to the four winds. And all over Egypt from Pharaoh to the swineherds, people broke out in boils. Pharaoh called on his priests for help, but they were too sore to move from their beds. And nobody was well enough to wait upon the others. The whole nation, except Goshen, groaned and suffered until Pharaoh sent for Moses and promised solemnly this time to let the Hebrews go. Egypt had suffered ten awful days and a great number of people muttered that the labor of the Israelites wasn't worth it. Why not let them go? But again Pharaoh changed his mind. The majority of the ruling class saw ruin in social change. So Moses went to him and said:

"I see that you think you are smarter than God. You have promised after each plague to let the Israelites depart to worship their God in their own way and in places of their own choosing, and each time you have double talked as soon as the trouble was taken off you. All right, tomorrow at this same time, I promise you a deadly storm of hail that shall kill people in the streets and in the fields; it shall strike down animals; it shall destroy crops and ruin houses."

"Hail?" asked Pharaoh of his court. "What is this man talking about? I never heard of such a thing."

So Moses told him what it was. And Pharaoh laughed out loud at that. "Hail!" he laughed. "Hail in a country where we

don't even have rain? You are not trying to amuse me now after all your other tricks?"

Pharaoh laughed some more and everybody helped him. They knew Moses had power because they had seen his signs and wonders but hail in Egypt was too much to believe. What! Water so cold that it turned to stone? This was really too much. And falling from the sky? How would Moses get the water up there in the first place? and even if he could, how would he get the coldness up to it to turn the water to stones and make it fall? Now, Moses has really overstepped his bounds. This must be a joke. They were relieved that he threatened hail instead of something that really could happen like a flood. Maybe it was like Pharaoh had said, Moses was bound to run out of tricks after a while and this looked like the end. The menace of Moses was gone for good. Pharaoh had worn him out.

"Meet me out on the battalion grounds outside of town tomorrow at this same time and see who is right and who is wrong," Moses challenged. "I may be lying. You better try me and see."

Everybody was coming to see this plague of hailstones for hardly anybody in Egypt had even seen ice. A few who had traveled tried to tell what it was like, but even they had not seen ice showers. All over the city people were making jokes about it. Such a nonsense. Ice out of the sky where everybody knew the hot sun lived.

This public interest was new. At first the battle of enchantments was between Moses, Pharaoh and the priests, but by now, from what they had seen and suffered, all Egypt was interested in that man who sent plagues. And a plague like hail that really couldn't happen was something to go to see. The people turned out by the thousands.

Pharaoh rolled in a little late with all of his priests behind him. As soon as he saw Moses he called, "Moses, are you ready to make ice fall out of the sky on us yet?"

Moses looked at the sky closely before he answered. "Not quite ready yet. I'll let you know in a little while."

"I'll bet you're not ready." So he told his priests to make some magic to entertain the people while Moses got ready, which they did for more than an hour.

All of a sudden Moses looked at the sky and walked out in the middle of the parade ground and took his stand. He lifted both hands high and spread them abroad and the hundred-prong lightning began to play across the sky, and thunder rolled behind it from east to west. Zig-zag fire darted from the sky to the earth and ran along the ground. Then while Moses still held up his hands, the hail began to fall. It fell and it fell and everybody fled the place but Moses. He stood as if he were cast in stone with the lightning playing about him and the hailstones falling like shot from heaven. The people fled with Pharaoh, but they did not escape the hail. It devastated Egypt as Moses had promised.

The chief scribe lifted himself from the ground where he had fallen when some younger man tripped him in flight and said, "There has been nothing like it since Egypt became a nation," and everybody else was saying the same thing.

They came with the east wind and went with the west wind. That is how the locust came into Egypt at the call of Moses. The hail storm had frightened Pharaoh while it lasted and he had said the people of Goshen could go. But as soon as it was over, he sent soldiers to guard the borders of Goshen so that not a soul could depart. He aggravated the matter by refusing the brickmakers straw, which had always been furnished to them. Now, he said, they must find straw for themselves and at the same time they must turn out just as many bricks. He was going hard.

So Moses lifted his right hand and the east wind woke up from where it was sleeping and romped across the narrow valley of Egypt all day and all night. And on the wind came the locusts in such hosts that daylight became dark. Their wings clashed out a din and their voices muttered of hunger. They came and muttered and trembled upon the wheat fields and muttered and ate and grumbled in their jaws until not a leaf was left standing in Egypt. Then when Egypt was eaten bare they attached themselves to a west wind that blew and went with the wind into the Red Sea.

The servants of Pharaoh gathered around him and asked him, "Pharaoh, how long is this man going to be set like a trap in Egypt to catch us? The nation can't stand this kind of

a thing much longer. We're just about ruined already. Aren't you ever going to do anything to stop it?"

"Then you will support me if I send these Hebrews out of my sight?"

"Do we have to go that far? Can't we compromise somehow?"

"We can see," Pharaoh said wearily.

"Give them a light vacation—a day or two ought not to ruin us."

"Call out the army, and send it down into Goshen."

"For what? Killing our slaves won't get our work done."

"Oh, let's leave it to Pharaoh. He is responsible for the country. He is conducting this on his own responsibility. Let's leave it to his intelligence."

Pharaoh wilted under this back-handed thrust and dismissed the council.

So Pharaoh sent for Moses and Aaron.

"Moses," he said, "I've about decided to let those people go out to worship like you asked me. But I can't let everybody go. You understand. If I did that my work would be at a standstill. Now if you all could let me know exactly who is going out to worship and just where they plan to go and how long they aim to be gone, I might give you some consideration."

"Pharaoh, if I told you any of those things you asked me, I would be telling you what I don't know myself. The Lord of Israel has ordered all the people to go out to a place which He will point out after we get on the way. That's all He told me, and I'm selling it just like I bought it."

"Before I let you go I will have to know when you are going, where you are going and how long you plan to stay."

"I can't tell you that, Pharaoh," Moses said stubbornly.

"Then nobody is going a step. Think I'm going to have all the help off the place at one time and I don't even know where they are at?"

"The time will come, Pharaoh, when they will go, and that soon, I'll bound you that."

"You say they will and I say they won't and I happen to be King of Egypt. And all Egypt will support me in my position."

"We'll see about that, King or no King. The god I repre-
sent is stronger than thrones."

The next Wednesday Moses got up early in the morning
and sent word around all over Goshen for the people to get
hold of every lamp they could get their hands on and lay in
a-plenty of oil. Gather up a-plenty lightwood and kindling
because they were going to need it mighty bad. Then he went
on over to the palace to talk with Pharaoh.

Moses noted that Pharaoh looked sunken and worn. His
haggard face was a grim, ashen mask. But his eyes glittered
like an asp at bay. Moses noted too that his right hand rested
on the hilt of his sword.

"Pharaoh," Moses began with a deceptive gentleness, "I
come this time to save you from yourself."

Pharaoh started at the sound of Moses' voice as if he had
been stabbed.

"Say what you have to say and leave here. I don't want to
see you. I don't want to hear your voice. I don't want to hear
your wretched name called again."

"I see that you are afraid, Pharaoh."

"A Pharaoh afraid?"

"That crown and that throne make you a Pharaoh, but in-
side of that frame you are a man. And you are afraid. And I
know you do not know what you are afraid of. Your fear is so
vast that it has crumbled you up inside. But for that you
would have killed me weeks ago."

"Liar!"

"Pharaoh," Moses went on calmly, "as I came along I saw
long trains of people fleeing Egypt—to the mountains, up
the river, anywhere so long as they got out of Egypt. Not
Hebrews, mind you, but your own people. They were afraid.
Whole villages and towns were empty. It seems that Egypt has
learned my name."

"Egypt knew your name before and nobody left but you."

"That was because I was not warring against Egypt then.
They had never suffered plagues. But now they flee away. You
can calm Egypt and restore your country to peace."

"If you have come to tell me to let those Hebrews go, I tell
you right now, No! I will not let them go."

"You mean you can't let them go. You wish you could. You

know and I know what it would cost you. You can't undo in a
few weeks what you took generations to do. So you don't
dare to do what would ease your position."

"Never mind about the affairs of Egypt. They do not con-
cern you. You came here to ask me to let the Hebrews go. I
tell you, No. So you have nothing to keep you here."

"But, Pharaoh, I can't go. My conscience wouldn't let me
until I warn you that my God says you must let His people go."

"Moses, I know nothing about this God. Nobody seems to
know anything about Him but you. I can't allow the welfare
of Egypt to be destroyed by your superstitions. You see that
your tricks have not moved me."

"Oh, yes, they have. You and Egypt will never be the same
after I am gone. And I warn you that I have other tricks, as
you call them in scorn, more terrible than those that you have
experienced. Don't make me use them to scourge you. Let
the Israelites go."

"You can't scare me, Moses. Out of the consciousness of
my might, I have been indulgent with you. Don't provoke me
any further."

"No, you have temporized with me because you are weak."

"Weak? Why, I have a million men under arms."

"And in your panic you contemplate sending a million men
against one man. I thought you said you were brave."

Pharaoh half rose from his seat in his anger. "You are get-
ting beyond your depth, Moses. I might forget my patience in
a moment."

"Oh, you will have your hour with me, when the time that
is set for it comes. In the meanwhile I am to tell you to let the
Hebrews go."

"And I tell you that I will not let them go. Nothing on
earth can make me change my mind."

"Nothing, Pharaoh?"

"Nothing, on my sacred oath, nothing. My very soul re-
volts at the thought."

"Then you have forgotten your past terrors."

"I never had any to forget."

"Perhaps not, but, Pharaoh, when you come to wind up
that last ball of sorrow, don't forget that I reasoned with
you."

"Fear is no part of me, say what you will."

"Pharaoh, have you ever seen darkness?"

"Of course I have! A night has followed every day I ever saw."

"But did a day always follow every night you ever saw, Pharaoh?"

"It never failed yet."

"It is just possible that a Pharaoh even is about to learn something new. You are going to have darkness in the broad open daylight. I am turning my back on you and the great invisible darkness that stands behind me shall make itself known. I am loosing the plague of darkness on Egypt."

Moses went out of the palace and lifted his right hand and the light began to thicken. There were no clouds in the sky. The world just began to grow dim. By the time Moses got home it was dusk in mid-afternoon. Then it went on from there. Egypt knew darkness, living crawling darkness that had a life of its own. It had body like the wind and it heaved in motion like the sea.

In Goshen, lamps burned in every house and at the doors. But in other Egypt the darkness smothered down upon the earth. Its pall silenced cries and choked back laughter. Even the beasts ceased groaning after the first hour. Egypt was soundless and motionless for three whole days. And outside of Goshen, nobody saw anybody else for the space of three days. It was a soundless vacuum like in heaven when the orchestra before the throne strikes silence for the space of half an hour once in every thousand years. When the three full days were over the darkness began to lift and to withdraw itself across the Red Sea into the land of Midian, into a certain mountain from which it had come.

In the druggy gray shadow of the departing darkness, children and parents groped toward each other and huddled together in silence a long while before they spoke. The lion that had fought off its own cubs in the terror of sightlessness hovered them again, and the asp had faith once more in its fangs.

"Horus is dead beneath the sundown horizon. His light will never come again," one priest whispered to the others. These were the first words spoken in Egypt since the reign of nights without days.

"Egypt will die in this coldness that has leaked out of the darkness," his brother whimpered. "How can we strain against a man who has killed our gods? Darkness strips everybody of everything. We can't live."

And everywhere in Egypt tongues began to move and say, "The pride and stubbornness of Pharaoh has destroyed us all."

And what they saw with their eyes was terrible. Old ones, sick and poor; children, women trampled to death during the darkness when the nation was stampeded by fear. Bodies on steps and in doorways.

The moment that he could see his hand before his face Pharaoh began to call out to his attendants to come closer to him. "I am King of a dead nation," he moaned. "Go beg Moses to come. The children of Israel can go. Find lamps and lanterns and go get me Moses."

But by the time that his messengers could grope their way to Goshen the light of a natural night had lightened Egypt. There was no moon, but the stars could be plainly seen. So Pharaoh haughtily refused to talk to Moses when he came, and put him off until morning and went off to bed.

"Moses," he said next morning, "as bad as I hate to see you in any form or fashion, I am a reasonable man. So I am prepared to let you go and take the children of Israel to go serve your God, but your flocks and your herds stay right here. You understand me, don't you?"

"I heard you, Pharaoh, but when we go out to worship, not a hoof will be left in Egypt."

"If you are only going out to worship your God as you say, what do you need livestock for?"

"We don't know what we might need to serve the Lord with until we get there. The flocks and the herds go with us or we don't go."

"Well, you don't go then. Egypt will not be robbed like that."

"Ta-Phar, I'm just as wore out with you as you are with me. I been just fooling along with you because I remember you're mean and stubborn, so I took advantage of it to let you make a fool out of yourself before Egypt. But I'm through playing with you now. I came back into Egypt to lead out the children of Israel. I am showing you my ugly laugh now."

"Don't you stand up here in my palace and talk to me like that, Moses. I am King in Egypt. Get out! And look out for yourself too. Don't look in my face again, for the day you do is the day you die. Get out!"

Moses laughed a laugh that he had been saving up for more than thirty years. "You told the truth then, Ta-Phar. I will certainly not see your face again—not that I ever got any pleasure out of it anyway. But you will hear from me again, and you sure won't like it when you do."

"It is my will not to see you again. Be warned."

"But I tell you, Pharaoh, that you will. I am talking for Israel now and you are talking for Egypt. But a time will come when you will seek me out so that Ta-Phar and Moses may stand face to face. You will seek me out to fight me. And I'll be there, Ta-Phar, and I'll be exulting like a stallion."

"And if that time ever comes, you be there like a stallion. I shall be there, a lion in his strength."

"Let us hope for the meeting," Moses said with restrained feeling. And he was gone.

XXVI

NIGHT came walking through Egypt swishing her black dress. The palace and the peasant slept. Pharaoh and the servants of Pharaoh had assured the Egyptians that the terrors of Moses were ended. He had said that Moses must cease and the word of a Pharaoh was enough. So the nation slept its sleep untroubled.

In Goshen the blind-eyed goddess of night huddled close, and families stayed inside their houses and waited. A bloody bunch of hyssop had swished against every door in Goshen three times—once on the lintel overhead and once on the door facing at either side. Then the people had gone inside and sat behind the blood and waited as Moses had ordered. Their new god, who had chosen them through Moses, was going to fight Pharaoh for their sake. He had asked the sign of the three bloody marks on the door and the people had done their part. The rest was for Moses and God to do. So the dark stillness in Goshen was not sleeping darkness. It meant waiting. The lamb had been sacrificed and eaten in every house in the land and his signal blood guarded the doors. The night went on its way.

Darkness balanced up on midnight looking both ways for day. Then the great cry arose in Egypt. They cried and died in Egypt. It was the great cry that had issued first from the throat of Israel years before and spread to the rim bones of the world and come back again. And now it poured out through the mouth of the Egyptian nation. It was such a cry that there was none like it since the morning stars sang together, and never shall be another like it as long as heaven is happy. Egypt cried out at the death of the first-born. Every house in Egypt was bloody. Blood outside the door in Goshen, blood inside every other house in Egypt.

Pharaoh looked upon his first-born and wept. His son was dead and the son of his son was dead in his own blood. There were snorts and bellows from his stables from the smell of animal blood. So Pharaoh cried for his dead with all of his voice. Every house in Egypt strained its voice trying to express

its bereavement. The noise of it struck the sky and came back to the Nile and ran with it to the sea, the Egyptian chorus of sorrow indoors.

Outside, the paths and pavements were full of soft, swift feet fleeing into Goshen with its listening ears. These were the sounds of the night, sounds without words.

With the sunrise, Princes and people said, "This is the hand, the right hand of Moses." They lifted their dead from beds and said in awe, "Moses and the God of the Israelites." They rolled their dead from straw mats and pallets and said, "Moses and his right hand." They crowded in and around the palace and shouted, "Get Moses and the Hebrews out of Egypt. If you don't, everybody in Egypt will be dead."

So Pharaoh sent for Moses to dismiss him, his God and his people from Egypt. He was no longer proud Pharaoh with the mask-like face. He was a man whose son was dead. But Moses refused to go see Pharaoh all that day. Burials went on and burials went out from houses all day in long lines and solemn weeping, and all Egypt was in tears. Pharaoh sent messengers to Moses again telling him not that the Hebrews might go, but that they must go.

Moses heard the message sitting in his house but he didn't say a word right then. The news was too big to speak at once. He had to sit with his feelings for a while. Afterwards he called his leaders to him and told them, "Your slavery is over. Pharaoh is broken at last. We march out of Egypt with a free people. We march out with a high hand."

XXVII

THE PEOPLE cried when Moses told them. He had ex-
pected wild clamor; the sound of cymbals and exultant
singing and dancing. But the people wept out of their eyes.
Goshen was very still. No songs and shouts.

"Free at last! Free at last! Thank God Almighty I'm free at
last! No more toting sand and mixing mortar! No more tak-
ing rocks and building things for Pharaoh! No more whip-
ping and bloody backs! No more slaving from can't see in the
morning to can't see at night! Free! Free! So free till I'm
foolish!" They just sat with centuries in their eyes and cried. A
few could express themselves like that. But the majority just
sat in the doors of their dwellings staring out at life.

But Moses put a stop to all of that. "You won't be free for
long if you keep that up. Stop that shouting, and stop that
sitting, people! Get everything you got together and let's go,
and that quick."

"Why, Moses?" some of them asked. "We're free now and
we can take our own time about everything."

"You people been around Pharaoh all this time and don't
know him no better than that? He is scared today and so he
says you can go. Tomorrow or next day he will realize what
he's losing and send his army into Goshen to put you back to
work. Grab up your things right now. Tonight we leave Egypt
forever."

"Good gracious!" somebody grumbled, "I was figuring on
going fishing tomorrow morning. I don't want to be both-
ered with no packing up today. It's too much like work and I
just got free this morning."

"That's the heaven's truth, too," plenty of others chimed
in. "Looks like we done swapped one bossman for another
one. I don't want nobody giving me no orders no more."

"But it was Moses that got us free," Joshua told them. "If
it hadn't been for him we would be hauling rocks right this
minute."

"Oh, I don't know about that. This God that done chose

us would have got us free anyhow. I never did much care for this Moses like some of you all."

"What's the matter with Moses? He got us free all right."

"Oh, I have every confidence in the man, I just don't trust him."

But Moses himself moved from place to place urging hurry and everybody, unwilling or not, did what he said. The women told Miriam's committee that they just couldn't get ready because it was baking day. "We got dough set to rise and we can't disturb it or it won't be light." Miriam went back and told Moses what they said and he went to see about it himself. "Mix your dough," Moses told them, "but don't put your seasoning in it so it won't spoil, and while you are at it, mix enough for a week. And that is just part of what I want done. Everybody roast a lamb so that everybody in Goshen can eat a full meal with some greens to settle the stomach. We got a long, hard march in front of us—tonight!"

Finally Moses got them ready in the spirit so everywhere in Goshen the people were saying, "Tonight!"

Everybody said it according to their thought and their feelings. Some talked it with the edge of their lips. Some rolled it deep in their throats. Some throbbed it inside their hearts and let their bodies move with the rhythm. Some said it with their eyes, with a gleam, with future-searching gazes. Some said it with a question, "Tonight?"

They fixed and they did around and got ready. Nothing was still. Children hunted the bitter herbs. Men slaughtered beasts and tied bundles. Women mixed dough and cooked. And all the time everybody thought back over the years and every now and then they breathed, "Tonight!" Moses had inspired them for the journey and they were going.

The God of the two horizons took flight beyond the western line and the frenzied hurry of the day took shape. Flocks and herds gathered and ready. Bundles tied. Every group had met its leader and been told.

"Now," Moses said to a group of men under Nun, "go quickly to the tomb of Joseph and bring me the casket with his bones. He brought Israel into Egypt and Israel must take him out of a land that is no longer fit for his dust. Hurry!"

The gorgeous carved and painted casket of Joseph rested on a pedestal before the house of Moses, and its bearers were appointed. So Moses told everybody to eat in haste, leaving nothing to eat behind them when they were ready to go.

They sang a song. Now that they were ready to go and going, it was triumphant but it was sad. It was a long time since Israel had done any singing much and they had forgotten how to shout. Moses noticed that their glad notes broke on wails. Israel was used to wailing now. They had forgotten how to laud. His heart hurt for them. So he said to himself that they should see glory mountains and shiny valleys and they should learn to sing.

He led them out of Goshen with a high hand. Out and out the tread of the tribes behind him. A great horde of mixed-blooded people grabbed up their things and joined the hosts of Israel. "Let us be free too," they begged and Moses said yes to them. His fighting men in front and behind with Joshua's volunteer boys in the center to give aid and assistance to women and children. Out and out he led. People cried and died and stayed where they fell. Aged ones hobbled and were partly carried, old ones, crippled by the generations behind them and blinded by the look ahead, grasped and clutched at young shoulders and gasped, "Don't leave me behind." Babies borned themselves and joined the procession out. Out was such a big word in Egypt to the Hebrews.

"Which way, Moses?" Aaron asked.

"By the wilderness of the Red Sea."

"It's a whole heap shorter through the land of the Philistines."

"I know, Aaron. But our people are leaving slavery. It takes free men for fighting. The Philistines might let us through without fighting but it's too much of a risk. If these people see an army right now they would turn right around and run back into Goshen. So let's head them for the Red Sea."

The soft murmur of sandals and bare feet kept up in the night without a moon as Moses and his hosts moved on.

"On our way at last," Aaron said happily to Nun.

"After four hundred and thirty years to the day. It still

seems like it ain't so to me, Aaron. Ain't but one thing I'm sorry about."

"What is that, Nun? I can't imagine any sorrows connected with the thing."

"I sure hate to miss seeing those Egyptians doing our work in all that hot sun."

"I hadn't thought of that, Nun, but it sure would be a lovely sight. I never want to even see a brick again—not even a brick house to live in."

"Me neither. Where we going now?"

"Out, Nun, out!"

"I don't mean that. I mean just exactly where we're going to live permanent when we get out?"

"Moses may know, but if he does he ain't told nobody yet."

"You reckon it's all right to ask him?"

"I guess so. You can ask him if you want to."

"Where is he now?"

"He was just ahead of us a few minutes ago."

The two men looked up and became conscious of a changed rhythm in the multitudes around them and behind them. It was a sort of spontaneous mass halt and they saw the reason right away. Ahead of them at a short distance was a column of fire. What it consumed was hard to understand for it towered up steady and solid as no flame they had ever seen. It was like an illumination that glowed but never flamed. It brightened the countryside, but never grew more nor less.

"What is that?" Nun asked in fear.

"It must be where Moses is. You think it is his right hand shining like that?"

"It could be. Is nothing impossible to Moses?"

"It don't look like it. Let's go ahead to see what it is."

The two leaders marching ahead of the host hurried nearer the fiery column and stopped. It was moving ahead as if it was borne but nothing was holding it up. Its many colored lights just moved along ahead of Moses like a vertical beam.

"Moses! Moses!" Aaron gasped. "What is that?"

"The pillar of fire that will always go in front of us at night.

It is the sign of the Presence. In the daytime it will be a cloud. Go tell the people not to be afraid."

With the fiery sign the people marched all night and camped next day far from the city of Rameses at Pihahiroth on the shore of the sea to rest and eat. Moses gazed across the water and exulted.

XXVIII

NEXT MORNING Pharaoh woke up and looked out of the window on the city, new and fine, its towers, its parks and streets, which the Hebrews had built for his father and him. He had a strange feeling of newness as if he had not seen these sights for a long time. As if he had awakened among familiar surroundings after a long, horrid dream. Then he noticed something. No work was going on around the half-finished public building near the palace grounds. He called a servant right away and asked about it. The servant didn't know.

"Well, go find out," Pharaoh snapped and ordered his breakfast. After a while the servant came back and said that no Hebrews had been seen that morning by anybody except a very sick old Hebrew found by the road by some fishermen. No work had been done for two whole days.

"Two days! You must be wrong."

"Send to Goshen and find out what's the matter. Some more foolishness out of that Moses, I reckon. If it is, I'm through playing with that man. He dies today, him and all his magic. I don't see why I stood him as long as I did."

The word came back, "A great song was heard, then the whole host of the Israelites were seen marching out, driving their flocks and herds, two days ago. Nobody has heard from them since."

"Oh, that worship they were talking about. I did say that they could go. I was too worried about the funeral of the first-born to notice things. It is a terrible thing to lose a son." Then Pharaoh became alarmed. "Do you suppose those Hebrews have run away?"

"A lot of people are saying the same thing, and they want their work done and they aren't getting a bit done today."

Pharaoh thought a minute and his blood jumped salty. He was angry with himself. He could have killed Moses and saved himself this trouble. But he had yearned to humble the man first. To outwit him and shame him. Then would have come death for Moses. But the man had made a fool of him instead

before the whole nation, and now he was gone with the Hebrews as he had threatened. Pharaoh was resolved on his death if he could lay hands on him now. He rose up with a great scowl on his face. "That's my trouble," he said, "I'm too good-natured."

"That's right, you certainly are," all the servants and courtiers agreed.

"I must have been out of my head to let those people go off and now we have nobody to work for us. That is, I mean that just because I was grieved down at the death of my son and my grandson and the first-born of all the other people and said things, this man Moses takes advantage of my good nature and runs off with our Hebrews."

"And why should we let them stop working for us and go off like that?" one of the courtiers asked. "It's a sin and a shame when you come to think about it. Them Hebrews off doing nothing and our work going undone."

"It's worse than that," one of the others agreed. "And they could be stopped, you know. They couldn't be very far by now, and them on foot, too."

"Get me my war chariots!" Pharaoh shouted. "Six hundred fighting chariots and men to fill them and have them ready in half an hour. I'm going after those Hebrews and I'm going to bring 'em back. And so far as that Moses is concerned I mean to kill him with my own hands. That rascal has been imposing on me for thirty-odd years. Always some trick up his sleeve. Get me my fighting chariots and do it now!"

People scurried in every direction and Pharaoh began to dress himself for war.

"My finest sword and javelin! I am a man of war today and it is the happiest day of my life. I have been tricked and tricked and made a fool of by that Moses ever since he was weaned from his nurse. He is facing me today for the last time. Where are my chariots and men?"

With a kill-mad cry, the six hundred chariots with Pharaoh in the lead thundered out of the city before a cloud of road dust, and raced down the road to way off.

XXIX

IT WAS late afternoon of the second day when Moses came
down to the sea. He ordered rest overnight and plenty
cooking and eating to keep up the strength of the hosts.
Some people grumbled about sore feet and some missed their
beds and houses. Moses let the Elders take care of that. He
went down to look at the sea. He studied the wind and sky
and looked at the sea and beyond.

That was the way things were when Joshua came running
and shouting, "Pharaoh! The Egyptians! They are coming
down behind us. Chariots!"

Moses hurried back to the Israelites. By now the thunder of
hoofs and the growl of chariot wheels were easy to hear.

Women screamed in open-mouthed terror and whimpered
in fear. Men cursed, cried out and milled about in great
whorls. Some tried to run away to the woods to hide, others
just stood or squatted on the ground in dumb fear. When
they saw Moses come among them they crowded about him.
Some clung to him while others screamed at him. He shook
them off roughly and kept marching towards the rear.

"I always told my husband not to bother with this mess,"
one woman sobbed. "I tried to tell him we was getting along
all right under the Egyptians. But he was so hard-headed he
had to go and get mixed up in it."

Voices broke out everywhere and all were sprung with fear.
The war chariots of Pharaoh were in plain view now though
distant on the plain. Moses could hear many things as he
shoved through the camp.

"Couldn't that man find graves enough in Egypt to bury us
all without dragging us out here in the wilderness to die?"

"Didn't I say all along that this Moses was some fake
prophet? That god he made up out of his own head—"

"Didn't I always tell you all that them Egyptians was nice
people to work for? You couldn't find better bossmen no-
where."

"The idea of coming and fooling people off from home and

leaving 'em with no protection. I mean to tell Pharaoh just how it was."

"Didn't I always say we was better off in slavery than we would be wandering all over the wilderness following after some stray man that nobody don't know nothing about? Tell the truth, didn't I always say that?"

"I told you all a long time ago that we had enough gods in Egypt without messing with some fool religion that nobody don't know nothing about but Moses. You all just let him make a fool out of you. I always knowed it was some trick in it. That man is a pure Egyptian and Pharaoh is his brother. He just toled us off so his brother could butcher us in the wilderness. I told you all so."

"You heard me at the meeting distinctly tell that man to leave us alone and let us serve our Egyptian masters in peace, didn't you? We was getting along fine—plenty to eat and a place to sleep and everything. We wouldn't be in the fix we're in right now if that Moses had of let us alone."

"Who asked him to butt in nohow? Our business didn't concern him, did it? It was our backs they was beating. It wasn't none of his and if we was satisfied he ought to been tickled to death. Now Pharaoh is going to kill us all."

"Great Ra! Great Horus! Great Thoth! Great Isis and the forty-two gods of the double justice! Save us."

Slowed down by the weight of the chariots over the rough ground, the horses were coming in a walk. Moses reached the rear of his great huddle of trembling humanity and took his stand, between danger and his charges. Again, he was one against all Egypt. Listening and thinking back, it was hard to keep his feelings from flying to his head. He had but to step aside and leave them to Pharaoh and his servants. But Pharaoh himself was driving the first chariot as the cavalcade approached, and he wanted to face him and beat him one last time. He laughed to himself as he thought, "Pharaoh thinks he's pursuing me, but it's the other way around. I been on his trail for thirty years, and now I got the old coon at last, as Jethro would say. Let me fuddle him all up for a night and then I will raise my hand. First and last, I'm showing him my ugly laugh."

As the chariots drew near the panic grew in Israel. They

committed every kind of folly and showed their inside weakness. Then Moses showed his power again. He turned his back on the Egyptian horde and spoke to his people. Spoke to them in their own dialect as one of them.

"Stand still!" he commanded in a sterner voice than they had ever heard before. "Stand still, every last one of you and stop that screaming and yelling. You haven't got a thing to be scared of. That ain't nobody but Pharaoh and his army and we done beat them too many times before. Don't get so excited about nothing! The Lord is going to fight for you just as He's been doing all along. Stand still and see the salvation of the Lord which He is going to show you today. See those Egyptians there? Take a good look at 'em, because those Egyptians that you are looking at today, you're never going to see *them* no more as long as you live. And nobody else won't be seeing them either. Stand still and keep quiet is all I ask you to do."

Moses didn't lift his hand while he talked but the command in his voice was calming. Suddenly everybody felt secure and brave.

Moses just stood and looked and the pillar of cloud that went before the host moved around from the sea and spread itself like a great plumey curtain between the Israelites and Pharaoh and hid each camp from the other. The Israelites felt shut in and safe. The Egyptians felt shut out and puzzled. They were afraid to attack until they could know what went on behind that cloud screen, so Pharaoh ordered his forces to camp until next day and then to attack with vigor.

"They can't get away from us so we might as well get some sleep. Our horses need freshening too," Pharaoh ordered. "We got them in a trap—between us and the sea. We'll close the trap in the morning." So they turned in and rested so they could have plenty of vim to butcher Hebrews in the morning.

But Moses never slept. The signal pillar of fire glowed behind the cloud screen and lighted the camp of Israel. Moses himself went back to the sea and stood. When the hour came he called up the east wind and stretched out his hand. They broke the head of the eastern drum and marched out on the sea. The retreating tidal waters did not creep on as was their

habit; they fell back from the strait on either side like two mighty armies in retreat. Both sides shrank away from the uplifted hand like lambs before a lion. The waters fled back and back and back and stood in a solid wall on either side and waited on the powers to close them up again.

Then Moses ordered the march. In the same order in which they had come down to the sea, Moses told his hosts to cross over. Flocks first, then women and children followed by the six hundred thousand men of fighting age armed with whatever Moses could find in Egypt to put in their hands—clubs, spears, javelins, old swords, sticks and anything that could wound and tear.

The bones of Joseph crossed over after the women and children. Then Moses challenged Pharaoh. The smoky cloud screen lifted. The fiery pillar again went before the hosts and the sentries of the Egyptian army saw that the children of Israel were escaping across the sea and ran to wake up the camp. "Wake up! The Hebrews have broke camp and are gone."

The camp woke up by degrees. Nobody could believe the sentry at first. They had to get to their feet and get their heads clear of dreams first, and then the peeping dawn did the rest. It was hard to believe, but the sea was really divided and the Hebrews were tramping across on dry land.

"Well, I'll be—" Pharaoh began, then sprang to action. "Get up and harness the horses! Don't let 'em get away! A palace and high houses to the man who overtakes Moses and hands him over to me alive! Get up and get after our slaves."

In a few minutes the camp was furiously alive. Leaping into chariots, shouts, cries, plunging and neighing of horses, clash of arms on shields, posing Pharaoh's chariot with its three Arabian horses in front of the forces and the furious charge to the sea crossing while the last ranks of the Hebrews were still in sight.

Moses heard the commotion in the Egyptian camp and knew that his movements had been seen as he intended them to be. He hurried across after the last man and waited. He saw the mad charge down the beach. He saw them hesitate there to debate the wisdom of trying the unusual crossing. Then he deliberately showed himself to Pharaoh and the

frenzied pursuit was on. The six hundred chariots dashed down into the sea ten and twenty abreast. The Egyptians shouted in triumph as they viewed the cowering Israelites on the opposite shore.

Then when the Egyptians had thoroughly committed themselves to the sea bed and wagered their lives and their vengeance on it, Moses stood on the opposite shore and looked hard at his pursuers. He could distinguish the royal chariot with its fiery Arabians well in the lead. Those were fine horses, Moses recognized, and a splendid chariot. But Ta-Phar had always thought too well of chariots. He could not see his uncle's face at that distance and read its expression, but he could feel it, the hatred, the bafflement and the lust for vengeance. Behind him the Israelites were already over their joy at the miraculous crossing and were beginning to cry out in fear.

"Moses! The Egyptians are coming after us! Ain't no more seas for us to cross."

"I see them. Don't worry."

What he knew must come, happened. Away from the smooth sand of the shore, the horses and the heavy chariots struck rough going. Horses began to flounder and fall as they stepped into holes and soft clay. Chariots swerved, overturned, and control was lost. Chariots coming after plunged into the tangle and were themselves overturned. Then Moses lifted his hand.

The gripping east wind loosed its mighty fingers and the sea water came rushing back to its bed. It was a moving time. There was the outspoken voice of the wind going east; the mad grumble and shout of the waves as they raced back to embrace each other over the clamor of men in fright, the scream of drowning horses, the last mad struggle of the chariots. That all made a boiling place in the sea for a space. Then there was just the heaving Red Sea with its two shores. Egypt on one side and Moses and his mission on the other. Moses stood and looked on the sea. It was a long time before he thought to change his rod from his right hand to his left and let the wind and the sea subside.

Behind him he heard the people exulting. "Didn't we outdo old Pharaoh, though?" Miriam was asking everybody.

"It was a great victory for our God," Aaron was saying. "The Lord is a man of war. The Lord is His name." "Old Pharaoh thought he knew who to fool with and who to let alone." "We showed him something. Yeah, he's dead out there in the ocean and there ain't no help for it. That's one old Pharaoh won't have no great big old tombstone over him."

"Well, he's got the great big sea over him, and I reckon that's big enough to suit anybody."

They made a song on that and danced it off. A man with a good voice got out in the center of the ring and sang.

"Old Pharaoh's dead!"

And the chorus answered, "How did he die?"

And the solo man went to dancing and said: "Well, he died like this!" and he danced that off. Then he sang another part and everybody went on dancing and shouting.

> "Oh, he died in his chariot and he died in the sea
> And he wouldn't have died at all if he let us be."

They sang that over and over and danced on it until they got tired. Then Miriam took the cymbal and some more women went behind her and they went all over the camp singing:

> "Oh, Miriam played the cymbal over the Red Sea
> Miriam played the cymbal over the Red Sea
> Miriam played the cymbal over the Red Sea.
> Oh, Miriam played the cymbal right over."

And they clapped time on that with their hands and danced and double clapped it off like they did the other song because everybody was happy and felt like clapping and dancing. Then Moses told them to make camp for the night.

Moses strolled down the beach a little way and sat down on the same boulder that he had sat down on after the first crossing so many years ago. It was another morning and another crossing and so he thought thoughts again. This time he had crossed over safely with a nation behind him and no weapon worth talking about but his right hand. Well, the present was an egg laid by the past that had the future inside its shell. So Moses sat on the rock and said, "You, Voice, you told me to lead out, and by the hardest, I did it. So I'm down here by

the Red Sea with these people. You know more about 'em than I do, Lord. What must I do with them now?"

A little tee-nincy voice raised up in the back of his mind and said: "Old Rameses is dead. Ta-Phar is dead. The set who bucked against you and hated you are dead. You know one time you were the idol of Egypt. The army still thinks you are the biggest man they ever made. Moses, you can go back to Egypt and be King. You can do even better than that. You can control the army which controls the King. The Voice told you to lead out and you have led out with a high hand. You have done your duty. The Israelites are out of Egypt and they are free. If they fall into slavery again somewhere else that's none of your business. You set them free. Moses, there is Egypt right over there and the King is dead in the sea."

Moses sat on the rock and thought back. He had sat on this rock when he fled from Pharaoh the first time and something had shown him clearly the futility of a life of war. Right on this rock he had forsworn the sword and glory. He got to his feet and looked earnestly at the camp for a while, then he said, "Which way, Lord, which way must I lead Your people?"

XXX

T HE NEXT MORNING everybody was around Moses' tent soon after sunrise. Joshua couldn't hold them back. "We just want to tell him what a great big man he is—bringing us off like that with his outstretched hand."

Another one said, "Joshua, go on, call him out so we can tell him how we feel. It just came to us in the night that nobody ain't thanked him yet. We was so excited yesterday on getting free and getting across the sea, that nobody ain't bowed down and nobody ain't turned him no thanks. Go wake him up, Joshua, so we can tell him."

"Mighty sorry," Joshua told them, "but I just can't do it. Fact of the matter is, he ain't asleep. He's been up a long time talking with God."

"With God?"

"Unhunh."

"Tell me how he sounds when he's talking with God."

"I didn't hear him. He goes off by himself to do that."

"Well, well, well! Is Aaron off talking with God too?"

"Nope, nobody can do that but Moses. God don't talk to everybody that comes slew-footing down the road. You know, there ain't but one Moses in the world. Never was one before and never will be one again."

"Well, well, well. Reckon we'll rock on down the road to the camp."

"Ain't you going to wait for him and tell him yourself?"

"Oh, no, you can just tell him for us. He ain't in the notion of putting out no plagues or nothing, is he?"

"Oh, no, he wouldn't be lifting his hand and stretching it out against us. He saves that for our enemies."

"Oh, much obliged to you, Joshua. Some of us was kind of worried. We didn't know if he might get us off and lift up that right hand and destroy us all."

"Nothing like that at all. Nothing he likes better than to see us prosper. That's what he led us out for, to better our condition from what it was."

"And he sure Lord is done it, too. He's a fine man, a noble

man! He's just like a lion. Look, Joshua, how about that thing he calls a cloud that moves in front of us in the daytime and that fiery thing at night—you reckon it's harmful?"

"No harm in it at all. It wouldn't harm a living soul. It's just there for our guide and leader, so we can know our Lord is with us. Of course, I wouldn't advise nobody to rush up to it and try to touch it. Stay your distance and it's just all right."

"I 'clare to my rest, Joshua, you sure is one smart young one. You done been round Moses so much till you talk just like him. Well, we'll be getting on back to camp. Where we headed to from here?"

"Moses will tell you when he gets ready."

The committee made their manners and went on back to their tents. They had found out what they came for—the intention of Moses towards Israel. Some feared him, and many doubted him. Thoughts had troubled many all night. They wanted some assurances.

But Moses was not talking with God as Joshua had said. Moses was down beside the sea gazing on the work of the waves.

The tide had strewn the beach with bodies. The dead bodies of the Egyptian soldiers were flung up along the shore in scores, flung helter-skelter like dolls.

Moses walked among them until he found the body of Ta-Phar, once Pharaoh of Egypt. As he looked down on the dead face, frozen in a gasp, he thought, "So powerful on one side of the Red Sea, so helpless on the other."

Standing there, Moses was torn by the pitiful sight of all the sudden dead, for a moment, and then he reflected that he had saved them from a fate much worse. They could not have overcome his strategy and carried the Hebrews back, and to return without them would have ruined them all politically and cost them their lives in a much more painful manner. As it was they would be heroes. They had tried to recapture Egypt's slaves and had lost their lives in the attempt.

Moses stooped and removed the great ring of state from Pharaoh's drowned hand and studied it in his own palm. It brought all his thoughts of peace and power and he weighed it in his hand for a long time. Then it was no longer the key

to the Egyptian palace to him. It was just so much gold, and so many gems. He thought of saving it for Jethro, then he smiled. Jethro wouldn't give a fig for it for his own use. He thought how proud and happy Zipporah would be to own the royal ring of Egypt, and it grew to be a sinister thing.

"Only something to stir up ambition and create unhappiness," Moses said out loud as he hurled it as far into the sea as he could. Then he hurried back to the camp and ordered the people to march.

And this was the way they formed to march: The stiff white billowy cloud first. Then Moses on his horse, then the tribe of Levi and the whole host of nearly two million people behind him. So Moses led and he led and he led in the general direction of Mount Sinai for three days and nights. Straight into the wilderness of Shur where there was next to no water and nothing to eat. It took him three days' march to make a full camp so everybody could rest. Moses remembered the numerous wells and springs he had seen in this vicinity when he passed through one time on a journey.

Soon as the people saw the water everybody went running to get a drink and to water their stock. Then they went to fussing and came running to Moses and crying:

"Moses, what you reckon we're going to drink for water?"

"There's plenty water round here, ain't it? Why you come running to me?"

"Call it water if you want to. If it ain't the nastiest and the bitterest stuff! Even my camel won't drink it. What you mean by tolling us off from all that good water for, to drag us out here to die wanting water?"

The words and the ferocity with which they were spoken caused Moses to inhale deeply before he tried to speak.

"Do you really think I want anybody to die out here?"

"Well, if you didn't, what did you bring us to any such of a God-forsaken place as this? Nobody don't know what you got up your sleeve."

"Let's don't talk about it any more. I'll go out and sample the water. Maybe we can do something about it. Come on, Joshua, and go with me."

Moses, with Joshua at his heels, went to the nearest stream to drink some of the water. People and beasts were lined up

around every piece of water there was and every eye either accused Moses or pleaded with him to do something. Moses could feel the hostility in their eyes attacking his skin as he walked through the multitudes to the water. They watched him while he tasted it and spat it out. Some people laughed when he did it. Others began to wail, "'Tain't no use! We're bound to all die in this desert, with our tongues all parched out of our mouths. We just can't make it to where good drinking water is. Maybe this is the way it was intended to be."

A great clamor went on all the time that Moses stood with the dipper in his hand, taking a sip of water, wallowing it around in his mouth and spitting it out. Where had he tasted water like that before and what had been done about it? All of a sudden he remembered a scene in a distant waste where he had found nothing but bitter water to drink and then he remembered the traveler who looked like an Arab who had gone to a certain tree, broken off a branch and thrust it into the spring, and instantly the composition of the water was changed. It was not marvelous drinking water after that but it was very drinkable. If only he could find a tree like that around here now!

So he told the people to make themselves comfortable for a few minutes. He had to go and question God. The people muttered and grumbled but there was nothing to do but wait. Moses walked off with Joshua and Aaron behind him and went walking in the woods. No more than a half an hour in the woods and Moses found a whole grove of the trees he was looking for. So he sent and had some tree-chopping done and sweetened the water. The people all drank and watered their stock and went to bed that night telling each other what a great man Moses was. He could even sweeten water that God had left bitter. There was no doubt about it, they had a great leader in front of them. Moses sat thinking, "Supposing I had not met that desert traveler way back yonder? Why was I chosen to lead these people instead of somebody else? They have revolted against me twice before we are fairly started on the journey. Why should I lead people whose ways are strange to me and who neither understand me nor trust me? How come, Voice?"

XXXI

THE NEXT DAY bright and early Moses was on the march. He led on to Elim because he knew there were a dozen huge springs of water in a grove of seventy palms. Moses decided to camp three nights so that the stock could be well watered and eat the grass growing around there.

He was pleased to see everybody in good humor again. But inside he was lonesome for Jethro and his family and all day his thoughts were in Midian. He took one of the mixed people who had come out of Egypt with him and sent him off on a camel to find the land of the Kenites and tell Jethro what had happened.* Joshua felt hurt that he was not given such a confidential mission, but when Moses told him, "Son, there's liable to be some fighting before long and young as you are, you are my man of war. I couldn't do without you that long."

Soon one morning, over the muttered protests of many who wanted to just stay on where they were, Moses struck camp and went. His road was roughly towards Mount Sinai and he meant to be there as soon as possible. When the people saw the holy mountain they were bound to believe in its God. They were bound to understand Him better. Maybe there, they would realize that they were really free people at last. Now they acted like they knew they were free by ear but they couldn't conceive of it. They did not believe they could take on any responsibility for themselves at all. They kept clamoring for somebody to act for them. But Moses had made up his mind to be patient until they should learn something. He was looking forward to Sinai and all it meant to him and them.

They struck out across the wilderness of Sin, and Moses marched them as hard as they could go to shorten both his time and his journey. To Moses, the quickest way to show the people to God, and God to the hosts, was the best. Besides he hoped that his messenger had reached Jethro and that his

*A multitude of mixed-blood people marched out of Egypt with the Hebrews.

519

friend and father would soon be meeting them somewhere along the way. So he led on across the barren waste called the Wilderness of Sin.

Joshua, mounted on a horse, rode up and down the line and passed out the orders as Moses gave them to him. While he was passing up and down and back and forth he would hear all that the people had to say and he let Moses know how they felt. So one night when the hosts were deep in the wilderness, he rode back and looked up Moses.

"The people are grumbling again," he told Moses gloomily.

"What's the matter this time?"

"They say they're hungry. They talk about splitting off. Some of them done formed a committee."

"Oh, they have, eh? Go tell 'em I say come here."

When Joshua went and told the committee what Moses said, they got mad with him and told all about his big mouth and his slew feet before they got through. "You up there running your mouth to that man Moses, and get us all killed with some kind of a plague. You ain't no good and you better quit lying on us, too."

"But you said all I told him and more besides. If you are dissatisfied how come you don't tell the man instead of doing all this talking and backbiting? He's here to help us and that's what he's trying to do."

"Listen at that long, tall young one that ain't quit wetting his diapers yet, trying to tell us what to do with our own mouths. Here we was talking before he was born and now he's going to come along and tell us how to talk. Course, we did mention that we ain't had nothing decent to eat since we been in this wilderness and that looks like this Moses ought to do better than he's doing if he makes out he knows all about God and can get anything he wants, more specially since he went and drug us off from our good homes in Egypt. But that ain't talking about nobody. That's just saying."

"Well, Moses is just saying that you come on up front and talk your big talk to him instead of to me and the rest of the people. And he's sitting in his tent and he's looking for you right now. Come on."

"We're going and see what he want with us, but don't you

be running up there putting out no lies on us no more, and we don't mean no Joe more, we mean no blamed more."

"I am the servant of Moses and his adopted son too, so don't let me hear nothing you don't want him to know. Anyhow, you all done talked this thing so much and so loud, till it's funny for you to make out it's any secret. I bet the folks way back in Egypt could hear your whooping and hollering for rations that you ain't bought."

"We ain't supposed to buy nothing. Moses is supposed to look out for us and take care of us. We left our good homes in Egypt for his sake, didn't we?"

"No. He wasn't the one in slavery. His back wasn't subject to no lash, you know. He was a Prince of the house of Pharaoh. He didn't have to pay us no mind if he didn't want to."

"Humph! I ain't saying nothing but there's a bug under that chip."

"Aw, don't change so many words with me. Bug under that chip! Why you so suspicious? Don't jaw at me. I ain't the boss. Come on and tell Moses about it."

Moses called Aaron to him. "Come on, Aaron, we got to sit on a case. The people are all hungry and mad."

"I done heard all about it. They been griping me since yesterday."

"You didn't say nothing to me about it, Aaron."

"Oh, it was just something that didn't need much attention. I figgered I could handle it myself. I'd naturally understand 'em better than you."

Moses didn't say anything for a minute. He looked at Aaron's face and he noticed the way he walked. His face looked like Ta-Phar's. There was the look of weak brains and strong pride. And he walked like he was conscious of the envy of men. "A beggar on horseback," Moses said to himself. "And first and last, something will have to be done about him." Out loud he said, "Well, Aaron, whatever it was you did and said to 'em, it don't seem to pacify 'em. Let's take our seats under that big tree over there, so all them that wants to can come before us."

So the committee of two hundred, selected from all of the tribes, came up to Moses and Aaron under the tree. "It's no use for me to try to talk any high court language to these

people. I might as well get right down with them, and you don't need to talk for me anymore, Aaron. I'll just talk to the people myself." So when the people crowded up before the two men, Moses spoke to them as a Hebrew.

"Eh, eh!" one old crone exclaimed with pleasure. "Moses is getting so he talks our language just like we talk it ourselves."

"Yeah, and the more Moses gets natural with us, the stiffer Aaron gets. He tries to sound like some high-toned Egyptian talking proper—when he don't forget to do it."

"And that's what makes it funny—he forgets."

"Yes, and Moses forgets too and goes back to talking his proper talk when he gets excited, too. I done took notice of that."

Nobody answered right away because everybody waited for somebody else to talk first. Then all of a sudden somebody started to beat his breast and wail and the whole crowd took it up and wailed. They cried out, "I wish to God we had of died whilst we was back in Egypt. There we was sitting down every day to a big pot of meat and bread. If this God you done got us mixed with just had to kill us, we sure wish He had of killed us down in Egypt on a full stomach. We don't care if they did work us some. We would much rather die tired than to die hungry."

"What makes you think you got to holler and cry about it?" Moses asked. "We're assembled and gathered here to find out what you all are grumbling and mumbling about and do what we can about it. We didn't come here to fuss and fight. Now what's the matter?"

"Not to be so much trouble, but we're hungry, boss."

"I'm mighty sorry to hear that, folkses. I realize myself that rations are none too plentiful around here."

"What we want to know is why you bring us off here where there ain't a thing to eat."

This put Moses on a deep thought and before he realized it he was thinking the thoughts and speaking the language of a cultivated man.

"I had the idea all along that you came out here hunting freedom. I didn't know you were hunting a barbecue. Freedom looks like the biggest thing that God ever made to me, and being a little hungry for the sake of it ought not to stop

you. Your wives and your children are your own now. I lift your eyes to the hills. I have been hungry a lot of times in places just like this, but I felt that getting what I went after was worth it, so I made myself satisfied. I found out want won't kill you half as quick as worry will."

"Where you get that good word from?" Aaron asked Moses in quick admiration.

"Oh, I don't know exactly. Just from living, I reckon, Aaron." Moses began to relax again. "Now you committee-men that's standing before me, where do you all figure I was going to find enough groceries to feed all of you all?"

"That we don't know and we figure it ain't none of our business. You brought us out there, didn't you? We want to know if this powerful God you talk about is here amongst us or if He ain't."

Moses was irritated but he tried not to show it. He took a long breath before he spoke.

"Well, if going a little hungry for your own sake is such a worry to you I'll have to do something about it. Go tell the people they are going to get bread and it's going to be bread from heaven. This evening the Lord is going to send you meat and meat a-plenty. Tomorrow morning, go look on the ground anywhere around here and pick up the bread to go with it. You are bound to hear some more qualifications about that bread later on. I'll send it out by my helpers. Now all of you go on about your business and let me think awhile."

So that's how the people had the great feast of quail that night and manna in the morning. Ten million quail came and lit all over the camp and the people caught them and quail meat was boiling so that they could smell it clear back to the Red Sea. Then the next morning they went out soon and early to pick up bread. They never had seen any bread like that. It wasn't a loaf and it wasn't rolls and it wasn't pone bread and it wasn't hoe-cake. It was in grains like seeds. So the people looked at it and called it manna because they didn't know what else to call it. Manna was a word that didn't mean anything in particular anyhow, so they called the grains of bread by that name. They ate aplenty of quail and manna and in the cool of the evening they sat around and said that

they knew that was a mighty good God that took up with them, and Moses was a fine man to come tell them about it.

When they praised Moses to his face, he merely said to Aaron, "Gather up a peck of that manna and put it on the altar for a souvenir to remember by. Nobody ever saw this kind of bread before, and nobody is going to see any more after this journey is over. Save some so your great-grandchildren will know what happened out here. They ought to know what dangers threatened us and how they were met."

Moses himself felt lonely and yearned for Jethro and his family. He felt more like an alien than he ever had felt in his life. But the mountain spoke to him from afar, and he answered it in his heart. And his worries and troubles shed off without really touching him because there was Sinai ahead. Here the people would find peace, God and a perfect understanding. These people were blind. It wouldn't do to mock them and leave them. He must put them on the right road. That was his difficult mission.

When they camped at Rephidim, several days' march closer to Sinai, and found that there was no water there, the committee did not wait on Moses respectfully. They rushed up to him with threatening gestures and told him, "Give us some water to drink, man. We ain't for no foolishness today. One time it's nasty water that not even a hog could drink. Then we ain't got nothing to eat. Now we ain't got no water at all. What kind of a leader is you anyhow?"

Moses said calmly, "You ain't talking to me, you know. It wasn't my idea to bring you out of Egypt. Your God commanded me to bring you. Go talk to Him. But I'm telling you now your attitude is a temptation to God to punish you, and punish you to death."

Nevertheless Moses went on off and talked with God. He said to Him, "Do you see these people of yours would just as soon stone me as not? What must I do about it?"

Then Moses saw an inner vision of a strong stream of clear water surging inside the cliff on the hillside. So he called the committee to him and touched the cliffside with his rod and the fountain of water gushed forth. While the people and the cattle drank, Moses called Joshua to him and told him, "Get

me a stone and mark it with a new name for this place. We done had such a big fuss here that the name of the place got to be something that fits the case. From now on, the name of this place is Massah, which means a big fuss."

Joshua told Moses, "I sure will attend to that first thing in the morning, but I got a message for you."

"What is it, Joshua? It must be serious from the look on your face."

"It is, Moses. The Amalekites, those folks who live on the other side of the ridge, aim to jump on us for a fight."

"I was afraid of that. When do they aim to strike?"

"Oh, in a day or so. They are sending out for their kinfolks and friends to come and help fight. As soon as they get here they mean to beat us and to take our stuff."

"Joshua, we are going to fight 'em tomorrow morning from sun-up on. Go get out all the fighting men we got right now."

"You don't think I'm too young for the men to follow me?"

"No. That makes no difference. Young or old men will follow you if you got that something to make 'em willing. You are going to be one of the great men of arms, watch my word. This will be good practice for you and it will be good for the people. Once they win a battle it will tend to lift up their heads. Now they are scared of everything and they think nothing is scared of them. They need to win something.

"Right now these Israelites are just like a passel of rabbits. You know, Joshua, one time the rabbits all met together in a convention and decided to kill themselves because nothing looked up to them and nothing was scared of them. So they all headed for the river to drown themselves. They hopped like an army down to the river bank. But just before they got to the river there was a marsh that the rabbits had to cross and while they were crossing it they ran over some frogs and the frogs hopped up crying, 'Quit it! Quit it!' So the rabbits said to one another, 'Those frogs are scared of us. We don't need to kill ourselves no more because something in the world is scared of us. Let's go on back home.' So they went on home happy again. Now that is just what the Israelites need—a victory. They just come out of slavery where they've

been stomped down and trampled on. So we got to fight them Amalekites, and, Joshua, we got to win. If we don't these people will go to pieces and all our hard work will be undone. We got to win tomorrow, Joshua, for them."

"We would have a better chance, Moses, if you led us. You're a great fighting man of experience."

"Joshua, I done laid down the sword altogether. It wouldn't do for me to be seen with a sword in my hand. I am the man of God. But I'm going to fight them just the same, and I don't aim to touch a sword. You'll get help from me."

"How you going to do it, then?"

"I'm going to mount that hill yonder with my rod in my hand and fight 'em with powers. I'm going to be there with the rod of God in my right hand and, Joshua, they can't win. Otherwise they would whip our raw fighting men before noontime. I got to be there with my rod."

The next morning Moses took Aaron and Hur with him and climbed the hill before dawn. The Israelites and the Amalekites were on opposite sides of another hill close by. The Amalekites hustled around getting ready to attack the Hebrews as soon as the former got enough men, not dreaming that the desperate Hebrews were ready to fight. Moses had instructed Joshua to have his men drawn up and ready before daylight. When he reached the top of the hill with Aaron and Hur, he would wave a torch of fire just once. Then Joshua must rush down the hillside and fall upon the enemy with fury. At that moment, Moses would lift his hands against the Amalekites and Israel must win that day or be Israel no more.

Joshua went among his six hundred thousand poorly armed fighting men and encouraged them as he woke up the camp. Then all was ready. He looked to his sword, balanced his heavy-handled spear and stood poised on the hilltop above the sleeping Amalekites and waited. The fiery signal came and Joshua charged down the hillside and began to crowd the enemy camp. The Amalekites were pushed back and back. And Moses stood with outstretched arms, fighting for Israel with his powers. He was calling on the invisible powers from Mount Sinai to fight and they fought for him. The untrained ex-slaves fought like old veterans and drove the hard-pressed Amalekites from point to point.

Then Moses began to feel the weight of his arms. Against his will they began to sink a little.

"Aaron," he said tensely, "my arms are falling. Our men will lose and they just can't lose now."

"Don't let 'em fall, Moses!" Hur and Aaron begged.

"You think I want 'em to fall?" Moses asked. "Trouble is they done got too heavy for me." With dismay, they saw his arms slowly sinking to his sides. But they saw something more. They saw the tide of battle turn. The Amalekites suddenly made a stand. They took the impact of the on-rushing Hebrews and hurled them back. Messengers came running to Moses from Joshua to ask him what to do. Moses sent back word what to do. Then his strength came back in his arms and he lifted and pointed his rod and strength flowed back into Israel again. The old men and women crowded hilltops and looked down on the battlefield and chanted. When the arms of Moses were up a high bragging chant filled the valley of strife. Then Moses' arms sank again and Israel was pressed hard, the nation of Israel muttered like sleeping thunder in the dark. And that was the way the fighting went all day. And Moses' strength was almost gone. He sat on the ground too tired to lift his head.

"Look and tell me, Aaron, how is Israel making out down there?"

"Pretty poorly, Moses. As far as I can make out from here, it looks like it's a big retreat."

"We can't lose, Aaron. We just can't lose. I keep on telling you. It'll be the breaking up of everything. We got to win. You all help me to my feet. I got to get my hands up as high as my head if it kills me. Help me up, you all!"

They got Moses up. The nation round about the fight was moaning low. Moses got up and his hands went high above his head and the Hebrews went to winning again, but they had lost a lot of blood. Then Moses felt his arms settling down and he looked through a dark cloud and saw the future of Israel. Beaten, disbanded and what was left of it, slaves again. The star of Israel sank with his hands. Suddenly he cried out to Aaron and said, "Come here, Aaron! Come here you two! Here, shove that big high rock under me so I can sit down. I just can't stand up no more. Now, Aaron, you stand

here at my right hand and Hur you come stand at my left. Hold up my hands and I'll send the powers to fight our battle."

Moses managed to stay on his tired feet until Hur and Aaron rolled the rock up behind him for a seat. "Now you all, prop me up on every leaning side. Don't let my hands fall. Aaron, you and Hur. We're holding up the world with these hands."

So the almost beaten and discouraged Israel staged a desperate rally to gain ground they had lost time and time again. Joshua stormed positions that seemed too strong to take and took them. He was thinking to himself, "I got to win for us else we won't be nobody. What's left of us will be less than we was in Egypt. There won't be no new God and no new nation if I don't win. I got to win for Moses. He done give all his life and his powers to us. Him and me got to win." So he led desperately and furiously and at darkfall stood master of a truly bloody battleground. And the surrounding chant of Israel was high and hoarse. Joshua surveyed the field and called his weary men to him and complimented them. "Rest yourselves the best way you can right where you are while I go up the hill and hear what else Moses wants us to do." So he climbed the hill to where Moses stood with his tired arms and shining eyes. Joshua took off his blood-soaked shoes when he stood before Moses and bowed his head.

"Nothing for you to hang your head about, Joshua," Moses told him. "You had a fight today that was a fight. Egypt's best general could not have beaten you today, not the way you fought and led."

"Thank you for your compliments, Moses. But if you hadn't of lifted up your arms—you whipped them Amalekites, Moses. All I did was to carry your sword for you." The two men stood face to face and embraced each other with eye-looks. Then they shook hands with a tight grip. "We brought them out from under Pharaoh with a high hand, Joshua. We crossed the sea on dry land. We have fought and conquered a nation today. So now we are ready for the mountain of God. Let's march to Sinai."

XXXII

MOSES spent the whole next day counting up and dividing the spoils taken from the Amalekites. Horses, cows, mules, camels, women, wine and jewelry, and household vessels of gold and silver. So Moses was tired when night fell and went to bed early. He sent word for everybody to get plenty of rest in the next three days because in that time the sick and wounded from the battle ought to be up and around again. Then they would once more be on the march. The next camp would be the wilderness of Sinai, at the foot of the shiny mountain, whose mists veiled the presence of God.

Soon one morning they broke camp and set out on the road to Sinai. Miriam and Aaron came knocking at Moses' door just before he stepped out to see about the line of march. They stood still and waited for him to say something first.

"Good morning, folks, you're around sort of early this morning."

"It's time we was around some place," Miriam said and flung her head and gave a sort of wink to her hips. "The way things is going round here we ought to done been round your tent door."

Moses looked at both of them very hard and let them talk.

Aaron saw Miriam looking at him right hard so he tightened his face up and said, "We ain't being treated right, Miriam and me. Ain't no ifs and ands about it. We just done had the hog run over us, that's all."

"I'm not surprised at either one of you talking like you do, but I wish *you* would tell me why you do."

"Don't try to make out you're dumb now, Moses. You ain't nobody's fool. And we ain't neither. Here we done whipped old Pharaoh down and took this nation of people away from him and brought 'em safe across the Red Sea and done I don't know what all in these three months, let alone whipping them Amalekites and here you don't give us no credit at all. You and Joshua is everything and me and Aaron

ain't nothing. And we're the very ones that got this thing together and kept it together all down the line."

"You done just fine down in Egypt, both of you."

"We're mighty glad to hear you own up to it," Aaron said in an ugly tone of voice. "Well, all right now, if we been all that help to you how come you don't show it by giving us more offices and honors? Looks like we could have a badge of some kind and some regalia to wear in front of the people so they could know we're the three head bosses of Israel."

"And another thing, Aaron forgot to mention, is this Joshua who got his mouth stuck in everything. You got to put that young rooster in his place and make him stay in it. He's getting too biggity and sassy for any good use. Him giving orders to men with whiskers just like he was some priest and prophet."

"Don't worry," Moses said calmly, "that Joshua is going to be put in his place and I'll see to it myself that he stays in it. Now down in Egypt I promised both of you places of preference and you are going to get just what I promised as soon as things can be organized. That will be after we get to Mount Sinai. Now what else you got to say, say it quick so we can go."

"Well," Aaron said, "you know back in Egypt, Miriam was a big prophet and people come to find out things from her. But since we been out here, she don't get no recognition no more."

"You can't hold me responsible for that, can you?"

"Looks like you could stand her up before the people and tell 'em that you back her up as a prophet and look on her as a great one on—er—on equality with the best. It would mean a whole lot to her."

"Well, I tell you all, it's like this. You will get all I promised you back in Egypt. I recognize that you need rich regalia to dress in to keep you from feeling like slaves again, and I will see to it in a lavish way. But don't look for too much else. The Lord usually gives a man what he is worth. The question before the house is, how much are you going to be worth to the people on this journey, not how much the people are going to be worth to you. And leaders have to be people who give up things. They ain't made out of people who grab things. Well, goodbye, see you after Sinai."

Three days later Israel was camped at the foot of Mount Sinai. And Moses pitched his tent exactly at the foot of the eminence with all of Israel behind him. They looked towards Moses and Moses looked towards the mountain.

Joshua asked Moses, "Will you go up this evening, Moses?"

"No, Joshua. The shiny mountain is there in front of me and there are the people behind me that the Voice from the mountain told me to bring. But I can't go up there till I get a sign."

So Israel camped in the wilderness before Sinai and waited for the Lord to speak. Way into the night as Moses sat in the door of his tent watching the top of the mountain, he said out loud, "Well, Lord, here is Israel." But the mountain was dark and silent. It seemed as if the first man had never been on earth, so far as the mountain knew.

The next day there was great excitement. The people saw a retinue coming mounted on camels, donkeys and horses. There were outriders and glimpses of glittering metal as the sun touched here and there on the caravan as it came in sight around the mountain. The people, fresh from one battle, wanted to know who the travelers were and what they wanted. Some rushed back after swords and spears when they saw the armed outriders and the splendor of the equipment. Joshua, lounging outside the tent, saw them and called Moses to come and look. "Must I choose out some fighting men and go challenge 'em before they get here and challenge us?" he wanted to know.

As soon as Moses could make out the white stallion at the head of the procession he knew who it was. Jethro had gotten his message and was coming to meet him. He could tell that was old Jethro on the racing camel right behind the white horse. He climbed up on a high rock and waved his hand in a certain way and Jethro broke out of the procession and came galloping up to Moses at top speed. Jethro put on a fierce scowl and came up looking every inch the stern patriarch, which was what he intended to do. He really wanted to grin from ear to ear when he caught sight of Moses but he thought that wouldn't do under the circumstances. And Moses had his company manners on, too. He jumped down off the rock and ran forward to the door of his tent. He had

Joshua to help Jethro to dismount, then he himself ran and knelt down so low before Jethro that his head touched the ground. That made Jethro feel big for Moses to kneel before him like that before all the people. But in a second he touched Moses on the shoulder and whispered, "Get up out of that dirt, Moses. I know that I'm your father-in-law and all that, but me and you don't have to put on all these airs with one another, do we? Not after all these years, do we?" The formality of it made Jethro feel cold and distant from his friend.

Moses got on up. "Of course we don't need no airs for each other, Jethro. I just didn't want these folks to think I didn't give my father-in-law the right respect."

"Oh, is that the way it was?" Jethro asked and laughed with relief. "Both of us putting on outside show to the world. Now let's be ourselves."

"Well, Jethro, I see you got my message and come. That makes me as happy as two men. How's my wife and children?"

"Just as fine as silk. I brought 'em all along because they wouldn't let me leave 'em behind."

"I'm mighty glad of that. I'm just dying to see my wife."

"Oh, she'll be glad to see you again, too. She all dressed up so till it would take a doctor to tell her how near she is dressed to death."

Moses laughed heartily, and Jethro went on. "Zipporah always was sort of queeny-like in her way. Just give her the least excuse and she'll put her trunk on her back and the lid on her head."

"I brought her some more jewelry out of Egypt and a few Amalekite pieces I saved for her from the stuff after the battle."

"I don't know where she's going to put it. She ain't got a finger nor a toe left uncovered. If all them necklaces she got on don't choke her to death I'd sure like to know the reason why. All her life, my daughter's been going around looking for a throne to sit on."

"Let me go greet her and make her welcome and get you all camped and everything. Then you and me can sit and talk like we used to, only I got plenty to tell you this time."

"Well, don't let Zipporah tie you up the way she always does. This is the greatest day we ever spent together and we got to talk."

Moses hurried off to where Zipporah and her attendants were gathered. The male attendants had dismounted and were standing by their mounts as rigid as ramrods. But Zipporah still sat her racing camel with its splendid accoutrements. Moses made a low bow before her and helped her to dismount.

"You look very beautiful, Zipporah," he told her.

"Still?" she asked him with great happiness in her voice.

"Still and always, Zipporah. Come on into my tent while your own is being set up."

He took her hand and they started towards his tent.

"But where did you get all the retainers and guards and what not?" he asked with a sly smile. "You are as elegant as Pharaoh."

"Oh, you know those are papa's servants with a few extra Kenites for show. But I wasn't coming here before all these people looking cheap. I'm the wife of Moses and Jethro's daughter."

She saw his face looking solemn and asked timidly, "You aren't mad with me, are you?"

"Oh, no, Zipporah, not at all."

"Well, what are you so frowned up about then?"

"You have come upon me in a solemn moment in my life. It's solemn for me, and for Jethro and for the people, and in a way for you too, Zipporah."

"Why? Oh, are you going to be King?"

"Oh, no, nothing like that. But you see, personally, my carefree days are over for a long, long time. I'm a leader now. It is a great hour for Jethro because his wish of a lifetime is fulfilled in part at least. For the people, an unsettled new life, and now they are here to meet a new God, and for the God to see them and pass on them. I don't suppose this ever happened before in the world and it might never happen again. And so far as you are concerned, you have lost the husband you used to have. I'm a leader now, and you'll have to suffer for it along with me."

"I'm still loving you, Moses. You see that I'm marching into your tent behind you just like that night—the night we got married, don't you? It's not all pride that keeps my bosom thrust out. There's some love there, too, Moses."

"That makes me real happy, Zipporah. We can talk about other things now. You can tell me about the children, and how Jethro is feeling about the great undertaking and everything tonight. Are these some of the clothes you bought recently? You wear your clothes better than Pharaoh's daughter. The womenfolks are admiring you too. Look all around you."

"I see them. Isn't that Miriam—that bitter-looking old woman over there?"

"That's right. She looks as if her face had fallen into disuse years ago."

"Oh, she just has the look of never having been loved. She has that terrible look of never having been nuded by a man. I don't want her near me if I can help it. What on earth is all that she's got on?"

"Don't take it too seriously. It's her idea of what a leading woman ought to look like. She's the leader of the women of Israel, you know."

"Oh, is she?"

"And she feels she should be Leader-in-Chief. She has more brains and more courage, too, than Aaron, but no talent for leadership. Too spiteful and bitter. Life has been cruel to her. Don't judge her."

"She looks as if she's already judging *me*. She's the one you ought to speak to, not me. Go tell her to take that look off of her face. She doesn't look like she's expecting to meet a God at all." She laughed and pinched Moses to make him laugh too. But he was solemn.

"Well, here we are at my tent. I'm sorry it can't be the jovial informal place that our tent is back home. This is the tent of the leader, with messengers and others running in and out all the time. But your own tent will be private."

At the door of the tent Zipporah looked back and saw that a great crowd, mostly women and children, were following them at a respectful distance. They had seen her come and watched her in growing numbers as she sat on her camel

waiting for Moses to welcome her. More had seen her dismount, and that was when Miriam elbowed her way through the crowd to glare at her.

When Miriam showed herself through the growing crowd of awe-struck women, it was her intention herself to welcome Zipporah and as the leader of Israel's womanhood, impress herself and her office upon the wife of Moses. But the glitter and glamour of Zipporah's entourage and the poise and elegance of Zipporah herself had balked Miriam. She burst through the crowd and just stood there staring and glaring. The sight of the daughter of Jethro in her finery carried Miriam back to that morning long ago when she had seen the daughter of Pharaoh bathing in the Nile.

Miriam was very unhappy at sight of Zipporah. She knew that all the feminine eyes of Israel saw the wife of Moses just as she did. They were bound to be impressed and to fall in behind her if she but beckoned. Miriam looked at her own rough clothing which was hung with jewelry that had been taken in battle, then turned her eyes away from the fine raiment of the woman on the camel. She looked again and saw well-cared-for hands and feet of Zipporah, and looked at her own gnarled fists and her square feet all twisted and coarsened by slavery, and almost snarled out loud. She, Miriam, had had so little in her life and now this place she had won by hard work and chance was being taken from her by the looks of a Prince's daughter who hadn't done anything but deck herself to come here and bewitch the eyes of foolish women! Miriam boiled with anger and a sense of injustice. So she snarled and said things to the women about her.

"Look at the hussy! Look what is getting down off that camel, will you! Somebody to come queen it over us poor people and rob us. Look at her trying to look like Mrs. Pharaoh! That Moses and his tricks. Fooling me and Aaron to do all the hard work for him down in Egypt and telling us all he meant to do for us as soon as he got to Sinai. Then soon as he got here, before he can talk to God, he got to send for that woman to put her over me! I'll show him. I'll show her too. I don't aim to be robbed out of my labor like that. Just look at her—the way she walks."

"I see her!" a woman at Miriam's elbow breathed in ecstasy.

"Oooh, ain't she elegant! Ain't she pretty, though? I'd give anything to look like that. She looks like Mrs. Leader."

Miriam turned and spat at the woman, but unwilling as her eyes were, she saw the admiration of Zipporah in thousands of faces and she felt utterly helpless in the presence of it. She was carried forward against her will by the slow wave of women that crept behind Moses and Zipporah as they walked. She could see women already trying to set down their broad bare feet in the same way that Zipporah set down her dainty sandals. Her walk and her gestures were catching. They were more than willing to take the wife of Moses for a pattern. So Miriam gave vent to her feelings in another way.

"Look at you!" she screamed. "Look at you! Running and gaping behind a woman and what she got on when we come here to this mountain to meet our God. Is that any way to act? You ought to be so glad that we got a God that made us free and now He is picking out a home for us and here you go running after somebody because they got on gold anklets and neck-rings and forget all about our new God in the mountain. Look at old Aunt Judy! Awringing and atwisting herself and grinning like she was some young gal! And she look like somebody slapped her in the face with a buzzard gut! All of you look like you done gone crazy! Get on back to your tents! Somebody in Israel got to have some sense."

Miriam changed the direction of their feet, but she did not change the direction of their thoughts. She went off to talk to Aaron about it.

Meanwhile Moses reached his tent door and ushered Zipporah inside. Then he stepped back outside to give final orders before he excluded himself from the public for the night. He told Joshua what to do and then saw Jethro approaching.

"You don't tell me you are turning in already, Moses," Jethro said with objection in his voice.

"Yes, I am. Got to talk with my wife."

"We got to talk some, too, Moses. Very important matters we got to talk over together."

"All right, you and I will talk all day tomorrow."

"But it's still daylight, Moses, we could go over a lot of things before dark if you would consider."

"Oh, well, it's so near sundown it's not worth bothering. See you tomorrow."

Jethro looked at Moses searchingly and said, "Moses, you are hurrying the sun across the sky to sleep with a woman."

"I believe I'm guilty, Jethro. It's your daughter's fault. It's a shame the way this woman keeps me running after her, but it looks like there ain't no help for it. I reckon I'll have to keep it up until I die."

"Don't forget you are called, Moses. You got a work to do that's going to take up about all of your time."

"Did the Voice say give up my wife too? I hope not."

"But, Moses, you have to consecrate yourself for work that you got to do. Women pull men aside, you know."

"You're right, I reckon, Jethro. In fact, I know you are right and maybe the day will come when I can go by your rule, but I will have to get a lot older than I am. Right now it's too hard for me. How come I can't have my wife with me to enjoy?"

"Moses, I reckon each one of us is talking from his own standpoint. Maybe you're right and I'm wrong. People put a whole lot of things on altars that they can't put inside of themselves, so there's a pile of things on altars that ain't in people, and then again, there's a lot of things in people that ain't on altars. So I reckon it was meant to be like that."

"Yes, Jethro, I have found all that out for myself. Everything in its time and place. Zipporah is waiting for me. See you tomorrow morning."

Next morning when Jethro came to the tent of Moses to look for him he was out and gone. Zipporah was being moved to a tent of her own with her several attendants, and thousands of women were crowded around staring at Zipporah and her trappings. Mrs. Moses was the greatest sensation the women had ever had.

Miriam came up to look and see because the whole nation of women was talking about nothing else, and she couldn't stay away. They had no more interest in prophecy and politics. They were still interested in the earrings of Mrs. Moses and her sandals, and the way she walked and her fine-twined colored linens. What she was doing was the way they all wanted to do. Anyhow they could all dream about it and talk,

even if they couldn't be like that. Miriam stood off at a short distance from the elaborate tent being put up for the exclusive use of Mrs. Moses and her saliva turned to venom in her mouth. She went up closer to finger the royal linen that Moses had brought out of Egypt for his wife. Then, as before, she looked down at her rough clothing and work-twisted feet and hands and she became aware of class. This woman of Moses' had been oiled with something from birth that she lacked and the futility of wishing for it made her more angry than ever. She whirled to find Aaron and Moses so she could empty herself out somehow.

She found Aaron and had another talk with him, but Moses was holding big court out under a shade tree. People by the thousands stood around for him to pass on their cases. They had been waiting for several weeks for Moses to set court, and law cases had accumulated. Moses listened to evidence and passed out judgment until his mouth was tired. Then Jethro called him to one side and spoke to him.

"Moses, what you got all these folks hanging around you like this for?"

"Big court has set, Jethro. I'm handling cases."

"Is that what you call yourself doing? I thought it was a dog-fight or something like that going on. If you're handling cases why don't you handle 'em right, Moses? You can't make out the way you are going."

"How you mean, Jethro?"

"Look at all these thousands of people standing around waiting for their cases to come up. You can't handle that many cases in one day."

"Well, you see, Jethro, we've been so busy with other things that I just haven't had time to sit on no cases. Naturally everybody comes to me when they have words over things and I have to lay a hearing on each case."

"Well, I'm telling you that you just can't do it, Moses. You got more than two million souls under you and you ain't but one lone man. You can't listen to every little jumped-up fuss that people get up. It will wear you out and kill you dead. And then again it ain't fair to the people to come stand round you all day like this without knowing whether you're going to find time to see 'em or not."

"What am I going to do then, Jethro? The folks just will law one another. Somebody's got to sit on the case."

"You sure are right there and I don't mind telling you so. But you can't listen to every case. It's much too much. Tell you what to do. You appoint good men to sit on all these small cases and get rid of 'em. You listen to the great big ones that nobody can settle but you. Then everything will work along smooth for everybody."

"All right, Jethro. That's a good idea you give me and I mean to carry it out just like you told me. You being a chief over people nearly all your life, you have learned something about how to handle 'em. I have been more of a military man."

"That is not your job in this case. You got to be something to these people that looks like God. That's a mighty big thing by itself. You appoint men to fight and men to judge, and men to wear the robes of priests and servants around the gathering place of the spirit. You have to be the something bigger and better than the robes and the outward signs. You have to stand between the people and God."

"That's a mighty big mouthful you said, Jethro. It's big like the womb of Time."

"I know it, Moses. But you can fill the bill. It's just one step higher up the shiny mountain for you, and you been climbing all the time. Be something pointing toward God to the folks, Moses. That's what you was born to be."

When Jethro's words went into the little door in Moses' ear, something else went inside besides. He felt that he had been embraced by Time itself. He was never to be the same man again.

"And if you don't mind, Moses, let me get on back home again."

"Oh, no, Jethro, I want you to stay with me all the time. I need you real bad to see this thing out to the end."

"You did need me, but now you don't. Let me go on home again. You got your wife and children now, and I done you all the good I could already. You know where home is any time you want to talk anything over. In fact it will be a help to you to come home and talk things over with me now and then. You know these woods and roads better than anybody else on

earth. Much as you done traveled 'em. Come home for a few days when you can. Sun-up tomorrow I reckon I'll hit the grit for home. Mighty lonesome there now without you and the children. Everybody married off and out of the house. It ain't much for me to do now but sit and think."

"I'll be there with you as often as I can get away. You know my heart is there, don't you?"

"Yes, Moses, I do. But this work done waited so long to get done, son. I hope you fulfill your birth-mission and do it right. Me and God neither one can't make out without you. We both realize you got an awful load to carry, but there wasn't no other way to get it done. Don't forget that when things get awful bad with you, me and God will both be sorry, but the mission, Moses, the mission." Jethro lifted his old hands up on the shoulders of Moses, gave him a powerful eye-look that lasted a long time; leaned his head on Moses' strong chest and hugged Moses very hard. In effect he had departed for home in spirit and at the same time pleaded for understanding. He was gone when Moses woke up in the morning.

XXXIII

NEXT DAY at a good hour, Moses went up on the mountain as if he had been called. The shining mountain. The mountain with a Voice. The mountain that cloaked the Presence. The mountain that had given Moses and Israel a God. The mountain that had given him his rod of God. The mountain that was the altar of the world. That was the way Moses was thinking when he climbed up its woody slopes with Joshua following behind him at a distance.

And from the cloud-ringed summit the Lord called out to Moses and told him who He was. To make Moses remember, the Lord called to mind the victories over Pharaoh in Egypt and the miracles since Israel had crossed the Red Sea. So Moses told Him right away that he remembered well.

"Moses, I see the people you brought here before me and I think well of them. Now, if they will listen to me when I speak, and keep the laws I'm going to hand down, I'm going to make a peculiar treasure out of those same people."

"Thank you, Lord," Moses said.

"Now, Moses, you go back to the people and see to it that they wash themselves all over today and tomorrow and wash their clothes, too, and generally clean up and then you sanctify them for two days and get them all ready for the third day. And I am coming down in the plain sight of everybody on Mount Sinai. And, Moses, I'm going to have a trumpet sound one long pull. And when you hear that, tell everybody to gather around the foot of the mountain. I'm coming."

Moses went on down and got all the people cleaned up and made all the arrangements. Then he told the people, "I know how forward and brash some of you people are, so I'm going to tell you right now that Mount Sinai is holy ground. Don't a one of you set foot on it, nor even put your hands on it. When the Lord appears to you on the top of the mountain, you stand still and listen because it is sure death to the one that touches that mountain. You hear me? Even your animals better not be caught grazing on it. And now don't nobody

sleep with your husbands and wives until God done been here and gone."

It was the third day and it was morning. Moses got up soon and put on the special new robe that Zipporah had had made for him. Everybody was clean and dressed. A low rumble of thunder from the mountain brought everybody out of their tents to gaze at the mountain and to listen. They saw the huge white cloud drop down and rest on the crest of the mountain like a Pharaoh assuming his throne. Something like lightning played in fiery figures, over and above the cloud-like visitor and great flashes darted from the interior of the mass and went back inside again. And the trumpet on the mountain sounded so long and so loud that everybody trembled.

"Come on, people!" Moses called out and told everybody. "Come on out. God wants to see you and talk to you. Everybody come stand right where I put you on this low part of the mountain and don't nobody try to go up. You are here to meet God and listen."

Dense white and black columns of smoke rose from the entire upper half of the mountain, and the great mass shook and quivered like a forest. The voice of the trumpet got louder and louder. Then Moses spoke to God and God answered him.

Moses said, "Here's Your people, Lord. Where are You?"

"I'm coming down on top of the mountain to meet you. Don't let nobody set foot on the mountain but you. But I want you to come on up to the top of the mountain. I want to talk with you."

Moses started on up the mountain and all of the people were scared for him. Some of them cried and begged him not to go. But most of them left their mouths just like the Lord found them. If they were open, they stayed open. If they were shut, they might just as well have had the lockjaw for all the use they made of their mouths. But right in front of everybody, Moses went on up into the smoke and flames and disappeared from sight.

And when Moses got up on the mountain top and vanished from the sight of the people, only one man had nerve enough to put his feet in the tracks of Moses. Joshua dashed from the multitude and began to run up the mountain the same way

that Moses had gone. People hollered to him to stop. Some of them began to wail for his death, but he kept right on.

"You going to drop dead, Joshua!" some of them hollered. "Don't go up there, Joshua!"

"My bossman and leader went up there, didn't he?" Joshua called back.

"He got that right hand of his and that rod, Joshua. He can walk out of the sight of men. He got the black cat bone and snake wisdom. He's a two-headed man. He ain't like nobody else on earth. Better come on back, Joshua, before that snake gets to you. We don't see no more of Moses. Maybe he's dead up there himself."

"Well, if he's dead up there with God, lemme go up and die too." So Joshua entered the smoke and fire and disappeared from the people like Moses did. But when he got near the top of the mountain, glory awed him to his knees. He saw Moses standing higher up and seven suns circling around him and the moon was under his feet. Moses held his rod in his left hand and elevated it towards the center of a whorl of light. His right hand was lifted and glowed like the firmament at sunrise. Therefore he knew Moses had more power than man because a voice spoke out of the equator of the moving light and Moses answered it back again. So that is how the people got laws and commandments from heaven, because Moses had power enough to take them out of the mouth of God and give them to the people. So Moses stayed up on the mountain and kept company with God for forty nights and days, and he didn't eat and he didn't get hungry. But he fed Joshua every day by a miracle. Therefore Joshua slept down below where Moses sat talking with God and saw Moses in a way that nobody else had ever seen him.

XXXIV

MOSES stayed up on the mountain so long because it takes a long time to learn God's secret words that have the power in them to make and to do. Moses learned ten words from God. So he took the ten words of power and he made ten commandments out of them. On the back side of the words there were seals and these seals had the power of all destructions. So Moses came down the mountain with plagues of death in his hands, besides more power to create and to do. And Joshua walked behind him in adoration and awe. Moses walked with the two tables of testimony in his hands and Joshua walked with worship.

But Moses had stayed within the aureate cloud for forty days and the people below had just about given him up. Most of them thought that Joshua and Moses were dead up there in the smoke. But some said, "Oh, he ain't dead. He just bit off more than he can chew so he done run off across the mountain and left us. We better begin to shift for ourselves."

They didn't say anything to Mrs. Moses because she seemed too much like a stranger to them to visit with her up close. Not that she tried to make them feel that way. But she looked like a ruler's wife to them and they kept off and looked at her tent and her servants and her clothes.

Aaron didn't give out any information at all. He kept on saying, "How would I know what that man is doing up there? He never tells me nothing. The Lord told me and him and Miriam to run this thing, but you see how he carries on. He goes up on the mountain to talk to God by himself and that leaves me and Miriam in the dark. I am beginning to think like a whole lot of people in Israel. You can't put no dependence at all in no Egyptian, don't care who it is."

Miriam said, "Yes, that no-count Egyptian come with his mealy mouth and talked me and Aaron into bringing you all off. We was the ones that done all the work because he ain't one of us sure enough. He couldn't have got nobody to follow him. Here I was a big prophetess in Israel and Aaron was a leader, so the people followed us on off and now he

done took full charge and full credit for everything. We ain't even good enough to go up with him and speak with the Lord. And look at that dark complected woman he done brought and put up to be a Queen over the rest of us women. Why, it's awful. I never seen such a caper cut in all my born days."

"Well, that being the case, let's we back the deal. We don't know nothing about where we headed for and nothing, and nobody don't know nothing about this new Lord in the mountain but Moses and Jethro." A bosom friend of Aaron's said this and looked to Aaron for the approval that he knew he would get.

"But we do know something about our gods back in Egypt," Miriam went on. "Maybe that's how come we having such a hard time, because we done give up our gods. Isis will sure help you if you pray to her and pray right. Did the Bull God Apis ever go back on us? No!"

"Well, then now, how come we can't have an altar to our real gods and maybe they will help us. It wouldn't be a bad idea, seeing the fix we're in. Aaron, you been used to working gold. How come you can't make us a golden calf for our altar?"

"I ain't telling you all to do nothing behind Moses' back that he wouldn't like. But if everybody will go and break off them dangles off your earrings and build me the right kind of a fire, I believe I could make a right good calf of gold for the altar. Then you can worship like you did in Egypt. Some of you go east and some go north and west and south and collect up all the ornaments you can get hold of. No telling what I might turn out if you all just will insist on me doing it. And while the image is being cast you all might just as well get ready to celebrate the service, you know what to do just as well as I do. Now everybody do around right smart and we might find something to consolate us out here in this wilderness where we been dragged for nothing."

The thing shook Israel like a wind. Suddenly the camp came alive. People stripped themselves and their children of ornaments and threw the things in the collection baskets with a smile. "A real old down home Egyptian ceremony getting ready to come off with Aaron at the altar. Just like old times

back home. And they tell me a breakdown and stomp is going to follow." People began to rush around and collect wines and drinkables and stuff to eat. Everybody oiled their whole bodies before they put on their Sunday clothes. For the first part of the ceremony they put on their best clothes. For the last part they were prepared to take them off. So they oiled themselves all over. The oil would do for a dress in the after dance.

"When you reckon it's going to be ready to worship, Aaron?" the people asked him about the golden calf he was making with engraving tools.

"Tonight some time. Be ready tomorrow for worship, since you all are forcing me to do this thing."

That night when the image was cooling, Aaron looked at his work and admired it exceedingly. "That sure is one fine piece of work, if I do say so myself. Believe I'll make an altar for it while it is cooling." And that's exactly what Aaron did. And the next morning when the finger of the eastern sun pointed in the face of the calf and set it to shining and shimmering, Aaron got behind the altar and the people worshipped.

"These be thy gods, O Israel, which brought thee up out of the land of Egypt. We don't know anything about no Lord in no mountain at all. Moses made Him up so let Moses keep Him."

Then they finished the altar part of it and got up to play. They cast off clothes and they cast off care. Drums and cymbals and harps and voices singing loud and happy. Shining bodies moved and turned and collided joyfully. Maidens danced in ecstasy with closed eyes and nobody looked too closely at faces. Joy was the feeling, joy!

XXXV

MOSES lifted the freshly chiseled tablets of stone in his hands and gazed down the mountain to where Israel waited in the valley. He knew a great exultation. Now men could be free because they could govern themselves. They had something of the essence of divinity expressed in order. They had the chart and compass of behavior. They need not stumble into blind ways and injure themselves. This was bigger than Israel itself. It comprehended the world. Israel could be a heaven for all men forever, by these sacred stones.

With flakes of light still clinging to his face, Moses turned down the mountain with the tablets of testimony in his hands. He heard nothing earthly nor sensed anything about him until he descended to where Joshua waited for him. With his eyes turned inward, he sat down on a stone opposite Joshua to rest.

"Joshua, I have laws. Israel is going to know peace and justice."

Moses indicated the sacred stones on his lap.

Then from far off a sound, a noise made up of many sounds came up to Moses and he listened. And his ears accepted what his soul refused. It was a wild and savage shout of voices and drums that Moses heard, but his spirit rejected it, because it injured his vision of destiny for Israel. It clashed with his exalted forty days. It soiled what had passed between him and God. So for a long time Moses sat silent and listened, hoping that he dreamed. Finally he asked Joshua, "Do I hear shouting and singing, Joshua, or is it just a ringing in my ears?"

"It's shouting and singing, Moses."

Moses sat sodden and sad for a long while and then a new hope crept into his voice.

"Do *you* hear anything that sounds like singing and cymbals, Joshua, or does it just sound like that to me because I'm tired and sort of frazzled out?"

Joshua looked at the face of Moses and pitied him.

"I hear a mighty loud noise down below," Joshua evaded.

Moses looked down at the stones in his lap and passed his

547

hand over the carved figures reverently and then he looked back up the mountain as if he would retreat up there. Then he brought his attention back to the tumult below.

"Does it sound like the voice of the people shouting for victory, Joshua? Maybe the Amalekites have come up against Israel while we've been up here with God."

"No, Moses, it's not the voice of mastery that I hear. It's the voice of Israel, but they are not shouting for conquering anybody."

Moses sat and listened for a while longer, shutting his heart against what he feared.

"Well, Joshua," he said haltingly, "do they sound to you like they are crying out for help? They could be overcome, you know, by some nation that might attack, with both of us away."

Joshua listened carefully for a moment. "No, it's not the voice of them that cry for being overcome."

"What do you reckon could have happened to Israel, Joshua?" Moses tried to persevere in his hopes.

"Oh, that's singing and dancing that I hear. Sounds like the dance songs to Apis, the Bull-god to me. Listen at those drums!"

Moses snatched his face away from Joshua and the last glimmer of light that had clung to his face from God, died to ashes.

"Oh, no, Joshua, they couldn't do a thing like that. Not after all we have been through from Egypt on! Not after they cried to God to deliver them from Egypt and its sorrows! Not after the God of the mountain sent me to save them from all harm and danger, and brought them here to the mountain to give them laws and pledges! No, Joshua, they wouldn't be back in unforgetfulness and ingratitude here at the foot of Sinai. They couldn't be howling in idolatry in the very ears of God."

"It certainly is the sound of drumming and chanting to Apis that I hear."

Moses stood up and closed his eyes with the tablets clasped tightly to his breast. Then he started slowly up the mountain-side again. "I better go back and talk to God again about Israel. He'd know better what to do than I would." He left Joshua behind him and struggled on back toward God.

But he didn't get far. At first he thought it was the wind scuffling around in the brush. Then he knew it was the Voice that spoke and halted him.

"Moses," it said like a strong breeze in the pine tops, "don't come up here to me. Hurry down!"

"Lord," Moses sobbed, "have they betrayed you?"

"They have betrayed me. They have betrayed you, and most of all they have dirtied their souls by betraying themselves. Go down, Moses, and halt them in their headlong flight. The people that you have brought out of Egypt have soiled themselves and tempted me to destroy them. They are worshipping a calf of gold and giving it the credit for bringing them out of the land of Egypt, and out of the house of bondage. Go stop them before I get too tired of their ingratitude and kill them."

The Voice was gone and the light was gone and Moses turned cold and heavy and went down the mountain like God descending into Eden. First it was the mountain top and then the high shoulder and then the heavy hips of the mountain and then the crumbling ankles of the mountain and then the plain where Israel waited for a sign from God.

So Moses stood before the altar of the golden calf with the tables of stone in his hands. Drunken shouts filled his ears; bodies drunk on the liquor of feeling rocked and reeled and contorted about him with eyes glazed and covered. Aaron with his bearded chin stuck out in front of him was presiding at the altar. His two oldest sons, Abihu and Nadab, chief acolytes in the dance and revel were shouting and leaping, and thumping their naked bodies and urging the people on.

"Aaron!" Moses cried at him with a stern voice. "Aaron, do you hear me?" Moses had to call three times before Aaron really saw him standing before the altar with the law from Sinai in his hands. Aaron took one long comprehending look and sunk behind the altar on his knees. The eyes of Moses had gutted him. Aaron hid himself behind the pagan altar while Moses towered tall and grim before it with the tablets of God in his hands. All around the spot the tumult boiled, for few had seen with their eyes or heard.

The calf and all its meaning and all the thoughts it collected glimmered and winked at Moses from its altar and suddenly

Moses raised one of the tablets with its fine writings and hurled it at the graven image and saw the golden calf topple over on its side. The force of the impact shattered the sacred stone and crumbled it in pieces. Moses lifted the other stone and hurled it, and the calf broke in pieces and the pieces scattered around the altar. But in breaking the calf, the tablets of testimony had been broken to crumbling stone. Moses stood in his wrath and considered. The law from Sinai had broken the idol of Egypt, but the sacred tablets had themselves been destroyed in the clash. Egypt against Sinai. It was going to be a hard struggle.

The crash of stone on metal had attracted attention. Drums faltered and stopped. Dancers paused and looked and saw Moses destroying Apis and froze to sculpture in poses, which broke into flight. Some ran heedless. Some crept off slowly with dazed faces to hiding places. Before Apis and Aaron they were clothed in joy and license. Before Moses and Sinai they were naked to their souls. They slunk into places of concealment as best they could. Moses strode over the huge vacant square of celebration with Joshua at his heels, looking, looking and seeing. Looking inside of people by their outward appearance and sickening at what he saw. He circled and circled and came back to the naked altar and stopped.

Moses found Aaron squatting down behind the altar trying to hide himself. Moses kicked over the altar and snatched Aaron to his feet and looked him dead in the eye. He looked at the man and saw him as he was, stripped of the imitation of dignity that he affected lately; saw him naked of the imitation of himself that he wore as best he might.

"Aaron," he said, "what on earth did these people do to you to make you bring such a sin on everybody like you did?"

Aaron tried to back off but Moses had him by his whiskers and he wouldn't let him go. So Aaron cringed and fawned and said, "Lord, Moses, you're my bossman, and I know it. I wouldn't think of putting myself on an equal with you. You're a great big high cockadoo and I ain't nothing. So you oughtn't to be wasting your time getting mad with me. You done been round these people long enough to know 'em. You know they ain't nothing and if you and God fool with 'em you won't be nothing neither."

"Aaron, you haven't said a thing yet to excuse yourself for what you have done. Tell me and tell me quick why you have betrayed God and the people in the way you have done."

Aaron lifted his hand as if to break Moses' grip on his beard, but the eye of Moses forbade him. He winced and said, "You oughtn't to hold my whiskers like that, Moses, the people are looking at us, and me being a leader—"

"The people are looking at you naked and capering around like an old goat, too. Let's forget about that while you answer me."

Moses did not miss the look of hatred born of hurt vanity in Aaron's eyes as he sought to placate Moses by dissembling.

"Now, Moses, you know these people is always up for something that ain't no good. They don't mean nobody no good including theirselves. Know what they did? When you didn't come back right away they was going round behind your back running you down and scandalizing your name and making out you was dead or done run on off and they took and brought me all them ornaments, just because they knowed I used to work in gold, and they told me, we don't know what become of that man Moses. Make us some gods to march in front of us instead of that cloud. And they shoved all them earrings and things in my hands and naturally I didn't want to be bothered with the things, so just to get 'em out of my hands I took and threw 'em in the fire and what you reckon, boss? All I did was to fling them earrings into the fire, and out come that calf."

"Aaron, you haven't said a thing yet and that is because you haven't thought a thing yet, nor felt anything except your own importance. Your whole body is nothing but a big bag to tote your littleness in."

Moses thrust Aaron from him so roughly that he all but fell. Then Moses strode away, noting as he went how many people who had taken no part in the ceremony to the bull. There was open disgust on the faces of many and that made Moses think. Some were here because of Sinai and all that it meant and some were just here. A divided people, and that would never do, not at this point in their history. So Moses made a decision. He straightened his shoulders and marched to the gate of the camp and lifted both hands in the air.

People saw Moses standing like a crucifix and came. Moses still stood and they kept coming and questioning each other and coming. When a great multitude stood before him, Moses began to speak and cried out, "Who is on the Lord's side? Who is on the Lord's side?" Moses kept crying until the words became a chant. "Who is on the Lord's side?" Israel's ears were wrung. "Who is on the Lord's side?" It woke up fear in the guilty. Israel was stung. "Who is on the Lord's side?" It freshened hope in the hearts of the just. Israel was called. "Who is on the Lord's side?" And some young Levites were the first to come closer and say, "We are, Moses, we are for the Lord of Sinai." Then others joined until thousands upon thousands stood by Moses. Then he said, "You who are on the Lord's side, take your swords in your hands and come to me." The surging multitudes of young men gathered around Moses with ready swords. So Aaron saw one of his sons, Eleazar, and all the other Levites go to Moses with swords and he was afraid to stay away. He came to Moses also with his sword and his censor in his hand and stood.

Moses said, "You all know what a foul thing has happened in Israel today. You know better than I do who the leaders and the agitators were. If this is to be a great nation, it must be purged of such evil-doers, or all Israel must perish. You have your eager weapons, men. Spare not a soul who is guilty." Their swords leaped out of their scabbards like day out of dawn.

The struggle began. Drunken people in hidden places roused from a stupor with their eyes wide open in judgment. Aaron saw two of his sons dragged forth and cut down before his eyes. He dropped his sword and swung his censor in wide arcs to call to the minds of the avengers that he was a priest. He stood between the living and the dead with his censor in his hand, weeping and quaking and cursing. He was afraid to fight, afraid to run and ashamed to cry out loud.

For hours there was fleeing and screaming and hiding and bloody swords. Then there was quiet again in the camp. It only remained to bury the dead. Aaron came creeping and looked down into the faces of Nadab and Abihu, his two dead sons, and wept. The men buried his sons with the other thousand leaders of the revolt slain by the sons of Levi. Aaron

started a little song in his heart that went like this: "It's your time now, be mine after while. Oh, it's your time now, but be mine after while, oh, it's your time now, but it'll be mine after while." And from that minute on till the hour he died Aaron kept his eyes on Moses in secret and waited his chance. All he needed was the strength to seize his hour for vengeance. His hate was strong but his heart was weak. From then on for forty years the underhand struggle went on. Sometimes he made an open attack upon Moses when Aaron thought he could succeed, but always the secret struggle went on to destroy him and have Aaron in the saddle. And always the strength of Moses trampled down the weak cunning of Aaron.

Moses was hard on Israel, after that. He felt that only discipline would save what he had begun and so he chastened the people severely. They suffered epidemics of ailments and many discomforts. It was then that he established the House of God. It was called the Tabernacle of the Congregation and Moses set it apart from all other tents, even his own. He pitched it far outside the camp. And when Moses went out to the tabernacle everybody saw him go and everybody was afraid. Would he lift his rod against them? Would he raise that right hand? As Moses went the people stood in their tent doors and watched him pass. And every eye in Israel followed him in fear.

They watched him go inside the door of the new tabernacle and they saw the shimmering cloudy pillar descend and they saw it stand at the door of the tabernacle and in awe they rose as one man and worshipped the God who had chosen to live among them. They heard the Lord talking to Moses from the cloud like two friends talking face to face. They heard Moses tell the Lord, "If you don't go with us, don't send me by myself, Lord. Other people will make a fool out of us."

So the Lord told him, "I'll always be there, Moses, because I love you and I know you by your name."

"Thank you, Lord. One favor more I want to ask you while I am still on pleading terms with mercy."

"What is it, Moses?"

"Lord, I done seen your pillar of fire and your pillar of cloud and heard your voice in rumbling thunder. I done seen

the cloudy cloak that hides your glory, but I ain't never seen your glory itself. Lord, be so pleased in your tender mercy as to show me your glory."

The Lord answered Moses and told him, "Moses, I will make all My goodness pass before you. And I will proclaim the name of the Lord before you and I will be gracious to whom I will be gracious, and show mercy unto whom I will show mercy, but, Moses, you just can't see My face, for no man can see My face and live. But, Moses, since it is you that ask me, look, see there is a place by Me and you go and stand upon that certain rock and when My Glory passes by, I'll take you and put you in a crack in the rock, and I will cover you with My hand while I pass by, then I will move My hand and you shall see the back parts of My Glory, but My face you shall never see."

So Moses thanked the Lord for letting him see that much and God told him, "Moses, get you two more nice smooth pieces of stone and bring it up to the top of the mountain so I can put those same laws that you broke upon that golden calf down again. These people need laws and rules to go by."

Moses got up early next morning and took the stones and went up to the top of the mountain and kept company with God again. And when he came down with the law in his hands, the skin of his face was iridescent and shining, but Moses didn't know it himself, that is, until the people gazed at him in awe and talked about his shining face. So they knew that God had covered Moses with His hand in the cleft of the rock and passed His Glory by Moses.

And Moses took the tables of testimony into the tabernacle and the pillar of cloud went in behind Moses and rested on the altar. So that was the first time that God had come inside the house to live with people.

XXXVI

"AND HOW is the black Mrs. Pharaoh making out this morning?"

"Who are you talking about, Miss Miriam?"

"Oh, you know I'm talking about that dark-complected woman that Moses done brought here trying to make out she's a lordgod sitting on a bygod. All dressed up every day like King Pharaoh's horse. She needn't think because her papa is some kind of a chief in Midian and she's married to Moses that she can come dictating to me."

"Is she done took to dictating, Miss Miriam? I didn't never hear of her saying nothing to nobody."

"She don't have to. But you seen her flourishing herself all over the place trying to get the influence of people's minds."

"You reckon?"

"No! I know it. She come here with the idea of getting control of the womenfolks and to root me out as a leader— after I done worked like a fool to get us free. Her idea is to get you all back into slavery again. You just swapped one Pharaoh for another one, to my notion. You don't want to go back into slavery, do you?"

"I sure don't. I used to get so tired of kneading dough for them rich Egyptians to eat. My knees was all wore out from kneeling down all day and half the night over them bread troughs. No, sir! I sure don't want no more slavery. Though I sure would love a loaf of that good old Egyptian bread."

"Well, you women better get together and do something or you will find that Ethiopian woman and that Moses will have us all out here in the woods using us for slaves."

"What can we do to head it off?"

"Get together as many women as you can and go stand around the tent of Moses and holler for him to get rid of that Ethiopian wife of his."

"Thought you said she was a Midianite?"

"Oh, don't try to take me up on every little point. Even if she was born and raised in Midian her folks could still come

from Ethiopia, couldn't they? Tell me! Look how dark her skin is. We don't want people like that among us mixing up our blood and all. That woman has got to go. Go get up some people to protest. When enough of you all get around this tent, my brother Aaron and me will go see Moses and demand him to get her off the place. Got us round here looking like her servants."

Miriam walked and talked all day so that by three o'clock that afternoon two or three thousand women were milling around the tent of Moses and muttering. Finally Moses sent Joshua out to demand what was wrong out there. Aaron and Miriam stepped out of the crowd and answered him. "It's no wonder the people is dissatisfied," they told Moses. "You got that strange woman around here—"

"What strange woman you talking about?" Moses asked shortly.

"That one in your tent," Miriam said perversely.

"She might be strange to you, but she sure ain't no stranger to me. She's been my wife more than twenty years. I hope you don't aim to tell me that I can't have my wife with me. I hope you ain't messing in my business to that extent."

"I mind my own business and I let other folks' business alone. Anybody that knows me can tell you that." Miriam evaded for the moment.

"Well, what do you think you got to do with my wife being here?" Moses insisted.

"Tell him, Aaron."

"That's right, Aaron, you tell me. I know you two ain't using up my time to try to break into my arrangements. Go on, Aaron, and tell me what you got to say about my wife."

"It ain't so much her being your wife as it is who she is."

"Jethro's daughter is good enough for anybody and any place. In fact, it is hard to find a place good enough for her. I could draw some harsh comparisons between you, but I won't do you that bad."

"It's her color, Moses. She's too dark to be around here."
"Why?"

"Well, you see the people, that is, the ladyfolks, don't want her ruling over them, dark as she is."

"In the first place she ain't ruling over nobody and in

the second place she's my wife and nobody ain't got nothing to do with how dark or how white she is but me."

"Oh, yes, we have. That's the very thing we don't like. You act like you're the boss of everything. God didn't call you, and you only, you know."

"Who else did He call, then?"

"He called me and Miriam too. All three of us is supposed to be on a equal balance."

"He didn't call you and you can't balance equal with me, but even if you could how come you think you got leave to stick your bill into my private business?"

"It's not us, it's the people. We don't care if she was black as tar. But the people come crying in our ears and we have to look out for what they want."

"That's a lie, Aaron. Nobody didn't come to neither one of you to complain about my wife's color. I got eyes in my head and ears on other people's heads. You two been proaging this camp over all day long working this thing up. Nobody here don't care anything about my wife's color. Haven't we had the mixed multitudes with us ever since we started from Egypt? Didn't they march out with us and not one soul in Israel has ever mentioned the subject. I know exactly what's the matter with you two. You want to stand in my shoes which they are much too big for your feet. The women all are making admiration over my wife and now Miriam is jealous and spiteful. I've given up everything else I wanted in life for the sake of this mission I have, but I mean to protect her against your littleness and malice."

"You wrong there, Moses. We ain't got no feeling against your wife. But we can't afford to look over the wants of the people, Moses. We got to consider the people."

"Aaron, you got ambition to be a leader without having anything else to go with it. I been noticing you tipping around and plotting and conniving. But you'll never be a leader. You are much too sensitive to the wishes of the people but you are too unconscious of their needs. And then again, you got a big idea of your own importance. I wish I could buy you for what you are really worth and sell you for what you think you're worth. I sure would make money on the deal."

"Don't let him holler you down, Aaron," Miriam jumped in.

"The Lord did call us just as much as He did Moses and it's about time we took our stand in front of the people. I was a prophetess in Israel while he was herding sheep in Midian. And that woman he done brought here to lord it over us, that black Mrs. Pharaoh got to leave here right now. She ain't going to lord it over me, after I done done all the hard part of it."

"Miss Miriam, your case is pitiful. The trouble with you is that nobody ever married you. And when a woman ain't got no man to look after, she takes on the world in place of the man she missed. You are one of those people who learn nothing in the long turnings and twistings of experience. But you better keep my wife's name out of your mouth. That's all I got to say."

Miriam lifted up her voice so all the women on the outside could hear what she said.

"Who you talking to, Moses? I know you ain't trying to tell me to shut up. The Lord don't speak through your mouth alone. He speaks through my mouth and Aaron's mouth just as much as He speaks through yours."

Moses rose in fury. "Come on over to the tabernacle, both of you, and we'll see who the Lord called and who He didn't. We might as well settle this thing in front of everybody once and for all."

So they three went to the Tent of Testimony with a great crowd following behind them and set the ceremony. And the Voice spoke out of the cloud and was angry with Miriam and Aaron. Then the cloud lifted and everybody saw that Miriam was a leper. Aaron fell on his knees and called Moses by all the praise-giving names, and begged for both of them. God! Miriam was a horrible sight in her leprous whiteness! Everybody shrank away from her in terror and disgust. So Moses put her outside of the camp as unclean for seven days. The camp remained stationary until she was healed again. All the rest of her days, Miriam was very silent. Whole days passed by at times in which she never uttered a word. Those seven days outside the camp seemed to put a veil between her and the world which never lifted. Now and then she would whisper to whoever happened to be close around. "He lifted his right hand. I saw him do it. He lifted his right hand and the thing come upon me. I felt it when it come. His right hand was clothed in light."

XXXVII

THE MONTHS and years went by. Moses had long ago sent his wife back home to Jethro, not because he no longer cared, but because this great thing that had grabbed hold of his life was doing things to their life together. Both of them changed under it. Moses became even less talkative than he had always been, and he had never had too many words to say. He lived in deep thought and reflection. He spent whole nights in the mountains alone except when Joshua followed him without his consent. Several times he crossed the mountain and spent a day or two with Jethro to talk things over and he always found help and comfort in the old man. The visits never failed to benefit both Moses and Israel.

Zipporah changed too. She was born the daughter of a powerful chief and though the fortunes of her father's house had gone down for a while, this was changed with the coming of Moses, and the wealth and prestige of Jethro's house was as great as any in all Midian. So she was used to ruling and seeing ruling done. To her, the most natural thing in the world would have been for Moses to assume the crown of Israel. She felt that the people expected it. And in fact they would have preferred it. They were used to Kings and rulers and felt lonesome and defenseless under this light pressure of leadership that Moses exerted. But Moses was stubborn on that point. He had no wish to impose his will on others and he said so every time the subject arose. So she looked towards what had been in men's relations to each other, and he faced towards what was to be, and a whole world stood between their two horizons. So after a while she was glad to leave the meager, hard fare of the camp and return to Jethro's tent. She understood herself there and felt that she knew the Moses who snatched a few days from Israel now and then to spend with her and Jethro. She took her younger son back with her to be company for her and to help Jethro, now that he was getting feeble with age. The oldest boy, Gershom, had stayed in the camp with Moses, and had become a Prince of Israel in the new order which Moses had set up, as a sop to certain

Elders in Israel. The hosts of the Hebrews were growing rich as they moved on by war and plunder, and the heads of families wanted some excuse to show their wealth. So titles and ranks had come to be, with the Levites outranking every other tribe. And Zipporah's son had become a Prince even though she never became a Queen. On the whole, however, Zipporah's mood lacked light.

But still Moses led the people. He thought and led. He prayed and led. He wrote and had his moments of philosophy and led, even when he knew that he would have been better loved as a King and more popular as a politician. But he chose to be a leader and he was. He stood in his high, lonely place and led. Jethro and Joshua glimpsed through the clouds that hid the peak where he stood from the common herd, but that was all. Joshua was so attached to him that he continued to serve about his person as often as he could despite his own leadership in the army. That pleased Moses and helped Joshua, for Moses spent hours at times teaching the younger man strategy and discipline of men.

This was not just sentiment on the part of Moses. Israel was going to have to fight and fight hard many times before the sons of Jacob should find and possess the place that was to be their home. So they needed military men to lead. Jethro had warned Moses that he must not take the risk of getting killed. Military officers could be made at any time, but the genius of Moses could never be replaced. So Moses taught Joshua and let him lead the army. It was easy to teach him, for Joshua had those things in him that make a great man of war.

There was something else about Joshua that encouraged Moses besides his unfailing loyalty to his chief and the cause. He had all those big virtues that command respect, and all those commonplace vices that make men understood. Men congregated about him. They respected his virtues and admired his vices. So he became the left hand of Moses, and Moses confided in him freely about his plans and after-thoughts. Joshua knew all of his hopes and disillusionments. All Israel had heard of the Promised Land, but only Joshua had heard the name of Canaan coupled with it.

"It's a mighty fine place for a homeland, Joshua," Moses confided to him, "but I don't know yet whether the people

have got back enough of what Pharaoh took out of them to go take it. We got the outside stuff to take it, but I ain't positively sure we got the insides yet."

"The way I see it, Moses, we ought to have it now. I'm ready if you're ready to tell me."

"No, we got to feel our way along, son. We got to go slow," Moses said, sliding into the mood and the expressions of the people as he liked to do at times. "You done seen how they blow up for nothing at all and fight against their own selves and all. I done found out from this that people can do an awful lot of feeling without doing a lick of thinking. And you and I know that we have some folks around here that loves to stir up feelings for their own benefit. I ain't naming no names. I'm letting things ride for a while longer till I see further."

"Well, Moses, I'll tell you like you told me once. Silence is all the genius a fool has and it is one of the things a smart man knows how to use when he needs it. You know what to do and how to do it better than anybody else but God."

"Thank you, Joshua, for your words and what I know is behind 'em. But, Joshua, with that other ear that I don't use for everyday listening, I hear a crowd coming here to talk. Go round the bend of the road there and meet whoever it is and see can't you straighten out the business they coming after. That will give me a chance to go on with my writing. I'm a week behind on my journal right now."

Joshua hurried on out and disappeared around the bend in the road and came face to face with the committee of seventy Elders on the way to confer with Moses. As soon as they saw Joshua, they hurried up to him and asked, "Is that man Moses in his quarters now or is he off hiding out in the mountain like he always does when we got something important to take up with him?"

"Don't waste up your time lying up some nerve to say what you ain't got guts enough to say otherwise. Tell me what you want and maybe I can get it for you."

"We didn't come to talk with Little Moses, we got business with the real thing. If we wanted to talk with substitutes we got Aaron right along here with us, and we wouldn't need you with him along."

"I ain't no Little Moses, even if you all done give me that nickname for spite. But just the same you better tell me what you want with the chief or else you won't see him at all. There's a few things I can do to save him some work and worry. Maybe if you'll tell me I can do you some good."

"All right, little leader, you go get us something to eat. We want plenty of everything and we want it right now. We want fresh meat and vegetables and fish and fruit and if we don't get it, we can get another leader that can take us back to Egypt. We ain't the helpless people we used to be."

"This talk is too serious for me to listen to."

"We thought so in the first place, but you just would dip in."

Joshua singled out Aaron and talked to him. "Aaron," he told him, "you know that Moses ain't got no provisions stored away nowhere. He eats the same as all the rest of us. Why don't you explain to these people so they can be satisfied and not worry Moses for nothing?"

Aaron stroked his long beard with a smug hand gesture and generally settled his priestly robes before he spoke.

"Oh, I can't say I know that much about the way Moses is running things. He don't count me enough to tell me nothing. How am I going to tell people something I don't know my own self?"

Joshua stood there for a minute feeling them stoning him with evil thoughts. Then he turned to go.

"Well, I'll go tell Moses that you are coming. But you all got the wrong idea about things."

Joshua re-entered the tent of Moses and stood and waited for Moses to recognize him, the way he always did. Moses looked up from his writing. "What's the matter, Joshua?" he asked.

"My people! My people!"

"What's wrong this time, Joshua?"

"I reckon you're going to have to take your rod and do something for 'em or something to 'em, one. My people just won't do. That complaint committee is outside to see you. The people are grumbling again."

"Over what?" Moses asked with a touch of impatience.

"Excuse me, chief, for talking with my mouth wide open.

The people is mumbling and grumbling about something to eat."

"Tell them seventy Elders to come on in, Joshua. Maybe I can make 'em understand why we are out here, but sometimes I doubt it."

The committee of seventy filed into the tent and stood gloomily behind Moses. He turned his chair to face them.

"All right, get it told. What's the matter now?"

"Moses, we're hungry."

"There's plenty manna. I see to that every day."

"But we're tired of manna. We want something else to eat."

"Why don't you find it then? Nobody is stopping you, are they?"

"We can't find nothing around here."

"If you can't find anything except the manna which I provide for you, how do you expect me to find anything?"

The committee began to boil like a pot. The spokesman whirled and made gestures with his hands. They acted out desperation, despair and futility. "Lawd, listen at that man! Here he done took and brought us out of Egypt where we was getting along just fine. We remember the nice fresh fish we used to get back there in Egypt every day. Nice sweet-tasting little pan-fish and a person could get all they could eat for five cents. Unhunh! and didn't we used to eat 'em, too. And the nice fresh cucumbers, and the watermelons, and the leeks and the onions and plenty garlic for seasoning! You could get a decent meal most anywhere before you could turn around. And now look where we're at—out here in this hungry wilderness with our souls all dried up and nothing but this manna before our eyes. Oh, we wish we had of died down there in Egypt instead of coming off like a pack of fools."

Moses listened until the end and then he said, "I'm sure sorry for you all, but not because you are crying after the fleshpots of Egypt. I'm sorry for you because you don't feel hungry nowhere else except in your bellies. You have lost sight of your high destiny in your scramble after food. You hate me at times for not being more interested in your stomachs than in your hearts. You are looking at this thing from one viewpoint and I'm looking at it from another. Here I am struggling to make a great nation out of you and you are

worrying about fried fish and cucumbers! Do you see me eating anything like that?"

"We don't know what you eat while you shut yourself up inside this great big old tent."

"Where do you reckon I would get it from?"

"Oh, you got that right hand of yours and that rod, ain't you? You got quails and this manna and water and a whole heap of other things with it. You could give us anything we wanted if you would."

"I see. You trust my ability, but you don't trust my judgment."

"We don't mean it that way exactly. But it's hard to love freedom if it keeps you hungry."

Moses saw a certain pleasure in Aaron's eye so he said, "Aaron, you could help out the people in a case like this."

"Oh, they know that if I had the power you got they wouldn't want for a thing. I been all through what they been through and I got some sympathy for 'em. They all know that."

"I see, Aaron. I see just what you mean, and it ain't what they think you mean, but we'll come to that part later on. Now, you Elders of the people, somebody done got you in the notion that I can get anything you want to eat and drink at a moment's notice. Supposing I could. But that ain't the question. I don't want to spend all my time and strength pulling miracles for the sake of your bellies. I'm here to make a nation out of you all, if you will work with me."

"Lord, the man come talking about making us a nation when we ain't even got garlic to season with! We want something besides this manna to eat."

Moses stood up and looked down on the committee and said, "It's a good thing your cattle can't talk or they would slur you as you do me, for your lack of interest in fodder. Well, go on home and I'll stop planning the future for you for the moment to satisfy your lusts. But it is getting a little tiresome, this always assailing me about trifles. You committeemen never come to help me, you come to complain."

They started on out and Moses let them go, all but Aaron. When they were alone Moses said to him, "Aaron, you ain't as helpful as you might be. I been noticing it right along.

Here I made you the high priest, and gave you all the pomp and regalia that I could but you still don't seem to feel your responsibility the way I would like."

Aaron fingered the jewelled girdle about his loins and stroked his beard. "Oh, well," he said, walking to the door, "maybe there's a lot of things you don't understand. Maybe sometime you'll find out you can't dog people around and dominate 'em as you see fit. That you can't use other folks for your stepping stones and then throw 'em away." Aaron flourished on out and around the bend of the road and left Moses in deep thought. Moses made two decisions and called Joshua.

"Joshua, get ready. I am going to send a representative from each tribe to spy out the Promised Land and you are going. Call a meeting of the Elders and find out who the other eleven men are by tomorrow night. I want this pilgrimage to end before long."

XXXVIII

THE OTHER DECISION Moses kept to himself. But with his plan all formed he felt better. The spies would come back with a favorable report. They were bound to. It was late August and all of the fruit trees would be loaded down. He had been in Canaan at this time of the year and knew what it looked like. They were bound to be favorably impressed. Then a swift, hard military thrust and the journey would be over. The Israelites would have a home, a God and a name. He would miss the mountains of Midian with Jethro's sheep trotting before him. The long exchange of thoughts with Jethro and the little comforts and delights with Zipporah. Jethro was getting mighty old. Maybe Moses would get back in time to spend a year or two with him. He hoped so very much. That night while the people feasted on quail which Moses had brought in to them on a big wind, Moses sat on the side of the mountain and fought with himself. He asked himself, "Why not go on home and leave these people to do whatever they want to? Aaron is stupid and full of conceit like all little men suddenly elevated to places of power. But if he wants to lead, why not go on and lead your life and let him lead? You brought them out of Egypt with the might of your right hand and you have done this thing up to now. Here they are in striking distance of Canaan with an army and with laws and statutes. Why not quietly go on home?" It was a tough battle, but Moses came down the mountain in the morning and went on with his plans for taking Canaan. For a period during the night he had had a vision of freedom but morning found him back in harness. He was a man who had been called.

Forty days passed and the spies came back. They came back with a bunch of grapes that it took two men to carry and they brought melons and cucumbers and various fruits and vegetables and the people were fired to go where things like that were growing.

Then they heard about the people they had to fight before they could own the land and another wind swept the camp. It

made no difference that two of the spies sent out said that they had a good chance to win. Not even the word of Joshua, the military leader of Israel, could talk down the fear inspired by the other ten.

"The land is rich," Joshua and Caleb told them. Caleb said, "All we got to do is to go take it. It's right there for us, ain't that right, Joshua?"

"It certainly is. We could lay down a hard campaign of two weeks and own every inch of Canaan from end to end. All it needs is some good hard fighting before they get time to double-teen us."

Another spy said, "Don't you all listen to Joshua and Caleb. Them two is crazy in the head. Just listen at them now and all of us will be dead. Them people live in stone houses and even the towns got walls around 'em. We couldn't never take 'em. And just look how many nations we got to fight! There's the Amalekites, and they live in the southern part there and they are stronger than they was when we fought 'em a few years back."

"But we are stronger too," Joshua cut in. "Don't forget that. And then another thing, we was just as green as grass when we whipped 'em last time. We ought to mop up for 'em this time. Shucks! They ain't no trouble."

"Don't tell me they ain't no trouble. And then there's some mountains all around and they just full of fighting folks. There's the Hittites and the Amorites and the Jebusites and, man, those folks can fight. And then over along the seacoast those Canaanites, and there sure is plenty of 'em to fight too."

Caleb said, "Aw, let's go on up and take the place. We can beat all those little nations one by one. Half a day to a nation and take that place. It sure is pretty country. Then we will have a place of our own that we can rule over and do as we please."

"Folks, don't you let Joshua and Caleb fool nobody. You ain't heard the worst yet. Do you know we passed through one place where everybody was giants? Yesirree, those men of Anak are sure enough big men. Why, they are so big we look like grasshoppers to ourselves beside them and that ain't the worst of it, we looked like grasshoppers to them, too. Don't

you let Caleb and Joshua fool you to run up against those people. Wouldn't nothing be left of Israel but a grease spot."

A few men wanted to follow Moses, Caleb and Joshua, but the big majority got scared and pulled back. They got so scared that they got mad.

"From one thing to another, that Moses keeps us in a strut. If it ain't one thing it's another. Now he wants us to go get ourselves killed just to make him a King and we just ain't agoing to do it. That man don't mean us no good at all. Let's go on back to Egypt where we belong, but first thing let's kill him for bringing us off."

Moses heard the mad clamor of the multitudes and knew the danger that he faced. Men circled him where he stood, snarling like animals. All they needed was a leader with courage enough to cross that small bare circle of ground that separated them from Moses. "Now is your time, Aaron," Moses thought to himself. "Now is your time if you only had the courage to seize it. But you are a snarling hyena, waiting for some lion to make your kill for you." But never for a moment did Moses forget that some unknown might find the spark that would destroy him, and more than that, destroy his mission. But in spite of it all he was cool enough to note the shuffle of the grass in the wind and the little dance of dust in a whirlwind. He realized that he was in great danger of being taken for a mere man where he stood. While in the Tabernacle of the Congregation they could scarcely think of him apart from the mysteries. So he turned suddenly and walked in that direction, wondering if he would live long enough to make it. And the clamoring mob, led by their Princes, followed him.

He invited the Princes and the Elders to enter and told the people to wait outside. He entered last and faced the angry Princes and Elders for a full minute in silence then fell on his face in the door.

A great gasp went up from the Princes and the people outside crowded back from the door in some nameless fear. The figure of Moses on the ground did not look helpless somehow. It inspired more terror than it would have even with the uplifted hand. Everybody shrunk away as far as they could.

Old Miriam outside crept forward a little in front of the

others and then backed away as fast as she could. Then she broke a silence of several months.

"Something awful will happen from this," she whispered from a throat so dry that it rattled. "It is a bad sign. He will lift that right hand and Israel will suffer terribly. It is better to do as he says."

The people and the Princes stood back and gazed on Moses. Not a man in Israel would have touched him. Their weapons were frozen to their hands, though the wish for his death was in the minds of many Princes and Elders. Moses sensed his victory and slowly stood erect.

Moses stood up and swept the nation with his eyes and they were scared.

"Lord," Moses said, "what kind of cowards are these You sent me to lead? You bring them out of slavery in Egypt with a high hand. You take care of them in the wilderness. You speak to them from Sinai and point out a beautiful rich country which You tell them is theirs. All they need to do is to show fight to a bunch of scrub nations and take the country and cease their wanderings in the wilderness. But will they do it, Lord? No! They are cowards. And none of these slave-minded cowards shall enter the land You promised them. They shall wander in this wilderness until they are all dead. That is, all those who are grown enough to know what they are talking about. Their carcasses shall rot in this wilderness. I am not talking about Joshua and Caleb, Lord. I am talking about these others. I can make something out of their children, but not out of them. They have the essence of greatness in them and I shall fight them and fight myself and the world and even God for them. They shall not refuse their destiny. In this wilderness shall they be consumed, and here they shall die."

When the people thought over-night about what Moses had said, they were more scared of him than they were of the fighting nations. So they got up soon in the morning and went up on the mountain and told Moses that they were ready to fight now, and they were willing to acknowledge to the fact that they talked too much the day before. But Moses told them, "It won't do you no good to come around talking about fighting today, because that ain't in my plans. You're

just breaking into my arrangements to be starting any war today. Go on home, all of you. The Lord ain't helping you do no fighting today. You go beyond that mountain and tackle those Amalekites and Canaanites and you'll get your whipping because I'm not going and the Ark of the Covenant is not going and Joshua is not going, so if you want to be hard-headed and go jump on those people, go right ahead."

But some of the Princes told the people to come on and fight, because, they argued, if they won it would prove that they didn't need Moses as much as they thought they did. In fact, if they won they could cut loose from him and God and everything else and be so free till they were foolish. So they went on to fight and the battle went against them from the beginning and they had to run it out for the most part, those who were able to run.

Therefore next day Moses turned the hosts of Israel back into the wilderness to serve their forty years and grow men and women in place of slaves. To wander and to fall down and to die in strange places where nobody lived and where nobody would live again for thousands of years. The Voice had said to take a nation across the Jordan, and the generation which he had brought out of Egypt had failed him. "The third generation will feel free and noble. Then I can mold a nation. Forty years is a long, long time, Joshua, but the Voice commanded me to lead." And Moses was very sad.

XXXIX

THEY WANDERED in the wilderness and wandered and sickened and died and gave birth and revolted again and again. So they came in their wanderings to Kadesh which is in the desert of Zin.

Moses was sitting in his tent writing when he looked up and saw Miriam standing over him. Everything about her was asserting itself that day. Her rusty gray hair that used to be a dry-looking red; her pale eye-lashes that had always been that way and her drooping jowls and shrunken-up figure.

"Well, Miss Miriam," Moses said, making a place for her to sit down, "this sure is a surprise, you coming to pay me a visit."

"Naw, it ain't," Miriam said without taking her eyes out of Moses' face nor changing a muscle in her own. "Nothing don't never surprise you. You know everything beforehand. You know, but you let things happen for reasons."

Moses looked at the mask of her face. It looked like nothing had moved in it for years. Nothing had gone in its portals and nothing had come out. It seemed to have finished with everything and just to have been waiting on time.

"Moses, I come here this evening to ask you to let me die."

"Why, Miss Miriam!"

"I ask you kindly, please, Moses, to let me die."

"What makes you think you got to get *my* consent to die?"

"Cause I know I can't die without it. That right hand of yours—it's got light in front of it and darkness behind. Moses, I come in the humblest way I know how to let you know I done quit straining against you. I done quit putting my poor little strength up against yours. I'm just a beat old woman and I want to die."

"But, Miss Miriam, you ain't had time to enjoy your freedom yet. You ought to want to live to enjoy it and to see Israel a nation."

"This freedom is more than a notion, Moses. It's a good thing. It's bound to be a good thing 'cause everybody wants it. But maybe I didn't know what to do with it, 'cause I ain't

been so happy. That ain't what I come to talk about, Moses. I come here to ask you to please let me die."

"That's something nobody ain't never asked me before. That ain't something that I can pass on like the vessels before the altar, Miriam. God got to tell you that and he is seldom known to even do that."

"I want to go on back home and lay down, Moses. Is you going to let me die or not?"

"Miss Miriam, you sure your mind is all right and everything?"

"Yes, I'm real sure, and I know I want to die. I reckon I done tackled something too big for me and it done throwed me like a bucking horse. I been through living for years. I just ain't dead yet."

"How long do you figure you been through living, Miss Miriam?"

"Ever since I spent that week outside the camp when, er— when I was a leper. When I was unclean and had the leprosy and looked at myself all over and I was shut out from everything and from the living. That was when I got to thinking with only certain places in my head and I got to fleeing all over with fear. And you showed me your hand, that shiny right hand of yours, every night while I was outside the camp there in the dark. You kept it held up over my head and I'd run and run all night long but I couldn't get away from it. You see, I was a prophetess back in Egypt and I had power, that is what the people told me, anyhow. So when you didn't do to suit me, I made up my mind to fight your power with mine. But I found out I was no more against you than a grain of sand against a mountain, because you beat me and then you bottled me up inside of my own body and you been keeping me in jail inside myself ever since. Turn me loose, Moses, so I can go on and die."

"I can't stop you from dying, Miss Miriam. This notion you got must come from a long way off because it is so strange."

"Moses, I'm going home to lay down to die. Don't let me see your hand over me like it's been every night for years. I don't need to drag my bones to Canaan to lay 'em down. This wilderness will do if you are through with me."

"Just what did you want me to do about your case, Miss Miriam?"

"You know just as well as I do, Moses. Just let your right hand fall from over me. You still punishing me about that wife of yours, Moses? Don't hold me here no more. Open your fingers, Moses, just a little bit and let the husks of a weak old woman escape out past 'em."

"Do you think that I am God, Miriam?"

"Indeed, I don't know, Moses. That's what I been trying to figure out for years. Sometimes I think you're just that Egyptian Prince that took up with us for some reason or other. Then again I would agree with some of them others that you was an Ethiopian. Once or twice I thought you was the sacred bull of Egypt with the known markings but the unknown history. Sometimes I thought God's voice in the tabernacle sounded mighty much like yours. But ever since you punished me with leprosy, I knew you had power uncommon to man. I been knowing ever since you healed me and took me back into the congregation that you wasn't through with me. You love that woman and we hurt her. You meant for us to punish and to punish well, didn't you? So you locked me up inside myself and left me to wait on your hour. Moses, ain't I done punished enough?"

"How do you know all of this?" Moses asked and studied her while she answered him.

"Oh, I don't know how I know, but I do. When I found out I couldn't do no more in Israel than you let me, I made up my mind to go on off and die, but I found out I couldn't even do that unless you let me. I saw all them people dead in the wilderness from snake-bites and disease and one thing and another and I looked at their bones and wished it was me. I waited and I waited, but death always avoided me. Aaron was waiting for the crown in Canaan, but I just been waiting to die. Now, I ask you please to leave me go. I done tried to be as stiff as you was stout, but I found out I got to come ask you to die. You knew it all along and you been waiting for me to come."

"I certainly didn't expect you to come here to say what you did."

"No, Moses, don't put me off like that. Talk to me straight.

I come here to you for something and I don't mean to go till you tell me yes or no. I don't mean to leave here until I get what I come after."

The repulsive old woman was tragic. She had been sent on a mission as he had been sent, and the burden had torn and twisted her. She had been petty, envious and mean, but she had served. But then fate had provided no compensations for making her a bearer. Miriam had lived on hopes where other women lived on memories. And that was bound to do something to her. She was not sent to be what she wanted to be, so she had wasted herself procuring pangs for people who had. Moses looked at her and through her with pity. She seemed to hold everything about herself very still until he got through looking. Then she got up and moved to the door.

"Much obliged, Moses. Now I can go."

"Much obliged for what, Miriam?"

"I felt your right hand fall from over me. I'm going on back to my tent now and rest. It's no sense in something like me being alive. I am going to die now, Moses. Keep that right hand of yours down."

Moses didn't say anything more. He just looked at her and watched her go. She went off a little brisk. Her face almost moved. She seemed to see something with her eyes. She made deep prints with her feet.

Miriam went back and laid down just like she said she would, and the next morning they found her dead with a bitter twist on her mask of a face.

Moses called a halt and told the people what it meant to lose a patriot like Miriam. The young ones were told what the old ones had forgotten—all about those days back in Egypt when the house of the prophetess Miriam was the meeting place of all those who were willing to work for freedom. How she had gathered folks together by twos and threes and changed weakness into resolution. Her dust weighed as much as all Israel. The people all listened and thought it was a great speech. They even mourned when Moses ordered them to mourn for thirty days. They held a great crying for Miriam. So Moses buried her with a big ceremony and ordered a great tomb of rocks to be piled up over her grave.

On the way back from the funeral Moses considered the life and death of Miriam. She was a woman, but he never had been able to quite think of her as such. What with her lack of female beauty and female attractions, and her loveless life with one end sunk in slavery and the other twisted and snarled in freedom. He wondered which had hurt her most. He thought how the threads of his life had gotten tangled with the threads of this homely slave woman. He wondered if she had not been born if he would have been standing here in the desert of Zin. In fact, he wondered if the Exodus would have taken place at all. How? If she had not come to the palace gates to ask for him and to claim him as a brother, would he have left Egypt as he did? He doubted it. He never would have known Jethro, nor loved Zipporah, nor known the shiny mountain, nor led out a nation with a high hand, nor suffered as he had done and was doomed to keep on doing. A mighty thing had happened in the world through the stumblings of a woman who couldn't see where she was going. She needed a big tomb so the generations that come after would know her and remember.

Well, Miriam was gone. There was Aaron left and himself. And there was the desert and the wilderness and the forty years and the people. This was the second going-out. He had led out Pharaoh's slaves. Now he must lead out a free and singing people from inside the cringing slaves. He turned from burying Miriam and set his face grimly for the task.

Then a running messenger came from Jethro telling Moses that he must come. Jethro was sick and wanted Moses' company. He mounted his white stallion in the night and rode hard back towards Midian, and was there on the third day.

The old chieftain was lying on his couch. On his face was a great stare that had not changed for days. But he saw Moses standing before him and smiled.

"Lift up his bed and carry him outdoors," Moses ordered at once.

They bore him out and Moses ordered them to place him under a tree with his face to the mountain and then he sat down beside him and touched his feeble hand. Life seemed to come back into the sunken face at once.

"That was right, Moses. That was right and good."

"Lying shut-in was no place for you, Jethro. You are a man without bounds."

"My eyes and my mind keep taking me where my old legs can't keep up. My old age is burdensome for that reason, now."

He rested awhile then he said, "I knew you were worked to death, and I wouldn't have sent for you except that I had to ask you a question, and I was afraid I couldn't wait for you to come."

"You know I would have been miserable if you hadn't sent for me—if you hadn't let me know in some way."

"Well, Moses, you never said so in too many words, but your love for me had something to do with your going back into Egypt to lead the Israelites, didn't it?"

"Perhaps it did, Jethro, but perhaps it was my destiny anyway."

The old man reached out and caught hold of Moses' hand and drew him closer. He lifted himself up and held the face of Moses between his hands and searched his face with his eyes.

"You don't hold it against me, Moses, do you?"

"Hold it against you? No, Jethro."

"I worried you so about my wish. You might have refused the call and been much happier here. Often and again I have blamed myself for urging you."

"You shouldn't have felt that way. You said yourself it was my destiny."

"Your friendship didn't shrink away from me in the least?"

"Not in the least, Jethro. Your friendship would have been worth ten times more."

Jethro embraced Moses with his skinny old arms and lay back smiling.

"I knew better all the time but I had to ask. If I had another night and day, you could tell me about the Israelites and the work. But as it is, about all you can do is to cover up my face for me. I didn't want anybody to do it but you."

That night the family and the tribe mourned around Jethro's body and the next day Moses buried him in the path that led up the side of the mountain and planted a grove of

trees to honor him. On the seventh day he set out for the camp of Israel again, sadder and more bereaved than he had ever been in his life before, or was ever to be again.

He wished that he could order a great crying in Israel for Jethro. He wished that the nation could know how much Jethro had meant to it. But he knew misunderstanding would come out of his act and so he mourned alone. He must keep on doing them good on the sly.

The years went on doing their slow drag over Israel and left it fat and strong. When Joshua marched out against a people he won. There was no longer famine and thirst among his army and always, now, the hosts moved nearer the Jordan, and Israel grew conscious of its might.

So at Jeshurun, the people offered Moses a kingly crown. "You brought our old folks out of slavery and you have led us from one degree of grace to another until now we are folks wherever our feet fall on dry land. We want to turn you some humble thanks so it ain't nothing but right for you to be our King and live rich. You done worked forty years for us for nothing. Therefore we took all the crowns that we beat off of the heads of Kings that we conquered and melted them all down and made them into one crown, something that's fitten for your conquering head. It ain't much, Moses, but it will give you some idea of how we feel."

Moses stood up and thanked everybody very kindly. But he went on to say that he wasn't sure that people ought to have Kings at all. It's pretty hard to find a man who wouldn't weaken under the strain of power and get biggity and over-bearing. He himself might not be any better than nobody else if he had the chance. So they better let this King business rest for a while. "This freedom is a funny thing," he told them. "It ain't something permanent like rocks and hills. It's like manna; you just got to keep on gathering it fresh every day. If you don't, one day you're going to find you ain't got none no more. I'm getting kind of old and I been with you like you say since back in Egypt. It's been kind of tough some-times, and maybe I neglected a lot of things I could have done off by myself. But if you just keep free and be a fine nation of folks I'll feel like I bought something with my life.

You done got free of Pharaoh and the Egyptian oppressors, be careful you don't raise up none among yourselves." Moses left with drooping heart.

The people had missed the whole point of his forty-odd years of work. He loved freedom and justice with a fierce love and he wanted Israel to be free and just. All that he had done to them and for them was intended to bring them to his view-point. And here they were wanting to be like other halted people that they touched along the way. They despised their high density. They misunderstood him so far that they even offered him a crown! As if he could not have had that from the very first. He could have led them to Midian and with Jethro to help him, set up a kingdom within a few weeks after leaving Egypt. He need not have experienced a wilderness, and deserts and hunger and thirst and misunderstanding and sacrifice to wear a crown. The hem of the sky ran in close around him and oppressed him. It took a long time to thrust it out again. Well, anyway, he could hope. He had produced the physical base for greatness.

These young Hebrews were something. They were bound to get somewhere if only they fell into the right hands after he was gone. And that put him to thinking back. The mood stayed on him for several days. Then the cloud of fire lifted from above the tabernacle and moved the Israelites to the plain at the foot of Mount Hor. And it rested there so Israel camped awhile.

As soon as they had gotten settled down, Aaron sent a del-egation of Levites to Moses to protest a decision Moses had made about the services. Moses listened until they were through and then he said, "The words you have brought here in your mouths are not your own. Somebody else made them and loaded your mouth up with 'em. Go back and tell Aaron to come and tell me what he's got to say his own self."

Aaron came, but he took his own time about it. He ex-plained to Moses that his beard-boy was looking after his beard so he could not come right away.

"Your beard-boy?" Moses exclaimed.

"Now, Moses, you know the Lord has given me as a sign of special favor the longest and the finest whiskers in all Israel. And me being who I am I don't really have time to do for it

like I should. So I had to sign up one of the young men around the altar to wait on my beard and tend to it. I give him the responsibility and if it gets out of shape and careless looking he'll have to suffer for it. The Lord don't want His gifts to be despised."

It all sank into the mind of Moses and he thought it over well before he spoke.

"Aaron, do you think that if you had of stayed back there in Egypt that the Lord would have bothered about whether your whiskers was greased or not?"

"We don't need to waste time over that because I ain't back there in Egypt. A smart man like me couldn't be kept down like that nohow. I got too much brains for people. You don't meet my kind every day. I let folks think they are using me for a tool when all the time I'm using them for a step-ladder."

Moses felt an acid wind from Aaron's words blowing across his face. He didn't need to look at the man to read him. He had been reading him for forty years or so. He didn't need to look for interpretation. He knew the meaning before he heard the words. So he went on to conclusions.

"Aaron, we're here at Mount Hor—not too far from the Jordan, but still a little distance off. I'm going up in the mountain to ask the Lord what He wants me to do next. Would you like to go up with me this time?"

"That's all goodness been begging righteous to do all these forty years. I should have been up there to meet God at Sinai. It made me look like a fool before Israel. The high priest his own self can't go to see God!"

"Well, you can go with me this time, Aaron. We won't have no hard words about all those other times you didn't go. But if God had of asked for you, Aaron, I would have come straight back and told you."

"I hope you would have, Moses."

"All right, come on and let's go. But let's take your oldest boy Eleazar along with us. God might want to see him and talk with him, too. No telling, he might make a fine priest when he gets a little older."

"I ain't got the least doubt about that, Moses. I done my best to bring him up right. He'd look noble in the robes, too—after I am gone."

The three men went up the mountainside together. Aaron and Moses walked a little ahead and Eleazar followed respectfully behind. Moses wore a short robe belted in at the waist with his traditional short sword at his side. He walked with his rod in his left hand, and now and then he helped Aaron over rough places with his right. They went up and round the mountain and then up. The huge camp of Israel below them began to take on a pattern. Moses saw that Aaron had stopped stroking his beard and was panting hard. So he paused and turned to Eleazar and told him, "Eleazar, you wait here until I call you. Your father is going higher up. He's got to listen to God."

Moses could see the tired old shoulders of Aaron stiffen with pride at that. He almost stood erect. They traveled on up the mountain for some time yet. Nobody tried to talk because both of them realized it was useless then. At last Moses stopped before a cool grotto in the mountainside with a rude stone seat inside. Aaron practically dragged himself to the seat and panted a long time before he could measure out his breath.

"Do you always have to climb this high to talk with God?" Aaron asked when he got his breath back.

"Higher than this, Aaron. Sometimes men have to push through the sky to reach Him. We stopped here to rest a minute, that's all."

Aaron groaned out loud.

"Supposing we talk awhile then, Aaron. I'm the leader of Israel and you're the high priest and we ain't had our heads together since way back there, Aaron, before Sinai."

"That's right, but it ain't no fault of mine. I been kept back in the background and I been kept in the dark about things. You don't never tell me nothing. Joshua is the only one that gets any information around here."

"Well, Canaan is right close now and we ain't got too much time to talk and plan. You know things won't be the same over there that it is out here in the wilderness."

"Don't I know it? I been waiting for it for forty years. I'm getting pretty old, but I think I can make it. It won't be so hard over there as it is in the wilderness nohow. Then Israel can reward me for my labors."

"But the Lord said, Aaron, that all the old folks who came out of Egypt had to die in the wilderness, all except Joshua and Caleb."

"Oh, I never took much stock in that, Moses. I'm not the people, you know. I believe I'm going to make it and when I do, I mean to be folks over there. The thought of it has kept me living or else I would have gone like Miriam. She fretted herself to death about who was going to get us there. That was foolish. I let who can get us there, then we can see about things after that. I know how to handle people."

"You think so, Aaron?"

"I sure do, unless I'm mighty mistaken." Aaron sat stroking his beard with a little gesture that was smug and flourishing at the same time. He knew he was important and he knew his clothes were fine. He looked just as satisfied as the snake that lives under God's foot-stool.

"Yet and still, Aaron, you have never done anything that I could not have prevented if I had wanted to and you never done a thing that I didn't undo."

"It's not too late, Moses. We're born but we ain't dead yet."

Moses stood up suddenly and looked Aaron straight in the eye. Aaron unveiled his eyes for the first time in front of Moses since the law was given at Sinai. There was neither love nor mercy in his look.

"You got your power and your brains, Moses, but you ain't never made the people happy like you said."

"I never said I'd make them happy people. I promised to make them great. Anyway, happiness is not something you can catch and lock up in a vault like wealth. Happiness is nothing but everyday living seen through a veil."

"Well, I can give 'em what they want better than you ever did, and I'll show you when we get over there. You can't scare people away from what they want over there. We won't need you any more. My time is coming just like I always knowed it would."

He gave Moses a look full of triumph and old hatred.

"Take off those robes, Aaron," Moses said shortly.

Aaron acted as if he didn't hear Moses right away. Then he gave Moses a scornful look. Then he chuckled slightly and

crossed his legs and smoothed the skirts of his priestly robe.

"Aaron, take off those robes."

"I ain't going to do it, Moses. God put these robes on me and He'll have to be the one to take 'em off. I know you been begrudging 'em to me for a powerful long time. I just wouldn't step down for you."

"God didn't put no robes on you, Aaron. I put 'em on you and I'm taking them off, because they don't fit you."

"You mean God never called me down there in Egypt at all?"

"No, Aaron."

"You told me He did."

"Yes, I did, Aaron. I thought I needed you for the big job I had to do because you were of the Hebrews. I did need you too, but you didn't do the job I picked out for you."

"You always held me back. You—"

"No, you got the wrong idea altogether. You held yourself back. You didn't think about service half as much as you did about getting served, Aaron. Your tiny horizon never did get no bigger, so you mistook a spotlight for the sun."

Aaron began to crumble. He didn't look at Moses any more. He began to finger his garments in different places all over himself and to dwindle and shrink.

"Those robes don't belong to you, Aaron. I planned them for a bigger man. Take 'em on off."

"What would I do without my robes?" Aaron wailed in anguish. "They're mine! They belong to the high priest. How do I know that God didn't call me? You said so yourself."

Moses snatched Aaron to his feet and Aaron looked into the eyes of Moses and lifted off his high headpiece and set it down on a stone in a soft, regretful way. Then piece by piece he shed his robes to his last undergarment and stood with his old corded arms and legs protruding from the short garment. Moses stooped and collected all of the rich regalia and laid them carefully on a rock. Aaron watched him without daring to move his feet out of his tracks until Moses turned back to him again.

"Aaron."

"Yes, Moses," Aaron whimpered.

"Aaron, you can't go over yonder with the people."

"Why, Moses? You know I always done the best I could."

"No. Not for the people, Aaron. You are blind. You didn't see Miriam and her face. You didn't see the graveyards in the wilderness. You didn't see the significance of the Ark of the Covenant nor the Tent of Testimony. All you saw was the gold and silver vessels and the robes and the power that goes with it. No, Aaron, you can't go over there and make a fool out of Israel's graves."

"What am I going to do then, Moses? You can't leave me looking like this. How can I go back before Israel?"

"You can't go back before Israel, Aaron."

Aaron looked hard in Moses' face and fell to his knees.

"Moses! Moses, please. I'll be a lot of help to you from now on. Moses, spare me, if you please."

Moses looked way off across the plain where the tents of Israel stretched for miles and held his eyes for a long pause. Then he said, "I haven't spared myself, Aaron. I had to quit being a person a long time ago, and I had to become a thing, a tool, an instrument for a cause. I wasn't spared, Aaron. No."

"No, and you didn't spare my two sons at Sinai—just for dancing and making a little ceremony before a god of Egypt which we had always known. My poor boys—you killed them!"

"I didn't kill your boys at Sinai, Aaron, though I know that you have always accused me of it, and hated me. But you know just as well as I do why they died. What they signified had to die if Israel was to be great."

"Let me be high priest over there, Moses, in the big new tabernacle with—"

"No, Aaron."

Aaron crawled to the knees of Moses and clasped them. "Moses, looks like pity and mercy would—"

"Aaron, the future of Israel is higher than pity and mercy. And why should I spare you? I did not spare the first-born. I did not spare Pharaoh. I did not spare myself. I did not spare my wife and my friend. Jethro is dead and I might have spent several more happy years with him instead of out in the wilderness leading a people and being reviled for doing what was best instead of what was popular. No, Aaron, nothing and nobody has been spared to make this nation great. And since

you wouldn't give yourself in any other way, Aaron, you will have to do something for Israel by denial."

"Moses, you don't need to take me along. Just let me go up here in the mountain and let me shift for myself. Please, Moses, don't kill me."

"You don't mean that, Aaron. You mean to double back and appeal to the people to back you up on account of your age and place. No, Aaron, fifty years of work can't be destroyed to give you a tomb in Canaan. God called you on Mount Hor. The tomb of Aaron the first high priest of Israel will be huge and fine, high up in this noble mountain. God has built you a pyramid greater than Pharaoh, and generations of Israelites will make pilgrimages to the grave of Aaron, the patriot. God will remember your sacrifice and guard your memories."

The knife descended and Aaron's old limbs crumpled in the dust of the mountain. Moses looked down on him and wept. He remembered so much from way back. "Is this my brother? Is this pitiful old carcass blood of my blood? Maybe this is me myself in other moods. Who am I to judge him?" Moses looked down the mountain at tented Israel and shook his head. "I have made a nation, but at a price." Then he buried Aaron and marked the place. "Poor Aaron, he died so hard for God!" Then he picked up the robes and walked firmly down the mountain to where Eleazar waited.

"Put on these robes, Eleazar. You are high priest now." The young man seized the robes eagerly. Then he halted for a moment and looked back up the mountain the way Moses had come down. He looked back the second time and then he looked into the face of Moses and began to undress himself. He dressed himself in the priestly scarlet and purple and set the breastplate of twelve stones upon his bosom. After that he never looked back again. He straightened his figure to set his garments well and fell in beside Moses and they started down the mountain side by side.

They descended to the camp and the people looked at Eleazar in the robes of Aaron, so Moses told them all, "God called Aaron in the mountain. You must build a big high tomb over him, and you must mourn for him thirty days. He was denied many pleasures for your sake."

XL

ISRAEL met nations and fought and conquered and moved on towards Canaan. Moses lifted his rod and made a way out of no way when it was needed and they moved on. They fought the giants of Bashan and conquered and moved on till one day they camped again on the River Jordan where their forefathers had been before.

"When are we crossing over?" That is what everybody wanted to know. "We are here! When do we cross over?"

Moses ordered Israel to camp and rest for two weeks. The battle against Bashan had been hard. Everybody needed a rest. So he sat in his tent day by day and wrote in his journal. The wanderings of Israel were there set down by his hand.

Joshua kept running in and out for first one thing and then another, so Moses told him to have a seat.

"Joshua, we been here at the river around two weeks, ain't that right?"

"Yes, sir, it sure is."

"How is the sick and the afflicted coming on?"

"If you talking about the soldiers, all them that was going to die are already dead. The rest of 'em will get well. Everything is in good shape, considering. Anyhow, chief, we ain't the same folks we was when we viewed the Jordan last time. We're a people now."

"It looks that way, Joshua. But when you was down at the Jordan last time you was such a lad of a boy that your moustache did not show. Your hair is all mixed with gray this time."

"Yeah, that's so, but I still don't feel no strain in a campaign. I'm able."

"That's good, because you are going to need everything you got in you on the other side. And that brings me to a subject I been wanting to take up with you a long time."

"What is it, Moses? You know I'm always ready to listen when you talk."

"Joshua, I'm old. I ain't getting old. I'm already old.

Supposing the Lord was to call me. What would become of Israel?"

"I'd do the very best I could in the same way that you would do it if you was there. But I don't want to be no secondhand ruler because I'm a first class fighting man. You must live and cross over and govern us till the rod just naturally falls out of your hand. Everybody in Israel is expecting you to be there."

"But sooner or later I'll have to go and you will have to govern in every way, Joshua, because there won't be nobody else to do it. Eleazar is a good and obedient servant, but that's all.

"Anyway, we done passed a lot of mileposts and we done come to the place where we need a fighting leader more than anything else. Israel has got her laws and her God. All she needs now is land and it takes fighting to get that."

"You know I'll fight, don't you?"

"Oh, yes, you're a general among generals. But now when Israel ain't fighting, you got to do something about governing the people. Now one thing I want you to get in your head: You can't have a state of individuals. Everybody just can't be allowed to do as they please. I love liberty and I love freedom so I started off giving everybody a loose rein. But I soon found out that it wouldn't do. A great state is a well-blended mash of something of all of the people and all of none of the people. You understand. The liquor of statecraft is distilled from the mash you got. How can a nation speak with one voice if they are not one? Don't forget, now. If you do, you encourage all the stupid but greedy and ambitious to sprout like toadstools and that's the end of right and reason in the state. Coddling and wheedling is not going to stop these destroyers. To a haughty belly, kindness is hard to swallow and harder to digest."

"I won't forget. I saw what you went through with some in Israel."

"And don't let the people take up too many habits from the nations they come in contact with and throw away what they got from God. They are blessed. Nobody else ever got a straight talk from God like we have. Don't let 'em throw it away. You know, Joshua, it ain't everybody who can go right

up and talk with God. And then, too, it's less than that who can talk with God and then bring back the right word from the talk. It is so easy to mix up what you are wishing with what God is saying. You might not get another good interpreter. You better hold on to what you got."

"Yes, sir, I'll do just like you tell me, as far as I am able."

"I got every faith in your good intentions, son. Just do the best you can. And, Joshua, patience and understanding helps out a whole lot. What we been trying to do all these forty-odd years was to channel the intentions of men. We got to fix their intentions. I'm wondering if the doings of the best of us will ever be good, but we can give 'em intentions to fumble their way back to God."

They talked on for some time. Then Joshua observed, "Moses, we been through thick and thin since we pulled out of Egypt that night. You seen plenty hard times, but did you ever have any pleasure since you been with us? It didn't look like it to me, except for the little time your wife was with us."

"The highest point of my feelings, Joshua, was when I spent the forty days on Mount Sinai talking with God and making plans for the people. And the highest feeling of that was when I had the laws in my hand ready to come down. The lowest feeling for me in these forty-odd years was when I come down and saw my Israel around that golden calf. I felt mighty sad, Joshua, when Jethro died. He meant more to me than anybody else in my whole life. Sometimes I feel he meant more to Israel than I do. He was a big man. A mighty big man if you look at him right. The worst time I ever had was when we fought those Amalekites. Oh! I was in plenty of trouble that time. We were out on a limb, Joshua, and we come pretty nigh getting sawed off. That fight showed me you were strong, Joshua, so it was worth it all right."

"Yes, that was a tight fight. Something like the monkey and the bulldog. The monkey told his bossman that he whipped the bulldog all right until it come time for him to sit down. Then he told his bossman he might have got the best of that bulldog, but the more he sit down, the more he doubted it."

"That puts me in mind of that tussle I had with Balaam and that mule of his. That was the best time I had on the whole trip up to now."

"Oh, I remember that time. He was that big hoodoo man from Pethor. He was coming down to put a curse on us and his mule turned around and sassed him good."

"Yes, that's the one. I fixed that old mule up for Balaam and made him say what he did. And then I fixed old Balaam up just like I did his mule and made him talk for our side."

"Seems like it was a donkey he was riding."

"That point don't seem important to me, Joshua, not from this distance. The point is, the fun I had with him. Here was old King Balak sicking Balaam on us to curse us and making big sacrifices of bulls and goats and things on seven altars at a time. Then when Balaam opens his mouth to curse us, out come a blessing on Israel. Old Balak got right in behind him for saying a blessing instead of a curse so Balaam moved the altars to another place and sacrificed seven times and got his mouth all full of curses again. But when he opened it, out come another blessing, and by that time Balaam was scratching his head and thinking sure enough. Well, the third time he tried it and got fooled, he made out he intended to do that all the time. But that was fun for me, outdoing Balaam like that. It was the first time since we left Egypt that I had a chance to strain against anybody that was trying to do something. It's good to sort of stretch yourself sometime. Power loves to meet power and strength loves strength."

"King Balak didn't know who he was sending Balaam up against. But the rest of us was scared, because we had heard all about how much power he had."

"He did have power, Joshua. He certainly did, but not enough."

"It's bad to have some power, but not enough."

"It certainly is, Joshua. It's a good thing for anybody to know just how much they have and when to stop."

Both men fell silent and thought on that awhile. Then Moses stood up.

"Joshua, I'm going up."

"Onto that mountain there—Mount Nebo?"

"Yes, Joshua. I love mountains. And then, too, I want to talk with God."

"Can I go up with you this time?"

"No, Joshua. I got to ask God some questions. You stay with the people. But you can go as far as the foot of the mountain with me and we can talk."

Moses took his rod and set out and the people saw him. And many feelings followed him as he went. Some thought ambitious thoughts and all of them thought awe. He halted at the very beginning of the climb and turned to Joshua.

"I know you want to follow me, Joshua, but not this time. If I don't come down in thirty days, you must come to search for me. God might call me up there, you know."

Moses put his arm around Joshua's shoulder briefly and began to climb.

Moses sat on the peak of Pisgah, looking both ways in time. He looked down first and saw the tents of Israel spread out like the pattern of a giant rug that moved and shimmered in the sunlight.

It was a sight such as the world had never seen before. A whole nation assembled together and under tents. Prominent in the front was the Tabernacle, the Tent of the Testimony that sheltered the Ark of the Covenant and the sacred mysteries that had made Israel a nation and set it apart from other nations. Inside were the gold and silver vessels, and candlesticks and basins. The rich and jewelled vestments of the priests and attendants and the instruments of worship. Outside, the cloudy pillar of the Guiding Presence hung serenely above the entrance as a sign and a promise to Israel. The Tabernacle sat brooding in the plain and hovering its mysteries like the sphinx.

There, eastward before the Tabernacle was his own roomy tent and the tents of the families of Aaron. The tents of Reuben were a large city to the south of the main tent as always. Ephraim's section in its allotted place to the west; the hosts of Dan to the north and Judah pitched to the rising sun. All good fighting men who would die for the glory of the tabernacle and Israel. A splendid and orderly sight—a magnificent spectacle. Moses lingered over it a long time with his eyes.

The sounds of Israel's existence came up to him. The lowing of herds, hammering of metal, sounds of strife, of crying and dying and sounds of song. Moses felt happy over that.

His dreams had in no way been completely fulfilled. He had meant to make a perfect people, free and just, noble and strong, that should be a light for all the world and for time and eternity. And he wasn't sure he had succeeded. He had found out that no man may make another free. Freedom was something internal. The outside signs were just signs and symbols of the man inside. All you could do was to give the opportunity for freedom and the man himself must make his own emancipation. He remembered how often he had had to fight Israel to halt a return to Egypt and slavery. Responsibility had seemed too awful to them time and time again. They had wanted to kill him several times for forcing them to be men. Only their awe and terror of his powers had saved his life. No man among the revolters had courage enough to touch his body or he would have died long ago. The few men, like Joshua who had courage, believed in his dream. So he had lived on and fought on through the wilderness and back again to the Jordan. And now he sat on Nebo's highest peak called Pisgah and gazed down on Israel and across at the Promised Land.

That carried him back in his mind to the earliest rocking of his cradle that he could remember, up until the present moment. Things thought and felt. Things done and undone. Joy, sorrow, defeat and triumph. What was and what might have been. Everything ended in riddles. He, Moses, who had never wanted to rule anyone had been thrust into the position of absolute rule- and law-giver. No man on earth had ever wielded so much power. He visited over Egypt and his various travels and studies and work, and the sun moved on and big pregnant-looking clouds wallowed past and eyed the solitary figure on the peak and moved on. Moses was fighting again all his wars, agonizing in wildernesses and deserts, facing revolts of Princes of Israel who had been slaves or the sons of slaves before he lifted his rod in Egypt. Ambitious men and women, stiff-necked with new pride. Wars, plagues of snakes and fevers and famine, misunderstanding and hatred. Only the short secret visits across mountains and plains to Jethro's house to light up his life. Something had made him endure it all, but he did not know what it was. Once or

twice he had felt that Jethro could have told him, but he never did. He did hover over him occasionally as if he felt for him, but he always stopped short of speech.

But here Israel was at the Jordan. If he had failed in his highest dreams he had succeeded in others. Perhaps he had not failed so miserably as he sometimes felt. Israel was at the Jordan inside as well as out. Perhaps he had done as much as it was possible for one man to do for another. He had put the future in their hands to do with it according to their hearts and their talents. Over the river they would till fields that they had not cleared and dwell in cities that they had not builded.

He had given Israel back the notes to songs. The words would be according to their own dreams, but they could sing. They had songs and singers.

They might not be absolutely free inside, but anyway he had taken from them the sorrow of serving without will, and had given them the strife of freedom. He had called to their memories the forgotten words of love and family. They had the blessing of being responsible for their own.

Moses lifted his eyes over Canaan. It was a good country and just as he had remembered it from his travels in his youth. He had known what the twelve spies would find before they got there. He merely wanted their interpretations for the people. If their representatives saw the benefits and not the difficulties, then Israel was ready for Canaan. If they saw the difficulties bigger than the benefits, they were unfit for citizenship and he would have to draw back and try again in another generation. The report of the twelve spies showed him somehow he had failed to stir the people to the full courage of responsibility in their first approach to the Jordan forty years before. They were still a horde of slaves, then. To his dying day he would always feel bad about this first great failure of his. But, well, anyway, this time Israel had her songs and her singers. Israel had a fine army of fighters. Israel had laws on tables of stone and Israel had a God. He had lifted their eyes to the mountain. Out of a rotting mass of creeds he had made a religion that had height and depth. Of course, he had made his mistakes and had his regrets. But every heart has its graveyard. But some things had been well done. Now God had a voice and glory.

So Israel was at the Jordan in every way. He had learned from his first failure and so looking on the nation beneath him, the gall of the numerous and senseless revolts grew less. You do not mock a man for being blind. You lead him.

The dimming sunlight gave him inside vision. He looked through time far and near. He saw the twelve priests, with Eleazar leading, descend into the shallow ford of the Jordan, bearing the sacred Ark of the Covenant on its staves. They must pick up twelve stones from the bed of the river as a sign forever. A strong front guard of fighting men would come down to the water's edge eight abreast and divide in midstream and pour four deep on either side of the Ark and mount up the other bank. They would go before to beat back any challenge to the crossing. Then the people and the herds would come down into the water the same way. Night and day, day and night, they would come down into the river and flow past the Ark and up into Canaan. Last would come the strong rear guard and last of all the priests would bear the Ark up the bank and the feet of Israel would be in Canaan. The high-lifted rod could be lowered.

And what would he, Moses, do over there? What could he do for Israel that he had not already done? Nothing but live in a palace and wear a crown. A deep frown settled on the face of Moses. He had known palaces and the shadows of crowns had fallen athwart his head. He recoiled inwardly and felt cold.

No, he didn't want to rule that way. He wanted freedom. He wanted to ask God and Nature questions. He wanted to revel in mountains. He wanted to sit on the slopes of Sinai and remember God's glory that he had glimpsed from the cleft in the rock. An altar high on Sinai where he had heard the Voice and seen the burning bush and had the rod thrust into his hands. Surely the Voice wouldn't trouble him again. He had answered and served his fifty years. Israel was at the Jordan and free. The Voice should welcome him and speak of other things like mysteries of sea and sky and air. There was his youngest son ruling the tribe in Jethro's place. He had seen next to nothing of his children and grandchildren. It would be nice to be among them. They wouldn't understand him any more than the Hebrews had, but at least he

wouldn't have to lead them. Zipporah was old and recon-
ciled. They could talk about simple things together like asking
about who was still living and who was dead and things like
that.

What about Israel? What would people think of him for
leaving them like that? Well, if he were dead they would make
out some way without him. He was still hale and strong.
None of his natural powers had failed him yet. He had ten
good active years ahead of him, barring accidents. Maybe
twenty years. He could go over the Jordan and spend them
straining against things that he had strained against for fifty
years. He could wear crowns and robes. But one day he must
die as other men died. And they looked upon him as different
from other men and followed him only through fear and awe.
When he sickened and crumbled like ordinary men, what
would become of his laws and statutes? No, Moses must not
die among the Hebrews. They must not see him die.

So Moses set to work to build a tomb on Nebo for himself.
The leader of Israel would be buried there. He would end in
mystery as he had come. Then his laws would stand and he
could spend those last years away from conniving politicians,
stupid, but stubborn pushers and suspicions and avarice. He
could dwell forever in the mountain without having to de-
scend and struggle with the sordid. He worked furiously for
hours piling stones over his relinquished power.

Under one stone he found an ancient lizard and asked him,
"What are you doing under there, old lizard?"

"Oh, just resting from living and thinking about the time
when my ancestors ruled the world. That was a glorious
time."

"How do you know your ancestors ruled the world? Your
life span isn't very long, you know," Moses said, sitting down
on a rock to listen and rest.

"Oh, we lizards don't try to keep our memories in our
bodies. We have a keeper of memories and when we want to
know what used to be, we go to him to find out."

"Do all lizards go to ask?"

"No, Moses, you don't have to know much to enjoy a fresh
batch of flies and worms or to have children. No, some lizards
never ask."

"Did you ever inquire?" Moses asked as he produced a small swarm of flies by lifting his right hand slightly. The lizard looked at him in surprise and pleasure and ate down a few flies before he answered.

"Oh, yes, I have been to ask. There was some dispute on this mountain about the month of the flood. So I traveled out to ask."

"Where did you have to go?"

"No need to wear myself out talking so much. I am an old lizard as you see and it's hard to be talking so much on a full stomach, though I'm much obliged to you for the favor of the flies. But if I told you where to go, it wouldn't do you any good. The keeper of our memories is hard to reach and hard to talk to. I'm getting sleepy now."

"Maybe I could reach him and could talk with him. You never can tell."

But the lizard was fast asleep. Moses got up and moved more rock upon the mound. Just then the lizard woke up and said, "You could try anyway. One who can produce fly-swarms might find a way. Listen: you must go east to a great mountain called Sinai and climb to the very top. There is a great flat stone on the very top and on that stone is another stone that is the very peak. And under that peak stone, and resting on the flat stone, is a bearded lizard who knows all the things that used to be."

"Would he know how the world was made, and the heavens?"

"Oh, yes, that is one of our important memories."

"I must go and talk with him. My work is finished but it is dark. I think I'll sleep on the mountain and start out soon in the morning. It is a long, long walk to Sinai. I have seen that mountain before."

But Moses did not sleep on the mountain. He sat on the mountain top for a while gazing at the dim shapes of things over Jordan in the night. He looked down at Israel's smoking, flaming stretch and turned away from his memories of fire-spitting mountains and night-vigils with God. "Lord, Your people are here." He took his rod in his right hand and lifted it and Nebo trembled. The moon in its reddest mood became to him a standing place for his feet and the sky ran down so

close to gaze on Moses that the seven great suns of the Universe went wheeling around his head. He stood in the bosom of thunder and the zig-zag lightning above him joined the muttering thunder. Fire and flame played all over the peak where the people could see. The voice of the thunder leaped from peak to plain and Moses stood in the midst of it and said "Farewell." Then he turned with a firm tread and descended the other side of the mountain and headed back over the years.

SERAPH ON THE SUWANEE

To
Marjorie Kinnan Rawlings
and
Mrs. Spessard L. Holland
With Loving Admiration

Chapter One

SAWLEY, the town, is in west Florida, on the famous Suwanee River. It is flanked on the south by the curving course of the river which Stephen Foster made famous without ever having looked upon its waters, running swift and deep through the primitive forests, and reddened by the chemicals leeched out of drinking roots. On the north, the town is flanked by cultivated fields planted to corn, cane potatoes, tobacco and small patches of cotton.

However, few of these fields were intensively cultivated. For the most part they were scratchy plantings, the people being mostly occupied in the production of turpentine and lumber. The life of Sawley streamed out from the sawmill and the "teppentime 'still." Then too, there was ignorance and poverty, and the ever-present hookworm. The farms and the scanty flowers in front yards and in tin cans and buckets looked like the people. Trees and plants always look like the people they live with, somehow.

This was in the first decade of the new century, when the automobile was known as the horseless carriage, and had not exerted its tremendous influence on the roads of the nation. There was then no U.S. 90, the legendary Old Spanish Trail, stretching straight broad concrete from Jacksonville on the Atlantic to San Diego on the Pacific. There was the sandy pike, deeply rutted by wagon wheels over which the folks of Sawley hauled their tobacco to market at Live Oak, or fresh-killed hog-meat, corn and peanuts to Madison or Monticello on the west. Few ever dreamed of venturing any farther east nor west.

Few were concerned with the past. They had heard that the stubbornly resisting Indians had been there where they now lived, but they were dead and gone. Osceola, Miccanope, Billy Bow-Legs were nothing more than names that had even lost their bitter flavor. The conquering Spaniards had done their murdering, robbing, and raping and had long ago withdrawn from the Floridas. Few knew and nobody cared that the Hidalgos under De Sota had moved westward along this

very route. The people thought no more of them than they did the magnolias and bay and other ornamental trees which grew so plentifully in the swamps along the river, nor the fame of the stream. They knew that there were plenty of black bass, locally known as trout, in the Suwanee, and bream and perch and cat-fish. There were soft-shell turtles that made a mighty nice dish when stewed down to a low gravy, or the "chicken meat" of those same turtles fried crisp and brown. Fresh water turtles were a mighty fine article of food anyway you looked at it. It was commonly said that a turtle had every kind of meat on him. The white "chicken meat," the dark "beef" and the in-between "pork." You could stew, boil and fry, and none of it cost you a cent. All you needed was a strip of white side-meat on the hook, and you had you some turtle meat.

But the people also knew that while the Suwanee furnished free meat, it furnished plenty of mosquitoes and malaria too. If you wanted to stay on your feet, you bought your quinine every Saturday along with your groceries. Work was hard, pleasures few, and malaria and hookworm plentiful. However, the live oaks set along the streets and in many yards grew splendidly and gave good shade. The Spanish moss hung down everywhere and seemed to interest travellers from the North, though these were few and far between. Nobody gave these Yankees any particular encouragement to settle around Sawley. The Reconstruction was little more than a generation behind. Men still living had moved into west Florida after Sherman had burned Atlanta and made his triumphant march to the sea. A dozen or more men who had worn the gray of the confederacy were local residents. Damn Yankees were suspect of foraging around still looking for loot; and if not that, gloating over the downfall of The Cause.

This was a Sunday and the sawmill and the 'still were silent. No Yankees passing through. The Negroes were about their own doings in their own part of town, and white Sawley was either in church or on the way. Less than a thousand persons inhabited the town, and more than half the white population belonged to Day Spring Baptist Church. The menfolks, as everywhere, were not too good on attendance, but they paid their dues more or less, and the women and children went.

On this particular Sunday, though, there was a large turn-out. Not that there was any revival meeting going on, which always brought everybody out, nor were they hurrying to the church because it was believed that the pastor, Reverend Carl Middleton, had anything new to say, or any new way of saying what he always said.

Sawley was boiling like a big red ants' nest that had been ploughed up. It was rumored that Arvay, the younger of the two Henson girls was a'courting at last. To be exact, Arvay was not a'courting so much as she was being courted, and what with Arvay's past record and everything, this was something that people had to see.

In the first place, Arvay was all of twenty-one, and according to local custom, should have been married at least five years ago. But at sixteen, shortly after the marriage of her older sister Larraine, commonly known as "Raine," to the Reverend Carl Middleton, Arvay had turned from the world. Such religious fervor was not unknown among white people, but it certainly was uncommon. During "protracted meeting," another name for the two weeks of revival that came around every summertime, most anybody was liable to get full of the spirit and shout in church and sing and pray. Backsliders and "sinner-folks" crowded the mourner's-bench and got religion over and over again. But it seldom lasted more than a month after the meetings closed. Nobody heard any more about it until the next time. A local wit put it this way: Sawley wore out the knees of its britches crawling to the Cross and wore out the seat of its pants back-sliding. Excessive ceremonies were things that the Negroes went in for. White folks just didn't go on like that.

So it was something when Arvay Henson, now, took her stand. Arvay could have done so different. In the first place, Arvay was still mighty young to take on self-denying. And then again, Arvay was pretty if you liked delicate-made girls. Her shape was not exactly in style in those parts, but that could easily be overlooked. She had breasts to her bosom, but elsewhere Arvay was lean-made in every way. No heavy-hipped girl below that extremely small waist, and her legs were long and slim-made instead of the much-admired "whiskey-keg" look to her legs that was common. She had

plenty of long light yellow hair with a low wave to it with Gulf-blue eyes. Arvay had a fine-made kind of a nose and mouth and a face shaped like an egg laid by a Leghorn pullet, with a faint spread of pink around her upper cheeks. True, she was said to be so slim that a man would have to shake the sheets to find her in bed, but there were many around Sawley who were willing to put themselves to the trouble of making a thorough search of the bed every night. Many a man felt that given the chance, he could put plenty of meat on Arvay's bones. So there was a feeling of shock and loss when Arvay gave up the world. It brought on plenty of talk.

Arvay, young and white, and teasing to the fancy of many men, had got up in church on First Sunday, Communion Day, and announced that she was through with the world and its sinful and deceitful ways. She solemnly said that she had given her whole heart and her life to the work of God. She planned to be a missionary and craved to be sent away off somewhere to take the Word to the heathens. Tell them of Christ and Him crucified, and warn them of the dangers in which they stood in their ignorance, of a burning and everlasting Hell. Also make them know that they had to die, and of the horrors of dying in their ignorance and sin.

Arvay's tearful speech followed the usual pattern, and everybody said it was just fine. There had been nothing about the heathens of China, India and Africa wallowing around on the heavenly chairs, nor ankling up and down the golden streets. None of her hearers could have imagined such a thing. Fancy meeting a Hindu, with his middle tied up in a dhoti and with white head-rag on, around the Throne, or singing in the Choir! It was too much, and nobody tried to imagine any such thing. He ought to consider himself pretty lucky to get saved from Hell. What became of him after that was just not talked about. The job of the missionaries was to save. So all of the women and a few of the older men cried tears of joy at the renunciation of the girl. She had to be full of The Spirit to talk that way, and so young, and therefore apt to be deviled and pestered by the flesh. It would be a mighty fine thing, the harried older women thought, if more girls felt as Arvay did. Therefore, on that day of Arvay's renunciation, when the girl had finished off by asking the prayers of the

congregation, their earnest prayers that she might hold out and never, never turn back but go on and on to greater grace, "Amens" burst out all over the church. The pastor himself had gotten to his feet and paid his young sister-in-law a great tribute.

"This young girl's devotion to the cause of Christ makes me feel ashamed," Reverend Middleton had said. "Here she is, too young to be sent into the field as yet, but ready and willing to go. Ready to go wherever the Spirit might send her. Her stand ought to make me and all of us grown folks feel ashamed. And if you, my flock feel that you can spare me, I will declare myself ready and willing to go."

The flock had cried some more at the thought of the pastor's offer to sacrifice himself, but it was felt that he could not be spared. Anyway, it would take a lot of money to send him. To compensate for this denial, the parsonage was repainted, and five dollars a month was added to his salary, bringing the total to an even seventy dollars a month.

Five years had passed since Arvay had turned her back on the world and all its sins and snares. Arvay still played the organ for the Sunday School, and she took an active part in church work. Otherwise, she kept strictly to herself. It was not too difficult for her, because the community soon put Arvay Henson down as queer, if not a little "tetched." Nothing like her sister 'Raine at all, who was robust, not to say a trifle lusty, and pretty in the ways that the rural community favored. Raine had a full head of curly reddish hair, big legs and a busty chest. Raine was lively and full of chat. Raine took after her father's side of the family, while Arvay looked like her mother's folks, and even had her mother's ways to an extent. Maria Henson was overly religious, not given to laughter, and was considered meek and mild. The old heads recalled that Maria Henson had been given to fits and spasms in her girlhood the same way that Arvay was right now. No one thought too much about the seizures. Fits were things that happened to some young girls, but they grew out of them sooner or later. It was usually taken as a sign of a girl being "highstrung." Marriage would straighten her out.

For the last three years, Arvay had been having hysterical seizures, classified in the local language as "having fits."

Sometimes they came upon her in church right after the sermon, but more often she was took down right after she got home from the service, and usually when some extra brash young gallant had forced himself upon her to the extent of seeing her home. It called for lots of persistence and a thick hide to "scorch" Arvay Henson home, but her looks and her unattainability nerved various young bucks to try it now and then. After the long walk in almost complete silence on Arvay's part, the venture invariably ended in an hysterical display as soon as the young man got inside the Henson parlor. Hardly did she get her hat off before she was sprawled out on the horse-hair sofa clenching hands and teeth and bobbling around and up and down, and with her mother running in with a small vial of spirits of turpentine and the sugar dish with a teaspoon in it to administer the dose of three "draps" of "teppentime on sugar" forced between the teeth of Arvay to bring her to. The embarrassed would-be suitor stumbled out, and that was the end of his hopes. One by one the more brash were discouraged, and the timid never tried.

But now, the rumor had flashed around that Arvay Henson had met her match. Arvay Henson was being courted in spite of all she could do and say and so the town and outlying country and districts, all were good and stirred up. And the news was so exciting that nobody wanted to be told about it. Everybody wanted to go to church and to be there and see for themselves.

And there were three prongs to stir up interest. The first was that Arvay was taking company at all. The second was who it was who was sparking Arvay; but the most hooking horn of all was the way it was being done.

The man was Jim Meserve, whose ancestors had held plantations upon the Alabama River before the War. In that respect, Jim Meserve differed from the rest of the inhabitants of Sawley, who had always been of the poor whites who had scratched out some kind of an existence in the scrub oaks and pines, far removed from the ease of the big estates.

Not that Jim Meserve had come among the people of Sawley with anything. He had brought little more than the suit he had on, the high laced boots, and the broad-brimmed felt hat, which he wore so rakishly on his curly head. The fortunes

of the War had wiped Jim's grand-father clean. His own fa-
ther had had no chance to even inherit. Jim had come to
town three months ago with only a small bundle, containing
his changing clothes. But Jim had a flavor about him. He was
like a hamstring. He was not meat any longer, but he smelled
of what he had once been associated with.

Jim Meserve was very handsome too, and had stirred the
hearts of practically every single girl in town. Caps were set to
catch the laughing stranger. He was obviously Black Irish in
his ancestry somewhere. He had the thick head of curly black
hair, deep blue eyes with long black lashes, so that they were
what the Irish called, "set in with a sooty finger," dimples in
his lean cheeks, white strong teeth set in a chaffing mouth.

Jim had the gift of gab, no doubt about it. Within a week
of his arrival in Sawley, he had talked himself into a job as
woodsman on a turpentine camp. That was a miracle in itself,
for "teppentime" folks are born, not made, and certainly not
over-night. They are born in teppentime, live all their lives in
it, and die and go to their graves smelling of teppentime. And
Brock Henson, Arvay's father, who was an over-rider for the
firm, and known to be a hard man to handle, had interceded
for Jim and got him the job. A man had to go some to out-
talk Brock Henson on anything. Brock Henson was a Cracker
from way back. Life had not been easy for him, and he had
cutting edges on his spirit, in spite of his love of jokes. Work-
ing that job out of the squat-shouldered, tobacco-chewing,
rusty-haired Brock was a feather in Jim's cap, and gave him a
standing.

Jim had the nerve of a brass monkey, everybody agreed.
But then, he made no bones about the fact that he was really
stuck on Arvay Henson. She just suited him, he said, and was
worth the trouble of breaking in. Too, Jim laughed off the
notion that Arvay was through with the world and had no use
for love. So it looked like the brash devil was a'courting Arvay
anyhow in spite of the well-known obstacles.

The Sunday before, Jim Meserve had rushed up to the
Henson home and had escorted Arvay to *and* from church
and people nearly split their sides at Jim walking along the
road holding Arvay's arm with every kind of politeness in
spite of all she could do and say. What would come off next?

That was what they all wanted to see and to know. The doings were something like a well-trained hound dog tackling a bob-cat, and everybody wanted to be in on the fun. So they were all on the way to church that Sunday morning, walking, in buggies, riding horse-back and some even straddling grass-gut mules or in double wagons pulled by mules.

Brock Henson had never made as much as a hundred dollars in any month in his life. The family lived in a clapboard house more than two miles east of the heart of Sawley, and nearly a mile from the Baptist church. The house had been a dark ugly red when Brock Henson, promoted to over-rider, had moved in ten years before. It had not been repainted since, and was now a rusty, splotchy gray-brown. Only one room in the house, the parlor, was ceilinged overhead. In the two bedrooms and the kitchen, the rafters were bare and skinny. Water for the household came from a well out back, and the privyhouse leaned a little to one side less than fifty feet from the kitchen door. A fig tree, two pear trees which bore pears that were only good for preserving, were scattered far apart in the field back of the house. There was a huge mulberry tree that redeemed the very back of the unkempt garden space.

The Sawley people, eager to be amused at Arvay's expense, had no idea who or what Arvay Henson was. They had no way of knowing that Arvay was timid from feeling unsafe inside. Nor had anyone, not even her parents, the answer to Arvay's reactions to people. They did not suspect that the general preference for Larraine, Arvay's more robust and aggressive sister, had done something to Arvay's soul across the years. They could not know, because Arvay had never told anyone how she felt and why.

Arvay had one comforting advantage over Larraine. Arvay could play music and Larraine just couldn't learn it. Arvay had been asked to spend a summer with her mother's sister in Madison one time, and this aunt could play on the organ some. Arvay had shown great interest and a quick ability and had surprised the family on her return to Sawley in the fall, by being able to pick out melodies, and to play a few songs with full harmony all the way through. The Henson parlor organ, which had been bought years ago for style and had seldom

been sounded, began to be used. Arvay was in there nearly every day practicing and practicing. She showed herself very apt with music.

But even this talent and comfort had laid a'road to ambush the timid Arvay. It had brought down upon her her most crushing blow so far, and this hurt had convinced Arvay Henson that happiness, love and normal relationships were not meant for her. Somehow, God had denied her the fate of sharing in the common happiness and joys of the world. Only she knew that her renunciation had been an acknowledgement of this conviction.

It had come about this way. Arvay was not quite sixteen when Carl Middleton, twenty-six, and newly ordained to the ministry, was called to Sawley to pastor Day Spring Baptist church. Middleton was five-feet-ten, deep-chested and husky, so that the godless Brock Henson snurled behind his back that Middleton ought to be mortally ashamed of himself to be dodging honest work like he was doing. Carl Middleton up in a pulpit beating on a Bible and hollering was nothing but a first-class teppentime-still hand going to waste.

The female Hensons disagreed with Brock. Maria and Larraine shouted and hollered Brock down that the new pastor was just wonderful. Brock laughed it off by saying that they would naturally say that because the new preacher was a bachelor and 'Raine and her mother were up to baiting a hook for the puzzle-gutted slob. Arvay said nothing in Middleton's favor or against him because she considered him too wonderful for her to ever have a chance with him. She listened to Larraine and the older girls rave over the way one lock of his brown hair dangled over his forehead when he got really active in the pulpit. How his gray eyes blazed and his face got all tied up with rage when he was giving general sin and sinners in general the very devil.

Arvay was secretly glorified then when the new pastor seemed to single her out. He made two or three attempts to talk with the shy and almost wordless girl. Then happening to hear that she could play the organ, he made her organist for the Sunday School out of hand. Then he suggested that he call at the Henson home on Friday afternoons to go over the songs with her for the following Sunday. There was not much

talk in the countrified parlor, but Arvay shone inside at Middleton's very presence. She fell in love, and began to live a sweet and secret life inside herself. The pastor leaning over her shoulder while she sat at the organ, little touches of his hand seemingly by accident, softness in his voice, and telling her that she was an exceptional young girl.

This went on for months, with Middleton paying Larraine and none of the older girls any attention. Then, all of a sudden, Larraine developed great interest in church affairs and in the program for the Children's Day exercises in particular. She was always on hand in the parlor or at the church. And Larraine was seventeen and had on long dresses and could take company. The Sunday after Children's Day, Middleton scorched Larraine home from the night service and the next day Larraine announced to Arvay that she and the pastor were engaged to be married.

Even with 'Raine married to Middleton, Arvay could not bring herself to feel that her instincts had deceived her. Ah, no! There had been a mistake somewhere. Maybe even at the bottom of Carl's sudden marriage with Larraine.

It was twice as hard for Arvay because she had no one to whom she could open her feelings. Not to her parents who were bragging over 'Raine catching the new pastor. And certainly not to her only sister whom Arvay felt had somehow toled her true love away from her.

Believing in her heart that she was secretly loved by Carl, it gradually came to Arvay that the next move was up to her. The best plan would be to get herself sent far off to some foreign land. Some day, and without doubt pretty soon, Carl would follow her there. She would be standing in a flower yard, and she would see Carl coming a long way off, tired and worn out and sad. He would kneel down on his knees, kiss the hem of her garment, tell her how it all happened and beg her to forgive and to forget. Larraine would be dead—of a broken heart because Carl had found her out and told her to her face that she had parted him from his true love by her double-tongued lies and deceitfulness.

Outside of her dreams Arvay could detect no weakening in Carl except for a kind of a look he gave her sometimes from the pulpit. Otherwise, Larraine seemed to have her husband

fetching and toting at her commands. But Arvay comforted herself that right was bound to win some old day, and dreamed and waited. The waiting was mighty hard, for Arvay found that it caused her to dream dreams that made her body plague her in miserable strange ways. For instance, what got the matter with her every time that Larraine got pregnant? It was something beyond Arvay's understanding. Some imp of Satan seemed to grab hold of her and drag her right into the darkened bedroom where Carl and 'Raine were, and made her look and see and hear from beginning to the end. It was after 'Raine's second announcement that Arvay felt her spasms coming on.

Not a soul in Sawley suspected this secret life of Arvay's. Most of them would have laughed at her if they had known about it. Carl Middleton had soon shot his bolt in Sawley. The new wore off him mighty quick. He never did say anything that had not been already said, and his repetitions were not very dramatic. His church members allowed that he would do, and that was the best that they could give him. He stayed home with his wife and had no loud kind of vices. Some complained that he couldn't lead a song worth talking about. Some wag went so far as to say that Reverend Middleton couldn't even raise a tune if you put a wagon-load of good compost under him and ten sacks of commercial fertilizer. They would have thought that a pretty young girl like Arvay was clean out of her head to be making so much out of nothing. But Arvay had felt wanted and warm and secure and important to someone for awhile, and it was hard for her to forget.

Chapter Two

THAT Sunday morning Arvay had no idea of the extent of interest in her affairs, but she did know how she felt. She fooled around and lingered over the breakfast table.

"Don't you reckon that you ought to be getting yourself fixed for Sunday School, Arvay?" Brock Henson asked sharply. "It's nearly nine o'clock."

Arvay jumped visibly and quivered. "That is, if I was going. I don't reckon I'll be going this morning."

"How come?" Brock demanded. "Before now, look like you couldn't get there soon enough. Why ain't you going this morning?"

"Oh, I just don't feel to be bothered, I reckon. Somebody else can preside at the organ one time, I reckon. I won't be so much missed."

"Call yourself trying to cold-shoulder Jim Meserve, I take it. If you had the sense that God give a june bug you'd feel glad that he feels to scorch you to and from. Ain't you never going to have sense enough to get yourself a husband? You intend to lay round here on me for the rest of your days and moan and pray?"

"I help you to say," Maria Henson agreed. "Arvay ain't acting with no sense at all. Here all these gals around here 'bout to bust they guts trying to git to him, and Arvay, that seems like she got the preference with him, trying to cut the tom fool."

"You all talk like I ain't got no feelings at all. You reckon I feel like pulling off down the road with him so he can make a fool out of me in front of everybody? Naw! I just ain't a'going."

But in the end she was driven from kitchen to her own room to dress. In sullen anger, she took as long as she could. She was no more than half dressed when she heard her father greeting Jim Meserve out on the porch. She became so nervous that she was useless to herself. It was a good thing that Maria ran in and helped her into the pink lawn dress at last, and put her accessories in her trembling hands. "Aw, good

gracious, Arvie! You ain't ready as yet? What in the nation you been doing all this time?" Maria made quick and anxious movements as she grumbled and rushed the dressing of her daughter along. "Got Mister Meserve out there waiting all this time. You don't even act with the sense you do have. Move! I'll button your frock for you. Make haste, Arvie! Don't comb and pull at that hair all day. Mister Meserve sure looks noble in his Sunday clothes. Make haste before he gits tired of waiting on you and leave you."

Arvay in the deeply flounced pink lawn dress, and with her flaxen hair swept up in front into a high pompadour, stood grim and panting before the looking-glass, her eyes stretched wide in fear like a colt that has been saddled for the first time; stood jerking at the body of her dress across her bust.

"You're all ready, now. I'll go tell him that you'll be right out. Naw, no need for you to grab up that Quarterly. Sunday School must be mighty nigh over by now. Here's a clean handkerchief for your pocketbook. Hurry on out to greet the young man."

Arvay heard her mother taking extra spry steps down the hallway and out on the front porch.

She halted with cold trembling hands in the doorway to brace herself. While she was doing this, she glanced around.

Just as Arvay had accused him to herself beforehand, Jim Meserve had a face full of grin. He was doing the talking, and her parents were seconding every word with nods and smiles of agreement. Currying favor, Arvay mentally scorned them, and acting two glad dogs in a meat-house!

She stepped out on the porch with a long fast step, made the briefest manners of her lifetime without halting, and was almost loping by the time her feet hit the ground. By not turning her head in the slightest, she could pretend to know nothing about the dismay in the faces of her parents, and to have no notion at all about what Jim Meserve was thinking. She had offered the grand insult, and now maybe she would be left in peace.

Halfway to the gate she felt her elbow being caught by a man's long and strong fingers, and the tall shape of Jim Meserve was walking along beside her.

"Why, Miss Arvay," Jim said in great concern, "you

wouldn't run off and leave me, would you?" They came to
the shabby gate and he swung it outwards with one hand,
while clinging to her arm with the other. "And I already
know your answer to that. . . . 'Not if you can keep up,' is
what you mean to tell me, ain't it, Miss Arvay?"

As they turned towards Sawley, Arvay heard a suppressed
guffaw from her father and her face flamed. She looked up
angrily into the young man's face and said nothing for several
steps. Then she could hold in no longer and said from be-
tween clenched teeth, "What you grinning all over yourself
like a chessy-cat for? You act like you found a mare's nest and
can't count the eggs."

Jim Meserve seemed to take enjoyment out of her burst of
rage and laughed some more.

"Grinning just like the Devil's doll-baby!" Arvay added as a
further insult.

"Wouldn't hurt your face to grin a little, would it, Miss
Arvay? You got yours all tied up in a winter-knot, or like you
been feasting off of green persimmons."

"That wouldn't be necessary at all, Mister Meserve. You'se
doing enough grinning and skinning back your gums for the
two of us. I'd give a good whoop and a holler, though, if you
was to go on about your business and leave me be."

"Why, Miss Arvay?"

"Why? Well, just because."

"That don't tell me nothing, Miss Arvay. I know that is a
woman's reason for most anything, but not being a woman, it
don't spell out a thing to me. Go ahead and tell me some-
thing that I can understand. I might be sort of chuckle-
headed, so don't chunk the whole pan of bread at me;
crumble it up fine so I can handle it."

Arvay stopped in her tracks and tried to release her arm by
a gentle jerk, but it did not work.

"Why do you want to come a'pestering and a'picking at me
for? You know that you just want to make game of me!"
There were tears in her voice if not in her eyes. "I never done
nothin' to you for you to come taking me for a figure of fun,
and making a laughing-stock out of me for folks to poke fun
at."

The laughter died off out of Jim Meserve's face, and he

stopped and stood looking down into her tortured eyes for a full minute.

"So you got notions like that about me, Miss Arvay?" Jim asked very soberly and kept studying the girl's face.

"You and everybody else," Arvay replied defiantly, but with something child-like and pathetic in her voice.

"But why, Miss Arvay? Why would anybody want to poke fun at you?"

"Because, because you don't, you couldn't mean what you say, that's how come."

"And why wouldn't I mean what I say? Why wouldn't I or most any man want you for your sweet little self?"

"Because you just wouldn't, that's all," Arvay stuttered out, and her face flushed red and she worked her eyelids rapidly to hold back the tears. At the point of failure, she shut her eyes tightly for a second and made a quick quarter turn to hide her face.

Instantly Jim seized her by her shoulders and whirled the slim girl back to face him, and Arvay's hand flew up and slapped Jim's face with all her might and main. "You leave me be!" Arvay tried to release herself and run away, but Jim held her too firmly. "I told you to quit bothering me!"

"No, Miss Arvay, that I can't do at all. You need my help and my protection too bad for that, I see." With a solemn kind of soberness, Jim drew the shrinking Arvay to him. "You have made me see into something that I don't reckon you understand your ownself. I have to stay with you and stand by you and give my good protection to keep you from hurting your ownself too much. No, I can't leave you be, not until you and me both can see further."

"Oh, you don't have to take it on yourself to worry about me, Mister Meserve," Arvay protested weakly.

"Oh, but I do! I have to because you don't understand your ownself, Miss Arvay, and somebody stronger than you, and that can see further than you, and somebody that feels your care, will have to be on hand to look after you. Now we got things all straightened out like. Come on." And Jim let go of Arvay's shoulders and took her companionably by her hand and faced up the road. "You'll get more used to me before long and see into things."

"See into what?" Arvay questioned shortly as she followed Jim along the road.

"Oh, a lot of things, Miss Arvay, that you ain't got the right ideas about as yet. It's bound to come to you in time. I'll be around to look out for you and point out things."

Arvay refused to comment further, and with eyes straight ahead of her, she walked determinedly on the sandy road. After a few paces, Jim shucked off his solemn manner, and returned to his laughing good humor in a marvellous way. He chuckled and squeezed Arvay's arm lightly.

"Didn't take me long to learn just how you're made, Miss Arvay, and now I know how to handle you. You and me are going to have a mighty high old time together."

The straight road waved along over the slight rises. On either side yellow and blue flowers were ornamenting the spring. They passed groves of live oak, scrub oak, scattering pines, and over towards the river, bay and magnolia in exotic white bloom. Deep curtains of gray moss hung from the trees and waved ever so slightly in the breeze. Budding wild grape-vines and briars tangled up trees and peeped out from upper branches. Possum persimmons spread their limbs among the rest.

But Arvay took these in through a gray veil of apprehension. Folks would be coming along this road and see her in the company of Jim, and she pictured them grinning slyly and making jokes about her. Her mind imaged up the picture of the future. After Jim had made a public show of her, he would naturally get himself a regular girl, and they would all laugh at her, Arvay, and say how Jim Meserve and whoever his wife might be had made her look like a fool at a funeral. If only nobody came along! Oh, but she was not born for luck. Somebody would be sure and certain to come along. Arvay walked in dread of that moment.

All of Arvay's fears were confirmed, as a shabby old buck-board came abreast of them, with the deep sand pouring from the rim of every wheel. There was no mistaking that one and all were extremely interested in her in company with Jim. Their necks craned out, and their eyes snapped in curiosity. Old Lady Minnie Brawley was so scared that her wrinkled-around old eyes might miss something that she reached up a

freckled old claw and flung back the bib part of her floppy calico bonnet the better to gaze and to peer. Grins and giggles broke out among the younger members of the clan. Her oldest son, who was at the reins, had to pull to a halt and scrape up some talk the best way that he could.

"Mawning, Miss Arvie, and Mister Jim. Hit's mighty hot and dusty walking for you all," he said. "You better hop in here with us and ride on to the church."

That grass-gut horse had more on him right then than he ought to have had, but Arvay suddenly saw a way out of her embarrassment.

"Yessuh, I thank you," Arvay said eagerly and made a motion to approach the buckboard. As crowded as it was, it would be almost a miracle if she was able to get in. There would certainly be no room for Jim.

"Mighty much obliged to you all for your kindness." Jim smiled his most charming, and swept off his hat to the Brawley females, while with his other hand, he held Arvay's arm so that she could not advance. "But I can't see room for the two of us, and knowing Miss Arvay as I do, I know that she would disfavor to part with my company, and so as not to disappoint her so much, I think that we'd better just walk."

Arvay could have screamed and fought, especially as she saw how Brawley whipped up his horse and wheeled off. Making haste to get to the church-grounds so they could talk and tell. She tried to disengage her arm, but just then she heard another rig coming up behind them and looked back in unhappy defeat.

"Let go of me!" she hissed. "Making a fool out of me right out here on the Big Road. Acting just like the Devil!"

"Don't know who told you, honey, but you sure got it right. Those who know me well call me by my right name, Peter Rip-Saw, the Devil's high sheriff and son-in-law."

Arvay looked over her shoulder and dwindled down in helpless misery. What could she do? She would die before she let folks see her out there on a public road tussling and scuffling with a man. It would cause all kinds of talk, say she was letting a man get common with her. There was nothing for her to do but to pass the time of day and swap manners with

the loaded-down carriage and the two double-team wagons that passed them in rapid succession.

But the unusual activity along the Big Road did not sufficiently prepare Arvay for the spectacle when she came in sight of the church-grounds. The place was thronged as she had seldom seen it before. Horses, mules, buggies, wagons, buckboards and carriages were crowded together out under the oak grove where the congregation usually collected and ate from baskets on Big Meeting Day. Many bicycles leaned against the trunks of trees. People were mingling and moving about. It was the social time between the letting out of Sunday School and the taking in of morning service. Arvay looked, and unconsciously clung to Jim's arm.

"Where in the world did all these folks come from?" Jim asked in surprise. "Everybody seems to be present from Joe Cry to Jimmy Giggle."

"Indeed, I sure don't know," Arvay mumbled.

As Jim boldly led her around and talked and joked with folks, Arvay had her ego nourished by the envious looks from single women and courting girls. Her vanity put on a little flesh, and she began to say a word or two herself to people. And besides, right in front of all those jealous girls, Jim was treating her like she was some precious play-pretty that might break in two. Bradford Cary III's wife could not have been handled more up to time than she was being handled. She was being helped over every little stick and root, and he fended that she was not bumped into and jostled around. It was a soul-satisfying mock-up. If only it could be so!

Arvay saw three girls in a bunch trying to look amused at her, but even Arvay could see that it was hardly big enough to reach across their thin-lipped mouths. It didn't taste near as good as they were trying to make out. They were the three ring-leaders in the social set of the poor. The most popular at all the square dances, barbecues and things like that. To make sure and crumple Arvay's feathers, they got themselves in the way so that she could overhear their comments as if by accident.

"That don't mean a thing. Mister Meserve is much too lively and used to things to waste up much time on missionaires."

"And what would he want with a skinny thing like that? He

being tall and spare-built hisself, he would naturally want somebody with some meat on they bones. Folks don't go to the butcher-shop to buy bones unless they aim to make lye-soap."

There was a blow of mirthless laughter at this piece of wit, and the chunky girl, giving a switch to her full hips, was encouraged to go on. "Can you imagine them married and in the bed together? I bet they would sound like a big dish-pan of crockery rattling together."

The three tickled themselves out loud at this and looked at Arvay.

"Oh, it won't never come to that," the third announced with assurance. "I got enough meat on my bones to straighten him out and put a stop to this. Don't you worry."

If Jim heard, he gave no notice. He accepted an invitation to a square dance for himself, and his especial company, Miss Henson, ten days later.

"Is that all right with you, Miss Arvay?" Jim asked with great solicitude.

"Most certainly!" Arvay replied and looked the three leaders of the sawmill set dead in the eyes.

But Arvay was sunk again when she and Jim went inside and beheld most of the young folks, married and single, packing into the center aisle pews behind them to comment and to be witnesses to what went on. She sank down into her seat, three rows from the front. Jim did not seem to notice a thing. He came parading like a king down the aisle behind her, stood until she had entered the pew, came in after her, stood and looked out over the fast filling church, hitched up his pants and sat down.

Suddenly Arvay became conscious of Carl's inspection from the back of the pulpit. It was funny, but she had forgotten all about the man she had thought that she had loved so hard and so hopelessly for six long years. But there was no mistaking. Every time that she looked off, when she brought her eyes back to the pulpit, she caught him watching her in a curious way from under the awning of his hand resting on his brows. It made Arvay nervous, and she squirmed.

And there was Jim Meserve brazenly leaning against her, shoulder to shoulder. It gave Arvay some kind of feeling of

being caught acting unfaithful by Carl Middleton. Why? Never had a word of love passed between them. Even so, his look seemed now to say that he had seized upon her secret, and he was sadly accusing her of defection. She inched away from Jim as far as she could, which was only a few inches, but Jim promptly closed the gap again. A loud whisper somewhere behind her applauded Jim.

"Go, gator, and muddy the water!"

"I'd give a spot cash one hundred dollars if Jim would up and buss her."

"Oh, he'll do it all right."

"Aw, aw! That Arvay would throw a acre of fits."

Along about the end of the uninspiring sermon, Arvay was startled by a quick but tender pressure on her arm by Jim. She turned her head in surprise and their eyes met head on. He was looking at her in some intense and hungry way. Some common pulse began to pump something from Jim to her. Arvay noticed for the first time that Jim was made out of flesh. It was too intense, and Arvay, flushing deeply, snatched her eyes away. She flung her eyes up to the choir stand, and in doing so, caught her sister's eyes upon her. Larraine must have been looking at her for some time, because the look was set, and it was as plain as day that Larraine was not pleased at what she was looking at. Her face was as naked as a jay-bird in whistling time. Her eyes went from Arvay to Jim and back again.

Arvay knew that look only too well. Just let Arvay get hold of something that gave her particular pleasure, and that look came over Larraine. Only today, there was an out-done look mixed up in Larraine's face, and Arvay knew why. There was no way in the world for 'Raine to handle Jim first and then fling him at Arvay when she was tired or he was damaged and scarred. She had Carl Middleton, and she had three children to boot. Let her pout and crave! Here was something that she could do nothing about. Something that Brock Henson could not snatch away from Arvay and hand over to Larraine. Jim Meserve, placed beside Carl Middleton, was like a slick race-horse beside a grass-gut mule. Was Larraine sitting up there being sorry that she had been in such a haste to grab Carl?

"Excuse me, Miss Arvay," Jim was murmuring as he got up from his seat. Jim was following the local custom. The collection was lifted right after the sermon. It was the habit of the young courting men to go outside immediately after the sermon, stretch their legs for a few minutes, and then just as the collection began, to swagger back in, and ostentatiously hand their lady-love a coin to put in the collection. It was a sure sign of who belonged to whom.

After the young men had bestowed their gifts, the girls arose proudly, and with their fellows swaggering after them, paraded up to the table, and dropped their coin with a ring. One young couple right after the other parading up, and returning simpering to their seats. It was hard on the girl or the fellow whose time had been beaten, but it was a triumph for the winners. Arvay cast her eyes up briefly at Larraine, and trembled as she realized what was about to happen. Never had she marched in the parade before.

The deacons took their places, the pastor made his appeal for money, the organ struck up *Pass Me Not O Gentle Saviour* at a lively pace, and the choir rose and led the singing. The young men waited until the old fogies had thinned out, then they came back in looking like conquerors, and began to rejoin their ladies, giving the money out before they took their seats. Jim pressed a quarter into Arvay's palm, hitched up his britches arrogantly and sat down. It only waited now until some couple began the parade.

"Come on, honey," Jim whispered to Arvay. "We might as well lead off."

Arvay got to her feet, feeling every eye upon her. They had hardly made the aisle, though, before fifteen to twenty other couples were struggling into the aisles. Arvay went back to her seat feeling an exhilaration that she had never known before. She belonged to something. They nodded and grinned at each other, these couples, as they met and passed going up and down the aisle. She looked up to see how Larraine was taking it. She could hardly sing along with the rest for watching Arvay, and she was not smiling either. Arvay looked and felt glad.

Surrounded by her new associations, Arvay lingered in front of the church with Jim, feeling like she had fed on

kings. Out of this feeling came a tremulous desire to take refuge in this man. To be forever warm and included in the atmosphere that he stirred up around him. The feel of his long-fingered hand on her arm, and the look from his eyes tingled her in a way that she had never felt before.

But with the intensity of desire stirred up in her came despair. This was the prettiest man that she had ever laid eyes on. He didn't have any great vast money, but this was no common Cracker boy whatsoever. Why, even the Carys had heard mention of his folks. What in the world did she have to win him with?

Ah, no, this pretty, laughing fellow was too far out of her reach. Things as wonderful as this were never meant for nobody like her. This was first-class, and she was born to take other people's leavings.

He had scorched her to church and back today to make good his bet. It had turned out very nice and happy for her in a way, but then again, it had given her something to wish for which she could never have. Nothing to do but submit herself to her fate.

But submission tazzled you all up inside. To cover up her feelings, Arvay began to try to be quick and care-free with answers, and began to talk at random. She hardly knew what she was saying and doing before she arrived at her gate.

"Oh, no indeed, Mister Meserve, you don't think my hair is the prettiest in the world, no such a thing." And Arvay affected a hollow laugh to show that she was not as simple as he might think. "I know that you just say things like that to pass the time. You think country folks like us ain't got no sense, I reckon."

"Why, Miss Arvay! You don't mean to tell me that you disbelieve me what I say?"

Arvay hung her head and refused to meet his eyes, even when he shook her elbow and tried to make her look.

"You do wish to get rid of me, don't you?"

Arvay still stumbled along and said nothing.

"Silence gives consent, Miss Arvay. Look like I hit the nail right on the head."

They were at the gate, and Arvay wanted to rush inside and away, but Jim detained her by holding her arm.

"But you might as well save yourself a whole heap of trouble in that line, Miss Arvay, because I'm going to marry you first and last."

Arvay was half in the gate. In spite of Jim's smiling way, there was something serious-sounding in his voice, and Arvay looked up into his face to see what his words really meant. Something in his eyes sent the blood rushing to her face, and involuntarily Arvay bowed her head and concealed her face on the top of the shaky gate-post.

"Oh, you know that you don't mean that, Mister Meserve." Arvay mumbled and lifted her face the slightest.

"Oh, but I do, Miss Arvay." Jim chuckled a little.

"You act like I, that is, somebody been just waiting around for you to ask 'em that. Supposing that I don't love you, or no other man, enough to marry 'em."

"That would mean that you didn't have all that belongs to you. I'd make a girl like *you* a damned fine husband." And Jim laughed at his own brashness.

"I been laying off to give my life to missionary work, Mr. Meserve. Even if you mean what you say, I'd have to take time to make up my mind."

"Oh, I mean it sure as you're born, and so far as making up your mind is concerned, that matters a difference. Women folks don't have no mind to make up nohow. They wasn't made for that. Lady folks were just made to laugh and act loving and kind and have a good man to do for them all he's able, and have him as many boy-children as he figgers he'd like to have, and make him so happy that he's willing to work and fetch in every dad-blamed thing that his wife thinks she would like to have. That's what women are made for."

"You reckon?"

"No, I know it. Since I been here in Sawley, I done got in the notion that I'd like to get hold of one of the useless things to keep for a play-pretty. I'm going on twenty-five, been knocking around the country for seven years now, seen a lot of women and places, and seen a lot of things. It's about time I settled down, get me a real pretty wife, and start to raise me a house full of young 'uns."

"Well, you don't have to worry." Arvay smiled with a corner of her mouth. "From all I can learn, plenty of these girls

around here would be only too glad to have you. It looks like you can just about take your pick."

Jim grinned. "That being the case, I'm picking you. I'm marrying you because I'm too tough for you to get shed of like you seem to be trying to do."

There it was, straight and simple. But this was like coming through religion, Arvay considered. Like your thoughts while you were out at the praying-ground in the depths of the woods, or being down at the mourners'-bench during pro-tracted meeting with the preacher, deacons and all the folks from the Amen corner standing around and over you begging and pleading with you to turn loose your doubting and only believe. Put your whole faith in the mercy of God and believe. Eternal life, Heaven and its immortal glory were yours if you only would believe. The hold-back was that it was not all that easy to believe. That was just the trouble. Bad luck, yes. That was easy to believe in from human experience, but a whole heap of happiness and good luck just didn't come to folks like that. Certainly, things had never turned out that way for her. Now, was she to believe that this very pretty man clothed in all the joys of Heaven and earth was for *her*, and all that she had to do was to part her lips and say "yes" to have him all for herself for life? Oh, no, this was just another hurting joke being played on her.

"You figger that you'se all that tough, Mister Meserve?" Arvay imagined that Jim's hand on her elbow trembled some as he assisted her through the gate. Naturally, she was mis-taken. How could this brash man, with everything in the world at his command, be nervous about anything? Knowing his power, he was just funning with her to show to the world that he could do what other boys hadn't been able to do. She glanced up at his face briefly and saw a deep grin beginning to spread out over his face.

"Sure do, Miss Arvay. What I'm about to tell you will give you some kind of idea. One time I was bossing a gang of lumberjacks and we was felling a big stand of cypress when a terrible thunderstorm come up all of a sudden. It was a mighty bad storm, Miss Arvay. Big wind a'blowing, heavy drops of rain, both chain and ball lightning forking from tree-top to tree-top and zig-zagging around something awful.

Well, a great big bolt of that lightning, red-hot and gritting its teeth, took off and headed straight at me. It's a habit of mine, Mis Arvay, when I catch a streak of lightning aiming at me, to stand in my tracks and slap it right back where it come from."

Arvay with the front of her skirts lifted slightly was mounting the steps side by side with Jim. She looked up at his face in buck-eyed astonishment.

"Slap lightning, Mister Meserve?"

"Yep, because I don't aim to be imposed on like that by nothing nor nobody. But this here streak of lightning must of been even faster than it's supposed to be, because the next thing I knowed, it had done got past my hand and struck me."

"Struck you, and you ain't dead?"

"That's right, Miss Arvay. I'm shamed to admit it, but it hit me, *kerwhammmmm!* and right in the head at that. All I could do to stay on my feet from that lick the lightning hit me. Man! But was I mad! Just as hot as Tucker when the mule kicked his Mammy. All them colored men that was working under me come running to see if I was killed. Outside of a slight headache, there was nothing wrong with me at all. Told 'em they might as well go on back to work. I wasn't hurt at all, but that sneaking bolt of lightning was done up pretty bad. Yes, Ma'am! Last I seen of it, it was going off through the woods a'limping."

Jim's face brimmed over with laughter like an orange being squeezed, and he stood with one hand resting on the jamb of the door holding back the explosion until Arvay joined him in it.

"Why, Mister Meserve!" Arvay flashed angry eyes up at him. "Telling that big old something-ain't-so, and on the Sabbath Day at that!"

Jim stood in utter amazement as she made to push past him and go inside. "Poking fun at people and taking 'em for dumb fools!" Arvay went on. "Nobody with any sense would put a bit of dependence in anything that you say. Always trying to make light of folks."

With that Arvay flounced angrily inside the house. Jim hesitated outside the door for a second. If he had not been specifically invited to partake of dinner by Brock Henson, warmly

seconded by Maria, and had not gladly accepted, he would have turned and left the place. But he followed Arvay. She was flinging her hat on the home-made hat-rack against the wall in the hall, and as Jim came up to her, was about to walk away without even offering to rest his hat. As he removed it, she snatched it out of his hand and hung it on one of the cow-horns without a word.

Maria, with an apron over her Sunday clothes, poked her head in the back door of the hall and beamed.

"Oh, so you all got back from church, did you? Walk right in the parlor, Mister Jim, and make yourself comfortable. Dinner'll be on the table tuhreckly."

"I thank you, Mrs. Henson." Jim replied as cheerfully as he could and walked on into the parlor ahead of Arvay. He sat down on one of the old parlor-rockers near the organ, and Arvay sank down on the horse-hair sofa on the other side of the room. She reached for a palm-leaf fan from the lower shelf of the table and began to fan herself nervously.

"You mean that you didn't see the joke in that tale, Miss Arvay?" Jim asked.

"Oh, so that was supposed to be a joke? I don't favor so many jokes, Mister Meserve. I don't like to be took for a fool. I admire for folks to talk plain and say just what they mean."

Arvay stole a look across the room and saw that something seemed to be troubling the man in his face, and she interpreted it from what she had inside her. Fear flew to her heart. Maybe Larraine knew her old feelings about Carl, and had maliciously said something to Jim about it. She remembered that Larraine had been talking to Jim for a few minutes on the church-grounds while she had been tied up elsewhere. It would be just like 'Raine to do a trick like that.

Jim, for his part, balked and puzzled, was trying to find an easier way with Arvay. While he sought, he entertained himself by taking stock of the room. There was the what-not in one corner loaded down with the usual things: sea-shells, a mustache cup and saucer with a motto on it in gilt letters, a cheap Japanese fan spread open, numerous other bits of cheap crockery with fanciful shapes and colors. There was the inevitable center table with the big family Bible on the under shelf. On top of the table was the parlor kerosene lamp, with a

decorated globe, and a strip of red flannel in the oil compartment for decoration. A cheap family album was on one corner of the table under the lamp, and a stereoptican lantern with pictures on the corner cater-cornered across. The remaining corners held fancy cups and saucers.

The four walls were crowded with ill-assorted pictures. All those in frames had nails beneath them so that the frame rested on these nails and leaned out from the wall at the top. The place of honor, over the mantlepiece was held by some artist's concept of General Robert E. Lee at Manassas. In that era, battle scenes were in high favor, and in these scenes, the generals all sat on rearing, fat-rumped horses. Though the enemy was always right up under the feet of the general's horse, he assumed that the men he led could not see them. Generals always pointed either their swords or their fingers to show his men the enemy. Lee, astride his famous Traveller, was pointing at the blue-clad Union soldiers and looking furious.

There were lithographs, unframed, depicting Bible scenes tacked plentifully around the walls. Peter was there in his unfortunate attempt to walk the waters like Christ. Acknowledging his lack of faith and his failure, he was pictured as squatting on the surface of the water, looking up guiltily into the face of his Master, who stood there calmly on the waves. It struck Jim that if Peter could squat like that without sinking, he could walk, and he started to comment on it, but remembered and held his peace. The other pictures, with the exception of a gaudy calendar advertising feed, seed, and fertilizers, were family pictures done in the prevalent crayon enlargements in showy frames. Brock Henson in a fierce mustache was on a bamboo easel in the corner by the sofa. There was one, obviously the wedding picture, in which Brock sat cross-legged in a chair with a stiff derby hat on his knees, and a young and pretty Maria standing beside the chair with one hand resting on his shoulder. Maria the mother, was in another frame, seated with a fat blob that must be Arvay on her lap, while another disfigurement that had to mean Larraine in a highly ruffled dress, leaned against her knee. This picture gave him an opening for conversation.

"That's you and your mother and your sister, ain't it?"

"Yes." Arvay answered, and ceased waving her fan for a moment. "That was took in Monticello one time when I wasn't nothing but a baby. A man come long two or three years back making enlargements, so Ma give it to him to get enlarged."

"Oh, I see." Jim pretended an interest that he did not feel, and now that he had an opening, he carried on. "Larraine looks so jolly in the picture, and even when you talk to her, that I'm surprised that she took up with that sorry preacher. How come that to come about, you reckon?"

"Why?" And Arvay's eyes flung wide open in a fright that Jim could not understand. "Why, how come you to ask a thing like that?"

"Oh, it's nothing to take so serious as all that, Miss Arvay. I just had the notion that your sister wasn't so full of religion as all that, and neither your pastor, so far as that is concerned. He looks like nothing but a big old humbug to me, and I wondered how she happened to get took in by something like that."

"Oh," Arvay sort of gasped, and the next thing Jim knew she was sprawled out on the sofa in the grip of a spasm.

"Good God, she's took with that again!" Jim jumped to his feet. "Mrs. Henson! Mrs. Henson!" He called out. "Come quick! Miss Arvay is having another spasm!"

Mrs. Henson came running, and she had the sugar dish with a teaspoon in it in one hand and a small flat bottle of spirits of turpentine in the other. The harshness of spirits of turpentine had earned it a high place as a cure-all.

"Oh, do, Jesus!" Maria Henson panted. "Look like she's took worse than usual. Help me with her, will you, Mister Jim?"

"Be only too glad to, if you'll show me what to do."

All the time, Jim was studying the behavior of the girl very closely.

"Hold her down, will you, whilst I drop three drops of this here teppentime on a spoonful of sugar. That always fetches her around."

Jim obligingly took hold of Arvay's shoulders, while Maria, with shaking hands, fixed the preparation.

"Got to git it to her mighty quick," Maria trembled out. "Git this spoon betwixt her teeth do she's liable to bite her

tongue off." She stooped and tried to force the spoon between the clenched teeth. Just then, Arvay flailed out with both arms, and the loaded spoon went flying across the room. "Oh, my Gawd, Mister Jim! She's liable to be done bit her tongue in two before I can git anymore fixed for her. Hold her for me tight as you can, please."

"Here, you're nervous your ownself, Mrs. Henson. You better take hold of her shoulders and lemme try to fix the medicine and get it in her mouth."

Jim's tone of authority gave Maria confidence, and she grabbed hold of the struggling girl, while Jim retrieved the spoon, dipped up fresh sugar, and standing directly over Arvay's head, took the little bottle and began to drop the turpentine. He was very deliberate.

"Make haste!" Maria screamed. "Git that spoon in her mouth before she bites her tongue! Do, my Maker!"

"She ever bit it as yet?" Jim asked calmly as he waited for the second drop to fall.

"Naw, but she's liable to. Hurry up!"

But Jim, standing there tall and composed over Arvay, would not be hurried. There were seconds, it seemed to Maria between each drop. Two of the drops were finally deposited on the sugar in the spoon. The mother looked anxiously, tracing the course of each drop. Jim looked from the bottle to the spoon, to Arvay's face and back again to the poised bottle and the spoon. Now for that last third drop. Suddenly his hand gave a nervous twitch, and the third, or maybe third and fourth drop together, missed the spoon entirely, and landed right in the outside corner of Arvay's right eye.

Then a hurricane struck the over-crowded parlor. Arvay gave a yell from the very bottom of her lungs and catapulted her body from that sofa. She was all over the room at one time, seemingly, knocking over and upsetting things. Jim thought that she was going to climb the wall like a cat, and all the time she was gasping out yells. Jim heard Brock's footsteps hurrying up the hall just as Arvay got her directions and split out of the door. She collided with her father, rushed on past the temporary obstruction, and vanished down the hall in a cloud of flying yellow hair and pink skirts. Nothing but

scream and screech in her wake as she made it to the back porch.

There was a frantic rattle of metal from the back porch.

"Poor, poor, thing!" Maria moaned. "Trying to git to some water to wash out her eye. I better go help her."

"We can all go help her with her eye," Jim offered as Brock Henson appeared in the parlor door. "Looks like she's sort of over her spasm by now." Jim and Brock Henson stood face to face and looked each other dead in the eye for a long moment. "We'll give what aid we can in washing out her pretty eye." With a dry grin smothering in his face, Jim led the way to the back porch.

Arvay was splashing cold water in her face frantically. Brock went and ranged himself against the wall. Jim took the half empty water pail and went out to the well and drew it full. Maria fluttered around like a hen with ducks for children at the edge of a pond and made little noises of sympathy.

"What took place in there, Arvay?" Brock asked unnecessarily, as Jim mounted the porch with the full bucket of fresh water.

"That varmint! Oooooooooh! He poured teppentime right in my eye! He done it a purpose, too." Arvay splashed and sobbed.

"Oh, I don't reckon he meant it to hurt you," Brock said casually. "Your eye ain't hurt none to mention. That being the case, you sure ought to thank him. Quickest cure for spasm-fits I ever did see. Yessiree!"

Arvay turned on Jim. "You long-legged scoundrel-beast, you! You and your no-count jokes. I got a good notion to take me a gun and kill you!"

"Aw, now, Miss Arvay," Jim drawled in good-humored unconcern. "You wouldn't take and kill you best-goodest would you?"

"Git away from me, sir! Git on away from me! Pouring teppentime in my eye for a joke. Git! Light a shuck offen this place!"

"Damn!" Brock breathed deeply impressed. "Jim, you sure done worked a miracle. I never knowed that Arvay had that much life in her."

"It's all right, Mr. Henson, I'll be able to handle all that. A

woman knows who her master is all right, and she answers to his commands. We'll make out good enough."

Arvay, egged on to greater rage, ran to the shelf and seized the bucket of water.

"Git from here, Jim Meserve! If you don't hurry up and git from here, I aim to dash this bucket of water on you. Git! And don't you dast to foot this place again."

Arvay was further maddened by the evidence that Jim was not sorry for what he had done. Not godly sorry anyway. He put on a sorry look on his face, but his eyes were grinning.

"Go ahead and fling that water on me, if you will and want to, Miss Arvay, but you ought to know that I wouldn't want to do a single thing to hurt *you*, not on purpose, anyhow. I beg your humble pardon for letting that little tetch of teppentime git into your eye. I wouldn't harm a hair on your pretty head. Fact is, I'd rather all the rest of the women in the world to be dead than for you to even have the toothache. That's the way I feel towards you."

Arvay had no more wish to throw water on Jim at all, but she stood there with the bucket in her hand, and not knowing how to get rid of it with dignity, just stood there. Jim helped her out. He stepped up, took the pail and put it back up on the shelf, then turned with an undisguised grin on his face this time.

"It was a good thing, Miss Arvay and you know it. Saved you a lot of spells of sickness, and me a whole lot of doctors bills."

Arvay got that, and right in front of her parents too. It gave her a stirring feeling inside, though she still held her mouth in an angry line.

"Anyhow," Jim went on and actually laughing now, "it got you to your feet long enough for me to talk to you and to tell you how I feel."

Arvay began to believe a little in Jim's sincerity, him talking like that right in the presence of her folks, and all. Then a terrible feeling of guilt came over her. Even if Jim meant it, she was not fitten. Here was the most wonderful man in all the world pomping her all up, and she had been living in mental adultery with her sister's husband for all of those wasted years. She was not fitten for a fine man like Jim. He

was worth more than she was able to give him. The Bible said plainly that you could sin inwardly just as much as if you had actually done the thing, and she had sinned. Nothing to do but to turn her back on her happiness and never let on that she had ever wanted Jim. But now that meant turning from the noonday of joy back into the dark mole holes that she had been living in so long. It was a terrible choice. But to be honest with Jim, there was nothing else for her to do. She acted on the conviction immediately. She brushed past him towards the door into the hall to retire to her room until Jim was gone.

"Where do you think you're going?" Jim demanded and grabbed her by her arm and jerked her backwards. "You can't leave here unlessen you say that I'm forgiven for what I did."

"I, I better go comb my hair, I reckon," Arvay said.

"Yeah, do," Maria urged. "It looks like a whoo-raw's nest. Dinner is all fixed, so don't be all day in there."

"And come ready to say the right thing soon as you get back," Jim ordered. "Shake a leg! The foundations of my patience gives way mighty easy."

Arvay went off meekly enough. She wanted to be by herself to think awhile anyway. She was falling into step with hope and she wanted to pick herself over inside just in case. As she combed out her hair and put it up again, she thought and asked questions of herself. If Jim really wanted her, what about herself?

Now, in the first place, was she really in love? She was beginning to feel that she was, or could be anyway. She might recede from this high point in the future, and retreat to the one of ruthlessness where only those things that count with the neighbors would seem worth fighting for, but right now she was smoking with illusions.

And the way Jim had talked coming along the road made things seem too easy. He had just as good as excused the woman he married from all worry and bother. In so many words he had said, "Love and marry me and sleep with me. That is all I need you for. Your brains are not sufficient to help me with my work; you can't think with me. Let's get this thing straight in the beginning. Putting your head on the same pillow with mine is not the same thing as mingling your

brains with mine anymore than crying when I cry is giving you the power to feel my sorrow. You can feel my sympathy but not my sorrow." All in all, that meant that if she married Jim Meserve, her whole duty as a wife was to just love him good, be nice and kind around the house and have children for him. She could do that and be more than happy and satisfied, but it looked too simple. There must be a catch in it somewhere. Being of high family, and having more book learning than she had, and being all that handsome, he could be as choosey as he pleased, and he was bound to be looking for something else. There was bound to come a time when he was going to feel outdone in not finding those other things in her.

Arvay took a long, tremulous breath. Her heart was leading her into the arms of Jim Meserve. The fearful future lying in ambush for her. Well, maybe God would have mercy and help her when it came. She might be able to hold onto Jim, and keep him from quitting her some way or another. Holding her breath in a fearful tenseness, she changed into a fresh dress, pinched her cheeks to make them pink, and slowly went out to join Jim and her father on the back porch.

Jim looked at her with admiration and came and stood in front of her and looked down earnestly into her face.

"All right now," he jollied, "what you got to say?"

"I got to forgive you, I reckon, Mister Meserve."

"You had better. I'm liable to take and frail you good."

Arvay smiled and cast her eyes to the floor. Then she reached out timidly and took his hand. "Come on. I got something pretty to show you before Maw can get dinner on the table. 'Tain't nothing but a mulberry tree, but I think it's fine."

Arvay pulled and they jumped off the porch into the yard. Just then Maria stuck her head out of the kitchen door.

"No time for that now, Arvie. I'm just putting dinner on the table."

"Won't take but a minute, Maw. I want to show him where I used to play doll-house."

"What in the nation for, Arvie? 'Tain't a thing out there for nobody to see at all. You ain't had no play-things out there for the last longest, and Mister Meserve done seen a many

mulberry tree before now, I 'speck. I wants to git out of this
hot kitchen over this cook-stove."

Arvay didn't talk back, but she led Jim on off determinedly.
She held on to Jim's hand and hurried him along. Her
mother had no idea about her at all, she was beginning to
believe. Before anything more could be said, she wanted a
cleansing of her sacred place. She wanted Carl and all her
thoughts about him to be gone from under that mulberry
tree. She wanted to feel that the temple was cleansed, and
that she herself was clean and worthy of what she was about
to receive. Only the strength that Jim radiated could drive out
the old things. Jim just had to come here and broom out
before she risked sitting down to the table with him and having
him say that he cared for her and ask her to marry him. Arvay
all but ran across the field, dragging Jim along with her.

They entered the place under the tree and stood there hand
in hand, almost hidden from the outside by the low-hanging,
supple limbs. It was a cool green temple of peace.

"Oh, but this is nice and pleasant," Jim exclaimed. "I don't
fault you for liking it here. Feels like we got the world all to
ourselves under here. Just you and me."

Arvay held tight to Jim's hand and said nothing. She led
him around the tree in a solemn walk till they came back to
the same spot again. She stood looking up through the new
green leaves, punctuated by tiny fuzzy things that looked like
green, stubby worms. Those were the young mulberries com-
ing on. She was just standing there clinging to Jim's hand and
feeling that everything little had been swept away by bigness
when she heard her mother bawling for them, sharply and
impatiently.

The feeling around the table was tense for a while. Every-
body thinking about the same thing and trying to act like
they were not. It was obvious that the tale Brock felt impelled
to tell about marriage customs in the backwoods of Arkansaw
was prompted by his thoughts.

"Girls marry off soon back in Arkansaw where I come
from," Brock began by way of ringing in his story, and both
Arvay and Maria jumped at the crudeness of the way Brock
was bringing out what they were all thinking about.

"You didn't come from no Arkansaw," Maria snapped by

way of heading off what she knew was coming. "You was borned back there in middle Georgia."

"Matters a difference about where I was borned, Maria. I'm talking about what I learned when I was visiting over there in the backwoods of Arkansaw. Now."

"You ain't even been nowhere near there, Brock, so you might as well squat that rabbit right now and jump another one. Anyhow, nobody don't want to hear that old-time lie. You done told it so many times that everybody is sick and tired of hearing it."

That was a way that Brock had for the last year or so. Everything that happened was in Arkansaw, influenced by a paper-backed book that had the rural South by the ears for the last few years and had become a sort of laughing Bible among them, called *A Slow Train Through Arkansas.*

"But I want to hear him tell it," Jim said. "Never been in them parts myself, and I'd favor to get some information on the marrying subject just as quick as I can. I needs any assistance I can get hold of along in here."

Arvay as well as her mother suffered. Act too anxious, and it might drive the man away. And just as things looked kind of hopeful, Brock had to flap his big mouth. Arvay sat stiff with misery. Maria suddenly remembered that she had not brought in the bowl of gravy and the pitcher of lemonade, and mentioning it, gave herself opportunity to not be present when the disaster struck her child.

But Brock, full of his purpose, was not hurried. He wallowed the thing around and waited for Maria to go and come. He watched Maria settle miserably into her seat again and then began:

"Oh, 'tain't much of a story, Jim, it's just the habit they got back there in them Arkansaw mountains. When a fellow sees a girl he figgers he'd love to marry, he goes to her Paw and asks for her. So the girl's Paw, if the fellow is agreeable to him, calls the girl to him, and they stand her up in a barrel. If her head sticks out, they figger that she's old enough to git married, and he turns her over to her new husband."

"Unhunh!" Jim chuckled. "That's a good system, but how about it if she ain't tall enough for her head to stick out the barrel? Do the fellow have to wait till she grows some more?"

"Not in Arkansaw." Brock laughed. "Naw, indeed. If her head don't stick out, they saws the barrel off some."

Both of the men burst out laughing loud at that, but Arvay felt stiff around her lips, and the fork fell from her fingers. Jim was going to think that she was much too old to marry from that. But she saw Jim with a serious face look at her as if he had caught her in some crime.

"Then they don't have no chance to do no missionarying around out there, eh?"

"Not a tap." Brock assured him positively, "And it's a damned good thing too, I figger."

"You got a barrel handy, Mr. Henson?" Jim asked with a serious face.

"Sure have."

Jim pretended to scramble to his feet. "Well, maybe it can wait till after dinner is over. Into the barrel Miss Arvay goes, and if her head sticks out, I'm marrying her just as sure as gun's iron."

"You sound like you got serious notions about courting, Jim."

"Look like none of you all don't understand me quite as yet," Jim replied very seriously. "I talk just like I spit. When I spit, it hits the ground, it never comes back to my mouth, does it?"

"Don't recollect that I ever knowed a thing like that to happen," Brock considered.

"Well then, when my word goes forth, I never rue back on it either. And I mean to say right here that I mean to marry Miss Arvay if she will have me. That's been my whole intention ever since the first time that I laid eyes on her. That's what I stayed here in Sawley for. If she can see her way clear to marry me, I mean to do all within my power to do to make her life comfortable and happy."

"Spoke like a natural man," Brock said quickly. "Nobody couldn't say no more than that. So far as I'm concerned, you have my consent. I couldn't wish her to be in better hands. Now, what you got to say on the subject, baby?"

Arvay took good notice. Her father was not in the habit of using pet names to her. Calling her "baby" now was his way of pleading with her to consent. She had known for a long

time that her father wanted her to be married and off his hands, so that was all right with her in a way. It was something different from that that made her fumble and twist the fringe of the tablecloth and drop her eyes while they all waited so anxiously for her answer.

"I thank you for your compliments, Mr. Meserve, and I'll accept if you feel that you really want me. That is, providing you make me a promise not to drop no more teppentime in my eye."

Chapter Three

"ARVAY, what in the world is got the matter with you?"

"How, Ma?"

"Out and gone nearly every blessed night. We ain't had but a month from the start off to get you ready for your wedding, and you ain't got no time to waste traipsing around with Jim from place to place. If it ain't a cane-grinding, it's a candy-pulling. If it ain't that, it's a peanut-biling. If it ain't a peanut-biling, it's a square dance, and you never used to dance. And you need all that time to get your sewing done. You got no time for all that."

"Jim, Ma. Look like he wants me with him."

Arvay did not choose to elaborate. It was true that Jim liked to attend all those social doings, but Arvay knew that she was not forced to go along with Jim. Her fear would not let her trust Jim off too much alone. Nobody was going to whisper anything to Jim while she was present. Being a preacher's wife, Larraine no longer danced, but she did attend many of the other doings. Arvay felt the need of getting her things ready even more than her mother did, but her unease would not permit her to risk letting Jim run into Larraine when she was not there.

Larraine had been rather nice, though. She had made Arvay a wedding nightgown trimmed with lace, and had bought the white kid slippers to go with the white dotted swiss that Arvay was to stand up in. Brock Henson had provided the money for the goods for the wedding dress and the Alice blue mull dress that Arvay was just finishing off this minute. She was to put it on for the reception. It was cut low in the neck with short puff sleeves.

Arvay was always with Jim in public, but she held away from him when they were alone. She did not feel fitten for him, never realizing how her contradictory behavior worried the man. Jim supposed that she would not go back on her promise, but that was not enough for Jim to marry on. He wanted things complete. His worries on that score followed him everywhere. To bed, at the table, and at his work. It was

like a sand-spur sticking in his skin. Particularly, he thought about it a great deal as he rode or walked through the "drifts" inspecting faces on the trees and checking generally on the work.

Two weeks of his marriage, Jim was down in the woods checking up for the pay-roll at the end of the week. Jim loved the silent chasms of the drifts. The growths, the birds and the sounds of the wind in the pines. A man could think down in there, and feel.

Jim Meserve was what was known as a woodsman in the turpentine plan of things. That meant that he was the resident head of a camp. He ran the commissary and kept the accounts of the workers and made out the time. It was his job to "ride the woods" before the semi-monthly pay-day and evaluate the work of the chippers and dippers. Their pay depended upon the number of trees streaked or dipped. The number of trees could be reduced by the number improperly worked. The limit of a "drift," a territory of one chipper, is known as the "butting-line or block," so as Jim rode his horse from drift to drift, he could enjoy both the beauty and the solitude of the pine woods. Free from the press of details around the camp, Jim came alive and stretched out his soul. Usually then, he could work out his problems. This day, he felt that he had something to bother over.

Jim was not so sure that that was what he wanted, but he found that he could not help himself. What was the matter with his engagement? He felt as if he had grabbed hold of a running man by the coat, and the man had run off, leaving Jim holding the empty jacket.

"Hands full of nothing, mouth full of 'much obliged.' " Jim heard somebody singing blues at a distance.

"Nobody but Joe Kelsey," Jim laughed. He ought to know that was Joe. He was in Joe's drift. Only two men working it, the chipper and the dipper, and he knew Joe's voice from Charlie's. He ought to know it anywhere, as he said. He had made a friend out of the Negro, or the Negro had made a friend out of him, one or the other.

"Good time to run up on Joe, too. Maybe Joe might know something that could help me just in here." He hurried back to his horse and mounted. He had spotted a few cups that Joe

had not cleaned out well, but he didn't care too much. That was not so good for the company, but he was not going to kick up a fuss with Joe Kelsey about it at all, because somehow, he liked the man tremendously. Joe Kelsey was a reddy brown Negro, ugly as sin, but with the best-looking smile that Jim had ever seen on a man. It always lit him right up. It always made Jim feel like playing and joking. Just seeing Joe put him into a playful mood and he decided at once to slip up on Joe and play some practical joke.

Now Joe had switched to that teppentime song:

"Oh, don't you see dat rider coming?"

The song went on to point out to dippers, chippers, wood-cutters and teamsters the perils of being caught fooling around on the job by the over-rider.

Jim got up close to Joe's back and made a sudden howl like an angry bob-cat on the kill. At the same time, he clawed his fingers and stuck them into Joe's broad back.

Joe jumped around, pretending great fright, and for a minute both men went into the act of pretending. Then they both broke into loud laughter.

"You *ought* to be skeered, Joe, even if you ain't. You ain't doing a goddamn thing down here in this drift but shamming."

"Why, you, Mister Jim! Why, I'm almost to the butting-line."

"And leaving nigh on to a barrel of gum behind you that you ain't dipped clean, you scoundrel-beast, you."

Joe did not defend himself by claiming perfection. He pointed out his family worries, the slick and tricky way that moonshine likker had a way of slipping up on him, and so on and so forth.

"I know, I know," Jim retorted in mock sternness. "It's Saturday nights that's your trouble Joe. Saturday pay-night, you spend all you got on likker and women. Before draw-day, you're pestering my life out of me for more money. Pretty nearly every man on the camp is the same way. Saturday night! Saturday night! Look like that's all you colored folks live for on this camp, Saturday night!"

Joe looked very serious while Jim was preaching. When the

woodsman had finished, Joe kept on looking serious. Finally he scratched his head and seemed to reach a conclusion.

"I speck youse right about that Saturday night business, Mister Jim. Fact of the matter is, I knows youse dead right. But if you ever was to be a Negro just *one* Saturday night, you'd never want to be white no more."

Jim looked at Joe in astonishment for a moment, then he burst out laughing and turned away.

"You're just all right, Joe. Maybe I could learn something from that."

Jim went on to where his horse was tied and mounted. Nearly a mile farther to the west he came upon another man chipping and dismounted. This was not Joe, so Jim was critical. He got into an argument with the chipper.

"Sink 'em in, there Charlie, sink 'em in! You ain't doing a thing but scratching that tree. Keep on scratching, and you'll be done scraped up kin. Sink 'em in!"

Charlie let his streaking iron rest on the ground for a minute as he turned a surly look on Jim. The known best chipper on the camp to be spoken to like that!

"I'm sinking 'em. What you want me to do, cut the tree down?"

"And looky there." Jim jumped from the depth of the streaks to something else. "You're drawing that face in. Keep on, it'll tossle afterwhile. And I noticed some trees back there where you put on some streaks too deep. You must be figgering on laying by timber instead of making gum. Work like that can kill off trees."

After more fault-finding, and leaving a surly Charlie behind him, Jim rode on off. He knew that he was too finicky with the man, and he knew that it was because he was not just satisfied with Arvay in a way. There seemed to be a hold-back to her love. Did she love some other man whom she could not get, and was just marrying him so as to be able to say that she had a husband of her own? Or was it that damn missionary business? Whichever one it was, it could be a lot of trouble later on. But what to do? He loved the girl too much by now to give her up! So what in hell to do? Whom could he turn to for advice? He could think of no one but Joe Kelsey, and possibly his wife, Dessie, who cooked and did for him

around his bachelor quarters on the camp. Joe had plenty experience with women, certainly. Maybe he could help.

But what Joe said that night on the commissary porch, after he had listened intently to Jim about his coming marriage, worried Jim even more.

"If it's like that, Boss, you got something to think about. Because if a woman don't get hold of the man she really wants, God help the man she do get. And if she don't get hold on none at all, God help the surrounding country!"

However, Joe did leave one shine of hope out of the things he said.

"Most women folks will love you plenty if you take and see to it that they do. Make 'em knuckle under. From the very first jump, get the bridle in they mouth and ride 'em hard and stop 'em short. They's all alike, Boss. Take 'em and break 'em."

Jim Meserve went to bed thinking hard.

Chapter Four

ARVAY and her mother were in the girl's bedroom sewing in a rush the next afternoon when Arvay heard somebody hail at the gate. It was Joe Kelsey astride a sweating horse. Recognizing him as one of Jim's men, Arvay told him to come on in.

He had a note from Jim, and Arvay tore it open and read it while he stood on the steps and waited.

It was a short note. All it said was that Jim would be there the next day right after dinnertime to take Arvay for a buggy-ride. She had better have on her good clothes, for they were going somewhere. Arvay told Joe to wait and took the note inside and handed it to her mother.

"That pesky Jim! Look like he don't intend to give you no chance to get your things ready at all. Might as well send him word to come ahead. You young folks ain't nothing like we was in my day. You ain't at all responsible. If it wasn't for me doing most of the work, you'd be in a pretty fix, I'm telling you."

Arvay turned on her heels and went on back to the porch and gave Joe the message for Jim.

Over her mother's outraged protests, Arvay put on the blue mull dress the next day. She thought that it was very becoming to her looks. She was ready away ahead of time, but ate no dinner. She was excited and curious about this buggy ride, and besides her corset was laced very tight. She put on the new leghorn-intention hat with the big pink rose on the floppy brim and waited. She could not help from wondering, and even worrying some. Maybe Jim had found out. She looked down at her high-buttoned white shoes and wondered. Two more weeks and she would be safely married. She wished that the time would hurry up and come.

Jim drove up just after one. He was dressed up in his suit of clothes, a new hard felt hat with a wide brim, and he had attempted to lay his thick black curls with water. Arvay watched him through the parlor window as he hitched the rig under the chinaberry tree near the gate.

"There's that Jim of your'n out there at the gate," Mrs. Henson observed unnecessarily. "And dressed up so it 'ud take ten doctors to tell how near he's dressed to death." Mrs. Henson grumbled it out, but there was pride in her manner. "Reckon you better hurry on out and meet him. Don't bring him inside this tore-up house."

"No, you go, Ma. If I bust right on out there it would look like I was dressed and waiting on him. Look like I was too anxious to get him." Arvay was reluctant to find out news if it should happen to be bad.

So Mrs. Henson went to the door, noting as Jim came down the walk that was lined on either side with quart bottles stuck neck-downwards in the ground that Jim Meserve was a well-built man. He made her wish that she was young again. Jim had it all over the square-built, stocky man with the red face that she had married. He had it over Carl Middleton too, so far as that was concerned. They called Arvay slow and poky, but she was doing mighty well for herself.

"Come right in, Jim, and have a chair."

"No, Ma'am, I thank you. Ain't got much time for setting. Got to hurry right along. Where's Arvay, Ma'am?"

"Putting on her last fixings. You know how these young gals is." She turned her head inside the door and called out to her daughter, then turned back to the young man standing impatiently on the porch and gave the opinion that Arvay would be along "tuhreckly." He knew how these courting gals was, she reckoned.

In another minute or so, Arvay stood in the door and smiled at Jim.

"Well, I guess I'm ready. Where you taking me today?"

"Oh, you find out in plenty time. You ready?"

"Much as I ever will be, I reckon."

"Then the two of us is ready and rearing to go. But before we drive off, I favor to see that playhouse you used to play in under that mulberry tree. Oh, hello, there, Mr. Henson! Didn't expect to find you around home this time of day."

"Bear got me and I knocked off. Got my pay-roll all fixed up and ready anyhow." Brock Henson explained as he came to the door and made a place beside his wife where he could see the young couple on the porch.

"The bear is out there all right. Mighty hot for this time of the year. Persimmons won't never get ripe if this kind of weather keeps on."

"Where you and Arvay headed for dressed up like that?" Mrs. Henson asked, but her husband nudged her into silence.

"Oh, just round and about, Ma'am," Jim answered and took Arvay by the arm and headed her off the porch. "First thing, I want Arvay to show me her playhouse. Just favor to see the place today."

Arvay led Jim around the house towards the back, and trembled as she went. Jim held the girl's arm all the way as they went along unevenly over clods that had grass grown over them, through patches of broom-straw and down to the back and bottom of the place where the huge mulberry tree stood in swaying majesty. There was a breeze, and the big leafy growth rolled in the arms of the wind.

"Well, here it is," Arvay said as they stooped under the low-hanging willowy limbs and straightened up in the wide shady area under the tree. It was like a green cave under there, or like being inside a big green tent. Arvay wanted to hear what she would hear.

"Mighty nice place to play house in. You must have had a high old time with your playthings under here."

"Reckon so. But I growed out of things like that long time ago. Don't even know what become of the last ones I used to have."

Jim went and leaned against the great trunk of the tree and fixed his eyes on the girl in blue. He studied her so long that she became embarrassed.

"That would be natural," Jim conceded at last. "But anyhow, you just go along acting like you was playing house again anyhow. I figger that you would look awful pretty at it. Go ahead."

After some embarrassment, Arvay tried to re-live the thing for Jim, wondering what on earth he wanted her to do it for.

"Pa made me and Larraine a playhouse, and it used to be right here. Over there by the tree we had some sea-shells and things. Oh, we about fetched anything under here that we felt to keep to play with. Bottles and jars, and oh, you know things like that."

"Yeah, I know. Something like in a boy's pockets."

"I reckon so. I never even had no brother. What I liked to do when I was under here playing by myself was to catch hold of two low limbs like this and play like I was in a swing, and lean way back and gaze way up into the top of the tree. It looks so cool-like and tender green away up there. And when the wind shakes the leaves some, you can see through to the sky." And Arvay caught hold of two limbs and bracing her heels against the ground, play-acted the thing out for Jim. Her body was stretched out so that she was almost reclining as she trusted her weight to the limbs above her. "And that's when I found out that Heaven was so far off."

"How, Arvay?"

"Well, I looked and I looked as hard as I could through the top of the tree, and I never could make out a thing. No angels moving around or nothing. I never could see a thing, so I knowed that Heaven was further away than folks made out it was."

Arvay pulled herself erect, took off her heavy hat, and deposited it on the roots of the tree. Then she returned to her reclining position and peered earnestly up to the very top of the tree. Her skirt slid up slightly, revealing the tops of her shoes, and a glimpse of the ruffled top petticoat beneath.

Looking upwards so intently, Arvay did not see Jim when he sprang away from the trunk of the tree. She only knew that he had moved when she felt his arms suddenly thrust beneath her, and his hands digging into her side.

"Let go!" Jim commanded shortly.

Arvay brought her head up shortly, and for a brief moment their eyes met and held. Arvay's eyes questioned fearfully. Instinct told Arvay something, and she held on to the limbs desperately.

It was no use. Jim took one hand from under her and tore her grip from the swinging limbs. In a fraction of the second she was snatched from the sky to the ground. Her skirts were being roughly jerked upwards, and Jim was fumbling wildly at her thighs.

"Jim! You——"

Jim was gritting his teeth fiercely on encountering the barrier of her tight-legged drawers, seeking an opening. Finding

none, Arvay felt one hand reach up and grasp the waistband. There was a "plop" and the girl knew that the button was gone. A tearing sound of starched fabric, and the garment was being dragged ruthlessly down her legs. Arvay opened her mouth to scream, but no sound emerged. Her mouth was closed by Jim's passionate kisses, and in a moment more, despite her struggles, Arvay knew a pain remorseless sweet.

Not until Jim lay limp and motionless upon her body, did Arvay return to herself and begin to think, and with thinking, all her old feelings of defeat and inadequacy came back on her. She was terribly afraid. She had been taken for a fool, and now her condition was worse than before. It was more than she could bear, to have been so lifted up for a few weeks only to be cast down like this. What was to become of her now? Where would she turn for refuge? Not to her folks, certainly. She would get no sympathy there. Larraine would put on airs, and pity her all the more.

Jim moved slowly and dreamily and began to kiss her on her mouth and all over her face.

"I love you a million times more, darling," Jim whispered and took his hand to brush back the fallen strands of her hair from her forehead, and to kiss her there too.

He got to his feet, modestly bringing her with him so that they both stood erect and covered at the same time. He held her at arms length for a long minute, and tried to look into her downcast eyes. When he released her, he turned his back for a minute, and rearranged his clothes.

"We got to, we better be going now, honey. Come on and let's make haste."

So he had all he wanted of her, and he was ready to go.

Arvay's eyes crept over to her torn garment lying far over to the right where Jim had flung it.

"If you would be so kind as to excuse me for a few minutes, I——"

Jim understood and walked to the edge of the green wall and turned his back.

Arvay went swiftly to her drawers and picked them up. She shook off the little dust and a dry leaf and looked them over. The starchy little ruffle around the legs still stood bravely, but Arvay realized that she could not put them on. The button

was gone, and the plaquette was ripped all the way down one leg to the ruffle. But if she did not put them on somehow, what was she to do? Not roll them up and take them into the house under her arm. Her mother's sharp eyes would never miss a thing like that. Come walking into the house after being off with a man with your drawers under your arm would never do with Maria Henson. The drawers would have to stay there under the tree until Arvay got a chance to sneak them into the house and sew them up again. Anyway no one ever came to the mulberry tree nowadays. Not wishing to leave such an intimate and revealing garment lying on the ground, Arvay looked around for a better place, and spied a dead snag of a limb at the level of her head, and she hung her drawers on that. Then she walked over in deep embarrassment and stood beside Jim.

Jim turned and looked her over carefully. He smiled as he picked a dead leaf and bits of trash out of the back of her head. He smiled because he realized that the poor innocent thing knew nothing about secret trysts. She had no idea about leaving tell-tale signs.

"I better get you your hat so we can hurry on," and strode to the trunk of the tree and picked up the hat.

"I had sort of forgot it," Arvay admitted, and Jim smiled again.

"Lemme place it back on your pretty head," Jim murmured, and set it too far back on her head, and studied the effect for a minute. He changed it two or three times, while Arvay stood passively with a faint smile of embarrassment on her face.

"Look like I ain't so good on placing hats," Jim admitted at last with a laugh. "You better hook it on your ownself, I reckon. But hold on a minute, I got to take another kiss before you move."

With that, Jim caught hold of either side of the wide brim and pulled Arvay's face close to his. He kissed her lightly once or twice, then let go of the hat and began to kiss her passionately and hold her tightly in his arms. Unconsciously, Arvay's own arms went up and were locked around Jim's neck.

"That's right, sugar." Jim murmured. "Hug my neck for me. Hug me tight."

Jim's urging was altogether unnecessary. Some unknown power took hold of Arvay. She pressed her body tightly against his, fitting herself into him as closely as possible. A terrible fear came over her that he might somehow vanish away from her arms, and she sought to hold him by the tightness of her embrace and her flood of kisses. It seemed a great act of mercy when she found herself stretched on the ground again with Jim's body weighing down upon her. Even then she was not satisfied. Somehow, she seemed not to be able to get close enough to him. Never, never, close enough. She must eat him up, and absorb him within herself. Then he could never leave her again.

When she was on her feet again, Arvay kissed Jim voluntarily and without words. Jim returned the kiss then grabbed her hand.

"Now I know we got to go, and we better hurry."

He grabbed her hat off the ground, and seized her hand and together they stooped and came out from under the mulberry tree. Over her shoulder as she stooped, Arvay glanced back at her drawers swinging ever so gently in the breeze. She took it as a kind of sign and symbol. Where this man was hurrying her off to, she had no idea, but she was going, and leaving her old life behind her. Left behind, but not forgotten, to be picked up another time, perhaps.

When they reached the house, Arvay turned her head to the left so that she could not see the back door. Her mother might be standing there and would read her like a book. Arvay held on to Jim's hand and went on around the house. Her parents had evidently seen them when they came out from under the tree, and were following their progress, for as they came abreast of the room where her parents slept, she spied them peeping through the sugar-sack half curtains at the window. Arvay started, and Jim, looking in the same direction to see the reason, saw them too. They were doing their best to see all they could and interpret. They snatched heads back guiltily, but the young couple had caught on to what was going on. Then Brock, to cover up, shoved the curtain aside to hail them through the window.

Jim looked, grabbed Arvay by the hand and began to run towards the gate and the buggy tied there. Their progress was

not fast enough for Jim evidently, for he stopped, grabbed up Arvay who was slightly behind him, and ran staggering for the gate. He was growling like a tiger which had just made a kill and was being challenged. With the weight of the girl in his arms, he kicked open the gate, made it to the side of the buggy and thrust Arvay in as Brock Henson reached the front door. He untied the reins in a frenzy and leaped in himself while Brock walked the width of the porch to the steps, with Mrs. Henson stooped shouldered in the door and her caved-in mouth wide open. Jim grabbed the reins, slapped them smartly on the rump of the horse and yelled, "Git up! Git up, there!" And Arvay found herself flying down the sandy road.

She could not hear Brock exclaim, "Well, I'll be god-damned!" as he gazed down the road after the flying buggy. "What the hell do you reckon is going on?"

Nor could Arvay hear her mother complain, "Something that don't mean us no good, I'll bound you. Could be dragging our girl off somewhere to rape her and then leave her here on our hands. A young 'un without no name for us to look after and to feed and raise. All that money, nigh on to forty dollars that we done spent already on things to marry her off in, too. Brock Henson, youse the biggest fool I ever did see in all my born days! If you was any man at all, you'd take that shot-gun and get on your horse and overtake 'em. Make him marry her before the sun go down."

"Aw, I wouldn't be in such a hurry, if I was you, Maria. Arvay wasn't hollering or nothing. We couldn't swear to a thing."

"Arvay not hollering!" Mrs. Henson snorted as she went to the steps and shaded her hands and looked down the road. "Nothing like Larraine. That Arvay ain't got the sense she was born with. According to my notion, you had better go get your gun."

"Better let well enough do," Brock admonished and reached for the back of a rocker turned to the wall, whirled it around and sat down. "Far as I can see, things is coming along just fine as it is. Don't reckon Jim Meserve is the kind to back out now, with the wedding day all set and all. It would take a mighty heap of gall."

"Gall! That Jim ain't nothing else but gall. Tell me!"

Brock sat down, scrooged the chair around so that he did not have to look at his wife, cut himself another chaw, chawed his tobacco and spit his juice. He could send it expertly clear over the bannister and into the yard.

Speeding down the road towards Sawley, Arvay was tugging with the same emotions as her mother. Jim was silent there beside her as if nothing much had happened. He kept the horse at a fast trot and paid attention to the road. Arvay kept a fearful silence because she did not know how to begin what she wanted to say in order to find out what she wanted so much to know.

They were passing the last open field before the straggling houses of Sawley began when Jim turned his face upon Arvay and grinned.

"Arvay Henson!" Jim hailed oratorically, "The apostle to the heathens!" Then he chuckled some more.

Arvay looked at him with quickly troubled eyes. Look like Jim was making fun of her. Something closed up inside of her.

Jim laughed again. "No need for you to go proaging clean around the world no more looking for no heathens to save, though."

"Why, Jim? Is they all done saved or died off?"

"Naw, indeed. That is, I reckon there's plenty of 'em still left to save. But their case don't come up in your court no more."

So after what went on under the mulberry tree, Jim figgers that I ain't fitten no more to tote the Word, Arvay thought. No getting away from what had happened. Her drawers hung on the mulberry tree, waving with the wind. Who was she now, to be telling folks how to live?

"Don't be looking so sick over it, and putting on a long face, Arvay. Missionary work is for old maids and preachers. Youse a married woman now. You ain't got no time for that."

"Married?" Jim was cruel to be making game of her at a time like this.

"Why, sure you're married, Arvay. Under that mulberry tree."

"All I know is that I been raped."

"You sure was, and the job was done up brown."

"I could have hollered for Pa."

"And it would not have done you a damn bit of good. Just a trashy waste of good time and breath. Sure you was raped, and that ain't all. You're going to keep on getting raped. You couldn't be hollering for your Pa every day for the rest of your life, could you?"

"Every day?" Arvay looked across and up at Jim in startled bewilderment. "You sure got plenty nerve."

"So I been told. But that's the way the cloth's been cut, and that's the way it's made. No more missionarying around for you. You done caught your heathen, baby. You got one all by yourself. And I'm here to tell you that you done brought him through religion and absolutely converted his soul. He been hanging around the mourner's bench for quite some time, but you done brought him through religion, and saved him from a burning hell. You are a wonderful woman, Arvay."

The elements opened above Arvay and she arose inside of herself. This must mean that she had been forgiven on high. Her secret sin was forgiven and her soul set free! Else why would Jim be talking like she thought he was? She had paid under that mulberry tree.

"You talking about me and you, ain't you, Jim?"

"You know so well that I ain't talking about nobody else."

"But, but, you just got through saying that you meant to keep on raping me. That . . ."

"You got that right, and I mean to tell you, rape in the first degree. We're headed for the courthouse now, just as fast as we can wheel and roll. And the minute we get there, we're going to take out some papers on it."

"Jim!"

"You didn't realize? Good Lord Almighty! Where else would we be headed for? Arvay, I got a letter from love today, and I'll go to Hell but what I answer it. Git up there, you good-for-nothing nag, you! Git along!"

Arvay was back at her father's house before sundown, a married woman. The news of the elopement had spread over town quickly, and by seven o'clock, people began to arrive to

wish them well. Her mother, balked of the wedding excite-
ment, was all put out at first, but of necessity made the best of
things as they were. Both parents joined in pleading with Jim
to stay the night and give people chance to come and make
merry. Jim compromised. They were around until nine
o'clock, then he drove the six miles out to the camp with his
bride.

Jim carried Arvay over the doorsill and kissed her as he set
her feet down in the turpentine shack.

"Well, honey, you're home, for two months anyhow."

"Two months?"

"Yep. You know that I ain't no teppentime man when it
comes right down to the thing, and then it don't bring in
enough now that I got me a wife. Two months is enough I
figger to fix us so we can go away from here and hunt up a
better-paying job."

Teppentime shacks are not built for beauty. They are tem-
porary shelters. In a few years usually the woods are worked
out, and the camp is moved. The houses are torn down and
put up again at the new location. But this house with its four
crude rooms looked beautiful to Arvay. The rooms were im-
maculately clean, but the most important thing to her was
that it was her own home. "This is ours," Arvay murmured as
she went about touching furniture and walls.

"Yep. Your dice, baby, to do just as you damn please.
Gimme a kiss now and hug my neck for me. We better go on
to bed. Pay-day tomorrow and I'll have a lot to do."

Jim himself began to get ready for bed immediately, and
Arvay timidly followed him. She found out the reason for
Jim's haste very soon. Less than ten minutes after the lamp
had been blown out, there was a gentle rustling outside the
bedroom window, and then the full tones of a guitar broke
out, playing in the way that only Negroes play that instru-
ment. Clear melody, full-bodied harmony, and added bass
that imitated drums.

Arvay leaped out of bed and stood at the window. She
could not be seen because of the darkness within aided by the
curtains at the window. She stood in her bare feet and wed-
ding nightgown and lived through the serenade. Instrumental
pieces, blues sung by men and some by women; spirituals, not

sad and forlorn, but sung with a drummy rhythm to them; work songs and ballads.

The music outside did something strange and new to Arvay. The strains induced pictures before her eyes. They conjured up odors and tastes. Streams of colors played across the sky for her, and she tasted exotic fruits. Looking out into the white moonlight of the night, she saw the trees and the woods for the first time from inside. The sky-scraping pines became feeling beings, standing there forever watching, and watching, and whispering with their branches in a rumbling song. They were the tree-men with the many toes probing into the earth. The giants who stood forever on one foot and waited.

The concert came to an end on an old ballad that Arvay had heard often, but had never really learned. It was being led by a female voice, a deep alto, backed up by the other mingled voices and the guitar. Arvay resolved that she would learn that song the very next day. The song was an old, old ballad and it haunted you. Sweet and bitter mixed up in just the right amounts.

> Love, Oh, love, Oh careless love
> Goes right to the head like wine
> Broken the heart of many a poor girl
> But you'll never break this heart of mine.
>
> Love, Oh, love Oh, careless love
> Love, Oh, love Oh, careless love
> You cause me to weep, you cause me to moan
> You cause me to leave my happy home.

The ballad went on for many more verses, and Arvay was all but moved to tears. After a few minutes, she noticed that the serenade was over.

"Oh, that was just too sweet and too wonderful, Jim. Don't expect to ever forget this night, the longest day I live."

"This is some of that damn Joe Kelsey's doings," Jim grumbled to hide his own emotion. "It would be just like that bastard to cut a caper like that."

He stooped over quickly and fetched a five gallon jug from under the bed and hurried to the window.

"Thank you, folks. Me and my wife both thank you for the music of welcome home."

There was great applause at this, and Jim had to wait a long time for it to die down. Then Arvay saw a male figure step nearer the window, strike a pose and begin to deliver an elaborate ramble of welcome to the newly wed couple. After a few sentences, the speaker got lost and scrambled in the jungle of florid syllables, and the crowd outside began to jeer and scream with laughter.

"That'll do, Joe Kelsey," Jim yelled out with mock seriousness. "You done lied enough for one time. Here, take this jug of moonshine and see that everybody gets some. Now, don't go on off and drink it all up your ownself, you buzzard, you! You know I know you, Joe."

There was loud laughter at this back-handed caress, and the crowd hurried off to the Jook to have themselves a time.

"You oughtn't to have spoke to the poor man like that, especially after he got up the serenade for us, Jim."

"Pay that no mind, honey. Joe knows where he stands with me. I would trust Joe Kelsey quicker than any man on earth I know of, and Joe knows it."

"Is he the same one that you been sending in messages by?"

"That's right. He's my right-hand man around this camp. Dessie, the woman who's been doing for me here, is his wife. Two nicest folks it has ever been my pleasure to meet. I made arrangements for Dessie to help around some. Hope you find her all right too. She's evermore easy to get along with."

Arvay was a daughter of the South. She knew exactly what to think from that.

"Joe is your pet, I'll bound you."

"Kee-reck! Different from every other Negro I ever did see. He's remarkable. Honest as the day is long. Just mighty damn fine, that's all."

Arvay sympathized and understood. Every Southern white man has his pet Negro. His Negro is always fine, honest, faithful to him unto death, and most remarkable. Indeed, no other Negro on earth is fitten to hold him a light, and few white people. He never lies, and in fact can do no wrong. If he happens to do what other people might consider wrong, it

is never his Negro's fault. He was pushed and shoved into it by some unworthy varmint. If he kills somebody else, the dead varmint took and run into the pet's knife or bullet and practically committed suicide just to put the pet in wrong, the low-life-ted scoundrel-beast! If the white patron has his way, the pet will never serve a day in jail for it. The utmost of his influence will be invoked to balk the law. Turn go *his* Negro from that jail!

Arvay had asked, and Jim had consented for her to help him out around the commissary. He conceded that it would be a help to him and the women on the camp for the store to be open all day.

So from time to time, Arvay could have been seen, if anybody watched her closely enough, weighing up a pound or so extra for Dessie and Joe on everything. She balanced this off by either cutting some body else light weight, or waiting until she was alone in the store and adding a pound or so to some other account. Side-meat added to one, sugar and coffee to another, snuff and tobacco to still other people, and growing very haughty and mad if anybody complained. She came to be very fond of Dessie, and Joe was her husband's man.

Her married life moved on smoothly and happily for Arvay except for one thing. Larraine and Carl drove out two or three times every week. Larraine came even when Carl did not, and Arvay wished so much that she wouldn't. She couldn't say a thing against it, and that made it very hard. Jim would think it funny if she ordered her own sister off the camp, but that was just what Arvay felt like doing.

Larraine was too bossy, Arvay felt. Dashing in and bossing around, and taking things in charge. It looked as if she could not bear for Arvay to be the head of a single thing.

Arvay objected to Carl, not because he dipped in her business at all, but because he stirred up memories, and kept her feeling of guilt alive and active. She wanted to forget the whole thing. To cast it in the sea of forgetfulness, where it would never rise to shame her in this world, or condemn her in the Judgment.

In this same connection, Larraine gave her a lot of worry. She was always calling Jim aside and giving him advice on

how to manage things. Arvay, fearing that Larraine knew of her secret passion of the past, feared that 'Raine might by accident or intention let her tongue slip. Jim would lose his faith in her, and then where would she be? She would be miserable every time that her sister managed to get Jim off to one side. She searched his face for signs after every session. So far, she had seen nothing, but she wished that Larraine would stay off the place. Oh, well, the two months would soon be up, and she and Jim would be off somewhere too far for Larraine to be around. Arvay shook and trembled, and saved her complete happiness for that day.

Then the blow fell. She had been married for only six weeks when she was almost knocked off her feet by Dessie.

They were in the kitchen together. Dessie often helped her out in more ways than she was being paid for. Dessie looked at her very hard and began to chuckle.

"What's wrong, Dessie?"

"I declare! That husband you done married is all parts of a man."

"What do you mean by that, Dessie?"

"Youse knocked up, that's what."

"Knocked up?" Arvay had heard the term too many times to misunderstand what was meant by it. Arvay just did not want to hear it.

"Going to have a young 'un, just as sure as youse born to die."

"No, Dessie. I'm sure that you're mistaken. I, I ain't noticed a thing."

"That's because it's a little early for signs just as yet. You ain't hardly more'n a month gone up right now. But you will. I can see that th'obbing in your neck. Youse up the creek, honey, and they ain't no iffs and ands about it."

"Dessie!" Arvay moaned.

"Oh, 'tain't nothing to be scared about. I done had five, and 'tain't nothing to the thing. You has birth-pains, naturally, but lemme tell you, them is the easiest forgotten pains they is in all the world. Oh, you remembers enough about it later on to tell about it, but that's about all you can do. Don't you worry none."

Arvay had every intention to keep the secret to herself until

after Jim had notified the owner that he was leaving, but she had no chance. Larraine drove up that very afternoon behind her little bay mare, and Dessie, not realizing what she did, hurried to tell "Miz' Middleton" the news. Jim came home to get a new hame to take out to the barns and Larraine had to up and blab her mouth to Jim.

Jim was glad and proud enough, but the upshot of it was that Jim said what Arvay had feared. It meant that they could not go away until the child was born. He wouldn't think of dragging his wife around from pillar to post in her condition.

In her nervous turmoil, brought on by disappointment and memories of other frustrations, somehow Arvay found her eyes fixed on Larraine's throat. That night Arvay had a strange dream. She saw 'Raine's white neck. It was huge like the stand-pipe at the water works, and down its long length blood was running and running from a huge gash near the top. Somehow she was impelled to look at her own hands, and in her right was a long sharp knife. Arvay woke up with a start, and scrouged up just as close to Jim as she could. She was almost afraid to go to sleep again.

Another night Arvay dreamed that she was in a beautiful forest of trees and very happy. Music and singing were coming to her from unseen voices. Suddenly the instruments and voices hushed as if in terrible fear. In the silence, Larraine came walking through the woods. A tiger leaped upon Larraine and tore her throat away. Great streams of blood ran down and some of it clotted between Larraine's breasts. Somehow Arvay was not afraid of the tiger. She looked on indifferently as the beast lapped Larraine's blood fiercely, and when he was sated, and moved away the music began again. Waking, Arvay shuddered with remorse. She knew then that she had been hating her own sister for years.

Jim himself began to notice how nervous Arvay was getting to be. He thought that the store was too much worry for her, and told her not to bother with it anymore. He would make out all right. But Arvay said no, it was just that she was tired of teppentiming, she guessed, and wanted to make a change.

"Jim, please! Take me on off. I won't care if we don't have much spending change for a while. I just crave to go away from here."

"Can't see my way clear to do that, Little-Bit. It wouldn't be the right thing for me to do. You're nervous on account of your condition. I wouldn't be no kind of a husband at all if I didn't look out for you no better than that. And then, Dessie is an A-number-one mid-wife. I'd rather for you to be where she could see after you."

"Couldn't we go and take Joe and Dessie with us?"

"That would be a hot come-off when we don't even know where we are going to be our ownselves. You just wait. The minute that you get able to move with the baby, I'll make a move."

"Six more months, maybe, Jim."

Can't be helped, Arvie. It ought not to seem so long. And then too, you got your folks close around to do for you. Your Mama and Larraine both. Naw, I can't see no sense in pulling out now, and running you into danger."

Arvay developed strange moods and appetites. A great craving for meat, and for clay. Arvay had seen many people in Sawley eat clay, but she had never touched it herself. Now she had a taste for clay, that fine, cream-colored clay which she had seen her mother eating all her life. There was not much clay in Florida, but there was a deposit not too far from Sawley, to the north of town. Many a time Arvay had gone with her mother and seen her eat it hungrily after a rain. She had even seen her mother bake it into little cakes and sigh with satisfaction afterwards. It had tasted so smooth and good!

But Jim exploded with disgust when Arvay asked him to get her some clay from the bank to eat. He pitched into Dessie hot and heavy when he found that Dessie had sent her twelve-year-old son for clay and smuggled it in to Arvay. He had better not find any more of the goddamned filthy, dirty stuff around the place. If he did, he was going around the ham-bone looking for meat! That was the word with the bark on it. Nothing but a notion anyway. No nourishment in the thing.

Arvay hungered and retreated inside of her self with her fears. She came to the place where she wished that Larraine would tell and have it over with. But, no, Larraine was acting cruel. Holding the thing back to keep Arvay in suspense.

There was nothing for Arvay to do but huddle with her eternal fear and wait.

The first quarrel arose over something which Jim contended later was trashy, and had nothing to do with them.

Arvay had gone back to reading a chapter in the Bible every night. Like many others, she had the habit of letting the Bible fall open and reading the chapter where it opened as a sort of message.

The night of the quarrel, the Book fell open in Genesis, and at the story of the killing of Abel by Cain. She read for quite a while; then Jim, beside her in the bed, asked her what she was reading, not because he was interested, but so as not to feel lonesome and excluded. Arvay told him.

"And it was an awful crime for Cain to do," Arvay commented. "It wasn't Abel's fault if God didn't accept Cain's sacrifice."

"And I don't blame God neither. I'd turn against a man that didn't have no better sense than to burn a stinking cabbage right under my nose."

"But what else could he have done, Jim? He tilled the fields, didn't he?"

"That's what I been told, Arvay. Cain's first crime was not killing his brother Abel, but in not having no sense of humor. The man was so chuckle-headed that he couldn't even take a joke."

"Joke?" Arvay was so outraged that she hurriedly propped herself up on one elbow and frowned down into Jim's face. "You must be crazy or awful wicked one, to be looking for jokes in the Bible."

"Well, if it's about the doings of people, it must be plenty jokes in there."

"Well, I never!" Arvay sighed and sank back on her pillow. "Jokes in the Word of God."

"Sure, Arvie, if you can see 'em like they is. Now, take this same man, Cain, that you been reading about. He never would have got into all that trouble if he could have seen a joke. He never would have up and scorched a stinking, rotten cabbage under God's nose for no sacrifice. Common sense ought to have told him God wouldn't stand for him stinking up Heaven and all like that. How come he couldn't have

made God a nice cool salad and took it to Him? That would have been something out of his garden too, wouldn't it? Tell me!"

The battle raged and roiled. The sacred quality of the Bible, sinner-people who could make mock of holy things. Folks given to jokes and the dumbness of those who couldn't see a joke, and on and on. Jim was not really annoyed at first, he just enjoyed teasing Arvay, but Arvay went further than Jim thought necessary, and he stung her somewhat with ridicule. For the first time, Arvay refused Jim's goodnight hug, turned her back on him and got as far away from him as she could.

It was three whole days before the house got warm and intimate again. But fights leave scars on people, no matter how slight, and both had revealed things inside them that they usually concealed. Jim found out that Arvay considered him a sinner and a scoffer. Arvay found out that Jim thought her a trifle dumb.

Chapter Five

IT WAS in the heat of summer when Arvay's baby came. With Dessie there giving expert aid, commanding Arvay to "Bear down! Bear down, I tell you!" making the girl get out of bed and kneel at the foot and strain against a sheet twisted into a rope and tied to the bed-post, Arvay came through easily.

After a while, Dessie brought Arvay's baby to her, all attended to and dressed. It had cried briefly when Dessie smacked the breath of life into it, then Arvay had heard no more. It was very quiet when Dessie put it in her arms, and Dessie was quiet too. Arvay was afraid that it might be dead.

Something must be wrong. She could tell from Dessie's kind eyes trying to lie to her and look enthusiastic. "It's a boy, and I know that his daddy will be glad."

Arvay looked at her baby, and then she understood. It was nothing like Jim at all. The hair and eyelashes were perfectly white. It would be a blond. That was disappointing but not serious. What else she saw made Arvay cry out in horror.

"Dessie! Dessie! What is the matter with my child's hands?"

"It would take a God to tell, Miz' Arvay. Them don't look much like fingers, do they?"

"Good gracious! They look more like strings. And his hands, Dessie. Why they look too little for his body."

Arvay passed her hand over the quiet baby's head as if to comfort it and then gave another cry. There was practically no forehead nor backhead on her child. The head narrowed like an egg on top. Arvay began to cry. Then when she had cried a while, she looked her baby all over and cried some more. The feet were long, and the toes well formed, but they looked too long for a new-born baby to have. And there was no arch to the tiny feet. They were perfectly flat, with a little lump of flesh huddled under what should have been the in-step. Arvay studied the little red bundle of flesh in her arms.

It certainly did not favor Jim. Who did it remind her of? Finally she knew. He looked like her Uncle Chester, her

mother's youngest brother. The one that they seldom talked about. The one who was sort of queer in his head. Oh, Jesus! How could she show this child to Jim? In what words could she explain? She handed the bundle off to one side, so as to be sure not to overlay it, and turned away and cried.

When Jim came, he acted like Dessie. He tried to say something nice. Arvay kept up with his face with her eyes. Jim was kind and asked her how she felt over and over again, but he did not enthuse at all. He kissed her and petted her much too much.

"What must we name him?" Arvay asked and prayed.

"Oh, no rush about that at all," Jim said casually. "We got plenty time to figger that out, Little-Bit. You just rest your self up good so we can move off from here."

Arvay was left alone with her child. Jim mentioned details of work. Too bad, but he was in a sort of a slow hurry. Had to look after things. He was a family man now, and had to make support for three.

Arvay could not keep from continually searching over the child. She was made conscious of the mouth at last. It was exceptionally small, and what there was of it was concentrated in the bottom lip. It was a tiny pink pug thrust out at the world. It did not hang loosely at all. Just a tiny half moon no bigger than Arvay's finger nail.

But the size of the mouth was no measure of the appetite of the child. He attacked ferociously when put to the breast. Arvay had to laugh at his eagerness. It was strange that the child seldom cried out demanding to be fed. Occasionally he made a low whimpering·sound and moved his limbs in complaint. But always he seized upon the breast; he did not simply accept it as most children did. Jim, watching one afternoon, looked on with astonishment.

"It's a damn lucky thing that you got plenty of milk, honey. If you didn't have it, I'm mighty scared that young 'un would eat you clean up. Look at him go to it!"

The baby's defects only increased Arvay's love for it. She mooned over it, caressed it with pity added to her love. She spent a long time morning and night bathing it, rubbing it over with sweet oil and massaging and manipulating the narrow head. She was doing her best to shape it into a more

agreeable form. Whether it was on account of her labors, or just nature, she was surprised every morning to note a little change. The head gradually ceased to be different enough to attract particular notice, and Arvay rejoiced with tears. Still, the bones of the string-like fingers did not appear to be gaining in size and strength. For a long time, the finger bones felt like limber cartilage to the touch. Arvay wondered if her son would ever be able to use his tiny hands. Nor was there any change in the shape of the baby's feet. It took on weight and grew decidedly better-looking if you did not examine the hands and the feet.

Arvay shut herself in the bedroom with her baby where she could talk aloud to herself for a while every day after Jim had been gotten off to work.

"Poor little thing, you! Mam is going to love you, don't care who else don't care. You couldn't help it. You ain't the blame at all. This is the punishment for the way I used to be. I thought that I had done paid off, but I reckon not. I never thought it would come like this, but it must be the chastisement I been looking for. You're Mama's precious honey, and don't you cry."

This was an unnecessary admonition, for the baby seldom cried. Even when he was several months old and a husky body, the child made few demands. It lay in the crude crib that Joe Kelsey had knocked together, calling on no one until he was picked up and fed or attended to. Neither did the child show any recognition or eagerness at the sight of anyone at all. He seized upon his food almost angrily, and when he was full, he could be put down again without a murmur. One thing only Arvay began to notice about him very early. The child seemed to be very much afraid. Any sudden movement, any strange object introduced into his presence brought screams of terror. Otherwise, Arvay's son was a world within himself.

When a week, ten days, and then two weeks went by and Jim had made no mention of a name for the child, Arvay gritted her teeth and put on a brave show of outwitting her husband. She included Dessie.

"Let's we bake a cake, Dessie, for the baby."

"Baby? He ain't near old enough to be eating no cake, Miss Arvie."

"I know, Dessie, but I want you to help me out with a cake for giving him a name."

Then Arvay smiled in a sly way. "I mean to get ahead of Jim and name the baby my ownself. It's natural for a man to want the first boy named after him, but I always loved the name of Earl David, and said that if I ever had a boy-child I was going to name him that. While Jim is laying low to fix up some big preparation to name the baby after him, I mean to get ahead and say it first. Supper tonight, I'll place the cake on the table with the name all wrote on top. You know how men folks are, and we women have to take advantage of 'em now and then."

Dessie agreed and the cake was made. Arvay was by no means sure that Dessie had been taken in, but that part did not matter. It was a case of saving face.

Jim made no objections to the choice of a name at all. Said it was very pretty, and a whole lot better than plain Jim Meserve. He didn't know as he wanted a child named after himself anyway. Let every man have a name all to himself.

That was a nice way of putting it, Arvay reflected at the other end of the table. Jim was putting on to keep from hurting her feelings. Before she went to bed that night, she opened the new family Bible, and on the lined page at the back, wrote *Earl David Meserve, born July 26, 1906.*

Jim was off somewhere in the quarters. Probably at Joe's house, where Arvay suspected Jim found the occasional drink that he took, and was taking more and more often here of late. He probably would not be home for some time.

So Arvay felt free to get on her knees and pray. First, she asked God for the health and welfare of her child, and please, let Earl David never be taken away from her. Then she prayed for Jim. Prayed for the saving of his soul; that he be moved to hurry up and take her away from the vicinity of Sawley and keep on loving her.

Chapter Six

Two months after Earl was born, Jim gave notice to the turpentine firm that he was leaving, and that announcement gave Arvay great satisfaction. Where they were going, how and why did not concern her. It did not matter so long as she was going away from Sawley. When they sat in the day coach, with the round-topped metal-bound trunk in the baggage car, and the telescope bag and the shabby old satchel in the rack over their heads, they had all their worldly possessions with them. Jim had around a hundred dollars in his pockets, mostly from the sale of their household goods, and his last pay-check. Her husband was beside her on the seat, and her baby was in her lap. They were headed east and south away from what she used to know and feel and Arvay was asking for nothing more.

They landed in Citrabelle, a bright-looking flowery town on the Florida ridge south of Polk County. By ways that Arvay knew nothing of, Jim had come to a decision to settle there, and had a job as foreman of a crew of fruit-pickers. She knew that she was settled in a light and airy cottage painted a bright yellow and trimmed with white. She did observe that folks down in these parts did seem to be powerful fond of painting houses and planting flowers. It was a very pretty habit, though, and Arvay put out to have herself a flower yard too. Outside of the miles and miles of orange groves, the people raised nothing but vegetables to eat. Not a speck of cotton or tobacco, or the things she was used to seeing growing. Things had a picnicky, pleasury look that, while it was pretty, made Arvay wonder if folks were not taking things too easy down in here. Heaven wasn't going to be any refreshment to folks if they got along with no more trouble than this. As far as she could see, the place was plumb given over to pleasure. Flower-yards looked as if folks had spent as much time fixing and attending them as they did back in west Florida to raise a crop of corn, peanuts, cotton or tobacco. It was the duty of man to suffer in this world, and these people round down here in south Florida were plainly shirking their

duty. They were living entirely too easy. There just didn't seem to Arvay to be any kind of honest work that kept folks bowed down from can't-see-in-the-morning till can't-see-at-night. Then too they could get hold of all the oranges, grapefruit and tangerines that they could lay under without spending a cent. What treat would a whole orange or tangerine in a Christmas stocking be to a person down in here? It just didn't seem right for folks to live as loose and as careless as all this. And look at the wages that were paid down in this vicinity! It was hard for her to believe. It worried Arvay so that finally she had to seek some information from Jim.

"When do these folks around here get down to work sure enough, Jim?" Arvay asked one day.

"Get to work, Arvay? Why, that's what they're doing all the time."

"You mean folks round here don't do no more'n this, and make all that money?"

"That's right. Fruit is the main thing, then truck-gardening. Ninety-day crops down in here. Three crops a year. Sell it to the commission houses, put your money in your pocket and put in another crop."

"Well suh! Nothing much to do but just wallow around. I don't know what's to become of folks. They'll be too lazy to draw they breath after while."

"Feel like you're being carried to the skies on flowery beds of ease, eh?" Jim laughed. "You married yourself a man, honey. I told you, like that old hymn says, marriage with me never was designed to make your pleasures less. Rest easy, you ain't seen nothing as yet. I aim to have you living so fine some day that this will look like a teppentime camp beside it. You're such a baby-child, Arvay. Maybe that's why I love you so hard." He kissed the back of her neck. "You don't have to worry about a thing. You got a man who can bring it when he come."

Therefore, Arvay knew nothing about the desperate struggle Jim was going through for their very existence. She did not know about those terrible three weeks when Jim, knowing nothing about citrus-fruit production, had stood around with his hands in his pockets feeling and turning over the little money he had, and casting about for some way to

get into the work. How he had finally decided that since the colored men did all of the manual work, they were the ones who actually knew how things were done, and how he had taken up around the jooks and gathering places in Colored Town, and swapped stories, and stood treats, and eased in questions in desperate hope, wondering if his money would hold out until he could get a footing, and how he had finally gotten information which landed him his job.

She did not know that fruit-cutters seldom worked at all from the end of the season early in June until it opened again around the middle of September when they began to cut grapefruit, however short of money they might be. But Jim had made an arrangement to look after the company groves during the summer months, seeing to the pruning, ploughing of the groves, fertilizing and hoeing. His pay envelope would be less, but it would be enough to keep them going, to save them from living on credit and having a big grocery bill facing him when the season opened. He had persuaded at least half of his crew to go along with him, and they worked all summer and opened up in the fall with money ahead.

During those summer months, Jim used his head too. Gaining a greater intimacy with his men, he subtly worked up the spirit of rivalry in fruit-cutting. Who was the best, sure enough? There got to be arguments and contests about it. The men took to bringing their bags and clippers along and any left-over fruit in the groves they were tending got cut in a fury of competition. There is always some fruit that gets overlooked and always sour-orange trees in every grove. They make a particularly fine-flavored lemonade. The men never left one with fruit on it now, and when the season opened up, they were rearing to go. They told him of the best cutters in other crews and for other companies, and Jim shifted around until he had nothing but experts under him, and augmented his crew by three men. By Christmas, they were "raising a fog" in any grove that they were thrown in, and the amount of fruit they cut had been duly taken note of at the packing-house. The manager stopped Jim and had a talk with him. He was particularly grateful because Jim had served during the off months when it was so hard to get work done, and his record since the season opened was impressive. It was now arranged

for Jim to get the same money all the year round and a bonus for exceeding a certain number of boxes a week. His men got their added money in the number of boxes they cut. They were the highest-paid men in that part of the state and getting known. To foster the spirit, the manager lined Jim and his men up on the loading-platform the day before Christmas, praised them to the highest in front of everybody, and presented each man with a Christmas turkey.

Arvay had the big turkey that Jim had received. She baked it and they ate it, but she never asked for the story behind it, and since the eager Jim, feeling no curiosity in her about his achievement, was that kind of a man, he did not offer her the information. He ate his dinner, and went off somewhere and came home drunk. Arvay was displeased about it and acted sullen, but she never sought the why of that either.

That did not mean that there were no high places in her existence. In spite of her silent resentment over Earl, and in spite of her lack of expression, there were times when they grabbed hands and mounted to Heaven together. They played music on the instrument of life. It was merely that two or three of the keys were out of fix, and there was a break in the tune when they were touched. There was no other child besides Earl, and neither of them dared mention it. Both were torn between longing and fear. A normal child would cancel out to an extent the disappointment over Earl, but then, supposing it came here another Earl? Arvay knew nothing of contraceptives, nor did Jim mention anything like that. She just noted that at certain times Jim found it convenient to stay out late, and come home tired. And he drank more than he used to. Arvay took what happiness she could in looking after Earl. She avenged herself on Jim by spending hours in his absence in teaching the slow-moving Earl to walk and to talk. It was slow and hard work, but by the time he was a year-and-a-half old, he could stay on his feet and take a few steps. A few months later, she was overjoyed to hear him lisp out a word. It was either "eat" or "meat," Arvay could not tell which, but it was a word and she was proud and glad.

She had worked on those feeble hands and feet so hard they had to respond some to the continual manipulations and oilings. Earl didn't look so odd now, and she was proud of

her work. He was still scary and showed no particular attach-ments. Secretly, it hurt Arvay to see that he did not show more preference for her, who gave all her time and energy to him, than he did for Jim, who bought him little toys and candies, but never played with him at all. So Arvay used to make up little fibs to tell Jim when he came home about the cute and loving things Earl said and did when they were there alone. Jim never believed a word of it, she could tell, but he never put himself to the trouble to make her out a liar. He took it for just what it was, her consolation, and let it go at that.

Who shall ascend into the hill of the Lord? And who shall stand in His holy place? Arvay thought that it would be her-self when and if she could birth Jim a perfect child and by this means tie him forever to her. Jim felt that he would stand on the mount of transfiguration when Arvay showed some appre-ciation of his love as expressed by what he was striving to do for her. Thus they fumbled and searched for each other in silent darkness.

Therefore, she was both exalted and torn with anxious fears when she passed her time and knew that she was pregnant. She looked at Earl, and day by day sloped around and could not find tongue to mention her condition to Jim. She had seen his terrible agony at the birth of Earl; he could not bear that again. He might just slip on his travelling-shoes, and she would never know where he made his last tracks. Well, Earl was two years old, and able to get around some, and if push came to the shove, she could go back up home to her parents and get some kind of work while her mother looked after Earl for her.

While she was bumbling around in this miasma of fear, Jim literally jumped into the house one afternoon, grinning proudly.

"Well, sugar, your husband's done got you a home."

"A home?"

"Yep. I done beat a man out of five acres of good land."

"Naw!"

"Yep. It's not right up in town, though. Out to the west of here, close to the Big Swamp. It's even been cleared, but not having no attention paid to it in seven years, it's growed up

some. Don't take long in a climate like this. Better throw on something, and let's go take a look at our land."

Arvay knew the general direction. The Big Swamp was a growth that ran north and south for eight or nine miles, and formed the western barrier of the town. They strolled on out there hand in hand in happiness. Jim led her to the place, and told her that they were now on the east line of their property.

"Why, Jim, this just fine! I bet you had to pay a plenty for all this land."

"Nope. I told you that I beat the fool out of the place. He ain't paid no taxes on it since he's had it, and he was about to lose it for taxes anyhow. So he said if I would give him two hundred cash, he'd make me out a clear deed to the place, then I paid up the taxes and it was mine. Of course he don't have nothing to do with that part no more. That's between me, the State, and County. But it's something less than a hundred all told."

"Naw, Jim!"

"That Cracker could have kept up his taxes, and made a good living out of this land besides, but he was too damn lazy and trifling. One crop of anything one time a year would have taken care of everything, but it was too much work for him. Come telling me that he had been trying to get money enough together to hire a nigger or two to put it in shape for him, but seemed as if he never could make it. When he got it, it was all fresh cleared. I don't know what more he wanted. Well, maybe that was the way it was meant to be so we could get hold of it. I'll bet you anything it'll be clean as a whistle a month from now, and I'll be planting me a grove."

"Oh, Jim! It do place us way up yonder, don't it?"

"Well, it gives us a toe-hold anyhow. My next young 'un is going to be born on his Daddy's place. I never did like the idea of no child of mine being born on borrowed land."

Arvay's heart began to beat very fast. My goodness! You couldn't never fool Jim about a thing. She might as well own up to it.

"You sure got the sharpest eyes, Jim. Here I ain't no more'n two months gone. How did you know it already?"

"Is that so, honey? You're mistaken, and I didn't know it,

but I'm ever so glad to get the news. Come on here and hug my neck."

"I'm so glad that you're glad, Jim. I . . ."

"Just give me something more to scuffle for. This one is bound to look like me. That means I'm in the ham-scram and got to hustle like hell to get a house up for him to be born in. I ain't been half doing, but I got to stretch out now and be a man."

They walked over the place hand in hand, Jim pointing out and stepping off and talking. Those two or three scattered palmetto palms, he was going to leave standing. They looked pretty scattered around in a grove. This east end of the place was good and sandy. Just the right kind of ground for a grove. The sandier the land, the thinner the skin and the juicier the orange. He was putting all but a half acre in grove. When it got to bearing good, it would more than take care of the place. The house site with the flower yard, the vegetable garden and barnyard would be that other half an acre. That would face towards the west, and the land began to slide off into muck up that way, which would make it more suitable for vegetables and flowers.

They wandered on up that way to give Arvay a chance to pick out where she wanted the house to be placed. There was a good-sized camphor tree about seventy feet back from the west line, and maybe fifty feet from the north line and Arvay decided that she wanted the house placed so that the tree would shade her kitchen door.

"A woman spends so much time around the back that it would be nice to have it cool and shady."

"You're right, Arvay. In fact, all the family passes more time out back than they do anywhere else, and it don't seem sensible to place everything out front for other folks to look at, and don't have nothing for comfort. We can say, then, ten feet from this tree is your kitchen door."

Everything was nice and agreeable until they faced towards the west, then Arvay stood still in her tracks and gasped.

"Jim! Looka there!" and she pointed dramatically at the swamp.

The swamp was so obvious, that Jim thought she must be pointing at something else.

"What is it, honey?"

"That Big Swamp."

"Ain't it noble? I just wish that I was in shape to take in right up to the edge of it. That's the finest stretch of muck outside the Everglades. And look at that stand of timber! If I just had the cash that five acres of that timber would bring, we wouldn't have to worry about a thing. Don't you fret, honey, some day I'm going to get it for you."

"Get it?" And Arvay's eyes flew open in terror. "I don't want no parts of that awful place. It's dark and haunted-looking and too big and strong to overcome. It's frightening! Like some big old varmint or something to eat you up."

"Why, honey, that ain't nothing but a lot of big trees and stuff growing together. Nothing to hurt you at all. They grows so thick and big and plentiful because the land is wet and rich. Some underground water breaking to the surface in spots along in there. Ain't never been disturbed and been growing like that for maybe thousands of years. That's what makes that land so rich. Plenty stuff done rotted into it, and none of it been used up for cropping. I sure would love to own it."

"Jim, it don't look safe to even be around. I know it's just full and running over with varmints, bears and pant'ers, and wild-cats and gators and rattlesnakes. . . ."

"Not hardly no rattlesnakes, Arvay. They likes clear high, dry ground. We run upon quite a few around in groves. Of course, there would be plenty of moccasins in a place like that, but since you don't have to go in there for nothing, you don't have to worry about that."

"But my child, Jim. Earl is too little to know how to look out for hisself, and he's liable to stray off in there, like young 'uns will, and get snake-bit, or tore to pieces by some varmint or other."

"Earl?" And Jim laughed harshly. "That scary thing ain't apt to stray nowhere at all. If that's all you got to worry about, you can put your mind at rest. He's scared to death of even a baby chicken, and then he ain't all that active."

"You can laugh, Jim but that place is frightening and awful. I wish that you wouldn't buy the place."

"You mean you want me to give up a lifetime start for a

notion like that? Naw, Arvay, it wouldn't be fair to you and my children to give in to a thing like that. Besides, I done passed my word to the man, and the deal is closed."

"Well, I reckon 'tain't nothing more to be said, Jim, but that swamp is a frightening thing."

"Oh, you'll get used to it after a while and pay no attention to it. Any varmint out of there that I catch trespassing on my property will wish that he had stayed at home. Don't you worry. It's a good half a mile off anyhow, and wild animals are more scared of men than we are of them. They ain't apt to bother around."

Jim went right to work clearing and planting his land, and laying the plans for his new home. He would have loved to tell Arvay how he managed on so little money, and let her laugh with him, but Arvay seemed very listless about it, and kept dwelling on the matter of the swamp every time he brought the matter up.

The cleaning up of the five acres had really cost him only ten gallons of moon-shine at a dollar and a half a gallon, ten pounds of sugar, two ten cent bags of salt, a quart of vinegar and some red pepper. There was a foot-note of a half a box of shot-gun shells. All he did was to mention his purchase among his crew and the necessity of getting the thing done, to be called aside by two of the men an hour later and be told that if the above mentioned supplies were furnished, the job could be taken care of the first slack Saturday that came along.

Jim furnished what was suggested, and was extra careful not to ask what would become of the shot-gun shells. Too many Crackers saved hog-feed by letting their hogs run wild in the woods until just before time to butcher for Jim to want to know too much. If a big barbecue was going to be held on his place to get it cleaned up, he knew nothing about where all that meat came from. Having provided what was suggested, he showed no further interest until late Sunday afternoon when he was urged to go take a look at the place.

No less than two hundred grown people could have gotten all that work done over the week-end. From fence-line to fence-line the place was thoroughly cleaned and even the

brush piled and burnt. As a gauge to the size of the gathering, Jim found a barrel under some trees that had been full of lemonade, but was empty now. Monday, downtown, the markets which usually got the colored trade were wondering what on earth had become of the colored folks. They had more than four hundred pounds of unsold meat on hand. His crew brought him many compliments and assured him that anytime he needed any further help, why all he needed to do was to let them know. He was a perfect gentleman, and they were only too glad to oblige him. It was the same every way he turned. Negroes whom he had never seen before were saying the same thing. Jim was laughing up his sleeve and wanted to take Arvay into the joke, then decided against it.

Once he was on the inside, he found that he got help in other ways. It seemed to be a sort of underground system in Colored Town that the whites did not know about. Two brothers who were good carpenters and did a good deal of work for the best real estate firm in town sought him out and made him a very reasonable figure to build his house, furnishing all the materials. They had, it seemed, connections with a big lumber company, and they could buy cheaper than he could himself. Jim decided to chance it and was more than satisfied with the results. Never did Jim go out to see how the work was coming along but what he took a jug along with him, and never did he go but what some others were around helping the carpenters work.

When the house and barn were declared finished, he took Arvay out to see her new home, and found all the trash cleaned up and hauled away.

"Jim," Arvay objected after the house was inspected, "it's nice and all, but they done toted off all that scrap lumber. It would of helped us out quite considerable for stove-wood. You ought to go make 'em put the last piece of it right back on this place."

"Then I wouldn't be no gentleman no more, Arvay, and that would cost me something. That's like broken food from the table. The help don't look for ladies and gentlemen to trace up a thing like that. If I act like I don't notice it, I got a lot of willing friends, and nobody will ever steal a thing off this place. I got this house built way under the regular figure

anyhow. All of 'em would feel hard towards me if I went around asking about those scraps of wood. Leave it be."

Arvay felt a comparison in this, and it hurt. Jim just as good as said that she wasn't used to things, and he had to teach her and tell her. But she had a child on the way, and only the Lord knew whether it would come right or not. If it was deformed, she would need all the good-will that she could get hold of to stay with Jim. So she pressed her teeth together and said no more.

Arvay just had no idea. She had no understanding to what extent she was benefiting from the good will that Jim had been building up ever since he had come to town. She knew nothing of his twisting and turning and conniving to make life pleasant for her sake. Neither had she any knowledge of the little arrangements he had made with the butcher-boys on the through trains to handle small lots of fancy fruit to bring in a little something extra. She never asked anything, and so Jim never volunteered to tell her.

She saw the young trees being set out in the grove, but she did not know that a friend of one of the men on his crew worked at a nursery, and had fixed it so that Jim was getting the benefit of every doubt, and the doubts were numerous. His grove was planted to the very finest and the most money-making trees. Only the oranges like Parson Browns, Pine-apples, Temples, Navels and Valencias went into the Meserve grove. The very early and the very late fruits when the prices would be high. The early fruit to one side and the late to the other with a broad band of grapefruit down the middle. The tangerine were set like a border trimming the grove on all sides towards the house. All budded stock so that Jim could look for a crop on the third year. Since he had the usual contract of six years to pay for his trees, he never actually paid a cent out of his own pocket. Before the time was up, the grove had paid for itself over and over.

Chapter Seven

ARVAY had planned the roomy bedroom in the northwest corner of the house for herself and Jim. It was across the hall from the front room, or parlor. In the old-fashioned double bed in this room her second child was born.

To the physical pain of her labor was added her secret worry as to whether the child would be normal or not. She gave birth to the squalling infant in an agony of uncertainty.

She kept her eyes closed as long as possible while the doctor and a woman friend attended to it, pretending to be in a swoon. But she opened her eyes as soon as she heard the doctor exclaim, "What a fine baby! Good set of lungs too. Just listen at her squall!"

"Do lemme see my baby, Doctor." Arvay struggled to one elbow with her eyes fixed on the fat child that the doctor was hefting. "I know it's got to be tended to, but lemme see it first, please."

It was a fine-looking infant, and active. Arvay looked at the reddy-brown down on its head and sighed. It reminded her of Larraine. Why couldn't it look more like Jim and been a boy? She let them take the child from her and sank back on her pillow. Where was Jim? He had been there before her last terrible pains. What would he say and do when he saw the little girl?

The bed had been changed, and she had been bathed and changed into a fresh nightgown when she heard Jim's voice outside the room door. Then he came in with the baby in his arms.

"A damn fine baby you had for me, honey."

"She looks a little like Larraine, don't you think?" And Arvay twisted her mouth in an apologetic kind of a way. She hoped that Jim could see his way to forgive her.

"Lorraine!" Jim snorted in scorn. "In the pig's eye! My child don't look like Larraine, nothing of the kind. She takes right after my mother, as you would know if you had ever seen her. She's got that same auburn hair and her mouth and eyes. They're light blue now, but them eyes will be a kind of

blue-gray in a little while. Larraine! I'm naming her Angeline, after my mother, too."

Arvay closed her eyes in happiness. She could have asked no more of God than this happiness and enthusiasm out of Jim. She hoped that Jim was right about who the child took after. She didn't want any child of hers taking after Larraine. Jim came and sat down on the side of the bed with the little bundle in one arm. With the other hand, he caught hold of hers and stroked up and down her arm tenderly.

"You better let me have the baby then while you go write in the Bible."

Jim reluctantly placed the bundle in her arms and crossed the hall to the living room and wrote: *"Angeline Meserve, Sunday morning, January 7, 1909, at 4:45. A pretty and healthy daughter."*

While Jim was writing, and in his enthusiasm wondering if he ought to add something more, Arvay was examining her new daughter from head to foot. The child was perfect. Not even a birthmark to mar the tender white skin. When Jim returned, she had the child at her breast.

From that hour on, Arvay found out what Jim was like as a father. He was hanging over the baby's crib practically all the time that he was in the house. He had to look at the child and touch it before he could leave for work in the morning. He came bolting in from work and made for wherever the baby was. It made her laugh to see him changing the baby's diapers, if the child happened to wet herself while Arvay was busy. He was afraid that her skin would get chafed if she had to wait a minute. Arvay kept to her bed a week, and the last day of her confinement, she had to smile at Jim's childishness. He came in with a little white box and hurried to the crib. Propping herself up on one elbow, Arvay could see him trying to put a little gold finger-ring on Angeline's finger. His disappointment was great when he found that the finger was too small as yet, and the ring kept slipping off.

"You ain't supposed to place that on until the child is older, Jim. What is that else you got?"

It was a little gold locket with Angeline's name carved on it. A tiny gold heart hung from a fine gold chain. Jim was dangling it in front of the baby's eyes and trying to delight it.

"Look like I got three babies on my hands," Arvay smiled. "It would be better if you laid it away, Jim, until she gets about three months old. That'll be time enough to start to ornamenting her up."

Then Arvay turned her face away. There had been no little ring nor anything for poor Earl. Already, she could see the pattern opening out. Her own childhood all over again, with Angeline favored like Raine always had been, and she made ready to resist. The lines were drawn, and she had become a partisan.

She was hardly up and around before she detected a new drive of energy in Jim. He began to make new plans. He turned and twisted every way to bring in more money, and to place it so it would grow. He bought a Jersey cow so that there could be plenty of milk and butter around the house. He came home one evening with two hundred strawberry plants and set them.

"By the time that big woman of mine gets so she can eat, I want her to have strawberries with cream all over 'em. The little rascal!"

Jim bragged on Angeline excessively, but even Arvay could see that the child was quick to catch on to things, and further, that the baby had a decided preference for her father. By the time that Angie was three months old, she could distinguish Jim by sight, and knew the sound of his voice, which puffed Jim up enormously. Arvay could be nursing her, with Jim across the room. The moment he spoke, Angeline would release the breast long enough to turn her little head quickly and show her toothless gums in a smile at Jim. She would go to him at any time from Arvay's arms. One afternoon, Arvay was changing Angie into clean things so that she would be nice and fresh when Jim got there. She had bathed and powdered the baby, and was folding a diaper to pin on her, when Jim arrived and began to call out. Immediately the little thing began to move her limbs about eagerly, and even tried to pull herself up to go to him. As Arvay kept on with the dressing and Jim did not appear, Angie first began to fret and then to scream in angry impatience.

"Shut up!" Arvay scolded as she jerked the baby into her

clothes. "I'm the one that's doing for you, and you squalling after Jim. Hush!"

Jim overheard her and flew into the room and snatched Angeline up in his arms. The little devil immediately behaved as if she had just been rescued from mortal danger. She snuggled her head up under Jim's chin and looked out at her mother in a most accusing way.

"You need that little rump of yourn blistered good for you, that's all," Arvay commented. "Give her back here, Jim, and lemme fling her dress over her head. That ain't nothing but a petticoat."

But the instant Arvay reached up her hands, Angeline scrambled and clung to Jim and pretended utter terror. Jim fended Arvay off and ran out of the backdoor laughing.

"You may think that's funny, Jim, but I sure don't. That child has got to be taught to mind. That very young'un is going to cause you to suck sorrow some of these days."

"Aw, naw she won't, because she loves her Daddy, and she's always going to do what her Daddy tells her to do." Then he laughed. "If she don't do like I tell her, then I'll do like she tells me and we'll be bound to get along. You ain't to hit her, well no more'n to slap her little hands. Please don't have me to come in and find no whelps on this child, Arvay. If I ever do, it's going to make a lot of difference between us. I mean that from my heart."

"Well, people!" Arvay gasped in amazement as she saw the serious look on Jim's face. "This is my first time to see a man cut the crazy over a child to that extent. Look like I done borned somebody to be over me in my own house. I don't count for nothing no more around here, I see. Angeline is the boss."

"Naw, honey, naw. You got the wrong understanding. Yes, I love the child with all that I'm able, but don't you see it's because she's yours that I love her so? I'm loving you through her and her through you."

Arvay was mollified to an extent, but still she wondered. She hated to be low enough to feel jealous of her own child.

Then Jim took to going off from home nearly every night. Once the baby was asleep, he found some excuse to go out nearly every night, and he usually came in with liquor on his

breath. That gave Arvay to wonder if the bonds between them were not slackening off.

What was more disturbing, Jim, usually so good-natured, began to get into fights. Arvay wondered what had got into the man. It was more puzzling because the fights were never serious. No pistol-whippings, no cutting-scrapes nor things like that. Just fist-fights that even left no marks on Jim worth mentioning. Furthermore, they always ended up in complete making-up with his opponent. Jim and his opponents were thicker after the battles than before. What was it all about? Oh, Arvay just knew that one of these nights, some desperado was going to kill her husband dead. She fretted and worried and begged Jim to desist. Jim took her solicitude for him with a pleased smile.

They had kept up a correspondence with Joe and Dessie Kelsey. Three or four letters a year each way, and now in her worry, Arvay called them to mind. Jim always liked having Joe around, and maybe if Joe was here, Jim could be broken of these new habits. She knew that Joe wanted to come, but had never been able to get enough money together to bring his family. Without giving her reason, Arvay broached the matter to Jim one evening.

"Damn, Arvay! I'm sure glad you mentioned Joe. Wonder why I didn't think of him before now? He's the very man I need. I can easily throw up a house back there in the grove for him, and have him right here. I'm going to send for him. You drop him a line and tell him to be ready to leave from there in a week. I'm sending his train-fare Monday week."

Arvay was very pleased at the way Jim had taken her suggestion. She felt that she could look forward and see her happiness ahead. It was as if she had been walking in the dark and come to a house where a light leaned out of the window and smiled.

But before Joe and his family could get there, Jim got into another fight that was a fight. It was to go down in local history as the Battle of the Horse's Behind.

Jim left home early that night, telling Arvay that he was going over into Colored Town to see about getting the house put up in the grove. She never did know if he reached his destination. She forgot to ask in the excitement afterwards.

The fight was with Hawley Pitts. The two men were not enemies, but certainly they were not exactly friends.

Hawley Pitts had the reputation of being the ugliest white man in the county, and probably that had something to do with his social outlook. He was tall on a broad-built frame, with a very red neck and ears. But it was Hawley's mouth that had made him his great reputation. His lips were unusually thick—thick at the corners of the mouth. He must have felt shy about his looks, for he had taken occasion to throw off on Jim Meserve's "pretty looks" more than once around the bar-rooms when he was sure that Jim could hear him.

Jim, seeing several of his cronies in the bar as he passed, hailed and decided to halt for a few minutes for a drink and an exchange of pleasantries. A score or more were lined up along the bar, and Jim made a place for himself and ordered.

Hawley Pitts had the floor. He was bearing down on Pearly Snead this time. Pearly was a harmless fellow, something under middle height, and slight of build. His wife had run off from him the week before with another man, and was said to be over to Lakeland living with him as man and wife. Some friend had seen her, and told Pearly where she was, and Pearly was so much in love that he had taken out over there and humbled himself enough to beg her to come back to him regardless. What made it bad, Pearly's wife had not only refused with scorn, but meeting someone from Citrabelle on the street in Lakeland, she had laughed and repeated Pearly's tearful plea and her answer. It was soon all over Citrabelle, and now Hawley was having himself a time ragging Pearly about it.

Hawley was too big for Pearly to fight to any advantage, and so he tried to make a laugh and leave the place, like he was humoring the joke.

"Where you trying to sneak off to?" Hawley demanded, and grabbing Pearly by the back of his shirt, hauled him back again. "I ain't had my proper amount of fun out of you yet. You stay right here till I tell you that you can go."

Pearly wanted to fight. Anybody could see that. His fists balled up and he eyed Hawley's face in a hungry way. But he decided that it would not pay, and tried to turn it off in a

grin. Hawley saw the same thing that Jim and the others did, and he laughed, and jerked Pearly's shirt out of his pants all the way around.

"You got a willing mind, Pearly, but too light behind. You're just as hot as little sister but scared to fight, eh?"

Jim moved in next to Pearly, and looked Hawley hard in the eye across Pearly's head. He looked so hard and so long that everybody got quiet.

"Hawley," Jim said finally, and with great deliberation, "I could object to a big, over-built man like you picking on a runt like Pearly. I could get mad because you was born a fool and tell you about it. But I pass all that up, and just take exception to your face." Jim spoke in a nasty quiet way that made his voice carry all over the place.

"What the hell you mean?" Hawley asked. "Taking exception to my face?"

"Yeah, your damn ugly face! I'm bound to take exception, Hawley Pitts. No scoundrel-beast can disrespect *my* wife without giving a strict account to me."

This was certainly exciting, and everybody drew in close.

"Your wife, Jim Meserve? What the hell *is* you talking about sure enough? Why, I ain't hardly ever even broke a breath with her on the streets. Accusing me of insulting your wife!"

"Naw, you ain't been talking to her, Hawley, and I give you full credit for having *that* much sense. But you been committing something worse than that."

"All right! All right! Now what can you claim that I ever done to your wife?"

"You been offering Mrs. Meserve the dirtiest kind of a disrespect. You been proaging out here in the public streets where she could come along and see you with a face like that."

"My face?" Hawley felt his face suspiciously. "I must say that I can't catch on to what you mean." Hawley kept looking from one man to another.

"Yeah, your natural goddamned face! Why, I'd just as soon for her to see you without your pants on as that face. It's a damn lie. It ain't no face at all. I can't consider that thing no face. And that mouth of yours just won't do at all. It's a horse's behind, and a female horse at that."

Spontaneous and raucous laughter broke out instantly. Even Pearly could take a part.

"You, you, say a thing like that to *me*? That's fighting talk."

"I mean it that way, Hawley. No man can insult my wife without giving me some satisfaction. If I allow you to get away with exposing a face like that on the public streets, next thing I know, you'll be out in broad daylight without your damn pants on. The only way you can get out of fighting me here and now is for you to hurry on home and ask your wife for a pair of her drawers and put 'em on that face of yours before you brazen out in public anymore. Git for home!"

The two men went together like lightning. The infuriated Pitts charged, and Jim met him halfway and straightened his head up with a powerful drive to his neck. Men scattered in every direction to be out of the way but at the same time be where they could take in all the battle.

There was no under-dog in this fight. The men were about the same height. Hawley had several pounds of advantage, but Jim was five years younger. It was hard blow for hard blow and neither man dodging away. Fists drumming against chests, and heads and teeth bared back in the frenzy of the battle. Take a blow and give as many as possible in return. So good a man, so good a man! Knock down and drag out, with the men on the side lines jumping up and down and cheering action. Up and down the room in rough and tumble; from the off wall to the bar and back again, panting, gasping, scuffling and smiting and being smitten. It was a close fight, and if Jim got more applause, it was due to his more nimble foot-work, and greater popularity around town. Hawley went down at last and stayed down, but Jim Meserve knew that he had been in a battle and that he had fought a man.

"Got enough?" Jim panted standing over Hawley. "You going to quit being so brazen and put some drawers on that face?"

Hawley did not have to answer, for just then the town marshal, who had been at the door for the greater part of the fight, ran in officially as if he had just arrived.

"What the hell is going on in here?" the law demanded and glared all around him.

"Jim Meserve picked a fight with me and jumped me," Hawley mumbled, getting slowly to his feet.

"He did?" The marshal glowered at Jim then looked around at everybody in the place. "Who saw what went on?" the officer evaded.

Nobody had seen a thing, it developed. Pitts appealed to first one and the other but not a soul would go as far as to witness to a thing. Oh, some kind of a scuffling had gone on, but not a man there could rightly swear to a thing. Who had started it, who had hit who was more than they could say.

"Hell! It was a fair fight wasn't it?" one irritated citizen blurted out at last. "What more can a man ask for than that? If Pitts had of won he would of felt that Jim was a sorry sport to have swore out a warrant against him, wouldn't he? I wouldn't go a step to testify for nothing."

Feeling mistreated and imposed upon, Hawley, with slumped-down shoulders, turned and started to leave the place. It was Jim who hurried forward and caught him and brought him back. Hawley jerked away angrily at first, then Jim charmed him with his eyes, and took his arm and drew him back to the bar.

"Set 'em up," Jim said to the bartender. "Me and my friend Hawley are having a drink together. What's yours, Hawley? It's on me. Come on all you jar-heads! This is to Hawley Pitts, a fair fighter and a true friend."

There was a moment of bewilderment, then every man in the place crowded up to the bar and began to lay down money and order and yell for Jim and Hawley to wait until they got theirs. Pearly tucked in his shirt-tail and joined the rest. A half hour later, no one who was not present would have known that there had been a fight. Jim led them to make over Hawley and to feed his ego. Jim slipped in something about Hawley's swell build and his loaded muscles, and Hawley swelled like a pouter pigeon. He swelled so that he had room inside for a big gesture. So he reached and got Pearly and placed his big arm around the little man's shoulder.

"Say, Pearly, you being luckier than the rest of us, not having no old hen to bother with, how about us all going over to your house and finishing off this thing?"

Pearly was so tickled that he almost split wide open, so they all went on over there and caroused for a couple of hours. Jim could see that they had done a good thing, for after an hour or so of the kind of stories men tell when they are off to themselves and a few more drinks, Pearly stood up and announced, "What the heck am I worrying about *his* hard luck for? What business I got feeling any sympathy for *him*? He got her on his hands, let him keep her."

Having secured himself some more partisans, Jim went on home in high fettle, but Arvay all but fainted when she saw his face and knuckles. She made a great demonstration of her sentiments, and Jim felt highly paid. He kept on being brusque and telling her not to fuss over him, but all the time he was leaning right into it. But Arvay did not understand.

"Jim, you got ways that I don't believe that I'm ever to understand. What you want to get into a fight for is more than I can see."

"Just put it down to me being a man and part Irish and let it go at that. You get so at times that you got to give vent to your muscles. Don't bother too much about understanding right now. Just hug my neck for me and call it square."

Chapter Eight

THE ARRIVAL of the Kelseys made life exactly right for Arvay. For some time Jim was kept close around the place getting Joe and them settled down and the work laid out. Joe and his three big boys were to look after the grove and the place. Dessie was to take care of the family washing. Arvay did not know enough about groves right then to realize that the grove would need no particular care for a year or more. She did not notice that because Jim had Joe and his boys broadcast black-eye peas over the entire grove. That crop served a three-fold purpose. It provided an enormous amount of additional food for the added mouths. The cows could eat the pea-vines for hay. It was a cover crop that added nitrate to the soil. That was all for the grove, and Arvay did not notice that Jim and Joe were off in a huddle a great deal, and that more often than not, Joe was not even on the place. His big boys did the milking, looked after the barn, the chicken-yard and the garden.

Arvay was not to pay too much attention because Dessie was up around the house most of the time. It was just as good as a visit to west Florida to hear Dessie talk. Arvay was brought up to date on everything that had happened since she left. Whose babies Dessie had caught, and who were supposed to be the fathers, but who they really favored, and so on and on as they set hens, being careful to put all the eggs but two of a setting in with the right hand to hatch out pullets and only two roosters to a batch. They took hens off the nests with their broods, housed them in coops and kept going over Sawley, Jim and Joe.

Dessie caught on to the signs right away, and Arvay saw them confirmed in her body. She was going to have another child. But thinking things over, she waited nearly a month more to speak of her condition to Jim.

The day, or to be more exact the night, that Arvay chose for the revelation was unfortunate for her.

Jim, eager to accumulate and prosper as well as to help Joe out, had set Joe up in a whiskey still. It was located about

685

three miles to the south in the very edge of the hammock. Joe could pay back the money that Jim had put out as he went along. All over a certain profit was to go to Jim after that. Both men considered that fair as Jim was to furnish the customers while Joe ran the still.

Joe had made his first run that night, with Jim and most of the important men of the community present. Everything had gone off swell, and a very good time had been had by all. They could look forward to good likker, because Joe really knew how to make it, charred barrels and all. There was no need for him to get rid of it in a hurry, so it could age. No law was going to touch that still. The law was present at the run. Moonshine likker was an old southern custom. Nothing wrong with it at all. So Jim had come home feeling fine.

As soon as Jim began to undress, Arvay stirred in bed and told Jim of her condition.

Jim was in a mood for wit and laughter, and Arvay's solemn eyes provoked him more. And when her eyes and her tone of voice plead with Jim to excuse her for what had happened, Jim just could not resist pulling Arvay's leg a bit. So he stood straddled legged, put on a stern face and pontificated.

"Now, as to that matter you just mentioned, Arvay, I'm agreeable, providing you promise me one thing."

"What is it, Jim?"

"You can have that baby, providing that you swear and promise me to bring it here a boy."

"Why, Jim! What a thing for you to make me swear to! How on earth can I tell what the child will be?"

"Easy enough. Just make up your mind to do, as I tell you, and have that child a boy. I never did want no girls around the house."

Arvay stretched her eyes, and looked at Jim a long time before she could say a word.

"That's a mighty funny thing for you to say, Jim. The way you makes over Angie nobody would think you didn't want no girl."

"Oh, I'm just putting on when I carry on like that, Arvay. I don't really want no girl, and don't you dare to have me no other one."

"Jim." Arvay gulped and swallowed. "That's no way to talk to me at all, and me in my condition too. It's cruel and mean, that's what it is. Cruel."

"Cruel? Why, what do you mean? If I got a cruel bone in me, this is my first of hearing about it. Why, I'm a mighty good-natured man, according to all that I can hear. Look how nice I acted when you up and had Angie on me. If I had of been cruel, I could of made you tie her up in a sack and chunk her into the lake, but I didn't do it. Or made you take her out in the swamp and lose her, but I never done that neither. I seen you was fond of the little thing, so I let you keep her for a pet. I'm a mighty good-natured man. Tell me!"

The stricken Arvay turned her face to the wall and said no more. Jim got into bed and blew out the light. After probably half an hour, Arvay murmured, "Jim."

"What is it, Arvay?"

"Supposing, supposing the child was to be born a girl."

"No use in supposing, Arvay. I know that you wouldn't have no girl after I done told you specifically to bring it here a boy." Then Jim went on off to sleep.

Arvay did not get to sleep until nearly morning, lying awake and supposing what could happen if the child happened to be a girl. And as she conjectured, she trembled.

Jim had evidently forgotten the teasing that he had given Arvay the night before, for he kissed her tenderly on waking and fondled her hair.

"You ain't to take no chances and run no risks, Arvay, in your condition. No lifting and stretching at all. Earl is big and old enough to keep you in wood and water. See to it that he keeps that bucket full in the kitchen, and keeps plenty of stove wood in the box."

"He ain't but seven, Jim."

"I could tote in wood and water long before that, Arvay. You let that boy do something and get manly. Naw, I don't want none of Dessie's young'uns doing it for Earl. I'll fill up the bucket and the box every morning before I go. Earl is to look after it for the rest of the day, you hear?"

"Yeah, Jim. He can't . . ."

"It's all cut and stacked, ain't it? More'n two strands of

good dry oak and pine out there for you to burn. All he got to do is tote in two or three pieces at a time and fill up that box before you start to cook supper. You understand?"

"Yes, Jim."

"In your condition, I want you to have every care. You ain't to worry about a thing. And don't look so sad and solemn, Arvie. You never got with this young'un out in no palmetto scrubs. You got it right here in the bed with Jim Meserve. You got full protection."

Arvay almost spoke and reminded Jim of what he had said the night before. But she could not bring herself to do so.

Jim went to work planning to make things better for Arvay in every way. With any luck at all with the still, by the time the child was born, he would have that carpet for the parlor and hall that Arvay wanted, and he would surprise her with a piano. Arvay played much better than she did when he married her, but that old second-hand organ was no help. He was going to deck her out with a brand new piano if things turned out as he hoped.

In her fear and desperation, Arvay fled back to her old time religion. Again and again she considered calling to Jim's mind his promise to love and protect her, but each time she failed of the courage to take her fate into her own hands and bring the matter to a head. Arvay could feel no faith in her own power over Jim, so she began again to take great stock in miracles. Arvay crept into the Bible and pulled down the lid. She made herself into parables and identified herself with Hannah before the conception of Samuel, and with Hagar, driven out into the desert by Abraham, and other sorrowful women. All day long during the hours that Jim was absent, Arvay went around muttering prayers for deliverance from her fancied danger.

Along with the habit of talking to herself, Arvay acquired the subconscious habit of keeping one hand on her abdomen. Any hand that was not busy at any time that she was awake went to her body. Round and round went the hand, round and round and round and round, as if she caressed the child inside her, and sought to placate it and persuade it to be a boy. In fact, she besought it aloud when she was sure that she would not be overheard.

"Be nice, honey. Be nice, now, and come here a boy-child for your Mama. You see the fix I'm in. Jim is liable to leave me if you ain't a boy. Me with three little hungry mouths to feed and to do for. I wouldn't have nowhere at all to go. Except to go pile up on Larraine, and I'd rather be dead and in my grave than to have to do a thing like that."

Arvay mentioned the same thing to the Lord several times a day.

Then, when she was seven months gone in pregnancy, Arvay discovered that Jim's demand had been only a joke. The day she found that out had been a trying one for her.

Angie was a great favorite with Bubber, Dessie's oldest boy, who was twenty, and working as yard man on the estate of a wealthy Yankee. Thoughtlessly, Bubber had brought home a mango for Angie and none for Earl, the night before. Arvay had put it away until morning. In mid-morning, Arvay had given it to Angie, and told her to divide with Earl. The children were out in the yard, and Arvay went on with her sewing.

Soon there were inhuman screams from the frontyard. Arvay's instant thought was that some wild beast had crept in from the swamp and was attacking Earl. The terrible snarly howls kept up as Arvay raced through the house to the front, grabbing the breech-loader from the head of the bed as she ran. She knew little about handling guns, but this did not occur to her as she ran.

The sight that met her eyes was far worse than if she had found a wild beast attacking her son.

Earl had the mango clutched in one hand as he lay drawn up in a knot on the ground. Angie was standing over him, hitting at the boy with a tiny branch of verbena, with the flowers still on it. Angie was striking at Earl with the spike of verbena, and Earl was on the ground clutching the mango and emitting those animal howls.

What had happened was obvious to Arvay on the porch. Earl had snatched the mango and attempted to flee to some safe place and eat it. He had run towards the corner of the yard and come up against a tangle of alaman bushes overrun by a Cherokee rose growing along the fence. There the little girl had overtaken him, and he had dropped to the ground.

The verbena bed was at hand, and Angie had broken off a branch no more than a foot long and was menacing her brother with it.

The scene told Arvay more than she wanted to know. The twig could not have hurt very much even in the hands of a grown man, and certainly three-year-old Angie could do him no harm with the thing. And the sounds! There was nothing human in them. She would never forget them the longest day that she lived. Earl had never made sounds like that before. Not in her hearing anyway.

Arvay leaned the gun against the porch with a shaking hand. A terrible anger took hold of her. For a confused minute, she did not know whether she was angry with Earl for his cowardice, or with Angie for teasing the poor child. Then she knew who was to blame. Bubber had no business to bring that mango on the place. She got off the porch and bent over the howling Earl and wrenched it from his hand and flung it over the fence.

"Hush up! Hush up, I tell you!" she cried as she hauled her son to his feet and shook him violently. She felt that if those sounds kept up another minute that she would lose her mind.

But while Arvay sought to cut off the sounds, Angie ran out of the gate and recovered her fruit, and was eating it. Earl saw her, and began to howl again. He kept it up until Arvay had dragged him clear around the house. Arvay had no time to take the mango from Angie again. She was too occupied with Earl. Those sounds had to cease at any cost. No doubt Dessie had heard them already. She must never learn that they had come from Earl's throat.

Arvay was shaken as she had never been before in all her life. Even the sight of the child at birth had not been as shocking as this.

"Oh, God, is my child going to be marked from this?"

After the noon dinner, the children were out in the yard, each amusing him and herself in their own way. Earl wandered on down to Dessie's and Arvay was glad. After a while, Angie lay down on the front porch and went to sleep.

It was time for Arvay to start the supper finally. She went out in the kitchen and put on the stew, washed some yams

and put them in the oven, and a pot of snap-peas and okra. While they were cooking, Arvay suffered as she washed the rice the regulation five waters and left it to soak. It would cook very quickly when she got to it.

There was no more wood in the box. She had no wish to call Earl to get the wood for her. If only some of Dessie's children would happen up.

Then a great anger and revolt seized upon her.

"I'm a'going out there and get me a turn of wood! Let Jim Meserve just try to help himself. If I overstrain and this child come here too soon, I don't care. It could be a blessing. I won't have to worry anymore. It's got to come here a boy, is it? I'll fix him! Let him worry like I been worried all this time."

Arvay went out into the yard, but she did not reach the wood-pile. Halfway there, she got to the pump and halted. No reason to it, her mind just wandered, and she halted. There was no water bucket on the broad shelf that Jim had built around the pump for Arvay's convenience, but Arvay took hold of the handle of the pump and started to pump. The pump had a strong suction, and the round handle went up in the air at the first stroke. Arvay let it stay there with her hand attached. She stood there for several minutes, her right hand hanging to the up-tilted pump handle, and her left hand going round and round over her abdomen. She hung there like a rag-doll and mumbled and suffered.

Then her eyes saw the sun in the west. It was just over the tops of the swamp trees. Some atavistic impulse arose in her, and suddenly the sun took on divine significance. She looked at it for several minutes, then slowly left the pump and advanced to a clear space facing the west and lifted her arms to pray.

"O, evening sun! You go where God is every night. Please take Him a message from me. Tell Him to take this child from me right now, or let me know that it's coming here a boy. Give me a sign by you. And, O evening sun, when you get on the other side, tell my Lord that I'm here praying. Tell Him . . ."

Arvay started violently, for just at that moment a shadow came between her and the sun. After a second she got it

straight and knew what it was. Jim had come around the corner of the house from the front.

"Oh!" Arvay let her arms come slowly to her sides.

"What's the matter, Little-Bits? Sending up a prayer for rain? I hope you get an answer, because the grove could certainly stand it along in here."

Arvay retreated before Jim for several steps. Backing back towards the pump but keeping her eyes fixed on Jim who had been smiling at first but was standing looking at her now with a worried look on his face.

"Naw! Naw, Jim Meserve, I wasn't praying for no rain. Know what I was praying for?" And now Arvay began to come forward again. "I was praying for God to take this child from me right now."

"My God, Arvay! What for? You know what that would mean, don't you?"

"I sure do. And that's exactly what I was praying for."

Jim was able to calm Arvay down after awhile, and find out what was the trouble. But not for long. When with difficulty Jim recalled the incident and told Arvay that it was a joke, she was not comforted at all.

"A joke! A joke and here I been suffering all this time! Jim, I'm never going to forget you for this thing."

Jim did not laugh it off as he had been inclined to do at first. He was quite serious, and apologized to Arvay most humbly. But when the only response he got was an indicting stare then a shamefaced hanging of her head, Jim dug deeper.

"But, Arvay, I thought that anybody at all would see through a joke like that. Anybody with even a teaspoonful of sense knows that you can't tell what a child'll turn out to be until it gets born. And furthermore, you know so well that I'd go to Hell for my daughter, and wade through solid rock up to my hips to do it. And then again, I'd be bound to love any child that you had for me."

Somehow, one of Arvay's braids had worked aloose, and Jim looked at her standing there with her head bowed and the yellow braid dangling over her shoulder and she looked pitiful and helpless to him. He did not want to talk about the thing any longer, nor to remember anything at all against her.

"You didn't act like it, Jim," Arvay accused sullenly. Then

the corners of her mouth went down and her voice trembled. "Looked to me like you just aimed to quit me, and was just fixing up any old kind of a shabby, sorry excuse to do it on." Arvay choked back a sob. "And me with three little bitty chillun on my hands to look after and do for. I was hurt-ed, Jim. Hurt-ed to my very heart, and felt like I was throwed clean away."

"Goddammit, why?" The sight of Arvay's drooping figure, the piteous tone of her voice made Jim see the months of pain and fear that Arvay had lived through in silence and so needlessly, and it was almost more than he could bear. It made him angry that Arvay should have suffered so uselessly, and through her belated revelation, make him agonize so. "What cause have you ever had to doubt me, Arvay? Have I ever mistreated you in any way whatsoever? Have I ever neglected to do my utmost for you and for my children?"

"Can't say as you have," Arvay murmured with her eyes still lowered.

"Then why would you put such an utmost application upon a silly thing like that? Where is your common, ordinary sense? Why did you want to twist a joke around like that?"

Jim whirled and loped off without waiting for an answer. He fled down into the peace and green calm of the grove to be alone in his anguish of feelings.

There was not sufficient understanding in his marriage, Jim said inside himself. It could not keep on like this. He was panging and paining far too much. What help for it except by parting from Arvay?

Minutes and possibly an hour passed with Jim controversing inside his mind. His thoughts and feelings made living pictures thrown against the white sand of the grove and the dark glossy foliage of the orange trees. He wouldn't be coming home anymore from work of evenings and finding Arvay doing around in the kitchen fixing him the kind of a supper that she figured he might choose and fancy. He wouldn't be grabbing up that sassy, impudent little piece of girl called Angeline. That bossy little chunk of prettiness that had the spunk to tussle and squall for what she wanted until she got it. And even poor helpless Earl. Who on earth would look after and protect him if his father was not around? And this

place, who would love it as he did and push it on to the
beauty and helpfulness that he saw in it? What would poor
helpless Arvay do with a place like this on her hands and no-
body to tell her and show her what to do about it? And Arvay
herself, what would become of the poor weak thing without
the proper person to give her the right care? She needed and
required the best that the world could afford. No one under-
stood that but himself. Some other dumb fool might come
along, find her forlorn and take the advantage and brutalize
her in some way or other.

With that thought, Jim leaped up from where he was
seated under a grapefruit tree as if he had found himself in
striking distance of a rattler, and headed back towards the
house. My God! What had got into him? Had he really been
wallowing around under that tree thinking about quitting his
wife? Arvay had acted dumb, but what more could you ex-
pect? She was a woman and women folks were not given to
thinking nohow. It was not in their make-up to do much
thinking. That was what men were made for. Women were
made to hover and to feel. He had gotten used to the com-
forts of a home through Arvay, and her tender and loving
care. He could not do without a woman now after that, and
what other woman on earth was he willing to suffer with and
do for? Why, she wasn't even born yet and her mama was
already dead. Arvay was his woman, and it was his privilege to
do for her. It was his part to put in the thinking. He had no
business pushing off nothing like that on her. He had played
the fool, not Arvay. As Jim neared the house the thing came
to him that had been dodging around in his mind for years.
There was something about Arvay that put him in mind of his
mother. They didn't favor each other in the face, but there
was something there that was the same. Maybe that was what
had caught his attention the first time that he had laid eyes on
Arvay. Maybe that was why he had never missed his family
since he had married her. All the agony of his lost mother was
gone when he could rest his head on Arvay's bosom and go
to sleep of nights.

That was just part of it, Jim went on, as he strode on
through the thriving young grove. There was something
about Arvay besides her good looks. Something like a vapor,

which reached to him and delivered him into her hands tied and bound. Now, supposing some other man should find out what he knew about Arvay, and be soothing his trashy head on Arvay's soft and comforting bosom, and breathing his breath in her face? Oh, but Jim would kill him dead wherever found.

In the kitchen Jim found Arvay switching around as fast as she could to finish his supper. And right away he became the loving and protecting husband, the ardent lover. He seized Arvay midway in a passage from the table to the stove and held her tight and kissed her and murmured sweet soothing things until the mysterious green light appeared in Arvay's blue eyes. Arvay's eyes had some strange power to change like that when she was stirred for him. Each time that she succumbed to his love making, Arvay's eyes gradually changed from that placid blue to a misty greenish-blue like the waters of the sea at times and at places. It warmed him, it burned him and bound him. But Jim did not consider himself weak in being overcome like that. He placed Arvay as having powers that few women on earth had. The strange thing was that she did not know her own strength. Maybe it was just as well. Knowing more, she might not have been so contented where she was. Twenty to twenty-five years later on, he could afford to let her know. No sense in crowding his luck.

Gradually, as the days went by, Arvay regained her composure, but she retained a residue of resentment. She felt like a fool for having suffered all those months so needlessly, and she stubbornly blamed Jim for making a fool of her.

And to add to that, the child was a boy, and as Dessie exclaimed, the spitting image of Jim. Couldn't have been anymore like Jim if Jim had spit him out of his mouth. Jim promptly named him James Kenneth Meserve, and he came to be called Kenny.

When Arvay was able to be up and around, she found a new carpet in the parlor and the hall, and there was a piano sitting where the old wheezy organ used to be. Next thing to be done, Jim said, was to have running water in the house. He aimed to put in electric lights some of these days.

The still that Arvay knew nothing about was doing well

indeed. Jim added another room to Joe's house and sunk a pump down that end of the grove. Dessie was going to have another baby herself, so Arvay thought that Jim was very good-hearted to get another woman to come in and take care of the washing so Dessie wouldn't have to strain. Arvay had to smile when Jim began to talk about buying an automobile. That back-gap was going to be widened into a driveway.

"Jim sure has got big notions," Arvay confided to Dessie. "It's nice to have all them big notions, but getting hold of the money is another thing."

"Oh, he's born lucky, you might say," Dessie answered mysteriously. "He's liable to stumble up on it. You never can tell."

Arvay had no idea about anything. But all the new improvements around the place lifted her up. From what she heard from west Florida, she was far and ahead of Larraine. Carl was still pastoring small charges. He had shifted twice since Arvay and Jim had married, and the changes were always for the worse. His youth was no longer a selling point.

What in the world had been the matter with her, Arvay wondered, wanting a man like Carl? Well, she had been young and ignorant then. Maybe she should tell Jim all about it now. But no, that would give him a stick to crack her over the head with. Better let sleeping dogs lie. Anyway, she'd never be able to feel resentment toward Larraine from now on.

Chapter Nine

KENNY MESERVE was a very lively child; everybody made over him. Arvay noticed that he would hang around the piano just as soon as he could walk. He was bold, and even more self-assured than Angie, but he had a cute smile to go with it.

Kenny got no public notice, and deserved none, until he was eight years old.

His favorite playmate and faithful follower was Belinda, three months younger than he was. Belinda was Dessie's baby.

Kenny was bossy like his father, and he preferred Belinda to all the other children he knew because Belinda was persuaded that he was very smart and showered admiration in various ways upon him. Then too, Belinda was right there on the place and handy. But Belinda's greatest charm for Kenny was her artistry. Belinda could stand on her head. Stand on her head with a better balance than Kenny had ever seen in any one. It was perfection, and Kenny admired her no end for it. He would even have been jealous, but he had taught it to her. Even though the pupil now surpassed her master, Kenneth was not jealous. She was a product of his skill.

Belinda contended that Kenny turned the best cart-wheels of anybody in the world. Kenny could always think up some scrape for them to get into, too. She could always help carry things through. It was a solid friendship.

It was through this friendship that Kenny came to public notice, and Arvay came to tears.

Kenny had led his expedition into town and wound up at the railroad station. The train came in, and Kenny particularly liked trains. It was the rhythm of movement and sound that entranced him, but he did not know that then. All he knew was that he loved trains. He got to see them seldom too, living out of town like that.

The train was a crack Pullman and parlor car affair—New York to Palm Beach and the Florida east coast in general. As the train blew for Citrabelle, Kenny with Belinda beside him,

lined up beside the track to enjoy the sight. Kenny was so overcome that he felt to worship. He wanted to do something in worship of the train. But what? A portly looking tourist came out on the platform between the coaches as the train slowed to a stop. He looked at the children and smiled. It was a nice smile, and that decided Kenny.

"Mister! Mister!" And as he finished shouting Kenny threw a perfect cartwheel. As he came up, he had another idea. He would offer the most perfect thing on earth to this train and the man who smiled on the platform. "Want to see Linda stand on her head?"

The smile got broader. The man misunderstood. He thought that Kenny was after making himself a little change. He tossed Kenny a quarter with an indulgent smile and said, "Sure thing. Let Belinda stand on her head."

Belinda needed no more than a flourish of the hand from Kenny. She made the proper approach, and in an instant, was standing on her head. Kenny looked raptly at first Belinda, and then at the man on the step.

"Ain't she wonderful? Nobody can't stand on their head that good. Nobody but Belinda. I showed her how myself."

Belinda's performance was attracting enormous interest among the passengers on the train. Kenny was about to burst his shirt with pride at the excitement Belinda created. He did not understand the reason. Belinda was innocent of underwear. She was there on her head, with her short percale skirt hanging over her face, with her shining little black behind glinting in the sun. Kenny was innocent, and besides he had seen it so often as he put his pupil through her paces that he paid no attention. As yet the two had no idea of nakedness.

Therefore, Kenny was outraged when he was heckled by a gray-haired chesty woman from the car ahead.

"Boy! You! You shameless little rascal, you! Turn that child down!"

Kenny was surprised and evermore hurt at such lack of appreciation of art. Here was the greatest artist of her time, and some fool hollering to turn her down. Kenny gave the outraged matron a snurling look, and ignored her after that. The excitement on the train was increased rather than diminished by the protest. Passengers from the off side of the cars

crowded over to see the show. There were smothered chuck-
les, and some unsmothered, running the whole length of the
train.

"Turn her down, I say!" the woman screamed again.

Kenny had not thought of gaining money by the show. It
was intended as a tribute. But the nice man had given him a
quarter to turn Belinda up. Two-bits was a heap of money
when you came right down to it. If it was worth all that much
to see Belinda stand on her head, it was worth double the
money to stop seeing it.

"Fifty cents to turn her down!" Kenny shouted, clothed in
innocence and arrogance.

The audience roared with laughter at this turn of affairs.
The heckler became more furious at being opposed, and then
made the butt of laughter by the dirty-faced little imp on the
ground with his frayed palmetto hat shoved far back on his
head.

"Fifty cents indeed!" the woman screamed. "You turn that
child down, I say!"

Kenny turned to Belinda like an impresario and directed:

"Wiggle your toes, Belinda!"

Belinda knew what was meant. She was to show that she
could move her lower extremities and still keep her balance.
That was the most technical part of the thing. Few could ac-
complish that. So the wrongside-up child proudly waved her
fat legs and wiggled her toes. Kenny flung his eyes up at his
audience. "What did I tell you? You have seen the most won-
derfullest thing on earth."

The train was about to pull off, but the woman, who was
evidently accustomed to being obeyed, gave another angry
and impatient command to turn Belinda down.

"You heard what I said. Fifty cents." And Kenny braced his
legs far apart and eye-balled his heckler belligerently.

The audience howled.

"Attaboy!" The smiling man who had donated the quarter
tossed another at Belinda. Somebody else flipped a coin, a big
round silver dollar.

"Hooray for Belinda!"

Silver money began to spout from every window and plat-
form.

The train began to move, and Kenny signified that Belinda could end the performance. She came down gracefully as the train pulled out of the station to more cheers. The last the passengers saw of the two children, they were standing and smiling and waving after the train.

When it had rounded the long curve to the south, and was no longer visible, the children searched around and collected the coins in Belinda's skirt. It was too much for them to count exactly, so they went across the street to the general store and Carl Galloway, the son of the proprietor, who waited on the people, counted it for them. Nine dollars and some odd cents.

"Whoo-eee! Belinda we're rich as we can be!" Kenny gloated and bought a dozen bananas for them to eat on as they walked homeward in clouds of triumph. Neither of them could make out what was wrong with that crazy woman.

"Tetched in the head," Kenny diagnosed.

"Tetched in her head," Belinda repeated as always.

The two children sankled on home eating bananas and feeling happy, never dreaming that the story of the performance was being told and laughed at all over town. That Kenny Meserve! He took after his Pappy all right. Nobody but a Meserve would have thought up such a thing.

Jim heard about it as he came through town after work. He was joshed and teased, and he laughed and replied in kind. He was rather proud of Kenny. A chip off the old block, all right.

So Jim was put out when he got home and found Arvay all upset over the incident. Kenny and Belinda had been whipped and were in deep disgrace. Jim took exception right away.

"What is it to be lawing and jawing about, Arvie? It was nothing but children's doings. They ain't got the least idea about nothing unless you done put into their heads. Let it be."

"I won't let it be, Jim! The way the twig is bent, the tree is bound to be inclined. I try to raise my children clean and right. I don't intend to have nobody around here toling a young'un of mine off and leading him astray. I don't intend to put up with it at all."

"Ha! Belinda leading Kenny! That's a joke. Nobody ain't apt to do no leading around Kenny Meserve. He's too much like his old man for that. I take it as a grand insult for you to even say such a thing. That was Kenny's own idea from stem to stern. Anyhow, what can be done about it now? It's done and over with."

Arvay looked up into Jim's positive eyes and gave a pained gasp. She slumped in silence for awhile before she spoke.

"Belinda being that no-count Joe's young'un, I reckon any caper that she might up and cut just have to be put up with. Look like Joe is the boss on this place."

"Now just what do you mean by that, Honey?" Jim asked in surprise and irritation. He made an impatient gesture, then comprehension came to him. He gave a big, clapping laugh and picked Arvay up and sat down with her in his lap.

"This baby-wife I got can't stand for her husband to think well of nobody but her." Jim caressed Arvay under her chin and cajoled her along. "Look, Little-Bits, I think as much of you as God does of Gabriel, and you know that's His pet angel. But . . ."

"But what?" Arvay pouted.

"But Joe is my helper. Sort of standing at my right hand. You don't know what a lot of help Joe has been to me, off and on. You're my wife, the most precious thing that I got, and nobody don't compare with you. What's between me and Joe is something different altogether and I wouldn't want you to take a pick at him. Just try to feel and believe that every move I make is in your interest, baby. Will you try to feel that without me always having to tell you so?"

Arvay nodded, then under Jim's kisses slipped one arm about his neck.

"Long as Joe ain't got more influence over you than I have, Jim, I ain't got a thing against him. I don't aim to make out that I like the notion of them young'uns being up around the depot naked and all, though. It ain't Christian. It's more like little heathens that ain't got nobody to teach 'em right from wrong. And Kenny . . ."

Jim realized what was before him. No amount of reasoning was going to do any good. Arvay lived by her feelings and not by conscious reasoning, so he fondled her and cajoled and

teased her and thus got her mind off the subject and left her
feeling assured.

The lifeless scare-crow that Arvay had set up herself had
been knocked down and trampled under foot, and Arvay had
a great feeling of power and victory. As much as Jim thought
of Joe, she had more power of her husband than Joe had. It
made her feel very good. So uplifted that she was extra nice to
Dessie and her children next day. She so far forgave Belinda's
little bare body that right after breakfast she dug out all of
Angeline's clothes that her daughter had outgrown and gave
them to Dessie for Belinda. The feeling of guilt drove her to
town to buy enough white lawn to make Belinda a dress for
Sunday School and a ribbon bow for her hair.

Something more than remorse was moving inside Arvay.
She found that it was a kind of gratitude for the happening.
Out of it had come her first glimmering of really being
Jim Meserve's wife, and while it was not anything like a full
realization, a hope, a possibility that it could be so. She
might come to win this great and perfect man some day.
That being the case, it was worth all the world to be right
there in the house with Jim and to have the privilege to do
for him the best that she knew how. It was a good thing
having Joe and his family on the place. They had brought
her luck.

So reconciled was Arvay, that she surprised herself by the
way she reacted to a small incident that happened a few days
later.

Jim had ordered some cement for the front walk, and the
white man who delivered it drove up with it under the cam-
phor tree in the back yard. Kenny and Belinda were playing
out around there, and came running up to see what was arriv-
ing. The driver saw the children as he jumped down from his
seat, and to make talk with them, pretended that he did not
know who they were. His face was all ready to smile at his
own teasing as he looked at Kenny first and asked, "Whose
little boy are you?"

Kenny gave him a look from under his long lashes that
called the man a dumb fool and retorted, "You know so well
that I'm Kenny, Jim Meserve's son."

The man looked at Arvay, who had come to the door and

winked his eye and chuckled. "And mighty proud about it, I see."

"Sure." Kenny braced himself and challenged the man with his eyes. "My Daddy can lick any man in the world."

"You don't tell me!" The truck-driver affected to be mightily impressed, and making no fun out of Kenny, turned to Belinda and asked her, "And whose little girl are you?"

Belinda wanted to come off as well as Kenny had, and was obviously stumped for an answer for a moment. She shuffled her bare feet in the sand, then flung up her head and said, "I'm Miss Arvay's little girl, that's who."

Both the truck-driver and Arvay had their mouths wide open for a minute and couldn't close them. Then the driver gave a great guffaw. He had gotten his laugh at last.

"Aw, gwan! Miss Arvay ain't your mother, nothing of the kind!" He rocked and rolled with laughter. He slapped his thigh, and looked to Arvay to join him in the joke.

"Yes I is Miss Arvay's little girl too," contended Belinda about to cry. "Yes I is, too. She gave me a pretty white dress for Sunday School," and Belinda spread her skirts to illustrate, "and a *pretty* pink ribbon for my head. Yes I is her little girl so!"

Arvay saw Belinda about to cry and understood. Belinda valued her and counted on her care and wanted to be loved by her. Arvay knew that feeling.

"Yes indeed, Belinda is my little girl," Arvay said with conviction as she came slowly down the steps to direct the delivery of the cement. "Born right here on the place, and I wouldn't take a play-pretty for her either, I'm a'telling you!"

It was worth something to Arvay to see Belinda's happy and triumphant look. With her head away up, Belinda marched around in a small circle with her soiled little skirt spread out on both sides.

"That *is* right," the driver agreed and fell in with the play. "Excuse me, Belinda. I just forgot." With that, Arvay pointed him to the wash-shed, and he began unloading the sacks of cement under there, while the two children looked on importantly.

Arvay felt very light-hearted for the rest of the afternoon, and told Jim about it as soon as they were alone in the bedroom.

"Knew from the very first time that I saw you, Little-Bits, that you was all heart," Jim remarked feelingly.

"You reckon?" Arvay blushed under Jim's approval.

"Naw, I know, honey, and that makes up for a lot of things. I can read your writing. Know you a lot better than you know your ownself, Arvay, and always have."

"I try to do what's right, Jim. Always did, to the best that I know how."

"And I believe you," Jim remarked after a pause. "You do the very best that you know how." Jim kissed her then and let it go at that. He went to bed feeling very encouraged. It looked as if Arvay was finding her way. The only snag was, could he make her understand that there was a way and that it was necessary for her to find it? How was he to bring a thing like that about? He had tried every way that he knew how and had only temporary results. Maybe it would just come all of a sudden some day. Then life would be perfect indeed.

Things went on very comfortably, Arvay thought, for two whole years. Many improvements of living took place around the house. Jim sank a deep well with a motor pump and there was running water in the house and a bathroom. The house was thoroughly screened and had a fresh coat of paint. Then came electric lights. Everything on the place reflected a greater degree of prosperity, and Arvay felt fine, but that was because she had no idea of the major source of Jim's income. Whenever she thanked Jim for some new comfort and inquired about possible raises in his salary, Jim always answered her in a parable, using a gambler's phrase, "Good dice are bringing the money!" As Arvay did little visiting around and encouraged few visitors, she knew nothing about the still.

Time and again when Jim made a big sale, he longed to run to Arvay and show her his pockets loaded down with money, but he knew his wife too well for that. Having anything to do with alcohol in any way whatsoever would outrage her religious principles. Jim was down in the grove talking over the work with Joe, or off somewhere on business, was all that she ever knew.

Then one day a dash of gossip fell in her ear while she was downtown on the streets, and Jim found a crying, outraged

woman when he got home. Arvay was still too unsure of her-self to lay down any ultimatums to her husband, so she took it out on Joe. He was leading her husband astray, and on top of that, she had a half-grown son, and he too was in danger of being ruined by Joe and his likkery ways.

Jim gritted his teeth and told Arvay that it was not Joe at all. He was the one who was responsible for the whole thing, and that she was not to tackle Joe on the subject at all. It was his still, and Joe was just running it for him. Let Joe right alone. Furthermore, it all had been done for her furtherance; she had and was enjoying the benefits from it. He had not meant for her to know, but now that she did, she was not to say a word to Joe about it. Joe had been careful to protect Jim, capable and ever so honest and faithful. Joe had run the risk of the chain-gang being faithful to him. It would be a very shabby return to place the blame on Joe.

With her hands tied like that, Arvay could not blaze out on Joe as she burned to do, but she showed her feelings by short-talking Joe everytime that she had occasion to speak to him. There were no more of those pleasant little exchanges of talk. It was a short "yes" or "no" or "what" and no more.

Arvay was throwing the rabbit in the briar patch without knowing it, and she would not have cared if she did. Under Jim's pressure, Joe had put some of his likker money into two lots in Colored Town. He had never admired working the grove, and now he felt that he had a sufficient accumulation of money to knock off. Only his feeling of loyalty had held Joe on the job for years. So now, under Arvay's short-talking, Joe claimed that his feelings were hurt-ed. He never liked to be around where he wasn't wanted. Miz' Arvay seemed like she would rather have his space than his company. It would be much more better if he took his family and got off the place. Which he did in a kind of a slow hurry. He had the shell of a six-room house thrown up on his lots and moved into the unfinished structure. That was as far as the house ever got. Joe bought himself a car and announced that he had got to be people in Citrabelle. Doing things on a high-toned scale. Heavy-set Daddy. If a woman asked him for a nickel, he gave her a ten-dollar bill. Ask him for a drink of likker, and he bought her a whiskey-still. Joe Kelsey was really some trouble.

Money coming in from the still and not too much work to do, Joe said that he was getting more like the rich folks every day. Living on premises and tending to groves was in the past.

Arvay was secretly joyful when Joe moved, but not for long. When the little house in the grove was empty, Arvay found that its silence left a vacancy in her days. Joe and Dessie and their children were a part of the pattern of her life. She was too proud to own it to Jim, but Arvay missed them, and wanted them back very much. It was denied her the simple way of just going to Dessie and telling her to move on back. Jim could do a thing like that, and would have done so but he believed that it would be against his wife's wishes. Therefore both of them glummed around and snapped at each other for other reasons.

Keeping her remorse to herself, Arvay could not know how Dessie wanted to return. With Joe cutting the tom-fool like he was, Dessie had small pleasure in being the mistress of her own home. A word of welcome from Arvay would have brought her and her children back. Joe would have been along in time.

The house in the grove was empty and Arvay was sorry and Jim was glum about it.

Chapter Ten

ARVAY could see Jim walking over the place and looking around, his thoughts reflected in his face. Things were getting to look shabby. Barn and chicken-yard not looked after, and fence-rows growing up in weeds. Arvay used to sit out under the camphor tree of afternoons and sympathize with the scenery, but now she avoided being caught out there. It might give Jim a chance to comment on the state of things, and the very thought of that put a squinge in her. She could see that Jim was aggravated and fretted about the way things were looking, because he was different from her father. Everything had to be neat and well-cared for around Jim.

He took to going off on fishing trips with men friends of Saturdays, coming back late of Sunday afternoons. Some of his men friends had cars, and he went off with them.

After months of days, Jim came back off of one of these trips and said to Arvay, "I've got somebody for the house in the grove."

"I'm mighty proud and glad about that, Jim. Who is it?"

"A white family."

"Would I know who they is?"

"Not hardly. He's a fisherman from over on the coast. That is, he was till he got a bad case of fish-poisoning and had to quit it for a while. He needs something to do to take care of his family till he can get well enough to go back to fishing."

"How many young'uns is he got?"

"Two. Girls. One is a little chap around seven or eight years old. The other one is almost a grown young lady. Around Earl's age, I reckon."

"Mighty far apart, I would say. How come that?"

"I ain't responsible, so I really wouldn't know. Didn't even feel that it was my business to ask."

A few days later the new family drove up in a truck. It was homemade from an old Ford car.

Arvay was annoyed because she felt that Jim had held things back from her. Jim had said that they were white folks, but the man turned out to be a Portuguese, and his name was

Corregio. That made them foreigners, and no foreigners were ever quite white to Arvay. Real white people talked English and without any funny sounds to it. The fact that his wife was a Georgia-born girl that he had married up around Savannah did not help the case one bit, so far as Arvay could see. The woman had gone back on her kind and fallen from grace.

But the sins of the parents certainly had not fallen on the children's looks. The older girl had dark brown hair and eyes, and the hair was lit up with golden glints. That would come from her mother's light brown hair. She was more American looking like her mother, but there was a sort of Latin overlay that made her exotic. She was already ripe-looking, and all in all, a very pretty girl. It seemed strange to Arvay for her to be named plain Lucy Ann with those looks. The younger girl was named Felicia, and her name fitted her. Great, soft mellow eyes with lashes so long that Arvay said that you could almost plait them. High arching eyebrows in a shiny black curve, that almost met over the bridge of her nose. Her hair was so thick and rich that Arvay thought with wonder that she must have ten hairs to every one of Angeline's and she had always considered that Angie had an extra thick head of hair. Young as she was, already it went curling to her waist. Her lips were red, red, and rosy.

Jim could have told her all these things at the start, but he had not done so, and Arvay couldn't say that she liked it at all. It was as if he called himself slipping something over on her. Come to think of it, what did this Gee know about tending a grove? And this Georgia Cracker woman who had lowered herself to marrying a foreigner, was not going to be one bit of service to her around the house. This was no laughing, obliging Dessie. There were two separate families now on the place.

Angeline and Kenny stood and gazed as the Corregios unloaded their things and toted them in the house. They too were disappointed. Lucy Ann was too old to interest them, and Angeline scorned Felicia off as much too young for her company. Kenny sidled around to Felicia to see if she was any use to him. When he found that she could neither skin the cat, throw cartwheels, stand on her head, walk on her hands, nor use a pop-gun, he was through. Anyway, he had arrived

at the stage where he was scornful of girls. The weakly things couldn't play ball, run or fight worth a cent. Just a waste of good material.

Earl was not at home when the new tenants arrived. Optimistically, and because she had no one else to send, Arvay had sent him after the clothes. He had been gone for two hours, and she did not expect him back for some time as yet. The distance to Colored Town was not great, but Earl always took a long time to go any place and return. His movements were so undecided and slow. It was around sundown when Earl came stumbling through the gate. The clothes were beginning to hang out of the bundle. Arvay was on the watch for him, and ran out to catch the dangling clean things. No use in scolding him. He couldn't do any better than that. She simply took the basket from him, and let him stumble on after her into the house. Arvay told him that he must be all tired out, and sent him on into his room, that he shared with Kenny, to lie down for a while before supper.

Arvay had the supper nearly ready, and hurried back to the kitchen to finish off things. In that way, she forgot to mention to Earl that they had folks down in the small house now. It didn't make any difference she thought, as she went about preparing the supper. He would know it soon anyway. She was making out a pan of biscuits when her attention was gradually caught by a peculiar kind of noise. A whimpering, whining, that broke into a kind of a yelp now and then as it grew more insistent. Something like a dog penned up in a strange place, or when a hunting dog sees its master take down the gun and is impatient to be off on the chase.

It seemed to Arvay to come from the vicinity of the boys' room. The thing was so puzzling that Arvay tipped through the hall to the door and listened.

It was coming from in there all right. She wondered if that devilish Kenny had toled somebody's dog off and got it shut up in there. Arvay was vexed with Kenny. He knew how scared Earl was of animals. So scared that he would not even go near a live chicken. Kenny was always pestering her for a dog, but no pets had ever been allowed on the place on account of Earl. Now, look like that Kenny had stolen a march on her, and slipped a puppy in there to frighten poor Earl to

death. She wanted to turn the door-knob and see, but her hands were in the biscuit dough and she couldn't. Then the sounds ceased, and Arvay turned away with relief.

"Maybe I was mistaken. Somebody could of passed along by the place with a dog."

She was shoving the big pan of biscuits into the bake-oven when she heard the sounds again. She could not be mistaken this time. She ran to the door of the boys' room and listened. Along with the whimpering yelps, there was a sound of running feet around inside the room. That would be poor Earl, too frightened of that puppy to even scream. Kenny was going to catch it, and catch it good for this. She took hold, and flung the door wide open.

Her eyes flung around angrily, but there was no dog in the room. Earl, with unseeing eyes, was doing the trampling and running around. She stood and he couldn't help seeing her there, but there was no recognition in his eyes. She became frightened and called his name, but it made no difference at all. He was bent over with his head and nose thrust forward and running and turning back on his course and running like a hound dog hunting for the scent. He found it, lost it again, and turned fast and hunted to pick it up again. Whining and whimpering and making growly noises in his throat from time to time. At last, he seemed to fix on it as coming through the window, and with a sound of triumph he flung himself against the screen. It was nailed around the window and didn't give, and the horrified Arvay saw him fling himself against it time and time again, and then begin to scratch and claw at it furiously. Arvay screamed at him to bring him to his senses. The only way she knew that her cries were heard was that he looked, and thereby his attention was directed to the open door. He didn't see his mother. He only saw the opening, and dashed and sprung for it, knocking Arvay down as he leaped past and over her, and by the time she could look, he was leaping out through the kitchen door.

Arvay jumped to her feet and ran after him calling him to halt. By the time she reached the kitchen door, though, she could spy him running down through the grove like a hunting dog on the trail. He turned and twisted frantically, but

finally headed dead for the house in the grove. Arvay sprang from the door and raced after him.

"Oh, my God! He'll go there in that condition, and I can't bear for them folks to see my boy that a'ways."

Arvay was in a good way to lose the race, but she was saved by seeing Jim, who she did not know had come home, coming from the direction of the house in the grove. He saw that something was wrong with Earl right away, and planted himself in the path of Earl's loping advance. When the boy was in reach, Jim tackled the slender frame and bore it easily to the ground. When he had subdued the thrashing and struggling to an extent, he slung Earl over his shoulder and hurried with him to the house, carried him back into the room and locked the door on him.

"What in the world's come over the boy, you reckon, Jim?" Arvay panted out, when Jim returned to the kitchen.

Jim dropped down into a chair at the table, and rested his forehead in his hands.

"It would take a God to tell, Arvay. Anyhow, now we know that we got to keep a sharp eye on him after this. No telling what might happen. Don't leave him out of your sight when I'm not on the place."

Arvay could see that Jim was mightily shaken. He had a grayish film over the skin of his face, and his eyes looked scared. His shoulders sagged and sagged, and he didn't feel to talk anymore, not even when they all sat down to eat.

Arvay was stirred up too, and agreed with Jim that he was right. But as the days passed by, she decided that she couldn't keep up with Earl all the time and get her housework attended to. Two weeks later, when Jim went off right after supper, she missed Earl around dusk-dark, and went all over the place in frantic search of him. She found him at last with his eyes glued to the kitchen window of the little house, hungrily watching the Corregio family gathered around the supper table. They were eating and laughing and talking mightily, and perhaps that was why none of them as yet had noticed the face pressed against the window. Arvay approached as quietly as she could, collared Earl, and clapped her hand over his mouth to prevent any betraying sounds, and dragged him away. The only way Earl resisted her was to

bite the hand that she had placed over his mouth. Otherwise, he let her lead him away.

Jim demanded to know how Arvay's hand got hurt like that, and she had to tell him. Two of her fingers were bitten too badly for her to hide.

Jim sat on the side of their bed and thought some time before he spoke. Then, taking Arvay's bloody hand in his own, he said, "Arvay, this can't go on. Earl has got to be put away."

Arvay's eyes flew wide open in terror.

"Why, why, what do you mean by that, Jim?"

"Just what I said. Chattahoochee, Arvay. Earl ain't in no condition to be aloose."

"Why you say a thing like that, Jim?"

"Now, don't ask me no dumb questions like that, honey. He's liable to hurt himself." And he stroked the wrist of her injured hand. "He'll do harm to other folks. We ought not to risk it. No later than sunrise in the morning, we ought to take steps to put the boy away."

"You set there and think that I'm a'going to agree to a thing like that?" And Arvay took her hand away angrily. "Putting my child in some crazy house? Nothing much wrong with Earl. He was all right, and you know it, until you fetched them furriners here on the place. They must have some different scent from regular folks and it maked Earl sick in some way or another. All you got to do is to get rid of 'em, and Earl will be all right."

"No, Arvay, you're ever so wrong about that. Something about one or the other of those girls has woke up something in the boy. They didn't put it there, though. It's been there all along. You see the boy can't control himself, and we had better take things in time."

"Jim, as I have said time and time again, there's things about you that I'm never to understand. Would you rather to place your own son in a crazy house than to do away with them people?"

"Those folks ain't got a thing to do with it, Arvay, I keep on trying to tell you and to show you," Jim snapped angrily. "Why can't we look at this thing in a sensible way and take steps to head off trouble? Why do we have to duck and dodge

and whip the Devil around the stump and lay ourselves open to sorrow and trouble? Why can't we just quietly put the boy away and provide for him, and let it go at that? I don't hold *you* responsible for his condition. It come through your father's folks, but you didn't have nothing to do with that. I'm trying to be fair about it all I know how, but look like you won't try to meet me at all."

"That's right, throw it up in my face!" Arvay blazed. "I know that you been had it in you to say all the time. I been looking for you to puke it up long time ago. What you stay with me for, I don't know, because I know so well that you don't think I got no sense, and my folks don't amount to a hill of beans in your sight. You come from some big high muck-de-mucks, and we ain't nothing but piney-woods Crackers and poor white trash. Even niggers is better than we is, according to your kind. Joe Kelsey's word stands higher than mine any old day. You can say it don't, but actions speak louder than words. You give him more credit for sense than you do me. All I'm good for is to lay up in the bed with you and satisfy your feelings and do around here for you. Naw, I'll never give my consent for Earl to be put away. Never so long as my head is warm. Earl is always wrong because he's like my folks. 'Tain't never nothing wrong with Angeline and Kenny because they take after your side. But I'm here to tell you that I'll wade in blood to my knees for him. He's not going to be put away."

"Well," Jim said quietly after a wait, "you've had your say, and I know a whole lot more than I used to. I reckon it wouldn't be no use for me to call to your attention that there was no compellment about us getting married, Arvay. I didn't have it to do. I knew what your folks were like before we got married, so I must have wanted to marry you."

"So you decided to put up with even so, eh? But you can't stand nothing that looks like my folks around the house. Since you hate the sight of Earl so bad, why don't you just quit me and lemme go on back where you got me from?"

"Because you're my wife, and I put in to spend the rest of my days with you. All right, Arvay, I won't be the one to break up our home. Henceforward, I got no more to say on the subject of Earl. I submit to your determination. One

thing you got to understand, and that thoroughly. I'm not telling Alfredo Corregio to move out. I have a reason for wanting him around, and here he stays till I see further. Suit your ownself about Earl. But bear in mind that anything bad that happens will be laid at your door."

"Satisfaction to me," Arvay snapped. "I know so well that Earl wouldn't hurt a living soul."

Jim looked at Arvay's injured hand significantly, then began to take off his shoes.

"I only wish that I was as sure about that as you seem to be, Arvay. I love Earl too, but I'm a man that's given to facts. And what makes it worse, I know, and you know too, that Earl's got some great craving after guns. Only thing I ever noticed that he wanted to play with. Goes hog wild just at the very sight of one. You know so well that I've had to keep my shot-gun, rifle and pistol hid away for the last three years, and daresent leave 'em loaded, just in case he might run upon one of 'em."

"Oh, I know what you're hinting at, Jim. Earl did aim that rifle at Kenny one time, but he was just playing, and you know it."

"Naw, I don't, Arvay. I do know that he pulled the trigger several times, but the gun just wasn't loaded. Kenny might have been blown to pieces. Naw, I don't know no such a goddamn thing that Earl was joking. I wouldn't swear to no lie like that, and I don't aim to take no chances."

"Things *is* come to a pretty place when you done got so you call me a liar to my face." Arvay began to cry. "And all because I try to take up for my child. The poor, pitiful thing ain't got nobody to care for him but me."

Jim sank wearily into bed and kept his mouth.

Chapter Eleven

MRS. CORREGIO was a handsome woman, a year or so
older than Arvay. Bright-eyed, a trifle full-bodied and
full of laughs and jokes. And hardly was she settled on the
place than she took to a habit that offended Arvay mortally.
Finding that Jim was fond of sea-food, she was forever—or
so it seemed to Arvay—cooking up batches of fried shrimp,
devilled crabs, fish in Savannah kinds of ways, and sending
one of her family up to invite the Meserves down to eat with
them. Arvay stood steadfast in her tracks and refused to go or
even to touch a mouthful of what she called "Geechy
messes," but Jim accepted with pleasure and came back tell-
ing how good it was. Jim even offered the grand insult of
urging Arvay to get the recipes from Alfredo's wife and fixing
some of those dishes her ownself. Jim had had no experience
in being a woman and he didn't understand. It kept Arvay
worried and hurt. She put the worst interpretation on it; that
Corregio woman was "fly" and doing her level best to bait
Jim Meserve in.

And if it was not the mother, then it could be that Lucy
Ann. Unfortunate as it was, you had to admit that the girl was
really pretty and ever so young and fresh, and Jim was too
much around that house in the grove. He claimed to be mak-
ing some kind of plans and talking things over with Alfredo,
but you never could tell. Arvay wanted to be fair about the
thing, and often and again she reminded herself that Jim was
old enough to be Lucy Ann's father. She called to mind the
girl's instant popularity on coming to Citrabelle. All the grass
was worn down on that little back road from the cars and the
feet of eager young local fellows. Jim laughed over it, so he
couldn't be thinking of the girl for himself. Jim was not that
kind of a man to take a back seat or ring a backing-bell for
any man. So she ought to feel satisfied, only she wasn't. No
matter how you twisted things around, Jim was spending too
much time down in there. Arvay felt double-teened and over-
powered by those Gees. So she contended about Earl. Her
aim was to hit a straight lick with a crooked stick. Jim, how-

ever, was acting mighty stubborn about it. He reminded her that the Corregios never would have been there if she had let Joe alone.

Instead of getting rid of them as she wished, Arvay was truly alarmed when Jim announced that he was closing down his still. He was selling out right away to a couple of men who had been trying to buy in with him for some time. Arvay's interpretation of the sale went like this: The Corregios had gotten such a hold over Jim that he had turned against Joe Kelsey. Any day now they might turn him against his own wife. If they could run off Joe Kelsey, God from glory! Anything was apt to come off next. They could run the hog over anything.

The truth of the matter was that Jim was getting out because an election was coming up and the man most likely to win the nomination for sheriff was doing a lot of speaking before women's clubs and church groups and swearing that he would enforce Prohibition even if he had to ring the entire county with deputies as close together as pickets on a fence. No use in playing the hog, Jim concluded. He had done mighty well. Better be satisfied with his profits and knock off. He had, in addition, put away enough to give him a start in another business. He sold out. The last run was celebrated hilariously by most of the prominent men in the county, and Jim gave Joe a lump sum, and the still went into the hands of its new owners. That last run had been the rooster, the boar, the bull, the stud and stallion of all stag parties. Jim had abdicated like a king.

Some time back, Jim had bought a strongbox and kept it in the closet. Arvay noted now that he was careful to keep it locked and the key on his ring. She had no idea how much was in there. That made her feel shut out. She accused the Corregios of being behind that too. Jim was so careful for fear that Earl would prowl upon it and get hold of weapons. The tension over Earl kept them from talking things out, and neither knew too much about what the other had in mind. The very air of the home was charged with opposition.

Arvay did a lot of communing with herself. Now, she thought, Jim's real feelings were exposed. He had never taken her for his equal. He was that same James Kenneth Meserve

of the great plantations, and looked down on her as the back-woods Cracker, the piney-woods rooter, and thought that he could just run the hog over her in anyway that he pleased. He could tell her to her face that those Gees were there to stay and she couldn't help herself. He could snatch her son from her, to accommodate those Gees, and stick her child in a crazyhouse. Well, she might not come from no high muck-de-mucks, but she would show him a thing or two. She was Little David to his mighty Goliath. He might go for a big cigar, but she would smoke him!

Jim went around feeling down-hearted. He could not understand why Arvay was acting so bull-headed and contrary about Earl. She had seen the signs just as plain as day. Why did she want to chance what could happen most any hour. What the hell was the matter with her nohow? Here he had got hold of Alfredo and was doing his level best to get into shrimping, a legal and profitable business to bring her more comforts and pleasures and she looked like she was pulling against him. She had reared and pitched against the still, yet she acted like it made her mad when he sold it. He didn't make her out at all. Didn't she want him anymore? He couldn't make heads nor tails out of that part either. She came to his embraces eagerly enough, but the very next day she was pouting around as usual. As much as it would hurt him, if she wanted to get shed of him, he would grant it. But she fended off any hint along that line too. What on earth was he to do? It all fumed up from Earl somehow, and Jim began to resent the boy. Then he would catch himself and reason over it. Earl was a pitiful thing and not responsible. If he could only make Arvay see things in the right way about the boy, they could be happy again.

All unconsciously, Jim was giving Arvay more cause for worry every day. Jim was fond of children and petted and played with Felicia too when he came upon her playing with Angeline and Kenny in the grove. Arvay noted with displeasure that within a week of the coming of the Corregios, her two younger children had made friends with Felicia and included her in everything, even begging her to eat with them when they were called to supper if she happened to be up around the house at the time. Arvay looked and listened, and

felt that she was losing ground all up and down the line. She blamed Jim for it all. He just would insist on having that family around. So everytime that she saw Felicia romping with her children; everytime that she heard blow-outs of laughter from the house in the grove of nights, and knew that Jim was down there taking part, and thought about Earl being in that room under watch-care, she boiled. She felt that she and Earl were shut off in loneliness by themselves. So from one thing to another, Arvay began to entertain a strange thought. She began to consider quitting Jim. She could not hold up her end against what she had to contend with. The great river plantations were too powerful for the piney woods, but never would she bow and buckle herself down and acknowledge it. She would march away from Jim and go back with her own kind.

First, she wrote a letter to her mother saying that she was coming to pay her a visit. She was bringing Earl along so her mother could see how he had grown. Two years before she had paid a short visit and carried all of her children, but this time, she was only bringing Earl.

As for support, Arvay figured that she could give music lessons, take in some plain sewing, and make enough to feed and clothe them anyway. She would be satisifed, for she would be where nobody looked down on her, and nobody would be talking about putting poor Earl away.

Still, Arvay wavered back and forth until she told Jim that she wanted to go see her mother, and take Earl along, and he handed her two hundred dollars, and did not question her about when she would be back. That decided her. In a cold fury she packed all of her best clothes and those of Earl's and went off to Sawley.

Arvay's ardent championship of her background and her family got a set-back as soon as she stepped off the train. Sawley looked poor and shabby and mean. Nothing like the bright flourishing look of Citrabelle. Things dragged around and houses looked like shacks and had no paint on them. Even the bank seemed narrow-contracted and silly. Beside the winter homes of the Yankees around Citrabelle, Bradford Cary's home no longer appeared so rich. Everything seemed to have shrunk up since she moved away.

Beside her own home and carefully tended grove, the Henson house and place looked just too awful for words. Inside and out, the place galled her. Before she was in the house two hours she found herself criticizing things.

"Mama, why don't you put on one of those housedresses that I sent you? Why you want to go around in them old raggedy things?"

She had not eaten out of cracked dishes in so long that her gorge rose at doing so now, and she hated to put the bent and rusty old cheap forks to her mouth.

But she braced herself to glory in her folks and keep up the fight. She spent the next day cleaning piles of old junk and mess out of the house and burning it over her mother's protest. It was no use at all that Arvay could see. Just junk for junk's sake. She had fallen over an old horse-collar as she came in the front door the first time. Then too, Arvay wanted things nice and clean for Earl. Rats, roaches and flies were simply taking the place. He could get hold of any kind of sickness at all from things like that. Why, her barn at home was better than this. Jim had bins lined with tin to keep out the rats and had screen wire on the doors and windows to keep biting flies away from his horse and cows. It had been so long that she had clean forgotten that some folks had flies and roaches and bed-bugs in their houses.

In her second day of dragging out junk and burning and scalding and scrubbing, Carl and Larraine and their five children jolted up in an old Ford and lit down. Arvay could not see that they were any improvement on the scenery at all. Some changes had been made. Either they had changed or she had.

"What awful gang of Crackers is that?" she asked herself as the car pulled up in the yard, and before she recognized who they were. True, Carl had been turned off from Day Spring for some years now, but they didn't have to look as poor and as common as all that. Common in the flesh and common in what they had on. It was all right seeing them here in Sawley, but Arvay was not sure that she would have liked to own them in Citrabelle. They were too poor for anybody to like them too much, and to have many friends. So common-cladded, and their poor-looking skins, and unbred feet and

legs, and the whole make of them. She was indeed glad that
Jim was not standing beside her now and seeing her folks as
she saw them. She wouldn't have a thing to rear back on.
They made Arvay angry, letting her down like that. It made
her feel to be cruel, and she let Larraine see all of her things.
It did her good to see Larraine letting her eyes get narrow at
the style and cut of her clothes, and see her fingering the
materials on the sly. Off-hand-like, she handed Earl five dol-
lars to go into town with his cousins and treat them to ice
cream and things. It did her good to see the look of gloating
pride on her mother's face. Maria gave Larraine a cut-eye
look as much as to say, "Now, how do like that come step-
ping up to you?" Arvay was not bringing up the tail end of
things any more.

Arvay could not make the house very comfortable or pretty,
but she did get it fairly clean and orderly. She went into town
and got some stuff for curtains, and fixed up what had been
her and Larraine's old room for Earl, and settled him down in
there. She herself slept in with her mother. She laid in a good
supply of staple groceries, and began to consider ways and
means.

If she was to give music lessons, she would need a piano.
Where was the money coming from for that? Then it was a
considerable distance for children to walk to take lessons. She
would need a new sewing machine to take in sewing, but the
same thing was in the way. How many folks would walk that
far to fit and try on a cheap dress? Ready-made things were
getting to be the style in Sawley like everywhere else. Arvay
decided to go out under the mulberry tree and think things
over.

The problems of making a living were immediately
swamped by her emotions when she got under the tree.
There was an old wooden box under there, probably left by
some children picking mulberries. Arvay sat down on it,
dazed by the feelings that swept over her. A memory inex-
pressibly sweet. No injury that she could conjure up could
stand up beside the ecstasy that she had felt here. God, please
have mercy on her poor soul, but she was a slave to that man!
How? Why? Those were answers that were hidden away from
her poor knowledge. All that she knew was that it was so.

Far, far up in the leafy haven of the tree, she spied a small gray body nestling close to the trunk of the tree. It was a screech owl sleeping during the daylight hours.

The screech owl was a lonesome creature, crying and shivering from housetops and nearby trees during the darkness for something or someone to come and drive away the lonesome feeling from its heart. Nobody that she ever knew of liked to hear that cry. They said that it meant the approach of death. Maybe they thought about death when they heard it because death was such a lonesome thing.

Sitting there, Arvay asked herself, would she have ever escaped from this ugly and lonesome place if Jim had not come along and just seized upon her and carried her off to the light? She doubted it. She could have spent all her days in that awful old house, her heart sleeping in the daylight of men, and crying lonesome in the night. Crying pitiful and lonesome like the screech owl.

Then what had got into her? Was she fighting Jim to get back to this?

Arvay went back to the house and wrote Jim a letter. It was the first one that she had written in the five days since she had been in Sawley. She would not, however, let on that she was backing water. What she wrote was that her father being dead now, and her mother getting old, would he mind if she left Earl up there with her mother for a while to keep her company? Maria really ought not to be there in the house all by herself. Please answer right away and let her know what he thought about it. His ever-loving wife, Arvay Meserve.

Jim answered by Special Delivery. He too thought that her mother was too old to be there alone. If she felt that she could spare Earl, why not let him stay there with his grandmother for a while? He could send five dollars a week for Earl's support as long as he stayed there, and anyway, he thought that they ought to look after Maria, now that Brock Henson was dead. He planned to send Maria ten dollars every month to take care of her groceries as long as she lived. Arvay was to find out about the taxes on the place and let him know. That was to make sure that Maria had some place to stay and take any worry off her mind. Let her last days be her best ones. He wanted Arvay to know that he missed her

presence, and hoped that she would not be away from him too long. Her ever devoted husband, Jim.

Out of the money she had on hand, Arvay paid up the taxes, and left word at the office that the tax bills from now on were to be sent to her husband in Citrabelle. Carl said that he didn't have the time, so Arvay paid a man to plough and harrow the place and put in a vegetable garden, so Earl could have plenty of fresh things to eat. Like he was used to at home.

The sacrifice of parting from Earl was almost more than she could bear, but the call of Jim could no more be resisted than the sun-flower can help turning its face to the sun. Her heart, her body, everything about her cried for the presence of that man. How in the world had she ever thought that she could stay away?

Chapter Twelve

Arvay's hackles got up just as soon as she reached home. She had been compelled and overpersuaded by her attachment to Jim to the compromise on Earl, and she resented her enslavement.

She observed that nobody bowed down, and not one soul repented because Earl was away from there. There was an air of triumph, and a sort of freedom-feeling that gave a big Amen to Earl's absence. Moving around in this atmosphere, Arvay got fiery mad.

"Earl's got just as much right to be here as anybody else, and a heap more than some that's flourishing around here so much," she told herself.

But Arvay was able to hold her feelings in for two whole weeks. After that, she began to wonder out loud if poor Earl was getting a sufficient to eat.

"Of course he is, honey. I sent the money ahead, and on top of that I sent a crate of fruit, and made arrangements to keep a good supply on hand up there. You know that your mother wouldn't neglect and mistreat Earl. From the way she wrote me, she's ever so glad to have him with her."

"Yeah, but I know, Jim. I feel and believe that Mama do love the boy, but she's getting old and apt to be careless about fixing regular meals."

Jim blunted that off and put the conversation to death by motioning to Angeline to pass him the dish of lima beans. From Arvay's point of view, he acted hateful that way every time she brought the subject up.

"Earl is liable to get to proaging around down there in the field and get hisself snake-bit," Arvay began to worry a week later.

"Didn't I understand you to say that you had the place ploughed up and put under cultivation?" Jim asked in an off-hand way.

"Yeah, but a snake could happen to be crossing the place to get to the woods and Earl could get bit and die like a dog up there with nobody to see after him right."

Jim let that lay right where Arvay had flung it and went on about something else. He encouraged Kenny to tell him all about a new tune that he had just learned from Joe, and how he had got it down perfect how to tune the box from the key of C into *Sebastopol*, called "Vasterpool" by Joe, and back again. Kenny asked for a quart whiskey bottle so he could break off the neck and keep it. Joe was going to start teaching him how to bottle-neck.

Arvay came to the breakfast table one morning relating a dream that she had had. That Suwanee river was no distance from the house at all. It was ever so deep and treacherous. In her dream she had seen poor Earl following some boys down to the river and being over-persuaded to go in swimming, and getting drowned. Arvay told how she saw his poor body go down and get hung on a snag way under the water and wasn't even found until it was much too late.

"That comes from that big mess of pig-tails that you had yesterday," Jim chuckled. "I tell you about eating all that heavy kind of stuff. You're liable to dream anything with something like that laying heavy on your stomach."

Nor, as weeks went by, could Jim be persuaded to sit down and worry over a dozen more gruesome possibilities. Every week, as Jim had requested, Maria dropped them a card saying how well Earl was getting along. Pretty occasionally, a boy who lived down the road a piece stopped by, and took Earl into Sawley with him to see the movies. Earl had a good appetite and was doing well. Didn't act homesick at all.

It was going into the sixth month since Arvay had left Earl up at Sawley that she decided she had been baffled around enough about her son. Without even bothering to pack a bag, she just caught the eleven o'clock train and went to Sawley, took the indifferent Earl from her protesting mother and brought him on back home. She had not even bothered to tell Jim that she was going. The next afternoon she was back and slamming things around in the kitchen defiantly.

Angie, beginning to pout out under her blouses and getting boy-conscious, merely said, "Oh, hello, Earl. I see you got back" and wetting her finger, tried to lay a fish-hook curl just in front of her ear. Kenny poured out on the indifferent Earl all about how he was learning to make that weeping

sound on the guitar with his bottle-neck. Gosh, but he was getting good! He had frammed *John Henry* behind Joe all the way. With Joe bottle-necking and carrying the tune, and him framming out a mean bass, it was something.

Jim got home an hour or so later, and without even giving him the time of day, Arvay whirled on him with, "You see that Earl is back home I reckon. I know you don't like it, but you can't help yourself."

"Why, good evening, Arvay. Did you hear me say a word against it? You come home with your behind stuck up your back like a black ant."

"Well, I just want to let you know in front that Earl is home, and he's here to stay. If he have to be drove away from his home, I'll go along with him."

"Aw, what the hell!" Jim exploded and went out and took pains to slam the door as he went.

Out on the front porch Jim halted and began to reason more than to feel.

"Now why the goddamn hell Arvay want to act so contrary for?" He walked out to the top step and took a stand. "But Arvay is a true mother, bless her heart! I can't fault her too much for what she's done, crazy as it is. Mother-meat never gives over, I reckon. They'll die and go to hell for their young."

With that conclusion, Jim simmered down. He was not blind, and shuddered at what might be ahead of him. Then his manhood and the obligation of it took hold of him.

"I'll have to throw my strong arm of protection around her the best that I can. Nothing else left for me to do."

Chapter Thirteen

ARVAY looked at the clock. It was just before nine o'clock in the evening. She looked because she hoped that it was late enough to tell Kenny to leave that piano alone and go to bed. Kenny had somehow transferred what he learned on the guitar to the piano and could drum out quite a few pieces. But it was all what Arvay called rag-time stuff and reels. Now he was in there, stomping and drumming out that tune on the piano called *Charleston!* and he and Angie were chanting it and dancing it off. "Hey, hey! Charles-ton! Charles-ton!" How Arvay had come to hate that tune. No matter which way she turned, she couldn't hear nothing else, unless it was *Shake That Thing*. Some Ethel Waters, who Kenny and Angeline thought was great. So Arvay was watching the clock. At nine-thirty, she was going to make them stop that racket.

It was on a Thursday night. Arvay had a little low rocking-chair in her room and she took up two shirts of Jim's and began to sew the buttons back on. This wash-woman she had didn't care how she wrung the buttons off of things. The wash came home with buttons missing, and rips and tears in clothes. Dessie wouldn't have let things like that happen. She would give a play-pretty to have Dessie back right now. Jim was off somewhere. Could be down there in the grove running off his mouth with Alfredo as usual for all she knew. Earl was in his room by his lonesome self. He had gone in soon after supper to go to bed. He had been home for over a month now, and went off by himself a lot. Just vanished off. Arvay always took for granted that he was around the place somewhere to himself, and never bothered. He seemed to have forgotten all about the house down in the grove since his return, and Arvay felt vindicated and glad.

"Now, just look at this shirt, will you?" Arvay broke out in anger. "That trifling woman's done shoved all the buttons off this shirt with the smoothening-iron. Dessie always took more care than that. Dessie is a good woman, don't care which way you take her. Wonder if I was to——"

A short shriek, full of terror, ripped the air. Then a long, long cry, and then more short screams as if somebody was suffering awful and mortal pains of danger. Arvay sprang to her feet and stood with her eyes flaring and the shirt dangling from her hand.

More shrieks, then a short howl kind of a sound and yelps mixed in with the screams. It sounded from the grove, and Arvay ran head-long towards the back door. From there she heard mingled voices yelling in excitement from down at the bottom of the grove. There were no more shrieks of pain, and no more yelps and growls.

"Gee whizz!" Kenny breathed back of Arvay's shoulder. "Sounds like Earl."

"Couldn't be," Arvay said shortly. "Earl's been gone to bed too long to talk about."

"It sounded like him to me too," Angeline insisted, and the three of them pitched out of the door into the darkness and went hurrying towards the source of excitement. The children ran faster than Arvay could.

Arvay was going fast, though, when she suddenly whirled and ran back to the house. She ran to the boys' room and flung open the door. Her fingers flew to the switch and drenched the room in light so as to make sure. Earl's bed was empty. He had never been in it at all.

"Do, my Jesus! Something has done hurt my boy!"

Arvay fled the room and the house and headed down through the grove. She was panting with fear and crying. That swamp! She had always known that some beast bred in there was going to hurt her child.

She turned back once again to grab the axe from the wood-pile, slung it over her shoulder and ran again. Be it a hundred panthers and bears, she would slay them all this night.

There was a small group gathered tight together, and somebody was holding a lantern and shedding light down on the ground, and they stood still and looked. She could make out Mrs. Corregio, Felicia, her own two children, and a man. She could hear more voices close at hand and running towards them.

"Where is he at?" Arvay screamed out of her fear as she rushed up.

Mrs. Corregio pointed in the general direction of south with her arm and hand, but never lifted her face from weeping to see who it was that asked.

Arvay was close enough now to see what they were looking at. It was Lucy Ann Corregio lying on the ground. Her heavy, glinty hair was spread out far beyond her head, and tangled like. Her eyes were closed and her mouth was open loosely. Blood was running down from a mangly spot on the side of her neck. The fingers of the white hand that lay limply across her body were chewed and bloody. The tubular maroon-colored skirt that she had on was up almost around her waist and there was a bleeding wound on one thigh. She was lying so quietly that for a long minute Arvay could not tell whether she was alive or dead.

Three men, seeing the light, came scrambling over the fence in their haste and joined the group.

"What's the matter? We heard screaming. Who's hurt?" Then they shoved their way into the circle and looked down, and the veins began to swell out in their necks. Arvay could hear running and shouting off to the south and the west in the grove.

"Help!" A shout came to her ears. "Head him off. He's gone thataway. Help!"

Arvay burned and turned to dry ashes inside as she heard a short series of triumphant yelps from the distance.

"That's Earl!" Kenny shouted. Arvay wheeled to the side and struck him hard on the side of his head.

"Shut up! Get on back to that house, the two of you. Git!" Arvay turned with the axe still over her shoulder and headed her children before her. They were cowed by her manner and ran ahead after a few steps homeward in the dark. They bolted inside ahead of her and disappeared. Arvay leaned the axe against the steps and went on in to seclude herself and think what steps to take. Then she realized how her coming off like that would look in case they were trying to make out that it was Earl, and went slowly but deliberately back down into the grove.

By that time many men had gathered. Lucy Ann was not there on the ground any more. She had been lifted and carried inside the house and her mother and sister were in there

with her. From the babble of talk Arvay learned that the girl was not dead. Somebody had gone to fetch a doctor. Somebody else had gone to notify the police.

"Aw, to hell with that!" Arvay heard one man say. "We know who did it. What we need is a posse to run the so-and-so down and string him up. Can't a clean-living, pretty white girl like Lucy Ann get no more protection than that? Don't need no damn Sheriff. Let's go, men!"

There was a muttering and a motion of a head, and the men quieted down to a grumble. They saw then that Arvay was present. They shifted around and said nothing to her at all. But their eyes and their ways made Arvay's flesh crawl all over her. She melted out and went on back to her house.

She found that she could walk the distance, but her feet were on the drag. The horizon to the south flashed intermittently with lightning, playing for some distant rainstorm that way. The faint echo of rumbling thunder sank way down in the west.

As she approached the steps, she found something for her mind to handle, to drive off the madness of fear. She must be sure to put the axe back at the wood-pile. Jim was extra particular about everything being where it was supposed to be. When he went to split kindling-wood in the morning, he would be mighty mad if that axe was not to his hand.

But the axe was not leaning against the steps as she had left it. Naturally. Jim had come along, and put it back where it belonged. That meant that he was back from town, and she was glad. Just to use up time, Arvay walked over to the wood-pile and looked. The axe was not stuck up in the chopping-block as Jim invariably left it. It was not leaning against the block as Kenny sometimes left it. Arvay looked all around the wood-pile, but the axe was nowhere around. That was very funny. Then the weak trembles ran all over Arvay. Maybe some man, thirsting for her son's blood, had passed there and picked it up. She rushed fearfully into the kitchen, and closed and bolted the door behind her. She was very glad that the children had neglected to turn off the light as they went through. Darkness held unspeakable terror for her this night.

She headed on across the room to get to her bedroom and wait there for Jim. She was almost at the door leading into the

hall-way, when she felt, more than heard, some movement under the table. The table cover that hung down on all sides made it shadowy under there. She flung her hands up to her breast, and gapped out a sound from her throat. Her eyes were compelled to the floor, and she saw the head of the axe being snatched under the table farther, and she heard a kind of a snarl.

Something rose up so suddenly under the table that it tilted and sent the salt cellar, pepper sauce bottle and vinegar crashing to the floor. A form began to spring away from the overturned table as Arvay leaped for the door, grabbed desperately for the light switch, and plunged the room in darkness so that she could not be so easily seen and make her escape.

The tall slight form of Earl fell on her back and tried to grab at her throat. Arvay fought the weak hands off after a short struggle and held them powerless to harm her there in the dark. Holding to the limp fingers for dear life, she shoved his head back violently twice to keep him from biting her hands.

"Don't lose no time, son, like this. Run! They aim to kill you just as quick as they can lay hands on you. Run! I don't aim to hurt you. Run, and run fast and get somewhere and hide. Now, run!"

She released the hands, and heard Earl's steps breaking for the back door, and his fumbling with the lock. Arvay flew over there and drew it back for him quickly.

"You ain't got no time to lose. Run just as fast as you can."

"Yes, Ma'am," Earl muttered. In a moment more, the form faded from the door, and Arvay heard fast steps padding around the south side of the house and away through the front. Arvay bolted the door again and hurried to her room at the front.

She had hardly reached it when men surged all around the house and grim and angry voices sounded outside of every window.

They wanted Earl. They wanted him, and they meant to have him. He might as well come on out peaceable, because if he didn't, they'd get him even if they had to burn the house down on him to get him.

Arvay tipped across the hall to peep out of the parlor win-

dows, but found her two children in there, their faces charged with terror. So Arvay, seeing her young, found the strength to stiffen herself and walk to the side window and speak to the men outside.

"Earl is not here," she told them. "I don't know no more where he's at than you do."

There was a sullen silence, then a muttered conference. Arvay knew that there could be few strangers out there. Most of them had to be men that she knew. They hated to face her and break right into the house. After a long while, the same voice spoke, a voice that was unknown to her.

"We'd like to talk to Jim if he is there."

"Jim ain't here neither. He went off right after supper. Said that he was going to step downtown."

There was another period of low mumbles. Then Arvay heard somebody say, "I saw him passing some time ago. I think I know where to find him."

But just at that minute, Jim came urgently through the front gate. Arvay saw the dark mass move to meet him, and close in around him near the gate. There was talk and talk, though Arvay could not distinguish a word. Both Kenny and Angeline wanted to run out there where Jim was, but Arvay made them keep quiet where they were. Finally, Jim walked down the path alone and mounted the steps.

"I'm going along with the men, honey," Jim said quietly, and took pains to place his arms around her waist and keep them there while he talked. "We're going to try to locate Earl. That is, if he's not hid around the house somewhere."

"No, he ain't here, Jim, and I don't know where he went to."

"Well, I certainly am sorry to my heart that he up and ran off. It makes things look mighty bad, and harder for me to handle. I hate worse than anything in the world that he did what he did."

"Oh, they done already persuaded you that Earl is guilty, eh?"

"Aw, honey, please don't. Them others don't need to know, but you and I know how he acted before he was took off to west Florida. Then tonight, there can't be a shadow of a doubt about the thing."

"Why can't there be, Jim?"

"Because, honey, the girl has come to now, and she says that she started out to the outhouse with a lighted lantern in her hand. She saw Earl when he jumped out from behind the corner of the house after her. She tried to run, but he was on her before she could get a start. She saw him, honey. Alfredo and them heard her hollering, and Alfredo leaped out of the door. Lucy Ann had dropped the lantern, but it's one of them ship lanterns, and it didn't go out. Alfredo could see Earl and recognize him. He had the girl down by then, and was biting at her legs. He never let go until Alfredo was almost on him, then he sprung up and took off through the grove with Alfredo after him, but he lost him. No, honey, no doubt about the thing. Alfredo and all of 'em realize that the boy is not just right in his head, and with me taking care of all doctors' bills and everything, Alfredo won't press the charges if Earl can just be found and give himself up."

"What good will that do, Jim?"

"What good will it do? Arvay, practically every man out there has got a wife, a sister or a daughter, and some all three. You ought to be able to see how they wouldn't want nobody like Earl loose on the community. You got a daughter. You know just how you would feel if it was somebody else, now don't you?"

"Yeah, but if I just thought that Earl was guilty."

"Aw, honey, please don't hurt me no more by giving me the idea that you feel I want to be unjust to my own son. Did you know that the screen wire is all tore loose from his window except at the top? That means that when he made out that he was so sleepy right after supper, he was being cunning enough to fool us and give himself time to tear loose that screen so he could get out without anybody missing him. For all we know, it might have been done before dark. Before I go off, I got to go and see that it's nailed down again good and tight. I don't want him doubling back and sneaking in through that window and maybe hurting you or Angeline or Kenny, or maybe all of you."

Arvay let him go without saying another word. She remembered that scene in the kitchen no more than an hour ago. The weak fingers feeling for her throat and the axe. The in-

tent was here, only the strength was lacking. But then, Arvay comforted herself quickly, poor Earl thought that she was somebody else.

Arvay heard men's voices and the pounding of the hammer as the screen wire was firmly nailed back in place. Two men whom she knew well came shamefaced through the house with Jim and spoke softly to her as they tramped around helping secure all the windows and doors. Jim cautioned Arvay and the children not to open them on any account until he returned. Then he went outside, placed himself in the midst of the posse of around a hundred men and they tramped off to search for her son.

As the hours stumbled past on rusty ankles and she heard nothing, Arvay began to hope that Earl had gotten clean away. Towards daylight, what was left of the mob came back to the house with Jim. They had a new lead. Jim thought that Earl might have taken refuge at Joe Kelsey's house, and they had been there just a short while ago. Earl was not there, and had not been there, Joe swore. But the Sheriff and some others thought that Joe was acting funny and guilty. Joe was holding back something that he knew, the Sheriff charged.

Joe was naturally terrified, and looked and looked at Jim with pleading eyes. Jim knew that Joe was hiding something, so he told Joe that it was all right. He must tell them anything that he might know.

"I don't know for sure, Mister Jim, but Earl could be down in the Big Swamp somewhere."

"Naw, Joe. You must be mistaken. Not Earl. Scary as he was, I can't see him rashing around in that swamp."

"But I have seen him going in there, Mister Jim, often and on." Joe looked at the Sheriff with a sly grin and continued. "When I used to have business down in there, I have seen him ducking and dodging down in there. I never hailed him because he never acted like he was slipping and I thought he called hisself playing sort of hide and seek and I would just ruin up the play by letting on that I seen him. Oh, yeah, I have seen him going in and coming out too many times."

They got the general directions from Joe of where Earl had been seen. Bloodhounds had been sent for. They were back at the house to get something of Earl's for the hounds to take

his scent from. Then they veered to the south and streamed off towards the swamp. The bell-toned dogs sang out on the trail before long, and the men marched forward to that.

The search went on and on. Now and then, Arvay could hear the distant baying. The day died behind the deep dark swamp, and still Jim did not come home. Hawley Pitts brought word about three o'clock the next afternoon that Earl had been located. They had trailed him to a place deep in the swamp that was almost opposite this house. Jim wanted her to know. He was staying to try and handle things. He wanted some hot coffee and something that he could eat.

Arvay rose up right away. She made Hawley eat, then she packed up a big mess of meat and bread and a dinner-bucket full of hot coffee all sweetened and with cream in it, and sent it back by Hawley.

"Tell Earl I say to come on home with you all, Hawley. Tell him I say so, please."

"Oh, I tell him, Mrs. Meserve, and don't you fret nor worry. Nobody don't want to hurt the boy."

Two hours later, Jim sent word by somebody else that Earl was surrounded and he would be home just as soon as he could persuade Earl to give himself up to the Sheriff. They were close enough to the boy to make themselves heard, but Earl, so far, acted as if he didn't hear them. He was in a spot that was hard for them to get to. They could see him as plain as day, but he was hard to rush, and they found out that he had a gun. A Winchester rifle, and just as soon as anybody tried to get near him, he levelled the gun and dared them to come on.

No sooner had the second messenger left than Arvay went to the parlor and peeped behind the piano. Yes, Jim's rifle was really gone.

Now when and how had Earl got that rifle out of the house? He certainly did not have it when he fled the house that night—and Arvay trembled as she remembered—or he would not have seized that axe. Arvay went back in her mind and recalled that Earl had often disappeared from around the house for long periods since his return from Sawley. He could have sneaked that gun out on any of those days. Well, it certainly was a lucky thing that the gun was not loaded. Then a

frightening thought came to Arvay. If he had searched around until he found the gun, maybe he had found the ammunition too. Arvay whirled and ran across the hall into the bedroom and to the pair of old boots in the back of the closet. Jim had had two boxes of long cartridges for that repeating rifle. Squatting on her heels, Arvay searched deep in the boots and found that both boxes were missing. With her face white and hands trembling, she was able to find comfort for a moment in the assumption that even if Earl did have the gun and the ammunition, he still did not know how to handle any kind of a gun, let alone that repeating rifle. But how could she swear to a thing like that? Off from her mother up there in Sawley, Earl might have asked and been taught something about handling guns by the boy who had been chumming around with him. All country boys knew something about guns. One hand fluttered to her breast, and still squatting on her heels, Arvay collapsed against the closet wall.

"My God, my God! It's a wonder somebody ain't been killed!"

Jim did not return to Arvay all that night. The word came that the posse were in a tight fix because the men dared not show themselves too plainly for fear of getting shot. Every time anybody showed himself, Earl upped with that rifle and levelled down. Coming at him from the rear meant cutting a way through two miles of dense swamp.

Jim staggered in home with a haggard face and told Arvay how it was. He saw the suffering in her own eyes and was very gentle with her.

"I know how you feel, Little-Bits, and I'm doing all I can to make things come off peaceable and right."

"Oh Jim, Jim! Why can't you holler out to Earl and let him know that you're there to help him and . . ."

"I haven't been doing a thing but begging and pleading with him, honey. I have told him and told him that nobody wanted to hurt him, and nobody was going to harm him if he would only come on out and give himself up. But, Arvay, Earl acts like he don't know me from nobody else." Jim hushed and bowed his head on his arms for a minute.

"He draws that gun on me every time I try to get near him, and the men are all getting wore out from fooling with him.

Nobody's said so in my hearing, but I know so well that if it wasn't for my presence, they would have killed Earl long time ago."

Arvay looked at the drooping figure of the man there at the table and a tender feeling went over her. But for too many years Arvay had thought of her husband as a being stronger than all others on earth. What God neglected, Jim Meserve took care of. Between the two, God and Jim, all things came to pass. They had charge of things. She had been praying ever since she had found out that Earl was surrounded in that swamp. So far, God had not made a move so it was up to Jim. So now, Arvay went to her husband and hung by her arms around his neck as she sank to her knees beside his chair.

"Jim! Jim! Don't let them men kill my boy. Just get him back safe one more time, please, Jim, so we can put him away." Arvay pressed her wet face tight against Jim's chest and whispered, "Please, Jim."

Jim hugged Arvay tenderly and tried to make her see the difficulties of the situation. To get to where Earl was, you had to watch your step mighty careful. Big roots humped up, and a slip of the foot, and over you would go into that deep spring that was running swiftly underground. Even a good swimmer would have all that he could do to keep from being carried away underground by that water. And there was no doubt that Earl would shoot while the man was struggling in the water. You had to creep along slow, and expose yourself to be shot at. The men were getting pretty tired, but he would do the best he could.

Jim went on back and joined the men. He had a promise that nothing would be done until he returned. He thanked them on his return for being so considerate of his feelings. He realized that this thing could not keep on forever.

So, calling soothingly to Earl, Jim started from the south border of the sink hole and began to pick along to where Earl stood braced between two great cypress trees. Earl's face was cold and unrecognizing. Jim caught hold to vines and shrubs to keep from slipping off the precarious footing into the water, and said nice things to Earl and kept going. He was a good half way along the dangerous route when Earl stepped forth and levelled the rifle and took aim.

Jim's Stetson leaped in the air and fell into the pool. A tiny trickle of blood started down his forehead as he fell on his face and tried to shield himself behind the bole of a tree. Earl, seeing his father where he had no chance of escape, advanced to get Jim exactly under his gun-sight again. Jim was helpless before him.

There was a shout of fury from the watching men. One gun, two guns, then two or three more blazed. The slight body jumped and fell forward with the rifle under it.

Chapter Fourteen

ARVAY saw some men coming late that Saturday afternoon—just a few men, with Jim, his hat in his hand, walking slowly in the lead. The rest of them followed Jim, and leaned together, carrying something between them. Arvay fled into the bedroom and slammed the door.

The men stopped out there in the yard at the foot of the steps, and stood there with their heads uncovered. Jim came into the bedroom and found Arvay leaning against the wall near the foot of the bed. The pain was showing in his face so that Arvay almost overlooked the little spot of dried blood above his right forehead. His broad shoulders hung down like a cape. He placed his arm about Arvay's waist and without speaking, led her to the front door.

The silent bareheaded men looked at Arvay, then looked down at what was at their feet.

"I'll go and have the bell tolled," Hawley Pitts offered, and all the others nodded solemn agreement. It was a relief that they could do something kind for Arvay and Jim.

"I'll thank you kindly, Hawley," Jim said. This was indeed a great kindness. The body of his son was not going to be handled like a criminal. Friends were going to accord it the ritual of a good Christian who had died in his sick-bed, with the pastor and the family and friends standing around the bed-side. Jim tucked his head a brief moment on Arvay's shoulder, then lifted it. "Yes, I'll thank you to toll the bell."

Hawley nodded, and turned his big frame towards the gate.

"Stop!" Arvay screamed, and tried to tear herself from Jim's embrace. "No you don't. Don't go tolling no bell for my boy. Earl ain't dead."

Hawley stopped dead in his tracks, and all the men looked from one to the other, then down at what was lying at the bottom of the steps.

"You needn't to look, and try to make out that's my boy dead there on the ground. It's somebody else. Oh, please don't toll the bell."

738

Jim took Arvay in his arms, and putting one hand firmly under her chin, lifted her face and made her eyes meet his.

"Look at me, darling. Look your Jim in the face. Our Earl is dead, honey. The poor thing was not sufficient for the world he was forced to live in. He has come to his peace at last. But the world ain't finished for you, honey. You've got me beside you. We got our two children and a world of loving friends. Our child, born out of our deep sweet love, is dead, honey, and laying out there on the ground. He's out there waiting for you to bid him in. You have always give him your love, haven't you? Well, out of that, go, darling, and give him the look of peace."

Arvay felt the power of Jim coming over her. She rested her head on his shoulders for a moment, then left the shelter of his arms and moved forward. She went down the five steps and stood over the body. She saw the many wounds in the chest. Slowly, she lifted the veil of Spanish moss that covered the face and gazed. Somehow, none of the bullets had struck Earl above his shoulders. The weak but handsome face was unmarred and was inhabited at last by a peace and a calm. Arvay passed her hand over it slowly as if to probe the mystery of the vanished life as well as to caress. Slowly now she stood erect and looked at Jim. She felt his arm beneath her shoulder just as plain as if he had been standing beside her. Arvay bowed her head and said softly, "Yes, now you can toll the bell. Toll the bell for my boy, somebody, please."

Chapter Fifteen

"HUG MY NECK for me honey," Jim drew near in the bed and pulled Arvay closer to him. "You haven't been sweet with me for a whole month now."

"Jim! And poor Earl dead and covered up in a four-sided grave!"

"But I'm still here, honey-pie, and still your husband."

"But I'm grieving so, Jim. I . . ."

"Naw, Arvay, you ain't grieving as much as you let on. You're mourning all right, but that ain't grief."

Arvay tensed herself to return a shocked and outraged answer, but just then Jim began to rub her shoulder as he talked, and then to slide his hand gently down towards her breasts in little circular motions.

"You just hate to own to yourself that a great burden done fell off your shoulders."

"Naw, Jim, I'm never to get over losing my boy, and losing him the way I did."

And at that moment, Arvay hated herself, because for the life of her, she could not move away from Jim, nor could she fling his hand away. She found herself softening, relaxing, and then throbbing under Jim's hand. She hated the man violently, and she hated him because he had so much power over her.

"Don't, Jim," Arvay murmured drowsily. "How in the world can I mourn for my boy with you feeling and hauling over me like that? Stop!"

But Jim did not stop, and Arvay did not resist him. Her body got warm and she seemed to be sinking, sinking, down through the mattress, through the floor and through the world on some soft cloudy material, and drifting off through the rim-bones of space. Passive, passive, receptive and dream-like, until she felt Jim's first kiss on her lips. It came as a great mercy and a blessing, and Arvay departed from herself and knew nothing until she came to earth again and found herself in the familiar bed.

Jim turned on his side, laid his head on her breast and went

right off to sleep with Arvay's fingers running through his hair, and she went to sleep herself with her hands tangled in his curls.

When morning came, Arvay knew that she must come back to her family somehow. She would have died rather than admit that Jim was telling the truth, but she knew it for herself. She acknowledged to herself that she had put on the greatest show of grief when she caught herself feeling relieved. A great, great burden *had* been wrenched off her shoulders, something that stood between her and Jim, and she hated to admit that anything that did that was worrisome. She had worn a shield and buckler for eighteen long years, and it had been very hard on her heart at times, but she had taken her stand, and stubbornly held it, because she had seen no way to retreat. Something must be wrong with her, for she knew that she could part with anything, even principles, before she could give up this man.

It was a Saturday, and the children were around the house and they worried her. She wanted to be alone to herself to feel and to think. They were so alive, and romped and played so noisily. Even at their Saturday tasks of helping out with a thorough cleaning, they found the energy and the occasion to chase each other back and forth through the house and around in the yard and yell and scream.

"What kind of a Devil am I?" Arvay asked herself, as with her head tied up in a towel, she swept down the cob-webs over the house. "I ain't got time to put up with my own young'uns while I think about Jim. Here I want 'em out of my way so I can give all my attention to what went on last night. That man's got me so that I'm just about as near nothing as anybody could be. Well, I just got to fight against it. I'll show him. When he comes home, I'm going to be mourning harder than I ever was, that's what I am."

Dinner was the mid-day meal. Jim got off early on Saturdays, but he was never home that early. By the time he knocked his men off and they got back to the packing-house and got paid off and all, it was always mid-afternoon. The whole house was clean, and her own room was just a little bit garnished. That vase full of pink oleander blooms on the small table by the head of the bed was not put there to tempt

Jim of course. It just made the room look more cheerful like. They had been through a lot of grief, and a few flowers made things look more brighter.

"Mama, we're through with the dinner dishes, and please can I go over to Joe's and practice some?" Kenny asked, and gave a pleading look up in her face. "You ought to let me go this time, Mama. I haven't been for a long time now. Maybe I'll be done forgot all I used to know on the box."

"Gwan, then, and stop bothering me, Kenny. But you better be back in this house before dark, else I'll attend to you, suh." Then an inspiration came to Arvay. "Angie better go 'long with you to see to it that you come home on time."

The two children screamed in joy and tore out. They went running and tussling out of the gate and away. Arvay took a long breath of relief and went about her thinking.

It led her to the boys' room. She went inside and looked around. In spite of her dedicated air, she knew exactly what she meant to do. She gathered up all of Earl's clothes and folded things one by one on the bed. She was going to put them somewhere out of sight. She was through going in there and sitting when the children were not at home and fingering Earl's things. Yes, Earl was dead. Nothing she could do would bring him back. She would store his things away out in the barn for a keep-sake. She could creep out there at times unbeknowings to Jim and handle them when she felt to. Arvay bundled everything up and tied the large package up neatly. She placed it on the floor by the door, then took time to place everything so that the room belonged to Kenny in full. It had taken her quite some time because she would not move hurriedly. It did not seem right to move like that. She looked at the package as she left the room. It could stay there until Jim or the children came home, and took it upstairs in the barn for her.

"I ain't giving in to Jim at all," Arvay told herself. "But it'll make a little more room for Kenny, him being so active and all."

Arvay came out and walked into the kitchen. She wanted to look over what she had to fix for supper. She might decide on something that took a long time. She felt for a good nice meal.

There was food in the house, but nothing that her taste called for in particular. Jim and the children might not care for what she had either. A nice bait of stew beef, browned down low with good gravy and rice and string beans out of the garden with that ham hock, with new potatoes dropped on top of the beans to steam, and maybe stir up a pan of ginger bread to eat with the buttermilk afterwards. That ought to be kind of nice for Saturday night. A baked chicken and sweet potatoes could be the main things for Sunday dinner. She would slip on something and go pick out the meat herself, instead of using the telephone, which Jim had fixed to save her steps. It was Saturday anyhow, and quite a few things had to be bought for the coming week. Jim favored his stomach.

Therefore Arvay was not at home when Jim arrived. She took the shortcut across the back of the place on her return, but saw nothing of her husband. So she went in by the back door, laid the package of meat on the table, and went on to the front of the house to take off her things before starting to cook the supper. Arvay halted long enough, though, to chunk up the dying fire with a piece of fat pine and two pieces of good dry oak. Then she decided that it might be better to get the stew on to simmer, while she changed and rested awhile.

Jim bragged on Arvay's beef stews. He said that he had never liked beef stew before he had married. It was really something wonderful the way his wife fixed it. So Arvay browned the chunks of red meat carefully, added salt and whole pepper corns with a little flour, added her water, then clamped down the pot lid and went on up front to change.

No sooner did she enter the bedroom than she heard Jim's voice out around the front gate. With her hands uplifted to take off her hat, Arvay went to the front window to look and see who it was that Jim was talking with.

She gave a great gasp. It was Fast Mary, a young woman whom folks made lots of jokes about.

Fast Mary had been crying, Arvay could see from the way her shoulders moved when she snuffled, and the way she wiped her eyes with her sleeve. The window was open, so Arvay stood in the shadow of the curtains and listened.

"You say that Kenny insulted you, Mary?"

"He sure did, and hurt me to my very heart, too, now." Some more sniffles. "I wasn't bothering him at all. I was sitting on the steps at the Long House, that's where I live, and he and his sister come along, and looked at me and begin to giggle and poke fun at me."

"That Kenny is a little limb of Satan. You musn't pay no attention to him. But just what did he do and say?"

"Stopped and looked up under my clothes and pointed, Mister Jim. It's kind of hot today, and I was kind of thin-cladded like, and . . ."

Arvay saw Jim pass his hand over his mouth for a moment, and she knew exactly why. According to the folklore of the town, the weather had nothing to do with the way Fast Mary dressed. She was well known, without having a real friend in the town. She had the misfortune to be too good-looking and too available for women to take to her, but not pretty enough for any man to excuse her generosity and want to protect her. Nor had she the avarice nor the hardness to turn her position to profit. Mary had an accumulation of poverties that worked against her. So Fast Mary had a room at what was known as "The Long House" because it was a one-story structure of about fifteen rooms, side by side, all facing on a common porch. A cheap homely unpainted building inhabited by such as Mary.

"So while I was setting up there on the top step of my house, trying to catch myself a sort of cool breeze off the gutter and looking around, your two children come along, and Kenny, he had to stop and point. He said that it looked like a mulberry pie. I wasn't bothering him nor nobody else."

Arvay saw Jim choking down a laugh while Mary buried her head in the crook of her arm and cried. Jim got his face fixed for sympathy and a serious consideration of the case just as Mary raised her eyes.

What do Jim mean by listening to all that rigmarole from that fan-foot, that street-walker, that brick-bat for? Arvay thought from her hiding place behind the curtain. They say any man can have her for a fish sandwich and a drink of gin. They claims that she takes men right up on the court-house lawn on dark nights, asks 'em for a dime apiece, lays down, grabs hold of the grass and tells 'em, "Let's go!"

"Well, Mary," Jim was saying with a half-hidden grin on his face, "you realize that Kenny ain't hardly twelve years old as yet. He couldn't be expected to know what he was talking about. It would take a man with experience to give you a sound opinion."

Mary's head and eyes came up quickly, and even from where Arvay stood she could see a different look in Mary's face.

"That's right, Mister Jim. Take for instance a man like you. You wouldn't say a thing like that about me, would you?"

"I couldn't say nothing one way or another, Mary, not unless I got hold of more information than I have. You could maybe give me a full description, and then I would know whether Kenny was lying or not."

Arvay almost forgot herself and hollered out through the window on hearing that and watching Jim's sly grin and Mary beginning to wring and twist herself. For a second, Arvay felt to burst right out there and jump on her. But Jim would say that she had lowered herself. But she had to let it be known that she was home somehow and get that woman away from her gate and that soon. Suddenly she knew what she was going to do. She flew back to the kitchen, grabbed her scrubbing-bucket, got some hot water, dumped some Gold Dust in it, grabbed her scrub-rag and brush and broke for the front porch. She remembered to halt at the door, and come out on the porch just as if she had no idea that anybody was around.

Mary, facing towards the house, saw her first, and Arvay could see the bad surprise in her face. Then that made Jim look around.

"Why, hello there, honey!" Jim looked and sounded as if he didn't care. "I didn't know that you had got back home as yet."

"Well, I'm here," Arvay stated most positively.

There was a bodied silence, then Jim said, "Mary here's been telling me that Kenny's been up to devilling her some way. Poking fun at her, and she come out to let us know about it."

"Kenny and Angie left here to go to Joe's house. Where would they come in contact with Mary?"

"She says that it was at her house, that is The Long House."

"What in the world would Kenny be doing at The Long House?" Arvay asked in a bruising way.

"Oh, they wasn't there, exactly, Miz' Arvay," Mary hurried to say, as ingratiatingly as possible. "They was just passing by and Kenny had to stop and meddle at me."

"Don't you worry, Mary, I'll really tend to him for meddling with *you*." Arvay snatched a rocking chair viciously and began to look it over for dust. "I'll mighty nigh beat him to death."

Mary didn't go for no weather prophet at all, but she knew when the climate got too cold for her clothes. Mary turned and went away, and went away so hurriedly that she took the wrong direction. Instead of turning north towards town, she turned south where there was nowhere to go except along the Meserve fence line. Jim decided not to use the front door just then, but went clear around the house, and Arvay heard him come in the back door and fool around for a minute or so before he came up the hall. Arvay was too mad to look right then. And now that she had come out there with that outfit under false pretense, she had to do something with it to fool Jim.

"That Kenny!" Arvay exclaimed out loud. "He won't do a single thing like you tell him to do. Sent him out here to scrub this porch, and these steps ain't seen a drop of water. Then had to sankle around that Long House. I aim to take me a bunch of peach hickories and use him up."

From back in the house, Jim chuckled amiably. "No more than to be expected, honey. You know how boys are about doing anything useful around a house. You just have to stand right over 'em to get anything done at all. Kenny had business to clean that porch and them steps for you," Jim hurried to be agreeable. "You ought to tan his hide for him when he gets back."

"Without a doubt," Arvay declared, though she knew very well she had no such intention. She was wondering about Jim, and as mad as fire with Mary. Jim was going to have to sense her into something about Mary and that quick. Maybe all this month past while she had been mourning, Jim had

been fooling around that Mary. She was just wondering how to tackle the subject when she saw Mary retracing her steps. Arvay had no intention of speaking to Mary, so she attacked the top step with a great flourish of soap-suds and scrubbing brush. To be sure not to look around she put plenty of muscle into the job.

"Humph!" Arvay heard behind her from the region of the gate. "Some of these old nice-nasty folks make me sick of my stomach. Putting on all them holy airs, and trying to slur at me."

Arvay raised up and looked over her shoulder at Mary, who was not passing the gate, but standing there, face all broken up with anger, and her arms akimbo. Arvay stood and looked with the brush in one hand and the cloth in the other and scorned the cheaply clad young woman with her eyes. She washed the face, the thin body, the cheap dress and the run-over high-heeled shoes with a look that was as good as hurling a bucket of solid sewage over the girl. Mary took it all in and reacted accordingly.

"Don't you be looking at me with your scorn like that!" Mary bellowed. "Making out I ain't nothing. With your cold-acting ways, nobody in town can't tell whether you're a man or a woman."

Jim had retreated somewhere inside. Arvay favored Mary with another scornful look, dropped the brush in the bucket, dipped her cloth, wrung it out with great deliberation, then said coolly, "That ain't *your* trouble, honey. They all know about *you* . . . exactly."

Arvay heard a smothered chuckle from Jim. He was in the bedroom.

"You, you!" Mary, in wild rage, floundered for an answer to that. "I, I, well, never mind. That's all right for you, Madam. I won't do nothing to you. I'll place you in the hands of the Lord. I'll pray for you, Miss Arvay. I'll get down on my knees for you! And when I get down on *my* knees and talk to God . . ."

Fast Mary kimboed herself again, wagged her head positively and angrily, and left the rest to Arvay's imagination. Anything was liable to happen from that. Arvay could even look for another Flood.

Arvay stroked her with her eyes again and slimed her over like a million snails. She dried the top steps with the big rag, then dropped it in the bucket and took the brush in her hands.

"*You* praying to God against anybody? Humph! That's a pretty come off. I'll bet you when you get down on them rusty knees and get to worrying God, He goes in His privy-house and slams the door. That's what He thinks about *you* and *your* prayers."

Maybe it was not what Arvay said and the way she said it that hurt Mary so much. It could have been that loud cackle that came out through the bedroom window. Jim was in there roaring with laughter. So Mary flirted her skirts and began to move off.

"That's all right for you, picking at me when I ain't done nothing to you." Mary halted for a moment and called back: "Just because I ain't got no whole heap of money like you, you think that you got a call to take and hurt my feelings. Treat me just like I was some old dog. I got feelings just like anybody else."

"You keep 'em away from my husband then, and you'll get along all right," Arvay yelled back. "Just let me catch you a'wringing and a'twisting your narrow self and grinning up in his face one more time if you dare, and I'll take me something and do my level best to salivate you! Rack on away from here!"

In her rage, Arvay did not bother to fake at the steps anymore. She dashed the bucket of water in the yard and went storming back through the house.

"You sure did give poor Mary a reading, honey." Jim was still chuckling as Arvay passed the bedroom door. "Come here."

"What do you want?" Arvay asked as she stood stiffly before him.

"You, as usual, but right now I want to know if you feel mad at me?"

"What I got to feel mad with you about, Jim? I don't reckon you told that heifer to come racking up here to grin up in your face. I don't believe that Kenny and Angie said or done a living thing to that fan-foot. Anyhow, it shows how

low she is to be setting in public with her no-count, trashy legs gapped open, knowing that she wasn't dressed for that. If they did even look at the slouchy wretch, she grabbed at the occasion to run to you hoping to get a trade out of the thing before it was over, the hongry-gut sow!"

"You reckon that was her idea?" Jim shied off.

"What else? But you wouldn't stoop to nothing like that, that is I don't reckon you would." And Arvay questioned Jim with her eyes.

"Well, I'd have to be pretty hard up and starved out to come to it, I reckon, Arvay. It would be tough titty at that."

"I help you to say!" Arvay encouraged the idea. "Now I reckon I better go fix you some supper." She looked at Jim hard, lying there across the bed, then slowly turned to go.

Arvay went into her kitchen. She took good pains about everything and fixed things well. The ginger bread was full of raisins and spices, and the crust glittered from plenty of butter, eggs and milk when she drew it out of the oven. Around the supper table neither Arvay nor Jim mentioned a thing about passing The Long House to the children. Let them keep their little secret, while their parents kept theirs.

Arvay took the supper things off the table, went to the big earthenware churn and filled first all the glasses, then an earthenware pitcher of fresh buttermilk and set it convenient to Jim's hand. He was very fond of fresh-churned buttermilk. She made generous squares of the thick hot ginger bread and piled up a plate of it on the table. Then she sat back down, accepted Jim's compliments on it and the children's cries of delight and arranged herself inside.

"You going to town I reckon after supper, Jim."

"Bound to. Saturday night, you know. You want to come along?"

"Not in particular, Jim."

"Something you forgot to get while you were downtown this evening and want me to bring it for you?"

"No, I reckon I about got everything. I just wanted to ask you if you run into Joe to mention to him to step here. I got a little few things that Dessie could make use of with that houseful of young'uns she's got. Tell Joe to step by here and get 'em."

"Saturday night, and Joe is bound to be downtown some-where, and I'll tell him sure. But if it ain't too heavy, I could just as easy take it along and hand it to him. What is it you plan on sending Dessie?"

"Earl's things. I got 'em all fixed up into a bundle and tied." Arvay bit into her ginger bread, chewed, swallowed, then fumbled with her fork before she lifted her eyes. "They wouldn't be fitten for nothing by the time Kenny growed up big enough to wear 'em. They's bound to fit somebody in Dessie's house. No need in letting 'em lay round here and rot when somebody could be getting some good out of 'em. They ain't a bit of use around here."

Arvay saw Jim's head come up and felt his searching gaze. The blood of her body began to climb to her head. She felt her ears getting hot and knew that her face was flushed. She lowered her face and began to poke at the tiny fragment of ginger bread on her plate like a maiden. Passionate pictures formed on her eyelids and faded and were instantly replaced by others. Earl lying dead there at the front steps. That first time that she had seen Jim Meserve, his broad felt hat shoved back from his tumbling curls and his white teeth flashing in a laugh as he talked with two other young men in Sawley. Their first visit to the mulberry tree. Earl as a new-born infant and her pangs of pain at the sight of him. Coming down the courthouse steps the day of her marriage. The moment that she knew that she was pregnant for her Jim. Wrapped in a glory cloud, she had walked to the window and looked out at the tall pines around the camp and heard them singing in the wind. The joyous moment when Jim had come running into the room with the newborn Kenny in his arms. Earl in his coffin. The pictures stopped and a bell was tolling, and tolling and tolling.

She looked up suddenly at Jim for help and he was there at the head of the table and the tolling ceased in her head. The same way that her agony had been bearable that day when she had looked from the dead face of Earl to Jim up on the porch by the door. Yes, Jim Meserve in his flesh was really there at the table with her. This was a miracle right out of the Bible. For some reason, still and as yet not revealed to Arvay, this miracle of a man had married her. She had been blessed be-

yond all other women of this world. How on earth had she ever risked losing his presence? Jim was there, but at any moment he might vanish from her sight, never to be seen again.

"You, you won't let them men keep you off from home too late tonight, will you please, Jim?" Arvay murmured without looking at Jim directly.

"No chance of that," Jim answered heartily. "I can attend to what little I got to do in no time, then I'll rattle my hocks on home."

Jim got up at once and hurried off. Arvay sat wrapped in a glory cloud of feeling while the children chattered on without her paying them the least attention. Arvay was off in a far country until she was recalled by Angie and Kenny contesting over the gingerbread. Both claimed the right to the still uncut other end of the dessert. Arvay came to herself with a jolt.

"Don't you!" she shouted as she sprang to her feet and snatched the pan from both of them. "I just dare you to touch that other end. You know that your Papa likes them corner pieces! Touch 'em if you dare and I'll salivate you!"

Chapter Sixteen

ANGELINE MESERVE was in her bedroom all by herself. It was a comfortable room, and fixed up with the oddities and little fripperies that a girl of seventeen would be apt to think attractive. Pennants of different high schools, souvenirs of school parties and dances.

The warm May sunshine came in through the two windows that faced the south this Sunday morning. Angeline shoved back the curtains so that the room was brightly lighted. She herself was utterly without clothing, planted before the long mirror in her dresser, admiring herself. Her thick, curly hair was loose and fell well below her shoulders and in the light looked like a flood of ribbon-cane syrup in a clear glass bottle with the sun shining through it. Angeline had the comb in her hand and was combing it with slow movements, and posing her hair first one way, then another: over her right shoulder, straight back from her face and down her back, then over her left shoulder, as she posed and smiled at herself.

"Wonder how Hatton would like to see me like this?" And Angeline smiled and smiled. "Or maybe he would rather see me like this," and she changed her hair and her position. She stood with both arms flung out languidly, her head far back, and her hair tumbling away from the back of her head as if it had been poured. Her feet were close together and her pubic hairs reflected back from the mirror like a triangle of bronzy gold pointed downward in the heart-shaped area of her pelvis. "But maybe he don't care about seeing me in no way at all." The smile fled away from her face. "Some of those older girls can beat my time with him." The girl looked sad and solemn. She stared at the creamy perfection of her body through smoky eyes. The stiff, out-thrust breasts with the old-rose nipples, the perfection of line down to her bare toes.

"Why? Why will Hatton turn me down for them? My shape is all right, and I'm not ugly in my face neither." Angeline's lips began to tremble. "It's just because I'm too young for him, and they won't let me take company."

Angeline went and flung her despised perfection across the bed and began to cry.

"What chance have *I* got against all those old grown girls that's after Hatton? I wish that I was dead."

Angeline had been crying and glooming for some time when she heard her mother calling her.

"Ma'am," she muttered through her pillow finally.

"With Jim and Kenny out the way, even though it's Sunday, I can work some on your graduating things. I can fit and try on this dress anyhow, and be ready to run it up and whip on the ruffles tomorrow. Get into that new white slip and I'll be right in there to try on this dress."

"Yessum." And Angeline got up sullenly, took the new slip out of the dresser drawer and snatched it angrily over her head.

Arvay crossed the hall and came into Angie's room with her arms full of billowy white, and her pin-cushion pinned to her bosom. Businesslike, she flung the unfinished dress over Angie's head and began to size up and pin here and there.

"My, goodness, Angie! This dress come near being too tight across in here." Arvay was too nice to mention breasts. It was just across in here. Her eyes popped, and she looked hard in her daughter's face. It was startling and shocking too. While she wasn't looking, her girl had taken on the shape of a woman. As she fitted on down, she took note that Angie had shaped out round her hips too. She worked on in silence, turning Angeline this way and that. Things went on very well until she got to the hem.

"Better step up on that chair, Angie. My knees gets too tired squatting down so long. Get up there so I can level this hem."

Angie got up on a wooden-bottomed chair. Now she could see only the lower half of herself in the glass. She could see her mother pinning a deep hem in the dress that let it hang just below her knees.

"Mama! Stop putting all that hem in my dress, making me look like I was some little old girl! No, Mama, no!"

The pitch and intensity of Angie's voice made Arvay jump.

"Why, Angie!" Arvay looked her surprise. "What in the world is done got into you?"

Angie was jumping up and down on the chair in a frenzy like she used to do when she was a little girl and determined to have her way. She was jumping, stomping her feet and screaming "No!" over and over like a chant.

"I'm not going to wear no short dress! I'm seventeen, and I'm not no little girl, and I'm not going to wear no short dress. I'm not going out there on that platform in no short dress like I was some little girl. I'm not going to . . ."

"Why, Angie, you act like you done gone clean crazy through your head. Look like you would feel proud for folks to think that you was schooling out so young. Plenty time for you to look like some full-grown woman. When you school out of college up there in Tallahassee later on, then you can be fixed up more like a woman. I . . ."

"I don't care if I don't never get to no Tallahassee!" Angeline grabbed her hands full of the dress and started to rip and tear. Arvay was just in time to prevent any damage being done by grabbing Angie's hands. "I don't care if I don't never go to no college at all. I'm not going out there to that exercise where folks can see me looking like no little child of a girl. I'm old enough to take company like other girls do, and I'm not going to be made out to be no child. Beat me if you want to, you can't kill me, and if you kill me, you sure Lord can't eat me. I'm not going to wear no short dress."

Arvay stood back and looked at the raging girl up on the chair for a long time before she could bring out what was in her mind.

"Oh, so you looks upon yourself as a grown woman now, I see." She said it very quietly and tightened her lips.

"Well, I am, ain't I?" Angeline retorted defiantly. "Some folks my age are married, and even got children."

"Call yourself hitting a straight lick with a crooked stick, I take it." Arvay murmured this equally quietly, while she looked up at the stranger standing on the chair. "The main idea you want understood is that you smell yourself and wants to take company. Boys and books don't mix, Angie, and I ever hoped that you would school out before you got a notion like that in your head."

"Think I aim to be some old maid sitting around teaching school or something?"

"Well, you said a while back, around Thanksgiving, that you wanted to go off to that college for girls up there in Tallahassee and school out, didn't you? Nobody didn't ask you for that. You said it your ownself. I ain't never had much schooling; never had the chance to rub the hair off of my head against no college walls, and I thought that it would be mighty nice for you to get hold of the advantage that I missed. All I know is my a b c's. Read some and figger a little. I thought that it would be nice, after you mentioned it, to have my girl come home with papers to hang on the wall."

"It would be nice too, Mama." Angeline spoke without heat in her voice now. "But, but, if I got to stay little for four more long years for that, Mama, I'd rather not. Fact is, I don't think I could live that long."

"Just what would rush you to a four-sided grave so soon, Angie? I wish that you would let me know."

"Because I want to take company, and . . ."

"Is it somebody particular that you so anxious to be with?" Arvay asked and trembled down her limbs.

"Yes, Ma'am. It's Hatton Howland, Mama."

"Hatton Howland? Ain't that that Yankee boy that drives that blue Chivvylay and works at the filling station?"

"That's right."

"But he's a Yankee, Angie, and you're born and raised up in the South, and to mingle up like that ain't——"

"I don't care!" Angie shouted passionately. "I don't care if he even come from Diddy-Wah-Diddy! I don't care nothing at all about no old Civil War. I don't care nothing about Jeff Davis nor Abraham Lincoln nor Lee nor nobody else if it's got to come between me and Hatton Howland. Compared with him, it comes before me just like a gnat in a whirlwind."

"You and this Hatton must of been seeing mighty much of one another to be feeling that a'way," Arvay remarked. "Though to my rest, I can't see when it could of been."

Angeline jumped down from the chair and sat on the bed.

"Mama, I been loving Hatton since way before Christmas, but he never noticed me at all. Treated me just like I was some little bitty girl. Flourishing around with all those twenty and so on years old women, and wouldn't do no more than

pass the time of day with me." Then an intense glow came from behind Angie's eyes. "But, Mama, all the boys around school are crazy about Hatton, and so they asked him to the Easter dance. And what you reckon? I asked him to dance with me, and he did, Mama! Hatton Howland danced with *me*! Then while we were dancing sort over in a corner around the potted palms, I kissed him, Mama, and then he asked me to dance with him next time. And ever since then, he's been noticing me a lot."

"I see," Arvay mumbled off. "But I never thought a girl of mine would put herself in the way of a man like that. I thought that she would look upon herself more than that. I'm hurt to my heart to hear it."

"But, Mama! You just don't catch on so good. You see, I knew that poor Hatton would love me if he only knew me, so I had to let the poor thing know, so he could come to be happy some day."

Then Angie was not a grown girl anymore. She rushed to her mother and began to cry with sobs.

"But you wouldn't let me take company when I asked you to, and you keep me looking like some little old twelve-year-old girl, and all them grown old girls are taking the advantage of me. Riding around in Hatton's car, and going to the show and to parties with him, and I can't go nowhere and can't do a thing, and they're going to take him away from me."

Arvay held the sobbing girl for a long time and let her cry. She had felt so warm and surrounded these last three years. Now the thing she had feared but refused to look at openly had come upon her. Her children were growing up. The little family circle could be broken up. A tall, loose-jointed, rusty-headed boy with gray eyes could make her daughter carry on like this. Angeline didn't need her. She was willing to give up all the care that she had given her, all the plans that she had made and had been made for her for that freckled boy from somewhere up in Michigan, who worked at a filling station to help support his widowed mother. Trying to keep Angie a child had done her no good. It was as if a crack had opened in the wall of her home and a cold damp draft was blowing through.

"Move, Angie. I got to get what I'm going to do on your dress for today off my hands and see about fixing dinner. Get back up on the chair one more time."

Angeline got back up on the chair with swollen eyes. With dead-feeling fingers, Arvay dropped the hem of the stiff organdy dress to Angie's ankles and pinned it all the way around.

Chapter Seventeen

"So I reckon we better leave her take company, you think, Jim?" Arvay asked in the privacy of their bedroom late that Sunday afternoon when she and Jim were both lying down, sluggish from the heavy meal.

"You know that I don't mind, honey. You was the one that was against it. I thought that it would have been all right the day she turned sixteen."

"Well, then, I can tell her that if she gets her di-plooma all right, we can let her have company a couple of nights a week. Maybe after the new wears off, she won't be so hog-wild over that Hatton Howland and all. You reckon?"

"How do I know, honey? It could be Angie just thinks she loves him because he's older than she is. Young girls are apt to feel that way. Or because she wants to have it that she took him away from those older girls. And then again, she might really care, for a while anyhow. Love is a funny thing, Little-Bits. Seems like that one person gets next to your heart, and you can't shake 'em loose no matter which way you twist and turn. You just got to go on serving 'em all your born days."

For a space, Arvay traveled the road that she had come for the last twenty years. Her love had mounted her to the tops of peaky mountains. It had dragged her in the dust. She had been in Hell's kitchen and licked out all the pots. She had stood for moments on the right hand side of God.

"I hope my child don't fall such a slave to nobody that they can just handle her anyway they will or may, and she be so under the influence that she can't help herself. I don't never want her to know the feeling of that."

Jim looked at Arvay very hard for a minute, then he let his head sink back down on the pillow and smiled a secret smile.

"I differ from you on that, Arvay. I want her to feel just like that. That is the only way to be in love. It ain't really love when you gamble with your stuff out the window. Leave all your best things outside and come in and get in the game, and soon as you win a little something, jump and run."

"But it's so compellment, Jim. When you'se so that any-

thing a person puts on you, you'se willing to take and swallow just so you can still be there."

"Love ain't nothing else *but* compellment, honey. 'Tain't love when you can help yourself. When you can chew but you can't swallow, you're just filling out an arrangement. I don't say that I'm rearing for my girl to jump in love so soon like this, and with Hatton neither, but when it do hit her, I want it to be the real thing."

Now, just what was real love? Arvay asked herself and sat in silence searching experience for the answer. She could find no one word to express what she felt was love. Maybe these high-bred, book-learnt kind of folks had been taught and told what it was, but nobody had taught her things like that. Arvay did come to a kernel of what she felt that love ought to be and to do. Love to her meant to possess as she was possessed. To be wrapped around and held in an embrace so warm and so tight that the Booger Man, the raw-head-and-bloody-bones of lonesomeness, could never come nigh her. An eternal refuge and everlasting welcome of heart to rest and rely on. Never had she been sure that she possessed anyone, though Jim had told her time and again that she owned him through and through. It was too wonderful to be so for her, but she hoped for that miracle for her daughter, and she was not too ready to believe that Angeline had found it in Hatton. How could it come to pass between a Yankee and her daughter? It might be, but Arvay felt to wait a long, long time and see.

Arvay was determined, and held onto to her own construction of things even after she saw that the moment the permission was given for Angeline to take company, Hatton Howland seemed to fairly infest the house. The Friday and Sunday nights arrangements didn't hold water, because other times he was there supposedly to talk about music with Kenny. Hatton just took up around the place, that was all. He came with a saxophone and pretended to practice with Kenny at the piano. But the graduating exercises the last Friday night in May, and getting ready and all, kept Arvay so busy that she could take comfort in that. Kenny was conducting the school band for the exercises, and what with seeing to a new suit for him and Angie's clothes, and rehearsals, things were not too obvious for her.

But Angie's infatuation was as plain as day after that. She laid her diploma on top of the piano and seemed to forget that she had it, but she took the bouquet that Hatton sent her for graduation into the bedroom clasped in her arms and gave those flowers every care. They were the new Talisman roses, and the way she found new things to exclaim about them every hour or so hurt Arvay to her heart.

The tocsin sounded for Arvay the Sunday night following Angie's graduation. Jim had climbed into his Buick sedan that morning with Alfredo and gone over to the coast. He had not returned at nine o'clock that night, and Arvay was in her bedroom with the door stretched wide open so she could hear what went on in the parlor across the hall. She had quietly worked her little rocker as near to the door as possible, and sat there pretending to devote herself to a Wine of Cardui almanac. She glanced at all the pictures of the women who wrote that it had done them so much good. Women who had yearned for children for years, but none came to bless their homes. This one had taken only ten bottles when a lovely child came to gladden her home. She recommended to all women in her same fix.

Arvay's ears caught a long silence, then some sort of quick and sudden movement, then Hatton's voice, husky and drugged like.

"Angie! Do that again, and so help me, I'll rape you!"

"So rape me, and I'll help you!" came just as fervently from her daughter's lips.

Arvay was on her feet in an instant, with the intention of rushing across the hall, denouncing Hatton as a low-down scamp and a scoundrel-beast, and no gentleman whatsoever, and driving him off the place. Hatton being gutted and shot with tacks, Angeline would be attended to for lowering herself to that extent. But with her feet at the bedroom door, she became confused as to just what to say when she got into the parlor.

"I don't mean to say a mumbling word! I'll kill him dead and then stomp his head, the Yankee scamp, the dirty Carpet-bagger! Done burnt out and robbed and murdered all over the South, and now come back to take the under-currents of my child! I'll get me a gun and go in there and shoot him dead."

Arvay ran on tip-toes to the closet, flung it open and laid her hand on the Winchester repeating rifle, and instantly, its association with Earl made it burn her hand. She snatched her hand away, fled to the dresser and fumbled desperately under Jim's handkerchiefs, ties and collars until she laid her hand on the revolver. Her fingers trembled so that she had trouble breaking the gun and shoving in the cartridges. She loaded it fully, then whirled and walked to the door.

At that moment the front door flew open and Jim came stalking in. Arvay was surprised. Her agitation was so great that she had not noticed the sound of the car entering the yard. Jim, with a good-natured look on his face, stood in the hall between the two doors and looked first into the parlor and then at Arvay with the gun gripped in her hand in the bedroom door. He started, then wordlessly shoved her back before him as he entered the bedroom and closed the door.

In hot, jerky phrases, Arvay told him the story. To her surprise, Jim chuckled.

"Nothing to laugh over, Jim Meserve. While you set here sniggling and giggling, that scamp is liable to be over there raping our child."

"You mean our child is liable to be over there raping Hatton, don't you?" He laughed some more. "If I know my daughter, this is one battle that the Yankees will never win."

Then Jim got very sober in the face. Fiddling with the revolver in his hand, he sat on the side of the bed and considered.

"I think I had better spend some time tomorrow looking up Hatton and finding out all I can about him. So far, I don't know nothing excepting that his Papa and Mama come down here from somewhere in Michigan eight or nine years back and settled. Since his old man died, his Mama's been renting rooms to tourists in the winter time. I reckon what little Hatton brings in since he got out of school helps along. I don't know a thing against his character, so far as I have heard. He does seem to be mighty popular with the young folks. Could be because he's got that nice-looking car. But anyhow, I'll look into things without delay."

"Look into things, Jim? What for? 'Tain't nothing to be looked into as I can see. His case don't need to come up in

our court at all. Just run him off the place and double-dog dare him to foot this place again. That's all that you need to do. Shoot him down like a mangy dog if he dast to shove his toe-nails across this doorway another time."

"Don't look like you're taking Angie into account. Her feelings have got to be considered. Unless I'm mighty mistaken, Angie's got her mind set on having the poor boy, and I'm mighty afraid that he's going to be had. If he don't want her, and is determined not to have her, if he got good sense he better grab the first thing smoking and make his left-here now. If he don't, and that mighty quick, he's a gone ginny."

"Well! If this don't take the rag clean off the bush! You mean to set there on your honkers and don't do nothing at all?"

"Nothing for me to do till I see more into things, Arvay. You know so well that Angie is my heart-string. I can't bring myself to take no steps that might hurt her feelings. Lemme search up this Hatton Howland and see if he will in any way do. If he won't, I'll have to try and seek some way to make her see that he won't do for her. Now, come on and let's go cross there and act nice with 'em and see can't we get some idea how the land is laying."

Arvay's experiences of love and passion told her things the moment that she stood in the parlor door. Angie and Hatton, being warned of their approach, were seated on either end of the sofa. Arvay stood and took in the situation with her experienced eye. Indeed, things had come to a critical fix. Angeline, drooping in her corner of the sofa looked to be under a heavy dose of laudanum. The long lashes of her eyes drooped to almost closing. Hatton, flushed in the face, was fidgeting like he had a hot stove lid in the seat of his pants. To Arvay's knowing eye, Hatton further betrayed his condition by throwing one arm about a pillow and patting and petting it with the fingers of his long, strong hand. Arvay smiled inwardly with a feeling of morbid triumph, and crossed the room slowly and took a seat opposite. This romance was unwelcome to her at this time, but it was not all one-sided, anyhow. Angeline was giving this long tall boy just as good as he sent. Angie had put Hatton on the linger, all right. Yes indeed!

Arvay was seated in a big chair close to the piano. She was so interested in watching and learning that she just sat and had nothing to say. Through her preoccupation she heard Jim, with the aid of a lot of jokes and sayings, skillfully lead Hatton to talk about himself and his plans.

Hatton made eighteen dollars a week at the filling-station regularly. Of course he picked up some tips, eight to ten dollars in the run of a week on an average. The Chevrolet, a little over a year old now, was paid for. The Howland home place was clean and clear. It had been about half paid for when his father died, and since then, he had managed to pay the debt off and the place was clear. His mother had nothing at all to worry her mind. She picked up a good deal on her rooms and meals during the season, and he could carry things over the summer months with ease.

"You Yankees can really find a dollar," Jim laughed. "I have to hand it to you. You really know how to hustle."

Hatton laughed with Jim. "Well, you know what they say about us Damnyankees down here. Come down with a dirty shirt and five dollars and never change either one and still manage to end up rich."

"So you intend to follow that example too, do you?"

"Well, I'll give in to the extent of changing my shirt, but I really am determined to get hold of something."

Neither Arvay nor Jim missed the sly glance at Angeline as Hatton talked. It was a prod for the girl to take notice.

"I want a wife and a home some day, and I don't want it to be too long off, either. A man ought to have something to give a wife after he takes her away from her home. If it costs me every drop of blood I own, I mean for *my* wife to have something."

"That's a nice thing to say, you child," Arvay stepped in, "but have you got anything besides yourself?"

Hatton, instead of being crushed, gave a mysterious smile. He cut one quick look at Angie, then at Jim and then put on a casual look.

"Oh, I'm not in any danger of starving to death right away. I think that I can say that I can get along. But the money that I handle now is not a drop in the bucket to what I intend to have a little later on. When and if I marry, I want it so that

my wife can toss a ten dollar bill in the penny collection in church, and if the usher looks surprised at her and frowns, take her finger and beckon him back and fling in a hundred and tell him to go with that. If she catches him frowning any more, she'll call him back and fling in a thousand.''

When the laughter died down, Jim worked his hips out eagerly to the edge of his chair and leaned forward towards Hatton.

"Spoken like a man, Howland. I don't favor nobody marrying for nothing but pure love, and when he comes to that, he ought to be able and willing to do the last thing on earth to look after his woman and the children they might have. That oath he took before God and man when he stood on the floor ought to come in front of everything else on earth. No excuses granted nor accepted. Come pay-day, leave your pretty wife sit on her front porch and look down the road and say with a smile, 'Well here come my husband and them.' ''

"Them what?" Arvay asked.

"Them dollars, fool. Let him be man enough to bring it when he comes. It might be so that you have to make your own rules, and ignore all the ready-made ones that folks already know about, but bring it when you come."

Jim at least did not miss the quick, bright and hopeful look that Hatton flashed him for a second.

"You look at things the same way I do, Mr. Meserve. When I get a wife, I mean to bring it or die in the attempt. Being a Damnyankee, I can't let business get away. Why don't you let us have your business, Mr. Meserve? I don't remember ever having the pleasure of servicing your car."

"You goddamned hustler," Jim chuckled. "All right, Hatton. You got a right to pull in all the business you can. I need a good grease job right now. I go to work pretty early, so it will have to be after I knock off tomorrow evening."

"It doesn't have to be that way, Mr. Meserve. If you stop by the station, I could drive you to work, bring the car back and service it, and pick you up any hour and any place that you say."

"You sound like somebody who means to get ahead. That's the ticket! I'll be there at seven o'clock sharp tomorrow morning."

The two men had made a date to talk, but the inning went over Arvay's head. She wondered why Angeline gave such a rustle and began to pick over herself. With a nervous gesture, the girl grabbed up a pillow and began pulling at the threads in the seams, and ripping them open without knowing what she was doing. Arvay reached over and took the pillow out of her hand and dropped it on the floor beside the piano.

Hatton arose abruptly. "Think that I better hit the hay. Be waiting for you at seven o'clock in the morning, sir. Good-night, Mrs. Meserve."

Angeline stood up with determination and went with Hatton to the door. While she lingered out on the dark porch for a few minutes in low conversation with Hatton, Arvay too saw a chance to speak.

"Well, what do make out of it, Jim?"

"But he sounds mighty promising, for a fellow as young as he is."

"Promising! Shucks! I like to see some of those things *done*. I'd rather *see* a promise than to hear about it any day."

Jim said nothing to that, and they sat awhile, both concerned with the unseen matter on the porch.

Arvay was on the lookout for Jim when he came home late the next afternoon, but Angeline was looking even harder. She had crept out to the front gate, and was there to run and jump on the runningboard when Jim slowed for the turn in.

"Daddy! The car's been washed and polished!"

"Yep, your Yankee put about the best servicing job on her that I've ever seen."

Angeline flung her arms around Jim's neck and practically choked him to a stop in the yard.

"Did I hear you say, *my* Yankee, Daddy?"

"Did I hear *you* say that?" Jim countered.

"Did you hear *Hatton* say that, Daddy?"

"Well, something to that effect."

Arvay, looking out of the kitchen window, heard it all, and saw her daughter fling the car door open in a frenzy, leap in Jim's lap and almost strangle him while she covered him with kisses.

"You got him for me, Daddy? You made him promise? Oh, Daddy, Daddy, Daddy, Daddy!"

"Hold on here, baby. I didn't make him promise me nothing. I thought that my girl could handle a thing like that herself."

Angeline got very quiet. Jim hugged her shoulder and laughed.

"I didn't need to, Angie. It didn't take but a minute or so for me to see that you had already laid poor Hatton under conviction. All I could do to keep him from crawling down my throat. From what I could learn, he's been holding off for fear that I wouldn't let him have you."

Angeline went into another frenzy of hugging and kissing her father and uttering senseless sounds.

"So I didn't need to bother about that end," Jim went on. "We just talked business together."

Jim shoved Angie out of the way and got out of the car and came on inside the house. Angie and Kenny had their usual tussle for the wheel to drive the car into the garage. Kenny beat Angie to the seat that time, she flirted her skirt at him, then ran on into the kitchen behind Jim.

Jim came in extra nice to Arvay. He had brought her a large bag of Japanese plums and forbade the children to touch a one unless their mother gave them permission.

"I know how you love the things, and there were three big trees on the place where we cut fruit today, so I made a couple of the men pick you some since they were so handy. I hope that our two trees will bear next year. Then you can have all that you want to eat."

They fooled around with off-hand talk and comments until they were around the supper table, then Jim got around to what he meant to say.

"That Hatton Howland is quite some hustler in this world." He cut into a baked yam and looked across at Arvay with a brightness in his face.

"I don't see where working at a filling station is nothing to brag over," Arvay said.

"And it ain't. It seems that he just holds onto that for a stall so he can't be picked up for vagrancy and have to tell where he really makes his living from."

"Well, how do he make his living?" Arvay asked wearily.

"He's no slough. He got that job as soon as he got out of school, but he seen that he would never get independent working like that. So he worked around and got in with the Boleta man, and started out to selling tickets for the Numbers. He made so good till a couple of years back, the head of the Big House up in Orlando sent for him, and put all the business in this county in Hatton's hands. He's really been making the money since then. On the quiet, naturally. No wonder he could pay for that car spot cash, pay off what was owed on his mother's house, wear the kind of clothes he wears, and to cap it all off, he's got some two to three thousand dollars stuck away. That ain't bad for a lad of twenty-two."

"Except that he's liable to be placed under arrest at any time and work it out on the chain-gang."

"Aw, naw. The Big House up in Orlando has seen to that. He's got all the protection from the law that he needs. Not only that, he don't have to run no risks in turning in his collections. They got a man with guards to come around and pick it up."

"I see, Jim. That Yankee is smarter than I give him credit for."

"Just what do you mean by that?"

"You done let him out-talk you, that's what, and you goes for smart. But he's took you right on in."

Arvay kept a close watch on the ardent courtship, but still the runaway marriage in mid-June was something that she was not prepared for. Kenny, who had gone along with Angie and Hatton called her around sundown that day and told her. Arvay turned from the telephone with slumping shoulders.

"Jim, my girl is married to Hatton." Arvay leaned against the jamb of the door and her lips trembled. "I, I just can't get it into me that my baby girl is old enough for nothing like that. And then, and then the way it was done, Jim. I, I . . ." Arvay twisted her mouth to keep from crying. "Her shoulders ain't old enough for a responsibility as heavy as that. Oh, Jesus!"

Arvay advanced into the kitchen making fumbling motions with her hands. "They're over to Hatton's Mama's house."

"Well, why don't you call 'em up and tell 'em to come on home, honey. That's all they're waiting for."

Arvay stood for a space in heavy silence, then she seemed to come alive again. She looked to Jim hopefully and touched him on his arm.

"You go call 'em, Jim. It's better for you to talk to 'em and tell 'em to come on home. Whilst you'se doing that I can fling some egg-nog together for 'em to drink. Go ahead and make 'em come on home."

Arvay was in a feverish frenzy as she switched around getting ready to receive the young couple. Rinsing out and polishing up the cut-glass punch bowl and cups that went with it. Jim had to run out and help her along.

"Run out to the hen-nests for me, Jim, please, and fetch me all the fresh eggs you can find. . . . Oh, I hope and pray that I got enough cow-cream to go in the egg-nog. I ever vominates poor-made egg-nog. . . . Hand me that bottle of whiskey here. . . . Now where in the world did I lay that nutmeg grater? Now I had that nutmeg in my hand just a while ago. Lord, I can't tell my head from my feet. . . . Dip me up another cup of sugar, there, Jim. . . . Thing like this just would have to come off when I ain't got nothing fitten to eat in the house. . . . You reckon that Angie's room could be fixed up good enough for 'em to stay in till they can do better, Jim? Hatton would be ever so welcome if he thinks the place is good enough for him. . . . Here take this egg-beater and whisk up them whites for me whilst I get down my cake plate and slice what's left over from that white pound cake I made for last Sunday. . . . Just lift up that punch-bowl for a second whilst I slide this Sunday tablecloth on the table. Things will look nice and clean. . . ."

The table was arranged with the brimming bowl of egg-nog so rich that it poured slowly, so yellow with egg yolks that it was a dark gold. The cake was sliced and arranged in a swirl on the fluted plate when they heard Hatton's car slowing down in the yard. Arvay put out her best napkins, and stacked her best plates to eat cake from.

Then Arvay stood trembling and with a fixed smile on her face looking towards the front door.

"Drag it on in here and get your whipping!" Jim yelled out as they heard the shuffling feet of the three on the front porch. "Come in with your britches down!"

Angeline flung open the door and led the others in with a laugh.

Jim grabbed Hatton and wrestled him around boisterously and hollered over his shoulder to Arvay. "I got this one, you grab the other one and frail her good! We'll show 'em how to run off and marry on us."

Arvay did catch hold of her daughter, hugged her first lest the fiery temper of Angeline prompt her to say the things that Arvay feared, then slapped her two or three times playfully across her buttocks.

"Now, Madam, get in that kitchen and taste that egg-nog I fixed for you. Git!"

Angeline looked at Arvay in astonishment for a minute, then ran for the kitchen pretending to cry loudly into the crook of her elbow. Arvay followed as if in pursuit.

In a minute or two everybody was around the table. Hatton pulled up a chair and sat as close as he could to Angie and placed his arm about her waist. Angie turned a look of such utter happiness upon him that a pain ripped up and down Arvay's body. She was presiding at the punch-bowl, and the hand with the ladle shook a little.

"Things sure can change in a hurry," Arvay said as cheerfully as she could as she dipped up egg-nog and filled cups. "This morning, Angie, you wasn't nothing but my little girl, and now this evening you're a married woman."

"That's right, Mama," Angie murmured with lowered eyes. "But I'm still your little girl, ain't I?"

Arvay dropped the ladle and rushed around and flung her arms about Angie's shoulders and buried her face in the back of the girl's neck. "To be sure and naturally, baby. Only I feel another gap, a kind of a vacant place in my arms. I . . ." Arvay choked back a sob and looked pitifully at Jim.

Hatton stood up and looked pleadingly at Arvay and spoke with emotion.

"Mrs. Meserve, I know that you feel hard towards me for stealing your daughter like I did, but I love her so much, and when she said that she would have me, I was scared to wait. Scared she might change her mind, so I rushed off and got papers for her while she was still in the notion. I intend to be good to her till the day I die, and I hope that some day you can forgive me, and look upon me as a son."

Neither Jim nor any of the family was ever to know what it cost Arvay to say what she did next. She took her seat again and spoke slowly.

"Time changes folks, Hatton, as they go along the road. Some things a person one time wouldn't do for big money, they get so they'll do 'em for nothing. If you love Angie like that, and feel to be my son along with it, I'm only too proud and happy to have you."

Hatton got up without a word and completed the conquest. He bent over Arvay's chair and kissed her respectfully. Tears began to run down her cheeks.

"What makes females cry so much?" Kenny looked from his father to Hatton in genuine bewilderment. "We just left Mrs. Howland crying, and come home and find Mama doing the same."

"Because we born children, take pains to raise 'em, and then they leave us for somebody else, Kenny." Arvay was sobbing full force now.

"Look like you would be glad to get rid of 'em some day or other and take some rest," Kenny pursued. "When I get grown and marry and have children, I don't intend to let mine lay around me but so long. I'm going to run mine off by the time they get half grown and let 'em go scuffle for themselves. I'll be sick and tired of 'em by that time."

They laughed a long time at that.

"Oh, you hush up, Kenny," Arvay chided. "Your last diapers ain't hardly dry yet, and you come telling grown folks what to do. Ain't you something?"

"But I think that's a darned good plan, Mama."

"Yeah, Kenny, but supposing they never come back to you? You would be hurting your ownself maybe more than them. A mother feels to keep in quotation with her child and don't care what it takes to do it."

"Table that!" Jim bellowed, "and let's open up the house for new business. Now that I got me a grown son, we got to make some arrangements."

"If you mean some place for Angie and Hatton to stay till they can see further, I don't see no reason why they can't stay right on in Angie's room. We could maybe get hold of a bigger bed."

Angeline and Hatton exchanged quick and embarrassed looks.

"Mother Howland is fixing us up a room over there," Angie said.

"Oh, that don't need to call for any long discussion," Hatton said. "Until we can build, which we intend to do just as soon as we can locate a lot that Angie likes, we got two homes, and we can stay at first one and then the other. We are in a shape where we don't need to be no burden on nobody, and soon as we can build, we'll get into a house of our own."

"Take your behind down off your shoulders, Hatton. You said that you wanted me to look upon you as a son, didn't you?"

"Yes sir, and I do."

"Well, you're at home here just as much as anywhere else, and if you listen to the advice I give you, you won't be building for quite some time as yet, and you won't be buying no lot right up in town. You willing for me to lead you and guide you?"

"In every way—Dad."

"Well then, let me place my wisdom tooth in your head, and put you on the road to something big. Don't never be afraid to try big things, Hatton. The time to get scared is when you mess with something little. That's where you get your whipping. Ready for the question?"

"Let her rip!"

"You have told me about your Number business and the money you got put away. There'll be another county election in a couple of years, and things might not be the same. Before that time, if you're as smart as I think you are, you'll put your money into something where no cheap and hungry politicians can't bleed it out of you in one way or another. Too many politicians look on their offices as a means of receiving what

they call stolen goods. Let some smart man make a pile in some illegal way, then bleed him for it. You take all the risk and they take all the money. Get me?"

"I guess I do."

"Well, before the next election comes around, I want you to hide all that money you make on Numbers in land. Then you can't be touched. Land is highly legal. You will be a realtor by then."

"I'm willing, that is, if you will show me how."

"It's something mighty big and hard that I got for you to do, but if you're willing to tackle it, it will give you a lifetime start so you don't never need to be in the ham-scram again. You and Angie can go right on from there to something really big."

"Gee, that sounds like something. Lead me to it is all I ask you to do."

"Okay, if you got guts in you, this is where it'll show. I want you to clear that swamp."

"Swamp?" Some kind of sound burst out of everybody. Jim was the only calm person in the room. He reached over, laid his hand on top of Arvay's and began to stroke it in a gentle and affectionate way.

"That's what I said, son, that swamp. There's a great big fortune hid in that dark old swamp. All it needs is the brains and the nerve to get it out. I been wanting to tackle it for nearly twenty years. Ever since I bought this place, but I wasn't in no position to handle it then, and anyhow the time wasn't right. The machinery necessary wasn't on hand in those days. Now it is, you're young and smart, and you can do the job that I been saving up for my sons to do. When you see daylight through that place from here, you're going to be a mighty well-off young man. Are you game?"

"You bet your bottom dollar if there's anything can be made out of it, and you show me how to go about it."

"It's so damn easy and soft that I hate to tell it. All these smart real estate operators done slept a good bet, and I don't want 'em woke up until you get things tied up so that they got to come in by you to get a smell."

"Keep on, Dad, my pockets are already crying for that money."

"Well, the truth is, that's all state land. The State of Florida and nobody else wants to be bothered with it in the fix it's in. Like Miami Beach before that guy from Indianapolis come along and filled it in and made it worth plenty millions. Then they were willing to pay a fortune for a home site on it."

"But my few thousands wouldn't be a drop in the bucket, Dad."

"That's where you're wrong. If you bite big enough, you can get a whale of a lot of cash right out of that swamp without hardly moving a muscle. If you take in two miles north to south on this side, then run a light straight through the swamp far enough to take in that lake back there in the woods about two miles from the swamp and square it all off into a rectangle, you get enough timber to bust a bank when you sell it off. Putnam, or any of those big fellows will buy a fine stand like that, and after you sign the contract, nothing more for you to do but to sit back while they go in there and take the lumber out and hand you the check. In fact, just as soon as they estimate the footage in there, you get your check in front. Then you can lay it aside until they get through, and have it on hand to develop your real estate with. You got to fill in the lowest part, and then you are ready to develop a new addition to this town. That swamp has held the town from growing west long enough."

To Arvay's astonishment, and somewhat to her dismay, Hatton took the proposition under consideration. A week later, Hatton said that he was willing to try it. She could not make herself believe that the thing was really going to be tackled, until Jim and Hatton drove up to Tallahassee for two days, secured the huge tract for a few cents an acre, and she saw the surveyors at work.

"What on earth did you want to sic that poor boy on that nasty old swamp for, Jim?" Arvay asked that night as they were getting ready to go to bed. "He could of made a living some other easier way."

Jim was unbuttoning his shirt, and he paused and looked at Arvay combing out her long hair in front of the dresser.

"Don't you have no idea, Arvay?"

"Why, no I don't, Jim. You done bought that boat for

fishing and all, and got Alfredo working on it for you. I don't see how come you couldn't take him in with you on that."

Jim dropped down and began to unlace his shoes. He got more quiet and took a long time before he looked up at Arvay again.

"So you really ain't got no notion why I wanted that swamp cleaned off, have you, honey?"

"Naw I told you. None at all."

Jim jerked off first one heavy shoe and then the other.

"Well, maybe it'll come to you some day."

They didn't talk about it anymore and went on to bed.

Chapter Eighteen

THE YEAR that followed Angie's marriage was to Arvay faintly melancholy, like twilight. Many things came to make her happy and proud, but the old familiar things in her life were fading away.

Arvay was alone much more than she used to be. Jim's shrimping business was on a safe enough basis now for Alfredo to move his family over to the coast with him so that there was no one living on the place now but Jim and Arvay, and Jim drove to the coast as often as possible these days. Kenny was up at the University of Florida at Gainesville. He wrote frequent and enthusiastic letters home, mostly about his activities in the University band, but that was not like his familiar presence around the house. Angeline was sweet and dutiful, but Angie was Hatton's wife first before she was anything else.

Arvay had ceased to worry about the success of the marriage. Angie and Hatton got along beautifully together, and neither he nor his mother did or said anything that Arvay could put down as a dirty Yankee trick. In fact, Arvay admitted to herself that she was jealous of that woman. By degrees Angie was becoming a Howland, being influenced by both Hatton and his mother. Arvay could see Angie's brisk new ways. Getting vigorous and thrifty increasingly, and proud about it. Putting up jams and jellies and running up housedresses for herself. This in spite of Hatton's fond indulgence of Angie to everything that she wanted. And financially, Hatton was doing remarkably well. Under Jim's tutelage many wealthy and able business men had been induced to buy into the project, and things were being done on a very big scale.

With a melancholy pride in the astonishing rise of her daughter's husband, Arvay watched the progress of things from the coming of the surveyors to the completion of the sumptuous club house of the country club in the new Howland Development.

As Jim had predicted, modern machinery and methods had cleared that swamp in an amazingly short time. Arvay, from

her seat on the front porch, watched the gangs of husky black roustabouts rumbling past in truck loads, singing, chanting, laughing as they went to the swamp and moved about in their high boots, and swinging shining axes to rhythm, felling the giant trees. Gnawing at the feet of the forest to make way for the setting sun.

Arvay was surprised at finding herself feeling a sympathy with the swamp. She was used to certain outlines against the sky and now it seemed a pity and a shame for those trees to be destroyed. She had hated and feared the swamp, but long association had changed her without her realizing it. She and the swamp had a generation of life together and memories to keep. She hated to see it go. But the horde of black men sang and chanted and swarmed and hacked, machinery rumbled and rattled, huge trucks grumbled and rolled until one day Arvay saw the sun setting behind the horizon of the world. The opening spread north and north before her eyes. The swamp monster retreated before the magic of man.

Arvay watched the conquest of her old enemy with the utmost fascination. It was very personal to her, though she never said so to anyone. She followed the progress of the men day by day. Now they were nearing the place of Earl's death. Who knew how many times Earl had been there before that fatal day! What had he done and felt there? Another day and they were about at the place. Arvay was so excited that she could scarcely sleep that night. The next morning she was in her rocking chair on the porch very early, as soon as Jim had gotten off to work. This morning, perhaps at this minute, those men must be felling those three big trees by the pool, and those others that surrounded the glade. Oh, do, Jesus!

Did that swarm of black men see or hear anything mysterious, or feel any strange presence? Were they halting, looking puzzled over some small something that she had failed to find on her secret visit to the place? Was there another place in there that she knew nothing about? Something that might reveal the unknown inner life of the son that she had borne. Arvay burned to halt the trucks loaded down with the miry, sweaty men as they rolled past her door at sundown, but then again, how could she ask them anything? She could watch

and feel and forever wonder, but she must keep such things to herself.

Where the loggers had been one day, the bulldozers followed the next, and right behind the big machines came the long train of dump-trucks pouring dry sand into the narrow, muddy gully that had been the lowest part of the swamp. Raw, dark gashes made by the bulldozers were streets stretching across the new fill and would soon be paved. Sewers, water-mains and electric lines rushed across to take the comforts of civilization to those who would make their homes over there. Influence had brought prompt action on the part of the county, and no sooner had the area opposite the Meserve place been filled in than Arvay saw the engineers laying out the ornate stone causeway that was to arch the low part of the land for the main highway. Tons of cement and steel were delivered and piled not too far from Arvay's front door, and she could watch the approaches of the causeway being laid. It began no more than a hundred feet from her front gate.

As Jim had predicted, the giving of the tract for the links and the club house had been a smart move for Hatton. The right people bought sites in the new development and it bloomed. The Howland Development exerted a tremendous effect on Citrabelle and the surrounding country. It came along and stratified the town. The original line of the swamp gave accent like a railroad track. Those who belonged moved west.

Hatton and Angie had one of the choicest sites on the big lake that was now known as Lake Charm, and Arvay felt pride in that. She saw her daughter friending with people whom she herself had never dreamed of associating with. The sons and daughters of first and second degree Yankees and wealthy southerners. Angie and Hatton played tennis and golf, went in swimming, canoed and motor-boated with the rest, and talked about getting sun-tanned.

Arvay took pride in all this, but underneath, it created a kind of lonesomeness in her. It made her wonder if she was needed anymore. She felt outside of this new life of her daughter. Kenny never seemed homesick either. What went on up there at the University seemed to fill his life. Jim was carried away with his shrimping and ran back and forth to the

coast. Arvay considered that she had only her hands to offer service with, and since nothing was required of her in that way anymore, she felt unnecessary most of the time. Her house was silent now, and her arms felt empty and useless. This Howland Development seemed infinitely more threatening to her than the dark gloom of the swamp had been. It was ever so personal to her, so she kept up her vigil on the porch, keeping track of every new change out there.

Jim watched it too, and with great satisfaction. When he did not prowl around over there of a Sunday, he took his newspaper and they sat on the porch and watched.

They sat there one Sunday and watched the cars glitter south from Citrabelle, swing around the huge half circle and sweep across the causeway.

"Just look at that!" Jim beamed at Arvay. "Hatton and the company are really selling and making money, but quiet as it's kept, we haven't been hurt a tap by the deal. This place is worth a whole lot more than it used to be on account of that development."

Jim was looking at her and beaming so that Arvay sensed that Jim was looking for her to say something, but for the life of her, she could not make out what was expected of her. She thrashed around for a while in her mind, then did the best that she could.

"I'll bound you," Arvay nodded and agreed. Then an alarming thought came to her. "But you don't aim to sell our home, do you, Jim?"

"Hell, no, Arvay! Not till Kenny gets through college anyhow. This place will be worth a whale of a lot more by then. You don't seem to realize how big this development is and what a change it has made in things around here."

Again Arvay could feel that Jim expected something of her but she still had no idea what he wanted her to say.

"Yeah, it's mighty nice, all right. But from the sums and amounts of money that folks have been spending over there it sure ought to be, Jim."

"Hatton's done mighty fine," Jim persisted. "Angie married her cup off when she landed that boy. Sensible, honest and with plenty push to him. I would of hated for her to miss a chap like that."

Arvay sat up and took a long look at Jim. Certain things were stirring in her mind.

"Well, she took good pains not to miss him, I notice. And that brings me to something that I have ever wondered about."

"For instance, honey?"

"Angie was under eighteen when she run off and got married, Jim."

"That's a fact, Arvay."

"It's always puzzled me how in the world she got a license to marry in Florida under age without neither one of us being there nor giving our consent."

Jim laid his folded paper in his lap and sat silent for a while. Then he braced himself and said evenly, "She wasn't by herself that day, Arvay. I was there." Jim waited a moment and spoke again. "She didn't go without consent at all. I was there."

Arvay's eyes took on that remote and unknowable look like the eyes of a python in repose. She had retreated within herself to her temple of refuge. Why, she asked herself, should she be surprised at being ignored like this? It had always been that way as long as she could remember. She had never been counted or necessary. Coming to know that she was born to be like that, she had finally found a refuge for herself from the whole round world. Not a happy, laughing place, but it was safe from all hurt, harm and danger. And who had toled and tricked her out of her refuge? That Jim Meserve who had come grinning with his teeth down the Big Road, and now to treat her like this. Making such a serious move with her own and only daughter and just as good as telling her that she couldn't help herself. All of a sudden Arvay whirled on Jim with clenched fists.

"So you can brag about you was there, eh?" Arvay accused hotly. "You, you deceiving scoundrel-beast!"

The house shook when Arvay slammed the front door behind her. She did not go into their communal bedroom. She felt then that she would never enter it again. She went into Angie's room and went to bed with her Bible. She stretched on her back and looked up at the ceiling. She tried to read again, but turned restlessly on her side. She kept on opening the Bible, but never finished a single verse. What had been

done to her was too tearing-down to bear. And the reason that she construed for it all was most hurting.

She didn't belong where she was, that was it. Jim was a Meserve. Angeline was a Meserve. Kenny was a Meserve, but so far as they were concerned, she was still a Henson. Sort of a handmaiden around the house. She had married a Meserve and borned Meserves, but she was not one of them. A handmaiden like Hagar, who had found favor in the master's sight. They didn't have to count her when anything important was to be done. Just go right ahead and ignore her. Took her for dumb and ignorant, and so narrow in her mind that she couldn't be expected to see that Hatton was a fine boy. Like she was ignorant and dumb enough to hold anything against the boy because he happened to be born up North! She could see as well as the next one that Yankees were like everybody else. She was as happy as the next one that Angie had married Hatton, and she would of freely give her consent if they had give her time to know the boy and get used to the idea. You couldn't find a nicer and more mannerable young man nowhere in the world, nor a better husband for her daughter. Oh, she might of said a off-hand word or two about Hatton being a Yankee, but they ought to of give her credit for being too sensible than to take it serious-like.

So now she would wash her hands of the whole mess. She would take no more pride in the development. It was Jim's ideas and Hatton's carrying 'em through. Let 'em have it! She couldn't turn her back on her children, but so far as Jim Meserve was concerned, she was through with him for good and all. This time she meant it. Never would she go back to his bed again.

Then Arvay turned over on her stomach and buried her face in the pillow. Arvay sobbed and wept. Her resolutions against Jim Meserve were just like the lightning-bugs holding a convention. They met at night and made scorning speeches against the sun and swore to do away with it and light up the world themselves. But the sun came up next morning and they all went under the leaves and owned up that the sun was boss-man in the world. Well, she would hold out until Jim came and carried her back across that hall by main force, which he did at midnight.

Chapter Nineteen

SINCE the fishing operations began, Jim was all new life and energy. He was back and forth to the coast sometimes twice a week.

"What you got to be running back and forth so much for?" Arvay asked petulantly. "You don't spend no time around your home at all these days. Can't that expert of yours that you place so much confidence in handle things?"

"Certainly! Alfredo don't fail to bring in the stuff if they can be found at all, and he's as honest a man as I ever expect to meet. I go up there as much just to be around boats and fishermen as I do to look after my business. Arvay, I love the sea!"

"I'm convinced that you must love something over there. You break your neck out of here every chance you get."

"We'll soon be living on the coast regular, I hope. I'm just hanging on at the packing-house till I get enough money ahead to see Kenny through the University up there in Gainesville, then I can afford to gamble just on my fishing. I don't want to draw out what I put in Hatton's firm so that the Meserve name can stay in there, and Kenny can have a share when he gets out of college. Though, from the way he talks, it might not be necessary at all. He claims that he's going to make his living with his box."

"I hope that you ain't paying that no mind. I been hearing the darkies picking boxes ever since I been old enough to know anything, and I got my first time to see any of 'em make a living at it. Just something for fun. It's all right to humor Kenny to an extent, but who you reckon is going to pay good money to hear anybody pick a box?"

"That's Kenny's business. Maybe he knows what he's talking about. He keeps up with that kind of a thing, and claims that white bands up North and in different places like New Orleans are taking over darky music and making more money at it than the darkies used to. Singers and musicians and all. You do hear it over the radio at times, Arvay. Kenny claims that it is just a matter of time when white artists will take it all

over. Getting so it's not considered just darky music and
dancing nowadays. It's American, and belongs to everybody.
Just like that swamp; so far they have slept over the darky
way of picking a box. He aims to be the first one to make it
something for the public, and he might be right for all we
know. Anyhow, just in case he might be wrong, I mean to
give him a good education so he can have something to fall
back on. That done, I can give my whole time and thoughts
to building me up a first-class fishing fleet. That's how I aim
to make your living from now on. Angeline is already well-
cared for."

"Think that you'll ever make it?"

"Without a doubt, Arvay. The last four trips, Alfredo has
come in with big-pay hauls. The last time, he took that boat
out and sunk her!" Jim's eyes glowed light with excitement
like a boy at a ball-game.

"My God, Jim! You mean that Alfredo done sunk your
boat?"

Jim laughed gaily. "Naw, indeed. When a shrimper says
that, he means that he come in loaded to the rails. From the
load on board, the stern of the boat is riding low down to the
water. Fishermen got their own way of saying things. Got
their own way of talking by signs too and a whole lot of crazy
things. You really ought to be along with me some times.
They'd make you laugh yourself to death. That's the only real
life to live, though my own folks would never have looked for
a Meserve to take to a thing like that. As I reckon I told you,
my father wanted me to take up law. If not that, the Army
out of West Point. He never said where the money was com-
ing from."

"Then you broke off, took to knocking around, worked in
teppentime, and married somebody like me."

"That's a fact. Seems like I had more sense than the rest of
my crowd." Jim grabbed Arvay by both corners of her mouth
and playfully stretched it across her face and kissed her in the
middle of it.

"I had too much sense to follow their lead. While my old
man was sitting around reading and taking notes trying to
trace up who did what in the Civil War, and my two brothers
were posing around waiting for the good old times that they

had heard went on before the War to come back again, I shucked out to get in touch with the New South. So far, I don't think that I have made out so bad, do you?"

"Can't say as you have, Jim. Fact is, from where we started off, you've spied noble. That's why I can't see why you always want to be tackling something new. We got a mighty good home, and with what you bring in, we don't want for a thing."

Jim looked at Arvay wistfully for a moment and said, "Maybe you will see into my reasons some day, Arvay. It ain't for me to point out some things for your information. I'll sure feel fine though when you come to realize for yourself."

"Seeing that I don't catch on to what you mean, Jim, look like you would tell me," Arvay replied after a pause.

"Naw, Arvay. That way wouldn't do me no good. Just search around inside yourself and some day you will understand what I mean." Jim's eyes wandered to a pair of fishing-boots over in one corner of the room and went and picked them up and looked them over carefully. "Alfredo is doing so fine with that boat that I feel like some kind of a king, only bigger and better. I just dare him to make six more trips like the last one! Damned if I won't haul off, reach back, and take that last piece of change that I still got stuck away and buy me another boat. That would make it the sooner for us to move to the coast for good."

"Get rid of our home?" Arvay asked in alarm.

"You ever known me to chunk money away like that?" Jim waved an arm towards the front of the house. "With the county paving a road south right in front of our door, and with all those new houses going up across the street there, that big development across the viaduct, this five acres is worth a young fortune now. It will be worth many times more a few years from now. I told you that I was saving it for Kenny. If he didn't have nothing else it would give him a good start in life. Give me one good year with my fishing and we won't need it for ourselves. We'll have the goddamn world by the tail with a down-hill pull."

"You really is set on moving to the coast, I see," Arvay murmured after a moment's thought. "How is Alfredo and all making out down there?" Arvay turned her head and looked

away off as if she were not really concerned with the answer. Just asking for politeness.

"Just fine! His wife is a mighty fine cook you know, and she's boarding some of the single men to help out, and they're coming along fine. I promised to bring you along with me sometime and have her fix us up a good sea-food dinner and generally have a grand time."

Arvay didn't say anything and Jim urged on. "When must I let 'em know?"

"I wouldn't want to put her to all that trouble, Jim."

"No trouble at all, honey. She would enjoy doing it and having you."

"I might be in your way."

"Aw, honey," Jim protested. "You never have been down there with me. Come on!"

"Naw."

"Well stay here then!" Jim shouted and slammed on out of the house and jumped into his car and drove off swiftly.

The shrimping fleet moved north for the summer and worked the Georgia and South Carolina coasts with Thunderbolt, Georgia, as a general base. Alfredo had gone up and Jim got regular reports, but was sorry that the distance was too great for him to make. That made him even more impatient to cut loose from his job and do nothing but fish. But when the fleet headed south in the fall, Alfredo brought him news of a good boat that he could get reasonable. The owner couldn't spare the time to fish it profitably by reason of women, whiskey and maybe too much whistling. Alfredo ran into the owner at just the right minute, and pledged Jim to buy the boat before anybody else found out that the man was willing to sell it so cheaply. It was really a bargain, and in better shape than the one Jim already had. More modern and all. Diesel powered and more icing-space.

Jim decided that this was too good a chance for him to miss, so he took the last two thousand dollars left over from his liquor venture, raked and scraped around otherwise, and laid the price of the boat on the line.

"You never got hold of such a bargain in your life, Boss, and you never will again in this world," Alfredo told him. "That damn fool sure did us a favor. He's gone crazy about

some woman here in Savannah, and all he's after is some ready cash to satisfy her mind. No notion of work at all no more. Well, his loss is our gain."

"You said it, Alfredo," Jim replied. "But I owe this chance of luck to you. Once more and again you have shown yourself to be a true friend to me, and taking care of my interest. I couldn't find a better friend nowhere. Anything that I can do for you at anytime, the favor is in me."

Alfredo asked for nothing, and that made Jim feel even more obligated. Therefore, some weeks later when Jim was at Alfredo's house for a business talk and one of Mrs. Corregio's meals, he was moved to offer something that he found that they prized more than money.

The fifteen-year-old Felicia, who was, as Arvay complained, well developed for her age, was looking at a newspaper in a wishful way.

"Oh," she sighed, "look like folks enjoy themselves so much at these football games. Gee, I wish I could go to one one time."

"Nothing to hinder you from going, is it?" Jim asked.

"You have to have different kind of clothes from what I got to go to a place like that, Mister Jim, and then, unless you belong to that college, you have to be asked to the social part, I mean. I don't have the clothes, and there's nobody to ask me to it."

Immediately Jim saw his chance. "Oh, I don't know about that, now Felicia. Kenny's up there at Gainesville, and almost like a brother to you. I don't have the least doubt that if he had any idea you wanted to go he would ask you."

"Oh, don't pay no attention to Felicia, Mister Jim," Mrs. Corregio hurried to say. "Some things is out of her reach and she might as well realize. She's been to her high school games and that ought to do her."

But Jim could see the wishfulness in the mother's eyes as well. She was merely afraid to ask anything of him.

"A person ought to do a few of the things they want to do in this world before they pass on, Felicia. You just leave it to your Uncle Jim, and he'll fix it for you."

"I was just talking, Mister Jim. Kenny wouldn't want to be bothered with nobody like me in a place like that."

"You don't know who Kenny wants to be bothered with. You let him talk his own chat."

Feeling that it was a very small thing that he could do for Alfredo, within twenty-four hours Jim had had a confidential talk with Angeline first, and then gotten off a letter to Kenny.

That was how it happened that Arvay saw Felicia at the football game. The Meserve family was bound to be there. Kenny was drum-major for the band, and they had to be there to see a thing like that at the big game on Thanksgiving Day. Kenny had reserved seats in a box for his family, and the number of friends whom Angeline specified. Prominent citizens of Citrabelle had the next box to gloat over their local boy.

They were all there early and in their places ahead of time to watch the huge grandstand fill up and greet old friends from other towns who would be sure to be there too. Angeline and Hatton seemed to know everybody. Jim and Arvay were kept busy accepting introductions and shaking hands. Prosperous looking young folks out of families that Arvay had never expected to pull level with.

"Our children might not be the bell-cows, but if they ain't they's right up in the gang," Arvay made a proud aside to Jim. "They seem to be right in with the best they is."

"Naturally," Jim boasted. "They got good manners, they got something, and they look like something. That's the stuff that makes for friends."

Jim and his party and everybody else became conscious of a young couple who had entered at one end of the field, and were parading down the other side. Everybody was asking, "Who is that?"

"Why, that's Kenny, my boy." Jim spoke so that he could be heard for several boxes around.

"Who is that pretty girl he's got with him?"

That was what everybody wanted to know. The girl attracted a lot of attention first, because she had an unbelievable mass of curly black hair that poured and tumbled nearly to her waist, and glittered in the sun, in a company of almost universal bobbed heads. Men like hair and they looked. Then she was so fresh and tender-looking. They noted that she was really built from her neck on down. The men looked at that and the women took in her clothes. She was dressed in a

white sweater suit, topped by a perky white tam over one eye, white buckskin oxfords, and a loose-fitting light-weight white coat. It was just the right thing for her dark hair and eyes. Brilliant big eyes, and a high natural pink in her cheeks. Kenny Meserve, ever the showman, was doing his stuff. He paraded along, pausing to make introductions, or when he was hailed by some yearning student who hoped for an introduction to his date. He had the eyes of the public, and he seemed to know it. It was a very eye-taking thing as he made his progress around three quarters of the grandstand, pretending to look for someone, till he arrived before the box where his party sat.

Arvay was not expecting, so she did not recognize Felicia until the couple was almost at the entrance to the box. She had no right to look for Felicia at a place like this, and certainly not in that kind of clothes. When she did make out who that was with Kenny, she was thunder-struck by lightning.

"Hey, folks!" Kenny hailed, and handled Felicia as proudly as if he had been escorting the Princess Royal. "Feliciana's here at last to use that seat I reserved in the family box." He went on to usher the smiling girl in to her seat. "Take care of her for me, kinfolks. I got to go. The band will parade in in a few minutes. Angie, I'm trusting you to look out after my interests. Feliciana is my date for the day. All of these college back-biters have had a look at her and their mouths are fairly drooling. Stand by me, Sis. Fight off the competition the best you can."

"We'll hold that line," Hatton promised.

"Satisfaction!" Kenny smiled and turned to go with a wave of his hand. "See you later and tell you straighter."

Arvay was entirely excused from keeping Felicia's company. Angeline's crowd took care of that. They made introductions, and kept up a great clatter until the teams marched in led by their respective bands. Kenny, now dressed in a showy uniform, and carrying a decorated baton, was the star of the piece. The Gators were on the home grounds, and the grandstand went wild when Kenny came prancing down the field. He shed more glory on his folks by saluting them as he passed the box in his tour around the field.

Kenny and the band brought up the drooping spirits of the students, alumni and fans at the half, when the visiting team had the Gators at 6–0. He ran over and spent some time in the box with them as the game took up again. Then he had to join the cheer-leaders and do his stuff. Jim was about to split his britches, but Arvay had no trouble at all in keeping quiet. She had never seen a football game before, anyway, so she could be excused for not going crazy when the Gators crushed across the enemy's goal line for a touchdown and then converted. In the last five minutes of the game, and on the third down, they did it again, and converted. It seemed to Arvay that over a million crazy people piled out onto the field and fell in behind the Gator band doing what they called the snake-dance. The bank president was a Gator grad, and he grabbed Jim and carried him out there too, and only the wives were left sitting there. The other women smiled indulgently, and Arvay acted it out as they did and chatted along, but she was going crazy in her own way.

Where and how did Felicia get those clothes that she had on? What was she doing here? Kenny had never mentioned Felicia in a single letter to her, so something underhand was going on. How much of Kenny's acting towards Felicia was put on and how much was real? Was Kenny bleeding them out of money that they could use otherwise to put clothes like that on that Felicia's back? Or was Jim crazy about something else in that Corregio home besides Alfredo's wife's cooking? Was it the mother or the daughter? Oh, that was too awful to think about. Laying around with the father and running after the son.

It turned out that Angeline and Hatton had good friends in Gainesville too. It was already arranged for Arvay and Jim to go to the home of one of these friends with them to dinner, and to rest and change their clothes.

The home was very good, and everything was done to make them comfortable, and Arvay tried to feel and act happy. She acted it out the best she could, but she couldn't feel that way. First and foremost, the presence of Felicia had her worried. She had no idea what it meant, but the rest of the family seemed to know. As in the case of Angie and Hatton, maybe Kenny would be married to this girl before she

knew anything about it at all. That made her miserable. The very name of Corregio called up sorrow and suffering to her mind. Why did that girl have to show up on a day like this, and in company with her son?

In addition, Arvay felt so out of place. All that this day meant in college circles was strange to her. She felt awkward and out of place. Listening to the people around her, she became terribly conscious of her way of speech. She hated to open her mouth for fear of making a balk, and putting her children to shame.

"Let's don't bother with the dance, Jim," Arvay suggested. "We got a long drive ahead of us, and it's getting late. Let's just say good-bye, thank the folks and go on home."

"But we can't do that, Arvay. Kenny is doing some special playing tonight at the dance, and he would feel mighty hurt if we wouldn't even wait to hear him."

Arvay found that she had to go. The family double-teened her and reluctantly she changed into a fresh dress and went to sit with Jim along the wall with a number of women who were chaperoning their daughters.

The sight that Arvay dreaded to see came before her eyes. Kenny came with his guitar around his neck and with Felicia on his arm. She created just as much excitement at the dance as she had at the game. She was dressed in a fluffy ruby-red tulle dress with a girdle of crushed cloth of gold. All of her decorations were gold. Gold kid slippers and a big gold flower in her flowing hair. She looked like the daughter of some foreign ruling-man. Almost instantly, she and Kenny were the center of things.

Angeline looked beautiful too. In a pale green something with silver-gilt touches, she and Felicia standing together had the floor. Angeline chummed up to Felicia and kept things looking like a pair of sisters.

Jim and the banker, who had stayed for the dance because his own niece was a guest, stood together near the wall chatting away when an important-looking man joined them and began to talk along. It turned out that he was the head of the Chamber of Commerce at Leesburg.

"Those are two really beautiful girls, yonder. The two standing together with that crowd of boys around them."

"Home town girls." The banker jumped in quickly and rocked back and forth on his heels. "Products of Citrabelle, prettiest little town in Florida, and grows nothing but pretty girls. Ain't that right, Jim?"

"Correct. Why, those two are about the ugliest in town. Fact is, they were run out of Citrabelle for the day so that the folks could enjoy their Thanksgiving dinner." The three men chuckled, and Jim went one better. "Just a couple of culls off of my place."

"I'll take your culls off of your hands and take 'em to Leesburg to ugly up the place."

"Aw, naw you don't, neither!" the banker objected. "Don't try to steal our samples. Come on down to Citrabelle and pick you a pair out of stock. This is Mr. James Kenneth Meserve, one of our first citizens, and that red-head is his daughter, and that black-haired one is his son's date."

"Congratulations, Meserve. You got a good thing all the way around."

"Yeah, but you haven't seen the best as yet. Turn around here and meet my pretty wife."

There was plenty to smile over, if Arvay had been in any notion to smile. Her face got cramps for the next hour while she tried her best to carry off everything nice. The orchestra assembled and the dance began. The parents took the chairs ranged around the wall and watched the young folks dance. A waltz, a fox-trot, and then Arvay and Jim grew proud as the drums opened up on Kenny's specialty, *House That Jack Built.* The way they had heard it at home was nothing to what this band could do with it. It was really *something.* The students seemed to be familiar with the piece enough to jump in every time they got to that line, "That milked that cow with the crumpled horn"—they all shouted it out.

The hall was full of exciting activity. The young folks were doing the Lindy Hop, and it seemed to Arvay that everything that could be done with a shin-bone was being done. Hundreds of young healthy boys were hurling pretty well-dressed girls around. Arvay noted that there was not a homely girl in the place, and a high percentage ranged to real beauty, and her own daughter was right up there in the front ranks. She could not enjoy anything, however, for Felicia Corregio was

there flashing around the room and stopping close to the band between every dance.

Jim and the rest insisted that the Corregios were as white as they were, but it made Arvay feel haunted to see any member of that family. Over the exciting rhythm of Kenny's composition Arvay could hear the mournful tolling of a bell. Pictures came before her eyes. Earl growling and hurling himself against the screen. Lucy Ann lying still and white and bleeding on the ground. The growling rumble of human men turned into a mob. Tolling, tolling, tolling sound of the bell. The siege in the swamp. Earl's quiet face in death. Tolling. Dead-and-gone. Dead-and-gone! The bell struck out with halting tongue.

Arvay struggled and tried to shake it off. Long ago she had brought herself to admit that the Corregios were not responsible for what happened, and as Jim said, Alfredo had acted a noble friend through it all. He had shown himself a faithful helper and friend since then, too. But the name called up that which she had tried hardest to forget. What human can desert his memories? The bell kept on tolling in her head. The heavy, slow-talking clapper seemed to be beating against her very skull. She waited and suffered between strokes. As the piece came to an end, Arvay leaped to her feet.

"Well, we done heard Kenny's special, Jim. It's time for us to go."

"Aw, what's the hurry, Arvay? I'd like to watch and hear some more of this thing."

"What for? This dance ain't for us. It's for these boys and girls."

"Yeah, but I want to watch and see. Looks like Kenny knows what he's talking about. Those white boys are playing that rag-time down to the bricks, and you saw that dancing, didn't you? I want to see as much as I can of it. You could almost think those were colored folks playing that music. I want to . . ."

Arvay was on her feet and had Jim by his arm. The band was resting for a minute or two, and Hatton, Angeline and Felicia were over there talking and laughing with Kenny. Arvay looked and wanted to go.

"I done begged you and begged you," Arvay gritted out in

a low tone. "I'm going, and I'm going this minute. You can take me if you want to, Jim. Suit yourself. If you don't come on this instant, I'm going anyhow. I'll go on out of here and grab the first thing smoking and go on home. You can stay here and gap at that Felicia until you get good and tired. I'm going!"

Jim backed the Buick out with a *zoosh*, wheeled around and headed through town in a hurry.

"You going too fast, Jim, with all these hundreds of cars on the streets. You're liable to hurt somebody."

Jim paid no attention. He cut through traffic like a razor and kept on going to the highway. No sooner did he hit it than he did what Angie and Kenny's crowd called washing his foot in the tank. That Buick squatted to the road and Arvay saw the needle moving up to fifty, sixty and beyond. She was terrified. She hated fast driving, and Jim so well knew it, but she was in no mind to ask him any favors. She gritted her teeth, held onto the door with one hand and put on brakes with her feet. East by south the car raced along with not one word being spoken between them.

Arvay was ever so glad when they approached Orlando. It was too big for Jim to dash through there, and this time of the year, Orange Avenue would be fairly working with north-ern cars. He would be slowed to a creep by the lights and traffic, and maybe by the time they got through there, Jim would have come to his sense.

But Arvay did not know the road. It was all strange to her coming from the direction they had. They came right into highway U. S. 17, which took them south without really en-tering the city. Also, there was that new three-lane stretch of twenty miles to Kissimmee. Jim stuck his foot in the tank and went from there. They were out on the Kissimmee Prairie, in the Florida cow-country, and little traffic. Arvay took one look and saw the needle slip past seventy, and closed her eyes. Before she knew it, they were in Kissimmee and approaching the bridge leaving town.

"Jim! Jim! Jim! Look out for that bridge! Don't kill me about that gnatty-tail gal! Jim! Oh, Lord have mercy!"

Jim took the bridge just like he did the rest of the road, and they flashed on past ranches with the trees and fence-posts

whirling in a mad dance past Arvay's eyes. Jim never said a word. "Wahooo!" the horn cried when Jim overtook a night-operating truck, and the wind yelled "whooo-ooom" as the Buick flashed past. Arvay screamed again when Jim passed a truck, and found another meeting him. He slashed between the two by a slight wiggle of the wheel almost rubbing hub-caps as he went with both. His hand was steady on the wheel, his face was grim and his foot was in the tank. Arvay screamed again as they entered Lakeland. The Buick dived down the slight hill to the ornamental lake, and for a second, it seemed to her that Jim would never be able to swerve to the right around the lake. It seemed as if it would plunge straight ahead into the water. Jim made the curve smoothly and kept on going. The car consumed on its way and Arvay screamed and cried. She had been sobbing and crying constantly for the last fifty miles when Jim pulled up into their drive with a sudden stop. Without a word, he reached across her, flung open the door on her side, and Arvay stumbled out crying very hard.

Jim made no effort to assist her up the steps as he usually did. He stomped up on the porch, unlocked the door, flung it open, switched on the hall light, and wheeled to go and put the car in the garage. Arvay staggered on into the bedroom, and sank down on the side of the bed in a lump, still shaking and crying.

Arvay would have felt better if Jim had stayed outside a while and given her a chance to collect herself, but he didn't. In no time, he came walking heavy over the floor. Hard-heeling and coming fast. He flung the bedroom door wide open and came and stood spraddle-legged in the middle of the floor. Instead of coming to her and trying to soothe her feelings, Jim just stood and looked down on her as if she were a chair. Arvay quit sobbing and leaped to her feet.

"Don't you stand there gapping at me, after you done done your best to kill me dead on that road! I got a good notion to take that gun and blow your infernal brains out!"

Jim went to taking off his clothes. He acted more like he had not heard what she said than anything else. Arvay stood there getting madder as he stripped and got into the pants of his pajamas.

"Oh, so you call yourself discounting me, do you?" Arvay screamed. "I think too much of myself to kill you like I ought to, but I'm through with you, Jim Meserve. I'm just as through with you as I is my baby-shirt."

She ran to the closet, snatched down her nightgown and headed for the door. Jim picked up the jacket of his pajamas, and let Arvay get as far as the door. Then he reached forward, caught her by the arm and flung her back into the room so forcibly that the back of her legs came up against the bed and she sat down without planning on it. Jim stood over her and glowered.

"Did I tell you that you could leave this room, Arvay?"

"N-n-no, Jim."

"Well, what did you start out of here for, then?"

"I-I thought that I had better go sleep——"

"You thought like Lit! Did I tell you to do any thinking?"

"No, Jim, you didn't."

"Well, don't let me hear none of your thinking unless I give you my command."

Jim stood and frowned down on the thoroughly frightened Arvay for a long time. She felt like a mouse under the paw of a cat. She looked up at him fearfully, caught his eyes on her, and then down quickly.

"Where I made my big mistake was in not starting you off with a good beating just as soon as I married you. I have never laid the weight of my hand on you in malice, and you done got beside yourself. What you mean by sitting there all drawed up into a winter knot? Get up from there and get out of those clothes."

Arvay got up timidly and Jim gave her a little shove towards the dresser, and Arvay's fighting blood got up. Besides, she was persuaded by now that Jim was not going to hit her. He never had so far. She whirled on him.

"Don't you dare to shove me, Jim Meserve! I'll wade knee deep in your blood. And I'm not a'going to take off . . . Jim! Jim! Don't hit me!"

Jim didn't hit her. He just grabbed the powder blue flat crêpe dress at the neck and ripped it off her, and flung the rags of it against the wall.

"Didn't I tell you to off with them rags? Off with 'em! Up

with that petticoat and down with them pants before you make me hurt you. Move!"

Arvay pulled at her underclothes in a desperate effort to get them off. Her slip stuck as she got it up to her shoulders, and she screamed as she felt Jim with a rough hand rip it off and hurl it away. She reached for her nightgown on the bed to cover herself, but Jim brought her up short.

"Did I command you to put on a gown, Madam? Leave it lay!"

Arvay stood with nothing on but her shoes and stockings, then remembered them and fairly clawed them off, and stood shivering with fright as naked as she had been born. She looked longingly at the closet door and took a step in that direction.

"Don't you move!" Jim bellowed harshly. "You're my damn property, and I want you right where you are, and I want you naked. Stand right there in your tracks until I tell you that you can move."

Arvay, her lips trembling to keep from crying, stood there with her legs close together and waited. Jim threw back the bed covers to the foot of the bed, then sat down in the little rocker, rested his hands on his thighs and looked Arvay over in a very cool way for awhile. Then he rested his face in his hands and sat silent and motionless for minutes. He was moved by love and pity, but Arvay could not know this from the way he spoke when he suddenly lifted his head.

"All right now," Jim commanded. "I reckon that you can go to bed. But move in a hurry before I change my mind."

Arvay leaped in and began to scramble the covers up over her to her very neck. With a springing jump, Jim was at the bedside and grabbing the upper corners, flung all the covers back over the foot of the bed.

"Who the hell told you to pull up any covers?" Jim demanded sternly. "You're too damned fast and previous! I'll let you know when I want you covered up, Madam."

Arvay laid there among her fears. But her fear of loss was much greater than her physical fear. Felicia and all the Corregios fell off Arvay's shoulder like a loose garment in her anxiety for reconciliation with this man who stood like a statue of authority beside the bed. No bells tolled; no memories could

find a place with her then. The hours of that morning before they had set out for Gainesville had seemed ordinary then. Looking back on that time from where she was now, they seemed to form a time of untellable bliss. If she could but have them back again! The most ordinary minute of peace with Jim in the past appeared like time spent in Paradise.

After what seemed like months to Arvay, Jim took his ample time and got in the bed with her. He stretched himself full length upon her, but in the same way that he might have laid himself down on a couch. After more years of suspense, Jim elevated himself from the shoulders up and looked down into Arvay's eyes.

"Hug my neck, Arvay," Jim said in the same way that he could have been telling her to pour him another cup of coffee.

Arvay flung her arms around Jim's neck with gladness. It could be that she had made her escape out of Hell. While she hugged and kissed her husband, Arvay prayed and promised God. Ah, but let these golden moments roll on a few years longer, please, God. She made vows and promises. If God would fix it so that she got over this greasy log, she would certainly sand the next one. That is, she would keep the Corregios out of her mouth and mind. Grant her this one favor of peace and agreement with Jim once more and again, and she would not bother God for no more favors. She would not even part her lips if the time should ever come when Kenny saw fit to court and marry Felicia, hard as the pill would be for her to swallow. By this time Arvay had hugged and hugged and kissed and kissed for what she decided was abundant and sufficient time. She lowered her arms and waited.

"Who told you to stop hugging my neck?" Jim demanded. "Get to hugging my neck and kiss me until I tell you it's time to knock off. I don't want no flabby kind of kissing neither. Go to work!"

Arvay hugged and she kissed and she kissed and she hugged.

"But Jim, you ain't acting mutual with me. That makes it hard work to do."

"You can't kiss me and talk at the same time, so hush talking."

Jim could feel Arvay's skin changing temperature, and the change in her breathing. The change became more and more pronounced. She kissed him violently and hungrily for a minute, then braced her hands against his shoulders and did all she could to shove him away from her.

"Go 'way from me, Jim, and leave me be!" Arvay began to scream and cry. "I can't stand this bondage you got me in. I can't endure no more! I can't never feel satisfied that I got you tied to me, and I can't leave you, and I can't kill you nor hurt you in no way at all. I'm tied and bound down in a burning Hell and no way out that I can see. I can't see never no peace of mind. It's a sure enough hard game when you got to die to beat it, but that's just what I aim to do—kill myself!"

Arvay ended on a high and agonizing scream of desperation.

Jim said nothing. Resting on his elbows, he took Arvay's face between his hands and looked down in her eyes which were running over with tears. Gradually, the features of her face relaxed and that calm Buddha mask that she always wore came over her face. But Jim was concentrating on her eyes. Once again he saw that greenish infusion creep in and mingle with the sky blue of her eyes. That peculiar thing about Arvay's eyes that he had a momentary glimpse of the first time that he had encountered her on the street at Sawley. He had seen it more fully when he had kissed her for the first time that Sunday at the table when they had become engaged. It had been daringly out in the open that flaming hour under the mulberry tree. It was an eternal and a compelling mystery how Arvay's face could stay as stiff as a false-face on Halloween while that something crept up like a tiger in the jungle peeping out through shielding leaves at its prey, and looked out through the eye-holes of the mask.

"No, I can't see no way out of my binding bondage but death, Jim. I aim to kill myself, so tomorrow I'll be dead and gone. I never is sure whether you love me or not, and I just can't endure no more."

For an answer, Jim kissed Arvay with a kind of happy arrogance, then snuggled his head down on her breast in that way he had that Arvay thought was so much like a helpless child, and went off into peaceful sleep.

Arvay buried her hand in his hair as she loved to do and stayed awake for awhile with her thoughts. And she had promised to escape this man by death tomorrow.

Tomorrow? When and what was that? Who ever has believed in the reality of death in the presence of vibrant life? It is a parable sometimes told by the old. Some man in a far country, whom you never knew, went off somewhere one time, and being a fool, laid down and died. But who, in love, ever paid any attention to a made-up tale like that?

Chapter Twenty

Y OU really mean to take her out, Boss?" Alfredo asked and looked for an answer in Jim's face.

"Hell, yes! Just got my pilot's license, took a week off from my job to be here, and then not go?"

"Okay. It's a little windy out there, and you not being too experienced, I didn't know whether you felt to take the risk. Quite a few boats ain't going out today. But then some are going right on. Even if you hadn't decided to go, I was going. This little wind is going to die down before night anyhow. From the northwest, and it won't blow real strong."

"Sure, Eddie Halliard and several more of the best men are going out," the Mate chimed in. "A little wind is even a help in getting the net over the side. Let's go, My Captain."

"Damn! But that sounds good!" Jim beamed. "First time in my life. Captain Meserve of the *Angeline*. Say it again, Stumpy, and lemme hear you."

"Gimme an order so I can answer you right."

"Wait, Stumpy, lemme get in the pilot-house with my hands on the wheel and look important. You and my Third Man stand there on deck and look scared. Alfredo, you get ashore and get aboard your own command, so everything'll look natural. All right now, let's go through it right."

Jim struck a pose, frowned ferociously at his crew, cleared his throat and bellowed.

"You Third Man, have you got all necessary stores on board?"

"Yes, My Captain, we are well provisioned."

"Mate!"

"Yes, My Captain!"

"Everything ship-shape below?"

"Yes, My Captain. We can cast off and head for the inlet."

"Well, why the hell don't you do it then, and let's go?"

They all broke into a laugh. The lines were cast off, and Jim moved the *Angeline* out safely from the dock and stood out in the stream. The *Arvay Henson*, Alfredo in command, waited long enough for the *Angeline* to clear sufficiently, then

came out to pair with the *Angeline*, and the two moved off, gaining speed gradually towards Mosquito Inlet.

When Jim had piloted his boat through the tricky inlet, and her bow slid out into the Atlantic, Jim waved at Alfredo gaily and said to Stumpy, who stood on deck by the pilot-house door: "Stumpy, Heaven can't be no treat to me after this. I got all the Heaven I want right now."

"It ought to feel fine to be captaining your own boat, but I don't ever expect to own one. I done swore on a stack of women so high that I was going to save up and own me a boat someday, but I knowed that I was lying when I said it. Too much good likker that needs drinking up, and everytime I see a pretty woman switching along, I got to stop and drop a flag on it."

They laughed, noted that the *Arvay Henson* had headed north, and swung that way. As the bow of the *Angeline* cut the choppy water, Jim looked to starboard over the seemingly limitless sea to the horizon where it curved away from sight in waving lines. He looked to port, at the dim line of the Florida coast, and forward at the three boats ahead, and was content.

"You're not afraid with a new captain like me, Stumpy?"

"No, indeed. You're doing just all right. I watched you how you brought her through the inlet. That was where the danger was. Anyhow, a fisherman got so many good chances to lose his life that if he stops to dwell on that, he'd be scared to death all the time. I ain't scared of a thing but old Bozo."

"Who in the hell is Bozo?"

"Nobody ain't told you who Bozo is as yet? Man, you ain't no real fisherman until you meet old Bozo and fight him."

"Who is he, and where can he be found, Stumpy?"

Stumpy laughed and summoned the Third Man from the galley.

"Come on up, Charlie. The Captain wants to locate Bozo. You fought him last, didn't you? Come on up and tell My Captain where Bozo can be found!"

The Third Man, who had been putting on breakfast, came up the steps, wiping his hand on a sugar sack towel, and put on a very serious face.

"I hate like everything that nobody never mentioned it to me while we was on the hill. We're way outside now, and you

have to wait until we go ashore again. Still and all, I figger that I can give you some idea where Bozo lives, and how he can be found. Then you can go and challenge him to a fight anytime you want to."

Before the Third Man got through with his fantastic directions, Jim caught on that this was some joke. With the state of Florida as flat as a flounder, he was told that he had to cross the Lick-and-Spit Mountains just back of New Smyrna. Then he turned short to port and went through the land of the Mollymoes. A Mollymoe was a peculiar kind of a bird. He never relieved himself but once a year, and when he did, why, you could smell him for a mile or more. That was how he came to have his name. Come through that country and you were right at a big plantation. That was where Bozo lived. Yes, sir! Big house and everything. Bozo seemed to have a plenty. Rich and well-to-do. All you had to do then was to go right up and knock on the door, and when Bozo opened it, challenge him to a fight. The man who whipped Bozo would be the king of the world.

"Did you whip him?" Jim asked to humor the joke.

"No, can't say as I did. Fact is, I never laid eyes on Bozo. Just like everybody else, all I ever saw was Bozo's cat."

"How was that, Charlie?"

"It was bad, Cap'n. As far as I seen it was mighty bad and more than I figgered that I could handle."

"Even being a fisherman?" Jim helped the story out.

"Even for a fisherman, and they can handle more'n anybody else in the world. You see, Cap'n, that cat was as big as a yearling calf to start off with. Then as things went along, when I seen that cat drink off a skillet full of hot boiling grease for coffee, and then take up a blazing li'dard knot out the fire and use it for toilet paper, I figgered that it was time for me to go! And man, I really went. I was running so fast till I had to turn sideways to keep from flying."

They laughed that off and then Jim asked, "So you never got a chance to see Bozo himself, eh?"

"What? Wait for Bozo? If his cat was that big and tough I didn't want to meet that Bozo riding nor walking. I went there feeling fit to fight, but my Mama always told me never to let my head start more than my behind could stand. If

Bozo is any tougher than his cat, I don't admire to meet him."

"Same thing happened to me," Stumpy nodded solemnly. "All the fishermen'll tell you the same. Don't care how you meet him he's the privileged vessel and you better treat him that way."

"Much obliged for the information," Jim said. "And now that I know about Bozo, I take it that I'm initiated."

"Kee-rect, My Captain," the Third Man grinned. "Reckon I'd better go finish off breakfast. Old Bozo is liable to board us any time and we ought to be in shape to tackle him."

Jim sat on his stool at the wheel and contemplated the ocean of sea around him. The colors charmed and pleased him. There was the delicate green close at hand, and flipping inward toward the faint outline of the Florida coast. To starboard and infinity, it took on a blue-green, and where the sun rested on it, it seemed to be over-laid by a silvery veil. A line of porpoises dipped and dived in a solemn parade between ship and shore. Portuguese Men-of-War sailed in purple glory. That was another thing that fascinated Jim about the sea, the seemingly infinity of form. No matter how much you saw, the sea had still other marvels of shape and color. He would never, never tire of the sea.

Jim had his breakfast and returned to the wheel. The small fleet went on northward. Jim and his crew cracked jokes and contentedly followed until they noticed signs of slowing down of the vessels ahead.

"Alfredo's going to fish, I believe. Okay, boys, let's try along."

The Mate went to the smaller winch, Third Man took the try-net in his hands, and as the strong steel cable was played out and out the net, shaped something like a wind-sleeve at an airport, went overboard and down for sixty fathoms. Jim sent the engine ahead, and the boat made a large slow circle for half an hour.

"Let's get it!" Jim sang out, and his eyes were filled with eagerness as the net came over the port side, and was dumped on the deck. There were numerous kinds of deep sea life spilled on the deck when the net was emptied, but the men

took little notice of it. The three of them were eagerly counting the shrimp.

"Nowhere near fifty there," Jim said in a flat voice when the count was over. "Not enough to be worth a drag."

The boat cruised for a half hour, then they tried again. As ever, the sea gulls appeared seeming from nowhere when a net was raised, and swarmed around, hungry for the rejected marine life that would be shovelled overboard when the shrimp was picked out. The men had not bothered to clear the deck before, but the try-net came up loaded this time. The birds were tired of waiting, and swarmed in.

"Near enough," Jim decided. "Let's go overboard."

The eager ritual was performed. Each man had a station and hurried to it. Jim to his wheel in the pilot-house. The Mate to the big winch. The Third Man took the bag of the big net in his hand and stood at the starboard rail and waited.

The mast was amidship, immediately aft of the pilot-house. The boom, to which the big rig was attached by pulleys and strong steel cables, was drawn up at around a hundred and sixty degree angle against the mast with its loose end pointing almost skyward like a cannon at rest. Now the boom was slowly lowered by means of the winch, swung to starboard to let the big drag-net slide into the sea. First, the long, coarse-fringy chafing-gear touched the surface of the water, got wet and began to sink. Then the whole of the mesh sank down and down until the boards, used for weights, were lying flat on the ocean like two big doors afloat on either side of the net.

"Is she spreading right?" Jim asked.

"Yep, she's just all right," the Mate answered. Immediately, the Third Man dropped the big bag over, and Jim sent the boat ahead. The cable ran out and out from the big drum to the sixty fathom line and the big net with its protecting chafing-gear was sweeping the bottom of the ocean. The drag was on. The Third Man went forward, picked up the bamboo stick that had a huge round cork fixed to it about eighteen inches from the butt end. Below that it was weighted. On the other end was a small triangular pennant of dark blue. This was the flag. They dropped that overboard, and it stood up like a buoy with the little pennant flying. It was a marker so

that the boat could stay over the shrimp, and drag back and forth through them.

The boat began the slow circling around that flag with the steel cable stretching out and down astern. The boat listed to port or to starboard from the weight of the big net sweeping the bottom according to the position of the boat in relation to the net. For two hours it would go on that way. Slow and easy around that flag.

As Alfredo had predicted, the wind was dying down. By the time the net was brought to the side, there was just enough sea to help lift the net over the side. They had almost had bad luck. The net was maneuvered around to port just in time to miss the stern and avoid fouling the propellers.

The bag was dumped on deck with its wealth of strange sea forms and the shrimp separated from the rest. The sea gulls miraculously appeared, as if spontaneously created out of the water and screamed to the crew to hurry.

"Not but eleven boxes," Jim said when the shrimp were measured up.

"Yeah," the Mate put in, "but that'll pay for ice and fuel. What we get after this will be gravy. We might sink her on the evening drag."

"Could be," Jim muttered. "Look, their feet are red. They're on the travel. Now if we just hit the right direction we might go in top boat."

"Let's make this a two-meal day and go over again, My Captain. I need some spending change. Anything I love is a big percentage."

"I'm more than ready, boys, if you don't mind the strain," Jim said and looked at the Third Man.

"Hell, yeah. Might be plenty nuggets at the bottom of this lake right under us. Let's go!"

They let the heading of what they had go until the drag was on again then the two men of the crew sat on the hatch cover and "cracked heads" and talked while the boat began again its slow circle.

"Wonder where do shrimp go when they disappear from the sea?" the Third asked. "Sometimes, don't care which way you go, they just can't be found."

"I believe that they get up under ledges close in shore, especially in bad weather."

"Well, we know that they travel down the coast in winter, go clean around the State of Florida and come into the Gulf. But where do they be when you can't find 'em at all?"

"You suppose that there's some underground, or undersea, passage across under Florida that connects the ocean and the Gulf and some of them know it and go that way?"

"Could be. Then, too, they travel at night sometimes. When you see 'em with red feet, they been travelling at night."

The net was brought over the side again, and this time they had had better luck. Forty boxes, after being headed, went into the hold. Jim felt good. The men began to get gay and talk about what they were going to do on the hill. "The hill" meant being ashore. Fernandina, St. Augustine, New Smyrna, whichever port they went in, the ladies were going to have a very interesting time. Oh, but they were!

Jim's first trip as a captain lasted three days. They went up and down the coast, but no boat made a record catch. Eddie Halliard came in top boat with two hundred and six boxes. Jim had one hundred and eighty-six in his hold. He had beaten Alfredo by five boxes and felt very good indeed.

He was thrilled when the boats began signalling that they were leaving the fishing ground. A chance to stick his head in a crown could not have given him the pleasure that he got from receiving his first sign language and answering it.

With the *Arvay Henson* nearly a hundred feet off his starboard, he saw Alfredo leave his pilot-house and come on deck. Jim hurried to do the same and looked across. Alfredo flung both his arms to his left about waist high, left palm facing out and right palm towards his body. With his hands and fingers out straight, he made the fluttering motion of fish tails swimming.

"Haul hips," Jim interpreted. Leaving the fishing ground. Jim did the same to indicate that he had the message.

Alfredo made a loose fist of his right hand as if he grasped a round cylinder, threw his head back, and placed the fist to his mouth.

"And going to have plenty to drink," Jim read the flash and returned it.

With the same right hand, held this time slightly to the right of his body on a level with his chest, Alfredo made the motion of winding a clock in a strenuous way.

"Going home to sleep with my wife." Winding the clock being the last thing before going to bed. Jim replied and the three signs were in. The boats were going into port.

They turned their bows south, paired off, and were under way. It was important for each boat to have a partner to afford assistance in case of trouble, and trouble can come swiftly and disastrously on the sea.

Proudly, after a five hours' run, Jim brought the *Angeline* through the inlet, and laid her dead beside the dock. Alfredo tied the *Arvay Henson* alongside when he got in a half hour later. According to arrangement, he sold his shrimp through Toomer, a "factory" with a fleet of seven boats, paid off his two crews and everybody headed uptown.

Jim jubilated from place to place for two or three hours, then stepped into a Jook that was very popular with the fishermen. The Jook organ was blaring out popular records, some few couples danced off and on, and the bar was crowded. Jim was congratulated and treated and he stood for drinks in return. Young women who were pretty, and some who merely had pretty intentions, were being very fond of the men with plentiful percentages. Five and ten dollar bills were laid down for two-bit drinks, and the ladies were allowed to keep the change. What kind of a fisherman was that who grabbed up change?

Stumpy was in there up against the bar with a girl with a moderately good-looking face and a shape like a partridge. He was treating and she was pocketing change. When Jim sat down at a table, Stumpy saw him and came over.

"My girl has got a friend who wants to meet you."

"Well, I'm not going to run from her. Might even drop a flag on it if it suits."

Stumpy, with the two girls, joined Jim at the table and he promptly stood treats. He played the game according to the rules up to a certain point, but he was gambling with his stuff out the window. Jim fancied pretty women, the kind that

gave him a tussle to get. This one was not ugly, just usual-looking, and was there to pick up change. But the girl didn't have to know what he was thinking, and she didn't.

"Who eats your white chicken?" Jim asked her. The girl bridled and looked flattered and took hope.

"Nobody, Captain Meserve. Haven't found nobody that I cares for."

"Then maybe there's a chance for me." His change came, and he put it in his pocket. The girl looked pained.

"Oh, you just ought to see the pretty new bed-spread that I bought yesterday. It's a dream!"

"I bet it is, too. Tell me how it looks." The girl thought that he was very dumb. She cuddled closer and began to try to put that thing on him. Jim petted and patted and looked impressed. "Go on and describe it to me. I'll bet it's got pretty flowers on it."

"Tell you what. You come on to my room and I'll let you see it."

"I'd just love to. But look at Stumpy over at the bar getting into a spending-duel with the Third Man from the *Savannah*. Let's watch him."

"Aw, yeah?" Stumpy was retorting. "We brought in plenty on the *Angeline*. I know that I can beat you spending."

"Aw, is that so? Well, make me know it. I don't believe nothing until I see it. I don't believe that the old sow had pigs. I don't even believe that lard is greasy."

Both called up their lady friends, bought rounds and let the girls pick up the change. They kept on until both of them were stony.

"Still I aim to beat you," Stumpy said. "I got my owner right here with me. Brought him along because I suspicioned some piker like you was going to get up in my face. Hell, it's plenty more shrimp out there in the ocean, and we sure know how to find 'em. Lemme have ten dollars, Boss, until the next trip."

Jim didn't grab at his pocket at all.

"Look, Stumpy, it ain't that I'm scared that you won't pay me back. But why do away with ten dollars you haven't even made yet? I paid you nearly a hundred dollars about six o'clock this evening."

"That's right, but it's all gone now."

"How about knocking off, and beginning to put something away for a rainy day?"

"Because that ain't no sensible way for a fisherman to do, Boss. I might get washed overboard crossing the bar the very next trip. A shark may get me before the next week is over. What do I need to put away money for somebody else to spend? I knowed a fisherman once who cut a caper like that and it brought him all kinds of bad luck. I knowed him mighty well. He was a good friend of mine."

Stumpy, high as a Georgia pine, made a gesture with his arm to call witnesses to his tale.

"Practically everybody in here knows who George Kemp was."

There was almost unanimous agreement. Those who did not know him personally, knew about him. One of those good fishermen who had fallen from grace. Good-hearted as he could be. A good boy, but a poor boy. Jim just had to hear George's pitiful story as a warning if nothing more.

George had been a regular fisherman, then all of a sudden something got the matter with him and he started to saving money. Stay out six, seven, ten days and never felt right unless he sunk his boat. Made a heap of money for his owner, a Portuguese factory outfit, and money for himself. Saved it all up and finally bought himself a boat of his own. Then he got to making himself some big money, but the poor fool didn't learn no better. Kept right on dodging good likker and hiding away from loving women and saving up money for hard times.

"So look what happened to the back-slider. A fly gal out to do herself some good gigged poor George on down to the courthouse and married him. And neither did she lose any time letting George know just what she married him for. I been told that love ain't nothing but the easy-going heart disease, but that she-eel made it quick. Had George working so hard till he soon come down with heart trouble. Doctor give him up for dead.

"You know, My Captain, lying is lying and joking is joking, but to stick a crooked stick like that up a straight man's behind is really too provoking. Knowing that he wouldn't be here long, George got to thinking. He admired to leave that

eel just like he found her, which was down and out. So he calls all of us who was his friends to his house, gives away every cent he had, drinks up all the likker that he can hold, makes the three leaving-the-fishing ground signs, and lays down on his bed and dies."

Jim doubted the story mightily, but practically every man there swore it was so. It was added that George found that he had two thin dimes on the back of the dresser, so he tossed them in his mouth and swallowed them with a drink of water. George had won the big pot after all. You just can't beat a fisherman.

"And what lesson do we learn from that?" Stumpy parodied a Sunday school teacher to the amusement of the crowd. "What do the Bible teach and tell a fisherman to do?"

"Spend it just like you make it!" came back in a roar from the crowd. "Don't leave a thing on the hill when you go to sea! Fatten no frogs for snakes!"

"Kee-reck!" Stumpy cried out, and looked at Jim in triumph. Jim laughed, reached in his pocket and handed Stumpy the ten.

Stumpy, who had been given his name for being tall, yelled for drinkers to treat, and to cheer him in his victory over his opponent. The ten-spot vanished in a blow.

Then in honor of the triumph of his crew-man, and of his new life, Jim stood the next round of drinks. For some time Jim had been yearning to feel his own deck under him, and that was his good-bye gift. Leaving Stumpy still "specifying," Jim drove back across the bridge to the shrimping docks and stood for a long time watching the life of the river, whose surface looked oily under the light of a cloudy moon. There was the fleet of boats tied up, two and three abreast; the shrimp factories, the swift life and death circle in the water traced out by phosphorescent streaks.

If he just didn't have to ever go back and be bothered with the packing-house! Kenny had two more years in college, and that seemed like an eternity to Jim now. Just thinking about the long wait got Jim so impatient that the spirit of profanity descended upon him. Leaning on the starboard rail Jim spoke in tongues and double-cussed all the way.

Chapter Twenty-One

TIME CAME when Arvay had a new addition to her house. It was a spacy and pretty sleeping-porch added onto the south side of the home. What had once been the side window of the living-room was now a pair of glass doors opening out onto the new porch.

Arvay was stunned by the newness of the idea, but she made no objections. She had seen that kind of porches attached to houses of people, but of a class of folks whom she thought of as too high-toned for her to compare with. For the used-to-be Arvay Henson, that kind of a thing was a mighty high kick for a low cow.

So Arvay was much relieved when Angie took charge of the empty new porch, forbidding any of the old porch chairs to be moved in. No, Angie declared, there had to be brand new things, and things meant especially for a porch like that. Things built for coolness, and bright and reclining-like. Angie selected wicker furniture with cretonne cushions and covers, a chaise longue for that corner to the right of the door. A pair of day-beds with good mattresses and bright covers and pillows fitted into spaces against the house wall for lounging by day and for sleeping on hot nights, with shaded lamps handy to read by. When Angie got through Arvay thought that the porch was prettier than anything that she had ever seen in her life. It put her in mind of an inside flower garden.

Arvay tried not to let on, but to save her soul she could not take up on that porch at first. She felt highly privileged to have it under her care, but she could not feel that she had any right to be there. She swept and dusted and petted and patted pillows and tended to the plants that Angie had spotted around in there for looks to make up for her uncomfortable feeling. A kind of outside show of ownership. She never sat down unless Jim insisted, and then she did not lean back in the deep, comfortable chairs. Arvay made excuses about the damp night air to keep from mussing up those day-beds until Jim declared that he would be damned if he was going to foot bills for a sleeping porch and good beds and then stick in the

same old room on warm nights. He was going to sleep out there. Arvay followed Jim meekly and found that she managed to sleep all right. It got easier every time that she tried it. After a week of that, Arvay took her mending out there one afternoon, and after a few minutes of trial, sat all the way back in a chair. She had not been settled like that very long before Hatton's mother called her on the phone, and in well-covered pride, Arvay invited her over to sit awhile and share a pitcher of cold lemonade with her.

Mrs. Howland made much over the porch, and over the lemonade. They chatted pleasantly, and afterwards Arvay decided that she had never passed a more agreeable afternoon. The porch belonged to her after that. She had noted a difference in Mrs. Howland's manner with her, she thought. She took to inviting other women friends to drop in and they all expressed envy of her porch. It built Arvay up and made her feel more inside of things. It was a kind of throne room, and out there, Arvay felt that she could measure arms and cope. Just looking around her gave her courage. Out there, Arvay had the courage to visit the graveyard of years and dig up dates and examine them cheerfully. It was a long, long way from the turpentine woods to her sleeping-porch.

Arvay's unsureness went away when she stepped out there. She had bright ideas and thought up things to say in answer to people. Arvay joked and laughed with Jim and they had a great deal of fun these days.

Every evening, as soon as supper was over, Arvay led the way out there to lounge around and wait for an event of her day. For the last year or so, she had been a little too bound for her usual good health. So her doctor had given her a routine to overcome this. He was a young new doctor that Angie had thrust upon her. He was against laxatives and the castor oil mixed with turpentine that Arvay had been raised to. Seven in the morning and eight at night had come to be Arvay's hours for her vigil. That gave her a good two hours after supper on the porch to enjoy her place with Jim.

Arvay had no fault to find with her routine. It was funny, she reflected more than once, how things could change around. Once upon a time, she would not have given what she was doing a second thought. But now she had to restrain

the impulse to make a victorious announcement and put herself in the way to receive compliments.

This particular evening was soon before Easter, but otherwise it was a good deal like others that Arvay already knew about. The differences were that Arvay heard the first whip-wills-widow of the year from somewhere outside in the dark. Then a bull alligator bellowed in rumbling thunder from a lake off towards the south. Jim lowered his newspaper and gloated.

"Spring is here!" He laid the paper down and lit his pipe. "When you hear a bull gator bellow and a whip-poor-will call, spring is here for sure. The weather man can't fool a gator."

"Sure sign," Arvay agreed. "Umm Jim! Just smell that night-blooming jessamine that Hatton and Kenny set out for me last Fall! Ain't it sweet?"

"Mighty, mighty nice. Mighty nice." Jim picked up his paper again.

"You mentioning the gators and spring and all puts me in the mind that Kenny and his foolishness will come loping up here before long."

"No more'n three more months now," Jim conceded cheerfully.

"With the house rammed and crammed with his cronies a'whooping and a'hollering and banging on that pianner and everything else they can get their hands on and eating up everything just as fast as I can get it cooked for 'em," Arvay complained happily. "Wonder how they's all making out over in New Orleans right now."

"That's right," Jim said. "You remember that Kenny mentioned in that last letter that they—the Gator band, I mean—was going to New Orleans to play at some kind of music-festival at that college up there. . . ."

"Tulane University," Arvay supplied with a touch of pride. "I declare to my rest, I never knowed that there was so many of these colleges in the world until Kenny got mixed up in one. Every time I turn around he's teaching me another name."

Jim yanked the hunting-case gold watch from his fob and snapped it open.

"That final concert was from three to six today, wasn't it? Yeah, they're all through playing now and on the way to

Gainesville, I reckon by now. Though the professor might let 'em stay over tonight and head back for Gainesville tomorrow sometime."

"What time is it now, Jim, near about eight?"

"Two minutes of."

"Then I reckon I better go." Arvay put her hands on the arms of the chair and got up. "I don't know what kind of a caper it is that Kenny cuts that makes folks act so crazy over his playing, but it sure is something or other."

Arvay moved leisurely towards the door into the house. As she went, the perfume from the flowers surged around her. The moon was rising, and some mocking-birds in a tangerine tree began to trill sleepily. The whip-poor-will was still sending out his lonesome call. Arvay paused in the door and looked back on the softly lighted porch. It was to her the most beautiful and perfect scene in all the world. She was as near to complete happiness as she had ever been in her life. The porch told her that she belonged. Slowly she turned away and went on to the bath.

Just then the telephone in the hall began to yell in long pulls. She heard Jim's solid tread down the hall, and the instrument rattle.

"Hello! Hello! Yeah, that's right . . . Yes, it is . . . Speaking."

Sounds like somebody sort of strange, Arvay decided.

"Long distance? . . . Did you say New Orleans?"

"Jim!" Arvay yelled through the closed door. "Didn't they say New Orleans? Do, My Maker! What's done happened to Kenny?"

"Just a minute, honey," Jim said quickly and impatiently through the door. "Oh, hello! Hello, Kenny boy! . . . Sure, I know your voice. Glad to listen to it any old time. What you got to say?"

Arvay leaned back, but she did not relax. Kenny couldn't be too bad off if he was able to come to the phone.

"Oh, he did, eh? That's just fine. How did you make out? . . . Gee, I'm proud to hear that. . . . You don't say! Oh, I knew all along that you could do it. Sure. . . . Oh, you did? . . . Well, if you've done put your name down on it, I don't see that's anything more to be said. Naturally, me and your

mother will feel sort of disappointed for you not to go ahead and finish school. Wait just a second, and I'll get her to the phone. . . ."

There was really no need for Jim to call Arvay. She had heard him through the door and was both eager and anxious to get to the phone, but found herself too seriously involved.

"Tell him to hold on for just a minute, Jim, then I'll be there."

Arvay heard Jim give her message over the wire.

"You got to catch the New York train in three minutes? Too bad. I'll tell her what you say. She says to give you her love. Wire us the minute you get there, and back it right up with a letter so that we'll know where to reach you. If you need anything, don't feel bashful about letting me know. I'm with you, son. Good-bye."

Arvay tried desperately to make it, but the click of the receiver found her scrambling to a standing position with her clothes up around her waist. Jim waited in silence until she came out of the door and told her.

A famous leader of a famous New York band had been playing an engagement at a celebrated New Orleans hotel. The engagement ended the very day that the Gator band had arrived at Tulane, but the bandleader had sent his men on ahead, and waited to scout the Gator band. He was there to hear Kenny play for three sessions. He liked Kenny's piece a lot. It was a rhumba and it went over swell. As soon as the concert was over that evening, he had managed to get Kenny to one side and make him an offer. Fifty dollars a week to start with, and double that in ninety days if Kenny took with the public in New York. So much for the exclusive use of Kenny's piece besides, and when it was published, Kenny would get something from that too. Kenny thought that it was a great opportunity, and he had grabbed it. The band was going into a famous nightclub in New York in two weeks.

A coldness as from outer space crept over Arvay as she listened. It stiffened her tongue and choked her throat so that it was a long time before she could speak.

"And you stood there and let him go?" Arvay managed to say at last.

"What else could I do, honey? He had done passed his

word and signed the contract. He couldn't go back on that. And then again as he said, he never has had any notion of doing nothing else but playing music for a living. It don't matter too much whether he finishes school or not. He figured on two or three years after he finished school to get to the very place that he got today. Looking at it from that standpoint, he's five or six years ahead of schedule. And if he don't make out up there in New York, he can come on back to school, can't he? I don't see no reason for you to feel so bad."

"I reckon you don't, Jim. I feel and believe that you'se telling the truth from your very heart. But just the same, I hope that you and nobody else don't never feel like I do right now. You never is known the feeling I got right now. All the little family I done got together is gone and done left me in one way or another."

Arvay sobbed and cried and leaned her head against the wall and shook. Jim reached out and warm-armed her up tight against his chest.

"You're ever so wrong, honey baby." Jim petted and tried to soothe. "You still got your children as much as ever. And even if you didn't, you still got me, ain't you?"

Arvay freed herself and pushed past Jim and towards the front of the house. Through the width of the living-room she could see the enchantment of the porch, but she saw it as from afar and in a vision. Like John on the island of Patmos. A golden land of refuge where all would be peace, but from which she was now expelled. Her power seemed broken. She stood looking, and new tears crept out from her eyes. Tears without sound that nevertheless flowed freely.

"Just like I always thought and feared . . . they all done turned from me and gone. . . . Why couldn't I have been setting quiet-like on my porch when my baby come to me and told me that he aimed to go off and leave me? So then I could of handled my feelings."

Arvay turned into her old bedroom and fell across the bed on her face. She was conscious that she had left Jim standing very still and looking after her with a heavy expression on his face. Behind the closed door of the room, she went forth to face the demon of waste and desert places and take him for her company.

Chapter Twenty-Two

Arvay had no idea how long it had been since she had left Jim standing open-armed in the hall. Lying on her face, she heard him enter the room and switch on the light. Out of the cracks of her eyes she saw him quietly changing into his night clothes. She began to charge him with not caring how she felt. He had loosed Kenny to leave home regardless of her feelings. Now, with her crying her heart out, he was going on out on the porch to sleep and leaving her to her misery and lonesomeness. But no, Jim came to the side of the bed and pulled her to a sitting position. Arvay did not help him, but she did nothing to resist him either. She let herself be hauled to her feet and hugged.

Without a sound Jim began to unloose her clothes and to handle her like she was a little child. Arvay was warmed and began to help out. In her nightgown, she stood looking diffidently at Jim for a while, then made the first step.

"Wouldn't you ruther us to go out on the porch to sleep, Jim? It feels kind of hot inside here to me. Come on."

Timidly, she took Jim's hand and led the way. Jim gripped her hand hard and followed her with lighter movements than he had used in the bedroom. Arvay believed in her porch again. Jim was still willing to be with her there. No sooner did she step through the French doors than she felt strong again, and went on to bed.

In the gentle darkness with the spring perfume drifting through, and the voices of nightbirds charming her ears, Jim near at hand on the other bed, and the comfort of her body, Arvay could hunt and find her way back to light and warmth.

Of course Kenny was a good and loving son to her. He would not have gone off sudden like that unless he had a reason. Kenny meant to be loving and kind. What was his reason then? Arvay searched and searched for a sacrifice and could find none unless she put it on the Corregios. She could not risk accusing them to Jim, but she could use and handle them as she pleased if she didn't talk out loud. She was free to

controverse all she wanted to in her mind. Kenny had jumped out and gone up North to be his own man.

That Felicia, no doubt put up to it and prompted by her mother, who would naturally want her to luck up on a good, nice white boy to marry to. And naturally she would go her length to tie up somebody like Kenny. Sure she would. Her Mama would make her see that she couldn't get to Kenny and handle him like she wanted to as long as he was under the influence of his Mama. So the first thing she had to do was to talk him into leaving school and going away off somewhere on his own. Handle his own money and do as he pleased. Then they could turn and twist his poor young mind any which a'way they pleased, which was to skull-drag him into marrying Felicia and letting her handle all his money. Oh, it was as plain as day!

Lying there in the dark on her day-bed, Arvay resolved to deal with Felicia and her mother and handle them anyway she pleased. In order to hate deeply and completely, one must have an image stripped of everything but that which lends itself to scorn and hate. Arvay had thought of herself since childhood as a soldier in the army of her Lord. A soldier of the Cross, and a follower of the Meek and Lowly Lamb, never once, in all these years, and hearing the expression as often as she had, the contradiction in the term. Who was the enemy to be assaulted without mercy and exterminated? Who else but the folks who did not accept the Prince of Peace and Him Crucified?

Felicia and her mother were nothing but heathen idolaters, and not to be treated white. Arvay proceeded to set up images of them among the African savages and heathen Chinee. They were not fellow-humans, nothing of the kind. She stripped them bald-naked and mocked at them. They were as stark-naked as a jay-bird in whistling time, and Christianity was the gospel of sufficient clothes.

She ought to know. She had heard the accounts of the foreign missionaries often and again, and she was one who had paid strict attention. She had sympathized with these martyrs for God who suffered themselves to be sent far, far away from a well-cladded Christian country to those heathen countries, where, for not knowing Christ in the pardon of their sins,

folks went brazenly around with all kinds of things right out in the open.

The poor suffering missionaries had not come right out with certain words, but they made it plain enough for anybody to understand that their sad duty was mostly in looking conditions over, praying over conditions, and then telling the benighted heathens for Christ's sake, to cover conditions up. Every letter that the missionary society got from the missionaries had a plea in it for more covers.

And right here, in these United States, a Bible land, and a praying and gospel country, were these two naked huzzy-heathens trying to pass themselves off as folks, white folks at that, and doing their level best to tole her son off from her. They were no different from that awful Herodias and her daughter Salome who had got John the Baptist killed for nothing. They had been put in the Bible to warn folks against just such sluts as Felicia and her Mama. Babylonian females with no God in their hearts, and no weapon against evil in their hands. Just out to bring ruin and destruction on widows and orphan-children. That back-sliding Corregio woman was no doubt right at this minute getting ready to drag her low-down self and her trashy daughter up to New York running after Kenny. Maybe the poor boy went off like that to get away from them. No telling. And go up there, like that Salome, dressed in nothing but veils to tempt the poor boy with her body. Arvay shuddered at the picture, for her interpretation of a veil was a skimpy piece of utterly transparent stuff pinned on a hat. And she wouldn't put it past Felicia to go dancing and prancing before Kenny and even chunk the scrap of veil away. A'jumping and a'wringing and a'twisting herself with her naked legs flinging every which a'way. You could be bound that they wouldn't be crossed at all. And no responsible person around to lay a halting-hand upon her. And his Mama not on hand to lead the poor boy away.

Arvay shook and shuddered at her home-made picture. It was horrifying to her, but strangely brought her comfort. She could reconcile. Her baby hadn't gone off from her of his own will and was distant from her only in the flesh. Furthermore, the wickedness of those Corregio females was too awful. God didn't like ugly, and neither did God eat okra. You

could get too slick for God to stomach you. Therefore, He was bound to take her part against wicked evil. He just wouldn't put up with a thing like that. Felicia and her Maw would catch it and catch it good! No doubt about it. Kenny would soon need his mother's care again and be back home. She could see him right now lounging around on her porch with his long-legged, good-looking and joking self.

Sure of her victory, Arvay felt better right away. She did not even hate the Corregios anymore. Foreseeing their sorrowful fate, she was inclined to feel sorry for them. They didn't count as her enemies anymore. To complete the banishment, Arvay reached up and turned on the light over her head and took a pleased look all around the porch. Hearing Jim stir a little from the influence of the light, Arvay cut it off quickly and went peacefully off to sleep.

Chapter Twenty-Three

Arvay woke up that morning in August feeling sluggish and irritated. She felt irritated because she felt empty-handed and sluggish. She had been feeling that way off and on ever since Kenny had gone up North. Arvay had no arrangements for spending idle time. She did not read things, and was not even given to fancy-work. Her life had been patterned to serve and now there was nobody for her to wait on and do for. Her impulses were balked and it made her sluggish in her mind. That called to her mind that she was not as young as she used to be.

Jim was up and out of doors a good half hour ahead of her. Even before she put her feet to the rag rug, she could hear Jim and Jeff Kelsey, Joe's third son, laughing boisterously out around the back door and it irritated her. The contrast to her own feelings this morning was painful.

What in the world did they find to skin back their gums and sniggle over to all of that, Arvay wondered, as she got into her underclothes. Giggle! Sniggle! Skin back their gums! Cackle! Must of found a mare's nest and couldn't count the eggs.

As she flung on her housedress, she made up her mind to go out in the kitchen, and by the way she acted, put a damper on all that. She hurried herself to get to it. Then she caught herself and walked slow. It would be better if she let on that they themselves had got her out of humor by the foolishness they were carrying on. She would go about her business of fixing breakfast just as usual, then wait till somebody said or did something that she could take exception to, and turn their dampers down for 'em good and proper.

Jim and Jeff were outside the kitchen door under the tree just as she had thought. Instead of going to the door and passing the time of day as she ordinarily would have, she made a great clatter of putting fresh water in the kettle, lighting the stove under it, and measuring out the cup of grits to cook.

"Mawning, Miss Arvay," Jeff ventured with a hesitant smile as Arvay came near the door. "You looking fine as silk."

Arvay more grunted than spoke, and Jim looked up at her in surprise. "What's the matter, honey?" Jim asked with some concern. "Don't look like you're feeling so good this morning."

"How can I when I get woke up with a whole lot of whooping and hollering around my back door?"

"Oh, that's too bad, Little-Bits. It wasn't intended. Fact of the matter, I had the idea that you was woke before I was, and was just laying there sort of resting. Jeff ain't been here but a very few minutes. But I'm ever so sorry if we woke you up."

Jeff said nothing. He looked uneasy, and fumbled around with the pruning tools that had been brought from the shed. He began to bunch them together to go away from the door. The laughter that had lit up his face faded from the hair-line and died out finally under his chin.

"Oh, then I'm a liar!" Arvay snapped. "I reckon that I ought to know whether I was asleep or not. Tell me!"

Jeff grabbed up the tools and went on away from there. As he neared the line of the grove, he cast a look over his chunky shoulders at Jim that said, "I ain't deserting you, Boss, but you know how things is. Around that back door ain't no place for me right at present."

"Hold on there, a minute, Jeff!" Jim called after him, and Jeff halted at the line of the grove and waited. "I ain't through telling you what I want done."

Jim joined the husky young Negro and after a moment of embarrassment on both sides, they began to laugh.

"Look like Ole Miss got up on the wrong side of the bed this mawning. Whew! I'm due to be scarce around your house today."

"Her feathers seem to be ruffled about something, though I ain't got the least idea what it is. But she'll be all right in a minute or so."

"Good mawning, Boss!" It came in a well-known baritone voice from behind, and Jim turned to see Joe inside the side gate and approaching in a good-humored roll.

"Come on over here, you trashy rascal, you! I got you fair

and square this time, and I aim to put you to work. Haul it on over here."

The men disappeared down in the grove somewhere. Arvay placed the bucket of fresh eggs handy, but before she broke any in the skillet of hot ham grease, she went to the door and called. She had got in her lick and she felt better already. She was fixing enough so that Joe and Jeff could have something too.

In a few minutes, Jim and Joe appeared at the door. Jim came straight on in, scraping his feet on the steps before he stepped into the kitchen. He pulled her ear playfully as he passed her and fled into the bathroom from her pretended lunge at him.

"Look out for yourself, Joe, the best way you can!" He yelled back in mock alarm over his shoulder. "It's a bear-cat aloose in there."

He returned in a few minutes with his hands washed and his hair combed a little, and took his place at the table. Arvay saw Jim and Joe exchange winks, then Joe's hat came scaling into the kitchen and landed under the table.

"If it don't get throwed back at me, I know that it's safe to hang around."

"Aw, come on in here and set down, Joe, and quit your foolishness!" Arvay scolded. "What become of Jeff? Don't he want nothing to eat today?"

"I'll go let him know," Joe said smilingly. "Jeff sure would feel hurted if I didn't. He ever favors his guts."

Jeff and Joe came back together after a while, and settled out under the camphor tree. Jim felt devilish and began to tease Joe again about working in the grove that day.

" 'Course I don't expect to get a lick of work out of you." Jim kept it up. "You ain't hit a lick of work since we closed down the still, and you don't want to see no work, nor even hear-smell of none."

"Well, you know, Mister Jim, I'm a business man, and keeps my arrangements in my hand."

"Naw!" Jim feigned great surprise and interest for the sake of the play. He glimpsed a faint grin running around the edges of Joe's aging face and was prepared to be amused. "Back your crap."

"Well, you recollect when we first shut down the still, always being more of a business man than anything else, I opened me up a grocery store to sell things."

"Before you start that lie, Joe," Arvay broke in, "you and Jeff come on inside and get yourselves a plate of breakfast. It'll be kind of cool there in the doorway."

The plates piled high with soft grits, fried ham and eggs, and the coffee pot on the floor by the door, and nothing more to eat in sight, Joe protested to Arvay that that was enough. Please don't offer them anything more. Jeff took his to the bench outside under the tree, but Joe sat down in the door. Taking whole fried eggs at a bite, and ramming them with chunks of grits, Joe smiled through his charge, set down his plate and went back to his narrative.

"Yeah, I remember when you opened that store," Jim pushed the tale along. "But if I remember correctly, it didn't last you very long."

"That sure is the evermore truth, you'se telling, Mist' Jim. What with folks trading in them big stores downtown, and me crediting so many that did buy from me, and my big family eating out of the store, I used that place up in no time at all."

"What you didn't swap off for coon-dick," Jeff flung in from the outside. "Case of canned tomatoes or corn for a gallon of moonshine. It couldn't last long that a'way, Paw."

"Hush up! You got that talk from your Maw. That's what Dessie claims, but I know better. I never done nothing like that at all . . . not more'n eight or nine times."

"So what finally become of your grocery-store, Joe?" Jim asked with exaggerated interest.

"Oh, well, when things got pretty low on the shelves, and with Dessie 'buking and dogging me all the time, when a Crack—I mean a white man from back of the woods over towards Davenport come along one day and offered to trade me a half a dozen shoats able to crack corn for what I had in the store. I swapped him, lock stock and barrel and he had the store and I had me some hogs. So then I was out of the store business and into the hog business, and figgered that I had done beat him outa some fine hogs, and could make me a independent living out of raising hogs."

"And that's a mighty good business, Joe, if it's handled right. You make much on your meat?"

"Funny thing, though, Mister Jim. Them hogs must of been crossed with hound-dog or gator once. Man, they could eat! I mean they could do a mean piece of biting, but look like they never put on no meat. 'Course, I found out that hog-shorts was kind of high, and I couldn't see my way to laying in too much at a time with the money that I was handling along in then. Them crossed-up hogs didn't gain none, but they lost a'plenty. They got to walking kind of lap-legged and squealing so till I couldn't get my night rest. First, they reared up and squealed. Then they stood still and squealed, then they took to laying down and squealing right on. Got me sick and tired of hearing them take on like that. So when the widow-'oman cross the railroad tracks but sort of on the outskirts, come over one day and offered to swap me a dozen fat chickens for a half a dozen poor hogs, I took her right up on it. Look like she didn't mind paying out money to pour shorts into them hound dogs on hog frames. So she had the hogs and I had the chickens. I was out of the hog business and right into the chicken business."

Jim threw back his head and laughed and laughed. Not a grin out of Joe though. He was acting out a drama of misfortune, and he had masked his face to fit the part. Until the curtain fell he was a modern Job, and suffering many things.

"So how did you make out with your chickens, Joe?" Jim asked it very seriously.

"Well, suh, look I must be born for bad luck. Here I was figgering on taking them twelve chickens and running 'em into a big chicken business. When them hens laid, I would set them eggs and hatch off a whole heap more and then from them hatch off still some more and really be in the business in a great big way. But first off, it seems like them devilish chickens was in a moult and wouldn't be laying no eggs for quite some time. Then somebody looked 'em over and told me that them white narrow-made chickens didn't have no habit of setting. All they did was lay eggs, that is, if they ever got around to doing some of it. They didn't had no feathers on 'em right then to amount to nothing, and they wasn't laying a frazzling egg, but they sure had they appetites along with

'em. By the time I found out how I had been beat out of my hogs, them greedy-gut devils had done et up all the feed I had on hand. They was eating up more feed than I could afford with the money I was handling just in then."

Joe remembered to feed himself heartily for a minute or so, then went on. Arvay was surprised how entertained she had become in a tale that she knew was not more than half so.

"So what become of those poor chickens?" she asked eagerly.

"Them chickens et like mules, Miss Arvay, but I say this for 'em, they had mighty good manners and nice behavior. Smart and sensible in they heads, too. You could make 'em understand. Without me even mentioning it to 'em, they seen that I was doing the very best I could to help 'em out. When I come across a nice green patch of grass out in the country like, I always went right home and took 'em out there and give 'em a chance to crap a nice mess of fresh grass. They could catch all the grasshoppers and worms around like some meat to go along with they greens. They seen that I was willing to divide with 'em what I had. It got so, that all I had to do was to go out in the yard, and they would lay down and cross they legs, making it convenient for me to tie 'em up and carry 'em to where I had done found something for 'em."

"Hush, Joe, hush!" Arvay commanded in all good nature. "I done heard a gracious plenty about you and your business head. You ain't going to hit a lick of work your ownself, so shut up and let Jeff do something."

Joe laughed and cleaned his plate, and poured himself another cup of coffee.

"No'm, I don't speck I will do much long in these dog days. I wouldn't exactly say that me and work had words, but we'se sort of at variance, you might say. Then too, I'm knocking along in years. I'm near abouts old enough for your daddy, Miss Arvay. Anyhow, I done raised Kenny and trained him to make a good living. I done done my share."

Arvay felt the same painful twist that she had felt years ago about Joe and Kenny. Then she took hold of herself. It wasn't right to feel jealous that way. She saw now why she had been so set against the music. It gave Joe a hold over her boy that made her feel excluded.

"Between me and you, Miss Arvie, we sure pulled that boy through, didn't us?"

Arvay shook her head slowly. "You mean you did, Joe. You learnt Kenny all that your ownself. I don't know the first pick on a box."

"That's where you'se ever so wrong, Miss Arvay. 'Tain't everybody that can learn music like that. Kenny took to it because he brought that talent in the world with him. He got that part from you. He just naturally worried and pestered me to death to teach him. I knowed that he couldn't help hisself. What's bred in the bones'll be bound to come out in the flesh. Yeah, that boy come here full of music from you."

"I always thought about Kenny as taking after Jim," Arvay said as if she were talking to herself. Joe looked at Jim and gave a great guffaw.

"Mister Jim? Why, Mister Jim couldn't even tote a tune if you put it in a basket for him. Looks, yeah, but that music part he takes right after you."

Arvay thought a minute, then her face lightened. "You could be right at that, Joe. I ever loved to hear and to play music. I took to it just like Kenny did when I was a chap of a child. And just like you say, Larraine never could learn none. Only different from Kenny, I had small chance to learn much of it. I ever wanted to learn more though. I know that I could of learnt a lot more than I know if I had of had a chance." Arvay sat quietly for a minute and her face lighted timidly. "Yeah, I guess, I hope, that Kenny did take his music after me."

"Couldn't be nobody else, Miss Arvay," Joe said positively. "And it sure is a noble gift to have. I learnt what I know by the hardest, but you and Kenny is just gifted to that. It's a shame and a pity that you didn't have more chance."

"I thank you, Joe," and Arvay smiled diffidently. "And I want you to know that I'm ever so proud about the way Kenny is making out. I'm glad too that he appreciates you and what you have done for him enough to send for you to be with him up North there. Kenny would look for you to come looking nice and clean, and I would want you to go that way too, Joe. How you fixed for something to put on up

North? Jim's got a shirt or two that he could spare, and I reckon we could see to it that you get a new suit of clothes."

"Thank you so much, Miss Arvie. You'se mighty kind and thoughtable like. I is sort of low on changing-clothes, since you make mention of it."

Jim snatched out his watch and brought the meeting to a close.

"Quarter to eight. You all through eating, Jeff?"

"Them few little mouthfuls *been* gone too long to talk about," Jeff laughed. "I'm ready for the question. Let's go!"

"You come on too, Joe. Come on and keep us company some. You ain't no good for nothing else."

"You gwan and leave Joe here with me. I got a few things to give him, and I got to hunt 'em up."

Arvay wasted no time. She was concerned about her son. Joe was to see to it that Kenny behaved. As she charged Joe to keep a stiff hand over Kenny, she moved around briskly searching through Jim's things and coming back with an accumulation of shirts, ties and underwear for Joe.

"You better take these, Joe. Jim's got more than he can wear out anyhow. And Joe, you being one in the family and knowing how I tried to raise my chillun, and how I want 'em to behave, maybe it would be better for Kenny if you was to stay up there with him until he takes the notion to come on home. See to it that he behaves himself and walks in the right way just like I would do, hear Joe?"

"Yes Ma'am. I'll sure hold his feet to the fire and keep him straight. Without a doubt, Miss Arvay. You know that Kenny ever would mind me. It'll be just like you was there."

Arvay made a slight dissenting movement of her body. It was not that she doubted Joe, but nobody and nothing could be the same as a mother's care.

"He's still a baby, Joe, and more particular, my baby-child. He ain't no hard grown man to be off by hisself like that. Don't care what he say, you go with him and stand by him, Joe, and prop him up on every leaning side. Don't allow him to forget his principles and his raising. And if he should mention anything about returning back home, you encourage him to it, Joe, will you please?"

"Sure will, Miss Arvay. It wouldn't do for him to be up there among strangers and out of work. Don't you worry none. We Meserves'll look after one another."

Arvay was comforted to think that "Uncle Joe" would be there with Kenny. She knew so well how much Joe loved her boy. Still and all, it was not the same as Kenny being where she could do for him herself. However comfortably Kenny might be making out up there, her arms were still empty and her hands had nothing to do. With Earl dead, Angeline married off and needing nothing, Kenny up there doing so well and not calling on her for a thing, Jim off from home so much with his boats, there was little for her serving hands to do. She felt like a dammed-up creek. Green scum was covering her over.

Thinking like that, the lift that Joe had given her was all but dissipated even before he left the house. She felt unnecessary. To take up the slack, Arvay decided to make a big potato pone for Jim. He ever loved it, and it took up a lot of time and called for work. She got out a big baking-pan, washed off a mound of sweet potatoes and started to grate them. The food-chopper would have done it easier and in a third of the time, but she wanted the feeling of doing. She peeled and grated with great care, fighting against that sluggish and lonesome feeling.

That was what Arvay was doing when she heard Jim yelling for her around three o'clock.

"Arvay! Arvay! Run here quick! I got something to show you! Run!"

Arvay did not run, but she walked very fast. From Jim's voice, it sounded like some kind of alarm.

Following the direction of his voice, Arvay hurried south through the grove. About midway, she saw Jim standing alone with his back almost to her. He was fooling with something that she couldn't make out until she was in twenty or thirty feet of him. Then she saw and stopped dead in her tracks.

Jim had the biggest diamond-back by the neck that she had ever seen, and the snake was trying to get aloose. Jim was holding it out at arms' length from him and laughing. The snake was trying to coil itself around his arm. It was eight feet

long if it was an inch, and being a rattler, thick according. Arvay had a deep-seated fear and dislike of snakes. Any kind of a snake. She shrank from worms even because they reminded her of snakes. She avoided touching the shed skin of a snake, even with her shoes.

"A snake! Jim! My God a'mighty, Jim! What you doing with that thing up in your hands?" Arvay screamed this out in jerks. Her heart was thumping so that she felt stifled.

Jim looked at her fright and chuckled. "Going to put him in a box and . . ." Jim had to halt to struggle with the reptile to keep it from coiling about his arm. "Jeff . . . gone to the barn . . . to get me a box."

Successful for the moment, Jim turned a bragging, triumphant face on Arvay. She could tell that he was expecting her to admire what he was doing. Just like a little boy turning cartwheels in front of the house where his girl lived. But this was nothing to be fooling with. Supposing that thing got a-loose. The thought of that possibility frightened Arvay so that she began to grow numb. She could see the lightning-like strike of the big head and feel in her own body the fiery pang from the long, curving fangs. And for a thing like that to happen to Jim. Oh, it was too horrifying! Then from her fear and pity, Arvay grew angry. Why would Jim do a thing like that, frightening her to death for nothing? It was all so unnecessary. If it happened, it would be her instant death. She could not bear to see it. Weak and trembling all over, she closed her eyes in dread.

But she could not refrain from looking, and she opened her eyes a moment later on a truly frightening scene. The writhing snake struck Jim's middle with the lower third of its body. Almost too quick to follow, it wrapped around and anchored. With horror Arvay saw more and more of the thick and powerful body ripple like water and crawl around Jim's waist. Two solid coils of awful beauty around Jim's middle, and Arvay, feeling faint, could see them tightening down.

With her mouth open and dry, Arvay's eyes flew to Jim's face to see what he was doing about it. Jim was no longer laughing. His lips began to slide back from his teeth. Arvay saw why. The tight coil about Jim's waist was terrible, but it was not the worst. The rattler was freeing its head, and Jim

was grimly putting every ounce of the strength in his hands and arms to hold onto the neck of that snake. It was unbelievably powerful, and Arvay saw the big flat head being almost imperceptibly but surely withdrawn through Jim's two clutching fists. The tip of the mouth slid down and disappeared within the upper hand. With a steady rhythm, the body of the snake quivered around Jim's waist as it exerted all its power backcrawling and straining to free its imprisoned head.

Jim's face was a straining, gasping horror now to Arvay. Hair falling over his forehead, big veins standing up in his face and neck, eyes dilated with fear and pain, and sweat pouring down in great drops.

Arvay never knew what happened to her then. She saw the imminent danger to her husband, her great love, the source of all the happiness that she had ever known, the excuse for her existence. And in this terrible danger, she went into a kind of coma standing there. Fear surrounded her about. She saw as through a casing of glass. She heard Jim faintly.

"Ar . . . vay! Help . . . me." It was breathed out on agonizing gasps.

In her consciousness Arvay flew to Jim and slew that snake and held Jim in her arms like a baby. Actually, Arvay never moved. She could neither run to the rescue nor flee away from the sight of what she feared would happen.

Then, after an endless time, Arvay heard the thump of running feet and heard Jeff scream, "My God, Mister Jim!" and Jim's agonized answer: "Jeff! . . . Oh, Jeff!"

Jeff was there and the covered box discarded on the ground. And Jeff, his prominent behind setting far out, had grabbed the snake by the tail. His strong white teeth, bordered by blue gums were snarled back in fear and rage as he threw his strength into pulling and unwinding the coils by stepping rapidly backwards around Jim and destroying the purchase of the reptile. Maybe two or three seconds that seemed like years to Arvay, and Jeff breathing loudly through nose and opened mouth asked, "Got a safe hold on his head now, Mister Jim?"

"Yeah . . . Jeff."

"I'm going to fling him. Get ready to leave go the same time I do."

Jim, with the pressure removed from his body, took a second to fill his lungs with air. Then he whispered more steadily, "Ready."

A quick and violent movement of the arms and bodies of both men in concert, and the huge rattler sailed through the air and thumped to the right, a good twenty feet away. Arvay was sure that it would be killed by the fall. A stunned minute, then it went into battle position with a movement so smooth and quick that the eye could scarcely follow. The quivering tail was sending out that ominous sound.

In her relief, Arvay felt to run and fling herself upon Jim and hug and cry in relief and thanksgiving, but Jeff was ahead of her. He looked at Jim, waving on his feet, and flung a brawny arm across Jim's back and steadied him until he could well steady himself. Two or three minutes at the outside while Jim breathed deeply. Arvay found herself, too, in that time and took a step forward to satisfy her mind of the miracle. If she touched Jim, then she would know that he was really alive and saved.

But Jeff gave her a look that halted her where she was. The look forbade her to approach the person of Jim Meserve. It called her unworthy of such an honor and pleasure and privilege by reason of cowardice and treason and trashiness. The look held. Jeff wanted her to know that she had been judged. Then he turned back to hovering and fussing around Jim. Arvay saw that Jim was not even looking at her. In that moment Arvay realized what fear had done to her, and how she looked to those who knew about it.

Neither Jeff nor Jim asked for her aid or assistance in any way. Jim leaned on Jeff, and Jeff never even looked in her direction. He talked, but he did all his talking to Jim.

"I better see you to the house and covered up in the bed. You ought to lay down just as quick as you can, Mister Jim." Jeff hovered and guarded just as if Jim had been an infant child. Just the way Arvay wanted to do. "Lawd have mussy, Boss! It's a wonder you ain't dead. Sure proud I got to you in time."

Jim, supporting himself with one arm about Jeff's stout shoulder, took a deep breath and patted Jeff feebly. "Don't believe that I could have held out another minute longer, Jeff.

You're all that stood between me and Old Stony Lonesome. Never had any idea a snake was all that strong."

"Mighty deceiving thing, Boss. Strong as a mule. Lemme get you to bed in the house so I can come back and kill that snake."

Arvay saw Jim remember to be himself. He saw her standing there forlorn with Jeff spitting on her in his mind, and he went to making Jeff's ears and eyes out to be liars.

"My poor wife, Jeff, ain't it too bad that women folks makes such a poor out at running?"

Arvay felt whipped all over with thorns. Jim had not really told a lie with his mouth, but the way he said it and tried to smile it off to fool Jeff was too pitiful. But Arvay could see that Jeff was not swallowing it down. He was nice and polite with Jim, and stretched his mouth both ways towards his ears in a smileless gesture to let on that he agreed. But his prominent eyeballs with the fat top lids purposely kept away from Arvay. The men kept coming slowly to where she stood and farther away from the snake all the time. About ten feet away from her, Jim straightened himself and grinned the best he could.

"I believe that the old man can make it now, Jeff. You must be just about as wore out as I am. Don't you dare to hit another lick of work today. Don't never forget, Jeff, that I got you folded away in the hip-pocket of my heart. Gwan home and get in the bed and make things tough for your wife."

"Thank you, Boss, but first I got to go back there and kill that old snake."

"Don't bother, Jeff."

"Boss! That damn thing is ever so vi-grous! Dangerous as he can lay in his rusty hide. He come durned near taking your life. He's got to go way from this world."

"Naw, Jeff. Leave him be. It wasn't no fault of his. He didn't try to tackle me. I was the one that tackled him. He acted the perfect gentleman in every way. A gentleman, Jeff, puts up the best fight that he's got in him to defend his life and what belongs to him. He spied noble in the fight. He put out the best he had, and it come mighty nigh being too damned much for me. Look back there! He ain't making the

first move to run away. I tip my hat to a fighter like that and leave him be."

"But, Boss, that's a rattlesnake!"

"So I hear, Jeff." Jim laughed lightly as he came up to Arvay. "Let him alone, I tell you! He's a gentleman who never picks a fight, and never is known to run from one that anybody picks with him. And till the day he dies, he is one general that never loses a battle. I like that kind of a heart. I tried him fair, and he was the best. Let's don't take a cowardly advantage and double-teen him. I don't want him to die calling me a coward, and less of a man than he is. I don't know whether you get my meaning or not, but you leave him be."

Jeff was unhappy about the snake, and it showed in his face. Jim looked at Jeff and chuckled.

"Here, Jeff, take this five dollars and gwan home and make your wife wish that you had of worked hard all day. Light a shuck out of here! See you bright and soon tomorrow."

Jeff brightened considerably at Jim, but never once turned his face towards Arvay.

"You sure you can make it on to the house from here, Mister Jim?"

"Just as sure as you snore. If I see myself giving out, my wife will help me along somehow. Bye, Jeff."

Arvay did not *hear* Jeff snort. He thought too much of Jim for that, but Arvay, happening to be looking at Jeff's barrel-like chest, saw it. She saw the print of that snort just as plain as day. The scorn and despisement in it cut Arvay so that she felt like killing him dead on the spot. She wanted to scream out to Jim and tell him, and make him kill Jeff then and there. But what could she say to Jim? Lynch this man for scorning me because I was right there when you were in danger of death, and I didn't even move my hand to come to your assistance, and now you got to make him stop scorning at me for that? No, no, that would never do.

"So long, Boss. See you in the morning."

"Bye, Jeff."

Then Arvay was alone with Jim in the strangeness of the familiar grove, and they had to get back to the house some

way or another, and then when they got there, they had to go inside, and be in there together.

Jim walked along all right. He didn't walk very fast, but he was steady on his feet. Jeff was gone now, and Jim was not smiling any more. They just walked along until they got to the house and went inside. Arvay halted in the kitchen. Jim never paused. He kept on through to the front of the house. Arvay stood around in the kitchen with her arms bent at the elbows, and her hands drooping off her wrists like damp clothes hanging from a nail. She took a few steps one way, and stood, and then after a while she took a step or so in some other direction and stood again. No use in trying to fool with the potato pudding anymore. She couldn't keep her mind on a thing long enough for that. She wanted to just go out on the porch and stretch out, but Jim was up there somewhere.

"Do, Jesus!" and Arvay moved herself a little. "Oh, my Maker! Do, Father!" and Arvay shifted a little here and there about the kitchen, for she didn't know how long. She baked off the potato pone in a mist of gloom. Maybe three times, but twice for sure, Arvay heard Jim at the telephone, but could not make out who he was talking with nor what he was saying. Maybe he was telling Angie what had happened. Maybe even talking to Kenny in New York. Then Jim got very quiet up there, and Arvay decided that he must be lying down.

Towards sundown, she took the fryer out of the ice-box that Jim had killed for her the day before, and put it on the stove to fry, and mixed up a mess of soda biscuits. She couldn't think of much to do, so she took some cold boiled sweet potatoes left over from the night before and sliced them and fried them brown in some bacon grease. Everything was all ready then. She had a good excuse to break a breath with Jim. In trembling fear she passed on through the narrow hall.

Arvay found Jim at last, across the bed in Angie's room. Oh, but it couldn't be so! She stood there in the open door and nothing was said. But Jim couldn't be asleep, because all the lights were on. For the very first time since she had known him, Jim was acting stiff and stout. She was on the point of backing off from the door when Jim sat up and looked straight at her.

"Jim," Arvay trembled out, and then she halted. That look that Jim was giving her, she couldn't make out. He wasn't mad, that she could easily see. One time it looked like he was hurt-ed deep inside, and then again it looked liked he was snurling at her. She tried for a minute, but for to save her ever-dying soul, she couldn't tell which it was. Anyhow, it was sharp. You could stab a breeze of wind with it and it would bleed. Arvay found herself breathing in those short quick breaths, that when dogs did it, the folks in west Florida said that they were "hassling." Arvay tried again. "Jim, I, maybe you . . ."

Jim cut her short. "Arvay, when folks have anything worth saying, they walks in noble and they talks bold." He had on his blue-striped pajamas, Arvay noted. He put his two hands down on the mattress on each side of him in a bracing way, and leaned forward ever so slightly and kept on eye-balling her and waiting.

"I—I just thought I better let you know that supper is on the table."

Jim looked at Arvay some more, and then he began to laugh in a slow, easy way. "All right, Arvay. You had the biggest chance in the world to make a great woman out of yourself. A Past Grand Noble chance. But you crapped out on it and lost the dice. So I reckon now that I will have to do the talking. Take a seat."

Arvay heard just what Jim said. It was not an invitation to rest her feet. It was a straight command. It was in the voice, in Jim's gray eyes, and Jim had rocks in his jaws. With her skirt wrapped tight about her legs, Arvay crooked timidly onto a chair by the wall and faced Jim. She saw that Jim's eyes, face and all over was so charged that involuntarily, she flung up her forearm to ward off a blow.

"Jim! Jim! You ought to give me a chance to say how sorry I is for what went on today. I'm sorry to my heart."

To Arvay's surprise, Jim made no move, and his voice was calm and low. But before he said anything, he gave a short laugh and rested his head in his hands.

"What happened today, Arvay?" And then he raised his head and looked at her and his eyes said that he bet she didn't know. That stung Arvay and she spoke according.

"You grabbing up that rattlesnake, and almost got snake-bit to death, and then just because I didn't know what steps to take . . ."

"See that, Arvay? That shows the difference between me and you. I see one thing and can understand ten. You see ten things and can't even understand one. A person can have very good eyesight, Arvay, and even wear glasses on top of that, but if they get in the habit of butting around with their eyes shut tight, they won't be able to see a thing."

"I was right there, Jim, and seen all that was there to see. Maybe now you aim to tell me that that wasn't no rattlesnake, and you never had him up in your hands. I maybe ain't got all the brains you carries, but I'm here to tell you that I'm not half as dumb as you all make me out to be."

"Naw, you ain't dumb, Arvay. You got plenty of sense if you would only use it. I guess you must be short on spirit in a way. Know what really took place today? No, so I'll have to tell you. Jim Meserve, the man that's been loving you so hard for twenty-odd years, thought that he saw a chance to do something big and brave and full of manhood, thinking maybe he might win admiration out of you and compliments and a big hug around his neck. He knowed all the time how dangerous it was, and that he had a chance to lose, but he was a man in love, so he took the chance. With Jeff around, Jim just barely broke even, that is, with the snake. He lost heavy otherwise. That was really what happened out there today, Arvay."

Arvay could not help from crying. "Jim, you have never known me to make a oath, but I swear that I didn't want you to get hurt by that old snake."

"And I believe you, Arvay, but that only makes things worse. Maybe you couldn't of done one thing to help me, but you could of showed what you was made out of by trying. Even if it was only to show me that you understood my intentions towards you by saying a word or two. I would of felt better even if you had let me know that you saw what I was after, but you hated my guts and then pitched in and helped the rattlesnake out. Not understanding is the part that I don't like."

"Maybe you done got the idea that I don't love you and

want you, Jim, but I declare I do. I don't know what come over me. . . ."

"I feel and believe that you do love me, Arvay, but I don't want that stand-still, hap-hazard kind of love. I'm just as hungry as a dog for a knowing and a doing love. You love like a coward. Don't take no steps at all. Just stand around and hope for things to happen out right. Unthankful and unknowing like a hog under a acorn tree. Eating and grunting with your ears hanging over your eyes, and never even looking up to see where the acorns are coming from. What satisfaction can I get out of that kind of a love, Arvay? Ain't you never stopped to consider at all?"

"A'plenty times. But all I could ever see was that the only holt I ever had on you was the way you craved after my body. Otherwise, I felt you looking down on me all the time."

"I heard that from you, Arvay, way back yonder, and it was a lie even when it was fresh. Look like you never have got over that old missionary distemper. Yes, I craved your body, and can't see a thing wrong with that. What the hell would I marry a woman for if I didn't want her like that? If it wasn't for that, I could just as well couple up with another man for a buddy."

"And you took the advantage of me that way, too. Keeping me ever feeling that way towards you, so you could handle me like you pleased. Yes you did!"

"You're a got-that-wrong, Arvay. You're a high-charged woman and you was born that way. That was all the matter with you before I come along. But in place of looking things in the face, you took and blinded your eyes and took up with that old missionary foolishness to make believe that you was much too nice to feel natural. Like I said, you just ain't given to looking at things, and that is a pity and a shame. Fighting back and holding a grudge against me because I filled the bill in the finest part of our life. I was your man, that's all, just like you was my natural woman. It's a mighty good idea to let God run things. He ain't give nobody a thing He didn't expect 'em to use, your goddamned lap-legged missionaries to the contrary."

"Jim, you say you been loving me so, and I wouldn't understand, but now, you show me and tell me how I——"

"You want to expose yourself by asking me that, Arvay? I used to hope that it wouldn't never be necessary, but you done convinced me that it is, if you're ever to see and know."

Jim leaned forward and rested his elbows on his knees again. His forehead was in his hands, and his shock of black hair fell forward over his fingers.

"I didn't have a damn thing when I married you, did I, Arvay?"

"Well, nothing much to speak of, Jim."

"But with you to care for, and loving you like I did, I got off of that teppentime still just as quick as I could, so as to make a better life for you. I knew that that was all that you had ever been used to, Arvay, but I saw you as due a much higher place. So I got out from there and moved you up a notch by coming down here. It was hard scrambling, Arvay, and I didn't mind that so much. All I ever wanted to hear from you was that you realized that I was doing out of love, and thought of you so high, that I wanted to see you pomped away up there. I never have seen you as a teppentime Cracker like you have thrown in my face time and again. I saw you like a king's daughter out of a story-book with your long, soft golden hair. You were deserving, and noble, and all I ever wanted to do was to have the chance to do for you and protect you. But never one time have I heard you mention that you understood all that."

"Oh, Jim! Jim! I . . ."

"Naw, Arvay. You've had your time to talk and you didn't do it. Let me finish what I got to say.

"You saw me in the ham-scram buying this place and making things as nice and as comfortable for you and our children as I could. I went in with Joe stilling likker, and run a heavy risk of going on the chain-gang to get hold of enough money to put you up closer to where I felt that *my* woman ought to be. I tried to keep it from you, knowing how you felt about things like that, so you'd think high of me and feel that you had done pretty fair in marrying me. When you did find out, you never came to me and flung your arms around me and told me you appreciated the length I was willing to go for you. Naw, you got jealous of the time I had to spend with Joe."

Arvay crumpled and fluttered one hand against her chest but Jim went right on.

"I did my level best to throw my long arm of protection around you to keep you from getting hurt about Earl. I could see what was on the way a long time before you did, but you wouldn't hear to a thing. It would of happened, even up there in west Florida, but that wouldn't have been near so bad as right there where you had to live, and I could see that. But no, you would let that be. Then when he was surrounded, I humbled myself among men to keep things from being worse than they turned out to save your feelings. But if you ever understood that, I never have been made wise of it. You have as good as accused me of helping to get him killed."

"Jim, oh, if . . ."

"And without saying anything to you, I took pains to tie Alfredo to me, so he wouldn't kick up no stink to fret and worry you more than you already was, but you couldn't even see through that. He stood by me like a major and kept down a whole lot of hard feelings and talk that would have been if he hadn't, and you been doing your damndest ever since to break things up. Yeah, I paid for that outfit that Felicia had on at Gainesville that time, and stood all expenses besides, and glad to do it. I was glad that Kenny had sense enough to ask her up there. I wouldn't have no shrimping business right now if it hadn't been for Alfredo being so faithful and pushing things ahead just like everything was his own. But it was all for your benefit that I was getting it done. You've never turned him nor his family a bit of thanks, and you never have had the feeling to even go down and see what I was doing, or trying to do, and you never have said once that you realized that I was scuffling like that to place you higher up."

"How could I, when you never let me know?"

"Some folks, Arvay, would have been awake enough to glimpse and see. And so far as that swamp is concerned, for twenty years it hung over my heart. I saw that it worried you, and I kept on working as hard as I could to get to the place where I could get it cleaned off for you. So when Hatton married Angie, and I seen how bad you felt over it, I put in to make them children pay you back. Hatton's made big money out of the deal, as I knew he was bound to do, but that

wasn't my main reason for sicking him on it. That was done as a honor and a comfort to you, but you soon let me see that you hadn't the least notion why. I had just done something else to fret you. Same way with Angie getting married. Same way with Kenny stepping out on his own. I could see that your glory would be added to, but you haven't give me one bit of credit for love."

There was a shapeless silence crowding around in the room. It was smothering Arvay, and she wanted to say something, do something to push and drive it away, and let her find some way to creep closer to Jim again. Finally, she said what she had said before.

"Jim, I love you. If I don't, I hope God will kill me right now."

For answer, Jim stood erect, flung wide his bath-robe and his body was bare to the line of his pelvis. Arvay screamed. From his short-ribs to his pelvis, was a band of raw-red abraded flesh. The crawling mechanics of the snake applied with such tremendous muscular tension that scoured Jim raw. Arvay saw Jim's lean belly trembling as he breathed.

"Your kind of love, Arvay, don't seem to be the right thing for me. My feelings inside is just how I look outside. Naw, Arvay. I done got my mind made up. I'm leaving you in the morning."

"Naw, Jim, Naw! You know I love you, Jim. So why you got to quit me like this?"

"Because I'm sick and tired of hauling and dragging you along. I'm tired of excusing you because you don't understand. I'm tired of waiting for you to meet me on some high place and locking arms with me and going my way. I'm tired of hunting you, and trying to free your soul. I'm tired."

"You mean to turn me loose to scuffle for myself after I done had children for you, and been with you all these years, and . . ."

"I didn't say that I was tired of taking care of you, Arvay. I'm leaving, yes, but this house, just like it stands, is yours to do with as you will or may. I'll send you something to live on every single week. You don't need to worry over that. I'm pushing fifty now, Arvay, and no use in me hoping no more. I

ever loved married life, but since I've missed it so far, no use in me hoping no further."

"Married life? Good gracious, Jim ain't we been married all this time?"

"Oh, we got the proper papers all right, and without a doubt, the folks around the court-house are more than satisfied. But to come right down to the fact of the matter, you and me have never been really married. Our bonds have never been consecrated. Two people ain't never married until they come to the same point of view. That we don't seem to be able to do, so I'm moving over to the coast tomorrow for good. My arrangements are done made. You can consider that me and you are parted, Arvay."

"Well," Arvay murmured out at last, "what you been pointing out about not loving me ought not to take me by surprise. I never is believed that you really loved me, Jim, so your saying it now ought not to hurt me so, but it do."

"I never said that I didn't love you. I told you just as plain as ever I could that I'm through and done with filling in where you choose to be insufficient. I eat high on the hog or nothing. I don't have no notion of breaking into my arrangements to leave here tomorrow morning, but if I ever see any signs of you coming to be the woman I married you for, why then I'll be only too glad and willing to try it again."

"So, if I'm ever to be with you again, I got to make the first move."

"My meaning exactly, that is, providing you make it inside of one year from this day. If it takes you any longer than that, I won't be expecting you at all. I'm gone like a turkey through the corn."

Somehow, Arvay got out on the porch, where she crumpled on her bed.

Chapter Twenty-Four

T HERE is always room in oblivion. That is one place that is never full. Since Jim had left her, Arvay sometimes felt herself lost in the edges of the wastes. Her days had nothing in them now but hours. Hours that somebody else had gotten all the light and service out of and chunked them away. Old, worn-out, lifeless marks on time. Like raw, bony, homeless dogs, they took to hanging around her doorway. They were there when she got up in the morning, and still whimpering and whining of their emptiness when she went to bed at night.

Only one day out of her week had any significance. Every Monday she received an envelope addressed in Jim's handwriting. It held a money order for fifteen dollars folded in a sheet of blank paper. The fall and the winter had about passed over, but not one word of writing had appeared on that sheet of paper as yet. She tore open the envelope and looked eagerly, but never any writing appeared.

So Arvay began to fear that her life with Jim was over. He had made no move towards her, and for the life of her, she could not seek out and discover what Jim expected of her. There was some hidden key to re-open the door of her happiness, but where and what it was, she could not discover it in spite of her torture.

God and the Devil can relieve their melancholy by the exercise of power. Men, therefore, feel themselves more or less god-like to the extent to which they can create happiness, tears and terror among their fellowmen.

Arvay felt now that she had this vanity stripped from among the nourishments of her life. Her living children were on their own. She had no control over either now. She could neither confer nor deny. Jim had made himself absent so that no act of hers did anything to his days. The day of his departure, he had moved Jeff and his wife, Janie, on the place to look after things, but Jeff let no opportunity pass to have it understood that he was working for *Mister* Meserve and taking orders only from him. This was not the Jeff Kelsey, with

the face like a cherub that had been built onto, when he was a child on this place. Since the day of the snake, Jeff seemed to have little use for her at all.

She went to sleep one afternoon out on the sleeping porch with her face turned towards the wall. When she somehow woke up suddenly and turned her face over her shoulders, there was Jeff standing with a "lazy boy" in one of his big brawny hands, the other hand on his hip, and his face pressed against the screen wire, staring at her. His face was pressed so hard against the screening that his nose was flattened, and his lips were distorted into purple blobs. His eyes were fixed on her and unmoving. Neither did he jump away when he saw her see him.

Traditionally, Arvay immediately thought of rape and murder. That look was so powerful and intense. But as she studied Jeff's face and eyes she got another shock. Jeff was not longing after her body. It was anger and dislike. If only he had his hands on her, he would tear her to little bitty pieces like a rag-doll.

When Jeff turned away it was with a savage abruptness. He walked a few steps and began to slash at the weeds viciously with the lazy boy. With her looking right at him, and Jeff knowing it, he slashed off the tops of some of her verbenas.

"Why, the impudent scoundrel-beast!" Arvay muttered from between pressed lips and jumped up from the day-bed and hurried into the house. "I don't aim to take his sass at all. I'll march right out there and run him off this place!"

But with her hand on the knob of the front door, Arvay halted. Jeff was going to give her a whole lot of back-talk and remind her that *Mister* Jim had put him on the place, paid his wages and gave him his orders. Every Monday, just as regular as pig-tracks, Jeff got a letter from Jim. On three different occasions Jeff had knocked off on Friday and gone to the coast, and Arvay had sense enough to know that it was at Jim's commands. She couldn't fire Jeff—nothing of the kind—and Jeff knew it. In his absence, Jim wouldn't just trust any and everybody on the place. She could only move Jeff by appealing to Jim, and Jeff had the place in the best shape that it had ever been. He took such good care of the grove that Arvay would not have been surprised to catch Jeff out there

with a curry comb dressing down the leaves. She had heard Jim what he told Jeff out there the day of the snake. No, no use in her flying out there. Jim was not going to get rid of Jeff at all.

"Jim's done quit me, and I don't believe that he wants me no more at all. If he did, he would tell me what it is he wants me to do so that we could go back together. That was just his way of doing things. So what am I doing hanging around here for? Just to get something to eat from a man that's done throwed me down? That don't make me out to be nothing. If I looked upon myself in the right way, I would pack my few things and go on back to west Florida where I reckon I belong."

But that was too drastic for Arvay's feelings. Any day, maybe tomorrow, Jim would come driving up and take her to the coast with him. Jim had left her in this house. She wanted to be where she would be easy to find when he came. He might not put himself to the trouble to proag all the way to west Florida. By her leaving, he might not consider it worth his while to even write a letter.

Arvay wished and wished from one point to the other every day. She would follow her pride and go back home to her mother. No, Jim was her husband and she would stay right where he put her. Back and forth. Light and cloud, and always wondering what Jim wanted her to do.

The door bell rang hard before she could hardly take her seat again, and Arvay went back to the door. A tall, skinny, pimply-faced boy had her signing for a message.

Arvay held the yellow envelope as if she was holding a snail. She was afraid that an enemy, a bad enemy, had gotten to her in that envelope. Jim was telling her not to bother. He was in love with another woman and wanted his divorce. No, Kenny was hurt or in some kind of trouble up North. It could be that Jim was sick or hurt and wanted her to come look after him. Lord have mercy! Lord have mercy! Arvay began to open the envelope with fumbling hands. Her relief made her whimper when she read the message:

MAMA SICK IN THE BED. LARRAINE MIDDLETON.

Arvay read it over several times. It seemed a funny kind of a message to her. It told her so little. It didn't say whether her mother was just poorly or ill-sick in the bed. It didn't tell how long Maria had been ailing, nor from what. It didn't say come or nothing. Not even whether Maria was in need of more money. Arvay sat down on the porch and pondered for some time. She wondered if she should wire or write for more information from Larraine. If she wired right back, in a day or so she would know better what to do.

Then Arvay decided. God worked in mysterious ways His wonders to perform. He planted His footsteps on the seas and rode upon the storms. Or so the old hymn said, and Arvay believed what she had heard sung in a church. God was taking a hand in her troubles. He was directing her ways. The answer was plain. He meant for her to go back home. This was His way of showing her what to do. The Bible said, "Everything after its own kind," and her kind was up there in the piney woods around Sawley. Her family, and the folks she used to know before she fooled herself and linked up with a man who was not her kind. Arvay tossed her head defiantly and rhymed out that she was a Cracker bred and a Cracker born, and when she was dead there'd be a Cracker gone. Jim's and even her own children's ways were not her ways. She had tried and tried but she did not fit in. Let Jim and them have their ways. She would go back and let Jim strain with his house and his impudent, biggity niggers his ownself.

Arvay was conscious at that moment that she had not really been trying to find the answer that Jim expected of her. As always, she had been trying to defend her background and justify it so that Jim could accept it and her along with it. She had been on the defensive ever since her marriage. The corroding poverty of her childhood became a glowing virtue, and a state to be desired. Arvay scorned off learning as a source of evil knowledge and thought fondly of ignorance as the foundation of good-heartedness and honesty. Peace, contentment and virtue hung like a rainbow over turpentine shacks and shanties. There love and free-giving abided and not on decorated sun-porches. Even Larraine and her family stood

glorified in this distant light. Arvay felt eager to get back in the atmosphere of her humble beginnings. God was showing favor to His handmaiden.

Arvay got brisk and phoned in a telegram to Kenny. Then she called Angeline and told her, and asked her to please let Jim know. Then she went excitedly about her packing. She was going *home*! Home to the good old times and simple, honest things, where greed after money and power had no place.

Arvay had gotten so used to ease and even a certain amount of luxury, that she took things for granted. She hauled out the luggage that Kenny had sent her as a present and began to pack her things in happy anticipation. Her wardrobe bag, over-night case and combination hat- and shoe-box were of dark-blue leather with her initials on every piece in raised silver. The trade-mark in the rich linings said *Mark Cross*. It did not occur to Arvay that the people she was raised with didn't even know about things like these. At the moment it did not enter her mind that this assembly of luggage had cost Kenny more than a turpentine worker ever handled in a year. That the people whom she was now gilding up had not the means to produce a son like Kenny. That the kind of father that they had had something to do with her children's good looks, and that beauty that everybody gave Angeline credit for was enhanced and made evident by her self-confidence which arose out of assurance brought on by means which Jim had provided. That her natural means had been pointed up by care, clothes and surroundings. Arvay was not analyzing. She was packing frantically to flee away, and to be gone from her married life for good. God was giving her another chance.

Nor did Arvay see the inconsistency in her exclamations when she got a taxi at the station. While the driver was loading her luggage, she stood on the sidewalk and admired around.

"Oh, I see several good changes since I been gone! What's that new building down the street there?"

"Our new and modern hotel, the Stephen Foster. We got two self-service grocery stores now, too, and with this national highway right through here, we even got some tourists

camps. One coming into town from the east and one on the west."

"Oh, that's just fine and noble!"

"Sure is. The lumber is all cut out, and no more saw-mills here now. The teppentime woods is all worked out too, and if you ask me, it's a damned good thing. The folks, white and colored, that follows that kind of work don't have the kind of money to spend to make good business. I'm glad to see 'em gone from here."

"Oh," Arvay said on a less happier note. "How do folks make they living around here now?"

"Well, new ways of using peanuts has been found, and peanuts is a big money crop around here now. They're raising tobacco in a better way and more of it, and a lots of folks are getting well-off at it. Then this new paved highway through here brings in a lot of business for the hotels and the eating places and rooming houses and taxis. We handle much more money than we used to."

"That's nice," Arvay mumbled.

"Certainly it is!" The taxi man was almost belligerent about it. "We got a Junior Chamber of Commerce now, and it's out to bring more business and more prosperity to Sawley. Why, we even got a daily paper now, and it's doing well. Since the Old Gentleman died and Young Brad Cary took hold of things, some good changes have been made, but a lot of these old fogies and dumb peckerwoods don't like it."

Arvay took sides with the peckerwoods in a timid way.

"Still and all, in the good old days, the folks in Sawley was good and kind and neighborly. I'd hate to see all that done away with."

"Lady! You must not know this town too good. I moved in here fifteen years ago and I done summered and wintered with these folks. I hauled the mud to make some of 'em, and know 'em inside and out. I ain't seen no more goodness and kind-heartedness here than nowhere else. Such another back-biting and carrying on you never seen. They hate like sin to take a forward step. Just like they was took out their cradles, they'll be screwed down in their coffins."

The taxi got under way and proceeded eastward and out of Sawley to where used to be the gate of her old home.

The taxi stopped, and one look at the place, and Arvay began to draw back from old times right away. With her own modest but modern home as a yard-stick, the Henson place was too awful to contemplate. And people who held to old ideas shocked her most unpleasantly in the person of her own sister, whom she identified in that ton of coarse-looking flesh sitting on the dilapidated old steps in a faded cheap cotton dress and dirty white cotton stockings.

Larraine was taking a dip of snuff as the taxi drove up, a habit that Arvay abominated, and which she had not seen for years. Larraine lowered her snuff-box, looked the taxi up and down and from end to end with a kind of distaste, and did not seem to recognize the passenger. Larraine just looked with sullen eyes. Her gray hair was bobbed and untidy. Her eyes said that there was nothing in the taxi that she wanted to see at all.

Arvay stood on the ground beside the taxi and revealed herself.

"Why, hello there, Larraine! Look like you don't know me."

Even so, Larraine did not greet Arvay directly. She turned her head off to the right and said, "Carl, Arvie done come. That's her."

A soiled, heavy-set man jerked his head out from under the hood of an unbelievably battered old Model T and flung his heavy features towards Arvay, standing beside the taxi. No! This drab creature could not be the once neat and self-assured Carl Middleton. His face marred and his body shaped by making too many humble motions. His face showed that he was not glad to see her for a moment, then was re-arranged to suit his words.

"Why, hello, little sister! So you did get here, eh?"

Arvay replied in kind, but she was thinking, "If that chuckle-head of yours was a hog head, I'd be willing to work for it for a solid year. Good God! I wonder if I have changed as bad as they have!"

"You want your things put off *here*?" the taxi-man asked and looked at the house and the people.

"Why, yes. Would you be so good and kind as to place 'em on the porch for me?"

Neither Carl nor Larraine said one word of encouragement. There was a loaded and waiting silence as their eyes watched the transfer of the luggage from the car to the dilapidated porch. Larraine did not move out of the way, except to slide a trifle to one side. The man had to scrouge past her.

Arvay had to do the same. Larraine looked upwards at her as she passed. Arvay went on into the narrow hallway, and stood looking in through the open door of the parlor when she heard shuffling steps back of her, and turned to see the shapeless mass and bulk of her sister coming heavily up the steps behind her, followed closely by Carl.

Arvay noted the museum-like arrangement of the parlor in the brief pause before she went on into her mother's room across the hall. She could see and recognize most of the things that she and her husband had sent Maria Henson in the last few years, arranged for display. The strange quiet made her fear that her mother was already dead, and that they hated to tell her. As she turned from the parlor door, she glimpsed two female faces peering at her from the back porch. Those would be Larraine's two daughters. They were mule-faced and ugly enough, Arvay decided as she stepped across the sill of her mother's room. Even in a croker-sack, Angeline would look like their mistress.

The room was very dim and still even in the bright light of early afternoon. Arvay could hear two things: the rattle of cook-pots in the kitchen, and the squeak and patter of rats in the walls. What was worse, she could smell the strong odor of rat-urine over everything. She flew a little angry that Larraine and all those grown children she had, had let things get into such a shape. Her mother was a yellowed picture of skull and skin sunk down in a deep feather pillow in the middle of the bed. She seemed to be asleep or dead. Arvay could detect no movement of any kind. She tipped to the head of the bed and leaned over.

"Mama!"

Instantly the old eyes flew open. One claw-like old hand came from under the cover. The face turned a little towards Arvay, and the old eyes peered.

"Arvie," came over eagerly, but unwilling to believe.

"It's me, Mama. Don't you know me?"

Just then, Larraine and Carl entered and took up positions at the foot of the bed. The old woman seemed not to see them, as she concentrated on the face bending over her. Then recognition, or rather assurance, came into her eyes. The old hand caught Arvay's lower arm, and the old head sank back on the pillow with a blissful smile.

"I winned! I winned!" Maria said weakly. "I lasted out until my baby child got to me. I begged my God to spare me, and He did. But every occasionally, I was skeered I wouldn't make it."

"Mama, you're mighty sick," Arvay exclaimed in alarm, looking down into the face intently. One hand felt the old forehead for fever. "How long you been sick like this?"

"Going on nearly a month, now, Arvie. I was took down awful sick."

"How come you didn't let me know before now, Mama?"

The old eyes looked towards the foot of the bed and then closed.

"I thought that you knowed all the time, and just couldn't see your way clear to come. I didn't feel no ways slighted about it, Arvie. You done took care of me so good ever since your Paw died, till I knowed it wasn't that you didn't care, you just couldn't spare no time to come."

"Why, I just got the wire yesterday evening, Mama, and caught that mid-night train. I'd of been here too long to talk about if I had of known you was sick and needed me."

"Them telegraph folks must be acting mighty loose and careless these days." Carl jumped in very quickly. "I sent you word over three weeks ago. Don't see how it could of missed you like that."

"Never mind," Maria muttered and closed her eyes again. "My baby is here with me now, and you and Larraine will kindly excuse yourselves so I can be with Arvie a spell. I'll call you if I need anything."

Larraine went out slowly, and Carl let her pass him, then followed sullenly, stretching the room door back to the wall as he left.

"Close to that door!" Maria ordered in the strongest voice that she had used so far. "I hates for folks to be standing around eavesdropping me."

Arvay closed the door and came back to the bed.

"I left a paper with Bradford Cary to place in your hands, Arvie, in case I might be gone when you got here."

"A paper?"

"Yeah, a paper fixing things so you could come into this place all by yourself without no trouble of any kind. Mr. Cary fixed it up for me as tight as bees-wax, and it's in his hands until it passes into yourn. He's sure been nice and kind."

"Bradford Cary?" Arvay's face and voice showed her surprise. "How on earth did he come to be helping you out so?"

"Now, 'tain't a thing stuck-up about Bradford Cary, Arvie. Just as easy to get along with as poor folks. Drove out to see me soon's he got back from New O'leans where Kenny played so good and told me all about it. His youngest boy was playing in that same band, and he went over there to hear it and come back bragging on Kenny. Set right down in my parlor and talked with me. Every time he seen anything in the paper about Kenny, he come out and read it to me, and talked with me."

"Well!" Arvay breathed out. "I never would of thought it of Bradford Cary, but I sure think it was mighty white of him to do it. I got to see him and thank him."

"Do that. And when he seen how Carl and Larraine was using me, hanging around just like turkey buzzards to get out of me any little change that I might git hold of, which was what you and Jim was sending me by the month, and then didn't do nothing for me, and I told him that I wanted you to have the place when I was gone, he took and fixed me up that paper so that they couldn't git hold of a thing. You go straight to him and git it when I'm gone."

"Thank you, Mama, that is, if I should happen to be the longest-liver. You might be the one to close my dying eyes."

"Naw, baby, I ain't here for long. All I could do to hold out till you could come. I know so well them limbs of Satan never sent you no word to come. They was laying round here waiting for me to die so they could move in here and take everything. Carl ain't made nothing worth mentioning for ever so many years. Long time ago folks let him know that they didn't want to hear him preach, and he won't do no kind of work, and so his family is terrible absent of things. Just

living off of me, all they was able. Disfurnishing me of the little money you sent me, and piling in here and destroying up the groceries I buy to carry me along from one time to the next one. That's all they's fitten for. Stuff they trashy guts and lay 'round like gators in the sun."

"I can't say that I feel good towards them for doing you like that, Mama. But if they's as hard up as all that, you can make over this place to Larraine if you want to. I can't say that I'm in any pressing need."

"Naw I ain't going to do it nothing of the kind. I wouldn't even give 'em air if they was stopped up in a jug, the no-manners way that they have treated me. Me here old and sick, and ain't able to do nothing for myself, and them with they hands out all the time to take from me. Larraine is done had more than her share. Naw."

"All right then, Mama, have your way. I sure can't feel good towards them for not letting me know."

The old woman tried to speak, hiccoughed several times instead, and nodded her head. When she was able to speak again, she beckoned Arvay to hold closer.

"Feel right here under this bed-tick, baby. Git it out and take it with you."

Arvay felt between the feather tick and the supporting shuck mattress, and drew out a large Manila envelope. She drew out first, two large, slick-printed unmounted photographs. One was of Kenny with his guitar in his hand standing beside a microphone. It was signed, *From Kenny to his darling Grandmother.* The other was a picture of Kenny with his guitar in a playing-position standing in front of the New York band. In both cases, he had that smile on his face. Dressed in a fine-fitting tuxedo and looking very rich. There was a blue rectangle of paper in there too. A money-order for twenty-five dollars made out to Maria Henson and signed by Kenny Meserve.

"This is noble of Kenny, Mama."

"Wasn't it though? Never forgot his old Grandma at all, up there with all them rich folks."

"When did you get it, Mama?"

"The day before I took down sick. No chance to do nothing with it. And I didn't want them gluttonous varmints to

git they hands on it, so I stuck it under me here in the bed. You take it and do what you see fit."

"All right, Mama."

"And he sent all that without me even asking him for a thing. All I done was to write him a loving letter. Mr. Cary wrote it off to Kenny for me, and he upped and done all that. Your chillun's got plenty soul and heart in 'em, Arvie. Look how Angie sends me things every Christmas, and fine things too. You and Jim sure is raised your chaps to be nice and kind. 'Tain't that a'way with Larraine nor none of her whelps."

The old woman gulped and hiccoughed again, and caught Arvay's arm and tried to pull herself into a sitting position, peering pleadingly into Arvay's eyes.

"Arvay, you been ever nice and good to me, but I got to beg one more favor of you whilst I'm still on pleading terms with mercy. I hope that you can see your way clear to grant it."

"If it's in my poor weak power, Mama, it's already granted. Tell me, and if I can do it, I sure will."

"Arvie, I know that I don't amount to much. Just one of them nothing kind of human things stumbling around 'mongst the toes of God. Ain't seldom had, nor neither done what I desired. It wasn't for me to have and to do. My footprints'll be erased off before my head is hardly cold. But, don't care for that, Arvay. I would dearly love to be put away nice, with a heap of flowers on my coffin and a church full of folks marching around to say me 'farewell.' I know that they won't care one way or another, baby, but I sure would love to die knowing that they'd be there just the same. To make pretend-like I'm mighty missed. And please, Arvie, baby, don't take me right from this house to the graveyard and finish with me. Take me to the church and pass me around."

"I'll do it, Mama, just like you say, that is, if I'm the longest-liver. You can put your dying dependence in me."

"Thankee, baby. It's four whole days till Sunday come next, and that's a mighty long time to hold anybody over. But working folks don't have no time during the week days to be at leisure. . . ."

"Don't care what day of the week you might die, Mama dear, you'll be held over and put away on a Sunday. I'll have

big services held over you on a Sunday so everybody that wills can come."

With Arvay perched by one hip beside the pillow and stroking her hand, Maria sank back down in the depths of her pillows with a look of utter rapture on her sunken face. Her toothless mouth had caved in so deeply that the nose and chin seemed about to meet. Arvay saw the thin lips work as if they tasted some delicious morsel as Maria closed her old eyes. There was a look of great triumph, as if the shabby old woman had vanquished life after all.

After a time the old woman stirred, and the second time she seemed to be trying to say something. Unable to understand the faint mumblings, Arvay tried to interpret for her mother.

"Want me to call Larraine for you, Mama?" And Arvay got up quickly to go, but the thin bony old hand clung to hers and held her back. Arvay sensed that it was some satisfaction at her presence that Maria was still trying to express. The muttering and gurgling went on for some minutes, then Maria belched, worked her lips for a moment and was very quiet. Stroking the old hand for a while, Arvay finally looked down and began to look for signs.

Arvay saw that the spark of life was gone, and quickly tipped to the door and called in Larraine. By the time that Larraine, Carl, and the three grown children who were with her assembled in the room of death, Arvay had solemnly folded her mother's tired arms, and was fishing two pennies out of her change purse to close the eyes. She sobbed as she leaned over and performed the rite, not for the passing of the old woman who was old and tired, but that the eyes she was closing forever had looked upon so little that had been joyful. Maria had passed a lonesome visit to this world.

Larraine joined in the crying and dropped down heavily on the foot of the bed, then got up hurriedly either from the thought of sacrilege or fear of the dead, and sat on the big wooden box that held Maria's quilts. Belatedly, her children joined in the keening. "Poor Double-Maw! Poor Grandmaw! Dead and gone! Done left us here behind! Dead and gone! Dead and gone!"

It was a measured mourning like the slow strokes of a

tolling bell for death, and without sing, like the slack head of a drum. It was the traditional chant.

Arvay began to straighen out the covers on the bed a little more and said in a kind of a whisper, "Next thing, we got to see about putting Mama away." The sobbing cut off instantly as if on signal, and they all moved slowly towards the door, as if afraid of being overheard by the shell of life on the bed with the two coppers holding down the eyelids. Arvay, being near the head of the bed, was the last to leave the room. She literally pursued the others outside in the backyard near the wash-pot where they had halted as around a family hearth.

Larraine began to cry hard and deep, and Arvay was touched to her heart. She ran towards 'Raine with open arms, and Larraine met her half way. They clung tight to each other and cried and patted each other with fondness.

"Don't cry so, 'Raine," Arvay consoled. "Mama lived out her time, and she's just gone to her rest. Don't cry after her so hard."

" 'Tain't that so much, Arvie, you child. It's the fix I'm in. I ain't got a thing to bury Maw with. Oh, Arvie, honey, you don't know what I been through! I ain't hardly got changing clothes. Not a dust of meal nor flour in the barrel. Out there in them scrub-oaks where we live ain't hardly fitten for a dog! But I didn't mean to leave Maw lay there and let the rats eat her whilst we went round begging up enough money to put her away. We might git hold of a few boards, and I could git Carl to knock together some kind of a box to bury Maw in. Make her a grave down there in the back of the place like."

"Aw, my God!" Arvay shuddered at the picture. "Don't fret about that part no more, 'Raine. I'm putting Mama away and putting her away very nice. You don't have to bother yourself at all."

"It sure is a help-out, Arvie. Things have been mighty hard with me."

Arvay remembered the mention of groceries, and went for the bill-fold tucked away in the slot in her hand-bag. Fired with sisterly concern and pity, Arvay opened the bill-fold, riffled through until she came to some smaller bills and impulsively handed Larraine a ten. From little economies, from Jim, from Kenny, from Angeline and Hatton, Arvay had over

a thousand dollars in her pocket-book. This was her stake for life when she had boarded the train in Citrabelle.

"Buy yourself some groceries with that, 'Raine. I reckon that'll be sufficient to carry you over the funeral. Then we can talk things over and figger out some better way for you."

Arvay smoothed down the pack of paper money to replace it. She paid no attention to the hungry way that Carl had stared at it, and the two or three steps that he had taken nearer her for a better look.

"Well then, Arvie, since you going to take care of all the expenses, you have the man to make you out a bill, and when Carl gets to pastoring another sizeable charge, we'll be only too glad to pay you back our part."

"We ain't got no part to pay, 'Raine. Your Mama saw fit not to leave you nothing, but to make over this whole place to your sister, so naturally it's her place to put her away. I ain't got nothing to do with the mess."

Arvay turned towards Carl. "I haven't asked 'Raine nor you to spend one cent on putting Mama away. I promised her that I would do it, and I'm not a'going to back out on my word. I'd rather to give 'Raine than to take from her."

"I hope that you don't call that little piece of change that you handed 'Raine money, not with all you got to do with. The more some folks gets their hands on, the more grasping and mean they gets. Naw, I'm clean out of this burial business and I aim to stay out of it. 'Raine, you can act with no sense at all. Give your sister leave to run into town and run up a bill for maybe over a hundred dollars, then look for me to pay half of it and more, when she's got vast money, and then this place on top of that. You take my name right out of it, and leave it out."

"Who asked you to go into any debt to bury Mama?" Arvay snapped. "I'm positive-certain I didn't, because I know so well that you ain't got nothing to do it with. I come prepared to do whatever was necessary to be done. I got a *husband*! He covers the ground he stands on. He ain't never let me know what a hard day means."

Arvay was halted by something that leaped up into Carl's brown eyes. Before, he had merely been peevish and surly. Now he looked insulted and fiery mad.

"As my sister's husband, all I thought of asking for you to do would be to drive in town and notify the funeral home to come and get Mama and prepare her for the burial. If you'll kindly do that, I won't ask nothing more of you."

"Then let that rich and noblefied husband of yours run into town for you. I sure ain't a'going to do it. And my wife ain't a'going and none of my children neither. We got to come under humble submission to you and take your orders I reckon. Put your foot in the road and walk if you want any messages toted."

Arvay stood wordless and amazed at the way things had turned out, and the fierce behavior of Carl. She looked from one to the other of the group to try and find the answer. Did she glimpse a quiet gloating look on Larraine's face? For a second she thought that Larraine looked ever so glad about the falling-out.

"I don't see no need for all this carrying on over nothing." Arvay spoke with calm out of her puzzlement. "I didn't come here to run the hog over nobody, and to hurt nobody's feelings. If I have, I didn't mean to, and I'm sorry to my heart."

"That's what I say," Larraine exclaimed heartily, and crossed to Carl and flung one arm about his shoulders. "With Mama laying in there on her cooling-board, you all ought not to be fussing and carrying on."

Arvay noted that 'Raine did not urge Carl to go to town, however. Instead, she began to drag him off towards the kitchen. Arvay felt too that her way of pacifying Carl exaggerated things. "Come on in here, sweet dumpling, and lemme fix you a cup of coffee and a little snack to eat. You know better than to let yourself get all fretted up like that! Don't care what nobody else do to you, you know that I'm always with you."

The exasperated Arvay stood and looked behind the two ungainly figures as they reached the back porch and creaked across the boards and disappeared into the kitchen.

"Well, people!" Arvay sighed as she looked around at the slyly grinning faces of her nephew and two nieces and felt her face getting hot. When she passed stomping through the back to get her hat, she saw 'Raine through the kitchen door with her arm about Carl's shoulders giving him pity. Carl was

weighing down an old kitchen chair with the back gone, and just taking it. Just like an image being made over. 'Raine acted as if she did not see or hear Arvay when she passed the door. But Carl seemed unable to ignore Arvay's nearness.

"Arvay!" Carl loosed his head from Larraine's fat arm and looked towards the door.

"What is it, Carl?" Arvay halted.

"When you get so that you can speak to me like you ought to, and not like I was some old throwed-away dog, and quit trying to throw up all Jim got in my face, I'll do what you ask me to do. If not, I ain't doing nothing at all."

"You shock my modesty, Carl Middleton, carrying on so ignorant like that, and your wife's Mama laying dead in the house and needing quick attention. Don't do me no favors at all. I can walk to town, and I want you to know that I don't mind doing it, neither. And you keep my husband's name right out of your mouth. Jim ain't got *you* to study about. So far as he thinks about you, you can kiss his high-toned, independent, money-making foot!"

If the look that Carl gave her then had been a bullet, it would have worked her three times before it killed her and five times after. Arvay whirled on off and went into the bedroom where Maria's body lay on the bed looking so peaceful in the face.

But the house was not peaceful around her. There was a mighty kind of scampering, rustling, pattering and gnawing in the walls and seeming from every direction around converging on the room. Placing on her hat, Arvay was struck with such horror that she started to run back to the kitchen and call on Larraine and them for help. Somebody to stand on the watch-wall and guard until she could get back with the undertaker. But she checked herself and began to consider what she could do to protect her mother's face and hands from mutilation while she was gone. Arvay pulled up the sheets, the three heavy quilts and the counterpane over Maria's head and tucked them all around under her body tightly and snugly until the corpse looked like a mummy in its wrappings.

Arvay took up her pocket-book and went on out to the gate with the creeping, jubilant noises in the wall behind her.

A long-nosed, black Cadillac sedan made an almost silent stop at the gap just as she reached it.

"Hello there, Arvay!" A quiet cultivated voice expressed sudden pleasure. After a minute, Arvay recognized that Bradford Cary II was greeting her like that.

"Oh, oh, howdey do, Banker Cary."

"Very glad to know that you're back in town. Thought that was you I saw in the taxi coming out this way, so I asked the driver and he told me. I have been in the habit of dropping out here now and then to see your mother, and as soon as I could get away after I heard that you were here, why I thought I'd make two visits in one."

Arvay thanked him shyly, and also for his past goodness to her mother. Then she told him the news, and of her destination. She was conscious too that by now, all the Middletons were up around the front of the house where they could look and listen.

"No need for you to put yourself to all that trouble, Arvay. We have known each other all *your* life, and we are friends, I'm sure. You just let me take all this bother off your hands. I'll make all the necessary arrangements and give you a chance to rest and settle your nerves. But for God's sake quit calling me Banker Cary like all these Crackers around here. I'm Brad to you, Arvay."

"Okay, Brad." Arvay smiled diffidently. "I leave everything in your able hands, and I thank you all I know how."

"And I know that you have no intention of spending a night in such an awful place as this, Arvay." Cary was looking her clothes and her accessories up and down. "Tell you what you do. I'm going to see the undertaker and make all other arrangements. But first thing, I'm sending that taxi out here to pick you up with your things. I'll speak for a suite at the Stephen Foster for you, and you can walk right in, have a nice hot bath and go to bed. My wife and I will get in touch with you this evening in some way or another. Now, just do as I tell you, and everything will be all right."

The Cadillac moved off smoothly but fast. It almost vanished by the time Arvay looked over her shoulder and back again. In the low voice that Brad used, it would have been next to impossible for any of them to have heard what had

been said, but Arvay knew so well that all of them had been looking as hard as they could. She went lightly up the steps and into the house. She looked in on the well-wrapped body, then across to the parlor where her luggage was piled.

Arvay was sad when she looked around the room in there. Her poor mother had been so proud of the presents that she, Jim, and her children had sent from time to time, that they had never been used. They were all there on display—that blue-worked chenille spread with the peacock in the center, the set of dishes that she had asked Jim for six years ago—rowed out on the mantelpiece, table and what-not to the most showy advantage. The bath-robe and bed-room slippers from Angeline. The set of plated silverware that she had sent in Kenny's name two years before because her mother had hinted that she had never owned a piece. House-dresses, tablecloths, bath towels, and things like that. As much as her mother made patch-work quilts, the sewing box with all its fixings had never been touched. The various photographs of the Meserves at different ages were arranged on top of the dilapidated old organ, and around the lamp on the center table.

There was only one object on display which Arvay did not recognize. It was a cheap celluloid soap dish on the lower shelf of the what-not. 'Raine or some of her family must have given Maria that.

Arvay was called from her mood of pity by the honking of the taxi at the door. She ran into the bedroom and retrieved the Manila envelope from Kenny to Maria from where she had hidden it and ran to the front door and asked the taxi-driver to take care of her luggage.

As Arvay was stepping into the taxi, the undertaker's conveyance arrived and Arvay took time to lead the two men into the bedroom and see Maria's body unwrapped and deposited in the basket. The owner of the funeral home was along himself, and most deferential.

"I won't hold you up for but just a minute, Mrs. Meserve. But if you would give us her birth date and such little information, we won't have to trouble you again. Banker and Mrs. Cary said that you were not to be put to no more disturbance than was necessary."

When Arvay had given the dates of birth, marriage and death, full name, maiden and married, the director was satisfied. He asked nothing about Maria's children at all. He acted as if he did not see the Middletons hovering around the front yard.

But suddenly Carl came forward to the edge of the yard.

"I ain't ordering no caskets and no coffins neither!" he announced in a most positive and an accusing way. "Don't be sticking my name on none of your bills. Let the folks pay for 'em that's doing all the flourishing around and talking."

"That they will! And the one that's making *this* bill can evermore do his paying. I don't reckon that Banker Cary will feel it necessary to call on you for no help, Reverend Middleton."

Arvay was astonished, but the sight of all the Middletons coming out from their listening posts at one time took her attention so that she couldn't find a word before Carl burst out.

"Mr. Banker Bradford Cary? I seen him here just a while ago talking with my wife's sister, but what's he got to do with it?"

The undertaker fairly reared back. "Banker Cary is a public-spirited citizen. The late Maria Henson is one of Sawley's oldest and one of its most *respected* citizens. He feels that her passing is more than a family affair. She is an honored and public citizen. Things will be carried out that way."

Arvay waved her sister good-bye and the taxi whirled her away. She had that last look of 'Raine looking wistfully after her, with one fat hand which had been lifted suddenly and spontaneously, being sort of arrested in the air and hanging there. Standing there in the weed-grown yard in her shabby dress, starting to be warm and friendly, then withdrawing herself.

Arvay felt grateful towards her sister as she flashed away. But for 'Raine's intervention, she might have been married to Carl. Been the mother of those awful-looking young men and women that he had fathered. Had to get in the bed with something like that! Do, Jesus! Arvay had no wish to go back out there and run any risk of another run-in with Carl. For some strange reason, he was very mean and bitter against her.

But 'Raine had heard where she would be until after the funeral. 'Raine would find some excuse to make it to the hotel. Then they would talk about old times, put hard feelings behind them and be sweet sisters together. Now that they were the only Hensons left, they ought to draw closer together.

But it was Carl whom Arvay saw next day at the hotel.

"Send him on up to my room," Arvay told the bell-hop.

"No Ma'am, Mrs. Meserve. I wouldn't risk that if I was you."

"How come? He's just my sister's husband."

"Yes Ma'am, I know, but he come in here acting and talking so funny that the Boss sent me ahead to bring you a message in private. He says that you better come on down in the lobby so you can have some kind of protection. Mrs. Banker Cary called up lessen an hour ago and said that you was to be looked after real careful and get the best of attention. The Boss don't aim to take no chances on nothing happening to you."

Arvay freshened up and went down and took a seat not far from the desk. She saw Carl rise to his feet from over near the front door. This was a Carl, shabby, but fairly neat. His thinning hair was brushed and laid down with water. Something of the old prideful Carl of nearly thirty years ago was about him. He came towards Arvay with the suspicion of a timid smile on his face.

"Hello, Arvay, I thought that I'd better take this chance of having a talk with you."

"About what?" Arvay asked coldly, the memory of the day before sharply in her mind.

She could see Carl's face change instantly. It got hard, and he sat down abruptly in a chair close by. The manager fiddled with a pen and paid attention.

Carl took a long time to answer. His forearms rested on the chair and his head was thrust forward in deep thought. Finally Carl seemed to whip himself up to a point and said, "I come here in the spirit of good will and compromise, but since you feel to be scornful, I'll let you have it raw. I want that thousand dollars you owe me."

"For what?" Arvay asked astounded. "I hope you don't

think that I aim to give you no thousand dollars to compromise on the place. It's mine to do with as I will or may, and I don't have to compromise."

"Oh, it's your place all right, and that's how come you're responsible in a case like this."

"Like what? I don't know what you're talking about."

"Me getting hurt so serious on your place last night."

"You hurt? How did it happen, Carl, and in what way can I be responsible. I wasn't even there."

"Matters a difference where you was. You're the owner just the same. I was walking across that old rottened-down back porch of yours that you neglected to fix and a board broke under me and I fell through and got crippled up pretty bad. Your own sister said that I ought to get double that, but I thought that I would come myself and make things easy on you. I'm ready and willing to compromise the thing for a thousand."

"A thousand?" Arvay sat there dumbfounded.

"A thousand hard dollars, and mighty reasonable at that. That ought not to be nothing for your high-toned rich husband to raise."

The manager cleared his throat to attract Arvay's attention, rustled some papers and shook his head for her to say nothing.

"Oh, er, Mrs. Meserve, not that I want to butt into your business, but as a hotel man I know something about liabilities. Now, for instance, is Middleton renting your place?"

"No."

"Is he a tenant, that is, working for you and living on your place?"

"No."

"Well, did he come there to visit at your invitation?"

"Naw indeed!" Arvay looked at Carl through narrow eyes. "From what I can learn, he and his family just come there and bunked on Mama."

"Then you don't have to worry about any claims that he might make at all. In fact, he's liable for trespassing on your premises. Turn the matter over to Banker Cary and let him handle things."

Arvay turned a very grateful face to the manager and smiled. "I thank you ever so much for your information." She

tensed her body to rise, but the sympathy for the defeated overcame her. Then there was the memory of the neat, virile, vigorous and confident young man that Carl Middleton had been when she first knew him set against the picture of him now. Arvay was full of pity, and fumbled for some way to make him the gift of a small sum. Say fifty dollars, maybe. She nodded her gratitude again at the desk and turned to Carl.

"You say that you're hurt powerful bad, Carl?" And Arvay began to look him over for the signs.

"I said so and I am," Carl snapped.

"I must say that you don't look it to me." Arvay became slightly tart.

"Naturally," Carl retorted sarcastically. "I been *trying* to treat you like a lady. Where I'm hurt at ain't to be exposed in public."

"Oh! I'm mighty sorry to hear that. But still you don't get around like you was hurt too bad nowhere. For me to take any steps at all I would have to know exactly."

"Well, if you'se determined for me to get common with you," Carl sneered and got to his feet, "it's my behind, and could be inside injuries besides for all I know." He took a step towards Arvay. "I guess now you want me to show it to you."

Arvay did not wilt as Carl seemed to expect of her. "Nope," she answered in a matter-of-fact voice. "My Mama always told me not to look on backlands. I'd rather you went to a doctor and let him tell me what is your condition."

"I been trying all I could to save you extra expense."

The manager snorted at that and the two bell-hops sniggered. That enraged Carl more and he glared around the lobby and announced, "I got me a good lawyer who says I don't have to go to all that rigmarole."

"Well then, Carl, you can just go back and tell that lawyer you got that I'm not giving you no thousand dollars, and he can law me for it all he wants to. I'm in no way responsible, but if you're in as bad a fix as you say, I can tell you something mighty good for a case like that. Get hold of some mutton tallow, then melt it and mix it together with some teppentime and grease yourself good back there."

The manager, the bell-hops and three male guests who were seated in the lobby sniggered.

"Teppentime and mutton-grease!" Carl exploded. "I come . . ."

"Yeah, it's mighty healing and dependable," Arvay confirmed earnestly and calmly. "Can't be beat in a case like that. Now, if it was a burn, you would need some baking soda and mix it good with some wet Octagon soap, and you take. . . ."

The laughter was more public this time. Nobody was pretending to hide it. Carl's anger and chagrin and Arvay's earnest manner made it twice as funny. Also it was plain that Arvay did not know that it was funny. She looked at Carl and all around her and went on.

"But I ain't joking. It really is mighty healing. Takes the soreness right out. I keep it on hand all the time. My husband and my . . ." The howls of laughter drowned her out and Carl's angry voice prevented Arvay's taking up again.

"You, you, female hypocrite you! I come here to get satisfaction for being mortal hurt on your rotten property! I didn't come here for you to teach and tell me how to grease my behind!"

"That'll do, Middleton!" the manager said sternly. A quick look passed between him and the burly porter who had been ostentatiously polishing the brass plates on the swinging doors that led into the dining-room. The porter straightened up and made ready to move forward. The bell-hops went on the alert. The manager came out from behind the desk and took a commanding stand. "I said *that will do!* You have got beside yourself, entirely. Mrs. Meserve is much too important to be handled carelessly, and anyhow, this hotel does not allow loose talk in front of ladies. You have worn out your welcome, and we'd much rather have your space than your company."

Carl glared and frowned at the manager and looked as if he felt to fight, but he went on out without another word. Arvay thought that Carl looked whipped and pitiful as he shuffled out through the big doors. She saw him walking slowly and with his head down as he passed the wide window. The manager stood like a victorious champion of protection until Carl was good and gone, then comforted Arvay.

"You don't need to fret about being sued, Mrs. Meserve.

You sued by him! That's a joke. When Banker Cary got through with him it would be manners and behavior. Ha!"

"I can't see what made him come here and carry on like that. To save my soul, I can't make him out," Arvay said in genuine confusion.

"Oh, the fool is stuck on you, Mrs. Meserve. Sweet on you and cutting the fool."

"Sweet on me?" Arvay looked around in astonishment. "He sure got a funny way of showing it."

"Oh, he just thought up that mention of money after you treated him so cold. Started to blabbing soon as he got in here about how he courted you when he first came to town."

"Courted *me*? Why, this is my first time even hearing of such a thing."

"Oh, nobody's paying his talk any mind, but that's what he claims. Said that you were so young that you might not understand and he tried to court you through your sister, but you sent word back and turned him down."

Arvay gave a gasp. "I sent word? Why, he's raving crazy." But the phrase said something to Arvay.

"He could be lying, or you never got the message one," the manager said off-hand. "Anyhow he claims that he lost interest in being a big man when he missed you, and lost interest in everything when you married. Makes out that he would have amounted to a whole lot if he could have married you." The manager's lips twisted in scorn and disbelief. "Oh, he ain't just started this whining about you. I've been told that he's been whispering it around for ever so many years. Must have made his poor wife feel mighty fine to hear a thing like that."

Arvay flushed to her hairline. "Never heard nothing as crazy as that in all my born days. Married to my own sister and acting like that. His feelings may be serving him all right, but his common sense must be gone astray."

"Crazy as a bed-bug," the manager agreed sympathetically. "So you see why I couldn't let him up to your suite and you be in there with him by yourself. No telling what the fool might try to do. I figure him out to be plumb crazy."

"I help you to say," Arvay chimed in with a nervous laugh and hurried off to her room.

Arvay fell on her face across the bed and laughed hysterically. It was too funny. Weak as she was, Carl believing that she could prop him up. Wanting to lean on her small strength! Larraine whom she had always looked upon as so self-satisfied feeling so frail of her chances that she needed to steal herself a husband from Arvay. Then both Carl and Larraine felt themselves less than she was. Maybe there were a lot of weak-feeling folks in the world. Weak as she herself was, it was strange to know that people had been depending on her. They must believe that she could hover them.

Still on her stomach across the bed, Arvay reached for a pillow and snuggled it under her head. So Carl claimed that he had sent her a message about marriage. Even if it was true, Arvay had no resentment nor felt any loss. Poor Larraine! No need at all for Carl to ever know the difference, but it was a pitiful thing. Now, he comes hunting her after all these years for a consolation and all she has on hand to give him is some teppentime and mutton-tallow to grease his behind. Teppentime and tallow. If Carl had loved her sure enough all these years as he said, it was a curious end to a long-time love affair. However, poor, poor Larraine! Poor Carl too. Life had funny ways.

Chapter Twenty-Five

NOTHING left for me to wish for except that I wish poor Mama could see how she's being put away."

Arvay looked at the glass-sided hearse, the lavender casket inside that opened out like a couch and the smother of floral pieces. And all the people that old Maria could have wished for were there to pass around and say her a last farewell.

Bradford Cary had really made a big thing of putting Maria Henson away. Arvay was touched and pleased. Her mother's dying wish had been realized. With wet eyes, Arvay went through the funeral with satisfaction and gratitude in her heart. She could not fathom the kindness and goodness of it all, but she was not probing and asking questions of herself nor anybody else. It was so, and that was enough for her. Arvay did not know that the urge to hold public office had been growing in Bradford Cary for the last two years. But he had to look like a man of the people and he was too well known as a monied aristocrat. The association of his youngest son with Kenny in the University band had given Cary an idea, and he had followed it up by cultivating Maria Henson. Months before her death it had spread around Sawley and the county in general of Cary's kindness to her and his attachment for her. Her grandson, Kenny, was assumed to be his product and protégé. Poor people began to think mighty well of Bradford Cary II. He was a big man who made himself one of them. That was ever so much better than one of them trying to make a big man of himself. They began to say that a man like that ought to be in office and looking after their affairs. Cary let on that he was surprised at such a thought and lingered back. Many people began to push and shove him forward.

Maria's death gave him his opportunity and he took it. The local paper gave great publicity to her passing as an old and worthy citizen. The kind of citizen who was the foundation and backbone of our great nation. Clean-living, plain, honest and a devoted Christian. The common people saw themselves glorified in Maria and they loved it. That Bradford Cary was

standing the expenses of the big funeral was spread by mouth. It went faster when it was understood that Cary had refused to let it be put in the paper. He was a good-hearted man who wanted no credit for what he had done.

But even if Arvay had known about the skillful manipulation, she would not have cared any more than Maria would have. Everything had been done in a fine and handsome way. Bradford Cary II had spread his prestige like a gold-worked coverlet over Maria Henson and sent her to rest as she had wished and more. Arvay was moved to her foundations and satisfied. If only her mother could see the hundreds of cars, the casket, the flowers, and the long, long line of people passing around her casket and looking down in her face!

Arvay felt sad at her mother's death, but she returned from the cemetery with happy satisfaction. A sacred promise had been kept. A dying plea had been granted. Maria, who had lived on scraps and crumbs all her life had been put away like a queen. It was some payment for all that she had missed. Bradford Cary, who had never noticed her when she was growing up, now chose to be her friend. The proof was all around her. Introductions to big and important people, dinners and taking all care and worry off her hands. Then putting her mother away the way he did. No, Arvay would not have welcomed any pulling-down whispers about the Bradford Carys.

And with her the feeling lasted. Nearly a year later she read of his entry in the gubernatorial race with great pride and pleasure. When he won, she looked upon it as a personal triumph. She had no idea what a part she had played in Florida politics. She did not realize that she had helped to make a governor of the state.

One thing she did know, however. She came away from her mother's funeral changed inside. Big, book-learnt people had seemed glad to know her and had treated her very nice. They said praising things to her and made her ever so welcome. They complimented her on being a fine wife and mother and seemed to find nothing wrong with her. Maybe she was not as bad off as she had thought she was. It made her feel to hold up her head and to look upon herself.

What put her ahead of Larraine and the other girls who had

come along with her? Seemed like it was Jim Meserve. She had caught the choicest man of them all. How had she managed to do it? The only thing that she could see was her face and her body, and maybe Jim liked her ways too. Then it could be that she wasn't too ugly after all, and her difference from the girls she used to envy was not a mistake as she had thought. Perhaps Jim's hankering after her was not such a burden to bear when she looked around at the lives of her old friends. Certainly the afternoon of her life was more pleasant than the morning had been.

Chapter Twenty-Six

M ONDAY had been in town many hours when Arvay opened her eyes. She saw that it was ten o'clock by her watch. Arvay had had a good sleep and sat up in bed at peace and agreement with the world. She was full of resolution. She was willing to take the blame for any variance with Larraine and Carl and shoulder the job of straightening things out.

With a breakfast of broiled country-cured ham, fried eggs, hot soda biscuits with country butter, and coffee inside her, Arvay set out to make a move. The tasty ham put her in the mind of something. She would make 'Raine the present of a big ham along with a pile of other groceries. Enough to do the family for a whole month and then slip her sister twenty-five dollars for spending change. No sense in two sisters not being thick friends and depending on one another. Arvay considered that she would be wrong to hold anything against 'Raine and Carl. Not having, and never having things made people do things and act in ways that they wouldn't if they ever had anything that they wanted. If she could make it up with Jim, maybe it would be a good thing to talk him into sending for the family and finding Carl and his two sons something to do. Why, they could live in the house in the grove! The very thing.

Arvay felt a happy giving off as she went into the store. She bought a large ham for Larraine and pictured 'Raine's face when she drove up with the load of good groceries that Arvay was taking to her. It was on a second thought that Arvay ordered three more hams to be shipped to her at Citrabelle. She explained to the clerk that you couldn't cure country meat down where she lived. Too warm all the year round. She ordered a bag of paper shell pecans as a present for Jeff and Janie. Let them know that she appreciated them too. Maybe Jeff was not snappy for just nothing. He was not that way with Jim and the children. The fault could be in her. She would show him that she meant him well. Then she ordered one packed for 'Raine and two more shipped to her home.

871

On top of the cases of canned goods and staples that she ordered delivered to 'Raine, Arvay bought a fat hen for chicken dumplings and a lot of fresh stuff to go along with it. She and 'Raine would fix a good dinner and they would all eat together for the first time in many years and have a good time together. Then Arvay remembered how they used to love fried round steak for Sunday morning breakfast and turned back and bought five pounds of top of the round to take with her.

A pleasant picture from her childhood came up before her. The Henson kitchen of a Sunday morning. A pot of soft grits on the back of the stove all ready and waiting. Big pan of biscuits made out and ready to shove into the bake-oven at the last minute. Quart bottle of molasses on the table and the dish of country butter. Big black iron skillet with grease in it waiting for Maria to get through pounding the steak with the hammer. The steak salted, sprinkled over heavy with black pepper and beat and beat until it was tender, then doused in flour and dropped into the hot pan to fry. Thick brown steak gravy with onions in it to go with the grits. Yes, they would have a good old-fashioned Sunday breakfast together. Then after that, she would make 'Raine come into town with her and pick out a couple of decent dresses, and a few other things to wear. 'Raine was bound to feel a lot better when she had silk stockings and got fixed up to look like something.

With the box of groceries loaded in the taxi, Arvay rode along the road happily noting the scene of things. The woods had not the lush, exotic look of south Florida, but there was a sturdy green fullness that was pleasing. Nowhere in the world, Arvay considered, did oak trees grow so fine. The dogwood that she missed in south Florida, the crêpe myrtle and rambler roses before a door. They didn't do well down south and she wished that they would.

"If you will be so kind as to set that box of groceries on the porch for me," Arvay told the driver at the gate, "you needn't never mind waiting for me." Arvay paid the man and tipped him. "I'm mighty much obliged to you."

The taxi drove off and left Arvay standing in the shabby yard and beaming towards the door.

Arvay waited for a sign of life, and seeing none decided that

the place looked mighty quiet, and that everything was closed up so. Carl's wreck of a car was nowhere to be seen, and no smoke coming out of the chimney. They must have run into town for something. She might as well go on in and start the cooking.

The door was closed, but it was not locked. There had been no key to it in Arvay's memory. She turned the doorknob and went inside. The first thing that she noticed was that the old sewing machine was gone out of the hall, and the hat-rack was missing. That made Arvay jerk her head around to look inside the parlor, and she could hardly believe her eyes.

There was nothing in there except that relic of an organ, which had been nothing for years but a rat's nest. Yes, there was something else, but it hurt Arvay's heart to see it. All the pictures of the Meserves were there, mutilated, and trompled on the floor.

The scene was the same in every room. The house had been cleaned out of everything. Even the backless chair in the kitchen was gone. One old fork with the tines bent was lying against the wall, probably overlooked.

The back porch was just a framework. All the sound boards had been ripped off and hauled away. Only the three or four rotten boards were left. The wash-pot was gone out of the backyard, and the three wooden wash-tubs from the wash-place.

In deep anguish, Arvay moved about, stumbling through the brittle dead weeds of the past summer, and suffering without words and without tears. Her soul was sunk in defeat. Her sense of accomplishment was gone. Both she and her dead mother had been robbed and defeated. All that fine funeral was in vain. Perhaps her mother had not got off in her high journey after all. Held back from her flight by such low-life-ted doings. No doubt Maria would get to creeping into 'Raine's shabby shack between midnight and day to frighten the fatal life out of the rascals. Arvay hoped that it would happen. Then no, she didn't. She didn't hope any such thing. She wanted her mother to be at rest at last. She had had enough of dirty, poverty-paralyzed places. Immortal Glory was where she ought to be, and setting down.

Arvay stumbled around, farther and farther away from the house crying, "Mama! Mama! Please don't fault me. I done the best that I know how." Then tears began to run from her eyes. She came to the pear tree that was the farthest to the west and looked down. There was trash piled up around it. She went to the other one, and the big fig tree and looked. They were all the same.

"They're gone, but they aim to come back, I see, and set these trees on fire."

Arvay was scattering the trash away from the trees when her neighbor to the east waved a hand at her and came through the fence. She was a woman about ten years younger than Arvay's mother, and had always been there next to them. She spoke to Arvay very warmly, and there was something peculiar in her eyes.

"You expecting to see your sister and her fambly, I reckon, ain't you?"

"Well, I sort of was."

"I reckon then that you didn't know that they moved out last Thursday. Sort of soon in the morning like. Got some man that raises hogs across the river to come with his truck and carry the things off for 'em. Bright and soon in the morning, it was."

With her hands propping up her lean shoulders by resting on her pelvic bones, the gray eyes bored at Arvay and told her that she understood things. Arvay didn't open up so the neighbor could talk, so she dropped another feeler.

"I was in to see your Maw pretty occasionally after she took down sick in the bed, fetching along a mouthful of chicken soup, and a few soft things that I figgered her stomach could handle. Every time she would be expecting you, and wishing for you to come. I was mighty glad when I seen that you was here."

"And I would of been here long time before if I had of been notified. I got the message that she was sick, and caught the train that very night."

The woman looked at Arvay with belief and pity, then glanced down at the pear tree.

"Look like somebody was getting ready to burn you out in case that you stayed around here and moved in." She wound

up the gray ball of hair at the back of her head. "But I don't reckon that it would happen if you was to go on home. They would treasure them pears and them figs after they was living on the place."

"But they'll never live here, Miss Hessie. Mama didn't want it, and she must of had her reasons, and I don't intend to allow it."

"Them was your Maw's wishes all right. I know it to be a fact. She loosed 'Raine and her fambly, long time before she took down sick. You wouldn't be doing the right thing to whip around and go against her wishes."

"Don't you worry, Miss Hessie. It'll never come to pass. I'll fix it so that even when I die they won't go over Mama's wishes like they please. I don't know just exactly how to go about it, but if any way can be found, they'll never make it."

"With the right kind of folks on this place, it could come to be real pretty, but not wishing to hurt your feelings about your folk . . . Oh, I can readily see that you'se different from them all the way. Don't seem like you was ever born in the same fambly. I hope and trust that they didn't take off Sister Maria's memory-things. She wanted so for them not to come nigh 'em. I know that they wasn't brash enough to take *them* outa that house."

Arvay nodded her head miserably without speaking, and Miss Hessie's eyes flew wide open. "Naw, Arvay, naw! You don't mean to tell me! I can't believe that unlessen I go see it with my own eyes."

Without a word, Arvay turned and led the way to the house. Miss Hessie groaned when she saw the back porch. She grunted and grunted as they went around the house and entered by the front door.

"This looks like groceries you fetched along, too. Umph! Umph! Umph! All that good eatings for folks to do you like that."

Miss Hessie was utterly outraged when she stood in the empty parlor.

"If it was me, nothing would do me but to call the high Sheriff and stuff they rusty hides in jail! That's good enough for 'em, and just what I would do, too."

"Oh, Miss Hessie, I feel so outdone I don't know exactly

what I aim to do. Come on back outside. I hate to look at it no more'n I can help. Poor, poor Mama! Her life-time memories being wallowed and dogged out in a hog-pen!"

"Send the high Sheriff to get 'em back. That's what I sure would do."

"But what would be the use, Miss Hessie? By now, I'll bet they ain't fitten to look at. Slums like them would just as soon scour the floor with Mama's tablecloths as not. It's just like my husband says. He says folks makes a bad mistake when they call places slums. He says folks are the slums instead of the places they live in. Places don't get nasty and dirty and low-down unlessen some folks make 'em like that. Place some folks in what is called slums and they'll soon make things look like a mansion. Place a slum in a mansion and he'll soon have it looking just as bad as he do. It ain't right to blame it on the place. Leave land alone by itself, and it'll grow up into trees and flowers. It don't grow up into slouchy people."

"You sure is telling the truth there, Arvay. Much as 'Raine and Carl and all them big grown children was around here, just look at this place! And it looks even worse now with this big highway passing right by here. This shackly old house tore down, and a little care, and your place could be made to look mighty pretty."

They were out on the porch again, and Miss Hessie stood over the box of groceries and looked down.

"You got fresh meat in here, ain't you, Arvay? I know that you was expecting for it to be used right away, but you got disappointed in them not being here. I better take it on over home with me and fix it for you. By the time you get through messing around over here, you might have a good appetite."

"That's a fine idea, Miss Hessie. Make use of everything except that ham and them pecans. I'll take them down home with me. I'll come and eat with you all, if you don't mind."

"You know so well that we'll be only too glad to have you. My grand-boy, Orrie is home right now. I'll send him to tote that box over for me."

Arvay liked Miss Hessie fine, but right at this time, she was glad for her to go and leave her alone to herself. She tore out immediately for the mulberry tree far down over the brown grass and dead weeds in the back. It was late February, and

the huge limbs and limber branches were nude of leaves. They made a pattern of dark lacings against the tepid sky. But soon now, three weeks at the most, tender green leaves would push out of those tight little brown bumps; badges that the tree put on every spring to show that it was in the service of the sun. Fuzzy little green knots would appear. These would turn out to be juicy, sweet, purple berries before the first of May. But most of all, this tree would become a great, graceful green canopy rolling its majesty against the summer sky. Here had been her dreams since early girlhood. Here, in violent ecstasy, had begun her real life.

Like her Mama's keep-sakes, this mulberry tree was her memory-thing. It brought back to her the happiest and most consecrated moments of her lifetime. As with other mortals, life is full of compromises and defeats with few clear victories to show. Here, Arvay, the woman, had triumphed, and with nothing more than her humble self, had won her a vivid way of life with love. This tree was a sacred symbol. She wished that she could use it like a badge and pin it like a bouquet over her heart.

Arvay flung a challenging look towards the highway. There was the world in shining cars; flying and flashing past. The nation crossing and re-crossing before her tree.

But between the tree and the world there stood that house. Now Arvay looked at it with a scrutiny, and darkened. Seeing it from the meaning of the tree it was no house at all. It was an evil, ill-deformed monstropolous accumulation of time and scum. It had soaked in so much of doing-without, of soul-starvation, of brutish vacancy of aim, of absent dreams, envy of trifles, ambitions for littleness, smothered cries and trampled love, that it was a sanctuary of tiny and sanctioned vices. Its walls were smoked over with the vapors from dead souls like smoky kerosene lamps.

By a lucky chance, she had been carried away from it at a fairly young age, but still, its fumes and vapors had stuck to her sufficiently to scar Jim and bruise her children. There was no getting away from it. It was a fact in truth. If it could still hurt and disease her at that distance and for so long a time, how then could she hold things against Larraine who had never been away? Look what it had done to her and to Carl

and to their children, and here was another crop about to come off from them. The house had caught a distemper from the people who had lived in it, and had then diseased up people. No, it was no longer just a building. It had caught a soul of its own now. It caught people and twisted the limbs of their minds. What was in its craw gave off a bad breath. It stood between her sign of light and the seeing world. It had just about stifled what the tree had given her. The tree, the servant of the sun, was being made out to be nothing by that ill-deformed brute of a thing. How much had it blinded her from seeing and feeling through the years!

Arvay got to her feet with great deliberation. She stood and looked up through the bare limbs of the tree once and then strode with purpose towards the house. Starting at the back, Arvay walked around it slowly and warily like a battler looking for an opening to charge in for the kill. She circled the place three times. Now and again she could hear frantic squealings and pattering as the dismal and disappointed denizens scurried around seeking something for their hunger. Arvay thought that the sounds just suited the place. It was the voice of the dark, the creeping, the gnawing and destroying. The old house was singing its song.

That determined and answered Arvay. She flung the back door wide with a clang and went inside. From room to room Arvay went gathering up and piling together the trash and rags that had been left behind. There was plenty everywhere. Then she went out in the yard and collected and shoved the masses under the sides of the house, particularly under Maria's old bedroom. Back in the house she started in Maria's bedroom and began to light fires. From room to room she went, and when she saw that they burned clear and swiftly, she ran out and set the piles underneath the house and watched them take on greedily with grim satisfaction. By the time that cars began to halt at a safe distance, and people collect on the highway to watch the fire, Arvay was seated under the mulberry tree. Looking at the conflagration, exultation swept over her followed by a peaceful calm. It was the first time in her life that she was conscious of feeling that way. She had always felt like an imperfect ball restlessly bumping

and rolling and rolling and bumping. Now she felt that she had come to a dead and absolute rest.

The dry old house burned furiously, and as Arvay watched the roaring and ascending flames, she picked herself over inside and recognized why she felt as she did now. She was no longer divided in her mind. The tearing and ripping and useless rending was finished and done. She had made a peace and was in harmony with her life. The physical sign of her disturbance was consuming down in flames, and she was under her tree of life. Arvay felt a piercing pain when she thought about her present terms with her husband. It could be that she had stumbled and fumbled around until it was too late to take in the slack. If that was the case, she would never be really happy in her lifetime. But even so, she knew her way now and could see things as they were. That was some consolation.

Arvay sat on and pictured images in the soaring flames. Evil, witchy-looking things formed, growling and twisting in agony, then perished in the cleansing fire and their thin remains were carried off by the smoke. The roof of their old den crashed in with a great roar and the victorious hosts of flames leaped and howled. After a while there was nothing but coals of embers lying low to the ground and panting out gusts of heat. Not a flicker of flame left at last.

Then Arvay got up and walked resolutely over to her neighbor's home. Miss Hessie looked at her for a moment and then told her in an off-hand voice, "Good you got here. Dinner's all ready and done."

"And I'm ready to eat it," Arvay answered and laid her hat and hand-bag on the bench on the back porch.

In the conspiracy of silence, Miss Hessie poured warm water in the wash-basin and handed Arvay a clean towel, then she turned away and put the dinner on the table. The grandson made a pitcher of ice water without asking a word about the fire. The three sat down to the table and helped their plates generously. Arvay shook her head with conviction after the first mouthful and accused Miss Hessie of being a fine cook. Miss Hessie challenged Arvay to try her and see if she was guilty. They all ate hungrily for a while.

"Appears like we had a fire in this vicinity," Miss Hessie

remarked casually and helped herself to some water-melon pickle.

"I reckon that I can stand the loss, though," Arvay answered just as off-hand.

"Without a doubt. When you planning to re-build?"

"Re-build? Never to my knowing, Miss Hessie. I can't see that I belong here no more."

"That's right. What would you need a house for here with your husband and your family otherwise. Be much more sensible to sell."

"Don't know as I want to be bothered with that either, Miss Hessie. Take up too much of my time."

"Just leave it lay there and eat you up in taxes?"

"No'm. It sort of come to me to make of it a better use. Brad Cary's got the welfare of this community at heart. . . ."

"He is that. Things have took on and bloomed since he put his shoulder to the wheel here recent. A honest and sincere man. Always looking out for Sawley's advancement. But what did you have in mind?"

"Him and Evelyn, his wife you know, was talking it over with me and some others last night about this town needing a play and a pleasure park, mostly for the young'uns. It come to me since I been setting here that Mama would feel glad to know that the place was all given over to pretty flowers and somewhere for folks to set down and rest. Believe I'll turn it over to Brad and them for what they want to do for a park."

"That would really be a great improvement for Sawley, Arvay. I can't help from wishing, though, that my grand-boy here was old enough to buy it in and handle it. So you cutting loose from Sawley, eh? Never expect to live here again?"

Arvay sat erect and looked Miss Hessie in the eyes.

"Miss Hessie, my husband come along and took me off from that place and planned and fixed bigger things for me to enjoy. Look like I ought to have sense enough to appreciate what he's done, and still trying to do for me, and not be always pulling back here. You've known me ever since I was a baby in my mother's arms. You know all about us. What would I be hanging on to that old place for?"

"Not a blessed thing that I can see, Arvay. Nothing ever was there for a girl like you. And from what I can learn, you

have really been blessed. But as I said to Maria over and again, no more than I expected, and no more than you deserve. No use at all in you pulling back here for that little piece of land."

"Oh, I won't, Miss Hessie, except for a visit with friends. Don't you worry about me hanging onto nothing here, more especially since Mama's gone. My last string has done been loosed. It would be a turning back on my travels."

"Yes indeed it would."

"Brad has been noble with me as a friend, and then putting poor Mama away like he did. So I aim to give this place to help out what he's trying to do. Only thing I ask and require is for them to save that mulberry tree and give it every care. I feel sure they'll grant me that."

"Without a doubt. You know I'm along with your Ma, Arvay. If I never see you no more after you leave here this time, I'll remember you in my prayers."

"Do that, Miss Hessie, and I'll do all in my power to take care of things my ownself. No need of wearing God out."

Chapter Twenty-Seven

IT WAS LATE in the afternoon when Arvay arrived home. She stood on the front porch and looked everything over with pleasure. Then she knew what she wanted to do first. Without taking off her hat or considering her luggage piled on the porch, she hurried straight down to the house in the grove. As she neared the house, she recalled the last time that she had been here. It was the night that she had seen Lucy Ann lying on the ground between the house and the privy. But it gave her no painful turn as she had always thought that it would do. Now it was just part of the life that had passed. A storm that she had weathered through. So she did not hesitate and halt. She hailed Jeff and Janie cheerfully as she ran.

They had been taking their comfort and came to the door in their bare feet and stood side by side. They looked at Arvay as she came and then at each other in puzzlement.

"Yeah it's me!" Arvay answered their looks with laughter. "Hello there, Jeff, you old rascal, you! Hi there, Janie!"

Arvay came to the steps and stood there looking up at them and smiling like a child. "You all look like new money in town to me. I sure am glad to see you."

Jeff was defrosted like lightning. He stammered from the rapid change of climate, but his face showed pleasure. "Why, Miss Arvay! We'se real glad to see you back." Jeff could hold out no longer and went all the way. "I was just telling Janie how I wished that you would come on back home."

"Sure was," Janie backed Jeff up, but Arvay could see the lie in Janie's eyes. But she could also see that they were both sincere now in saying that they were glad to see her. To see this kind of Miss Arvay home again.

Arvay braced her hands on her hips and looked up at them.

"Well, you no-manners thing! I so well know that Dessie never taught you no kind of manners like that, Jeff. I know Dessie too well for that. You haven't had manners enough about you to ask me in, and if you don't make room in that door, I ain't going to give you what I brought you."

Loving play-acting, they made a great show of making way

for Arvay to enter. She stepped in, laughing, shoved Jeff, smacked Janie on her hips and sat down near the door. They were eager to know all about the burial and what all had gone on up there.

Arvay gave them an animated account of the funeral, but left out what she did not wish to remember, that was about how Larraine and Carl had behaved towards her. She dwelt more on the visits and the meals and other entertainments which the Carys had furnished. They were extremely interested, but suddenly Jeff cut her off.

"Who lifted your things inside for you, Miss Arvay?"

"Why, come to think about it, Jeff, nobody did. They're still out on the front porch."

"Oh Lawd, Miss Arvay! Maybe somebody done took 'em already."

"Do, Jesus! I sure hope not, Jeff. Kenny's present to me. You reckon anybody would bother 'em?"

"Sure would. Things ain't like they used to be around here, Miss Arvay. Never no more. Folks passing and re-passing all the time now. I have to watch this grove like a hawk now. Several attempts been made to steal fruit."

"Naw! You don't mean it, Jeff."

"Yes, Ma'am! Only day before yistiddy, three men together was in there just helping theyselves, and to my King oranges at that. With that new settlement right here at us, and that club and all them folks across the bridge, I got my hands full these days. You better gimme the keys to the house and I'll run and see about your things. Be right back."

Arvay was so embarrassed that she had not left the keys with Jeff when she went off, that she hung her head and colored.

"I was so worried about Mama's condition that I clean forgot to hand 'em to you before I went off," Arvay dissembled.

"I thought you must of," Jeff conceded cheerfully. "I had sense enough to know that you wasn't locking up against us, because us Meserves don't mistrust one another. I made mention of it to Janie."

All of the turmoil and uncertainty that Arvay had felt before she went away visited her swiftly for a moment. Jeff hurried off through the sunset, and Arvay sat and fiddled with the

edge of the tablecloth for a minute or so before she came to herself and began to describe her mother's casket and the flowers, all of which Janie was more than eager to hear about. Jeff was back very shortly, but Arvay had command of herself by then.

"Jeff, why do you want to make things hard on yourself? You could just as easy have brought the present that I fetched you while you were coming."

"It clear slipped my mind, Miss Arvay. I was too worried about your things and glad to see that they was still there. I put 'em in your bedroom for you. Then again, I didn't know what it was that you wanted us to have."

Then Arvay took an attitude that she would have died before adopting before she went away.

"My dumbness, Jeff. Common sense would of told me that you couldn't read my mind." Arvay stood up gaily. "Come on, you all. Let's all go up to the house and I'll show you what I brought you. I can finish off about the funeral up there."

Arvay watched with a glow while Jeff and Janie made great admiration over the ham and the bag of pecans. Janie was a good-looking brown girl. She turned large soft eyes on Arvay with deep emotions.

"I declare, Miss Arvay, but you sure is folks."

"Sure is," Jeff added sincerely. "Just like Mister Jim, ain't she, Janie? And everybody knows that Mister Jim is quality first-class. Knows how to carry hisself, and then how to treat everybody. Miss Arvay's done come to be just like him."

The reflection upon her past condition escaped Arvay in the shine and the gleaming of the present. Her face flushed, and tears came to her eyes.

"Jeff, Janie!" Arvay turned her eyes away to try and hide her feelings. "Why, that's just about the nicest thing that I ever heard in all my born days! It is! I thank you so much for telling me that."

"But it's the living truth," Jeff confirmed with feeling. "You felt for us and remembered us. Made us feel like we amount to something with you. We feel proud and glad to work around you. You'se quality all the way."

Arvay was touched and sat down abruptly in one of the wicker chairs. She looked all around the porch and her throat worked painfully. She was glad that she had had Jeff to bring the box out on the porch to open it. After a long wait, she spoke.

"You all, going back up there in Sawley learnt me more than I'm able to tell you about. I done seen and felt things that I don't want to never see and to feel no more. I don't want to find it in me, and I don't want to find it nowhere around me. If I got any narrow-hearted littleness in me, I hope to God to cut myself and let it run out."

Arvay did not use many words, but she told them that she had burned the house, and turned her back on what it stood for for good and all. She had found that she did not belong there after all. Without realizing, she had come to prefer Jim's way of handling things.

There was a feeling silence. Arvay took in the pleasure of her porch, and a long look southward through the grove. This was her life and she loved everything about it. Jim had said that she loved like a coward and he had been telling the truth. If ever she was to be with him again, it was her move. She stiffened herself internally and said casually, "And Jeff, as soon as I rest up for a day or two, I'm going to the coast and spend a few days with my husband."

"That's ever so fine and nice, Miss Arvay. I'm proud and glad to hear you say it. You just say what day you aim to go, and I'll have the car here and all ready for you."

"The car, Jeff? Why, Jim's got it on the coast with him, ain't he?"

"That one, yes, Ma'am." Jeff fumbled around nervously. "But it's another one—I mean that I can get hold of one for your convenience."

"You bought yourself a car since I been gone, Jeff?"

"No'm."

"Then I can just get on the train, Jeff."

"No, Ma'am. You ain't to—no, I mean it's too much trouble for you to be fooling with the train. Have to go up to Palatka and lay over, and then take another train to get to the coast. Then you have to change at St. Augustine to get to

New Smyrna. No'm, I can have the car here at the door any day you see fit to make the trip. You had much better go by car."

Arvay sat there and looked at Jeff and thought. There was a bug under this chip. Jeff was as good as giving her an order not to go by train. This was a roundabout order from Jim Meserve and nobody else. The faithful Jeff was carrying out an order. The thought gave Arvay some hope. Maybe he had not forgotten her then.

"All right, Jeff. If you think that that is the best way for me to go, then I place myself in your hands. I got a few dirty clothes on hand that need to be done up. Some of those pieces I would like to take with me. I would love to be there day after tomorrow, but getting those things done up . . ."

"Oh, that's no trouble, Miss Arvay," Janie spunked up. "Gather up all you feel you need, and I can suds 'em out first thing in the morning and they'll be dry in no time. I can have 'em all pressed off by dinner time. I can go in there with you right now, and whilst I'm helping you to unpack your things, you can pick out what you want freshened up."

"Why, Janie, I would thank you from the bottom of my heart if you was to help me out like that. I'll thank you until you're better paid."

Arvay woke up next morning with hope and determination. Nothing beats trial but a failure, Arvay decided. She might not win Jim back, but she meant to give it a poor man's trial. That is the best that she could do. If she failed, it was not going to be because she never tried.

The place felt like Dessie's best days all that day. Good will and cheerful willingness all around her. Janie was in the kitchen ironing by eleven o'clock. Arvay had volunteered to cook enough lunch for everybody.

"I'll bet that old east coast is something to see," Janie said wistfully as she shoved the iron back and forth busily. "And them boats. I never is seen nothing like that myself, but Jeff claims that it's something wonderful to see."

Arvay looked quickly at Janie and understood. She had not thought about Janie going along before, but now, why not?

"Why, ain't you going along with me tomorrow? Jeff told me that it was a nice big sedan car that he was getting. I

thought that it was understood that you would be going with us."

"Oh, Miss Arvay! Oh, Miss Arvay! I'm so glad and happy. 'Tain't nothing that I wouldn't do for you. You'se so nice and kind."

"You still got to use your influence on Jeff, Janie, to get him to kill and pick up some frying-size chickens to fix and take along with us. I think that it would be much nicer if we fixed us up something to eat to take along. See can't you talk Jeff into killing and cleaning four chickens for us. We got plenty turning round to do. While he's doing that, you and I can be stirring up a tater prone to take along. We got plenty here to eat, no need in us going off empty-handed and depending on eating hot dogs along the road, now is it?"

"No ma'am!"

"And then there's my husband. Jim ever favors his stomach, and he just dotes on my tater pone."

The two women did a lot of turning and fixing for the trip. Arvay kept herself so busy that she had no time to fear the outcome of her journey. She steeled herself and refused to anticipate. Let tomorrow speak for itself. She got out an old cheap suitcase and lined it with white paper to hold the lunch. She and Janie laughed at the amount that they were taking. There was the big potato pone, four fried chickens, buttered biscuits, two dozen hard-boiled eggs, potato salad, and the gallon thermos jug full of hot coffee with cream and sugar in it.

Jeff, bathed and soaped so till the skin of his face looked tight and stretched and dressed in his Sunday suit of blue serge, had the car at the door at six o'clock the next morning. With his change of clothes went a formal manner. Jeff stood stiffly as he held the back door for Arvay to get in. He carefully stowed the lunch and Arvay's over-night case in the back with her. Janie, looking as if she had wallowed in a rainbow, beamed and gleamed as she leaped into the front seat beside Jeff, and the car rolled off. Arvay's hands were cold and moist in the palms as the car turned into the highway, but no one could have told it from her face.

At first, Arvay kept her mind off her mission by studying Janie and Jeff. That innocent-looking face that Jeff had, with a

surprising earnestness and dependability behind it. He had never failed Jim in any particular, and in spite of all the laughing and talking that he was doing with Janie up there, was never likely to do so. He seemed never to forget the slightest thing around the place, and never neglected to take care of it.

Janie now, that mixture of colors that she had on. Nothing that Angeline would have thought about picking out to wear at all. But strangly, they did not look funny on Janie. That cheap silk dress became her looks very well indeed. Her short hair was as straight as anybody's today and the way she had it fixed, it improved her looks. Janie was a pretty colored girl and good-hearted. Jeff had made a very lucky pick. If she did not move to the coast, they would be mighty comfortable to have around. How did colored people get their hair straightened? There were no kinky-haired women these days.

As the car turned into U. S. Highway 1 and sped north towards Melbourne, Arvay began to look at the scenery. This was a different Florida than she had known. This Indian River was a beautiful thing. The groves of leaning palms that bordered it, the beautiful homes scattered along its western bank, the arrangements of the flower yards, and the signs of free-spending wealth impressed her. So many kinds of palms, flowers, pleasure boats out on the river with happy-looking people in them, and fish leaping up and splashing back. And cars, cars, cars, flashing past heading south, and cars behind and in front of them going north. And they all were "really trotting" as Jeff said. Many of them passed Arvay as Jeff never went over forty-five. Arvay smiled because she knew that must have come from Jim. He knew that she was nervous at fast driving.

That thought was encouraging, and then again it was not. Jim was the kind who would take care of her whether he wanted her again or not. Her great trial was still before her.

The car began to slow, and Jeff pointed out the ancient Turtle Mounds, kitchen middens of a people who had disappeared ages before the coming of the Spaniards; rusting old iron pots left over from the indigo industry of the Minorcans; foundations of an old fort left by the Spaniards. Jeff was very proud of his information, but Arvay was not paying him as much attention as she seemed. She was straining forward, drawing back from what was before her. Then before she

knew it, Jeff was swinging the car across a high wooden bridge. The Halifax River was before them. This was the waterfront of New Smyrna. They were there.

A short drive down a narrow road seaward, and Jeff swung the car off, and parked in a wide, grassy space before a big shed-looking building that had its backside in the river.

"Here we is, Miss Arvay. We'se at the shrimping docks."

Arvay sat looking at the structure and the activities around it. Several cars and trucks were parked around. On the river side she saw many boats berthed single, double and triple alongside the warehouses and open docks. Her feet felt heavy and cold, but Arvay decided that it was too late to run now. She had come thus far and she might as well wade on in. She lifted one hand to the handle of the door.

"Just keep your seat, Miss Arvay. I'll jump out and run in and ask if our boats is in," Jeff volunteered importantly.

"Well, all right, Jeff," Arvay murmured wearily, "but I reckon I ought to get on out and stretch my legs."

Janie jumped out behind Jeff and went with him into the dusky interior of the building marked with the name of a shrimping "factory." There were four more big dark doors with other names beside them, but Jeff headed into the one that had Toomer on it. In a very few minutes, he was out again.

"I asked for Captain Jim, Miss Arvay. Miss Mary Toomer, that takes care of all the business in the office, says that our boats is really in, and that Captain Meserve's done sold his shrimp and set led up, and drove off uptown. Want me to go hunt him up?"

"No, Jeff. He'll be back sometime or nother. Yeah, I reckon you better. No telling what time he might come. Tell him, tell him, oh, you can just tell him that I'm waiting here."

Arvay made to get out of the car. She did not want to meet Jim with Jeff or anybody else present. She would rather get out of the car and walk around by herself and wait. As she made to alight, a smiling, middle-aged white woman came out of the door and introduced herself. She was Mrs. Toomer, and said that Arvay's chauffeur had told her that Captain Meserve's madam was present. She knew that Captain Meserve would want to be told as soon as possible that his

wife had come. One of the fishermen was going uptown. If Arvay wished, she would send him along with Jeff to locate Captain Jim. While they were gone, she would be pleased if Mrs. Meserve would step inside the office and have a seat.

Arvay went inside and smiled and answered something back when Miss Mary said something. Miss Mary was nice and pleasant, and Arvay was sure that she would like her fine, only she was too tense right now to say and do the right thing in company. Fearing that she might be acting dumb and saying the wrong things, Arvay said that she would love to look around the place and excused herself. Out of the office, Arvay walked up and down the dock, looked off over the woods and around, but saw nothing at all with her eyes.

Then Arvay saw Jim coming. He was driving his usual fast but certain way as he swung expertly into the parking space. He was parked and striding towards the building before the car with Jeff and Janie came trailing in and stopped.

"Oh, hello, Jim!" Arvay tried to be brisk and off-handed, but flushed and faltered. Her eyes could not stay where she wanted them to.

"Hello, Arvay," Jim said casually, but looked her over boldly.

"Oh, I got so much to tell you about, Jim," Arvay chattered in nervous haste. "I know you'll want to hear how everything went off in Sawley." Arvay saw Jeff and Janie hovering around, obviously waiting for orders. They must be gotten rid of. If Jim turned her down, how could she ever go back to the house in Citrabelle if Jeff and Janie had witnessed her downfall? She turned to Jeff.

"I reckon that you want show Janie over the town, don't you, Jeff? It's all new to her, and she wanted to come see it so bad. Tell you what to do. We'll whack up the lunch. You and Janie take all you want, and leave some for me to eat. Then you won't have to hurry back."

"Hold on a minute, there," Jim interrupted. "Just what is in this lunch you're talking about?"

Glad for a chance for conversation, Arvay told Jim. Jim started at once for the borrowed car, and went into the lunch. He grabbed up a chicken wing and ate it with appreciation.

Then he partitioned it out himself, and transferred the suit-cases to his own car.

"That's enough for Jeff and Janie. They're going straight back home where there's plenty more. Give a man that needs it a chance. Me for instance. And potato pone, too. My favorite groceries."

Arvay was pleased that Jim wanted her cooking. She opened her eyes wide and asked, "Oh, you want Jeff to take the car on back?"

"He better get away from here. Who's going to look after things while he's off fooling around? Hit the grit, Jeff, and get on back home. Give that road a cold fever."

With the lunch on the seat between them, and eating as they pulled off, Jeff really tore out and left Arvay standing before Jim and feeling weak. Her easy retreat was cut off. She would have to deal with things one way or another, and she didn't know where nor how to start. They stood there in silence until the car was long out of sight, then Arvay looked up at Jim and said diffidently, "I'm just dying to see the boats."

"You haven't seen 'em yet?" Jim asked in surprise.

"Why, no, Jim. That is, I would rather for you to show 'em to me yourself."

"Oh, so that's the way it is, eh? Well, come ahead. Wait a minute till I grab that lunch box. I'm hungry as a dog for some of that tater pone."

With Jim lugging the suitcase, Arvay followed him through the shed and out on the river side of the building. Jim walked ahead a piece and stopped. Arvay could tell that he meant for her to look around and she did.

"Oh, Jim! You got three boats already! And, my goodness! You got one named after me."

"That was my very first one, Arvay. The *Angeline* was next. That trashy Kenny scraped up the money for that last one, so I named it after him. I aim for the next one to be the *Hatton Howland*. The fifth one will be named after that baby that Angeline is about to have. Next one after that will be named the *Big Jim*, meaning me."

"Oh, Jim, but you are doing well. Can we go on board now and look around? This is my first time to even see a boat as big as this."

With his pride well shuttered, Jim helped Arvay aboard the *Arvay Henson*, and they inspected the others too. He stuck to showing and explaining the boats. Nothing personal at all. When Arvay was tired of climbing around, they went back to the *Arvay Henson* and sat down in the cabin.

"Let's eat!" was all the encouragement that Arvay got out of Jim. If there was any talking coming off, Arvay saw that she would have to do it herself. As they ate, Arvay fenced by telling Jim what had happened in Sawley. With him, however, she did not leave out the part about Larraine and Carl. She did not damn them, though. She surprised Jim by making allowances and excuses. They were really not to be blamed. But Jim's jaws got grim.

"Did Carl cut a caper like that because he had some idea that you had no kind of protection?"

"No. That is, I don't see how he could of got a notion like that."

"Oh," Jim said and waited some time before he spoke again. "I wouldn't quit my business to go hunt up that toad-fish, but he'd better have sense enough not to never come in my sight. I hope that you didn't back off because you felt helpless at all."

"No, it wasn't that way, Jim. I just felt that they were so far back that I was sorry for 'em."

"Well, then that's okay. Say, it's some mighty nice boats tied up here, Arvay. I'd take you on board and let you see 'em and introduce you around, but you ain't dressed for nothing like that. Them high heels and that narrow skirt ain't suitable."

Arvay flashed out with light and leaned forward. "But I really want to do that, Jim. Where can I get something to put on so that I can go along?"

Jim looked at her for a minute, thrust his hands deep into his pockets and finally said as if he were talking to himself, "It would be a kind of waste of money to buy a outfit just for that. It wouldn't be needed any further, and——"

"But why can't I go out on the trip with you, Jim? I'm so proud and pleased with how you have done, that I want to go along with you and see you handle things if you'll let me."

"You really mean that, Arvay?" Jim asked after a pause.

"Jim, I'm so proud, I'm so pleased, that just a little bit more and I'd bust wide open right here. All I wish is that I had of been here with you all along and helping you out like Miss Mary does for her husband. I know that I got the smartest husband in the world, so why wouldn't I feel proud?"

Jim didn't kiss her. He just took hold of her arm very firmly and led her across the deck to the rail.

"Come on then, honey, and let's go uptown and fix you up with something to put on. But mind you now, it's tough out there. Well, you can go along this time anyhow."

Jim bought a pair of the blue jeans that the fishermen wore, two blue shirts, and the tall rubber sea-boots, and Arvay changed into them in the back of the store. Jim told her that the Third Man bought the stores for the galley, but Arvay would go into a grocery and come out with several things that a wife would naturally buy. Jams, and jellies, salad dressing, lettuce and tomatoes, in fact several dollars worth of extras for the galley which she kept on calling the kitchen and Jim kept on correcting her. Then they crossed the bridge again and pulled up in front of the shrimping docks.

That night they visited several boats and Arvay was introduced around. Alfredo was captain of the *Angeline*, and a husky Negro around twenty-five was in command of the *Kenny M*. Arvay was surprised at that, but soon learned that it was a common thing. There were as many if not more colored captains than white. It was who could go out there and come back with the shrimp. And nobody thought anything about it. White and Negro captains were friendly together and compared notes. Some boats had mixed crews. They all talked about the same things, and they all cursed out the owners. Everything that went wrong on a boat was named after the owner. Did the fuel pump on the engine go bad? It was a Toomer, Meserve or whatever the owner's name so-and-so of a bastard! It was that way about everything. Arvay found that Jim knew all about it, as did the other owners and laughed it off.

"The men got to have some outlet for their feelings. They don't mean a bit of harm. They run the risk of their lives out there, and they got a right to some fun. Cussing the boss out

behind his back is a lot of pleasure. I forget that I'm the owner and cuss my ownself out at times. I heard the captain of the *Kenny M.* cussing the winch to every kind of a Meserve so-and-so that he could lay his tongue to this morning when we were berthing. I just let on I didn't hear him."

Jim laughed and Arvay joined in with him. They made the rounds of the Jooks and it was the same way about getting their heads bad. Jim watched Arvay closely as he explained that life was mighty uncertain on a shrimping boat. So many ways that a man could go. Get swept overboard in rough weather; go overboard to cut the net loose when it got fouled in the propeller and a shark happen along; get a bad case of fish-poisoning, and other chances to lose his life. A man had to enjoy himself while he could. The very next trip might be his last. So if they bought likker and love recklessly, what of it? Arvay noted that he relaxed when she agreed that they had a point there. Even though most of them spent their money right away, and depended on going out there and getting more. If they never came back, how could they enjoy money in the bank anyway?

To point this up, they ran into Captain Dutch Smith of the *Savannah.* Last trip, he had lost a man going over the St. Augustine Bar and Dutch was very sad about it. The bar was always risky, and this time it was extra rough, and somehow the man had gone on deck without a line around his waist and had been swept overboard by a big sea.

"He must have been death-struck," somebody consoled Dutch. "I can't imagine what he was thinking about to have done like that. He sure knew better."

But Dutch just wouldn't be consoled. "I sure hate to lose a man," he kept on saying over and over.

"Well, Dutch," Jim put in, "he'll come to beach pretty soon and get a decent burial. That is, unless he met up with a shark. They all come to the beach sooner or later. We all do, I mean. Every man comes to the beach at last. Even if it's a shark, that's your beach, ain't it?"

All the fishermen agreed. Everybody comes rolling home to the beach some old day. No telling when you might come rolling in.

Arvay slept on board the *Arvay Henson* that night in Jim's

narrow cabin. Jim saw her comfortable, then went below. Neither Mate nor Third Man slept on board that night. The Negro had a wife to go to, and the Mate had found love for the night.

They ate and had visitors all the morning. Fishermen dropping in to meet Jim's wife, or just dropping in to pass off time. Stripped to the waist, Jim went over his Diesel engine and got it to running the way he wanted it. That afternoon, Jim took on fuel and ice. Arvay was thrilled watching the five tons of crushed ice cascading down into the hold. There was laughing and talking as other boats drew up one by one and took on ice. The *Ramos*, with Fritz Toomer, son of the owner, in command, the *Savannah*, the *Thunderbolt*, the *Rosalie I*, which was called the *Rosalie Eye* with Sapelo, a popular Negro, as captain. They all seemed to like Sapelo, which was not his real name; he had got it from the island off the Georgia coast where he hailed from.

They were all getting set to cross the bar on the first tide which would cover the treacherous New Smyrna Bar around six o'clock the next morning. Jim was in the notion of heading for the Cape, that is Carnaveral, where he had done mighty well this last trip. But some of the captains talked north, off St. Augustine or Fernandina. The *Kenny M.* was going that way. Alfredo was undecided.

The rest of the day was spent very pleasantly, but it was a form of torture to Arvay, because she did not know whether she was merely a guest on board and still parted from her husband, or whether she was part of the thing.

She was awakened about five o'clock in the morning by the throbbing of the engine beneath her. She got up and peeped down and saw that Jim was the first man up. He was warming up his engine and seeing to everything. Then the other two men began to stir around down there. There was activity all around her now as engines warmed up, men moved about on the decks of other vessels and there was a general bustle, and a calling back and forth from boat to boat.

Somebody came aboard cursing. The Third Man had gotten his head so bad that he had neglected to buy canned milk. A couple of cans were borrowed, and the man hurried on off.

A gray mist was sheeting the water when the lines were cast

off and the *Arvay Henson* eased slowly off from the dock.
She had not moved many lengths before the *Savannah*
paired with her and they throbbed outwards towards the
bar. Arvay hurriedly dressed and went out on deck. She saw
boats pairing and falling in line behind the *Arvay Henson*,
though none were very close. The Mate explained to her
that there would not be enough water over the bar for
nearly an hour yet. They were slowing along to cross it at its
best, which was none too good at that. The *Arvay Henson*
would get there ahead of time, but would anchor and wait
for a while. Be in the first boat over, no doubt, but wait till
it was safe.

"Want me to fix you some breakfast?" Arvay asked Jim,
who was at the wheel inside the pilothouse just in front of the
door to the cabin where she had slept.

"Nope. We'll wait for that until we get outside."

The boat roved on down the river gracefully enough. Arvay
saw for the first time the forests of mangrove swamps that
lined the water on each side. Flocks of white herons perched
among them like great white blooms among the dark leaves.
She pointed at the swarms of sea gulls moving overhead.

"They fly pretty, Jim, but from what I heard so far, they
got mighty poor voices for singing."

Jim laughed. "Eating fish must be against good singing.
None of these birds that live around the water got any voices
for singing worth talking about."

"But look at them big-mouthed things, Jim!"

"Pelicans."

"Ain't they crazy, though? Look how they lights on the
water! Stick out their feet and land on their heels!"

"He's putting on brakes to skid to a stop."

"And look at his head, Jim! Shaped like a pair of big sewing
scissors, got a grin running all the way around that long bill
from one side to the other. Oh, I like to look at 'em. They're
crazy as they can be, but cute!"

Away off somewhere ahead, Arvay began to detect a thun-
der and a growling roar. It got plainer all the time. The Mate
who was standing on deck in front of the door to the pilot-
house looked at Jim a time or two, but Jim had his eyes
straight ahead. Something was the matter, Arvay knew from

the way the Mate kept looking at Jim. The thunder and roar kept getting closer and louder all the time.

Looking over Jim's shoulder through the glass of the housing, Arvay made out the dim shape of a boat coming to meet them. The sun was not up yet, and the boat was a dark mass against the grayness of the mist. The approaching vessel cut a white pompadour with its bow as it came ahead. When its bow was abreast of the bow of the *Arvay Henson*, the captain, a chestnut-colored Negro, stepped out of his pilot-house and stood on deck looking over at the *Arvay Henson*. Jim left his wheel at once and stepped on deck. The two boats were probably fifty feet apart. Jim made some mysterious motions with his hands, and the captain of the other boat doubled his two black fists, and struck one on top of the other rapidly several times. They smiled and waved at each other, and both went back to their wheels.

"Everything fast above and below?" Jim called out, and Mate and Third Man began looking around hastily for a check-up, on deck and below. Two low stools and a pail were brought in and carried below. Jim got up off the high stool that he had been sitting on to steer and shoved it into the cabin. There was a rope fixed to the bulkhead near the floor, and Jim secured the stool to the bulkhead by passing the line tightly around the legs of the stool and tying it securely. He closed the four windows in the cabin and looked around to see that nothing was left that could shift. Then he went back and stood at the wheel and peered straight ahead of him. The Mate was standing on deck in front of the door, and gave Jim a hard questioning look over his shoulder, then fixed his eyes ahead. Arvay could see that he was not pleased about something.

The grumbling thunder ahead increased in power, and the Mate turned and spoke.

"He said that it was pounding on the bar."

Jim seemed not to hear. He kept his eyes straight ahead, and the boat held on her course.

"He said that he turned back to wait until there was more water over that bar."

For all the attention that Jim paid, the Mate might as well have saved his breath. Now amid the rumbling and roaring

ahead, Arvay could distinguish a sound like a whale letting out its breath. *Shhhaaaaaow!* It came now and then and mingled in with the tumult and the roar.

Now a misty moisture began to cloud the windows of the pilot-house. Jim spoke over his shoulder.

"You better get inside there, Arvay. Lay down in the berth so you won't get flung off your feet and maybe get hurt."

Jim acted calm, but Arvay could feel the excitement in him just the same. Standing in the cabin door, whose level was a good foot higher than the decking of the pilot-house, she looked ahead over Jim's shoulder and her eyes stared out in sudden fear. Perhaps ten boat lengths ahead was a colossal boiling and tumbling, grumbling and rumbling of the sea that sent a white spray mounting like somebody shaking a world-sized veil. Havoc was there with her mouth wide open.

The Mate came in from the deck, fastened the door securely after him, gave Jim a sullen look and stumbled on down the stairs. Arvay closed her door to shut out the sight ahead, and lay down in the bunk.

Suddenly, the *Arvay Henson* reared up and then stumbled. The shock was so violent that Arvay leaped to her feet in fright. Through the forward window she saw waves, gray-headed from their birth, leap up around the boat, and come storming over her bow. A hand, powerful enough to have formed creation, grabbed the boat and flung her halfway around to port. She listed way over, and for a second it seemed that she would pitch-pole over. Arvay was hurled back against the berth, but scrambled up and peered out to see about Jim. His face was set and his jaw-muscles bunched. With his feet braced far apart, Jim was fighting a battle with the wheel. Twisting his body halfway to the floor on the right, he brought the bow around and dead on course again.

The Mate came plunging up from below. "Captain! My Captain! You gone crazy? Turn back! This bar is too rough to cross right now. Oh, Captain!"

Jim never turned his head nor even seemed to hear the terrified shouts of his Mate. The boat shuddered and swung violently to starboard.

"Captain! Goddammit, you're going to lose the boat and kill us all! Captain! Captain!"

The frightened Mate, a stocky, butt-end of a man, noting that Jim paid no attention, fell on his knees and wrapped his arms about Jim's left leg, and begged Jim with his eyes. In this struggle where Jim was fighting for the life of his boat and all on board, he tried to shift his leg, but was held fast by the Mate. Arvay saw and acted almost instinctively. She flung the door open, leaped upon the Mate and grabbed him by his hair to pull him away from Jim's leg.

"Let go my husband's leg!" She pounded the man about the face with her fists then yanked and pulled again. "You want to make him wreck his boat? Turn loose!"

In the struggle, Jim was able to kick the hysterical man loose and brace his body and fight the elements.

The Mate, in a lump against the outside door, began to cry and pray. Jim twisted his body slightly to the left and lashed him with his tongue.

"Don't you be praying on my damn boat, you bastard you! Get up off of your damn rusty knees!"

But the Mate mumbled and prayed incoherently. Jim paid him no more attention for a minute or so. Arvay, standing behind Jim, fierce with anger at the Mate who had done such a senseless and dangerous thing, was like a she-bear in her rage. Jim seemed not to know that she was there. His body strained, contorted, with his eyes ahead and his jaw-muscles showing. Arvay thought that the going was getting a little easier. Anyhow, with both hands gripped on the wheel, Jim whirled his body around to face the Mate.

"Pray, you goddamned white-livered bastard, you! Pray! I'm crossing this bar if I land you slap in Hell! Pray! Oh, you can pray on my damn boat, eh? Why you didn't pray last night while you were crawling that barrel of whores? Why you didn't pray while you was guzzling rotgut likker? You didn't have time to pray then, did you? All right now, pray your damn prayer now! Pray, goddamn you, pray!"

The boat shook and shuddered once more, and the Mate's voice was lifted again. Jim whirled on him again.

"Don't you pray another lick on this damn boat, you puking-drunk, seven-sided son of a so-and-so! Get below!"

The Mate looked at Jim's face and fairly tumbled down. Jim kept his furious face straight ahead, and the boat held her

course. He said nothing to Arvay, and she said nothing to him. She stood just back of him and looked fearfully over his shoulder. She had never been so frightened in her life as she was now. The boat gave another shudder and then a leap, and glided out onto the calm waters of the Atlantic.

The contrast was utterly startling. No waves, just an undulating motion that made the distant horizon seem to go up and down slowly and gently. The sun was not up yet, but he had sent his messengers on ahead. A diffused pinkness lit up the sky to the east, then suddenly the rim of the great ball rushed up from the east of the ocean, and laid a red sword westward across the swaying water. Arvay was enchanted.

"Oh, Jim! I never have seen the ocean before. Oh, it's just too pretty for anything. Look how it's changing colors from gray to blue! I'm so proud you brought me with you."

"I thought you might like it, Arvay. Biggest thing that God ever made. It's pretty like you say, and then it can be ugly. It's good and it's bad. It's something of everything on earth."

"Oh, but it is!" Arvay looked and gasped in awe and admiration. The sea vastness, the unobstructed glory of the rising sun, the delicate and forming colors on horizon and sea made new sensations for Arvay. She felt herself stretching and extending with her surroundings. Her eyesight seemed better, and her hearing more keen. The fear that she had experienced while crossing the bar was like a birth-pain. It was already forgotten and gone. In this mood a happy suspicion visited Arvay. She moved so that she could study Jim's profile and asked diffidently, "Jim, it would have been a whole lot easier for you to have crossed the bar later on, wouldn't it?"

Jim looked at Arvay and his eyes were set for battle.

"Maybe so, Arvay. What do you want to know for?"

"Well," and Arvay spoke in a soft maiden voice. "Because the notion just come to me that you took that awful chance so that I could see the sunrise out here on my first sight of the ocean. That right?"

"Yes." Jim bit it off shortly.

"Then, Jim, you're the boldest and the noblest man that ever forked a pair of pants. You'se a monny-ark, Jim, and that's something like a king, only bigger and better. I'm proud enough to die."

"If it reached from me to you, Arvay, I'm glad." He looked ahead for a long minute, then turned his head to the left and yelled down below.

"Cup-Cake!"

"Yes, my Captain!"

"Shake your rusty-dusty down there! I'm hungry as hell."

"It's on the fire and your name's done called. You don't come now you needn't to come at all."

"Copasetty! I'm rearing to go. You and the Mate hurry up and eat so he can come take the wheel for a while so my wife and I can come eat."

"I heard you, my Captain!" The Negro yelled back up.

Fifteen minutes later, the Mate, now calm but shame-faced, came up and took the wheel.

"Take it easy." Jim spoke as if nothing had happened between them. "We're headed for the Cape, but give some of the other boats a chance to catch up with us."

"Okay, my Captain," the Mate said cheerfully, and Jim and Arvay went below.

Cup-Cake, the Third Man, had done himself proud. Hotcakes, bacon and eggs, syrup and butter on the table and hot coffee in plenty. He beamed and smiled as Arvay downed a heavy breakfast.

"Something about this ocean must bring on a big appetite," she excused herself for eating so heartily. "Or else it's Cup-Cake's cooking one. Look like I can't hardly get enough."

A half second later she knew that she had said just the right thing. Jim smiled and opened his eyes wide and looked at her with pleasure. Cup-Cake grinned all over himself.

"You just wait till I pitch you a dinner," he said. "I never do feel right to do when we'se tied up. But outside now, I can be myself in a galley. Ain't I telling it right, my Captain?"

"Oh, you'll do in a rush, Cup-Cake. I hope that my wife don't take and spoil you too rotten, bragging on your cooking. You got to be useful on deck, you know."

Cup-Cake laughed that off and rinsed out a big pot, dropped a ham hock in it, and put it on the fire. He brought out the big bundle of turnip greens from the ice box and began to pick them over.

"Sure glad you bought these, Mrs. Captain. Lay a good poultice of these, seasoned down with ham, against a man's ribs, and it'll just about cure him of whatever might ail him. Make a dead man set up on the cooling-board."

When they came top-side again, a dozen or more boats were in the offing, and more approaching from the west. The sun had become a light yellow yolk and was walking with red legs across the sky. Jim stood out on deck, and made sign language back and forth from boat to boat. Now and then at Arvay's insistence, he translated for her. She made great admiration over their being able to talk to each other like that.

Finally, the *Arvay Henson* paired off with the *Rosalie I*, and put on power for the seven-hour run down to the Cape. Now and then they slowed and tried along. Finding nothing, they held on towards the Cape.

It was late when the fleet anchored off Cape Carnavarel, and none of the boats were disposed to begin operations that day. They would eat, have a good rest, and get set for two drags the next day, a three-meal day. A drag right after breakfast, one right after dinner and head and ice shrimp after supper.

Arvay and Jim sat out on deck on the hatch for a long time that night. The talk was too impersonal for her happiness, but she put on a happy face.

"Jim, I just can't get over the ocean. It's too big for me to even imagine. And night or day, it's something wonderful to look at. I feel like I never want to go away from it no more. Seems like I been off somewhere on a journey and just got home."

"Funny, Arvay, but I ever had that feeling. That's why I was bent and bound to go back to fishing. Once I had seen and been on the sea, it got inside me, and I ever longed for it like a drop of water."

"Like a drop of water, Jim?"

"Sure, Arvay. Don't you realize that the sea is the home of water? All water is off on a journey unlessen it's in the sea, and it's homesick, and bound to make its way home some day."

"Oh, I never thought about a thing like that, Jim."

"You ought to, though. You can't kill it. Mix it up in any-thing, and in anyway that you will or may, but sooner or later it separates itself out and heads back home to the sea. Falls on the ground, soaks down, gets to a tiny branch maybe, and that heads into a creek that runs into a river that maybe runs into a bigger river and all that millions-times multiplied drops of water marches like an army back to the sea. Some gets soaked way down in the ground in rivers and pools so far down in the rocks that folks walking along don't even know that it's there under 'em. Maybe it might get stopped up in a place like that for thousands and thousands of years, but the water never gives up. It gnaws and gnaws at them rocks till they finally gives way, and then the water gets loose and runs as fast as it can back home to the sea. Maybe, in an hour after it gets home, the sun and wind might draw it up again in a cloud and the cloud travels out over the land, and that drop is on another journey, but don't worry, it will arrive back home again. The very same water that you see out there was right here when the world was formed. Changed places and forms too many thousands of times for you to imagine, been off from home and come back just that many times. It'll always be water, though, and always come back home. It's a million times stronger and more durable than anything that ever lived in it nor passed over it. I look at it and think about it, and I never get tired of looking and thinking."

"That's something to think about, Jim. It's never entered my mind before. Maybe it's like that with everything and everybody. If it's in there, it will return to its real self at last."

"That's well-spoken, Arvay. If it's there, it'll come out some old day. Like the water in the underground cave like Silver Springs. Underground for nobody knows how many hundreds of miles, and for nobody knows for how many cen-turies of years, to break through in that crystal clear spring at last. That's the way life is, when you come to think about it. Some folks are surface water and are easily seen and known about. Others get caught underground, and have to cut and gnaw their way out if they ever get seen by human eyes."

That was as near as they came to anything personal, and right after that Jim stretched himself and stood up.

"We ain't doing nothing but rocking and rolling out to-

night, but tomorrow we got to get them nuggets off the bottom and on ice. No, I wouldn't trust you to set out here after I'm gone in. Rail too low. Once you start to falling off of a boat you can't stop. Motion of the boat will pitch you on the way it's going. Come on in and stay in the cabin till you hear somebody stirring in the morning."

Soon the next morning things were astir. The engine was pulsing when she woke up. There was a great to-do with nets and winches on the after deck. Right after breakfast the fishing was to begin. The excitement invaded the galley, and the minute that it was over, the men left her below and went top-side. By the time that Arvay had washed up the dishes, and reached the deck, they were going over with the try-net. Jim at the wheel sang out, "All right, boys, let's try along!"

The sleeve-like net, operated from the smaller winch, went over the side, and Jim sent the boat slowly ahead. A half hour later it was reeled up, and lifted over the side, and the contents dumped on the deck. A lot of curious-looking strange things were in it, but only twenty-odd shrimp. Jim tried to look casual, but Arvay could see that he was disappointed.

"Don't seem to be many, but let's go overboard anyhow."

The Mate went to the big winch. Cup-Cake got the big bag of the net in his hands and stood to the starboard rail to drop it overside after the big net went over and was spreading right.

"All right, let's go overboard!" Jim called out from his place at the wheel. Down came the boom, swung to starboard, and the big net went sinking down and down. The Mate watched closely to see if it was spreading evenly and right. When the boards disappeared under the water, the Third Man dropped the bag overboard, and Jim sent the boat ahead. It went round and round in a big circle slowly, listing to port or starboard from the pull of the heavy net sixty fathoms down on the bottom of the ocean. The steel cable attached to the mast made a straight line to the net below, and moved back and forth like a slow pendulum across the stern as the boat circled and circled. Things got quiet on board as the two-hour drag went on.

"All right, let's get it!" Jim called at last, and the Mate and

the Third Man ran to take up their positions. Finally, the big net was brought to the side and lifted by the winch to the deck.

A cloud of gulls and pelicans appeared from nowhere, making their dissonant call-cries, and hovered for prey. They swooped and swirled as the bag was emptied on deck.

Turtles, numerous kinds of fish, a leopard shark, strange unimaginable-shaped things from the bottom of the sea cascaded out on the deck. Things in shells, soft-looking queer-shaped things; four octopi, about four feet across, bent their arms like swastikas and rolled about the deck trying to find their way back to the water. Jim stood with his hands on his hips looking down gloomily on the mass. Plenty of stuff, but few shrimp in all that mass. Arvay saw several things that looked to her like living pin-cushions and thought to get one to save and take home with her. As she stooped to pick it up, everybody yelled at her at the same time to leave it alone.

"That's a damn whore's-egg!" Jim cautioned. "Ruin you if only one spine of it gets into your hand." Arvay jumped back from the sea-nettle and stood far off to the side.

The men went in killing things. First that astonishingly limber-bodied shark. It could whip its body around as if it hadn't a bone in it. With shovels and the axe, they fell upon it cursing the whole shark family as improperly born cutters of nets, and hefted it overside, where it was immediately fallen upon by other sharks and disappeared in a few minutes down their under-slung, saw-toothed mouths.

"A basket and a half of shrimp in all that mess," Jim said in deep disappointment, and the men were just as gloomy.

"If this kind of luck keeps up, no percentage for nobody worth mentioning," the Mate said in a heavy voice. Cup-Cake said nothing, but he did not smile as usual.

"All right, clean up the deck," Jim muttered, and went back in the pilot-house.

With shovels, the men scooped up the mass of strange life on deck, and tossed it back into the water. The sea birds screamed and swooped, picking up the dead, and catching the weakened creatures before they could dive out of reach. Turtles, sea-nettles and things with shells had nothing to worry about. Few soft-bodied things had a chance. Arvay

watched the slaughter with pity. As Jim had said, the sea was good and it was cruel too. It was thing eat thing out here. She turned her head away until the struggle was over.

Arvay thought that Jim avoided her after that. He had little to say at the dinner table, and got busy down in the hold somewhere back of the engine. She went and stretched out in the cabin, but she could hear him below being surly and snappish with the men.

"It's me," Arvay wept up there in the cabin alone. "He don't want me here nohow, and now, he's blaming me for a Jonah. I know that he wishes that I was dead and off his hands, and I wish so too."

There was an old coverless *Adventure* magazine on the table beside the head of the bunk, and Arvay picked it up and tried to read it some. All she did was to turn pages from front to back and then the other way. She looked out of first one window and then another, at the peaceful, waving horizon, at the distant boats circling and circling around flags. She could tell when the nets were taken on board by the swarms of birds and their hungry, unmusical cries.

Arvay felt even worse when Jim came and stood on deck just outside the pilot-house and she heard him mutter, "It certainly is funny. Everybody catching something but me."

Half an hour later, she heard him say in a lifeless way, "Supposing we try again, men." He took his place at the wheel, and finally gave the order to "get it." Arvay didn't bother to follow him on deck when the try-net came over the side. The kind of silence that prevailed out there told her enough. Only the hungry birds had anything to make noise about. The shovels scraped on the decks in a dispirited way. Then buckets of sea water sloshed over the deck and ran off chortling through the scuppers. Jim came nowhere near her to say nor to do a thing.

An hour later, though, she heard him swearing out there like anything. At the end of the long catalogue of damns and other trimmings, he shouted, "We're going over without a try. There's shrimp in this goddamned ocean and we got to get 'em."

Jim sat unsmiling at the wheel, never once turning his head to look at Arvay shrinking like a Portuguese man o' war on

the beach, for the entire two hours. He kept looking at his watch towards the end, and finally yelled, "Goddamn it, let's get it!"

Before the net came over the side Arvay knew that the luck had changed. It was something like three savage warriors out there on the deck shouting, jumping, swearing and working the machinery.

"The stuff is here!" The Mate screamed.

"We're going to sink her!" Jim crowed.

"Going in high boat!" Cup-Cake bellowed.

"You're damn tooting!" Jim added, "or report to Hell the reason why."

There was furious action out there, and Arvay raised herself to peer out of the window over the bunk that gave on the after deck.

"The bailing-net!" Jim shouted. "We got to bail before we can bring her over the side. Look at the goddamned sharks grabbing at the fish gilled in the net and cutting my goddamned net to pieces!" Arvay had always known that Jim was a cursing man, but she had never heard him to this extent as he called the sharks every kind of low, unprincipled thing that he could lay his tongue to, and plenty seemed to be available. He played the dozens with them and went way back in their ancestry. Never had a shark's mother been married or begot a shark in a decent bed. And as for their pappies, they were thus-and-sos. "Liable to cut up this net so that all our catch gets away!"

But the furious and quick work saved the day. Very little got away. However, a huge silver-grey man-killing shark was inside the net and was dumped on the deck. With shouts of vengeful joy the three men fell upon it with the axe, shovel and gig. Its head was a bloody mess in no time, and it lay like dead. The men were stooping to pick up the carcass and dump it overboard by means of the winch and cables, when the limber thing whipped around all of a sudden and almost got Jim's right foot. The shark actually did take off the heel of his boot. Arvay, watching through the window, involuntarily let out a scream. There was more blaspheming the honor of female sharks, and the men fell upon the monster again. When it lay still again, they hacked through the tough

hide and ripped open the belly. Arvay ran outside to see what they were looking at with so much interest. There were little live sharks inside inclosed in transparent sacs.

"Let's heave the whole she-bang over the side and let the little bastards drown!" Jim cursed.

The cables were hooked on and the huge sea-beast splashed bloodily overboard, but the men were put out to see the baby sharks free themselves of their envelopes and swim off. The men expressed the shame and the pity that they had gotten away, and Arvay thought, carried on like little boys.

They turned back to the huge mass of sea life piled on the deck and began to separate the shrimp out with zeal.

"Over two tons, I'd say," Jim estimated with satisfaction. "This gives us the start to sink her tomorrow and go in high boat."

"Just look at the money piled up there!" The Mate gloated. He sat down on a stool to look and admire some more. "I can see myself on the hill soon as we get in making some fool fisherman go broke trying to beat me spending money."

"Okay," Jim muttered, "we got 'em, let's fall to cracking heads."

"Yes, my Captain!" the crew answered and sat down to heading shrimp. No matter how late it might be, there would be no sleeping aboard until all the shrimp were headed and on ice. Good humor prevailed. The men remembered funny stories and told them to each other.

Arvay felt glad about the haul herself. She could not be looked upon as a Jonah, and Jim was in such good humor now. But then again, a winning Jim might easily be farther away from her grasp than a losing Jim. She turned around and leaned her back against the rail and looked at the three men working away. Jim was sitting on the hatch cover and looking as male as a coconut tree. What woman wouldn't be glad to get hold of a man like that? The tiny lines from the outside corners of his eyes, and around his mouth took nothing away from his looks and appeal in Arvay's eyes. Naturally, all the other females on earth were bound to see his wonders. They could not help themselves. Arvay sankled around and reached a spot close to Jim and stood and looked on for a few minutes.

"Could I give you all any help in any way?"

Jim looked up at Arvay sharply and the look flustered her.

"Maybe I could cook some supper for you, or . . ." Arvay added in a desperate hurry lest Jim tell her that there was nothing that she could do for him.

"Now that's a fine idea, Arvay. A most grand noble notion. Of course, I know that old Cup-Cake don't want to hear the news. Nothing would suit him better than to sneak off down there into the galley and pass an easy time ruining up groceries while me and Titty-Nipple squat up here heading shrimp, and getting our hands all stuck up on their horns. Now, with you being so cool and kind as get us some supper, we got old Cup-Cake's trashy hide dead in the works."

Arvay laughed from happiness and fluttered her eyelids up and down.

"What you all reckon you want me to fix for you to eat, boys?"

"You eat them few stone crabs that I picked out and laid aside for you," Jim helped out. "Fix them for your ownself. I want a great big mess of these shrimp fried to a turn with fried potatoes, and, oh, just anything more that you feel to fix. You ought to know how to feed me by now. You sure know how to cook, so suit yourself."

They all wanted the same. Whatever Mrs. Captain took a notion to fix. Fried shrimp, however, was the preference.

Then a great grin spread clear across Cup-Cake's face. "I'll have to leave you all heading by yourself for awhile. I got to hull them shrimp for Mrs. Captain. That's too hard a work for her to do."

Jim, in mock fury jumped up, and grabbed up a stool as if he meant to haul off and lam Cup over the head with it.

"What did I tell you, Titty?" Jim shouted triumphantly. "That sooner's too slick and slippery to handle. Naturally the shrimp ought to be cleaned first, but I'll show the hammerhead that I'm just as slick as he is greasy. We all will shuck shrimp for cooking, and rush that no-count jar-head back to heading shrimp."

Jim jumped up and filled a pail with the fresh, grey-green shrimp and beckoning to the crew, headed for the galley on the lope. Cup and Titty followed him laughing. By the time

that Arvay descended to the galley, they were laughing and cleaning the shrimp, and indulging in horse-play. Arvay looked on and noted how like little boys they acted. Didn't men ever get grown? Arvay asked herself indulgently. It was nice to see how they could play like that. It made her feel good and like taking care of them.

She fixed the dinner in a warm family atmosphere and was glad when they all praised her and said how good it was. They ate so Arvay could believe them, and it made her feel very good. She shooed them on back to their heading and cleaned up the galley as she would her own kitchen.

With nothing more to occupy her hands, Arvay went back to her personal probing. She could not rest easy. What she had come to do was still ahead.

Arvay could hear the three men laughing and joking over their work on the after deck as she came up from the galley. She stood in the pilot-house for several minutes listening. They sounded so happy and free of care together. It made her wonder if Jim was thinking seriously as she was. How was she to get out what she wanted to tell him? The sea was calm and nice. She decided to go out on the forward deck and feel the breeze and think.

Numerous were the eyes of the night. Clear and bright before the rise of the moon. She took a seat on a coil of anchor rope and began to back over things. She went back over her life from the day she had first met Jim up until the day of the snake. Frankly and with truth she counted up and put values on things. Jim was right. She had pulled back and halted, and must have tried his patience something awful at times. And what made her halting and doubting so bad—Jim had given her no cause to doubt him. Her case was not the same as many women that she knew. So far as she knew, Jim had never messed around with another woman. She had never had to put on a play like some she knew had to do. They flashed around what their husbands had given them to cover up the fact that they had fine clothes and rings and things, but couldn't lay their hands on their husbands after dark most of the time. Jim gave her too, and then he was present in her bed. Why then had she doubted herself? What more did she want than she had already received?

She had been a good mother, that she could swear to. She had taken good care of Jim in every way. What more then would he be expecting out of her? What had he demanded? Not whom she had descended from. Jim had never said a word along that line. He knew her folks, and if he was satisfied, what had she been whining over? Then in a flash it came back to Arvay what Jim had said to her that Sunday when they had got engaged to marry. He had told her exactly what he wanted in a wife. She had clean forgotten about it and had made herself touchy and miserable all this time for nothing. Love and be sweet to him. She had done that to the best of her ability. Certainly she had loved Jim all that she was able to love anybody. Her whole heart and mind was his and had always been so. Have him children. She had done that too. Look pretty. She had certainly kept herself looking the best that she knew how. Whether she was pretty or not was according to Jim's own eyes. He had told her often and again that she was pretty, so he must have been satisfied.

So much for the foundations and the past. What could she learn from that to help her out right now? Jim could have made up his mind to do without her.

Arvay thought some more and took a stand. According to Jim's own words, he had a good right to take her back and give her a chance to show that she had changed. She had been weak and cowardly in the past, never realizing what he had done for her, and making not anything of being his wife. But then on the other hand, she had suffered about everything that a woman could suffer through loving and clinging to Jim. From where she had come from, Jim could never realize what it had cost her to scramble and struggle along to keep alongside of him the way he travelled in life. The battle had been awful, but she had fought down the things that had made the difference between them. She had suffered a sad birth and a sadder death from her love. Now, after all the pressing pain of the journey and winning against herself in order to stand beside him, she certainly ought to be allowed to receive her crown of victory. Since she had rejoined Jim, she had tried to show him the change in her by signs, but so far he hadn't seemed to take a bit of notice. Maybe since they had parted that day in August, some other woman had come in between.

At that thought, more fighting blood than Arvay thought she had in her rushed to her heart. Her temples throbbed and her ears felt hot.

No, she told herself. It was not going to be that way at all if she could help herself. She did not aim to step aside and let no other woman take her place with Jim Meserve. She was going to have her husband back or die in the attempt. Whatever it took to bring it about she was going to do it. And she did not mean next year sometime either. She meant right here and now.

Arvay felt so intense that she could not keep her seat. She stood erect and her hands were clinched.

She was going to deal with things. Oh, yes she was! And she was not going to fool around with a try-net. She was going overboard with the drag and sweep the very bottom.

Arvay was eager to rush in and settle her fate, but she could hear the men still talking and laughing over their work. She would have to wait until that was over with.

The white, white, Florida moon rose up and began to gild the ocean. The calm surface rose and fell like the breast of a sleeping woman. Other boats twinkled off in the distance to right and left of her. A school of fish flashed silver sides as they broke surface and hurled themselves in the air to fall back, and flash again and again. Arvay saw what they were fleeing, when the fin of a huge shark rushed along in their wake. The shark too disappeared under when a school of porpoises came ploughing and diving and re-appearing on the route of the shark. The moonlight lit up her pale gold hair coiled in thick braids around her head.

Arvay let the scene swamp her. She felt privileged to be there. It was like being taken into a new lodge. The fellowship of beauty-seers. Jim had made all this. Well, anyhow, he had provided this ocean-sea for her to look at. Well, to bring it down a little more, she would never have known anything about such as this by hearsay if it wasn't for Jim.

So was some other woman to receive such things from Jim? Would she stand on the front of Jim's boat and see and feel what she now saw and felt? The thought was not to be put up with. Maybe she would be young and ever so pretty, and of high family and learned in books and ways. Arvay crimped her

mouth and accepted the challenge. Be she who and what she would or may, Arvay grimmed herself to go up against her. That woman would have to beat what she could do and be, and that was going to be a gracious plenty. If and when she got hold of Jim, it was not going to be a gracious gift from Arvay. Not because she had backed off from her. Her scars would always keep her in mind that she had been in a battle. Win or lose, Arvay was determined to trot out the best horse she had in her stable, to never turn her back on the enemy, and if she lost, not to go off crying.

A great freedom and calm came to Arvay with her determination. Nothing ahead of her but war, and she was ready and eager for it to start. She sat down again on the coil of rope and pleasured herself with the night. She sat and fed her senses with the light, the movement of the sea and the march of the stars across the sky. This was all hers until death if only she had the courage and the strength to hold it, and that she meant to do. Finally, it came to her just how to begin with Jim. Now, there was Isaac and Rebecca at the well and smiling lovingly at each other. No, that wouldn't do. They had already done that part years ago. She and Jim were a married couple, even if at variance. What Ruth said to Naomi fitted things more better, but put into words that fitted just her and Jim.

"Jim, your loving Arvay has throwed off every hindering weight so as to follow you along in a easy way. Whither thou goest, I will go along too. Thy kind of people shall be my kind of people, and thy God, my God."

Reciting this over and over so as not to forget it, Arvay went in the cabin and went to bed. The men were still working outside, but they were not chattering so much now. Their words were few and sounded tired to Arvay. They ought to be near about through. That being the case, her time was close at hand.

But how was she to get Jim off to himself to talk in private? The shrimp headed and put on ice down in the hold, Jim would go below with the crew as usual. He would pass close to the door of the cabin it was true, but not halt his steps.

Why not change what she had been doing since she had been on board and leave the door open? Jim would notice that. Well, she could attract his notice more easily anyway.

Arvay heard the movements of finishing off out on the after deck and she tensed herself and found that her limbs were trembling. She became conscious of how she was dressed. She had no silk female things on board to adorn herself with. Nothing to sleep in but one of the blue work shirts that Jim had bought her. It stopped half way between her hips and her knees. With the sound of the men dragging and scuffling baskets of shrimp as they carried them below, Arvay got up and brushed her hair and fixed her face. That was all that she could do for her looks. She opened the door about a third of the way and lay down again to wait in agitation. Now that the action was at hand, she found herself tense and trembling.

Arvay traced every movement outside with her ears. The men got through icing. She heard the hatch cover close finally, and the crew going below with tired steps, mumbling a little as they went. But she missed the well-known steps of Jim Meserve. All was quiet below when she heard Jim enter the pilot-house. She could hear him moving back and forth softly out there, and glimpse his form each time that he passed the open door. Jim did not turn on the light out there. He seemed to be fumbling back and forth as if he were searching for something. Arvay got so that she could not stand the suspense any longer. She closed her eyes and called out softly, "Jim?"

"Yeah, Arvay," Jim answered wearily, and stood in the crack of the door.

"Come here, Jim. I got something to tell you."

Quickly, Jim pushed the opening a little wider and stuck his head inside the cabin. Lying there on top of the covers, Arvay felt shamefaced about her clothes. Jim was looking at her very hard from her head to her feet. Most particularly from where her shirt-tail stopped on down.

"What is it, Arvay?" Jim asked after a long time, Arvay thought.

Arvay gritted her teeth and plunged on.

"You can't go down below to sleep tonight, Jim, that is, not until I have a talk with you nohow. You can't go. . . ."

"Who says I can't?"

"I say so, Jim. You're not going down there and crawl into no bunk, not until I get through with what I want with you."

Jim's face went very tense, and his eyes narrowed down. Boldly, he stepped inside the cabin and closed the door firmly behind him. He leaned his back against it and folded his hands behind him. Not a word was exchanged between them for a minute or so. Arvay's eye-lids had lowered while Jim just stood looking at her.

"You called me, Arvay, so here I am." He looked at Arvay for a long and a searching time with his eyes still narrowed down. Only Arvay thought that his head drooped a little bit.

Arvay realized that she had the floor, and it threw her into a vast panic. That chance that she had yearned for through long terrible months was in her hand. But her speech of explanations and review had flown out of her presence and was blowing off somewhere over the big ocean. She didn't have any ideas. She didn't even have any words. She was on the point of crying.

"You can't go below," Arvay stumbled out. "You got to . . ."

"Arvay, do you realize that you are giving orders to the captain of a ship? And on the high seas at that? That's mutiny, which is a high crime punishable by death, and instant death if I feel like it. And then on top of that, it's pretty damned biggity and imposing."

"Captain or no captain, Jim, you're my husband, ain't you?"

"Even so, all that cheek and brass that you're acting with, you must think that you've found some weapon to your hand since I seen you last."

Arvay's blue eyes flew wide open at that. If she sounded biggity to Jim, then he didn't realize how scared she was. She mounted to the pulpit and took her text from that.

"Do I need any more weapon than I already got? Did I ever need any different?" Arvay shot an impudent and challenging look at Jim. "Maybe the reason you never see no bear-cat with hip-pockets is because he don't have no need to tote no pistol with him. I was born with all I ever needed to handle your case."

Jim's eyes now flew wide open. His body gave a jerk.

"There now! The mule done kicked Rucker!" Jim exploded, and Arvay caught him eye-balling her in a new way.

"You're mighty plague-goned impudent and sassy these days."
He gave Arvay a strong under-eye look. "Who's been pomp-
ing you up so? Who's been telling you that you're pretty?"

"Jim Meserve, that's who."

"Oh, is *that* the case? When did I tell you all that, Arvay?"

"Every since I knowed you . . . in one way or another. Aw,
I ain't near so dumb as I used to be. I can read your writing.
Actions speak louder than words."

Arvay had every intention to keep on talking and acting flip
until she got out all that was in her to say, but her eyelids
fluttered and drooped before that look that Jim was giving
her. She just couldn't help herself. But a sound of movement
made them fly open again. There was Jim coming towards the
bunk like he was stalking a prey. Involuntarily, Arvay flinched.

"Don't you holler!" Jim growled. "Putting me on the lin-
ger like you did! I ought to take my belt to you and run your
backside crazy!" All of a sudden, Jim stood over Arvay on the
bunk and offed with his jacket and flung it from him without
looking to see which way it went. He tore at the buttons of
his shirt frantically and threw it as if it had done something to
him. "Holler if you dare! You had better not even cheep!"

It was a moment of great revelation for Arvay. She got a
glimpse of something which she would never have believed
possible before. Jim, Jim Meserve, Lord, had his doubts
about holding her as she had hers about him. She was not the
only one who had trembled. All these years and time, Jim had
been feeling his way towards her and grasping at her as she
had been towards him. This was a wonderful and powerful
thing to know, but she must not let him know what she had
perceived. Arvay trembled visibly and looked up innocently
afraid and scared at Jim. But one time in her life, she wanted
to fully express herself in words and let Jim know how she
had improved and changed.

"Just lemme tell you one thing more, Jim. You—I want
you to overlook how dumb I used to be. But, Jim, I just
wasn't wise of things. Like Mama used to say, being dumb
never kilt nobody. All it did was to make you sweat, and Jim,
since I've been with you, I done sweated mightily."

"Aw, hush up!" Jim hurled his shoes, one after the other
against the forward bulkhead. "No need for any long explana-

tions. I can read your writing, Arvay." He stood up and shucked his pants. "You took long enough to stumble round the tea-cup to get to the handle." Jim dropped suddenly down on the side of the bunk and snatched off his socks. "And don't try to get cute and resist me, neither." He fairly flung himself at full length on the bunk, grabbed Arvay by her ears and shook her head fretfully. "Kiss me, Arvay!"

Arvay really kissed him. Jim took her face between his hands and looked into her eyes for some time.

"You had a damned good chance to be rid of me, Arvay. Me *and* my habits for good and all. Just live off apart from me with full support, but you didn't have sense enough to make good of it. And that's your hard luck, baby."

"Why, Jim?"

"Why? Because you'll damn sure never get a chance like that again. Never no more in this world, nor even in Georgia, will I act the goddamn fool for your benefit like that again. If being with me don't suit you, you got nobody but your own-self to blame. You bought this on yourself. You could have stayed away from me, but you didn't. So you're planted here now forever. You're going to do just what I say do, and you had better not let me hear you part your lips in a grumble. Do you hear me, Arvay?"

"Yes, Jim, I hear you."

The sweetness of the moment swept over Arvay so that she almost lost consciousness. Jim shook her roughly and growled.

"Well, hell! You don't act like it. What the hell you think I got a neck for if it ain't for you to be hugging?"

Arvay's arms went up in a languorous curve and clasped tightly around Jim's neck, and without being urged, she kissed him fondly time and again. Jim was gripping her shoulders so hard until it hurt her, and trembling all over his body like a child trying to keep from crying. Like a little boy who had fled in out of the dark to the comfort of his mother. After a while, Jim sighed deeply, and his head slid down and snuggled on her breast. From long habit, Arvay's fingers began to play through his hair in a gentle way. Almost immediately, Jim sighed and went off into a deep and peaceful sleep.

The *Arvay Henson* rode gently on the bosom of the Atlan-

tic. It lifted and bowed in harmony with the wind and the sea. It was acting in submission to the infinite, and Arvay felt its peace. For the first time in her life, she acknowledged that that was the only way. She shifted her body sufficiently to lie on her right side, and with her arms still about the sleeping Jim, snuggled him more comfortably in the narrow bunk and held and hovered him as if he had been her little boy.

The movement of the boat was soothing and drowsy-like, but Arvay could not sleep. A great exaltation had come upon her, and her mind spoke in voices to her. She heard them as plain as day.

All that had happened to her, good or bad, was a part of her own self and had come out of her. Within her own flesh were many mysteries. She lifted her left hand before her eyes and studied it in every detail with wonder. With wonder and deep awe like Moses before his burning bush. What all, Arvay asked of herself, was buried and hidden in human flesh? You toted it around with you all your life time, but you couldn't know. If you just could know, it would be all the religion that anybody needed. And what was in you was bound to come out and stand.

Earl was in her and had to come out some way or another. Arvay looked back and shuddered. Then a new feeling came. Yes, Earl had been bred in her before she was even born, but his birth had purged her flesh. He was born first. It was meant to be that way. Somebody had to pay off the debt so that the rest of the pages could be clean. God must have thought that she was the one who could shoulder the load and bear it. He had not trusted it to her mother, nor yet to Larraine. God had made her a mother to give peace and comfort around. Earl had served his purpose and was happily removed from his sufferings. It was pitiful that she had not seen things in the right way from his birth. She had been purged out, and the way was cleared for better things.

Then it was like the Resurrection. The good that was in her flesh had taken form. Angeline, female beauty, had come out of her, and Kenny, as handsome a boy as you would find anywhere. Kenny had come bringing the music part inside her that she had never had a chance to show herself. It had to be there or it could never have come out as it did. He repre-

sented those beautiful sounds that she used to hear from nowhere as she played around with her doll under the mulberry tree. But give credit where credit was due. Jim was the other part. Joined together, they had made these wonders. Human flesh was full of mysteries and a wonderful and unknown thing.

Arvay bent her neck and kissed Jim tenderly on top of his head. Jim Meserve was her man and her care. Naturally, children would grow up and seek for partners just as she had done. It was the thing to do. It was meant to be that way. Arvay hoped fervently that her two children would find the same kind of fullness that she had found. Angeline seemed to have it already. She hoped and prayed that Kenny would find the same. It was not for her to worry about how and with whom they found what she had found. Jim was her business. Arvay bent and kissed his hair again. It was funny that she had never known Jim in full until this night. Jim was not the overpowering general that she had took him for. Oh, he had that way with other folks and things. No matter of doubt about it. From a teppentime shack to his own fleet on the ocean was a long, long road to travel. But that was the outside Jim. Inside he was nothing but a little boy to take care of, and he hungered for her hovering. Look at him now! Snuggled down and clutching onto her like Kenny when he wore diapers. Arvay felt such a swelling to protect and comfort Jim that tears came up in her eyes. So helpless sleeping there in her arms and trusting himself to her.

And just like she had not known Jim, she had known her own self even less. What she had considered her cross, she now saw as her glory. Her father and Larraine had taken from her because they felt that she had something to take from and to give out of her fullness. Her mother had looked to her for dependence. Her children, and Jim and all. Her job was mothering. What more could any woman want and need? No matter how much money they had or learning, or high family, they couldn't do a bit more mothering and hovering than she could. Holy Mary, who had been blessed to mother Jesus had been no better off than she was. She had been poor and unlearnt too. Even poor Carl had felt her need and care. Maybe as he said, he would have come to more than he had if he had had her beside him.

Thinking and feeling that way, Arvay could not sleep. The few hours left of the darkness passed away with Jim held in her arms. Jim was hers and it was her privilege to serve him. To keep on like that in happiness and peace until they died together, giving Jim the hovering that he needed.

A breeze of dawn sprang up, and the boat rocked gently with it. The slightly increased motion made Arvay look out upon the sea. She saw that the sun was rising. It seemed to her that the big globe of light leaped up from a bed fixed on the eastern horizon and mounted, trailing the red covers of his bed behind him. Arvay pictured that he looked and saw the *Arvay Henson* with her and Jim on board and laid that rosy path across the crinkling water straight to it to look and see if she was carrying out her work. The sunlight rose higher, climbed the rail and came on board. Arvay sat up as best she could without disturbing Jim and switched off the artificial light overhead, and met the look of the sun with confidence. Yes, she was doing what the big light had told her to do. She was serving and meant to serve. She made the sun welcome to come on in, then snuggled down again beside her husband.

SELECTED STORIES

Contents

Contents

John Redding Goes to Sea

T HE VILLAGERS said that John Redding was a queer child.
His mother thought he was too. She would shake her
head sadly, and observe to John's father: "Alf, it's too bad our
boy's got a spell on 'im."

The father always met this lament with indifference, if not
impatience.

"Aw, woman, stop dat talk 'bout conjure. Tain't so nohow.
Ah doan want Jawn tuh git dat foolishness in *him*."

"Cose you allus tries tuh know mo' than me, but Ah ain't
so ign'rant. Ah knows a heap mahself. Many and manys the
people been drove outa their senses by conjuration, or rid tuh
deat' by witches."

"Ah keep on telling yuh, woman, tain's so. B'lieve it all you
wants tuh, but dontcha tell mah son none of it."

Perhaps ten-year old John *was* puzzling to the simple folk
there in the Florida woods for he was an imaginative child
and fond of day-dreams. The St. John River flowed a scarce
three hundred feet from his back door. On its banks at this
point grow numerous palms, luxuriant magnolias and bay
trees with a dense undergrowth of ferns, cat-tails and rope-
grass. On the bosom of the stream float millions of delicately
colored hyacinths. The little brown boy loved to wander
down to the waters edge, and, casting in dry twigs, watch
them sail away down stream to Jacksonville, the sea, the wide
world and John Redding wanted to follow them.

Sometimes in his dreams he was a prince, riding away in a
gorgeous carriage. Often he was a knight bestride a fiery
charger prancing down the white shell road that led to distant
lands. At other times he was a steamboat captain piloting his
craft down the St. John River to where the sky seemed to
touch the water. No matter what he dreamed or who he fan-
cied himself to be, he always ended by riding away to the
horizon; for in his childish ignorance he thought this to be
farthest land.

But these twigs, which John called his ships, did not always
sail away. Sometimes they would be swept in among the

weeds growing in the shallow water, and be held there. One day his father came upon him scolding the weeds for stopping his sea-going vessels.

"Let go mah ships! You ole mean weeds you!" John screamed and stamped impotently. "They wants tuh go 'way. You let 'em go on!"

Alfred laid his hand on his son's head lovingly. "What's mattah, son?"

"Mah ships, pa," the child answered weeping. "Ah throwed 'em in to go way off an' them ole weeds won't let 'em."

"Well, well, doan cry. Ah thought youse uh grown up man. Men doan cry lak babies. You musn't take it too hard 'bout yo' ships. You gotta git uster things gittin' tied up. They's lotser folks that 'ud go on off too ef somethin' didn' ketch 'em an' hol' 'em!"

Alfred Redding's brown face grew wistful for a moment, and the child noticing it, asked quickly: "Do weeds tangle up folks too, pa?"

"Now, no, chile, doan be takin' too much stock of what ah say. Ah talks in parables sometimes. Come on, les go on tuh supper."

Alf took his son's hand, and started slowly toward the house. Soon John broke the silence.

"Pa, when ah gets as big as you Ah'm goin' farther than them ships. Ah'm goin' to where the sky touches the ground."

"Well, son, when Ah wuz a boy Ah said Ah wuz goin' too, but heah Ah am. Ah hopes you have bettah luck than me."

"Pa, Ah betcha Ah seen somethin' in th' wood-lot you ain't seen!"

"Whut?"

"See dat tallest pine tree ovah dere how it looks like a skull wid a crown on?"

"Yes, indeed!" said the father looking toward the tree designated. "It do look lak a skull since you call mah 'tention to it. You 'magine lotser things nobody else evah did, son!"

"Sometimes, Pa dat ole tree waves at me just aftah th' sun goes down, an' makes me sad an' skeered, too."

"Ah specks youse skeered of de dahk, thas all, sonny. When you gits biggah you won't think of sich."

Hand in hand the two trudged across the plowed land and

up to the house, the child dreaming of the days when he should wander to far countries, and the man of the days when he might have—and thus they entered the kitchen.

Matty Redding, John's mother, was setting the table for supper. She was a small wiry woman with large eyes that might have been beautiful when she was young, but too much weeping had left them watery and weak.

"Matty," Alf began as he took his place at the table, "Dontcha know our boy is different from any othah chile roun' heah. He 'lows he's goin' to sea when he gits grown, an' Ah reckon Ah'll let 'im."

The woman turned from the stove, skillet in hand. "Alf, you ain't gone crazy, is you? John kain't help wantin' tuh stray off, cause he's got a spell on 'im; but *you* oughter be shamed to be encouragin' him."

"Ain't Ah done tol' you forty times not tuh tahk dat low-life mess in front of mah boy?"

"Well, ef tain't no conjure in de world, how come Mitch Potts been layin' on his back six mont's an' de doctah kain't do 'im no good? Answer me dat. The very night John wuz bawn, Granny seed ole Witch Judy Davis creepin outer dis yahd. You know she had swore tuh fix me fuh maryin' you, 'way from her darter Edna. She put travel dust down fuh mah chile, dat's whut she done, tuh make him walk 'way fum me. An' evuh sence he's been able tuh crawl, he's been tryin tuh go."

"Matty, a man doan need no travel dust tuh make 'im wanter hit de road. It jes' comes natcheral fuh er man tuh travel. Dey all wants tuh go at some time or other but they kain't all get away. Ah wants mah John tuh go an' see cause Ah wanted to go mah self. When he comes back Ah kin see them furrin places wid his eyes. He kain't help wantin' tuh go cause he's a man chile!"

Mrs. Redding promptly went off into a fit of weeping but the man and boy ate supper unmoved. Twelve years of married life had taught Alfred that far from being miserable when she wept, his wife was enjoying a bit of self-pity.

Thus John Redding grew to manhood, playing, studying and dreaming. He attended the village school as did most of the youth about him, but he also went to high school at the

county seat where none of the villagers went. His father shared his dreams and ambitions, but his mother could not understand why he should wish to go strange places where neither she nor his father had been. No one of their community had ever been farther away than Jacksonville. Few indeed had even been there. Their own gardens, general store, and occasional trips to the county seat—seven miles away—sufficed for all their needs. Life was simple indeed with these folk.

John was the subject of much discussion among the country folk. Why didn't he teach school instead of thinking about strange places and people? Did he think himself better than any of the "gals" there about that he would not go a-courting any of them? He must be "fixed" as his mother claimed, else where did his queer notions come from? Well, he was always queer, and one could not expect the man to be different from the child. They never failed to stop work at the approach of Alfred in order to be at the fence and inquire after John's health and ask when he expected to leave.

"Oh," Alfred would answer, "Jes' as soon as his mah gits reconciled to th' notion. He's a mighty dutiful boy, mah John is. He doan wanna hurt her feelings."

The boy had on several occasions attempted to reconcile his mother to the notion, but found it a difficult task. Matty always took refuge in self-pity and tears. Her son's desires were incomprehensible to her, that was all. She did not want to hurt him. It was love, mother love, that made her cling so desperately to John.

"Lawd knows," she would sigh, "Ah nevah wuz happy an' nevah specks tuh be."

"An' from yo' actions," put in Alfred hotly, "You's determined *not* to be."

"Thas right, Alfred, go on an' 'buse me. You allus does. Ah knows Ah'm ign'rant an' all dat, but dis is mah son. Ah bred an' born 'im. He kain't help from wantin' to go rovin' cause travel dust been put down fuh him. But mebbe we kin cure 'im by disincouragin' the idee."

"Well, Ah wants mah son tuh go; an' he wants tuh go too. He's a man now, Matty. An' we mus' let John hoe his own

row. If it's travelin' twon't be foh long. He'll come back to us bettah than when he went off. What do you say, son?"

"Mamma," John began slowly, "It hurts me to see you so troubled over my going away; but I feel that I must go. I'm stagnating here. This indolent atmosphere will stifle every bit of ambition that's in me. Let me go mamma, please. What is there here for me? Why, sometimes I get to feeling just like a lump of dirt turned over by the plow—just where it falls there's where it lies—no thought or movement or nothing. I wanter make myself something—not just stay where I was born."

"Naw, John, it's bettah for you to stay heah and take over the school. Why don't you marry and settle down?"

"I don't *want* to, mamma. I want to go away."

"Well," said Mrs. Redding, pursing her mouth tightly, "You ainta goin' wid *mah* consent!"

"I'm sorry mamma, that you won't consent. I am going nevertheless."

"John, John, mah baby! You wouldn't kill yo' po' ole mamma, would you? Come, kiss me, son."

The boy flung his arms about his mother and held her closely while she sobbed on his breast. To all of her pleas, however, he answered that he must go.

"I'll stay at home this year, mamma, then I'll go for a while, but it won't be long. I'll come back and make you and papa oh so happy. Do you agree, mama dear?"

"Ah reckon tain' nothin' tall fuh me to do else."

Things went on very well around the Redding home for some time. During the day John helped his father about the farm and read a great deal at night.

Then the unexpected happened. John married Stella Kanty, a neighbor's daughter. The courtship was brief but ardent —on John's part at least. He danced with Stella at a candy-pulling, walked with her home and in three weeks had de-clared himself. Mrs. Redding declared that she was happier than she had ever been in her life. She therefore indulged in a whole afternoon of weeping. John's change was occasioned possibly by the fact that Stella was really beautiful; he was young and red-blooded, and the time was spring.

Spring-time in Florida is not a matter of peeping violets or bursting buds merely. It is a riot of color in nature—glistening green leaves, pink, blue, purple, yellow blossoms that fairly stagger the visitor from the north. The miles of hyacinths lie like an undulating carpet on the surface of the river and divide reluctantly when the slow-moving alligators push their way log-like across. The nights are white nights for the moon shines with dazzling splendor, or in the absence of that goddess, the soft darkness creeps down laden with innumerable scents. The heavy fragrance of magnolias mingled with the delicate sweetness of jasmine and wild roses.

If time and propinquity conquered John, what then? These forces have overcome older men.

The raptures of the first few weeks over, John began to saunter out to the gate to gaze wistfully down the white dusty road; or to wander again to the river as he had done in childhood. To be sure he did not send forth twig-ships any longer, but his thoughts would in spite of himself, stray down river to Jacksonville, the sea, the wide world—and poor home-tied John Redding wanted to follow them.

He grew silent and pensive. Matty accounted for this by her ever-ready explanation of "conjuration." Alfred said nothing but smoked and puttered about the barn more than ever. Stella accused her husband of indifference and made his life miserable with tears, accusations and pouting. At last John decided to bring matters to a head and broached the subject to his wife.

"Stella, dear, I want to go roving about the world for a spell. Would you stay here with papa and mama and wait for me to come back?"

"John, is you crazy sho' nuff? If you don't want me, say so an' I kin go home to mah folks."

"Stella, darling, I do want you, but I want to go away too. I can have both if you'll let me. We'll be *so* happy when I return . . ."

"Naw, John, you cain't rush me off one side like that. You didn't hafta marry me. There's a plenty othahs that would have been glad enuff tuh get me; you know Ah wan't educated befo' han'."

"Don't make me too conscious of my weakness, Stella. I

know I should never have married with my inclinations, but it's done now, no use to talk about what is past. I love you and want to keep you, but I can't stifle that longing for the open road, rolling seas, for peoples and countries I have never seen. I'm suffering too, Stella, I'm paying for my rashness in marrying before I was ready. I'm not trying to shirk my duty—you'll be well taken care of in the meanwhile."

"John, folks allus said youse queer and tol' me not to marry yuh, but Ah jes' loved yuh so Ah couldn't help it, an' now to think you wants tuh sneak off an' leave me."

"But I'm coming back, darling . . . listen Stella."

But the girl would not. Matty came in and Stella fell into her arms weeping. John's mother immediately took up arms against him. The two women carried on such an effective war against him for the next few days that finally Alfred was forced to take his son's part.

"Matty, let dat boy alone, Ah tell you! Ef he wuz uh home-buddy he'd be drove 'way by you all's racket."

"Well, Alf., dat's all we po' wimmen kin do. We wants our husbands an' our sons. John's got uh wife now, an' he ain't got no business to be talkin' 'bout goin' nowheres. I lowed dat marrin' Stella would settle him."

"Yas, dat's all you wimmen study 'bout—settlin' some man. You takes all de get-up out of 'em. Jes' let uh fellah mak uh motion lak gettin' somewhere, an' some 'oman'll begin tuh hollah 'Stop theah! where's you goin'? Don't fuhgit you b'longs tuh me.' "

"My Gawd! Alf! Whut you reckon Stella's gwine do? Let John walk off an' leave huh?"

"Naw, git outer huh foolishness an' go 'long wid him. He'd take huh."

"Stella ain't got no call tuh go crazy 'cause John is. She ain't no woman tuh be floppin' roun' from place tuh place lak some uh dese reps follerin' uh section gang."

The man turned abruptly from his wife and stood in the kitchen door. A blue haze hung over the river and Alfred's attention seemed fixed upon this. In reality his thoughts were turned inward. He was thinking of the numerous occasions upon which he and his son had sat on the fallen log at the edge of the water and talked of John's proposed travels. He

had encouraged his son, given him every advantage his own poor circumstances would permit. And now John was home-tied.

The young man suddenly turned the corner of the house and approached his father.

"Hello, papa."

" 'Lo, son."

"Where's mama and Stella?"

The older man merely jerked his thumb toward the interior of the house and once more gazed pensively toward the river. John entered the kitchen and kissed his mother fondly.

"Great news, mamma."

"What now?"

"Got a chance to join the Navy, mama, and go all around the world. Ain't that grand?"

"John, you shorely ain't gointer leave me an' Stella, is yuh?"

"Yes, I think I am. I know how both of you feel, but I know how *I* feel, also. You preach to me the gospel of self-sacrifice for the happiness of others, but you are unwilling to practice any of it yourself. Stella can stay here—I am going to support her and spend all the time I can with her. I am going—that's settled, but I want to go with your good will. I want to do something worthy of a strong man. I have done nothing so far but look to you and papa for everything. Let me learn to strive and think—in short, be a man."

"Naw, John, Ah'll nevah give mah consent. I know yous hard-headed jes'l-ak yo' paw; but if you leave dis place ovah mah head, Ah nevah wants you tuh come back heah no mo. Ef Ah wuz laid on de coolin' board, Ah doan want yuh standin' ovah me, young man. Doan even come neah mah grave, you ongrateful wretch!"

Mrs. Redding arose and flung out of the room. For once, she was too incensed to cry. John stood in his tracks, gone cold and numb at his mother's pronouncement. Alfred, too, was moved. Mrs. Redding banged the bed-room door violently and startled John slightly. Alfred took his son's arm, saying softly: "Come, son, let's go down to the river."

At the water's edge they halted for a short space before seating themselves on the log. The sun was setting in a purple

cloud. Hundreds of mosquito hawks darted here and there, catching gnats and being themselves caught by the lightning-swift bullbats. John abstractly snapped in two the stalk of a slender young bamboo. Taking no note of what he was doing, he broke it into short lengths and tossed them singly into the stream. The old man watched him silently for a while, but finally he said: "Oh, yes, my boy, some ships get tangled in the weeds."

"Yes papa they certainly do. I guess I'm beaten—might as well surrender."

"Nevah say die. Yuh nevah kin tell what will happen."

"What *can* happen? I have courage enough to make things happen; but what can I do against mamma! What man wants to go on a long journey with his mother's curses ringing in his ears? She doesn't understand. I'll wait another year, but I am going because I must."

Alfred threw an arm about his son's neck and drew him nearer but quickly removed it. Both men instantly drew apart, ashamed for having been so demonstrative. The father looked off to the wood-lot and asked with a reminiscent smile: "Son, do you remember showin' me the tree dat looked lak a skeleton head?"

"Yes, I do. It's there still. I look at it sometimes when things have become too painful for me at the house, and I run down here to cool off and think. And every time I look at it, papa, it laughs at me like it had some grim joke up its sleeve."

"Yuh wuz always imagin' things, John; things that nobody else evah thought on!"

"You know, papa, sometimes—I reckon my longing to get away makes me feel this way. . . . I feel that I am just earth, *soil* lying helpless to move myself, but *thinking*. I seem to hear herds of big beasts like horses and cows thundering over me, and rains beating down; and winds sweeping furiously over— all acting upon me, but me, well, just soil, *feeling* but not able to take part in it all. Then a soft wind like love passes over and warms me, and a summer rain comes down like understanding and softens me, and I push a blade of grass or a flower, or maybe a pine tree—that's the ground thinking. Plants are ground thoughts, because the soil can't move itself. When-

ever I see little whirls of dust sailing down the road I always step aside — I don't want to stop 'em 'cause they're on their shining way — moving! Oh, yes, I'm a dreamer. . . . I have such wonderfully complete dreams, papa. They never come true. But even as my dreams fade I have others."

"Yas, son, Ah have them same feelings exactly, but Ah can't find no words lak you do. It seems lak you an' me see wid de same eyes, hear wid de same ears an' even feel de same inside. Only thing you kin talk it an' Ah can't. But anyhow you speaks for me, so whut's the difference?"

The men arose without more conversation. Possibly they feared to trust themselves to speech. As they walked leisurely toward the house Alfred remarked the freshness of the breeze.

"It's about time the rains set in," added his son. "The year is wearin' on."

After a gloomy supper John strolled out into the spacious front yard and seated himself beneath a China-berry tree. The breeze had grown a trifle stronger since sunset and continued from the southeast. Matty and Stella sat on the deep front porch, but Alfred joined John under the tree. The family was divided into two armed camps and the hostilities had reached that stage where no quarter could be asked or given.

About nine o'clock an automobile came flying down the dusty white road and halted at the gate. A white man slammed the gate and hurried up the walk toward the house, but stopped abruptly before the men beneath the China-berry. It was Mr. Hill, the builder of the new bridge that was to span the river.

"Howdy John, Howdy Alf. I'm mighty glad I found you. I am in trouble."

"Well now, Mist' Hill," answered Alfred slowly but pleasantly. "We'se glad you foun' us too. What trouble could *you* be having now?"

"It's the bridge. The weather bureau says that the rains will be upon me in forty-eight hours. If it catches the bridge as it is now, I'm afraid all my work of the past five months will be swept away, to say nothing of a quarter of a million dollars worth of labor and material. I've got all my men at work now and I thought to get as many extra hands as I could to help

out tonight and tomorrow. We can make her weather tight in that time if I can get about twenty more."

"I'll go, Mister Hill," said John with a great deal of energy. "I don't want papa out on that bridge—too dangerous."

"Good for you, John!" cried the white man. "Now if I had a few more men of your brawn and brain, I could build an entirely new bridge in forty-eight hours. Come on and jump into the car. I am taking the men on down as I find them."

"Wait a minute. I must put on my blue jeans. I won't be long."

John arose and strode to the house. He knew that his mother and wife had overheard everything, but he paused for a moment to speak to them.

"Mamma, I am going to work all night on the bridge."

There was no answer. He turned to his wife.

"Stella, don't be lonesome. I will be home at day-break."

His wife was as silent as his mother. John stood for a moment on the steps, then resolutely strode past the women and into the house. A few minutes later he emerged clad in his blue overalls and brogans. This time he said nothing to the silent figures rocking back and forth on the porch. But when he was a few feet from the steps he called back: "Bye, mamma; bye, Stella," and hurried on down the walk to where his father sat.

"So long, papa. I'll be home around seven."

Alfred roused himself and stood. Placing both hands upon his son's broad shoulders he said softly: "Be keerful son, don't fall or nothin'."

"I will, papa. Don't *you* get into a quarrel on my account."

John hurried on to the waiting car and was whirled away.

Alfred sat for a long time beneath the tree where his son had left him and smoked on. The women soon went indoors. On the night breeze were borne numerous scents: of jasmine, of roses, of damp earth of the river, of the pine forest near by. A solitary whip-poor-will sent forth his plaintive call from the nearby shrubbery. A giant owl roared and boomed from the wood lot. The calf confined in the barn would bleat and be answered by his mother's sympathetic "moo" from the pen. Away down in Lake Howell Creek the basso profundo of the alligators boomed and died, boomed and died.

Around ten o'clock the breeze freshened, growing stiffer until midnight when it became a gale. Alfred fastened the doors and bolted the wooden shutters at the windows. The three persons sat about a round deal table in the kitchen upon which stood a bulky kerosene lamp, flickering and sputtering in the wind that came in through the numerous cracks in the walls. The wind rushed down the chimney blowing puffs of ashes about the room. It banged the cooking utensils on the walls. The drinking gourd hanging outside by the door played a weird tattoo, hollow and unearthly, against the thin wooden wall.

The man and the women sat silently. Even if there had been no storm they would not have talked. They could not go to bed because the women were afraid to retire during a storm and the man wished to stay awake and think with his son. Thus they sat: the women hot with resentment toward the man and terrified by the storm; the man hardly mindful of the tempest but eating his heart out in pity for his boy. Time wore heavily on.

And now a new element of terror was added. A screech-owl alighted on the roof and shivered forth his doleful cry. Possibly he had been blown out of his nest by the wind. Matty started up at the sound but fell back in her chair, pale and trembling: "My Gawd!" she gasped, "dat's a sho' sign uh death."

Stella hurriedly thrust her hand into the salt-jar and threw some into the chimney of the lamp. The color of the flame changed from yellow to blue-green but this burning of salt did not have the desired effect—to drive away the bird from the roof. Matty slipped out of her blue calico wrapper and turned it wrong side out before replacing it. Even Alfred turned one sock.

"Alf," said Matty, "What do you reckon's gonna happen from this?"

"How do Ah know, Matty?"

"Ah wisht John hadn't went away from heah tuh night."

"Humh."

Outside the tempest raged. The palms rattled dryly and the giant pines groaned and sighed in the grip of the wind. Flying leaves and pine-mast filled the air. Now and then a brilliant

flash of lightning disclosed a bird being blown here and there with the wind. The prodigious roar of the thunder seemed to rock the earth. Black clouds hung so low that the tops of the pines were among them moving slowly before the wind and made the darkness awful. The screech owl continued his tremulous cry.

After three o'clock the wind ceased and the rain commenced. Huge drops clattered down upon the shingle roof like buckshot and ran from the eaves in torrents. It entered the house through the cracks in the walls and under the doors. It was a deluge in volume and force but subsided before morning.

The sun came up brightly on the havoc of the wind and rain calling forth millions of feathered creatures. The white sand everywhere was full of tiny cups dug out by the force of the falling raindrops. The rims of the little depressions crunched noisily underfoot.

At daybreak Mr. Redding set out for the bridge. He was uneasy. On arriving he found that the river had risen twelve feet during the cloudburst and was still rising. The slow St. Johns was swollen far beyond its banks and rushing on to sea like a mountain stream, sweeping away houses, great blocks of earth, cattle, trees—in short anything that came within its grasp. Even the steel framework of the new bridge was gone!

The siren of the fibre factory was tied down for half an hour, announcing the disaster to the country side. When Alfred arrived therefore he found nearly all the men of the district there.

The river, red and swollen, was full of floating debris. Huge trees were swept along as relentlessly as chicken coops and fence rails. Some steel piles were all that was left of the bridge.

Alfred went down to a group of men who were fishing members of the ill-fated construction gang out of the water. Many were able to swim ashore unassisted. Wagons backed up and were hurriedly driven away loaded with wet shivering men. Two men had been killed outright, others seriously wounded. Three men had been drowned. At last all had been accounted for except John Redding. His father ran here and there asking for him, or calling him. No one knew where he was. No one remembered seeing him since daybreak.

Dozens of women had arrived at the scene of the disaster by this time. Matty and Stella, wrapped in woolen shawls, were among them. They rushed to Alfred in alarm and asked where was John.

"Ah doan know," answered Alfred impatiently. "That's what Ah'm trying to fin' out now."

"Do you reckon he's run away?" asked Stella thoughtlessly. Matty bristled instantly.

"Naw," she answered sternly, "he ain't no sneak."

The father turned to Fred Mimms, one of the survivors and asked him where John was and how had the bridge been destroyed.

"Yuh see," said Mimms, "when dat turrible win' come up we wuz out 'bout de middle of de river. Some of us wuz on de bridge, some on de derrick. De win' blowed so hahd we could skeercely stan' and Mist' Hill tol' us tuh set down fuh a spell. He's 'fraid some of us mought go overboard. Den all of a sudden de lights went out—guess de wires wuz blowed down. We wuz all skeered tuh move for slippin' overboard. Den dat rain commenced—an' Ah nevah seed such a downpour since de flood. We set dere and someone begins tuh pray. Lawd how we did pray tuh be spared! Den somebody raised a song an' we sung, you hear me, we sung from de bottom of our hearts till daybreak. When the first light come we couldn't see nothin' but fog everywhere. You couldn't tell which wuz water an' which wuz lan'. But when de sun come up de fog begin to liff, an' we could see de water. Dat fog wuz so thick an' heavy dat it wuz huggin' dat river lak a windin' sheet. And when it rose we saw dat de river had rose way up durin' the rain. My Gawd, Alf! it wuz runnin' high—so high it nearly teched de span of de bridge—an' red as blood! So much clay, you know from lan' she done overflowed. Comin' down stream, as fas' as 'press train wuz three big pine trees. De first one wuzn't fohty feet from us and there wasn't no chance to do nothin' but pray. De fust one struck us and shook de whole works an' befo' it could stop shakin' the other two hit us an' down we went. Ah thought Ah'd never see home again."

"But, Mimms, where's John?"

"Ah ain't seen him, Alf, since de logs struck us. Mebbe he's

swum ashore, mebbe dey picked him up. What's dat floatin' way out dere in de water?"

Alfred shaded his eyes with his gnarled brown hand and gazed out into the stream. Sure enough there was a man floating on a piece of timber. He lay prone upon his back. His arms were outstretched, and the water washed over his brogans but his feet were lifted out of the water whenever the timber was buoyed up by the stream. His blue overalls were nearly torn from his body. A heavy piece of steel or timber had struck him in falling for his left side was laid open by the thrust. A great jagged hole wherein the double fists of a man might be thrust, could plainly be seen from the shore. The man was John Redding.

Everyone seemed to see him at once. Stella fell to the wet earth in a faint. Matty clung to her husband's arm, weeping hysterically. Alfred stood very erect with his wife clinging tearfully to him, but he said nothing. A single tear hung on his lashes for a time then trickled slowly down his wrinkled brown cheek.

"Alf! Alf!" screamed Matty, "Dere's our son. Ah knowed when Ah heard dat owl las' night. . . ."

"Ah see 'im, Matty," returned her husband softly.

"Why is yuh standin' heah? Go git mah boy."

The men were manning a boat to rescue the remains of John Redding when Alfred spoke again.

"Mah po' boy, his dreams never come true."

"Alf," complained Matty, "Why doantcher hurry an' git my boy—doantcher see he's floatin' on off?"

Her husband paid her no attention but addressed himself to the rescue-party.

"You all stop! Leave my boy go on. Doan stop 'im. Doan' bring 'im back for dat ole tree to grin at. Leave him g'wan. He wants tuh go. Ah'm happy 'cause dis mawnin' mah boy is goin' tuh sea, *he's goin' tuh sea*."

Out on the bosom of the river, bobbing up and down as if waving good bye, piloting his little craft on the shining river road, John Redding floated away toward Jacksonville, the sea, the wide world—at last.

Drenched in Light

"YOU Isie Watts! Git 'own offen dat gate post an' rake up dis yahd!"

The little brown figure perched upon the gate post looked yearningly up the gleaming shell road that led to Orlando, and down the road that led to Sanford and shrugged her thin shoulders. This heaped kindling on Grandma Potts' already burning ire.

"Lawd a-mussy!" she screamed, enraged—"Heah Joel, gimme dat wash stick. Ah'll show dat limb of Satan she kain't shake huhseff at *me*. If she ain't down by de time Ah gets dere, Ah'll break huh down in de lines" (loins).

"Aw Gran'ma, Ah see Mist' George and Jim Robinson comin' and Ah wanted to wave at 'em," the child said petulantly.

"You jes wave dat rake at dis heah yahd, madame, else Ah'll take you down a button hole lower. You'se too 'oomanish jumpin' up in everybody's face dat pass."

This struck the child in a very sore spot for nothing pleased her so much as to sit atop of the gate post and hail the passing vehicles on their way South to Orlando, or North to Sanford. That white shell road was her great attraction. She raced up and down the stretch of it that lay before her gate like a round eyed puppy hailing gleefully all travelers. Everybody in the country, white and colored, knew little Isis Watts, the joyful. The Robinson brothers, white cattlemen, were particularly fond of her and always extended a stirrup for her to climb up behind one of them for a short ride, or let her try to crack the long bull whips and yee whoo at the cows.

Grandma Potts went inside and Isis literally waved the rake at the "chaws" of ribbon cane that lay so bountifully about the yard in company with the knots and peelings, with a thick sprinkling of peanut hulls.

The herd of cattle in their envelope of gray dust came alongside and Isis dashed out to the nearest stirrup and was lifted up.

"Hello theah Snidlits, I was wonderin' wheah you was,"

said Jim Robinson as she snuggled down behind him in the saddle. They were almost out of the danger zone when Grandma emerged.

"You Isie-s!" she bawled.

The child slid down on the opposite side from the house and executed a flank movement through the corn patch that brought her into the yard from behind the privy.

"You lil' hasion you! Wheah you been?"

"Out in de back yahd," Isis lied and did a cart wheel and a few fancy steps on her way to the front again.

"If you doan git tuh dat yahd, Ah make a mommuk of you!" Isis observed that Grandma was cutting a fancy assortment of switches from peach, guana and cherry trees.

She finished the yard by raking everything under the edge of the porch and began a romp with the dogs, those lean, floppy eared 'coon hounds that all country folks keep. But Grandma vetoed this also.

"Isie, you set 'own on dat porch! Uh great big 'leben yeah ole gal racin' an' rompin' lak dat—set 'own!"

Isis impatiently flung herself upon the steps.

"Git up offa dem steps, you aggavatin' limb, 'fore Ah git dem hick'ries tuh you, an' set yo' seff on a cheah."

Isis petulently arose and sat down as violently as possible in a chair, but slid down until she all but sat upon her shoulder blades.

"Now look atcher," Grandma screamed. "Put yo' knees together, an' git up offen yo' backbone! Lawd, you know dis hellion is gwine make me stomp huh insides out."

Isis sat bolt upright as if she wore a ramrod down her back and began to whistle. Now there are certain things that Grandma Potts felt no one of this female persuasion should do—one was to sit with the knees separated, "settin' brazen" she called it; another was whistling, another playing with boys, neither must a lady cross her legs.

Up she jumped from her seat to get the switches.

"So youse whistlin' in mah face, huh!" She glared till her eyes were beady and Isis bolted for safety. But the noon hour brought John Watts, the widowed father, and this excused the child from sitting for criticism.

Being the only girl in the family, of course she must wash

the dishes, which she did in intervals between frolics with the dogs. She even gave Jake, the puppy, a swim in the dishpan by holding him suspended above the water that reeked of "pot likker"—just high enough so that his feet would be immersed. The deluded puppy swam and swam without ever crossing the pan, much to his annoyance. Hearing Grandma she hurriedly dropped him on the floor, which he tracked up with feet wet with dishwater.

Grandma took her patching and settled down in the front room to sew. She did this every afternoon, and invariably slept in the big red rocker with her head lolled back over the back, the sewing falling from her hand.

Isis had crawled under the center table with its red plush cover with little round balls for fringe. She was lying on her back imagining herself various personages. She wore trailing robes, golden slippers with blue bottoms. She rode white horses with flaring pink nostrils to the horizon, for she still believed that to be land's end. She was picturing herself gazing over the edge of the world into the abyss when the spool of cotton fell from Grandma's lap and rolled away under the whatnot. Isis drew back from her contemplation of the nothingness at the horizon and glanced up at the sleeping woman. Her head had fallen far back. She breathed with a regular "snark" intake and soft "poosah" exhaust. But Isis was a visual minded child. She heard the snores only subconsciously but she saw straggling beard on Grandma's chin, trembling a little with every "snark" and "poosah". They were long gray hairs curled here and there against the dark brown skin. Isis was moved with pity for her mother's mother.

"Poah Gran-ma needs a shave," she murmured, and set about it. Just then Joel, next older than Isis, entered with a can of bait.

"Come on Isie, les' we all go fishin'. The perch is bitin' fine in Blue Sink."

"Sh-sh—" cautioned his sister, "Ah got to shave Gran'ma."

"Who say so?" Joel asked, surprised.

"Nobody doan hafta tell me. Look at her chin. No ladies don't weah no whiskers if they kin help it. But Gran'ma gittin' ole an' she doan know how to shave like me."

The conference adjourned to the back porch lest Grandma wake.

"Aw, Isie, you doan know nothin' 'bout shavin' a-tall—but a *man* lak *me*——"

"Ah do so know."

"You don't not. Ah'm goin' shave her mahseff."

"Naw, you won't neither, Smarty. Ah saw her first an' thought it all up first," Isis declared, and ran to the calico covered box on the wall above the wash basin and seized her father's razor. Joel was quick and seized the mug and brush.

"Now!" Isis cried defiantly, "Ah got the razor."

"Goody, goody, goody, pussy cat, Ah got th' brush an' you can't shave 'thout lather—see! Ah know mo' than you," Joel retorted.

"Aw, who don't know dat?" Isis pretended to scorn. But seeing her progress blocked for lack of lather she compromised.

"Ah know! Les' we all shave her. You lather an' Ah shave."

This was agreeable to Joel. He made mountains of lather and anointed his own chin, and the chin of Isis and the dogs, splashed the walls and at last was persuaded to lather Grandma's chin. Not that he was loath but he wanted his new plaything to last as long as possible.

Isis stood on one side of the chair with the razor clutched cleaver fashion. The niceties of razor-handling had passed over her head. The thing with her was to *hold* the razor—sufficient in itself.

Joel splashed on the lather in great gobs and Grandma awoke.

For one bewildered moment she stared at the grinning boy with the brush and mug but sensing another presence, she turned to behold the business face of Isis and the razor-clutching hand. Her jaw dropped and Grandma, forgetting years and rheumatism, bolted from the chair and fled the house, screaming.

"She's gone to tell papa, Isie. You didn't have no business wid his razor and he's gonna lick yo hide," Joel cried, running to replace mug and brush.

"You too, chuckle-head, you, too," retorted Isis. "You was

playin' wid his brush and put it all over the dogs—Ah seen you put it on Ned an' Beulah." Isis shaved some slivers from the door jamb with the razor and replaced it in the box. Joel took his bait and pole and hurried to Blue Sink. Isis crawled under the house to brood over the whipping she knew would come. She had meant well.

But sounding brass and tinkling cymbal drew her forth. The local lodge of the Grand United Order of Odd Fellows led by a braying, thudding band, was marching in full regalia down the road. She had forgotten the barbecue and log-rolling to be held today for the benefit of the new hall.

Music to Isis meant motion. In a minute razor and whipping forgotten, she was doing a fair imitation of the Spanish dancer she had seen in a medicine show some time before. Isis' feet were gifted—she could dance most anything she saw.

Up, up went her spirits, her brown little feet doing all sorts of intricate things and her body in rhythm, hand curving above her head. But the music was growing faint. Grandma was nowhere in sight. She stole out of the gate, running and dancing after the band.

Then she stopped. She couldn't dance at the carnival. Her dress was torn and dirty. She picked a long stemmed daisy and thrust it behind her ear. But the dress, no better. Oh, an idea! In the battered round topped trunk in the bedroom!

She raced back to the house, then, happier, raced down the white dusty road to the picnic grove, gorgeously clad. People laughed good naturedly at her, the band played and Isis danced because she couldn't help it. A crowd of children gather admiringly about her as she wheeled lightly about, hand on hip, flower between her teeth with the red and white fringe of the table-cloth—Grandma's new red tablecloth that she wore in lieu of a Spanish shawl—trailing in the dust. It was too ample for her meager form, but she wore it like a gipsy. Her brown feet twinkled in and out of the fringe. Some grown people joined the children about her. The Grand Exalted Ruler rose to speak; the band was hushed, but Isis danced on, the crowd clapping their hands for her. No one listened to the Exalted one, for little by little the multitude had surrounded the brown dancer.

An automobile drove up to the Crown and halted. Two white men and a lady got out and pushed into the crowd, suppressing mirth discreetly behind gloved hands. Isis looked up and waved them a magnificent hail and went on dancing until—

Grandma had returned to the house and missed Isis and straightway sought her at the festivities expecting to find her in her soiled dress, shoeless, gaping at the crowd, but what she saw drove her frantic. Here was her granddaughter dancing before a gaping crowd in her brand new red tablecloth, and reeking of lemon extract, for Isis had added the final touch to her costume. She *must* have perfume.

Isis saw Grandma and bolted. She heard her cry: "Mah Gawd, mah brand new table cloth Ah jus' bought f'um O'landah!" as she fled through the crowd and on into the woods.

II

She followed the little creek until she came to the ford in a rutty wagon road that led to Apopka and laid down on the cool grass at the roadside. The April sun was quite hot.

Misery, misery and woe settled down upon her and the child wept. She knew another whipping was in store for her.

"Oh, Ah wish Ah could die, then Gran'ma an' papa would be sorry they beat me so much. Ah b'leeve Ah'll run away an' never go home no mo'. Ah'm goin' drown mahseff in th' creek!" Her woe grew attractive.

Isis got up and waded into the water. She routed out a tiny 'gator and a huge bull frog. She splashed and sang, enjoying herself immensely. The purr of a motor struck her ear and she saw a large, powerful car jolting along the rutty road toward her. It stopped at the water's edge.

"Well, I declare, it's our little gypsy," exclaimed the man at the wheel. "What are you doing here, now?"

"Ah'm killin' mahseff," Isis declared dramatically, "Cause Gran'ma beats me too much."

There was a hearty burst of laughter from the machine.

"You'll last sometime the way you are going about it. Is this the way to Maitland? We want to go to the Park Hotel."

Isis saw no longer any reason to die. She came up out of the water, holding up the dripping fringe of the tablecloth.

"Naw, indeedy. You go to Maitlan' by the shell road—it goes by mah house—an' turn off at Lake Sebelia to the clay road that takes you right to the do'."

"Well," went on the driver, smiling furtively, "Could you quit dying long enough to go with us?"

"Yessuh," she said thoughtfully, "Ah wanta go wid you."

The door of the car swung open. She was invited to a seat beside the driver. She had often dreamed of riding in one of these heavenly chariots but never thought she would, actually.

"Jump in then, Madame Tragedy, and show us. We lost ourselves after we left your barbecue."

During the drive Isis explained to the kind lady who smelt faintly of violets and to the indifferent men that she was really a princess. She told them about her trips to the horizon, about the trailing gowns, the gold shoes with blue bottoms—she insisted on the blue bottoms—the white charger, the time when she was Hercules and had slain numerous dragons and sundry giants. At last the car approached her gate over which stood the umbrella China-berry tree. The car was abreast of the gate and had all but passed when Grandma spied her glorious tablecloth lying back against the upholstery of the Packard.

"You Isie-e!" she bawled. "You lil' wretch you! come heah *dis instant.*"

"That's me," the child confessed, mortified, to the lady on the rear seat.

"Oh, Sewell, stop the car. This is where the child lives. I hate to give her up though."

"Do you wanta keep me?" Isis brightened.

"Oh, I wish I could, you shining little morsel. Wait, I'll try to save you a whipping this time."

She dismounted with the gaudy lemon flavored culprit and advanced to the gate where Grandma stood glowering, switches in hand.

"You're gointuh ketchit f'um yo' haid to yo' heels m'lady. Jes' come in heah."

"Why, good afternoon," she accosted the furious grand-

parent. "You're not going to whip this poor little thing, are you?" the lady asked in conciliatory tones.

"Yes, Ma'am. She's de wustest lil' limb dat ever drawed bref. Jes' look at mah new table cloth, dat ain't never been washed. She done traipsed all over de woods, uh dancin' an' uh prancin' in it. She done took a razor to me t'day an' Lawd knows whut mo'."

Isis clung to the white hand fearfully.

"Ah wuzn't gointer hurt Gran'ma, miss—Ah wuz jus' gointer shave her whiskers fuh huh 'cause she's old an' can't."

The white hand closed tightly over the little brown one that was quite soiled. She could understand a voluntary act of love even though it miscarried.

"Now, Mrs. er—er—I didn't get the name—how much did your tablecloth cost?"

"One whole big silvah dollar down at O'landah—ain't had it a week yit."

"Now here's five dollars to get another one. The little thing loves laughter. I want her to go on to the hotel and dance in that tablecloth for me. I can stand a little light today—"

"Oh, yessum, yessum," Grandma cut in, "Everything's alright, sho' she kin go, yessum."

The lady went on: "I want brightness and this Isis is joy itself, why she's drenched in light!"

Isis for the first time in her life, felt herself appreciated and danced up and down in an ecstasy of joy for a minute.

"Now, behave yo'seff, Isie, ovah at de hotel wid de white folks," Grandma cautioned, pride in her voice, though she strove to hide it. "Lawd, ma'am, dat gal keeps me so frackshus, Ah doan know mah haid f'um mah feet. Ah orter comb huh haid, too, befo' she go wid you all."

"No, no, don't bother. I like her as she is. I don't think she'd like it either, being combed and scrubbed. Come on, Isis."

Feeling that Grandma had been somewhat squelched did not detract from Isis' spirit at all. She pranced over to the waiting motor and this time seated herself on the rear seat between the sweet, smiling lady and the rather aloof man in gray.

"Ah'm gointer stay wid you all," she said with a great deal of warmth, and snuggled up to her benefactress. "Want me tuh sing a song fuh you?"

"There, Helen, you've been adopted," said the man with a short, harsh laugh.

"Oh, I hope so, Harry." She put her arm about the red draped figure at her side and drew it close until she felt the warm puffs of the child's breath against her side. She looked hungrily ahead of her and spoke into space rather than to anyone in the car. "I want a little of her sunshine to soak into my soul. I need it."

Spunk

A GIANT of a brown-skinned man sauntered up the one street of the Village and out into the palmetto thickets with a small pretty woman clinging lovingly to his arm.

"Looka theah, folkses!" cried Elijah Mosley, slapping his leg gleefully. "Theah they go, big as life an' brassy as tacks."

All the loungers in the store tried to walk to the door with an air of nonchalance but with small success.

"Now pee-eople!" Walter Thomas gasped. "Will you look at 'em!"

"But that's one thing Ah likes about Spunk Banks—he ain't skeered of nothin' on God's green footstool—*nothin'!* He rides that log down at saw-mill jus' like he struts 'round wid another man's wife—jus' don't give a kitty. When Tes' Miller got cut to giblets on that circle-saw, Spunk steps right up and starts ridin'. The rest of us was skeered to go near it."

A round-shouldered figure in overalls much too large, came nervously in the door and the talking ceased. The men looked at each other and winked.

"Gimme some soda-water. Sass'prilla Ah reckon," the new-comer ordered, and stood far down the counter near the open pickled pig-feet tub to drink it.

Elijah nudged Walter and turned with mock gravity to the new-comer.

"Say, Joe, how's everything up yo' way? How's yo' wife?"

Joe started and all but dropped the bottle he held in his hands. He swallowed several times painfully and his lips trembled.

"Aw 'Lige, you oughtn't to do nothin' like that," Walter grumbled. Elijah ignored him.

"She jus' passed heah a few minutes ago goin' thata way," with a wave of his hand in the direction of the woods.

Now Joe knew his wife had passed that way. He knew that the men lounging in the general store had seen her, moreover, he knew that the men knew *he* knew. He stood there silent for a long moment staring blankly, with his Adam's apple twitching nervously up and down his throat. One could

actually *see* the pain he was suffering, his eyes, his face, his hands and even the dejected slump of his shoulders. He set the bottle down upon the counter. He didn't bang it, just eased it out of his hand silently and fiddled with his suspender buckle.

"Well, Ah'm goin' after her to-day. Ah'm goin' an' fetch her back. Spunk's done gone too fur."

He reached deep down into his trouser pocket and drew out a hollow ground razor, large and shiny, and passed his moistened thumb back and forth over the edge.

"Talkin' like a man, Joe. Course that's *yo'* fambly affairs, but Ah like to see grit in anybody."

Joe Kanty laid down a nickel and stumbled out into the street.

Dusk crept in from the woods. Ike Clarke lit the swinging oil lamp that was almost immediately surrounded by candle-flies. The men laughed boisterously behind Joe's back as they watched him shamble woodward.

"You oughtn't to said whut you did to him, Lige—look how it worked him up," Walter chided.

"And Ah hope it did work him up. 'Tain't even decent for a man to take and take like he do."

"Spunk will sho' kill him."

"Aw, Ah doan't know. You never kin tell. He might turn him up an' spank him fur gettin' in the way, but Spunk wouldn't shoot no unarmed man. Dat razor he carried outa heah ain't gonna run Spunk down an' cut him, an' Joe ain't got the nerve to go up to Spunk with it knowing he totes that Army .45. He makes that break outa heah to bluff us. He's gonna hide that razor behind the first likely palmetto root an' sneak back home to bed. Don't tell me nothin' 'bout that rabbit-foot colored man. Didn't he meet Spunk an' Lena face to face one day las' week an' mumble sumthin' to Spunk 'bout lettin' his wife alone?"

"What did Spunk say?" Walter broke in—"Ah like him fine but 'tain't right the way he carries on wid Lena Kanty, jus' cause Joe's timid 'bout fightin'. "

"You wrong theah, Walter. 'Tain't cause Joe's timid at all, it's cause Spunk wants Lena. If Joe was a passle of wile cats Spunk would tackle the job just the same. He'd go after *any-*

thing he wanted the same way. As Ah wuz sayin' a minute ago, he tole Joe right to his face that Lena was his. 'Call her,' he says to Joe. 'Call her and see if she'll come. A woman knows her boss an' she answers when he calls.' 'Lena, ain't I yo' husband?' Joe sorter whines out. Lena looked at him real disgusted but she don't answer and she don't move outa her tracks. Then Spunk reaches out an' takes hold of her arm an' says: 'Lena, youse mine. From now on Ah works for you an' fights for you an' Ah never wants you to look to nobody for a crumb of bread, a stitch of close or a shingle to go over yo' head, but *me* long as Ah live. Ah'll git the lumber foh owah house to-morrow. Go home an' git yo' things together!'

" 'Thass mah house,' Lena speaks up. 'Papa gimme that.'

" 'Well,' says Spunk, 'doan give up whut's yours, but when youse inside don't forgit youse mine, an' let no other man git outa his place wid you!'

"Lena looked up at him with her eyes so full of love that they wuz runnin' over, an' Spunk seen it an' Joe seen it too, and his lip started to tremblin' and his Adam's apple was galloping up and down his neck like a race horse. Ah bet he's wore out half a dozen Adam's apples since Spunk's been on the job with Lena. That's all he'll do. He'll be back heah after while swallowin' an' workin' his lips like he wants to say somethin' an' can't."

"But didn't he do *nothin'* to stop 'em?"

"Nope, not a frazzlin' thing—jus' stood there. Spunk took Lena's arm and walked off jus' like nothin' ain't happened and he stood there gazin' after them till they was outa sight. Now you know a woman don't want no man like that. I'm jus' waitin' to see whut he's goin' to say when he gits back."

II

But Joe Kanty never came back, never. The men in the store heard the sharp report of a pistol somewhere distant in the palmetto thicket and soon Spunk came walking leisurely, with his big black Stetson set at the same rakish angle and Lena clinging to his arm, came walking right into the general store. Lena wept in a frightened manner.

"Well," Spunk announced calmly, "Joe come out there wid a meatax an' made me kill him."

He sent Lena home and led the men back to Joe—Joe crumpled and limp with his right hand still clutching his razor.

"See mah back? Mah cloes cut clear through. He sneaked up an' tried to kill me from the back, but Ah got him, an' got him good, first shot," Spunk said.

The men glared at Elijah, accusingly.

"Take him up an' plant him in 'Stoney lonesome,' " Spunk said in a careless voice. "Ah didn't wanna shoot him but he made me do it. He's a dirty coward, jumpin' on a man from behind."

Spunk turned on his heel and sauntered away to where he knew his love wept in fear for him and no man stopped him. At the general store later on, they all talked of locking him up until the sheriff should come from Orlando, but no one did anything but talk.

A clear case of self-defense, the trial was a short one, and Spunk walked out of the court house to freedom again. He could work again, ride the dangerous log-carriage that fed the singing, snarling, biting, circle-saw; he could stroll the soft dark lanes with his guitar. He was free to roam the woods again; he was free to return to Lena. He did all of these things.

III

"Whut you reckon, Walt?" Elijah asked one night later. "Spunk's gittin' ready to marry Lena!"

"Naw! Why, Joe ain't had time to git cold yit. Nohow Ah didn't figger Spunk was the marryin' kind."

"Well, he is," rejoined Elijah. "He done moved most of Lena's things—and her along wid 'em—over to the Bradley house. He's buying it. Jus' like Ah told yo' all right in heah the night Joe wuz kilt. Spunk's crazy 'bout Lena. He don't want folks to keep on talkin' 'bout her—thass reason he's rushin' so. Funny thing 'bout that bob-cat, wan't it?"

"Whut bob-cat, 'Lige? Ah ain't heered 'bout none."

"Ain't cher? Well, night befo' las' was the fust night Spunk an' Lena moved together an' jus' as they was goin' to bed, a

big black bob-cat, black all over, you hear me, *black*, walked round and round that house and howled like forty, an' when Spunk got his gun an' went to the winder to shoot it, he says it stood right still an' looked him in the eye, an' howled right at him. The thing got Spunk so nervoused up he couldn't shoot. But Spunk says twan't no bob-cat nohow. He says it was Joe done sneaked back from Hell!"

"Humph!" sniffed Walter, "he oughter be nervous after what he done. Ah reckon Joe come back to dare him to marry Lena, or to come out an' fight. Ah bet he'll be back time and agin, too. Know what Ah think? Joe wuz a braver man than Spunk."

There was a general shout of derision from the group.

"Thass a fact," went on Walter. "Lookit whut he done; took a razor an' went out to fight a man he knowed toted a gun an' wuz a crack shot, too; 'nother thing Joe wuz skeered of Spunk, skeered plumb stiff! But he went jes' the same. It took him a long time to get his nerve up. 'Tain't nothin' for Spunk to fight when he ain't skeered of nothin'. Now, Joe's done come back to have it out wid the man that's got all he ever had. Y'll know Joe ain't never had nothin' nor wanted nothin' besides Lena. It musta been a h'ant cause ain' nobody never seen no black bob-cat."

"'Nother thing," cut in one of the men, "Spunk wuz cussin' a blue streak to-day 'cause he 'lowed dat saw wuz wobblin'—almos' got 'im once. The machinist come, looked it over an' said it wuz alright. Spunk musta been leanin' t'wards it some. Den he claimed somebody pushed 'im but 'twant nobody close to 'im. Ah wuz glad when knockin' off time come. I'm skeered of dat man when he gits hot. He'd beat you full of button holes as quick as he's look atcher."

IV

The men gathered the next evening in a different mood, no laughter. No badinage this time.

"Look, 'Lige, you goin' to set up wid Spunk?"

"Naw, Ah reckon not, Walter. Tell yuh the truth, Ah'm a lil bit skittish. Spunk died too wicket—died cussin' he did. You know he thought he wuz done outa life."

"Good Lawd, who'd he think done it?"

"Joe."

"Joe Kanty? How come?"

"Walter, Ah b'leeve Ah will walk up thata way an' set. Lena would like it Ah reckon."

"But whut did he say, 'Lige?"

Elijah did not answer until they had left the lighted store and were strolling down the dark street.

"Ah wuz loadin' a wagon wid scantlin' right near the saw when Spunk fell on the carriage but 'fore Ah could git to him the saw got him in the body—awful sight. Me an' Skint Miller got him off but it was too late. Anybody could see that. The fust thing he said wuz: 'He pushed me, 'Lige—the dirty hound pushed me in the back!'—He was spittin' blood at ev'ry breath. We laid him on the sawdust pile with his face to the East so's he could die easy. He helt mah han' till the last, Walter, and said: 'It was Joe, 'Lige—the dirty sneak shoved me . . . he didn't dare come to mah face . . . but Ah'll git the son-of-a-wood louse soon's Ah get there an' make hell too hot for him. . . . Ah felt him shove me . . . !' Thass how he died."

"If spirits kin fight, there's a powerful tussle goin' on somewhere ovah Jordan 'cause Ah b'leeve Joe's ready for Spunk an' ain't skeered any more—yas, Ah b'leeve Joe pushed 'im mahself."

They had arrived at the house. Lena's lamentations were deep and loud. She had filled the room with magnolia blossoms that gave off a heavy sweet odor. The keepers of the wake tipped about whispering in frightened tones. Everyone in the village was there, even old Jeff Kanty, Joe's father, who a few hours before would have been afraid to come within ten feet of him, stood leering triumphantly down upon the fallen giant as if his fingers had been the teeth of steel that laid him low.

The cooling board consisted of three sixteen-inch boards on saw horses, a dingy sheet was his shroud.

The women ate heartily of the funeral baked meats and wondered who would be Lena's next. The men whispered coarse conjectures between guzzles of whiskey.

Sweat

IT WAS eleven o'clock of a Spring night in Florida. It was Sunday. Any other night, Delia Jones would have been in bed for two hours by this time. But she was a washwoman, and Monday morning meant a great deal to her. So she collected the soiled clothes on Saturday when she returned the clean things. Sunday night after church, she sorted them and put the white things to soak. It saved her almost a half day's start. A great hamper in the bedroom held the clothes that she brought home. It was so much neater than a number of bundles lying around.

She squatted in the kitchen floor beside the great pile of clothes, sorting them into small heaps according to color, and humming a song in a mournful key, but wondering through it all where Sykes, her husband, had gone with her horse and buckboard.

Just then something long, round, limp and black fell upon her shoulders and slithered to the floor beside her. A great terror took hold of her. It softened her knees and dried her mouth so that it was a full minute before she could cry out or move. Then she saw that it was the big bull whip her husband liked to carry when he drove.

She lifted her eyes to the door and saw him standing there bent over with laughter at her fright. She screamed at him.

"Sykes, what you throw dat whip on me like dat? You know it would skeer me—looks just like a snake, an' you knows how skeered Ah is of snakes."

"Course Ah knowed it! That's how come Ah done it." He slapped his leg with his hand and almost rolled on the ground in his mirth. "If you such a big fool dat you got to have a fit over a earth worm or a string, Ah don't keer how bad Ah skeer you."

"You aint got no business doing it. Gawd knows it's a sin. Some day Ah'm gointuh drop dead from some of yo' foolishness. 'Nother thing, where you been wid mah rig? Ah feeds dat pony. He aint fuh you to be drivin' wid no bull whip."

"You sho is one aggravatin' nigger woman!" he declared

and stepped into the room. She resumed her work and did not answer him at once. "Ah done tole you time and again to keep them white folks' clothes outa dis house."

He picked up the whip and glared down at her. Delia went on with her work. She went out into the yard and returned with a galvanized tub and set it on the washbench. She saw that Sykes had kicked all of the clothes together again, and now stood in her way truculently, his whole manner hoping, *praying*, for an argument. But she walked calmly around him and commenced to re-sort the things.

"Next time, Ah'm gointer kick 'em outdoors," he threatened as he struck a match along the leg of his corduroy breeches.

Delia never looked up from her work, and her thin, stooped shoulders sagged further.

"Ah aint for no fuss t'night Sykes. Ah just come from taking sacrament at the church house."

He snorted scornfully. "Yeah, you just come from de church house on a Sunday night, but heah you is gone to work on them clothes. You ain't nothing but a hypocrite. One of them amen-corner Christians—sing, whoop, and shout, then come home and wash white folks clothes on the Sabbath."

He stepped roughly upon the whitest pile of things, kicking them helter-skelter as he crossed the room. His wife gave a little scream of dismay, and quickly gathered them together again.

"Sykes, you quit grindin' dirt into these clothes! How can Ah git through by Sat'day if Ah don't start on Sunday?"

"Ah don't keer if you never git through. Anyhow, Ah done promised Gawd and a couple of other men, Ah aint gointer have it in mah house. Don't gimme no lip neither, else Ah'll throw 'em out and put mah fist up side yo' head to boot."

Delia's habitual meekness seemed to slip from her shoulders like a blown scarf. She was on her feet; her poor little body, her bare knuckly hands bravely defying the strapping hulk before her.

"Looka heah, Sykes, you done gone too fur. Ah been married to you fur fifteen years, and Ah been takin' in washin' fur fifteen years. Sweat, sweat, sweat! Work and sweat, cry and sweat, pray and sweat!"

"What's that got to do with me?" he asked brutally.

"What's it got to do with you, Sykes? Mah tub of suds is filled yo' belly with vittles more times than yo' hands is filled it. Mah sweat is done paid for this house and Ah reckon Ah kin keep on sweatin' in it."

She seized the iron skillet from the stove and struck a defensive pose, which act surprised him greatly, coming from her. It cowed him and he did not strike her as he usually did.

"Naw you won't," she panted, "that ole snaggle-toothed black woman you runnin' with aint comin' heah to pile up on *mah* sweat and blood. You aint paid for nothin' on this place, and Ah'm gointer stay right heah till Ah'm toted out foot foremost."

"Well, you better quit gittin' me riled up, else they'll be totin' you out sooner than you expect. Ah'm so tired of you Ah don't know whut to do. Gawd! how Ah hates skinny wimmen!"

A little awed by this new Delia, he sidled out of the door and slammed the back gate after him. He did not say where he had gone, but she knew too well. She knew very well that he would not return until nearly daybreak also. Her work over, she went on to bed but not to sleep at once. Things had come to a pretty pass!

She lay awake, gazing upon the debris that cluttered their matrimonial trail. Not an image left standing along the way. Anything like flowers had long ago been drowned in the salty stream that had been pressed from her heart. Her tears, her sweat, her blood. She had brought love to the union and he had brought a longing after the flesh. Two months after the wedding, he had given her the first brutal beating. She had the memory of his numerous trips to Orlando with all of his wages when he had returned to her penniless, even before the first year had passed. She was young and soft then, but now she thought of her knotty, muscled limbs, her harsh knuckly hands, and drew herself up into an unhappy little ball in the middle of the big feather bed. Too late now to hope for love, even if it were not Bertha it would be someone else. This case differed from the others only in that she was bolder than the others. Too late for everything except her little home. She had

built it for her old days, and planted one by one the trees and flowers there. It was lovely to her, lovely.

Somehow, before sleep came, she found herself saying aloud: "Oh well, whatever goes over the Devil's back, is got to come under his belly. Sometime or ruther, Sykes, like everybody else, is gointer reap his sowing." After that she was able to build a spiritual earthworks against her husband. His shells could no longer reach her. *Amen.* She went to sleep and slept until he announced his presence in bed by kicking her feet and rudely snatching the cover away.

"Gimme some kivah heah, an' git yo' damn foots over on yo' own side! Ah oughter mash you in yo' mouf fuh drawing dat skillet on me."

Delia went clear to the rail without answering him. A triumphant indifference to all that he was or did.

The week was as full of work for Delia as all other weeks, and Saturday found her behind her little pony, collecting and delivering clothes.

It was a hot, hot day near the end of July. The village men on Joe Clarke's porch even chewed cane listlessly. They did not hurl the cane-knots as usual. They let them dribble over the edge of the porch. Even conversation had collapsed under the heat.

"Heah come Delia Jones," Jim Merchant said, as the shaggy pony came 'round the bend of the road toward them. The rusty buckboard was heaped with baskets of crisp, clean laundry.

"Yep," Joe Lindsay agreed. "Hot or col', rain or shine, jes ez reg'lar ez de weeks roll roun' Delia carries 'em an' fetches 'em on Sat'day."

"She better if she wanter eat," said Moss. "Syke Jones aint wuth de shot an' powder hit would tek tuh kill 'em. Not to *huh* he aint."

"He sho' aint," Walter Thomas chimed in. "It's too bad, too, cause she wuz a right pritty lil trick when he got huh. Ah'd uh mah'ied huh mahseff if he hadnter beat me to it."

Delia nodded briefly at the men as she drove past.

"Too much knockin' will ruin *any* 'oman. He done beat huh 'nough tuh kill three women, let 'lone change they

looks," said Elijah Mosely. "How Syke kin stommuck dat big black greasy Mogul he's layin' roun' wid, gits me. Ah swear dat eight-rock couldn't kiss a sardine can Ah done thowed out de back do' 'way las' yeah."

"Aw, she's fat, thass how come. He's allus been crazy 'bout fat women," put in Merchant. "He'd a' been tied up wid one long time ago if he could a' found one tuh have him. Did Ah tell yuh 'bout him come sidlin' roun' *mah* wife—bringin' her a basket uh pee-cans outa his yard fuh a present? Yessir, mah wife! She tol' him tuh take 'em right straight back home, cause Delia works so hard ovah dat washtub she reckon everything on de place taste lak sweat an' soapsuds. Ah jus' wisht Ah'd a' caught 'im 'roun' dere! Ah'd a' made his hips ketch on fiah down dat shell road."

"Ah know he done it, too. Ah sees 'im grinnin' at every 'oman dat passes," Walter Thomas said. "But even so, he useter eat some mighty big hunks uh humble pie tuh git dat lil' 'oman he got. She wuz ez pritty ez a speckled pup! Dat wuz fifteen yeahs ago. He useter be so skeered uh losin' huh, she could make him do some parts of a husband's duty. Dey never wuz de same in de mind."

"There oughter be a law about him," said Lindsay. "He aint fit tuh carry guts tuh a bear."

Clarke spoke for the first time. "Taint no law on earth dat kin make a man be decent if it aint in 'im. There's plenty men dat takes a wife lak dey do a joint uh sugar-cane. It's round, juicy an' sweet when dey gits it. But dey squeeze an' grind, squeeze an' grind an' wring tell dey wring every drop uh pleasure dat's in 'em out. When dey's satisfied dat dey is wrung dry, dey treats 'em jes lak dey do a cane-chew. Dey thows 'em away. Dey knows whut dey is doin' while dey is at it, an' hates theirselves fuh it but they keeps on hangin' after huh tell she's empty. Den dey hates huh fuh bein' a cane-chew an' in de way."

"We oughter take Syke an' dat stray 'oman uh his'n down in Lake Howell swamp an' lay on de rawhide till they cain't say 'Lawd a' mussy.' He allus wuz uh ovahbearin' niggah, but since dat white 'oman from up north done teached 'im how to run a automobile, he done got too biggety to live—an' we oughter kill 'im," Old Man Anderson advised.

A grunt of approval went around the porch. But the heat was melting their civic virtue and Elijah Moseley began to bait Joe Clarke.

"Come on, Joe, git a melon outa dere an' slice it up for yo' customers. We'se all sufferin' wid de heat. De bear's done got *me*!"

"Thass right, Joe, a watermelon is jes' whut Ah needs tuh cure de eppizudicks," Walter Thomas joined forces with Moseley. "Come on dere, Joe. We all is steady customers an' you aint set us up in a long time. Ah chooses dat long, bow-legged Floridy favorite."

"A god, an' be dough. You all gimme twenty cents and slice away," Clarke retorted. "Ah needs a col' slice m'self. Heah, everybody chip in. Ah'll lend y'll mah meat knife."

The money was quickly subscribed and the huge melon brought forth. At that moment, Sykes and Bertha arrived. A determined silence fell on the porch and the melon was put away again.

Merchant snapped down the blade of his jackknife and moved toward the store door.

"Come on in, Joe, an' gimme a slab uh sow belly an' uh pound uh coffee—almost fuhgot 'twas Sat'day. Got to git on home." Most of the men left also.

Just then Delia drove past on her way home, as Sykes was ordering magnificently for Bertha. It pleased him for Delia to see.

"Git whutsoever yo' heart desires, Honey. Wait a minute, Joe. Give huh two bottles uh strawberry soda-water, uh quart uh parched ground-peas, an' a block uh chewin' gum."

With all this they left the store, with Sykes reminding Bertha that this was his town and she could have it if she wanted it.

The men returned soon after they left, and held their watermelon feast.

"Where did Syke Jones git dat 'oman from nohow?" Lindsay asked.

"Ovah Apopka. Guess dey musta been cleanin' out de town when she lef'. She don't look lak a thing but a hunk uh liver wid hair on it."

"Well, she sho' kin squall," Dave Carter contributed.

"When she gits ready tuh laff, she jes' opens huh mouf an' latches it back tuh de las' notch. No ole grandpa alligator down in Lake Bell ain't got nothin' on huh."

Bertha had been in town three months now. Sykes was still paying her room rent at Della Lewis'—the only house in town that would have taken her in. Sykes took her frequently to Winter Park to "stomps." He still assured her that he was the swellest man in the state.

"Sho' you kin have dat lil' ole house soon's Ah kin git dat 'oman outa dere. Everything b'longs tuh me an' you sho' kin have it. Ah sho' 'bominates uh skinny 'oman. Lawdy, you sho' is got one portly shape on you! You kin git *anything* you wants. Dis is *mah* town an' you sho' kin have it."

Delia's work-worn knees crawled over the earth in Gethsemane and up the rocks of Calvary many, many times during these months. She avoided the villagers and meeting places in her efforts to be blind and deaf. But Bertha nullified this to a degree, by coming to Delia's house to call Sykes out to her at the gate.

Delia and Sykes fought all the time now with no peaceful interludes. They slept and ate in silence. Two or three times Delia had attempted a timid friendliness, but she was repulsed each time. It was plain that the breaches must remain agape.

The sun had burned July to August. The heat streamed down like a million hot arrows, smiting all things living upon the earth. Grass withered, leaves browned, snakes went blind in shedding and men and dogs went mad. Dog days!

Delia came home one day and found Sykes there before her. She wondered, but started to go on into the house without speaking, even though he was standing in the kitchen door and she must either stoop under his arm or ask him to move. He made no room for her. She noticed a soap box beside the steps, but paid no particular attention to it, knowing that he must have brought it there. As she was stooping to pass under his outstretched arm, he suddenly pushed her backward, laughingly.

"Look in de box dere Delia, Ah done brung yuh somethin'!"

She nearly fell upon the box in her stumbling, and when she saw what it held, she all but fainted outright.

"Syke! Syke, mah Gawd! You take dat rattlesnake 'way from heah! You *gottuh*. Oh, Jesus, have mussy!"

"Ah aint gut tuh do nuthin' uh de kin'—fact is Ah aint got tuh do nothin' but die. Taint no use uh you puttin' on airs makin' out lak you skeered uh dat snake—he's gointer stay right heah tell he die. He wouldn't bite me cause Ah knows how tuh handle 'im. Nohow he wouldn't risk breakin' out his fangs 'gin *yo'* skinny laigs."

"Naw, now Syke, don't keep dat thing 'roun' heah tuh skeer me tuh death. You knows Ah'm even feared uh earth worms. Thass de biggest snake Ah evah did see. Kill 'im Syke, please."

"Doan ast me tuh do nothin' fuh yuh. Goin' 'roun' tryin' tuh be so damn asterperious. Naw, Ah aint gonna kill it. Ah think uh damn sight mo' uh him dan you! Dat's a nice snake an' anybody doan lak 'im kin jes' hit de grit."

The village soon heard that Sykes had the snake, and came to see and ask questions.

"How de hen-fire did you ketch dat six-foot rattler, Syke?" Thomas asked.

"He's full uh frogs so he caint hardly move, thass how Ah eased up on 'm. But Ah'm a snake charmer an' knows how tuh handle 'em. Shux, dat aint nothin'. Ah could ketch one eve'y day if Ah so wanted tuh."

"Whut he needs is a heavy hick'ry club leaned real heavy on his head. Dat's de bes 'way tuh charm a rattlesnake."

"Naw, Walt, y'll jes' don't understand dese diamon' backs lak Ah do," said Sykes in a superior tone of voice.

The village agreed with Walter, but the snake stayed on. His box remained by the kitchen door with its screen wire covering. Two or three days later it had digested its meal of frogs and literally came to life. It rattled at every movement in the kitchen or the yard. One day as Delia came down the kitchen steps she saw his chalky-white fangs curved like scimitars hung in the wire meshes. This time she did not run away with averted eyes as usual. She stood for a long time in the doorway in a red fury that grew bloodier for every second that she regarded the creature that was her torment.

That night she broached the subject as soon as Sykes sat down to the table.

"Syke, Ah wants you tuh take dat snake 'way fum heah. You done starved me an' Ah put up widcher, you done beat me an Ah took dat, but you done kilt all mah insides bringin' dat varmint heah."

Sykes poured out a saucer full of coffee and drank it deliberately before he answered her.

"A whole lot Ah keer 'bout how you feels inside uh out. Dat snake aint goin' no damn wheah till Ah gits ready fuh 'im tuh go. So fur as beatin' is concerned, yuh aint took near all dat you gointer take ef yuh stay 'roun' *me.*"

Delia pushed back her plate and got up from the table. "Ah hates you, Sykes," she said calmly. "Ah hates you tuh de same degree dat Ah useter love yuh. Ah done took an' took till mah belly is full up tuh mah neck. Dat's de reason Ah got mah letter fum de church an' moved mah membership tuh Woodbridge—so Ah don't haftuh take no sacrament wid yuh. Ah don't wantuh see yuh 'roun' me atall. Lay 'roun' wid dat 'oman all yuh wants tuh, but gwan 'way fum me an' mah house. At hates yuh lak uh suck-egg dog."

Sykes almost let the huge wad of corn bread and collard greens he was chewing fall out of his mouth in amazement. He had a hard time whipping himself up to the proper fury to try to answer Delia.

"Well, Ah'm glad you does hate me. Ah'm sho' tiahed uh you hangin' ontuh me. Ah don't want yuh. Look at yuh stringey ole neck! Yo' rawbony laigs an' arms is enough tuh cut uh man tuh death. You looks jes' lak de devvul's doll-baby tuh *me.* You cain't hate me no worse dan Ah hates you. Ah been hatin' *you* fuh years."

"Yo' ole black hide don't look lak nothin' tuh me, but uh passle uh wrinkled up rubber, wid yo' big ole yeahs flappin' on each side lak uh paih uh buzzard wings. Don't think Ah'm gointuh be run 'way fum mah house neither. Ah'm goin' tuh de white folks bout *you,* mah young man, de very nex' time you lay yo' han's on me. Mah cup is done run ovah." Delia said this with no signs of fear and Sykes departed from the house, threatening her, but made not the slightest move to carry out any of them.

That night he did not return at all, and the next day being Sunday, Delia was glad that she did not have to quarrel before she hitched up her pony and drove the four miles to Wood-bridge.

She stayed to the night service—"love feast"—which was very warm and full of spirit. In the emotional winds her domestic trials were borne far and wide so that she sang as she drove homeward,

> *"Jurden water, black an' col'*
> *Chills de body, not de soul*
> *An' Ah wantah cross Jurden in uh calm time."*

She came from the barn to the kitchen door and stopped.

"Whut's de mattah, ol' satan, you aint kickin' up yo' racket?" She addressed the snake's box. Complete silence. She went on into the house with a new hope in its birth struggles. Perhaps her threat to go to the white folks had frightened Sykes! Perhaps he was sorry! Fifteen years of misery and suppression had brought Delia to the place where she would hope *anything* that looked towards a way over or through her wall of inhibitions.

She felt in the match safe behind the stove at once for a match. There was only one there.

"Dat niggah wouldn't fetch nothin' heah tuh save his rotten neck, but he kin run thew whut Ah brings quick enough. Now he done toted off nigh on tuh haff uh box uh matches. He done had dat 'oman heah in mah house, too."

Nobody but a woman could tell how she knew this even before she struck the match. But she did and it put her into a new fury.

Presently she brought in the tubs to put the white things to soak. This time she decided she need not bring the hamper out of the bedroom; she would go in there and do the sorting. She picked up the pot-bellied lamp and went in. The room was small and the hamper stood hard by the foot of the white iron bed. She could sit and reach through the bedposts—resting as she worked.

"Ah wantah cross Jurden in uh calm time." She was singing again. The mood of the "love feast" had returned. She threw back the lid of the basket almost gaily. Then, moved by both

horror and terror, she spring back toward the door. *There lay the snake in the basket!* He moved sluggishly at first, but even as she turned round and round, jumped up and down in an insanity of fear, he began to stir vigorously. She saw him pouring his awful beauty from the basket upon the bed, then she seized the lamp and ran as fast as she could to the kitchen. The wind from the open door blew out the light and the darkness added to her terror. She sped to the darkness of the yard, slamming the door after her before she thought to set down the lamp. She did not feel safe even on the ground, so she climbed up in the hay barn.

There for an hour or more she lay sprawled upon the hay a gibbering wreck.

Finally she grew quiet, and after that, coherent thought. With this, stalked through her a cold, bloody rage. Hours of this. A period of introspection, a space of retrospection, then a mixture of both. Out of this an awful calm.

"Well, Ah done de bes' Ah could. If things aint right, Gawd knows taint mah fault."

She went to sleep—a twitchy sleep—and woke up to a faint gray sky. There was a loud hollow sound below. She peered out. Sykes was at the wood-pile, demolishing a wire-covered box.

He hurried to the kitchen door, but hung outside there some minutes before he entered, and stood some minutes more inside before he closed it after him.

The gray in the sky was spreading. Delia descended without fear now, and crouched beneath the low bedroom window. The drawn shade shut out the dawn, shut in the night. But the thin walls held back no sound.

"Dat ol' scratch is woke up now!" She mused at the tremendous whirr inside, which every woodsman knows, is one of the sound illusions. The rattler is a ventriloquist. His whirr sounds to the right, to the left, straight ahead, behind, close under foot—everywhere but where it is. Woe to him who guesses wrong unless he is prepared to hold up his end of the argument! Sometimes he strikes without rattling at all.

Inside, Sykes heard nothing until he knocked a pot lid off the stove while trying to reach the match safe in the dark. He had emptied his pockets at Bertha's.

The snake seemed to wake up under the stove and Sykes made a quick leap into the bedroom. In spite of the gin he had had, his head was clearing now.

"Mah Gawd!" he chattered, "ef Ah could on'y strack uh light!"

The rattling ceased for a moment as he stood paralyzed. He waited. It seemed that the snake waited also.

"Oh, fuh de light! Ah thought he'd be too sick"—Sykes was muttering to himself when the whirr began again, closer, right underfoot this time. Long before this, Sykes' ability to think had been flattened down to primitive instinct and he leaped—onto the bed.

Outside Delia heard a cry that might have come from a maddened chimpanzee, a stricken gorilla. All the terror, all the horror, all the rage that man possibly could express, without a recognizable human sound.

A tremendous stir inside there, another series of animal screams, the intermittent whirr of the reptile. The shade torn violently down from the window, letting in the red dawn, a huge brown hand seizing the window stick, great dull blows upon the wooden floor punctuating the gibberish of sound long after the rattle of the snake had abruptly subsided. All this Delia could see and hear from her place beneath the window, and it made her ill. She crept over to the four-o'clocks and stretched herself on the cool earth to recover.

She lay there. "Delia, Delia!" She could hear Sykes calling in a most despairing tone as one who expected no answer. The sun crept on up, and he called. Delia could not move— her legs were gone flabby. She never moved, he called, and the sun kept rising.

"Mah Gawd!" She heard him moan. "Mah Gawd fum He-ben!" She heard him stumbling about and got up from her flower-bed. The sun was growing warm. As she approached the door she heard him call out hopefully, "Delia, is dat you Ah heah?"

She saw him on his hands and knees as soon as she reached the door. He crept an inch or two toward her—all that he was able, and she saw his horribly swollen neck and his one open eye shining with hope. A surge of pity too strong to support bore her away from that eye that must, could not, fail

to see the tubs. He would see the lamp. Orlando with its doctors was too far. She could scarcely reach the Chinaberry tree, where she waited in the growing heat while inside she knew the cold river was creeping up and up to extinguish that eye which must know by now that she knew.

The Bone of Contention

EATONVILLE Florida is a colored town and has its colored interests. It has not now, nor ever has had anything to rank Brazzle's yellow mule. His Yaller Highness was always mentioned before the weather, the misery of the back or leg, or the hard times.

The mule was old, rawbony and mean. He was so rawbony that he creaked as he ambled about the village street with his meanness shining out through every chink and cranny in his rattling anatomy. He worked little, ate heartily, fought every inch of the way before the plow and even disputed with Brazzle when he approached to feed him. Sale, exchange or barter was out of the question, for everybody in the county knew him.

But one day he died. Everybody was glad, including Brazzle. His death was one of those pleasant surprises that people hope for, but never expect to happen.

The city had no refuse plant so H.Y.H. went the way of all other domestic beasts who died among us. Brazzle borrowed Watson's two grey plugs and dragged the remains out to the edge of the cypress swamp, three miles beyond the city limits and abandoned them to the natural scavengers. The town attended the dragging out to a man. The fallen gladiator was borne from the arena on his sharp back, his feet stiffly raised as if in a parting gesture of defiance. We left him on the edge of the cypress swamp and returned to the village satisfied that the only piece of unadulterated meanness that the Lord had ever made was gone from among us forever.

Three years passed and his bones were clean and white. They were scattered along the swamp edge. The children still found them sufficiently interesting to tramp out to gaze upon them on Sunday afternoons. The elders neglected his bones, but the mule remained with them in song and story as a simile, as a metaphor, to point a moral or adorn a tale. But as the mean old trouble-making cuss, they considered him gone for good.

II

It was early night in the village. Joe Clarke's store porch was full of chewing men. Some chewed tobacco, some chewed cane, some chewed straws, for the villager is a ruminant in his leisure. They sat thus every evening ostensibly waiting for the mail from Number 38, the south-bound express. It was seldom that any of them got any but it gave them a good excuse to gather. They all talked a great deal, and every man jack of them talked about himself. Heroes all, they were, of one thing or another.

Ike Pearson had killed a six-foot rattler in a mighty battle that grew mightier every time Ike told about it; Walter Thomas had chinned the bar twenty times without stopping; Elijah Moseley had licked a "cracker"; Brazzle had captured a live catamount; Hiram Lester had killed a bear; Sykes Jones had won the soda-cracker eating contest; AND JOE CLARKE HAD STARTED THE TOWN!

Reverend Simms, the Methodist preacher, a resident of less than a year, had done nothing to boast of, but it was generally known that he aspired to the seat of Joe Clarke. He wanted to be the mayor. He had observed to some of his members that it wasnt no sense in one man staying in office all the time.

"Looka heah," Clarke cut across whoever it was that was talking at the time, "When Ah started dis town, Ah walked right up to de white folks an' laid down TWO HUN'DED DOLLAHS WID DIS RIGHT HAND YOU SEE BEFO' YOU AN' GOT MAH PAPERS AN' PUT DIS TOWN ON DE MAP! It takes uh powerful lot uh sense an' grit tuh start uh town, yessirree!"

"Whut map did you put it on, Joe?" Lindsay disrespectfully asked. "Ah aint seed it on no map."

Seeing Clarke gored to his liver, Rev. Simms let out a gloating snicker and tossed a cane knot to Tippy, the Lewis' dejected dog frame hovering about the group hoping for something more tempting to a dog's palate than cane chews and peanut shells might drop. He tossed the knot and waited for Clarke to answer. His Honor ignored the thrust as being too low for him to stoop to and talked on. Was he not mayor,

postmaster, storekeeper and Pooh Bah general? Insults must come to him from at least the county seat.

"Nother thing," Clarke continued, giving Simms a meaning look, "There's a heap goin' on 'round heah under the cover dat Ahm gointer put a stop to. Jim Weston done pro-aged through mah hen house enough. Last Sat'day Ah missed three uh mah bes' layin' hens, an' Ah been tol' he buried feathers in his backyard the very next day. Cose Ah caint prove nothin', but de minute he crooks his little finger, he goes 'way from mah town. He aint de onliest one Ah got mah eye on neither."

Simms accepted the challenge thrown at him.

"Fact is, the town aint run lak it might be. We oughta stop dat foolishness of runnin' folks outa town. We oughta jail'em. They's got jails in all de other towns, an' we oughta bring ours up to date."

"Ah'll be henfired! Simms, you tries to know mo' 'bout runnin' de town than me! Dont you reckon a man thats got sense enough to start uh town, knows how tuh run it. Dont you reckon if de place had uh needed uh jailhouse Ah would have got one built 'long befo' you come heah?"

"We do so need a jail," Lindsay contended. "Jus' cause you stahted the town, dat dont make yo' mouf no prayer book nor neither yo' lips no Bible. They dont flap lak none tuh *me*."

Lindsay was a little shriveled up man with grey hair and bow-legs. He was the smallest man in the village, who nevertheless did the most talk of fighting. That was because the others felt he was too small for them to hit. He was harmless, but known to be the nastiest threatener in the county.

Clarke merely snorted contemptuously at his sally and remarked dryly that the road was right there for all those who were not satisfied with the way he was running the town.

"Meaning to insult me?" Lindsay asked belligerently.

"Ah dont keer HOW yuh take it. Jus' take yo' rawbony cow an' gwan tuh de woods, fuh all I keer," Clarke answered.

Lindsay leaped from the porch and struck his fighting pose. "Jus' hit de ground an' Ah'll strow yuh all over Orange County! Aw, come on! Come on! Youse a big seegar, but Ah kin smoke yuh!"

Clarke looked at the little man, old, and less that half his size and laughed. Walter Thomas and 'Lige Moseley rushed to Lindsay and pretended to restrain him.

"That's right," Lindsay panted, "you better hold me offen him. Cause if I lay de weight uh dis right hand on him, he wont forget it long as he live."

"Aw, shet up, Lin'say, an' set down. If you could fight as good as you kin threaten, you'd be world's champeen 'stead uh Jack Dempsey. Some uh dese days when youse hollerin' tuh be let loose, somebody's gointer take you at yo' word, then it will be jus' too bad about yuh," Lester admonished.

"Who? — "

The war was about to begin all over on another front when Dave Carter, the local Nimrod, walked, almost ran up the steps of the porch. He was bareheaded, excited and even in the poor light that seeped to the porch from the oil lamps within, it was seen that he was bruised and otherwise unusually mussed up.

"Mist' Clarke, Ah wants tuh see yuh," he said. "Come on inside."

"Sholy, Dave, sholy." The mayor responded and followed the young man into the store and the corner reserved for City Administration. The crowd from the porch followed to a man.

Dave wiped a bruise spot on his head. "Mist' Clarke, Ah wants uh warrant took out fuh Jim Weston. Ahm gointer law him outa dis town. He caint lam me over mah head wid no mule bone and steal mah turkey and go braggin' about it!"

Under the encouraging quiz of the mayor, Dave told his story. He was a hunter and fisherman, as everybody knew. He had discovered a drove of wild turkeys roosting in the trees along the edge of the cypress swamp near the spot where Brazzle's old mule had been left. He had watched them for weeks, had seen the huge gobbler that headed the flock and resolved to get him.

"Yes," agreed Clarke, "you said something to me about it yesterday when you bought some shells."

"Yes, and thats how Jim knowed Ah was goin' turkey huntin'. He was settin' on de store porch and heard me talkin' to you. Today when Ah started out, jes 'bout sun-

down—dats de bes' time tuh get turkeys, when they goes tuh roost—he ups and says he's goin' long. Ah didnt keer 'bout dat, but when them birds goes tuh roost, he aint even loaded, so Ah had shot dat gobbler befo' he took aim. When he see dat great big gobbler fallin' he fires off his gun and tries tuh grab him. But Ah helt on. We got tuh pushin' and shovin' and tusslin' 'till we got to fightin'. Jim's a bully, but Ah wuz beatin' his socks offa him till he retched down and picked up de hock-bone of Brazzle's ol' mule and lammed me ovah mah head wid it and knocked me out. When Ah come to, he had done took mah turkey and gone. Ah wants uh warrant, Mist' Clarke. Ahm gointer law him outa dis town."

"An' you sho gointer get, Dave. He oughter be run out. Comes from bad stock. Every last one of his brothers been run out as fast as they grow up. Daddy hung for murder."

Clarke busied himself with the papers. The crowd looking on and commenting.

"See whut you Meth'dis' niggahs will do?" asked Brazzle, a true Baptist. "Goin' round lammin' folks ovah the head an' stealin they turkeys."

"Cose everybody knows dem Westons is a set uh bullies, but you Baptists aint such a much," Elijah Moseley retorted.

"Yas, but Ah know yuh know," put in Lindsay. "No Baptis' aint never done nothin' bad as dat. Joe Clarke is right. Jail is too good fuh 'em. The last one uh these heah half-washed christians oughta be run 'way from heah."

"When it comes tuh dat, theres jus' as many no count Baptists as anybody else. Jus' aint caught 'em," Thomas said, joining the fray.

"Yas," Lindsay retorted, "but we done kotched yo' Meth'dis' niggah. Kotched him knockin' people ovah de head wid mule bones an' stealin' they turkeys, an' wese gointer run him slap outa town sure as gun's iron. The dirty onion!"

"We dont know whether you will or no, Joe Lindsay. You Baptists aint runnin' this town exactly."

"Trial set for three oclock tomorrow at de Baptis' church, that being the largest meetin' place in town," Clarke announced with a satisfied smile and persuaded the men to go back to the porch to argue.

Clarke, himself, was a Methodist, but in this case, his in-

terests lay with the other side. If he could get Jim to taste the air of another town, chicken mortality of the sudden and un-explained variety, would drop considerably, he was certain. He was equally certain that the ambitious Simms would champion Jim's cause and losing the fight, lose prestige. Be-sides, Jim was a troublesome character. A constant disturber of the village peace.

III

It was evident to the simplest person in the village long before three oclock that this was to be a religious and political fight. The assault and the gobbler were unimportant. Dave was a Baptist, Jim a Methodist, only two churches in the town and the respective congregations had lined up solidly.

At three the house was full. The defendant had been led in and seated in the amen corner to the left of the pulpit. Rev. Simms had taken his place beside the prisoner in the role of defense counsel. The plaintiff, with Elder Long, shepherd of the Baptist flock in the capacity of prosecution, was seated at the right. The respective congregations were lined up behind their leaders.

Mutual glances of despisement and gloating are exchanged across the aisle. Not a few verbal sorties were made during this waiting period as if they were getting up steam for the real struggle.

Wize Anderson (Meth) Look at ole Dave tryin' to make out Jim hurt his head! Yuh couldnt hurt a Baptist head wid a hammer—they're that hard.

Brother Poke (Bapt.) Well, anyhow we dont lie an' steal an' git run outa town lak de softhead Meth'dis niggahs.

Some Baptist wag looked over at Jim and crowed like a rooster, the others took it up immediately and the place was full of hen-cackling and barnyard sounds. The implication was obvious. Jim stood up and said, "If I had dat mule bone heah, Ahd teach a few mo' uh you mud-turtles something."

Enter His Honor at this moment. Lum Boger pompously conducted him to his place, the pulpit, which was doing duty as the bench for the occasion. The assembly unconsciously moderated its tone. But from the outside could still be heard

the voices of the children engaged in fisticuffy trials of the case.

The mayor began rapping for order at once. "Cote is set. Cote is set! Looka heah, DIS COTE IS DONE SET! Ah wants you folks tuh dry up."

The courtroom grew perfectly still. The mayor prepared to read the charge to the prisoner, when Brother Stringer (Meth.) entered, hot and perspiring with coat over his arm. He found a seat near the middle of the house against the wall. To reach it, he must climb over the knees of a bench length of people. Before seating himself, he hung his coat upon an empty lamp bracket above his head.

Sister Lewis of the Baptist persuasion, arose at once, her hands akimbo, her eyes flashing.

"Brothah Stringah, you take yo' lousy coat down off dese sacred walls! Aint you Methdis got no gumption in the house uh washup?"

Stringer did not answer her, but he cast over a glance that said as plain as day, Just try and make me do it!

Della Lewis snorted, but Stringer took his seat complacently. He took his seat, but rose up again as if he had sat on a hot needle point. The reason for this was that Brother Hambo on the Baptist side, a nasty scrapper, rose and rolled his eyes to the fighting angle, looking at Stringer. Stringer caught the look, and hurriedly pawed that coat down off that wall.

Sister Taylor (M) took up the gauntlet dropped like a hot potato by Stringer. "Some folks" she said with a meaning look, "is a whole lot mo' puhtic'lar bout a louse in they church than they is in they house." A very personal look at Sister Lewis.

"Well" said that lady, "mah house mought not be exactly clean. But nobody caint say *dat*"—indicating an infinitesimal amount on the end of her finger—"about my chaRACter! They didnt hafta git de sheriff to make Ike marry ME!"

Mrs. Taylor leaped to her feet and struggled to cross the aisle to her traducer but was restrained by three or four men. "Yas, they did git de sheriff tuh make Sam marry me!" She shouted as she panted and struggled, "And Gawd knows you

sho oughter git him again and make *some* of these men marry yo' Ada."

Mrs. Lewis now had to be restrained. She gave voice and hard, bone-breaking words flew back and forth across the aisle. Each was aided and abetted by her side of the house. His Honor was all the time beating the pulpit with his gavel and shouting for order. At last he threatened to descend in person upon the belligerents.

"Heah! You moufy wimmen! Shet up. Aint Ah done said cote was set? Lum Boger, do yo' duty. Make them wimmen dry up or put 'em outa heah."

Marshall Boger who wore his star for the occasion was full of the importance of his office for nineteen is a prideful age; he hurried over to Mrs. Taylor. She rose to meet him. "You better gwan 'way from me, Lum Boger. Ah jes' wish you would lay de weight of yo' han' on me! Ahd kick yo' cloes up round yo' neck lak a horse collar. You impident limb you."

Lum retreated before the awful prospect of wearing his suit about his neck like a horse-collar. He crossed the aisle to the fiery Della and frowned upon her. She was already standing and ready to commence hostilities. One look was enough. He said nothing, but her threats followed him down the aisle as he retreated to the vestibule to shoo the noisy children away. The women subsided and the Mayor began.

"We come heah on very important business," he said. "Stan' up dere, Jim Weston. You is charged wid 'ssaultin' Dave Carter here wid a mule bone, and robbin' him uh his wild turkey. Is you guilty or not guilty?"

Jim arose, looked insolently around the room and answered the charge: "Yas, Ah hit him and took de turkey cause it wuz mine. Ah hit him and Ahll hit him agin, but it wasnt no crime this time."

His Honor's jaw dropped. There was surprise on the faces of all the Baptist section, surprise and perplexity. Gloating and laughter from the Methodists. Simms pulled Jim's coat-tail.

"Set down Jim," he cooed, "youse one of mah lambs. Set down. Yo' shepherd will show them that walks in de darkness wid sinners and republicans de light."

Jim sat down and the pastor got to his feet.

"Looka heah, Jim, this aint for no foolishness. Do you re-alize dat if youse found guilty, youse gonna be run outa town?"

"Yeah" Jim answered without rising. "But Ah aint gonna be found no guilty. You caint find me." There was a pleasur-able stir on his side of the house. The Baptists were still in the coma which Jim's first statement had brought on.

"Ah say too, he aint guilty," began Rev. Simms with great unction in his tones. "Ah done been to de cot-house at Or-lando an' set under de voice of dem lawyers an' heard 'em law from mornin' tell night. They says you got tuh have a weepon befo' you kin commit uh 'ssault. Ah done read dis heah Bible fum lid tuh lid (he made a gesture to indicate the thorough-ness of his search) and it aint in no Bible dat no mule bone is a weepon, an' it aint in no white folks law neither. Therefo' Brother Mayor, Ah ast you tuh let Jim go. You gotta turn 'im loose, cause nobody kin run 'im outa town when he aint done no crime."

A deep purple gloom settled down upon the Mayor and his followers. Over against this the wild joy of the Methodists. Simms already felt the reins of power in his hands. Over the protest of the Mayor he raised a song and he and his followers sang it with great gusto.

> "Oh Mary dont you weep, dont you mourn
> Oh Mary, dont you weep dont you mourn
> Pharaoh's army got drownded,
> O-O-oh Mary, dont you weep"

The troubled expression on the face of the Baptist leader, Elder Long, suddenly lifted. He arose while yet the trium-phant defense is singing its hallelujah. Mayor Clarke quieted the tumult with difficulty. Simms saw him rise but far from being worried, he sank back upon the seat, his eyes half closed, hands folded fatly across his fat stomach. He smirked. Let them rave! He had built his arguments on solid rock, and the gates of Baptist logic could not prevail against it!

When at last Long got the attention of the assembly, he commanded Dave to stand.

"Ah jus want you all tuh take a look at his head. Anybody

kin see dat big knot dat Jim put on dere." Jim, the Rev. Simms and all his communicants laughed loudly at this, but Long went on calmly. "Ah been tuh de cote-house tuh Orlando an' heard de white folks law as much as any body heah. And dey dont ast whether de thing dat a person gits hurt wid is uh weepon or not. All dey wants tuh fin' out is, 'did it hurt?' Now you all kin see dat mule bone did hurt Dave's head. So it must be a weepon cause it hurt 'im."

Rev. Simms had his eyes wide open now. He jumped to his feet.

"Never mind bout dem white folks laws at O'landa, Brother Long. Dis is a colored town. Nohow we oughter run by de laws uh de Bible. Dem white folks laws dont go befo' whuts in dis sacred book."

"Jes' hold yo' hot potater, Brother Simms, Ahm comin' tuh dat part right now. Jes lemme take yo' Bible a minute."

"Naw indeed. You oughter brought one of yo' own if you got one. Furthemo' Brother Mayor, we got work tuh do. Wese workin' people. Dont keep us in heah too long. Dis case is through wid."

"Oh, naw it aint" the Mayor disagreed, "you done talked yo' side, now you got tuh let Brother Long talk his. So fur as de work is concerned, it kin wait. One thing at a time. Come on up heah in yo' pulpit an' read yo' own Bible, Brother Long. Dont mind me being up heah."

Long ascended the pulpit and began to turn the leaves of the large Bible. The entire assembly slid forward to the edges of the seat.

"Ah done proved by de white folks law dat Jim oughter be run outa town an' now Ahm gointer show by de Bible—"

Simms was on his feet again. "But Brother Mayor—"

"Set down Simms" was all the answer he got. "Youse *entirely* outa order."

"It says heah in Judges 15:16 dat Samson slewed a thousand Philistines wid de jaw-bone of a ass" Long drawled.

"Yas, but this wasnt no ass, this was a mule" Simms objected.

"And now dat bring us to de main claw uh dis subjick. It sho want no ass, but everybody knows dat a donkey is de father of every mule what ever wuz born. Even little chillen

knows dat. Everybody knows dat dat little as a donkey is, dat
if he is dangerous, his great big mule son is mo' so. Every-
body knows dat de further back on a mule you goes, de mo'
dangerous he gits. Now if de jawbone is as dangerous as it
says heah, in de Bible, by de time you gits clear back tuh his
hocks hes rank pizen."

"AMEN!! Specially Brazzle's ol' mule," put in Hambo.

"An' dat makes it double 'ssault an' batt'ry," Long contin-
ued. "Therefo' Brother Mayor, Ah ast dat Jim be run outa
town fuh 'ssaultin Dave wid a deadly weepon an' stealin' his
turkey while de boy wuz unconscious."

It was now the turn of the Baptists to go wild. The faint
protests of Simms were drowned in the general uproar.

"I'll be henfired if he aint right!" the Mayor exclaimed
when he could make himself heard. "This case is just as plain
as day."

Simms tried once more. "But Brother Mayor—"

"Aw be quiet, Simms. You done talked yo'self all outa joint
already." His Honor cut him short. "Jim Weston, you git
right outa *mah* town befo sundown an' dont lemme ketch
you back heah under two yeahs, neither. You folks dats so
rearin' tuh fight, gwan outside an' fight all you wants tuh. But
dont use no guns, no razors nor no mule-bones. Cote's dis-
missed."

A general murmur of approval swept over the house. Clarke
went on, unofficially, as it were. "By ziggity, dat ol' mule
been dead three years an' still kickin'! An' he done kicked
more'n one person outa whack today." And he gave Simms
one of his most personal looks.

Book of Harlem

1. A pestilence visiteth the land of Hokum, and the people cry out. 4. Toothsome, a son of Georgia returns from Babylon, and stirreth up the Hamites. 10. Mandolin heareth him and resolveth to see Babylon. 11. He convinceth his father and departs for Babylon. 21. A red-cap toteth his bag, and uttereth blasphemy against Mandolin. 26. He lodgeth with Toothsome, and trieth to make the females of Harlem, but is scorned by them. 28. One frail biddeth him sit upon a tack. 29. He taketh council with Toothsome and is comforted. 33. He goeth to an hall of dancing, and meeting a damsel there, shaketh vehemently with her. 42. He discloseth himself to her and she telleth him what to read. 46. He becometh Panic, and quoteth poetry. 51. Toothsome cometh to him with a question, and is satisfied.

1. And in those days when King Volstead sat upon the throne in Hokum, then came a mighty drought upon the land, and many cried out in agony thereof.

2. Then did the throat parch and the tongue was thrust into the cheek of many voters.

3. And men grew restless and went up and down in the land saying, "We are verily the dry-bones of which the prophet Ezekiel prophesied."

4. Then returned one called Toothsome unto his town of Standard Bottom, which is in the province of Georgia. And he was of the tribe of Ham.

5. And his raiment was very glad, for he had sojourned in the city of Babylon, which is ruled by the tribe of Tammany. And his garments putteth out the street lamps, and the vaseline upon his head, yea verily the slickness thereof did outshine the sun at noonday.

6. And the maidens looked upon him and were glad, but the men gnasheth together their bridgework at sight of him. But they drew near unto him and listened to his accounts of the doings of Babylon, for they all yearned unto that city.

7. And the mouth of Toothsome flapped loudly and fluently in the marketplace, and the envy of his hearers increased an hundredfold.

8. Then stood one youth before him, and his name was called Mandolin. And he questioned Toothsome eagerly, asking 'how come,' and 'wherefore' many times.

9. And Toothsome answered him according to his wit. Moreover he said unto the youth, "Come thou also to the city as unto the ant, and consider her ways and be wise."

10. And the heart of Mandolin was inflamed, and he stood before his father and said, "I beseech thee now, papa, to give unto me now my portion that I may go hence to great Babylon and see life."

11. But his father's heart yearned towards him, and he said, "Nay, my son, for Babylon is full of wickedness, and thou art but a youth."

12. But Mandolin answered him saying, "I crave to gaze upon its sins. What do you think I go to see, an prayer-meeting?"

13. But his father strove with him and said, "Why dost thou crave Babylon when Gussie Smith, the daughter of our neighbor, will make thee a good wife? Tarry now and take her to wife, for verily she is a mighty biscuit cooker before the Lord."

14. Then snorted Mandolin with scorn and he said, "What care I for biscuit-cookers when there be Shebas of high voltage on every street in Harlem? For verily man liveth not by bread alone, but by every drop of banana oil that drippeth from the tongue of the lovely."

15. Then strove they together all night. But at daybreak did Mandolin touch the old man upon the hip, yea verily upon the pocket-bearing joint, and triumphed.

16. So the father gave him his blessing, and he departed out of Standard Bottom on his journey to Babylon.

17. And he carried with him of dreams forty-and-four thousand, and of wishes ten thousands, and of hopes ten thousands.

18. But of tears or sorrows carried he none out of all that land. Neither bore he any fears away with him.

19. And journeyed he many days upon the caravan of steel, and came at last unto the city of Babylon, and got him down within the place.

20. Then rushed there many upon him who wore scarlet caps upon the head, saying "Porter? Shall I tote thy bags for thee?"

21. And he marvelled greatly within himself, saying, "How charitably are the Babylonians, seeing they permit no stranger to tote his own bag! With what great kindness am I met!"

22. And he suffered one to prevail and tote his bag for him. Moreover he questioned him concerning the way to Harlem which is a city of Ham in Babylonia.

23. And when he of the scarlet cap had conducted Mandolin unto a bus, then did Mandolin shake hands with him and thank him greatly for his kindness, and stepped upon the chariot as it rolled away, and took his way unto Harlem.

24. Then did the bag-toter blaspheme greatly, saying, "Oh, the cock-eyed son of a wood louse! Oh, the hawg! Oh, the sea-buzzard! Oh, the splay-footed son of a doodle bug and cock-roach! What does he take me for? The mule's daddy! The clod-hopper! If only I might lay my hands upon him, verily would I smite him, yea, until he smelt like onions!"

25. But Mandolin journeyed on to Harlem, knowing none of these things.

26. And when he had come unto the place, he lodged himself with Toothsome, and was glad.

27. And each evening stood he before the Lafayette theatre and a-hemmed at the knees that passed, but none took notice of him. Moreover flashed he the chicken feed which he possessed, but none turned the head except to snigger at him.

28. Moreover, one frail of exceeding sassiness bade him go to and cook an radish, and seat himself upon an tack, which being interpreted is slander.

29. Then went he unto his roommate and saith, "How now doth the damsel hink me? Have I not a smiling countenance, and coin in my jeans? My heart is heavy for I have sojourned in Harlem for many weeks, but as yet I have spoken to no female."

30. Then spoke Toothsome, and answered him saying, "Seek not swell Shebas in mail-order britches. Go thou into the marketplace and get thee Oxford bags and jacket thyself likewise. Procure thee shoes and socks. Yea, anoint thy head with oil until it runneth over so that thou dare not hurl thyself into bed unless thou wear Weed chains upon the head, lest thou skid out again.

31. Moreover lubricate thy tongue with banana oil, for from the oily lips proceedeth the breath of love."

32. And Mandolin hastened to do all that his counsellor bade him.

33. Then hied him to the hall of dancing where many leaped with the cymbal, and shook with the drums.

34. And his belly was moved, for he saw young men seize upon damsels and they stood upon the floor and "messed around" meanly; moreover many "bumped" them vehemently. Yea, there were those among them who shook with many shakings.

35. And when he saw all these things, Mandolin yearned within his heart to do likewise, but as yet he had spoken to no maiden.

36. But one damsel of scarlet lips smiled broadly upon him, and encouraged him with her eyes, and the water of his knees turned to bone, and he drew nigh unto her.

37. And his mouth flew open and he said, "See now how the others do dance with the cymbal and harp, yea, even the saxophone? Come thou and let us do likewise."

38. And he drew her and they stood upon the floor. Now this maiden was a mighty dancer before the Lord; yea of the mightiest of all the tribe of Ham. And the shakings of the others was as one stricken with paralysis beside a bowl of gelatine. And the heart of the youth leaped for joy.

39. And he was emboldened, and his mouth flew open and the banana oil did drip from his lips, yea even down to the floor, and the maiden was moved.

40. And he said, "Thou sure art propaganda! Yea, verily thou shakest a wicked ankle."

41. And she being pleased, answered him, "Thou art some sheik thyself. I do shoot a little pizen to de ankle if I do say so myself. Where hast thou been all my life that I have not seen thee?"

42. Then did his mouth fly open, and he told her everything of Standard Bottom, Georgia, and of Babylon, and of all those things which touched him.

43. And her heart yearned towards him, and she resolved to take him unto herself and to make him wise.

44. And she said unto him, "Go thou and buy the books

and writings of certain scribes and Pharisees which I shall name unto you, and thou shalt learn everything of good and of evil. Yea, thou shalt know as much as the Chief of the Niggerati, who is called Carl Van Vechten.

45. And Mandolin diligently sought all these books and writings that he was bidden, and read them.

46. Then was he sought for all feasts, and stomps, and shakings, and none was complete without him. Both on 139th street and on Lenox avenue was he sought, and his fame was great.

47. And his name became Panic, for they asked one of the other, "Is he not a riot in all that he doeth?"

48. Then did he devise poetry, and played it upon the piano, saying

> "Skirt by skirt on every flirt
> They're getting higher and higher
> Day by day in every way
> There's more to admire
> Sock by sock and knee by knee
> The more they show, the more we see
> The skirts run up, the socks run down
> Jingling bells run round and round
> Oh week by week, and day by day
> Let's hope that things keep on this way
> Let's kneel right down and pray.

49. And the women all sought him, the damsels and the matrons and the grandmothers and all those who wear the skirt, and with them his name was continually Panic.

50. And the men sought him because his raiment was such that all knew from them the styles which would come to pass.

51. And he roomed no more with Toothsome, but had unto himself swell lodgings. But one day Toothsome sought him and asked,

52. "How now dost thou come to Harlem and become Panic unto the virgin, and the matron, and the grandmatron, and unto the sheik and the Niggerati (which being interpreted means Negro literati) and unto all those above 125th street? In all my years in Babylon none has called me thus."

53. And Mandolin who is called Panic, answered him, "In

my early days in Babylon was I taught to subscribe to Vanity Fair, and to read it diligently, for no man may know his way about Babylon without it."

54. Then did a great light dawn upon him called Tooth-some, and he rushed forth to subscribe to the perfect maga-zine.

55. And of his doings and success after that, is it not written in the Book of Harlem?

The Gilded Six-Bits

IT WAS a Negro yard around a Negro house in a Negro settlement that looked to the payroll of the G and G Fertilizer works for its support.

But there was something happy about the place. The front yard was parted in the middle by a sidewalk from gate to door-step, a sidewalk edged on either side by quart bottles driven neck down into the ground on a slant. A mess of homey flowers planted without a plan but blooming cheerily from their helter-skelter places. The fence and house were whitewashed. The porch and steps scrubbed white.

The front door stood open to the sunshine so that the floor of the front room could finish drying after its weekly scouring. It was Saturday. Everything clean from the front gate to the privy house. Yard raked so that the strokes of the rake would make a pattern. Fresh newspaper cut in fancy edge on the kitchen shelves.

Missie May was bathing herself in the galvanized washtub in the bedroom. Her dark-brown skin glistened under the soapsuds that skittered down from her wash rag. Her stiff young breasts thrust forward aggressively like broad-based cones with the tips lacquered in black.

She heard men's voices in the distance and glanced at the dollar clock on the dresser.

"Humph! Ah'm way behind time t'day! Joe gointer be heah 'fore Ah git mah clothes on if Ah don't make haste."

She grabbed the clean meal sack at hand and dried herself hurriedly and began to dress. But before she could tie her slippers, there came the ring of singing metal on wood. Nine times.

Missie May grinned with delight. She had not seen the big tall man come stealing in the gate and creep up the walk grinning happily at the joyful mischief he was about to commit. But she knew that it was her husband throwing silver dollars in the door for her to pick up and pile beside her plate at dinner. It was this way every Saturday afternoon. The nine

dollars hurled into the open door, he scurried to a hiding place behind the cape jasmine bush and waited.

Missie May promptly appeared at the door in mock alarm.

"Who dat chunkin' money in mah do'way?" she demanded. No answer from the yard. She leaped off the porch and began to search the shrubbery. She peeped under the porch and hung over the gate to look up and down the road. While she did this, the man behind the jasmine darted to the china berry tree. She spied him and gave chase.

"Nobody ain't gointer be chunkin' money at me and Ah not do 'em nothin'," she shouted in mock anger. He ran around the house with Missie May at his heels. She overtook him at the kitchen door. He ran inside but could not close it after him before she crowded in and locked with him in a rough and tumble. For several minutes the two were a furious mass of male and female energy. Shouting, laughing, twisting, turning, tussling, tickling each other in the ribs; Missie May clutching onto Joe and Joe trying, but not too hard, to get away.

"Missie May, take yo' hand out mah pocket!" Joe shouted out between laughs.

"Ah ain't, Joe, not lessen you gwine gimme whateve' it is good you got in yo' pocket. Turn it go, Joe, do Ah'll tear yo' clothes."

"Go on tear 'em. You de one dat pushes de needles round heah. Move yo' hand Missie May."

"Lemme git dat paper sack out yo' pocket. Ah bet its candy kisses."

"Tain't. Move yo' hand. Woman ain't got no business in a man's clothes nohow. Go way."

Missie May gouged way down and gave an upward jerk and triumphed.

"Unhhunh! Ah got it. It 'tis so candy kisses. Ah knowed you had somethin' for me in yo' clothes. Now Ah got to see whut's in every pocket you got."

Joe smiled indulgently and let his wife go through all of his pockets and take out the things that he had hidden there for her to find. She bore off the chewing gum, the cake of sweet soap, the pocket handkerchief as if she had wrested them

from him, as if they had not been bought for the sake of this friendly battle.

"Whew! dat play-fight done got me all warmed up," Joe exclaimed. "Got me some water in de kittle?"

"Yo' water is on de fire and yo' clean things is cross de bed. Hurry up and wash yo'self and git changed so we kin eat. Ah'm hongry." As Missie said this, she bore the steaming kettle into the bedroom.

"You ain't hongry, sugar," Joe contradicted her. "Youse jes' a little empty. Ah'm de one whut's hongry. Ah could eat up camp meetin', back off 'ssociation, and drink Jurdan dry. Have it on de table when Ah git out de tub."

"Don't you mess wid mah business, man. You git in yo' clothes. Ah'm a real wife, not no dress and breath. Ah might not look lak one, but if you burn me, you won't git a thing but wife ashes."

Joe splashed in the bedroom and Missie May fanned around in the kitchen. A fresh red and white checked cloth on the table. Big pitcher of buttermilk beaded with pale drops of butter from the churn. Hot fried mullet, crackling bread, ham hock atop a mound of string beans and new potatoes, and perched on the window-sill a pone of spicy potato pudding.

Very little talk during the meal but that little consisted of banter that pretended to deny affection but in reality flaunted it. Like when Missie May reached for a second helping of the tater pone. Joe snatched it out of her reach.

After Missie May had made two or three unsuccessful grabs at the pan, she begged, "Aw, Joe gimme some mo' dat tater pone."

"Nope, sweetenin' is for us men-folks. Y'all pritty lil frail eels don't need nothin' lak dis. You too sweet already."

"Please, Joe."

"Naw, naw. Ah don't want you to git no sweeter than whut you is already. We goin' down de road a lil piece t'night so you go put on yo' Sunday-go-to-meetin' things."

Missie May looked at her husband to see if he was playing some prank. "Sho nuff, Joe?"

"Yeah. We goin' to de ice cream parlor."

"Where de ice cream parlor at, Joe?"

"A new man done come heah from Chicago and he done got a place and took and opened it up for a ice cream parlor, and bein' as it's real swell, Ah wants you to be one de first ladies to walk in dere and have some set down."

"Do Jesus, Ah ain't knowed nothin' 'bout it. Who de man done it?"

"Mister Otis D. Slemmons, of spots and places—Memphis, Chicago, Jacksonville, Philadelphia and so on."

"Dat heavy-set man wid his mouth full of gold teethes?"

"Yeah. Where did you see 'im at?"

"Ah went down to de sto' tuh git a box of lye and Ah seen 'im standin' on de corner talkin' to some of de mens, and Ah come on back and went to scrubbin' de floor, and he passed and tipped his hat whilst Ah was scourin' de steps. Ah thought Ah never seen *him* befo'."

Joe smiled pleasantly. "Yeah, he's up to date. He got de finest clothes Ah ever seen on a colored man's back."

"Aw, he don't look no better in his clothes than you do in yourn. He got a puzzlegut on 'im and he so chuckle-headed, he got a pone behind his neck."

Joe looked down at his own abdomen and said wistfully, "Wisht Ah had a build on me lak he got. He ain't puzzle-gutted, honey. He jes' got a corperation. Dat make 'm look lak a rich white man. All rich mens is got some belly on 'em."

"Ah seen de pitchers of Henry Ford and he's a spare-built man and Rockefeller look lak he ain't got but one gut. But Ford and Rockefeller and dis Slemmons and all de rest kin be as many-gutted as dey please, Ah'm satisfied wid you jes' lak you is, baby. God took pattern after a pine tree and built you noble. Youse a pritty man, and if Ah knowed any way to make you mo' pritty still Ah'd take and do it."

Joe reached over gently and toyed with Missie May's ear. "You jes' say dat cause you love me, but Ah know Ah can't hold no light to Otis D. Slemmons. Ah ain't never been no-where and Ah ain't got nothin' but you."

Missie May got on his lap and kissed him and he kissed back in kind. Then he went on. "All de womens is crazy 'bout 'im everywhere he go."

"How you know dat, Joe?"

"He tole us so hisself."

"Dat don't make it so. His mouf is cut cross-ways, ain't it? Well, he kin lie jes' lak anybody else."

"Good Lawd, Missie! You womens sho is hard to sense into things. He's got a five-dollar gold piece for a stick-pin and he got a ten-dollar gold piece on his watch chain and his mouf is jes' crammed full of gold teethes. Sho wisht it wuz mine. And whut make it so cool, he got money 'cumulated. And womens give it all to 'im."

"Ah don't see whut de womens see on 'im. Ah wouldn't give 'im a wink if de sheriff wuz after 'im."

"Well, he tole us how de white womens in Chicago give 'im all dat gold money. So he don't 'low nobody to touch it at all. Not even put dey finger on it. Dey tole 'im not to. You kin make 'miration at it, but don't tetch it."

"Whyn't he stay up dere where dey so crazy 'bout 'im?"

"Ah reckon dey done made 'im vast-rich and he wants to travel some. He say dey wouldn't leave 'im hit a lick of work. He got mo' lady people crazy 'bout him than he kin shake a stick at."

"Joe, Ah hates to see you so dumb. Dat stray nigger jes' tell y'all anything and y'all b'lieve it."

"Go 'head on now, honey and put on yo' clothes. He talkin' 'bout his pritty womens—Ah want 'im to see *mine*."

Missie May went off to dress and Joe spent the time trying to make his stomach punch out like Slemmons' middle. He tried the rolling swagger of the stranger, but found that his tall bone-and-muscle stride fitted ill with it. He just had time to drop back into his seat before Missie May came in dressed to go.

On the way home that night Joe was exultant. "Didn't Ah say ole Otis was swell? Can't he talk Chicago talk? Wuzn't dat funny whut he said when great big fat ole Ida Armstrong come in? He asted me, 'Who is dat broad wid de forte shake?' Dat's a new word. Us always thought forty was a set of figgers but he showed us where it means a whole heap of things. Sometimes he don't say forty, he jes' say thirty-eight and two and dat mean de same thing. Know whut he tole me when Ah wuz payin' for our ice cream? He say, 'Ah have to hand it to you, Joe. Dat wife of yours is jes' thirty-eight and two. Yessuh, she's forte!' Ain't he killin'?"

"He'll do in case of a rush. But he sho is got uh heap uh gold on 'im. Dat's de first time Ah ever seed gold money. It lookted good on him sho nuff, but it'd look a whole heap better on you."

"Who, me? Missie May youse crazy! Where would a po' man lak me git gold money from?"

Missie May was silent for a minute, then she said, "Us might find some goin' long de road some time. Us could."

"Who would be losin' gold money round heah? We ain't even seen none dese white folks wearin' no gold money on dey watch chain. You must be figgerin' Mister Packard or Mister Cadillac goin' pass through heah."

"You don't know whut been lost 'round heah. Maybe somebody way back in memorial times lost they gold money and went on off and it ain't never been found. And then if we wuz to find it, you could wear some 'thout havin' no gang of womens lak dat Slemmons say he got."

Joe laughed and hugged her. "Don't be so wishful 'bout me. Ah'm satisfied de way Ah is. So long as Ah be yo' husband, Ah don't keer 'bout nothin' else. Ah'd ruther all de other womens in de world to be dead than for you to have de toothache. Less we go to bed and git our night rest."

It was Saturday night once more before Joe could parade his wife in Slemmons' ice cream parlor again. He worked the night shift and Saturday was his only night off. Every other evening around six o'clock he left home, and dying dawn saw him hustling home around the lake where the challenging sun flung a flaming sword from east to west across the trembling water.

That was the best part of life—going home to Missie May. Their whitewashed house, the mock battle on Saturday, the dinner and ice cream parlor afterwards, church on Sunday nights when Missie out-dressed any woman in town—all, everything was right.

One night around eleven the acid ran out at the G. and G. The foreman knocked off the crew and let the steam die down. As Joe rounded the lake on his way home, a lean moon rode the lake in a silver boat. If anybody had asked Joe about the moon on the lake, he would have said he hadn't paid it any attention. But he saw it with his feelings. It made

him yearn painfully for Missie. Creation obsessed him. He thought about children. They had been married more than a year now. They had money put away. They ought to be making little feet for shoes. A little boy child would be about right.

He saw a dim light in the bedroom and decided to come in through the kitchen door. He could wash the fertilizer dust off himself before presenting himself to Missie May. It would be nice for her not to know that he was there until he slipped into his place in bed and hugged her back. She always liked that.

He eased the kitchen door open slowly and silently, but when he went to set his dinner bucket on the table he bumped it into a pile of dishes, and something crashed to the floor. He heard his wife gasp in fright and hurried to reassure her.

"Iss me, honey. Don't git skeered."

There was a quick, large movement in the bedroom. A rustle, a thud, and a stealthy silence. The light went out.

What? Robbers? Murderers? Some varmint attacking his helpless wife, perhaps. He struck a match, threw himself on guard and stepped over the door-sill into the bedroom.

The great belt on the wheel of Time slipped and eternity stood still. By the match light he could see the man's legs fighting with his breeches in his frantic desire to get them on. He had both chance and time to kill the intruder in his helpless condition—half in and half out of his pants—but he was too weak to take action. The shapeless enemies of humanity that live in the hours of Time had waylaid Joe. He was assaulted in his weakness. Like Samson awakening after his haircut. So he just opened his mouth and laughed.

The match went out and he struck another and lit the lamp. A howling wind raced across his heart, but underneath its fury he heard his wife sobbing and Slemmons pleading for his life. Offering to buy it with all that he had. "Please, suh, don't kill me. Sixty-two dollars at de sto'. Gold money."

Joe just stood. Slemmons looked at the window, but it was screened. Joe stood out like a rough-backed mountain between him and the door. Barring him from escape, from sunrise, from life.

He considered a surprise attack upon the big clown that stood there laughing like a chessy cat. But before his fist could travel an inch, Joe's own rushed out to crush him like a battering ram. Then Joe stood over him.

"Git into yo' damn rags, Slemmons, and dat quick."

Slemmons scrambled to his feet and into his vest and coat. As he grabbed his hat, Joe's fury overrode his intentions and he grabbed at Slemmons with his left hand and struck at him with his right. The right landed. The left grazed the front of his vest. Slemmons was knocked a somersault into the kitchen and fled through the open door. Joe found himself alone with Missie May, with the golden watch charm clutched in his left fist. A short bit of broken chain dangled between his fingers.

Missie May was sobbing. Wails of weeping without words. Joe stood, and after awhile he found out that he had something in his hand. And then he stood and felt without thinking and without seeing with his natural eyes. Missie May kept on crying and Joe kept on feeling so much and not knowing what to do with all his feelings, he put Slemmons' watch charm in his pants pocket and took a good laugh and went to bed.

"Missie May, whut you cryin' for?"

"Cause Ah love you so hard and Ah know you don't love *me* no mo'."

Joe sank his face into the pillow for a spell then he said huskily, "You don't know de feelings of dat yet, Missie May."

"Oh Joe, honey, he said he wuz gointer give me dat gold money and he jes' kept on after me——"

Joe was very still and silent for a long time. Then he said, "Well, don't cry no mo', Missie May. Ah got yo' gold piece for you."

The hours went past on their rusty ankles. Joe still and quiet on one bed-rail and Missie May wrung dry of sobs on the other. Finally the sun's tide crept upon the shore of night and drowned all its hours. Missie May with her face stiff and streaked towards the window saw the dawn come into her yard. It was day. Nothing more. Joe wouldn't be coming home as usual. No need to fling open the front door and sweep off the porch, making it nice for Joe. Never no more

breakfast to cook; no more washing and starching of Joe's jumper-jackets and pants. No more nothing. So why get up?

With this strange man in her bed, she felt embarrassed to get up and dress. She decided to wait till he had dressed and gone. Then she would get up, dress quickly and be gone forever beyond reach of Joe's looks and laughs. But he never moved. Red light turned to yellow, then white.

From beyond the no-man's land between them came a voice. A strange voice that yesterday had been Joe's.

"Missie May, ain't you gonna fix me no breakfus'?"

She sprang out of bed. "Yeah, Joe. Ah didn't reckon you wuz hongry."

No need to die today. Joe needed her for a few more minutes anyhow.

Soon there was a roaring fire in the cook stove. Water bucket full and two chickens killed. Joe loved fried chicken and rice. She didn't deserve a thing and good Joe was letting her cook him some breakfast. She rushed hot biscuits to the table as Joe took his seat.

He ate with his eyes in his plate. No laughter, no banter.

"Missie May, you ain't eatin' yo' breakfus'."

"Ah don't choose none, Ah thank yuh."

His coffee cup was empty. She sprang to refill it. When she turned from the stove and bent to set the cup beside Joe's plate, she saw the yellow coin on the table between them.

She slumped into her seat and wept into her arms.

Presently Joe said calmly, "Missie May, you cry too much. Don't look back lak Lot's wife and turn to salt."

The sun, the hero of every day, the impersonal old man that beams as brightly on death as on birth, came up every morning and raced across the blue dome and dipped into the sea of fire every evening. Water ran down hill and birds nested.

Missie knew why she didn't leave Joe. She couldn't. She loved him too much, but she could not understand why Joe didn't leave her. He was polite, even kind at times, but aloof.

There were no more Saturday romps. No ringing silver dollars to stack beside her plate. No pockets to rifle. In fact the yellow coin in his trousers was like a monster hiding in the cave of his pockets to destroy her.

She often wondered if he still had it, but nothing could have induced her to ask nor yet to explore his pockets to see for herself. Its shadow was in the house whether or no.

One night Joe came home around midnight and complained of pains in the back. He asked Missie to rub him down with liniment. It had been three months since Missie had touched his body and it all seemed strange. But she rubbed him. Grateful for the chance. Before morning, youth triumphed and Missie exulted. But the next day, as she joyfully made up their bed, beneath her pillow she found the piece of money with the bit of chain attached.

Alone to herself, she looked at the thing with loathing, but look she must. She took it into her hands with trembling and saw first thing that it was no gold piece. It was a gilded half dollar. Then she knew why Slemmons had forbidden anyone to touch his gold. He trusted village eyes at a distance not to recognize his stick-pin as a gilded quarter, and his watch charm as a four-bit piece.

She was glad at first that Joe had left it there. Perhaps he was through with her punishment. They were man and wife again. Then another thought came clawing at her. He had come home to buy from her as if she were any woman in the long house. Fifty cents for her love. As if to say that he could pay as well as Slemmons. She slid the coin into his Sunday pants pocket and dressed herself and left his house.

Half way between her house and the quarters she met her husband's mother, and after a short talk she turned and went back home. Never would she admit defeat to that woman who prayed for it nightly. If she had not the substance of marriage she had the outside show. Joe must leave *her*. She let him see she didn't want his gold four-bits too.

She saw no more of the coin for some time though she knew that Joe could not help finding it in his pocket. But his health kept poor, and he came home at least every ten days to be rubbed.

The sun swept around the horizon, trailing its robes of weeks and days. One morning as Joe came in from work, he found Missie May chopping wood. Without a word he took the ax and chopped a huge pile before he stopped.

"You ain't got no business choppin' wood, and you know it."

"How come? Ah been choppin' it for de last longest."

"Ah ain't blind. You makin' feet for shoes."

"Won't you be glad to have a lil baby chile, Joe?"

"You know dat 'thout astin' me."

"Iss gointer be a boy chile and de very spit of you."

"You reckon, Missie May?"

"Who else could it look lak?"

Joe said nothing, but he thrust his hand deep into his pocket and fingered something there.

It was almost six months later Missie May took to bed and Joe went and got his mother to come wait on the house.

Missie May was delivered of a fine boy. Her travail was over when Joe came in from work one morning. His mother and the old women were drinking great bowls of coffee around the fire in the kitchen.

The minute Joe came into the room his mother called him aside.

"How did Missie May make out?" he asked quickly.

"Who, dat gal? She strong as a ox. She gointer have plenty mo'. We done fixed her wid de sugar and lard to sweeten her for de nex' one."

Joe stood silent awhile.

"You ain't ast 'bout de baby, Joe. You oughter be mighty proud cause he sho is de spittin' image of yuh, son. Dat's yourn all right, if you never git another one, dat un is yourn. And you know Ah'm mighty proud too, son, cause Ah never thought well of you marryin' Missie May cause her ma used tuh fan her foot round right smart and Ah been mighty skeered dat Missie May wuz gointer git misput on her road."

Joe said nothing. He fooled around the house till late in the day then just before he went to work, he went and stood at the foot of the bed and asked his wife how she felt. He did this every day during the week.

On Saturday he went to Orlando to make his market. It had been a long time since he had done that.

Meat and lard, meal and flour, soap and starch. Cans of corn and tomatoes. All the staples. He fooled around town

for awhile and bought bananas and apples. Way after while he went around to the candy store.

"Hello, Joe," the clerk greeted him. "Ain't seen you in a long time."

"Nope, Ah ain't been heah. Been round in spots and places."

"Want some of them molasses kisses you always buy?"

"Yessuh." He threw the gilded half dollar on the counter. "Will dat spend?"

"Whut is it, Joe? Well, I'll be doggone! A gold-plated four-bit piece. Where'd you git it, Joe?"

"Offen a stray nigger dat come through Eatonville. He had it on his watch chain for a charm—goin' round making out iss gold money. Ha ha! He had a quarter on his tie pin and it wuz all golded up too. Tryin' to fool people. Makin' out he so rich and everything. Ha! Ha! Tryin' to tole off folkses wives from home."

"How did you git it, Joe? Did he fool you, too?"

"Who, me? Naw suh! He ain't fooled me none. Know whut Ah done? He come round me wid his smart talk. Ah hauled off and knocked 'im down and took his old four-bits way from 'im. Gointer buy my wife some good ole lasses kisses wid it. Gimme fifty cents worth of dem candy kisses."

"Fifty cents buys a mighty lot of candy kisses, Joe. Why don't you split it up and take some chocolate bars, too. They eat good, too."

"Yessuh, dey do, but Ah wants all dat in kisses. Ah got a lil boy chile home now. Tain't a week old yet, but he kin suck a sugar tit and maybe eat one them kisses hisself."

Joe got his candy and left the store. The clerk turned to the next customer. "Wisht I could be like these darkies. Laughin' all the time. Nothin' worries 'em."

Back in Eatonville, Joe reached his own front door. There was the ring of singing metal on wood. Fifteen times. Missie May couldn't run to the door, but she crept there as quickly as she could.

"Joe Banks, Ah hear you chunkin' money in mah do'way. You wait till Ah got mah strength back and Ah'm gointer fix you for dat."

The Fire and the Cloud

Moses sat upon his new-made grave on Mount Nebo. His back stooped wearily, but his strong gaze leaped the Jordan and travelled over the land of Canaan.

A lizard popped out of a hole under a rock directly before Moses.

"Good morning, O brother-of-insufficient walking legs. I find you at waking where I left you at sun-rest." So the reptile greeted Moses.

With his eyes still in Canaan, Moses answered. "Ah yes, little kin who-uses-all-his-legs-for-walking, the labor has been long. This is the thirtieth day that I have sojourned upon this mountain." He waved at the mound of stone. "Behold, friend, it is finished."

From the top of a low bush near the left foot of Moses the lizard studied the work. "It is good. But you have been a long time in the building of your nest. Your female must be near death from retaining her eggs."

"No fecund female awaits this labor."

"A male alone?"

"A male alone."

"Perhaps you are a widower also. It is very sad, but you must know that fat lizards have many sudden-striking enemies." A tear dewed the leaf beneath him.

"I am alone, O lizard, because I am alone."

The lizard felt that Moses' answer lacked reason and he would have taught him how to make answer as do the great ones in the council of lizards, but when he lifted his head to speak, he beheld the head of Moses enveloped in a dense white cloud. "The gods have borne away the head of the rock-lifter," he thought aloud, and scurried to his hole in quivering awe. He slept and memory fled away. So soon he emerged and looked into the benign eyes of the nation-maker from the same bush.

"The lizard says that the present hour is much hotter than the tender ones of morning," he began abruptly.

"The lizard is wise," Moses answered casually.

"The words of lizards are full of truth," the reptile went on cunningly. "But even so, O friend-who-digs-his-hole-above-ground, the greatest among us has no rod that can summon fly-swarms at will." The lizard said this and looked at Moses under-eyed.

"That is true," Moses agreed with his thoughts at a distance.

"All your works accumulate praise. Twenty and nine days you have been with me upon this mountain, and each day you have called forth a swarm of flies at the hour, when I am most hungry."

"Pardon me, friend," Moses said humbly. "The thirtieth day shall be as the twenty-nine." He lifted his rod ever so slightly and flies swarmed over the bush upon which the lizard rested. "Sup."

The lizard ate. The last fly of the swarm was just enough. Every day it had been so. He looked at Moses in admiration.

"Whence do you come, O Master?"

Moses pointed to the plain of Moab where the tents of Israel crowded the horizon.

"How do you say that you are alone if of your kind such hosts of multitudes be at hand?"

"I am that I am and so I am alone. I am Moses, The-drawn-out. It is given me to call God by his power-compelling names. I bear his rod. The blind and the mute have companionship, but I am a leader."

"I see that your leadership has galled your shoulders. Why then did you go before?"

"I went because I was sent. In my agony I cried into nothingness and enquired 'Why am I called?' There was no answer. Only the voice that again said 'Go!' "

"How long O mighty Moses, have you led?"

"Forty years and more. From the mountain of God I returned to Eygpt, and with my stretched-out arm I confounded the Pharaoh, and led my people forth with a mighty hand. From the Nile, where we were bondsmen, to beyond the Jordan, where they shall rule."

"Ah Moses, because you have so exalted your kind and kindred, their love for you must exceed this great mountain in thickness and the height would not be less."

"Lizard, love is not created by service to mankind. But if the good be deemed sufficiently great, man sometimes erects little mountains of stone to the doer called monuments. They do this so that in the enjoyment of the benefit they forget not the benefactor. The heart of man is an ever empty abyss into which the whole world shall fall and be swallowed up."

"Do none of the hosts love their deliverer?"

"Who shall know? However, Joshua is strong in soul and body. He shall follow me. He gives thought to me. If I do not return to my tent before another day begins, he will ascend this mountain in search of me."

"Your labors have brought little joy."

"Lizard, forty years ago I led a horde of slaves out of Egyptian bondage and held them in the wilderness until I grew men. Look now upon the plain of Moab. A great people! They shall rule over nations and dwell in cities they have not builded. Yet they have rebelled against me ever. A stiff-necked race of people. They murmur against me anew because I have held them before the Jordan for forty days. Their taste would humble them before the armies of Canaan. They must wait yet another thirty days. I have not striven with God, with the wilderness, with rebellion and my own soul for forty years to bring them to a new bondage in the land beyond the Jordan. They shall wait for strength."

"How then, Moses will you hold your horde of murmurers on the brink of the Jordan when their eyes already feast on the good land?"

"If a leader dies in Israel, the hosts mourn thirty days."

Again the head of Moses disappeared in cloud and a sleep fell upon the lizard. But the cloud-splitting eye of Moses carried to the silver gilt hills of Canaan lying half in the late light, and half in shadows of the setting sun, and his soul wandered beyond the Jordan for the space of half an hour. When it returned to him upon Nebo he gazed down upon the tented nation beneath him, and the nation-maker sorrowing, wept over Israel. But Israel, unknowing, sang and danced, hammered its swords, milked its cows, got born and died.

"Ah Moses," the lizard observed on waking. "You shall yet rejoice. Soon your hosts will triumph beyond the Jordan, and you shall be called king of kings."

"I have already known the palaces of the Pharaohs, lizard, but I was not happy in the midst of them."

"You were an alien in the Egyptian palaces, but the mansions in Canaan shall be of your kindred."

"When the Israelites shall erect palaces, God shall raise up abundant palace-dwellers to fill them. I have taught them statutes and judgments fit for the guidance of kings and shepherds alike."

"But will they remember your laws?"

"If I tarry within this that I have erected on Nebo, then shall they remember my laws in Canaan. People value monuments above men, and signs above works."

The lizard travelled around the tomb and studied its contours.

"But Moses, your splendid new dwelling has no hole by which you may enter. A queer dwelling. A hole above ground—no entrance."

"This is no dwelling, lizard. It is a place of burial."

"I am no longer young, Moses, perhaps I nodded. What buried you there?"

"No, you did not witness it, but here is interred the voice of Sinai, the stretched-out arm of Moses, the law-giver, the nation-maker."

"Those are your words, but I behold you sitting as you sat at sunrise."

"Those are your thoughts, but you see the old man of the wilderness sitting upon the tomb of Moses."

Whereupon Moses arose and took one long look at the tented nation in the valley, and his face shone as it had done at Sinai when even Aaron had feared to look upon it. He took one dragging look beyond the Jordan, then wrapped his mantle closely about him.

"Sun is set," he said in low rumbles. "I depart."

He laid his rod upon the new-made tomb, set his face sternly towards the wilderness and walked away, leaning lightly on a new-cut staff.

"But wait, O Moses!" the lizard squeaked after him. "You have left your rod behind."

"Oh, Joshua will pick it up," he called back and strode on.

Story in Harlem Slang

WAIT till I light up my coal-pot and I'll tell you about this Zigaboo called Jelly. Well, all right now. He was a sealskin brown and papa-tree-top-tall. Skinny in the hips and solid built for speed. He was born with this rough-dried hair, but when he laid on the grease and pressed it down overnight with his stocking-cap, it looked just like that righteous moss, and had so many waves you got seasick from looking. Solid, man, solid!

His mama named him Marvel, but after a month on Lenox Avenue, he changed all that to Jelly. How come? Well, he put it in the street that when it came to filling that long-felt need, sugar-curing the ladies' feelings, he was in a class by himself and nobody knew his name, so he had to tell 'em. "It must be Jelly, 'cause jam don't shake." Therefore, his name was Jelly. That was what was on his sign. The stuff was there and it was mellow. Whenever he was challenged by a hard-head or a frail eel on the right of his title he would eye-ball the idol-breaker with a slice of ice and put on his ugly-laugh, made up of scorn and pity, and say: "Youse just dumb to the fact, baby. If you don't know what you talking 'bout, you better ask Granny Grunt. I wouldn't mislead you, baby. I don't need to—not with the help I got." Then he would give the pimp's* sign, and percolate on down the Avenue. You can't go behind a fact like that.

So this day he was airing out on the Avenue. It had to be late afternoon, or he would not have been out of bed. All you did by rolling out early was to stir your stomach up. That made you hunt for more dishes to dirty. The longer you slept, the less you had to eat. But you can't collar nods all day. No matter how long you stay in bed, and how quiet you keep, sooner or later that big gut is going to reach over and grab that little one and start to gnaw. That's confidential right

*In Harlemese, *pimp* has a different meaning than its ordinary definition as a procurer for immoral purposes. The Harlem pimp is a man whose amatory talents are for sale to any woman who will support him, either with a free meal or on a common law basis; in this sense, he is actually a male prostitute.

from the Bible. You got to get out on the beat and collar yourself a hot.

So Jelly got into his zoot suit with the reet pleats and got out to skivver around and do himself some good. At 132nd Street, he spied one of his colleagues on the opposite sidewalk, standing in front of a café. Jelly figured that if he bullskated just right, he might confidence Sweet Back out of a thousand on a plate. Maybe a shot of scrap-iron or a reefer. Therefore, Jelly took a quick backward look at his shoe soles to see how his leather was holding out. The way he figured it after the peep was that he had plenty to get across and maybe do a little more cruising besides. So he stanched out into the street and made the crossing.

"Hi there, Sweet Back!" he exploded cheerfully. "Gimme some skin!"

"Lay de skin on me, pal!" Sweet Back grabbed Jelly's outstretched hand and shook hard. "Ain't seen you since the last time, Jelly. What's cookin'?"

"Oh, just like de bear—I ain't nowhere. Like de bear's brother, I ain't no further. Like de bear's daughter—ain't got a quarter."

Right away, he wished he had not been so honest. Sweet Back gave him a top-superior, cut-eye look. Looked at Jelly just like a showman looks at an ape. Just as far above Jelly as fried chicken is over branch water.

"Cold in hand, hunh?" He talked down to Jelly. "A red hot pimp like you *say* you is, ain't got no business in the barrel. Last night when I left you, you was beating up your gums and broadcasting about how hot you was. Just as hot as July-jam, you told me. What you doing cold in hand?"

"Aw, man, can't you take a joke? I was just beating up my gums when I said I was broke. How can I be broke when I got de best woman in Harlem? If I ask her for a dime, she'll give me a ten dollar bill; ask her for drink of likker, and she'll buy me a whiskey still. If I'm lying, I'm flying!"

"Gar, don't hang out dat dirty washing in my back yard! Didn't I see you last night with dat beat chick, scoffing a hot dog? Dat chick you had was beat to de heels. Boy, you ain't no good for what you live."

"If you ain't lying now, you flying. You ain't got de first thin. You ain't got nickel one."

Jelly threw back the long skirt of his coat and rammed his hand down into his pants pocket. "Put your money where your mouth is!" he challenged, as he mock-struggled to haul out a huge roll. "Back your crap with your money. I bet you five dollars!"

Sweet Back made the same gesture of hauling out non-existent money.

"I been raised in the church. I don't bet, but I'll doubt you. Five rocks!"

"I thought so!" Jelly crowed, and hurriedly pulled his empty hand out of his pocket. "I knowed you'd back up when I drawed my roll on you."

"You ain't drawed no roll on me, Jelly. You ain't drawed nothing but your pocket. You better stop dat boogerbooing. Next time I'm liable to make you do it." There was a splinter of regret in his voice. If Jelly really had had some money, he might have staked him, Sweet Back, to a hot. Good Southern cornbread with a piano on a platter. Oh, well! The right broad would, or might, come along.

"Who boogerbooing?" Jelly snorted. "Jig, I don't have to. Talking about *me* with a beat chick scoffing a hot dog! You must of not seen me, 'cause last night I was riding round in a Yellow Cab, with a yellow gal, drinking yellow likker and spending yellow money. Tell 'em 'bout me, tell 'em!"

"Git out of my face, Jelly! Dat broad I seen you with wasn't no pe-ola. She was one of them coal-scuttle blondes with hair just as close to her head as ninety-nine is to a hundred. She look-ted like she had seventy-five pounds of clear bosom, guts in her feet, and she look-ted like six months in front and nine months behind. Buy you a whiskey still! Dat broad couldn't make the down payment on a pair of sox."

"Sweet Back, you fixing to talk out of place." Jelly stiffened.

"If you trying to jump salty, Jelly, that's your mammy."

"Don't play in de family, Sweet Back. I don't play de dozens. I done told you."

"Who playing de dozens? You trying to get your hips up on

your shoulders 'cause I said you was with a beat broad. One of them lam blacks."

"Who? Me? Long as you been knowing me, Sweet Back, you ain't never seen me with nothing but pe-olas. I can get any frail eel I wants to. How come I'm up here in New York? You don't know, do you? Since youse dumb to the fact, I reckon I'll have to make you hep. I had to leave from down south 'cause Miss Anne used to worry me so bad to go with me. Who, me? Man, I don't deal in no coal. Know what I tell 'em? If they's white, they's right! If they's yellow, they's mellow! If they's brown, they can stick around. But if they come black, they better git way back! Tell 'em bout me!"

"Aw, man, you trying to show your grandma how to milk ducks. Best you can do is to confidence some kitchen-mechanic out of a dime or two. Me, I knocks de pad with them cack-broads up on Sugar Hill, and fills 'em full of melody. Man, I'm quick death and easy judgment. Youse just a home-boy, Jelly. Don't try to follow me."

"Me follow *you*! Man, I come on like the Gang Busters, and go off like The March of Time! If dat ain't so, God is gone to Jersey City and you know He wouldn't be messing 'round a place like that. Know what my woman done? We hauled off and went to church last Sunday, and when they passed 'round the plate for the *penny* collection, I throwed in a dollar. De man looked at me real hard for dat. Dat made my woman mad, so she called him back and throwed in a twenty dollar bill! Told him to take dat and go! Dat's what he got for looking at me 'cause I throwed in a dollar."

"Jelly, de wind may blow and de door may slam; dat what you shooting ain't worth a damn!"

Jelly slammed his hand in his bosom as if to draw a gun. Sweet Back did the same.

"If you wants to fight, Sweet Back, the favor is in me."

"I was deep-thinking then, Jelly. It's a good thing I ain't short-tempered. 'T'aint nothing to you, nohow. You ain't hit me yet."

Both burst into a laugh and changed from fighting to lounging poses.

"Don't get too yaller on me, Jelly. You liable to get hurt some day."

"You over-sports your hand your ownself. Too blamed astorperious. I just don't pay you no mind. Lay de skin on me!"

They broke their handshake hurriedly, because both of them looked up the Avenue and saw the same thing. It was a girl and they both remembered that it was Wednesday afternoon. All of the domestics off for the afternoon with their pay in their pockets. Some of them bound to be hungry for love. That meant a dinner, a shot of scrap-iron, maybe room rent and a reefer or two. Both went into the pose and put on the look.

"Big stars falling!" Jelly said out loud when she was in hearing distance. "It must be just before day!"

"Yeah, man!" Sweet Back agreed. "Must be a recess in Heaven—pretty angel like that out on the ground."

The girl drew abreast of them, reeling and rocking her hips.

"I'd walk clear to Diddy-Wah-Diddy to get a chance to speak to a pretty lil' ground-angel like that," Jelly went on.

"Aw, man, you ain't willing to go very far. Me, I'd go slap to Ginny-Gall, where they eat cow-rump, skin and all."

The girl smiled, so Jelly set his hat and took the plunge.

"Baby," he crooned, "what's on de rail for de lizard?"

The girl halted and braced her hips with her hands. "A Zigaboo down in Georgy, where I come from, asked a woman that one time and the judge told him 'ninety days.' "

"Georgy!" Sweet Back pretended to be elated. "Where 'bouts in Georgy is you from? Delaware?"

"Delaware?" Jelly snorted. "My people! My people! Free schools and dumb jigs! Man, how you going to put Delaware in Georgy? You ought to know dat's in Maryland."

"Oh, don't try to make out youse no northerner, you! Youse from right down in 'Bam your ownself!" The girl turned on Jelly.

"Yeah, I'm *from* there and I aims to stay from there."

"One of them Russians, eh?" the girl retorted. "Rushed up here to get away from a job of work."

That kind of talk was not leading towards the dinner table.

"But baby!" Jelly gasped. "Dat shape you got on you! I bet the Coca Cola Company is paying you good money for the patent!"

The girl smiled with pleasure at this, so Sweet Back jumped in.

"I know youse somebody swell to know. Youse real people. You grins like a regular fellow." He gave her his most killing look and let it simmer in. "These dickty jigs round here tries to smile. S'pose you and me go inside the café here and grab a hot?"

"You got any money?" the girl asked, and stiffened like a ramrod. "Nobody ain't pimping on me. You dig me?"

"Aw, now, baby!"

"I seen you two mullet-heads before. I was uptown when Joe Brown had you all in the go-long last night. Dat cop sure hates a pimp! All he needs to see is the pimps' salute, and he'll out with his night-stick and whip your head to the red. Beat your head just as flat as a dime!" She went off into a great blow of laughter.

"Oh, let's us don't talk about the law. Let's talk about us," Sweet Back persisted. "You going inside with me to holler 'let one come flopping! One come grunting! Snatch one from de rear!' "

"Naw indeed!" the girl laughed harshly. "You skillets is trying to promote a meal on me. But it'll never happen, brother. You barking up the wrong tree. I wouldn't give you air if you was stopped up in a jug. I'm not putting out a thing. I'm just like the cemetery—I'm not putting out, I'm taking in! Dig?"

"I'll tell you like the farmer told the potato—plant you now and dig you later."

The girl made a movement to switch on off. Sweet Back had not dirtied a plate since the day before. He made a weak but desperate gesture.

"Trying to snatch my pocketbook, eh?" she blazed. Instead of running, she grabbed hold of Sweet Back's draping coat-tail and made a slashing gesture. "How much split you want back here? If your feets don't hurry up and take you 'way from here, you'll *ride* away. I'll spread my lungs all over New York and call the law. Go ahead, Bedbug! Touch me! And I'll holler like a pretty white woman!"

The boys were ready to flee, but she turned suddenly and rocked on off with her ear-rings snapping and her heels popping.

"My people! My people!" Sweet Back sighed.

"I know you feel chewed," Jelly said, in an effort to make it appear that he had had no part in the fiasco.

"Oh, let her go," Sweet Back said magnanimously. "When I see people without the periodical principles they's supposed to have, I just don't fool with 'em. What I want to steal her old pocketbook with all the money I got? I could buy a beat chick like her and give her away. I got money's mammy and Grandma change. One of my women, and not the best one I got neither, is buying me ten shag suits at one time."

He glanced sidewise at Jelly to see if he was convincing. But Jelly's thoughts were far away. He was remembering those full, hot meals he had left back in Alabama to seek wealth and splendor in Harlem without working. He had even forgotten to look cocky and rich.

GLOSSARY OF HARLEM SLANG

Air out—leave, flee, stroll

Astorperious—haughty, biggity

Aunt Hagar—Negro race (also Aunt Hagar's chillun)

Bad hair—Negro type hair

Balling—having fun

Bam, and down in Bam—down South

Battle-hammed—badly formed about the hips

Beating up your gums—talking to no purpose

Beluthahatchie—next station beyond Hell

Big boy—stout fellow. But in the South, it means fool and is a prime insult.

Blowing your top—getting very angry; occasionally used to mean, "He's doing fine!"

Boogie-woogie—type of dancing and rhythm. For years, in the South, it meant secondary syphilis.

Brother-in-black—Negro

Bull-skating—Bragging

Butt sprung—a suit or a skirt out of shape in the rear

Coal scuttle blonde—black woman

Cold—exceeding, well, etc., as in "He was cold on that trumpet!"

Collar a nod—sleep

Collar a hot—eat a meal

Color scale—high yaller, yaller, high brown, vaseline brown, seal brown, low brown, dark black

Conk buster—cheap liquor; also an intellectual Negro

Cruising—parading down the Avenue. Variations: *oozing*, *percolating*, and *free-wheeling*. The latter implies more briskness.

Cut—doing something well

Dark black—a casually black person. Superlatives: *low black*, a blacker person; *lam black*, still blacker; and *damn black*, blackest man, of whom it is said: "Why, lightning bugs follows him at 12 o'clock in the day, thinking it's midnight."

Dat thing—sex of either sex

Dat's your mammy—same as, "So is your old man."

Diddy-wah-diddy—a far place, a measure of distance. (2) another suburb of Hell, built since way before Hell wasn't no bigger than Baltimore. The folks in Hell go there for a big time.

Dig—understand. "Dig me?" means, "Do you get me? Do you collar the jive?"

Draped down—dressed in the height of Harlem fashion; also *togged down*.

Dumb to the fact—"You don't know what you're talking about."

Dusty butt—cheap prostitute

Eight-rock—very black person

Every postman on his beat—kinky hair

First thing smoking—a train. "I'm through with this town. I mean to grab the first thing smoking."

Frail eel—pretty girl

Free schools—a shortened expression of deprecation derived from "free schools and dumb Negroes," sometimes embellished with "free schools, pretty yellow teachers and dumb Negroes."

Function—a small, unventilated dance, full of people too casually bathed

Gator-faced—long, black face with big mouth

Getting on some stiff time—really doing well with your racket

Get you to go—power, physical or otherwise, to force the opponent to run

1008

Ginny Gall—a suburb of Hell, a long way off

Git up off of me—quit talking about me, leave me alone

Go when the wagon comes—another way of saying, "You may be acting biggity now, but you'll cool down when enough power gets behind you."

Good hair—Caucasian-type hair

Granny Grunt—a mythical character to whom most questions may be referred

Ground rations—sex, also *under rations*

Gum beater—a blowhard, a braggart, idle talker in general

Gut-bucket—low dive, type of music, or expression from same

Gut-foot—bad case of fallen arches

Handkerchief-head—sycophant type of Negro; also an *Uncle Tom*

Hauling—fleeing on foot. "Man! He cold hauled it!"

I don't deal in coal—"I don't keep company with black women."

I'm cracking but I'm facking—"I'm wisecracking, but I'm telling the truth."

Inky dink—very black person

I shot him lightly and he died politely—"I completely outdid him."

Jar head—Negro man

Jelly—sex

Jig—Negro, a corrupted shortening of zigaboo

Jook—a pleasure house, in the class of gut-bucket; now common all over the South

Jooking—playing the piano, guitar, or any musical instrument in the manner of the Jooks (pronounced like "took") (2) Dancing and "scronching" ditto.

Juice—liquor

July jam—something very hot

Jump salty—get angry

Kitchen mechanic—a domestic

Knock yourself out—have a good time

Lightly, slightly and politely—doing things perfectly

Little sister—measure of hotness: "Hot as little sister!"

Liver-lip—pendulous, thick, purple lips

Made hair—hair that has been straightened

Mammy—a term of insult. Never used in any other way by Negroes.

Miss Anne—a white woman

Mister Charlie—a white man

Monkey chaser—a West Indian

Mug man—small-time thug or gangster

My people! My people!—Sad and satiric expression in the Negro language: sad when a Negro comments on the backwardness of some members of his race; at other times, used for satiric or comic effect

Naps—kinky hair

Nearer my God to Thee—good hair

Nothing to the bear but his curly hair—"I call your bluff," or "Don't be afraid of him; he won't fight."

Now you cookin' with gas—now you're talking, in the groove, etc.

Ofay—white person

Old cuffee—Negro (genuine African word for the same thing)

Palmer House—walking flat-footed, as from fallen arches

Pancake—a humble type of Negro

Park ape—an ugly, underprivileged Negro

Peckerwood—poor and unloved class of Southern whites

Peeping through my likkers—carrying on even though drunk

Pe-ola—a very white Negro girl

Piano—spare ribs (white rib-bones suggest piano keys)

Pig meat—young girl

Pilch—house or apartment; residence

Pink toes—yellow girl

Playing the dozens—low-rating the ancestors of your opponent

Red neck—poor Southern white man

Reefer—marijuana cigaret, also a *drag*

Righteous mass or *grass*—good hair

Righteous rags—the components of a Harlem-style suit

Rug-cutter—originally a person frequenting house-rent parties, cutting up the rugs of the host with his feet; a person too cheap or poor to patronize regular dance halls; now means a good dancer.

Russian—a Southern Negro up north. "Rushed up here," hence a Russian.

Scrap iron—cheap liquor

Sell out—run in fear

Sender—he or she who can get you to go, i.e., has what it takes. Used often as a compliment: "He's a solid sender!"

Smoking, or *smoking over*—looking someone over

Solid—perfect

Sooner—anything cheap and mongrel, now applied to cheap clothes, or a shabby person.

Stanch, or *stanch out*—to begin, commence, step out

Stomp—low dance, but hot man!

Stormbuzzard—shiftless, homeless character

Stroll—doing something well

Sugar Hill—northwest corner of Harlem, near Washington Heights, site of newest apartment houses, mostly occupied by professional people. (The expression has been distorted in the South to mean a Negro red light district.)

The bear—confession of poverty

The big apple, also *the big red apple*—New York City

The man—the law, or powerful boss

Thousand on a plate—beans

Tight head—one with kinky hair

Trucking—strolling. (2) dance step from the strolling motif

V and X—five-and-ten-cent store

West Hell—another suburb of Hell, worse than the original

What's on the rail for the lizard?—suggestion for moral turpitude

Whip it to the red—beat your head until it is bloody

Woofing—aimless talk, as a dog barks on a moonlight night

Young suit—ill-fitting, too small. Observers pretend to believe you're breaking in your little brother's suit for him.

Your likker told you—misguided behavior

Zigaboo—a Negro

Zoot suit with the reet pleat—Harlem style suit, padded shoulders, 43-inch trousers at the knee with cuff so small it needs a zipper, to get into, high waistline, fancy lapels, bushels of buttons, etc.

Chronology

1891 Born Zora Lee Hurston January 7 in Notasulga, Macon County, Alabama, fifth child of Lucy Ann Potts, born December 1865, and John Hurston, born January 1861, a Baptist preacher, farmer, and carpenter. (Parents are both from Notasulga. Mother's father, Richard Potts, became a landowner after the Civil War. Father's family worked on cotton plantations. Both grandfathers were born in Georgia; both grandmothers are from Alabama.) Siblings are Hezekiah Robert (Bob), born November 1882, John Cornelius, born January 1885, Richard William, born January 1887, and Sarah Emmeline, born December 1889.

1893 Brother Joel (later known as "Clifford Joel") born March 4.

1894 Family moves to Eatonville, Florida, a small town five miles north of Orlando that was incorporated in 1886 (Hurston later describes it as the first incorporated black community in America; in 1900 its population is 125). Most men work as day laborers; women find domestic jobs in nearby towns of Maitland and Winter Park, both of which are popular with northern tourists. (Parents will eventually own five acres of land and eight-room house; father becomes pastor of the Zion Hope Baptist Church and the Macedonia Baptist Church, and will serve as moderator of the South Florida Baptist Association.)

1895 Brother Benjamin Franklin born December 7.

1897 Father is elected mayor of Eatonville (will serve three terms).

1898 Brother Edward Everett born October 26.

1900 Hurston attends Hungerford School in Eatonville, founded by Mary and Russell Calhoun, former students of Booker T. Washington at Tuskegee Institute. Helped in studies by mother, a former country school teacher and superintendent of the Sunday school. Loves verbal playfulness and the "lies" (stories) adults tell on the porch of Joe Clarke's store ("the heart and spring of the town").

1901 Impresses two visiting northern white women with her
 ability to read; they give her books, including the
 Grimms' and Andersen's fairy tales, Greek and Roman
 myths, Norse legends, *Gulliver's Travels*, and works by
 Rudyard Kipling and Robert Louis Stevenson.

1904 Mother dies on September 18. Hurston is sent in October
 to school in Jacksonville where Sarah is a student; Bob
 attends the Florida Baptist Academy in Jacksonville (later
 Florida Memorial College at St. Augustine).

1905 Hurston continues in school in Jacksonville; when her
 school bill is not paid she scrubs stairs on Saturdays and
 cleans kitchens after school. Wins spelling competition
 held among all the Negro schools in Jacksonville. Learns
 from Sarah that father has remarried. Sarah marries and
 moves to Palmetto, Florida, taking Everett with her.
 School officials pay for Hurston's return home several
 weeks after end of term when father fails to send for her.

1906–11 After brothers John and Richard leave home, Hurston
 and her younger siblings are sent to live with friends and
 relatives of their mother. Hurston dislikes her stepmother
 intensely and blames her for the dispersion of the family.
 Moves from one house to another and attends school in-
 termittently. Works as a domestic.

1912 Lives with brother Dick and his wife in Sanford, Florida,
 until her father tells her to come home. Has physical
 fight with her stepmother. Hurston leaves to find work
 in another town.

1914–15 Moves into home of brother Bob, now a doctor in Mem-
 phis, who promises to send her to school; is disappointed
 when he tells her that she must first help his wife take care
 of their three children and the home.

1915–16 Travels with a Gilbert & Sullivan troupe as maid to the
 lead singer. Falls ill in Baltimore and is unable to continue
 touring; has appendix removed in free ward of Maryland
 General Hospital.

1917–18 Works as waitress in Baltimore. Attends night high school
 (tells school officials year of her birth is 1901). Inspired by

teacher Dwight O. W. Holmes. Father dies in automobile accident on August 10. Enters Morgan Academy (high school division of what is now Morgan State University) in September 1917, and is aided by Dean William Pickens, who finds her domestic work in exchange for room and board in home of one of the white trustees of the school. Graduates in June 1918 and moves to Washington, partly at the suggestion of May Miller, daughter of mathematician and essayist Kelly Miller, dean of the College of Arts and Sciences at Howard University. Works during summer as waitress at the Cosmos Club, and then as manicurist in a black-owned barber shop that serves whites only. Enters the preparatory school at Howard University in September.

1919–20 Begins courses in the college department at Howard; receives an associate degree in 1920 (will attend Howard intermittently through 1924 but does not receive B.A.). Majors in English; studies with pioneering black linguist Lorenzo Dow Turner (later author of *Africanisms in the Gullah Dialect*) and Dwight O. W. Holmes, who has since moved to Howard. Joins Zeta Phi Beta sorority. Meets Herbert Sheen, a student from Decatur, Illinois.

1921 Joins literary club sponsored by philosophy professor Alain Locke and Montgomery Gregory, professor of English and drama. Publishes her first story, "John Redding Goes to Sea" (set in Eatonville), and a poem, "O Night," in the May number of club magazine *Stylus*. Regularly attends literary salon held by poet Georgia Douglas Johnson, which attracts local and visiting writers such as Locke, Bruce Nugent, Jean Toomer, W.E.B. Du Bois, essayist and fiction writer Marita Bonner, journalist and poet Alice Dunbar-Nelson, novelist and poet Jessie Fauset (literary editor of NAACP magazine *The Crisis*), poet Angelina Grimké, and Hurston's friend May Miller (who later becomes an educator, playwright, and poet).

1922 Publishes poems "Night," "Journey's End," and "Passion" in *Negro World*, the official newspaper of Marcus Garvey's Universal Negro Improvement Association.

1924 Publishes short story "Drenched in Light" in *Opportunity*, literary journal sponsored by the Urban League. Begins correspondence with journal's editor, Charles S. Johnson.

1925 With Johnson's encouragement, moves to New York City in January. Submits two stories, "Black Death" and "Spunk," and a play, *Color Struck*, to literary contest sponsored by *Opportunity*. Wins two second-place prizes and attends the magazine's awards dinner, where she meets poets Langston Hughes and Countee Cullen and novelists Carl Van Vechten, Annie Nathan Meyer, and Fannie Hurst. Accepts job with Hurst as personal secretary, but does not have adequate clerical skills and works instead as a chauffeur and companion (continues job until the end of 1926; friendship with Hurst continues for decades). Begins working occasionally as a domestic for Meyer, who secures her a scholarship to Barnard College for the fall (Meyer is one of the college's founders). Publishes story "Spunk" in the June number of *Opportunity* (it is reprinted later in the year in the signal anthology of the Harlem Renaissance, *The New Negro*, edited by Alain Locke). Enters Barnard in September as its only African-American student; studies anthropology with Franz Boas (anthropology faculty also includes Ruth Benedict and Gladys Reichard). Publishes article "The Hue and Cry about Howard University," criticizing students' negative attitude toward Negro spirituals, in the September number of *The Messenger*, Harlem journal co-founded by labor leader A. Philip Randolph.

1926 Begins field work for Boas in Harlem, measuring the skulls of passersby to disprove theories of racial inferiority. Moves to apartment at 43 West 66th Street, not far from Fannie Hurst; it is furnished with donations from friends. Submits story "Muttsy" and comic play *The First One*, based on the biblical legend of Ham, to the *Opportunity* contest ("Muttsy" wins second-place award and is published in August). In the summer begins meeting with Langston Hughes, poet Gwendolyn Bennett, painter Aaron Douglas, bohemian writer and artist Bruce Nugent, and novelist Wallace Thurman to plan *Fire!!*, a quarterly "devoted to the younger Negro artists." First and only number is published in November; Hurston

contributes "Sweat" and play *Color Struck*. In September folktale "Possum or Pig" is published in *Forum* and the first installment of "The Eatonville Anthology" appears in *The Messenger*.

1927 Publishes *The First One* in *Ebony and Topaz*, edited by Charles S. Johnson. With Boas' help, receives $1,400 research fellowship from the Association for the Study of Negro Life and History, founded and directed by African-American historian Carter G. Woodson. Leaves New York in February to collect folklore in the South. After a visit to Eatonville goes to Jacksonville to begin work. Visits brother John and buys used car for $300, which she names "Sassy Susie." Marries Herbert Sheen, now a medical student, in St. Augustine, Florida, on May 19. Visits brothers Bob and Ben, a pharmacist and owner of a drugstore, in Memphis (brother Dick is a traveling chef on the East Coast; Joel is the principal of the Negro high school in Decatur, Alabama; Everett is working in the post office in Brooklyn, N.Y; Sarah is married to a man the family does not like). Sheen returns in August to Rush Medical School in Chicago. Hurston accidently meets Langston Hughes in Mobile, Alabama. Drives him to New York, stopping in Tuskegee, Alabama, where they visit the grave of Booker T. Washington with Jessie Fauset, and in Macon, Georgia, where they see blues singer Bessie Smith perform and visit her in her hotel room. Hurston drives along southern back roads, and tells Hughes, who has never been South before, about her research in black folkways. Seeking financial help to create opera based on southern black folk material, Hurston meets Charlotte Mason (Mrs. Rufus Osgood Mason) in September through Alain Locke. (Mason, born Charlotte van der Veer Quick in Princeton, New Jersey, in 1854, had previously lived among the Plains Indians while sponsoring the field work of Natalie Curtis. At Locke's urging, she offered financial assistance to black artists, including Hughes, Claude McKay, sculptor Richmond Barthe, painter Aaron Douglas, and choirmaster Hall Johnson. Hurston later wrote that a "psychic bond" existed between her and "Godmother" who "was just as pagan as I.") Publishes two articles in *Journal of Negro History* in October: "Communication," transcriptions from archives in St. Augustine, Florida, about Fort

Moosa, a 17th-century black settlement, and "Cudjo's Own Story of the Last African Slaver," based partly on interviews with Cudjo Lewis, reputed to be sole survivor of the last slave ship to land in the United States, but heavily supplemented by passages taken from *Historic Sketches of the Old South* by Emma Langdon Roche (plagiarism is not detected until 1972). Returns to interview Lewis several times in December and completes book-length manuscript inspired by his life. Signs contract with Mason on December 8; under its terms, Mason employs Hurston as an independent agent to compile and collect information concerning "the music, poetry, folk-lore, literature, hoodoo, conjure, manifestations of art and kindred subjects relating to and existing among the North American negroes . . ." Contract gives ownership of collected material to Mason and forbids Hurston to make material known to anyone not designated in writing by Mason; for her services, Hurston receives stipend of $200 per month (contract is eventually extended through March 1931).

1928 Relationship with Sheen ends in January (they are divorced on July 7, 1931). Resumes collecting folklore and in March goes to sawmill camp operated by Everglades Cypress Lumber Company near Loughman, Polk County, Florida, that draws workers from across the South. Finds camp a rich source of material, including folktales, work songs, proverbs, sermons, children's rhymes, and blues. Meets "Big Sweet," who becomes a central figure in *Mules and Men* and *Dust Tracks on a Road*. Travels throughout Florida, staying in and near the towns of Mulberry, Pierce, and Lakeland (carries a pearl-handled revolver while traveling alone). Publishes "How It Feels To Be Colored Me" in the May number of *World Tomorrow*; declares that she is not "tragically colored." Fee goes to pay creditors for *Fire!!*. Writes but does not publish essay "The Emperor Effaces Himself," satirizing Marcus Garvey. Receives B.A. degree from Barnard College in May. Rests in Eatonville, then travels through Alabama; plans a volume of work songs with music for piano and guitar. Arrives in New Orleans in August to begin investigation of hoodoo. Makes friends with the community of believers and followers of legendary priestess Marie Leveau (died c. 1875). Remains in Louisiana through the winter.

1929 Stays with brother John in Jacksonville in April while organizing field notes (has by then collected more than 95,000 words of stories, games, and material on conjure and religion, along with numerous photographs). Rents a small house in Eau Gallie, hamlet north of Melbourne, Florida. Transcribes sermon preached by the Reverend C. C. Lovelace on May 3 (it will become part of first novel, *Jonah's Gourd Vine*). Falls ill with a liver ailment and is hospitalized in St. Augustine. Moves to Miami and has second and third drafts of folklore manuscript typed. Writes Hughes with ideas for a play on which they will collaborate, proposing they call it "Jook." Travels to Nassau, Bahamas, in October to collect more material, convinced by encounters with Bahamians in Florida that links exist between African-American and African-Caribbean folklore. In Nassau discovers strong African elements in Bahamian culture, including knowledge that some Bahamians had about where their ancestors came from in Africa. Experiences powerful five-day hurricane during stay. Returns to Miami after two weeks because of lack of money. Leaves for New Orleans on October 23 to continue research, as well as to help Boas' Columbia University colleague Otto Klineberg collect material (Mason has forbidden her to do so); remains in New Orleans until December. Finds that Mason's demands complicate relationship with Boas, particularly requirement that Mason's identity not be revealed.

1930 Spends January and February in the Bahamas. Writes "Dance Songs and Tales from the Bahamas" (published in July–September *Journal of American Folklore*). Lives in a rooming house in Westfield, New Jersey, from March to June; works clandestinely on play *Mule Bone: A Comedy of Negro Life* with Hughes, dictating to typist Louise Thompson, who is also receiving money from Mason. (Based on folktale "The Bone of Contention," which Hurston had collected and set in Eatonville, *Mule Bone* presents a series of oral and musical performances.) Hurston works on dialogue while Hughes concentrates on play construction and plot revisions. Returns to Florida in June, promising to complete the second act. In October, files for copyright as the sole author.

1931 Moves back to 43 West 66th Street; continues to organize

field notes for folklore manuscript. Engages Elizabeth Marbury as literary agent. Takes part in bitter dispute with Hughes over rights to *Mule Bone*. Despite sporadic efforts at continued collaboration and reconciliation, the play is not produced and their friendship ends. Employment by Mason ends officially in March, but Hurston continues to receive $100 monthly stipend. Sends folklore manuscript (which will become *Mules and Men*) to friend and editor Harry Block, who likes the material but advises that it will need to be shaped into a sustained narrative for a general audience. Tries to place the monograph on Cudjo Lewis (variously titled "Kossula" and "Barracoon"). After it is rejected by Harper Brothers and Covici-Friede, withdraws it from Viking "for extensive revisions." Writes for theatrical revue *Fast and Furious*, featuring music by composers J. Rosamund Johnson and Porter Grainger and performances by black vaudevillians Jackie (Moms) Mabley and Tim Moore (who later plays "Kingfish" on television show *Amos and Andy*). Revue opens on September 15 and closes within a week; begins work on another show, *Jungle Scandals*, also with music by Grainger; the show never opens. Begins to work on *The Great Day*, a folk concert loosely structured around a single day in the life of a railroad camp; the show features much of the material later published in *Mules and Men* (Mason has refused permission to include conjure material). Gathers a group of performers and dancers and begins rehearsals. "Hoodoo in America" appears in December *Journal of American Folklore*.

1932 Special performance of *The Great Day* presented on January 10 at the John Golden Theatre on Broadway. Hurston sells her car to pay theater rental deposit and her radio to pay for performers' carfare, and borrows $530 from Mason, promising her entire box-office receipts in return. Program notes, written by Locke, emphasize the material's authenticity. Though reviews are favorable, no Broadway producer offers to take the show. Borrows more money from Mason, who has a legal document drawn itemizing material Hurston can use for "theatrical purposes." Excerpts from the show are presented at the New School for Social Research in New York on March 29, and at a cabaret at the Hotel Vanderbilt, sponsored by the Folk Dance Society, on

April 22. Too few engagements force the disbanding of the troupe. Exhausted and suffering from intestinal illness, Hurston persuades Mason to pay her fare home and leaves for Eatonville on April 28. Meets Hamilton Holt, president of whites-only Rollins College in Winter Park, and Edwin O. Grover, a Rollins professor, who invite her to visit the campus. Mason ends support permanently. Works with Robert Wunsch of Rollins English department on production of the show, now called *From Sun to Sun*, recruiting most cast members from friends and relatives in Eatonville.

1933 Suffers severe intestinal pain and conducts rehearsals on an automobile cushion. Writes one-act play, "The Fiery Chariot," for inclusion in the show. First performance is given in small experimental theater in January and then in main auditorium at Rollins in February. Schedules shows in other Florida cities; performances are given to segregated audiences. Special performance is held in Eatonville later in February. Hopes that with resources from Rollins she will realize dream of building a Negro theater. Learns that Charlotte Mason had entered New York Hospital on February 22 (she will remain there until her death on April 15, 1946). Writes "The Gilded Six-Bits," which Wunsch submits to *Story*; it appears in August. When publisher Bertram Lippincott, impressed with her story, writes to her, Hurston replies that she is working on a novel. Moves to nearby Sanford, rents house with bed and stove for $1.50 a week and, with 50 cents a week for food, given by cousin, begins to write *Jonah's Gourd Vine*. Mails the completed manuscript on October 3. Receives telegram on October 16 from Lippincott accepting it with offer of a $200 advance.

1934 Publishes essays "Characteristics of Negro Expression," "Spirituals and Neo-Spirituals," "Conversions and Visions," "Shouting," "Mother Catherine," and "Uncle Monday" in anthology *Negro*, edited by Nancy Cunard. Joins the faculty of Bethune-Cookman College in Daytona Beach, Florida, in January, expecting to establish a school of dramatic arts "based on pure Negro expression." Finds herself in disagreement with the school's president, Mary McLeod Bethune (soon to be founder of the National Council of Negro Women and an adviser to

President Roosevelt). Hurston resents the college's social obligations and low pay. After producing another version of *From Sun to Sun*, Hurston leaves the faculty. Takes group of performers to St. Louis to participate in National Folk Festival, April 29–May 2. Corresponds regularly with James Weldon Johnson, Locke, and Van Vechten. *Jonah's Gourd Vine* published in May. Lippincott agrees to publish *Mules and Men*. Spends the summer revising the manuscript while living in a cabin near the sawmill camp in Loughman, Florida, where she had collected much of her material. In September "The Fire and the Cloud," short story based on the biblical Moses, is published in *Challenge*, black literary journal edited by Dorothy West. Continues to produce folklore concerts, including one at Fisk University; Fisk's president, Thomas Jones, invites Hurston to apply for position as a drama professor, with the suggestion that she enroll for a year at Yale, at Fisk's expense, to study dramatic arts. Publishes review of *God Shakes Creation*, by David M. Cohn, in *New York Herald Tribune Books*, November 3. *Singing Steel*, a version of *Great Day*, is performed in Chicago in late November with cast made up of students Hurston met while staying at the Chicago South Parkway YWCA. Officials of the Julius Rosenwald Foundation see the performance and invite Hurston to apply for fellowship to pursue Ph.D. in anthropology at Columbia. Writes in her application that "it is almost useless to collect material to lie upon the shelves of scientific societies. . . . The Negro material is eminently suited to drama and music. In fact it *is* drama and music and the world and America in particular needs what this folk material holds." The Foundation offers Hurston $3,000 over two years, and she goes to New York to enroll for spring semester. Publishes article "Race Cannot Become Great Until It Recognizes Its Talent," a plea to blacks to recognize the value of African-American folklore, in the *Washington Tribune* on December 29.

1935 Proposes to study general ethnology and then prepare for field work in Haiti. Although plan is endorsed by Boas, the Rosenwald Foundation disapproves of her doing fieldwork and withdraws its original support, instead offering Hurston $100 a month for total fellowship of $700. Hurston enrolls in Columbia, but does not attend

class. Begins writing novel and submits draft to Lippincott in the late spring. Gives interviews discussing *Jonah's Gourd Vine* and the forthcoming *Mules and Men*. Joins folklorists Alan Lomax and Mary Elizabeth Barnicle in June and travels with them through the South recording material for the Music Division of the Library of Congress. Gains access to rural black communities; Lomax credits her with being "almost entirely responsible for the success" of the first part of the expedition. Returns to New York in August. Takes job as a dramatic coach for the Works Progress Administration Federal Theatre Project in Harlem. *Mules and Men* is published in October to good reviews.

1936 Awarded a Guggenheim Fellowship in March to study Obeah practices in the West Indies. Arrives in Kingston, Jamaica, on April 14, after making a brief stopover in Haiti. Travels throughout the island, visiting all of its parishes; spends much time with a community of Maroons, descendants of people legendary for their resistance to slavery. Researches surviving African elements in Jamaican religious practices. Departs for Haiti on September 22 to continue her research. Finds a surfeit of material in Haiti and learns Creole. Begins novel *Their Eyes Were Watching God* and completes it on December 19.

1937 Returns to the United States in March. After receiving fellowship renewal from Guggenheim, goes back to Haiti in May. Suffers "violent gastric disturbance" in late June; frightened, believes it is related to studies of voodoo. Spends two weeks in bed, then continues to travel through Haiti while recuperating, but does not resume intensive research. Suggests that the Guggenheim Foundation fund a college of African-American music, with lectures by Duke Ellington, Fats Waller, Louis Armstrong, singer Ethel Waters, and tap dancer Bill Robinson. Returns to Florida in September, then travels to New York for the publication of *Their Eyes Were Watching God* on September 18. Novel is well received by most reviewers, although Richard Wright in *New Masses* on October 5 faults it for its lack of ideas and use of "minstrel technique." Hurston publishes a profile of Fannie Hurst in *The Saturday Review* October 9, and a review of *The Hurricane's Chil-*

dren by Carl Carmer in *New York Herald Tribune Books*, December 26.

1938 Reacts angrily to Locke's commentary on *Their Eyes* in January *Opportunity*, in which he asked when she would begin writing "social document fiction"; writes "The Chick With One Hen" in response, which *Opportunity* declines to publish. Returns to Florida in February. Completes manuscript based on her Caribbean research in Maitland in mid-March. Reviews Wright's *Uncle Tom's Children* in *Saturday Review*, April 2, criticizing it for its rendering of black southern speech and its violent representations of black life. Joins the Federal Writers' Project in Jacksonville, Florida, in April as an editor for the Florida volume in the American Guide series. Becomes involved in another Project book, "The Florida Negro" (never completed), patterned on Federal Writers' Project volume *The Negro in Virginia*. Becomes supervisor of the Negro unit of the Florida Federal Writers' Project. Travels to Washington to argue for salary increases and equipment. Leads choir sponsored by the Rollins College Folklore Group at the National Folk Festival in Washington. Visits black communities in the Everglades with a recording machine in July. Often takes time off to work on novel, *Moses, Man of the Mountain*, telling no one where she is. Caribbean book, *Tell My Horse*, is published in October to disappointing reviews.

1939 Writes essay "Now Take Noses," caricaturing biological rationalizations of racial differences (later published in *Cordially Yours*, volume of essays written by participants in the 1939 Boston Book Fair). Receives an honorary Doctor of Letters degree from Morgan State College in June. Returns to Florida, where she records 18 songs, stories, and explanations for the Library of Congress and the Folk Arts Committee of the WPA on June 18. Marries Albert Price III, a 23-year-old WPA playground worker, on June 27, in Fernandina, Nassau County, Florida (gives her year of birth as 1910). Leaves Price in Florida to join faculty of North Carolina College for Negroes in Durham (later North Carolina Central University). Intends to start a drama program but becomes dissatisfied with conditions at the college and quarrels with the school's founder and president, James Edward Shepard, a leading black

educator (remains for the academic year but does not stage any plays). Lectures to white drama group in Chapel Hill on black drama and meets Paul Green, Pulitzer Prize–winning playwright and professor of drama at the University of North Carolina. Attends Green's weekly seminar and makes plans to collaborate with him on a play. In October *Tell My Horse* is published in England as *Voodoo Gods: an Inquiry into Native Myths and Magic in Jamaica and Haiti*; sales earn back $500 advance within a week. *Moses, Man of the Mountain* is published in November to mixed reviews.

1940 Files for divorce from Price in February, but they briefly reconcile and travel together to Beaufort, South Carolina, in summer, where Hurston does research on religious trances in "sanctified" churches and other topics, and helps produce a film as part of project led by anthropologist Jane Belo. (Film from expedition is deposited at the Museum of Natural History in New York.) Contracts malaria. Writes essay "Ritualistic Expression from the Lips of the Communicants of the Seventh Day Church of God, Beaufort, South Carolina" (unpublished). Returns to New York in late summer. Lectures, renews old friendships, and considers book projects; publisher Bertram Lippincott suggests she write an autobiography.

1941 Moves in late spring to Los Angeles at the invitation of Katharine Mershon, a wealthy friend; works on autobiography, *Dust Tracks on a Road*. Unsuccessfully tries to arrange for singer and actress Ethel Waters to give a benefit concert for the Hungerford School in Eatonville. Publishes short story "Cock Robin, Beale Street" in the *Southern Literary Messenger* in July. Begins work in October as story consultant at Paramount Pictures (continues until January 1942). Works on revisions of autobiography; removes critique of American imperialism after Japanese attack on Pearl Harbor on December 7.

1942 Lectures at black colleges throughout the South. Moves to St. Augustine to complete revisions of *Dust Tracks*. Spends summer collecting folklore in Florida. Publishes "Story in Harlem Slang" in July *American Mercury*. Profiles Lawrence Silas, an African-American cattleman in Florida, in *The Saturday Evening Post*, September 5

("Negro" is printed under her by-line). Returns to St.
Augustine; teaches creative writing part-time at Florida
Normal, a local black college, and collects data on the
Seminole Indians. Begins friendship with author Marjorie
Kinnan Rawlings. *Dust Tracks* is published in November
to generally good reviews. Hurston is profiled in *Who's
Who in America*, *Current Biography*, and *Twentieth Cen-
tury Authors*, where she lists her favorite authors as Ana-
tole France, Gorky, Shaw, Hugo, Mark Twain, Dickens,
Robert Nathan, Cather, Irvin Cobb, Anne Morrow Lind-
bergh, and Sinclair Lewis.

1943 Moves to Daytona Beach, Florida. Purchases the *Wanago*,
a 32-foot houseboat with 44 horsepower engine (will live
on houseboats for the next four years). Joins Florida
Negro Defense Committee, local civil rights group that
Hurston favors because it does not see blacks as victims.
Gives talks to segregated audiences of GIs as part of Rec-
reation in War program, sponsored by Florida governor's
wife, Mary Holland. *Dust Tracks* is awarded the $1,000
Anisfield-Wolf Book Award for the best book on race re-
lations and Hurston is featured on the cover of *Saturday
Review*, sponsor of the award, on February 20. Quoted in
the *New York World Telegram* on February 1 as asserting
that blacks are much better off in the South than in the
North: "In other words the Jim Crow system works."
After Roy Wilkins, assistant executive secretary of the
NAACP, attacks her in the New York *Amsterdam News*
on February 27 for talking "arrant and even vicious non-
sense" for the purpose of selling her book, Hurston
claims that she was misquoted. Travels to Washington in
March to receive the annual Distinguished Alumni Award
from Howard University and speaks to a meeting of Zeta
Phi Beta. Publishes three articles in *American Mercury*:
"The 'Pet Negro' System" in May, "High John de Con-
quer" in October, and "Negroes Without Self-Pity" in
November. Divorce from Price granted November 9.

1944 Engagement to James Howell Pitts of Cleveland is an-
nounced in New York *Amsterdam News* on February 5,
but marriage never takes place. Publishes "The Last
Slave Ship" in *American Mercury* in March. Stays at
Harlem's Hotel Theresa in the spring. Collaborates on a
musical comedy with Dorothy Waring, a white writer

whose husband, Stephen Kelen d'Oxylion, is a theatrical producer. Tentatively titled "Polk County," the play is to use material from "High John de Conquer," *Mules and Men*, and *Mule Bone*. Finishes play despite differences in artistic viewpoint with Waring. Contributes to the ongoing series "My Most Humiliating Jim Crow Experience" in June number of *Negro Digest*, recounting her treatment by expensive Brooklyn medical specialist who examined her in a laundry closet rather than his office. Returns to Florida, then sails back to New York on the *Wanago*. Arrives in November hoping to secure backing for production of "Polk County." After Reginald Brett, English adventurer and gold miner, tells her of unexplored Mayan ruins on the Patuca River in Honduras, Hurston applies unsuccessfully to the Guggenheim Foundation and the Library of Congress for support to do ethnographic fieldwork there.

1945 Returns to Daytona Beach and purchases new houseboat, *Sun Tan*. Publishes "The Rise of the Begging Joints," attacking "inferior" black colleges and secondary schools, in *American Mercury* in March. Makes plans to go to Honduras on schooner of Miami adventurer and friend Fred Irvine, but postpones trip to work on novel. Suffers severe intestinal pains. Writes *Mrs. Doctor*, novel about upper-class blacks, which is rejected by Lippincott in September. Finishes novel set in Eatonville, incorporating elements of myth and legend, but it is also rejected. Publishes "Crazy For This Democracy," attacking failure of the United States to extend freedom to blacks at home and to people of color abroad, in the *Negro Digest* in December.

1946 After efforts to raise money for Honduras trip fail, goes to New York to work on unsuccessful political campaign of Grant Reynolds, Republican who is running for Congress in Harlem against Democrat Adam Clayton Powell, Jr. Stays in New York after campaign, living in a rented room on 124th Street. Organizes "block mothers plan," community self-help program offering child care to Harlem women. Feeling depressed, does not look up old acquaintances; considers New York generally to be "a basement to hell," due to the impact of national, class, and race hatreds. Reviews *How God Fix Jonah* by Lorenz Graham on November 24, and *Shining Trumpets* by Rudi Blesh

on December 22, for the *New York Herald Tribune Weekly Book Review*.

1947 Reviews *Journey to Accompong* by Katherine Dunham on January 12 and *Trinidad Village* by Melville and Frances Herskovits on March 9 for the *New York Herald Tribune Weekly Book Review*. Through Rawlings' introduction, Hurston signs contract with Scribner's and receives $500 advance; Maxwell Perkins is to be her editor, but he dies in June. Sails for Honduras on May 4. Stays at the Hotel Cosenza in Puerto Cortés, travels along the coast, admires its widely contrasting scenery, and regrets lack of money to do fieldwork in the interior. Receives a second advance from Scribner's and remains in Puerto Cortés, writing *Seraph on the Suwanee* (earlier titles are "Good Morning Sun" and "Sign of the Sun"). Mails draft to New York in September, then continues making revisions through December. *Caribbean Melodies for Chorus of Mixed Voices*, with arrangements by William Grant Still, is published by Oliver Ditson in Philadelphia. Negatively reviews Robert Tallant's *Voodoo in New Orleans* in the October–December *Journal of American Folklore*.

1948 Leaves Honduras on February 20 for editorial meeting with Scribner's. Completes final manuscript on March 17. Spends the summer at Constance Seabrook's home in Rhinebeck, New York. Takes a room at 140 West 112th Street in Harlem. After being falsely accused of molesting a ten-year-old boy, the son of the landlady who had rented her the room on 124th Street in 1946, Hurston is arrested on September 13. Moves to an apartment in the Bronx, leaving no forwarding address. Assisted with legal representation by Scribner's and her editor, Burroughs Mitchell. Devastated by her indictment in early October, based on charges supported solely by the word of young accuser. Story is printed in the press in mid-October as the result of tip from a black court employee. Hurston denies charges, presenting passport to prove she was in Honduras when the alleged crime occurred; wonders whether racism is responsible for court's acceptance of the child's accusations, and vows "to fight this horrible thing to the finish and clear my reputation." *Seraph* is published on October 11 to generally favorable reviews. Feels completely betrayed by her country and race when the Balti-

more *Afro-American*, a nationally distributed newspaper, publishes story on October 23 headlined "Boys, 10, Accuse Zora," with subheading "Novelist Arrested on Morals Charge. Reviewer of Author's Latest Book Notes Character Is 'Hungry for Love' " (story falsely claims there are three boys involved). Hurston writes Van Vechten that she has "resolved to die."

1949 Case against Hurston is dismissed in March after investigation by Manhattan District Attorney's office shows that the boy is "disturbed" (Hurston had earlier advised his mother to have him tested at Bellevue Hospital). Reviews *New Day* by Victor Stafford Reid in the *New York Herald Tribune Weekly Book Review* on March 20. Returns to Florida. Sails with Fred Irvine on a cruise to the Bahamas. Lives on Irvine's boat in Miami and makes plans to return to Honduras. Despair subsides. Begins a new novel. Writes story "Conscience of the Court," about the trial of a black woman accused of assaulting a white man in an effort to protect her white female employer.

1950 Takes a job as a maid on Rivo Island, an affluent Miami neighborhood. When "Conscience of the Court" is published in *The Saturday Evening Post*, employer discovers Hurston is author and on March 27 article appears in the *Miami Herald* headlined "Famous Negro Author Working as Maid Here Just 'to Live a Little.' " National wire services pick up the story, which quotes Hurston as saying that she is "written out" and has taken job to do research with intention of starting a magazine "for and by domestics." Continues to work on new novel, "The Lives of Barney Turk," about the adventures of a white Floridian who travels to Central America and Hollywood (novel later rejected by Scribner's). In April *Negro Digest* publishes "What White Publishers Won't Print," attacking policies that allow only "exceptional" or "quaint" blacks to be portrayed. Leaves Rivo Island to work for conservative George Smathers, who is running against liberal Claude Pepper in the Democratic Senate primary (Smathers wins). "I Saw Negro Votes Peddled," published in November *American Legion Magazine,* offends many blacks, including moderate civil-rights leaders such as Lester Granger of the Urban League. Moves in with

friends in Belle Glade, Florida. Buys used car to explore the Everglades.

1951 Works on novel "The Golden Bench of God," based on the life of Madame C. J. Walker (1867–1919; born Sarah Breedlove), who invented and manufactured products for straightening black women's hair and became the first black woman millionaire. Writes her literary agent, Jean Parker Waterbury, that she plans to make it a "truly indigenous Negro novel," written from inside the black American world. Publishes "Mourner's Bench, Communist Line: Why the Negro Won't Buy Communism" in the June *American Legion Magazine,* arguing that blacks resent and reject the patronizing appeals of the Communist Party. Moves to Eau Gallie in mid-June, renting for $5 a week the same one-room cabin she had lived in when finishing *Mules and Men* (will live there for five years). Works happily repairing house and planting vegetable and flower gardens. Learns that Scribner's has rejected "The Golden Bench of God." Publishes "A Negro Voter Sizes Up Taft" in *The Saturday Evening Post,* December 8, favorable profile of Ohio Senator Robert Taft, a leading candidate for the 1952 Republican presidential nomination.

1952 Lives contentedly in Eau Gallie, where her beautiful gardens attract sightseers. Begins sequel (never finished) to *Dust Tracks,* writes stories about her pet dog Spot, adapts biblical tales, researches articles on Florida cattle and colonialism in Southeast Asia, and considers writing about career women returning to work in the home. Has increasing difficulty selling work. Gives five folk concerts in six weeks to earn money. Declines invitation to speak at Taft *vs.* Eisenhower forum in Boston in March because she has no winter coat. Increasingly plagued by health problems, including a tropical virus contracted from drinking impure water in Honduras, gall bladder infection, irritated colon, and the effects of obesity. Hired by the *Pittsburgh Courier* to cover the trial of Ruby McCollum, a black woman charged with the murder of a prominent white doctor who had been her lover. Unable to gain permission to interview McCollum, Hurston asks William Bradford Huie, a journalist and one of the South's best-known white anti-segregationists, to intercede. Hurston's stories defending McCollum appear in

the *Courier* from October 11, 1952, to May 2, 1953. (Mc-
Collum was sentenced to death; after the sentence was
overturned on appeal, she was declared mentally incom-
petent and committed to a state hospital where she re-
mained for 20 years; Huie published a book on the case
in 1956, *Ruby McCollum: Woman in the Suwanee Jail*,
which included Hurston's reporting.)

1953 Works on biography of Herod the Great, project she has
 contemplated for many years. Reads about Herod in
 works of Flavius Josephus, Livy, Eusebius, Strabo, and
 Nicolas of Damascus. Perceives Herod to have been a
 great soldier, statesman, and lover and hopes that dra-
 matic treatment of his life will interest Cecil B. DeMille,
 Hollywood producer and director of biblical epics.

1954 Continues to work on Herod the Great, which she ac-
 knowledges has become her "great obsession"; invites
 Winston Churchill to write the book's introduction and
 commentary.

1955 Writes letter to the Orlando *Sentinel* in August condemn-
 ing the 1954 Supreme Court decision in *Brown* v. *Board of
 Education*, which ruled segregated schools unconstitu-
 tional; Hurston criticizes the Court's implication that
 black children could learn only when they went to school
 with whites. Letter is widely reprinted in southern news-
 papers and produces a sensation that surprises Hurston
 and angers civil-rights leaders. Scribner's rejects the
 Herod manuscript, which has grown to encompass Jewish
 history and the origins of a "movement" which produced
 Christianity and Western civilization. Despite the rejec-
 tion, Hurston continues to work on the book.

1956 Engages a "book hunting agency" to find copies of *Dust
 Tracks* and *Their Eyes Were Watching God* to send to
 Dutch translator Margrit Sablonière. Receives eviction
 notice in March from landlord, who is selling the house.
 Moves out in mid-May. Receives award for "education
 and human relations" at the Bethune-Cookman College
 commencement in late May. Takes job in June as library
 clerk at Patrick Air Force Base in Cocoa Beach, Florida,
 and is paid $1.88 an hour for filing technical literature.
 Hates job.

1957 Fired from job in May (supervisor explains that she is "too well educated"). Receives unemployment insurance. Moves to Merritt Island and lives in a house trailer and drives an old station wagon. Suffers from stomach ulcer, but continues to work on "Herod." After C. E. Bolen, publisher of the *Fort Pierce Chronicle*, a local black newspaper, invites her to write for his publication in December, Hurston moves to Fort Pierce and for the next two years writes articles on various subjects and contributes a column on "Hoodoo and Black Magic."

1958 Works as substitute teacher at Lincoln Park Academy, the segregated public school for blacks in Fort Pierce. Rents small cinder-block house at 1734 School Court. Plants azaleas, gardenias, morning glories, collard greens, and tomatoes. Works on "Herod" and tries to find another publisher. Becomes good friends with her landlord and physician, Dr. C. C. Benton, who visits often and occasionally buys her groceries. Health deteriorates: suffers from high blood pressure, as well as intestinal pains.

1959 Suffers stroke and is left weak and mentally distracted. Applies to the county welfare office in May for money to pay for medicine; begins receiving food vouchers in June. Writes occasionally for the *Chronicle*. Condition continues to deteriorate and on October 29 Hurston enters the Saint Lucie County Welfare Home. Refuses to contact members of family; has long been out of touch with friends and acquaintances from earlier years of her life.

1960 Dies January 28 in the Saint Lucie County Welfare Home from "hypertensive heart disease." Following funeral on February 7 paid for by collection from local friends and acquaintances, Hurston is buried in an unmarked grave in the Garden of Heavenly Rest, a segregated cemetery in Fort Pierce.

Note on the Texts

This volume contains all four of the novels published by Zora Neale Hurston (*Jonah's Gourd Vine*; *Their Eyes Were Watching God*; *Moses, Man of the Mountain*; and *Seraph on the Suwanee*), which are printed here from the first and only editions published during Hurston's lifetime. A selection of nine short stories, arranged in the order they were written, is included following the novels.

Hurston began work on her first novel, *Jonah's Gourd Vine*, in July 1933 after the publisher Bertram Lippincott, who had read Hurston's story "The Gilded Six-Bits" in the August number of *Story*, asked her if she was working on a novel. She mailed the manuscript to Lippincott on October 3. The novel was published in Philadelphia by J. B. Lippincott, Inc., in May 1934.

Their Eyes Were Watching God was written while Hurston was doing anthropological fieldwork in Haiti. She began writing the novel late in September 1936 and completed it on December 19, 1936. The novel was published by J. B. Lippincott on September 18, 1937.

In December 1935, Hurston told a friend that she was writing a book about Moses, but she did not complete *Moses, Man of the Mountain* until early in 1939, while she was employed by the Florida Federal Writers' Project. The novel was published by J. B. Lippincott in November 1939.

After the editors at the Lippincott firm rejected several proposals she had submitted to them, Hurston signed a contract for a novel with Charles Scribner's Sons in April 1947. With a $500 advance from Scribner's, she went to Honduras in May and began work on her new novel. She sent a draft to her editor in September and received an additional $500, which enabled her to stay in Honduras while she continued writing. During her work on the novel, she considered various titles, including "Angel in the Bed," "Sang the Suwanee in the Spring," "The Seraph's Man," "Good Morning Sun," and "Sign of the Sun." She sent a completed version to Scribner's in December 1947 and returned to New York in February 1948 to work on final revisions with Burroughs Mitchell, her editor at Scribner's. The novel, now titled *Seraph on the Suwanee*, was published in New York by Charles Scribner's Sons on October 11, 1948.

Hurston never published a collection of short stories. Seven of the stories presented here were published in periodicals during her lifetime; the two others remained in typescript at her death.

"John Redding Goes to Sea," Hurston's first published story, was written when she was an undergraduate at Howard University; it was

published in *Stylus*, the campus literary magazine, in May 1921. She republished it, with some alterations, in *Opportunity* for January 1926. The text printed here is that of the 1926 version.

"Drenched in Light" (posthumously published as "Isis") was Hurston's first story to be published by *Opportunity*, appearing in the December 1924 number. The story was later included in two anthologies, *Readings from Negro Authors for Schools and Colleges* (1931) and *Within Our Gates: Selections on Tolerance and the Foreign Born of Today* (1940), but Hurston did not revise it for these publications. The text of the 1924 periodical version is printed here.

"Spunk" was published in *Opportunity* in June 1925, and was included in *The New Negro: An Interpretation*, an anthology edited by Alain Locke (New York: Albert & Charles Boni, 1925). There is no difference in wording between these nearly simultaneous texts; because *The New Negro* text contains no errors, that text is printed here.

"Sweat" was published in the only number of the Harlem journal *Fire!!* in November 1926. The story was never published again during Hurston's lifetime.

"The Bone of Contention" (written about 1929) was not published during Hurston's lifetime. The text printed here is from Langston Hughes and Zora Neale Hurston's *Mule Bone: A Comedy of Negro Life*, edited by George Houston Bass and Henry Louis Gates, Jr. (New York: Harper Perennial, 1991). Reprinted by permission of HarperCollins, Inc.

"The Book of Harlem" (written about 1921) was never published during Hurston's lifetime. The text printed here is that of the typescript in the James Weldon Johnson collection in the Beinecke Library, Yale University.

"The Gilded Six-Bits" was published in *Story* for August 1933, and later collected in *Story in America* (1934). The text printed here is that of the periodical version.

"The Fire and the Cloud" was published in the *Challenge* number of September 1934, the only version printed in Hurston's lifetime.

"Story in Harlem Slang" appeared in the *American Mercury* in July 1942; it was not published again in Hurston's lifetime.

This volume presents the texts of the original printings and typescript chosen for inclusion here but does not attempt to reproduce features of their typographic design, such as display capitalization of chapter openings. The texts are printed without change, except for the correction of typographical errors. Spelling, punctuation, and capitalization are often expressive features, and they are not altered, even when inconsistent or irregular. The following is a list of typographical errors corrected, cited by page and line number: 7.17,

Beaseley; 63.40, so won't; 85.13, inward.; 91.7, live; 93.13, foilage; 97.35, Foriduh; 110.36, stuck; 110.37, wont; 117.24, 'buse; 121.8, Mattie; 129.23, its; 133.26, y'll; 148.3, will all; 181.6, at."; 222.24, breakast; 241.4, Phoeby; 246.8, houses; 305.18, cut up; 315.30, mo.'; 319.14, days."; 331.18, somethin'."; 350.15, substances; 372.5, county; 383.34, moment; 404.21, oveseers; 420.2, sorrow; 420.6, hearing; 420.34, things; 423.18, Its; 442.11, seroius; 452.3, mountan; 481.20, go,'; 527.36, dishanded; 530.6, show by; 562.10, "We; 567.15, town's; 602.33, not just; 611.18, you; 619.20, lead; 620.28, things that; 625.40, it?'; 641.15, sent; 643.18, willowly; 650.17, shell; 662.26, picked and; 668.25, migh; 669.14, it was it was; 672.18, brough; 673.11, see; 679.14, smiled; 696.4, a take; 699.18, The; 708.7, fallen of; 717.6, an; 724.10, Suwannee; 726.10, Charls-ton; 745.34, here.; 747.11, look; 749.12, idea,; 754.35, youself; 782.33, sense the; 785.17, "Oh"; 789.11, wtih; 794.12, you to that; 795.3, Arvay,; 800.13, swiching; 801.10, peculair; 804.11, over side; 804.20, in, but; 804.21, "What; 804.38, The; 810.4, dise window; 812.24, averything; 812.28, right."; 814.21, angagement; 830.15, of of; 843.37, everbody; 847.6, demned; 856.18, Carl; 860.10, age; 866.15, he he; 867.2, hysterically It; 873.10, was was; 875.29, Mis; 878.40, impefect; 884.17, got up; 888.22, may; 893.14, gallery; 896.27, big-mouthed,; 911.12, abiilty; 926.6, on!'"; 927.15, him.'; 928.14, muss; 929.18, nevertheless.; 929.23, answerd; 931.11, 'But; 931.32, Stellah; 932.7, 'Lo; 932.12, mamma.'"; 932.38, 'Come; 933.3, bullhats; 933.31, fell; 934.14, 'It's; 934.28, bulider; 934.30, Howdy; 934.32, 'Well; 935.3, 'I'll; 935.14, "Mamma,"; 935.33, jassamine; 938.13, when; 938.26, lan'."; 938.40, 'Ah; 940.7, Patts'; 940.37, "Hello; 941.9, yahd"; 944.20, Grandma nowhere; 944.39, listed; 956.6, sit; 959.22, He; 959.39, to biggety; 260.28, botles; 963.31, years.; 963.34, up paih; 965.1, he; 966.38, is one; 971.19, yuh, Me; 974.19, day 'Just; 975.38, wil; 987.3, up."; 993.28, aud; 999.13–14, Eygptian; 1008.B5, midnight.

Notes

In the notes below, reference numbers denote page and line of this volume (the line count includes chapter headings). No note is made for material included in standard desk-reference books such as Webster's *Collegiate*, *Biographical*, and *Geographical* dictionaries. The glossaries on pages 169–71 and 1008–10 and the footnotes in the text are Hurston's own. Biblical references are keyed to the King James Version. For further background than is contained in the Notes and the Chronology, see Robert E. Hemenway, *Zora Neale Hurston: A Literary Biography* (Urbana: University of Illinois Press, 1977); Karla Holloway, *The Character of the Word: The Texts of Zora Neale Hurston* (Westport: Greenwood Press, 1987); Lillie Pearl Howard, *Zora Neale Hurston* (Boston: Twayne Publishers, 1980); and N. Y. Nathiri, *Zora! Zora Neale Hurston: A Woman and Her Community* (Orlando: Sentinel Communications Co., 1991).

JONAH'S GOURD VINE

6.15 proagin'] Or prog, proague: to prowl, poke, or search about, to forage, to hunt out, to progress.

25.15 Raw-Head-and-Bloody-Bones] A bogeyman whose raw head sweats blood. Hurston relates tales of Raw Head, a legendary doctor of conjure, and the bloody bones in *Mules and Men*, Chapter X.

29.4 brought to America . . . drum] Prohibited from using drums in most of the South, slaves relied on hand-clapping and foot-stomping to produce the percussion effects and polymeter characteristic of African music.

35.34–37 "A chieftain . . . longest pieces] "Lord Ullin's Daughter," 56-line ballad by Scottish poet Thomas Campbell (1774–1814).

41.5 bulldozia.] Boastful and threatening language.

46.13 mommucked] Ruined, messed (from "mommick"—to maul, chop up, mangle).

51.36–37 woman-jessie] Woman-flogger (jessie is a rod in Isaiah 11:1).

65.8 uh lark . . . settin'?"] In the traditional African-American courting riddle, a flying lark is a woman in search of a mate, while a setting dove is a woman who has found one.

70.31 stump-knocker] Unlicensed traveling preacher.

71.2 jump . . . broomstick] Get married. Dating from the antebellum period when slave marriages had no legal standing, the ritual of jumping the

broomstick was the symbolic enactment of a couple's commitment to each other.

84.24 sugar-tit] Sugar wrapped in a cloth and shaped like a nipple.

93.35 crocus] Or croker: burlap, or coarse, loosely woven brown hemp.

98.3 A. C. L.] Atlantic Coast Line Railroad.

98.11–13 gran' march . . . step."] To conform with religious prohibitions against dancing, Christianized slaves invented new rituals such as the Grand March, which they adapted from West African traditions. However ardent their movements, they were not considered to be dancing as long as their feet did not cross.

98.22 Saul and David] Cf. 1 and 2 Samuel for the rivalry between Saul, first king of Israel, and the shepherd soldier David.

106.3 Palma Christi] The castor oil plant *ricinus communis.*

107.9 war water] Conjuring solution made with filtered oil of tar and used to create domestic chaos.

117.37–38 John-de-conquer root] The most powerful root used in conjure, named for the mythical hero High John de Conquer who, according to Hurston, accompanied Africans on the Middle Passage and remained a symbol of spiritual sustenance and hope in African-American folklore.

121.6 bug . . . chip."] An ulterior or hidden motive or cause.

123.38–39 Jonah's gourd vine] Jonah 4:6–10. As Hurston summarized the passage in a letter to Carl Van Vechten dated February 28, 1934, the prophet Jonah had sat up under a gourd vine that had grown up overnight. In the morning a worm cut it down. One act of malice destroyed great and sudden growth. The vine withered and died.

124.18 two-headed men."] Or "two-headed doctors" (meaning, according to Hurston in *Mules and Men*, "twice as much sense"): practitioners of conjure.

126.7 bookooin'] Loud talking, bragging (from the French *beaucoup*).

132.26 his "Dry Bones" sermon] A variation on one of the best-known sermons in the African-American oral tradition, based on Ezekiel 37:1–4.

141.2 death puddin'] A kind of sausage.

144.19–20 Oh . . . dove!] Refrain of a Negro spiritual "Sing a-ho, if I had the wings of a dove,/I'd fly away and be at rest" (Psalm 55:6).

144.27–28 "He . . . me."] Judas receives the sop from Jesus, a sign that he will betray him (John 13:26).

144.31–36 "Beloved . . . is."] 1 John 3:2.

145.8–151.29 "Our theme . . . Amen.] Hurston heard this sermon preached by the Rev. C. C. Lovelace in Eau Gallie, Florida, May 3, 1929; she published her transcription of it in *Negro* (1934), an anthology edited by Nancy Cunard.

166.28 rabbit . . . patch.] In the folktale, the cornered rabbit tricks the creatures he has cheated into hurling him into a dense brier patch (where he was actually born and bred) by begging for any fate but that, then mocks them from among its protecting thorns.

THEIR EYES WERE WATCHING GOD

174.2 HENRY ALLEN MOE] Moe (b. 1894) was secretary of the John Simon Guggenheim Memorial Foundation and a lecturer at Columbia University School of Law.

176.6 bander log] The Bandar-log are a nation of monkeys in Rudyard Kipling's *Second Jungle Book* (1895); the term came to mean "vacuous, irresponsible chatterers." In Hindi, *bander* (also transliterated *bandar*, *bandur*) means "rhesus monkey" and *log* means "people."

179.18 zigaboos] Slang reference to African-Americans.

184.23–24 palma christi] See note 106.3.

186.13–19 Honey, . . . womenfolks.] This folktale was recorded by Hurston under the title "Why the Sister in Black Works Hardest" in *Mules and Men*, Chapter IV.

199.38 diasticutis] Buttocks (pseudo-Latin formation probably based on "ass").

210.1–2 dry long so] Without embellishment, plainly, "just like that."

219.4 Miccanopy] City in northern Florida, about 10 miles south of Gainesville.

228.25–35 Big . . . Ole John] For John de Conquer, see note 117.37–38. Old John (an extension of John de Conquer) is the slave protagonist who outwits the master in a cycle of folktales.

231.9 class leader] Lay officer in the Methodist church.

238.38 playin' de dozens] Verbal game of figurative, ritual insult.

239.7 Saul's daughter . . . David.] 2 Samuel 6:20.

240.12 eat . . . spoon] "He must have a long spoon [i.e., all his wits about him] who sups with the devil," an old proverb.

241.16 still-bait] Bait used for still-baiting (fishing in one spot with a long line, as distinguished from trawling).

254.6–7 cut . . . air."] To "cut a hog" is to make an embarrassing mistake; to "catch air" is to run.

264.19–20 coon-can . . . flip] Card games.

284.17 "woof"] Defined in *Mules and Men* as a kind of aimless talk, e.g., semi-serious flirtation or bragging (from the purposeless barking of dogs at night).

284.21 skin game] A card game, also called Georgia Skin Game and Florida Flip.

302.33–38 Yo' . . . *Draws*] An example of playing the dozens (see note 238.38), here, the dirty dozens.

MOSES, MAN OF THE MOUNTAIN

338.3–4 *The Sixth . . . Moses*] By Johann Scheible (Stuttgart, 1840); an American edition (New York, 1890) is subtitled: *or Moses' magical spirit-art, known as the wonderful arts of the old wise Hebrews, taken from the Mosaic books of the Cabala and the Talmud, for the good of mankind. Translated from the German, word for word, according to old writings.* Moses is the traditional author of the Pentateuch, the first five books of the Bible.

387.7 forty-two . . . Maati] In ancient Egyptian religion, at the judgment before Osiris in the Hall of the Double Maat (Truth and Justice), the deceased denied the commission of 42 evil acts to the 42 assessor gods, then his or her heart was weighed against the feather of Maat (Truth). If the heart was not weighted with evil, eternal life among the gods was attained; if it tipped the scale, it was devoured by the crocodile-lion-hippopotamus god Amati.

387.9 book of Thoth] Thoth, god of wisdom, learning, magic, and the arts, and scribe and adviser of the gods, was considered the author of works of powerful magic and the occult, including funerary texts known as "The Coming Forth by Day" or, more commonly, "Book of the Dead."

388.11 Koptos] Or Coptos, a city on the right bank of the Nile north of Karnak, now the location of Qift (or Kift, Kuft).

392.9 Ka] A spiritual entity, an aspect of the individual believed to live within the body during life and to survive it in the tomb after death.

509.12 toled] Variant of tolled: lured off, as an animal for the purpose of capturing.

567.11 double-teen] Variant of "double-team": to gang up on.

SERAPH ON THE SUWANEE

599.32–33 Osceola, . . . Bow-Legs] Osceola was a war leader and Miccanope and Billy Bow Legs chiefs of the Seminole during the Second Seminole War (1835–42).

601.23 mourner's-bench] The front seats at revivalist meetings, reserved for those who publicly repent their sins.

608.25 toled] See note 509.12.

633.15 *A Slow . . . Arkansas.*] Thomas W. Jackson, *On a Slow Train Through Arkansas* (1903), joke book also known for its "hillbilly" illustrations.

642.37 "Bear got me] I was overcome by the heat.

688.28–29 Hannah . . . Abraham] 1 Samuel 1:2–19; Genesis 21:14.

705.22 throwing . . . briar patch] See note 166.28.

707.9 squinge] Squeeze, squelch, crimp.

708.38–39 skin the cat] Gymnastic stunt, performed while grasping the bar or rings, in which the legs are swung up, over the back between the arms, then lowered straight down.

715.35 double-teened] See note 567.11.

717.2 piney-woods rooter] A wild hog of the Florida swamps; a razorback hog.

759.17 Booger . . . bones] See note 25.15.

767.5 Boleta] A numbers game played with consecutively numbered balls enclosed in a sack (*bolita* means "little ball").

773.3–4 guy from Indianapolis] Carl Fisher, who around 1913 loaned $50,000 to a group of financially pressed entrepreneurs developing a residential colony at Miami Beach (incorporated 1915), then a wilderness area. Fisher received 200 acres of land, mostly under water, as security; eventually sand pumped in from the bottom of Biscayne Bay turned his acreage into several small islands and a yacht basin.

806.35–36 drop a flag on it] Spend a little money on her.

806.39–40 gambling . . . window] Defined in *Mules and Men* as "risking nothing, i.e., hat, coat and shoes out the window so the owner can run if he loses."

815.25 John . . . Patmos.] St. John wrote the Book of Revelation on the island of Patmos (Revelation 1:9).

818.40 neither . . . okra.] See page 171.13–14.

835.5 snurling] Turning up his nose in disdain (a snurle is a nostril).

844.18 proag] See note 6.15.

849.22 croker-sack] See note 93.35.

888.36 Minorcans] About 1200 Minorcans were brought to Florida to

colonize New Smyrna (now New Smyrna Beach) in 1767; they raised indigo for trade with England.

901.9 Copasetty] Or copacetic: excellent, fine, very satisfactory.

SELECTED STORIES

941.8 hasion] A mischievous or unruly child.

941.11 mommuk] See note 46.13.

960.5–6 bear's got *me*!"] See note 642.37.

960.8 eppizudicks] Used humorously for an imaginary or bogus human illness or ailment (from epizootic, a disease of livestock of an undetermined nature).

972.25–26 half-washed christians] Methodist baptism involves having the forehead wetted; Baptists are completely immersed.

981.21 Lafayette theatre] Famous Harlem theater, from 1916 to 1923 home of a stock company whose productions ranged from English classics to popular Broadway plays performed for almost exclusively black audiences. It then became a vaudeville house known for its boisterous audiences and Friday night shows. After a short run as a movie theater, it was sold and became a house of worship. It burned down in 1968.

981.30 hink] Snub.

995.30 fan . . . round] To run around (to seek sexual relations).

996.29 sugar tit] See note 84.24.

Cataloging Information

Hurston, Zora Neale.
 [Selections. 1995]
 Novels and stories / Zora Neale Hurston.
 Edited by Cheryl A. Wall.
 p. cm. — (The Library of America ; 74)
 Contents: Jonah's gourd vine—Their eyes were watching God—
Moses, man of the mountain—Seraph on the Suwanee—Selected stories.
 1. Afro-Americans—Fiction. I. Title. II. Jonah's gourd vine.
III. Their eyes were watching God. IV. Moses, man of the mountain.
V. Seraph on the Suwanee. VI. Series.
PS3515.U789A6 1995 94-25757
813'.52—dc20
ISBN 0-940450-83-6

THE LIBRARY OF AMERICA SERIES

This book is set in 10 point Linotron Galliard,
a face designed for photocomposition by Matthew Carter
and based on the sixteenth-century face Granjon. The paper is
acid-free Ecusta Nyalite and meets the requirements for permanence
of the American National Standards Institute. The binding
material is Brillianta, a woven rayon cloth made by
Van Heek-Scholco Textielfabrieken, Holland.
The composition is by The Clarinda
Company. Printing and binding by
R. R. Donnelley & Sons Company.
Designed by Bruce Campbell.